GREAT STORIES
OF ALL NATIONS

GREAT STORIES
OF ALL NATIONS

*One Hundred Sixty Complete Short
Stories from the Literatures of All
Periods and Countries*

EDITED BY
MAXIM LIEBER

&

BLANCHE COLTON WILLIAMS, PH. D.
Head of Department of English, Hunter College, New York

NEW YORK
TUDOR PUBLISHING CO.
MCMXXXIV

CONTENTS

ANCIENT EGYPT

    INTRODUCTION . . . . PAGE

    INTRODUCTION 3

    THE DOOMED PRINCE—*Anonymous* 3

ANCIENT GREECE

    INTRODUCTION 9

    ARES AND APHRODITE—*Homer* 9

    CANDAULES' FOLLY—*Herodotus* 12

    CNEMON'S STORY—*Heliodorus* 14

ANCIENT INDIA

    INTRODUCTION 19

    THE TALKATIVE TORTOISE—*Anonymous* 19

    THE BUTTER-BLINDED BRAHMAN—*Anonymous* . . . 21

    DEVASMITA—*Somadeva* 23

BIBLICAL LITERATURE

    INTRODUCTION 28

    THE BOOK OF ESTHER—*Old Testament* 28

    BEL AND THE DRAGON—*The Apocrypha* 37

ANCIENT ROME

    INTRODUCTION 40

    PYRAMUS AND THISBE—*Ovid* 40

    TRIMALCHIO'S DINNER—*Petronius* 43

    THE THREE ROBBERS—*Apuleius* 49

PERSIA

    INTRODUCTION 56

    FERIDUN AND HIS THREE SONS—*Abul Firdawsi* . . . 56

    THE TREASURE OF MANSUR—*Anonymous* 68

ARABIA

    INTRODUCTION 74

    THE JAR OF OLIVES AND THE BOY KAZI—*Anonymous* . . 75

FRANCE

    INTRODUCTION 82

    OUR LADY'S TUMBLER—*Anonymous* 83

    THE HUSBAND WHO WAS BLIND OF AN EYE—*Marguerite De Navarre* 91

vij

PAGE

Blue Beard—*Charles Perrault* 93
Jeannot and Colin—*Voltaire* 97
Soliman II—*J. F. Marmontel* 105
The Executioner—*Honoré De Balzac* 116
The Taking of the Redoubt—*Prosper Merimée* 125
Omphale: A Rococo Story—*Théophile Gautier* 129
The Heroism of Dr. Hallidonhill—*Villiers de L'Isle Adam* . 137
The Ensign—*Alphonse Daudet* 141
The Maid of the Dauber—*Émile Zola* 144
The Lost Stars—*Catulle Mendès* 148
Constant Guinard—*Jean Richepin* 150
The Dowry—*Guy De Maupassant* 154
The Horse of Genghis Khan—*Paul Morand* 160

SPAIN

INTRODUCTION 167
The Man Who Tamed the Shrew—*Juan Manuel* . . . 168
How Lazaro Served a Priest—*Diego Hurtado De Mendoza* . . 172
The Mock Aunt—*Miguel Cervantes* 181
Paul Turns Beggar—*Francisco De Quevedo* 192
Bella-Flor—*Fernan Caballero* 195
Cordovans in Crete—*Don Juan Valera* 199
The Stub-Book—*Pedro Antonio Alarcón* 204
The First Prize—*Emilia Bazan* 209

ITALY

INTRODUCTION 214
The Stone of Invisibility—*Giovanni Boccaccio* . . . 215
The Usurer's Will—*Giovan-Francesco Straparola* . . . 219
The Jealous Wife—*Anton-Francesco Grazzini* 223
Love Triumphant—*Giovanbattista Giraldi Cinthio* . . . 231
Story of the Saint Joseph's Ass—*Giovanni Verga* . . . 238
The Orderly—*Edmondo de Amicis* 247
Turlendana Returns—*Gabriele d'Annunzio* 254
A Mere Formality—*Luigi Pirandello* 261
Mirrors—*Massimo Bontempelli* 282
The Slap—*Raffaele Calzini* 285

GREAT BRITAIN

INTRODUCTION 293
The Pardoner's Tale—*Geoffrey Chaucer* 294
Sir Simon Eyer—*Thomas Deloney* 297

PAGE

IN DEFENCE OF HIS RIGHT—*Daniel Defoe* 309
TOM VARNISH—*Richard Steele* 318
WANDERING WILLIE'S TALE—*Sir Walter Scott* . . . 320
PADDY AT SEA—*Samuel Lover* 335
THE HALF-BROTHERS—*Elizabeth C. Gaskell* 342
THE CONVICT'S RETURN—*Charles Dickens* 352
"BLOW UP WITH THE BRIG!"—*Wilkie Collins* 359
MARKHEIM—*Robert Louis Stevenson* 369
THE CLERK'S QUEST—*George Moore* 382
THE SPHINX WITHOUT A SECRET—*Oscar Wilde* . . . 386
IL CONDE—*Joseph Conrad* 391
THE STOLEN BACILLUS—*H. G. Wells* 403
MARY WITH THE HIGH HAND—*Arnold Bennett* . . . 409
QUALITY—*John Galsworthy* 420
TWO BLUE BIRDS—*D. H. Lawrence* 425
MRS. BEELBROW'S LIONS—*Stacy Aumonier* 438
THE APPLE-TREE—*Katherine Mansfield* 445
HUBERT AND MINNIE—*Aldous Huxley* 447

GERMANY
  INTRODUCTION 458
  EULENSPIEGEL CARRIES OFF THE PARSON'S HORSE—*Anonymous* . 459
  DR. FAUST ARRANGES A MARRIAGE—*Anonymous* . . . 461
  THE NEW-YEAR'S NIGHT OF AN UNHAPPY MAN—*Jean Paul Richter* 463
  THE BROKEN PITCHER—*Heinrich Zschokke* 465
  THE FRIENDS—*Johann Ludwig Tieck* 479
  RUMPELSTILTSKIN—*Jacob and Wilhelm Grimm* . . . 488
  THE VIRGIN AND THE NUN—*Gottfried Keller* 491
  THE VICTIM—*Hermann Sudermann* 497
  FLOWERS—*Arthur Schnitzler* 505
  THE BEAST—*Jacob Wassermann* 511
  A RAILWAY ACCIDENT—*Thomas Mann* 513

UNITED STATES
  INTRODUCTION 522
  PETER RUGG, THE MISSING MAN—*William Austin* . . . 524
  THE STOUT GENTLEMAN—*Washington Irving* 546
  RAPPACCINI'S DAUGHTER—*Nathaniel Hawthorne* . . . 554
  THE CASK OF AMONTILLADO—*Edgar Allan Poe* . . . 578
  WHAT WAS IT?—*Fitz-James O'Brien* 584
  A TALE OF NEGATIVE GRAVITY—*Frank R. Stockton* . . 595

PAGE

THE CELEBRATED JUMPING FROG OF CALAVERAS COUNTY—*Mark Twain* 612
THE POSTMISTRESS OF LAUREL RUN—*Francis Bret Harte* . . . 617
AN OCCURRENCE AT OWL CREEK BRIDGE—*Ambrose Bierce* . . 631
ZENOBIA'S INFIDELITY—*H. C. Bunner* 639
DRIFTING CRANE—*Hamlin Garland* 648
A NEW ENGLAND NUN—*Mary Wilkins Freeman* 653
A MUNICIPAL REPORT—*O. Henry* 664
THE DEBT—*Edith Wharton* 677
PAPAGO WEDDING—*Mary Hunter Austin* 688
THE ONE HUNDRED DOLLAR BILL—*Booth Tarkington* . . . 692
THE DOOMDORF MYSTERY—*Melville Davisson Post* 706
DEATH IN THE WOODS—*Sherwood Anderson* 716
BLUE MURDER—*Wilbur Daniel Steele* 727

RUSSIA

INTRODUCTION 744
THE COFFIN-MAKER—*Alexander Pushkin* 745
THE RASPBERRY WATER—*Ivan Turgenev* 751
THE BEGGAR BOY AT CHRIST'S CHRISTMAS TREE—*Feodor Dostoievsky* 759
THE EMPTY DRUM—*Leo Tolstoy* 763
THE DARLING—*Anton Chekhov* 769
THE WHITE DOG—*Feodor Sologub* 777
HER LOVER—*Maxim Gorky* 782
CAPRICE—*Alexander Kuprin* 787
THE LIE—*Leonid Andreyev* 792

POLAND

INTRODUCTION 800
THE LEGEND—*Zygmunt Krasinsky* 800
DO YOU REMEMBER?—*Eliza Orzeszkowa* 809
TWILIGHT—*Wladyslaw Reymont* 813

HUNGARY

INTRODUCTION 816
THE ASSIGNATION—*Karoly Kisfaludi* 816
THE ROOM WITH FORTY-EIGHT STARS—*Maurus Jokai* . . . 820
THE GRASS OF LOHINA—*Koloman Mikszath* 824
THE DANCING BEAR—*Etienne Bársony* 835
DARKENING SHADOWS—*Louis Biro* 841

CONTENTS

PAGE

YIDDISH
INTRODUCTION 846
A Reincarnated Melody—*Isaac Loeb Peretz* 846
Eva—*Sholom Aleichem* 851
A Livelihood—*Judah Steinberg* 863
Military Service—*Micah Joseph Berdyczewski* . . . 868
The Black Cat—*David Pinski* 874
A Jewish Child—*Sholom Ash* 882
Winter Wolves—*Joseph Opatoshu* 887

BELGIUM
INTRODUCTION 892
The Glass House—*Camille Lemmonier* 892
The City Hunter—*Georges Rodenbach* 895
The Horse Fair at Opdorp—*Emile Verhaeren* . . . 899

HOLLAND
INTRODUCTION 903
Johannes Attends a Party—*Frederick W. Van Eeden* . . 903
About Myself and Others—*Louis Couperus* . . . 913
Chicken—*Herman Heijermans* 922

LATIN AMERICA
BRAZIL
The Farm Magnate—*Monteiro Lobato* 926
ARGENTINA
The Healer—*Manuel Ugarte* 937
MEXICO
Rip-Rip—*Manuel Gutiérrez-Nájera* 943
SANTO DOMINGO
The Marble Bust—*Fabio Fiallo* 948
CHILE
Nights in Talca—*Armando Zegri* 950

CZECHOSLOVAKIA
INTRODUCTION 954
A Lodger for the Night—*Jan Neruda* 954
The Apple-Tree—*Svatopluk Čech* 957
The Island—*Karel Čapek* 965

BULGARIA
INTRODUCTION 973
Happiness—*Tedor Panov* 973

JUGOSLAVIA   PAGE
   INTRODUCTION 979
   VOUYA GOES A-WOOING—*Milovan Glishich* 979
   FERID—*Vladimir Trescec* 988
   THE MAN WITH THE RAGGED SOUL—*Francis Xavier Meško* . 991

CHINA
   INTRODUCTION 1000
   THE SACRIFICE OF YANG CHIAO-AI—*Anonymous* 1000
   THE DONKEY'S REVENGE—*P'u Sung-Ling* 1011

JAPAN
   INTRODUCTION 1017
   OF A DANCING GIRL—*Lafcadio Hearn* 1018
   TSUGARU STRAIT—*Shimazaki Toson* 1033
   THE BILL-COLLECTING—*Nagai Kafu* 1042

THE SCANDINAVIAN COUNTRIES
   INTRODUCTION 1051
   ICELAND
   THE BIRTH OF SINFJOTLI, THE SON OF SIGMUND—*Anonymous* . 1052
   DENMARK
   WHAT THE OLD MAN DOES IS ALWAYS RIGHT—*Hans Christian Andersen* 1054
   THE PLAGUE AT BERGAMO—*Jens Peter Jacobsen* . . . 1058
   IRENE HOLM—*Hermann Joachim Bang* 1065
   NORWAY
   FIDELITY—*Björnstjerne Björnson* 1074
   THE STORY OF A CHICKEN—*Jonas Lie* 1077
   AT THE FAIR—*Alexander Kielland* 1081
   SWEDEN
   A FUNERAL—*August Strindberg* 1086
   THE OUTLAWS—*Selma Lagerlöf* 1091
   THE FIG-TREE—*Verner Von Heidenstam* 1105
   BEAR SOLOMON—*Pelle Molin* 1106

ROUMANIA
   INTRODUCTION 1114
   A GREAT INVENTION—*I. L. Caragiale* 1114
   THE WANDERERS—*Michael Sadoveanu* 1117

GREAT STORIES
OF ALL NATIONS

ANCIENT EGYPT

Introduction

WHEN, in 1852, the first Egyptian story was discovered and deciphered, even scholars, who were presumed to know most about Ancient Egypt, were surprised. In 1864 there was found in the tomb of a Coptic monk a collection of manuscripts, among which was a very curious tale of magic. Since then many similar discoveries have been made, all purporting to prove that the Egyptians had a literature of their own.

These Egyptian stories, preserved on papyrus, date back to what is known as the Middle Kingdom, that is, the IXth Dynasty, or the thirteenth century, B.C. While some are very sober and somewhat biographic, there are other tales of a highly imaginative nature. They may be truly called the first known folk tales, for they give very faithful pictures of domestic and social life. If the stories sometimes border on the marvellous, it must be remembered that the Egyptians, in common with other early peoples, were very superstitious.

The Egyptian tales are of particular interest to us inasmuch as they are the earliest known examples of the story teller's art. It may be conjectured whether the groundwork of these stories is foreign, but the form is definitely Egyptian.

* * *

THE DOOMED PRINCE
(Anonymous: About 1600 B.C.)

THIS tale is one of the works contained in the *Harris Papyrus No. 500*, of the British Museum. It is said that the manuscript was intact when it was found, and that it was injured in Egypt, several years later, by the explosion of a powder magazine, which partially destroyed the house in which it was.

The Doomed Prince is an imaginative story, dealing with the destiny of an unfortunate prince. Destiny was born with the man, grew with him, and, it may be said, cast his entire life in the unalterable mould that the gods had prepared. The Hâthors, the Egyptian goddesses of destiny, were like the fairy godmothers of the Middle Ages.

3

The translation here used is that by Mrs. C. H. W. Johns from *Popular Tales of Ancient Egypt*, by Maspero, published in 1915 by G. P. Putnam's Sons, by whose permission it is here reprinted.

THE DOOMED PRINCE

THERE was once a king to whom no man child was born. His heart was very sad thereat; he asked for a boy from the gods of his time, and they decreed that one should be born to him. He lay with his wife during the night, and she conceived; when the months of the birth were accomplished lo, a man-child was born. When the Hâthors came to decree him a destiny, they said, "He shall die by the crocodile, or by the serpent, or indeed by the dog." When the people who were with the child heard this, they went to tell His Majesty, l.h.s., and His Majesty, l.h.s., was sad at heart thereat. His Majesty, l.h.s., had a stone house built for him on the mountain, furnished with men and all good things of the dwelling of the king, l.h.s., for the child did not go out of it, and when the child was grown, he went up on to the terrace of his house, and he perceived a greyhound who ran behind a man walking on the road. He said to his page who was with him: "What is it that runs behind the man passing along the road?" The page said to him, "It is a greyhound." The child said to him, "Let one be brought to me exactly like it." The page went to repeat this to His Majesty, l.h.s., and His Majesty, l.h.s., said, "Let a young running dog be taken to him, for fear his heart should be saddened." And lo, the greyhound was taken to him.

And after the days had passed in this manner, when the child had acquired age in all his limbs, he sent a message to his father, saying, "Come! why be like the sluggards? Although I am doomed to three grievous destinies, yet I will act according to my will. God will not do less than he has at heart." One listened to that which he spake, one gave him all kinds of weapons, and also his greyhound to follow him, and transported him to the eastern coast. One said to him, "Go where thou desirest." His greyhound was with him; he went therefore as he fancied across the country, living on the best of all the game of the country. Having arrived to fly to the prince of Naharinna, behold there was no son born to the prince of Naharinna, only a daughter. Now, he had built a house with seventy windows which were seventy cubits above the ground. He caused all the sons of the princes of the country of Kharu to be brought, and he said to them, "To him who shall reach the window of my daughter, she shall be given him for wife."

Now, many days after these things were accomplished, while the princes of Syria were engaged in their occupation of every day, the prince of Egypt, having come to pass into the place where they were, they conducted the prince to their house, they brought him to the bath, they gave provender to his horses, they did all manner of things for the prince, they perfumed him, they anointed his feet, they gave him of their loaves, they said to him, by way of conversation, "Whence comest thou, goodly youth?" He said to them, "I am the son of a soldier of the chariots of the land of Egypt. My mother died, my father took another wife. When children arrived, she hated me, and I fled before her." They pressed him in their arms, they covered him with kisses. Now, after many days had passed in this way, he said to the princes, "What are you doing here?" They said to him, "We pass our time doing this: we fly, and he who shall reach the window of the daughter of the prince of Naharinna, she shall be given him for wife." He said to them, "If it please you, I will conjure my limbs, and I will go and fly with you." They went to fly, as was their occupation of every day, and the prince stood afar off to behold, and the face of the daughter of the prince of Naharinna was turned to him. Now, after the days had passed in this manner, the prince went to fly with the sons of the rulers, and he flew, and he reached the window of the daughter of the chief of Naharinna; she kissed him, and she embraced him in all his limbs.

They went to rejoice the heart of the father of the princess, and said to him, "A man has reached the window of thy daughter." The prince questioned the messenger, saying, "The son of which of the princes?" They said to him, "The son of a soldier of chariots who comes as a fugitive from the country of Egypt to escape his step-mother when she had children." The prince of Naharinna became very angry; he said, "Shall I give my daughter to a fugitive from the land of Egypt? Let him return there!" They went to say to the prince, "Return to the place from whence thou art come." But the princess seized him, and she sware by God, saying, "By the life of Phrâ Harmakhis! if he is taken from me, I will not eat, I will not drink, I will die immediately." The messenger went to repeat all that she had said to her father, and the prince sent men to slay the young man while he was in her house. The princess said to them, "By the life of Phrâ! if he is killed, by sundown I shall be dead; I shall not spend one hour of life apart from him." They went to tell her father. The prince caused the young man to be brought with the princess. The young man was seized with terror when he came before the prince, but the prince embraced him, he covered him with kisses, he said to him, "Tell me who thou art, for behold thou art to me as a son." The young man said, "I am the son of a soldier of chariots of the country of Egypt. My mother died, and my father took another wife. She hated me, and I fled before her." The chief gave him his daughter to wife; and he gave him a house, vassals, fields, also cattle and all manner of good things.

Now, when the days had passed thus, the young man said to his wife, "I am doomed to three destinies, the crocodile, the serpent, the dog." She said to him, "Let the dog be killed that runs before thee." He said to her, "If it please thee, I will not kill my dog that I brought up when it was little." She feared for her husband greatly, greatly, and she did not let him go out alone. Now it happened that one desired to travel; the prince was escorted to the land of Egypt, to wander about the country. Now behold, the crocodile of the river came out of the river, and he came into the midst of the town where the prince was; they shut him up in a dwelling where there was a giant. The giant did not let the crocodile go out, but when the crocodile slept the giant went out for a stroll; then when the sun arose, the giant returned every day, for an interval of two months of days. And after that the days had passed in this manner, the prince remained to divert himself in his house. When the night came, the prince lay down on his bed, and sleep took possession of his limbs. His wife filled a vase with milk and placed it by her side. When a serpent came out of its hole to bite the prince, behold, his wife watched over her husband with close attention. Then the maid-servants gave milk to the serpent; it drank of it, it became drunk, it lay on its back, and the wife cut it in pieces with blows of her hatchet. Her husband was awakened, who was seized with astonishment, and she said to him, "Behold, thy god has given one of thy fates into thy hand; he will give thee the others." He presented offerings to the god, he adored him, and exalted his power all the days of his life. And after the days had passed in this manner, the prince came out to walk near his domain, and as he never came out alone, behold, his dog was behind him. His dog started in pursuit of the game, and he ran after the dog. When he reached the river, he went down the bank of the river behind his dog, and the crocodile came out and dragged him to the place where the giant was. He came out and saved the prince; then the crocodile said to the prince "Lo, I am thy destiny that pursues thee; whatever thou mayest do, thou wilt be brought back on to my path to me, thou and the giant. Now behold, I am about to let thee go; if the. . . . thou wilt know that my enchantments have triumphed, and that the giant is slain; and when thou seest that the giant is slain, thou seest thy death." And when the earth lightened, and the second day was, then came. . . .

"Thou wilt swear to me to slay the giant; if thou dost refuse this, thou shalt see death." And when the earth lightened, and a second day

[The prophecy of the crocodile is so much mutilated that I cannot guarantee its exact meaning; we can only guess that the monster set some kind of fatal dilemma before his adversary; or that the prince fulfilled a certain condition, and succeeded in overcoming the crocodile, or that he did not fulfil it, and that *he saw his death.*]

was, the dog came up and saw that his master was in the power of the crocodile. The crocodile said again, "Wilt thou swear to slay the giant?" The prince replied, "Why should I slay him who has watched over me?" The crocodile said to him, "Then shall thy destiny be accomplished. If at sundown, thou wilt not make the oath that I demand, thou shalt see thy death." The dog, having heard these words, ran to the house, and found the daughter of the prince of Naharinna in tears, for her husband had not reappeared since the day before. When she saw the dog alone, without its master, she wept aloud, and she tore her breast; but the dog seized her by her robe, and drew her to the door, as asking her to come out. She arose, she took the hatchet with which she had killed the serpent, and she followed the dog to that part of the shore where the giant was. She then hid herself in the reeds, and she neither drank nor ate; she did nothing but pray the gods for her husband. When evening arrived the crocodile said again, "Wilt thou swear to slay the giant? if not, I will take thee to the shore, and thou shalt see thy death." And he replied, "Why should I slay him who has watched over me?" Then the crocodile took him to the place where the woman was, and she came out of the reeds, and behold, as the crocodile opened its jaws, she struck it with her hatchet, and the giant threw himself on it and killed it. Then she embraced the prince, and she said to him, "Behold, thy god has given the second of thy fates into thy hands; he will give thee the third." He presented offerings to the god, he adored him, and exalted his might all the days of his life.

And after this enemies entered the country. For the sons of the princes of the country of Kharu, furious at seeing the princess in the hands of an adventurer, had assembled their foot-soldiers and their chariots, they had destroyed the army of the chief of Naharinna, and they had taken him prisoner. When they did not find the princess and her husband, they said to the old chief: "Where is thy daughter, and that son of a soldier of chariots from the land of Egypt, to whom thou hast given her as wife?" He answered them: "He is gone with her to hunt the beasts of the country—how should I know where they are?" Then they deliberated, and they said one to another: "Let us divide into small bands, and go hither and thither over the whole world, and he who shall find them, let him slay the young man, and let him do as pleases him with the woman." And they departed, some to the east, and some to the west, to the north, to the south; and those who had gone to the south reached the land of Egypt, at the same time that the young man was with the daughter of the chief of Naharinna. But the giant saw them; he hastened to the young man, and said to him: "Behold, seven sons of the princes of the country of Kharu come to seek thee. If they find thee, they will slay thee, and will do with thy wife as it pleases them. They are too many for thee to resist; flee from them, and for me, I will return to my brothers." Then the prince called his wife, he took his dog with him, and they all hid themselves in a cave of the mountain. They had been there two days and two nights when the sons of the princes of Kharu arrived with many soldiers, and they passed before the mouth of the cave without any of them perceiving the prince; but as the last of them came near, the dog went out against him and began to bark. The sons of the princes of Kharu recognized him, and they came back and went into the cave. The wife threw herself before her husband to protect him, but, behold, a lance struck her, and she fell dead before him. And the young man slew one of the princes with his sword, and the dog killed another with his teeth, but the rest struck them with their lances, and they fell to the ground unconscious. Then the princes dragged the bodies out of the cave, and left them stretched on the ground to be devoured by wild beasts and birds of prey, and they departed to rejoin their companions and divide with them the lands of the chief of Naharinna.

And, behold, when the last of the princes had departed, the young man opened his eyes, and he saw his wife stretched on the ground by his side, as dead, and the dead body of his dog. Then he trembled, and he said: "In truth, the gods fulfil immutably that which they have decreed beforehand. The Hâthors have decided, from my infancy, that I should perish by the dog, and behold, their sentence has been executed, for it is the dog which has betrayed me to mine enemies. I am ready to die, because, without these two beings, who lie beside me, life is intolerable to me." And he raised his hands to the sky, and cried: "I have not sinned against you O ye gods! Therefore grant me a happy burial in this world, and to be true of voice before the judges of Amentît." He sank down as dead, but the gods had heard his voice, the Ennead of the gods came to him, and Râ-Harmakhis said to his companions: "The doom is fulfilled; now let us give a new life to these two wedded people, for it is good to reward worthily the devotion which they have shown one to the other." And the mother of the gods approved with her head the words of Râ-Harmakhis, and she said: "Such devotion deserves very great reward." The other gods said the same; then the seven Hâthors came forward, and they said: "The doom is fulfilled; now they shall return to life." And they returned to life immediately.

ANCIENT GREECE

Introduction

IT is probable that the beginnings of Greek literature had their source in the songs and stories sung by minstrels wandering from court to court who thrilled their audiences with the traditions of their race. It is not unlikely that the epics of Homer were strung together from the many stories that had been woven about legendary heroes, and which had been recited long before they had assumed their present form.

Hesiod, who flourished about 800 B.C., was the son of a small land-holder. He employed the epic form; but no longer as merely a story of great deeds. His books were designed to instruct the common man in the pursuit of everyday life. Epic, lyric and dramatic poetry had reached perfection before prose was achieved. Herodotus, who was not only the father of history but the first great prose writer, lived from about 480 to 424 B.C. His history is interpolated with many delightful tales which make his work most readable.

Some of the other important writers of prose were Achilles Tatius, Lucian, Longus, and Heliodorus. While none of these wrote short stories as such, they nevertheless incorporated complete and unified tales in their books.

❋ ❋ ❋

HOMER
(About 1000 B.C.)

GREEK literature begins with the poems of Homer. Nothing definite is known about him, except that seven cities claim the honour of having given birth to him. The *Odyssey*, in which we find the lovely story of *Ares and Aphrodite*, presents one of a number of legends concerned with the return of the heroes from captured Troy to their homes in Greece.

The present version has been prepared by the editors. The story has no title in the original.

9

ARES AND APHRODITE

(From *The Odyssey* Book VIII)

THE minstrel twanged the chords of his lyre in prelude to his lay and sang of the love of Ares and Aphrodite, of the fair crown, how first they secretly lay together in the house of Hephæstus; and Ares gave her many gifts, and dishonoured the bed of the lord Hephæstus. But soon there came to him one with tidings, even Helius, who had seen them as they made love together. And when Hephæstus heard the bitter news, he went his way to his smithy, feeling evil in his heart, and set on the anvil block the great anvil and forged fetters which none might break or loosen, that the lovers might remain fast where they were. But when he had wrought the snare in his wrath against Ares, he went to the chamber where his bed was set, and round about the bed-posts he spread the bonds, and many too were hung aloft, from the roof-beams, cunning as spiders' webs, so that no one even of the blessed gods could see them, so craftily were they forged. And when he had strewed all his snare about the bed, he made as though he would go to Lemnos, that well-built castle, which in his eyes was far the dearest of all lands. But no blind watch did Ares of the golden rein keep, when he saw Hephæstus, famous for his craftsmanship, departing. He went his way to the house of the renowned Hephæstus, eager for the love of Cytherea of the fair crown. Now she had but lately come from her father, the mighty son of Cronos, and had sat her down. And Ares came into the house and clasped her hand and spake to her:

"Come, beloved, let us to bed and take our joy of love. For Hephæstus is no longer here, but has now departed, methinks, to Lemnos, to visit the Sintians of savage speech."

So he spake, and a happy thing it seemed to her to lie with him. So they went to the couch, and lay them down to sleep, and about them clung the subtle bonds of the crafty Hephæstus, nor could they in any manner move their limbs or raise them. Then at last they knew there was no escape. Now approaching them came the famous god of the mighty arms, having turned back ere he reached the land of Lemnos; for Helius had kept watch for him and reported. So he went to his house with a troubled heart, and stood at the gateway, and a furious rage seized him. And terribly he shouted out to all the gods:

"Father Zeus, and ye other blessed gods that endure forever, come hither that ye may see a mirthful matter and a monstrous, for Aphrodite, daughter of Zeus, contemns me because of my lameness and enamoured of treacherous Ares since he is fair and strong of limb, whereas I was born deformed. How be it there is none to reproach other than my parents—would they had never begotten me! But ye shall see where these twain have gone up into my bed and sleep together in love; and I am troubled at the sight. Yet methinks, they will not care to lie thus longer, no, not for a moment, in spite of their great love. Soon shall they both lose all desire of sleep; but the snare and the bonds shall hold them until her father returns to me all the gifts of wooing that I gave him for the hand of his wanton girl; for she is fair but restrains not her passion."

So he spake and the gods gathered to the house of the brazen floor. Poseidon came, the embracer of the earth, and Hermes came, and the Prince Apollo came. Now the goddesses abode for shame each in her own house, but the gods, the bestowers of good things, stood in the entrance; and gave way to unquenchable laughter as they beheld the guile of artful Hephæstus. And thus would one speak, glancing at his neighbour:

"Ill deeds thrive not. The slow catches the swift; even as now Hephæstus, slow though he is, has outwitted Ares albeit he is the swiftest of the gods who hold Olympus. Lame though he be, he has caught him by craft, wherefore Ares owes the fine of the adulterer."

Thus they spoke to one another. But to Hermes the lord Apollo, son of Zeus, said:

"Hermes, son of Zeus, messenger, giver of good things, wouldst thou in sooth be willing, even though enmeshed by strong bonds, to lie on a couch alongside of golden Aphrodite?"

Then the messenger, Argeïphontes, answered him: "Would that this might befall, lord Apollo, thou archer-god—that thrice as many bonds inextricable might engirdle me about and all ye gods, and goddesses might witness this, still would I lie by the side of golden Aphrodite."

So he spake and laughter arose among the deathless gods. Yet Poseidon smiled not, but implored Hephæstus, the famous craftsman, to liberate Ares; and he spoke and addressed him with winged words:

"Free him, and I promise, as thou biddest, that he shall himself pay thee all that is due in the presence of the immortal gods."

Then the famous god of the two strong arms answered him: "Demand not this of me, Poseidon, thou earth-embracer. A sorry thing to be sure of is the surety for a sorry knave. How could I keep thee in bonds among the immortal gods, if Ares were to depart and avoid both the debt and the bonds?"

Then again, Poseidon, the earth-shaker, answered him: "Hephæstus, even if Ares avoid the debt and flee, I myself will pay thee all."

Then the famous god of the strong arms answered him: "It may not be that I should say thee nay, nor were it seemly."

So saying the mighty Hephæstus loosed the bonds and the twain, when they were freed from that bond so strong, leapt up forthwith. And Ares departed to Thrace, but laughter-loving Aphrodite, went to Cyprus to

Paphos, where is her domain and fragrant altar. There the Graces bathed her and anointed her with immortal oil, such as gleams upon the deathless gods. And they clad her in lovely raiment, a wonder to behold.

* * *

HERODOTUS
(484-424 B.C.)

HERODOTUS, the Father of History, was a native of Halicarnassus in Asia Minor. He left his native city and turned traveller, in which capacity he collected a mass of material at first hand. He was the first to give artistic form to what had so far been a dry recital of events, and coloured all he wrote with the imagination of an epic poet. *Candaules' Folly* may partake more of gossip than history, but it is a rare story which modern authors have frequently retold.

The present version is a slightly modified one of the translation by B. R., first published in 1584. There is no title in the original.

CANDAULES' FOLLY
(From the *History*, Book I)

CANDAULES was passing well affectioned to his wife, in so much that for the singular love he bare her, he thought her to excel all women in the comely features of the body. And hereof, being himself fully persuaded, he fortuned to fall in talk with Gyges, son of Dascylus, one of the chief and principal men of his guard (whom also he especially favoured and not seldom employed him in matters of great weight) advancing unto him the seemly shape of his wife above mentioned. In a short space after (for the evil hap haunted him) meeting with the aforesaid Gyges, he began thus:

"My faithful servant Gyges, whereas thou seemest not to credit the large vaunts and often brags which I make of my lady's beauty and comeliness (the ears of men being much more incredulous than their eyes) behold I will so bring to pass, that thou shalt see her naked." Whereat the poor gentleman great abashed and in no wise willing to assent thereto, made answer as follows:

"My lord," quoth he, "what manner of speech is this which unadvisedly you use in persuading me to behold my lady's secrets. For a woman, you know, the more in sight, the less in shame. Who together with her garments layeth aside her modesty. Honest precepts have been devised by our elders which we ought to remember, whereof this is one;

that every man ought to behold his own. For my own part I easily believe you, that of all women in the world, there is none comparable unto her in beauty. Wherefore I beseech your Grace to have me excused, if in a case so heinous and unlawful, I somewhat refuse to obey your will."

Gyges having in this sort acquitted himself, fearing the danger that might ensue, the King began afresh to reply saying:

"My good Gyges, take heart at grace and fear not, lest either myself do go about to examine and feel thy meaning by the coloured gloss of feigned speech, or that the Queen, my lady take occasion to work thy displeasure hereby. Pull up thy spirits and leave all to me. It is I that will work the means whereby she shall never know any part of herself to have been seen by any creature living. Listen then awhile and give ear to my counsel.

"When night is come the door of the chamber wherein we lie being wide set open, I will covertly place thee behind the same: straight at my entrance thereinto, her custom is not to be long after me, directly at her coming in there standeth a bench, whereat unclothing herself, she is accustomed to lay her garments upon it, propounding her divine and angelical body, to be seen and viewed for a long space, this done as she turns from the bench to bedward, her back being toward thee, have care to slip privily out of the doors lest happily she espy thee."

The gentleman seeing himself taken in a trap, that in nowise he could escape without performance of his Lord's folly, gave his assent, and at an hour appointed stood in a readiness, whom Candaules closely brought into his chamber: and immediately after came the Queen: whom Gyges having beheld at his pleasure, when her back was turned crept out of the door, yet not so secretly, but that the Queen had a glimpse of him, and perceived, who he was.

The lady seeing the fond and undiscreet treachery of her husband made little ado, and seemed as though she had seen nothing. Albeit fully minding to be revenged of the shameless foolish fact of her espoused Lord.

For with the Lydians, and well nigh also with the rest of the Barbarians, it is a great reproach even for a man to be seen unclothed. Howbeit for the present time she kept silence, making no semblance of any displeasure.

The day following, having assembled certain of her household servants in whom she had especial affiance, Gyges was sent for, who suspecting nothing less than that his deceipt was known: speedily and with all diligence addressed him to come: being wont also at other times to come to the Queen as oft as it pleased her to send for him. Being entered the chamber, she began to assail him in these words: "Now Gyges, of two present ways I give thee free choice which of them both thou wilt take;

either to slay the King Candaules and enjoy me with the Kingdom of Lydia: or thy self presently to lease thy life. Lest in obeying thy Lord in that thou oughtest not, thou be henceforth privy to that which thou shouldest not. There is no remedy that one of you both must to the pot, either the master or the man, either he which led thee hereunto, or thyself that sawest me naked, and didst those things that were unlawful to be done."

Gyges herewith amazed began first to beseech her humbly, entreating her not to bind him to so hard a condition. Nevertheless being not able to persuade her, and seeing it necessary either to murder his Lord, or to be murdered by other; he deemed it the better choice to live himself, addressing his speech to the Queen in this wise: "My Sovereign Lady," quoth he, "since of necessity you compel me to become guilty of the blood of my King, let me hear by what means we shall set upon him." "Of a truth," said she, "our treason shall proceed from the same place from whence he betrayed my shame. The assault shall be given when he is asleep." The wretched Gentleman driven to so hard a strait, that either he must slay or be slain, made no delay but followed the Queen into her bed chamber, whom with a naked dagger in his hand, she privily placed behind the same door, from whence Gyges afterwards arising bereaved Candaules of his life and obtained both his wife and his kingdom.

❋ ❋ ❋

HELIODORUS
(3rd Century, A.D.)

HELIODORUS was born in Syria and, upon conversion to Christianity, became Bishop of Tricca in Thessaly. According to Saintsbury, he is almost the Homer of prose fiction. His *Æthiopian Romance*, the most finished and earliest full-size romance, is interspersed with tales, among which *Cnemon's Story* stands out as a model for plot and structure.

The present version is slightly modified from the translation by Thomas Underdowne, 1587. The story is without a title in the original.

CNEMON'S STORY
(From *The Æthiopica*, Book I)

MY father's name was Aristippus, he was born in Athens, one of the upper Senate, as rich as any Commoner in the City, he, after the decease of my mother, applied his mind to marry again, thinking it an unreasonable thing for me, his only son's sake, still to be of an uncertain and doubtful mind. He doth therefore bring home a little woman somewhat fine, but passing malicious, named Demeneta: as soon as she was married, she reclaimed my father all to her own lure, and made him do what she list, enticing the old man with her beauty, and was very curious in many other points, for if any woman ever knew how to make a man mad of her, she was better skilled in that art than any man would think, but especially when my father went forth she would be sorrowful, and run to him when he came home and blame him much for his long tarrying, and not stick to tell him, that she would have died if he had tarried never so little longer: At every word would she embrace him, and moist her kisses with tears, with which means my father was so bewitched that he never was well but when he either had her in his arms, or else looked upon her: above all other, she would have me in her sight, as if I had been her own son, by this means also making Aristippus to love her the better. Sometimes would she kiss me, often-times, would she wish, that she might pastime herself with me, wherewith I was well content, mistrusting nothing less, than that she went about marvelling also that she bare such a motherly affection toward me. But when she came to me more wantonly, and that her kisses were more hot than beseemed an honest woman, and her countenance passed modesty, then many things caused me to suspect her, therefore I conveyed myself away, and would nothing regard her fair words. I will let other things pass, which would be too long to tell, by what means she went about to win me, what proffers she made, how sometime she would call me her pretty boy, sometime her sweetheart, then her heir, after, her own life, last of all to these her fair names, would she add many enticements with especial consideration what I liked best: so that in grave affairs she would behave herself like my mother, but if she chose to dally, then would she manifestly declare her love. At length such a chance befell when Pillas high feast called Quinquatria was celebrated, on which the Athenians were accustomed to consecrate a ship by land, and I (for I was not then sixteen years old) had sung the usual hymn of her praise, and done other ceremonies, and rites due to the same, even as I was attired in my robes, and my crown on my head, I came home, she, as soon as she espied me, was by and by distraught of her wits and not able with policy to cover her love any longer, but for very desire ran to me, and took me in her arms and said: "Oh, my young Hippolitus, and my dear Theseus." In what case was I then think you, who even now am ashamed to tell you the same. That night my father supped in the castle, and as it often happened in such company, and public resort, he determined to lie there all night: that night she came to me, and strived to have an unlawful thing at my hand. But I with all my power withstood her, and regarded, neither her flattering words, nor fair promises, no, nor her threatenings: wherefore, fetching a sigh from the bottom of her heart, for that time departed, but within two nights after, like a mischievous queen she sought

all means possible to entrap me. And first of all, she kept her bed, and
when my father came home, and asked her how she fared, made him
answer, that she was sick, but when he was very importunate, and desirous to know what she ailed: The goodly young man (said she) that
loved me so well, son to us both, whom I, the Gods know, loved a great
deal better than you, when he perceived by certain tokens that I was great
with child by you, which thing I concealed from you (until I knew the
certainty myself) and waiting for your absence, when I counselled him
as my manner was, and persuaded him to leave haunting of harlots; and
too much drinking (which things I knew well enough, but would never
tell you of them, least thereby I should incur the cruel suspicion of a
stepmother with you) while I say I talked with him of these things alone,
no more but he and I, least he should be ashamed, I will not tell the worst,
for I am abashed so to do, nor in what manner he reviled both you and
me, lastly spurned me on the belly, and hath caused me to be in such
case as you see. As soon as he heard this, he said nothing, nor asked me
no questions, neither gave me leave to speak for myself, but persuading
himself, that she, who loved me so well, would by no means belie me,
as soon as he found me in a certain corner of the house, boxed me with
his fists, and calling his servants together, scourged me with rods, and
would not suffer me to know (which all men do) why I was cruelly
beaten. When his anger was well cooled, and he came to himself again,
I said to him, father, yet now at length I pray you tell me why I have
had thus many stripes, wherewith he was much more incensed, oh cleanly
dissembler, (said he) he would know his owne misdeed of me, he went
in again to Demeneta, but she had not content with this, devised such another sleight against me. She had a maid called Thisbe which could play
well on the virginals, and was otherwise fair, and a very proper wench.
Her, she made a stale for me and commanded her to love me, and by and
by she did so in deed, and where she refused me, oftentimes attempting
her before, now she allured me with countenance, becks, and many other
signs. Now was I somewhat proud, for that of a sudden I was become
beautiful, and in deed on a night, when she came to my bed, thought no
scorn to make her room. She liked her entertainment so well, that she
came again and continually haunted my bed. At length when I gave her
counsel to use circumspection in this matter, and take heed that her mistress found her not with me, Cnemon (said she) you seem to be too
simple, if you count it a dangerous matter, for me being a bond maybe
bought with money, to be taken abed with you, what punishment think
you her worthy that professing herself a free woman, and lawfully
married hath a husband, and yet playeth the naughtipack: Peace (quoth I)
I cannot believe that. Yes (said she) if you will, I will deliver the
adulterer to you, even in the deed doing. If you will so do (quoth I)
you shall do me a pleasure. With all my heart (said she) not only for

your own sake, who hath been injured by her before, but for mine also, who for that she hath me in jealousy, am used of her very extreemly: wherefore, if thou be a man, apprehend him. I promised her I would so do, and she for that time went her way. About three nights after, she came, and waked me out of my sleep, and told me that an adulterer was come in, and that my father upon occasion suddenly was gone into the country, and he according to appointment, was gone to bed to Demeneta, therefore it was expedient for me to haste to be revenged, and put on my sword that the knave might not escape. I did so, and taking my sword in my hand, followed those which carried a candle before and went to the bed chamber. When I came near the door, and perceived the glimmering of a candle through the slivers and the doors locked: Very angry as I was, brake up the doors, and ran in crying out, where is that same villain, the worthy lover of this chaste dame? Which when I had said, I came to the bed in mind to slay them both, but therewith my Father (O God) leapt out of the bed, and falling on his knees, before me, said: My son, have pity upon thy father, spare his white hairs that hath brought thee up. We have done thee wrong in deed, yet not so great that therefore with death thou shouldst be revenged on me. Give not so much to thy wrath, neither by thy father's blood imbrue thy hands. This with much more spake my father, humbly upon his knees desiring me to save his life. But I, as I had been stricken with a thunderbolt, stood still amazed, and looked round about after Thisbe, who had, I know not how, conveyed herself away, neither had one word to say, neither could I tell, what was best to do, and in this case my sword fell out of my hands, which Demeneta straight way caught up, and my father then out of danger, laid hands upon me, and commanded me to be bound, Demeneta in the meanwhile many ways moving, and setting him on, Did I not tell you this before (cried she) that it was best to look to the princocks: which would no doubt if time served attempt somewhat. I looked in her face and perceived her mind well enough. And he answered: You told me indeed but I believed you not. And thus was I in bonds, and he would not give me leave to tell him, how the matter was handled. As soon as it was day, he brought me bound, as I was, before the people, and strewing ashes on his head, said, I brought not up my son (yee men of Athens) to see him come to this end, but trusting he would be a staff to stay mine age upon: as soon as he was born, I brought him up gentlemanlike, and set him to school, and when I had well placed him among our kinsfolk and written him in the number of other young men, his equals and according to the laws of this city, made him one of our citizens: lastly I led not a very quiet life for his sake, he hath not only forgotten all these things but also diversely injured me, and beaten this woman, who according to our law is my second wife. At length he came to me by night with a sword in his hand, and was no further from being a parricide, but that Fortune hindered him, and by a sudden fear, his sword fell out of his hand. I flee to you and tell you thereof. And although by the law I might with mine own hand slay him, yet I would not: therefore remit I my whole cause to your discretion, thinking that I shall do better, if I punish my son, rather by public law; than private bloodshed: and therewithal he wept, so did Demeneta also, and feigned herself to be very sorrowful for my mishap, calling me an unhappy creature, as truly she might, being in danger to die before my natural time whom evil sprites had stirred against my parents. Not only did she so much outwardly lament as she testified the same with her tears, and as though her accusation had been true, with weeping she confirmed the same. And when I craved license to speak for myself, the scribe came to me, and propounded this straight question, whether I came to my father, or not, with a sword in my hand, I did (quoth I) but I will tell you how. Therewith every man cried out, and said, that I ought not to speak for myself: wherefore some judged me worthy to be stoned to death, others to be hanged, and some to be cast headlong into the dungeon. All this while that they were consulting of my punishment, I cried out, Oh my cruel stepmother, alas, for my stepmother's sake am I thus troubled, my stepmother killeth me without judgment, and many marked my words very well, and began to suspect as it was indeed, but for all that at that time, could I not be heard such was the tumult, and noise of the people. And when the voices were reckoned, those, who condemned me to die, were a thousand seven hundred, whereof, the one half would have me stoned, the other cast into the dungeon, the other, of whom was about a thousand crediting somewhat the suspicion they had conceived of my stepmother, gave sentence that I should be banished for ever, yet those prevailed, for although they were fewer than the whole number of the rest, yet forasmuch as the other voices differed, severally compared with every one alone, a thousand was the greatest number, and thus was I banished from my father's house and native country.

ANCIENT INDIA

Introduction

THE ancient literature of the Hindus known as Sanskrit, has been made known to us in comparatively modern times. In spite of a great deal of scholarship that has been devoted to its study, students have only been able to conjecture as to when certain masterpieces had been produced and who were their authors. Aside from the *Rig-Veda*, the collection of the most ancient Indian thought, we have the *Jātaka*, or Buddhist "birth-stories", and the *Panchatantra*, each of these a storehouse of stories and fairy tales, and many of which have found their way into European literature. These last two works probably date from about the fourth century B.C.

The Hindus were not without their epics. The *Mahābhārata* and the *Rāmāyana*, composed about the beginning of the Christian era, are full of splendour, romance and adventure. But the two great collections of tales are the *Brihat-kathā-manjarī*, or "great cluster of story" written by Kshemendra about 1030, and the far superior work of Somadeva done in the early part of the twelfth century, known as the *Kathā-sarit-sāgara*, or the "ocean of the streams of story." Both these works are based on a presumably lost work, Gunādhya's *Brihat-kathā*, or "great story", which is supposed to have been done about the first century of our era.

❋ ❋ ❋

THE TALKATIVE TORTOISE

(Anonymous: about 500 B.C.)

ACCORDING to T. W. Rhys Davids the Buddha was accustomed to comment on the events happening around him by telling of similar events that had occurred in his own previous births. These commentaries in the form of tales were gathered after his death into a collection of 550, called the *Jatakas* or Birthlets.

This story is reprinted from the Jataka Tales, translated by T. W. Rhys Davids, London, 1880.

THE TALKATIVE TORTOISE
(From the *Játaka*)

ONCE upon a time when Brahma-datta was reigning in Benares, the future Buddha was born in a minister's family; and when he grew up, he became the king's adviser in things temporal and spiritual.

Now this king was very talkative: while he was speaking, others had no opportunity for a word. And the future Buddha, wanting to cure this talkativeness of his, was constantly seeking for some means of doing so.

At that time there was living, in a pond in the Himalaya mountains, a tortoise. Two young hangsas (i.e. wild ducks) who came to feed there, made friends with him. And one day, when they had become very intimate with him, they said to the tortoise:

"Friend tortoise! the place where we live at the Golden Cave on Mount Beautiful in the Himalaya country is a delightful spot. Will you come there with us?"

"But how can I get there?"

"We can take you, if you can only hold your tongue, and will say nothing to anybody."

"O! that I can do. Take me with you."

"That's right," said they. And making the tortoise bite hold of a stick, they themselves took the two ends in their teeth, and flew up into the air.

Seeing him thus carried by the hangsas, some villagers called out, "Two wild ducks are carrying a tortoise along on a stick!" Whereupon the tortoise wanted to say, "If my friends choose to carry me, what is that to you, you wretched slaves!" So just as the swift flight of the wild ducks had brought him over the king's palace in the city of Benares, he let go of the stick he was biting, and falling in the open courtyard, split in two! And there arose a universal cry: "A tortoise has fallen in the open courtyard, and has split in two!"

The king, taking the future Buddha, went to the place surrounded by his courtiers, and looking at the tortoise, he asked the Bodisat: "Teacher! how comes he to be fallen here?"

The future Buddha thought to himself: "Long expecting, wishing to admonish the king, have I sought for some means of doing so. This tortoise must have made friends with the wild ducks; and they must have made him bite hold of the stick, and have flown up into the air to take him to the hills. But he, being unable to hold his tongue when he hears anyone else talk, must have wanted to say something, and let go the stick, and so must have fallen down from the sky and thus lost his life." And

saying "Truly, O King! those who are called chatter-boxes—people
whose words have no end—come to grief like this," he uttered these
verses:

> "Verily the tortoise killed himself
> Whilst uttering his voice;
> Though he was holding tight the stick,
> By a word himself he slew.

> "Behold him then, O excellent by strength!
> And speak wise words, not out of season,
> You see how, by his talking overmuch,
> The tortoise fell into this wretched plight!"

The king saw that he was himself referred to, and said: "O Teacher!
are you speaking of us?"

And the Bodisat spake openly, and said: "O great king! be it thou,
or be it any other, whoever talks beyond measure meets with some mishap like this."

And the king henceforth refrained himself and became a man of
few words.

❋ ❋ ❋

THE BUTTER-BLINDED BRAHMAN
(Anonymous: 2nd Century b.c.)

THE individual stories of *The Panchatantra,* or the Five Books,
of great and unknown antiquity, were gathered into a collection about
200 b.c. In the original, each of the five books is independent,
consisting of a framing story with numerous inserted stories, a most
familiar example of this style being the Arabian Nights. These
stories are characterised by the beautiful and witty epigrammatic
verses employed by the beasts. These ancient tales are presumed
to have been arranged by a wise and learned man desirous of reforming certain princes who showed themselves hostile to less attractive
educational methods.

The present story is from *The Panchatantra. Translated from
the Sanskrit*, by Arthur W. Ryder, 1925, and is here reprinted by
permission of the translator and the publishers, University of Chicago
Press. It has no title in the original.

THE BUTTER-BLINDED BRAHMAN
(From *The Panchatantra*)

THERE was once a Brahman named Theodore. His wife, being unchaste and a pursuer of other men, was forever making cakes with sugar and butter for a lover, and so cheating her husband.

Now one day her husband saw her and said: "My dear wife, what are you cooking? And where are you forever carrying cakes? Tell the truth."

But her impudence was equal to the occasion, and she lied to her husband: "There is a shrine of the blessèd goddess not far from here. There I have undertaken a fasting ceremony, and I take an offering including the most delicious dishes." Then she took the cakes before his very eyes and started for the shrine of the goddess, imagining that after her statement, her husband would believe it was for the goddess that his wife was daily providing delicious dishes. Having reached the shrine, she went down to the river to perform the ceremonial bath.

Meanwhile her husband arrived by another road and hid behind the statue of the goddess. And his wife entered the shrine after her bath, performed the various rites—laving, anointing, giving incense, making an offering, and so on—bowed before the goddess, and prayed: "O blessèd one, how may my husband be made blind?"

Then the Brahman behind the goddess' back spoke, disguising his natural tone: "If you never stop giving him such food as butter and butter-cakes, then he will presently go blind."

Now that loose female, deceived by the plausible revelation, gave the Brahman just that kind of food every day. One day the Brahman said: "My dear, I don't see very well." And she thought: "Thank the goddess."

Then the favored lover thought: "The Brahman has gone blind. What can he do to me?" Whereupon he came daily to the house without hesitation.

But at last the Brahman caught him as he entered, seized him by the hair, and clubbed and kicked him to such effect that he died. He also cut off his wicked wife's nose, and dismissed her.

SOMADEVA

(The early part of the 12th Century A.D.)

LITTLE is known about Somadeva, except that, because of his literary skill, we are enabled to enjoy his large collection of stories, *The Ocean of the Streams of Story*. This celebrated volume is based on an earlier collection of tales.

DEVASMITA

(From the *Katha-sarit-sagara*)

THERE is a city in the world famous under the name of Támraliptá, and in that city there was a very rich merchant named Dhanadatta. And he, being childless, assembled many Bráhmans and said to them with due respect, "Take such steps as will procure me a son soon." Then those Bráhmans said to him: "This is not at all difficult, for Bráhmans can accomplish all things in this world by means of ceremonies in accordance with the Scriptures. To give you an instance, there was in old times a king who had no sons, and he had a hundred and five wives in his harem. And by means of a sacrifice to procure a son, there was born to him a son named Jantu, who was like the rising of the new moon to the eyes of his wives. Once on a time an ant bit the boy on the thigh as he was crawling about on his knees, so that he was very unhappy and sobbed loudly. Thereupon the whole harem was full of confused lamentation, and the king himself shrieked out 'My son! my son!' like a common man. The boy was soon comforted, the ant having been removed, and the king blamed the misfortune of his only having one son as the cause of all his grief. And he asked the Bráhmans in his affliction if there was any expedient by which he might obtain a large number of children. They answered him, 'O king, there is one expedient open to you; you must slay this son and offer up all his flesh in the fire. By smelling the smell of that sacrifice all thy wives will obtain sons.' When he heard that, the king had the whole ceremony performed as they directed; and he obtained as many sons as he had wives. So we can obtain a son for you also by a burnt-offering." When they had said this to Dhanadatta, the Bráhmans, after a sacrificial fee had been promised them, performed a sacrifice: then a son was born to that merchant. That son was called Guhasena, and he gradually grew up to man's estate. Then his father Dhanadatta began to look out for a wife for him.

Then his father went with that son of his to another country, on the pretence of traffic, but really to get a daughter-in-law. There he asked an excellent merchant of the name of Dharmagupta to give him his daughter named Devasmitá for his son Guhasena. But Dharmagupta, who was tenderly attached to his daughter, did not approve of that connection, reflecting that the city of Támraliptá was very far off. But when Devasmitá beheld that Guhasena, her mind was immediately attracted by his virtues, and she was set on abandoning her relations, and so she made an assignation with him by means of a confidante, and went away from that country at night with her beloved and his father. When they reached Támraliptá they were married, and the minds of the young couple were firmly knit together by the bond of mutual love. Then Guhasena's father died, and he himself was urged by his relations to go to the country of Katáha for the purpose of trafficking; but his wife Devasmitá was too jealous to approve of that expedition, fearing exceedingly that he would be attracted by some other lady. Then, as his wife did not approve of it, and his relations kept inciting him to it, Guhasena, whose mind was firmly set on doing his duty, was bewildered. Then he went and performed a vow in the temple of the god, observing a rigid fast, trusting that the god would show him some way out of his difficulty. And his wife Devasmitá also performed a vow with him; then Siva was pleased to appear to that couple in a dream; and giving them two red lotuses the god said to them, "Take each of you one of these lotuses in your hand. And if either of you shall be unfaithful during your separation, the lotus in the hand of the other shall fade, but not otherwise." After hearing this, the two woke up, and each beheld in the hand of the other a red lotus, and it seemed as if they had got one another's hearts. Then Guhasena set out, lotus in hand, but Devasmitá remained in the house with her eyes fixed upon her flower. Guhasena for his part quickly reached the country of Katáha, and began to buy and sell jewels there. And four young merchants in that country, seeing that that unfading lotus was ever in his hand, were greatly astonished. Accordingly they got him to their house by an artifice, and made him drink a great deal of wine, and then asked him the history of the lotus, and he being intoxicated told them the whole story. Then those four young merchants, knowing that Guhasena would take a long time to complete his sales and purchases of jewels and other wares, planned together, like rascals as they were, the seduction of his wife out of curiosity, and eager to accomplish it set out quickly for Támraliptá without their departure being noticed. There they cast about for some instrument, and at last had recourse to a female ascetic of the name of Yogakarandiká, who lived in a sanctuary of Buddha; and they said to her in an affectionate manner, "Reverend madam, if our object is accomplished by your help, we will give you much wealth." She answered them: "No doubt, you young men desire some woman in this city, so tell me all about it, I will procure you the object of your desire. What woman do you desire? I will quickly procure her for you." When they heard that they said, "Procure us an interview with the wife of the merchant Guhasena named Devasmitá." When she heard that, the ascetic undertook to manage that business for them, and she gave those young merchants her own house to reside in. Then she gratified the servants at Guhasena's house with gifts of sweetmeats and other things, and afterwards entered it with her pupil. Then, as she approached the private rooms of Devasmitá, a hound, that was fastened there with a chain, would not let her come near, but opposed her entrance in the most determined way. Then Devasmitá seeing her, of her own accord sent a maid, and had her brought in, thinking to herself, "What can this person be come for?" After she had entered, the wicked ascetic gave Devasmitá her blessing, and, treating the virtuous woman with affected respect, said to her, "I have always had a desire to see you, but to-day I saw you in a dream, therefore I have come to visit you with impatient eagerness; and my mind is afflicted at beholding you separated from your husband, for beauty and youth are wasted when one is deprived of the society of one's beloved." With this and many other speeches of the same kind she tried to gain the confidence of the virtuous woman in a short interview, and then taking leave of her she returned to her own house. On the second day she took with her a piece of meat full of pepper dust, and went again to the house of Devasmitá, and there she gave that piece of meat to the hound at the door, and the hound gobbled it up, pepper and all. Then owing to the pepper dust, the tears flowed in profusion from the animal's eyes, and her nose began to run. And the cunning ascetic immediately went into the apartment of Devasmitá, who received her hospitably, and began to cry. When Devasmitá asked her why she shed tears, she said with affected reluctance: "My friend, look at this hound weeping outside here. This creature recognised me to-day as having been its companion in a former birth, and began to weep; for that reason my tears gushed through pity." When she heard that, and saw that hound outside apparently weeping, Devasmitá thought for a moment to herself, "What can be the meaning of this wonderful sight?" Then the ascetic said to her, "My daughter, in a former birth, I and that hound were the two wives of a certain Bráhman. And our husband frequently went about to other countries on embassies by order of the king. Now while he was away from home, I lived at my good will and pleasure, and so did not cheat the elements, of which I was composed, and my senses, of their lawful enjoyment. For considerate treatment of the elements and senses is held to be the highest duty. Therefore I have been born in this birth with a recollection of my former existence. But she, in her former life, through ignorance, confined all her attention to the preservation of her character, therefore she has been degraded and born again as one of the canine race, however, she too remembers her former birth." The wise Devasmitá said to herself, "This is a novel conception of duty; no doubt this woman has laid a treacherous snare

for me"; and so she said to her, "Reverend lady, for this long time I
have been ignorant of this duty, so procure me an interview with some
charming man." Then the ascetic said, "There are residing here some
young merchants that have come from another country, so I will bring
them to you." When she had said this, the ascetic returned home delighted, and Devasmitá of her own accord said to her maids: "No doubt
those scoundrelly young merchants, whoever they may be, have seen that
unfading lotus in the hand of my husband, and have on some occasion
or other, when he was drinking wine, asked him out of curiosity to tell
the whole story of it, and have now come here from that island to
deceive me, and this wicked ascetic is employed by them. So bring
quickly some wine mixed with Datura, and when you have brought it,
have a dog's foot of iron made as quickly as possible." When Devasmitá
had given these orders, the maids executed them faithfully, and one of
the maids, by her orders, dressed herself up to resemble her mistress. The
ascetic for her part chose out of the party of four merchants (each of
whom in his eagerness said—"Let me go first"—) one individual, and
brought him with her. And concealing him in the dress of her pupil,
she introduced him in the evening into the house of Devasmitá, and coming out, disappeared. Then that maid, who was disguised as Devasmitá,
courteously persuaded the young merchant to drink some of that wine
drugged with Datura. That liquor, like his own immodesty, robbed him
of his senses, and then the maids took away his clothes and other equip-
ments and left him stark naked; then they branded him on the forehead
with the mark of a dog's foot, and during the night took him and pushed
him into a ditch full of filth. Then he recovered consciousness in the last
watch of the night, and found himself plunged in a ditch, as it were the
hell *Avíchi* assigned to him by his sins. Then he got up and washed
himself and went to the house of the female ascetic, in a state of misery,
feeling with his fingers the mark on his forehead. And when he got
there, he told his friends that he had been robbed on the way, in order
that he might not be the only person made ridiculous. And the next
morning he sat with a cloth wrapped round his branded forehead, giving
as an excuse that he had a headache from keeping awake so long, and
drinking too much. In the same way the next young merchant was maltreated, when he got to the house of Devasmitá, and when he returned
home stripped, he said, "I put on my ornaments there, and as I was coming out I was plundered by robbers." In the morning he also, on the plea
of a headache, put a wrapper on to cover his branded forehead.

　　In the same way all the four young merchants suffered in turn brand-
ing and other humiliating treatment, though they concealed the fact.
And they went away from the place, without revealing to the female
Buddhist ascetic the ill-treatment they had experienced, hoping that she
would suffer in a similar way. On the next day the ascetic went with her

disciple to the house of Devasmitá, much delighted at having accomplished what she undertook to do. Then Devasmitá received her courteously, and made her drink wine drugged with Datura, offered as a sign of gratitude. When she and her disciple were intoxicated with it, that chaste wife cut off their ears and noses, and flung them also into a filthy pool. And being distressed by the thought that perhaps these young merchants might go and slay her husband, she told the whole circumstance to her mother-in-law. Then her mother-in-law said to her, "My daughter, you have acted nobly, but possibly some misfortune may happen to my son in consequence of what you have done."

So the wise Devasmitá forthwith put on the dress of a merchant. Then she embarked on a ship, on the pretence of a mercantile expedition, and came to the country of Katáha where her husband was. And when she arrived there, she saw that husband of hers, Guhasena, in the midst of a circle of merchants, like consolation in external bodily form. He seeing her afar off in the dress of a man, as it were, drank her in with his eyes, and thought to himself, "Who may this merchant be that looks so like my beloved wife?" So Devasmitá went and represented to the king that she had a petition to make, and asked him to assemble all his subjects. Then the king full of curiosity assembled all the citizens, and said to that lady disguised as a merchant, "What is your petition?" Then Devasmitá said, "There are residing here in your midst four slaves of mine who have escaped, let the king make them over to me." Then the king said to her, "All the citizens are present here, so look at everyone in order to recognise him, and take those slaves of yours." Then she seized upon the four young merchants, whom she had before treated in such a humiliating way in her house, and who had wrappers bound round their heads. Then the merchants, who were there, flew in a passion, and said to her, "These are the sons of distinguished merchants, how then can they be your slaves?" Then she answered them, "If you do not believe what I say, examine their foreheads which I marked with a dog's foot." They consented, and removing the head-wrappers of these four, they all beheld the dog's foot on their foreheads. Then all the merchants were abashed, and the king, being astonished, himself asked Devasmitá what all this meant. She told the whole story, and all the people burst out laughing, and the king said to the lady, "They are your slaves by the best of titles." Then the other merchants paid a large sum of money to that chaste wife, to redeem those four from slavery, and a fine to the king's treasury. Devasmitá received that money, and recovered her husband, and being honoured by all good men, returned then to her own city Támraliptá, and she was never afterwards separated from her beloved.

BIBLICAL LITERATURE

Introduction

WHILE it is strictly outside the province of this volume to consider the inspirational value of the Bible, we can not ignore the fact that for sheer beauty, poetry and wisdom—not to mention historicity—it is unsurpassed by any other single volume. Because of its universal appeal, primarily created by churches and their missionaries, the Bible has permeated the very structure of our language and has even influenced our thoughts. The masters of literary style have sedulously studied the Bible for it was and still is the intellectual and poetic treasurehouse.

The *Old Testament*, the basis of Hebrew literature and the Jewish religion, consists of thirty-nine books. While some of these are at times a trifle dull, such as the lengthy genealogies, we are compensated by such tales as those about the tragic Samson, the heroic Deborah; or the Book of Ruth, with its motive of homesickness exercising a universal appeal.

The *New Testament* concerns itself with the biography of Jesus. Among the gospels are to be found the parables which, while they do not possess the form of the short story, are pregnant with rare beauty. The *Talmud* is a collection of laws held sacred by orthodox Jews and serves as a commentary on the *Old Testament*. It contains a great many tales of a moral nature, which were no doubt used to illustrate a theological contention.

❊ ❊ ❊

THE BOOK OF ESTHER
(From the *Old Testament*)

THE *Book of Esther* may be justifiably considered as an early example of historical romance. At any rate we have here all the elements for such a romance, namely, plot and counter-plot with plenty of bloodshed, and an exceedingly beautiful and witty woman whose appeal to her royal husband prevents a massacre of her people. The narrative is remarkable for its swift and succinct literary style.

Only the first eight chapters are used here, and the version is that of the King James translation except that the verses have been merged into paragraphs.

ESTHER

NOW it came to pass in the days of Ahasuerus, (this is Ahasuerus which reigned, from India even unto Ethiopia, over an hundred and seven and twenty provinces;) that in those days, when the king Ahasuerus sat on the throne of his kingdom, which was in Shushan the palace, in the third year of his reign, he made a feast unto all his princes and his servants; the power of Persia and Media, the nobles and princes of the provinces, being before him: when he shewed the riches of his glorious kingdom and the honour of his excellent majesty many days, even an hundred and fourscore days. And when these days were expired, the king made a feast unto all the people that were present in Shushan the palace, both unto great and small, seven days, in the court of the garden of the king's palace; where were white, green, and blue hangings, fastened with cords of fine linen and purple to silver rings and pillars of marble: the beds were of gold and silver, upon a pavement of red, and blue, and white, and black, marble. And they gave them drink in vessels of gold, (the vessels being diverse one from another,) and royal wine in abundance, according to the state of the king. And the drinking was according to the law; none did compel: for so the king had appointed to all the officers of his house, that they should do according to every man's pleasure. Also Vashti the queen made a feast for the women in the royal house which belonged to king Ahasuerus.

On the seventh day, when the heart of the king was merry with wine, he commanded Mehuman, Biztha, Harbona, Bigtha, and Abagtha, Zethar, and Carcas, the seven chamberlains that served in the presence of Ahasuerus the king, to bring Vashti the queen before the king with the crown royal, to shew the people and the princes her beauty: for she was fair to look on. But the queen Vashti refused to come at the king's commandment by his chamberlains: therefore was the king very wroth, and his anger burned in him.

Then the king said to the wise men, which knew the times, (for so was the king's manner toward all that knew law and judgment: and the next unto him was Carshena, Shethar, Admatha, Tarshish, Meres, Marsena, and Memucan, the seven princes of Persia and Media, which saw the king's face, and which sat the first in the kingdom;) "What shall we do unto the queen Vashti according to law, because she hath not performed the commandment of the king Ahasuerus by the chamberlains?"

And Memucan answered before the king and the princes:—"Vashti the queen hath not done wrong to the king only, but also to all the princes, and to all the people that are in all the provinces of the king Ahasuerus. For this deed of the queen shall come abroad unto all women, so that they shall despise their husbands in their eyes, when it shall be reported,

The king Ahasuerus commanded Vashti the queen to be brought in before him, but she came not. Likewise shall the ladies of Persia and Media say this day unto all the king's princes, which have heard of the deed of the queen. Thus shall there arise much contempt and wrath. If it please the king, let there go a royal commandment from him, and let it be written among the laws of the Persians and the Medes, that it be not altered, That Vashti come no more before king Ahasuerus; and let the king give her royal estate unto another that is better than she. And when the king's decree which he shall make shall be published throughout all his empire, (for it is great,) all the wives shall give to their husbands honour, both to great and small."

And the saying pleased the king and the princes; and the king did according to the word of Memucan: for he sent letters into all the king's provinces, into every province according to the writing thereof, and to every people after their language, that every man should bear rule in his own house, and that it should be published according to the language of every people.

After these things, when the wrath of king Ahasuerus was appeased, he remembered Vashti, and what she had done, and what was decreed against her. Then said the king's servants that ministered unto him:— "Let there be fair young virgins sought for the king: and let the king appoint officers in all the provinces of his kingdom, that they may gather together all the fair young virgins unto Shushan the palace, to the house of the women, unto the custody of Hegai the king's chamberlain, keeper of the women; and let their things for purification be given them: and let the maiden which pleaseth the king be queen instead of Vashti." And the thing pleased the king; and he did so.

Now in Shushan the palace there was a certain Jew, whose name was Mordecai, the son of Jair, the son of Shimei, the son of Kish, a Benjamite; who had been carried away from Jerusalem with the captivity which had been carried away with Jeconiah king of Judah, whom Nebuchadnezzar the king of Babylon had carried away. And he brought up Hadassah, that is, Esther, his uncle's daughter: for she had neither father nor mother, and the maid was fair and beautiful; whom Mordecai, when her father and mother were dead, took for his own daughter.

So it came to pass, when the king's commandment and his decree was heard, and when many maidens were gathered together unto Shushan the palace, to the custody of Hegai, that Esther was brought also unto the king's house, to the custody of Hegai, keeper of the women. And the maiden pleased him, and she obtained kindness of him; and he speedily gave her things for purification, with her portions, and the seven maidens, which were meet to be given her, out of the king's house: and he preferred her and her maids unto the best place of the house of the women. Esther had not shewed her people nor her kindred: for Mordecai had charged her that she should not shew it. And Mordecai walked every day before the court of the women's house, to know how Esther did, and what should become of her.

Now when every maid's turn was come to go in to king Ahasuerus, after that she had been twelve months, according to the manner of the women, (for so were the days of their purifications accomplished, to wit, six months with oil of myrrh, and six months with sweet odours, and with other things for the purifying of the women;) then thus came every maiden unto the king; whatsoever she desired was given her to go with her out of the house of the women unto the king's house. In the evening she went, and on the morrow she returned into the second house of the women, to the custody of Shaashgaz, the king's chamberlain, which kept the concubines: she came in unto the king no more, except the king delighted in her, and that she were called by name.

Now when the turn of Esther, the daughter of Abihail the uncle of Mordecai, who had taken her for his daughter, was come to go in unto the king, she required nothing but what Hegai the king's chamberlain, the keeper of the women, appointed. And Esther obtained favour in the sight of all them that looked upon her. So Esther was taken unto king Ahasuerus into his house royal in the tenth month, which is the month Tebeth, in the seventh year of his reign. And the king loved Esther above all the women, and she obtained grace and favour in his sight more than all the virgins; so that he set the royal crown upon her head, and made her queen instead of Vashti. Then the king made a great feast unto all his princes and his servants, even Esther's feast; and he made a release to the provinces, and gave gifts, according to the state of the king. And when the virgins were gathered together the second time, then Mordecai sat in the king's gate. Esther had not yet shewed her kindred nor her people; as Mordecai had charged her: for Esther did the commandment of Mordecai, like as when she was brought up with him.

In those days, while Mordecai sat in the king's gate, two of the king's chamberlains, Bigthan and Teresh, of those which kept the door, were wroth, and sought to lay hand on the king Ahasuerus. And the thing was known to Mordecai, who told it unto Esther the queen; and Esther certified the king thereof in Mordecai's name. And when inquisition was made of the matter, it was found out; therefore they were both hanged on a tree: and it was written in the book of the chronicles before the king.

After these things did king Ahasuerus promote Haman the son of Hammedatha the Agagite, and advanced him, and set his seat above all the princes that were with him. And all the king's servants, that were in the king's gate, bowed, and reverenced Haman: for the king had so commanded concerning him. But Mordecai bowed not, nor did him reverence. Then the king's servants, which were in the king's gate, said

unto Mordecai:—"Why transgressest thou the king's commandment?"
Now it came to pass, when they spake daily unto him, and he hearkened
not unto them, that they told Haman, to see whether Mordecai's matters
would stand: for he had told them that he was a Jew. And when
Haman saw that Mordecai bowed not, nor did him reverence, then was
Haman full of wrath. And he thought scorn to lay hands on Mordecai
alone; for they had shewed him the people of Mordecai: wherefore
Haman sought to destroy all the Jews that were throughout the whole
kingdom of Ahasuerus, even the people of Mordecai.

In the first month, that is, the month Nisan, in the twelfth year of
king Ahasuerus, they cast Pur, that is, the lot, before Haman from day
to day, and from month to month, to the twelfth month, that is, the
month Adar. And Haman said unto king Ahasuerus:—"There is a certain people scattered abroad and dispersed among the people in all the
provinces of thy kingdom; and their laws are diverse from all people;
neither keep they the king's laws: therefore it is not for the king's profit
to suffer them. If it please the king, let it be written that they may be
destroyed: and I will pay ten thousand talents of silver to the hands of
those that have the charge of the business, to bring it into the king's treasuries." And the king took his ring from his hand, and gave it unto
Haman the son of Hammedatha the Agagite, the Jews' enemy. And the
king said unto Haman:—"The silver is given to thee, the people also,
to do with them as it seemeth good to thee."

Then were the king's scribes called on the thirteenth day of the first
month, and there was written according to all that Haman had commanded
unto the king's lieutenants, and to the governors that were over every
province, and to the rulers of every people of every province according
to the writing thereof, and to every people after their language; in the
name of king Ahasuerus was it written, and sealed with the king's ring.
And the letters were sent by posts into all the king's provinces, to destroy,
to kill, and to cause to perish, all Jews, both young and old, little children
and women, in one day, even upon the thirteenth day of the twelfth
month, which is the month Adar, and to take the spoil of them for a prey.
The copy of the writing for a commandment to be given in every province was published unto all people, that they should be ready against that
day. The posts went out, being hastened by the king's commandment,
and the decree was given in Shushan the palace. And the king and
Haman sat down to drink; but the city Shushan was perplexed.

When Mordecai perceived all that was done, Mordecai rent his
clothes, and put on sackcloth with ashes, and went out into the midst of
the city, and cried with a loud and a bitter cry; and came even before the
king's gate: for none might enter into the king's gate clothed with sackcloth. And in every province, whithersoever the king's commandment
and his decree came, there was great mourning among the Jews, and

fasting, and weeping, and wailing; and many lay in sackcloth and ashes. And Esther's maids and her chamberlains came and told it her. Then was the queen exceedingly grieved; and she sent raiment to clothe Mordecai, and to take away his sackcloth from him: but he received it not. Then called Esther for Hatach, one of the king's chamberlains, whom he had appointed to attend upon her, and gave him a commandment to Mordecai, to know what it was, and why it was. So Hatach went forth to Mordecai unto the street of the city, which was before the king's gate. And Mordecai told him of all that had happened unto him, and of the sum of the money that Haman had promised to pay to the king's treasuries for the Jews, to destroy them. Also he gave him the copy of the writing of the decree that was given at Shushan to destroy them, to shew it unto Esther, and to declare it unto her, and to charge her that she should go in unto the king, to make supplication unto him, and to make request before him for her people. And Hatach came and told Esther the words of Mordecai.

Again Esther spake unto Hatach, and gave him commandment unto Mordecai:—"All the king's servants, and the people of the king's provinces, do know, that whosoever, whether man or woman, shall come unto the king into the inner court, who is not called, there is one law of his to put him to death, except such to whom the king shall hold out the golden sceptre, that he may live: but I have not been called to come in unto the king these thirty days." And they told to Mordecai Esther's words. Then Mordecai commanded to answer Esther:—"Think not with thyself that thou shalt escape in the king's house, more than all the Jews. For if thou altogether holdest thy peace at this time, then shall there enlargement and deliverance arise to the Jews from another place; but thou and thy father's house shall be destroyed: and who knoweth whether thou art not come to the kingdom for such a time as this?"

Then Esther bade them return Mordecai this answer:—"Go, gather together all the Jews that are present in Shushan, and fast ye for me, and neither eat nor drink three days, night or day: I also and my maidens will fast likewise; and so will I go in unto the king, which is not according to the law: and if I perish, I perish." So Mordecai went his way, and did according to all that Esther had commanded him.

Now it came to pass on the third day, that Esther put on her royal apparel, and stood in the inner court of the king's house, over against the king's house: and the king sat upon his royal throne in the royal house, over against the gate of the house. And it was so, when the king saw Esther the queen standing in the court, that she obtained favour in his sight: and the king held out to Esther the golden sceptre that was in his hand. So Esther drew near, and touched the top of the sceptre. Then said the king unto her:—"What wilt thou, queen Esther? and what is thy request? it shall be even given thee to the half of the kingdom." And

Esther answered:—"If it seem good unto the king, let the king and Haman come this day unto the banquet that I have prepared for him." Then the king said:—"Cause Haman to make haste, that he may do as Esther hath said." So the king and Haman came to the banquet that Esther had prepared.

And the king said unto Esther at the banquet of wine:—"What is thy petition? and it shall be granted thee: and what is thy request? even to the half of the kingdom it shall be performed." Then answered Esther, and said:—"My petition and my request is: if I have found favour in the sight of the king, and if it please the king to grant my petition, and to perform my request, let the king and Haman come to the banquet that I shall prepare for them, and I will do to-morrow as the king hath said."

Then went Haman forth that day joyful and with a glad heart: but when Haman saw Mordecai in the king's gate, that he stood not up, nor moved for him, he was full of indignation against Mordecai. Nevertheless Haman refrained himself: and when he came home, he sent and called for his friends, and Zeresh his wife. And Haman told them of the glory of his riches, and the multitude of his children, and all the things wherein the king had promoted him, and how he had advanced him above the princes and servants of the king. Haman said moreover:—"Yea, Esther the queen did let no man come in with the king unto the banquet that she had prepared but myself; and to-morrow am I invited unto her also with the king. Yet all this availeth me nothing, so long as I see Mordecai the Jew sitting at the king's gate." Then said Zeresh his wife and all his friends unto him:—"Let a gallows be made of fifty cubits high, and to-morrow speak thou unto the king that Mordecai may be hanged thereon: then go thou in merrily with the king unto the banquet." And the thing pleased Haman; and he caused the gallows to be made.

On that night could not the king sleep, and he commanded to bring the book of records of the chronicles; and they were read before the king. And it was found written, that Mordecai had told of Bigthana and Teresh, two of the king's chamberlains, the keepers of the door, who sought to lay hand on the king Ahasuerus. And the king said:—"What honour and dignity hath been done to Mordecai for this?" Then said the king's servants that ministered unto him:—"There is nothing done for him." And the king said:—"Who is in the court?" Now Haman was come into the outward court of the king's house, to speak unto the king to hang Mordecai on the gallows that he had prepared for him. And the king's servants said unto him:—"Behold, Haman standeth in the court." And the king said:—"Let him come in." So Haman came in. And the king said unto him:—"What shall be done unto the man whom the king delighteth to honour?" Now Haman thought in his heart:— "To whom would the king delight to do honour more than to myself?"

And Haman answered the king:—"For the man whom the king delighteth to honour, let the royal apparel be brought which the king used to wear, and the horse that the king rideth upon, and the crown royal which is set upon his head: and let this apparel and horse be delivered to the hand of one of the king's most noble princes, that they may array the man withal whom the king delighteth to honour, and bring him on horseback through the street of the city, and proclaim before him, Thus shall it be done to the man whom the king delighteth to honour."

Then the king said to Haman:—"Make haste, and take the apparel and the horse, as thou hast said, and do even so to Mordecai the Jew, that sitteth at the king's gate: let nothing fail of all that thou hast spoken." Then took Haman the apparel and the horse, and arrayed Mordecai, and brought him on horseback through the street of the city, and proclaimed before him:—"Thus shall it be done unto the man whom the king delighteth to honour."

And Mordecai came again to the king's gate. But Haman hasted to his house mourning, and having his head covered. And Haman told Zeresh his wife and all his friends every thing that had befallen him. Then said his wise men and Zeresh his wife unto him:—"If Mordecai be of the seed of the Jews, before whom thou hast begun to fall, thou shalt not prevail against him, but shalt surely fall before him." And while they were yet talking with him, came the king's chamberlains, and hasted to bring Haman unto the banquet that Esther had prepared.

So the king and Haman came to banquet with Esther the queen. And the king said again unto Esther on the second day at the banquet of wine:—"What is thy petition, queen Esther? and it shall be granted thee: and what is thy request? and it shall be performed, even to the half of the kingdom." Then Esther the queen answered and said:—"If I have found favour in thy sight, O king, and if it pleases the king, let my life be given me at my petition, and my people at my request: for we are sold, I and my people, to be destroyed, to be slain, and to perish. But if we had been sold for bondmen and bondwomen, I had held my tongue, although the adversary could not have compensated for the king's damage."

Then the king Ahasuerus answered and said unto Esther the queen: —"Who is he, and where is he, that durst presume in his heart to do so?" And Esther said:—"The adversary and enemy is this wicked Haman." Then Haman was afraid before the king and the queen. And the king arising from the banquet of wine in his wrath went into the palace garden: and Haman stood up to make request for his life to Esther the queen; for he saw that there was evil determined against him by the king. Then the king returned out of the palace garden into the place of the banquet of wine; and Haman was fallen upon the bed whereon Esther was. Then said the king:—"Will he force the queen also before me in the house?" As the word went out of the king's mouth, they covered Haman's face. And Harbonah, one of the chamberlains, said before the king:—"Behold also, the gallows fifty cubits high, which Haman had made for Mordecai, who had spoken good for the king, standeth in the house of Haman." Then the king said:— "Hang him thereon." So they hanged Haman on the gallows that he had prepared for Mordecai. Then was the king's wrath pacified.

On that day did the king Ahasuerus give the house of Haman the Jews' enemy unto Esther the queen. And Mordecai came before the king; for Esther had told what he was unto her. And the king took off his ring, which he had taken from Haman, and gave it unto Mordecai. And Esther set Mordecai over the house of Haman. And Esther spake yet again before the king, and fell down at his feet, and besought him with tears to put away the mischief of Haman the Agagite, and his device that he had devised against the Jews. Then the king held out the golden sceptre toward Esther. So Esther arose, and stood before the king, and said:—"If it please the king, and if I have found favour in his sight, and the thing seem right before the king, and I be pleasing in his eyes, let it be written to reverse the letters devised by Haman the son of Hammedatha the Agagite, which he wrote to destroy the Jews which are in all the king's provinces: for how can I endure to see the evil that shall come unto my people? or how can I endure to see the destruction of my kindred?"

Then the king Ahasuerus said unto Esther the queen and to Mordecai the Jew:—"Behold, I have given Esther the house of Haman, and him they have hanged upon the gallows, because he laid his hand upon the Jews. Write ye also for the Jews, as it liketh you, in the king's name, and seal it with the king's ring: for the writing which is written in the king's name, and sealed with the king's ring, may no man reverse."

Then were the king's scribes called at that time in the third month, that is, the month Sivan, on the three and twentieth day thereof; and it was written according to all that Mordecai commanded unto the Jews, and to the lieutenants, and the deputies and rulers of the provinces which are from India unto Ethiopia, an hundred twenty and seven provinces, unto every province according to the writing thereof, and unto every people after their language, and to the Jews according to their writing, and according to their language. And he wrote in the king Ahasuerus' name, and sealed it with the king's ring, and sent letters by posts on horseback, and riders on mules, camels, and young dromedaries: wherein the king granted the Jews which were in every city to gather themselves together, and to stand for their life, to destroy, to slay, and to cause to perish, all the power of the people and province that would assault them, both little ones and women, and to take the spoil of them for a prey, upon one day in all the provinces of king Ahasuerus, namely, upon the thirteenth day of the twelfth month, which is the month Adar. The copy of the writing for a commandment to be given in every province was published unto all people, and that the Jews should be ready against that day to avenge themselves on their enemies. So the posts that rode upon mules and camels went out, being hastened and pressed on by the king's commandment. And the decree was given at Shushan the palace.

And Mordecai went out from the presence of the king in royal apparel of blue and white, and with a great crown of gold, and with a garment of fine linen and purple: and the city of Shushan rejoiced and was glad. The Jews had light, and gladness, and joy, and honour. And in every province, and in every city, whithersoever the king's commandment and his decree came, the Jews had joy and gladness, a feast and a good day. And many of the people of the land became Jews; for the fear of the Jews fell upon them.

* * *

BEL AND THE DRAGON
(From *The Apocrypha*)

BEL and the Dragon occurred originally in the Book of Daniel, the most adventurous and most popular of the major prophets. This perfect little story is an episode in the life of Daniel who had won a high place in Nebuchadnezzar's government. It shows how through his wit, Daniel was able not only to maintain his religious views, but to convert the King to monotheism.

BEL AND THE DRAGON

AND king Astyages was gathered to his fathers, and Cyrus of Persia received his kingdom. And Daniel conversed with the king, and was honoured above all his friends. Now the Babylonians had an idol, called Bel, and there were spent upon him every day twelve great measures of fine flour, and forty sheep, and six vessels of wine. And the king worshipped it, and went daily to adore it: but Daniel worshipped his own God.

And the king said unto him:—"Why dost not thou worship Bel?" Who answered and said:—"Because I may not worship idols made with hands, but the living God, who hath created the heaven and the earth, and hath sovereignty over all flesh." Then said the king unto him:— "Thinkest thou not that Bel is a living god? seest thou not how much he eateth and drinketh every day?" Then Daniel smiled, and said:—"O king, be not deceived: for this is but clay within, and brass without, and did never eat or drink any thing." So the king was wroth, and called for his priests, and said unto them:—"If ye tell me not who this is that devoureth these expences, ye shall die. But if ye can certify me that Bel devoureth them, then Daniel shall die: for he hath spoken blasphemy against Bel." And Daniel said unto the king:—"Let it be according to thy word."

Now the priests of Bel were threescore and ten, beside their wives and children. And the king went with Daniel into the temple of Bel. So Bel's priests said:—"Lo, we go out: but thou, O king, set on the meat, and make ready the wine, and shut the door fast, and seal it with thine own signet; and to-morrow when thou comest in, if thou findest not that Bel hath eaten up all, we will suffer death: or else Daniel, that speaketh falsely against us." And they little regarded it: for under the table they had made a privy entrance, whereby they entered in continually, and consumed those things. So when they were gone forth, the king set meats before Bel. Now Daniel had commanded his servants to bring ashes, and those they strewed throughout all the temple in the presence of the king alone: then went they out, and shut the door, and sealed it with the king's signet, and so departed.

Now in the night came the priests with their wives and children, as they were wont to do, and did eat and drink up all. In the morning betime the king arose, and Daniel with him. And the king said:— "Daniel, are the seals whole?" And he said:—"Yea, O king, they be whole." And as soon as he opened the door, the king looked upon the table, and cried with a loud voice:—"Great art thou, O Bel, and with thee is no deceit at all." Then laughed Daniel, and held the king that he should not go in, and said:—"Behold now the pavement, and mark well whose footsteps are these." And the king said:—"I see the footsteps of men, women, and children." And then the king was angry, and took the priests with their wives and children, who shewed him the privy doors, where they came in, and consumed such things as were upon the table. Therefore the king slew them, and delivered Bel into Daniel's power, who destroyed him and his temple.

And in that same place there was a great dragon, which they of Babylon worshipped. And the king said unto Daniel:—"Wilt thou also say that this is of brass? lo, he liveth, he eateth and drinketh; thou canst not say that he is no living god: therefore worship him." Then said Daniel unto the king:—"I will worship the Lord my God: for He is the living God. But give me leave, O king, and I shall slay this dragon without sword or staff." The king said:—"I give thee leave." Then Daniel took pitch, and fat, and hair, and did seethe them together, and made lumps thereof: this he put in the dragon's mouth, and so the dragon burst in sunder: and Daniel said:—"Lo, these are the gods ye worship."

When they of Babylon heard that, they took great indignation, and conspired against the king, saying:—"The king is become a Jew, and he hath destroyed Bel, he hath slain the dragon, and put the priests to death." So they came to the king, and said:—"Deliver us Daniel, or else we will destroy thee and thine house." Now when the king saw that they pressed him sore, being constrained, he delivered Daniel unto them: who cast him into the lion's den: where he was six days. And in the den there were seven lions, and they had given them every day two carcases, and two sheep: which then were not given to them, to the intent they might devour Daniel.

Now there was in Jewry a prophet, called Habakkuk, who had made pottage, and had broken bread in a bowl, and was going into the field, for to bring it to the reapers. But the angel of the Lord said unto Habakkuk:—"Go, carry the dinner that thou hast into Babylon unto Daniel, who is in the lions' den." And Habakkuk said:—"Lord, I never saw Babylon; neither do I know where the den is." Then the angel of the Lord took him by the crown, and bare him by the hair of his head, and through the vehemency of his spirit set him in Babylon over the den. And Habakkuk cried, saying:—"O Daniel, Daniel, take the dinner which God hath sent thee." And Daniel said:—"Thou hast remembered me, O God: neither hast Thou forsaken them that seek Thee and love Thee." So Daniel arose, and did eat: and the angel of the Lord set Habukkuk in his own place again immediately.

Upon the seventh day the king went to bewail Daniel: and when he came to the den, he looked in, and, behold, Daniel was sitting. Then ›cried the king with a loud voice, saying:—"Great art Thou, O Lord God of Daniel, and there is none other beside Thee." And he drew him out, and cast those that were the cause of his destruction into the den: and they were devoured in a moment before his face.

ANCIENT ROME

Introduction

THE Greek influence was largely the determining factor for Roman literature. Some of the first teachers the Romans had were Greeks that had been taken prisoners after the capture of southern Italy. During the first period of Roman literature we first see the growth of poetry, drama and history; and since we are essentially concerned with the short story, we need not go into the works of Ennius, Plautus, Terrence, Livy and the many others who contributed to the development of Latin literature.

In the Augustan period we find some of the greatest poets, Virgil, Horace and Ovid. The latter was not only a brilliant poet, but he also had the power of continuous narrative, which is best seen in his *Metamorphoses*. In this collection of myths we find some delightful stories.

The *Satyricon* of Petronius is the first sustained prose work produced in Latin. It has a genuine literary quality, is most sincere in its representation and is most penetrating in its satire. The period that follows is somewhat more sober and drier. Pliny the Elder writes his *Natural History*, Statius his *Epics*, and Martial his *Epigrams*. It is in these *Epigrams* that the age of Domitian is forever preserved for us. Here we meet the familiar personages as they go about their daily life. Later, under Trajan, were produced the famous *Histories* of Tacitus and the *Satires* of Juvenal. Both of these authors have summed up in their respective works the experiences of the Roman world from the accession of Tiberius to the death of Domitian. Though Pliny the Younger did not contradict the indignation and the scorn found in Tacitus and Juvenal, he nevertheless toned down their tragic implication in his *Letters*.

After the death of Juvenal, it may be said that Latin literature, with the exception of Suetonius and Apuleius, began rapidly to decline.

❊ ❊ ❊

OVID

(43 B.C.-18A.D.?)

OVID, born in the eastern part of central Italy, began his career as a brilliant and successful poet, and was forced, by imperial command, to spend the later part of his life in exile. *Metamorphoses* is among his best known titles. In this work Ovid successfully completed the task of retelling the stories of Greek mythology. Pyramus and Thisbe is one of the lovely stories in this volume.

The present version is based upon a metrical translation.

PYRAMUS AND THISBE

(From *Metamorphoses*, Book 4)

PYRAMUS, a handsome youth, and Thisbe, a most beautiful maiden, dwelt in Babylon which had been surrounded with walls of brick by Semiramis. Being neighbours, they became acquainted. This developed into friendship and soon ripened to a love, which would have been crowned by marriage, had not their parents forbade it. But they could not hinder the fierce flames which burned young Pyramus and which were returned by grateful Thisbe. They dared not speak aloud their love, but the more they repressed it the more were they consumed by its passion.

In the party-wall that separated their houses a chink had been left undiscovered through all the years. This cranny was ever so slight, but what escapes the eyes of love? They soon found it and made it the channel of speech. Safely they whispered their joys and sorrows, and often strove to catch each other's breath. "O spiteful wall," they would say, "to stand thus between lovers. Why can't you stand aside and permit us to embrace, or if this be too much, grant us at least the pleasure of a kiss. We are not ungrateful, for we owe to you the privilege of exchanging our words." Thus they would petition to no purpose, until night, and then softly said adieu, first printing a kiss on the wall, which died untasted.

As soon as the morning had extinguished the stars of night, and the sun's rays had dried the dew on the grass, the lovers returned to the accustomed place, to bitterly lament their plight. At last they resolve to steal away from their homes that very night, and leave the town. And to avoid the risk of missing one another as they wandered about in the dark, they agree to meet at the tomb of Ninus where they could rest secure in the shade of the fruit-laden boughs of a mulberry tree near the edge of a purling brook. This plan pleased them, and now they waited impatiently for the friendly dusk. At last the sun plunged into the waves from which the night emerged.

With caution Thisbe now unlocks the door, veils her face, swiftly departs, and soon arrives at the trysting-place. Love has made her bold. But lo! a lioness, besmeared with the blood of slain cattle, rushes to slake her thirst at the neighbouring spring. By the light of the moon Thisbe sees her and swiftly flees into a cave, losing her veil behind. When the savage lioness, her thirst sated with copious draughts, scours back into the woods, she chances upon the veil and tears the lifeless thing with her bloody jaws.

Pyramus, coming a little later, notes by the glimmering moon the tracks of the beast printed on the ground and grows pale. But when he spied the blood-stained veil, he cried, "One night shall bring two lovers to death. But she was deserving of long life. I am guilty, and have caused thy death by asking thee here to this dangerous place while I did not come sooner. O, ye lions, repair from your neighbouring dens and rend my guilty body. But only cowards pray idly thus for death." He gathers up the veil and carries it to the appointed tree, kissing it and washing it with his tears, and exclaims, "Drink now of my blood also." Then he plunged his shining sword into his breast, and fell on the ground, drawing the blade from his wound. As he did so, the hot blood spouted upward, just as a conduit-pipe bursting, shoots a gushing stream of water skyward. The fruit of the tree, stained with blood, showed a dark colour, while the roots, soaked with the flowing gore, tinged the berries with the same purple hue.

Meantime Thisbe, fearing that her lover might miss her, comes, trembling, from her hiding-place and seeks for him with eager eyes and ardent soul, anxious to tell him what destruction she had escaped. And while she perceives the tree and recognises its form, the colour of the fruit leaves her in doubt. As she hesitates, she sees a body on the ground gasping and quivering in death, at sight of which she starts back horrified and shivers like the smooth surface of the sea when ruffled by a rising breeze. But when she finally recognises her lover, she shrieks, tears her hair and beats her breast in grief; then embracing his body she bathes his wound with her tears. And as she pressed her lips to his cold face, she wailed, "My Pyramus, what cruel fate has caused this deed? Pyramus, answer me! 'Tis thy dearest Thisbe calling thee. Speak but one word, I implore." At Thisbe's name, Pyramus opened his dying eyes, looked upon her face, and closed them again.

Now when she found her veil and the sheathless sword, she said, "Thy own hand and thy love took thy life. I too can show a bold hand, and love shall give me strength and guide the fatal blow. I will follow thee in death. The world may say that I am the cause of thy death but I shall be the comrade of thy fate. Though death divide us, it shall not have the power to part me from thee. O wretched parents, hear the prayer I offer for us both, that we, whom love at first and ultimately fate has joined, should be laid together at rest. And thou, O tree, who now shade one lifeless corpse, and ere long will shade another, keep thou the marks of our death, and bear thy purple fruit in token of our blood."

She spoke, and plunged the sword, still warm with her lover's blood, below her breast. The prayer of dying Thisbe moved the gods and the parents to compassion; for the whiteness of the mulberry has turned to a dusky red, and the remains of both rest in a common urn.

❊ ❊ ❊

PETRONIUS
(Died 66 A.D.)

GAIUS PETRONIUS was one of many distinguished Romans who were forced to commit suicide by Nero, because this monarch could not tolerate men whom he suspected of being superior to himself. Tacitus speaks of Petronius as the artist in luxury. "He was enrolled among Nero's boon companions as the Arbiter of Elegance, his judgment being the sole criterion of style and taste." *Trimalchio's Banquet* is the most famous section of the *Satyricon*, the novel on which rests the literary fame of Petronius. Written in an admirable style, it gives a remarkably vivid picture of the middle-class life in the provinces. Trimalchio is the typical vulgar and ostentatious *parvenu* who has risen to his position because trade was held in contempt by Romans of good birth.

The present version is a slight modification of an old translation.

TRIMALCHIO'S DINNER
(From *The Satyricon*)

AT last we were seated and boys from Alexandria poured iced water over our hands. Others knelt down at our feet, and began, with remarkable skill, to pare our hangnails. Even this unpleasant operation did not silence them, but they sang during their work. I desired to learn whether the whole household was able to sing, so I asked for a drink. A slave repeated my request in a shrill chant. They did all things to the accompaniment of a tune. It was more like a comic opera than a gentleman's dining-room.

But some rich and tasty *hors d'œuvres* were brought on in due course. Every one had now been seated except Trimalchio, who, being quite modern, had the first place reserved for him. A donkey of Corinthian bronze, on the side-board, was laden with panniers holding olives, white in one tray, black in the other. Two dishes, engraved with Trimalchio's name and their weight in silver, also encumbered the donkey. There were also dormice steeped in honey and poppy-seed, on iron frames that looked like little bridges. Then, on a silver grill, there were hot sausages and beneath it were plums and sliced pomegranates.

While we were relishing these delicacies, Trimalchio was borne into the hall to the sound of music, propped on tiny cushions. A laugh escaped the surprised guests. His shaven head popped out of a scarlet cloak, and over his well wrapped neck he had put a napkin with a broad stripe and fringes dangling all round. On the little finger of his left hand he wore a huge gilt ring, and on the last joint of the next finger was a smaller ring which appeared to me to be solid gold, but was really set with star-shaped bits of steel. And to show that this display of wealth was but part of his possession, he bared his right arm, encircled by a golden bracelet and an ivory bangle clasped with a plate of gleaming metal.

Then, picking his teeth with a silver quill, he said, "It is inconvenient for me to appear at dinner so soon, my friends, but I did not like to stay away any longer and keep you from your enjoyment. But you will allow me to finish my game?"

A boy followed him carrying a table of terebinth wood and crystal pieces, and I noticed a curious thing. Instead of black and white counters he used gold and silver coins. Trimalchio kept swearing as he played and we were still occupied with the *hors d'œuvres*, when a tray was brought in with a basket on it, in which there was a wooden hen with outspread wings as if in the act of laying an egg. While the music grew loud, two slaves came up to the tray and began to search in the straw. They pulled out peahen's eggs and distributed them to the guests. Trimalchio observed this procedure and said, "I have ordered, my friends, to put peahen's eggs under this hen. And upon my word I hope they are not yet hatched. But let us try them and see whether they are still fresh." We took our spoons, weighing at least half-a-pound, and beat the eggs, which were made of a fine paste. I was on the point of throwing away my share, believing that a chick had already formed. But hearing an experienced diner exclaim, "What dainty have we here?" I broke the shell and found a fat becafico smothered in yolk spiced with pepper.

Trimalchio had now finished his game, and began to partake of all the same dishes. In a loud voice he invited any of us who might so desire, to drink a second glass of mead. Suddenly the music crashed forth, and the appetizers were swept away by a host of chanting waiters. A dish happened to fall in the confusion and a boy gathered it up from the floor. Trimalchio saw him, and had his ear boxed, and directed him to throw down the dish again. A litter-man appeared and swept out the silver with the other wasted contents. Then entered two long-haired Ethiopians with small wineskins, just like those used for scattering sand in an amphitheatre, and poured wine on our hands, for no one thought of offering us common water.

We complimented our host on his excellent taste. "Mars loves fair play," said he, "and therefore I ordered that every one should have a separate table. This will give us room and these filthy slaves will not make us uncomfortable by pressing upon us."

While he was speaking, some glass jars carefully sealed were brought on, the necks of which were labelled

FALERNIAN,

OPIMIUS' VINTAGE,

ONE HUNDRED YEARS OLD.

As we were poring over the inscriptions Trimalchio clapped his hands and cried, "Ah me, wine lives longer than miserable man. So let us be merry, for wine is life. I treat you to real wine of Opimius' year. I provided some inferior stuff yesterday, although there was a more distinguished set of people to dinner." As we drank and appreciated with gusto each luxury, a slave brought in a silver skeleton, so constructed that its limbs and spine could be moved at will. He put it down several times on the table so that the flexible joints flopped into various attitudes, and Trimalchio mused appropriately: "Alas for us poor mortals, our life is pretty mean and poor. So shall we be, after the world below takes us away. Let us then enjoy ourselves while we may."

After we had applauded this sentiment, another course was brought in, not quite as sumptuous as we expected; but its novelty attracted every eye. This was a round plate with the signs of the Zodiac circling the edge, and on each one the chef had placed some food in keeping with the symbol; over the Ram, ram's-head peas, a piece of beef on the Bull, kidneys over the Twins, over the Crab a crown, an African fig over the Lion, a barren sow's udder over Virgo, over Libra a pair of scales with a tart on one side and a cake on the other, over Scorpio a small sea-fish, over Sagittarius a bull's eye, over Capricornus a lobster, over Aquarius a goose, over Pisces two mullets. In the center lay a honeycomb on a bit of grassy turf. An Egyptian boy offered us bread kept hot in a silver chafing-dish. Nor did he fail to amuse us with a song, excruciatingly rendered.

Such a poor course depressed our spirits. "Now," said Trimalchio, "let us begin. This is merely the beginning of the dinner." As he spoke, four slaves ran up keeping time with the music and removed the top part of the tray, revealing in its hollow fat fowls and sow's bellies, and in the middle a hare prepared with wings to resemble Pegasus. We also perceived figures of Marsyas at the corners of the dish, from which a spiced sauce ran over the fish, swimming about in a kind of canal. We all took up the applause which the slaves started, and heartily assailed these viands. Trimalchio was delighted with this cunning dish, and said, "Now, Carver." Whereupon the man approached at once, and flourishing his instruments in time with the music, carved the dainty in pieces, like a gladiator in a chariot fighting to the accompaniment of a barrel-organ. As Trimalchio kept repeating softly, "Oh, Carver, Carver," I pondered on the meaning of this word, believing it to be a jest, and I made bold to ask the man who sat on my left what it meant. (He had seen such performances before.) "Do you see the fellow carving the meat? Well, his name is Carver. So whenever Trimalchio says the words, he calls him by name, and gives him his orders."

When I had eaten my fill, I turned to my neighbour to get as much gossip as possible. I inquired who the woman was who kept running about the hall. "She is Trimalchio's wife Fortunata," he said, "and she counts her money by the bushel." "And what was she before?" I asked. "You will pardon me if I say that you would not have taken a piece of bread from her hand. Now, who knows why or wherefore, she is queen of Heaven, and Trimalchio's all in all. Fact is, if she tells him that it is dark at midday, he will believe her. He is so enormously wealthy that he himself does not know all he possesses; but his lynx-eyed wife has a plan for everything, even where you least suspect it. She is temperate, sober and thrifty, but she has a shrewish tongue, and henpecks him in his own home. Whom she likes, she likes; whom she dislikes, she dislikes. Trimalchio has estates greater than a kite can fly over in a day, and has uncounted millions. There is more plate in his steward's cupboard than other people have in the whole world. And his legion of slaves! My word! I really don't believe that one in ten knows his master by sight! Why, he can knock any of these young wretches into a cocked hat.

"You must not suppose that he buys anything. Everything is produced by him; wool, citrons, pepper; even pigeon's milk. Just to show you, his sheep were growing a poor quality of wool, so he bought rams from Tarentum to improve his flocks. He had bees consigned from Athens to give him Attic honey on the spot; the Roman bees incidentally will be improved by breeding with the Greeks. A few days ago he sent to India for a cargo of mushroom spawn. And every mule he has is the child of a wild ass. Note these cushions: every one has purple or scarlet stuffing. He is nothing if not extravagant.

"But do not be contemptuous of his fellow freedmen. They are saturated with money. Do you see that one lying at the bottom of the end sofa? Well, he has his eight hundred thousand. He was quite a nobody. He started by carrying loads of wood on his back. People do say—I can't vouch for it but I have heard—that he pulled off a goblin's cap and found a hidden treasure. I am jealous of nobody receiving favours of providence. He still shows the marks of his master's fingers, but he has an exalted opinion of himself. So he has just put up a sign on his door:

THIS ATTIC,
THE PROPERTY OF GAIUS POMPEIUS DIOGENES,
TO LET FROM THE 1ST OF JULY,
THE OWNER HAVING PURCHASED A MANSION.

"As for that person sprawling with such a satisfied air in the freed-man's place, he had money at one time. I do not blame him, poor fellow. He had his million in his hands, but he has had a bad shaking. I believe he cannot call his hair his own, and that through no fault of his. Here is a fine chap; but these damned freedmen pocketed everything he had. You know how it is: when the pot stops boiling, or business takes a bad turn your friends desert you. Now you see him in this reduced state. He was an undertaker. He used to dine like a prince; boars cooked in a cloth, wonderful pastry, game; chefs innumerable and confectioners! There used to be more wine spilt in his house than many a man has in his cellars. He was a fairy prince, not a mortal. When his business was falling to pieces, and he feared his creditors might suspect that he was going bankrupt, he advertised an auction:

GAIUS JULIUS PROCULUS
WILL OFFER FOR SALE SOME SURPLUS STOCK."

Trimalchio interrupted this delightful chat, for the meat had now been removed, and the cheerful guests began to turn their attention to the wine and general conversation. He reclined on his couch and remarked: "Now you must sparkle as much as this wine. A fish must naturally swim. But say, did you suppose I would be content with the dinner you saw in the hollow of that dish—'Is this the old Ulysses whom ye knew—?' well, well, one must exhibit one's culture even at dinner. My patron, may God rest his soul, wanted me to be an equal among men. There is little one can teach me, as that last dish demonstrated. The sky where the twelve gods inhabit is divided into as many symbols. Let us take the Ram. Anyone who is born under that sign has many flocks and abundance of wool, a hard head and a brazen forehead and a fine brain. Many professors and young rams are born under this sign."

We applauded the cleverness of his astrological utterance, while he went on: "Then the sky turns into a young bull. Men who kick with their heels, and oxherds and people who have to scout their own food are born under it. Under the Twins two-wheeled chariots are born, and oxen, and debauchees, and those who serve many masters. I was born under the Crab. Therefore I have many feet to stand on, and immense estates by sea and land; for either of these elements suits your crab. And that was why I put nothing on top of the Crab, for fear of weighing down my good star. Under the Lion gluttons and masterful men are born; under Virgo women, and runaway slaves, and criminals; under

Libra butchers, and perfumers, and various tradesmen; poisoners and assassins under Scorpio: under Sagittarius cross-eyed men, who take the bacon while they look at the cabbage; under Capricornus the poor toilers whose troubles cause horns to sprout on them; under Aquarius, innkeepers and men with water on the brain; under Pisces chefs and orators. So the world turns round like a mill, and always brings evil in one form or another, causing the birth of men or their death. And you saw the green turf in the middle surmounted by the honeycomb? Even that has significance. Mother Earth lies in the world's midst rounded like an egg, within which all blessings are contained as in a honeycomb."

"Excellent!" we all cried, vowing with our hands uplifted that even Hipparchus and Aratus were inferior to him. Just then servants appeared and spread over the couches coverlets embroidered with scenes of nets and hunters lying in wait with spears, and all the instruments of the chase. We were still wondering what next to expect when a deafening shout arose outside the dining-room and in rushed some Spartan hounds, leaping round the tables. A tray was brought in after them with a wild boar of huge proportions upon it, wearing a cap of freedom; two little baskets woven of palm-twigs were hanging from its tusks, one full of dry dates and the other of fresh. Round it lay sucking-pigs made of pastry with their snouts to the teats, thereby showing that we had a sow before us. These sucking-pigs were for the guests to take away. Carver, who had dealt with the fowls, did not carve the boar, but a tall bearded man with leggings round his legs, and a spangled silken hunting-cape, who drew a hunting-knife and plunged it hard into the boar's side. Whereupon a number of thrushes flew out and were immediately caught by fowlers standing with limed twigs. Trimalchio ordered each guest to be given one, and added: "Now you see what fine acorns our boar has been eating." Then boys came and took the baskets which hung from its tusks and distributed fresh and dry dates to the guests.

Meantime I had got a quiet corner to myself, and had begun to ponder,—why the pig had come in decorated with a cap of freedom. After speculating on the problem without arriving at a satisfactory conclusion, I ventured to put the question which was troubling me to my old informant. "Your humble servant can explain that too," he said. "There is no mystery, the thing is as clear as daylight. Yesterday when this animal was served as *pièce de résistance* at dinner, the guests turned him down; and so today he comes back to dinner as a freedman." I cursed my stupidity and determined to ask no more questions, for fear of showing that I had never dined among decent people.

As we were speaking, a lovely boy crowned with vineleaves and ivy impersonating Bacchus in ecstasy, Bacchus full of wine, Bacchus dreaming, brought round grapes in a little basket, and rendered one of Tri-

malchio's verses in a piercing voice. Trimalchio turned at the noise
and said, "Dionysus, rise and be free." The boy clutched the cap of
freedom off the boar, and put it on his own head. Then Trimalchio
continued: "I am sure you will agree that the god of liberation is my
father." We applauded Trimalchio's phrase, and kissed the boy heartily
as he passed round.

❋ ❋ ❋

APULEIUS
(Born about 125 A.D.)

THE METAMORPHOSES, otherwise known as *The Golden Ass*,
was written by Lucius Apuleius who was born and educated in Africa.
This book, which is probably based upon a Greek original of Lucian,
is a fascinating tale of a dabbler in magic who by a curious chance
is transformed into an ass. This bizarre and highly imaginative
romance has been so keenly appreciated that even Boccaccio and
Cervantes availed themselves of many of its comic passages. The
present version is from an early English translation.

THE THREE ROBBERS
(From *The Golden Ass*)

A S Telephron reached the point of his story, his fellow revellers,
befuddled with their wine, renewed the boisterous uproar. And
while the old topers were clamouring for the customary libation
to laughter, Byrrhæna explained to me that the morrow was a day religiously observed by her city from its cradle up; a day on which they
alone among mortals propitiated that most sacred god, Laughter, with
hilarious and joyful rites. "The fact that you are here," she added,
"will make it all the merrier. And I do wish that you would contribute
something amusing out of your own cleverness, in honour of the god, to
help us duly worship such an important divinity."

"Surely," said I, "what you ask shall be done. And, by Jove! I
hope I shall hit upon something good enough to make this mighty god of
yours reveal his presence."

Hereupon, my slave reminding me what hour of night it was, I
speedily got upon my feet, although none too steadily after my potations,
and, having duly taken leave of Byrrhæna, guided my zigzag steps upon
the homeward way. But at the very first corner we turned, a sudden
gust of wind blew out the solitary torch on which we depended, and left
us, plunged in the unforeseen blackness of night, to stumble wearily

and painfully to our abode, bruising our feet on every stone in the road.

But when at last, holding each other up, we drew near our goal, there ahead of us were three others, of big and brawny build, expending the full energy of their strength upon our doorposts. And far from being in the least dismayed by our arrival, they seemed only fired to a greater zeal and made assault more fiercely. Quite naturally, it seemed clear to us both, and especially to me, that they were robbers, and of the most dangerous sort. So I forthwith drew the blade which I carry hidden under my cloak for such emergencies, and threw myself, undismayed, into the midst of these highwaymen. One after another, as they successively tried to withstand me, I ran them through, until finally all three lay stretched at my feet, riddled with many a gaping wound, through which they yielded up their breath. By this time Fotis, the maid, had been aroused by the din of battle, and still panting and perspiring freely I slipped in through the opening door, and, as weary as though I had fought with the three-formed Geryon instead of those pugnacious thieves, I yielded myself at one and the same moment to bed and to slumber.

Soon rosy-fingered Dawn, shaking the purple reins, was guiding her steeds across the path of heaven; and, snatched from my untroubled rest, night gave me back to day. Dismay seized my soul at the recollection of my deeds of the past evening. I sat there, crouching on my bed, with my interlaced fingers hugging my knees, and freely gave way to my distress; I already saw in fancy the court, the jury, the verdict, the executioner. How could I hope to find any judge so mild, so benevolent as to pronounce me innocent, soiled as I was with a triple murder, stained with the blood of so many citizens? Was this the glorious climax of my travels that the Chaldean, Diophanes, had so confidently predicted for me? Again and again I went over the whole matter bewailing my hard lot.

Hereupon there came a pounding at our doors and a steadily growing clamour on the threshold. No sooner was admission given than, with an impetuous rush, the whole house was filled with magistrates, police, and the motley crowd that followed. Two officers, by order of the magistrates, promptly laid hands upon me, and started to drag me off, though resistance was the last thing I should have thought of. By the time we had reached the first cross street the entire city was already trailing at our heels in an astonishingly dense mass. And I marched gloomily along with my head hanging down to the very earth—I might even say to the lower regions below the earth.

At length after having made the circuit of every city square, in exactly the way that the victims are led around before a sacrifice meant to ward off evil omens, I was brought into the forum and made to confront the tribunal of justice. The magistrates had taken their seats upon the raised platform, the court crier had commanded silence, when suddenly everyone present, as if with one voice, protested that in so vast a gathering there was danger from the dense crowding, and demanded that a case of such importance should be tried instead in the public theatre. No sooner said than the entire populace streamed onward, helter-skelter, and in a marvellously short time had packed the whole auditorium till every aisle and gallery was one solid mass. Many swarmed up the columns, others dangled from the statues, while a few there were that perched, half out of sight, on window ledges and cornices; but all in their amazing eagerness seemed quite careless how far they risked their lives. After the manner of a sacrifice I was led by the public officials down the middle of the stage, and was left standing in the midst of the orchestra. Once more the voice of the court crier boomed forth, calling for the prosecutor, whereupon a certain old man arose, and having first taken a small vase, the bottom of which ended in a narrow funnel, and having filled it with water, which escaping drop by drop should mark the length of his speech, addressed the populace as follows:

"This is no trivial case, most honoured citizens, but one which directly concerns the peace of our entire city, and one which will be handed down as a weighty precedent. Wherefore, your individual and common interests equally demand that you should sustain the dignity of the State, and not permit this brutal murderer to escape the penalty of the wholesale butchery that resulted from his bloody deeds. And do not think that I am influenced by any private motives, or giving vent to personal animosity. For I am in command of the night watch, and up to this time I think there is no one who will question my watchful diligence. Accordingly I will state the case and faithfully set forth the events of last night.

"It was about the hour of the third watch, and I was making my round of the entire city, going from door to door with scrupulous vigilance, when suddenly I beheld this bloodthirsty young man, sword in hand, spreading carnage around him; already, no less than three victims of his savagery lay writhing at his feet, gasping forth their breath in a pool of blood. Stricken, as well he might be, with the guilt of so great a crime, the fellow fled, and, slipping into one of the houses under cover of the darkness, lay hidden the rest of the night. But, thanks to the gods who permit no sinner to go unpunished, I forestalled him at daybreak, before he could make his escape by secret ways, and have brought him here for trial before your sacred tribunal of justice. The prisoner at the bar is a threefold murderer; he was taken in the very act; and, furthermore, he is a foreigner. Accordingly, it is your plain duty to return a verdict of guilty against this man from a strange land for a crime which you would severely punish even in the case of one of your own citizens."

Having thus spoken, the remorseless prosecutor suspended his vindictive utterance, and the court crier straightway ordered me to begin my defence, if I had any to make. At first I could not sufficiently control my voice to speak, although less overcome, alas, by the harshness of the accusation than by my own guilty conscience. But at last, miraculously inspired with courage, I made answer as follows:

"I realise how hard it is for a man accused of murder, and confronted with the bodies of three of your citizens, to persuade so large a multitude of his innocence, even though he tells the exact truth and voluntarily admits the facts. But if in mercy you will give me an attentive hearing, I shall easily make clear to you that far from deserving to be put on trial for my life, I have wrongfully incurred the heavy stigma of such a crime as the chance result of justifiable indignation.

"I was making my way home from a dinner party at a rather late hour, after drinking pretty freely, I won't attempt to deny—for that was the head and front of my offence—when, lo and behold! before the very doors of my abode, before the home of the good Milo, your fellow-citizen, I beheld a number of villainous thieves trying to effect an entrance and already prying the doors off from the twisted hinges. All the locks and bolts, so carefully closed for the night, had been wrenched away, and the thieves were planning the slaughter of the inmates. Finally, one of them, bigger and more active than the rest, urged them to action with these words:

"'Come on, boys! Show the stuff you are made of, and strike for all you are worth while they are asleep! No quarter now, no faint-hearted weakening! Let death go through the house with drawn sword! If you find any in bed, slit their throats before they wake; if any try to resist, cut them down. Our only chance of getting away safe and sound is to leave no one else safe and sound in the whole house.'

"I confess, citizens, that I was badly frightened, both on account of my hosts and myself; and believing that I was doing the duty of a good citizen, I drew the sword which always accompanies me in readiness for such dangers, and started in to drive away or lay low those desperate robbers. But the barbarous and inhuman villains, far from being frightened away, had the audacity to stand against me, although they saw that I was armed. Their serried ranks opposed me. Next, the leader and standard-bearer of the band, assailing me with brawny strength, seized me with both hands by the hair, and bending me backward, prepared to beat out my brains with a paving stone; but while he was still shouting for one, with an unerring stroke I luckily ran him through and stretched him at my feet. Before long a second stroke, aimed between the shoulders, finished off another of them, as he clung tooth and nail to my legs; while the third one, as he rashly advanced, I stabbed full in the chest.

"Since I had fought on the side of law and order, in defence of public safety and my host's home, I felt myself not only without blame but deserving of public praise. I have never before been charged with even the slightest infringement of the law; I enjoy a high reputation among my own people, and all my life have valued a clear conscience above all material possessions. Nor can I understand why I should suffer this prosecution for having taken a just vengeance upon those worthless thieves, since no one can show that there had ever before been any enmity between us, or for that matter that I had ever had any previous acquaintance with the thieves. You have not even established any motive for which I may be supposed to have committed so great a crime."

At this point my emotion again overcame me, and with my hands extended in entreaty, I turned from one to another, beseeching them to spare me in the name of common humanity, for the sake of all that they held dear. I thought by this time they must be moved to pity, thrilled with sympathy for my wretchedness; accordingly I called to witness the Eye of Justice and the Light of Day, and intrusted my case to the providence of God, when lifting up my eyes I discovered that the whole assembly was convulsed with laughter, not excepting my own kind host and relative, Milo, who was shaking with merriment. "So much for friendship!" I thought to myself, "so much for gratitude! In protecting my host, I have become a murderer, on trial for my life; while he, far from raising a finger to help me, makes a mock of my misery."

At this moment a woman clad in black rushed down the centre of the stage, weeping and wailing and clasping a small child to her breast. An older woman, covered with rags and similarly shaken with sobs, followed her, both of them waving olive branches as they passed around the bier on which lay the covered bodies of the slain, and lifted up their voices in mournful outcry: "For the sake of common humanity," they wailed, "by all the universal laws of justice, be moved to pity by the undeserved death of these young men! Give to a lonely wife and mother the comfort of vengeance! Come to the aid of this unhappy child left fatherless in his tender years, and offer up the blood of the assassin at the shrine of law and order."

Hereupon the presiding magistrate arose and addressed the people: "The crime for which the prisoner will later pay the full penalty, not even he attempts to deny. But still another duty remains to be performed, and that is to find out who were his accomplices in this wicked deed; since it does not seem likely that one man alone could have overcome three others so young and strong as these. We must apply torture to extract the truth; and since the slave who accompanied him has made his escape, there is no other alternative left us than to wring the names of his companions from the prisoner himself, in order that we may effectually relieve the public of all apprehension of danger from this desperate gang."

Immediately, in accordance with the Greek usage, fire and the wheel were brought forth, together with all the other instruments of torture. Now indeed my distress was not only increased but multiplied when I saw that I was fated to perish piecemeal. But at this point the old woman, whose noisy lamentations had become a nuisance, broke out with this demand:

"Honoured citizens, before you proceed to torture the prisoner, on account of the dear ones whom he has taken from me, will you not permit the bodies of the deceased to be uncovered in order that the sight of their youth and beauty may fire you with a righteous anger and a severity proportioned to the crime?"

These words were received with applause, and straightway the magistrate commanded that I myself should with my own hand draw off the covering from the bodies lying on the bier. In spite of my struggles and desperate determination not to look again upon the consequences of my last night's deed, the court attendants promptly dragged me forward, in obedience to the judge's order, and bending my arm by main force from its place at my side stretched it out above the three corpses. Conquered in the struggle, I yielded to necessity, and much against my will drew down the covering and exposed the bodies.

Great heavens, what a sight! What a miracle! What a transformation in my whole destiny! I had already begun to look upon myself as a vassal of Proserpine, a bondsman of Hades, and now I could only gasp in impotent amazement at the suddenness of the change; words fail me to express fittingly the astounding metamorphosis. For the bodies of my butchered victims were nothing more nor less than three inflated bladders, whose sides still bore the scars of numerous punctures, which, as I recalled my battle of the previous night, were situated at the very points where I had inflicted gaping wounds upon my adversaries. Hereupon the hilarity, which up to this point had been fairly held in check, swept through the crowd like a conflagration. Some gave themselves up helplessly to an unrestrained extravagance of merriment; others did their best to control themselves, holding their aching sides with both hands. And having all laughed until they could laugh no more, they passed out of the theatre, their backward glances still centred upon me.

From the moment that I had drawn down that funeral pall I stood fixed as if frozen into stone, as powerless to move as any one of the theatre's statues or columns. Nor did I come out of my stupor until Milo, my host, himself approached and clapping me on the shoulder, drew me away with gentle violence, my tears now flowing freely and sobs choking my voice. He led me back to the house by a roundabout way through the least frequented streets, doing his best meanwhile to soothe my nerves and heal my wounded feelings. But nothing he could say availed to lessen my bitter indignation at having been made so undeservedly ridiculous. But all at once the magistrates themselves, still wearing their insignia of office, arrived at the house and made personal amends in the following words:

"We are well aware, Master Lucius, both of your own high merit and that of your family, for the renown of your name extends throughout the land. Accordingly, you must understand that the treatment which you so keenly resent was in no sense intended as an insult. Therefore, banish your present gloomy mood and dismiss all anger from your mind. For the festival, which we solemnly celebrate with each returning year in honour of the God of Laughter, must always depend upon novelty for its success. And so our god, who owes you so great a debt to-day, decrees that his favouring presence shall follow you wherever you go, and that your cheerful countenance shall everywhere be a signal for hilarity. The whole city, out of gratitude, bestows upon you exceptional honours, enrolling your name as one of its patrons, and decreeing that your likeness in bronze shall be erected as a perpetual memorial of to-day."

PERSIA

Introduction

PERSIA has, more than any other Oriental nation, enriched the poetry of the world. The great epic poet of Persia, Firdawsi, who lived in the tenth century A.D., wrote the *Shah Nameh*, or *Book of Kings*, an account of the glories of Persia from the earliest times. The best known of the Persian poems is the Rubaiyat of Omar Khayyam, no doubt due to its classic translation by Edward FitzGerald. Beside this gem of Omar, we have the famous lyrics of Saadi in his *Gulistan* (*Rose-Garden*) and *Bustan* (*Fruit-Garden*).

The short stories in Persia owe their origin to wandering literateurs who invented their tales for the amusement of patrons. These tales were invariably concerned with treasure or love; in either instance the motive being to acquire, treasure or lady love, by accident or stratagem, by fair means or foul. The story teller was not concerned with psychology or psychoanalysis. His object was simply to create a hero whose mission in life was to procure immense wealth or the most beauteous damsel in the world, solely for the sake of possession. Inasmuch as the Persian story-teller's audience had been suckled on superstitions, it is not surprising that he frequently introduces, in a most nonchalant manner, denizens of the supernatural world.

❈ ❈ ❈

ABUL KASIM MANSUR FIRDAWSI
(935-1025 A.D.)

FIRDAWSI, born in Tus, composed the greatest Persian Epic, the *Shah Nameh*, or Book of Kings. This celebrated epic compares favorably in scope and beauty with the *Nibelungenlied*. He was exceedingly encouraged in his work by Mahmud of Ghazna who admired Firdawsi's brilliant mind, profound knowledge of ancient history, and poetic genius; to such an extent that he ordered his treasurer to pay the poet a thousand gold pieces for every thousand verses. The task was not completed for forty years, and by that time, the story has it, the monarch forgot his promise of payment. *Feridún and His Three Sons* is one of the episodes that make up this marvellous epic of the splendours of ancient Persia.

The present version is from a translation by James Atkinson, published by the Oriental Translation Fund of Great Britain and Ireland, 1832.

FERIDUN AND HIS THREE SONS
(From the *Shah Nameh*)

FERIDÚN had three sons. One of them was named Sílim, the other Túr, and the third Irij. When they had grown up, he called before him a learned person named Chundel, and said to him: "Go thou in quest of three daughters, born of the same father and mother, and adorned with every grace and accomplishment, that I may have my three sons married into one family." Chundel departed accordingly, and travelled through many countries in fruitless search, till he came to the King of Yemen, whose name was Sarú, and found that he had three daughters of the character and qualifications required. He therefore delivered Feridún's proposition to him, to which the King of Yemen agreed. Then Feridún sent his three sons to Yemen, and they married the three daughters of the king, who gave them splendid dowries in treasure and jewels. It is related that Feridún afterwards divided his empire among his sons. To Sílim he gave Rúm and Kháwer; to Túr, Túrán; and to Irij, Irán or Persia. The sons then repaired to their respective kingdoms. Persia was a beautiful country, and the garden of spring, full of freshness and perfume; Túrán, on the contrary, was less cultivated, and the scene of perpetual broils and insurrections. The elder brother, Sílim, was therefore discontented with the unfair partition of the empire, and displeased with his father. He sent to Túr, saying: "Our father has given to Irij the most delightful and productive kingdom, and to us, two wild uncultivated regions. I am the eldest son, and I am not satisfied with this distribution,—what sayest thou?" When this message was communicated to Túr, he fully concurred in the sentiments expressed by his brother, and determined to unite with him in any undertaking that might promise the accomplishment of their purpose, which was to deprive Irij of his dominions. But he thought it would be most expedient, in the first instance, to make their father acquainted with the dissatisfaction he had produced; "for," he thought to himself, "in a new distribution, he may assign Persia to me." Then he wrote to Sílim, advising that a messenger should be sent at once to Feridún to inform him of their dissatisfaction, and bring back a reply. The same messenger was dispatched by Sílim accordingly on that mission,

> Charged with unfilial language. "Give," he said,
> "This stripling Irij a more humble portion,
> Or we will, from the mountains of Túran,

From Rúm, and Chín, bring overwhelming troops,
Inured to war, and shower disgrace and ruin
On him and Persia."

When the messenger arrived at the court of Feridún, and had obtained permission to appear in the presence of the king, he kissed the ground respectfully, and by command related the purpose of his journey. Feridún was surprised and displeased, and said, in reply:

"Have I done wrong, done evil? None, but good.
I gave ye kingdoms, that was not a crime;
But if ye fear not me, at least fear God.
My ebbing life approaches to an end,
And the possessions of this fleeting world
Will soon pass from me. I am grown too old
To have my passions roused by this rebellion;
All I can do is, with paternal love,
To counsel peace. Be with your lot contented;
Seek not unnatural strife, but cherish peace."

After the departure of the messenger Feridún called Irij before him, and said: "Thy two brothers, who are older than thou art, have confederated together, and threaten to bring a large army against thee for the purpose of seizing thy kingdom, and putting thee to death. I have received this information from a messenger, who further says, that if I take thy part they will also wage war upon me." And after Irij had declared that in this extremity he was anxious to do whatever his father might advise, Feridún continued: "My son, thou art unable to resist the invasion of even one brother; it will, therefore, be impossible for thee to oppose both. I am now aged and infirm, and my only wish is to pass the remainder of my days in retirement and repose. Better, then, will it be for thee to pursue the path of peace and friendship, and like me throw away all desire for dominion.

For if the sword of anger is unsheathed,
And war comes on, thy head will soon be freed
From all the cares of government and life.
There is no cause for thee to quit the world,
The path of peace and amity is thine."

Irij agreed with his father, and declared that he would willingly sacrifice his throne and diadem rather than go to war with his brothers.

"Look at the Heavens, how they roll on;
And look at man, how soon he's gone.
A breath of wind, and then no more;
A world like this, should man deplore?"

With these sentiments Irij determined to repair immediately to his brothers, and place his kingdom at their disposal, hoping by this means to merit their favour and affection, and he said:

> "I feel no resentment, I seek not for strife,
> I wish not for thrones and the glories of life;
> What is glory to man?—an illusion, a cheat;
> What did it for Jemshíd, the world at his feet?
> When I go to my brothers their anger may cease,
> Though vengeance were fitter than offers of peace."

Feridún observed to him: "It is well that thy desire is for reconciliation, as thy brothers are preparing for war." He then wrote a letter to his sons, in which he said: "Your younger brother considers your friendship and esteem of more consequence to him than his crown and throne. He has banished from his heart every feeling of resentment against you; do you, in the like manner, cast away hostility from your hearts against him. Be kind to him, for it is incumbent upon the eldest born to be indulgent and affectionate to their younger brothers. Although your consideration for my happiness has passed away, I still wish to please you." As soon as the letter was finished, Irij mounted his horse, and set off on his journey, accompanied by several of his friends, but not in such a manner, and with such an equipment, as might betray his rank or character. When he arrived with his attendants in Turkistán, he found that the armies of his two brothers were ready to march against him. Silim and Túr, being apprised of the approach of Irij, went out of the city, according to ancient usage, to meet the deputation which was conveying to them their father's letter. Irij was kindly received by them, and accommodated in the royal residence.

It is said that Irij was in person extremely prepossessing, and that when the troops first beheld him, they exclaimed: "He is indeed fit to be a king!" In every place all eyes were fixed upon him, and wherever he moved he was followed and surrounded by the admiring army and crowds of people.

The courtiers of the two brothers, alarmed by these demonstrations of attachment to Irij continually before their eyes, represented to Sílim and Túr that the army was disaffected towards them, and that Irij alone was considered deserving of the supreme authority. This intimation exasperated the malignant spirit of the two brothers; for although at first determined to put Irij to death, his youth and prepossessing appearance had in some degree subdued their animosity. They were therefore pleased with the intelligence, because it afforded a new and powerful reason for getting rid of him. "Look at our troops," said Sílim to Túr, "how they assemble in circles together, and betray their admiration of him. I fear they will never march against Persia. Indeed it is not improbable that

even the kingdom of Túran may fall into his hands, since the hearts of
our soldiers have become so attached to him."

Again, Sílim said to Túr: "Thou must put Irij to death, and then his
kingdom will be thine." Túr readily undertook to commit that crime,
and, on the following day, at an interview with Irij, he said to him:
"Why didst thou consent to be the ruler of Persia, and fail in showing a
proper regard for the interests of thy elder brothers? Whilst our barren
kingdoms are constantly in a state of warfare with the Turks, thou art
enjoying peace and tranquillity upon the throne of a fruitful country?
Must we, thy elder brothers, remain thus under thy commands, and in
subordinate stations?

> Must thou have gold and treasure,
> And thy heart be wrapt in pleasure,
> Whilst we, thy elder born,
> Of our heritage are shorn?
> Must the youngest still be nursed,
> And the elder branches cursed?
> And condemned, by stern command,
> To a wild and sterile land?"

When Irij heard these words from Túr, he immediately replied,
saying:

> "I only seek tranquillity and peace;
> I look not on the crown of sovereignty,
> Nor seek a name among the Persian host;
> And though the throne and diadem are mine,
> I here renounce them, satisfied to lead
> A private life. For what hath ever been
> The end of earthly power and pomp, but darkness?
> I seek not to contend against my brothers;
> Why should I grieve their hearts, or give distress
> To any human being? I am young,
> And Heaven forbid that I should prove unkind!"

Notwithstanding, however, these declarations of submission, and
repeated assurances of his resolution to resign the monarchy of Persia,
Túr would not believe one word. In a moment he sprung up, and furiously seizing the golden chair from which he had just risen, struck a
violent blow with it on the head of Irij, calling aloud, "Bind him, bind
him!" The youth, struggling on the ground, exclaimed: "O, think of
thy father, and pity me! Have compassion on thy own soul! I came for
thy protection, therefore do not take my life: if thou dost, my blood will
call out for vengeance to the Almighty. I ask only for peace and retirement. Think of my father, and pity me!

Wouldst thou, with life endowed, take life away?
Torture not the poor ant, which drags the grain
Along the dust; it has a life, and life
Is sweet and precious. Did the innocent ant
Offend thee ever? Cruel must he be
Who would destroy a living thing so harmless!
And wilt thou, reckless, shed thy brother's blood,
And agonize the feelings of a father?
Pause, and avoid the wrath of righteous Heaven!"

But Túr was not to be softened by the supplications of his brother.
Without giving any reply, he drew his dagger, and instantly dissevered
the head of the youth from his body.

With musk and ambergris he first embalmed
The head of Irij, then to his old father
Dispatched the present with these cruel words:—
"Here is the head of thy beloved son,
Thy darling favourite, dress it with a crown
As thou wert wont; and mark the goodly fruit
Thou hast produced. Adorn thy ivory throne,
In all its splendour, for this worthy head,
And place it in full majesty before thee!"

In the meantime, Feridún had prepared a magnificent reception for
his son. The period of his return had arrived, and he was in anxious
expectation of seeing him, when suddenly he received intelligence that
Irij had been put to death by his brothers. The mournful spectacle soon
reached his father's house.

A scream of agony burst from his heart,
As wildly in his arms he clasped the face
Of his poor slaughtered son; then down he sank
Senseless upon the earth. The soldiers round
Bemoaned the sad catastrophe, and rent
Their garments in their grief. The souls of all
Were filled with gloom, their eyes with flowing tears,
For hope had promised a far different scene;
A day of heart-felt mirth and joyfulness,
When Irij to his father's house returned.

After the extreme agitation of Feridún had subsided, he directed all
his people to wear black apparel, in honour of the murdered youth, and
all his drums and banners to be torn to pieces. They say that subsequent
to this dreadful calamity he always wore black clothes. The head of
Irij was buried in a favourite garden, where he had been accustomed
to hold weekly a rural entertainment. Feridún, in performing the last
ceremony, pressed it to his bosom, and with streaming eyes exclaimed:

"O Heaven, look down upon my murdered boy;
His severed head before me, but his body
Torn by those hungry wolves! O grant my prayer,
That I may see, before I die, the seed
Of Irij hurl just vengeance on the heads
Of his assassins; hear, O hear my prayer."
—Thus he in sorrow for his favourite son
Obscured the light which might have sparkled still,
Withering the jasmine flower of happy days;
So that his pale existence looked like death.

Feridún continued to cherish with the fondest affection the memory of his murdered son, and still looked forward with anxiety to the anticipated hour of retribution. He fervently hoped that a son might be born to take vengeance for his father's death. But it so happened that Mahafríd, the wife of Irij, gave birth to a daughter. When this daughter grew up, Feridún gave her in marriage to Pishung, and from that union an heir was born who in form and feature resembled Irij and Feridún. He was called Minúchihr, and great rejoicings took place on the occasion of his birth.

The old man's lips, with smiles apart,
Bespoke the gladness of his heart.
And in his arms he took the boy,
The harbinger of future joy;
Delighted that indulgent Heaven
To his fond hopes this pledge had given.
It seemed as if, to bless his reign,
Irij had come to life again.

The child was nourished with great tenderness during his infancy, and when he grew up he was sedulously instructed in every art necessary to form the character, and acquire the accomplishments of a warrior. Feridún was accustomed to place him on the throne, and decorate his brows with the crown of sovereignty; and the soldiers enthusiastically acknowledged him as their king, urging him to rouse himself and take vengeance of his enemies for the murder of his grandfather. Having opened his treasury, Feridún distributed abundance of gold among the people, so that Minúchihr was in a short time enabled to embody an immense army, by whom he was looked upon with attachment and admiration.

When Sílim and Túr were informed of the preparations that were making against them, that Minúchihr, having grown to manhood, was distinguished for his valour and intrepidity, and that multitudes flocked to his standard with the intention of forwarding his purpose of revenge, they were seized with inexpressible terror, and anticipated an immediate invasion of their kingdoms. Thus alarmed, they counselled together upon the course it would be wisest to adopt.

> "Should he advance, his cause is just,
> And blood will mingle with the dust,
> But heaven forbid our power should be
> O'erwhelmed to give him victory;
> Though strong his arm, and wild his ire,
> And vengeance keen his heart inspire."

They determined, at length, to pursue pacific measures, and endeavour by splendid presents and conciliatory language to regain the good-will of Feridún. The elephants were immediately loaded with treasure, a crown of gold, and other articles of value, and a messenger was dispatched, charged with an acknowledgment of guilt and abundant expressions of repentance. "It was Iblis," they said, "who led us astray, and our destiny has been such that we are in every way criminal. But thou art the ocean of mercy; pardon our offences. Though manifold, they were involuntary, and forgiveness will cleanse our hearts and restore us to ourselves. Let our tears wash away the faults we have committed. To Minúchihr and to thyself we offer obedience and fealty, and we wait your commands, being but the dust of your feet."

When the messenger arrived at the court of Feridún he first delivered the magnificent presents, and the king, having placed Minúchihr on a golden chair by his side, observed to him, "These presents are to thee a prosperous and blessed omen—they shew that thy enemy is afraid of thee." Then the messenger was permitted to communicate the object of his mission.

> He spoke with studied phrase, intent to hide,
> Or mitigate the horror of their crime;
> And with excuses plausible and bland
> His speech was dressed. The brothers, he observed,
> Desired to see their kinsman Minúchihr,—
> And with the costliest gems they sought to pay
> The price of kindred blood unjustly shed—
> And they would willingly to him resign
> Their kingdom for the sake of peace and friendship.
>   The monarch marked him scornfully, and said,
> "Canst thou conceal the sun? It is in vain
> Truth to disguise with words of shallow meaning.
> Now hear my answer. Ask thy cruel masters,
> Who talk of their affection for the prince,
> Where lies the body of the gentle Irij?
> Him they have slain, the fierce, unnatural brothers,
> And now they thirst to gain another victim.
> They long to see the face of Minúchihr!

> Yes, and they shall, surrounded by his soldiers,
> And clad in steel, and they shall feel the edge
> Of life-destroying swords. Yes, they shall see him!"

After uttering this indignant speech, Feridún shewed to the messenger his great warriors, one by one. He shewed him Kavah and his two sons, Shalpúr, and Shírúeh, and Kárun, and Sám, and Naríman, and other chiefs—all of admirable courage and valor in war,—and thus resumed:

> "Hence with your presents, hence, away,
> Can gold or gems turn night to day?
> Must kingly heads be bought and sold,
> And shall I barter blood for gold?
> Shall gold a father's heart entice,
> Blood to redeem beyond all price?
> Hence, hence with treachery; I have heard
> Their glozing falsehoods, every word;
> But human feelings guide my will,
> And keep my honours sacred still.
> True is the oracle we read:—
> 'Those who have sown oppression's seed
> Reap bitter fruit; their souls, perplext,
> Joy not in this world or the next.'
> The brothers of my murdered boy,
> Who could a father's hopes destroy,
> An equal punishment will reap,
> And lasting vengeance o'er them sweep.
> They rooted up my favourite tree,
> But yet a branch remains to me.
> Now the young lion comes apace,
> The glory of his glorious race;
> He comes apace, to punish guilt,
> Where brother's blood was basely spilt;
> And blood alone for blood must pay;
> Hence with your gold, depart, away!"

When the messenger heard these reproaches, mingled with poison, he immediately took leave, and trembling with fear, returned to Sílim and Túr with the utmost speed. He described to them in strong and alarming terms the appearance and character of Minúchihr, and his warriors; of that noble youth who with frowning eyebrows was only anxious for battle. He then communicated to them in what manner he had been received, and repeated the denunciations of Feridún, at which the brothers were exceedingly grieved and disappointed. But Sílim said to Túr:

> "Let us be first upon the field, before
> He marshals his array. It follows not,
> That he should be a hero bold and valiant,

> Because he is descended from the brave;
> But it becomes us well to try our power,—
> For speed, in war, is better than delay."

In this spirit the two brothers rapidly collected from both their king-doms a large army, and proceeded towards Irán. On hearing of their progress, Feridún said: "This is well—they come of themselves. The forest game surrenders itself voluntarily at the foot of the sportsman." Then he commanded his army to wait quietly till they arrived; for skill and patience, he observed, will draw the lion's head into your toils.

As soon as the enemy had approached within a short distance, Minú-chihr solicited Feridún to commence the engagement,—and the king hav-ing summoned his chief warriors before him, appointed them all, one by one, to their proper places.

> The warriors of renown assembled straight
> With ponderous clubs; each like a lion fierce,
> Girded his loins impatient. In their front
> The sacred banner of the blacksmith waved;
> Bright scimitars were brandished in the air;
> Beneath them pranced their steeds, all armed for fight,
> And so incased in iron were the chiefs
> From top to toe, their eyes were only seen.
>   When Kárun drew his hundred thousand troops
> Upon the field, the battle-word was given,
> And Minúchihr was, like the cypress tall,
> Engaged along the centre of the hosts;
> And like the moon he shone, amid the groups
> Of congregated clouds, or as the sun
> Glittering upon the mountain of Alberz,
> The squadrons in advance Kabád commanded,
> Garshasp the left, and Sám upon the right,
>   The shedders of a brother's blood had now
> Brought their innumerous legions to the strife,
> And formed them in magnificent array:
> The picquet guards were almost thrown together,
> When Túr sprung forward, and with sharp reproach,
> And haughty gesture, thus addressed Kabád:
> "Ask this new king, this Minúchihr, since Heaven
> To Irij gave a daughter, who on him
> Bestowed the mail, the battle-axe, and sword?"
> To this insulting speech, Kabád replied:
> "The message shall be given, and I will bring
> The answer, too. Ye know what ye have done;
> Have ye not murdered him who, trusting, sought
> Protection from ye? All mankind for this
> Must curse your memory till the day of doom;

> If savage monsters were to fly your presence,
> It would not be surprising. Those who die
> In this most righteous cause will go to Heaven,
> With all their sins forgotten!" Then Kabád
> Went to the king, and told the speech of Túr:
> A smile played o'er the cheek of Minúchihr
> As thus he spoke: "A boaster he must be,
> Or a vain fool, for when engaged in battle,
> Vigour of arm and the enduring soul,
> Will best be proved. I ask but for revenge—
> Vengeance for Irij slain. Meanwhile, return;
> We shall not fight today."
>
>   He too retired,
> And in his tent upon the sandy plain,
> Ordered the festive board to be prepared,
> And wine and music whiled the hours away.

When morning dawned the battle commenced, and multitudes were slain on both sides.

> The spacious plain became a sea of blood;
> It seemed as if the earth was covered o'er
> With crimson tulips; slippery was the ground,
> And all in dire confusion.

The army of Minúchihr was victorious, owing to the bravery and skill of the commander. But Heaven was in his favour.

In the evening Sílim and Túr consulted together, and came to the resolution of effecting a formidable night attack on the enemy. The spies of Minúchihr, however, obtained information of this intention, and communicated the secret to the king. Minúchihr immediately placed the army in charge of Kárun, and took himself thirty thousand men to wait in ambuscade for the enemy, and frustrate his views. Túr advanced with a hundred thousand men; but as he advanced, he found every one on the alert, and aware of his approach. He had gone too far to retreat in the dark without fighting, and therefore began a vigorous conflict. Minúchihr sprung up from his ambuscade, and with his thirty thousand men rushed upon the centre of the enemy's troops, and in the end encountered Túr. The struggle was not long. Minúchihr dexterously using his javelin, hurled him from his saddle precipitately to the ground, and then with his dagger severed the head from his body. The body he left to be devoured by the beasts of the field, and the head he sent as a trophy to Feridún; after which, he proceeded in search of Sílim.

The army of the confederates, however, having suffered such signal a defeat, Sílim thought it prudent to fall back and take refuge in a fort. But Minúchihr went in pursuit, and besieged the castle. One day a warrior named Kakú made a sally out of the fort, and approaching the centre of the besieging army, threw a javelin at Minúchihr, which however fell harmless before it reached its aim. Then Minúchihr seized the enemy by the girdle, raised him up in air, and flung him from his saddle to the ground.

> He grasped the foe-man by the girth,
> And thundering drove him to the earth;
> By wound of spear, and gory brand,
> He died upon the burning sand.

The siege was continued for some time with the view of weakening the power of Sílim; at last Minúchihr sent a message to him, saying: "Let the battle be decided between us. Quit the fort, and boldly meet me here, that it may be seen to whom God gives the victory." Sílim could not, without disgrace, refuse this challenge: he descended from the fort, and met Minúchihr. A desperate conflict ensued, and he was slain on the spot. Minúchihr's keen sword severed the royal head from the body, and thus quickly ended the career of Sílim. After that, the whole of the enemy's troops were defeated and put to flight in every direction.

The leading warriors of the routed army now sought protection from Minúchihr, who immediately complied with their solicitation, and by their influence all the forces of Sílim and Túr united under him. To each he gave rank according to his merits. After the victory, Minúchihr hastened to pay his respects to Feridún, who received him with praises and thanksgivings, and the customary honours. Returning from the battle, Feridún met him on foot; and the moment Minúchihr beheld the venerable monarch, he alighted and kissed the ground. They then, seated in the palace together, congratulated themselves on the success of their arms. In a short time after, the end of Feridún approached; when recommending Minúchihr to the care of Sám and Narímán, he said: "My hour of departure has arrived, and I place the prince under your protection." He then directed Minúchihr to be seated on the throne:

> And put himself the crown upon his head,
> And stored his mind with counsel good and wise.

Upon the death of Feridún, Minúchihr accordingly succeeded to the government of the empire, and continued to observe strictly all the laws and regulations of his great grandfather. He commanded his subjects to be constant in the worship of God.

> The army and the people gave him praise,
> Prayed for his happiness and length of days;
> Our hearts, they said, are ever bound to thee;
> Our hearts, inspired by love and loyalty.

THE TREASURE OF MANSUR

THE author of the following story is not known. It was inscribed in the margins of a valuable work on Mongol history which, with other literary collections, was presented to the Bodleian Library by travellers in Persia. It aptly illustrates the chief subject matter of the Persian story-teller.

The present version is from a translation by Reuben Levy, M.A., of MS. Ouseley 187, page 187 (margin), Bodleian Library. Copyright, 1923, by Humphrey Milford, Oxford University Press, by whose permission it is here reprinted.

THE TREASURE OF MANSUR

THERE was once a prince of Baghdad, famed for his richness and the vastness of his treasures. He had one son, Mansur, whom he loved dearly, and whom he had reared with the greatest care. He engaged the wisest philosophers and the most learned tutors to teach him, so that he understood the languages of east and west. With the passage of time, the prince became aware that the day of his death was near. Therefore, summoning Mansur, he spoke to him as follows: 'My son, I am about to depart and you will be left alone to deal with the great treasures which I bequeath to you. Spend it not except by measure, and ponder well on all you do.'

The next day the prince died, and Mansur mourned for him. So eager, however, was he to behold his father's treasures that at the end of three days he cast off his mourning, and, taking the keys of the treasure-house with him, he made his way into it. He remained astonished at the sight of the gold and jewels which were heaped there, and thought to himself: 'Why did my father warn me so earnestly, for here is more than I can ever spend?' He therefore commanded his servants to bring out chests full of gold and jewels, and the next day he set about planning the building of gardens and palaces which would excel in splendour all that had ever been built before. His gardens were filled with the finest fruit-trees, and under each was set a couch of precious wood inlaid with gold and jewels.

Thus Mansur continued, until at last his treasurehouses were empty. By degrees he was compelled to sell his gardens and fine houses until only one remained, and soon he decided that he would sell this too. With the money he would buy merchandise and travel into foreign countries, where he could acquire wealth again.

This he did. He sold his last house, loaded a caravan, and set out for Mosul, where he arrived after a long journey. He found it a fine city with splendid palaces and pleasant gardens, but his business there did not prosper. After a month he decided to travel farther to Syria, and accordingly, leaving Mosul with a caravan, he journeyed from city to city until Damascus was reached. He found a town full of people, surrounded by beautiful gardens and containing many great buildings. Filled with delight, he remained in the town until his merchandise was all sold and the money he had obtained for it was all eaten up. Then he departed, leaving on foot with a caravan, and gaining a livelihood by bringing water for sale to merchants at any place where they alighted.

It happened one day that he fell sick; his clothes were worn out and he had no money wherewith to buy food. Faint and weak after a long journey, he fell down in the bazaar of a town where he had arrived. A crowd gathered round him, and took pity on him when they saw that he was young and a foreigner. They offered him food and drink, but he refused it, until one, more wealthy and understanding than the rest, took him to the hammam, and gave him clothes and brought him to his house. There Mansur ate and drank, and related his history to his benefactor. When he had concluded, his host asked him whither he now intended to go, and he replied that he wished to go to Egypt. This kindly man, therefore, gave him a sum of gold for his journey and dismissed him, praying that God would favour him with fortune.

Mansur set his face towards Egypt, and after a long journey arrived in the great city of Cairo. There he beheld a magnificent spectacle of great bazaars and rich shops; on every side were palaces reaching into the blue sky. On both banks of the Nile were fine buildings and beautiful gardens. For long he marvelled, and with the money that remained to him he bought such delectable foods as his heart desired. Many days he wandered in the bazaars, beholding and marvelling at the people and the palaces. It happened that every day he passed by a place on the riverside where women draw water, and there was one that came regularly and greatly pleased Mansur by her appearance. One day he made acacquaintance with her, and for several days afterwards he met her at the watering place. Then one day as he came she saw that he was downcast and gloomy, and, when she asked the reason, he told her that his money was almost at an end, and that he did not know how he was to live in the future. She said to him: 'Many people pass by here bent on pleasure. Buy some fruits and sweetmeats and lay them in a tray or on the grass. I, too, will help you and give you food. When people sit down here to eat, enter into conversation with them, amuse them with witticisms and become friendly with them.' Mansur approved of this plan. That very moment he departed, and brought fruits and sweets and offered them to people that came down to the water.

This he continued to do for some time, so that people became well acquainted with him and always bought from him, and every night he carried home a sum of money. One day, two Indians, richly dressed, came to sit down near him. They called to him to bring them some of his wares, and he set his tray before them. They made him sit down with them, telling him to remain with them to amuse them for the whole day, and not to go to any one else. Mansur said that he would place himself at their service, and sat down with them to eat and drink.

Very soon the two Indians were drunk, and, holding out some gold dinars, told Mansur to play and sing and amuse them with stories. When at last they were too dazed with wine to hear more, they began to speak to each other in the Indian tongue, not knowing that Mansur could understand them. He heard one of them say, 'The gold which we brought is finished, we must go out to-night and find sufficient for our needs.' The other, however, replied: 'No, I brought enough for a month.' This filled Mansur with the thought that the two men must in some place have a store of gold, and he therefore determined to discover what further information he could concerning the two men, and so find out whence they got their gold and their wealth. He remained in their company until one hour after sunset, then taking up the accoutrement which they had brought with them, they departed.

Mansur hastened to his friend and told her that he intended to go to his own lodging that night. 'The way is long,' said he, 'and if you have a sword I pray you give it to me.' The woman gave him a sword, and Mansur hastened away in pursuit of the two men. He followed them outside the town and into the desert. There they sat down, and he heard them say to each other that they must go warily and see that no one followed them. Mansur at this crept into a hole which he found, fortunately for himself, for one of the two Indians turned back a little way to see if any one was about. Again they proceeded until they reached a certain tree, under which they halted. Mansur saw them engaged in digging for a little while, then suddenly they disappeared from view. Very cautiously he approached and at last he saw the mouth of a hole, and, inside it, a door. He was just about to descend, when one of the Indians appeared with a bag upon his back. As soon as he emerged Mansur sprang upon him with his sword and hacked off his head. The bag fell to the ground, but as Mansur was about to bend down to open it, the other Indian appeared, also carrying a bag. Swiftly Mansur turned upon him, sword in hand, and slew him too. Then he opened both bags and found them filled with pearls.

In great haste he descended into the hole and beheld before him a vestibule, very long and dark. As he proceeded along it, it began to grow lighter, and he made his way towards the spot whence the light came. Soon he beheld an enormous palace, in the midst of which was a great fountain surrounded by ten gold pillars, ornamented with jewels. By each pillar was set a jewel-encrusted throne and great vats full of jewels and wealth beyond counting. Being driven almost to madness by what he had seen, Mansur rushed out into the open, locking the door after him. Then, taking up the two bags, which he had filled with gold coins, he made his way back to his lodging.

The next day Mansur set about spending his newly-gotten wealth. Summoning his neighbours, he bought from them at a great price all the houses in that district, and there began to build a palace, the like of which no prince or vizier in all Egypt possessed. When it was completed, he had it spread with carpets befitting its richness. Night after night he went to the underground palace and brought back some of the treasure. But if one man had worked night and day for a thousand years he could never have completed the task.

At last the people of Cairo began to talk among themselves about Mansur, and said: 'This Baghdadi, who used to sell fruits and sweets and to wander from tavern to tavern, is now richer than any one in Cairo, though there are many owners of great treasure here. Whence does he acquire all the wealth to enable him to build so fine a palace and maintain his household so lavishly? Also, does he pay his due tenth to the prince of Cairo?' This talk reached the ears of the chief of the police, who thereupon made his way to the palace of Mansur. He was amazed at the sight that met his gaze, and, turning to Mansur, he said: 'The people of this city remember that when you came here you were a beggar, but now your affairs have reached this prosperous state. Will you not inform me whence you have obtained all this wealth and splendour? Whatever it be, I bid you tell me the truth.' When Mansur asked him what office he held, he replied that he was chief of the police. This alarmed Mansur greatly, and he was much agitated. The officer, however, told him not to be afraid, and added that if Mansur dealt generously with him, he in his turn would be generous also. 'How much must I pay?' asked Mansur. When he was told a hundred dirhams of silver he laughed aloud, and offered a hundred dinars of gold, whereat the officer was much pleased, and said: 'Even if you have found a hundred treasures you are welcome to them, in so far as concerns me.'

Soon afterwards the story reached the ears of the vizier also. He summoned Mansur, and, treating him with great regard, said: 'I understand that when you came here you were a beggar, penniless and friendless, but that now you have become possessed of great treasure. It has come to our sovereign's ears that the royal dues are not being paid by you. I advise you therefore, my friend, to pay these dues; but, in addition, you may expend what you please.'

Upon hearing this, Mansur understood what was expected of him, and said: 'I admit that I have found a treasure, but it is in a place where no man can cast an eye. I am a foreigner and will not pay a grain to the Sultan, even if he tears me limb from limb; but to you I will pay a thousand dirhams every day, and that is sufficient to defray all the expenditure of Cairo. I say this, however, on condition that you are content with what I pay and do not demand more.' The vizier swore an oath that he would not demand more, thinking that if he slew Mansur he would derive no profit. He therefore dismissed him, saying: 'For my part, if you have found a thousand treasures you are welcome to them.' But he sent a messenger to Mansur to bring back the first day's payment.

Some time elapsed and then the story of the treasure was brought to the Sultan. He summoned the vizier and asked him concerning Mansur, and then he called Mansur before him. He treated him with great condescension, and said: 'Young man, if you discover to me this treasure which you have found, I will take but one fifth of it and leave the rest to you.' Mansur replied: 'An oath has been laid upon me not to disclose my secret to a living soul, and if I were to be cut into a thousand pieces I would not speak of it. I will pay, however, daily, the sum of twelve thousand dinars in gold.' The matter was thus arranged, and the Sultan bade the vizier to put on Mansur a robe of honour, and to publish his name abroad with great ceremony as a public benefactor.

When Mansur had departed, the Sultan began to consider how great the treasure of Mansur must be if he could afford to pay twelve thousand dinars every day in addition to other great sums. He pondered long, therefore, on the means whereby he could lay his hands on the source of this wealth. As he sat thus engrossed in thought, a favourite slave-girl beheld him and asked what schemes possessed him. He told her what he had in mind, and she replied that she would gain for him what he desired. He promised that if she succeeded he would give her one of his palaces for her own, and would keep her with him always.

Now it happened that Mansur's custom was to sit in his courtyard every day, with a chest of gold by his side. Beggars and other needy persons came in streams to ask his aid, and, being given what they desired, passed on. On the day after Mansur had visited the Sultan, a maiden joined the stream of people at Mansur's house, and, as she passed by him, she uncovered her face and smiled at him bewitchingly, saying that she had a request to make in private. Mansur, greatly delighted with her beauty, bade her go into the house, and he followed. There he bade food and wine to be brought, and, while they ate and drank, Mansur became more and more enamoured of her. At last he asked what her need was, and she replied: 'I have heard that you have found a rich treasure, and I am consumed with desire to behold it.' Mansur laughed aloud at this, but after much persuasion he at last consented. He put on a cloak, took a sword, and bade the girl accompany him. When they arrived outside the city, he blindfolded his companion securely with a kerchief, and led her to the underground chamber. There he uncovered her eyes again and showed her all that there was to see. She was amazed at the sight, and said, 'Show me whence you obtain all the gold coins which you pay out every day.' He pointed to the tank, which was full of gold coins up to two fingers' breadth from the top. 'Here,' he said, 'I have sufficient to last me the whole of my life, and need never touch the rest of the treasure.'

After going about for some time, Mansur and his companion desired to rest, and they proceeded towards an alcove where there stood a couch. As they entered they saw another couch on one side, and upon it a man asleep, with a maiden by his side. Over the head of the sleeping man hung a golden tablet, upon which was written: 'I, that gathered all this treasure, took cities, and stormed fortresses, and overcame all mine enemies. When death descended upon me, this wealth was of no avail to me that created it. If it falls into the hand of any man, let him spend it lavishly, for it will not diminish. In me, that gathered it all, desires are at an end. Let him that beholds me be warned, and let him not be deceived by worldly wealth.'

After reading this Mansur looked again at the sleeping pair, and saw that they were dead. Around the dead maiden's neck was a necklace of jewels. This Mansur unclasped and gave it to his companion, whose eyes he again covered with the kerchief. This time she cried out, and begged that she might be allowed to see where she was going. But Mansur asked her if she was tired of life that she spoke thus, and she remained silent.

They then returned to the city, Mansur going to his home, and the slave-girl back to the palace. There she told the Sultan all that had occurred and confessed her failure. In great wrath thereat he told her to go back to Mansur, to whom he said he had presented her. When she arrived, Mansur bid her to rejoice, for he would deal with her a thousand times more graciously than ever her royal master had done. With great ceremony he married her, and with her lived long and happily. But, when he died, he told the secret of his treasure to no one, so that it disappeared from the world.

ARABIA

Introduction

PROFESSOR CLEMENT HUART gives a very interesting account of the origins of Arabic poetry. The camel's steady swing in his pace across the monotonous desert bent the rider's body almost double and taught him to sing rhymes. The Arab soon noted that as he hurried the pace of his recitation, the string of camels would raise their heads and step out with quickened pace. Thus we have the *hidâ,* the song of the leading camel-driver of the caravan. It is quite a step from the *hidâ* to the works of the famous pre-Mahommedan poets, such as Imru'u'l-Qais, Tarafa, and 'Antara, whose poems had been collected by Asma'ī about the beginning of the ninth century. But this is explained by the fact that the desert Arabs were of a nomadic temperament whose poets merely recited their poems without putting them on paper. In the inter-tribal wars many of the poets were slain, and their works were, except in rare cases, forgotten. So that while there had been a gradual development of poetic literature we have only the works of the transcribed poets to gauge this development.

The most remarkable collection of Arabian stories, or for that matter any other Oriental which has delighted the civilised world is contained in the *Thousand and One Nights,* or *Arabian Nights' Entertainment.* Some of the celebrated stories that go to make this masterly compendium of Oriental life,—town life as differentiated from the desert life portrayed in the epic poems previously mentioned,—have probably been taken from the Sanscrit through the Persians, but the Arab story-tellers have contributed so much glamour, such vivid colour to their tales that the reader need not be troubled about original sources. What is surprising, however, is that while the Arabian Nights had appeared as far back as the fourteenth century (certain parts of it as early as the tenth), it was not until the eighteenth century that a translation was made into the French by Antoine Galland.

THE JAR OF OLIVES
(Anonymous. 10th-14th Century)

THE THOUSAND AND ONE NIGHTS has brought joy to innumerable readers; and justly so, for it is a collection of stories with a universal charm. And Harun al-Rashid, the most beloved monarch in fiction, again renders justice in the case of *The Jar of Olives and the Boy Kazi*, a yarn of mystery and adventure.

The present version is translated by Sir Richard F. Burton, London, 1888.

THE JAR OF OLIVES AND THE BOY KAZI
(From *The Thousand and One Nights*)

UNDER the reign of the Caliph Harun al-Rashid there dwelt in the city of Baghdad a certain merchant, 'Ali Khwajah hight, who had a small stock of goods wherewith he bought and sold and made a bare livelihood, abiding alone and without a family in the house of his forbears. Now so it came to pass that each night for three nights together he saw in vision a venerable Shaykh who bespake him thus, "Thou art beholden to make a pilgrimage to Meccah; why abidest thou sunk in heedless slumber and farest not forth as it behoveth thee?" Hearing these words he became sore startled and affrighted, so that he sold shop and goods and all that he had; and, with firm intent to visit the Holy House of Almighty Allah, he let his home on hire and joined a caravan that was journeying to Meccah the Magnified. But ere he left his natal city he placed a thousand gold pieces, which were over and above his need for the journey, within an earthen jar filled up with Asafiri or Sparrow-olives; and, having made fast the mouth thereof, he carried the jar to a merchant-friend of many years' standing and said, "Belike, O my brother, thou hast heard tell that I purpose going with a caravan on pilgrimage to Meccah, the Holy City; so I have brought a jar of olives the which, I pray thee, preserve for me in trust against my return." The merchant at once arose and handing the key of his warehouse to Ali Khwajah said, "Here, take the key and open the store and therein place the jar anywhere thou choosest, and when thou shalt come back thou wilt find it even as thou leftest it." Hereupon Ali Khwajah did his friend's bidding and locking up the door returned the key to its master. Then loading his travelling goods upon a dromedary and mounting a second beast he fared forth with the caravan. They came at length to Meccah the Magnified, and it was the month Zu al-Hijjah wherein myriads of Moslems hie thither on pilgrimmage and pray and

prostrate before the Ka'abah-temple.   And when he had circuited the
Holy House, and fulfilled all the rites and ceremonies required of
palmers, he set up a shop for sale of merchandise.   By chance two merchants passing along that street espied the fine stuffs and goods in Ali
Khwajah's booth and approved much of them and praised their beauty and
excellence.   Presently quoth one to other, "This man bringeth here most
rare and costly goods: now in Cairo, the capital of Egyptland, would he
get full value for them, and far more than in the markets of this city."
Hearing mention of Cairo, Ali Khwajah conceived a sore longing to visit
that famous capital, so he gave up his intent of return Baghdad-ward
and purposed wayfaring to Egypt.   Accordingly he joined a caravan and
arriving thither was well-pleased with the place, both country and city;
and selling his merchandise he made great gain therefrom.   Then buying other goods and stuffs he purposed to make Damascus; but for one
full month he tarried at Cairo and visited her sanctuaries and saintly
places, and after leaving her walls he solaced himself with seeing many
famous cities distant several days' journey from the capital along the
banks of the River Nilus.   Presently, bidding adieu to Egypt he arrived
at the Sanctified House, Jerusalem, and prayed in the temple of the Banu
Isra'il which the Moslems had re-edified.   In due time he reached
Damascus and observed that the city was well builded and much peopled,
and that the fields and meads were well-watered with springs and channels and that the gardens and vergiers were laden with flowers and fruits.
Amid such delights Ali Khwajah hardly thought of Baghdad; withal he
ceased not to pursue his journey through Aleppo, Mosul, and Shiraz,
tarrying some time at all of these towns, especially at Shiraz, till at length
after seven years of wayfaring he came back to Baghdad.

For seven long years the Baghdad merchant never once thought of
Ali Khwajah or of the trust committed to his charge; till one day as his
wife sat at meat with him at the evening meal, their talk by chance was
of olives.   Quoth she to him, "I would now fain have some that I
may eat of them"; and quoth he, "As thou speakest thereof I bethink
me of that Ali Khwajah who seven years ago fared on a pilgrimage to
Meccah, and ere he went left in trust with me a jar of Sparrow-olives
which still cumbereth the storehouse.   Who knoweth where he is or
what hath betided him?   A man who lately returned with the Hajj-
caravan brought me word that Ali Khwajah had quitted Meccah the
Magnified with intent to journey on to Egypt.   Allah Almighty alone
knoweth an he be still alive or he be now dead; however, if his olives
be in good condition I will go bring some hither that we may taste them:
so give me a platter and a lamp that I may fetch thee somewhat of them."
His wife, an honest woman and an upright, made answer, "Allah forbid
that thou shouldst do a deed so base and break thy word and covenant.
Who can tell?   Thou art not assured by any of his death; perchance he

may come back from Egypt safe and sound to-morrow or the day after; then wilt thou, an thou cannot deliver unharmed to him what he hath left in pledge, be ashamed of this thy broken troth, and we shall be disgraced before man and dishonoured in the presence of thy friend. I will not for my part have any hand in such meanness nor will I taste the olives; furthermore, it standeth not to reason that after seven years' keeping they should be fit to eat. I do implore thee to forswear this ill-purpose." On such wise the merchant's wife protested and prayed her husband that he meddle not with Ala Khwajah's olives, and shamed him of his intent so that for the nonce he cast the matter from his mind. However, although the trader refrained that evening from taking Ali Khwajah's olives, yet he kept the design in memory until one day when, of his obstinacy and unfaith, he resolved to carry out his project; and rising up walked toward the store-room dish in hand. By chance he met his wife who said, "I am no partner with thee in this ill-action: in very truth some evil shall befall thee an thou do such deed." He heard her but heeded her not; and, going to the store-room opened the jar and found the olives spoiled and white with mould; but presently he tilted up the jar and pouring some of its contents into the dish, suddenly saw an Ashrafi fall from the vessel together with the fruit. Then, filled with greed, he turned out all that was within into another jar and wondered with exceeding wonder to find the lower half full of golden coins. Presently, putting up the moneys and the olives he closed the vessel and going back said to his wife, "Thou spakest sooth, for I have examined the jar and have found the fruit mouldy and foul of smell; wherefore I returned it to its place and left it as it was aforetime." That night the merchant could not sleep a wink for thinking of the gold and how he might lay hands thereon; and when morning morrowed he took out all the Ashrafis and buying some fresh olives in the Bazar filled up the jar with them and closed the mouth and set it in its usual place. Now it came to pass by Allah's mercy that at the end of the month Ali Khwajah returned safe and sound to Baghdad; and he first went to his old friend, to wit, the merchant who, greeting him with feigned joy, fell on his neck, but withal was sore troubled and perplexed at what might happen. After salutations and much rejoicing on either part Ali Khwajah bespake the merchant on business and begged that he might take back his jar of Asafiri-olives which he had placed in charge of his familiar. Quoth the merchant to Ali Khwajah, "O my friend, I wot not where thou didst leave the jar of olives; but here is the key, go down to the store-house and take all that is thine own." So Ali Khwajah did as he was bidden and carrying the jar from the magazine took his leave and hastened home; but, when he opened the vessel and found not the gold coins, he was distracted and overwhelmed with grief and made bitter lamentation. Then he returned to the merchant and said, "O my friend,

Allah, the All-present and the All-seeing, be my witness that, when I went on my pilgrimage to Meccah the Magnified, I left a thousand Ashrafis in that jar, and now I find them not. Canst thou tell me aught concerning them? An thou in thy sore need have made use of them, it mattereth not so thou wilt give them back as soon as thou art able." The merchant, apparently pitying him, said, "O good my friend, thou didst thyself with thine hand set the jar inside the store-room. I wist not that thou hadst aught in it save olives; yet as thou didst leave it, so in like manner didst thou find it and carry it away; and now thou chargest me with theft of Ashrafis. It seemeth strange and passing strange that thou shouldst make such accusation. When thou wentest thou madest no mention of any money in the jar, but saidst that it was full of olives, even as thou hast found it. Hadst thou left gold coins therein, then surely thou wouldst have recovered them." Hereupon Ali Khwajah begged hard with much entreaty, saying, "Those thousand Ashrafis were all I owned, the money earned by years of toil: I do beseech thee have pity on my case and give them back to me." Replied the merchant, waxing wroth with great wrath, "O my friend, a fine fellow thou art to talk of honesty and withal make such false and lying charge. Begone: hie thee hence and come not to my house again; for now I know thee as thou art, a swindler and impostor." Hearing this dispute between Ali Khwajah and the merchant all the people of the quarter came crowding to the shop; and thus it became well known to all, rich and poor, within the city of Baghdad how that one Ali Khwajah had hidden a thousand Ashrafis within a jar of olives and had placed it on trust with a certain merchant; moreover how, after pilgrimaging to Meccah and seven years of travel the poor man had returned, and that the rich man had gainsaid his words anent the gold and was ready to make oath that he had not received any trust of the kind. At length, when naught else availed, Ali Khwajah was constrained to bring the matter before the Kazi, and to claim one thousand Ashrafis of his false friend. The Judge asked, "What witnesses hast thou who may speak for thee?" and the plaintiff answered, "O my lord the Kazi, I feared to tell the matter to any man lest all come to know of my secret. Allah Almighty is my sole testimony. This merchant was my friend and I recked not that he would prove dishonest and unfaithful." Quoth the Judge, "Then must I needs send for the merchant and hear what he saith on oath"; and when the defendant came they made him swear by all he deemed holy, facing Ka'abah-wards with hands uplifted, and he cried, "I swear that I know naught of any Ashrafis belonging to Ali Khwajah." Hereat the Kazi pronounced him innocent and dismissed him from court; and Ali Khwajah went home sad at heart and said to himself, "Alas, what justice is this which hath been meted out to me, that I should lose my money, and my just cause be deemed unjust! It hath been truly said: He loseth the lave who sueth before a knave." On the next day he drew out a statement of his case; and, as the Caliph Harun al-Rashid was on his way to Friday-prayers, he fell down on the ground before him and presented to him the paper. The Commander of the Faithful read the petition and having understood the case deigned give order saying, "To-morrow bring the accuser and the accused to the audience-hall and place the petition before my presence, for I myself will inquire into this matter." That night the Prince of True Believers, as was his wont, donned disguise to walk about the squares of Baghdad and its streets and lanes and, accompanied by Ja'afar the Barmaki and Masrur the Sworder of his vengeance, proceeded to espy what happened in the city. Immediately on issuing forth he came upon an open place in the Bazar when he heard the hubbub of children a-playing and saw at scanty distance some ten or dozen boys making sport among themselves in the moonlight; and he stopped awhile to watch their diversion. Then one among the lads, a goodly and a fair-complexioned, said to the others, "Come now and let us play the game of Kazi: I will be the Judge; let one of you be Ali Khwajah and another the merchant with whom he placed the thousand Ashrafis in pledge before faring on his pilgrimage: so come ye before me and let each one plead his plea." When the Caliph heard the name of Ali Khwajah he minded him of the petition which had been presented to him for justice against the merchant, and bethought him that he would wait and see how the boy would perform the part of Kazi in their game and upon what decision he would decide. So the Prince watched the mock-trial with keen interest saying to himself, "This case hath verily made such stir within the city that even the children know thereof and re-act it in their sports." Presently, he among the lads who took the part of Ali Khwajah the plaintiff and his playmate who represented the merchant of Baghdad accused of theft, advanced and stood before the boy who as the Kazi sat in pomp and dignity. Quoth the Judge, "O Ali Khwajah, what is thy claim against this merchant?" and the complainant preferred his charge in a plea of full detail. Then said the Kazi to the boy who acted merchant, "What answerest thou to this complaint and why didst thou not return the gold pieces?" The accused made reply even as the real defendant had done and denied the charge before the Judge, professing himself ready to take oath thereto. Then said the boy-Kazi, "Ere thou swear on oath that thou hast not taken the money, I would fain see for myself the jar of olives which the plaintiff deposited with thee on trust." Then turning to the boy who represented Ali Khwajah he cried, "Go thou and instantly produce the jar that I may inspect it." And when the vessel was brought the Kazi said to the two contentious, "See now and say me: be this the very jar which thou, the plaintiff, leftest with the defendant?" and both answered that it was one and the same. Then said the self-constituted Judge, "Open now the

jar and bring hither some of the contents that I may see the state in which
the Asafiri-olives actually are." Then tasting of the fruit, "How is this?
I find their flavor is fresh and their state excellent. Surely during the
lapse of seven twelve-months the olives would have become mouldy and
rotten. Bring now before me two oil-merchants of the town that they
may pass opinion upon them." Then two other of the boys assumed the
parts commanded and coming into court stood before the Kazi, who asked,
"Are ye olive-merchants by trade?" They answered, "We are and this
hath been our calling for many generations, and in buying and selling
olives we earn our daily bread." Then said the Kazi, "Tell me now,
how long do olives keep fresh and well-flavoured?" and said they, "O
my lord, however carefully we keep them, after the third year they
change flavour and colour and become no longer fit for food, in fact
they are good only to be cast away." Thereupon quoth the boy-Kazi,
"Examine me now these olives that are in this jar and say me how old
are they and what is their condition and savour." The two boys who
played the parts of oil-merchants pretended to take some berries from
the jar and taste them and presently they said, "O our lord the Kazi,
these olives are in fair condition and full-flavoured." Quoth the Kazi,
"Ye speak falsely, for 'tis seven years since Ali Khwajah put them in
the jar as he was about to go a-pilgrimaging"; and quoth they, "Say
whatso thou wilt, those olives are of this year's growth, and there is not
an oil-merchant in all Baghdad but who will agree with us." Moreover
the accused was made to taste and smell the fruits and he could not but
admit that it was even so as they had avouched. Then said the boy-Kazi
to the boy-defendant, " 'Tis clear thou art a rogue and a rascal, and thou
hast done a deed wherefor thou richly deservest the gibbet." Hearing
this the children frisked about and clapped their hands with glee and
gladness, then seizing hold of him who acted as the merchant of Baghdad,
they led him off as to execution. The Commander of the Faithful,
Harun al-Rashid, was greatly pleased at this acuteness of the boy who
had assumed the part of judge in the play, and commanded his Wazir
Ja'afar saying, "Mark well the lad who enacted the Kazi in this mock-
trial and see that thou produce him on the morrow: he shall try the case
in my presence substantially and in real earnest, even as we have heard
him deal with it in play. Summon also the Kazi of this city that he may
learn the administration of justice from this child. Moreover send word
to Ali Khwajah bidding him bring with him the jar of olives, and have
also in readiness two oil-merchants of the town." Thus as they walked
along the Caliph gave orders to the Wazir and then returned to his palace.
So on the morrow Ja'afar the Barmaki went to that quarter of the town
where the children had enacted the mock-trial and asked the schoolmaster
where his scholars might be, and he answered, "They have all gone away,
each to his home." So the Minister visited the houses pointed out to him

and ordered the little ones to appear in his presence. Accordingly they were brought before him, when he said to them, "Who among you is he that yesternight acted the part of Kazi in play and passed sentence in the case of Ali Khwajah?" The eldest of them replied, " 'Twas I, O my lord the Wazir"; and then he waxed pale, not knowing why the question was put. Cried the Minister, "Come along with me; the Commander of the Faithful hath need of thee." At this the mother of the lad was sore afraid and wept; but Ja'afar comforted her and said, "O my lady, have no fear and trouble not thyself. Thy son will soon return to thee in safety, Inshallah—God willing—and methinks the Sultan will show much favour unto him." The woman's heart was heartened on hearing these words of the Wazir and she joyfully dressed her boy in his best attire and sent him off with the Wazir, who led him by the hand to the Caliph's audience-hall and executed all the other commandments which had been issued by his liege lord. Then the Commander of the Faithful, having taken seat upon the throne of justice, set the boy upon a seat beside him, and as soon as the contending parties appeared before him, that is Ali Khwajah and the merchant of Baghdad, he commanded them to state each man his case in presence of the child who should adjudge the suit. So the two, plaintiff and defendant, recounted their contention before the boy in full detail; and when the accused stoutly denied the charge and was about to swear on oath that what he said was true, with hands uplifted and facing Ka'abah-wards, the child-Kazi prevented him, saying, "Enough! swear not on oath till thou art bidden; and first let the jar of olives be produced in court." Forthwith the jar was brought forward and placed before him; and the lad bade open it; then, tasting one he gave also to two oil-merchants who had been summoned, that they might do likewise and declare how old was the fruit and whether its savour was good or bad. They did his bidding and said, "The flavour of these olives hath not changed and they are of this year's growth." Then said the boy, "Methinks ye are mistaken, for seven years ago Ali Khwajah put the olives into the jar: how then could fruit of this year find their way therein?" But they replied, " 'Tis even as we say: an thou believe not our words send straightway for other oil-merchants and make inquiry of them, so shalt thou know if we speak sooth or lies." But when the merchant of Baghdad saw that he could no longer avail to prove his innocence, he confessed everything; to wit, how he had taken out the Ashrafis and filled the jar with fresh olives. Hearing this the boy said to the Prince of True Believers, "O gracious Sovereign, last night in play we tried this cause, but thou alone hast power to apply the penalty. I have adjudged the matter in thy presence and I humbly pray that thou punish this merchant according to the law of the Koran and the custom of the Apostle; and thou decree the restoring of his thousand gold pieces to Ali Khwajah, for that he hath been proved entitled to them."

FRANCE

Introduction

MEDIÆVAL France was divided not only geographically into north and south, but also in the matter of its literature: in the north, the *trouvères* composed or sang the epic, lyric and the *fabliaux;* in the south, the more gallant and aristocratic troubadours composed their lyric melodies of love with which the *jougleurs* or *jongleurs*, professional entertainers, would entertain the populace in the market place or the nobility in the hall.

The earliest French poetry to influence European literature is the *chanson de geste*, or song of deed, the foremost of which is the *Chanson de Roland*. Another form of poetry, which might be called story in verse form, is the *lay*, a form greatly cultivated by Marie de France who wrote about 1175. A much more famous individual and contemporary was Chrétien de Troyes, who is important in the development of the French Arthurian cycle.

It is not until the Renaissance that we discover the development of prose. In much of it we can trace the influence of Boccaccio. Particularly is this true of Marguerite de Navarre, Bonaventure des Périers, Noël du Fail, and others who, in keeping with the period, wrote exceedingly racy tales. But this century produced a far greater master in Rabelais, who more than any other author helped to create French prose.

With the exception of Perrault and Madame d'Aulnoy, who wrote delightful fairy tales that have since become children's classics, the seventeenth century was given over mainly to the drama. In the following century, the moral tale which found its counterpart in the works of Addison, Steele, and Goldsmith, was cultivated, and was especially practised by Marmontel. At the same time the novel was further developed, the outstanding masterpieces of the period being *Gil Blas*, by Le Sage, and *Manon Lescaut*, by Abbé Prévost. But most of the great writers of the time were essayists. In spite of an apparent frivolity and licentiousness, this was truly an age of reason, and its strength was not in its fiction but rather in its mighty thinkers, Diderot, Rousseau, and Voltaire. These did not, however, limit themselves to any particular form of expression, and we find that Voltaire, who wrote voluminously, is best remembered for his little satiric gem, *Candide*, and some deliciously ironic tales.

The nineteenth century is, without doubt, the richest period of French prose. It also witnessed the full fruition of the short story. It is nearly impossible, within the limits of this sketchy outline, to do more than merely mention some of the authors who have contributed to this magnificent literature. At the beginning of the century, we have Balzac, Dumas, Hugo, Stendhal, and George Sand. These were followed by Flaubert, Zola, and Maupassant, the last of these a master of the short story. Mérimée, Gautier, Daudet, Coppée, Richepin, Catulle Mendès are but a few of the many authors who have enriched the short-story literature, not only of France but of the world.

✷ ✷ ✷

OUR LADY'S TUMBLER
(Anonymous: 12th Century)

THIS beautiful tale that has been rewritten by Anatole France with exquisite perfection is a specimen of an immense literature devoted to the service of the Blessed Virgin, a service that distinguished the religion of the Middle Ages just as the worship of woman was the social note of the same period.

The present version is translated by Eugene Mason, in the volume *Aucassin and Nicolette and Other Medieval Romances and Legends*, published in Everyman's Library, E. P. Dutton & Co., by whose permission it is here reprinted.

OUR LADY'S TUMBLER

AMONGST the lives of the ancient Fathers, wherein may be found much profitable matter, this story is told for a true ensample. I do not say that you may not often have heard a fairer story, but at least this is not to be despised, and is well worth the telling. Now therefore will I say and narrate what chanced to this minstrel.

He erred up and down, to and fro, so often and in so many places, that he took the whole world in despite, and sought rest in a certain Holy Order. Horses and raiment and money, yea, all that he had, he straightway put from him, and seeking shelter from the world, was firmly set never to put foot within it more. For this cause he took refuge in this Holy Order, amongst the monks of Clairvaux. Now, though this dancer was comely of face and shapely of person, yet when he had once entered the monastery he found that he was master of no craft practised therein. In the world he had gained his bread by tumbling and dancing and feats of address. To leap, to spring, such matters he knew well, but of greater things he knew nothing, for he had never spelled from book—

nor Paternoster, nor canticle, nor creed, nor Hail Mary, nor aught concerning his soul's salvation.

When the minstrel had joined himself to the Order he marked how the tonsured monks spoke amongst themselves by signs, no words coming from their lips, so he thought within himself that they were dumb. But when he learned that truly it was by way of penance that speech was forbidden to their mouths, and that for holy obedience were they silent, then considered he that silence became him also; and he refrained his tongue from words, so discreetly and for so long a space, that day in, day out, he spake never, save by commandment; so that the cloister often rang with the brothers' mirth. The tumbler moved amongst his fellows like a man ashamed, for he had neither part nor lot in all the business of the monastery, and for this he was right sad and sorrowful. He saw the monks and the penitents about him, each serving God, in this place and that, according to his office and degree. He marked the priests at their ritual before the altars; the deacons at the gospels; the sub-deacons at the epistles; and the ministers about the vigils. This one repeats the introit; this other the lesson; cantors chant from the psalter; penitents spell out the Miserere—for thus are all things sweetly ordered—yea, and the most ignorant amongst them yet can pray his Paternoster. Wherever he went, here or there, in office or cloister, in every quiet corner and nook, there he found five, or three, or two, or at least one. He gazes earnestly, if so he is able, upon each. Such an one laments; this other is in tears; yet another grieves and sighs. He marvels at their sorrow. Then he said, "Holy Mary, what bitter grief have all these men that they smite the breast so grievously! Too sad of heart, meseems, are they who make such bitter dole together. Ah, St. Mary, alas, what words are these I say! These men are calling on the mercy of God, but I—what do I here! Here there is none so mean or vile but who serves God in his office and degree, save only me, for I work not, neither can I preach. Caitif and shamed was I when I thrust myself herein, seeing that I can do nothing well, either in labour or in prayer. I see my brothers upon their errands, one behind the other; but I do naught but fill my belly with the meat that they provide. If they perceive this thing, certainly shall I be in an evil case, for they will cast me out amongst the dogs, and none will take pity on the glutton and the idle man. Truly am I a caitif, set in a high place for a sign." Then he wept for very woe, and would that he was quiet in the grave. "Mary, Mother," quoth he, "pray now your Heavenly Father that He keep me in His pleasure, and give me such good counsel that I may truly serve both Him and you; yea, and may deserve that meat which now is bitter in my mouth."

Driven mad with thoughts such as these, he wandered about the abbey until he found himself within the crypt, and took sanctuary by the altar, crouching close as he was able. Above the altar was carved the statue of Madame St. Mary. Truly his steps had not erred when he sought that refuge; nay, but rather, God who knows His own had led him thither by the hand. When he heard the bells ring for Mass he sprang to his feet all dismayed. "Ha!" said he; "now am I betrayed. Each adds his mite to the great offering, save only me. Like a tethered ox, naught I do but chew the cud, and waste good victuals on a useless man. Shall I speak my thought? Shall I work my will? By the Mother of God, thus am I set to do. None is here to blame. I will do that which I can, and honour with my craft the Mother of God in her monastery. Since others honour her with chant, then I will serve with tumbling."

He takes off his cowl, and removes his garments, placing them near the altar, but so that his body be not naked he dons a tunic, very thin and fine, of scarce more substance than a shirt. So, light and comely of body, with gown girt closely about his loins, he comes before the Image right humbly. Then raising his eyes, "Lady," said he, "to your fair charge I give my body and my soul. Sweet Queen, sweet Lady, scorn not the thing I know, for with the help of God I will essay to serve you in good faith, even as I may. I cannot read your Hours nor chant your praise, but at the least I can set before you what art I have. Now will I be as the lamb that plays and skips before his mother. Oh, Lady, who art nowise bitter to those who serve you with a good intent, that which thy servant is, that he is for you."

Then commenced he his merry play, leaping low and small, tall and high, over and under. Then once more he knelt upon his knees before the statue, and meekly bowed his head. "Ha!" said he, "most gracious Queen, of your pity and your charity scorn not this my service." Again he leaped and played, and for holiday and festival, made the somersault of Metz. Again he bowed before the Image, did reverence, and paid it all the honour that he might. Afterwards he did the French vault, then the vault of Champagne, then the Spanish vault, then the vaults they love in Brittany, then the vault of Lorraine, and all these feats he did as best he was able. Afterwards he did the Roman vault, and then, with hands before his brow, danced daintily before the altar, gazing with a humble heart at the statue of God's Mother. "Lady," said he, "I set before you a fair play. This travail I do for you alone; so help me God, for you, Lady, and your Son. Think not I tumble for my own delight; but I serve you, and look for no other guerdon on my carpet. My brothers serve you, yea, and so do I. Lady, scorn not your villein, for he toils for your good pleasure; and, Lady, you are my delight and the sweetness of the world." Then he walked on his two hands, with his feet in the air, and his head near the ground. He twirled with his feet, and wept with his eyes. "Lady," said he, "I worship you with heart, with body, feet and hands, for this I can neither add to nor take away. Now am I your very minstrel. Others may chant your praises in the church, but here in the crypt will I tumble for your delight. Lady, lead me truly in your way, and for the love of God hold me not in utter despite." Then he smote upon his breast, he sighed and wept most tenderly, since he knew no better prayer than tears. Then he turned him about, and leaped once again. "Lady," said he, "as God is my Saviour, never have I turned this somersault before. Never has tumbler done such a feat, and, certes, it is not bad. Lady, what delight is his who may harbour with you in your glorious manor. For God's love, Lady, grant me such fair hostelry, since I am yours, and am nothing of my own." Once again he did the vault of Metz; again he danced and tumbled. Then when the chants rose louder from the choir, he, too, forced the note, and put forward all his skill. So long as the priest was about that Mass, so long his flesh endured to dance, and leap and spring, till at the last, nigh fainting, he could stand no longer upon his feet, but fell for weariness on the ground. From head to heel sweat stood upon him, drop by drop, as blood falls from meat turning upon the hearth. "Lady," said he, "I can no more, but truly will I seek you again." Fire consumed him utterly. He took his habit once more, and when he was wrapped close therein, he rose to his feet, and bending low before the statue, went his way. "Farewell," said he, "gentlest Friend. For God's love take it not to heart, for so I may I will soon return. Not one Hour shall pass but that I will serve you with right good will, so I may come, and so my service is pleasing in your sight." Thus he went from the crypt, yet gazing on his Lady. "Lady," said he, "my heart is sore that I cannot read your Hours. How would I love them for love of you, most gentle Lady! Into your care I commend my soul and my body."

In this fashion passed many days, for at every Hour he sought the crypt to do service, and pay homage before the Image. His service was so much to his mind that never once was he too weary to set out his most cunning feats to distract the Mother of God, nor did he ever wish for other play than this. Now, doubtless, the monks knew well enough that day by day he sought the crypt, but not a man on earth—save God alone—was aware of aught that passed there; neither would he, for all the wealth of the world, have let his goings in be seen, save by the Lord his God alone. For truly he believed that were his secret once espied he would be hunted from the cloister, and flung once more into the foul, sinful world, and for his part he was more fain to fall on death than to suffer any taint of sin. But God considering his simplicity, his sorrow for all he had wrought amiss, and the love which moved him to this deed, would that this toil should be known; and the Lord willed that the work of His friend should be made plain to men, for the glory of the Mother whom he worshipped, and so that all men should know and hear, and receive that God refuses none who seeks His face in love, however low his degree, save only he love God and strive to do His will.

Now think you that the Lord would have accepted this service, had it not been done for love of Him? Verily and truly, no, however much this juggler tumbled; but God called him friend, because he loved Him much. Toil and labour, keep fast and vigil, sigh and weep, watch and pray, ply the sharp scourge, be diligent at Matins and at Mass, owe no man anything, give alms of all you have—and yet, if you love not God with all your heart, all these good deeds are so much loss—mark well my words—and profit you naught for the saving of your soul. Without charity and love, works avail a man nothing. God asks not gold, neither for silver, but only for love unfeigned in His people's hearts, and since the tumbler loved Him beyond measure, for this reason God was willing to accept his service.

Thus things went well with this good man for a great space. For more years than I know the count of, he lived greatly at his ease, but the time came when the good man was sorely vexed, for a certain monk thought upon him, and blamed him in his heart that he was never set in choir for Matins. The monk marvelled much at his absence, and said within himself that he would never rest till it was clear what manner of man this was, and how he spent the Hours, and for what service the convent gave him bread. So he spied and pried and followed, till he marked him plainly, sweating at his craft in just such fashion as you have heard. "By my faith," said he, "this is a merry jest, and a fairer festival than we observe altogether. Whilst others are at prayers, and about the business of the House, this tumbler dances daintily, as though one had given him a hundred silver marks. He prides himself on being so nimble of foot, and thus he repays us what he owes. Truly it is this for that; we chant for him, and he tumbles for us. We throw him largesse: he doles us alms. We weep his sins, and he dries our eyes, Would that the monastery could see him, as I do, with their very eyes; willingly therefore would I fast till Vespers. Not one could refrain from mirth at the sight of this simple fool doing himself to death with his tumbling, for on himself he has no pity. Since his folly is free from malice, may God grant it to him as penance. Certainly I will not impute it to him as sin, for in all simplicity and good faith, I firmly believe, he does this thing, so that he may deserve his bread." So the monk saw with his very eyes how the tumbler did service at all the Hours, without pause or rest, and he laughed with pure mirth and delight, for in his heart was joy and pity.

The monk went straight to the Abbot and told him the thing from beginning to end, just as you have heard. The Abbot got him on his feet, and said to the monk, "By holy obedience I bid you hold your peace, and tell not this tale abroad against your brother. I lay on you my strict command to speak of this matter to none, save me. Come now, we will go forthwith to see what this can be, and let us pray the Heavenly King, and His very sweet, dear Mother, so precious and so bright, that in her gentleness she will plead with her Son, her Father, and her Lord, that I may look on this work—if thus it pleases Him—so that the good man be not wrongly blamed, and that God may be the more beloved, yet so that thus is His good pleasure." Then they secretly sought the crypt, and found a privy place near the altar, where they could see, and yet not be seen. From there the Abbot and his monk marked the business of the penitent. They saw the vaults he varied so cunningly, his nimble leaping and his dancing, his salutations of Our Lady, and his springing and his bounding, till he was nigh to faint. So weak was he that he sank on the ground, all outworn, and the sweat fell from his body upon the pavement of the crypt. But presently, in this his need, came she, his refuge, to his aid. Well she knew that guileless heart.

Whilst the Abbot looked, forthwith there came down from the vault a Dame so glorious, that certainly no man had seen one so precious, nor so richly crowned. She was more beautiful than the daughters of men, and her vesture was heavy with gold and gleaming stones. In her train came the hosts of Heaven, angel and archangel also; and these pressed close about the minstrel, and solaced and refreshed him. When their shining ranks drew near, peace fell upon his heart; for they contended to do him service, and were the servants of the servitor of that Dame who is the rarest Jewel of God. Then the sweet and courteous Queen herself took a white napkin in her hand, and with it gently fanned her minstrel before the altar. Courteous and debonair, the Lady refreshed his neck, his body and his brow. Meekly she served him as a handmaid in his need. But these things were hidden from the good man, for he neither saw nor knew that about him stood so fair a company.

The holy angels honour him greatly, but they can no longer stay, for their Lady turns to go. She blesses her minstrel with the sign of God, and the holy angels throng about her, still gazing back with delight upon their companion, for they await the hour when God shall release him from the burden of the world, and they possess his soul.

This marvel the Abbot and his monk saw at least four times, and thus at each Hour came the Mother of God with aid and succour for her man. Never doth she fail her servants in their need. Great joy had the Abbot that this thing was made plain to him. But the monk was filled with shame, since God had shown His pleasure in the service of His poor fool. His confusion burnt him like fire. "Dominus," said he to the Abbot, "grant me grace. Certainly this is a holy man, and since I have judged him amiss, it is very right that my body should smart. Give me now fast or vigil or the scourge, for without question he is a saint. We are witnesses to the whole matter, nor is it possible that we can be deceived." But the Abbot replied, "You speak truly, for God has made us to know that He has bound him with the cords of love. So I lay my commandment upon you, in virtue of obedience, and under pain of your person, that you tell no word to any man of that you have seen, save to God alone and me." "Lord," said he, "thus I will do." On these words they turned them, and hastened from the crypt; and the good man, having brought his tumbling to an end, presently clothed himself in his habit, and joyously went his way to the monastery.

Thus time went and returned, till it chanced that in a little while the Abbot sent for him who was so filled with virtue. When he heard that he was bidden of the Abbot, his heart was sore with grief, for he could think of nothing profitable to say. "Alas!" said he, "I am undone; not a day of my days but I shall know misery and sorrow and shame, for well I trow that my service is not pleasing to God. Alas! plainly doth He show that it displeases Him, since He causes the truth to be made clear. Could I believe that such work and play as mine could give delight to the mighty God! He had no pleasure therein, and all my toil was thrown away. Ah me, what shall I do? what shall I say? Fair, gentle God, what portion will be mine? Either shall I die in shame, or else shall I be banished from this place, and set up as a mark to the world and all the evil thereof. Sweet Lady, St. Mary, since I am all bewildered, and since there is none to give me counsel, Lady, come thou to my aid. Fair, gentle God, help me in my need. Stay not, neither tarry, but come quickly with Your Mother. For God's love, come not without her, but hasten both to me in my peril, for truly I know not what to plead. Before one word can pass my lips, surely will they bid me 'Begone.' Wretched that I am, what reply is he to make who has no advocate? Yet, why this dole, since go I must?" He came before the Abbot, with the tears yet wet upon his cheeks, and he was still weeping when he knelt upon the ground. "Lord," prayed he, "for the love of God deal not harshly with me. Would you send me from your door? Tell me what you would have me do, and thus it shall be done." Then replied the Abbot, "Answer me truly. Winter and summer have you lived here for a great space; now, tell me, what service have you given, and how have you deserved your bread?" "Alas!" said the tumbler, "well I knew that quickly I should be put upon the street when once this business was heard of you, and that you would keep me no more. Lord," said he, "I take my leave. Miserable I am, and miserable shall I ever be. Never yet have I made a penny for all my juggling." But the Abbot answered, "Not so said I; but I ask and require of you—nay, more, by virtue of holy obedience I command you—to seek within your conscience and tell me truly by what craft you have furthered the business of our monastery." "Lord," cried he, "now have you slain me, for this commandment is a sword." Then he laid bare before the Abbot the story of his days, from the first thing to the last, whatsoever pain it cost him; not a word did he leave out, but he told it all without a pause, just as I have told you the tale. He told it with clasped hands, and with tears, and at the close he kissed the Abbot's feet, and sighed.

The holy Abbot leaned above him, and, all in tears, raised him up, kissing both his eyes. "Brother," said he, "hold now your peace, for I make with you this true covenant, that you shall ever be of our monastery. God grant, rather, that we may be of yours, for all the worship you have brought to ours. I and you will call each other friend. Fair, sweet brother, pray you for me, and I for my part will pray for you. And now I pray you, my sweet friend, and lay this bidding upon you, without pretence, that you continue to do your service, even as you were wont heretofore—yea, and with greater craft yet, if so you may." "Lord," said he, "truly is this so?" "Yea," said the Abbot, "and verily." So he charged him, under peril of discipline, to put all doubts from his mind; for which reason the good man rejoiced so greatly that, as telleth the rhyme, he was all bemused, so that the blood left his cheeks, and his knees failed beneath him. When his courage came back, his very heart thrilled with joy; but so perilous was that quickening that therefrom he shortly died. But theretofore with a good heart he went about this service without rest, and Matins and Vespers, night and day, he missed no Hour till he became too sick to perform his office. So sore was his sickness upon him that he might not rise from his bed. Marvellous was the shame he proved when no more was he able to pay his rent. This was the grief that lay the heaviest upon him, for of his sickness he spake never a word, but he feared greatly lest he should fall from grace since he travailed no longer at his craft. He reckoned himself an idle man, and prayed God to take him to Himself before the sluggard might come to blame. For it was bitter to him to consider that all about him knew his case, so bitter that the burden was heavier than his heart could bear, yet there without remedy he must lie. The holy Abbot does him all honour; he and his monks chant the Hours about his bed, and in these praises of God he felt such delight that not for them would he have taken the province of Poitou, so great was his happiness therein. Fair and contrite was his confession, but still he was not at peace; yet why say more of this, for the hour had struck, and he must rise and go.

The Abbot was in that cell with all his monks; there, too, was company of many a priest and many a canon. These all humbly watched the dying man, and saw with open eyes this wonder happen. Clear to their very sight, about that lowly bed, stood the Mother of God, with angel and archangel, to wait the passing of his soul. Over against them were set, like wild beasts, devils and the Adversary, so they might snatch his spirit. I speak not to you in parable. But little profit had they for all their coming, their waiting, and their straining on the leash. Never might they have part in such a soul as his. When the soul took leave of his body, it fell not in their hands at all, for the Mother of God gathered it to her bosom, and the holy angels thronging round, quired for joy, as the bright train swept to Heaven with its burthen, according to the will of God. To these things the whole of the monastery was witness, besides such others as were there. So knew they and perceived that God sought no more to hide the love He bore to His poor servant, but rather would that his virtues should be plain to each man in that place; and very wonderful and joyful seemed this deed to them. Then with meet reverence they bore the body on its bier within the abbey church, and with high pomp commended their brother to the care of God; nor was there monk who did not chant or read his portion that day within the choir of the mighty church.

Thus with great honour they laid him to his rest, and kept his holy body amongst them as a relic. At that time spake the Abbot plainly to their ears, telling them the story of this tumbler and of all his life, just as you have heard, and of all that he himself beheld within the crypt. No brother but kept awake during that sermon. "Certes," said they, "easy is it to give credence to such a tale; nor should any doubt your words, seeing that the truth bears testimony to itself, and witness comes with need; yea, without any doubt have we full assurance that his discipline is done." Great joy amongst themselves have all within that place.

Thus endeth the story of the minstrel. Fair was his tumbling, fair was his service, for thereby gained he such high honour as is above all earthly gain. So the holy Fathers narrate that in such fashion these things chanced to this minstrel. Now, therefore, let us pray to God—He Who is above all other—that He may grant us so to do such faithful service that we may win the guerdon of His love.

Here endeth the Tumbler of Our Lady.

❊ ❊ ❊

MARGUERITE DE NAVARRE
(1492-1542)

MARGUERITE, sister of Francis I, was the second wife of the King of Navarre. Having intellectual ambitions, and being inclined to favor advancement of learning, she was enabled, because of her high position, to accomplish much. She herself aspired to be a poet, but as such she achieved mediocrity. The work which is chiefly responsible for her fame is the *Heptameron*, a collection of stories patterned after the *Decameron*, and dealing largely with questions of social intrigue and polite love.

The present version of the tale that follows is reprinted from the *Heptameron*, translated by Walter K. Kelly, London, no date.

THE HUSBAND WHO WAS BLIND OF AN EYE
(From the *Heptameron*, Novel 6)

CHARLES, the last Duke of Alençon, had an old valet-de-chambre who was blind of an eye, and who was married to a woman much younger than himself. The duke and duchess liked this valet better than any other domestic of that order in their household, and the consequence was that he could not go and see his wife as often as he could have wished, whilst she, unable to accommodate herself to circumstances, so far forgot her honour and her conscience as to fall in love with a young gentleman of the neighbourhood. At last the affair got wind, and there was so much talk about it, that it reached the ears of the husband, who could not believe it, so warm was the affection testified to him by his wife. One day, however, he made up his mind to know the truth of the matter, and to revenge himself if he could on the person who put this affront upon him. With this view he pretended to go for two or three days to a place at some little distance; and no sooner had he taken his departure, than his wife sent for her gallant. They had hardly been half an hour together when the husband came and knocked loudly at the door. The wife knowing but too well who it was, told her lover, who was so astounded that he could have wished he was still in his mother's womb. But while he was swearing and confounding her and the intrigue which had brought him into such a perilous scrape, she told him not to be uneasy, for she would get him off without its costing him anything; and that all he had to do was to dress himself as quickly as possible.

Meanwhile the husband kept knocking and calling to his wife as loud as he could bawl, but she pretended not to know him. "Why don't you get up," she cried to the people of the house, "and go and silence those who are making such a noise at the door? Is this a proper time to come to honest people's houses? If my husband was here he would make you know better." The husband, hearing her voice, shouted louder than ever. "Let me in, wife; do you mean to keep me at the door till daylight?" At last, when she saw that her lover was ready to slip out, "Oh, is that you, husband?" she said; "I am so glad you are come! I was full of a dream I had that gave me the greatest pleasure I ever felt in my life. I thought you had recovered the sight of your eye." Here she opened the door, and catching her husband round the neck, kissed him, clapped one hand on his sound eye, and asked him if he did not see better than usual. Whilst the husband was thus blindfolded the gallant made his escape. The husband guessed how it was, but said "I will watch you no more, wife. I thought to deceive you, but it is I who have been the dupe, and you have put the cunningest trick upon me that ever was invented. God mend you! for it passes the act of man to bring back a wicked woman from her evil ways by any means short of putting her to death. But since the regard I have had for you has not availed to make you behave better, perhaps the contempt with which I shall henceforth look upon you will touch you more, and have a more wholesome effect." Therefore he went away, leaving her in great confusion. At last, however, he was prevailed upon by the solicitations of relations and friends, and by the tears and excuses of his wife, to live with her again.

✳ ✳ ✳

CHARLES PERRAULT
(1628-1703)

PERRAULT, born in Paris, was one of four sons, each of whom was a man of some distinction. Charles studied for the law at Orleans, was called to the Bar at Paris, but ceased practice after a short time. In 1663, he was chosen by Colbert as his secretary to assist him in matters relating to art and literature. In 1671, Perrault was admitted to the Académie française. While he wrote a number of things, the only works of his which continued to be read with great pleasure are his famous fairy tales which appeared in a volume in 1697.

The present version is translated for this collection by Maxim Lieber.

BLUE BEARD
(From *Tales of Perrault*)

THERE lived once upon a time a man who had lovely houses in town and country, an abundance of gold and silver plate, embroidered furniture and gilded coaches. But, unfortunately, he had a blue beard, which made him so frightfully ugly, that there was neither dame nor maiden that did not fly at sight of him.

One of his neighbours, a lady of quality, had two perfectly beautiful daughters; and he asked the lady for the hand of one of these, leaving the matter of choice to her. Neither of the two wanted him, and they sent him from one to the other, not being able to make up their minds to take a husband with a blue beard. What particularly disgusted them was the fact that he had already married several wives, and, moreover, no one knew what had become of them.

Blue Beard, in order to make their acquaintance, invited them, with their mother and three or four of their lady friends as well as several young men of the neighbourhood, to one of his country houses, where they spent a whole week. One round of pleasure succeeded another, walking, hunting, fishing, feasting, dancing. They never slept, but rather passed the hours of night joking and teasing one another. In short all went so smoothly, that the younger daughter began to find that their host did not have so blue a beard after all, and that he was indeed a very honest man. As soon as they returned to town, the marriage was concluded.

At the end of a month, Blue Beard told his wife that he was obliged to take a journey into the provinces, for some six weeks at least, for some business of serious consequence. He begged her to divert herself during his absence by inviting some of her friends, to take them to the country if she so desired; and above all, to make good cheer.

"Here," said he, "are the keys to the two great store-chambers. This one opens the room of my gold and silver plate, which is but seldom used; these are the keys of my jewel coffers, and here is the master-key to all of the apartments. As for this little key, that is for the cabinet at the end of the great gallery of the ground floor apartment. Open all the doors; go everywhere, but I forbid you to enter that little cabinet. And I forbid you so strongly, that if you should open it, there is nothing you may not expect from my anger."

She promised to obey all his orders exactly; and after embracing her, he got into his coach and departed on his journey.

Her friends and kind neighbours scarcely waited for the young bride's invitation, so impatient were they to see all the riches of her home, having never dared to come while her husband was in, because of his blue beard which terrified them. They ran through the entire house, the chambers, the closets, the wardrobes, each one proving to be more beautiful than the last. They went into the store-rooms, where they could not sufficiently admire the number and beauty of the tapestries, beds, sofas, consoles, tables, and mirrors, in which one could see oneself from head to foot, with their frames of glass and silver and silver-gilt, the most magnificent ever seen. They did not cease to extol and to envy the good fortune of their friend who, meanwhile, was not in the least amused by the sight of all these riches, being impatient to open the little cabinet on the ground floor.

She was so pressed by her curiosity, that, without considering how uncivil it was to leave her guests, she ran down a back staircase with such haste that she thought she would break her neck. When she reached the door of the cabinet, she hesitated for a moment, thinking of her husband's order, and considering what ill fate might befall her if she disobeyed it. But the temptation was so powerful, that she could not overcome it. She therefore took the little key, and, trembling, opened the door.

At first she could see nothing, because the window-shutters were closed. After some moments, she began to perceive that the floor was covered with clotted blood in which was reflected the corpses of several dead women hanging along the wall. These were the women whom Blue Beard had married, and whose throats he had slit, one after the other. She thought to die of fear, and the key, which she had pulled from the lock, fell from her hand.

After having regained her senses a little, she picked up the key, locked the door, and went up to her room to recover herself. This was very difficult, because she was so wrought up. Having observed that the key was smeared with blood, she wiped it two or three times; but the blood would not come off. She tried to wash it, even scrubbed it with sand and pumice-stone, but the blood still remained; for the key was a magic one, and there was no means of making it quite clean; when the blood was scoured off on one side, it came back on the other. . . .

Blue Beard returned that same evening. He told her that he had received letters on the road which had apprised him that the business he had gone about had been settled to his advantage. His wife did all she could to give him proof that she was delighted at his speedy return.

The next morning he asked her to return the keys; which she gave him, but with such a trembling hand, that he easily guessed what had transpired.

"Why is not the key to the cabinet among the rest?" he asked.

"I must have left it upstairs on my table," she replied.

"Do not fail to let me have it at once," said Blue Beard.

Not being able to delay any longer, she finally brought the key. Blue Beard, having scrutinised it, asked his wife, "Why is there blood on this key?"

"I know nothing at all about it," replied the poor woman, paler than death.

"You know nothing about it?" cried Blue Beard. "But I know very well. You have chosen to enter the cabinet. Well, madam, you shall enter it and take your place among the ladies you saw there."

She flung herself at her husband's feet, weeping and begging his pardon with every sign of truly repenting her disobedience. She would have melted a rock, so beautiful and distressed was she; but Blue Beard had a heart harder than a rock.

"You must die, madam," said he, "and immediately."

"Since I must die," she answered, looking at him with her eyes bathed in tears, "give me a little time to pray."

"I give you fifteen minutes," replied Blue Beard, "but not a moment more."

On being left alone, she called her sister and exclaimed, "My dear Anne," (for that was the other's name) "ascend, I implore you, to the top of the tower, to see if my brothers are approaching. They promised to come and see me today. And when you see them, beckon them to make haste."

Sister Anne ran up to the roof of the tower; and from time to time, the afflicted one cried up to her, "Anne, Sister Anne, do you see anyone coming?"

And Sister Anne answered her, "I see nothing but the noon dust a-blowing and the green grass a-growing."

Meanwhile, Blue Beard, holding a huge sabre in his hand, cried with all his might, "Come down quickly, or I will go up to you!"

"Another moment, I pray you," his wife replied. And then she called softly to her sister, "Anne, Sister Anne, do you see anyone coming?" And Sister Anne answered, "I see nothing but the noon dust a-flying and the green grass a-growing."

"Come down quickly," shouted Blue Beard, "or I will go up to you!"

"I am coming," answered his wife. And then she cried, "Anne, Sister Anne, do you see anyone coming?"

"I see," replied Sister Anne, "a great cloud of dust coming from yonder."

"Is it my brothers?"

"Alas! no, sister. I see a flock of sheep. . . ."

"Will you not come down?" shouted Blue Beard.

"Yet another moment," pleaded his wife. And again she called, "Anne, Sister Anne, do you see nobody coming?"

"I see two knights approaching, but they are yet a long way off. . . . God be praised," she cried out a moment after, "they are our brothers. I'll signal them to make haste."

Then Blue Beard began to roar so terribly that he made the whole house tremble. The poor lady came down and cast herself at his feet, all in tears and dishevelled. "This shall not help you," said Blue Beard. "You must die!" Then clutching her hair in one hand and flourishing the sabre in the other, he was going to strike off her head. The poor lady wriggled about and looked up at him with dying eyes, imploring him to grant her just a moment to fix her thoughts on devotion.

"No, no," said he, "recommend thyself to God," and he lifted his arm. . . .

In that moment there came so loud a knocking at the gate, that Blue Beard's arm abruptly paused, midair. The gate was opened, and two cavaliers ran in with drawn swords and rushed at Blue Beard. He had recognised them as his wife's brothers,—one was a dragoon, the other a musketeer,—and he ran to save himself. But the two brothers pursued him so swiftly, that they overtook him before he could reach the perron. They passed their swords through his body, and left him there for dead. The poor lady was nearly as dead as her husband, and had not the strength to rise and embrace her brothers.

It transpired that Blue Beard had no heirs, and thus his wife became mistress of his estates. She employed a part of her wealth to marry her young Sister Anne to a young gentleman who had loved her a long while. Another part she used to purchase captain's commissions for her two brothers; and the rest to marry herself to a very honest man, who made her forget the unhappy time she had passed with Blue Beard.

✳ ✳ ✳

VOLTAIRE
(1694-1779)

FRANCOIS MARIE AROUET, better known as Voltaire, was born at Paris, and received his education at the Collège Louis-le-Grand, which was conducted by the Jesuits. He was possibly the greatest man of thought during the eighteenth century, half of which he almost completely dominated with his ironic pen. He wrote voluminously, in every field of literature, getting himself into difficulties by his vigorous attacks on church and state. One of his most delightful books is *Candide*, a satire on optimism. Besides his longer works, he wrote a number of short stories which, ironically enough, will probably endure longer than any of his other writings. Saintsbury says, "It may be doubted whether any of his works displays his peculiar genius more fully and more characteristically." Of these stories *Jeannot and Colin* is one of the most artistic of Voltaire's fiction. The present version appears in *Zadig and Other Tales*, translated by R. Bruce Boswell, published in Bohn's Standard Library.

JEANNOT AND COLIN

MANY trustworthy persons have seen Jeannot and Colin when they went to school at Issoire in Auvergne, a town famous all over the world for its college and its kettles. Jeannot was the son of a dealer in mules, a man of considerable reputation; Colin owed his existence to a worthy husbandman who dwelt in the outskirts of the town, and cultivated his farm with the help of four mules, and who, after paying tolls and tallage, scutage and salt-duty, poundage, poll-tax, and tithes, did not find himself particularly well off at the end of the year.

Jeannot and Colin were very handsome lads for natives of Auvergne; they were much attached to each other, and had little secrets together and private understandings, such as old comrades always recall with pleasure when they afterwards meet in a wider world.

Their schooldays were drawing near their end, when a tailor one day brought Jeannot a velvet coat of three colours with a waistcoat of Lyons silk to match in excellent taste; this suit of clothes was accompanied by a letter addressed to Monsieur de la Jeannotière. Colin admired the coat, and was not at all jealous; but Jeannot assumed an air of superiority which distressed Colin. From that moment Jeannot paid no more heed to his lessons, but was always looking at his reflection in the glass, and despised everybody but himself. Some time afterwards a footman arrived post-haste, bringing a second letter, addressed this time to His Lordship the Marquis de la Jeannotière; it contained an order from his father for the young nobleman, his son, to be sent to Paris. As Jeannot mounted the chaise to drive off, he stretched out his hand to Colin with a patronising smile befitting his rank. Colin felt his own insignificance, and wept. So Jeannot departed in all his glory.

Readers who like to know all about things may be informed that Monsieur Jeannot, the father, had rapidly gained immense wealth in business. You ask how those great fortunes are made? It all depends upon luck. Monsieur Jeannotière had a comely person, and so had his wife; moreover her complexion was fresh and blooming. They had gone to Paris to prosecute a lawsuit which was ruining them, when Fortune, who lifts up and casts down human beings, at her pleasure, presented them with an introduction to the wife of an army-hospital contractor, a man of great talent, who could boast of having killed more soldiers in one year than the cannon had destroyed in ten. Jeannot took the lady's fancy, and Jeannot's wife captivated the gentleman. Jeannot soon became a partner in the business, and entered into other speculations. When one is in the current of the stream it is only necessary to let oneself drift, and so an immense fortune may sometimes be made without any trouble. The beggars who watch you from the bank, as you glide along in full sail, open their eyes in astonishment; they wonder how you have managed to get on; they envy you at all events, and write pamphlets against you which you never read. That was what happened to Jeannot senior, who was soon styled Monsieur de la Jeannotière, and, after buying a marquisate at the end of six months, he took the young nobleman his son away from school, to launch him into the fashionable world of Paris.

Colin, always affectionately disposed, wrote a kind letter to his old schoolfellow in order to offer his congratulations. The little marquis sent him no answer, which grieved Colin sorely.

The first thing that his father and mother did for the young gentleman was to get him a tutor. This tutor, who was a man of distinguished manners and profound ignorance, could teach his pupil nothing. The marquis wished his son to learn Latin, but the marchioness would not hear of it. They consulted the opinion of a certain author who had obtained considerable celebrity at that time from some popular works which he had written. He was invited to dinner, and the master of the house began by saying:

"Sir, as you know Latin, and are conversant with the manners of the Court——"

"I, sir! Latin! I don't know a word of it," answered the man of wit; "and it is just as well for me that I don't, for one can speak one's own language better, when the attention is not divided between it and foreign tongues. Look at all our ladies; they are far more charming in conversation than men, their letters are written with a hundred times more grace of expression. They owe that superiority over us to nothing else but their ignorance of Latin."

"There now! Was I not right?" said the lady. "I want my son to be a man of wit, and to make way in the world. You see that if he were to learn Latin, it would be his ruin. Tell me, if you please, are plays and operas performed in Latin? Are the proceedings in court conducted in Latin, when one has a lawsuit on hand? Do people make love in Latin?"

The marquis, confounded by these arguments, passed sentence, and it was decided that the young nobleman should not waste his time in studying Cicero, Horace, and Virgil.

"But what is he to learn then? For still, I suppose, he will have to know something. Might he not be taught a little geography?"

"What good will that do him?" answered the tutor. "When my lord marquis goes to visit his country-seat, will not his postillions know the roads? There will be no fear of their going astray. One does not want a sextant in order to travel, and it is quite possible to make a journey between Paris and Auvergne without knowing anything about the latitude and longitude of either."

"Very true," replied the father; "but I have heard people speak of a noble science, which is, I think, called *astronomy*."

"Bless my soul!" rejoined the tutor. "Do we regulate our behaviour in this world by the stars? Why should my lord marquis wear himself out in calculating an eclipse, when he will find it predicted correctly to a second in the almanac, which will moreover inform him of all the movable feasts, the age of the moon, and that of all the princesses in Europe?"

The marchioness was quite of the tutor's opinion, the little marquis was in a state of the highest delight, and his father was very undecided.

"What then is my son to be taught?" said he.

"To make himself agreeable," answered the friend whom they had consulted; "for, if he knows the way to please, he will know everything worth knowing; it is an art which he will learn from her ladyship, his mother, without the least trouble to either of them."

The marchioness, at these words, smiled graciously upon the courtly ignoramus, and said:

"It is easy to see, sir, that you are a most accomplished gentleman; my son will owe all his education to you. I imagine, however, that it will not be a bad thing for him to know a little history."

"Nay, madame—what good would that do him?" he answered. "Assuredly the only entertaining and useful history is that of the passing hour. All ancient histories, as one of our clever writers * has observed, are admitted to be nothing but fables; and for us moderns it is an inextricable chaos. What does it matter to the young gentleman, your son, if Charlemagne instituted the twelve Paladins of France, or if his successor † had an impediment in his speech?"

"Nothing was ever said more wisely!" exclaimed the tutor. "The minds of children are smothered under a mass of useless knowledge; but of all sciences that which seems to me the most absurd, and the one best adapted to extinguish every spark of genius, is geometry. That ridiculous science is concerned with surfaces, lines, and points which have no existence in nature. In imagination a hundred thousand curved lines may be made to pass between a circle and a straight line which touches it, although in reality you could not insert so much as a straw. Geometry, indeed, is nothing more than a bad joke."

The marquis and his lady did not understand much of the meaning of what the tutor was saying; but they were quite of his way of thinking.

"A nobleman like his lordship," he continued, "should not dry up his brain with such unprofitable studies. If, some day, he should require one of those sublime geometricians to draw a plan of his estates, he can have them measured for his money. If he should wish to trace out the antiquity of his lineage, which goes back to the most remote ages, all he will have to do will be to send some learned Benedictine. It is the same with all the other arts. A young lord born under a lucky star is neither painter, nor a musician, nor an architect, nor a sculptor; but he may make all these arts flourish by encouraging them with his generous approval. Doubtless it is much better to patronise than to practise them. It will be quite enough if my lord the young marquis has taste; it is the part of artists to work for him, and thus there is a great deal of truth in the remark that people of quality (that is, if they are very rich) know everything without learning anything, because, in point of fact and in the long run, they are masters of all the knowledge which they can command and pay for."

The agreeable ignoramus then took part in the conversation, and said: "You have well remarked, madame, that the great end of man's exis-

* Bernard Fontenelle, who died in the year 1757.—[ED.]
† Louis le Bègue, i. e., the Stammerer, was third in succession from Charlemagne.—[ED.]

tence is to succeed in society. Is it, forsooth, any aid to the attainment of this success to have devoted oneself to the sciences? Does any one ever think in select company of talking about geometry? Is a well-bred gentleman ever asked what star rises to-day with the sun? Does any one at the supper-table ever want to know if Clodion the Long-Haired crossed the Rhine?"

"No, indeed!" exclaimed the Marchioness de la Jeannotière, whose charms had been her passport into the world of fashion; "and my son must not stifle his genius by studying all that trash. But, after all, what is he to be taught? For it is a good thing that a young lord should be able to shine when occasion offers, as my noble husband has said. I re-member once hearing an abbé remark that the most entertaining science was something the name of which I have forgotten—it begins with a *b*."

"With a *b*, madame? It was not botany, was it?"

"No, it certainly was not botany that he mentioned; it began, as I tell you, with a *b*, and ended in *onry*."

"Ah, madame, I understand! It was blazonry or heraldry. That is indeed a most profound science; but it has ceased to be fashionable since the custom has died out of having one's coat of arms painted on the carriage-doors; it was the most useful thing imaginable in a well-ordered state. Besides, that line of study would be endless, for at the present day there is not a barber who is without his armorial bearings, and you know that whatever becomes common loses its attraction."

Finally, after all the pros and cons of the different sciences had been examined and discussed, it was decided that the young marquis should learn dancing.

Dame Nature, who disposes everything at her own will and pleasure, had given him a talent which soon developed itself with prodigious success; it was that of singing street-ballads in a charming style. His youthful grace accompanying this superlative gift, caused him to be regarded as a young man of the highest promise. He was a favourite with the ladies, and, having his head crammed with songs, he had no lack of mistresses to whom to address his verses. He stole the line, "Bacchus with the Loves at play," from one ballad; and made it rhyme with "night and day" taken out of another, while a third furnished him with "charms" and "alarms." But inasmuch as there were always some feet more or less than were wanted in his verses, he had them corrected at the rate of twenty sovereigns a song. And The Literary Year placed him in the same rank with such sonneteers as La Fare, Chaulieu, Hamilton, Sarrasin, and Voiture.

Her ladyship the marchioness then believed that she was indeed the mother of a genius, and gave a supper to all the wits of Paris. The young man's head was soon turned upside down, he acquired the art of talking without knowing the meaning of what he said, and perfected himself in the habit of being fit for nothing. When his father saw him so eloquent, he keenly regretted that he had not had him taught Latin, or he would have purchased some high appointment for him in the Law. His mother, who was of more heroic sentiments, took upon herself to solicit a regiment for her son; in the meantime he made love—and love is sometimes more expensive than a regiment. He squandered his money freely, while his parents drained their purses and credit to a lower and lower ebb by living in the grandest style.

A young widow of good position in their neighbourhood, who had only a moderate income, was well enough disposed to make some effort to prevent the great wealth of the Marquis and Marchioness de la Jeannotière from going altogether, by marrying the young marquis and so appropriating what remained. She enticed him to her house, let him make love to her, allowed him to see that she was not quite indifferent to him, led him on by degrees, enchanted him, and made him her devoted slave without the least difficulty. She would give him at one time commendation and at another time counsel; she became his father's and mother's best friend. An old neighbour proposed marriage; the parents, dazzled with the splendour of the alliance, joyfully fell in with the scheme, and gave their only son to their most intimate lady friend. The young marquis was thus about to wed a woman whom he adored, and by whom he was beloved in return. The friends of the family congratulated him, the marriage settlement was on the point of being signed, the bridal dress and the epithalamium were both well under way.

One morning our young gentleman was on his knees before the charmer whom fond affection and esteem were so soon to make his own; they were tasting in animated and tender converse the first fruits of future happiness; they were settling how they should lead a life of perfect bliss, when one of his lady mother's footmen presented himself, scared out of his wits.

"Here's fine news which may surprise you!" said he; "the bailiffs are in the house of my lord and lady, removing the furniture. All has been seized by the creditors. They talk of personal arrest, and I am going to do what I can to get my wages paid."

"Let us see what has happened," said the marquis, "and discover the meaning of all this."

"Yes," said the widow, "go and punish those rascals—go, quick!"

He hurried homewards, he arrived at the house, his father was already in prison, all the servants had fled, each in a different direction, carrying off whatever they could lay their hands upon. His mother was alone, helpless, forlorn, and bathed in tears; she had nothing left her but the remembrance of her former prosperity, her beauty, her faults, and her foolish extravagance.

After the son had condoled with his mother for a long time, he said at last:

"Let us not despair; this young widow loves me to distraction; she is even more generous than she is wealthy, I can assure you; I will fly to her for succour, and bring her to you."

So he returns to his mistress, and finds her conversing in private with a fascinating young officer.

"What! Is that you, my Lord de la Jeannotière? What business have you with me? How can you leave your mother by herself in this way? Go, and stay with the poor woman, and tell her that she shall always have my good wishes. I am in want of a waiting-woman now, and will gladly give her the preference."

"My lad," said the officer, "you seem pretty tall and straight; if you would like to enter my company, I will make it worth your while to enlist."

The marquis, stupefied with astonishment, and secretly enraged, went off in search of his former tutor, confided to him all his troubles, and asked his advice. He proposed that he should become, like himself, a tutor of the young.

"Alas! I know nothing; you have taught me nothing whatever, and you are the primary cause of all my unhappiness." And as he spoke he began to sob.

"Write novels," said a wit who was present; "it is an excellent resource to fall back upon at Paris."

The young man, in more desperate straits than ever, hastened to the house of his mother's father confessor; he was a Theatine * monk of the very highest reputation, who directed the souls of none but ladies of the first rank in society. As soon as he saw him, the reverend gentleman rushed to meet him.

"Good gracious! My lord marquis, where is your carriage? How is your honoured mother, the marchioness?"

The unfortunate young fellow related the disaster that had befallen his family. As he explained the matter further the Theatine assumed a graver air, one of less concern and more self-importance.

"My son, herein you may see the hand of Providence; riches serve only to corrupt the heart. The Almighty has shown special favour then to your mother in reducing her to beggary. Yes, sir, so much the better! —she is now sure of her salvation."

"But, father, in the meantime are there no means of obtaining some succour in this world?"

"Farewell, my son! There is a lady of the Court waiting for me."

*The Theatines are a religious brotherhood now confined to Italy, formed in 1524. Their first superior was one of the four founders of the order, Caraffa, Bishop of Theate (Chieti); hence their name.—[Ed.]

The marquis felt ready to faint. He was treated after much the same manner by all his friends, and learned to know the world better in half a day than in all the rest of his life.

As he was plunged in overwhelming despair, he saw an old-fashioned travelling-chaise, more like a covered tumbril than anything else, and furnished with leather curtains, followed by four enormous waggons all heavily laden. In the chaise was a young man in rustic attire; his round and rubicund face had an air of kindness and good temper. His little wife, whose sunburnt countenance had a pleasing if not a refined expression, was jolted about as she sat beside him. The vehicle did not go quite so fast as a dandy's chariot, the traveller had plenty of time to look at the marquis, as he stood motionless, absorbed in his grief.

"Oh! good Heavens!" he exclaimed; "I believe that is Jeannot there!"

Hearing that name the marquis raised his eyes—the chaise stopped.

"'Tis Jeannot himself! Yes, it is Jeannot!"

The plump little man with one leap sprang to the ground, and ran to embrace his old companion. Jeannot recognised Colin; signs of sorrow and shame covered his countenance.

"You have forsaken your old friend," said Colin; "but be you as grand a lord as you like, I shall never cease to love you."

Jeannot, confounded and cut to the heart, told him with sobs something of his history.

"Come into the inn where I am lodging, and tell me the rest," said Colin; "kiss my little wife, and let us go and dine together."

They went, all three of them, on foot, and the baggage followed.

"What in the world is all this paraphernalia? Does it belong to you?"

"Yes, it is all mine and my wife's; we are just come from the country. I am at the head of a large tin, iron, and copper factory, and have married the daughter of a rich tradesman and general provider of all useful commodities for great folks and small. We work hard, and God gives us his blessing. We are satisfied with our condition in life, and are quite happy. We will help our friend Jeannot. Give up being a marquis; all the grandeur in the world is not equal in value to a good friend. You will return with me into the country; I will teach you my trade, it is not a difficult one to learn; I will give you a share in the business, and we will live together with light hearts in that corner of the earth where we were born."

Jeannot, overcome by this kindness, felt himself divided between sorrow and joy, tenderness and shame; and he said within himself:

"All my fashionable friends have proved false to me, and Colin, whom I despised, is the only one who comes to my succour. What a lesson!"

Colin's generosity developed in Jeannot's heart the germ of that good disposition which the world had not yet choked. He felt that he could not desert his father and mother.

"We will take care of your mother," said Colin; "and as for the good man your father, who is in prison—I know something of business matters—his creditors, when they see that he has nothing more, will agree to a moderate composition. I will see to all that myself."

Colin was as good as his word, and succeeded in effecting the father's release from prison. Jeannot returned to his old home with his parents, who resumed their former occupation. He married Colin's sister, who, being like her brother in disposition, rendered her husband very happy. And so Jeannot the father, and Jeannotte the mother, and Jeannot the son came to see that vanity is no true source of happiness.

❋ ❋ ❋

JEAN-FRANCOIS MARMONTEL
(1723-1799)

MARMONTEL was educated for the priesthood, but he grew too liberal and became a professional writer. He wrote plays, memoirs, romances, articles for the *Encyclopedia*, and a collection of *Moral Tales*, in which, by a curious paradox, the morals are frequently absent. The merit of these famous tales lies in the delicate finish of the style, as well as in the graphic pictures of French society under Louis XV. Occasionally, Marmontel conveys his readers to an Oriental scene, as happens in *Soliman II*.

The present version is from a translation of the *Moral Tales*, published in London, no date.

SOLIMAN II.

IT is pleasant to see grave historians racking their brains, in order to find out great causes for great events. Sylla's *valet-de-chambre* would perhaps have laughed heartily to hear the politicians reason on the abdication of his master; but it is not of Sylla that I am now going to speak.

Soliman II. married his slave in contempt of the laws of the Sultans. It is natural at first to paint to ourselves this slave as an accomplished beauty, with an elevated soul, an uncommon genius, and a profound skill in politics. No such thing; the fact was as follows:—

Soliman grew splenetic in the midst of his glory: the various but ready pleasures of the seraglio were become insipid to him. "These slaves move my pity. Their soft docility has nothing poignant, nothing flattering. It is to hearts nourished in the bosom of liberty that it would be delightful to make slavery agreeable."

The whims of a Sultan are laws to his ministers. Large sums were instantly promised to such as should bring European slaves to the seraglio. In a short time there arrived three, who, like the three Graces, seemed to have divided among themselves all the charms of beauty.

Features noble and modest, eyes tender and languishing, an ingenuous temper, and a sensible soul, distinguished the touching Elmira. The entrance to the seraglio, the idea of servitude, had chilled her with a mortal terror: Soliman found her in a swoon in the arms of his women. He approaches; he recalls her to life; he encourages her; she lifts towards him a pair of large blue eyes, bedewed with tears; he reaches forth his hand to her; he supports her himself; she follows him with a tottering step. The slaves retire; and as soon as he is alone with her—"It is not with fear, beautiful Elmira," said he to her, "that I would inspire you. Forget that you have a master; see in me only a lover." "The name of lover," said she to him, "is not less unknown to me than that of master; and both the one and the other make me tremble. They have told me (and I still shudder at the thought) that I am destined to your pleasures. Alas! what pleasure can it be to tyrannise over weakness and innocence! Believe me, I am not capable of the compliances of servitude; and the only pleasure possible for you to taste with me is that of being generous. Restore me to my parents and my country; and in the respect you show for my virtue, my youth, and my misfortunes, merit my gratitude, my esteem, and my regret."

This discourse from a slave was new to Soliman; his great soul was moved by it. "No," said he, "my dear child, I will owe nothing to violence. You charm me! I will make it my happiness to love and please you; and I will prefer the torment of never seeing you more to that of seeing you unhappy. However, before I restore you to liberty, give me leave to try, at least, whether it be not possible for me to dissipate that terror which the name of slave strikes into you. I ask only one month's trial: after which, if my love cannot move you, I will avenge myself of your ingratitude in no other way than by delivering you up to the inconstancy and perfidy of mankind." "Ah! my lord!" cried Elmira, with an emotion mixed with joy, "how unjust are the prejudices of my country, and how little are your virtues known there! Continue such as I now see you, and I no longer reckon this day unfortunate."

Some moments after, she saw slaves enter, carrying baskets filled with stuffs and valuable trinkets. "Choose," said the Sultan to her; "these are clothes, not ornaments, that are here presented to you; nothing can adorn you." "Decide for me," said Elmira to him, running her eyes over the baskets. "Do not consult me," replied the Sultan; "I hate without distinction everything that can rob me of one of your charms." Elmira blushed, and the Sultan perceiving she preferred the colours most favourable to the character of her beauty, he conceived a pleasing hope from that circumstance: for care to adorn one's self is almost a desire to please.

The month of trial passed away in timid gallantries on the part of the Sultan, and on Elmira's side in complaisance and delicate attentions. Her confidence in him increased every day without her perceiving it. At first he was not permitted to see her till after the business of the toilette and on condition to depart when she prepared to undress again. In a short time he was admitted both to her toilet and dishabillé. It was there that the plan of their amusements for that day and the next was formed. Whatever either proposed was exactly what the other was going to propose. Their disputes turned only on the stealing of thoughts. Elmira, in these disputes, perceived not some small slips which escaped her modesty. A pin misplaced, or a garter put on unthinkingly, etc., afforded the Sultan pleasures which he was cautious not to testify. He knew (and it was much for a Sultan to know) that it was impolitic to advertise modesty of the dangers to which it exposes itself; that it is never fiercer than when alarmed; and that in order to subdue it one should render them familiar. Nevertheless, the more he discovered of Elmira's charms the more he perceived his fears increase, on account of the approach of the day that might deprive him of them.

The fatal period arrives. Soliman causes chests to be prepared, filled with stuffs, precious stones, and perfumes. He repairs to Elmira, followed by these presents. "It is to-morrow," said he, "that I have promised to restore you to liberty, if you still regret the want of it. I now came to acquit myself of my promise, and to bid adieu to you for ever." "What!" said Elmira trembling, "is it to-morrow? I had forgot it." "It is to-morrow," resumed the Sultan, "that, delivered up to my despair, I am to become the most unhappy of men." "You are very cruel, then, to yourself, to put me in mind of it!" "Alas! it depends only on you, Elmira, that I should forget it for ever." "I confess," said she to him, "that your sorrow touches me; that your proceedings have interested me in your happiness; and if, to show my gratitude, it were necessary only to prolong the time of my slavery—" "No, madam, I am but too much accustomed to the happiness of possessing you. I perceive that the more I shall know of you, the more terrible it would be to me to lose you. This sacrifice will cost me my life; but I shall only render it the most grievous by deferring it. May your country prove worthy of it! May the people whom you are going to please deserve you better than I do! I ask but one favour of you, which is that you would be pleased cordially to accept these presents, as the feeble pledges of a love the most pure and tender that yourself, yes, that yourself, are capable of inspiring." "No," said she to him, with a voice almost smothered, "I will not accept your presents. I go; you will have it so! But I shall carry away from you nothing but your image." Soliman lifting up his eyes to Elmira, met hers bedewed with tears. "Adieu, then, Elmira!" "Adieu, Soliman!" They bid each other so many and such tender adieus, that they concluded by swearing not to separate for life. The avenues of pleasure through which he had passed so rapidly with his slaves from Asia appeared to him so delicious with Elmira that he found an inexpressible charm in going through them step by step; but arrived at the happiness itself, his pleasures had from that time the same defect as before. They became too easy of access, and in a short time after too languid. Their days, so well filled up till then, began to hang heavy. In one of these moments, when complaisance alone retained Soliman with Elmira—"Would it be agreeable to you," said he, "to hear a slave from your own country, whose voice has been greatly commended to me?" Elmira, at the proposal, plainly perceived that she was lost; but to put any constraint on a lover who begins to grow tired is to tire him still more. "I am for anything," said she, "that you please"; and the slave was ordered to enter.

Delia (for that was the singer's name) had the figure of a goddess. Her hair exceeded the ebony in blackness, and her skin the whiteness of ivory. Two eyebrows, boldly arched, crowned her sparkling eyes. As soon as she began singing, her lips, which were of the finest vermilion, displayed two rows of pearl set in coral. At first she sung the victories of Soliman, and the hero felt his soul elevated at the remembrance of his triumphs. His pride hitherto, more than his taste, applauded the accents of that thrilling voice, which filled the whole saloon with its harmony and strength.

Delia changed her manner, to sing the charms of pleasure. She then took the theorbo, an instrument favourable to the display of a rounded arm, and to the movements of a delicate and light hand. Her voice, more flexible and tender, now resounded none but the most touching sounds. Her modulations, connected by imperceptible gradations, expressed the delirium of a soul intoxicated with pleasure, or exhausted with sentiment. Her sounds, sometimes expiring on her lips, sometimes swelled and sunk with rapidity, expressed by turns the sighs of modesty and the vehemence of desire; while her eyes still more than her voice animated these lively descriptions.

Soliman, quite transported, devoured her both with his ears and eyes. "No," said he, "never before did so beautiful a mouth utter such pleasing sounds. With what delight must she, who sings so feelingly of pleasure, inspire and relish it! How charming to draw that harmonious breath, and to catch again in their passage those sounds animated by love!" The Sultan, lost in these reflections, perceived not that all the while he kept beating time on the knee of the trembling Elmira. Her heart oppressed with jealousy, she was scarce able to breathe. "How happy is Delia," said she in a low voice to Soliman, "to have so tuneful a voice! Alas! it ought to be the organ of my heart! everything that she expresses, you have taught me to feel." So said Elmira, but Soliman did not listen to her.

Delia changed her tone a second time to inconstancy. All that the changeful variety of nature contains, either interesting or amiable, was recapitulated in her song. It seemed like the fluttering of the butterfly over roses, or like the zephyrs losing themselves among the flowers. "Listen to the turtle," said Delia; "she is faithful but melancholy. See the inconstant sparrow. Pleasure moves his wings; his warbling voice is exerted merely to return thanks to love. Water freezes only in stagnation; a heart never languishes but in constancy. There is but one mortal on earth whom it is possible to love always. Let him change, let him enjoy the advantage of making a thousand hearts happy; all prevent his wishes, or pursue him. They adore him in their own arms; they love him even in the arms of another. Let him give himself up to our desires, or withdraw himself from them, still he will find love wherever he goes, wherever he goes will leave the print of love on his footsteps."

Elmira was no longer able to dissemble her displeasure and grief. She gets up and retires. The Sultan does not recall her; and while she is overwhelming herself with tears, repeating a thousand times, "Ah, the ungrateful! ah, the perfidious man!" Soliman, charmed with his divine songstress, prepares to realise with her some of those pictures which she had drawn so much to the life. The next morning the unhappy Elmira wrote a billet filled with reproach and tenderness, in which she puts him in mind of the promise he had made her. "That is true," said the Sultan, "let us send her back to her country, laden with marks of my favour. This poor girl loves me dearly, and I am to blame on her account."

The first moments of his love for Delia were no more than an intoxication; but as soon as he had time for reflection he perceived that she was more petulant than sensible, more greedy of pleasure than flattered in administering it—in a word, fitter than himself to have a seraglio at command. To feed his illusion, he sometimes invited Delia, that he might hear that voice which had enchanted him; but that voice was no longer the same. The impression made by it became every day weaker and weaker by habitude; and it was now no more than a slight emotion, when an unforeseen circumstance dissipated it for ever.

The chief officer of the seraglio came to inform the Sultan that it was impossible to manage the untractable vivacity of one of the European slaves, that she made a jest of his prohibitions and menaces, and that she answered him only by cutting railleries and immoderate bursts of laughter. Soliman, who was too great a prince to make a state affair of what merely regarded the regulation of his pleasures, entertained a curiosity of seeing this young madcap. He repaired to her, followed by the eunuch. As soon as she saw Soliman—"Heaven be praised!" said she, "here comes a human figure! You are without doubt the sublime Sultan, whose slave I have the honour to be? Do me the favour to drive away this old knave, who shocks my very sight." The Sultan had a great deal of difficulty to refrain from laughing at this beginning. "Roxalana," said he to her, for so she was called, "show some respect, if you please, to the minister of my pleasures; you are yet a stranger to the manners of the seraglio; till they can instruct you in them, contain yourself and obey." "A fine compliment!" said Roxalana. *"Obey!* Is that your Turkish gallantry? Sure you must be mightily beloved, if it is in this strain you begin your addresses to the ladies! *Respect the minister of my pleasures!* You have your pleasures, then? and, good Heaven! what pleasures, if they resemble their minister! an old amphibious monster, who keeps us here, penned in, like sheep in a fold, and who prowls round with his frightful eyes always ready to devour us! See here the confidant of your pleasures, and the guardian of our prudence! Give him his due, if you pay him to make yourself hated, he does not cheat you of any of his wages. We cannot take a step but he growls. He forbids us even to walk, and to receive or pay visits. In a short time, I suppose, he will weigh out the air to us, and give us light by the yard. If you had seen him rave last night, because he found me in these solitary gardens! Did you order him to forbid our going into them? Are you afraid that it should rain men? and if there should fall a few from the clouds, what a misfortune! Heaven owes us this miracle."

While Roxalana spoke thus, the Sultan examined, with surprise, the fire of her looks and the play of her countenance. "By Mahomet!" said he to himself, "here is the prettiest looking romp in all Asia. Such faces as these are made only in Europe. Roxalana had nothing fine, nothing regular in her features; but, taken all together, they had that smart singularity which touches more than beauty. A speaking look, a mouth fresh and rosy, an arch smile, a nose somewhat turned up, a neat and well-made shape; all these circumstances gave her giddiness a charm which disconcerted the gravity of Soliman. But the great, in his situation, have the resource of silence; and Soliman, not knowing how to answer her, fairly walked off, concealing his embarassment under an air of majesty.

The eunuch asked him what orders he would be pleased to give with respect to this saucy slave. "She is a mere child," replied the Sultan, "you must pass over some things in her."

The air, the tone, the figure, the disposition of Roxalana had excited in the soul of Soliman an anxiety and emotion which sleep was not able to dispel. As soon as he awoke he ordered the chief of the eunuchs to come to him. "You seem to me," said he, "to be but little in Roxalana's good graces; in order to make your peace, go and tell her I will come and drink tea with her." On the arrival of the officer, Roxalana's women hasten to wake her. "What does the ape want with me?" cried she, rubbing her eyes. "I come," replied the eunuch, "from the Emperor, to kiss the dust off your feet, and to inform you that he will come and drink tea with the delight of his soul." "Get away with your strange speeches! My feet have no dust, and I do not drink tea so early."

The eunuch retired without replying, and gave an account of his embassy. "She is in the right," said the Sultan; "why did you wake her? You do everything wrong." As soon as it was broad day with Roxalana, he went thither. "You are angry with me?" said he. "They have disturbed your sleep, and I am the innocent cause of it. Come, let us make peace; imitate me. You see that I forget all that you said to me yesterday." "You forget it! so much the worse. I said some good things to you. My frankness displeases you, I see plainly; but you will soon grow accustomed to it. And are you not too happy to find a friend in a slave? Yes, a friend who interests herself in your welfare, and who would teach you to love. Why have not you made a voyage to my country? It is there that they know love. It is there that it is lively and tender; and why? Because it is free. Sentiment is involuntary, and does not come by force. The yoke of marriage amongst us is much lighter than that of slavery; and yet a husband that is beloved is a prodigy. Everything under the name of duty saddens the soul, blasts the imagination, cools desire, and takes off that edge of self-love which gives all the relish and seasoning to affection. Now, if it be so difficult to love a husband, how much harder is it to love a master, especially if he has not the address to conceal the fetters he puts upon us!" "And I," replied the Sultan; "I will forget nothing to soften your servitude; but you ought in your turn—" "I *ought!* nothing but what one *ought!* Leave off, I prythee, now, these humiliating phrases. They come with a very ill grace from the mouth of a man of gallantry, who has the honour of talking to a pretty woman." "But, Roxalana, do you forget who I am, and who you are?" "*Who you are, and who I am?* You are powerful, I am pretty; and so we are even." "Maybe so," replied the Sultan haughtily, "in your country; but here, Roxalana, I am master, and you a slave." "Yes, I know you have purchased me; but the robber who sold me could transfer to you only those rights over me which he had himself, the rights of rapine and violence—in one word, the rights of a robber; and you are too honest a man to think of abusing them. After all, you are my master, because my life is in your hands; but I am no longer your slave, if I know how to despise life, and truly the life one leads here is not worth the fear of losing it." "What a frightful notion!" cried the Sultan; "do you take me for a barbarian? No, my dear Roxalana, I would make use of my power only to render this life delightful to yourself and me." "Upon my word," said Roxalana, "the prospect is not very promising. These guards, for instance, so black, so disgusting, so ugly, are they the smiles and sports which here accompany love?" "These guards are not set upon you alone. I have five hundred women, whom our manners and laws oblige me to keep watched." "And why five hundred women?" said she to him, with an air of confidence. "It is a kind of state which the dignity of Sultan imposes upon me." "But what do you do with them, pray? for you lend them to nobody." "Inconstancy," replied the Sultan, "has introduced this custom. A heart void of love stands in need of variety. Lovers only are constant, and I never was a lover till I saw you. Let not the number of these women give you the shadow of uneasiness. They shall serve only to grace your triumph. You shall see them all eager to please you, and you shall see them attentive to no one but yourself."

"Indeed," said Roxalana, with an air of compassion, "you deserve better luck. It is pity you are not a plain private gentleman in my country. I should then be weak enough to entertain some sort of kindness for you, for, at the bottom, it is not yourself that I hate; it is that which surrounds you. You are much better than ordinary for a Turk. You have even something of the Frenchman about you; and, without flattery, I have loved some who were not so deserving as yourself." "You have loved!" cried Soliman with horror. "O Heavens, what do I hear! I am betrayed!—I am lost! Destruction seize the traitors who meant to impose upon me!" "Forgive them," said Roxalana; "the poor creatures are not to blame. The most knowing are often deceived. And then the misfortune is not very great. Why do not you restore me to my liberty if you think me unworthy of the honours of slavery?" "Yes, yes, I will restore you to that liberty, of which you have made so good use." At these words the Sultan retired in a rage, saying to himself, "I plainly foresaw that this little turned-up nose had made a slip."

It is impossible to describe the confusion into which this imprudent avowal of Roxalana's had thrown him. Sometimes he had a mind to have sent her away, sometimes that they should shut her up, next that they should bring her to him, and then again that she should have been sent away. The great Soliman no longer knows what he says. "My lord," remonstrated the eunuch, "can you fall into despair for a trifle? One girl more or less; is there anything so uncommon in her? Besides, who knows whether the confession she has made be not an artifice to get herself sent back to her own country?" "What say you? How! can it be possible? It is the very thing! He opens my eyes. Women are not used to make such confessions. It is a trick—a stratagem! Ah, the perfidious hussy! Let me dissemble in my turn; I will drive her to the last extremity. Hark ye! go and tell her that I invite her to sup with me this

evening. But no; order the songstress to come here. It is better to
send her."

Delia was charged to employ all her art to engage the confidence of
Roxalana. As soon as the latter had heard all that she had got to say—
"What!" said she, "young and handsome as you are, does he charge you
with his messages, and have you the weakness to obey him? Get
you gone; you are not worthy to be my countrywoman! Ah! I see
plainly that they spoil him, and that I alone must take upon me to
teach this Turk how to live. I will send him word that I keep you to
sup with me; I must have him make some atonement for his impertinence." "But, madam, he will take it ill." "He! I should be glad to
see him take anything ill of me." "But he seemed desirous of seeing you
alone." "Alone, ah! it is not come to that yet; and I shall make him go
over a good deal of ground before we have anything particular to say to
each other."

The Sultan was as much surprised as piqued to learn that they should
have a third person. However, he repaired early to Roxalana's. As soon
as she saw him coming, she ran to meet him with as easy an air as if
they had been upon the best footing in the world together. "There,"
said she, "is a handsome man come to sup with us! Do you like him,
madam? Confess, Soliman, that I am a good friend. Come, draw near,
salute the lady. There; very well. Now, thank me. Softly; I do not
like to have people dwell too long on their acknowledgments. Wonderful! I assure you he surprises me. He has had but two lessons, and see
how he is improved! I do not despair of making him one day or other
an absolute Frenchman."

Do but imagine the astonishment of a Sultan; a Sultan!—the conqueror of Asia!—to see himself treated like a school-boy by a slave of
eighteen. During supper her gaiety and extravagance were inconceivable.
The Sultan was beside himself with transport. He questioned her concerning the manners of Europe. One picture followed another. Our
prejudices, our follies, our humours, were all laid hold of, all represented.
Soliman thought himself in Paris. "The witty rogue!" cried he; "the
witty rogue!" From Europe she fell upon Asia. This was much
worse; the haughtiness of the men, the weakness of the women, the
dulness of their society, nothing escaped her, though she had only seen but
cursorily.

She was preparing to enlarge upon the honour that the circumstance
of his reign would do him in history; but he begged her to spare him.
"Well," said she, "I perceive that I take up those moments which Delia
could fill up much better. Throw yourself at her feet, to obtain from
her one of those airs which they say she sings with so much taste and
spirit." Delia did not suffer herself to be entreated. Roxalana appeared
charmed; she asked Soliman, in a low voice, for a handkerchief; he gave

her one, without the least suspicion of her design. "Madam," said she to Delia, presenting it to her, "I am desired by the Sultan to give you the handkerchief; you have well deserved it." "Oh, to be sure!" said Soliman, carried away with anger; and presenting his hand to the songstress, retired along with her.

As soon as they were alone—"I confess," said he to her, "that this giddy girl confounds me. You see the style in which she treats me. I have not the courage to be angry with her. In short, I am mad, and I do not know what method to take to bring her to reason." "My lord," said Delia, "I believe I have discovered her temper. Authority can do nothing. You have nothing for it but extreme coldness or extreme gallantry. Coldness may pique her; but I am afraid we are too far gone for that. She knows that you love her. She will enjoy the pain that this will cost you; and you will come to sooner than she. This method, besides, is disagreeable and painful; and if one moment's weakness should escape you, you will have all to begin again." "Well then," said the Sultan, "let us try gallantry."

From that time there was in the seraglio every day a new festival, of which Roxalana was the object; but she received all this as an homage due to her, without concern or pleasure, but with a cool complaisance. The Sultan sometimes asked her, "How did you like those sports, those concerts, those spectacles?" "Well enough," said she, "but there was something wanting." "And what?" "Men and liberty."

Soliman was in despair; he had recourse to Delia. "Upon my word," said the songstress, "I know nothing else that can touch her; at least, unless glory have a share in it. You receive to-morrow the ambassadors of your allies; cannot I bring her to see this ceremony behind the curtain, which may conceal us from the eyes of your court?" "And do you think," said the Sultan, "that this would make any impression on her?" "I hope so," said Delia; "the women of her country love glory." "You charm me!" chied Soliman; "yes, my dear Delia, I shall owe my happiness to you."

At his return from this ceremony, which he took care to render as pompous as possible, he repaired to Roxalana. "Get you gone," said she to him, "out of my sight, and never see me more." The Sultan remained motionless and dumb with astonishment. "Is this, then," pursued he, "your art of love?" "Glory and grandeur, the only good things worthy to touch the soul, are reserved for you alone; shame and oblivion, the most insupportable of all evils, are my portion; and you would have me love you! I hate you worse than death!" The Sultan would fain have turned his reproach into raillery. "Nay, but I am serious," resumed she; "if my lover had but a hut, I would share his hut with him, and be content. He has a throne; I will share his throne, or he is no lover of mine. If you think me unworthy to reign over the Turks, send me back to my own country, where all the handsome women are sovereigns, and much more absolutely than I should be here; for they reign over hearts." "The sovereignty of mine, then, is not sufficient for you?" said Soliman, with the most tender air in the world. "No, I desire no heart which has pleasures that I have not. Talk to me no more of your feasts, all mere pastimes for children! I must have embassies." "But, Roxalana, you are either mad or you dream!" "And what do you find, then, so extravagant, in desiring to reign with you? Am I formed to disgrace a throne? and do you think that I should have displayed less greatness and dignity than yourself in assuring our subjects and allies of our protection?" "I think," said the Sultan, "that you would do everything with grace; but it is not in my power to satisfy your ambition, and I beseech you to think no more of it." "Think no more of it! Oh! I promise you I shall think of nothing else; and I will from henceforward dream of nothing but a sceptre, a crown, an embassy." She kept her word. The next morning she had already contrived the design of her diadem, and had already settled everything, except the colour of a ribbon which was to tie it. She ordered rich stuffs to be brought her for her habits of ceremony; and as soon as the Sultan appeared, she asked his opinion on the choice. He exerted all his endeavours to divert her from this idea; but contradiction plunged her into the deepest melancholy; and to draw her out of it again he was obliged to flatter her illusion. Then she displayed the most brilliant gaiety. He seized these moments to talk to her of love; but, without listening, she talked to him of politics. All her answers to the harangues of the deputies, on her accession to the crown, were already prepared. She had even formed projects of regulations for the territories of the Grand Seignor. She would make them plant vines and build opera houses; suppress the eunuchs because they were good for nothing; shut up the jealous because they disturbed society; and banish all self-interested persons because sooner or later they become rogues. The Sultan amused himself for some time with these follies; nevertheless he still burned with the most violent love, without any hope of being happy. On the least suspicion of violence she became furious, and was ready to kill herself. On the other hand, Soliman found not the ambition of Roxalana so very foolish—"For, in short," said he, "is it not cruel to be alone deprived of the happiness of associating to my fortune a woman whom I esteem and love? All my subjects may have a lawful wife; an absurd law forbids marriage to me alone." Thus spoke love, but policy put him to silence. He took the resolution of confiding to Roxalana the reasons which restrained him. "I would make it," said he, "my happiness to leave nothing wanting to yours; but our manners—" "Idle stories!" "Our laws—" "Old songs!" "The priests—" "What care they!" "The people and the soldiery—" "What is it to them? Will they be more wretched when you shall have me for your comfort? You have very little love if you have so little courage!" She prevailed so far that Soliman was ashamed of being so timid. He orders the Mufti, the Vizier, the Camaican, the Aga of the Sea, and the Aga of the Janissaries, to come to him; and he says to them, "I have carried, as far as I was able, the glory of the crescent; I have established the power and peace of my empire; and I desire nothing by way of recompense for my labours, but to enjoy, with the good-will of my subjects, a blessing which they all enjoy. I know not what law, but it is one that is not derived down to us from the Prophet, forbids the Sultans the sweets of the marriage-bed; thence I perceive myself reduced to the condition of slaves, whom I despise; and I have resolved to marry a woman whom I adore. Prepare my people, then, for this marriage. If they approve of it, I receive their approbation as a mark of their gratitude; but if they dare to murmur at it, tell them that I will have it so." The assembly received the Sultan's orders with a respectful silence, and the people followed their example.

Soliman, transported with joy and love, went to fetch Roxalana, in order to lead her to the mosque; and said to himself in a low voice, as he was conducting her thither, "Is it possible that a little turned-up nose should overturn the laws of an empire?"

❋ ❋ ❋

HONORE DE BALZAC
(1799-1850)

BALZAC'S great ambition was to be a famous writer. That he lived to realise his ambition is witnessed in his herculean achievement known as the *Comédie humaine*, a series of connected novels which drew all aspects of life. This enormous undertaking was not quite completed when Balzac died from overwork in an effort to pay off huge debts resulting from business troubles. The strange thing about Balzac was that he created a multitude of remarkable characters in his realistic novels, despite his leading a life of forced seclusion. While he is essentially a novelist, Balzac has also written several short stories, the best of which are some of the finest in French. *The Executioner* certainly ranks high and as a tale of violent horror stands supreme.

The present version, anonymously translated, is reprinted from the Works of Honoré de Balzac.

THE EXECUTIONER

MIDNIGHT had just sounded from the belfry tower of the little town of Menda. A young French officer, leaning over the parapet of the long terrace at the further end of the castle gardens, seemed to be unusually absorbed in deep thought for one who led the reckless life of a soldier; but it must be admitted that never was the hour, the scene, and the night more favourable to meditation.

The blue dome of the cloudless sky of Spain was overhead; he was looking out over the coy windings of a lovely valley lit by the uncertain starlight and the soft radiance of the moon. The officer, leaning against an orange tree in blossom, could also see, a hundred feet below him, the town of Menda, which seemed to nestle for shelter from the north wind at the foot of the crags on which the castle itself was built. He turned his head and caught sight of the sea; the moonlit waves made a broad frame of silver for the landscape.

There were lights in the castle windows. The mirth and movement of a ball, the sounds of the violins, the laughter of the officers and their partners in the dance were borne towards him and blended with the far-off murmur of the waves. The cool night had a certain bracing effect upon his frame, wearied as he had been by the heat of the day. He seemed to bathe in the air, made fragrant by the strong, sweet scent of flowers and of aromatic trees in the gardens.

The castle of Menda belonged to a Spanish grandee, who was living in it at that time with his family. All through the evening the oldest daughter of the house had watched the officer with such a wistful interest that the Spanish lady's compassionate eyes might well have set the young Frenchman dreaming. Clara was beautiful; and although she had three brothers and a sister, the broad lands of the Marqués de Légañès appeared to be sufficient warrant for Victor Marchand's belief that the young lady would have a splendid dowry. But how could he dare to imagine that the most fanatical believer in blue blood in all Spain would give his daughter to the son of a grocer in Paris? Moreover, the French were hated. It was because the Marquis had been suspected of an attempt to raise the country in favor of Ferdinand VII. that General G——, who governed the province, had stationed Victor Marchand's battalion in the little town of Menda to overawe the neighbouring districts which received the Marqués de Légañès' word as law. A recent despatch from Marshal Ney had given ground for fear that the English might ere long effect a landing on the coast, and had indicated the Marquis as being in correspondence with the Cabinet in London.

In spite, therefore, of the welcome with which the Spaniards had received Victor Marchand and his soldiers, that officer was always on his guard. As he went towards the terrace, where he had just surveyed the town and the districts confided to his charge, he had been asking himself what construction he ought to put upon the friendliness which the Marquis had invariably shown him, and how to reconcile the apparent tranquility of the country with his general's uneasiness. But a moment later these thoughts were driven from his mind by the instinct of caution and very legitimate curiosity. It had just struck him that there was a very fair number of lights in the town below. Although it was the Feast of Saint James, he himself had issued orders that very morning that all lights must be put out in the town at the hour prescribed by military regulations. The castle alone had been excepted in this order. Plainly here and there he saw the gleam of bayonets, where his own men were at their accustomed posts; but in the town there was a solemn silence, and not a sign that the Spaniards had given themselves up to the intoxication of a festival. He tried vainly for a while to explain this breach of the regulations on the part of the inhabitants; the mystery seemed but so much the more obscure because he had left instructions with some of his officers to do police duty that night, and make the rounds of the town.

With the impetuosity of youth, he was about to spring through a gap in the wall preparatory to a rapid scramble down the rocks, thinking to reach a small guard-house at the nearest entrance into the town more quickly than by the beaten track, when a faint sound stopped him. He fancied that he could hear the light footstep of a woman along the graveled garden walk. He turned his head and saw no one; for one moment his eyes were dazzled by the wonderful brightness of the sea, the next he saw a sight so ominous that he stood stock-still with amazement, thinking that his senses must be deceiving him. The white moonbeams lighted the horizon, so that he could distinguish the sails of ships still a considerable distance out at sea. A shudder ran through him; he tried to persuade himself that this was some optical delusion brought about by chance effects of moonlight on the waves; and even as he made the attempt, a hoarse voice called to him by name. The officer glanced at the gap in the wall; saw a soldier's head slowly emerge from it, and knew the grenadier whom he had ordered to accompany him to the castle.

"Is that you, commandant?"

"Yes. What is it?" returned the young officer in a low voice. A kind of presentiment warned him to act cautiously.

"Those beggars down there are creeping about like worms; and, by your leave, I came as quickly as I could to report my little reconnoitring expedition."

"Go on," answered Victor Marchand.

"I have just been following a man from the castle who came round this way with a lantern in his hand. A lantern is a suspicious matter with a vengeance! I don't imagine that there was any need for that good Christian to be lighting tapers at this time of night. Says I to myself, 'They mean to gobble us up!' and I set myself to dogging his heels; and that is how I found out that there is a pile of faggots, sir, two or three steps away from here."

Suddenly a dreadful shriek rang through the town below, and cut the man short. A light flashed in the commandant's face, and the poor grenadier dropped down with a bullet through his head. Ten paces away a bonfire flared up like a conflagration. The sounds of music and laughter ceased all at once in the ballroom; the silence of death, broken only by groans, succeeded to the rhythmical murmur of the festival. Then the roar of cannon sounded from across the white plain of the sea.

A cold sweat broke out on the young officer's forehead. He had left his sword behind. He knew that his men had been murdered, and that the English were about to land. He knew that if he lived he would be dishonoured; he saw himself summoned before a court-martial. For a moment his eyes measured the depth of the valley, the next, just as he was about to spring down, Clara's hand caught his.

"Fly!" she cried. "My brothers are coming after me to kill you. Down yonder at the foot of the cliff you will find Juanito's Andalusian. Go!"

She thrust him away. The young man gazed at her in dull bewilderment; but obeying the instinct of self-preservation, which never deserts even the bravest, he rushed across the park in the direction pointed out to him, springing from rock to rock in places unknown to any save the goats. He heard Clara calling to her brothers to pursue him; he heard the footsteps of the murderers; again and again he heard their balls whistling about his ears; but he reached the foot of the cliff, found the horse, mounted, and fled with lightning speed.

A few hours later the young officer reached General G——'s quarters, and found him at dinner with the staff.

"I put my life in your hands!" cried the haggard and exhausted commandant of Menda.

He sank into a seat, and told his horrible story. It was received with an appalling silence.

"It seems to me that you are more to be pitied than to blame," the terrible general said at last. "You are not answerable for the Spaniard's crimes, and, unless the marshall decides otherwise, I acquit you."

These words brought but cold comfort to the unfortunate officer.

"When the Emperor comes to hear about it!" he cried.

"Oh, he will be for having you shot," said the general, "but we shall see. Now we will say no more about this," he added severely, "except to plan a revenge that shall strike a salutary terror into this country, where they carry on war like savages."

An hour later a whole regiment, a detachment of cavalry, and a convoy of artillery were upon the road. The general and Victor marched at the head of the column. The soldiers had been told of the fate of their comrades, and their rage knew no bounds. The distance between headquarters and the town of Menda was crossed at a wellnigh miraculous speed. Whole villages by the way were found to be under arms; every one of the wretched hamlets was surrounded and their inhabitants decimated.

It so chanced that the English vessels still lay out at sea, and were no nearer the shore, a fact inexplicable until it was known afterwards that they were artillery transports which had outsailed the rest of the fleet. So the townsmen of Menda, left without the assistance on which they had reckoned when the sails of the English appeared, were surrounded by French troops almost before they had had time to strike a blow. This struck such terror into them that they offered to surrender at discretion. An impulse of devotion, no isolated instance in the history of the Peninsula, led the actual slayers of the French to offer to give themselves up; seeking in this way to save the town, for from the general's reputation for cruelty it was feared that he would give Menda over to the flames, and put the whole population to the sword. General G—— took their offer, stipulating that every soul in the castle from the lowest servant to the Marquis should likewise be given up to him. These terms being accepted, the general promised to spare the lives of the rest of the townsmen, and to prohibit his soldiers from pillaging or setting fire to the town. A heavy contribution was levied, and the wealthiest inhabitants were taken as hostages to guarantee payment within twenty-four hours.

The general took every necessary precaution for the safety of his troops, provided for the defense of the place, and refused to billet his men in the houses of the town. After they had bivouacked, he went up to the castle and entered it as a conqueror. The whole family of Légañès and their household were gagged, shut up in the great ballroom, and closely watched. From the windows it was easy to see the whole length of the terrace above the town.

The staff was established in an adjoining gallery, where the general forthwith held a council as to the best means of preventing the landing of the English. An aide-de-camp was despatched to Marshal Ney, orders were issued to plant batteries along the coast, and then the general and his staff turned their attention to their prisoners. The two hundred Spaniards given up by the townsfolk were shot down then and there upon the terrace. And after this military execution, the general gave orders to erect gibbets to the number of the prisoners in the ballroom in the same place, and to send for the hangman out of the town. Victor took advantage of the interval before dinner to pay a visit to the prisoners. He soon came back to the general.

"I am come in haste," he faltered out, "to ask a favour."

"*You!*" exclaimed the general, with bitter irony in his tones.

"Alas!" answered Victor, "it is a sorry favor. The Marquis has seen them erecting the gallows, and hopes that you will commute the punishment for his family; he entreats you to have the nobles beheaded."

"Granted," said the general.

"He further asks that they may be allowed the consolations of religion, and that they may be unbound; they give you their word that they will not attempt to escape."

"That I permit," said the general, "but you are answerable for them."

"The old noble offers you all that he has if you will pardon his youngest son."

"Really!" cried the commander. "His property is forfeited already to King Joseph." He paused; a contemptuous thought set wrinkles in his forehead, as he added, "I will do better than they ask. I understand what he means by that last request of his. Very good. Let him hand down his name to posterity; but whenever it is mentioned, all Spain shall remember his treason and its punishment! I will give the fortune and his life to any one of the sons who will do the executioner's office. There, don't talk any more about them to me."

Dinner was ready. The officers sat down to satisfy an appetite whetted by hunger. Only one among them was absent from the table—that one was Victor Marchand. After long hesitation, he went to the ballroom, and heard the last sighs of the proud house of Léganès. He looked sadly at the scene before him. Only last night, in this very room, he had seen their faces whirl past him in the waltz, and he shuddered to think that those girlish heads with those of the three young brothers must fall in a brief space by the executioner's sword. There sat the father and mother, their three sons and two daughters, perfectly motionless, bound to their gilded chairs. Eight serving-men stood with their hands tied behind them. These fifteen prisoners, under sentence of death, exchanged grave glances; it was difficult to read the thoughts that filled them from their eyes, but profound resignation and regret that their enterprise should have failed so completely was written on more than one brow.

The impassive soldiers who guarded them respected the grief of their bitter enemies. A gleam of curiosity lighted up all faces when Victor came in. He gave orders that the condemned prisoners should be unbound, and himself unfastened the cords that held Clara a prisoner. She smiled mournfully at him. The officer could not refrain from lightly touching the young girl's arm; he could not help admiring her dark hair, her slender waist. She was a true daughter of Spain, with a Spanish complexion, a Spaniard's eyes, blacker than the raven's wing beneath their long curving lashes.

"Did you succeed?" she asked, with a mournful smile, in which a certain girlish charm still lingered.

Victor could not repress a groan. He looked from the faces of the three brothers to Clara, and again at the three young Spaniards. The first, the oldest of the family, was a man of thirty. He was short, and somewhat ill made; he looked haughty and proud, but a certain distinction was not lacking in his bearing, and he was apparently no stranger to the delicacy of feeling for which in olden times the chivalry of Spain was famous. His name was Juanito. The second son, Felipe, was about twenty years of age; he was like his sister Clara; and the youngest was a child of eight. In the features of little Manuel a painter would have discerned something of that Roman steadfastness which David has given to the children's faces in his Republican *genre* pictures. The old Marquis, with his white hair, might have come down from some canvas of Murillo's. Victor threw back his head in despair after this survey; how should one of these accept the general's offer! nevertheless he ventured to intrust it to Clara. A shudder ran through the Spanish girl, but she recovered herself almost instantly, and knelt before her father.

"Father," she said, "bid Juanito swear to obey the commands that you shall give him, and we shall be content."

The Marquesa trembled with hope, but as she leaned towards her husband and learned Clara's hideous secret the mother fainted away. Juanito understood it all, and leaped up like a caged lion. Victor took it upon himself to dismiss the soldiers, after receiving an assurance of entire submission from the Marquis. The servants were led away and given over to the hangman and their fate. When only Victor remained on guard in the room, the old Marqués de Légañès rose to his feet.

"Juanito," he said. For all answer Juanito bowed his head in a way that meant refusal; he sank down into his chair, and fixed tearless eyes upon his father and mother in an intolerable gaze. Clara went over to him and sat on his knee; she put her arms about him, and pressed kisses on his eyelids, saying gaily—

"Dear Juanito, if you but knew how sweet death at your hands will be to me! I shall not be compelled to submit to the hateful touch of the hangman's fingers. You will snatch me away from the evils to come and—— Dear, kind Juanito, you could not bear the thought of my belonging to any one—well, then?"

The velvet eyes gave Victor a burning glance; she seemed to try to awaken in Juanito's heart his hatred for the French.

"Take courage," said his brother Felipe, "or our wellnigh royal line will be extinct."

Suddenly Clara sprang to her feet. The group round Juanito fell back, and the son who had rebelled with such good reason was confronted with his aged father.

"Juanito, I command you!" said the Marquis solemnly.

The young Count gave no sign, and his father fell on his knees; Clara, Manuel, and Felipe unconsciously followed his example, stretching out suppliant hands to him who must save their family from oblivion, and seeming to echo their father's words.

"Can it be that you lack the fortitude of a Spaniard and true sensibility, my son? Do you mean to keep me on my knees? What right have you to think of your own life and of your own sufferings? Is this my son, madame?" the old Marquis added, turning to his wife.

"He will consent to it," cried the mother in agony of soul. She had seen a slight contraction of Juanito's brows which she, his mother, alone understood.

Mariquita, the second daughter, knelt, with her slender clinging arms about her mother; the hot tears fell from her eyes, and her little brother Manuel upbraided her for weeping. Just at that moment the castle chaplain came in; the whole family surrounded him and led him up to Juanito. Victor felt that he could endure the sight no longer, and with a sign to Clara he hurried from the room to make one last effort for them. He found the general in boisterous spirits; the officers were still sitting over their dinner and drinking together; the wine had loosened their tongues.

An hour later, a hundred of the principal citizens of Menda were summoned to the terrace by the general's orders to witness the execution of the family of Légañès. A detachment had been told off to keep order among the Spanish townsfolk, who were marshaled beneath the gallows whereon the Marquis' servants hung; the feet of those martyrs of their cause all but touched the citizens' heads. Thirty paces away stood the block; the blade of a scimitar glittered upon it, and the executioner stood by in case Juanito should refuse at the last.

The deepest silence prevailed, but before long it was broken by the sound of many footsteps, the measured tramp of a picket of soldiers, and the jingling of their weapons. Mingled with these came other noises— loud talk and laughter from the dinner-table where the officers were sitting; just as the music and the sound of the dancers' feet had drowned the preparations for last night's treacherous butchery.

All eyes turned to the castle, and beheld the family of nobles coming forth with incredible composure to their death. Every brow was serene and calm. One alone among them, haggard and overcome, leaned on the arm of the priest, who poured forth all the consolations of religion for the one man who was condemned to live. Then the executioner, like the spectators, knew that Juanito had consented to perform his office for a day. The old Marquis and his wife, Clara and Mariquita, and their two brothers knelt a few paces from the fatal spot. Juanito reached it, guided by the priest. As he stood at the block, the executioner plucked him by the sleeve, and took him aside, probably to give him certain instructions. The confessor so placed the victims that they could not witness the executions, but one and all stood upright and fearless, like Spaniards, as they were.

Clara sprang to her brother's side before the others.

"Juanito," she said to him, "be merciful to my lack of courage. Take me first!"

As she spoke, the footsteps of a man running at full speed echoed from the walls, and Victor appeared upon the scene. Clara was kneeling before the block; her white neck seemed to appeal to the blade to fall. The officer turned faint, but he found strength to rush to her side.

"The general grants you your life if you will consent to marry me," he murmured.

The Spanish girl gave the officer a glance full of proud disdain.

"Now, Juanito!" she said in her deep-toned voice.

Her head fell at Victor's feet. A shudder ran through the Marquesa de Légañès, a convulsive tremor that she could not control, but she gave no other sign of her anguish.

"Is this where I ought to be, dear Juanito? Is it all right?" little Manuel asked his brother.

"Oh, Mariquita, you are weeping!" Juanito said when his sister came.

"Yes," said the girl; "I am thinking of you, poor Juanito; how unhappy you will be when we are gone."

Then the Marquis' tall figure approached. He looked at the block where his children's blood had been shed, turned to the mute and motionless crowd, and said in a loud voice as he stretched out his hands to Juanito.

"Spaniards! I give my son a father's blessing. Now, *Marquis*, strike 'without fear;' thou art 'without reproach.' "

But when his mother came near, leaning on the confessor's arm— "She fed me from her breast!" Juanito cried, in tones that drew a cry of horror from the crowd. The uproarious mirth of the officers over their wine died away before that terrible cry. The Marquesa knew that Juanito's courage was exhausted; at one bound she sprang to the balustrade, leaped forth, and was dashed to pieces on the rocks below. A cry of admiration broke from the spectators. Juanito swooned.

"General," said an officer, half-drunk by this time, "Marchand has just been telling me something about this execution; I will wager that it was not by your orders."

"Are you forgetting, gentlemen, that in a month's time five hundred families in France will be in mourning, and that we are still in Spain?" cried General G——. "Do you want us to leave our bones here?"

But not a man at the table, not even a subaltern, dared to empty his glass after that speech.

In spite of the respect in which all men hold the Marqués de Légañès, in spite of the title of *El Verdugo* (the executioner) conferred upon him as a patent of nobility by the King of Spain, the great noble is consumed by a gnawing grief. He lives a retired life, and seldom appears in public. The burden of his heroic crime weighs heavily upon him, and he seems to wait impatiently till the birth of a second son shall release him, and he may go to join the Shades that never cease to haunt him.

❊ ❊ ❊

PROSPER MÉRIMÉE
(1803-1870)

WHILE Mérimée spent a good part of his life in the government service, he, nevertheless, succeeded in writing a number of short stories which, for sheer artistry, are unsurpassed in French fiction. Mérimée possessed a style, clear and colourful, added to which was a remarkable brevity that lent his stories the sharpness of an etching. *The Taking of the Redoubt* is the best example of this quality. *Carmen* and *Colomba* are his two longer stories.

The present version is translated for this collection by Maxim Lieber.

THE TAKING OF THE REDOUBT

A MILITARY friend, who died of the fever in Greece several years ago told me one day about the first action in which he had engaged. His tale so impressed me that I wrote it down from memory as soon as I had the leisure. Here it is:

I joined the regiment in the evening of the fourth of September. I found the colonel in camp. He greeted me rather roughly; but when he had read General B——'s recommendation, his manner changed and he spoke a few courteous words to me.

I was presented by him to my captain, who had just returned from a reconnaissance. This captain, with whom I scarcely had time to become acquainted, was a tall, dark man, with a harsh repellent face. He had been a private, and had won his epaulets and his cross on the battle-field. His voice, which was hoarse and feeble, contrasted singularly with his almost gigantic stature. I was told that he owed that peculiar voice to a bullet which had pierced him at the battle of Jena.

Learning that I was fresh from the school at Fontainebleau, he made a wry face and said:

"My lieutenant died yesterday."

I understood that he wanted to say: "You ought to take his place, and you are not capable of it." A sharp retort came to my lips, but I restrained myself.

The moon rose behind the redoubt of Cheverino, about two gunshots from our bivouac. It was large and red, as it usually is when it rises. But on that evening it seemed to me of extraordinary size. For an instant the redoubt stood sharply out in black against the brilliant disk of the moon. It resembled the crater of a volcano at the moment of an eruption.

An old soldier beside whom I chanced to be, remarked upon the colour of the moon.

"It is very red," said he; "that's a sign that it will cost us dear to take that famous redoubt!"

I have always been superstitious, and that augury especially at that moment affected me. I lay down, but I could not sleep. I rose and paced about for some time observing the immensely long line of camp-fires that covered the heights above the village of Cheverino.

When I thought that the fresh, biting night air had sufficiently cooled my blood, I returned to the fire; I wrapped myself carefully in my cloak and closed my eyes, hoping not to open them before dawn. But sleep refused to come. Insensibly my thoughts assumed a dismal colour. I said to myself that I had not a friend among the hundred thousand men who covered that plain. If I were wounded I should be taken to a hospital and treated by ignorant surgeons. All that I had heard of surgical operations assailed my mind. My heart beat violently, and I mechanically arranged my handkerchief, and the wallet that I had in my breast pocket, as a sort of cuirass. I was worn out with fatigue, I dozed every moment and every moment some sinister thought returned with renewed force and roused me with a start.

Meanwhile, weariness had triumphed, and when they sounded reveille, I was fast asleep. We were drawn up in battle array, the roll was called, then we stacked arms, and everything indicated that we were to have a quiet day.

Toward three o'clock an aide-de-camp appeared, bringing an order. We were ordered under arms again; our skirmishers deployed over the plain; we followed them slowly, and after about twenty minutes, we saw all the advanced posts of the Russians fall back and take cover behind the redoubt.

A battery of artillery came into position at our right, another at our left, but both well in advance of us. They began a very hot fire at the enemy, who replied vigorously, and the redoubt of Cheverino soon disappeared beneath dense clouds of smoke.

Our regiment was almost protected from the Russian fire by a rise in the ground. Their balls, rarely aimed at us, for they preferred to fire at our gunners, passed over our heads, or, at the worst, spattered us with dirt and small stones.

As soon as the order to advance had been given, my captain looked at me with a scrutiny which compelled me to run my hand over my budding moustache twice or thrice, with all the composure at my disposal. Besides I had no fear, and the only dread I suffered was that he should believe that I was frightened. Those harmless cannon-balls contributed to maintain my heroic calm. My self-esteem told me that I was really in danger, as I was at last under the fire of a battery. I was overjoyed to be so entirely at my ease, and I thought of the pleasure of relating the capture of the redoubt of Cheverino in Madame de B———'s salon on Rue de Provence.

The colonel passed our company; he spoke to me: "Well, you are going to see some sharp work for your début."

I smiled with quite a martial air while brushing my coat-sleeve, on which a shot, that struck the ground thirty paces away, had spattered a little dust.

It seems that the Russians perceived the ill success of their cannon-balls; for they replaced them with shells, which could more easily reach us in the hollow where we were posted. A large piece of one took off my shako and killed a man near me.

"I congratulate you," said my captain, as I picked up my shako; "you're safe now for to-day."

I was acquainted with the military superstition which believes that the axiom, *Non bis in idem,* has the same application on a field of battle as in a court of justice. I proudly replaced my shako.

"That is making a fellow salute rather unceremoniously," I said as gaily as I could. That wretched joke was considered first-rate, in view of the circumstances.

"I congratulate you," resumed the captain; "you will get nothing worse, and you will command a company this evening; for I feel that the oven is being heated for me. Every time that I have been wounded the officer nearest me has been hit by a spent ball; and," he added in a low and shameful tone, "their names always began with a P."

I feigned incredulity; many men would have done the same; many men too would have been, as I was, profoundly impressed by those prophetic words. Conscript as I was, I felt that I could not confide my sensations to any one, and that I must always appear cool and intrepid.

After about half an hour the Russian fire sensibly diminished; thereupon we emerged from our shelter to march upon the redoubt.

Our regiment consisted of three battalions. The second was ordered to turn the redoubt on the side of the ravine; the other two were to make the assault. I was in the third battalion.

As we came out from behind the species of ridge which had protected us, we were received by several volleys of musketry, which did little damage in our ranks. The whistling of the bullets surprised me; I kept turning my head, and thus drew upon myself divers jests of my comrades, who were more familiar with that sound.

"Take it all in all," I said to myself, "a battle isn't such a terrible thing."

We advanced on the double-quick, preceded by skirmishes; suddenly the Russians gave three hurrahs, three distinct hurrahs, then remained silent and ceased firing.

"I don't like this silence," said my captain; "it bodes us no good."

I found that our men were a little too noisy, and I could not forbear making a mental comparison between their tumultuous clamour and the enemy's imposing silence.

We speedily reached the foot of the redoubt; the palisades had been shattered and the earth torn up by our balls. The soldiers threw themselves at these newly-made ruins with shouts of "Vive l'Empéreur!" louder than one would have expected to hear from men who had already shouted so much.

I raised my eyes, and I shall never forget the spectacle that I saw. The greater part of the smoke had risen, and hung like a canopy about twenty feet above the redoubt. Through a bluish haze one could see the Russian grenadiers behind their half-destroyed parapet, with arms raised motionless as statues. I believe I can still see each soldier, with his left eye fastened upon us, the right hidden by the levelled musket. In an embrasure, a few yards away, a man stood beside a cannon, holding a fusée.

I shuddered, and I thought that my last hour had come.

"The dance is going to begin," cried my captain. "Bon-soir!"

Those were the last words I heard him utter.

A rolling of drums resounded within the redoubt. I saw all the muskets drop. I closed my eyes, and I heard a most appalling crash, followed by shrieks and groans. I opened my eyes, surprised to find myself still among the living. The redoubt was once again filled with smoke. I was surrounded by dead and wounded. My captain lay at my feet; his head had been shattered by a cannon-ball, and I was covered with his brains and his blood. Of all my company only six men and myself were left on our feet.

This carnage was succeeded by a moment of stupefaction. The colonel, placing his hat on the point of his sword, was the first to scale the parapet, shouting *"Vive l'Empereur!"* He was followed instantly by all the survivors. I have a very dim remembrance of what followed. We entered the redoubt; I don't know how. We fought hand to hand, amid smoke so dense that we could not see one another. I believe that I struck, for my sabre was all bloody. At last I heard shouts of "Victory!" and, the smoke growing less dense, I saw blood and corpses completely covering the surface of the redoubt. The guns especially were buried beneath piles of bodies. About two hundred men, in the French uniform, were standing about in groups, with no pretence of order, some loading their muskets, others wiping their bayonets. Eleven hundred Russian prisoners were with them.

The colonel, covered with blood, was lying on a shattered caisson near the ravine. A number of soldiers were bustling about him. I approached.

"Where is the senior captain?" he asked a sergeant.

The sergeant shrugged his shoulders most expressively.

"And the senior lieutenant?"

"Monsieur here, who arrived last night," said the sergeant, in a matter-of-fact tone.

The colonel smiled bitterly.

"Well, monsieur," he said, "you command in chief; order the entrance to the redoubt to be strengthened with these waggons, for the enemy is in force; but General C—— will see that you are supported."

"Colonel," I said, "are you severely wounded?"

"Finished, my boy, but the redoubt is taken!"

※ ※ ※

THÉOPHILE GAUTIER
(1811-1872)

GAUTIER'S early training was in the direction of painting, an influence which he carried into literature. Harassed by financial troubles, he used to grind out literary and dramatic criticisms. He wrote vividly, colourfully, in a flawless style, though his work lacks any profundity. His famous collection of poetry, *Émaux et Camées*, displaying a jewelled perfection, made him the leader of the Parnassians, the new school of poetry. It was not his poetry, but rather his famous *Mlle. de Maupin*, which established his reputation on an imperishable basis. He also wrote a number of short stories, among which we find, *Omphale: A Rococo Story*. These have a brilliant literary quality that is equalled only by Mérimée.

The present version, translated by Lafcadio Hearn, is reprinted from the volume, *One of Cleopatra's Nights*, by permission of the publishers, Brentano's. Copyright, 1899.

OMPHALE: A ROCOCO STORY

MY uncle, the Chevalier de ——, resided in a small mansion which looked out upon the dismal Rue de Tournelles on one side, and the equally dismal Boulevard St. Antoine upon the other. Between the Boulevard and the house itself a few ancient elmtrees, eaten alive by mosses and insects, piteously extended their skeleton arms from the depth of a species of sink surrounded by high black walls. Some emaciated flowers hung their heads languidly, like young girls in consumption, waiting for a ray of sunshine to dry their half-rotten leaves. Weeds had invaded the walks, which were almost undistinguishable, owing to the length of time that had elapsed since they were last raked. One or two goldfish floated rather than swam in a basin covered with duck-weed and half-choked by water plants.

My uncle called that his garden!

Besides all the fine things above described in my uncle's garden, there was also a rather unpleasant pavilion, which he had entitled the *Délices*, doubtless by antiphrasis. It was in a state of extreme dilapidation. The walls were bulging outwardly. Great masses of detached plaster still lay among the nettles and wild oats where they had fallen. The lower portions of the wall surfaces were green with putrid mould. The woodwork of the window-shutters and doors had been badly sprung, and they closed only partially or not at all. A species of decoration, strongly suggestive of an immense kitchen-pot with various effluvia radiating from it, ornamented the main entrance, for in the time of Louis XV., when it was the custom to build *Délices*, there were always two entrances to such pleasure houses for precaution's sake. The cornice, overburdened with ovulos, foliated arabesques, and volutes, had been badly dismantled by the infiltration of rain-water. In short, the *Délices* of my uncle, the Chevalier de ——, presented a rather lamentable aspect.

This poor ruin, dating only from yesterday, although wearing the dilapidated look of a thousand years' decay—a ruin of plaster, not a stone, all cracked and warped, covered with a leprosy of lichen growth, mosseaten and mouldy—seemed to resemble one of those precociously old men worn out by filthy debauches. It inspired no feeling of respect, for there is nothing in the world so ugly and so wretched as either an old gauze robe or an old plaster wall, two things which ought not to endure, yet which do.

It was in this pavilion that my uncle had lodged me.

The interior was not less rococo than the exterior, although remaining in a somewhat better state of preservation. The bed was hung with yellow lampas, spotted over with large white flowers. An ornamental shell-work clock ticked away upon a pedestal inlaid with ivory and mother-of-pearl. A wreath of ornamental roses coquettishly twined around a Venetian glass. Above the door the Four Seasons were painted in cameo. A fair lady with thickly powdered hair, a sky-blue corset, and an array of ribbons of the same hue, who had a bow in her right hand, a partridge in her left, a crescent upon her forehead, and a leverette at her feet, strutted and smiled with ineffable graciousness from within a large oval frame. This was one of my uncle's mistresses of old, whom he had had painted as Diana. It will scarcely be necessary to observe that the furniture itself was not of the most modern style. There was, in fact, nothing to prevent one from fancying himself living at the time of the Regency, and the mythological tapestry with which the walls were hung rendered the illusion complete.

The tapestry represented Hercules spinning at the feet of Omphale. The design was tormented after the fashion of Vanloo, and in the most Pompadour style possible to imagine. Hercules had a spindle decorated with rose-coloured favours. He elevated his little finger with a peculiar and special grace, like a marquis in the act of taking a pinch of snuff, while turning a white flake of flax between his thumb and index finger. His muscular neck was burdened with bows of ribbons, rosettes, strings of pearls, and a thousand other feminine gew-gaws, and a large *gorge-de-pigeon* coloured petticoat, with two very large panniers, lent quite a gallant air to the monster-conquering hero.

Omphale's white shoulders were half covered by the skin of the Nemean lion. Her slender hand leaned upon her lover's knotty club. Her lovely blonde hair, powdered to ash-colour, fell loosely over her neck—a neck as supple and undulating in its outlines as the neck of a dove. Her little feet, true realisations of the typical Andalusian or Chinese foot, and which would have been lost in Cinderella's glass slippers, were shod with half-antique buskins of a tender lilac colour, sprinkled with pearls. In truth, she was a charming creature. Her head was thrown back with an adorable little mock swagger, her dimpled mouth wore a delicious little pout, her nostrils were slightly expanded, her cheeks had a delicate glow—an *assassin* * cunningly placed there relieved their beauty in a wonderful way; she only needed a little moustache to make her a first-class mousquetaire.

There were many other personages also represented in the tapestry—the kindly female attendant, the indispensable little Cupid—but they did not leave a sufficiently distinct outline in my memory to enable me to describe them.

In those days I was quite young—not that I wish to be understood as saying that I am now very old; but I was fresh from college, and was to remain in my uncle's care until I could choose a profession. If the good man had been able to foresee that I should embrace that of a fan-

* Beauty-spot.

tastic story-writer, he would certainly have turned me out of doors forthwith and irrevocably disinherited me, for he always entertained the most aristocratic contempt for literature in general and authors in particular. Like the fine gentleman that he was, it would have pleased him to have had all those petty scribblers who busy themselves in disfiguring paper, and speaking irreverentially about people of quality, hung or beaten to death by his attendants. Lord have mercy on my poor uncle! He really esteemed nothing in the world except the epistle to Zetulba.

Well, then, I had only just left college. I was full of dreams and illusions. I was as naïve as a *rosière* of Salency, perhaps more so. Delighted at having no more pensums to make, everything seemed to me for the best in the best of all possible worlds. I believed in an infinity of things. I believed in M. de Florian's shepherdess with her combed and powdered sheep. I never for a moment doubted the reality of Madame Deshoulière's flock. I believed that there were actually nine muses, as stated in Father Jouvency's *Appendix de Diis et Heroïbus*. My recollections of Berquin and of Gessner had created a little world for me in which everything was rose-coloured, sky-blue, and apple-green. Oh, holy innocence!—*sancta simplicitas!* as Mephistopheles says.

When I found myself alone in this fine room—my own room, all to myself!—I felt superlatively overjoyed. I made a careful inventory of everything, even the smallest article of furniture. I rummaged every corner, and explored the chamber in the fullest sense of the word. I was in the fourth heaven, as happy as a king, or rather as two kings. After supper (for we used to sup at my uncle's—a charming custom, now obsolete, together with many other equally charming customs which I mourn for with all the heart I have left), I took my candle and retired forthwith, so impatient did I feel to enjoy my new dwelling-place.

While I was undressing I fancied that Omphale's eyes had moved. I looked more attentively in that direction, not without a slight sensation of fear, for the room was very large, and the feeble luminous penumbra which floated about the candle only served to render the darkness still more visible. I thought I saw her turning her head toward me. I became frightened in earnest, and blew out the light. I turned my face to the wall, pulled the bed-clothes over my head, drew my night-cap down to my chin, and finally went to sleep.

I did not dare to look at the accursed tapestry again for several days.

It may be well here, for the sake of imparting something of verisimilitude to the very unlikely story I am about to relate, to inform my fair readers that in those days I was really a very pretty boy. I had the handsomest eyes in the world, at least they used to tell me so; a much fairer complexion than I have now, a true carnation tint; curly brown hair, which I still have, and seventeen years, which I have no longer. I needed only a pretty stepmother to be a very tolerable cherub. Unfortunately mine was fifty-seven years of age, and had only three teeth, which was too much of one thing and too little of the other.

One evening, however, I finally plucked up courage enough to take a peep at the fair mistress of Hercules. She was looking at me with the saddest and most languishing expression possible. This time I pulled my nightcap down to my very shoulders, and buried my head in the coverlets.

I had a strange dream that night, if indeed it was a dream.

I heard the rings of my bed-curtains sliding with a sharp squeak upon their curtain-rods, as if the curtains had been suddenly pulled back. I awoke, at least in my dream it seemed to me that I awoke. I saw no one.

The moon shone full upon the window-panes, and projected her wan bluish light into the room. Vast shadows, fantastic forms, were defined upon the floor and the walls. The clock chimed a quarter, and the vibration of the sound took a long time to die away. It seemed like a sigh. The plainly audible strokes of the pendulum seemed like the pulsations of a young heart, throbbing with passion.

I felt anything but comfortable, and a very bewilderment of fear took possession of me.

A furious gust of wind banged the shutters and made the window-sashes tremble. The woodwork cracked, the tapestry undulated. I ventured a glance in the direction of Omphale, with a vague suspicion that she was instrumental in all this unpleasantness, for some secret purpose of her own. I was not mistaken.

The tapestry became violently agitated. Omphale detached herself from the wall and leaped lightly to the carpet. She came straight toward my bed, after having first turned herself carefully in my direction. I fancy it will hardly be necessary to describe my stupefaction. The most intrepid old soldier would not have felt very comfortable under similar circumstances, and I was neither old nor a soldier. I awaited the end of the adventure in terrified silence.

A flute-toned, pearly little voice sounded softly in my ears, with that pretty lisp affected during the Regency by marchionesses and people of high degree:

"Do I really frighten you, my child? It is true that you are only a child, but it is not nice to be afraid of ladies, especially when they are young ladies and only wish you well. It is uncivil and unworthy of a French gentleman. You must be cured of such silly fears. Come, little savage, leave off these foolish airs, and cease hiding your head under the bedclothes. Your education is by no means complete yet, my pretty page, and you have not learned so very much. In my time cherubs were more courageous."

"But, lady, it is because——"

"Because it seems strange to you to find me here instead of there," she said, biting her ruddy lip with her white teeth, and pointing toward the wall with her long taper finger. "Well, in fact, the thing does not look very natural, but were I to explain it all to you, you would be none the wiser. Let it be sufficient for you to know that you are not in any danger."

"I am afraid you may be the—the——"

"The devil—out with the word!—is it not? That is what you wanted to say. Well, at least you will grant that I am not black enough for a devil, and that if hell were peopled with devils shaped as I am, one might have quite as pleasant a time there as in Paradise."

And to prove that she was not flattering herself, Omphale threw back her lion's skin and allowed me to behold her exquisitely moulded shoulders and bosom, dazzling in their white beauty.

"Well, what do you think of me?" she exclaimed, with a pretty little air of satisfied coquetry.

"I think that even were you the devil himself I should not feel afraid of you any more, Madame Omphale."

"Ah, now you talk sensibly, but do not call me madame, or Omphale. I do not wish you to look upon me as a madame, and I am no more Omphale than I am the devil."

"Then who are you?"

"I am the Marchioness de T——. A short time after I was married the marquis had this tapestry made for my apartments, and had me represented on it in the character of Omphale. He himself figures there as Hercules. That was a queer notion he took, for God knows there never was anybody in the world who bore less resemblance to Hercules than the poor marquis! It has been a long time since this chamber was occupied. I naturally love company, and I almost died of *ennui* in consequence. It gave me the headache. To be only with one's husband is the same thing as being alone. When you came I was overjoyed. This dead room became reanimated. I had found some one to feel interested in. I watched you come in and go out, I heard you murmuring in your sleep, I watched you reading, and my eyes followed the pages. I found you were nicely behaved, and had a fresh, innocent way about you that pleased me. In short, I fell in love with you. I tried to make you understand. I sighed. You thought it was only the sighing of the wind. I made signs to you. I looked at you with languishing eyes, and only succeeded in frightening you terribly. So at last in despair I resolved upon this rather improper course which I have taken, to tell you frankly what you could not take a hint about. Now that you know I love you, I hope that——"

The conversation was interrupted at this juncture by the grating of a key in the lock of the chamber door.

Omphale started and blushed to the very whites of her eyes.

"Adieu," she whispered, "till to-morrow." And she returned to her place on the wall, walking backward, for fear that I should see her reverse side, doubtless.

It was Baptiste, who came to brush my clothes.

"You ought not to sleep with your bed-curtains open, sir," he remarked. "You might catch a bad cold. This room is so chilly."

The curtains were actually open, and as I had been under the impression that I was only dreaming, I felt very much astonished, for I was certain that they had been closed when I went to bed.

As soon as Baptiste left the room, I ran to the tapestry. I felt it all over. It was indeed a real woollen tapestry, rough to the touch like any other tapestry. Omphale resembled the charming phantom of the night only as a dead body resembles a living one. I lifted the hangings. The wall was solid throughout. There were no masked panels or secret doors. I only noticed that a few threads were broken in the groundwork of the tapestry where the feet of Omphale rested. This afforded me food for reflection.

All that day I remained buried in the deepest brown study imaginable. I longed for evening with a mingled feeling of anxiety and impatience. I retired early, resolved on learning how this mystery was going to end. I got into bed. The marchioness did not keep me waiting long. She leaped down from the tapestry in front of the pier-glass, and dropped right by my bed. She seated herself by my pillow, and the conversation commenced.

I asked her questions as I had done the evening before, and demanded explanations. She eluded the former, and replied in an evasive manner to the latter, yet always after so witty a fashion that within a quarter of an hour I felt no scruples whatever in regard to my liaison with her.

While conversing she passed her fingers through my hair, tapped me gently on the cheeks, and softly kissed my forehead.

She chatted and chatted in a pretty mocking way, in a style at once elegantly polished and yet familiar and altogether like a great lady, such as I have never since heard from the lips of any human being.

She was then seated upon the easy-chair beside the bed. In a little while she slipped one of her arms around my neck, and I felt her heart beating passionately against me. It was indeed a charming and handsome real woman, a veritable marchioness whom I found beside me, poor student of seventeen! There was more than enough to make one lose his head, so I lost mine. I did not know very well what was going to happen, but I felt a vague presentiment that it would displease the marquis.

"And Monsieur le Marquis, on the wall up there—what will he say?"

The lion's skin had fallen to the floor, and the soft lilac-coloured buskins, filigreed with silver, were lying beside my shoes.

"He will not say anything," replied the marchioness, laughing heartily. "Do you suppose he ever sees anything? Besides, even should he see, he is the most philosophical and inoffensive husband in the world. He is used to such things. Do you love me, little one?"

"Indeed I do, ever so much!—ever so much!"

Morning dawned. My mistress stole away.

The day seemed to me frightfully long. At last evening came. The same things happened as on the evening before, and the second night left no regrets for the first. The marchioness became more and more adorable, and this state of affairs continued for a long time. As I never slept at night, I wore a somnolent expression in the daytime which did not augur well for me with my uncle. He suspected something. He probably listened at the door and heard everything, for one fine morning he entered my room so brusquely that Antoinette had scarcely time to get back to her place on the tapestry.

He was followed by a tapestry-hanger with pincers and a ladder.

He looked at me with a shrewd and severe expression which convinced me that he knew all.

"This Marchioness de T—— is certainly crazy. What the devil could have put it into her head to fall in love with a brat like that?" muttered my uncle between his teeth. "She promised to behave herself.

"Jean, take that tapestry down, roll it up, and put it in the garret."

Every word my uncle spoke went through my heart like a poniard-thrust.

Jean rolled up my sweetheart Omphale, otherwise the Marchioness Antoinette de T——, together with Hercules, or the Marquis de T——, and carried the whole thing off to the garret. I could not restrain my tears.

Next day my uncle sent me back in the B—— diligence to my respectable parents, to whom, you may feel assured, I never breathed a word of my adventure.

My uncle died; his house and furniture were sold; probably the tapestry was sold with the rest.

But a long time afterward, while foraging the shop of a bric-à-brac merchant in search of oddities, I stumbled over a great dusty roll of something covered with cobwebs.

"What is that?" I said to the Auvergnat.

"That is a rococo tapestry representing the amours of Madame Omphale and Monsieur Hercules. It is genuine Beauvais, worked in silk, and in an excellent state of preservation. Buy this from me for your study. I will not charge you dear for it, since it is you."

At the name of Omphale all my blood rushed to my heart.

"Unroll that tapestry," I said to the merchant in a hurried, gasping voice, like one in a fever.

It was indeed she! I fancied that her mouth smiled graciously at me, and that her eye lighted up on meeting mine.

"How much do you ask?"

"Well, I could not possibly let you have it for any less than five hundred francs."

"I have not that much with me now. I will get it and be back in an hour."

I returned with the money, but the tapestry was no longer there. An Englishman had bargained for it during my absence, offered six hundred francs for it, and taken it away with him.

After all, perhaps it was best that it should have been thus, and that I should preserve this delicious souvenir intact. They say one should never return to a first love, or look at the rose which one admired the evening before.

And then I am no longer so young or so pretty that tapestries should come down from their walls to honour me.

❋ ❋ ❋

VILLIERS DE L'ISLE ADAM
(1838-1889)

VILLIERS DE L'ISLE ADAM, born in Brittany, may be said to have inaugurated the Symbolist movement in French literature. He wrote several plays, novels, and, in 1883, a series of stories called the *Contes Cruels,* which contains his best work. In these stories "may be found every classic quality of the French *conte,* together with many of the qualities of Edgar Allan Poe and Ernest Hoffman," says Arthur Symons. *The Heroism of Doctor Hallidonhill* is one of the stories that appears in the fantastic *Contes Cruels.*

The present version, translated by E. O'Neil, is reprinted from *The Pagan* magazine, by permission of the editor.

THE HEROISM OF DOCTOR HALLIDONHILL

To kill in order to cure!
Official adage of Broussais

THE unusual case of Doctor Hallidonhill will shortly come before the London Assizes. Here are the facts:

The twentieth of last May, the two vast ante-chambers of the illustrious specialist, the healer quand-même of all affections of the lungs, overflowed with clients, as was habitually the case,—their appointment-cards in their hands.

At the entrance, in a long black frock-coat, stood the receiver of money: he took from each one the required two guineas, tested them, with a single blow of the hammer upon an anvil de luxe, automatically crying out, "All-right!"

In the glassed-in office,—bordered all around by large tropical plants in their great pots from Japan,—had just seated himself before his desk, the erect little Doctor Hallidonhill. At his side, next to a round table, his secretary took down brief prescriptions in short-hand. On the steps leading up to a door, draped in red velvet, with gold clasps, stood an attendant of monstrous size, whose duty it was to transport the staggering consumptives to the landing-place,—from which they were taken down in the elevator in special lounges (all this after the sacramental "Next!" had been pronounced).

The patients entered, eyes glassy and veiled, torso naked, their clothes over their arm; they received, on the instant, upon the back and chest, the application of the pessimeter and tube.

"Tik! tik! plaff! Breathe!. . . . Plaff. . . . Good."

Followed a medication dictated in few seconds, then the famous "Next!" And, for three years, every morning, the commonplace procession filed away like this, from nine o'clock until precisely twelve.

Suddenly, upon that day, the twentieth of May, nine o'clock was striking, when a sort of tall skeleton with enlarged pupils, the hollows of his cheeks touching under his palate, the torso bare, resembling a cage around which was twisted a flabby parchment, uplifted by the inhalation of a broken cough,—briefly, one who was doubtfully alive, a piece of blue fox fur folded over one of his emaciated fore-arms, elongated the compass of his femurs in the doctor's office, while holding himself up by the large leaves of the plants.

"Tik! tik! plaff! Nothing to do!" grumbled Doctor Hallidonhill; "am I a coroner, good for pronouncing upon the deceased? Within a week, the greater growth of this left lung will be discharged: and the right is a sieve! . . . Next!"

The attendant was about to "remove the client," when the eminent therapeutist, slapping himself on the forehead, brusquely added, with a complex smile:

"Are you rich?"

"An arch-millionaire!", croaked, all in tears, the unfortunate personage whom Hallidonhill had just so succinctly dismissed from the planet.

"In that case, have your carriage leave you at Victoria Station! Eleven o'clock express to Dover! . . . Then the boat! . . . Then from Calais to Marseilles, sleeping-car with stove! . . . And then on Nice! There, six months of water-cress, day and night, without bread, or wine, or fruits, or meats. A spoonful of rain-water, well iodined, every other day. And water-cress, water-cress, water-cress! . . . ground, pounded in its juice . . . only chance . . . and even then!—— This pretended cure, with which they besiege my ears, appears to me more than absurd. I offer it to a desperate man, but without believing in it for a second. Well everything is possible . . . Next!"

The tubercular Crœsus, once delicately placed in the canopied enclosure of the elevator, the usual procession of consumptive, scorbutic, and bronchial patients began.

Six months later, the third of November, nine o'clock was striking, when a species of giant with a formidable and joyous voice, the timbre of which made the panes of glass in the office vibrate, and the leaves of the tropical plants tremble, a chubby-cheeked colossus, in rich furs, having hurled himself like a human bomb through the lamentable ranks of the clientele of Doctor Hallidonhill, penetrated, without appointment-card, into the sanctum of the Prince of Science, who, cold, in his black suit, had just seated himself as usual in front of his table. Seizing his body in his arms, he lifted him like a feather, and bathing,—in silence,—the withered and sallow cheeks of the practitioner with tender tears, kissed them, and kissed them again, in a sonorous fashion, in the manner of a paradoxical Norman nurse . . . then replaced him, half in a coma, and almost suffocated, in his green arm-chair.

"Two millions? Do you want them? Do you want three?" vociferated the giant, a terrible and living advertisement. "I owe to you the breath of life, the sun, good meals, the unbounded passions, existence, everything! Claim, therefore, from me unheard-of remuneration! I have a thirst for making recompense!"

"Well! really, who is this madman? . . . Have him put out!" . . . feebly articulated the doctor after a moment's prostration. "But no, but no!", scolded the giant, with the look of a boxer, which made the attendant draw back. "In reality, I understand that you, even you, my saviour, do not recognise me. I am the man of the water-cress! The skeleton that was done-for, lost! Nice! water-cress, water-cress, water-cress! . . . I have finished my semester, and here is what you have accomplished. Look here; listen to this!"

And he beat upon his thorax with fists capable of breaking the skulls of prime Middlesex bulls.

"Hein!" cried the doctor, leaping to his feet,—"you are . . . what! This is the moribund who . . ."

"Yes, a thousand times yes, it is I!" shouted the giant:—"Since last evening, scarcely had I left the steamer, when I ordered your statue in bronze, and I will know how to manage to have some funeral ground bestowed on you at Westminster!"

Letting himself fall upon a vast sofa, the spring of which creaked and groaned: "—Ah, but life is good!" he sighed with the beatific smile of placid ecstasy. Upon two rapid words pronounced in a low voice by the doctor, the secretary and the attendant withdrew. Once alone with his resuscitated patient, Hallidonhill, stiff, wan and icy, with a nervous eye, looked upon the giant, during several seconds, in silence—then, all of a sudden:

"Permit me, in the first place," he murmured in a strange tone, "to remove this fly from your temple!" and precipitating himself forward, the doctor, taking from his pocket a short bull-dog revolver, discharged it twice, very rapidly into the artery of the left temple.

The giant fell, the skull fractured, bespattering with his grateful brain, the rug of the room, which he beat with the palms of his hands for a minute.

With ten cuts of the scissors, fur great coat, clothes, and under clothes, slashed at random, left bare his chest,—which the grave surgeon, with a single stroke of his large bistoury, cleft immediately from bottom to top.

A quarter of an hour later, when the constable had entered the office to beg Doctor Hallidonhill to be so good as to follow him, the latter, calm, seated before his table, his powerful magnifying glass in his hand, scrutinised a pair of enormous lungs laid out flat upon his sanguinary desk. The genius of Science was trying, in the person of this man, to find an explanation of the arch-miraculous action of the water-cress, at once lubricating and relieving.

"Constable," said he, as he rose, "I judged it opportune to immolate this man,—his immediate autopsy being able to reveal a salutary secret for the degenerating tree of the human species: that is why I did not hesitate, I admit it, to sacrifice, in this instance, my conscience to my duty."

Needless to add that the illustrious doctor was released upon purely formal bail, his liberty being more useful to us than his detention. This strange affair will now come before the British assizes. Ah! what marvellous legal appeals Europe will read!

Everything leads us to hope that this sublime attempt will not cost its hero the gallows of New Gate, the English being people to understand, just as well that *the exclusive love of future humanity to the point of perfect disregard of the present individual is, in our day, the unique motive which must absolve the magnanimous outrages of Science.*

ALPHONSE DAUDET
(1840-1897)

DAUDET, born at Nîmes, suffered a depressing boyhood. In 1857 he came to Paris to try his hand at literature, and, in the following year, he published a collection of poems which, consequently, led to his appointment on the staff of the *Figaro*. This started him on the road to success, and he subsequently published a number of novels and short stories. *Fromont Junior and Risler Senior* is the novel that established Daudet's fame. The *Tartarin* trilogy, now accepted as little classics, followed and increased his popularity. Daudet has been compared to Dickens for his pathos, humour and sympathy with the downtrodden.

The *Ensign* is from a volume, *In the Midst of Paris*, translated by Céline Bertault, published by Platt, Bruce & Co. Copyright, 1895.

THE ENSIGN

THE regiment was engaged on the banks of a railway, and served as a target to the whole Prussian army massed in an opposite wood. They were firing on each other at a distance of eighty yards. The officers shouted, "Lie down!" but no one would obey, and the proud regiment remained standing gathered round their colours. In the great horizon of the setting sun, of cornfields, of pasture land, this confused group of men, enveloped in smoke, were like a flock of sheep surprised in the open country by the first whirlwind of a terrific storm.

It rained iron on that slope! Nothing was heard but the crackle of the volleys and the prolonged vibration of the balls which flew from one end of the battle-field to the other. From time to time the flag, which waved overhead in the wind of the mitrailleuse, disappeared in the smoke, then a voice grave and steady, dominating the firing, the struggles of the dying, the oaths of the wounded, would cry: *"Au drapeau, mes enfants, au drapeau!"* Instantly an officer, vague as a shadow in the red mist, would spring forward, and the standard, once more alive as it were, showed again above the battle.

Twenty-two times it fell. Twenty-two times its staff, still warm, slipping from a dying hand, was seized and upheld, and when, at sunset, what remained of the regiment—scarce a handful of men—retreated slowly firing as they went, the colours were mere rags in the hands of Sergeant Hornus, the twenty-third ensign of the day.

Sergeant Hornus was a crusty old war-dog, who could hardly write his own name, and who had taken twenty years to gain his sergeant's stripes. All the miseries of a foundling, all the brutalising effects of barrack-life, could be traced in the low projecting forehead, the back beneath the knapsack, that air of careless self-neglect acquired in the ranks.

Besides all this he stammered, but then eloquence is not essential to an ensign. On the evening of the battle, his colonel said to him, "You have the colours, my brave fellow; keep them." And on his coarse hood, frayed by war and weather, the vivandière stitched the gold band of a sub-lieutenant.

This had been the one ambition of his humble life. From that moment he drew himself up; he who was wont to walk with bent head and eyes fixed on the ground, henceforth looked proudly upwards to the bit of stuff which he held very straight, high above death, treachery and defeat. Never was there a happier man than Hornus on days of battle, holding his staff firmly in its leather socket with both hands.

He neither spoke nor moved, and was as serious as a priest guarding some sacred thing. All his life, all his strength, were concentrated in the fingers grasping that gilded rag upon which the balls beat so persistently, and in his defiant eyes looking the Prussians full in the face, as if saying, "Try, if you dare, to take it from me!"

No one did try, not even death.

After Borny, after Gravelotte, those murderous battles, the colours came out, tattered, in holes, transparent with wounds, but it was still old Hornus who carried them.

Then came September with the army around Metz, the investment, and that long pause when the cannon rusted in the mud, and the finest troops in the world, demoralised by inaction, want of food and want of news, died of fever and *ennui* beside their piled arms. No one, neither chiefs nor soldiers, had faith in the future; Hornus alone was still confident. His ragged *tricolor* was all in all to him, and as long as he could see that, nothing seemed lost.

Unfortunately, as there was no more fighting, the colonel kept the colours at his house in one of the suburbs of Metz, and poor Hornus was much like a mother whose child is out to nurse. He thought of it constantly. Then when the yearning was too much for him, he went off to Metz, and having seen it still in the same place, leaning against the wall, he returned full of courage and patience, bringing back to his dripping tent dreams of battle and of advancing marches, with flying colours floating over the Prussian trenches. An order of the day from Marshal Bazaine put an end to these illusions. One morning Hornus on awakening found the whole camp clamorous, groups of soldiers in great excitement, uttering cries of rage, all shaking their fists towards one side of the town as though their anger were roused against some criminal. There were shouts of "Away with him!" "Let him be shot!" And the officers did nothing to prevent them. They kept apart with bent heads as if ashamed of being seen by their men. It was indeed shameful. The marshal's order had just been read to 150,000 fighting men, well armed and efficient—an order which surrendered them to the enemy without a struggle!

"And the colours?" asked Hornus, growing pale. The colours were to be given up with the rest, with the arms, with what was left of the munitions of war—everything.

"*To-To-Tonnerre de Dieu!*" stuttered the poor man. "They shan't have mine." And he started at a run towards the town.

Here also there was great disturbance: National Guards, civilians, gardes mobiles shouting and excited, deputations on their way to the Marshal; but of all this Hornus saw and heard nothing. All the way up the Rue du Faubourg he kept saying to himself:

"Take my flag from me indeed! It is not possible. They have no right to it! Let him give the Prussians what is his own, his gilded carriages, his fine plate brought from Mexico! But that, it is mine. It is my honour. I defy any one to touch it."

These fragments of speech were broken by his rapid pace and by his stammer, but the old fellow had his idea notwithstanding; a very clear and defined idea—to get the standard, carry it to the regiment, and cut his way through the Prussians with all who would follow him.

When he reached his destination he was not even allowed to enter the house. The colonel, furious himself, would see no one; but Hornus was not to be put off thus. He swore, shouted, hustled the orderly!

"My flag, I want my flag." At last a window opened.

"Is it you, Hornus?"

"Yes, Colonel; I——"

"The colours are all at the arsenal—you have only to go there and you will get an acknowledgment."

"An acknowledgment! What for?"

"It is the Marshal's order."

"But Colonel——"

"Leave me alone," and the window was shut.

Old Hornus staggered like a drunken man.

"An acknowledgment, an acknowledgment," he repeated mechanically, moving slowly away, comprehending only one thing, that the flag was at the arsenal, and that he must get it again, no matter at what price.

The gates of the arsenal were wide open, to allow the passage of the Prussian waggons which were drawn up in the yard. Hornus shuddered. All the other ensigns were there, fifty or sixty officers silent and sorrowful; those sombre carts in the rain, with the men grouped bareheaded behind them, had all the aspect of a funeral.

In a corner the colours of Bazaine's army lay in a confused heap on the muddy pavement. Nothing could be sadder than these bits of gay-coloured silks, these ends of gold fringe and of ornamented hafts, all this glorious paraphernalia thrown on the ground, soiled by rain and mud. An officer took them one by one, and as each regiment was named, its ensign advanced to receive an acknowledgment. Two Prussian officers, stiff and unmoved, superintended the ceremony.

And must you go thus, oh sacred and glorious flags!—displaying your brave rents, sweeping the ground sadly like broken-winged birds, with the shame of beautiful things sullied? With each of you goes a part of France. The sun of long marches hid in your faded folds. In each mark of a ball you kept the memory of the unknown dead falling at random around the standard, the enemy's mark!

"Hornus, it is your turn, they are calling you; go for your receipt."

What did he care about a receipt?

The flag was there before him. It was his, the most beautiful, the most mutilated of all. And seeing it again, he fancied himself once more on that railway bank. He heard the whistling balls and the colonel's voice, *"Au drapeau, mes enfants!"* He saw his twenty-two comrades lying dead; himself, the twenty-third, rushing forward in his turn to support the poor flag which sank for want of an arm. Ah! that day he had sworn to defend it to the death—and now!

Thinking of all this made his heart's blood rush to his head. Distracted, mad, he sprang on the Prussian officer, tore from him his beloved standard, tried to raise it once more straight and high, crying, *"Au dra———"* But the words stuck in his throat—he felt the staff tremble, slip through his hands. In that paralysing atmosphere, that atmosphere of death which weighs so heavily on capitulated towns, the standard could no longer float, nothing glorious could live, and old Hornus, too, choked with shame and rage, fell dead.

※ ※ ※

ÉMILE ZOLA
(1840-1903)

ZOLA was the most prolific of the naturalist group of writers. After his *Contes à Ninon*, a collection of fairy tales, and several other books he projected with characteristic energy a series of novels that were to relate the history of a family of the Second Empire. This collossal creation, larger than Balzac's *Comédie humaine*, is powerful as a mass, though it lacks the charm and grace of the best French style. *The Maid of the Dauber*, appearing in the volume, *Le Vœu d'une Morte*, is one of Zola's best short stories.

The present version is translated for this collection by Maxim Lieber.

THE MAID OF THE DAUBER

SHE is still in bed, half nude, smiling, her head sunk in the pillow and her eyes heavy with sleep. One of her arms is hidden in her hair, and the other dangles over the edge of the bed. The count, in his slippers, stands before one of the windows and pulls up the shade. He is smoking a cigar and seems absorbed in thought.

You all know her. She was twenty yesterday, but looks barely sixteen. She wears the most magnificent crown that heaven has ever granted to one of its angels, a crown of brown gold, soft and strong as a horse's mane, glossy as a skein of silk. The curling flame rolls, all about her neck. Each wisp straightens itself and then runs out very long. The curls fall, the tresses slide and roll; the entire mass glows resplendent. And under the burning mass, in the midst of its splendour, appears the nape of a white and delicate neck, creamy shoulders and full breasts. Irresistible seduction dwells on that snowy throat, peeping out discreetly from beneath the fiery red hair. Passion kindles and burns when your eyes explore that neck of tender lights and golden shadows. Here mingle wild beast and the child, boldness and innocence, intoxication invoking ardent kisses.

Is she beautiful? It is hard to say; her face is hidden by masses of hair. She must have a low forehead; greyish eyes, narrow and long. Her nose is doubtless irregular, capricious; her mouth somewhat large with rosy lips.

What matter for the rest? You could not analyse her features or determine the contour of her face. She intoxicates you at first sight, as a strong wine does at the first glass. All you see is a whiteness amidst a red flame, a rosy smile; and her eyes are like the flash of silver in the sunlight. She turns your head and you are already too captivated to study her perfections one by one. She is of medium height—a little slow and heavy in her movements. Her hands and feet are those of a little girl. Her whole body expresses indolent voluptousness. One of her bare arms, rounded and dazzling, provokes a thrill of desire. She is queen of May evenings, queen of loves that last but for a day.

She reclines on her left arm, which is slightly bent. Presently she will rise. Meanwhile she half opens here eyelids to accustom them to the daylight, and looks at the pale blue bed-curtains.

She lies lost in the lace of her pillows. She seems engulfed in perspiration and the delicious lassitude of awakening. Her body is stretched out, white and motionless, barely stirring with gentle breathing. Rosy flesh appears here and there, where the batiste nightgown opens. Nothing could be more luxurious than this bed and the woman lying upon it. The divine swan has a nest worthy of her.

The chamber is a marvel of delicate blue. The colours and the perfume are refreshing. The air is enervating, thrilling and cool. The curtains hang in lazy folds. The carpet lies indolently on the floor, deaf and mute. The silence of this temple, the softness of the lights, the discreetness of the shadows, the purity of the furnishings remind one of a goddess, who unites in herself all the grace and elegance with the soul of an artist and that of a duchess. Surely she was reared on milk baths. Her delicate limbs bespeak the noble indolence of her life. It is amusing to fancy that her soul has all the purity of her body.

The count is finishing his cigar, deeply interested in a horse which has just fallen in the Champs Elysée and which they are trying to set again on its legs. The poor beast has fallen on his left flank, and the shaft must be breaking his ribs.

At the back of the bedroom, on her perfumed bed, the beautiful creature is slowly awakening. Now she has her eyes wide open, but remains motionless. The mind is awake, the body asleep. She is dreaming. To what luminous space has she been soaring? What angelic legions are passing before her and bringing a smile to her lips? What project, what task is she pondering? What curious idea, dawn of her awakening, has just surprised her? Her wide-open eyes are fixed on the curtain. She has not yet stirred. She is absorbed in vagaries. She lies thus nursing her dreams.

Then briskly, as if obeying an irresistible call, she stretches forth her feet and leaps lightly to the carpet. She flings back her hair which tumbles in flaming curls about her snowy shoulders. She gathers up her laces, slips into her blue velvet slippers, crosses her arms in a graceful pose; then, half-stooping, her shoulders arched, pouting like a sullen child, she trots off swiftly, noiselessly, and opening a door, disappears.

The count throws away his cigar with a sigh of satisfaction. The horse in the street has been raised. A lash of a whip brought the poor beast to its feet. The count turns and sees the empty bed. He looks at it a moment; then advancing leisurely, and sitting on the edge, begins in his turn to contemplate the pale blue curtains.

The woman's face is brazen: a man's is like a clear spring which reveals all the secrets of its limpidity. The count is studying the curtain, and figures mechanically how much a yard it may have cost. He adds and multiplies and concludes with a huge figure. Then involuntarily, carried away by the chain of ideas, he proceeds to set a valuation on the whole bedchamber, and arrives at an enormous total.

His hand rests on the bed, elbow the pillow. The spot is warm. The count becomes oblivious to the temple and begins to think of the idol. He examines the bed, that voluptuous disorder which every beautiful sleeper leaves behind her; and at the sight of a golden hair, glistening on the whiteness of the pillow, he grows absorbed in thought of this woman. Then two ideas unite: he thinks of the woman and of the chamber synchronously. In his fancy he compares the woman and the furniture, the draperies and the carpet. Everything is in harmony.

Here the count's revery strays, and by one of those inexplicable mysteries of human thought, his boots claim his attention. Suggested by nothing, the idea of boots suddenly invades his whole mind. He recalls that for about three months every morning when he has left this room he has found his boots cleaned and brilliantly polished. He ruminates over this recollection.

The chamber is magnificent. The woman simply divine. The count glances again at the sky-blue curtains and the single golden hair on the sheet. He compliments himself, declaring that he repaired an error of Providence when he clad in satin this queen of grace, whom destiny caused to be born to a sewer-cleaner and a concierge near Fontainebleau. He praises himself for having given a soft nest to this marvel for the insignificant sum of five or six hundred thousand francs. He rises and takes a few steps forward. He is alone. He recalls that he has been left alone thus every morning for a full quarter of an hour. And then, without curiosity, merely to be doing something, he opens the door and disappears in his turn.

The count passes through a long suite of rooms, without encountering anybody. But returning, he hears in a closet a violent and continued sound of brushing. Thinking that it is a servant, and wishing to question her as to her mistress' absence, he opens the door and puts his head in. And he stops on the threshold, gaping, stupefied.

The closet is small, painted yellow, with a brown base the height of a man. In one corner there is a pail and a large sponge, in another a broom and a duster. A bay-window throws an imperfect light on the bareness of this store-room, very high and narrow. The air is damp and chilly.

In the centre, on a door-mat, with her feet tucked under her, sits the beauty with golden hair. On her right is a pot of boot-blacking, with a brush blackened from use, still thick and damp. On her left is a boot, shining like a mirror, masterpiece of the bootblack's art. About her are spattered dabs of dirt and a fine grey dust. A little further off lies the knife used to scrape the mud off the soles. She is holding the other boot on her hand. One of her arms is quite lost in its interior. Her little fingers clutch an enormous brush with long, stiff bristles, and she is scrubbing furiously at the heel, which refuses to shine.

She has swathed her laces about her legs which she holds apart. Drops of perspiration roll down her cheeks and shoulders; and now and then she must stop to impatiently thrust back her tresses, which fall over her eyes. Her alabaster bosom and arms are covered with spots, some tiny as pinheads, some large as lentils: the blacking, as it flies from the bristles, has flecked that dazzling whiteness with black stars. She compresses her lips, and her eyes are moist and smiling. She bends lovingly over the boot, appearing rather to caress than to brush it. She is absorbed in her task and forgets herself in her infinite pleasure, shaken by her rapid movements. Through the bay-window a cold light shines on her. A wide ray falls across her, kindling her hair, enhancing the rosy tint of her skin and turning her laces blue; and reveals this marvel of grace and delicacy in the mud.

She is eager and happy. She is the daughter of her father, the true child of her mother. Every morning, upon awakening, she thinks of her childhood spent on the filthy staircase, in the midst of the old shoes of all the lodgers. She dreams of them; and a wild desire possesses her to clean something, even if it is only a pair of boots. She has a passion for polishing, as other people have a passion for flowers. This is her secret, the thing of which she is ashamed, but in which she finds strange delights. And so, she rises and goes every morning in her luxury, in her immaculate beauty, to scrape the soles with the tips of her white fingers, and to bedraggle the delicacy of a great lady in the dirty task of a bootblack.

The count touches her lightly on the shoulder: and when she raises her head in surprise he takes his boots from her, puts them on, tosses her five sous and quietly withdraws.

Later in the day the maid of the dauber is vexed and outraged. She writes to the count. She claims an indemnity of a hundred thousand francs. The count replies that he does recall owing her something. Polishing his boots at twenty-five centimes a day makes twenty-three francs at the end of three months. So he sends her twenty-three francs by his man.

✳ ✳ ✳

CATULLE MENDÈS
(1841-1909)

MENDÈS, born at Bordeaux, was a brilliant poet and one of the moving spirits of the Parnassians. He was a very versatile writer, seeking self-expression in the novel, drama and short story. His work has a sensuous quality, besides being delightfully fantastic. *The Lost Stars*, displaying meticulous craftmanship, is cast in that fanciful vein so characteristic of Mendès.

The present version is translated by Walter Brooks, and is reprinted from his volume, *Retold in English*, by permission of the publishers, Brentano's, copyright, 1905.

THE LOST STARS

MONSIEUR," said my *valet de chambre*, just as I was completing the fifth verse of a sonnet, "there are two angels without who wish to speak with Monsieur."

"Have they given you their cards?" I asked.

"I have them here, Monsieur."

On one I read "Helial," on the other "Japhael." Two angels without question!

"Ask them to enter," I said.

It was not without pleasure that I received these visitors of quality. They were clad in large wings, each made of seven plumes, on which scintillated through a soft down, light as the mist of an early morning, the seven colors of the rainbow. What one could see of their bodies resembled transparent snow faintly tinged with pink. I begged them, with a wave of the hand, to be seated, and inquired politely the motive which gave me the honour of their acquaintance.

"We will be brief," said Helial. "Sixteen years ago, one beautiful night in July, we were playing at billiards, Japhael and myself, on the green carpet of the sky."

"Pardon," I interrupted, "I thought the sky was blue!"

"It is blue in certain parts of its immensity; but in others, particularly in those which border upon the towns and the open country of Persia, it is of a green most agreeable to the eye."

I did not reply.

Helial continued:

"We had for balls, stars, the most beautiful we could find."

"And for cues?" I inquired.

"The tails (queues) of comets. Naturally, the game was most interesting. I was on the point of winning, when with a violent stroke I sent two balls over the edge."

"Over the edge?"

"Yes, of the horizon. It was a sad misfortune, for you can well understand that two stars less in heaven is a matter of grave importance. We were warned by the ruler of the heavens that we would no more be permitted to participate in the joys of paradise until we had recovered and put back into place the two lost stars.

"You can imagine the search we have made these sixteen years, up and down the earth, where to all appearance the stars had fallen. But all our quests have, alas, been in vain.

"We were going to resign ourselves to eternal exile, when we heard of the incomparable eyes of a young girl, who is your sweetheart, if one can believe rumours which are abroad. Everything seemed to indicate that in place of mortal eyes she had the celestial lights we sought, and let us hope she will be willing to return them."

I felt myself strangely perplexed. The mere idea that any one should take from me the eyes of my dearly beloved one caused me an alarming inquietude. But it was in my power to aid two angels to recover their divine patrimony! I summoned Mademoiselle Mesange and explained to her in few words the situation.

She neither appeared surprised nor troubled, but after having reflected a few seconds, she turned toward the visitors and, raising her eyelids as much as possible, said, "Look, beautiful angels, and tell me if you recognize your stars."

They drew near. They examined, with the greatest care, the clear eyes of Mesange. For some moments they communicated one with the other in a low voice, as judges who exchange their opinions. Then Helial said: "No, these are not the luminaries which disappeared sixteen years ago. Ours, although they were at their best that July night, were neither as brilliant nor as sparkling."

Thereupon they departed with a truly dejected air. I pitied them with all my heart, delighted as I was that they had not robbed me of my love.

And Mesange? She burst into laughter. "Have I not tricked them well?" she said. "It is true—my mother has told it me a hundred times —how, shortly after my birth, two stars fell through the open window straight between my eyelids. But while the angels were observing me, I thought of that moment when for the first time, my love, you imprinted a kiss upon my lips, and I knew full well that the recollection of that delight would make my eyes, those stars of former times, more brilliant than the most beautiful among the heavenly bodies."

❋ ❋ ❋

JEAN RICHEPIN
(1849-1926)

RICHEPIN was born at Medea, Algeria, and, while yet at school, gave evidence of brilliant, if somewhat undisciplined powers. In his poems, reflecting his erratic genius, he first found an outlet for his colourful life. A volume of poems entitled *Chanson des Gueux* (1876) resulted in his being imprisoned for outraging public morals. This did not deter him from his fearless purpose of describing life as he saw it. This quality is present in his later work, although his novels have developed in style and psychological treatment. *Constant Guinard*, from *Les Morts bizarres*, is almost brutal in its irony.

The present version is translated by Sylvia Eldridge. It appeared originally in *The Pagan* magazine, and is here reprinted by permission of the editor.

CONSTANT GUINARD

A l'action! au mal! le bien reste ignoré . . . .
A. De Musset.

THE couple Guinard, having married for love, passionately desired a son; and this longed-for little being, wishing to hasten the realization of their yearning, came into the world before his time. His mother died; and his father, unable to bear the grief, hung himself . . .

Constant Guinard's childhood was exemplary, but unfortunate. At school he was frequently punished, though undeservedly, and was given extra tasks to do; also was he the recipient of blows intended for other boys, and fell ill on test-days. He finished his studies with the reputation of being a hypocrite and a dunce.

At the examination for his Bachelor's Degree, he wrote the Latin version for his neighbour, which was accepted, while he was expelled for having copied.

Such unlucky débuts in life would have rendered an ordinary person ill-natured, but Constant Guinard had a noble soul, and being persuaded that happiness is the reward of virtue, he resolved to conquer ill-fortune through heroism.

The business-house where he was employed took fire one morning. When he saw the disconsolate look on the face of his employer, he threw himself into flames in order to save the valuables in the safe. His hair was singed and his arms and hands burned, but he succeeded, at the risk of his life, in breaking the box and taking out all the valuables.

Suddenly he felt himself being dragged out. Two policemen were pulling him by the collar.

A month later he was condemned to five years' imprisonment for having tried to appropriate the contents of the safe.

A revolt took place in the prison, and wishing to rescue one of the attacked keepers, he unwittingly tripped the latter, who fell, and was killed by the rebels.

Without more ado, Constant Guinard was sent to the dungeon of Cayenne. Strengthened by his innocence, however, he escaped, and returned to France under a different name. Thinking he had outwitted Fate, he once more began his good deeds.

One day, at a fair, he saw a runaway horse dragging a carriage which was about to fall into a ditch. Incontinently he throws himself in front of the horse, has his wrists twisted, a leg broken, and one rib crushed, but succeeds in warding off the fall. The animal, however, turns about, rushes into the crowd and tramples upon an old man, two women, and three children. There was nobody in the carriage. . . .

Disgusted with acts of heroism, Constant Guinard now decides to do good humbly, and he consecrates himself to assuaging miseries. But the money which he brings to poor women is recklessly spent in the wine-shops by their husbands. The sweaters which he distributes to workers, already accustomed to hard weather, only makes them catch cold in the chest. A stray dog which he gladly welcomes, gives hydrophobia to six persons in the neighborhood. And an interesting youth, for whom he buys a commission in the army, afterwards sells the plans of the fortress to the enemy.

Constant Guinard thought that money works more havoc than good; so instead of squandering his philanthropy, he decided to concentrate it on a single being. He therefore adopted a young orphan who was not at all pretty, but who was endowed with rare qualities.

He raised her with all the tenderness that a father could bestow on a child. Alas! he was so good, so devoted, so gentle to her, that one evening she threw herself at his feet and confessed her love for him. He tried to make her understand that he always thought of her as his daughter, and that he would feel guilty of committing a crime if he should yield to the temptation she was offering him.

He argued and pleaded with her in paternal fashion to prove to her that what she mistook for love was only the awakening of her senses. He promised, nevertheless, that he would look for a husband for her as soon as possible.

The next morning he found her stretched across his threshold, dead.

Thereupon, Constant Guinard renounced his rôle of "Good Fairy," and swore to himself, that from now on, in order to do good, he would content himself by simply avoiding evil.

Some time after the last occurrence he was by chance put on the track of a crime which one of his friends was about to commit.

He could easily have denounced him to the police, but he preferred to thwart the crime without ruining the criminal. He therefore prepared to seize all the threads of the plot, and awaited the precise moment when he should frustrate it. But the rascal whom he wished to overreach saw clearly into his game, and continued the affair in such a way, that the crime was committed, the criminal escaped, and Constant Guinard was arrested.

The speech of the District Attorney against Constant Guinard was a masterpiece of logic. He recalled the whole life of the accused, his deplorable childhood, his punishments, his expulsion from the examination, the audacity of his first theft, his odious conspiracy in the prison-revolt, his escape from Cayenne, his return to France under a different name. . . .

From that moment on, the orator ascended to the pinnacle of judiciary eloquence. He stigmatised the accused as a hypocrite of goodness, a corruptor of honest homes, who in order to gratify his passions, sent the husband to the wine-shops to squander money, . . . a false benefactor who, by means of presents, gained low-brow notoriety, . . . a monster disguised in the mantle of philanthropy.

He analysed with horror the refined perversity of the rogue, who welcomed mad dogs only to let them loose on people; a Satan who, loving evil for the sake of evil, risked crippling himself by stopping a runaway horse,—what for? Only to experience the appalling joy of letting the beast break into the crowd to crush old men, women, and little children.

Ah, such a creature was capable of anything! Without a shadow of doubt he had committed many other crimes of which we would never know. There were a thousand and one reasons for believing that he was the accomplice in that commission to betray France; and as for the orphan whom he had raised, and who was found killed one morning at his door, who other but himself could have assassinated her? That murder was certainly the bloody epilogue to one of those infamous dramas of shame, debauchery, and vileness that one dares hardly speak of.

After so many transgressions, there was no need of dwelling upon the last crime. Here, despite the impudent denials of the accused, there was absolute evidence. And he should be sentenced to the fullest extent of the law. Thus, he would be punished justly and not too severely. For he was not merely an ordinary criminal but a veritable demon of crime; one of those monsters of malice and hypocrisy who make us almost doubt virtue and become despairing of humanity.

Before such a requisition, the lawyer of Constant Guinard had no alternative to plead insanity for his client. He did his best . . . spoke of pathologic cases, expounded learnedly on the "nervous disturbances of criminals," presented his client as an irresponsible monomaniac, a sort of unconscious automaton, and concluded by saying that such anomalies are treated at Charenton * rather than in prison.

Constant Guinard was unanimously condemned to death.

Virtuous men, rendered ferocious by the hatred of this crime, were transported with joy, and cried bravo! bravo! bravo!

The death of Constant Guinard was like his childhood, exemplary but unfortunate. He ascended the scaffold without fear and without pose, his face as peaceful as his conscience, with the serenity of a martyr,— which everyone mistook for a brute's unconcern.

At the supreme moment, knowing that the hangman was poor and the father of a family, he whispered softly that he had left him all his

* Hospital for insane.

fortune. The executioner, startled by this last phrase, was obliged to strike three times before his benefactor's head fell. . . .

Three months later, a friend of Constant Guinard having returned from a distant voyage, learned of the sad end of that honest man, whose merits he alone knew. In order to repair as much as he could the injustice of Destiny, he ordered a beautiful monument of marble and wrote the epitaph for his friend. Fate willed it that his friend should die the next day of a hemorrhage. The expenses, however, having been paid in advance, the tombstone was sure to be placed over the grave of the unfortunate Guinard.

The workman charged with carving the epitaph took it upon himself to correct a letter which he thought was wrongly formed in the manuscript. And the poor man of good deeds, misunderstood during his lifetime, lies for all time with the following inscription above him:

HERE LIES CONSTANT GUINARD

HOMME DE RIEN
(A no-account man)

The engraver had corrected the original epitaph from HOMME DE BIEN (Man of good deeds) to HOMME DE RIEN (A no-account man).

* * *

GUY DE MAUPASSANT
(1850-1893)

DE MAUPASSANT, born at the Château de Miromesnil, became, under the tutelage of Flaubert, a master of the short story. Although he wrote a number of novels, it is his shorter fiction that ranks him as one of the best French writers of the nineteenth century. He had that rare quality of being able to tell a story without seeming to direct his characters or events. *The Dowry* is an excellent example of his style,—simple, strong, direct, and an economy of detail.

The present version, translated by Lafcadio Hearn, appeared in the New Orleans *Times-Democrat*.

THE DOWRY

NOBODY was surprised by the marriage of Maître Simon Lebrument and Mademoiselle Jeanne Cordier. Maître Lebrument had just purchased the notary-practice of Maître Papillon:—of course a good deal of money had to be paid for it; and Mademoiselle Jeanne had three hundred thousand francs ready cash,—in bank notes and money at call.

Maître Lebrument was a handsome young man, who had style,—a notarial style, a provincial style,—but anyhow style, and style was a rare thing at Boutigny-le-Rebours.

Mademoiselle Cordier had natural grace and a fresh complexion;— her grace may have been a little marred by awkwardness of manner, and her complexion was not set off to advantage by her style of dressing; but for all that she was a fine girl, well worth wooing and winning.

The wedding turned all Boutigny topsy-turvy.

The married pair, who found themselves the subject of much admiration, returned to the conjugal domicile to hide their happiness,— having resolved to make only a little trip to Paris, after first passing a few days together at home. . . .

At the end of four days, Madame Lebrument simply worshipped her husband. She could not exist a single moment without him; she had to have him all day near her to pet him, to kiss him, to play with his hands, his beard, his nose, etc. Sitting on his lap, she would take him by both ears and say: "Open your mouth and shut your eyes!" Then he would open his lips with confidence, half close his eyes, and receive a very tender and very long kiss, that would make a sort of electrical shiver run down his back. And he, for his part, did not have caresses enough, lips enough, hands enough—did not have enough of himself, in short, to adore his wife with from morning till evening and from evening until morning.

*   *   *   *   *   *   *   *

After the first week passed, he said to his young companion:

"If you like, we'll start for Paris next Tuesday. We'll do like lovers before they get married:—we'll go to the restaurants, the theatres, the concert halls, everywhere, everywhere."

She jumped for joy.

"Oh! yes,—oh! yes; let us go just as soon as possible!"

He continued:

"And then, as we must not forget anything, tell your father in advance to have your dowry all ready;—I will take it with us, and while I have the chance to see Maître Papillon, I might as well pay him."

"I'll tell him first thing to-morrow morning."

And then he seized her in his arms to recommence that little petting game which she had learned to love so much during the previous eight days.

The following Tuesday the father-in-law and mother-in-law went to the railroad depot with their daughter and their son-in-law, who were off for Paris.

The step-father said:

"I swear to you it is not prudent to carry so much money in your pocketbook."

The young notary smiled:

"Don't worry yourself at all, *beau-papa;*—I'm used to these things. You must understand that in this profession of mine it sometimes happens that I have nearly a million on my person. As it is, we can escape going through a heap of formalities and delays. Don't worry yourself about us."

An employee shouted:

"All aboard for Paris!"

They rushed into a car where two old ladies were already installed. Lebrument whispered in his wife's ear:

"This is annoying;—I shan't be able to smoke."

She answered in an undertone:

"Yes, it annoys me too,—but not on account of your cigar."

The engine whistled, and the train started. The trip lasted a full hour, during which they said little or nothing to each other, because the two old women would not go to sleep. As soon as they found themselves in the Saint-Lazare station, Maître Lebrument said to his wife:

"If you like, darling, we'll first breakfast somewhere on the boulevard,—then we'll come back leisurely for our baggage and have it taken to the hotel."

She consented at once.

"Oh! yes—let us breakfast at the restaurant. Is it far?"

He answered:

"Yes; it's rather far; but we'll take the omnibus."

She was surprised.

"Why not take a hack?"

He scolded her smilingly:

"And that is your idea of economy, eh? A hack for five minutes' ride at the rate of six sous a minute! You could not deny yourself anything,—eh?"

"You are right," she murmured, feeling a little confused.

A big omnibus, drawn by three horses, came along at full trot. Lebrument shouted:

"Driver!—hey, driver!"

The ponderous vehicle paused. And the young notary, pushing his wife before him, said to her in a very quick tone:

"Get inside! I'm going on top to smoke a cigarette before breakfast."

She did not have time to answer. The conductor, who had already caught her by the arm in order to help her up the step, almost pitched her into the vehicle: and she fell bewildered upon a bench, looking through the rear window, with stupefaction, at the feet of her husband ascending to the top of the conveyance.

And she sat there motionless between a big fat man who stunk of tobacco, and an old woman who smelled of dog.

All the other passengers, sitting dumbly in line—(a grocery boy; a working woman;—an infantry sergeant;—a gold-spectacled gentleman, wearing a silk hat with an enormous brim, turned up at each side like a gutter-pipe;—two ladies with a great air of self-importance and a snappy manner, whose very look seemed to say, "We are here; but we do not put ourselves on any level with this crowd!"—two good Sisters;—a girl with long hair; and an undertaker)—all had the look of a lot of caricatures, a museum of grotesques, a series of ludicrous cartoons of the human faces—like those rows of absurd puppets at fairs, which people knock down with balls.

The jolts of the vehicle made all their heads sway, shook them, made the flaccid skin of their cheeks shake, and as the noise of the wheels gradually stupefied them, they seemed so many sleeping idiots.

The young wife remained there, inert:

"Why did he not come in with me?" she kept asking herself. A vague sadness oppressed her. Surely he might very well have afforded to deny himself that one cigarette!

The two good Sisters signed to the driver to stop, and got out, one after the other. The omnibus went on, and stopped again. And a cook came in, all red-faced and out of breath. She sat down, and put her market basket on her knees. A strong odour of dishwater filled the omnibus.

"Why, it is much further away than I thought," said Jeanne to herself.

The undertaker got out, and was succeeded by a coachman who smelled of stables. The long-haired girl had for successor a messenger whose feet exhaled an odour of perspiration. The notary's wife felt ill-at-ease, sick, ready to cry without knowing why.

Other persons got out; others got in. The omnibus still rolled on through interminable streets, stopping at stations, and proceeding again on its way.

"How far it is!" said Jeanne to herself. "Suppose that he forgot or went to sleep! He was very tired anyhow. . . ."

Gradually all the passengers got out. She alone remained.

The driver cried out:

"Vaugirard!"

As she did not stir, he called again:

"Vaugirard!"

She stared at him, vaguely comprehending that he must be addressing her, since there was no one else in the omnibus. For the third time the driver yelled:

"Vaugirard!"

She asked him:

"Where are we?"

He answered in a tone of irritation:

"We're at Vaugirard, *parbleu!*—that's the twentieth time I've been hollering it!"

"Is it far from the boulevard?" she asked.

"What boulevard?"

"The Boulevard des Italiens."

"We passed that ages ago!"

"Ah! . . . Please be so kind as to let my husband know."

"Your husband?—Where's he?"

"Up on top——"

"Up on top! There hasn't been anyone outside for ever so long!"

She threw up her hands in terror:

"How is that? It can't be possible! He came with me, on the omnibus. Look again, please!—he must be there!"

The driver became rude:

"Here, here! that's enough talk for you, little one. One man lost, —ten to be found. Scoot now!—the trip's over. You'll find another man in the street if you want one." Tears came to her eyes:—she persisted:

"Oh, sir, you are mistaken,—I assure you, you are mistaken. He had a great big pocketbook under his arm. . . ."

The employee began to laugh:

"A great big pocketbook. Ah! yes—he got down at La Madeleine. It's all the same,—he's dropped you pretty smartly—ha! ha! ha! . . ."

The vehicle stopped. She got out, and in spite of herself glanced up instinctively at the roof of the omnibus. It was absolutely deserted.

*   *   *   *   *   *   *   *

Then she began to cry loud, without thinking that everybody would hear and see her. She sobbed:

"What is going to become of me?"

The superintendent of the station approached, and demanded:

"What is the matter?"

The driver responded in a mischievous tone:

"It's a lady whose husband gave her the slip on the trip."

The other replied:

"Well, that has nothing to do with you—you just mind your own business!"

And he turned on his heel.

Then she began to walk straight ahead,—too much bewildered and terrified to even comprehend what had happened to her. Where was she to go? What was she to do? What on earth could have happened to him? How could he have made such a mistake?—how could he have so ill-treated her?—how could he have been so absent-minded?

She had just two francs in her pocket. Whom could she go to? All of a sudden she thought of her cousin Barral, assistant superintendent in the naval department office.

She had just enough to pay for a hack; and she had herself driven to his residence. And she met him just as he was leaving the house to go to the office. He had just such another big pocketbook under his arm as Lebrument had.

She jumped from the hack.

"Henry!" she cried.

He stopped in astonishment.

"What! Jeanne!—you here? all alone? . . . why what is the matter?—where have you come from?"

She stammered out, with her eyes full of tears:

"I lost my husband a little while ago."

"Lost him—where?"

"On an omnibus."

"On an omnibus? . . . oh!"

Then she told him all her adventure, with tears.

He listened thoughtfully. He asked:

"Well, was his head perfectly clear this morning?"

"Yes."

"Good! Did he have much money about him?"

"Yes,—he had my dowry——"

"Your dowry?—the whole of it?"

"Yes, the whole of it . . . to pay for his practice."

"Well! well; my dear cousin, your husband must at this very moment be making tracks for Belgium."

Still she did not understand. She stammered:

"You say my husband . . . is, you say? . . ."

"I say that he has swindled you out of your—your capital . . . that's all there is about it!"

She stood there panting, suffocating;—she murmured:

"Then he is . . . he is . . . he is a scoundrel!"

And completely overcome by emotion, she hid her face against her cousin's vest, sobbing.

As people were stopping to look at them, he pushed her very gently inside the house, and guided her up the stairs, with his arm about her waist. And, as his astonished housekeeper opened the door, he said: "Sophie, go to the restaurant at once, and order breakfast for two. I shall not go to the office today."

❋ ❋ ❋

PAUL MORAND
(1888-   )

MORAND is the chief representative of the impressionist school today. His cosmopolitan stories are immensely interesting studies of present times. He writes vividly in a vivacious and witty vein. *The Horse of Gengis Khan* appears in his most recent volume of short stories, *East India and Company*, which has been characterised as a mingling of bizarre oriental adventures with the most ultra-modern European spices.

The Horse of Gengis Khan is reprinted here from the volume, *East India and Company*, by kind permission of the author and its publishers, Albert and Charles Boni, copyright, 1927.

THE HORSE OF GENGIS KHAN
(*Mysterious Mongolia Leaves Its Imprint in the Life of a Parisian Traveller*)

ERIK LA BONN crossed the Great Wall of China at P'ing Fu and headed in the direction of Leng K'on Pass. Mongolia lay unfolded before him, flat as a board into which, twisting like a corkscrew, the little caravan was entering. This caravan was made up of horses, mules, two blue carts drawn by mules, carriers, teamsters and the traveller himself. Erik La Bonn was an eccentric young wanderer, as independent as his long nose proclaimed him to be, and passionately devoted to the open road. He was on his way from Peking back to Europe on horseback, for he was much less afraid of perishing from the cold than suffocating in the heat of the Trans-Siberian railroad coaches. For days he had thus been on the march, all alone, singing *Parsifal* to himself at the top of his lungs, his long legs dangling from the flanks of his Mongolian pony; and since his was not a costume such as one might expect to be worn on a trip like this, but a city-cut overcoat, tight at the waistline, long trousers, a starched, stand-up collar and a grey derby hat (which he wore on principle) he caused a great deal of astonishment among the Chinese he met, and, of course, was taken for a very high personage.

The caravan crossed rivers which proved great obstacles, being so sinuous that they had to be forded as often as fifteen times. Finally, they entered the Gobi Desert. They met Bactrian camels, whose thickening fur already heralded the approaching winter; soldiers on furlough, without pay; and who had eyes like wolves', merchants sitting in their traps, accompanied by their wives, placidly drawing puffs of smoke through their waterpipes, missionaries of the Foreign Bible Society, sharpers who displayed great dexterity in the shell game at which the Mongolians stand ready to lose their souls and their dollars. One evening, being a little bored with these sights, which were always the same, Erik La Bonn had pushed ahead of his escort to visit a hunting pavilion, halfway up a hill which had been built for the great emperor Kien Lung. He lost his way and found that he was alone in a desolate valley strewn with stones and boulders. For days, to be sure, there had not been any trees, but never until this moment had he felt the vast and naked grandeur of Asia. Even the beaten path had disappeared: It seemed that after several smaller paths had become entangled with it and spread it out in several different directions, the path had stopped of its own accord on the edge of a void—on the very brink of an underworld.

La Bonn did not know what fear was. He carried no weapons on his travels, except mustard, with which, as he used to say, he defended himself during the day against the vile taste of the native cooking, and he sprinkled it on his bed at night to keep the vermin away. He had been told that bandits only held the rich Nomad families for ransom and hardly ever molested Europeans, so that he really dreaded nothing but the tenacity of the beggars and the smell of the Mongolian women. He stopped: around him nothing but debris of porphyrous rock, shafts of abandoned coal mines, and a blinding sun which set the dry autumn air on fire. Suddenly, some twenty or thirty yards away, he noticed a striking object lying on the ground; at first he took it to be a mirror. He went up to it and found it to be the skull of a horse. There was no sign of a skeleton. This skull was so white, so highly polished by many winds and rains, so perfect in substance, so strangely shaped, with its sloping indentation of the nose, and the empty, horrible looking hollows of the eyes—so religious almost in its stripped barrenness, that it seemed to date from the very first years of the existence of this earth. Erik La Bonn alighted from his horse and took the object into his hands; it was terribly heavy. For a long time this modern Hamlet, having placed the skull on his knees, lost himself in thoughts. Were these the last remains of some caravan, which, overtaken by the fierce, salty winds, had perished there of thirst? Was this the last vestige of the moment of

some departed Mongolian prince, in a red robe, repulsive and goitrous, a
standard bearer or klan chieftain perhaps, sent to guard one of the outer
bastions of the Great Wall? Or perhaps the sole surviving witness of
some great battle fallen here, cornered by the wolves? A horse! La
Bonn thought of the days of Sung, when the horse was king, celebrated
by all the poets, immortalised by the best artists, and to be found, either in
clay effigies or in its natural state, in every tomb. The horse, without
which none of the great migrations could have taken place! This immense stony valley was only deserted now because its former inhabitants,
the Mongols, the Huns and the Turks, had been able, thanks to their
horses, to gain and conquer China, India and Europe. Gengis Khan had
been the master of the world then, but the master of Gengis Khan's was
his horse.

Softness of the skin is a sign of youth, but the polish on the skeleton
is proof of its great age. From the horse's skull, which had taken on
the lustre of ivory, the flesh had, no doubt, dropped centuries ago. La
Bonn let his imagination run riot, and, exalted by his solitude and the
nimbus of such grand relics, he lost sense of time and space and fell
asleep. He dreamed that he had found the head of Gengis Khan
horse and that he could never part with it again.

He was at last torn out of his dream by the arrival of his escort which
joined him just about as night was falling and which he found prostrated on the ground as he awakened. The sight of that skull filled
those men with a holy terror. He had his precious find lifted into the
cart, and the march was resumed. The howls of wild dogs could already
be heard; the smell of goatskins and smoke, carried over to them by the
wind, proclaimed that a village was near. And in fact, a long wall of
dried mud was outlined against the horizon, punctuated by dim lights.
They were approaching Jehol, "The Town of Complete Virtue."

He had to stop at a fourth-rate hotel—one of the kind that are called
pork-taverns in China—because it was market day and all the other
hostelries were filled. Goatskins were drying in the open air; their
smell hardly obscured the stench of manure and sewage which ran openly
down the middle of the only street. Pelts from Dzingary were being
lifted onto the backs of camels by great big devils in blue tunics; a
Chinese checker in yellow coat and hat traced characters in Chinese
ink on the reverse sides, directing the pieces to a port on the Pacific Ocean,
en route to America.

The servants prepared the bed in the guest room. La Bonn was waiting for his dinner to be cooked, which consisted of millet cakes. He
had affixed the horse's skull outside of his room; it was soon surrounded
by a crowd of curious people who contemplated it awestruck and with
fright. Women with flat and otherwise deformed feet came to have a
look at it; beggars' dogs with a scowling expression, their hair standing

on end, yellow lamas with shaven heads remained to mill about the strange fetish of the white man.

It was plain that the indifferent and skeptical Chinese had been left far behind, that one was in the midst of those superstitious and wild Mongolians, sons of a country particularly given to magic and all sorts of devilish practices. Soon the crowd became so large that the court-yard of the inn was completely filled. The pork bladders, which served as lamps, were lighted. At just about that time the clandestine opium vendors and the managers of the Jehol theatre sent a delegation to make a complaint that the resorts of pleasure were empty and to re-quest that the stranger go to his room and kindly remain there.

The next day, after having left his calling card at the governor's— leaving one's calling card is regarded in the Orient as a propitious rite and is a rigid requirement of good form—Erik La Bonn went to the temple. This was another monument of dried mud, of no definite epoch, located outside the town, in the midst of a dirt and refuse dump. There Buddha smiled. La Bonn was received by a priest who was half doctor, half sorcerer, clad in yellow silk; quite a pleasant person. In the usual roundabout fashion La Bonn put several questions to him. He had him asked if in these parts any particular faith or belief was attached to animal bones, more specially a horse's skull. The answer that he received was that every kind of skeleton was a dangerous abomination because the greedy souls of a body are always hovering about it in order to reincarnate themselves. A horse's skull had often enriched its find, but caused his male progeny to perish. Women pregnant more than five months should stand in fear of it. However, everything depended on the day on which the object had been found.

Last night . . . ?

That was one of the very worst days, said the lama. One of the most dreaded on the whole calendar. Although prayers might yet be said, be-fore nightfall, still there was little hope. There was really nothing else to do but to fly before the invisible, to fool the demons, or to burn the skull. La Bonn shrugged his shoulders at all this nonsense and gave orders to have his find attached to his saddle. And from then on the horse's skull never left that place.

Thus he travelled through central Asia. An invisible protection seemed to emanate from the skull: Bandits never came near the caravan; nowhere was hospitality refused. La Bonn was allowed to wash in the sacred hot springs, and when he reached the country of the great pastures he always had his share of fresh meat and almost every night he found a wooden bed under those strange tents of the nomadic Mongolians, quar-ters made of such thick felt that they were as hot inside as one of those Norwegian cookers in which food can be boiled without fire. When he met lamas, bent on pilgrimages to Thibet, they honoured him by offering him tea. Every evening La Bonn hung the skull outside of his tent on a pole driven into the ground.

The reception was not only cordial in Mongolia, but was equally friendly in Turkestan, in Kokand and Bokkara. The religions, the customs and the colour of the skins changed, but the horse's skull continued to receive the respect of everyone. The population become gradually Moslem, welcomed La Bonn as no European had been received since the arrival of the Bolsheviks. Even the customs inspectors let him pass duty-free.

One evening La Bonn arrived at the *Gare de l'Est* in Paris with the skull of Gengis Khan's horse under his arm. Sentimental effusions, accompanied by verbose lyricism, gushed from him whenever he talked about it. However, he spoke of it seldom, for those people who were slaves of petty habits, jostled about in narrow streets, boxed up in ugly, tall houses, have not the least understanding for the beauties of the steppes and the life of the nomad. La Bonn could not find an apartment and so had to content himself with a small hotel room in the *Quartier Latin*. In it there was a Louis Philippe bed—much too large—and a mirrored cabinet, so that he could hardly open his wardrobe trunks. First he put the skull under the dressing table, then on the mantelpiece. This relic, as majestic and provoking as it had been when he found it back there in the Gobi Desert, had become nothing more than a piece of refuse from a butcher shop, in Paris, a skeleton for a rag-picker; the dust had made a shabby object of it, turned it a grey colour. But La Bonn did not have the nerve to get rid of it, nor even confess that its possession embarrassed him considerably.

An Englishwoman, Lady Cynthia D., heard about the horse of Gengis Khan and became exceedingly interested in the subject. As a matter of fact, she was only interested in the young Frenchman, but she begged La Bonn to entrust to her that which remained of the Mongolian courser; she said that she would hang the skull over her bed. Through the eyes of the skull she put blue ribbons which came out by the nostrils, thus robbing the dramatic relic of its last mystery. La Bonn had to restrain her from gilding it. Two days after she had hung the horse's head over her bed, Lady Cynthia was lying down when a great noise was heard in her room. People entered and found her bathed in her blood. The cursed thing had detached itself from the wall and had split the head of the young Englishwoman in two. She only recovered after a great amount of suffering. She did not want to hear any more of the horse's head nor of its owner, and after this accident the horse of Gengis Khan went back to *Quartier Latin*. La Bonn kept it for some time, but on the eve of a journey entrusted it to a retired deep-sea captain, who was an invalid. This simple man—although grown more imaginative since he had been compelled to lead a sedentary life—had waxed enthusiastic over La Bonn's tale and had asked for the privilege of keeping the skull during the absence of his friend. The much-travelled La Bonn then began to receive strange letters from the captain which became disquieting, and finally totally demented. He was just preparing to return when he learned that the old mariner had been found one morning suspended from the window fastening. On the table, in plain view, was the horse's head. La Bonn hoped that the captain's heirs would inherit it and took pains not to give a sign of life. But on the very next day after his return, he received a call from a notary who informed him that he had been made the captain's sole heir, and that the skull would be returned to him so soon as the seals had been broken. Then these things happened: A little later La Bonn gave it to a painter for a still life, but the latter's studio burned down. He gave it to a raffle, but the number that should have won it was never presented. People began to know the history of the skull. The servants did not dare enter the room any more on account of the "haunted head," as they called it. It seemed indeed that all the mishaps which the heavens had spared La Bonn and which, without dropping, had remained suspended over his head, and the strange immunity which he enjoyed, were suddenly interrupted as soon as the skull left his hands. He did not dare destroy it for fear of some curse befalling him. He could no longer risk giving it away for fear of participating in a crime.

"Alas! You, the last remains of the companion of the greatest conqueror the world has ever known," thought La Bonn, "perhaps there is nothing you fear more than rest. Perhaps you are anxious to escape from among these sedentary lives where I have put you, to regain your freedom? And is that the reason why you perpetrate all these crimes? Perhaps what you like in me is a taste similar to your own, for a life which is a continuous journey, a passion for moving on to always new countries, and climates which are never the same?"

It was night, and La Bonn, thus soliloquising, looked from his bed at the horse's skull which the light of the moon was illuminating with a soft silver glow which had nothing earthly in it and seemed to resemble the colour of infinite space.

La Bonn knew the moment had come. It would be now or never. He put an overcoat on over his pajamas, took the skull on his shoulders and went down to the street; it weighed a great deal. Soon it was necessary to carry it in both hands. Finally La Bonn reached the bridge *de l'Alma.* A cold wind was blowing, which reminded him of the great winds of the steppes, the Seine curved gently as it flowed past the *Trocadero,* the two towers of which were outlined against the sky, darker than the night. After ceasing to be royal a little further up, as it passed in front of the Louvre, the Seine now abandoned itself to romantic gracefulness as it flowed on to Passy. Erik La Bonn placed the skull on the railing of the bridge. He was thinking of the great Siberian streams, of the torrents of the Chinese river *Altai,* of the Mongolian tributaries swallowed up by the salty and thirsty sand. . . . How small the Seine was, how shallow for such an adventure—such an end! But is there ever an end to anything?

The electric lights lit up the river and gave it a rose colour, like those face lotions they sell in beauty parlours. . . . La Bonn thrust the skull out into the black void. . . . There was a silence. Then a splash. Evidently its great weight will make it sink straight to the bottom. . . . But no. . . . A miracle! The skull floated! Yes, that heavy object actually floated, carried along by the current like a piece of paper. La Bonn saw distinctly how it took the middle of the stream, then gently sheered off to the left, following the bend of the river.

Gengis Khan's horse, that gem of the Mongolian steppes, had started out again. Where would it go? Perhaps it would be stopped to-morrow by some obstacle, by a fisherman, by the hands of a child? Or perhaps, free to gain the open sea, it would become a strange sea-horse. Would it ride about the dungeons of the sea,—with the taste of salt,—the same taste as that of the great Mongolian desert, which still clings to the memory that it was once a sea?

SPAIN

Introduction

LIKE most of the early literatures, that of Spain has its beginnings in minstrelsy; and the first great epic that has survived through the ages is the *Chronicle of the Cid*, dating from the middle of the twelfth century. This is a series of episodes relating the adventures of Rodrigo Diaz de Bivar (d. 1099), the national hero, surnamed the Cid by the Arabs.

In the latter part of the thirteenth century prose tales began to be cultivated, and we find Juan Manuel, the nephew of Alphonso X., among the chief writers of mediæval Castilian prose. His best known work is the collection of stories entitled *El Conde Lucanor* and sometimes named the *Book of Examples*. Each story points a moral and ends "when Don Johan heard this example he found it good, ordered it to be set down in this book, and added these verses."

With the appearance of *Lazarillo de Tormes*, a new form of literature is introduced, namely, the picaroon novel, dealing with rogues and scoundrels in a very amusing manner. The novel consists of a number of incidents held together by virtue of a central character. Other examples of this species, and equally interesting are Quevedo's *Paul the Sharper*, and Aleman's *Guzman de Alfarache*.

The most celebrated Spanish writer, Cervantes, lived at the period when Spain had achieved the peak of her power and glory, her golden age. His *Don Quixote* is one of the most humorous, satirical and, at times, poignantly wistful books in all of literature. It simultaneously bridges and dominates mediæval and modern Spanish literature. Cervantes, among other things, also wrote twelve stories known as the *Examplary Novels*, which alone would have sufficed to establish his reputation.

The defeat of the Armada brought in its wake a complete decline of Spanish literature, and throughout the seventeenth and eighteenth centuries it loses its vigour, colour and originality. In the first part of the last century French influence is evident, although, curiously enough, Spanish writers escape almost entirely the romantic movement that sweeps all of Europe.

The renaissance of Spanish fiction is ushered in by Fernan Caballero, a serious realist, and Alarcon, an able story-teller. Pereda is remarkable at describing the life of peasants and fishermen, while Valera is much more of a cosmopolitan and his stories treat of city life. A woman of no mean artistic ability is Emilia Pardo-Bazan who has achieved great popularity with her graphic descriptions of nature and sympathetic treatment of characters.

Of the more recent writers Baroja has given us some remarkable short stories. A more popular writer than any of the other moderns, although not taken seriously in Spain, is Blasco Ibañez.

❊ ❊ ❊

JUAN MANUEL
(1282-1349)

JUAN MANUEL, born at Escalona, led a very active life. In his fourteenth year he served against the Moors at Granada, and later acted as guardian of the king, Alphonso XI. During his stormy political and military career, he found time to turn to the field of letters, and consequently established for himself a most eminent position as a writer of Castilian prose. His masterpiece, *Count Lucanor*, consists of a series of moral tales, spiced with irony and occasional sarcasm, all very skilfully told. *The Man Who Tamed a Shrew*, one of these delightful stories, contains, according to Fitzmaurice-Kelly, the germ of Shakespeare's *Taming of the Shrew*.

The present version is reprinted from Thomas Roscoe's *Spanish Novelists*, London, no date. The title in the original is *Concerning What Happened to a Certain Young Man Upon the Day of His Marriage*.

THE MAN WHO TAMED A SHREW
(From *Count Lucanor*, XLV)

ONE day the Conde Lucanor, speaking with his counsellor Patronio, said, "Patronio, I have a servant who informs me that he has it in his power to marry a very wealthy woman, but who is higher in station than himself. It would, he says, be a very advantageous match for him, only for one difficulty which stands in the way, and it is this. He has it on good authority, that this woman is one of the most violent and wilful creatures in the world; and now I ask for your counsel, whether I ought to direct him to marry this woman, knowing what her character is, or advise him to give up the match?" "My Lord Conde Lucanor," said Patronio, "if your man hath any resemblance to the son of a certain good man, who was a Moor, I advise him to marry at all venture, but if he be not like him, I think he had better desist." And the Conde then enquired how that affair had been?

THE HISTORY

Patronio said, that "in a certain town there lived a noble Moor, who had one son, the best young man ever known perhaps in the world. He was not, however, wealthy enough to enable him to accomplish half the many laudable objects which his heart prompted him to undertake, and for this reason he was in great perplexity, having the will and not the power to perform it.

"Now in that same town there dwelt another Moor, far more honoured and rich than the youth's father; and he, too, had an only daughter, who offered a strange contrast to this excellent young man; her manners being as violent and bad as his were good and pleasing, insomuch that no man liked to think of an union with such an infuriate shrew.

"Now that good youth one day came to his father and said 'Father, I am well assured that you are not rich enough to support me according to what I conceive becoming and honourable. It will, therefore, be incumbent upon me to lead a mean and indolent life, or to quit the country; so that if it seem good unto you, I should prefer for the best to form some marriage alliance by which I may be enabled to open myself a way to higher things.' And the father replied, that it would please him well if his son should be enabled to marry according to his wishes. He then said to his father, that if he thought he should be able to manage it, he should be happy to have the only daughter of the good man given him in marriage. Hearing this, the father was much surprised, and answered, that as he understood the matter, there was not a single man whom he knew, how poor soever he might be, who would consent to marry such a vixen. And his son replied, that he asked it as a particular favour that he would bring about this marriage; and so far insisted, that, however strange he thought the request, his father gave his consent.

"In consequence of this, he went directly to seek the good man, with whom he was on the most friendly terms, and having acquainted him with all that had passed, begged that he would be pleased to bestow his daughter's hand upon his son, who had courage enough to marry her. Now, when the good man heard this proposal from the lips of his best friend, he said to him:—'Good God, my friend, if I were to do any such thing, I should serve you a very bad turn; for you possess an excellent son, and it would be a great piece of treachery on my part, if I were to consent to make him so unfortunate, and become accessory to his death by marrying such a woman. Nay, I may say worse than death, for better would it be for him to be dead than to be married to my daughter! and you must not think that I say thus much to oppose your wishes; for as to that matter, I should be well pleased to give her to your son, or to anybody's son, who would be foolish enough to rid my house of her.' To this his friend replied, that he felt very sensibly the kind motives which led to speak thus; and yet entreated that, as his son seemed so bent upon the match, he would be pleased to give the lady in marriage. He agreed, and accordingly the ceremony took place. The bride was brought to her husband's house, and it being a custom with the Moors to give the betrothed a supper, and to set out the feast for them, and then to take leave and return to visit them on the ensuing day, the ceremony was performed accordingly. However, the fathers and mothers, and all the relations of the bride and bridegroom, went away with many misgivings, fearing that when they returned the ensuing day, they should either find the young man dead or in some very bad plight indeed. So it came to pass, that as soon as the young people were left alone, they seated themselves at the table, and before the dreaded bride had time to open her lips, the bridegroom, looking behind him, saw stationed there his favourite Mastiff dog, and he said to him somewhat sharply:—'Mr. Mastiff, bring us some water for our hands, and the dog stood still, and did not do it. His master then repeated the order more fiercely, but the dog stood still as before. His master then leaped up in a great passion from the table, and, seizing his sword, ran towards the mastiff, who, seeing him coming, ran away, leaping over the chairs and tables, and fire-place, trying every place to make his escape, with the bridegroom hard in pursuit of him. At length, reaching the dog, he smote off his head with his sword; he then hewed off his legs, and cut up all his body, until the whole place was covered with blood. He then resumed his place at table, all covered as he was with gore; and soon casting his eyes around, he beheld a lap-dog, and commanded him to bring him water for his hands, and because he was not obeyed, he said: 'How, false traitor! see you not the fate of the mastiff, because he would not do as I commanded him? I vow that if you offer to contend one moment with me, I will treat thee to the same fate as I did the mastiff. And when he found it was not done, he arose, seized him by the legs, and dashing him against the wall, actually beat his brains out; showing even more rage than against the poor mastiff.

"Then, in a great passion, he returned to the table, and cast his eyes about on all sides, while his bride, fearful that he had taken leave of his senses, ventured not to utter a word. At length he fixed his eyes upon his horse, that was standing before the door, though he had only that one belonging to him; and he commanded him to bring him water, which the horse did not do. 'How now, Mr. Horse,' cried the husband, 'do you imagine because I have only you, that I shall suffer you to live, and not do as I command you? No! I will inflict as hard a death upon you as upon the others; yea, there is no living thing I have in the world which I will spare, if I am not to be obeyed!' But the horse stood where he was, and the master, approaching with the greatest rage, smote off his head, and cut him in pieces, in the same way, with his sword. Well! And when his wife saw that he had actually killed his horse, having no other, and now heard him declare that he would do the same to any creature that ventured to disobey him, she found that he had by no means done it by way of jest, and took such an alarm, that she hardly knew whether she were dead or alive. Then, all covered with gore as he was, he again seated himself at table, swearing that though he had a thousand horses, or wives, or servants, if they refused to do his behest he would not scruple to kill them all; and he once more began to look around him, with his sword in his hand. And after he had looked well round him, and found no other living thing near him, he turned his eyes fiercely upon his wife, and said in a great passion, 'Get up, and bring me some water to wash my hands'; and his wife, expecting nothing less than to be cut to pieces, rose in a great hurry, and giving him water for his hands, said to him,— 'Ah, how I ought to return thanks to God, who inspired you with the thought of doing as you have just done! for, otherwise, owing to the wrong treatment of my foolish friends, I should have behaved in the same way to you as I did to them.'

"After this he commanded her to help him to something to eat, and this in such a tone, that she felt as if her head were on the point of dropping off upon the floor; so that there was a perfect understanding settled between them during that night; and she never spoke, but only did everything which he required her to do. After they had reposed some time, the husband said,—'The passion I have been put into this night has hindered me from sleeping: get you up, and see that nobody comes to disturb me, and prepare me something well cooked to eat!'

"When it came full day, and the fathers, mothers, and other relatives arrived at the door, they all listened; and hearing no one speak, at first concluded that the unfortunate man was either dead or mortally wounded by his ferocious bride. In this they were the more confirmed, when they saw her standing at the door and the bridegroom not there. But when the lady saw them advancing, she stepped gently on tip-toe towards them, and whispered, 'False friends, as you are, how dared you to come up to the door in that way, or even to breathe a word? Be silent, as you value your lives or mine;—hist, and awake him not.'

"Now when they were all made acquainted with what she said, they greatly marvelled at it; but when they learnt all that had passed during the night, their wonder was changed into admiration of the young man, for having so well known how to manage what concerned him, and to maintain order in his house. From that day forth, so excellently was his wife governed, and so well conditioned in every respect, that they led a very pleasant sort of life together. Such indeed was the good example set by the son-in-law, that a few days afterwards, the father-in-law, desirous of the same happy change in *his* household, also killed a horse; but his wife only observed to him, 'By my faith, Don Foolano, you have thought of this plan somewhat too late in the day; we are now too well acquainted with each other.'

"And you, my Lord Conde Lucanor, if that servant of yours wish to marry such a woman, and hath as great a heart as this youth, in God's name, advise him to take her, for he will surely know how to manage in his house. But should he be of another kidney, and not so well know what is most befitting, then let him forego it, or run a bad chance. And I do further advise you, with whatever manner of men you have to do, you always give them well to understand on what footing they are to stand with you." And the Conde held this for a good example; made it as it is, and it was esteemed good. Also, because Don Juan found it a good example, he ordered it to be written in this book, and made these verses, which follow it:—

> If at first you don't shew yourself just what you are,
> When you afterwards wish it, your fortune 'twill mar.

❋ ❋ ❋

DIEGO HURTADO DE MENDOZA
(1503-1575)

MENDOZA, born of a noble family at Granada, played an important part in the politics and literature of Spain. He served under Charles V. in the Italian wars, at the same time devoting himself to classical studies at the universities of Bologna, Padua and Rome. Although his authorship of *Lazarillo de Tormes* is questioned by a number of critics, Fitzmaurice-Kelly seems to believe there is something to be said in favor of Mendoza's claim. If so, he produced the first picaresque novel and the best of its many rivals. It is packed with a sharp wit and a cynicism that betrays a seasoned observer of life in the raw.

The present version is reprinted from Roscoe's *Spanish Novelists*, London, no date. The title of the chapter is *How Lazaro Entered into the Service of a Priest, and What Ensued.*

HOW LAZARO SERVED A PRIEST
(From *Lazarillo de Tormes*)

THE next day, not considering myself quite safe where I was, I went to a place called Maqueda, where, as it were in punishment of my evil deeds, I fell in with a certain priest. I accosted him for alms, when he enquired whether I knew how to assist at mass. I answered that I did, which was true, for the old man, notwithstanding his ill treatment, taught me many useful things,—and this was one of them. The priest therefore engaged me on the spot.

There is an old proverb which speaks of getting out of the frying pan into the fire, which was indeed my unhappy case in this change of masters. The old blind man, selfish as he was, seemed an Alexander the Great, in point of magnificence, on comparison with this priest, who was, without exception, the most niggardly of all miserable devils I have ever met with. It seemed as though the meanness of the whole world was gathered together in his wretched person. It would be hard to say whether he inherited his disposition, or whether he had adopted it with his cassock and gown. He had a large old chest, well secured by a lock, the key of which he always carried about him, tied to a part of his clothing. When the charity bread came from the church, he would with his own hands deposit it in the chest, and then carefully turn the key.

Throughout the whole house there was nothing to eat. Even the sight of such things as we see in other houses, such as smoked bacon, cheese, or bread, would have done my heart good, although I might have been forbidden to taste them. The only eatable we had was a string of onions, and these were locked up in a garret. Every fourth day I was allowed *one*; and when I asked for the key to take it, if anyone chanced to be present, he would make a serious matter of it, saying, as he gave me the key, "Take it, and return quickly; for when you go to that tempting room, you never know when to come out of it;"—speaking as though all the sweets of Valencia were there, when I declare to you, as I said before, the devil a bit of anything was there but this string of onions hung on a nail, and of these he kept such an account, that if my unlucky stars had tempted me to take more than my allowance, it would have cost me very dear.

In the end, I should in fact have died of hunger, with so little feeling did this reverend gentleman treat me, although with himself he was rather more liberal. Five farthings' worth of meat was his allowance for dinner and supper. It is true that he divided the broth with me; but my share of the meat I might have put in my eye instead of my mouth, and have been none the worse for it: but sometimes, by good luck, I got a little morsel of bread. In this part of the country it is the custom on

Sundays to eat sheeps' heads, and he sent me for one that was not to come to more than three farthings. When it was cooked, he ate all the tit-bits, and never left it while a morsel of the meat remained; but the dry bones he turned over to me saying,—"There, you rogue, eat that; you are in rare luck; the Pope himself has not such fare as you." "God give him as good!" said I to myself.

At the end of the three weeks that I remained with him, I arrived at such an extreme degree of exhaustion, from sheer hunger, that it was with difficulty I stood on my legs. I saw clearly that I was in the direct road to the grave, unless God and my own wit should help me out of it. For the dexterous application of my fingers there was no opportunity afforded me, seeing there was nothing to practise on; and if there were, I should never have been able to have cheated the priest as I did the old man, whom God absolve, if by my means it went ill with him after his leap. The old man, though cunning, yet wanting sight, gave me now and then a chance; but as to the priest, never had anyone so keen a sight as he.

When we were at mass, no money came to the plate at the offering that he did not observe: he had one eye on the people and the other on my fingers. His eyes danced about the money-box as though they were quicksilver. When offerings were given, he kept an account, and when it was finished, that instant he would take the plate from my hands, and put it on the altar. I was not able to rob him of a single maravede in all the time I lived with him, or rather all the time I starved with him. I never fetched him any wine from the tavern, but the little that was left at church he locked up in his chest, and he would make that serve all the week. In order to excuse all this covetousness, he said to me, "You see, my boy, that priests ought to be very abstemious in their food. For my part, I think it a great scandal to indulge in viands and wine as many do." But the curmudgeon lied most grossly, for at convents or at funerals, when we went to pray, he would eat like a wolf, and drink like a mountebank; and now I speak of funerals—God forgive me, I was never an enemy to the human race but at that unhappy period of my life, and the reason was solely, that on those occasions I obtained a meal of victuals.

Every day I did hope, and even pray, that God would be pleased to take his own. Whenever we were sent for to administer the sacrament to the sick, the priest would of course desire all present to join in prayer. You may be certain I was not the last in these devout exercises, and I prayed with all my heart that the Lord would compassionate the afflicted, not by restoring him to the vanities of life, but by relieving him from the sins of this world; and when any of these unfortunates recovered—the Lord forgive me—in the anguish of my heart I wished him a thousand times in perdition; but if he died, no one was more sincere in his blessings than myself.

During all the time I was in this service, which was nearly six months, only twenty persons paid the debt of nature, and these I verily believe that I killed, or rather that they died, by the incessant importunity of my particular prayers. Such was my extreme suffering, as to make me think that the Lord, compassionating my unhappy and languishing condition, visited some with death to give me life. But for my present necessity there was no remedy; if on the days of funerals I lived well, the return to my old allowance of an onion every fourth day seemed doubly hard; so that I may truly say, I took delight in nothing but death, and oftentimes I have invoked it for myself as well as for others. To me, however, it did not arrive, although continually hovering about me in the ugly shape of famine and short commons. I thought many times of leaving my brute of a master, but two reflections disconcerted me; the first was, the doubt whether I could make my way by reason of the extreme weakness to which hunger had reduced me; and the second suggested, that my first master, having done his best to starve me, and my next having succeeded so far in the same humane object as to bring me to the brink of the grave, whether the third might not, by pursuing the same course, actually thrust me into it.

These considerations made me now pause, lest, by venturing a step further, it would be my certain fate to be a point lower in fortune, and then the world might truly say, "Farewell, Lazaro."

It was during this trying and afflicting time, when, seeing things going from bad to worse, without anyone to advise with, I was praying with all Christian humility, that I might be released from such misery, that one day, when my wretched, miserable, covetous thief of a master had gone out, an angel, in the likeness of a tinker, knocked at the door—for I verily believe he was directed by Providence to assume that habit and employment—and enquired whether I had anything to mend? Suddenly a light flashed upon me, as though imparted by an invisible and unknown power. —"Uncle," said I, "I have unfortunately lost the key of this great chest, and I'm sadly afraid my master will beat me; for God's sake, try if you can fit it, and I will reward you." The angelic tinker drew forth a large bunch of keys, and began to try them, while I assisted his endeavours with my feeble prayers; when lo, and behold! when least I thought it, the lid of the chest arose, and I almost fancied I beheld the divine essence therein in the shape of loaves of bread. "I have no money," said I to my preserver, "but give me the key and help yourself." He took some of the whitest and best bread he could find, and went away well pleased, though not half so well as myself. I refrained from taking any for the present, lest the deficiency might be noticed; and contented myself with the hope, that, on seeing so much in my power, hunger would hardly dare to approach me.

My wretched master returned, and it pleased God that the offering my angel had been pleased to accept, remained undiscovered by him. The next day, when he went out, I went to my farinaceous paradise, and taking a loaf between my hands and teeth, in a twinkling it became invisible; then, not forgetting to lock the treasure, I capered about the house for joy to think that my miserable life was about to change, and for some days following, I was as happy as a king. But it was not predestined for me that such good luck should continue long; on the third day symptoms of my old complaint began to shew themselves, for I beheld my murderer in the act of examining our chest, turning and counting the loaves over and over again. Of course I dissimulated my terror, but it was not for want of my prayers and invocations that he was not struck stone-blind like my old master,—but he retained his eyesight.

After he had been some time considering and counting, he said, "If I were not well assured of the security of this chest, I should say that somebody had stolen my bread; but, however, to remove all suspicion, from this day I shall count the loaves; there remain now exactly nine and a piece."

"May nine curses light upon you, you miserable beggar," said I to myself—for his words went like an arrow to my heart, and hunger already began to attack me, seeing a return to my former scanty fare now inevitable.

No sooner did the priest go out, than I opened the chest to console myself even with the sight of food, and as I gazed on the nice white loaves, a sort of adoration arose within me, which the sight of such tempting morsels could alone inspire. I counted them carefully to see, if, perchance, the curmudgeon had mistaken the number; but, alas! I found he was a much better reckoner than I could have desired. The utmost I dared do, was to bestow on these objects of my affection a thousand kisses, and, in the most delicate manner possible, to nibble here and there a morsel of the crust. With this I passed the day, and was not quite so jovial as on the former, you may suppose.

But as hunger increased, and more so in proportion as I had fared better the few days previously, I was reduced to the last extremity. Yet, all I could do was to open and shut the chest, and contemplate the divine image within. Providence, however, who does not neglect mortals in such an extreme crisis, suggested to me a slight palliation of my present distress. After some consideration, I said within myself, "This chest is very large and old, and in some parts, though very slightly, is broken. It is not impossible to suppose that rats may have made an entrance, and gnawed the bread. To take a whole loaf would not be wise, seeing that it would be missed by my most liberal master; but the other plan he shall certainly have the benefit of." Then I began to pick the loaves, on some table cloths which were there, not of the most costly sort, taking one loaf and leaving another, so that in the end, I made up a tolerable supply of crumbs, which I ate like so many sugar plums; and with that I in some measure consoled myself and contrived to live.

The priest, when he came home to dinner and opened the chest, beheld with dismay the havoc made in his store; but he immediately supposed it to have been occasioned by rats, so well had I imitated the style of those depredators. He examined the chest narrowly, and discovered the little holes through which the rats might have entered; and calling me, he said, "Lazaro, look what havoc has been made in our bread during the night." I seemed very much astonished, and asked, "what it could possibly be?" "What has done it?" quoth he, "why, rats; confound 'em, there is no keeping anything from them." I fared well at dinner, and had no reason to repent of the trick I played, for he pared off all the places which he supposed the rats had nibbled at, and, giving them to me, he said, "There, eat that, rats are very clean animals." In this manner, adding what I thus gained to that acquired by the labour of my hands, or rather my nails, I managed tolerably well, though I little expected it. I was destined to receive another shock, when I beheld my miserable tormentor carefully stopping up all the holes in the chest with small pieces of wood, which he nailed over them, and which bade defiance to further depredations. "Oh, Lord!" I cried involuntarily, "to what distress and misfortunes are we unhappy mortals reduced; and how short-lived are the pleasures of this our transitory existence. No sooner did I draw some little relief from the measure which kind fortune suggested, than it is snatched away; and this last act is like closing the door of consolation against me, and opening that of my misfortunes."

It was thus I gave vent to my distress, while the careful workman, with abundance of wood and nails, was finishing his cruel job, saying with great glee, "Now, you rascals of rats, we will change sides, if you please, for your future reception in this house will be right little welcome."

The moment he left the house, I went to examine his work, and found he had not left a single hole unstopped by which even a musquito could enter. I opened the chest, though without deriving the smallest benefit from its contents; my key was now utterly useless; but as I gazed with longing eyes on the two or three loaves which my master believed to be bitten by the rats, I could not resist the temptation of nibbling a morsel more, though touching them in the lightest possible manner, like an experienced swordsman in a friendly assault.

Necessity is a great master, and being in this strait, I passed night and day in devising means to get out of it. All the rascally plans that could enter the mind of man, did hunger suggest to me; for it is a saying, and a true one, as I can testify, that hunger makes rogues, and abundance fools. One night, when my master slept, of which disposition he always gave sonorous testimony, as I was revolving in my mind the best mode of renewing my intimacy with the contents of the chest, a thought struck me, which I forthwith put in execution. I arose very quietly, and taking an old knife, which, having some little glimmering of the same idea the day previous, I had left for an occasion of this nature, I repaired to the chest, and at the part which I considered least guarded, I began to bore a hole. The antiquity of the chest seconded my endeavours, for the wood had become rotten from age, and easily yielded to the knife, so that in a short time I managed to display a hole of very respectable dimensions. I then opened the chest very gently, and taking out the bread, I treated it much in the same manner as heretofore, and then returned safe to my mattress.

The next day my worthy master soon spied my handiwork, as well as the deficiency in his bread—and began by wishing the rats at the devil. "What can it mean?" said he; "during all the time I have been here, there have never been rats in the house before." And he might say so with truth; if ever a house in the kingdom deserved to be free from rats, it was his, as they are seldom known to visit where there is nothing to eat. He began again with nails and wood; but when night came, and he slept, I resumed my operations, and rendered nugatory all his ingenuity.

In this manner we went on; the moment he shut one door, I opened another: like the web of Penelope, what he spun by day, I unravelled by night; and in the course of a few nights the old chest was so maltreated, that little remained of the original that was not covered with pieces and nailing. When the unhappy priest found his mechanical ability of no avail, he said, "Really, this chest is in such a state, and the wood is so old and rotten, that the rats make nothing of it. The best plan I can think of, since what we have done is of no use, is to arm ourselves within, against these cursed rats." He then borrowed a rat-trap, and baiting it with bits of cheese which he begged from the neighbours, set it under the chest. This was a piece of singular good fortune for me, for although my hunger needed no sauce, yet I did not nibble the bread at night with less relish, because I added thereto the bait from the rat-trap. When in the morning he found not only the bread gone as usual, but the bait likewise vanished, and the trap without a tenant, he grew almost beside himself. He ran to the neighbours, and asked of them what animal it could possibly be that could positively eat the very cheese out of the trap, and yet escape untouched. The neighbours agreed that it could be no rat that could thus eat the bait, and not remain within the trap, and one more cunning than the rest observed,—"I remember once seeing a snake about your premises, and depend on it that is the animal which has done you this mischief, for it could easily pick the bait from the trap without entering entirely, and thus too it might easily escape." The rest all agreed that such must be the fact, which alarmed my master a good deal.

He now slept not near so soundly as before, and at every little noise, thinking it was the snake biting the chest, he would get up, and taking a cudgel which he kept at his bed's head for the purpose, began to belabour the poor chest with all his might, so that the noise might frighten the reptile from his unthrifty proceedings. He even awoke the neighbours with such prodigious clamour, and I could not get a single minute's rest. He turned me out of bed, and looked amongst the straw, and about the blanket, to see if the creature was concealed anywhere; for, as he observed, at night they seek warm places, and not infrequently injure people by biting them in bed. When he came, I always pretended to be very heavy with sleep, and he would say to me in the morning, "Did you hear nothing last night, boy? The snake was about, and I think I heard him at your bed, for they are very cold creatures, and love warmth." "I hope to God he will not bite me," returned I, "for I am very much afraid." He was so watchful at night, that, by my faith, the snake could not continue his operations as usual, but in the morning, when the priest was at church, he resumed them pretty steadily as usual.

Looking with dismay at the damage done to his store, and the little redress he was likely to have for it, the poor priest became quite uneasy from fretting, and wandered about all night like a hobgoblin. I began very much to fear that, during one of these fits of watchfulness, he might discover my key, which I placed for security under the straw of my bed. I therefore, with a caution peculiar to my nature, determined in future to keep this treasure by night safe in my mouth; and this was an ancient custom of mine, for during the time I lived with the blind man, my mouth was my purse, in which I could retain ten or twelve maravedies in farthings, without the slightest inconvenience in any way. Indeed, had I not possessed this faculty, I should never have had a single farthing of my own, for I had neither pocket nor bag that the old man did not continually search. Every night I slept with the key in my mouth without fear of discovery; but, alas! when misfortune is our lot, ingenuity can be of little avail.

It was decreed, by my evil destiny, or rather, I ought to say, as a punishment for my evil doings, that one night, when I was fast asleep, my mouth being somewhat open, the key became placed in such a position therein, that my breath came in contact with the hollow of the key, and caused—the worst luck for me!—a loud whistling noise. On this my watchful master pricked up his ears, and thought it must be the hissing of the snake which had done him all the damage, and certainly he was not altogether wrong in his conjectures. He arose very quietly, with his club in his hand, and stealing towards the place whence the hissing sound proceeded, thinking at once to put an end to his enemy, he lifted his club, and with all his force discharged such a blow on my unfortunate head, that it needed not another to deprive me of all sense and motion. The moment the blow was delivered, he felt it was no snake that had received it; and guessing what he had done, called out to me in a loud voice, endeavouring to recall me to my senses. Then touching me with his hands, he felt the blood, which was by this time in great profusion about my face, and ran quickly to procure a light. On his return, he found me moaning, yet still holding the key in my mouth, and partly visible, being in the same situation which caused the whistling noise he had mistaken for the snake. Without thinking much of me, the attention of the slayer of snakes was attracted by the appearance of the key, and drawing it from my mouth, he soon discovered what it was, for of course the wards were precisely similar to his own. He ran to prove it, and with that, at once, found out the extent of my ingenuity.

"Thank God," exclaimed this cruel snake hunter, "that the rat and the snakes which have so long made war upon me, and devoured my substance, are both at last discovered."

Of what passed for three days afterwards, I can give no account; but that which I have related I heard my master recount to those who came there to see me. At the end, however, of the third day, I began to have some consciousness of what was passing around me, and found myself extended on my straw, my head bound up, and covered with ointment and plasters.

"What is the meaning of all this?" I cried, in extreme alarm. The heartless priest replied, "I have only been hunting the rats and the snakes which have almost ruined me." Seeing the condition in which I was, then guessed what had happened to me. At this time an old nurse entered, with some of the neighbours, who dressed the wounds on my head which had assumed a favourable appearance; and as they found my senses were restored to me, they anticipated but little danger, and began to amuse themselves with my exploits, while I, unhappy sinner, could only deplore their effects.

With all this, however, they gave me something to eat, for I was almost dying with hunger; and at the end of fourteen or fifteen days was able to rise from my bed without danger, though not even then without hunger, and only half cured. The day after I got up, my worthy and truly respectable master took my hand, and opening the door, put me into the street, saying, "Lazaro, from this day look out for yourself; seek another master, and fare you well. No one will ever doubt that you have served a blind man; but for me, I do not require so diligent nor so clever a servant." Then shaking me off, as though I was in league with the Evil One, he went back into his house and shut the door.

MIGUEL CERVANTES
(1547-1616)

CERVANTES, born at Alcala de Henares, is the foremost literary figure of Spain's golden age. His was a spectacular life of adventure that included wars against the Turks; capture by Moorish pirates who held him in captivity for five years during which he divided his time between writing plays and attempting escape; constant imprisonment in Spain for irregularities in connection with government funds. Nevertheless, and in spite of perpetual poverty, he managed to write his *Don Quixote*, one of the greatest books ever conceived. It is a masterpiece of irresistible humour, unlimited sympathy, and a penetrating analysis of human frailty.

In 1613, about eight years after the appearance of *Don Quixote*, Cervantes published the *Novelas Exemplares*, twelve remarkable stories which contain some of his best work. In these he shows a mastery of Spanish prose which he seldom excels elsewhere. *The Mock Aunt*, given in this collection, did not appear in the *Examplary Novels* until 1814, since when it has been included in all editions.

The present version is reprinted from Roscoe's *Spanish Novelists*, London, no date

THE MOCK AUNT

AS two young law-students, natives of La Mancha, were one day passing along the streets of Salamanca, they happened to see over the window of a certain shopkeeper, a rich Persian blind, drawn closely down,—a novelty which attracted their attention. Fond of adventure, and more deeply read in the noble science of attack and defence, than the laws of Bartolus or Baldus, they felt a strong curiosity to know why the articles the shop contained were kept, being marked on sale, so studiously out of view. Why not exhibited in the window as well as at the door? To remove their perplexity, they proceeded to make inquiries— not at the shop, but at one some little distance off, where they observed a babbling old shopkeeper, busily serving his neighbours, and, at the same time, retailing the latest news and scandal of the place. In answer to their questions, he ran on with the same volubility. "My young gentlemen, you are very inquisitive; but if you must know, there is a foreign lady now resides in that house, at least half a saint, a very pattern of self-denial and austerity, and I wish you were under her direction. She has with her, also, a young lady of extraordinary fine appearance and great spirit, who is said to be her niece. She never goes out without an old squire, and two old duennas, young gentlemen; and, as I think, they are a family from Granada, rich, proud, and fond of retirement. At least, I have not seen a single soul in our city (and I have watched them well) once pay them a visit. Nor can I, for the life of me, learn from what place they last came hither. But what I do know is, that the young lady is very handsome and very respectable, to all appearance; and from the style of living and high bearing of the aunt, they belong to none of the common sort, of that I am sure."

From this account, pronounced with no little emphasis and authority, by the garrulous old gentleman, the students became more eager than ever to follow up their adventure. Familiar as they were with the topographical position of the good citizens, the names of the different families and dwellings, and all the flying reports of the day, they were still in the dark as to the real quality of the fair strangers, and their connections in the University. By dint of industry and perseverance, however, they hoped soon to clear up their doubts, and the first thing they ascertained was, that, though past the hour of noon, the door of the mansion was still closed, and there seemed no admittance, even upon business. From this they naturally inferred, that, if no tradesmen were admitted, the family could not well take their meals at home; and that if, like other mortals, they eat at all, they must soon make their appearance on their way to dinner.

In this conjecture they were not deceived, for shortly they saw a staid and reverend looking lady issue from the dwelling, arrayed all in white, with an immense surplice, wider than a Portuguese canon's, extending over her head, close bound round her temples, and leaving only just space enough for her to breathe. Her fan was in her hand, and a huge rosary with innumerable beads and bells about her neck—so large indeed, that, like those of Santinuflo, they reached down to her waist. Her mantle was of fine silk trimmed with furs; her gloves of the whitest and newest, without a fold; and she had a walking-stock, or rather an Indian cane, delicately wrought and tipped with silver. A venerable old squire, who seemed to have belonged to the times of Count Fernan Gonzales, escorted his honoured mistress on the left hand. He was dressed in a large wide coat of velvet stuff, without any trimming—ancient scarlet breeches—moorish hose—a cloak trimmed with bands—and a cap of strong netted wool, which produced rather a quizzical effect, but which he wore because he was subject to cold and a dizziness in his upper story; add to which a larger shoulder-belt and an old Navarrese sword.

These respectable-looking personages were preceded by another of very different exterior; namely, the lady's niece, apparently about eighteen, graceful in her deportment, and of a grave but gracious aspect. Her countenance was rather of the oval—beautiful and intelligent; her eyes were large and black as jet, not without a certain expression of tenderness and languor; arched and finely marked eyebrows, long dark eyelashes, and on her cheeks a delicate glow of carnation. Her tresses, of a bright auburn, flowed in graceful curls round brows of snowy whiteness, combined with a fine delicate complexion, &c., &c.; and she had on a sarcenet mantle; a bodice of Flemish stuff; her sandals were of black velvet, enriched with gilt fastenings and silver fringe; fine scented gloves, not only fragrant with common essence, but with the richest amber.

Though her demeanour was grave, her step was light and easy: in each particular she appeared to advantage, and in her *tout ensemble* still more attractive. In the eyes of the young scholars she appeared little less than a goddess, and, with half the dazzling charms she boasted, would have riveted her fetters on the hearts of older and most experienced admirers. As it was, they were completely taken by surprise—astonished, stupefied, overwhelmed, and enchanted. They stood gazing at so much elegance and beauty as if their wits had left them; it being one of the prerogatives of beauty, like the fascination of the serpent, first to deprive its victims of their senses, and then to devour them.

Behind this paragon of perfection walked two ugly old duennas (like maids of honour), arrayed, if we only allow for their sex, much in the obsolete manner of their knight companion, the ancient squire.

With this formal and imposing escort, the venerable chaperon at length arrived at the house,—the good squire took his station at the door, and the whole party made their entrée. As they passed in, the young students doffed their caps with extraordinary alacrity and politeness; displaying in their air and manner, as much modesty and respect as they could muster for the occasion.

The ladies, however, took no notice of them, shutting themselves in, and the young gentlemen out: who were left quite pensive and half in love, standing in the middle of the street. From this want of courtesy they ingeniously came to the conclusion, that these fair disturbers of their peace had not come to Salamanca for the purpose of studying the laws of politeness, but studying how to break them. In spite, however, of their ingratitude, they agreed to return good for evil, and to treat them on the following night to a little concert of music, in the form of a serenade,— for this is the first and only service which poor students have it in their power to offer at the windows of her who may have smitten them.

Seeking some solace, however, for their disappointment just at present, they repaired to a restaurateur's; and having partaken of what little they could get, they next betook themselves to the chambers of some of their friends. There they made a collection of all the instruments of musical torture they could find; such as old wire-worn guitars, broken violins, lutes, flutes, and castanets; for each of which they provided suitable performers, who had at least one eye, an arm, and a leg among them. Not content, however, with this, being determined to get everything up in the most original style, they sent a deputation to a poet, with a request that he would forthwith compose a sonnet. This sonnet was to be written for, and precisely upon, the name of *Esperanza;* such being the Christian appellation of the hope of their lives and loves; and it was to be sung aloud on that very same night. The poet undertook the serious charge; and in no little while, by dint of biting his lips and nails, and rubbing his forehead, he manufactured a sonnet, weaving with his wits just as an operative would weave a piece of cloth.

This he handed to the young lovers; they approved it, and took the author along with them to repeat it to the musicians as they sung it, there being no time to commit it to memory.

Meantime the eventful night approached—and at the due hour, there assembled for the solemn festival, nine knights of the cleaver, four vocal performers with their guitars, one psaltery, one harper, one fiddler, twelve bell-ringers, thirty shield-sounders, and numerous other practitioners, divided into several companies; all, however, better skilled in the music of the knife and fork than in any other instrument. In full concert they struck up, on entering the street, and a fresh peal on arriving at the lady's house; the last of which made so hideous a din as to rouse all within hearing from their quiet slumbers, and bring them to their windows half dead with wonder and alarm. This was continued some time just under the lady's window, till the general concert ceased, to give room for the harp and the recital of the poet's sonnet. This was sung by one of those musicians who never wait to be invoked; nor was the poet less on the alert as prompter on the occasion. It was given with extreme sweetness and harmony of voice, and quite accorded with the rest of the performance.

Hardly had the recitation of this wonderful production ceased, when a cunning rogue, among the audience, turning to one of his companions, exclaimed in a loud, clear voice, "I vow to Heaven I never heard a viler song worse sung, in all my born days! Did you note well the harmony of the lines, and that exquisite adaptation of the lady's name; that fine invocation to Cupid, and the pretty mention of the age of the adored object,—the contrast then between the giant and the dwarf—the malediction—the imprecation—the sonorous march of the whole poem. I vow to God, that if I had the pleasure of knowing the author, I would willingly, to-morrow morning, send him a dozen pork sausages, for I have this very day received some from the country." At the word sausages, the spectators were convinced that the person who had just pronounced the encomium, meant it in ridicule; and they were not mistaken; for they afterwards learnt that he came from a place famous for its practical jokers, which stamped him in the opinion of the bystanders for a great critic, well qualified to pass judgment upon poets, as his witty analysis of this precious morsel had shown.

Notwithstanding all their endeavours, the windows of the house they were serenading seemed the only ones that remained closed, a circumstance at which our young adventurers were not a little disappointed. Still, however, they persevered; the guitars were again heard, accompanied by three voices, in a romantic ballad chosen for the occasion. The musicians had not proceeded far, before they heard a window opened, and one of the duennas whom they had before seen, made her appearance. In a whining hypocritical tone, she addressed the serenaders: "Gentlemen, my mistress, the Lady Claudia di Astudillo y Quinones, requests that you will instantly repair to some other quarter, and not bring down scandal upon this respectable neighbourhood by such violent uproar; more particularly as there is now at her house a young lady, her niece, my young mistress, Lady Esperanza di Torralva Meneses y Pachico. It is very improper, therefore, to create such a disturbance among people of their quality. You must have recourse to other means, of a more gentlemanly kind, if you expect to meet with a favourable reception."

On hearing these words, one of the young gallants quickly retorted, "Do me the favour, most venerable mistress, to request your honoured Lady Donna Esperanza, to gladden our eyes by presenting herself at the window. I wish to say a few words, which may prove of the greatest consequence." "Oh, shocking?" exclaimed the duenna, "is it the Lady Esperanza you mean? You must know, my good sir, she is not thus lightly to be spoken of,—she is a most honourable, exemplary, discreet, modest young person, and would not comply with such an extravagant request, though you were to offer her all the pearls of the Indies."

During this colloquy with the ancient duenna, there came a number of people from the next street; and the musicians, thinking the alguazils were at hand, sounded a retreat, placing the baggage of the company in the centre; they then struck up some martial sounds with the help of their shields, in the hope that the captain would hardly like to accompany them with the sword dance, as is the custom at the holy feast of San Fernando at Seville; but would prefer passing on quietly to risking a defeat in the presence of his emissaries.

They therefore stood their ground, for the purpose of completing their night's adventure; but one of the two masters of the revels refused to give them any more music, unless the young lady would consent to appear at the window. But not even the old duenna again honoured them with her presence there, notwithstanding their repeated solicitations; a species of slight which threw the whole company into a rage, and almost incited them to make an attack upon the Persian blinds, and bring their fair foes to terms. Mortified as they were, they still continued their serenade, and at length took their leave with such a volley of discordant sounds, as to make the very houses shake with their hideous din.

It was near dawn before the honourable company broke up, to the extreme annoyance and disappointment of the students, at the little effect their musical treat seemed to have produced. Almost at their wits' end, they at last hit upon the expedient of referring their difficulties to the judgment of a certain cavalier, in whom they thought they could confide. He was one of that high-spirited class termed in Salamanca *los generosos.*

He was young, rich, and extravagant, fond of music, gallant, and a great admirer of bold adventures; in short, the right sort of advocate in a cause like theirs. To him they recounted very minutely their prodigious exertions and their ill-success; the extreme beauty, grace, and attractions of the young, and the imposing and splendid deportment of the old lady; ending with the small hope they had of ever becoming better acquainted with them. Music, it was found, boasted no charm for them, "charmed they ever so wisely;" nay, they had been accused of bringing scandal upon the whole neighbourhood.

Now their friend, the cavalier, being one who never blinked danger, began to reassure them, and promised that he would soon bring their uncourteous foes to conditions, *coute qui coute;* and that, as he was himself armed against the keenest shafts of the little archer-god, he would gladly undertake the conquest of this proud beauty on their account.

Accordingly, that very day he despatched a handsome and substantial present to the lady-aunt, with his best services; at the same time offering all he was worth—life, his person, his goods and chattels, and—his compliments. Such an offer not occurring every day, the elder duenna took on her the part of the Lady Claudia, and, in her mistress's name, was curious to hear from the page something of the rank, fortune, and qualifications of his master. She inquired especially as to his connections, his engagements, and the nature of his pursuits, just as if she were going to take him for a son-in-law. The page told her everything he knew, and the pretended aunt seemed tolerably well satisfied with his story.

It was not long ere she went, in person, in her mistress's name, as the old duenna, with an answer to the young cavalier, so full and precise, that it resembled an embassy rather than a letter of thanks. The duenna arrived, and proceeded to open the negotiation; she was received by the cavalier with great courtesy. He bade her be seated in a chair near his own; he took off her cloak with his own hands, and handed her a fine embroidered handkerchief to wipe the perspiration from her brow, for she seemed a little fatigued with her walk. He did more; and before permitting her to say a single word on the nature of her errand, he ordered sweetmeats and other delicacies to be set before her, and helped her to them himself. He then poured out two glasses of exquisitely flavoured wine, one for her and one for himself. In short, so delicate and flattering were his attentions, that the venerable guardian of youthful virtue could not have received more genuine pleasure if she had been made a saint upon the spot.

She now opened the object of her embassy, with the most choice, demure, and hypocritical set of phrases she could command; though ending with a most flat falsehood to the following purport. "She was commissioned," she said, "by her excellent young mistress, Donna Esperanza di Torralva Meneses y Pachico, to present to his excellency her best compliments and thanks. That his excellency might depend, that, though a lady of the strictest virtue, Donna Esperanza would never refuse to receive so excellent and accomplished a gentleman upon an honourable footing, whenever he were inclined to honour her aunt's house with his presence." The cavalier replied, "that he had the most perfect faith in all he had heard respecting the surpassing beauty, virtue, and accomplishments of her young mistress, qualities which made him only the more eager to enjoy the honour of an interview."

After an infinite variety of reservations and circumlocutions, this proposal was acceded to by the good duenna, who assured him there could be no possible objection on the part of either of the ladies; an assertion, than which, however, nothing could be farther from the truth. In short, desirous of discharging her duennal duty in the strictest manner, and not content with intercepting the cavalier's presents, and personating Donna Claudia, the wily old lady resolved to turn the affair to still further account. She ended the interview, therefore, with assuring him that she would, that very evening, introduce him to the ladies; and first, to the beautiful Esperanza, before her aunt should be informed of his arrival.

Delighted with his success, the young cavalier dismissed his obliging guest with every expression of esteem, and with the highest compliments to her fair mistress; at the same time putting a purse into the old duenna's hand, enough to purchase a whole wardrobe of fine clothes. "Simple young man," muttered the cunning old lady, as she left the house; "he thinks it is all finely managed now; but I must touch a little more of his money; he has certainly more than he knows what to do with. It is all right; he shall be welcome to my lady's house, truly; but how will he go out again, I wonder. The officers will see him home, I dare say, but not till after he has paid me well again for being admitted; and my young lady has made me a present of some handsome gowns for introducing so pretty a young gentleman; and her foolish old aunt rewarded me well for discovering the secret."

Meantime, the young cavalier was impatiently expecting the appointed hour; and as there is none but sooner or later must arrive, he then took his hat and cloak, and proceeded where the ancient duenna was expecting him.

On his arrival she nodded to him out of a window, and having caught his eye, she threw him the empty purse he had presented her with, well filled in the morning. Don Felix was at no loss to take the hint, and on approaching the door, he found it only a little open, and the claws of the old beldame ready to clutch the offered bait before she granted him admittance. It was then opened wide, and she conducted him in silence up stairs, and through a suite of rooms into an elegant little boudoir, where she concealed him behind a Persian screen, in a very skilful and cautious manner. She bade him remain quite still; her young lady, Esperanza, was informed of his arrival, and from HER favourable representation of his high rank, fortune, and accomplishments, she was prepared to give him an interview, even without consulting her aunt. Then giving her hand as a token of her fidelity, she left Don Felix couched behind the screen, in anxious expectation of the result.

Meanwhile, the artful old wretch, under the strictest promise of secrecy, and a handsome present of new gowns, had communicated to the aunt the important intelligence of the discovery of so unpleasant an affair, relating to the unsullied reputation and high character of her niece. She then whispered her mistress in the ear that she had actually discovered a man concealed in the house, and what was worse, by appointment with her young lady, as she had learnt from a note she had intercepted; but that she dared not disturb the intruder, as he appeared armed at all points. She therefore intreated her mistress to make no noise, lest he should perpetrate some deadly deed, before the officers of justice, to whom she had sent notice, should arrive to secure him. Now the whole of this statement was a new tissue of lies, as the old beldame intended to let the cavalier very quietly out, and had never yet ventured to acquaint her young lady with his presence at all. Having thus carried her point with the old lady, she declared that if she would promise to stay without disturbing herself in that room, she would go in search of Esperanza, and conduct her to her aunt immediately. This being agreed upon, the duenna proceeded to look for her young lady up stairs, and was not a little puzzled to find her seated in her boudoir, and Don Felix near her, with an expression of the utmost pleasure and surprise in his countenance. What had been his astonishment on Esperanza's entrance, to behold the beloved girl from whom he had been separated by her aunt's cruelty not many months before. What an ecstatic meeting for both; what a dilemma for the treacherous old duenna, should an explanation have already taken place! She had not been many weeks in the Lady Claudia's service, and she would certainly not be many more if the lovers should be thus discovered together. What was to be done? Ere they could decide, her mistress's step was heard on the stairs; she was calling Esperanza, in those sharp, bitter tones to which her niece was too well accustomed, and she had already reached the ante-room ere Don Felix was safely ensconced behind the screen. Esperanza hastened towards her, and found her seated in an easy arm-chair, in a sad flurry of mingled rage and alarm.

She cast ominous and perturbed glances towards the boudoir whence her niece had just issued, and then looked out of the window, impatient for the arrival of the police. She did not venture to allude to the cause of her dismay; bidding her niece sit down, a portentous silence ensued. It was now late, the whole household, even their protector, the ancient squire, had retired to rest. Only the old duenna and her young mistress were wide awake, and the latter was particularly anxious for her aunt to retire. Though only nine, she declared she believed the clock had struck ten; she thought her aunt looked jaded and unwell; would she not like to go to bed? No reply; but dark, malignant glances, sufficiently attested what it would have been, had she dared to speak out. Though unable, however, to deal in particulars, she could not refrain from making some general observations which bore upon the case. In a low tone, therefore, she addressed her niece as follows:—"I have often enough warned you, Esperanza, not to lose sight of the exhortations I have invariably made it my business to give you. If you valued them as you ought, they would be of infinite use to you, as I fear time and experience will, ere long, sufficiently show;" and here she again looked out of the window. "You must not flatter yourself we are now at Placentia, where you were born; nor yet at Zamora, where you were educated, no, nor at Toro, where you were first introduced. The people of those places are very different to what they are here; there is no scandal, no jealousies, no intriguing, my dear; and (in a still lower tone) no violence and uproar such as we heard in the street last night. Heaven protect us from all violent and deceitful men; from all house-breaking, robbery, and assassinations. Yes, I say, I wish we were well out of Salamanca! You ought to be aware in what a place you are; they call it the mother of sciences, but I think it is the mother of all mischief; yes, of everything bad, not excepting some people whom I know; but I mention no names just now," she added, with a look of suppressed malice and vexation; "though I could if I pleased. But the time will come!" and she here muttered some low unintelligible threats about grates and convents. "We must leave this place, my dear; you perhaps don't know there are ten or twelve thousand students here; young, impudent, abandoned, lost, predestined, shameless, graceless, diabolical, and mischievous wretches, the scum of all parts of the world, and addicted to all evil courses, as I think we had pretty good proofs only last night. Though avaricious as misers, when they set their eyes upon a young woman, my dear, they can be extravagant enough. The Lord protect us from all such, I say! Jesu Maria save us from them all!"

During this bitter moral lecture, Esperanza kept her eyes fixed upon the floor, without speaking a word, and apparently quite resigned and obedient, though without producing its due effect upon her aunt. "Hold up your head, child, and leave off stirring the fire; hold up your head and look me in the face, if you are not ashamed, and try to keep your eyes open, and attend to what I say. You require all the senses you have got, depend upon it, to make good use of my advice; I know you do." Esperanza here ventured to put in a word: "Pray, dear aunt, don't so fret yourself and me by troubling yourself to say any more. I know all you would say, and my head aches shockingly—do spare yourself, or I think my head will split with pain." "It would be broken with something else, perhaps, if you had your deserts, young miss, to answer your affectionate aunt in such a way as that! To say nothing of what I know— yes, what I know, and what others shall know, when somebody comes;" and she glanced very significantly towards the door.

Of this edifying conversation Don Felix had partly the benefit, as it occurred so near his place of concealment. The old duenna, meantime, being desirous, after the discovery that had taken place, of ingratiating herself with the lovers, and finding there was no hope of Donna Claudia retiring to rest till the arrival of the police, thought it high time to bring the young cavalier out of his dilemma. It was her object to get him safe out of the house, and yet preserve the good opinion of her venerable mistress, who might wait, she thought, till doomsday for the police. As it was impossible to speak to Don Felix, she hit upon the following expedient to make him speak for himself, trusting to her own and her young lady's discretion for bringing him off safely. She took her snuff-box, and approaching his hiding-place very slyly, threw a good handful into his face, which taking almost immediate effect, he began to sneeze with such a tremendous noise, that he might be heard in the street. She then rushed, in apparent alarm, into the next room, crying out: "He is coming! he is here;—guns and pistols—pistols and guns—save yourselves, my dear ladies! Here, you go into this closet;" she pushed the old aunt into it, almost dead with fright, and closed the door. "You come with me," she continued to Esperanza, "and I will see you safe here." Saying which, she took the young lady with her, and joined her lover, who had already found his way down stairs.

Unluckily, however, to make the scene more complete, and to impose the better upon her old mistress, she opened the window, and began to call out, "Thieves! thieves! help! help!" though in as subdued a tone as possible. But at the very first cry, the corregidor, who happened to be walking close to the house, entered the door, followed by two of his myrmidons, just as Don Felix opened it to go out. They instantly pounced upon and secured him, before he had time either to explain or defend himself; and, spite of the entreaties of Esperanza and the duenna, he was borne away.

They followed, however, to represent the affair to the chief alguazil; and they had gone only a little way when they were met by a strong party, headed by the identical two students, who came prepared for a fresh serenade, on the strength of their friend the cavalier's support and assistance. What was their surprise and dismay to behold him in such hands, and followed by the lovely Esperanza herself, the cause of all their anxiety and exertions. Love and honour at once fired their breasts, and their resolution was taken in a moment. Six friends, and an army of musicians, were behind them. Turning to them, out flew their own swords, as they called on them to draw in aid of honour and beauty, and rescue them from the hands of the vile alguazils. All united in the cry of rescue,—the musicians in the rear struck up the din of war; and a hideous peal it was,—while the rest rushed on with as much haste and spirit as if they had been going to a rich banquet. The combat was not long doubtful; the emissaries of justice were overpowered by the mere weight of the crowd which bore upon them; and unable to stir either hand or foot, they were mingled in the thick of the engagement, pressed on all sides by halt, and maimed, and blind, and stunned with the din of battle from the rear.

While this continued, Don Felix and his fair companion had been the especial care of the students and their friends, by whom they had been early drawn off into a place of comparative safety. Here a curious scene took place:—after the first congratulations upon their victory, the two students took their friend Don Felix by the hand, expressing the deep gratitude they both felt for the eternal obligation he had conferred upon them, having so nobly redeemed his pledge of bringing the lady to terms, and placing her in their hands. The speaker then continued, that *he* having had the good fortune to bear her away in safety from the crowd, was justly entitled to the prize, which he hoped would not be disputed, as he was then ready to meet any rival. The other instantly accepted the challenge, declaring he would die sooner than consent to any such arrangement. The fair object of their strife looked at Don Felix, uttering exclamations of mingled terror and surprise, while the young cavalier, just as the students were proceeding to unsheath their weapons, burst into a fit of uncontrollable mirth. "Oh, miracle of love! mighty power of Cupid!" he exclaimed. "What is it I behold? Two such sworn friends to be thus metamorphosed in a moment! Going to fight; after I have so nobly achieved the undertaking! Never,—I am the man you must both run through the body, for verily I am about to forfeit my pledge. I too am in love with this lady; and with Heaven's permission and her own, to-morrow she will be mine—my own wedded wife; for, by Heaven! she returns no more to Aunt Claudia and her duennas. He then explained to the astonished students the story of their love; how, when, and wherefore they had wooed,—their separation and sufferings,—with the happy adventure that had crowned their hopes. Then imitating the language of the students, he took their hands, assuring them of his deep gratitude for the eternal obligation they had conferred upon him.

On the ensuing day, Esperanza gave her hand to Don Felix, and the venerable Aunt Claudia was released from her hiding place, and all further anxiety on her niece's account.

FRANCISCO DE QUEVEDO Y VILLEGAS
(1580-1645)

QUEVEDO, born at Madrid, was educated at the University of Alcalá, and soon distinguished himself as a scholar and linguist. In consequence of a duel which ended disastrously for his adversary, Quevedo fled to Italy and thence travelled many years throughout Europe. He was later recalled and given an honorary post in the palace of Philip IV. He wrote a great deal, gaining a reputation as an excellent poet and satirist, second only to Cervantes as a master of fiction in the seventeenth century. His *Paul, the Sharper* is "one of the cleverest books in the world." The book describes the life of Paul, son of a barber and a loose woman, who goes from one exciting adventure to another.

The present version is reprinted from Roscoe's *Spanish Novelists*, London, no date.

PAUL TURNS BEGGAR
(From *Paul, the Sharper*, Chapter 6)

THE next morning, by break of day, my landlady appeared at my bed side. She was a choice old woman, at the years of discretion, past fifty-five, a great pair of beads in her hand, and a face like a chitterlin, or a walnut shell, it was so full of furrows. She was always very fond of proverbs, and began her speech after this manner; "A drop of water, continually falling on a stone, makes a hole in time; as you sow, so will you reap; if you walk barefoot among thorns, you must expect to be scratched. My child, Don Philip, to deal plainly, I do not understand you, nor can I conceive how you live. You are young, and it is no wonder you should be somewhat wild, without considering, that even whilst we sleep, we are travelling to our end. I, who have now one foot in the grave, have the privilege to tell you so much. It is very odd I should be told that you spent so much money, and nobody knows how; that you have, since you came to town, sometimes appeared like a scholar, sometimes a sharper, and sometimes like a gentleman. All this comes of keeping company, for, my child, tell me where you herd, and I'll tell you what you are, and birds of a feather flock together, and many a good bit is lost between the lip and the dish. Go, you fool, if you had a hankering after women, did you not know that I had always a good stock of that commodity by me, and that I have them ready at my beck? What occasion have you to be drawn away by one scoundrel to-day, and by another rascal to-morrow; picking up a dirty drab here, and a pickled jade there, who fleece you to keep another? By my father's soul, and as I hope for mercy, I would not have asked you now for what is due for lodging, but that I want it for some private uses, and to make a little ointment." Perceiving that all her discourse and long speech ended in a dun, for though that was her text, she did not begin with it as others do, but made it her conclusion; when I found that I was not at all to seek for the occasion of her loving visit, which was the first she had made me whilst I lodged in her house, excepting only one day, when she came to answer for herself, because she heard that I had been told some story about her witchcraft, and that when the officers came to seize her she had cast such a mist before their eyes, that they could neither find the house nor the street; she came then to tell me it was all a mistake, for they meant another of her name, and no wonder, for there were more of the name and profession,—I paid her down the money, and as I was telling it out, ill fortune, which always attends me, and the devil, who never forgets to plague me, so ordered it, that the officers came to seize her for a scandalous liver, and had information that her gallant was in the house. They came directly into my room, and seeing me, and her by me, they laid hold of us both, gave me half a score good bangs, and dragged me out of bed. Two others held her fast, saluting her with all kind of ill titles. Who would have thought of it, a woman that lived as I have said? The noise the constables made, and my cries, gave the alarm to the gallant, who was a fruiterer, and lay in the next room within; he set a running; they observing it, and being informed by another lodger in the house that I was not the man, scoured after, and laid hold of him, leaving me well beaten, and my hair torn off; yet, for all I had endured, I could not forbear laughing, to hear how the dogs complimented the old woman. One cried, "How gracefully you will look in a cart, mother; by my troth, it will be a great satisfaction to me, to see a thousand or two rotten oranges and turnip tops fly after you." Another said, "There is care taken that you shall make a good shew, and be well attended." At last they caught her bully, bound them both, begged my pardon, and left me to myself.

I lay eight days in the house under the surgeon's hands, and was scarce able to go abroad at the end of them, for they were fain to stitch up my face, and I could not go without crutches. By this time my money was spent, for the hundred royals all went in lodging, diet, and cure; so that to avoid further expenses, when my treasure was gone I resolved to go abroad on crutches, and sell my linen and clothes, which were very good. I did so, and with part of the money bought an old leather jerkin, a canvas waistcoat, a patched beggar's great coat down to my ankles, gamashes on my legs, and great clouted shoes, the hood of the great coat on my head, a large brass crucifix about my neck, and a pair of beads in my hand. A mummer, who was a master at his trade, taught me the doleful tone and proper phrases for begging, so I began immediately to practise it about the streets. Sixty royals I had left I sewed up in my doublet, and so set up for a beggar, much confiding in my cant. I went about the streets for a whole week, howling in a dismal tone, and repeating my lesson after this manner:—"Merciful Christians of the Lord, take pity on a poor, distressed, miserable, wounded, and maimed creature, that has no comfort of his life." This was my working day note; but on Sundays and holidays I altered my voice, and said, "Good charitable people, for Christ Jesus' sake, give one farthing or a halfpenny to the poor cripple whom the Lord has visited." Then I stood a little, which does good service, and went on again, "See my poor limbs were blasted, unhappy wretch that I am, as I was working in a vineyard; I lost the use of all my precious limbs, for I was as strong and as sound as any of you are, the Lord be for ever praised, and preserve your health and limbs." Thus the farthings came dropping in by shoals; I got abundance of money, and was in a way of getting much more, had I not been thwarted by an ill-looking lusty young fellow, lame of both arms, and with but one leg, who plied my very walks in a wheelbarrow, and picked up more pence than I did, though he begged not half so genteelly; for he had a hoarse voice which ended in a squeak, and said, "Faithful servants of Jesus Christ, behold how the Lord hath afflicted me for my sins; give one farthing to the poor, and God will reward you:" and then he added, "For the sweet Jesu's sake." This brought him a mighty revenue, and I observed, and for the future I cut off the *s*, and said only *Jesu*, because I perceived that it took with the simple people. In short, I altered my phrases as occasion served, and there was no end of my gettings; I had both my legs bound up in a leather bag, and lay in a surgeon's porch, with a beggar that plied at the corner of a street, one of the arrantest knaves that ever God put life into, and who was, as it were, our superior, and earned as much as all of us. He was broken bellied, and it hung out in a bunch; besides, he bound up his arm hard with a rope above the shoulder, which made his hand look as if it were lame, swelled, and had an inflammation. He lay flat on his back, with all the rupture naked, which was as big as his head, and cried, "Behold my misery, see how the Lord chastises his servants." If a woman happened to pass by, "Sweet beautiful lady, the Lord bless your dear soul." Most of them would give him an alms for calling them handsome, and would make that their way to their visits, though never so much about. If any ragged soldier came by, he called him, "Noble captain;" if any other sort of man, "Good worthy gentleman;" if he saw anybody in a coach, "Right honourable lord," and if a clergyman on a mule, "Most reverend archdeacon." In short, he was a most intolerable flatterer, and had particular ways for begging on holidays. I contracted such intimacy with him, that he acquainted me with a secret, which in a few days made us rich; which was that he kept three little boys who begged about the streets, stole everything that came in their way, brought it to him, and he was the receiver; besides, he had two small children that learned to pick pockets, and he went halves with them. Being so well instructed by such an able master, I took to the same courses, and he provided me with fit instruments for my purpose. In less than a month's time, I had got above forty crowns clear, besides all extravagant expenses; and at last designing that we should go away together, he disclosed to me the greatest secret and cunningest design that ever beggar had in his head, which we both joined in; and was, that between us we every day stole four or five children, which being cried, we presently appeared, inquired what marks they had to be known by, and said, "Good God, sir, I found this child at such a time, and had I not come as I did, a cart had run over it, but I have taken care of it." They readily paid us the reward, and it throve so well that I got above fifty crowns more, and by this time my legs were well, though I still wore them wrapped in clouts. I resolved to leave Madrid and go away to Toledo, where I knew nobody, and nobody knew me. Having made this resolution, I bought an old suit of grey clothes, a sword and bands, took leave of Valcazar, the beggar I last mentioned, and went about the inns to find some conveniency to go to Toledo.

❋ ❋ ❋

FERNAN CABALLERO
(1796-1877)

THIS name was the pseudonym of Cecilia Bohl de Faber, daughter of the erudite German authority on Spain, Juan Nicolas Bohl de Faber, and of Dona Francisca Larrea. She was born in Bern, and studied in Germany, returning to Spain in 1816. Fernan Caballero is one of the great figures of the novel of manners in Spain during the nineteenth century. She also wrote a great number of fairy tales. The characteristics of her work are a simple sententious style, clarity of exposition, and in general a tendency to moralize on her theme. Among her best-known works are: *La Gaviota*, *Clemencia*, *La Famila de Alvareda*, and her collection of fairy tales.

Bella-Flor, one of Caballero's charming fairy tales, was translated for this volume by Armando Zegri.

BELLA-FLOR

ONCE upon a time there was a father who had two sons: the older became a soldier and went to America, where he remained for a number of years. When he returned, his father had died, and his younger brother was enjoying the use of the fortune, and had grown rich. He called at the house of his brother, whom he found descending the stairs.

"Don't you know me?" he asked.

The brother answered ill-humouredly.

Whereupon the soldier announced himself. His brother told him there was an old trunk in the barn; that it was the inheritance left by his father. So saying, he went on his way, refusing to notice his brother.

He went to the barn and found a very ancient trunk. To himself, he said:

"What can I do with this dilapidated trunk? By God! At least I can make a fire out of it and warm my bones, for it's quite cold."

He shouldered it and carried it to his lodgings, where he began to chop it into pieces with an axe. Some pieces of paper fell out of a secret drawer. He picked the paper up, read it and observed it to be a legal document for a large amount of money that was due his father. This amount he collected, and became rich.

One day, as he walked through the street, he encountered a woman weeping bitterly. He asked her the reason. She told him that her husband was very sick. Not only was she without any money to buy medicine, but her husband was in danger of being sent to jail to satisfy his creditors.

"Do not worry," Jose said. "They will not put your husband in jail, neither will they sell your possessions, for I will arrange matters. I will pay his debts, the cost of his sickness, and even give him a fine funeral, if he happens to die."

These very things he carried out. But he found that after the man had died, and he had paid the cost of burial, he was left without a *real*, having expended all his inheritance on this good deed.

"And what am I to do now?" he asked himself. "Now, I have not enough money to buy myself a meal. Ah, I shall go to a court, and hire myself out as a servant."

This he did, entering the service of the King as a servant.

He bore himself so well and the King appreciated him to such a degree, that he was quickly promoted, and soon was honoured with the rank of "first gentleman".

Meanwhile his villainous brother had become poor and wrote to him, entreating assistance; and because Jose had such a good heart, he did assist him, petitioning the King to give his brother employment, and this the King granted.

So he came, but instead of feeling gratitude toward his brother, he experienced envy when he beheld him the favourite of the King, and planned mischief. With this end in view, he proceeded to ascertain those things needful to his plot, and learned that the King was enamoured of the Princessa Bella-Flor who, seeing that the King was old and ugly, refused to retaliate his affection, and so hid herself in a palace situated in some wild inaccessible region, the exact place of which no one knew.

The brother informed the King that Jose knew the Princess' whereabouts and corresponded with her. Whereupon the King, in high dudgeon, sent for Jose, and ordered him to leave instantly and bring back the Princessa Bella-Flor, with the threat that he would be hanged if he failed.

The poor disconsolate fellow went to the stable for a horse, and then went forth to adventure, without knowing which road to take in order to find Bella-Flor. He observed a white horse, very old and lean, that said:

"Take me and do not worry."

Jose was astonished to hear a horse address him; but he mounted and rode forth, taking with him three loaves of bread which the horse had told him to get.

After they had travelled a long stretch, they came on an ant-colony. The horse said:

"Scatter the three loaves of bread so that the ants can eat them."

"Why?" asked Jose. "We need them ourselves."

"Throw them," the horse insisted, "it always pays to be good."

They proceeded on their way and then came on an eagle, caught in a hunter's trap.

"Dismount," the horse said, "cut the meshes and set the poor bird free."

"But won't we lose time, if we stop?" Jose asked.

"Have no fear. Do as I tell you and never tire of doing good."

They advanced, and in time reached a river, where they beheld a fish that had been cast on dry land, and try as it would, could not get back to the current.

"Alight," the white horse told Jose. "Take that fish and throw it back into the water."

"We haven't time to lose," Jose insisted.

"There is always time to do a good deed," the white horse answered. "Never tire of doing good."

Shortly after, they came to a castle, hidden in a sombre forest, and beheld the Princessa Bella-Flor, scattering bran to her chickens.

"Wait," the white horse ordered Jose. "Now I am going to leap and pirouette, which will delight Bella-Flor. She will remark that she would like to ride me for a while, and you will invite her; then I will kick about and snort. She will be frightened, whereupon you will tell her that the reason is because I am not accustomed to women, and that if you mount her, I will be quieted. You will mount me, and I will gallop straight to the King's palace."

Everything fell out according to the strategy, and only when the horse was rushing away did Bella-Flor realise that she was the victim of a plot.

Then she dropped the bran which she had been holding in her hands, and told her companion that she had dropped it, and would he be good enough to pick it up for her.

"Where we are bound for," Jose assured her, "is plenty of bran."

Then, as they passed a tree, she threw her handkerchief in the air; it caught on the topmost branches. She asked Jose to dismount and climb the tree to get her handkerchief.

"There are lots of handkerchiefs in the place we are bound for," Jose answered.

Then they crossed a river, and she let a ring fall into it. She asked Jose to dismount and find it. But he answered that in the place to which they were bound were many rings.

At last they reached the King's palace, and the King was delighted to behold his beloved Bella-Flor. But she shut herself up in a room and refused to open it to anybody. The King entreated her to open it; but she vowed that she would not open it until the three objects she had let fall on the way here were recovered.

"There is nothing else to do, Jose," the King told him, "but for you, who know about these matters, to go and find them. And if you fail, you shall be hung."

The poor Jose was quite dejected, and went to convey the news to the white horse.

The white horse said:

"Have no fear. Mount me and we will go and find them."

They proceeded on their journey and came to the ant-colony.

"Would you like to have the bran?" the horse asked.

"Certainly," Jose answered.

"Then call on the ants and ask them to bring the bran to you. And if they cannot find it, they will at least bring you the bread you gave them."

So it fell out. The ants, grateful to him, fetched him bran.

"You see," remarked the horse, "that anyone who does good will reap the rewards, sooner or later."

They came upon the tree on which Bella-Flor had thrown her handkerchief; there it was, flapping in the breeze, like a flag, on one of the topmost branches.

"How can I get that handkerchief?" Jose asked. "To get it, I would need Jacob's ladder."

"Don't worry," the white horse answered. "Call the eagle that you liberated from the hunter's net, and she will get it for you."

And so it came to pass. He called the eagle, who caught the handkerchief in its beak and delivered it to Jose.

They reached the river, which was quite turbid.

"How can I get the ring from the bottom of this deep river, since I cannot see it, and I do not even know the spot where Bella-Flor threw it?" Jose questioned.

"Do not worry," the horse answered. "Call the fish you saved, and he will get it for you."

And so it came to pass. The fish dived down and came up happy, wagging its fins, and bearing the ring in its mouth.

Then, extremely happy, Jose returned to the palace. But when the objects were restored to Bella-Flor, she said that she would not budge from her retreat before the rogue who had kidnapped her from her palace had been fried in oil.

The King was so cruel that he acquiesced to this, and informed Jose that there was no other way out of the difficulty, and that he would have to die, fried in oil.

Jose, plunged in grief, entered the stable and informed the white horse of what was transpiring.

"Do not worry," said the horse. "Mount me, we will gallop so fast that I will begin to sweat. Cover your body with my sweat, and then let yourself be fried. Nothing will happen to you."

And so it fell out. And when he came out of the cauldron, he had changed into such a beautiful and elegant young man, that everybody gasped with astonishment, and no one more than Bella-Flor, who fell in love with him.

Then the King, who was very old and ugly, upon seeing what had happened to Jose, believed the identical change would come over him, and that Bella-Flor would then fall in love with him. So he threw himself into the cauldron and was fried to death.

Then they all proclaimed the chamberlain King, and he married Bella-Flor.

When he went to give thanks to the white horse, to whom he owed his good-fortune, he was told:

"I am the soul of that poor man, for whose illness and funeral you expended your whole fortune. And when I saw you so afflicted and endangered, I asked permission of God to come to your help, and thus pay back your kindness. For as I have told you before, and as I repeat now, never tire of doing good to people."

❊ ❊ ❊

DON JUAN VALERA
(1827-1905)

BORN in Cabra, son of the Marqueses de la Paniega. He pursued a diplomatic career, and while still young, travelled to Naples, accompanying the Duke of Rivas. He then visited other countries of Europe as a Spanish representative. He was dispatched as ambassador to Washington, Lisbon and Brussels. In his last years he grew blind. He was erudite in classic culture, a true humanist in the style of the Renaissance. A partisan of art for art's sake, his work is noted for its clarity of style, exactitude of description, and the cosmopolitanism of many of his themes. In his time, he opposed the tendencies of romanticism and naturalism, remaining faithful to the classical tradition, to the academic bias of his spirit. He wrote novels, poetry, criticism and dramas. Among his best-known works are: *Pepita Jimenez, Juanita la larga, El Comendador Mendoza.*

Cordovans in Crete was translated for this volume by Armando Zegri.

CORDOVANS IN CRETE

IN the reign of Alhakem I., in the year 218 of the Hegira, there was a rich merchant in Cordova called Abu Hafaz el Goleith, who lived in the environs of Fohs Albolut. In his bazaar, situated in one of the most central streets, could be seen the most precious objects of human industry, both those produced in our Peninsula, as well as those imported from remote regions; from Bagdad, Damascus, Bucharia, Samarcand, Persia, India, and the little known, immense empire of Cathay. Abu Hafaz possessed his own ships, which voyaged to the Levant to secure merchandise.

One afternoon in Spring, a veiled lady, accompanied by her servant, entered Abu Hafaz's bazaar. Although he could not see her face, he admired the grace and carriage of her walk, the slenderness and elegance of her form, the positive and ineffable seductiveness she exhaled, as though a luminous nimbus enveloped her, and the aristocratic beauty of her white, pretty well-cared hands.

The lady wished to inspect the richest objects in the bazaar. Abu Hafaz, complacency itself, offered to her eyes, and placed on the counter, a thousand and one exquisite items in jewels and cloth. She could not tire of gazing on them. She was very curious. The merchant remarked:

"I have not yet shown you, sultana, the most splendid and rare things which my bazaar possesses."

"Why then do you hide them and now show them to me?" she asked.

"Because I am selfish and do not care to work for nothing. Show me your face, and in payment I shall show you my rarest treasures."

The lady did not have to be coaxed. She lifted her veil, and revealed the most lovely and graceful face that the merchant had ever seen, or even dreamed of, in all his life. Filled with gratitude and enthusiasm, he then brought forth pearls from Ormuz, diamonds from Golconda, and silken weaves that came from Cathay, and embroidered with such care and mastery that they did not seem to be the work of human beings as much as of fairies and genii.

The unknown lady fell in love with the best and most elaborate of these embroidered weaves, wished to purchase it, and asked the price.

"It is so expensive," said the merchant, "that you will perhaps not wish or be able to pay for it. But if you are agreeable, the stuff will cost you very little."

"Done! Tell me what the cloth will cost me."

"A kiss from your mouth," the merchant answered.

Irritated by such disrespectful audacity, the lady covered her face, turned her back on Abu Hafaz, and left the bazaar, followed by her servant.

The merchant wished to follow her, so as to ascertain where she lived and who she was. But the lady had disappeared in the labyrinths of the narrow streets.

After five days, the servant came to the bazaar and told the merchant that her mistress had been unable to sleep, or secure tranquillity, so much had she been preoccupied with the cloth, so much had she wished to own it; that she yielded to his terms, and that on the following day, when night fell, she would come to the bazaar discreetly, and pay for the cloth the price that had been demanded.

And in fact the lady did come to the rendezvous. The merchant then learned that she was in the harem of the sultan, from which she had secretly issued, while the sultan was hunting wild boar in the mountains. Her name was Glafira. She came from a small village situated on the slope of Mount Ida. Although her family was poor, it belonged to a high and old nobility. Her ancestors went back to mythical ages. Among them were numbered poets and priests from Mount Ida, who, weaving war dances to the sound of the clarions and to the clangour of shields struck with sword handles, surrounded Zeus, when he was still a boy, and thus prevented Cronos from hearing and devouring him.

In this remote retreat, the family of Glafira had resisted the encroachments of Christianity and had preserved, fresh and pure, the traditions and memories of paganism. It even prided itself on possessing magical powers and supernatural gifts, acquired through initiation, in venerable and primitive mysteries. Glafira affirmed that one of her progenitors had been Epimenides, sage, legislator, poet and prophet, cunning in the art of suspending life, and remaining in a state of coma, in profound caves, in order to learn by experience the tortuous movements and courses occurring through the centuries in human events.

Glafira had lost the secret of the magic arts, but nonetheless she possessed no small abilities in this direction. She could sing or recite a thousand and one ancient legends in verse of the divine ages, of heroes and demigods; of the coming of Europa to her island, of the passion of Pasiphæ, and of the triumph and perfidy of Theseus. She could still dance, she affirmed, the same ingenious dance which Dedalus created for the Princess Ariadne of the golden tresses.

Accused of witchcraft and paganism, and fleeing the intolerant religious persecution, the father of Glafira left Crete with his daughter. He wandered through different countries and at last died, leaving her friendless and alone. Wandering like Io, Glafira reached Hesperia, without Argos detecting her, and without being bitten either by gad-flies or inspiration. She had no other inspiration than her ambitious will.

Alhakem, enchanted and seduced by her talents and loveliness, had given her shelter in his palace. She dreamed of being the favourite and the queen in the empire of the Omniadas.

The irresistible caprice of possessing the cloth, and a certain dim half-conscious desire which the young merchant had awakened in her, had attracted Glafira and impelled her to pay the price which he had asked.

The kiss, instead of satisfying and quieting Abu Hafaz, flamed and grew ardent in his heart. He was daring, able to risk and adventure all things, confident in the power of his brain, and conceiving himself able to overcome mountains of difficulties. He accordingly resolved to keep Glafira in his house as his own property, without freeing the slave, who might reveal the hiding place of her mistress.

Upon learning of the determination of Abu Hafaz, Glafira was furious. She declared that, hoping to be queen of Hesperia, of the adjacent islands and of a part of Magreb, she could not resign herself to be the spouse or mistress of an insignificant merchant, who was a plebeian renegade of the vanquished and dominated Spanish race. She also considered as crazy that which Abu Hafaz proposed doing. Before long the sultan would find how matters stood, and would wreak cruel vengeance. In her fury, Glafira insulted Abu Hafaz, and tried to stab him with a dagger which she concealed in her girdle. He disarmed her, and returned her insults with a vampire-like kiss. He imprinted that kiss on her snow-white neck, and by the light of a lamp, in a mirror of polished steel, he made her inspect the mark he had left thereon.

"It is the mark," he told her, "that shows you are my slave."

There was a purple circle the size of a *dirhem*.

"It will take more than a year," Abu Hafaz said, "to erase that mark. How can you have the courage to return to the presence of your old master? You are mine already. But before this mark with which I have branded you shall have healed, I will win a throne and you shall be queen with me."

Not long after, Alhakem had his son, Abderahman, sworn in as Vali-alahdi, or successor to the throne. His son managed everything, the while the father devoted himself to pleasure, and only intervened in the government whenever his two most dominating passions were involved: anger and avarice. The people groaned, burdened by enormous taxes, harassed, and humiliated by the personal guard of the prince, composed of mercenary slaves, of negro eunuchs, and of three thousand Andalusian Mozarabs. A fracas between some of the people and various tribute collectors, supported by guards of the king, provoked a riot that was put down the while Alhakem was hunting. Returning from the hunt, and giving full rein to his cruelty, he ordered crucified the ten chief leaders of the riot.

For some little time, a conspiracy had been plotted against Alhakem. The horrible spectacle of the ten persons executed, excited the compassion and the fury of the people. The plot proved premature. The rebellion was vigorous. Nearly all the *muladies*, or Spanish renegates, participated. Abu Hafaz led them as their captain. It happened on the day following the kidnapping of Glafira. The king's guard and the other armed soldiers of the garrison were vanquished and repelled two or three times, finally being forced to take refuge in the *alcazar*. The mob surrounded it and was making ready to attack it. Alhakem feared that this would prove the end of his reign, and the end of his life. He called his favourite page, ordered him to sprinkle his hair and beard with fragrant perfumes, so that, through this fragrance, he might be identified among the dead, and then issued either to die or vanquish the rebels.

By the order of Alhakem, a goodly number of his warriors crossed the Guadalquivir River; these went and overran the section which was on the other side of the river, began a sack, and started a devastating conflagration. The renegades saw the flame and smoke; thinking that their houses were on fire, and their wives and children endangered, they abandoned the fight in order to succour their beloved ones. The battle was instantly converted to a rout and a frightful carnage and butchery of the renegades, attacked on all sides, both by those commanded by Alhakem, and by those who, crossing the bridge, returned from the quarter they had set on fire.

Vanquished, Abu Hafaz had enough good luck and presence of mind to succeed in escaping with a number of his followers, taking the greater part of his treasures, and Glafira. Encountering a thousand and one dangers, and vanquishing innumerable obstacles, Abu Hafaz finally reached Adra. There, he had ten of his large ships. He embarked in them and abandoned Spain forever.

Following the victory, Alhakem continued to fiercely punish the rebels. More than four hundred heads belonging to those who had been captured alive, appeared severed and nailed on poles, by the banks of the Guadalquivir. Then he wished to show his clemency, because he could not put thousands of persons to death; but he expelled thousands from Spain. Some went to Morocco and populated a large section of the town of Fez. Others emigrated farther and established themselves in Egypt.

Meanwhile, Abu Hafaz, with his ships, and with the most valiant of his followers, turned pirate.

There now began for him a series of adventures and incursions in Provence, in Sardinia, in the coasts of Calabria, and other places.

Abu Hafaz, laden with booty and with a greater number of ships and men who had enlisted in his service, set sail for Alexandria. Assisted by the civic disorders then occurring, he was able to capture that magnificent city, and held it for some time. The Caliph of Bagdad sent a powerful army against him. Abu Hafaz defended, and finally surrendered and abandoned the city, following an honourable and lucrative capitulation, in which he received a large sum of money for permitting the Caliph to retake the town.

With twenty ships and several hundred warriors, Abu Hafaz finally betook himself to Crete. He always took Glafira with him, maintaining his bombastic promise to make her queen, and now he hoped to install her as queen in her own country, long before the time when the badge of slavery, which he had imprinted on her neck, should be removed. Crete was under the rule of the Byzantines when the Andalusian outlaws disembarked on their coasts.

After sacking several towns of the island, the warriors of Abu Hafaz wished to abandon it, so as to avoid an engagement with the army of the Emperor of Greece. And Abu Hafaz, long before the action of the Catalinians at Galipoli and of Hernan Cortes in Mexico, set fire to his score of ships, so that there would be no other recourse for his warriors but to vanquish or be slain.

In the war that ensued, the soldiers of the Grecian Empire were vanquished.

Abu Hafaz then made himself lord of the island and established the throne and capital of his dominions in a fortress, established by him, and which he called Candax. Thus he erased, for a number of centuries, the ancient name of the island, which came to be called Candia.

Glafira was queen, as Abu Hafaz had promised her. The mark on her face did not disappear till long after she had mounted the throne. Glafira's son, grandson and great-grandson reigned in Crete, since her dynasty lasted two or three centuries.

❋ ❋ ❋

PEDRO A. ALARCON
(1833-1891)

BORN in Guadax, Granada, the son of a distinguished family. For some time he studied law and theology, but abandoned both the university and his home to go from Granada to Madrid with a group of writers. In Madrid he followed journalism. During the war with Africa in 1859, Alarcon took part in the campaign as a volunteer. His valour in the war won him the San Fernando Cross. Returning to Spain, he published his *Diary of an Eyewitness of the African War*. Others of his works are: *La Prodiga, El Sombrero de tres Picos, El Capitan Venono*, and his celebrated *Historietas Nacionales*, a collection of short-stories in which *The Stub-Book* is found. He wrote dramas, novels and poetry. He is one of the representative figures of Spanish literature in the nineteenth century. One of his principal characteristics is an aphoristic brusque style, and a certain humour typical of the land.

The *Stub-Book* was translated for this volume by Armando Zegri.

THE STUB-BOOK

"UNCLE" Buscabeatas's back began to curve during the period of which I am going to relate, and the reason was that he was sixty years old, forty of which had been spent working a piece of ground that bordered the banks of the Costilla.

That year he had cultivated on his farm a crop of prodigious pumpkins, as large as those decorative balls on the railings of monumental bridges; and these pumpkins had attained an orange colour, both inside and outside, which fact signified that it was now the month of June. "Uncle" Buscabeatas knew each one of them most perfectly by its form, its state of ripeness, and even by its name, especially the forty specimens that were fattest and richest in colour, and which seemed to be saying, "Cook us!" And he spent all his days gazing on them tenderly, and sadly exclaiming:

"Soon we shall have to part!"

In the end, he decided, one fine afternoon, on the sacrifice, and pointing to the ripest among his beloved pumpkins, which had cost him so much effort, he pronounced the terrible sentence:

"To-morrow," he said, "I will cut this forty, and bring them to the Cadiz market. Happy that man who will eat them!"

And he walked back into his house with slow steps, and spent the night with the anguish of a father who is going to marry off his daughter on the following day.

"My poor dear pumpkins!" he sighed time and time again, unable to fall asleep. But he then reflected and came to a decision with these words:

"What else can I do but sell them? I cultivated them with that end in view. At least I will realise fifteen *duros* on them."

Imagine, then, his extreme astonishment, his unmitigated fury, and his desperation when, going the following morning to the farm, he discovered that he had been robbed during the night of his forty pumpkins. To save further explanation, I will merely say that, like Shakespeare's Jew, he attained the most sublimely tragic fury, frantically repeating those terrible words of Shylock:

"Oh, if I catch you, if I catch you!"

Then he began to reflect, coldly, and decided that his beloved objects could not yet be in Rota, his native village, where it would be impossible to put them on sale, without risking their being recognised, and where, in addition, pumpkins fetch a very low price.

"They are in Cadiz, as sure as I live!" he deduced, after pondering. "The infamous rogue, the robber, robbed me last night at nine or ten o'clock and escaped with them at midnight in the cargo boat. I will leave this very morning for Cadiz in the hour boat, and I will be very much surprised if I do not catch the robber and recover the daughters of my labour."

So saying, he yet remained about twenty minutes in the vicinity of the scene of the catastrophe, as though caressing the mutilated plants, or counting the missing pumpkins, or planning a species of dire punishment on the culprit, until it was eight o'clock, and he left in the direction of the pier.

The hour boat was almost ready to sail. This humble boat leaves every morning for Cadiz promptly at nine o'clock, conducting passengers, just as the cargo boat leaves every night at midnight, with a cargo of fruit and vegetables.

It is called the first hour boat, because in this space of time, and sometimes even in forty minutes, when the wind is at the stern, it makes the three leagues that separate the ancient town of Duque de Arcos and the old town of Hercules.

That morning at ten-thirty, "Uncle" Buscabeatas paused in front of a vegetable counter in the Cadiz market-place, and said to a bored policeman who was standing by:

"Those are my pumpkins. Arrest that man!"

And he pointed to the merchant.

"Arrest me!" exclaimed the merchant, utterly surprised and enraged. "Those pumpkins are mine. I bought them. . . ."

"You'll be able to tell that to the *alcalde*," answered "Uncle" Buscabeatas.

"I won't."

"You will."

"You are a thief."

"You're a rascal."

"You should speak with more politeness, less indecency. Men should not talk to each other in this fashion," the policeman said with extreme calm, punching each of the contestants on the chest.

Meanwhile a crowd had collected, and it was not long before there appeared the police inspector of the public market, the judge of provisions.

The policeman resigned his charges to his superior, and informed the latter of the matter at issue. With a pompous expression, the judge questioned the merchant.

"From whom did you buy those pumpkins?"

"From 'Uncle' Fulano, the old man from Rota," the merchant answered.

"That would be the man!" cried "Uncle" Buscabeatas. "That's the fellow I suspected! When his farm, which is poor, produces little, he begins to rob his neighbours."

"But admitting the theory that you have been robbed last night of forty pumpkins," pursued the judge, turning to the old farmer, "how could you prove that these, and no others, are yours?"

"Why?" replied "Uncle" Buscabeatas. "Because I know them as well as you know your daughters, if you have any. Don't you see that I have raised them? Look here! this one is called 'the round one,' that one, 'the fat fellow,' and this one, 'the big-belly,' that one, 'the red one,' that one, 'Manuela' . . . because she resembles my youngest daughter."

And the poor old man began to cry bitterly.

"All this is very good," answered the judge. "But the law does not rest satisfied with the fact that you recognise your pumpkins. It is necessary that authority should be convinced at the same time of the preexistence of the thing in question, and that you should identify it with indisputable proofs. . . . Señores, you needn't smile. I'm a lawyer."

"Well, you will soon see the proofs, without leaving this place, that these pumpkins were raised in my farm!" said "Uncle" Buscabeatas, to the great astonishment of the spectators.

And dropping on the ground a package which he had been carrying in his hand, he knelt till he was able to sit on his feet, and then tranquilly began to untie the knots of the handkerchief that had held the package.

The astonishment of the judge, the merchant and the bystanders reached its climax.

"What is he going to take out?" everybody asked.

At the same time, the crowd was augmented by a new curiosity seeker. Seeing him, the merchant exclaimed:

"I am glad you are here, 'Uncle' Fulano! This man says that the pumpkins which you sold me last night, and which are on this very spot, were stolen. You can explain. . . ."

The newcomer turned more yellow than wax, and tried to escape; but circumstances materially prevented him, and in addition the judge suggested that he remain.

Meanwhile, "Uncle" Buscabeatas confronted the supposed thief, and said:

"You will now see what is good!"

"Uncle" Fulano recovered his composure and explained:

"We will see which of us can prove what he is trying to prove. For if you cannot prove, and you will not be able to prove, your charge, I will have you sent to prison for libel. These pumpkins were mine. I raised them on my *Egido* farm as I did all the rest I brought this year to Cadiz, and no one can prove the contrary."

"Now you will see!" repeated "Uncle" Buscabeatas, finishing the untying of the handkerchief, and opening it.

Then he scattered on the floor a quantity of pumpkin stalks, still green and exuding sap, the while the old farmer, seated on his feet, and half dead with laughter, addressed the following speech to the judge and the spectators:

"Gentlemen, have you ever paid taxes? If you have, have you seen that green book that the tax-collector carried, from which receipts are cut, leaving a stub by which it can be proved if such and such a receipt is counterfeit or not?"

"What you are talking about is the stub-book," gravely observed the judge.

"That is what I am carrying with me. The stub-book of my garden, that is, the stalks that were attached to these pumpkins before they were stolen from me. And if you do not believe me, look at them. This stalk belonged to this pumpkin. Nobody can doubt it. This other one, as you can easily see, belonged to this one. This one, which is wider, must belong to this other one. Exactly! And this one. . . . And that one. . . . And that one!"

And as he said these words, he fitted a stalk to the hollow remaining in the pumpkin when it was plucked, and with astonishment the spectators perceived that the irregular base of the stem exactly fitted the white and small form of the concavity, which represented what we might call the scars of the pumpkins.

Then all the spectators, including the policemen and the judge himself, crouched low, and began to assist "Uncle" Buscabeatas in this singular verification, all saying at one and the same time, with childish glee:

"Yes, yes! It is certainly so! Don't you see? This one belongs here? This one is here. That one there! That one there!"

And the laughter of the men blent with the whistling of the street gamins, with the imprecations of the women, with the tears of triumph and happiness of the old farmer, and the shoves given the robber by the policemen anxious to lead him off to jail.

It is unnecessary to say that this pleasure was granted them; that "Uncle" Fulano was obliged to return to the merchant the fifteen *duros* he had received; that "Uncle" Buscabeatas returned to Rota with deep satisfaction, though he kept saying all the way:

"How beautiful they looked in the market-place! I should have brought back *Manuela*, so that I might eat her to-night and keep the seeds."

* * *

EMILIA PARDO BAZAN
(1852-1921)

BAZAN was one of the most eminent Spanish leaders of Naturalism and of the Regional Novel. She was born in Coruna, a daughter of the Count of Pardo Bazan. During her lifetime she ardently defended the cause of feminism. She possessed an encyclopædic culture. In literature, she adopted the principles of the Zola school, conforming them, however, to the character of her race. Like the Goncourts, she was enamoured of colour. Her style is spontaneous, though some of her work is characterised by an archaic tone. Her favourite type in fiction was the man of action, and she devoted the last years of her life to planning a book on Hernan Cortez, in which she hoped to give a résumé of the strength of her race. Among her best-known works are: *Insolacion y Morrina*, *Los Pasos de Ulloa*, *San Francisco de Asis*, and *La Madre Naturaleza*.

The First Prize was translated for this volume by Armando Zegri.

THE FIRST PRIZE

IN the time of Godoy, the fortune of the Torres-nobles de Fuencar was placed among the most powerful of the Spanish monarchy. Political vicissitudes and other reverses reduced their revenues and put an end to the dissolute mode of living of the last Marques de Torres-nobles, a dissolute spendthrift whose conduct had induced much gossip in the court when Narvaes was young. He was close to seventy years when the Marques de Torres-nobles adopted the resolution to retire to his farm at Fuencar, the only remaining property which was unmortgaged. There he devoted himself to the task of building up his body, which was no less ruined than his house; and as Fuencar was able to let him enjoy a modicum of comfort, he organized his life so that nothing was wanting. He had a priest who, in addition to saying mass on Sundays and conducting the festivals, played cards with him and would read and comment to him on the most reactionary political periodicals; a major-domo, in charge of the estate, who skilfully directed the crops; an obese coachman who solemnly drove the two mules of his carriage; a reserved and solicitous governess, too old to tempt him and yet not sufficiently old to be repulsive in his eyes; a butler that he brought from Madrid, the only remaining relic of his past dissolute life, and now converted to the master's reformed life, as discreet and punctual now as in the past; and finally, a female cook, clean as gold, with delicate hands for all the plates of the ancient national kitchen, who could satisfy the stomach without irritating it, and could delight the palate without perverting it. With such excellent wills, the Marques' house functioned like a well-wound clock, and the master more and more congratulated himself on having left the Gulf of Madrid and found port in Fuencar, where he might dock for repairs. His health recuperated; the sleep and digestion of that poor threadbare tunic which serves as the jail to the spirit, was renovated; and in a few months the Marques de Torres-nobles grew fat without losing his agility, his back straightened a bit, and his fresh breath testified to the fact that his ferocious gastric malady no longer bothered his stomach.

But if the Marques lived well, so did his servants. In order to keep them in his service, he paid them more generously than any one else in the province, and frequently gave them presents. So they were quite happy: little work to do, but that little, methodical and unchanging; a high salary, an occasional pleasant surprise from the generous Marques.

The month of December, the year before last, was colder than usual, and the farm and environs of Fuencar were covered with about five inches of snow. Bored with the solitude of his huge study, the Marques descended one night to the kitchen, instinctively seeking sociability—the companionship of fellow-men. He drew near to the fire, warmed the palms of his hands, snapped his fingers, and even laughed at the tales of Andalusian humour narrated by the major-domo and the shepherd. He even observed that the eyes of the cook were most attractive. Among other talk, more or less of a rustic nature, that amused him, he heard that all his servants were planning to club together so as to buy a tenth of a ticket in the Navidad lottery.

The following day, very early, the Marques dispatched his butler to the next town. And that same night the condescending señor entered the kitchen, waving a number of papers, and announced to the domestics, with a benign expression, that he had carried out their wishes, by purchasing a whole ticket for the coming lottery, of which he meant to present them with a two-tenth share, reserving for himself the remaining eight-tenths, so as to tempt his luck. Upon hearing the news, everyone in the kitchen burst out into loud bravos and extravagant blessings; all save the shepherd, an old white-haired fellow, low-speaking and sententious, who shook his head, and affirmed that no good could come of playing with gentlemen, and that it killed luck. This so enraged the Marques, that he forbade the shepherd from sharing in the two-tenth share of the ticket in question.

That night the Marques slept less soundly than he had done since coming to Fuencar; some of those ideas which mortify bachelors kept him awake. He had not relished the grasping avidity with which his servants spoke of the money they might win. "These fellows," the Marques reflected, "are only waiting to fill their pockets, before they forsake me. And what plans they have! Celedonio (the coachman) talked of setting up a tavern . . . probably to get drunk on his own wine. And that dolt of a Doña Rita (she was the governess) is thinking of nothing else but of keeping a boarding house! Jacinto (the butler) kept mighty silent, but I could see him squinting in the direction of that Pepa (the cook) who, let us be frank, has some charm. . . . I would swear that they are planning to get married. Bah!" As he uttered this exclamation, the Marques de Torres-nobles turned in his bed the better to cover himself, for a cold gust of wind had attacked his neck. "And after all, what is all this to me? We won't win the big prize . . . and if we do, they will have to wait till I leave them the money in my will."

A moment later, the good man was snoring.

Two days later, the lottery was held, and Jacinto, who was more resourceful than Celedonio, arranged matters so that his master should send him to town in order to purchase some needed items. Night fell, there was a heavy fall of snow, and Jacinto had not yet returned, in spite of the fact that he had left the house at dawn.

The servants were gathered in the kitchen, as usual; suddenly they heard the muffled hoof-beats of a horse over the new-fallen snow, and a man, whom they recognised as their friend Jacinto, entered like a bomb. He was pallid, trembling and transformed, and with a catch in his voice, let fall these words:

"The first prize!"

At this precise moment, the Marques was in his study and, his legs wrapped in a thick poncho and smoking a fragrant cigar, was listening to the priest reading the political gossip of *El Siglo Futuro*. Both suddenly paused and listened to the outburst issuing from the kitchen. At first the Marques thought there was a row among his servants, but ten minutes of listening convinced him that these were voices of jubilation, so unmeasured and crazy were the sounds; and the Marques, angry and feeling that his dignity was compromised, dispatched the priest to learn what was happening, and to command silence. Within three minutes the messenger returned, and falling on the divan, huskily exclaimed, "I am choking!" Then he wrenched his collar loose and tore his vest in the effort to open it.

The Marques ran to his assistance and, fanning his face with *El Siglo Futuro*, finally succeeded in forcing a few fragmentary phrases out of the priest's mouth.

"The first prize! We have won . . . n . . . the prize . . .!"

In spite of his years, the Marques rushed to the kitchen with unwonted agility; reaching the door, he suddenly stopped, stupefied by the unusual scene that presented itself to his eyes. Celedonio and Doña Rita were dancing—I don't know if it was the *jaleo* or the *cachucha*—, with a thousand and one different stampings, leaping about like mannikins that have been electrified. Jacinto, amorously embracing a chair, was waltzing round and round the room. Pepa was drumming with a pan handle on a frying pan, producing a horrible cacophony, and the major-domo, stretched out on the floor, was rolling around, shouting, or rather ullulating: "Long live the Virgin!" Hardly did they perceive the Marques than the crazy loons rushed at him with outstretched arms and, before he could offer any resistance, they hoisted him on their shoulders, and singing and dancing and passing him around from one to the other, like a rubber ball, they gave him a free ride all round the kitchen, until they perceived that he was in a towering rage, and put him back on the ground. And then things grew worse, for the cook, Pepa, seizing the Marques by the waist, willy-nilly rushed him into a dizzying gallop, while the major-domo, presenting a bottle of wine, insisted that he sample it, assuring his employer that the liquor was very fine, since he had sent most of the blood of the bottle into his stomach, and therefore knew what he was talking about.

As soon as the Marques could make his escape, he rushed to his room, anxious to divulge to some one the terrible happenings; to the priest he described the audacities of his servants, and then discussed the matter of the first prize. To his grand surprise, he observed that the priest was ready to leave the house, wrapped in his cape, and putting on his cap.

"Where can you be going, Don Calixto, for the love of God?" the astonished Marques exclaimed.

Well, with his permission, Don Calixto was going to Seville to visit his family, give them the glad tidings, and collect in person his share of the tenth of the prize, a matter of several thousand *duros*.

"And you are going to leave me now? And the mass? And . . ."

While he was still talking, the butler introduced his face through the door. If the Marques would let him, he also wished to go and collect his part of the prize. The Marques raised his voice, and told them they must be unnatural monsters to wish to leave the house at such an ungodly hour, and with so much snow on the ground; to this both Don Calixto and Jacinto answered that the train would be leaving at midnight, at the next station, to which place they would wend on foot, as best they could. The Marques was about to open his mouth, to declare: "Jacinto will remain here, for I have need of him," when just then the ruddy face of the coachman appeared framed in the door, and without authorisation, and with insolent joy, came to bid adieu to his master, since he too was about to collect his winnings.

"And the mules?" shouted the master. "And pray tell me, who will take care of the coach?"

"Any one your grace wishes to put on the job. I'm not going to drive any more!" the coachman answered, presenting his back, and making room for Doña Rita who entered, not as was her wont, as if she were gingerly treading over eggs, but with dishevelled hair, an excited manner, and a smile on her mouth. Brandishing a heavy bunch of keys, she handed them to the Marques, with these words:

"Your Grace must know that these belong to the pantry . . . this to the closet . . . and that one . . ."

"That one is the key of the devil who will get you and your family, you witch of hell! You want me to fetch the bacon, the beans, eh? Go to the . . ."

Doña Rita failed to hear the final imprecation, for she sailed out whistling, and behind her went the others, and after all of them went the Marques himself, angrily following them through the rooms and almost overtaking them in the kitchen; but he could not muster up enough courage to follow them into the courtyard, for fear of the cold. By the light of the moon that silvered the snowy expanse, the Marques beheld them depart: first came Don Calixto, then Celedonio and Doña Rita arm in arm, and last of all Jacinto walking close to a feminine form which he made out to be Pepa, the cook. "Pepilla, too!" The Marques gazed into the abandoned kitchen, and saw the dying embers, and heard a sort of animal grunt. At the foot of the chimney, sprawling his full length, the major-domo was sleeping off his spree.

The following morning, the shepherd, who had not cared "to kill his luck," prepared a mess of soup, made out of bread and garlic, for the Marques de Torres-nobles de Fuencar, so that the noble señor might have something to eat on the day he awoke a millionaire.

It is unnecessary for me to describe the sumptuous installation of the Marques in Madrid, but I must relate that he acquired a cook whose dishes were gastronomical poems. It is declared that the delicacies of this excellent artist, whose offerings were relished so much by the Marques, produced that illness which sent him to the grave. Nevertheless, I believe that his death was caused by his fright, when he fell from a magnificent English horse, that became panicky; this happened shortly after he came to live in the palace he furnished in the Alcala Street.

When they opened the Marques' will, they found that he made the shepherd of Fuencar his heir.

ITALY

Introduction

IF we permit a flexibility of terms, we may say that the glorious Renaissance was ushered in by Dante, although he was born in the thirteenth century, while the Rebirth of Learning is officially dated from the fourteenth. Florence, for the next three centuries, was destined to be the centre of literary as well as artistic activity.

Boccaccio was the first master of Italian narrative prose, and one of the world's greatest masters of the short story. He was followed by a number of writers like Bandello, Grazzini, Straparola, and others who pursued the *novella* as the popular medium of expression, although none of these surpassed their master, Boccaccio. In the fifteenth century, Machiavelli, a politician as well as a writer, "forged Italian prose into a keen instrument of exposition and analysis". A great romantic epic of the period, *Orlando Furioso*, by Ariosto, became one of the most popular romances through the fifteenth and sixteenth centuries.

Thereafter, with the exception of Tasso, the most brilliant poet of the sixteenth century, we witness the decline of the golden age of Italian literature, which was not to be revived until the nineteenth century. This decline is quite possibly connected with the internal strife and continual warfare which battered and exhausted Italy until its creative spirit was destroyed.

The nineteenth century saw a revival of the romantic spirit in *The Betrothed*, a first-rate novel by Manzoni, but the period produced rather more poetry than fiction. Verga, the first distinguished writer of short stories, is best known for his *Cavalleria Rusticana* which is the basis of Mascagni's famous opera. He ushers in the modern movement in Italian literature which, as in other countries, concerns itself with social problems. Other outstanding authors who have cultivated the short story are Edmondo de Amicis, Matilde Serao, Pirandello and, to a lesser degree, d'Annunzio.

Among the contemporary writers Bontempelli, Ada Negri and Calzini are doing much to lift Italian literature from a purely provincial or national position to a European significance.

GIOVANNI BOCCACCIO
(1313-1375)

BOCCACCIO, besides being one of the great scholars and prolific poets of his time, was a writer of remarkable tales. In his incomparable *Decameron*, he overshadowed all his other achievements. And while the range of his stories is extraordinary, not one of them is dull. Some of these stories Boccaccio invented, some he reshaped and others he borrowed from French *fabliaux*. *The Decameron* became so popular that it was translated into most of the European literatures, and became a source for Chaucer, Shakespeare, and other famous writers.

The present version has been modernised by the editors from an old English translation.

THE STONE OF INVISIBILITY
(From *The Decameron*, 8th Day, Novel 3)

There dwelt in our city of Florence, always full with people of different tempers and characters, a painter called Calandrino, a man of simple mind, and one that dealt much in novelties. He was often in the company of two other painters, the one named Bruno, the other Buffalmacco, both satiric, cheerful persons, and quite subtle. They liked to be with Calandrino on account of his naïveté. At the same time there also lived in the city a most engaging and artful young man called Maso del Saggio, who, hearing reports of Calandrino's simplicity, determined to amuse himself at his expense by exciting his curiosity with some strange and monstrous tales. Meeting him by chance one day in St. John's Church, and observing him engaged in examining the sculpture and painting of the tabernacle, which had just been placed over the altar, he thought he had found the desired opportunity. Acquainting one of his friends of his intention, they approached the place where Calandrino was seated, and, pretending to be unaware of his presence, began to discuss the qualities of various precious stones, of which Maso spoke with the air of an expert lapidary. Calandrino began to listen and, perceiving that their conversation was not private, he joined them. Maso was delighted at this, and as he pursued his discourse, Calandrino asked him where these stones were to be found. Maso replied, "They are mostly to be found in Berlinzone, near the city of Baschi, in a country called Bengodi, where they tie the vines with sausages, a goose is bought for a penny and the gosling thrown into the bargain; where there is also a mountain of grated Parmesan cheese, and the people dwelling thereon do nothing else but make macaroni and other delicacies which they boil in capon broth which they afterwards throw down to those who choose to catch them: and nearby flows a river of white wine, the best ever tasted, without a drop of water in it."

"Indeed," exclaimed Calandrino, "that must be a delightful country. But tell me, what becomes of the capons after they are boiled?" "The people," replied Maso, "eat them." "Were you ever there?" asked Calandrino. "A thousand times, at least," replied Maso. "And how many miles away is this land?" Calandrino questioned. "In truth, beyond number," quoth Maso. "Then, it must be further off than Abruzzi." "But a trifle," replied Maso.

Calandrino observing that Maso had told this tale with a grave countenance, considered the matter to be true, wherefore he uttered with simplicity, "Believe me, sir, it is too great a journey for me, else I should like to go and see them make this macaroni. But allow me to ask, sir, are any of the precious stones you were just speaking of in that country?" Maso replied, "Indeed there are two kinds to be found there, both possessing special virtues. One of these, coming from Montisci, makes excellent mill-stones, from which arises the saying, that grace comes from God and mill-stones from Montisci. Such plenty is there of these mill-stones, and yet so lightly esteemed among us as emeralds are with them, of which there are whole mountains of them shining resplendently at midnight. They set these stones in rings and send them to the great Sultan, who gives them whatever price they ask. The other is a stone which our lapidaries call the Heliotrope, which has the virtue of rendering the one who carries it invisible." "That is wonderful," said Calandrino. "And where else may this stone be found?" To which Maso replied, "Frequently on our plains of Mugnone." Quoth Calandrino, "Of what size and color is this stone?" And Maso replied, "Of various sizes, but invariably black."

Calandrino, memorizing this information, and pretending urgent business, he departed, determining to seek for this stone. But first he resolved to consult with his two friends, whom he sought the entire morning. Recollecting that they were working at a convent at Faenza, he ran to them in haste and said to them, "If you will follow my advice, we will become the richest men in all of Florence, for I have learned from a trustworthy person that there can be found a stone in Mugnone which renders those who carry it invisible. If you will come with me, we will seek for it before any one else finds it. We are certain to find it, because I know its description; and once we have it, we have but to put it in our pockets and go to the bankers and help ourselves to all the money we please. No one will see us, since we shall be invisible, and thus we shall become rich without toiling all our lives in painting these church walls." Bruno and Buffalmacco on hearing this, suppressed their laughter and looked at each other with surprise, and greatly commended Calandrino's advice. When Buffalmacco asked the name of the stone, Calandrino, who had a dull memory, had forgotten it, and therefore said, "What do we need its name so long as we are assured of its virtues. Let us go off in search of it without delay." "What is its shape?" asked Bruno. "They have various shapes, but always black, thus in picking all the black stones, we shall find the right one. Let us hasten then."

"Quite right," Bruno agreed, "but this is not a fit time for our quest, for the sun is now hot and shines so brightly, that all the black stones will appear white. Besides there are many people on the plain who, seeing us occupied in that manner, may guess the reason and find the stone before we do, and our labour will then have been in vain. We had therefore better go in the morning when colours can more easily be distinguished, and a holiday would be best, for then there will be no people about to see us. They then and there agreed to seek the stone the ensuing Sunday morning. Meantime, Calandrino begged them to keep the matter secret, as it had been imparted to him in strict confidence. Then he also told them of the wonders he had heard about the land of Bengodi, assuring them solemnly that it was all true.

When Calandrino had departed, the other two agreed on a course of action. Calandrino waited impatiently for Sunday, when he arose and called upon his companions. The three went out through the Gate of St. Gallo and continued until they came to the plain of Mugnone where they began to hunt for the stone. Calandrino stole on before the other two and looking carefully about him, picked up every stone that looked black and put them into his pockets. He then tucked up his apron with a belt thus forming it into a sack and began filling it with stones. Buffalmacco and Bruno observing that Calandrino was now quite loaded, and the dinner hour now approaching, one said to the other, "Where is Calandrino?" "I do not know," quoth Buffalmacco, "though I saw him here just now." "Then," said Bruno, "he must have gone home to dinner and left us here to make fools of ourselves picking black stones." "He has served us right," said Buffalmacco, "for permitting ourselves to be duped. Who but ourselves could believe in such stones?" Calandrino, hearing them speak thus while he stood near them, imagined that he had found the true stone, and was, by its virtue, invisible. He was overjoyed, and resolved to return home, leaving his friends to follow if so they would. Buffalmacco perceiving his intent, said to Bruno, "Why stay any longer? Let us also go back." To which Bruno replied, "Yes, let us return, but I vow Calandrino shall play no more tricks on me; and were I now as near to him as I was this morning, I would give him such a knock on the heel with this stone that he would have cause to remember it." And while still speaking, he struck him a blow on the heel; and though it was painful, Calandrino maintained his silence and his pace. Buffalmacco then selecting another stone, said to Bruno, "And I would give him one on the back with this." Then he pelted Calandrino severely. This they kept doing all the way to the gate of San Gallo where they threw away the rest of their stones and acquainted the guards with their secret, who were amused at it and feigned not to see Calandrino as he passed them. Without tarrying he went on to his house which was near the mills. Fortune so favoured this jest, that as he passed through the city no one paused to speak to him, as everybody was then at dinner. Sinking under his burden, Calandrino arrived home and met his wife standing at the top of the stairs, who, being provoked at his long absence, exclaimed angrily, "The devil must have possessed you not to come home till everyone has dined." When Calandrino heard this, he realised that he was not invisible to his wife, and in a fit of rage he cried, "Thou wretched woman, thou hast undone me. But I will be revenged." Ridding himself of his stones, he ran at her, seized her by the hair and beat her unmercifully. Meantime, Bruno and Buffalmacco, having laughed with the guards at the gate, followed Calandrino to his house; and arriving at the door, heard the disturbance. They called out to Calandrino who, looking out of the window, asked them to come up. This they did, seeming the while greatly surprised; and seeing the floor strewn with stones, his bruised wife sitting in one corner, and he himself exhausted in another, they said, "How now, Calandrino, art thou building a house, that thou hast provided so many stones? And what has happened to you, madame? You are so dishevelled?" Calandrino, vexed and fatigued, could speak no word. Whereupon Buffalmacco continued, "Calandrino, if you were angry with any one, you ought not to have mocked your friends as you have done today, in leaving us out on the plains like a couple of fools, where you left us without saying a word. But rest assured, you shall never serve us in this fashion again." Somewhat recovered, Calandrino replied, "My friends, do not be offended, the case is very different from what you imagine. I found the precious stone. When you first asked each other what had become of me, I was very near; and when I perceived that you did not see me, I walked before you;" and he related all that had happened, adding, "As I came through the gates, I saw you standing with the guards who, by virtue of the stone in my possession, did not molest me. And in the streets I met many friends who are in the habit of stopping me, yet none saw me. At length, coming home, I met this fiend of a woman who saw me at once, because, as you well know, women have a way of making things lose their virtue. So that I who might have been the happiest man in Florence, am now the most unfortunate. And that is why I beat her and would gladly tear her to pieces." When Buffalmacco and Bruno had heard this, they were ready to burst with laughter. But when they saw him try to beat his wife again, they interfered, protesting that his wife was not to blame but rather he who should have commanded her to keep out of his presence all that day; and that doubtless Providence had deprived him of this good fortune for deceiving his friends and not allowing them to share in the discovery of the stone. With great difficulty they finally reconciled him to his wife, and leaving him yet grief stricken for his loss, they departed.

❊ ❊ ❊

GIOVAN-FRANCESCO STRAPAROLA
(Sixteenth Century)

STRAPAROLA was born at Caravaggio, and is ranked among the Venetian writers, having chiefly resided and composed his works at Venice. He is to be esteemed rather a useful than a happy novelist, inasmuch as he furnished a large collection of stories for the benefit of his successors. Together with Boccaccio, he may be considered the great storehouse from which the French, and occasionally English, dramatists have drawn their subjects. His *Piacevoli Notti* was completed and published at Venice in 1554.

The present version of *The Usurer's Will* is translated by Thomas Roscoe, and reprinted from his *Italian Novelists*, London, no date. The story has no title in the original.

THE USURER'S WILL
(From *Piacevoli Notti*, 10th Night, Novel 4)

IN Como, a little city of Lombardy not very far from Milan, there once dwelt a citizen of the name of Andrigetto da Sabbia, whose immense possessions, surpassing those of any other individual, did not, however, prevent him from adding to them by every means in his power. Being perfectly secure against the attacks of conscience in all his dealings, he was never known to suffer remorse for the most unjustifiable actions. He was in the habit of disposing of the produce of his large estates to the poorer citizens and peasantry, instead of selling it to merchants and others who could command ready money; not from any charitable motives, but in order to obtain possession of their little remaining property, still uniting field after field to the great possessions he had already acquired. It happened that so great a scarcity began to prevail in the city and its vicinity, that many persons actually perished of want, while numbers had recourse to our old usurer for assistance, to whom, from the urgent pressure of circumstances, they were compelled to make over, in return for the necessaries of life, such interest as they might possess either in houses or lands. The concourse of people in his neighbourhood was so great as almost to resemble a jubilee or a public fair. Now there was a certain notary, Tonisto Raspante by name, a most notorious and wily practitioner of his art, and more successful than any other of his brethren in emptying the pockets of the poor villagers. He had still, however, so much regard for an ancient law in Como relating to usurious contracts, which required the money lent to be counted in the presence of proper witnesses, as to refuse to draw up such instruments as Andrigetto often directed him to prepare, observing that they were altogether against the form of the statute, and he would not venture to risk the penalty. But such were the overbearing manners of the old miser, and so great was his authority in the city, that sometimes threatening him with ruin, and at other times bribing him to his purpose, he compelled the attorney to obey his commands. The time for confessing himself being at hand, before presenting himself at the confessional, Andrigetto took care to send to the priest an excellent dinner, with as much of the finest cloth as would make a pair of hose for himself and his servant, announcing at the same time his intention to confess on the ensuing day, when he thought that he was sure of meeting with a favourable hearing. The priest undertook with pleasure the task of absolving from his sins so eminent and rich a citizen, and received his penitent with the utmost cordiality. Andrigetto fell on his knees before his spiritual father, accusing himself with very little ceremony of various sins and errors, not forgetting his usurious and illegal contracts, all which he recounted in the most minute manner. The priest, who had sense enough to perceive the enormous nature of his offences, conceiving himself bound to make some representations on the subject, ventured certain gentle hints on the impropriety of their repetition, and in the meanwhile strongly recommending restitution to the injured parties. Instead of taking this in good part, Andrigetto turned very sharply round upon his confessor, observing that he was at a loss to understand what he meant, and that he had better go, and return no more until he had learned how to confess persons in a more rational manner. The priest owing his preferment in a great measure to Andrigetto, and fearful lest he might lose his favour altogether, began to retract as well as he could, gave him absolution, and then imposing as slight a penance as possible, received a florin for his reward, after which Andrigetto took his leave in very excellent spirits.

Not long after this interview, our old usurer, while rejoicing in this absolution from all his sins, fell ill of a mortal distemper, and the physicians shortly despaired of his life. His friends and relatives having gathered round his bed, took the liberty of suggesting that it was now time to think of a sincere confession, to receive his last spiritual consolation, and make a final arrangement of his affairs, like a good Catholic and a Christian. But the old gentleman, who had hitherto devoted all his thoughts and exertions, both day and night, to the hoarding of his wealth, instead of being at all impressed by the awfulness of his situation, only replied with great levity to their arguments, still amusing himself with arranging the most trifling concerns, and evincing not the least uneasiness at his approaching end. After long entreaties and persuasions, he was at last prevailed upon to comply with their request, and agreed to summon to his assistance his old agent, Tonisto Raspante the notary, and Father Neofito, his confessor.

On the arrival of these personages, they addressed the patient with a cheerful countenance, telling him to keep up his spirits, for that with God's help he would soon be a sound man again. Andrigetto only replied that he feared he was too far gone for that, and that he had perhaps better lose no time in first settling his worldly affairs and then arranging his ghostly concerns with his confessor. But the good priest, exhorting and comforting him to the best of his ability, advised him first of all to place his sole trust in the Lord, humbly submitting himself to His will, as the safest means of obtaining a restoration to health. To this, however, Andrigetto replied only by ordering seven respectable men to be called in as witnesses of his nuncupative last will and testament. These individuals having been successively presented to the patient, and taken their seats, he proceeded to inquire from his friend Tonisto the very lowest charge which he was in the habit of making for penning a will. "According to the strict rules of the profession," replied Tonisto, "it is only a florin; but in general the amount is decided by the feelings of the testator." "Well, well, then," cried the patient, "take two florins, and set down what I tell you." The notary having invoked the divine name, drew out the preliminaries in the usual manner, bequeathing the body of the testator to the earth and his soul to the hands of God who gave it, with humble thanks for the many favours vouchsafed by Him to His unworthy creature. This exordium being read to Andrigetto, he flew into a violent rage, and commanded the notary to write down nothing but his own words, which he dictated as follows: "I, Andrigetto di Valsabbia, being of sound mind, though infirm of body, do hereby declare this to be my last will and testament: I give and bequeath my soul into the hands of the great Satan, the prince of devils." Hearing these words, the witnesses stood aghast; Raspante's quill started from the paper, and, in evident horror and perturbation, he stopped. Looking the testator very earnestly in the face, he interposed: "Ah! Messer Andrigetto, these are the words of a madman!" "How!" exclaimed Andrigetto, in a violent passion, "what do you mean? How dare you stop? Write word for word as I direct you, and nothing more, or you shall never be paid for a will of mine: proceed, I tell you!" Struck with the greatest horror and surprise, his friends attempted to remonstrate with him, lamenting that he should make use of language so opposite to his usual good sense, language which only madmen or blasphemers could be capable of using on such a subject and in so awful a situation as his. "Desist, then," they continued, "for

Heaven's sake, and consult your honour and the safety of your poor soul.
Think of the scandal such a proceeding would bring upon your family,
if you, who were esteemed so prudent and so wise, were to make yourself
an example of all that is perfidious, ungrateful, and impious towards
Heaven."

But Andrigetto paid no further attention to their reproaches than by
observing that his business was with his attorney, and that as he had not
yet finished his will, they had better take care what they were about; on
which there was soon a respectful silence throughout the room. He then
turned towards his attorney, requesting to know, in a voice of suppressed
passion, whether he was prepared to go on, as he had already offered to
pay double the usual charge for his labours. Apprehensive that Andrigetto might expire before he had made a disposition of his property, the
notary promised to do as he was required, more especially when he heard
the patient beginning to hiccup with the violence of his emotions; so that
he was compelled to make a solemn vow to fulfil his client's instructions.

"Item," continued Andrigetto, "I hereby bequeath the wretched soul
of my wicked agent, Tonisto Raspante, to the great Satan, in order that
it may keep company with mine when it leaves this world, as it shortly
must." "The Lord have mercy on me!" cried the poor attorney, shocked
at the deep solemnity with which these last words were uttered; "the
Lord have mercy on my soul!" and the pen dropped from his hand.
"Recall," he continued, "my honoured patron, recall those wicked words;
do anything but destroy my eternal interests, my last, my dearest hopes."
"Go on, you rogue!" cried the testator, "and do not venture to interrupt
me again; do not tell me about your soul. You have your pay, and that
is enough; so proceed quickly as I shall direct you. I leave my said attorney's soul to the devil, for this reason, that if he had not consented to
draw up so many false and usurious contracts, but had driven me from
his presence as soon as I proposed them, I should not now find myself
reduced to the sad extremity of leaving both our souls to the king of hell,
owing entirely to his shameful cupidity and want of common honesty."
The attorney, though trembling at the name of the king of hell, yet
fearful lest his patron might enter into further particulars far from
creditable to him, wrote as he was commanded.

"Item," continued the patient, "I bequeath the soul of Father Neofito,
my confessor, into the claws of Lucifer; aye, to thirty thousand pair of
devils." "Stop, Messer Andrigetto, pray stop," cried the priest; "and do
not think of applying those dreadful words to me. You ought to put
your trust in the Lord, in the Lord Jesus, whose mercies always abound,
who came to save sinners, and is still inviting them, night and day, to
repentance. He died for our sins, and for your sins, Messer Andrigetto;
you have only to beseech pardon, and all will yet be well. The road is
still open to restitution; hasten to make restitution, then; for the Lord

does not wish the death of a sinner. You have great wealth; remember the Church; you will have masses said for your soul, and may yet sit in the seats of paradise." "Oh, thou wicked and most wretched priest!" retorted the patient, "by thy vile avarice and simony thou hast helped thine own soul, as well as mine, into the pit of perdition. And dost thou now think of advising me to repent? Confusion on thy villainy! Write, notary, that I bequeath his soul to the very centre of the place of torments; for had it not been for his bold and shameless conduct in absolving me from my numerous and repented offences, I should not now find myself in the strange predicament in which I am placed. What! does the rogue think it would be now just to restore my evil-gotten gains, and thus leave my poor family destitute? No, no; I am not quite such a fool as to do that; so please to go on. Item, To my dear lady Felicia I leave my pretty farm, situated in the district of Comacchio, in order to supply herself with the elegancies of life, and occasionally treat her lovers as she has been hitherto in the habit of doing, thus preparing the way further to oblige me with her company in the other world, sharing with us the torments of eternity. The remainder of my property, as well personal as real, with all future interest and proceeds accruing thereon, I leave to my two legitimate and beloved sons, Commodo and Torquato, on condition that they give nothing for a single mass to be said for the soul of the deceased, but that they feast, swear, game, and fight, to the best of their ability, in order that they may the sooner waste their substance so wickedly acquired, until, driven to despair, they may as speedily as possible hang themselves. And this I declare to be my last will and testament, as witnesseth all present, not forgetting my attorney." Having signed this instrument and put his seal to it, Andrigetto turned away his face, and uttering a terrific howl, finally surrendered his impenitent soul to Pluto.

❄ ❄ ❄

ANTON-FRANCESCO GRAZZINI

(1503-1583)

GRAZZINI was born at Florence of a well-to-do family. He was brought up to the medical profession which he soon abandoned for the more agreeable pursuit of letters. Grazzini possessed a strange and whimsical talent, and a remarkably lively disposition runs through his whole style and manner. His principal works are *La Cene,* a collection of stories in the manner of Boccaccio. In *The Jealous Wife* we have an example of his copious and flexible style which carries with it the force and freshness of popular Tuscan speech.

The present version is translated by Thomas Roscoe, and reprinted from his *Italian Novelists*, London, no date. The story has no title in the original.

THE JEALOUS WIFE
(From *La Cene*, 1st Evening, Novel 5)

IN the annals of Pisa is found the name of Guglielmo Grimaldi, who came to settle in Pisa from the confines of Genoa. He was then a youth of about two-and-twenty, with very few resources, and living in a hired apartment; yet, with saving habits and some ability, he was at length enabled to lend little sums of money upon usury. And in this way, by hoarding his gains while he spent little, he became in no very long time a rich man, without losing his desire of adding to his wealth. He lived alone, and, with the most unremitting diligence and secrecy, amassed and concealed his increasing stores, until growing old at length, he found himself in possession of thousands, of which he would not have parted with a single crown to save the life of a friend or to redeem the whole world from eternal punishment. On this account he was detested by all his fellow-citizens, and paid dearly enough for it in the end. Having one evening supped out with some of his miserly acquaintance, he was returning late to his own house when he was assaulted by an unknown hand, and feeling himself wounded in the breast, he cried out and fled for help. Just at this moment came on a terrific storm of hail and wind and thunder, which increased his distress and compelled him to look out for shelter. Becoming faint from the loss of blood, he ran into the first house that he found open, belonging to one Fazio, a goldsmith, attracted by the blaze of a large fire at which he, the said Fazio, was making chemical experiments, having for some time past devoted the whole of his earnings to these pursuits, attempting to convert the dull metals of lead and tin into fine silver or gold. For this purpose had he now made so glorious an illumination that he was compelled to open the door to admit air while he melted down his metals; but hearing the sound of footsteps, he turned round, and beheld Guglielmo Grimaldi, the miser. "What are you doing here, friend," he inquired, "at such an hour and in such a night as this?" "Alas!" answered the miser, "I am ill; I have been attacked and wounded; I know not why nor by whom;" and he had no sooner uttered these words, than he sat down and died upon the spot.

Fazio was greatly surprised and alarmed on beholding him fall dead at his feet, and opening his bosom to receive air, he tried to recall him to life, believing at first that the poor miser was dying of pure exhaustion and inanition by denying himself food. But on discovering the wound in his breast, and finding that his pulse no longer beat, he concluded that his visitor had really departed this life. Running to the door, he was about to alarm the neighbourhood, when hearing the terrific raging of the storm, he again drew back and sought refuge in his house. Now his wife Pippa and twin boys happened just at this time to be on a visit to his father-in-law, who was likewise about to take his leave of the world. Instead of calling a physician, then, he suddenly changed his measures and closed the door; examining next the body of the deceased, he found only four florins in his purse. Then, hid in a heap of old rags, he discovered a great bunch of keys, which from their appearance belonged to the house and chambers, the chests and strong boxes, of the miser, who, if report were true, had hoarded up immense wealth, especially in ready cash, secured in his own house.

The moment the idea flashed across Fazio's mind, being of a keen and penetrating genius, he determined to turn it to his own account, and to aim a bold stroke at fortune, whatever were the event. "Why not hasten," he said, "to his stronghold at once? I am sure to find it in his house, without a living creature near to say me nay. Why not transport it quietly, I say, into my own dwelling? I think no one will hinder me, such a night as it is, thundering as if the sky would fall! Besides, it is past midnight, and every living soul is either sheltering or asleep. I am alone here, too, and the assassin of the poor miser must by this time, I think, have taken to flight, without stopping to see where he took refuge. So, if I can only keep my own counsel, who will ever suspect that Grimaldi the miser ran into my house thus grievously wounded and died? This is surely, then, an unlooked-for blessing; and were I to go about telling the real truth, who knows whether I should be believed? People might say I had robbed and murdered him, and I should infallibly be taken and put to the question; and how should I be able to clear myself? I dread to encounter the ministers of justice, for most probably I should never come alive out of their hands. What, therefore, will be the best? Why, Fortune is said to aid the bold; bold, then, will I be, and try to rescue myself at once from a lot of penury and pain." Saying these words, he thrust the keys into his bosom, and throwing a fur cloak over his shoulders, his face half buried in a huge slouched hat, he issued forth with a dark lantern in his hand, offering his bosom to the pelting of the pitiless storm with a secure and joyous air. Arriving at the miser's house, that stood at no great distance, he seized two of the largest keys, and soon made good his entrance; then advancing at once to the most secret chamber he could find, he gained admittance by double keys, and beheld a large chest, which after much difficulty he succeeded in opening. This contained others which were equally well secured, and which he had still more difficulty in unlocking; but what treasures opened upon his view when his task was completed! One contained all kinds of gold rings, chains, and jewels, with other ornaments, the most massy and valuable in their nature. In another were bags almost bursting with gold ducats, all regularly numbered and parcelled. Fazio, overpowered with joy, relinquished the bags filled with chains and jewels, saying, "As these may perhaps be recognised, I will stick to the solid gold." Having secured the last, then, under his arm, he departed with the keys in his belt towards his own house, without meeting a single person by the way; such were the pealing thunders and the flashes of terrific light which redoubled the terrors of the storm. Fazio, however, reached his house, and having secured the treasure, changed his dress; and being stout and active, he took the dead body of the miser in his arms, and bore it into his cellar. There he proceeded to make in the floor an excavation sufficiently large to contain his remains, into which, dressed exactly as he was, with the keys of all his treasures in his pocket, Fazio now thrust the body at least six feet below the earth, and covering it up, he fixed the whole firmly down with certain pieces of lime and tiles, in such a way that no one could perceive the place had been at all disturbed. Having thus disposed of the old miser, he proceeded very leisurely to count over the bags of money to which he had thus become the heir; and such was the sudden blaze of gold that opened on his eyes, that it was with difficulty he could support the sight. Each bag contained exactly three thousand ducats, as it had been marked which he deposited in a large chest of drawers secured by a secret lock. His next care was to consume the trunk and bags in which he had brought the treasure in the great fire prepared for the transmutation of his metals; and to these he added his crucibles, his bellows, and his base metals, having no further use for them; and having thus completed his labours, he went to rest.

By this time the storm had abated, and it was already daybreak; Fazio, therefore, continued to sleep and recruit his exhausted strength until near vespers. He then rose and went as far as the piazza and upon the Exchange, in order to learn whether there were any reports yet afloat in regard to the disappearance of the deceased, but he heard nothing either that day or the following. On the third day, however, the miser being no longer seen about his usual affairs, people began to make remarks, more especially when they saw his house shut up, suspecting some evil must have befallen him. Several of his friends with whom he had last been in company then made their appearance relating everything they knew; but no further intelligence could in any way be elicited. Upon this the court issued an order that his dwelling should be forcibly entered, where everything was found apparently as he had left it, to the surprise of the spectators, and the whole of his property was taken possession of in the name of the government. Books, writings, jewels, and furniture, everything was found as it ought to be, in such a way as to preclude the idea of any attempt at robbery. Advertisements, however, were immediately issued, offering high rewards for the production of his person, either dead or alive. All inquiries were in vain; and though the subject excited considerable noise and alarm, nothing whatever transpired. At the end of three months the government, being at war with Genoa, and no relatives advancing their claims, the whole of Grimaldi's goods were confiscated for the use of the state; but it was considered an extraordinary circumstance that there was no appearance of ready money.

Fazio in the meanwhile continued quiet and unmolested, rejoiced to perceive how well the affair went off, and leading a happy life with his wife and family, who were now returned to him. To them he did not venture to breathe a syllable of his good fortune; and had he fortunately persisted in this resolution he would have avoided the utter downfall and ruin of his family. For the affair had already begun to be forgotten, gradually dying away for ever, and Fazio had given out that he was about to take a journey into France for the purpose of disposing of several bars of silver which he had recently made; a report ridiculed by many who were aware that he had already thrown away his time, his labour, and money in forging the precious metals, while his friends strongly dissuaded him from leaving the place, observing that he might carry on his experiments at Pisa as well as at Paris. But our goldsmith had adopted his plan very well knowing that he had plenty of good silver to dispose of; though, pretending that he had not money enough for his journey, he mortgaged a little farm for one hundred florins, half of which he took with him, and left the other half for his wife. He then took his passage in a vessel to Marseilles, deaf to all the tears and entreaties of his wife, who besought him not to throw away the last of their little substance, and abandon her and her little ones to penury and to woe. "When," she said, "were we happier or better than when you pursued your own trade, bringing us daily enough for all our wants? Leave us not, then, to solitude and despair!" Fazio, tenderly soothing her, promised on his return to throw such a golden harvest into her lap as would console her for all past sufferings; but still in vain. "For," she she continued, "if all this fine silver really exists, it will surely be as valuable here as in France; but I fear you want to desert us for ever; and when once these fifty ducats are spent, what will become of me, wretch that I am? Alas! must I go begging with these helpless little ones? Must I lose you, and be left to solitude and tears?" Her husband, who loved her most affectionately, unable to behold her affliction, determined to acquaint her with his good fortune, and kissing her tenderly, he took her one day after dinner into the chamber where he had concealed his newly acquired wealth, and related to her the particulars that had occurred. He then exhibited the whole of the riches he possessed, bags of ducats, silver and gold without end; and such was the astonishment and delight of his now happy wife, that she flung her arms in an ecstasy of pleasure round his neck, and weeping, begged forgiveness for all the complaints and reproaches she had used. Insisting upon her promise of secrecy, Fazio then acquainted her with his future plans, explaining how shortly he meant to return to her, and what a joyful and uninterrupted course of happiness would thenceforward be theirs. She no longer objected to his departure; but taking a tender farewell, bade him to think of her, and hasten as soon as possible his return.

The next morning, accordingly, having well secured the valuable metals he was taking along with him, double-locked and barred, and leaving a large portion of his treasures with his wife, he went on board, accompanied by the regrets and reproaches of all his friends, in which, his wife, the better to conceal her feelings, affected to join. Indeed, the whole city united in ridiculing his enterprise, and some who had known him in his better days expressed their opinion that he ought to be taken care of, for that he was certainly inclined to run mad. Others said that they had long been aware what would be the consequence, and he would very soon share the fate of his mad predecessors in the accursed art of alchemy, that ruined instead of enriching its followers. In spite of all, however, Fazio set sail, and with prosperous breezes soon arrived at Marseilles, taking care by the way to throw the whole of his chemical apparatus into the sea, reserving only the more valuable articles he had obtained from the miser's house, with which he landed, and proceeded with the carriers as far as Lyons. In a few days after he emptied the contents of his money-bags, depositing a large sum at one of the first banks, for which he received letters of exchange on Pisa, some at the house of Lanfranchi, and others at that of Gualandi; after which he sat down to write to his wife, acquainting her that he had disposed of his silver, and intended shortly to return to Pisa. This letter the lady showed to her father, as well as to the rest of Fazio's friends and relations, some of whom expressed themselves much surprised, while others declared that he was a ruined man, the truth of which would speedily appear. Soon after, having received his letters of credit, Fazio left Lyons for Marseilles, and thence taking ship for Leghorn, he had the pleasure in a short time of again beholding his wife and children. Embracing them again and again, he declared that he had succeeded beyond his utmost expectations, while the tidings quickly spread among his acquaintance that he had returned home rich with the products of his metals. He lost no time in presenting his letters of credit, on which he received nine thousand gold ducats, which were immediately sent to his house, exciting the joy and congratulations of all his relatives and friends.

Thus finding himself one of the richest men in his trade, and with the credit of having realised his fortune by his own ingenious experiments, Fazio began to think of living in a more splendid manner, and of sharing some of his happiness with his friends. In the first place, therefore, he bought an estate, and then a handsome house, besides making several other rich purchases; and investing his money in such advantageous concerns as offered, he soon assumed the manners and establishment of a prince. He added to the number of his domestics, and set up two equipages, the one for himself and the other for his lady; his sons were distinguished for the richness of their apparel; and he continued to live on the happiest terms with his wife, enjoying together the luxuries and pleasures which they had at command. Pippa, to whom such a life was wholly new, became somewhat vain of the change, and was in the habit of inviting her acquaintance to witness it, among whom was an old lady with her fair daughter, whom she invited to come and stay some time with her. Fazio, to whom she said that they would be of use to her in a variety of ways, was induced to give his consent, happy to perceive that they assisted his wife in the cares of her establishment, and that they all lived on the best terms together.

But Fortune, the constant enemy of any long-continued enjoyment and content, was preparing to change the colour of their fate, and turn this summer sweetness and glory of their days into the chilling winter of sorrow and despair. For it was the cruel lot of Fazio to become enamoured of the young charms of the fair Maddelena, the daughter of their guest; and such was his continued and violent passion, that he at length succeeded, by the most consummate art, in leading her from the paths of innocence. Their intercourse continued for some time unknown to his poor wife, and he conferred on his unhappy victim the most lavish proofs of his regard. But as they became bolder with impunity, the unsuspicious Pippa could not at length fail to be aware of the truth, and displayed the indignation of her feelings on the subject in no very gentle terms. She reproached her fair guest with still more bitterness, and one day took occasion, in Fazio's absence, to drive her with the utmost fury and opprobrium from her house. Fazio, on returning home, was greatly incensed at these proceedings, and continued with the same infatuation to lavish the same favours upon the young Maddelena as before. On this account scenes of the most cruel and distressing nature were continually occurring between him and his wife; the demon of jealousy had taken possession of her bosom, and family peace and love were thenceforward banished alike from their bed and board. It was in vain that Fazio now attempted to soothe or to subdue her irritated feelings. She spurned his divided affection, and she met his threats with still more violent passion, treating them with merited indignation and contempt. In order to avoid these reproaches, her husband went to one of his villas at some distance, whither he invited his young mistress, and continued to lead the same abandoned course of life, while his wife remained plunged in the profoundest wretchedness and despair. These feelings, however, were soon absorbed in rage and jealousy, when she found after some months that her husband did not return, and was lavishing still greater proofs of tenderness and favour upon her rival. Thus dwelling with ceaseless anxiety and pain upon one hateful idea, the sense of her wrongs became too great to bear, and in a short time she came to the resolution of accusing her faithless and abandoned husband to the state, by revealing the transaction which had led to his sudden elevation and prosperity. And this appearing the only resource she had left to revenge her injuries upon the authors of them, without further warning or consultation she proceeded alone to consult a magistrate, who, holding an office similar to that of the Council of Eight in our own city, took down her deposition, comprehending everything she knew relative to the affairs of her husband. She, moreover, directed them to the exact spot where the remains of the miser had been buried in the cellar of their former house, and where the officers of justice accordingly found them. Then, still retaining her in custody, the magistrate despatched the captain of the band to the residence of her husband, where they found him enjoying himself in the society of his fair Maddelena. Immediately seizing him as a prisoner of the state, they conducted him back to Pisa, overwhelmed with the most abject despair; and when brought up for examination he refused to utter a syllable. But his wife being ordered to appear against him, he cried out with a loud voice, at the sight of her, "This is justice, indeed!" and then turning towards her, he added, "My too great affection for you has brought me to this;" and taking one of the magistrates aside, he freely revealed to him the truth of the affair, exactly as it had occurred. With one accord, however, the whole Council refused to give credit to the story, asserting that there was every appearance of his having himself robbed and murdered the unfortunate Guglielmo, and threatening instantly to put him to the torture if he did not confess. This, upon his maintaining his own story, they proceeded to do, and by dint of repeated trials they at length compelled him to say what they pleased, and afterwards proceeded to sentence him to be broken alive upon the wheel, while the state appropriated the whole of his possessions. The remains of the miser, Grimaldi, were then ordered to be removed and interred in sacred ground; the beautiful Maddelena and her mother were driven with ignominy from the villa to their former abode, and the establishment of Fazio was completely broken up; his wife, with her family and domestics, being compelled to take refuge wherever they could. On being released from court, where she had appeared as evidence against her own husband, the wretched Pippa returned home, but to a home desolate and deserted by all but her children. In the agony of her grief, she wept, she raved, she tore her hair, too late perceiving, with feelings of remorse, the grievous error she had committed.

The tidings spread rapidly throughout all Pisa, and the people joined in expressing their astonishment, no less at the supposed enormity and deceit of which Fazio was accused, than at the strange treachery and ingratitude of his wife. Even her own relatives and friends, who assisted her, unanimously agreed in condemning her conduct, reproaching her bitterly for the degradation and ruin which she had brought upon her family, besides the inhumanity of having thus betrayed her husband to a painful and ignominious death. Having said this, they left her weeping bitterly and overpowered with intolerable remorse. On the ensuing day the wretched Fazio was led forth, and drawn through the streets of Pisa on a sledge, and after being thus exhibited to the people, he was conducted to the place of execution. There, having been first broken upon the wheel, he was executed in the presence of the people, and left on the same spot, by way of example, during the rest of the day.

The tidings of this terrific scene coming to the ears of his wife, whom he had continued cursing and reviling to his latest hour, in a fit of desperation she resolved to take vengeance upon herself. About dinner-time, then, there being few people to observe her, she seized her two little boys by the hand, and led them, weeping, towards the great square, the scene of the execution, while such as met her by the way only bestowed their maledictions on her, and allowed her to pass on. When she arrived at the foot of the platform where the body lay, few spectators being present, she proceeded, still weeping bitterly, to ascend the steps of the platform, with the children along with her, no one around offering the least resistance. There, affecting to lament over the wretched fate of her husband, she was sternly and severely upbraided by all who stood near, who said aloud, "See how she can weep now that it is done! It is her own work; she would have it so; and let her therefore despair!" The wretched wife then tearing her hair, and striking her lovely face and bosom with her clenched hands, while she pressed her burning lips to the cold features of her husband, next bade her little boys kneel down to kiss their father; at which sight the surrounding spectators, forgetting their anger, suddenly burst into tears. But their distracted mother, drawing a knife from her bosom, with remorseless fury hastily plunged it into the breasts of her sons, and before the people were prepared to wrest the deadly weapon from her hand, she had already turned it against herself, and fallen upon the lifeless bodies of her husband and her children.

* * *

GIOVANBATTISTA GIRALDI CINTHIO
(1504-1573)

CINTHIO was born at Ferrara of noble lineage, and flourished during the sway of Ercole da Este II., Duke of Ferrara whom he served as secretary. Cinthio was one of the most voluminous novelists of his century, his famous work being the *Hecatomithi*, or Hundred

Fables, first published in 1565. In spite of a laboured and painfully involved style, he is yet a fine and powerful writer. He threw energy and passion into his narratives that usually treated some terrific subject contrived to awaken a strong dramatic interest.

Love Triumphant, which follows, is a rare example of connubial fidelity under distressing circumstances. Curiously enough, the strategem of procuring the husband's liberty, has been successfully achieved in actual life, one memorable instance being that of the Earl of Nithsdale, who by this ruse escaped from the Tower in 1716.

The present version is translated by Thomas Roscoe, and reprinted from his *Italian Novelists*, London, no date. The story has no title in the original.

LOVE TRIUMPHANT
(From *Hecatomithi*, 5th Decade, Novel 4)

AT the period when the celebrated Giovanni Trivulzi was appointed by the king of France governor of Milan, the capital city of Lombardy, a certain noble youth resided there of the name of Giovanni Panigarola, whose bold and fiery temper involved him in frequent disputes, both with the soldiers and the citizens, to the no slight interruption of the public peace. This unruly disposition having more than once caused him to be brought before the governor at the instance of several individuals with whom he had been engaged, he would probably have incurred the punishment due to his indiscretion, had not the venerable Trivulzi been more desirous of reforming offenders than of punishing them. Discharging him merely with a severe reprimand, out of regard to the feelings of the youth's family and friends, he trusted that he should hear of him no more. But this unfortunately was not the case; the perverse and ungrateful youth still pursuing the same perilous career in spite of the entreaties and reproaches of his best friends. Even his union with a pleasing and accomplished young lady of Lampognani, named Filippa, failed to convince him of the folly of his conduct: her tenderness and anxiety were lavished upon him in vain, and she lived in daily expectation of hearing of some calamitous event. Though he always treated her with the utmost kindness and affection, she would rather have been herself the victim of his quarrelsome and unhappy disposition, than have heard of his indulging it at the expense of others, and at the imminent risk of his own life. Unable to support this incessant anxiety, the fond Filippa would frequently conjure him to abstain from thus wantonly hazarding his reputation and her own repose, for the sake of encouraging so idle and dangerous a propensity, which cost her so many tears. Then throwing her fair arms around him, she declared that she could not long live under the torments she endured on his behalf, being in hourly dread of beholding him borne homewards a lifeless corpse. "I had rather," she exclaimed, "that you would at once pierce my bosom with your sword than listen to the sad accounts I am daily expecting to hear of you; so derogatory to your own honour and the name you bear, and frequently, I fear, so unjust towards the objects of your resentment. I entreat you, therefore, by our long attachment, by all my unutterable love and devotion to you, that, if you have any pity or gentleness in your nature, you will henceforth become more reasonable, and avoiding occasions of embroiling yourself with others, consent to lead the blameless and honourable life for which your abilities and your connections are in every way so well calculated to qualify you. Then, and then only, shall I consider myself truly happy, blest with your society, and enjoying the honour and respectability of your name."

Whilst listening to the kind and judicious words of her he loved, Giovanni sincerely promised reformation, and believed that he could renounce all his errors, and never more give her reason to complain. But when he was again exposed to temptations, when his boon companions repeatedly invited him, and, half mad with wine, he received imaginary insults from the guests, borne away by the force of his habitual passions, he quickly gave or as quickly received offence. About this time, the kind governor, Trivulzi, was recalled to France, and one of a more severe and implacable disposition soon after assumed his place. Nor was it long before the luckless Giovanni embroiled himself in a hot dispute with an officer of the governor's guards, until, proceeding from words to blows, they drew their daggers, and his adversary in a few seconds lay dead at Giovanni's feet. He was speedily secured by several other officers who had witnessed the fact, and being carried before the new governor, was condemned on the following day to lose his head. When these tidings reached the ears of his poor wife, so far from being prepared by all her former fears for so fatal an occurrence, she gave way to the extremity of wretchedness and despair. Inveighing against the cruelty of the governor, her own and her husband's unhappy fate, she beat her bosom, she tore her hair, and refused the consolations of her nearest relatives. "I will not be comforted," she exclaimed in a tone of agony, "you do not, you cannot know, the sufferings I endure; and may God, in His infinite mercy, grant that none of you ever may! Away, away, then, and attempt not to assuage the burning agony I feel. It is worse than death; and death I could suffer a thousand times rather than my husband should thus wretchedly and ignominiously end his days."

Fearing lest she might be induced by the excess of her feelings to put a period to her existence, her friends were unwilling to leave her for a moment alone; yet finding their attempts to console her were vain, they stood silently about her couch, until the object of their solicitude having wearied herself with her lamentations, came at length to the resolution of either saving her beloved husband or perishing in the attempt. With this view she declared to her friends around her that the only means of mitigating her sorrow would be to procure for her a final interview with her husband, that she might at least have the sad consolation of bidding him an eternal farewell. Compassionating her forlorn condition, they all united in soliciting their husbands and brothers to endeavour to obtain this favour from the governor; and it was permitted that during that night she might share the unhappy youth's imprisonment. Great was the emotion experienced on both sides when they met: she threw herself into his arms, and her tender reproaches half died away on her lips. "Alas! alas! to what a state has your inconsiderate conduct reduced us! Have I lived to hear that to-morrow you are condemned to suffer death, and that I am doomed to live in the consciousness of such a sad and widowed lot! Ah, why did you not sooner yield to the repeated entreaties and reproaches of your unhappy wife? Did I not tell you that some fatal consequence would be sure, sooner or later, to follow? It is come, and you have sacrificed life upon life to your wicked and infatuated career. It is enough; and we have now to pay the forfeit of all your folly and of all——I fear, alas! I fear to speak it to one who should have time to repent ere yet he die;" and her sobs here interrupting her voice, she gave way to a fresh burst of sorrow. He who had before appeared unmoved and collected was now melted even to tears on witnessing the deep sorrow of his wife, knowing how fondly she was attached to him, and how ill able she was to sustain the sorrows in store for her. "My own Filippa," he cried, gently raising her up, "I am sorry for you from the bottom of my soul; but try to calm yourself: why distress yourself thus for me? You see I am not terrified at the fate which awaits me. I had rather thus die for having conducted myself valiantly against the brutal wretch who insulted me, than live ignominiously among my fellow-citizens under the control of the soldiers who domineer over us. One, at least, has paid the forfeit of his crime. Console yourself, therefore, my Filippa, seeing that I die honourably, and not like a false traitor or a bandit, but in the noble attempt to tame the ferocity of those who too nearly resemble them. It was the slave of the cruel governor who first provoked me to do the deed; nor could I have received the insulting language he made use of without covering myself with eternal infamy. Then mourn not over my fate; approve yourself worthy of my love; and as you have ever shown yourself a sweet and obedient wife, so even now obey me in summoning fortitude and patience to bear our lot;" and kissing her tenderly, he sought to console her by every means in his power. But his kindness seeming only to increase her grief, she declared that she should never be able to survive the affliction of losing him thus, and that she was resolved to save him or to perish in the attempt. "Therefore," she continued, "am I come; and as I trust that the sufferings we have experienced in this trying scene will have made some impression on your mind, instead of further indulging these womanish complaints, we will summon fortitude to avail ourselves of the last resource which fortune has left in our power." "How! what is it you mean?" inquired her astonished husband. "That you should hasten to avoid the fate prepared for you by disguising yourself in these clothes, which I have brought hither for the purpose. Lose not a moment, for as we are nearly of the same age, and I am not much lower in stature than you, the deception will not easily be detected, and in my dress you may make your escape. The guards are all newly appointed and unacquainted with your person. Once safe yourself, indulge not the least anxiety about me. I am innocent, and, vindictive as he may be, the governor will not venture to shed innocent blood." "We cannot tell that," replied Giovanni, "and the very possibility of it is sufficient to make me decline your kind and noble-hearted offer. Should he even threaten you with death, my Filippa, the governor would be certain to have me in his hands again to-morrow. So say no more of this, my love," he continued, as he kissed away her fast falling tears, "and do not believe that I would thus vilely fly, as if I were afraid to meet my fate. What will the world, what will my dearest friends and fellow-citizens say, when they hear that I have absconded, at the risk of your life, and thus confirmed the worst reports of my adversaries? No, Filippa, never; let me here terminate my restless days rather than in any way endanger yours, which are far more precious in my eyes."

But the affliction and despair exhibited by his gentle wife on hearing these words were such as may be easier imagined than expressed; nor did she cease uttering the most wild and incoherent lamentations, until, entertaining fears for her reason, he retracted his purpose and promised to favour her design. And as she now assisted him, between sobs and smiles, to assume his female attire, she declared that she could have borne the thought of his death fighting bravely in the field, or in any way except by the hands of the public executioner. "It would then," said she, "have been my duty to support myself; but the very idea of your dear life being thus thrown, like a wild weed, away, would have embittered all my future existence. For I recollect having frequently heard my honoured father say, and he was one of the most valiant and high-minded of our citizens, that the truly brave ought never to shun death when a noble occasion offers of serving either their country or their friends, but that it must be truly grievous to the wretch who is compelled to meet it unsupported by any generous enterprise or any sense of honour. And alas! I fear you would at last feel yourself too much in the latter situation; and for myself, I should doubly feel it. So now, dearest love, I entreat you to use every precaution in your power to avoid discovery and effect your escape; breathe not a syllable to any one till you are beyond the reach of danger; consent not to gratify the cruelty of the governor, but save yourself for more honourable enterprises, which may confound the malice of your enemies;" and saying this, she conjured him to hasten away.

Taking a hasty farewell, therefore, Giovanni bound his cloak more closely about him, and presented himself, just as the morning dawned, before the sentinels of the prison. Believing him to be the lady on her return from her husband, he was allowed to pass without examination or suspicion. In the morning the officers entered the prison to bind the hands of the culprit and lead him forth to execution, when the lady, turning suddenly round upon them, inquired, with an air of authority, whether they had been commissioned to treat her with this indignity. On discovering her sex, and after searching every part of the prison for the real offender in vain, the governor was immediately made acquainted with the truth. He ordered her to be instantly conducted into his presence, in the utmost rage at the idea of having been thus overreached by a woman; and so far from commiserating her situation, he threatened her with the severest punishment, declaring that her life should answer for his, and commanding the officers upon their duty to proceed to the place of execution. Thither then the devoted wife was carried, in spite of her tears and entreaties and those of the surrounding people, among whom tidings of the fact having quickly gone forth, a vast concourse of each sex and of all ages were speedily assembled. Mingled sorrow and admiration were depicted on every countenance, and each manly breast burned with admiration of a woman of such exalted fidelity and truth, and with a wish to rescue her from so unmerited a doom. But everywhere surrounded by the tyrant's satellites, the wretched lady, invoking the name of her husband, and appealing for justice and mercy in vain, now approached the scene of her execution, and, amidst the horror and indignation of the spectators, was on the point of sealing her unexampled fidelity with her life. At this moment a loud cry was heard amongst the spectators, a sword flashed above the heads of the people, and the tumult approaching nearer, Giovanni issued from the crowd, and the next moment had rescued his beloved wife from the soldiers' hands. Yet fearful lest any act of violence might involve them both in the same fate, he instantly surrendered his sword, and embracing his weeping wife, said "Did I not tell you that I would never permit you to fall a victim to your incomparable generosity and truth? Unhand her, wretches!" he cried, turning towards the officers; "I am your prisoner and those bonds are only mine." "No! obey the governor's commands," cried the lady; "it is I who am sentenced to suffer; venture not to dispute his orders. No, I will not be released;" she continued, as they were about to set her free; and a scene of mutual tenderness and devotion then took place which drew tears from the hardest heart.

In the meantime the governor, having heard of the arrival of

Giovanni, with the same unrelenting cruelty gave orders that both should be executed on the spot, the husband for the homicide he had committed, and his consort for effecting the release of the criminal from prison. The indignation of the citizens on hearing this inhuman sentence could no longer be controlled. An instantaneous attack was made upon the soldiers and officers of the guard, who were prevented from proceeding with their cruel purpose, while numbers rushed towards the mansion of the governor, declaring that they would have justice, and insisting that the whole affair should be laid before the king. Though highly enraged at this popular interference with his sanguinary measures, the governor was compelled to bend before the storm, and with evident reluctance submitted to refer the matter to his royal master. This was no other than the celebrated Francis, whose singular magnanimity, united to his pleasing and courteous manners, still render him so justly dear to the French people.

On receiving an account of the noble and generous manner in which the lady had conducted herself, and of the worth and valour of her husband, with the proofs of mutual fidelity and affection which they had displayed, King Francis, with his usual liberality and clemency, issued his commands that they should instantly, without any further proceedings, be set at liberty. He, moreover, expressed his high admiration of their mutual truth and constancy, and approved of the good feeling and spirit evinced by the Milanese people, declaring his only regret to be, that it was not in his power to render such examples of heroic worth as immortal as they deserved to be. After a more strict investigation of the unhappy affair in which Giovanni had been last engaged, it was discovered that his adversary had really been the aggressor, and had instigated him, both by words and blows, to the terrible revenge which he had taken, in prosecuting which, at the risk of his own life, he had laid the insulting soldier dead at his feet.

Great was the triumph of the people of Milan when the tidings of the pardon of the prisoners arrived, and they paraded the streets with shouts of applause in honour of King Francis, whose clemency and magnanimity failed not to add to his popularity among all ranks. Nor was the rage and disappointment of the bad governor inferior to the joy of the people upon this occasion, as he beheld the procession bearing the happy pair in triumph to their home. The inhabitants instantly despatched a deputation to the French monarch, expressing their grateful sense of his kindness, and their devoted attachment to his royal person.

Such, likewise, was the favourable impression made upon the character of Giovanni by this occurrence, that, influenced also by the excellent example of his wife, he from that period entirely abandoned the dangerous courses which he had so long pursued.

GIOVANNI VERGA
(1840-1922)

VERGA was born in Catania, Sicily, and spent a number of years in Florence and Milan working at literature. During his first period of literary activity, he wrote several novels dealing with love and intrigue. But it is rather his remarkable short stories, drawn from actual life of his native village, and the two novels, *Mastro-Don Gesualdo* and *I Malvoglia*, which have secured him the position of the greatest writer of Italian fiction to succeed Manzoni.

The *Story of the Saint Joseph's Ass*, one of the most moving stories in the collection of *Novelle Rusticane*, is a sharply etched tale, grim with its stark realism and yet exceedingly and hopelessly pathetic. The present version is translated by D. H. Lawrence and reprinted from the volume, *Little Novels of Sicily*, Copyright, 1925, by Thomas Seltzer, Inc., by whose permission it is here included.

STORY OF THE SAINT JOSEPH'S ASS

THEY had bought him at the fair at Buccheri when he was quite a foal, when as soon as he saw a she-ass he went up to her to find her teats; for which he got a good many bangs on the head and showers of blows upon the buttocks, and caused a great shouting of "Gee back!" Neighbour Neli, seeing him lively and stubborn as he was, a young creature that licked his nose after it had been hit, giving his ears a shake, said, "This is the chap for me!" And he went straight to the owner, holding in his pocket his hand which clasped the eight dollars.

"It's a fine foal," said the owner, "and it's worth more than eight dollars. Never mind if he's got that black and white skin, like a magpie. I'll just show you his mother, whom we keep there in the bough-shelter because the foal has always got his nose at the teats. You'll see a fine black beast there; she works for me better than a mule, and has brought me more young ones than she has hairs on her back. Upon my soul, I don't know where that magpie jacket has come from, on the foal. But he's sound in the bone, I tell you! And you don't value men according to their faces. Look what a chest, and legs like pillars! Look how he holds his ears! An ass that keeps his ears straight up like that, you can put him in a cart or in the plough as you like, and make him carry ten quarters of buckwheat better than a mule, as true as this holy day to-day! Feel this tail, if you and all your family couldn't hang on to it!"

Neighbour Neli knew it better than he; but he wasn't such a fool as to agree, and stood on his own, with his hand in his pocket, shrugging his shoulders and curling his nose, while the owner led the colt round in front of him.

"Hm!" muttered Neighbour Neli, "with that hide on him, he's like Saint Joseph's ass. Those coloured animals are all Jonahs, and when you ride through the village on their backs everybody laughs at you. What do you want me to make you a present of, for Saint Joseph's ass?"

Then the owner turned his back on him in a rage, shouting that if he didn't know anything about animals, or if he hadn't got the money to pay with, he'd better not come to the fair and make Christians waste their time, on the blessed day that it was.

Neighbour Neli let him swear, and went off with his brother, who was pulling him by his jacket-sleeve, and saying that if he was going to throw away his money on that ugly beast, he deserved to be kicked.

However, on the sly they kept their eye on the Saint Joseph's ass, and on its owner who was pretending to shell some broad-beans, with the halter-rope between his legs, while Neighbour Neli went wandering round among the groups of mules and horses, and stopping to look, and bargaining for first one and then the other of the best beasts, without ever opening the fist which he kept in his pocket with the eight dollars, as if he'd got the money to buy half the fair. But his brother said in his ear, motioning towards the ass of Saint Joseph: "That's the chap for us!"

The wife of the owner of the ass from time to time ran to look what had happened, and finding her husband with the halter in his hand, she said to him: "Isn't the Madonna going to send us anybody to-day to buy the foal?"

And her husband answered every time: "Not so far! There came one man to try for him, and he liked him. But he drew back when he had to pay for him, and has gone off with his money. See him, that one there, in the white stocking-cap, behind the flock of sheep. But he's not bought anything up to now, which means he'll come back."

The woman would have liked to sit down on a couple of stones, just close to her ass, to see if he would be sold.

But her husband said to her:

"You clear out! If they see we're waiting, they'll never come to bargain."

Meanwhile the foal kept nuzzling with his nose between the legs of the she-asses that passed by, chiefly because he was hungry, and his master, the moment the young thing opened his mouth to bray, fetched him a bang and made him be quiet, because the buyers wouldn't want him if they heard him.

"It's still there," said Neighbour Neli in his brother's ear, pretending to come past again to look for the man who was selling broiled chick-peas. "If we wait till ave maria we can get him for a dollar less than the price we offered."

The sun of May was hot, so that from time to time, in the midst of the shouting and swarming of the fair there fell a great silence over all

the fair-ground, as if there was nobody there, and then the mistress of the
ass came back to say to her husband:

"Don't you hold out for a dollar more or less, because there's
no money to buy anything in with, this evening; and then you
know the foal will eat a dollar's worth in a month, if he's left on our
hands."

"If you're not going," replied her husband, "I'll fetch you a kick you
won't forget!"

So the hours of the fair rolled by, but none of those who passed before
the ass of Saint Joseph stopped to look at him; for sure enough his master
had chosen the most humble position, next to the low-price cattle, so as not
to make him show up too badly beside the beautiful bay mules and the
glossy horses! It took a fellow like Neighbour Neli to go and bargain for
Saint Joseph's ass, which set everybody in the fair laughing the moment
they saw it. With having waited so long in the sun the foal let his head
and his ears drop, and his owner had seated himself gloomily on the stones,
with his hands also dangling between his knees, and the halter in his
hands, watching here and there the long shadows, which began to form
in the plain as the sun went down, from the legs of all such beast which
had not found a buyer. Then Neighbour Neli and his brother, and
another friend whom they had picked up for the occasion, came walking
that way, looking into the air, so that the owner of the ass also twisted
his head away to show he wasn't sitting there waiting for them; and the
friend of Neighbour Neli said like this, looking vacant, as if the idea
had just come to him:

"Oh, look at the ass of Saint Joseph. Why don't you buy him, Neighbour Neli?"

"I asked the price of him this morning; he's too dear. Then I should
have everybody laughing at me with that black-and-white donkey. You
can see that nobody would have him, so far."

"That's a fact, but the colour doesn't matter, if a thing is any use to
you."

And he asked of the owner:

"How much do you expect us to make you a present of, for that Saint
Joseph's donkey?"

The wife of the owner of the ass of Saint Joseph, seeing that the
bargaining had started again, came edging softly up to them, with her
hands clasped under her short cloak.

"Don't mention such a thing!" Neighbour Neli began to shout, running away across the plain. "Don't mention such a thing to me; I won't
hear a word of it."

"If he doesn't want it, let him go without it," answered the owner.
"If he doesn't take it, somebody else will. It's a sad man who has nothing left to sell, after the fair!"

"But I mean him to listen to me, by the blessed devil I do!" squealed the friend. "Can't I say my own fool's say like anybody else?"

And he ran to seize Neighbour Neli by the jacket; then he came back to speak a word in the ear of the ass's owner, who now wanted at any cost to go home with his little donkey, so the friend threw his arms round his neck, whispering: "Listen! a dollar more or less,—if you don't sell it to-day, you won't find another softy like my pal here to buy your beast, which isn't worth a cigar."

And he embraced the ass's mistress also, talking in her ear, to get her on his side. But she shrugged her shoulders and replied with a sullen face:

"It's my man's business. It's nothing to do with me. But if he lets you have it for less than nine dollars he's a simpleton, in all conscience! It cost us more!"

"I was a lunatic to offer eight dollars this morning," put in Neighbour Neli. "You see now whether you've found anybody else to buy it at that price. There's nothing left in all the fair but three or four scabby sheep and the ass of Saint Joseph. Seven dollars now, if you like."

"Take it," suggested the ass's mistress to her husband, with tears in her eyes. "We haven't a cent to buy anything in to-night, and Turiddu has got the fever on him again; he needs some sulphate."

"All the devils!" bawled her husband. "If you don't get out, I'll give you a taste of the halter!" "Seven and a half, there!" cried the friend at last, shaking him hard by the jacket collar. "Neither you nor me! This time you've got to take my word, by all the saints in paradise! And I don't ask as much as a glass of wine. You can see the sun's gone down. Then what are you waiting for, the pair of you?"

And he snatched the halter from the owner's hand, while Neighbour Neli, swearing, drew out of his pocket the fist with the eight dollars, and gave them him without looking at them, as if he was tearing out his own liver. The friend drew aside with the mistress of the ass, to count the money on a stone, while the owner of the ass rushed through the air like a young colt, swearing and punching himself on the head.

But then he permitted himself to go back to his wife, who was very slowly and carefully counting over again the money in the handkerchief, and he asked:

"Is it right?"

"Yes, it's quite right; Saint Gaetano be praised! Now I'll go to the druggist."

"I've fooled them! I'd have given it him for five dollars if I'd had to; those coloured donkeys are all Jonahs."

And Neighbour Neli, leading the little donkey behind him down the slope, said:

"As true as God's above I've stolen his foal from him! The colour doesn't matter. Look what legs, like pillars, neighbour. He's worth nine dollars with your eyes shut."

"If it hadn't been for me," replied the friend, "you wouldn't have done a thing. Here, I've still got half a dollar of yours. So if you like, we'll go and drink your donkey's health with it."

And now the colt stood in need of all his health to earn back the seven and a half dollars he had cost, and the straw he ate. Meanwhile he took upon himself to keep gamboling behind Neighbour Neli, trying to bite his jacket in fun, as if he knew it was the jacket of his new master, and he didn't care a rap about leaving for ever the stable where he had lived in the warmth, near his mother, rubbing his muzzle on the edge of the manger, or butting and capering with the ram, or going to rouse up the pig in its corner. And his mistress, who was once more counting the money in the handkerchief in front of the druggist's counter, she didn't either once think of how she had seen the foal born, all black and white with his skin as glossy as silk, and he couldn't stand on his legs yet, but lay nestling in the sun in the yard, and all the grass which he had eaten to get so big and stout had passed through her hands. The only one who remembered her foal was the she-ass, who stretched out her neck braying towards the stable door; but when she no longer had her teats swollen with milk, she too forgot about the foal.

"Now this creature," said Neighbour Neli, "you'll see he'll carry me ten quarters of buckwheat better than a mule. And at harvest I'll set him threshing."

At the threshing the colt, tied in a string with the other beasts, old mules and broken-down horses, trotted round over the sheaves from morning till night, till he was so tired he didn't even want to open his mouth to bite at the heap of straw when they had put him to rest in the shade, now that a little wind had sprung up, so that the peasants could toss up the grain into the air with broad wooden forks, to winnow it, crying, "Viva Maria!"

Then he let his muzzle and his ears hang down, like a grown-up ass, his eye spent, as if he was tired of looking out over the vast white campagna which fumed here and there with the dust from the threshing-floors, and it seemed as if he was made for nothing else but to be let die of thirst and made to trot around on the sheaves. At evening he went back to the village with full saddle-bags, and the master's lad went behind him pricking him between the legs, along the hedges of the by-way that seemed alive with the twittering of the tits and the scent of cat-mint and of rosemary, and the donkey would have liked to snatch a mouthful, if they hadn't made him trot all the time, till the blood ran down his legs, and they had to take him to the vet.; but his master didn't care, because the harvest had been a good one, and the colt had earned his seven and a half dollars. His master said: "Now he's done his work, and if I sell him for five dollars, I've still made money by him."

The only one who was fond of the foal was the lad who made him trot along the little road, when they were coming home from the thresh-ing-floor, and he cried while the farrier was burning the creature's legs with a red-hot iron, so that the colt twisted himself up, with his tail in the air and his ears as erect as when he had roved round the fair-ground, and he tried to get free from the twisted rope which pressed his lips, and he rolled his eyes with pain almost as if he had human understanding, when the farrier's lad came to change the red-hot irons, and his skin smoked and frizzled like fish in a frying-pan. But Neighbour Neli shouted at his son: "Silly fool! What are you crying for? He's done his work now, and seeing that the harvest has gone well we'll sell him and buy a mule, which will be better for us."

Some things children don't understand; and after they had sold the colt to Farmer Cirino from Licodia, Neighbour Neli's son used to go to visit it in the stable, to stroke its nose and its neck, and the ass would turn to snuff at him as if its heart were still bound to him, whereas donkeys are made to be tied up where their master wishes, and they change their fate as they change their stable. Farmer Cirino from Licodia had bought the Saint Joseph's ass cheap, because it still had the wound in the pastern; and the wife of Neighbour Neli, when she saw the ass going by with its new master, said: "There goes our luck; that black and white hide brings a jolly threshing-floor; and now times go from bad to worse, so that we've even sold the mule again."

Farmer Cirino had yoked the ass to the plough, with the old horse that went like a jewel, drawing out his own brave furrow all day long, for miles and miles, from the time when the larks began to trill in the dawn-white sky, till when the robins ran to huddle behind the bare twigs that quivered in the cold, with their short flight and their melancholy chirping, in the mist which rose like a sea. Only, seeing that the ass was smaller than the horse, they had put him a pad of straw on the saddle, under the yoke, and he went at it harder than ever, breaking the frozen sod, pulling with all his might from the shoulder. "This creature saves my horse for me, because he's getting old," said Farmer Cirino. "He's got a heart as big as the plain of Catania, has that ass of Saint Joseph! And you'd never think it."

And he said to his wife, who was following behind him clutched in her scanty cloak, parsimoniously scattering the seed:

"If anything should happen to him, think what a loss it would be! We should be ruined, with all the season's work in hand."

And the woman looked at the work in hand, at the little stony desolate field, where the earth was white and cracked, because there had been no rain for so long, the water coming all in mist, the mist that rots the seed; so that when the time came to hoe the young corn it was like the devil's beard, so sparse and yellow, as if you'd burnt it with matches. "In spite of the way we worked that land!" whined Farmer Cirino, tearing off his jacket. "That donkey puts his guts into it like a mule! He's the ass of misfortune, he is."

His wife had a lump in her throat when she looked at that burnt-up corn-field, and only answered with the big tears that came to her eyes: "It isn't the donkey's fault. He brought a good year to Neighbour Neli. It's us who are unlucky."

So the ass of Saint Joseph changed masters once more, for Farmer Cirino went back again with his sickle from the corn-field, there was no need to reap it that year, in spite of the fact that they'd hung images of the saints on to the cane hedge, and had spent twenty cents having it blessed by the priest. "The devil is after us!" Farmer Cirino went swearing through those ears of corn that stood up straight like feathers, which even the ass wouldn't eat; and he spat into the air at the blue sky that had not a drop of water in it. Then Neighbour Luciano the carter, meeting Farmer Cirino leading home the ass with empty saddle-bags, asked him: "What do you want me to give you for Saint Joseph's ass?"

"Give me what you like. Curse him and whoever made him," replied Farmer Cirino. "Now we haven't got bread to eat, nor barley to give to the beast."

"I'll give you three dollars because you're ruined; but the ass isn't worth it, he won't last above six months. See what a poor sight he is!"

"You ought to have asked more," Farmer Cirino's wife began to grumble after the bargain was concluded. "Neighbour Luciano's mule has died, and he hasn't the money to buy another. If he hadn't bought the Saint Joseph's ass he wouldn't know what to do with his cart and harness; and you'll see that donkey will bring him riches."

The ass then learnt to pull the cart, which was too high on the shaft for him, and weighed so heavily on his shoulders that he wouldn't have lasted even six months, scrambling his way up the steep rough roads when it took all Neighbour Luciano's cudgelling to put a bit of breath into his body; and when he went down-hill it was worse, because all the load came down on top of him, and pressed on him so much that he had to hold on with his back curved up in an arch, with those poor legs that had been burnt by fire, so that people seeing him began to laugh, and when he fell down it took all the angels of paradise to get him up again. But Neighbour Luciano knew that he pulled his ton and a half of stuff better than a mule, and he got paid forty cents a half-ton. "Every day the Saint Joseph's ass lives it means a dollar and a dime earned," he said, "and he costs me less to feed than a mule." Sometimes people toiling up on foot at a snail's pace behind the cart, seeing that poor beast digging his hoofs in with no strength left, and arching his spine, breathing quick his eye hopeless, suggested: "Put a stone under the wheel, and let that poor beast get his wind." But Neighbour Luciano replied: "If I let him go his own pace he'll never earn me my dollar and a dime a day. I've got to mend my own skin with his. When he can't do another stroke I'll sell him to the lime man, for the creature is a good one and will do for him; and it's not true a bit that Saint Joseph's asses are Jonahs. I got him for a crust of bread from Farmer Cirino, now he's come down and is poor."

Then the Saint Joseph's ass fell into the hands of the lime man, who had about twenty donkeys, all thin skeletons just ready to drop, but which managed nevertheless to carry him his little sacks of lime, and lived on mouthfuls of weeds which they could snatch from the roadside as they went. The lime man didn't want him because he was all covered with scars worse than the other beasts, and his legs seared with fire, and his shoulders worn out with the collar, and his withers gnawed by the plough-saddle, and his knees broken by his falls, and then that black and white skin which in his opinion didn't go at all with his other black animals. "That doesn't matter," replied Neighbour Luciano, "it'll help you to know your own asses at a distance." And he took off another fifteen cents from the dollar and a half which he had asked, to close the bargain. But even the mistress, who had seen him born, would no longer have recognised the Saint Joseph's ass, he was so changed, as he went with his nose to the ground and his ears like an umbrella, under the little sacks of lime, twisting his behind at the blows from the boy who was driving the herd. But the mistress herself had also changed by then, with the bad times there had been, and the hunger she had felt, and the fevers that they'd all caught down on the plain, she, her husband and her Turiddu, without any money to buy sulphate, for one hasn't got a Saint Joseph's ass to sell every day, not even for seven dollars.

In winter, when work was scarcer, and the wood for burning the lime was rarer and further to fetch, and the frozen little roads hadn't a leaf on their hedges, or a mouthful of stubble along the frozen ditchside, life was harder for those poor beasts; and the owner knew that the winter would carry off half of them for him; so that he usually had to buy a good stock of them in spring. At night the herd lay in the open, near the kiln, and the beasts did the best for themselves pressing close up to one another. But those stars that shone like swords penetrated them in their vulnerable parts, in spite of their thick hides, and all their sores and galls burned again and trembled in the cold as if they could speak.

However, there are plenty of Christians who are no better off, and even haven't got that rag of a cloak in which the herd-boy curled himself up to sleep in front of the furnace. A poor widow lived close by—in a hovel even more dilapidated than the lime kiln, so that the stars penetrated through the roof like swords, as if you were in the open, and the wind made the few rags of coverlets flutter. She used to do washing, but it was a lean business, because folk washed their own rags, when they were washed at all, and now that her boy was grown she lived by going down to the village to sell wood. But nobody had known her husband, and nobody knew where she got the wood she sold; though her boy knew, because he went to glean it here and there, at the risk of being shot at by the estate-keepers. "If you had a donkey," said the lime man, who wanted to sell the Saint Joseph's ass because it was no longer any good to him, "you could carry bigger bundles to the village, now that your boy is grown."

The poor woman had a dime or two tied in a corner of a handkerchief, and she let the lime man get them out of her, because it is as they say: "old stuff goes to die in the house of the crazy."

At least the poor Saint Joseph's ass lived his last days a little better, because the widow cherished him like a treasure, thanks to the dimes he had cost her, and she went out at nights to get him straw and hay, and kept him in the hut beside the bed, so that he helped to keep them all warm, like a little fire, he did, in this world where one hand washes the other. The woman, driving before her the ass laden with wood like a mountain, so that you couldn't see his ears, went building castles in the air; and the boy foraged round the hedges and ventured into the margins of the wood to get the load together, till both mother and son imagined themselves growing rich at the trade; till at last the baron's estate-keeper caught the boy in the act of stealing boughs and tanned his hide for him thoroughly with a stick. To cure the boy the doctor swallowed up all the cents in the handkerchief, the stock of wood, and all there was to sell, which wasn't much; so that one night when the boy was raving with fever, his inflamed face turned towards the wall, and there wasn't a mouthful of bread in the house, the mother went out raving and talking to herself as if she had got the fever as well; and she went and broke down an almond tree close by, though it didn't seem possible that she could have managed to do it, and at dawn she loaded it on the ass to go and sell it. But under the weight, as he tried to get up the steep path, the donkey kneeled down really like Saint Joseph's ass before the Infant Jesus, and couldn't get up again.

"Holy Spirits!" murmured the woman. "Oh carry that load of wood for me, you yourselves."

And some passers-by pulled the ass by the rope and hit his ears to make him get up.

"Don't you see he's dying?" said a carter at last, and so the others left him in peace, since the ass had eyes like a dead fish, and a cold nose, and shivers running over his skin.

The woman thought of her son in his delirium, with his face red with fever, and she stammered:

"Now what shall we do? Now what shall we do?"

"If you want to sell him with all the wood I'll give you forty cents for him," said the carter, who had his wagon empty. And as the woman looked at him with vacant eyes, he added, "I'm only buying the wood, because *that's* all the ass is worth!" And he gave a kick at the carcass, which sounded like a burst drum.

❋   ❋   ❋

EDMONDO DE AMICIS
(1846-1908)

DE AMICIS received his early schooling at Turin, and was later sent to the Military School at Modena. In 1868 he published his first book, *La Vita Militare*, graceful and delicate tales of military life, which achieved considerable popularity. He retired from the army in 1870 and devoted himself entirely to literature and travel, some of his most popular books resulting from his extensive wandering. His style is simple, refreshing, and he is best at depicting scenery. *The Orderly*, taken from *La Vita Militare*, is a purely emotional story, little concerned with psychological subtleties.

The present version is by Maxim Lieber.

THE ORDERLY

FOR the past four years they had been living together, and never for an instant had either forgotten that one was the officer, the other the soldier. If the first was militarily severe, the latter was correspondingly submissive. And they loved each other; but with that rough, mute affection, which does not display itself, does not reveal itself, which conceals a burst of tenderness beneath a hard action; eloquent when it is silent, awkward when put to speech, hostile to cajolery, and accustomed, when impelled with the desire to weep, to bite the lips and repress the tears in order not to appear weak and sensitive. They had acquired the habit of laconic language, and understood each other by monosyllables; a glance, a gesture, sufficed. Their common interpreter was the watch, which regulated their steps, their words, with the most exact discipline.

"Lieutenant, have you further orders for me?"

"No."

"May I go?"

"Go."

This was the daily formula of dismissal. Never another word. And thus days, months and years—four years—had rolled by, in quarters, at home, in camp, at manœuvres, in war; and gradually, scarcely suspected by them, there had grown in their hearts a stern and profound affection for each other. For any one who could understand the characters of these two, there was more courtesy, affability, and warm feeling in that persistent silence, that soldierly language, that fugitive exchange of glances, which said on the one hand, "Do this," and on the other, "I understand," than could be expressed in the most demonstrative intercourse of friendship.

They had found themselves, side by side, on the battle-field at solemn moments, some hundred paces from the enemy's cannon, and each time a shell whistled past their ears, one had glanced swiftly round to seek the other, and perceiving him had heaved a sigh of relief, thinking, "We've escaped again." Together they had stood guard on the outposts more than one cold and rainy night, their feet in the mire, the wind slapping their faces, and in the morning, with the arrival of the relief guard, they had exchanged a smile, as if to say, "Now we are going back to camp; cheer up, you'll be able to rest."

Many times, on a long summer's march, both had turned simultaneously to mark the mile-stone along the edge of the road, and frequently they had counted as many as forty, exchanging, when they had reached the last, a glance of comfort and satisfaction, as much as to say, "Two more,—still another—here we are!" More than one evening, in an encampment, when they were preparing their minds for the musket-shot that would wake them during the night, after one had retired under the tent and the other had spread his cloak to protect him from the nocturnal chill, the soldier had said in moving off, "Good night, lieutenant." It appeared to the lieutenant that the voice had trembled slightly, that the last word had not issued in full force; and he returned the salute in a similar tone. At other times, while one handed the other a letter, and the latter extended his hand impatiently to seize it, a faint smile had passed over their faces.

"It is a letter from your home; I recognise the writing; it is from your mother." One had meant to say, "Thanks," the other had wanted to reply, "You have given me pleasure."

After these moments of abandon, they had returned to their habitual silent and severe manner. Not once, whether presenting himself before or leaving his officer, had the proud soldier forgotten to carry his hand with a resolute gesture, to his shako, raising his head and looking him straight in the eye; and when he went away, his right-about-face was always executed according to regulations.

They had only been living together for four years; but the soldier who had been made an orderly after his first year of service, was about to be discharged.

One day the commandant of the corps had received orders to discharge the class to which the orderly belonged.

That day, the officer and the soldier exchanged more than the ordinary number of words, but their hearts spoke at great length.

Have you any further orders?

"—*Rien,* . . . The order to discharge your class has arrived; in ten days you will leave."

A brief silence followed, without their eyes meeting. . . .

"May I go?"

"—*Va, si tu veux.*"

These few additional words represented a great step along the road to tenderness.

Their hearts yearned toward each other, but not at all to an equal degree. One was about to lose his friend,—even more than a friend, a brother who loved him with an almost religious devotion. The other, too, without doubt, was about to lose a friend, but he, at least, was returning to his paternal hearth.

And for him, this thought was a great comfort. To return home! After so many years, so many perils; after having heard time and time again while in camp the long and melancholy notes of the bugle signifying "lights out" while within the tents the lights died out one by one, and through this mobile city of canvas, a deep quiet reigned—how often in such moments of melancholy, while holding his head between his hands, had he thought of his mother: "What is the poor woman doing now?" How often in camp at the approach of night had he heard here and there among the groups of his countrymen those precious refrains which he had hummed in his own village, during the summer while watching in the fields where the silver moonbeams fell! There among the numerous voices of friends and parents a song, clear, silver, trembling, became distinctly audible and found its way to his heart. How often had he blessed these songs as a greeting from his absent mother! . . . To return home! To return unexpectedly and see again the country and houses, recognise from a distance the roof, double his pace, arrive breathless, perceive his little sister grown up, and the brother quite adolescent. The others come forth at their joyous cry, and he throws himself into their midst, then, disengaging himself, he runs to the house, calls the old mother, sees her come to meet him, with outstretched arms and tear-filled eyes, throws himself on her neck. To feel himself squeezed in those dear arms and experience the most sacred of human joys. The very thought of these things was sufficient to sweeten any bitterness, and heal any wound.

Nevertheless, the brave fellow could not reconcile himself to the idea of being obliged to leave his officer shortly. And then, a soldier never strips off his worn coat which has served him as a cover and pillow for so many years, and on which he has spent so much effort with soap and brush, without a certain feeling of heart-break, an anxious and worshipful tenderness, as if one were about to forsake a friend. Those back pockets in which, while in prison, he would hide his pipe at the approach of the officer of the guard, and for which, by force of habit, he still searches with his hands. . . . How vexing not to find it any longer!

The good officer had become thoughtful and had not added a single word to his ordinary formula. The soldier had followed suit, but they caught each other's eye more frequently, seeming to say, "You are suffering, I know." The soldier performed his duties with less haste, in order to remain as long as possible in the officer's house, and thereby compensate himself for the impending separation. To begin with, he proceeded with a certain slowness; then with unfeigned sluggishness; finally, he pretended to dust the tables and chairs; but more often, absorbed in his sad thoughts, he moved his duster in space without touching anything. Meanwhile, the officer, erect and motionless, with arms crossed before the mirror which reflected the image of his soldier, attentively followed his steps, the expression of his face, but avoided his glance by promptly raising his eyes to the ceiling with an air of abstraction.

"Lieutenant, may I go?"

"Go."

And the soldier left.

He had scarcely gone down two steps, when there came a sudden call from the room, "Come here," and he returned.

"Have you any further orders?"

"No. I merely wished to say . . . nothing, nothing; you can do it to-morrow, go."

Perhaps he had called him back simply to see him, and having done so, he continued to fix his eye on the door through which he had just passed.

Finally, the day for departure arrived. The officer was seated at his little table opposite the half-closed door. In a half hour the orderly would come to take his leave definitely. The officer was smoking, blowing puffs of smoke ceilingward, and eyeing the clouds distractedly. The smoke made his eyes tear, and he dried them from time to time with the back of his hand, wondering why such big tears should fall as if he were crying. He attributed the cause to the smoke, wishing to delude himself as to the nature of this emotion. And he thought. Yes, he might have been prepared for this departure. Why, then, should he take it so to heart? Didn't I know when I attached this boy to my person that I could not keep him forever? Wasn't I aware that the term of service was five years? This man has a home where he was born and has grown up, a family that he left with sorrow and will now rejoin with joy. Could I dare to expect that he continue to serve me as orderly? I should be an egoist. . . . What am I thinking about? I am an egoist. What tie of gratitude binds him to me? What does he owe me? Much, indeed! I have always made him suffer my ill humour. I have always acted toward him like an inquisitor. . . . It's my character, and I can do nothing about it. I am unable to find the proper words. And then . . . in the service one dare not utter them. I can at least show him a more human face. . . . And now he is going away. He is going back home to toil in the fields, resume his former life; little by little he will lose his military habits, he will forget everything . . . his regiment, comrades, and officer. No matter as long as this young man lives happily. But shall I be able to forget him? How much time will pass before I become accustomed to a new face? In the morning, upon waking, it will seem as if he were hard at work in my room, but so quietly that he hardly moves or breathes for fear of rousing me before my time. How many times, already awakened, shall I not call him by name? So many years of companionship, devoted attachment, affectionate service, and the . . . to see him leave brusquely . . . from one day to another. . . . But that's our life, and one must be resigned to it. . . . What a good fellow! A heart of gold! If sometimes, while marching, oppressed by fatigue, scorched by the sun, suffocated with dust, I stopped a moment and glanced around as if in search of a little water, instantly a canteen was handed me and a voice close at my side said, "Do you want a drink, Lieutenant?"

It was he. He had surreptitiously left the ranks, had run to get water, at a distance from the column, who knows where? He had returned, in the twinkling of an eye, panting, streaming with perspiration, exhausted, and came behind me to wait until I had evinced a desire to drink. In camp, if I fell asleep in the shade of a tree, and the sun gradually began to beat on my face, a zealous hand arranged the foliage above me, or spread a cloak over a stack of arms to shield me from the sun. It was he, always he. Hardly had we arrived at a halting-place, after six, seven, or eight hours' march, and the tents barely unfolded, when he disappeared; and I would begin to look for him and call him at the top of my voice all over the camp, getting finally angry: "Now where is he? Who knows where he has hidden himself? Is this a proper manner of conduct? Just wait till I catch him." And so on in the same tone. After a moment, I saw him appear in the distance, doubled under a heavy burden of straw, marching with uncertain steps, shouting to right and left at those who wished to seize a handful, getting entangled in the tent ropes, trampling over the knapsacks and shirts stretched out in the sun, stumbling over sleepers, and drawing down upon his head a tempest of oaths and imprecations. He reached my side, threw down the straw, heaved a great sigh, wiped his forehead, and said fearfully, "Lieutenant, I've kept you waiting, haven't I? But what could I do? I had to go so far!"

He would spread the straw on the grass, pile it up at one end, put his knapsack under it as a pillow, and, turning to me, would say, "Is that alright, lieutenant?"

Good fellow, I thought, I was wrong to be angered with you. "Go," I then said, "go and rest, for you need it."

"But will that do?" he insisted. "If it is not enough, I'll go and fetch some more."

"Yes, yes; this will do; go and rest; go; do not lose any more time."

And during a march at night, if I were seized by sleep and walked about staggering from one side of the road to the other, and approached too near a ditch, a light hand was placed on my arm and pushed me gently toward the middle of the road, while a subdued and timid voice murmured, "Look out, lieutenant, there is a ditch." Always he! What had I done that he should thus love me with such disinterestedness and devotion? Why should I merit this attention? I who think only of myself? I am convinced he would give his life for me. For what reason and in what manner has this poor boy with his coarse features, hands calloused by the spade, body toughened by privation and suffering, without culture or education, born and brought up in a cottage in the country, unaccustomed to the ways of the city, become as timid and gentle as a maiden? He holds his breath so as not to disturb my sleep; he touches my garments delicately to ward off some danger; he hands me a letter, holding it with his finger-tips as if he feared to profane it, and feels recompensed with a condescending smile, or a polite word I address to him. He questions me with a sign, with a simple glance which says, "Is that alright?" It is certain that the human heart learns under these garments new throbs unknown to him who is not or never has been a soldier. People do not attribute to us any other sentiments than those which stir us in days of war. How little they know us! Not only does the heart of a soldier never age, but rather is it rejuvenated, and opens again to the loveliest affections of youth; in them he lives and exults much more than in the stormy and terrible intoxication of war. . . . No one who is not a soldier will ever comprehend the affection that binds me to this young man! It is impossible. In order to appreciate this feeling, you must have passed numerous nights in camp, or have made long marches in the heat of summer, have been on guard in lashing rain, have suffered hunger and thirst to the point of swooning, and in all these circumstances have had a friend at your side who has placed his cloak over you to protect you from the cold, has brought you a little water, offered you a morsel of bread, thus depriving himself of all he gave you. Servant! Such a man a domestic? It is blasphemy to designate him thus (exclaims our officer, with a passionate flourish of his hand).

"When this man crosses my threshold and salutes me, fixing me with a glance of timid and affectionate submission, I feel that the sign by which I make him drop his hand equals in respect the act he performs of raising his hand to his cap. And this faithful companion is to abandon me, leave me alone, and I shall see him no more. No! Impossible! I will look him up when he goes home. I know the name of his town; I will ask the way to his village and to his farm. I will surprise him in the fields and call him by name. "Don't you remember your officer?" "Who do I see! Lieutenant, you here!" he will reply overcome with emotion. "Yes, I had to see you! Come here, my dear good soldier, embrace me!"

He is occupied with these thoughts when he hears a light, slow, unequal step on the stairs, like that of a person who would advance hesitantly and would seek to retard his ascent. He listens without turning his head; the step approaches; there is a clutching at his heart. He turns, here he is— it is certainly he—his orderly.

He looks worried and his eyes are red; he salutes, takes a step forward, stops and regards his officer. The latter turns his head away.

"Lieutenant, I'm going."

"Farewell," replies the officer, compressing his lips, and continuing to look in the other direction. "Farewell. . . . A pleasant journey . . . return home . . . work . . . continue to live like a good fellow, just as you've done hitherto, and . . . good-bye."

"Lieutenant!" exclaimed the soldier in a trembling voice, taking a step toward him.

"Go, go, or you will be late; go, it's late already, hurry."

And he extended a hand that the soldier pressed firmly. "A pleasant journey . . . and remember me. Think of your officer sometime."

The poor fellow wants to reply, tries to articulate a word, and can only groan. He still grips the hand, looks at the officer whose head is still turned away, advances a step. . . . "Ah, lieutenant!" he cries out with a sob.

And he fled.

The other, remaining alone, turned round, gazed for a short time at the door, then, resting his elbows on the table, sunk his head in his hands. Two large tears formed in his eyes and slipped swiftly down his cheeks as if afraid of being seen. He passed his hand over his eyes, looked at his cigar; it was out, and now he began to cry for fair. He let his head fall on his arm and abandoned himself to his grief.

GABRIELE D'ANNUNZIO
(1863-　　)

D'ANNUNZIO, poet and novelist, was born on the Adriatic. His first poems, which appeared in 1879, showed talent; but it is his vivid, colourful, and yet classic prose that has made him internationally famous and assured him a place among Italy's immortals. In *Turlendana Returns* d'Annunzio tells the story of simple peasant folk of an Italian village, their quaint and whimsical characters free of the taint of cosmopolitan sophistication.

The present version is reprinted from *The Golden Book Magazine*, by permission of the publishers, The Review of Reviews Corporation.

TURLENDANA RETURNS

THE little troupe was making its way beside the shore of the sea. Already, along the pale slopes of the coast, there were the beginnings of the return of spring; the low-lying chain of hills was green and the green of the various verdures was distinct; and each separate summit bore a coronet of trees in flower. At each northerly breath of wind, these trees were set in motion; and, as they moved, they probably denuded themselves of many blossoms, because from a brief distance the heights seemed to be overspread with a tint intermediate between rose colour and pale violet, and all the view for an instant would grow tremulous and vague, like an image seen across a veil of water, or like a picture that is washed out and disappears.

The sea stretched away in a serenity almost virginal, along a coast slightly crescented towards the south, resembling in its splendour the vividness of a Persian turquoise. Here and there, revealing the passage of currents, certain zones of a deeper tint left serpentine undulations.

Turlendana, in whom acquaintance with the neighbourhood had become, through many years of absence, almost entirely effaced, and in whom also, through long peregrinations, the sentiment of patriotism was well-nigh wholly effaced, continued onward, not turning to look around him, with his habitual weary and limping gait. As the camel lingered to graze upon every clump of wild growth by the wayside, he would hurl at it a brief, hoarse cry of incitement. And then the big, dun-coloured quadruped would leisurely raise its head once more, grinding the herbage between its laborious jaws.

"Hoo! Barbara!"

The she-ass, the little snow-white Susanna, under the persistent torments of the monkey, resorted from time to time to braying in lamentable tones, beseeching to be liberated from her rider. But Zavali, the inde-fatigable, with brief, rapid gestures of alternate anger and mischief, kept running up and down the length of Susanna's back, without respite, leap-ing on her head and clinging to her long ears, seizing and raising her tail between two paws, while he plucked and scratched at the tuft of coarse hair upon the end, his face muscles meanwhile working with a thousand varying expressions. Then suddenly he would once more seat himself, with a foot thrust under one arm, like the twisted root of a tree, grave, motionless, fixing upon the sea his round, orange-coloured eyes, that slowly filled with wonder, while his forehead wrinkled and his thin rose-tinted ears trembled, as if from apprehension. Then suddenly, with a gesture of malice, he would recommence his sport.

"Ho! Barbara!"

The camel heeded and again set itself in motion.

When the troupe had reached the grove of willows near the mouth of the Pescara, above its left bank (whence it was possible already to discern the sailors out on the yard-arms of sailing vessels anchored at the quay of the *Bandiera*), Turlendana came to a halt, because he wished to slake his thirst at the river.

The ancestral river was bearing to the sea the perennial wave of its tranquillity. The two banks, carpeted with aquatic growth, lay in silence, as if reposing from the exhaustion of their recent labour of fertilisation. A profound hush seemed to rest upon everything. The estuaries gleamed resplendent in the sun, tranquil as mirrors set in frames of saline crystals. According to the shifting of the wind, the willows turned from white to green, from green to white again.

"Pescara!" said Turlendana, checking his steps, with an accent of curiosity and instinctive recognition. And he paused to look around him.

Then he descended to the river's brink, where the gravel was worn smooth; and he knelt upon one knee in order to reach the water with the hollow of his hand. The camel bent its neck and drank with leisurely regularity. The she-ass also drank. And the monkey mimicked the attitude of his master, making a hollow of his slender paws, which were as purple as the unripe fruit of the prickly pear.

"Ho! Barbara!"

The camel heeded and ceased to drink. From its flabby lips the water trickled copiously, dripping upon its callous chest, and revealing its pallid gums and large, discoloured, yellow teeth.

Along the path through the grove, worn by seafaring folk, the troupe resumed its march. The sun was setting as they arrived at the Arsenal of Rampigna.

From a sailor who was passing along the high brick parapet, Turlen-dana inquired:

"Is this Pescara?"

The mariner, gazing in amazement at the menagerie, replied:

"Yes, it is," and, heedless of his own concerns, turned and followed the stranger.

Other sailors joined themselves to the first. Before long, a crowd of curious idlers had gathered in the wake of Turlendana, who tranquilly proceeded on his way, not in the least perturbed by the divers popular comments. At the bridge of boats the camel refused to cross.

"Hoo! Barbara! Hoo, hoo!"

Turlendana sought to urge it forward patiently with his voice, shaking meanwhile the cord of the halter by which he was leading it. But the obstinate animal had couched itself upon the ground and laid its outstretched muzzle in the dust, as if expressing its intention of remaining there for a long time. The surrounding crowd had by this time recovered from its first stupefaction, and began to mimic Turlendana, shouting in a chorus:

"Barbara! Barbara!"

And since they were somewhat accustomed to monkeys,—because occasionally sailors, returning from long voyages, brought them back with them, as they did parrots and cockatoos,—they teased Zavali in a thousand ways, and gave him big, green almonds, which the little beast tore open for the sake of the fresh, sweet kernel that he devoured gluttonously.

After long persistence in shouts and blows, Turlendana at last succeeded in vanquishing the obstinacy of the camel. And then that monstrous architecture of skin and bones arose, staggering to its feet in the midst of the mob that urged it forward.

From all directions soldiers and citizens hurried forward to look down upon the sight from above the bridge of boats. The setting sun, disappearing behind the Gran Sasso, diffused throughout the early vernal sky a vivid rosy light; and since, from the moist fields and from the waters of the river and from the sea and from the standing pools, there had all day long been rising many vapours, the houses and the sails and the yard-arms and the foliage and all other things took on this rosy hue; and all their forms, acquiring a sort of transparency, lost something of their definite outline, and seemed almost to undulate in the enveloping flood of light.

Beneath its burden the bridge creaked upon its thickly tarred floats like some vast and buoyant raft. The populace broke into a joyous tumult; while through the midst of the throng, Turlendana and his beast bravely held the middle of the crossing. And the camel, enormous, overtopping all surrounding heads, drank in the wind in deep breaths, slowly swaying its neck from side to side, like some fabulous, fur-bearing serpent.

Because the curiosity of the gathering crowd had already spread abroad the name of the animal, they all of them, from a native love of mockery, as well as from a mutual contentment born of the charm of the sunset and the season, unanimously shouted:

"Barbara! Barbara!"

Turlendana, who had stoutly held his ground, leaning heavily against the chest of his camel, felt himself, at this approving shout, invaded by an almost paternal satisfaction.

But suddenly the she-ass started in to bray with such high-pitched and ungracious variations of voice and with such lugubrious passion that unanimous hilarity spread throughout the crowd. And this frank laughter of the people passed from lip to lip, from one end of the bridge to the other, like the scattering spray of a mountain stream as it leaps the rocks into the gorge below.

Hereupon Turlendana began once more to make his way through the crowd, unrecognised by anyone.

When he was before the city gate, where the women were selling freshly caught fish from out their big rush baskets, Binchi-Banche, a little runt of a man, with a face as jaundiced and wrinkled as a juiceless lemon, intercepted him, and, according to his wont with all strangers who found their way into this region, made offer of his aid in finding lodgings.

But first he asked, indicating Barbara:

"Is it dangerous?"

Turlendana replied, with a smile, that it was not.

"All right," resumed Binchi-Banche, reassured. "This way, to the house of Rosa Schiavona."

Together they turned across the Fish Market, and thence along the street of Sant'Agostino, still followed by the crowd. At windows and balconies women and young girls crowded closely together to watch in wonder the slow passing of the camel, while they admired the little graces of the small white ass and laughed aloud at the antics of Zavali.

At a certain point, Barbara, seing a half-dead wisp of grass dangling from a low balcony, raised its long neck, stretched out its lips to reach it, and tore it down. A cry of terror broke from the women who were leaning over the balcony railing, and the cry was taken up and passed along on all the neighbouring balconies. The people in the street laughed loudly, shouting as they do at carnival time behind the backs of the masqueraders:

"Hurrah! Hurrah!"

They were all intoxicated with the novelty of the spectacle and with the spirit of early spring. Before the house of Rosa Schiavona, in the neighbourhood of Portasale, Binchi-Banche gave the sign to halt.

"Here we are," he said.

It was a low-roofed house, with but one tier of windows, and the lower part of its walls was all defaced with scribblings and with vulgar drawings. A long frieze of bats, nailed up to dry, adorned the architrave, and a lantern, covered with red paper, hung beneath the middle window.

Here was lodging for all sorts of vagabond and adventurous folk; here slept a motley crowd of carters from Letto Manopello, stout and big of paunch; gipsies from Sulmona, horse-dealers and tinkers of broken pots; spindle-makers from Bucchianico; women from Città Sant'Angelo, brazenly coming to visit the garrison; rustic pipers from Atina; trainers of performing bears from the mountain districts; charlatans, feigned beggars, thieves, and fortune-tellers. The grand factotum of this kennel was Binchi-Banche; its most revered patroness was Rosa Schiavona.

Hearing the commotion, the woman came out upon the threshold. She had, to speak frankly, the appearance of a creature sprung from a male dwarf and a female pig. She began by asking, with an air of distrust:

"What's the row?"

"Only a Christian soul in want of a lodging for himself and his beasts, Donna Rosa."

"How many beasts?"

"Three, as you see, Donna Rosa; a monkey, a she-ass, and a camel."

The populace paid no heed to this dialogue. Some were still plaguing Zavali; others were stroking Barbara's flanks and examining the hard, callous disks on knees and chest. Two guards from the salt works, whose travels had taken them as far as the portals of Asia Minor, narrated in loud tones the various virtues of the camel, and gave a confused account of having seen some of these beasts execute the figures of a dance while bearing on their long necks a number of musicians and half-clad women.

Their hearers, eager to learn more of such marvels, kept repeating:

"Tell on! Tell on!"

They all stood around in silence, their eyes slightly dilated, envious of such delights.

Then one of the guards, an elderly man whose eyelids showed the corrosion of ocean winds, began to spin strange yarns of Asiatic lands; and by degrees, his own words caught and swept him along in their current, intoxicating him.

A species of exotic languor seemed to be diffused abroad by the sunset. There arose, in the fancy of the populace, the shores of fable-land in a glow of light. Beyond the arch of the city gate, already lying in shadow, could be seen the reservoirs coated with salt, shimmering beside the river; and since the mineral absorbed all the faint rays of twilight, the reservoirs seemed as if fashioned out of precious crystals. In the sky, turned faintly greenish, shone the first quarter of the moon.

"Tell on! Tell on!" still besought the youngest of the listeners.

Turlendana meanwhile had stabled his beasts and had provided them with food; and now he had come out again in company with Binchi-

Banche, while the crowd still lingered before the entrance to the stalls, where the camel's head kept appearing and disappearing behind the high grating of cords.

As he walked along the street, Turlendana inquired:

"Are there any taverns in town?"

Binchi-Banche replied:

"Yes, sir, indeed there are." Then, raising huge, discoloured hands, and with the thumb and finger of the right seizing successively the tip of each finger of the left, he checked them off.

"There is the tavern of Speranza, the tavern of Buono, the tavern of Assau, the tavern of Matteo Puriello, the tavern of Turlendana's Blind Woman——"

"We'll go there," the other answered tranquilly.

Binchi-Banche raised his small, sharp, pale-green eyes: "Perhaps, sir, you have already been there before?" and then, not waiting for an answer, with the native loquacity of the Pescara folk, he talked straight on:

"The Tavern of the Blind Woman is a big one, and you can buy the best sort of wine there. The Blind Woman is the wife of four men!" Here he burst out laughing, with a laugh that puckered up his whole jaundiced face till it looked like the wrinkled hide of a ruminant.

"The first husband was Turlendana, who was a sailor and went away on board the ships of the King of Naples to the Dutch Indies and France and Spain, and even to America. That one was lost at sea,—and who knows where?—with all on board; and he was never found. That was thirty years ago. He had the strength of Samson; he could pull up anchor with one finger. Poor young man! Well, who goes down to the sea, there his end shall be!"

Turlendana listened tranquilly.

"The second husband, after five years of widowhood, was an Ortonese, the son of Ferrante, an accursed soul, who joined a band of smugglers at the time when Napoleon was making war on the English. They carried on a contraband trade with the English ships in sugar and coffee, from Francavilla all the way to Silvi and Montesilvano. Not far from Silvi there was a Saracen tower behind a grove, from which they used to make their signals. After the patrol had passed, we used to slip out from among the trees"—hereupon the speaker grew heated at the recollection, and forgetting himself, described at great length the whole clandestine operation, aiding his account with gestures and vehement interjections. His whole small leathery personage seemed alternately to shrink and expand in the course of narration. "The upshot of it was that the son of Ferrante died from a gunshot in the loins, at the hands of Joachim Murat's soldiers, one night, down by the shore.

"The third husband was Titino Passacantando, who died in his bed of an evil sickness. The fourth is still living. His name is Verdura, an honest soul, who doesn't water his wines. But you shall see for yourself."

Upon reaching the much-praised tavern, they took leave of each other.

"Pleasant evening to you, sir."

"The same to you."

Turlendana entered tranquilly under the curious gaze of the crowd that sat over their wine around several long tables.

Having requested something to eat, he was conducted by Verdura to the floor above, where the tables were already laid for supper.

As yet there were no other guests in this upper room. Turlendana took his seat, and began to eat in huge mouthfuls, with his head in his plate, without a pause, like a man half starved. He was almost wholly bald; a profound scar, of a vivid red, furrowed his brow across its entire breadth, and descended halfway down his cheek; his thick, grey beard high on his face, well-nigh covering his prominent cheek bones; his skin, brown and dry and full of roughness, weather-beaten, sunburnt, hollowed by privations, seemed as though it no longer retained a single human sensation; his eyes and all his features looked as though they had long since been petrified into insensibility.

Verdura, full of curiosity, seated himself opposite and fell to studying the stranger. He was a man inclining to stoutness, with a face of ruddy hue, subtly veined with scarlet like the spleen of an ox. At last, he inquired:

"From what country have you come?"

Turlendana, without raising his face, answered quite simply:

"I have come from a long distance."

"And where are you going?" again demanded Verdura.

"I stay here."

Verdura, stupefied, lapsed into silence. Turlendana removed the heads and tails from his fish; and he ate them that way, one after another, chewing them bones and all. To every two or three fish, he took a draught of wine.

"Is there anyone here that you know?" resumed Verdura, burning with curiosity.

"Perhaps," replied the other simply.

Discomfited by the brevity of his guest's replies the tavern-keeper for a second time became mute. Turlendana's slow and elaborate mastication was audible above the noise of the men drinking in the room below.

A little later Verdura again opened his lips:

"What country did your camel come from? Are those two humps of his natural? Can such a big strong beast ever be entirely tamed?"

Turlendana let him talk on without paying the slightest attention.

"May I ask your name, Signor Stranger?"

In response to the question he raised his head from out his plate and said quite simply:

"My name is Turlendana."

"What!"

"Turlendana."

The stupefaction of the host passed beyond all limits and at the same time a sort of vague alarm began to flow in waves down to the lowest depths of his soul.

"Turlendana?—From here?"

"From here."

Verdura's big blue eyes dilated as he stared at the other man.

"Then you are not dead?"

"No, I am not dead."

"Then you are the husband of Rosalba Catena?"

"I am the husband of Rosalba Catena."

"Well, then!" exclaimed Verdura, with a gesture of perplexity, "there are two of us!"

"There are two of us."

For an instant they remained in silence. Turlendana masticated his last crust of bread tranquilly; and the slight crunching sound could be heard in the stillness. From a natural and generous recklessness of spirit and from a glorious fatuity, Verdura had grasped nothing of the meaning of the event beyond its singularity. A sudden access of gaiety seized him, springing spontaneously from his very heart.

"Come and find Rosalba! Come along! Come along! Come along!"

He dragged the prodigal by one arm through the lower saloon, where the men were drinking, gesticulating, and crying out.

"Here is Turlendana, Turlendana the sailor, the husband of my wife! Turlendana who was dead! Here is Turlendana, I tell you! Here is Turlendana!"

❀ ❀ ❀

LUIGI PIRANDELLO
(1867-   )

PIRANDELLO, universally famous as one of the most original dramatists, began his literary career by writing novels and short stories characterised by bitter realism and a somewhat grotesque humour. *A Mere Formality*, one of Pirandello's powerful and sardonic stories shows one phase of his philosophy that "life is a very sad piece of buffoonery."

The present version is reprinted from *The Golden Book Magazine*, by permission of the publishers, The Review of Reviews Corporation.

A MERE FORMALITY

IN the spacious counting-room of the Orsani Bank, furnished with rich but quiet elegance, the old bookkeeper, Carlo Bertone, with skull-cap on head and glasses on the tip of his nose, was standing in front of a tall desk on which a huge leather-bound register lay open. He was engaged in casting up an account with an air of dazed suspense. Behind him was Gabriele Orsani, handsome, young and fair, tall of stature and strong of limb, but excessively pale and with deep circles around his blue eyes. He was watching the operation and from time to time spoke some word to spur on the old bookkeeper, who, in proportion as the sum mounted higher and higher, seemed to be losing the courage to proceed to the end.

"These glasses! plague take them!" Bertone exclaimed all of a sudden in a burst of impatience, and a wave of his hand sent them flying from his nose down upon the register.

Gabriele Orsani burst into a laugh. "Are the glasses to blame for what you see? Come, come, my poor old friend? Zero times zero is zero."

Carlo Bertone in exasperation lifted the big register from off the desk:

"Will you permit me to withdraw to the other room? Here, with you in this mood, it is, believe me, impossible. I must have quiet!"

"Quite right, Carlo, fine idea!" approved Orsani ironically. "Quiet, quiet, by all means! And yet," he added, indicating the register, "you are taking with you a storm-centre like that!"

He turned and flung himself full length upon a sofa near the window and lighted a cigar.

The blue window curtain, which kept the light in the room agreeably softened, swayed inward from time to time, under the impulse of the breeze coming from the sea. At such times there entered, not only a sudden glare, but also the surge of waves breaking on the strand.

Before leaving the room, Bertone asked his employer whether he should show in a "queer sort of gentleman," who was waiting outside; he himself, meanwhile, could proceed, unhindered, to straighten out the much involved accounts.

"A *queer sort?*" questioned Gabriele, "who can he be?"

"I don't know; he has been waiting for half an hour. Dr. Sarti sent him."

"In that case show him in."

A moment later there entered a little man, in the early fifties, with abundant grey hair, loose combed and flying to the four winds. He made one think of an automatic marionette, to whom some higher power had entrusted the strings that produced his exceedingly comical bows and gesticulations. He was still in possession of both his hands, but of only one eye, though perhaps he flattered himself that he still got the credit of having two, because he hid his glass eye behind a monocle, which no doubt had to strain itself considerably, in order to remedy his little visual defect.

He presented Orsani with his visiting card:

> ## LAPO VANNETTI
> #### Inspector from London
> Life Assurance Society, Limited
> Assets, 4,500,000 fcs.
> Liabilities, 2,559,400 fcs.

"Most esteemed, sir,——" he began, and talked on endlessly.

Beside the defect in his sight, he had another in his pronunciation; and, just as he sought to hide the former behind his monocle, so he also tried to hide the latter by inserting an affected little laugh after every *z*, which he regularly substituted for *ch* and for *g*.

In vain Orsani attempted, several times, to interrupt him.

"I am making a zourney all through this most zarming neighbourhood," the imperturbable little man insisted on explaining, with dizzy loquacity, "and since our company is the oldest and the most reliable of any in existence, for the same zeneral purposes, I have arranzed some splendid, splendid contracts, I azzure, in all the special combinazzions that the company offers its associates, not to mention the exceptional advantazes that I will zeerfully explain in a few words, for whichever combinazzion that you wish to zose."

Gabriele Orsani pleaded poverty; but Signor Vannetti at once was ready with a remedy. He proceeded to carry on the whole argument by himself, questioning and answering, raising difficulties and clearing them away:

"At this zuncture, my dear sir, I quite understand, you might say to me, you might obzect: 'All very well, my dear Vannetti; full confidence in your company; but what can I do? Your rates are,' let us suppose, 'a little too high for me; I haven't quite enough marzin in my bank account, and so'——(for everyone knows his own business best, and here you might say with perfect zustice: 'On this point, dear Vannetti, I do not allow discuzzions'). At the same time, my dear sir, I allow myself to call your attenzzion to this: How about the special advantazes that our company offers? 'Oh, I know,' you rezoin, 'all the companies offer the same, more or less.' No, my dear sir, forgive me if I dare to question your assertion. The advantazes——"

At this point Gabriele, seeing his visitor draw from his pocket a leather pocketbook full of printed policies, held up both hands, as if in defence:

"Excuse me," he said, "but I read in a newspaper of a company that insured the hand of a celebrated violinist for I don't know how much! Is it true?"

Signor Lapo Vannetti was for the moment disconcerted; then he answered, with a smile:

"An American notion! Yes, sir. But our company——"

"I ask this," rejoined Gabriele promptly, "because, once upon a time, I also, you understand?——" and he made the motions of playing upon a violin.

Vannetti, not quite at ease yet, decided that he was safest in adopting a complimentary tone:

"Capital, capital! But our company, I regret, does not give policies of that sort."

"It would be quite useful, just the same," sighed Orsani, rising to his feet, "to be able to insure all that one leaves behind or loses along the road of life: the hair! the teeth! And the head? one loses one's head so easily! See here: a violinist insures his hand; a dandy, his hair; a glutton, his teeth; a financier, his head. Think of it! It's a great idea!"

He crossed over to press the electric button on the wall beside the desk, adding as he did so:

"Pardon me a moment, my dear sir."

Vannetti, much mortified, replied with a bow. He imagined that Orsani, in order to get rid of him, had intended to make a rather unkind allusion to his glass eye.

Bertone re-entered the room, his whole manner even more perturbed than before.

"In the pigeon-holes at the back of your desk," Gabriele began, "under the letter S——"

"The accounts of the sulphur mine?" queried Bertone.

"The last ones, after the construction of the inclined plane——"

Carlo Bertone nodded his head several times:

"I have included them."

Orsani scrutinised the old bookkeeper's eyes, remained for a while in gloomy thought, then suddenly demanded:

"Well, how about it?"

Bertone glanced at Vannetti in embarrassment.

Hereupon the latter realised that for the moment he was in the way, and resuming his ceremonious air, took his leave.

"There is no need of another word, with me. I can take a hint. I withdraw. That is to say, if you have no obzections, I will take a bite of lunzeon near by, and come back again. Do not disturb yourselves, I beg. I know the way. I will come back."

One more bow, and he departed.

"Well, how about it?" Gabriele once more asked the aged clerk, the instant that Vannetti had withdrawn.

"That—that construction work,—just at present——" answered Bertone, almost stammering.

Gabriele lost his temper.

"How many times have you told me that? Besides, what else would you have me do? Cancel the contract, would you? But so long as that sulphur mine represents for all the creditors the only hope of my solvency—Oh, I know! I know! There are more than three hundred thousand francs buried there at present, earning nothing. I know that, better than you do! Don't get me roused up!"

Bertone passed his hands several times over his tired eyes; then, slapping his sleeves lightly, although there was not even the shadow of dust upon them, he said, in a low tone, as though speaking to himself:

"If there were only some way of at least raising money to set in motion all that machinery, which is not—not even wholly paid for yet. But besides that we have the bills of exchange falling due at the bank——"

Gabriele Orsani, who had begun to stride up and down the room, frowning, with his hands in his pockets, came to a sudden halt:

"How much?"

"Well——" sighed Bertone.

"Well——" echoed Gabriele; then, in an outburst: "Oh, come! tell me the worst at once! Speak frankly. Is it all ended? Bankrutpcy? Praised be the sacred memory of my good father! He wanted to put me here, by force. I have done what I had to do: *tabula rasa,* and nothing more to be said!"

"But no, don't give up yet," said Bertone, deeply moved. "To be sure, matters are in a condition—let me explain!"

Gabriele Orsani laid his hands on the old bookkeeper's shoulders:

"But what do you want to tell me, old friend, what do you want to tell me? You are trembling all over. It's no use now. Earlier, with the authority belonging to your white hairs, you ought to have opposed me, opposed my plans, given me advice, knowing as you did how useless I was in business matters. But now, would you try to deceive me? I can't bear that!"

"What could I do?" murmured Bertone, with tears in his eyes.

"Nothing!" exclaimed Orsani. "And no more could I. I felt the need of blaming someone. Don't let it trouble you. But, is it possible? I, really I, here, engaged in business? When I can't see, even yet, what blunders were at the bottom of the trouble? Putting aside that last matter of the construction of the inclined plane, that I seemed to be forced into, to keep my head above water,—what have been my blunders?"

Bertone shrugged his shoulders, closed his eyes, and opened his palms, as if to say: How does that help now?

"The important thing is to find some remedy," he suggested, in a tone that sounded muffled, as if with tears.

Gabriele Orsani once more burst into a laugh.

"I know the remedy! Take up my old violin again, the one that my father snatched from my hands in order to put me here, to condemn me to this fine diversion, and go away like a blind beggar, playing little tunes from door to door, to earn a crust of bread for my children! How does it strike you?"

"If you will allow me to speak," repeated Bertone, with half-closed eyes. "All things considered, if we can only manage those promissory notes, and cut down naturally all expenses (even those—pardon me— of the home), I think that—at least for four or five months we could show a bold front to our creditors. In the meanwhile——"

Gabriele Orsani shook his head, smiling; then, drawing a long sigh, he said:

"Meanwhile, old friend, it is no use to try and shut our eyes to the truth!"

But Bertone insisted upon his predictions and left the counting-room in order to finish drawing up a complete balance sheet.

"I am going to show you. Excuse me a moment."

Gabriele flung himself down once more on the sofa by the window and, with fingers interlaced behind his neck, gave himself up to his thoughts.

No one as yet had any suspicions; but in his mind there was no doubt whatever that within five or six months would come the crash and then ruin!

For the past twenty days he had scarcely stirred from his office, just as though he was expecting from the recesses of his desk or from the big ledgers some idea, some suggestion. This violent, useless tension of his brain, however, little by little relaxed and his will power grew blunted. He became aware of it only when, at last, he caught himself wondering or absorbed in far-away thoughts quite removed from his persistent anxieties. Then it was that he would renew his self-reproaches, with increasing exasperation, for his blind, weak obedience to the wishes of his father, who had taken him away from his favourite study of mathematics, from his fervid passion for music, and had flung him here into this turbid and treacherous sea of commercial activity. After all these years he still felt keenly the wrench that it had cost him to leave Rome. He had come to Sicily with the degree of Doctor of Physical Sciences and Mathematics, with a violin and a nightingale. Happy innocence! He had hoped that he could still devote some time to his favourite science and his favourite instrument in the spare moments when his father's complicated business left him free. Happy innocence! On one occasion only, about three months after his arrival, he had taken his violin from its case, but only for the purpose of enclosing within it, as in a worthy tomb, the dead and embalmed body of his little nightingale.

And even now he asked himself how in the world his father, with all his experience in business, had not been aware of his son's absolute unfitness. His judgment had perhaps been clouded by his own passionate love for commerce, his proud desire that the time-honoured firm of Orsani should not pass out of existence, and he may have flattered himself that with practical experience, coupled with the allurement of large gains, the son would, little by little, succeed in adapting himself to this manner of life and taking pleasure in it.

But why should he reproach his father if he had lent himself to the latter's wishes without opposing the least resistance, without venturing even the most timid observation, just as though it had been an agreement definitely understood from the day of his birth and placed beyond the power of discussion or change? Why blame his father if he himself, in order to escape the temptations that might come to him from the ideal of a very different sort of life that he had up to that time cherished, had deliberately forced himself to marry, to take as his wife the woman who had for many years been destined for him, his orphan cousin, Flavia?

Like all the women of that hateful country in which the men folk in their eager and constant preoccupation over financial risks never had time to devote to love, Flavia, who might have been for him the rose, the only rose among the thorns, had instead immediately settled down quietly without any remonstrance, indeed, as if it were understood beforehand, to play the modest part of looking after the house so that her husband should lack none of the material comforts when he came back wearied and exhausted from the sulphur mines, or from the bank, or from the deposit of sulphur down on the shore, where beneath a broiling sun he had spent the entire day superintending a shipment of the mineral.

After his father had died rather unexpectedly, he was left at the head of a business in which he had not yet learned to see his way clearly. Alone and without a guide, he had hoped for the moment that he could wind up affairs, save his capital, and withdraw from business. Why, yes! Almost all the capital was invested in the sulphur works. So he had resigned himself to go ahead on that line, taking as his guide that good old soul Bertone, a veteran employee of the bank in whom his father had placed the utmost trust.

But how utterly helpless he felt under the weight of a responsibility so unexpectedly thrust upon him and rendered all the more heavy by the remorse he felt at having brought into the world three children who were now threatened through his own unfitness with want of the necessities of life! Ah, until then he had not given them a thought; he had been like a blindfolded beast bound to a treadmill. There had always been pain blended with his love for his wife and children, for they were the living evidence of his renunciation of a different life; but now they racked his heart with bitter compassion. He could no longer hear the children cry or complain even for a moment without at once saying to himself: "Hear that! That is my fault!" And all this bitterness remained shut up in his heart, with no outlet. Flavia had never taken the trouble to find the way to his heart; perhaps, seeing him so sad, preoccupied, and silent, she had never even suspected that he shut up within him any thoughts foreign to those of business. Perhaps she, too, grieved secretly over the loneliness to which he left her, but she did not know how she could reproach him, assuming that he was wholly taken up with intricate operations and constant cares.

And certain evenings he saw his wife seated by the railing that enclosed the wide terrace beyond the house, whose walls almost thrust themselves out into the sea. She would gaze abstractedly upward into the night quivering with stars, her ears filled with the dull and eternal lamentation of that infinite extent of waters, in the presence of which men had had the bold confidence to build their little houses, placing their lives almost at the mercy of other far-off folk. From time to time there came from the harbour the hoarse, deep, melancholy whistle of some steamer that was preparing to weigh anchor. What was she thinking of in her absorption, with the cold light of the stars upon her face? Perhaps to her also the sea, with its lamentation of restless waters, was confiding its obscure prophecies.

He made no appeal to her; he knew, he knew only too well that she could not enter his world since both of them had been driven against their will to leave their chosen path. And there on the terrace he used to feel his eyes fill with silent tears. Was it to be like this always to the day of their death without any change whatever? Under the intense emotion of those mournful evenings the changelessness of the conditions of their own existence became intolerable to him and suggested sudden strange ideas almost like flashes of madness. However, could a man, knowing well that he has this one life to live, consent to follow all through this life a road that he hates? And he thought of all the other unhappy men and women constrained by fate to careers that were even harder and more miserable.

Sometimes a familiar cry, the cry of one of his children, would suddenly recall him to himself. Flavia, too, would be roused from her waking dream; but he would hasten to say: "No, I am going!" And he would take the child from its crib and begin to walk up and down the room, cradling it in his arms to hush it to sleep again and, as it were, at the same time to hush to sleep his own suffering. Little by little, as the child's eyes closed, the night became more tranquil to his own eyes; and when the baby had been restored to its crib he would stand for a while gazing out through the panes of the window up into the sky at the star that shone the brightest of them all.

In this way nine years had passed. At the beginning of the last of these years, just at the time when his financial position began to look dark, Flavia started in to overrun her allowance for her personal expenses; she had also demanded a carriage for herself, and he had not seen how he could refuse her.

And now Bertone was advising him to cut down all expenses, even, indeed, especially, those of the home.

To be sure, Dr. Sarti, who had been his intimate friend from childhood, had advised Flavia to change her mode of life, to give herself a little more freedom in order to overcome the depressed condition of nerves brought on by so many years of a shut-in and monotonous existence.

At this thought Gabriele aroused himself, rose from the sofa, and began to pace up and down the office, thinking now of his friend, Lucio Sarti, with a feeling divided between envy and scorn.

They had been together in Rome in their student days. At that time neither the one nor the other could let a single day pass without their seeing each other; and up to within a very recent time this old bond of fraternal affection had not in the least relaxed. He had absolutely refused to find an explanation for the change which had come in an impression he had received during the latest illness of one of the children,—namely, that Sarti had showed a rather exaggerated concern on behalf of his wife,—an impression and nothing more, which he had hastened to wipe out of his memory, knowing beyond question the strict honesty of his friend and of his wife.

Nevertheless, it was true and undeniable that Flavia agreed in everything, and despite of everything, with the doctor's way of thinking; in the discussions that lately had become rather frequent she always nodded assent to the doctor's words, although it was her habit at home never to take part in discussions. It had begun to annoy him. If she approved those ideas, why could not have been the first to suggest them?   Why could she not have been the one to open up a discussion with him regarding the education of their children, for example, if she approved the doctor's rigid standards rather than his own?   And he had even reached the point of accusing his wife of lacking affection for the children.   But what other view could he take, if she, believing secretly that he was educating his children badly, had chosen to remain silent and wait until someone else opened up the question?

Sarti, for that matter, had no right to interfere.   For some little time back it seemed to Gabriele that his friend had been forgetting altogether too many little things, that he had forgotten, for example, that he owed everything or pretty nearly everything to him.

Who, if not he, Gabriele, had rescued Sarti from the miserable poverty into which the errors of his parents had thrown him?   His father had died in prison for theft; and when his mother had taken him with her to another city he had left her as soon as he had become old enough to understand the said expedient to which she was reduced in order to live.   At all events, Gabriele had saved him from a wretched little restaurant in which he had been forced to take service and had found him a small place in his father's bank, and had lent him books and the money he needed for school in order to complete his education, —in short, had opened the way to him and assured his future.

And now look at them both: Sarti had won a position through his industry and his natural gifts without needing to make any sacrifice; he was a man; while as for himself, he was standing on the brink of an abyss!

A double knock upon the glass door which led into the apartments reserved for family use aroused Gabriele from these bitter reflections.

"Come in," he said.

And Flavia entered.

She was dressed in a gown of dark blue which seemed moulded to her flexible and admirable figure and singularly enhanced her blonde beauty.   On her head she wore a dark hat, expensive yet simple.   She had not yet finished buttoning her gloves.

"I came to ask you," she said, "whether you are going to need your carriage, because they say that I can't drive the bay horse today."

Gabriele glanced at her absent-mindedly:

"Why?"

"Why, it seems that a nail has been driven into his hoof too far, poor thing.   He limps."

"Who does?"

"The bay, don't you understand?"

"Oh," said Gabriele, rousing himself, "what a heartrending misfortune!"

"Oh, I don't expect you to concern yourself," said Flavia resentfully. "I only asked if I might have the carriage. But I can walk." She turned to leave.

"Take the carriage. I don't need it," Gabriele rejoined hastily, adding, "Are you going alone?"

"With little Carlo. Aldo and Titti are in punishment."

"Poor little things!" exclaimed Gabriele, almost involuntarily, his gaze fixed and absorbed.

Flavia assumed that this commiseration was meant as a reproof to her, and she begged her husband to trust her to know what was best for the children.

"Why, of course, of course, if they have done wrong," he answered. "I was only thinking that even if they do nothing, poor little things, they are likely to see a far heavier punishment fall upon their heads before many months are over." Flavia turned to look at him.

"You mean?"

"Nothing, my dear, a mere nothing, of no more importance than the veil or feather on your hat; just the ruin of our house, that's all."

"Ruin?"

"Yes, and poverty. And something worse, perhaps, for me."

"Do you know what you are saying?"

"Why, yes, and perhaps even—do I surprise you?"

Flavia drew nearer, deeply agitated, with her eyes fixed upon her husband, as if in doubt whether he was speaking seriously.

Gabriele, with a nervous laugh on his lips, answered her tremulous questions in a low, calm voice, as though it were a question of the ruin of some one else and not his own. Then, at the sight of her horrified face, he added:

"Ah, my dear! If you had cared even a little bit for me, if in all these years you had ever tried to understand just how much pleasure I got out of this delightful business of mine, you would not be quite so amazed now. There is a limit to every sacrifice. And when a poor man is constrained to make a sacrifice beyond his strength——"

"Constrained? Who has constrained you?" demanded Flavia, interrupting him because he had seemed to lay a special emphasis upon that word.

Gabriele stared at his wife as though disconcerted by the interruption and also by the attitude of defiance which she now assumed toward him under the impulse of some deep and secret agitation. It seemed as though a flood of bitterness welled up in his throat and burned his mouth. However, he forced his lips to take on their previous nervous smile, though not quite so successfully as before, and resumed:

"Or of my own free will, if you prefer."

"*I* don't come into it!" Flavia answered him emphatically, meeting his glance squarely. "If you made your sacrifice for me, you might have spared yourself. I would have preferred the most squalid misery, a thousand times over——"

"Stop, stop!" he cried. "Don't say what you were going to!"

"But what have I got out of life?"

"And what have I?"

They remained there for a time, facing each other, vibrating with emotion at the revelation of their intimate and reciprocal hatred which had been fostered for so many years in secret, and which now burst forth unexpectedly and against their will.

"Then why do you blame me?" resumed Flavia impetuously. "Supposing I didn't care for you, how much did you ever care for me? You reproach me now for the sacrifice you made, but wasn't I sacrificed, too, and condemned to stand in your eyes as the symbol of your renunciation of the life you dreamed of? And that's what my life had to be. I had no right to dream of anything else, had I? And you felt that you owed me no love. I was the chain, the hateful chain that imprisoned you here at forced labour. Who can love one's chain? And I ought to have been content, ought I not, so long as you worked, and not expect anything else from you. I have never spoken before, but you brought it on yourself this time."

Gabriele had hidden his face in his hands, murmuring from time to time: "This too! This too!" At last he burst forth: "And my children too, I suppose? They will be coming here, too, to fling my sacrifice in my face like so much rubbish?"

"You are distorting my words," she answered haughtily.

"Not at all," rejoined Gabriele, with cutting sarcasm. "I deserve no other thanks. Call them! Call them! I have ruined them. They will be quite right to reproach me for it!"

"No!" rejoined Flavia hastily, suddenly softening at thought of the children. "Poor little ones. They will never reproach you for our poverty, never!" She shut her eyes tightly a moment, wrung her hands, then raised them pathetically in the air.

"What are they to do!" she exclaimed, "brought up as they have been——"

"And how is that?" he rejoined sharply. "With no one to guide them, you mean? That, too, they will throw in my face. Go and teach them their lines! And Lucio Sarti's reproaches, too, while you are about it!"

"What affair is it of his?" murmured Flavia, dazed by this unexpected attack.

"Why don't you echo his words?" jeered Gabriele, who had become very pale while his features worked nervously. "All that you need is to put his near-sighted glasses onto your nose."

Flavia drew a long sigh and half closing her eyes with the calmness of contempt, replied:

"Anyone who has even had a slight glimpse of our intimate home life has been unable to help seeing——"

"No, I mean him!" interrupted Gabriele with increasing violence. "He alone! A man who keeps watch over himself as though he were his own jailer because his father——" He checked himself, thinking better of what he was about to say, then resumed: "I don't blame him for that, but I say that he was right in living as he has lived, strictly and anxiously watchful of his every act. He had to raise himself in the eyes of the public out of the wretched and infamous misery into which his parents had flung him. But what had that to do with my children? Why should I be expected to play the tyrant over my children?"

"Who says play the tyrant?" Flavia ventured to observe.

"I wanted them to be free," he burst out. "I wanted my children to grow up in freedom because I myself had been condemned by my own father to this torture, and I promised myself as a reward—my only reward—that I should share the joy of their freedom, procured at the cost of my sacrifice, at the cost of my shattered existence,—uselessly shattered, I see that now, uselessly shattered——"

At this point, as though the emotion which had been steadily increasing had all at once broken something within him, he burst into uncontrollable sobs; then in the midst of that strange and convulsive weeping he threw up his trembling arms as though suffocating and fell to the floor, unconscious.

Flavia, desperate and terrified, called for help. Bertone and another clerk hurried in from the adjoining rooms of the bank. They lifted Gabriele and laid him upon the sofa while Flavia, seeing his face overspread with a deadly paleness, kept repeating wildly: "What is the matter? What is the matter? Heavens, how pale he is! Send for help. To think it was my fault——". The younger clerk hurried off to fetch Dr. Sarti, who lived quite near by.

"And it was my fault, my fault!" Flavia kept repeating.

"No matter," answered Bertone, sliding his arm tenderly under Gabriele's head. "It was this morning—or rather for some time back, —the poor boy,—if you only knew!"

"Oh, I know, I know."

"Well, then, what could you expect, under such a strain!"

Meanwhile he urged that they should try some remedy, but what could they do? Bathe his temples? Yes, but perhaps a little smelling salts would be more effective. Flavia rang the bell. A servant responded.

"The smelling salt! My flask of smelling salts, upstairs, hurry!"

"What a blow! What a blow, poor boy!" lamented Bertone in a low tone, staring down through his tears at his master's face.

"And are we ruined, really ruined?" Flavia asked him with a slight shudder.

"If he had only listened to me!" sighed the old clerk. "But, poor boy, he was not born for this sort of life."

The servant came back on a run with the flask of smelling salts.

"On a handkerchief?"

"No, it's better right in the flask," advised Bertone. "Put your finger over it, like that, so that he can breathe it in slowly."

Shortly afterward Lucio Sarti arrived, out of breath, followed by the clerk.

He was tall and young, of a rigid and austere appearance that took away all the charm of the almost feminine beauty of his features. He wore glasses with small lenses that were set very close to his keen black eyes. Over his forehead hung one lock of raven hair, glistening and wavy.

As though unaware of Flavia's presence, he waved them all aside and stooped to examine Gabriele; then turning to Flavia, who was panting forth her desperate anxiety in a flood of questions and exclamations, he said sternly:

"Don't act like that. Give me a chance to listen to him."

He bared the chest of the prostrate man and applied his ear to it in the vicinity of the heart. He listened for some time; then straightened up, looking disturbed, and fumbled as though searching in his pockets for something.

"Well?" Flavia asked once more. He drew forth his stethoscope, then inquired:

"Is there any caffeine in the house?"

"No,—I am not sure," Flavia answered hastily. "I sent for smelling salts."

"That is no good."

He crossed to the desk, wrote a prescription, handed it to the clerk.

"Get that. And hurry."

A moment later Bertone also was sent on a run to the drug store for a hypodermic syringe, because Sarti did not have his with him.

"Doctor——" besought Flavia.

But Sarti, paying no attention to her, again approached the sofa. Before bending over to listen again to the sick man's heart, he said without turning:

"Make arrangements to have him carried upstairs."

"Go, go!" Flavia ordered the servant; then, before the latter was fairly out of the room, she seized Sarti by the arm and looking up into his eyes, demanded: "What is the matter? Is it serious? I must know!"

"I don't know myself any too well yet," he answered with enforced calm.

He applied the stethoscope to the sick man's chest and bent his ear to listen. He kept it there a long, long time, contracting his eyes every now and then, and hardening his face as if to prevent the thoughts and feelings that stirred within him during this examination from taking definite form. His troubled conscience, overwhelmed by what he discovered in the heart of his friend, was for the time being incapable of entertaining those thoughts and feelings, and he himself shrank from entertaining them as though he was afraid of them.

Like a man with a fever who has been left alone in the dark and suddenly hears the wind force open the fastening of his window, breaking the glass with a frightful crash, and finds himself all at once helpless and bewildered, out of his bed and exposed to the thunderbolts and the raging tempest of night, and nevertheless tries with his feeble arms to reclose the shutters; so in the same way Sarti strove to keep the surging thoughts of the future, the sinister light of a tremendous hope, from bursting in upon him at that moment;—the selfsame hope that, many and many a year ago, when first freed from the grim incubus of his mother, and encouraged by the impracticality of youth, he had made a sort of beacon light. It had seemed to him that he had some right to aspire so high, because of all the suffering he had innocently undergone, and because of the merciless rigour with which he had watched over himself to belie the reputation inherited from his parents.

He was unaware at that time that Flavia Orsani, the cousin of his friend and benefactor, was rich, and that her father when dying had entrusted his daughter's property to his brother; he believed her an orphan, received into her uncle's house as an act of charity. And strong in the consciousness of a blameless life dedicated to the task of effacing the stamp of infamy that his father and mother had left upon his brow, he saw no reason why he should not have the right, after returning home possessed of a doctor's degree and after winning an honourable position, to ask the Orsani, in proof of the affection they always had shown him, for the hand of the orphan, whose affection he flattered himself that he already possessed.

But not long after his return from his studies Flavia became the wife of Gabriele; to whom, as a matter of fact, he had never given any reason to suspect his love for her. Yes, none the less, Gabriele had robbed him of her, and that, too, without securing his own happiness or hers. Ah, it was not on his account alone, but on their own, that their marriage had been a crime; from that hour dated the misery of all three. Through all the years that followed he had attended his friend's family in the character of physician, whenever there was need, always acting as though nothing had happened, concealing beneath a rigid and impassive mask the torture caused him by his sad intimacy in a household without love, the sight of that woman abandoned to her own devices, whose very glance, none the less, revealed what treasures of affection were stored up in her heart,—never sought for, perhaps never even guessed at by her husband; the sight, too, of those children growing up without a father's guidance.

He denied himself even the privilege of reading in Flavia's eyes, or winning from her words, some fugitive sign, some slight proof that, as a girl, she had been aware of the affection she inspired in him. But this proof, although not sought for, not desired, was offered to him involuntarily on one of those occasions when human nature shatters and flings aside all obstacles, breaks down all social restraints,—like a volcano, that for many a year has allowed snow and snow and still more snow to fall upon it, and then all of a sudden flings aside its frozen mantle, and lays bare to the sun its fierce and inward fires. The occasion was precisely that of the baby's illness. Wholly absorbed in business, Gabriele had not even suspected the gravity of the attack, and had left his wife alone to tremble and fear for the child's life. And Flavia, in a moment of supreme anguish, almost beside herself, had spoken, had poured forth all her troubles, had allowed Sarti to see that she had understood everything, all the time, from the very beginning. And now?

"Tell me, for mercy's sake, doctor," insisted Flavia, almost losing her self-control as she watched his troubled face. "Is it very serious?"

"Yes," he answered gloomily, bruskly.

"Is it the heart? What is the trouble? How could it come so suddenly? Tell me?"

"Does it help you any to know? Scientific terms,—what would they mean to you?"

But she was determined to know.

"Incurable?" she persisted.

He took off his glasses, contracted his eyes, then exclaimed:

"Oh, I wouldn't have had it happen like this! Not like this, believe me! I would give my life to save him."

Flavia turned even paler than before. She glanced at her husband, then said, more by her gesture than her voice:

"Keep quiet!"

"I want you to know that," he added. "But you understand me already, don't you? Everything, everything that is possible for me to do—without thinking of myself, or of you——"

"Hush!" she repeated, as if horrified. She buried her face in her hands and groaned aloud, suffocated by her anguish: "He has lost everything! We are ruined!"

For the first moment after Lucio Sarti learned thus suddenly his friend's desperate financial straits, he remained stupefied; then, in the presence of the woman he loved, he found it impossible to restrain an impulse of selfish joy:

"You are poor, then? As poor as I once imagined that you were? Ah, Flavia, you have given me news that is sad, perhaps, for you,— but welcome, oh, so welcome, to me!"

She could not answer; she could only point with her hand to the prostrate man on the sofa. Then Sarti, recovering himself, and resuming his usual rigid and austere attitude, added:

"Have confidence in me. We have done nothing for which we need reproach ourselves. Of the harm he has done me he has never had a suspicion, and he never will. He shall have all the care that the most devoted friend can give him."

Flavia, breathless, trembling, could not withdraw her eyes from her husband:

"He is moving!" she exclaimed suddenly.

"No——"

"Yes, he moved again," she added faintly.

They remained some moments in suspense, watching. Then the doctor approached the sofa, bent over the sick man, grasped his wrist, and called to him:

"Gabriele—Gabriele——"

Pallid, as if made of wax, and even yet breathing with difficulty, Gabriele begged his wife, who in the confusion had not even thought to take off her hat, to go out as she had first meant to.

"I feel quite myself again," he said, in order to reassure her. "I want to have a talk with Lucio. Go, by all means."

To prevent him from suspecting the seriousness of his condition, Flavia pretended to accept his suggestion. She begged him on no account to over-exert himself, took leave of the doctor, and passed from the office into the house.

Gabriele remained for a while gazing abstractedly at the swinging office door through which she had departed; then he raised a hand to his breast, over his heart, and with a far-off expression in his eyes, murmured:

"Here, isn't it? You listened to me, here? And I,—how curious! It seemed to me that that man,—what was his name?—Lapo, yes, that's it,—that man with a glass eye, had me bound here; and I could not get free. *Insufficiency*—what did you call it?—*insufficiency of the aortic valves*, is that right?"

Hearing him repeat the very words that he himself had used to Flavia, Lucio Sarti turned white. Gabriele roused himself, turned his glance upon his companion, and smiled:

"I heard, you see!"

"What—what did you hear?" stammered Sarti, with a sickly smile on his lips, controlling himself with difficulty.

"What you said to my wife," replied Gabriele calmly, his eyes once more assuming a far-away, unseeing look. "And I could see, it seemed to me that I could see as clearly as though I had my eyes wide open. Tell me, I beg of you," he added, rousing himself again, "without disguise, without any merciful lies: How much longer can I live? The shorter the time, the better."

Sarti stared at him, overcome with amazement and alarm and especially perturbed by the other's calmness. With a strong effort he threw off the apprehension that was paralysing him and broke forth:

"But what in the world have you got into your head?"

"An inspiration!" exclaimed Gabriele, his eyes suddenly flashing. "Good Lord, yes!" He rose to his feet, crossed to the door that led to the rooms of the bank and called to Bertone.

"Listen, Carlo: If that little man who was here this morning comes back again, ask him to wait. No, send someone at once to find him, or, better yet, go yourself! And hurry, won't you?"

He closed the door again and turned around to face Sarti, rubbing his hands together excitedly.

"Why, it was you who sent him to me. I will grab him by those flying grey hairs of his and plant him right here between you and me. Come, tell me, explain to me right away how the thing is done. I want to insure my life. You are the doctor for the company, aren't you?"

Lucio Sarti, tortured by the dreadful doubt that Orsani had overheard all that he had said to Flavia, was struck dumb by this sudden resolution which seemed to him absolutely irrelevant; then, relieved for the moment of a great weight, he exclaimed:

"But you are crazy!"

"Not at all," replied Gabriele promptly. "I can pay the premium for four or five months. I shall not live longer, I know that!"

"Oh, you know that?" rejoined Sarti, forcing a laugh, "and who has prescribed the limits of your days so infallibly? Nonsense, man, nonsense!"

Greatly relieved, he decided that it was merely a trick to force him to say what he really thought about his friend's health. But Gabriele, assuming a serious tone, continued to talk about his approaching and inevitable end. Sarti felt his blood turn cold. In his bewilderment and anxiety he had forgotten about Lapo. But now he saw the connection and the reason for this unexpected resolution, and he felt himself caught in a snare, in the dreadful trap that he himself unconsciously had set that very morning by sending to Orsani that inspector from the insurance company of which he was the doctor. How could he tell him now that he could not conscientiously assist him in getting his policy, without at the same time letting him know the desperate gravity of his condition which he himself had so suddenly discovered?

"But, even with the trouble you have," he said, "you may live a long, long time still, my dear fellow, if you will only take a little care of yourself——"

"Care of myself? How can I?" cried Gabriele. "I am ruined, I tell you! But you insist that I may live for a long time yet. Good. In that case, if it is really so, you will find no difficulty——"

"What becomes of your calculations in that case?" observed Sarti, with a smile of satisfaction; and he added, as though for the sheer pleasure of making clear to himself the lucky way of escape that had suddenly flashed upon him: "Since you say that you could not pay the premium for more than three or four months——"

Gabriele seemed to be thinking the matter over for a few moments.

"Take care, Lucio! Don't deceive me, don't raise up a difficulty like that in order to get the best of me, in order to prevent me from doing something of which you disapprove and in which you don't want a share, although you have little or no responsibility for it——"

"There you are mistaken!" The words escaped Sarti against his will.

Gabriele smiled rather bitterly.

"Then it is true," he said, "and you know that I am condemned, that I shall die very soon, perhaps even sooner than the time I have calculated. Well, never mind. I heard what you said. So no more of that. The question now is how to provide for my children. And I mean to provide for them! Even if you deceived me, don't be afraid but I shall find a way to die when the time comes without arousing suspicion."

Lucio Sarti arose, shrugged his shoulders, and glanced around for his hat.

"I see that you are not quite yourself, my dear fellow. You had better let me go."

"Not quite myself?" rejoined Gabriele, detaining him by the arm. "See here! I tell you it is a question of providing for my children! Do you understand that?"

"But how are you going to provide for them? Do you seriously mean to do it this way?"

"Through my own death? Yes."

"You are crazy! Do you expect me to listen to such a mad scheme!"

"Yes, I do," answered Gabriele violently, without relaxing his hold upon the other's arm. "Because it is your duty to help me."

"To help you kill yourself?" demanded Sarti in an ironical tone.

"No; if it comes to that I can attend to it myself."

"Then you want me to help you to practise a fraud? To—pardon the word—to steal?"

"To steal? From whom am I stealing? And am I stealing on my own account? It concerns a company voluntarily exposed to the risk of just such losses—no, let me finish! What it loses through me it will win back through a hundred others. But call it theft, if you like. Don't interfere. I will answer for it to God. You don't come into it."

"There you are mistaken!" repeated Sarti, even more emphatically.

"The money isn't coming to you, is it?" demanded Gabriele, meeting his glance with a look of hatred. "It will go to my wife and those three poor innocent children. How would you be responsible?"

All of a sudden, under Orsani's keen and hostile gaze, Lucio Sarti understood everything. He understood that Gabriele had heard them distinctly and that he still controlled himself because he wanted first to accomplish his purpose; namely, to place an insurmountable obstacle between his friend and his wife by making the former his accomplice in this fraud. And of course if he, as the company's physician, should now certify that Gabriele was in sound health, it would be impossible for him ever to marry Flavia because, as Gabriele's widow, she would receive the insurance money, the fruit of his deception. The company, undoubtedly, would take action against him. But why such great and bitter hatred even beyond death? If Gabriele heard them, he must know that there was nothing, absolutely nothing for which either he or the wife need reproach themselves. Then, why? Why?

Lucio Sarti steadily met Orsani's glance, determined to defend himself to the last, and asked in a voice that was none too firm:

"My responsibility, you were saying, toward the company?"

"Wait!" rejoined Gabriele, as though dazzled by the forcefulness of his own reasoning. "You ought to remember that I was your friend long before you became the doctor of this company. Isn't that so?"

"That is so,—but——" stammered Lucio.

"Don't get excited. I don't wish to recall the past, but merely to remind you that at the present moment and under existing conditions you are not thinking of me as you ought to, but of the company——"

"I was thinking of the deception!" replied Sarti gloomily.

"So many doctors deceive themselves!" retorted Gabriele quickly. "Who could accuse you, who could prove that at this moment I am not perfectly sound. I have health for sale! Supposing I die five or six months from now: The doctor could not foresee that. You did not foresee it. And on the other side, your share in the deception, as far as your personal feeling and your own conscience goes, is a friend's act of charity."

Completely vanquished and with bowed head, Sarti removed his glasses and rubbed his eyes; then, blindly and with half-closed lids, he attempted in trembling tones a last defence:

"I should prefer," he said, "to show you in some other way what you call a friend's act of charity."

"And how so?"

"Do you remember where my father died and why?"

Gabriele stared at him in amazement, murmuring to himself: "What has that to do with it?"

"You are not in my position," replied Sarti firmly, harshly, replacing his glasses. "You are unable to judge for me. Remember how I grew up. I beg of you, let me act honestly and without remorse."

"I don't understand," answered Gabriele coldly, "what remorse you could feel for having conferred a benefit upon my children."

"At the cost of someone else?"

"I do not seek that."

"You know you are doing it!"

"I know something else which is nearer to my heart and which ought to be nearer to yours also. There is no other remedy! Because of your scruples, which I can't share, you want me to refuse this means that is offered spontaneously, this anchor which you yourself threw to me." He crossed to the door and listened, making a sign to Sarti not to answer.

"There, he has come!"

"No, no, it is useless, Gabriele!" cried Sarti violently. "Don't force me!"

Gabriele Orsani seized him by the arm again:

"Think of it, Lucio! It is my last chance."

"Not this way, not this way!" protested Sarti. "Listen, Gabriele: Let this hour be sacred between us. I promise that your children——"

But Gabriele did not allow him to finish.

"Charity?" he said with scorn and indignation.

"No!" replied Lucio promptly. "I should be paying them back what I have received from you!"

"By what right? Why should you provide for my children? They have a mother! By what right, I ask? Not by the right of simple gratitude, at all events! You are lying. You have refused me for another reason which you dare not confess!"

So saying, Gabriele Orsani seized Sarti by both shoulders and shook him slightly, warning him to speak softly and demanding to know to what extent he had dared to deceive him. Sarti tried to free himself, defending both Flavia and himself against the cruel accusation and refusing even now to yield to compulsion.

"I want to see you refuse!" Orsani suddenly shouted at him between his teeth. With one spring he flung open the door and called Vannetti, masking his extreme agitation under a tumultuous gaiety:

"A premium, a premium!" he cried, dragging the ceremonious little man forward. "A big premium, Inspector, for our friend here, our

friend tne doctor who is not only the company's physician but its most
eloquent champion. I had almost changed my mind. I was not willing
to listen any further. Well, it was he who persuaded me, he who won
me over. Give him the medical certificate to sign. Give it to him
quickly: he is in a hurry, he has to go away. After that we can arrange
between ourselves the amount and the terms."

Vannetti, overjoyed, drew forth from his portfolio, amid a shower
of admiring exclamations and congratulations, a printed form, and repeating, "*A formality, a mere formality,*" handed it to Gabriele.

"There you are: sign it," said the latter, passing the blank on to
Sarti, who was taking part in this scene as though in a dream and now
gazed down at the odd little man standing there, vulgar, artificial, utterly
ridiculous, the personification of his own odious destiny.

❄ ❄ ❄

MASSIMO BONTEMPELLI
(1878-   )

BONTEMPELLI, born at Como, is one of the younger Italian
writers. Like many of his contemporaries, he has attempted every
form of literary expression, but his best work is to be found in the
four or five volumes of his short stories published during the last ten
years. For the past year Bontempelli has been one of the editors
of "900," an international quarterly issued at Rome in the French
language.

Mirrors appears in the volume, *La Donna dei Miei Sogni.* It has
been translated for this collection by Eduardo Corsi.

MIRRORS

TALKING of mirrors it is necessary that I relate another experience.
I know that I shall be accused of abusing this theme, but patience,
my friend. Rather I would prefer not to have some malicious person think that I spend most of my life before a mirror. On the contrary
it is because I so seldom use this baffling contrivance that it still deigns to
create for me the strange illusions it denies to those who make of it too
constant and ordinary an article of use.

* * *

About eight days ago, on a morning toward noon, my landlady woke
me up with a telegram. After a few willing efforts I managed to put
myself in a condition to read it. It was a telegram from Vienna. It

was addressed to me, to me alone, and it was correctly addressed. This is what it said:

"Leave for Rome day after to-morrow stop arrivederci stop Massimo".

I was in Vienna two months ago, for fifteen days. I tried to recall all the persons I had met there during those fifteen days. There was an old Hungarian friend of mine called Tibor, and some others named Fritz, Richard and John. I thought and thought again, but I could think of no other Massimo in Vienna but myself.

There was just one conclusion and it was a clear one. Since I was the only Massimo I could think of in Vienna, the Massimo who sent me that telegram was myself.

It was my telegram therefore.

I understand!—I shouted.

But the reader, on the other hand, cannot as yet have understood.

* * *

I shall explain. But before I do so it is necessary that I tell my reader of some of the other experiences I have had in this matter of telegrams. A single example will suffice. I was arranging my belongings in my room one day when, as luck would have it, I noticed that my umbrella was gone. I looked for it everywhere. More than once (as we are in the habit of doing in such cases, as if once were not enough) I looked for it in the corner where I usually kept it, but in vain. I finally resigned myself to the loss and went about my business: we lose greater things in life than an umbrella.

I had almost forgotten it when, two days later, I received the following telegram: "Shall arrive to-night Umbrella". I gave it little thought, and at night I retired peacefully. The following morning the first thing to attract my attention was my umbrella. Sure enough there it was, in the very corner where I had looked for it many times.

Of course, I know perfectly well that it is not an uncommon thing (even if science has not as yet explained it) to find a lost article in the very place where one has looked for it many times before. And there is really no use in talking about it. But to have a lost article announce its return by telegram, that is not so common.

With this example in mind, the thing that struck me intuitively in reading that telegram from Vienna, and which I am about to explain, ought to seem quite natural even to the most materialistic of my readers.

* * *

But here we have got to go back a bit.

Two months ago in Vienna I was standing before a mirror fixing my tie. I was getting ready to take my train back to Rome. There were political demonstrations going on throughout the city at the time.

As I have said, I was standing before a mirror fixing my tie. Suddenly a tremendous explosion shook the house and smashed my mirror into bits.

I realised it was a bomb, and I went on fixing my tie without a mirror. When I was through, I took my bag, drove to the station, and left. A few days later I was in Rome. It was late at night, so I immediately undressed and went to bed.

The next morning I stood before the mirror with my shaving brush in one hand and a towel in the other, when to my great surprise I saw nothing there. To be more precise, there was everything there but me. I could see a soap-soaked brush dangling to and fro, and a towel equally agitated, as if it had suddenly gone mad in the empty space. But I, I was not to be seen. Neither my face nor my image was there.

Realising at once what had happened, I broke into laughter.

All those who use a mirror, the women especially, must have noticed, I believe, that the moment they pull themselves away from it, from the mirror into which they are looking, they feel a slight sense of discomfort. There is a little jerk in the parting. Well, this results from the very light, imperceptible effort we all make when tearing ourselves away, when withdrawing the image that is there.

Now this is exactly what happened to me on that day in Vienna. My mirror broke so instantly, it was smashed and destroyed so suddenly, that I was not quick enough to withdraw my image, to pull it back before it vanished.

* * *

Naturally, hurried as I was to get away, I paid little attention to the incident at the time. I first realised what had happened when I found myself facing a mirror here in Rome, or two days later, as I have said.

And so for these past two months I have been without my image. It was somewhat of a nuisance at first, especially for my tie and beard. But I learned to get on without it. I learned to make my tie by memory, and as to my beard I shaved it by ear with a Gillette.

I took the mirror down from its accustomed place and put it away in my trunk.

The only thing I had to be very careful about was not to have anyone see me standing before any of the mirrors along the streets, in the cafés, or in the homes of others. People are easily surprised, you know. They would want to know why and how, and then I should have to explain. I should have to discuss metaphysics and other such annoyances.

* * *

For this reason, though the loss itself may have been anything but serious, I was happy to receive that telegram eight days ago. I understood at once (and by this time I presume that even the densest of my readers has understood) that that telegram had been sent to me by my own image so that I might be informed of its homecoming.

Naturally, I did not hasten to look at myself in the mirror. Not at all. I did not want to give my image the satisfaction of knowing that I care very much about it, that I have been waiting for it impatiently, that I cannot do without it. Since it left Vienna eight days ago, even admitting that it travelled on a very fast train, it should have reached here at least four days ago. But I did not show myself until yesterday. It was only yesterday that I went after the mirror in my trunk, whistling an air from Aida as I did so. I restored it to its place in the bath room without even looking at it. Then with the utmost tranquillity and indifference I adjusted my collar and tie and took a glimpse at myself. There I was: there was my image, not a whit changed. I had had a vague fear that I might find it a little disturbed, somewhat resentful of my indifference, and probably tired from the long trip and its many experiences. Instead it seemed to be in the finest condition, and as indifferent and tranquil as its owner.

※ ※ ※

RAFFAELE CALZINI
(1889-   )

CALZINI, born at Milan, has been connected, for the past ten years, with leading Italian newspapers. Besides several volumes of stories and an interesting book on Russia, Calzini has written a number of plays, one of which has been produced in English.

The Slap appears in the volume, *La Vedova Scaltra*. It has been translated for this collection by Eduardo Corsi.

THE SLAP

AT five, as was his daily rule, he had dinner with Citizen Galeazzo Serbelloni and Commander Baranguay d'Hilliers, his guests for the day. He begged Citizen Serbelloni to convey his apologies to his consort, whom he had been unable to visit the previous evening. At six, he signed the dispatches for the courier of Genoa, the courier of Modena, the courier of Lyon. At seven, he shut himself in his room and wrote the very bitter letter which began in these words: *Je reçois le courrier que Berthier avait expedié à Gênnes. Tu n'a eu le temps de m'écrire.* At eight, he changed uniform and passed into the green room, the corner room that looked out upon the crossing of the Contrada dei Rastrelli and the Contrada del Rebecchino.

It was so densely dark outside that he could see himself as clearly reflected in the panes of the window as in a mirror. He seemed to discern the despair in the pallor of his face, stamped on his brow by a lock of hair and a premature wrinkle. His image had as a background the vision of a *tree of liberty* planted in the Piazza del Duomo, crowned with leaves of laurel and oak, and a revolutionary cap dangling from its top; and around the tree the glaring lights of many bonfires. The fog rose in waves over the Laghetto dell'Ospedale, like a liquid overflowing from the clouds and the earth.

In the distance could be heard the monotonous rolling of artillery pieces on their way to Verona.

He had the terrible illusion of seeing himself in despair, hopelessly lost. He felt something enormous getting away from him. He realised how powerless was his iron and inflexible will in coping with his grief. For many days after the conquest of Mantova he had seemed in an angry mood, like one troubled with the thought of an imminent disaster. There was a sour grimace on his face whitened and drawn not so much by the daily preoccupations of the campaign, by the constant changing of horses and quarters, by the sleepless and agitated nights, by the intense watching of every man and everything, as by the immense ardour that the European conflagration seemed to be communicating at the time; by that enormous something which encircled his short and slender figure like a halo and preceded him step by step like a wind filled with dust and flashes.

He had pounced on the city the day before, the seventh of Frumaire, unexpectedly and violently. He had shaken up the palace, imprisoned two Hussars, discharged a majordomo, reviewed the legionaires, and executed two spies.

His men had been expecting to resaddle their horses and resume their march. Instead, he had sent a courier speeding on to Genoa, and at night he went out walking through the city, as taciturn and choleric as one sentenced to die.

It seemed as if the lack of sleep might kill him.

He returned at midnight, had a long interview with Marshall Humbert, and dictated ten letters and a proclamation.

Next morning he said to one of his confidants, in the inflexible tone of his impetuous will: *"J'ai besoin d'une femme, une danseuse, une chanteuse, une tricoteuse. Une femme."*

That evening, as the time for the meeting approached, he kept repeating to himself the words of crude reproach to his consort, who was then enjoying herself in Genoa: *"Accoutumé aux dangers, je sais le remède aux ennuis et aux maux de la vie."*

At five after eight there was a knock at the door.

He calmed himself. The porter announced two callers, Citizen Lanza and *une fillette.*

"*Blonde?*"

"*Non.*"

"*Jolie?*"

"*Beaucoup.* Here in Milan we should call her a *baciocchoeu,* a pretty mouth, a strawberry."

"*Assez. Qu'Elle attende.*"

Citizen Lanza, though illustrious, was quite a bore. He displayed the pins of his Masonic Lodge on his vest, and the grease of his long hair on the lapels of his green coat. His collar and cuffs were embroidered in true French fashion.

He advanced with the humility of a liberated slave, and launched at once into an interminable querimonious twaddle on the misfortunes of his "Political Thermometer," which had only a few readers. Considering its highly patriotic purpose, he pleaded, the Government should buy two or three hundred copies and have them distributed in the homes of the aristocrats, in the cafés, and in the churches.

"In the Caffe dell'Orto, opposite the Teatro Grande, for example. That is the nest of the aristocrats. Or in the Caffe del Mazza, where there are impudent ex-noblemen who address each other thus: 'Good morning, my dear ex-Marquis,' and 'Good-bye, my dear ex-Count'—with a complimentary dialogue which is unworthy, Sir."

A cavalry patrol galloped through the Piazza del Duomo.

"Unworthy," Lanza repeats, "for they are satisfied with an ex instead of receiving and communicating the title of Citizen, like me Lanza, like you, Citizen General."

Citizen Lanza, the illustrious bore with long hair and Masonic pins, was dismissed with the promise of a subsidy, a pat on the shoulder, and a terribly ironic smile.

The General remained alone, standing with his legs somewhat apart, his hands crossed back of him. He was immersed in silent contemplation of the portrait that Gros was painting at the time.

The hustle and bustle of the city rose deafeningly. The singing of hoarse and inebriated voices could be heard above the din:

> —Allons, chantons de ça et de là
> *La Marsigliesa con el ça ira!*

The door opened slowly as if a ghost or a wind were coming through. She advanced very timidly, one hand over her heart and the other on her waist, just as her petite figure demanded, and her head tilted slightly, as Cleofe, the modiste, had advised her to do. Her big black eyes betrayed the fear, and yet the desire, of coming so near to the General.

Hearing the creaking of the knob, the General turned to meet his caller. He tendered his hands cordially, his face serene and smiling:

"*Bonsoir, citoyenne; je suis heureux. . . .*"

And as the girl, watching him with her great bewildered eyes, pretended not to understand, he paused abruptly, somewhat piqued and surprised.

"*Vous ne parlez pas français, Mamzelle?*"

"No, Citizen General, I even speak Italian badly."

"And yet they say here in Italy that Italian is the language of love!"

"The language of love, sir, is silence."

He changed subject at once, unaccustomed as he was to flat and open contradictions.

"Have you come alone?"

"No, Citizen General, the hairdresser of the Teatro accompanied me to the door."

"Ah, you are an actress. Do you play? Do you sing?"

"I sing in the chorus of the Teatro Grande della Scala. I sang in the first act of the *Cosa Rara*, when you, Citizen General, were . . . Pardon me sir."

"But do they pay you well?"

"I do not know. My mother takes all my earnings."

He was rather amazed to find himself face to face with a young lady who had the shyness of a schoolgirl and yet spoke so impassably. He scrutinised her for a moment, squinting his eyes to sharpen his view. He was afraid to be deceived. Meanwhile she eyed him fixedly, her hands playing with her fan.

"How many sweethearts have you, *citoyenne?*"

She stared at him silently.

"At your age; *avec vos charmes et vos talents!* Surely you have one sweetheart."

"Yes, an artist who is following in the footsteps of Appiani. . . . He will be famous some day."

"Appiani belongs to the school of David. And your artist . . . how often do you betray him?"

"*Jamais.*"

"Then you do speak French!"

"When I want to be understood."

"*Bien! et les petits chiens? Aimez vous les petits chiens qui frôlent les jupes et couchent dans le lit de leur maîtresse?*"

"No, I have brothers and sisters."

"*Moi aussi.* In poverty?"

"Yes, Citizen General."

"*Dans une grande maison morne, dans l'ombre des arbres et des chagrins, avec une douce mère tyrann'que, sereine et bourgeoise. Je m'y connais, citoyenne. Je m'y connais, citoyenne. Je suis passé par là.* Your life is sad, dear one, is it not?"

"I do not know. At times it is. When the stage manager, for in-

stance, fines me for making a mistake, or for looking at the people in the
boxes, or for talking with Rachel."

"Who?"

"One of the *danseuses*. The dressmaker makes me wear the old
dresses."

"*Vraiment!*"

"My sister wears my new shoes. My mother will not give me supper
if I go dancing in the hostelries of the town, in the Cascina dei Pomi for
instance."

"*Après?*"

He was standing by the hearth, nervously poking the tongs into the
glowing embers.

"*Après. . . . Je suis bien triste lorsque Claudio s'en va:* he is fresco-
ing the ceilings of a village on Lake Como for an old singer. He stays
away two or three weeks. I fear he may be betraying me."

"Yes, my dear, that thought comes with all other thoughts. It creeps
into the heart like a snake."

"*Oui, citoyen.*"

"It is like a floating cork which keeps on coming to the surface."

"*C'est vrai.*"

"But we thrive on these secret innermost pains. They are an incentive
to live; for life, my dear, is more apt to cling to a sorrow than to a joy.
It is easier to master a desire than a grief. It was Jean-Jacques Rousseau
who wrote . . ."

"But you, Citizen General, who are omnipotent . . . !"

"I have not a moment of peace in this journey of despair, in this
struggle against everybody and everything. I have ventured into the darkness seeking fortune or misfortune, life or death, and it is this maddest
of all jealousies that spurs me on. And it may be this very jealousy that
has made me struggle all the more, kill all the more, conquer all the
more."

She was not listening. The sight of that lonely, broken hearted man
struggling in a whirlpool of passion gripped her singularly. She had come
to meet an immortal, but she had met a sufferer like herself, a mere man
in the clutches of the same immaterial enemy.

"I reach Milan by marches, forced marches," he continued, "taking
prisoners by the thousands and wresting flags everywhere. But she is not
here. My broken health demands the peace of family life and the care
of a woman. My insomnia needs but the sound of a voice, the face of a
woman. But she is not with me. I write, but she does not answer.

"Why is it that while I am night and day on horseback or sleeping on
an army cot on the eve of a battle or during bivouac, she should be listening to the flattery of a silly sparrow, or playing *colin-maillard* in the
salons of the villas? Do you play *colin-maillard?*"

"No, Citizen General, I don't."

He felt the atrocious, biting need of having to betray his jealousy at all cost, of revealing the sadness that was in his heart, to shout it to the four winds as it were. He felt the desire of having someone share that consuming fire. It was like a poison coursing through his veins, and he wanted to poison others, corrode the hearts and violate the souls of others. The morbid taciturnity with which he had been guarding his pride was giving away under the impetus of a delirious verbosity flowing like a current from his usually cold and obstinate soul.

He talked more than he wished. The feeling of torture, the pangs of pain, and the thought of *that woman*, drove him on irresistibly, as they had driven him on when on the road to Treviglio, many steps ahead of Massena's horse, his wailing echoed over the squalid plain thick with poplars crackling in the rain.

He tore the black cravat that held him by the throat and threw it on the floor.

"*Vous me trouvez malheureux . . . peut-être . . . ou ridicule?*"

"There is nothing ridiculous in love, Citizen General."

"*Pas dans l'amour, chérie; mais dans le mariage.*"

Realising the inopportunity of his confession and the vanity of his words he changed subject and behaviour with the swiftness of a wind. He became humble again, almost smiling, and began praising her dress with an improper terminology and an embarrassing cheerfulness.

"I have not offered you anything, have I? Will you accept some refreshments? I know that you Milanese are fond of sweets. What is the Italian for *glacés?*"

"*Gelati.*"

"No, not that."

"*Sorbetti.*"

She laughed sonorously, throwing back her curly head and showing a beautiful white throat in which her laughter quivered with the transparency of water. He caressed her gently, his fingers toying with her luscious locks.

"Last summer some of my officers walked five or six leagues at a time for one of your *sorbetti*. They would abandon their benches outside the Porta and spend their afternoons at the Caffe della Corsia dei Servi."

"Really?"

"Yes, Italy is sweetened indeed. It is all a *gâteau*."

"Not too small a *gâteau* for those who are very hungry."

He let the insolence go by. He had other things in mind. He put his arm around her shoulder and began playing with her necklace. He seemed happy. But it was not she that he would have preferred at his side. It was rather the woman who had held him affectionately on her knees while he posed for the portrait of Ponte d'Arcole.

The *citoyenne* moved away from him with a very chaste gesture. Holding the ends of her bodice, which had unlaced because of a fatality common to the garments of all women in all ages, she covered her eyes with her arm, pointing to the candelabra glowing over the fireplace.

"*À l'école de Brienne*," said the strange metallic voice in a forcibly gay tone, "we used to put out the candles with our boots and shoes. We were good shots those days."

She chuckled with a slight shiver in her shoulders which untied one of her tresses and made her hairpin fall. He picked it up gallantly. Then taking her by the hand, he swung her as in a dance around the room, raised her bodily to the height of the candelabra, and with a military sharpness barely attenuated by a smile, ordered her to blow.

Feu!

There was no trembling of the ground, no recoiling of artillery guns, no rattling of musketry, no clouds of smoke and death. But in the silence the girl's breath, as light as a sigh, fell upon the lights, as upon a flower, and blew them all out. All but one, and then the gay laughter broke out again, drowning the noise of heavy steps, of the spurs and boots passing through the hallways back of the closed doors.

There was a throbbing fever in his temples and in his pulses. He watched the shifting phantoms on the walls, contemplated the flickering agony of the remaining light.

Out on the Piazza hoarse and tired voices were still singing:

—Allons, chantons de ça et de là
La Marsigliesa con el ça ira!

A bloody glow cast its reflection fanlike over the mosaic floor, adding a touch of deep red to the bare feet of the *citoyenne*, who was gripped in the arms of the General as a dove in the clutches of a falcon.

He pulled her on his knees and held her madly like some prey. She felt her lips kissed violently, two terrible hands squeezing her impatiently and brutally. Her half closed eyes beheld the sudden shadow of a lock of hair that obscured her view, that covered his forehead. The mad figure gripped her, squeezed her, tortured her. There was a moment of deadly silence, and then she heard him cry in her face, in her hair, in her ears, in her throat, in a painful, passionate, sorrowful tone, a strange and foreign name:

"*Josephine! Josephine! Josephine! toi, toi, Josephine.*"

She broke loose from the General who, with his marvellous face transfigured by desire and folly, pursued her in the dark, still crying the strange name. A sudden sense of rebellion took hold of her. There was a rush of blood to her temples, a feeling of anger in her heart, and she slapped him.

He released his prey and calmed himself.

He went to the window and opened it so violently that the panes seemed to be breaking. An icy gust swept through the room, followed by a cloud of thick fog. The last candle blew out, the curtains swelled, and a door slammed. The enraged *citoyenne* was gone.

He saw the lamplighter coming through the Contrada dell'Arcivescovado, a sooty, greasy, broken figure limping under the weight of an old ladder and a box of wicks; and it occurred to him that the service was not well performed if the lamps were lit every night at that hour. He decided to have the Municipality do better the next day.

He was moving away when he heard the tumultuous and thunderous rumbling of an artillery regiment on its way to join Massena's army in Verona.

The rumbling and the roaring became louder and louder. The sleepy provincial city was shaken to its foundations. He seemed to hear the servants and the children weeping in their homes.

The heavy air seemed charged with the deep and laborious rolling in which a trained ear could distinguish the pounding of the howitzers, the tossing of the cannons, the trotting of horses, and the cracking of the whips.

One of the soldiers looked up and pointed to the sleepless shadow of General Bonaparte watching his migrating army.

GREAT BRITAIN

Introduction

ONLY a broad outline, in most condensed form, can here be given of the development of the English short story. As with all other national literatures, the history of the English short story parallels the growth of the nation and its changing tastes, so that with each new period we see new elements introduced into the story.

We first have the tale in verse form, the best examples of which are to be found in Chaucer. While his culture was French, he actually wrote in English. Chaucer drew his material from many sources, chiefly Italian, and with the skill of great artistry gave the world a masterpiece, the *Canterbury Tales*. This collection of stories, told by characters on a pilgrimage, betrays a rare humour, a profound knowledge of humanity in its mellow characterisation, and an inexhaustible versatility.

For a time after Chaucer, the short story languished. We have the *Gesta Romanorum*, a collection of dull, moral tales, translated from the Latin; and the lovely lyrics of Henryson as well as his *Testament of Cresseid*, a collection of stories in verse form. Towards the end of the fifteenth century Malory wrote his *Morte d'Arthur*. In the sixteenth century the Italian *novella*, or short story, was introduced, frequently from French translations; and these soon assumed the character of the English scene. Collections were produced by Painter, Green, Deloney, Rich and others, which became quite popular. But presently, the short story disappears and is not revived until the latter part of the seventeenth century, used by Addison, Steele; later, in the eighteenth century, by Hawkesworth and Goldsmith, who employ the story as a moral essay. We now see the novel ushered in, for the development of incident and character assumes proportions that cannot conveniently be limited to the short story. Nevertheless, fine distinctions had not yet been established and, consequently, we are frequently greeted with a short story that breaks up the thread of a long narrative, as, for example, Fielding or Sterne.

While the eighteenth century was the century of great prose, there were comparatively few who turned to the short story. This decline continued until the middle of the nineteenth century, when the story gradually began to develop and finally flourish into the form it has now achieved.

GEOFFREY CHAUCER
(1340-1400)

CHAUCER was born in London, the son of a wine-merchant. He did not attend a university, but he made up for his lack of scholasticism by extensive reading and a native mental activity. He was always connected with the court of Edward III. and held office in various capacities, as well as appointments on embassies to Italy. Chaucer's principal literary work is his *Canterbury Tales,* a series of stories within a story, on which he worked the last twelve years of his life. Apparently he never finished this masterpiece, for his original design was planned for a work about five times its present length. *The Pardoner's Tale* which follows is one of two perfect little stories in the *Canterbury Tales.* The present version is retold in prose by the editors.

THE PARDONER'S TALE
(From *Canterbury Tales*)

THERE dwelt one time in Flanders a company of young folk who followed such folly as riotous living and gaming in stews and taverns, where with harps, lutes and citerns they danced and played at dice both day and night, and ate and drank without restraint. Thus they served the Devil in cursed fashion within those Devil's temples by abominable superfluity.

These rioters, three, of whom I speak, long ere any bell had rung for prime had sat down in a tavern to drink. And as they sat, they heard the tinkle of a bell that was carried before a corpse to his grave. One of them called to his boy. 'Be off with you, and ask straightway what corpse is passing by; and mind you report his name aright.'

'Sir,' quoth the boy, 'that needs not be. It was told me two hours before you came here; he was an old fellow of yours, by God, and he was suddenly slain tonight, as he sat very drunk on his bench. There came a privy thief men call death, that slays all people in this countryside, and with his spear he smote his heart in two, and went his way without a word. A thousand he has slain in this pestilence; and master, ere you come into his presence, methinks it were best to be warned of such an adversary. Be ready to meet him ever; thus my mother taught me, I say no more.'

'By St. Mary,' said the taverner, 'the child speaks truth, for over a mile hence, in a large village, he has slain both woman, child, servant and knave. I trow his habitation be there. It were great wisdom to be advised ere he do injure a man.'

'Yea, God's arms!' quoth this rioter, 'is it such peril to meet with him? I will seek him in the highways and byways, I vow by God's bones. Hearken, fellows, we three be like; let each hold up his hand to the other and become the other's brother, and we will slay this false traitor, Death. He that slays so many shall be slain ere night, by God's Dignity!'

Together these three plighted their troth each to live and die for the rest as though he were their sworn brother, and up they then started in this drunken rage, and forth they went toward that village of which the taverner had spoken; and many a grisly oath they swore, and rent Christ's blessed body. —'Death shall be dead if they can but catch him.'

When they had gone not quite a mile just as they were about to go over a stile, an old man and poor met them and greeted them full meekly, and said, 'Lordings, God be with you!'

The proudest of the three rioters answered, 'What, churl, bad luck to you! Why are you all wrapped up save your face? Why live you so long to so great an age?'

This old man began to peer into his visage, and said, 'Because I cannot find a man, though I walked to India, neither in hamlet nor in city, who will change his youth for mine age. And therefore must I keep mine old age as long as it is God's will. Death, alas will not have me! Thus I walk like a restless caitiff, and early and late I knock with my staff upon the ground which is my mother's gate, and say, "Beloved Mother, let me in. Lo, how I wane away, flesh and blood and skin! Alas when shall my bones be at rest? Mother, with you I would exchange my chest, that has been long time in my chamber, yea for an hair-cloth to wrap me in!" But yet she will not do me that favour; wherefore my face is full pale and withered.—But sirs, it is not courteous to speak churlishly to an old man, unless he trespass in word or deed. You may yourselves read in Holy Writ, "Before an old hoary-head man ye shall arise;" wherefore I counsel you, do no harm now to an old man, no more than you would that men did to you in your old age if it be that you abide so long. And God be with you, wherever you go or be; I must go whither I have to go.'

'Nay old churl, you shall not go, by God,' said the second gamester straightway. 'You part not so lightly by St. John! You spoke right now of that traitor Death who slays all our friends in this country side. By my troth, you are his spy! Tell where he is, or by God and the Holy Sacrament you shall die. Truly you are of his consent to slay us young folk, false thief.'

'Now, sirs,' quoth he, 'if you be so lief to find Death, turn up this crooked way; for by my faith I left him in that grove under a tree, and there he will abide, nor for all your boasting will he hide him. See you that oak? Right here you shall find him. May God, Who redeemed mankind, save you and amend you!' Thus said this old man.

And each of these rioters ran till he came to the tree, and there they found florins coined of fine round gold well nigh seven bushels, as they thought. No longer sought they then after Death, but each was so glad at the sight that they sat them down by the precious hoard. The youngest of them spoke the first word. 'Brethren,' he said, 'heed what I say; my wit is great, though I jest oft and play. This treasure has been given us by Fortune that we may live our lives in mirth and jollity, and lightly as it comes, so we will spend it. Eh! God's precious dignity! Who would have weened today that we should have so fair a grace! But could this gold be carried to my house or else to yours,—for you know well all this gold is ours,—then were we in high felicity! But truly by day it may not be done. Men would say we were sturdy thieves and hang us for our treasure. This treasure must be carried by night, as wisely and as slyly as may be. Wherefore I advise that we draw cuts amongst us all, and he that draws the shortest shall run with a blithe heart to the town and that full swift and privily bring us bread and wine. And two of us shall cunningly guard this treasure, and at night, if he will not tarry, we will carry it where we all agree is safest.'

One of them brought the cuts in his fist and bade them draw and look where the lot should fall. It fell to the youngest of them and he went forth toward the town at once. So soon as he was gone one said to the other, 'You well know you are my sworn brother, and you will profit by what I tell you. Here is gold and plenty of it, to be divided amongst us three. You know well our fellow is gone. If I can shape it so that it be divided betwixt us two, had I not done you a friendly turn?'

The other answered, 'I wot not how that may be. He knows well the gold is with us two. What shall we do? What shall we say?'

'Shall it be a secret?' said the first wicked fellow. 'I shall tell you in a few words what we shall do to bring it about.'

'I agree,' quoth the other, 'not to betray you, by my troth.'

'Now,' quoth the first, 'you know well we be two and that two should be stronger than one. Look when he is set down; do you arise as though you would play with him, and I will rive him through the two sides while you struggle with him as in sport; and look that you do the same with your dagger. And then shall all this gold be shared, dear friend, betwixt you and me. Then may we both fulfil all our lusts, and play at dice at our will.' And thus, as you heard me say, were these two villains accorded to slay the third.

The youngest, who went to town, revolved full often in his heart the beauty of those bright new florins. 'Oh Lord,' quoth he, 'if so be I could have all this gold to myself, no man living under God's throne should live so merry as I!' And at last the fiend, our enemy, put it into his thought to buy poison with which he might slay his two fellows; for the fiend found him in such a way of life that he had leave to bring him to sorrow, for this was his full intention namely to slay them both and never to repent. And forth he went without tarrying into the town to an apothecary, and prayed him to sell him some poison that he might kill his rats; and there was also a pole-cat in his yard, which he said, had killed his capons and he would fain wreak him upon the vermin that destroyed him by night. The apothecary answered, 'And you shall have such a thing, that, so may God save my soul, no creature in all this world can eat or drink of this composition the amount of a grain of wheat, but he shall at once forfeit his life. Yea, die he shall, and that in less time than you can walk a mile, this poison is so strong and violent.'

This cursed man clutched the box of poison in his hand and then ran into the next street to a man and borrowed of him three large bottles. Into two of them he poured his poison, but the third he kept clean for his drink, for all night long he planned to labour in carrying away his gold. And when this rioter, the Devil take him! had filled his three great bottles with wine, he repaired again to his fellows.

What need to speak about it more? for just as they had planned his death, even so they slew him, and that anon. And when this was done, one spake thus, 'Now let us sit and drink and make merry, and then we will bury his body.' And then by chance, he took one of the bottles where the poison was, and he drank and gave his fellow to drink also. Wherefore anon they both died. And Certes Avicenna wrote never in any canon or any chapter more wondrous sufferings of empoisoning than these two wretches showed ere they died. Thus ended these two murderers as well as the poisoner.

❋ ❋ ❋

THOMAS DELONEY
(1543-1600)

DELONEY worked as a silk-weaver in Norwich, and came to London by 1586, where he began writing ballads that involved him in difficulties. He then turned to prose, writing in a simple, natural and direct manner of middle-class citizens and tradesmen. Each of his novels concerns itself with a different trade, and *The Gentle Craft* is dedicated to the praise of shoemakers. *Sir Simon Eyer*, which appears in *The Gentle Craft*, is conceived in a pleasant humour and shows that even a shoemaker may be a good subject for a story; a thought which might have sounded heretical before the days of Deloney. But we must remember that he wrote at a time when the Gilds were a respected power.

SIR SIMON EYER

(From *The Gentle Craft*)

IT came to pass, that Simon having at length worn out his years of apprenticeship, that he fell in love with a maiden that was near neighbour unto him, unto whom at length he was married and got him a shop, and laboured hard daily, and his young wife was never idle, but straight when she had nothing to do, she sat in the shop and spun: and having lived thus alone a year or thereabout, and having gathered something together, at length he got him some prentises, and a journey-man or two, and he could not make his ware so fast as he could have sold it, so that he stood in great need of a journey-man or two more.

At the last, one of his servants spying one go along the street with a fardell at his back, called to his master, saying, "Sir, yonder goes Saint Hugh's bones, twenty pounds to a penny."

"Run presently," quoth he, "and bring him hither."

The fellow, being a Frenchman that had not long been in England, turning about, said, "Hea? what you sea? Will you speak wed me Hea? What you have? tell me, what you have, Hea?" And with that coming to the stall, the good man asked him if he lacked work, "We pay ma foy," quoth the Frenchman.

Hereupon Simon took him in, and to work he went merrily, where he behaved himself so well, that his master made good account of him, thinking he had been a bachelor, but in the end it was found otherwise.

This man was the first that wrought upon the low cut shoe, with the square toe, and the latchet overthwart the instep, before which time in England they did wear a high shoe that reached above the ankles, right after the manner of our husbandmen's shoes at this day, save only that it was made very sharp at the toe, turning up like the tail of an Island dog or as you see a cock carry his hinder feathers.

Now it is to be remembered, that while John Denevale dwelt with Simon Eyer, it chanced that a ship of the Isle of Candy was driven upon our coast, laden with all kinds of lawns and cambrics and other linen cloth: which commodities at that time were in London very scant, and exceedingly dear: and by reason of a great leak the ship had got at sea being unable to sail any further, he would make what profit he could of his goods here.

And being come to London, it was John Denevale's chance to meet him in the streets, to whom the merchant (in the Greek tongue) demanded where he might have lodging: for he was one that had never been in England before, and being unacquainted, did not know where to go: but while he spoke in Greek, John Denevale answered him still in French, which tongue the merchant understood well: and therefore being glad that he had met with one that could talk to him, he declared unto him what tempests he endured at sea, and also how his ship lay upon the coast with such commodities as he would sell.

"Truly, sir," quoth John, "I am myself but a stranger in this country and utterly unacquainted with merchants, but I dwell with one in this city that is a very honest man, and it may be that he can help you to some that will deal with you for it, and if you think it good, I will move him in it, and in the meantime, I'll bring you where you may have a very good lodging; tomorrow morning I will come to you again."

"Sir," said the merchant, "if you please to do me that favour, I'll not only be thankful unto you for the same, but also in most honest sort will content you for your pains:" and with that they departed.

Now as soon as John the Frenchman came home, he moved that matter unto his master, desiring him that he would do what he could for the merchant. When his master had heard each circumstance, noting therewith the want of such commodities in the land, cast in his mind as he stood cutting up his work, what were best to be done in this case, saying to his man John, "I will think upon it between this and the morning, and then I will tell you my mind:" and therewithall casting down his cutting knife, he went out of his shop into his chamber, and therein walked up and down alone very sadly, ruminating hereon: he was so far in his muse, that, his wife sending for him to supper two or three times, he nothing regarded the maid's call, hammering this matter in his head.

At last his wife came to him, saying, "Husband, what mean you that you do not come to supper? Why speak you not, man? Hear you? good husband; come away, your meat will be cold!" But for all her words he stayed walking up and down still, like a man that had sent his wits a wool-gathering, which his wife seeing, pulled him by the sleeve, saying, "Why, husband, in the name of God, why come you not? Will you not come to supper tonight? I called you a good while ago."

"Body of me, wife," said he, "I promise thee I did not hear thee."

"No, faith, it seems so," quoth she, "I marvel whereupon your mind runneth."

"Believe me, wife," quoth he, "I was studying how to make myself Lord Mayor and thee a lady."

"Now God help you," quoth she, "I pray God make us able to pay every man his own, that we may live out of debt and danger, and drive the wolf from the door, and I desire no more."

"But, wife," said he, "I pray thee now tell me, dost thou not think that thou couldest make shift to bear the name of a lady, if it should be put upon thee?"

"In truth, husband," quoth she, "I'll dissemble with you, if your wealth were able to bear it, my mind would bear it well enough."

"Well, wife," replied he, "I tell thee now in sadness, that, if I had

money, there is a commodity now to be bought, the gains whereof wou[
be able to make me a gentleman forever."

"Alas, husband, that dignity your trade allows you already, being
squire of the Gentle Craft, then how can you be less than a gentlema
seeing your son is a prince born?"

"Tush, wife," quoth he, "those titles do only rest in name, but not i
nature: but of that sort had I rather be, whose lands are answerable 1
their virtues, and whose rents can maintain the greatness of their mind.

"Then, sweet husband, tell me," said his wife, "tell me, what com
modity is that which you might get so much by? I am sure yourself hat
some money, and it shall go very hard, but I'll procure friends to borro
one forty shillings, and beside that, rather than you should lose so goc
a bargain, I have a couple of crowns that saw no sun since we were fir
married, and them also shall you have."

"Alas, wife," said Simon, "all this comes not near that matter:
confess it would do some good in buying some backs of leather, but i
this thing it is nothing, for this is merchandise that is precious at th
time, and rare to be had; and I hear that whosoever will have it mu
lay down three thousand pounds ready money. Yea, wife, and y
thereby he might get three and three thousand pounds profit."

His wife hearing him say so was inflamed with the desire thereof, ;
women are (for the most part) very covetous: that matter running sti
in her mind, she could scant find in her heart to spare him time to go 1
supper, for very eagerness to animate him on, to take that bargain upc
him. Wherefore so soon as they had supped, and given God thank
she called her husband, saying, "I pray you, come hither, I would spea
a word with you: that man is not always to be blamed that sometim
takes counsel of his wife; though women's wits are not able to compr
hend the greatest things, yet in doubtful matters they oft help on
sudden."

"Well, wife, what mean you by this?" said her husband.

"In truth," quoth she, "I would have you to pluck up a man's hear
and speedily chop up a bargain for these goods you speak of."

"Who I?" quoth he, "which way should I do it, that am not able fc
three thousand pounds, to lay down three thousand pence?"

"Tush man," quoth she, "what of that? every man that beholds
man in the face, knows not what he hath in his purse, and whatsoeve
he be that owes the goods, he will no doubt be content to stay a mont
for his money, and three weeks at the least: And, I promise you, to pa
a thousand pounds a week is a pretty round payment, and, I may say t
you, not much to be misliked of.

"Now, husband, I would have you in the morning with John th
Frenchman to the Grecian merchant, and with good discretion drive
sound bargain with him for the whole freight of the ship, and thereupc

ive him half a dozen angels in earnest, and eight and twenty days after
he delivery of the goods, condition to deliver him the rest of his money."

"But, woman," quoth he, "dost thou imagine that he would take my
vord for so weighty a mass of .money, and to deliver his goods upon no
etter security?"

"Good Lord," quoth she, "have you no wit in such a case to make
hift? I'll tell you what you shall do: Be not known that you bargain
or your own self, but tell him that you do it in the behalf of one of
ie chief aldermen in the city; but beware in any case, that you leave
ith him your own name in writing; he being a Grecian cannot read
.nglish: and you have no need at all to show John the Frenchman, nor
f you should, it were no great matter, for you can tell well enough
iat he can neither write nor read."

"I perceive, wife," quoth he, "thou wouldst fain be a lady, and
vorthy thou art to be one, that dost thus employ thy wits to bring thy
usband profit: but tell me, if he should be desirous to see the alderman
) confer with him, how shall we do then?"

"Jesus have mercy upon us," quoth she. "You say women are fools,
ut me seemeth men have need to be taught sometimes. Before you come
way in the morning, let John the Frenchman tell him that the alderman
imself shall come to his lodging in the afternoon: and, receiving a note
f all the goods that be in the ship, he shall deliver unto him a bill of
is hand for the payment of his money, according to that time. Now,
veetheart," quoth she, "this alderman shall be thine own self, and I'll
o borrow for thee all things that shall be necessary against that time."

"Tush," quoth her husband, "canst thou imagine that he, seeing me
1 the morning, will not know me again in the afternoon?"

"Oh, husband," quoth she, "he will not know thee, I warrant thee:
or in the morning thou shalt go to him in thy doublets of sheeps' skins,
ith a smuched face, and thy apron before thee, thy thumb-leather and
and-leather buckled close to thy wrist, with a foul band about thy neck,
nd a greasy cap on thy head."

"Why, woman," quoth he, "to go in this sort will be a discredit to
le, and make the merchant doubtful of my dealing: for men of simple
ttire are (God wot) slenderly esteemed."

"Hold your peace, good husband," quoth she, "it shall not be so with
ou, for John the Frenchman shall give such good report to the merchant
or your honest dealing (as I praise God he can do no less) that the
recian will rather conceive the better of you than otherwise: judging
ou a prudent discreet man, that will not make a show of that you are
ot, but go in your attire agreeable to your trade. And because none of
ur folks shall be privy to our intent, tomorrow we'll dine at my cousin
ohn Barber's in Saint Clements Lane, which is not far from the George
1 Lumbard Street, where the merchant strangers lie. Now I'll be sure

that all things shall be ready at my cousin John's that you shall put on
in the afternoon. And there he shall first of all with his scissors snap
off all the superfluous hairs, and fashion thy bushy beard after the alderman's grave cut: then shall he wash thee with a sweet camphor ball, and
besprinkle thine head and face with the purest rose-water; then shall
thou scour thy pitchy fingers in a basin of hot water, with an ordinary
washing ball; and all this being done, strip thee from these common
weeds, and I'll put thee on a very fair doublet of tawny satin, over the
which thou shalt have a cassock of branched damask, furred round about
the skirts with the finest foynes, thy breeches of black velvet, and shoes
and stockings fit for such array: a band about thy neck as white as the
driven snow, and for thy wrists a pretty pair of cuffs, and on thy
head a cap of the finest black, then shalt thou put on a fair gown, welted
about with velvet, and overthwart the back thwart it shall be with rich
foyne, with a pair of sweet gloves on thy hands, and on thy forefinger
great seal-ring of gold.

"Thou being thus attired, I'll intreat my cousin John Barber, because
he is a very handsome young man, neat and fine in his apparel (as indeed
all barbers are) that he would take the pains to wait upon you unto the
merchants, as if he were your man, which he will do at the first, because
one of you cannot understand the other, so that it will be sufficient with
outward curtesie one to greet another, and he to deliver unto you his notes
and you to give him your bill, and so come home.

"It doth my heart good, to see how trimly this apparel doth become you, in good faith, husband, me seems in my mind, I see you in
already, and how like an alderman you will look, when you are in the
costly array. At your return from the merchant, you shall put off all
these clothes at my cousin's again, and come home as you did go forth.
Then tell John the Frenchman, that the alderman was with the merchant
this afternoon, you may send him to him in the morning, and bid him to
command that his ship may be brought down the river: while she is coming about, you may give notice to the linen drapers, of the commodities
you have coming."

"Enough, wife," quoth he, "thou hast said enough; and, by the grace
of God, I'll follow thy counsel, and I doubt not but to have good
fortune."

Anon, after supper time drew near, she, making herself ready in
the best manner she could devise, passed along with her husband unto my
Lord Mayor's house: and being entered into the great hall, one of the
officers there certified my Lord Mayor that the great, rich shoemaker and
his wife were already come. Whereupon the Lord Mayor in courteous
manner came into the hall to Simon, saying, "You are most heartily welcome good Master Eyer, and so is your gentleman bed-fellow." Then
came forth the Lady Mayoress and saluted them both in like manner

aying, "Welcome, good Master Eyer and Mistress Eyer both:" and
aking her by the hand, set her down among the gentlewomen there
resent.

"Sir," quoth the Lord Mayor, "I understand that you are a shoe-
naker, and that it is you that hath bought up all the goods of the great
Argozy."

"I am indeed, my lord, of the Gentle craft," quoth he, "and I praise
God, all the goods of the great Argozy are mine own, when my debts
re paid."

"God give you much joy of them," said the Lord Mayor, "and I trust
ou and I shall deal for some part thereof."

So the meat being then ready to be brought in, the guests were placed
ach one according to their calling. My Lord Mayor holding Simon by
he hand, and the Lady Mayoress holding his wife, they would needs have
hem sit near to themselves, which they then with blushing cheeks refus-
ng, my lord said unto them, holding his cap in his hand.

"Master Eyer and Mistress Eyer, let me intreat you not to be trouble-
ome, for I tell you it shall be thus: and as for those gentlemen here
resent, they are all of mine old acquaintance, and many times we have
een together, therefore I dare be the bolder with them: albeit you are
ur neighbours also, yet I promise you, you are strangers to my table,
nd to strangers common courtesy doth teach us to show the greatest
avour, and therefore let me rule you in mine house, and you shall rule
ae 'n yours."

When Simon found there was no remedy, they sat them down, but
he poor woman was so abashed, that she did eat but little meat at the
able, bearing herself at the table with a comely and modest countenance:
ut what she wanted in outward feeding, her heart yielded to, with inward
elight and content.

Now, so it was, many men that knew not Simon, and seeing him in so
mple attire sit next to my lord, whisperingly asked one another what
e was. And it was enough for Simon's wife, with her eyes and her
ars, to see and hearken after everything that was said or done.

A grave, wealthy citizen, sitting at the table, spoke to Simon, and said,
Sir, in good will I drink to your good health, but I beseech you pardon
ae, for I know not how to call your name."

With that my Lord Mayor answered him, saying, "His name is
Iaster Eyer, and this is the gentleman that bought all the goods that came
a the *Black Swan* of Candy, and, before God, though he sit here in
mple sort, for his wealth I do verily believe he is more sufficient to bear
ais place than myself. This was a man that was never thought upon,
ving obscure amongst us, of no account in the eyes of the world, carry-
ag the countenance but of a shoemaker, and none of the best sort neither,
nd is able to deal for a bargain of five thousand pounds at a clap."

"We do want many such shoemakers," said the citizen. And so wit other discourse drew out supper.

At what time, rising from the table, Simon and his wife, receivin sundry salutations of my Lord Mayor and his lady, and of all the res of the worshipful guests, departed home to their own house: at wha time his wife made such a recital of the matters; how bravely they wer entertained, what great cheer was there, also what a great company o gentlemen and gentlewomen were there, and how often they drank to he husband and to her, with divers other circumstances, that I believe, i the night had been six months long, as it is under the north pole, the would have found talk enough till morning.

"Of a truth," quoth she, "although I sat closely by my ladies' side, could eat nothing for very joy, to hear and see that we were so muc made of. And ever give me credit, husband, if I did not hear th officers whisper as they stood behind me, and all demanded one of anothe what you were, and what I was: 'Oh,' quoth one, 'do you see this man Mark him well, and mark his wife well, that simple woman that si next my lady, what are they?' 'What are they?' quoth another. 'Marr this is the rich shoemaker that bought all the goods in the great Argozy I tell you there was never such a shoemaker seen in London since the ci was builded.' 'Now by my faith,' quoth the third, 'I have heard much o him today among the merchants in the street, going between the tw chains.' Credit me, husband, of mine honesty, this was their communica tion. Nay, and do you not remember, when the rich citizen drank you (which craved pardon because he knew not your name) what m Lord Mayor said? 'Sir,' quoth he, 'his name is Master Eyer,' did yc mark that? And presently thereupon he added these words: 'This is th gentleman that bought,' and so forth. The gentleman understood yo did you hear him speak that word?"

"In truth, wife," quoth he, "my lord uttered many good words c me, I thank his honour, but I heard not that."

"No," quoth she. "I heard it well enough: for by and by he pr ceeded further, saying, 'I suppose though he sit here in simple sort, he more sufficient to bear this charge than myself.' Yea," though I, "I may thank his wife for that, if it come so to pass."

"Nay," said Simon, "I thank God for it."

"Yea, and next him you may thank me," quoth she. And it did h so much good to talk of it, that I suppose, if she had lived till this da she would yet be prating thereof, and if sleep did not drive her from

And now seeing that Simon the shoemaker is become a merchant, v will temper our tongues to give him that title, which his customers we wont to do, and from henceforth call him Master Eyer, who, while had his affairs in hand, committed the government of his shop to Jo the Frenchman, leaving him to be guide of his other servants, by mea of which favour John thought himself at that time to be a man of no small reputation.

In this space Master Eyer following his business, had sold so much of his merchandise as paid the Grecian his whole money: and yet had resting to himself three times as much as he had sold, whereof he trusted some to one alderman, and some to another, and a great deal amongst substantial merchants; and for some had much ready money, which he employed in divers merchandises: and became adventurer at Sea, having, (by God's blessing) many a prosperous voyage, whereby his riches daily increased.

It chanced upon a time, that being in his study, casting up his accounts, he found himself to be clearly worth twelve or thirteen thousand pounds, which he finding to be so, called his wife to him, and said:

"The last day I did cast up my accounts, and I find that Almighty God of his goodness hath lent me thirteen thousand pounds to maintain us in our old age, for which his gracious goodness towards us, let us with our whole hearts give his glorious Majesty eternal praise, and therewithall pray unto him, that we may so dispose thereof, as may be to his honour, and the comfort of his poor members on earth, and above our neighbours may not be puffed up with pride, that, while we think on our wealth, we forget God that sent it to us, for it hath been an old saying of a wise man, that abundance groweth from riches, and disdain out of abundance: of which God give us grace to take heed, and grant us a contented mind."

So soon as he had spoken this, they heard one knocking hastily at the door, whereupon he sent Florence to see who it was; the maiden, coming again, told her master it was one of my Lord Mayor's officers that would speak with him. The officer being permitted to come in, after due reverence, he said, "Sir, it hath pleased my Lord Mayor with the worshipful aldermen his brethren, with the counsel of the whole communaltie of the honourable city, to choose your worship Sheriff of London this day, and have sent me to desire you to come and certify your mind therein, whether you be contented to hold the place or no."

Master Eyer hearing this, answered he would come to his honour and their worships incontinent, and resolve them what he was minded to do; and so the officer departed.

His wife, which all this while listened to their talk, hearing how the case stood, with a joyful countenance meeting her husband, taking him about the neck with a loving kiss, said, "Master Sheriff, God give thee joy of thy name and place!"

"Oh, wife," quoth he, "my person is far unworthy of that place, and the name far exceeds my degree."

"What, content yourself, good husband," quoth she, "and disable not yourself in such sort, but be thankful unto God for that you have, and

do not spurn at such promotion as God sendeth unto you: the Lord b
praised for it, you have enough to discharge the place whereunto you ar
called with credit: and wherefore sendeth God goods, but therewithall t
do him and your country service?"

"Woman," quoth he, "soft fire makes sweet malt: For such as tak
things in hand rashly, repent as suddenly: to be Sheriff of London is n
little cost.　Consider first," quoth he, "what house I ought to have, an
what costly ornaments belong thereunto, as: hanging tapestry cloth o
Arras, and other such like, what sort of plate and goblets of gold, wha
costly attire, and what a chargeable train, and that which is most of all
how greatly I stand charged beside, to our Sovereign Lord, the King, fo
the answering of such prisoners as shall be committed to my custody, wit
a hundred matters of such importance, which are to such an office be
longing."

"Good Lord husband," quoth she, "what need of all these repetitions
You need not tell me it is a matter of great charge: notwithstanding,
verily think many heretofore have with great credit discharged the place
whose wealth hath not in any sort been answerable to your riches, an
whose wits have been as mean as your own: truly sir, shall I be plain
I know not anything that is to be spoken of, that you want to perform i
but only your good will: and to lack good will to do your king an
country good were a sign of an unworthy subject, which I hope you wi
never be."

"Well, wife," said the husband, "thou dost hold me here with prittl
prattle, while the time passes on; 'tis high time I were gone, to Guild
Hall, I doubt I shall appear too unmannerly in causing my Lord Mayo
and the rest to stay my leisure."

And he having made himself ready, meet to go before such an a
sembly as he went unto, he went out of doors, at what time his wife calle
after him, saying: and holding up her finger, "Husband, remember, yo
know what I have said: 'take heed you dissemble not with God and th
world', look to it, husband."

"Go to, go to, get you in," quoth he, "about your business."　An
so away he went.

So soon as he was gone out of sight, his wife sent one of his me
after him to Guild-Hall, to hearken and hear, whether her husband he
his place or no: "And if he do," she said, "bring me word with all possib
speed."

"I will, mistress," quoth her man.

Now, when Master Eyer came to Guild-Hall, the Lord Mayor a
his brethren bade him heartily welcome, saying, "Sir, the community
the city, having a good opinion of you, have chosen you for one of ou
Sheriffs for this year, not doubting but to find you a man fit for th
place."

"My good Lord," quoth he, "I humbly thank the city for their courtesy and kindness, and I would to God my wealth were answerable to my good will, and my ability were able to bear it. But I find myself insufficient; I most humbly desire a year's respite more, and pardon for this present."

At these words, a grave commoner of the city standing up, with due reverence spoke thus unto the Mayor: "My good Lord, this is but a tender excuse for Master Eyer to make; for I have often heard him say, and so have divers others also, that he hath a table in his house whereon he breaks his fast every day, that he will not give for a thousand pounds. Wherefore (under your Lordship's correction) in my simple judgment, I think he that is able to spare a thousand pounds in such a dead commodity is very sufficient to be Sheriff of London."

"See you now," quoth my Lord, "I muse, Master Eyer, that you will give so lame an excuse before us, as to take exceptions, at your own wealth, which is apparently proved sufficient; you must know, Master Eyer, that the commons of London have searching eyes, and seldom are they deceived in their opinion, and, therefore looke what is done, you must stand to it."

"I beseech you, my Lord," quoth Master Eyer, "give me leave to speak one word. Let it be granted, that I will not give my table whereon I break my fast for a thousand pounds, that is no consequence to prove it is worth so much, my fancy to the thing is all: for doubtless no man more would give me a thousand shillings for it when they see it."

"All is one, for that," quoth my Lord Mayor, "yet dare I give you as much wine as you will spend this year in your shrivaltie to let me have "

"My good Lord," quoth he, "on that condition I will hold my place, and rest no longer troublesome to this company."

"You must hold," said my Lord, "without any condition or exceptions, at all in this matter;" and so they ended.

The assembly being then broken up, the voice went, "Master Eyer is Sheriff, Master Eyer is Sheriff." Whereupon the fellow that Mistress Eyer sent to observe how things framed, ran home in all haste, and with leaping and rejoicing said: "Mistress, God give you joy, for you are now a gentlewoman."

"What?" quoth she. "Tell me, sir sawce, is thy master Sheriff, or ? and doth he hold his place?"

"Yes, mistress, he holds it now as fast as the stirrup doth the shoes while we sew it."

"Why then," quoth she, "I have my heart's desire, and that I so long looked for." And so away she went.

Within a while after came her husband, and with him one of the aldermen, and a couple of wealthy commoners, one of them was he that

gave such great commendations of his table, and coming to his door, h
said, "You are welcome home, good master Sheriff."

"Nay, I pray you, come in and drink with me before you go." The
said he, "Wife, bring me forth the pasty of venison, and set me here m
little table, that these gentlemen may eat a bit with me before they go.

His wife, which had been oft used to this term, excused the matte
saying; "The little table! Good Lord, husband, I do wonder what yo
will do with the little table now, knowing that it is used already? I pra
you, good husband, content yourself, and sit at this great table this once.
Then she whispered him in the ear, saying; "What, man, shall we sham
ourselves?"

"What shame?" quoth he. "Tell me not of shame, but do thou
thou art bidden; for we are three or four of us, then what do w
troubling the great table?"

"Truly," answered she, "the little table is not ready now, good hu
band, let it alone."

"Trust me we are troublesome guests," said the alderman, "but y
we would fain see your little table, because it is said to be of such prize.

"Yea, and it is my mind you shall," quoth Master Eyer. Therefo
he called his wife again, saying, "Good wife, dispatch and prepare t
little table: for these gentlemen would fain have a view of it."

Whereupon his wife, seeing him so earnest, according to her wont
manner, came in: and setting herself down on a low stool, laid a fa
napkin over her knees, and set the platter with the pasty of venison ther
upon, and presently a chair was brought for master alderman, and a coup
of stools for the two commoners, which they beholding, with a sudd
and hearty laughter, said: "Why, Master Sheriff, is this the table yo
held so dear?"

"Yes truly," quoth he.

"Now verily," quoth they, "you herein have utterly deceived o
expectation."

"Even as did you mine," quoth he, "in making me Sheriff: but y
are right welcome, and I will tell you true, had I not thought wondro
well of you, you had not seen my table now. And I think, did my Lo
Mayor see it as you do, he would repent his bargain so hastily mac
Notwithstanding I account of my table never the worse."

"Nor have you any cause," quoth they, and so after much pleasa
talk, they departed, spreading the fame of Master Sheriff's little tab
over the whole city.

DANIEL DEFOE
(1659?-1731)

DEFOE, the son of a butcher, was born in London. His father being
a Dissenter, he was educated at a Dissenting College for the Presby-
terian ministry. This being distasteful to him, he joined the army
of Monmouth, and on its defeat was fortunate to escape punishment.
Before settling down as a pamphleteer, Defoe had been engaged as
a hosier, a merchant adventurer and a brick-maker, all with so little
success that he had to fly from creditors. As a result of writing
The Shortest Way With the Dissenters, he suffered imprisonment for
two years. He finally gave up political writing and took to fiction,
producing his first and most famous novel, *Robinson Crusoe,* in 1719.
These were followed by his other well-known novels and shorter
fiction. In all, he wrote, including his political pamphlets, some 250
works. His fiction is distinguished by a clear, nervous style and by
a naturalness of incident. *In Defence of His Right* is an unusual
example of Defoe's realism and exhibits many of the characteristics
of the modern story.

IN DEFENCE OF HIS RIGHT

A GENTLEMAN of a very good estate married a lady of also a
good fortune, and had one son by her, and one daughter, and no
more, and after a few years his lady died. He soon married a
second venter; and his second wife, though of an inferior quality and
fortune to the former, took upon her to discourage and discountenance
his children by his first lady, and made the family very uncomfortable,
both to the children and to their father also.

The first thing of consequence which this conduct of the mother-in-
law produced in the family, was that the son, who began to be a man,
asked the father's leave to go abroad to travel. The mother-in-law,
though willing enough to be rid of the young man, yet because it would
require something considerable to support his expenses abroad, violently
opposed it, and brought his father also to refuse him after he had freely
given him his consent.

This so affected the young gentleman, that after using all the dutiful
applications to his father that he could possibly do, as well by himself as
by some other relations, but to no purpose; and being a little encouraged
by an uncle, who was brother to his mother, his father's first lady, he
resolved to go abroad without leave, and accordingly did so.

What part of the world he travelled into I do not remember; it seems
his father had constantly intelligence from him for some time, and was

prevailed with to make him a reasonable allowance for his subsistence, which the young gentleman always drew bills for, and they were honourably paid; but after some time, the mother-in-law prevailing at home, one of his bills of exchange was refused, and being protested, was sent back without acceptance; upon which he drew no more, nor did he write any more letters, or his father hear anything from him for upwards of four years, or thereabout.

Upon this long silence, the mother-in-law made her advantage several ways; she first intimated to his father that he must needs be dead; and consequently, his estate should be settled upon her eldest son (for she had several children). His father withstood the motion very firmly, but the wife harassed him with her importunities; and she argued upon two points against him, I mean the son.

First, if he was dead, then there was no room to object, her son being heir at law.

Secondly, if he was not dead, his behaviour to his father in not writing for so long a time was inexcusable, and he ought to resent it, and settle the estate as if he were dead; that nothing could be more disobliging, and his father ought to depend upon it that he was dead, and treat him as if he was so; for he that would use a father so, should be taken for one dead as to his filial relation, and be treated accordingly.

His father, however, stood out a long time, and told her that he could not answer it to his conscience; that there might happen many things in the world, which might render his son unable to write; that he might be taken by the Turks, and carried into slavery; or he might be among the Persians or Arabians (which it seems was the case), and so could not get any letters conveyed; and that he could not be satisfied to disinherit him till he knew whether he had reason for it or no, or whether his son had offended him or no.

These answers, however just, were far from stopping her importunities, which she carried on so far, that she gave him no rest, and it made an unquiet family; she carried it very ill to him, and in a word, made her children do so too; and the gentleman was so wearied out with it, that once or twice he came to a kind of consent to do it, but his heart failed him, and then he fell back again, and refused.

However, her having brought him so near it, was an encouragement to her to go on with her restless solicitations, till at last he came thus far to a provisional agreement, that if he did not hear from his son by such a time, or before it, he would consent to a re-settling the estate.

She was not well satisfied with the conditional agreement, but being able to obtain no other, she was obliged to accept of it as it was; though as she often told him, she was far from being satisfied with it as to the time, for he had fixed it for four years, as above.

He grew angry at her telling him so, and answered, that she ought to be very well satisfied with it, for that it was time little enough, as his son's circumstances might be.

Well, she teased him however so continually, that at last she brought him down to one year: but before she brought him to that, she told him one day in a heat, that she hoped his ghost would one time or other appear to him, and tell him that he was dead, and that he ought to do justice to his other children, for he should never come to claim the estate.

When he came, so much against his will, to consent to shorten the time to one year, he told her that he hoped his son's ghost, though he was not dead, would come to her, and tell her he was alive, before the time expired. "For why," says he, "may not injured souls walk while embodied, as well as afterwards?"

It happened one evening after this, that they had a most violent family quarrel upon this subject, when on a sudden a hand appeared at a casement, endeavouring to open it; but as all the iron casements used in former times opened outward, but hasped and fastened themselves in the inside, so the hand seemed to try to open the casement, but could not. The gentleman did not see it, but his wife did, and she presently started up, as if she was frighted, and, forgetting the quarrel they had upon their hands: "Lord bless me!" says she, "there are thieves in the garden." Her husband ran immediately to the door of the room they sat in, and opening it, looked out.

"There's nobody in the garden," says he; so he clapped the door to again, and came back.

"I am sure," says she, "I saw a man there."

"It must be the devil then," says he; "for I'm sure there's nobody in the garden."

"I'll swear," says she, "I saw a man put his hand up to open the casement; but finding it fast, and I suppose," adds she, "seeing us in the room, he walked off."

"It is impossible he could be gone," says he; "did not I run to the door immediately? and you know the garden walls on both sides hinder him going."

"Pry'thee," says she angrily, "I an't drunk nor in a dream, I know a man when I see him, and 'tis not dark, the sun is not quite down."

"You're only frighted with shadows," says he (very full of ill-nature): "folks generally are so that are haunted with an evil conscience: it may be 'twas the devil."

"No, no, I'm not soon frighted," says she; "if 'twas the devil, 'twas the ghost of your son: it may be come to tell you he was gone to the devil, and you might give your estate to your eldest bastard, since you won't settle it on the lawful heir."

"If it was my son," says he, "he's come to tell us he's alive, I warrant you, and to ask how you can be so much a devil to desire me to disinherit him;" and with these words: "Alexander," says he aloud, repeating it twice, starting up out of his chair, "if you are alive, show yourself, and don't let me be insulted thus every day with your being dead."

At those very words, the casement which the hand had been seen at by the mother, opened of itself, and his son Alexander looked in with a full face, and staring directly upon the mother with an angry countenance, cried "Here," and then vanished in a moment.

The woman that was so stout before, shrieked out in a most dismal manner, so that the whole house was alarmed; her maid ran into the parlour, to see what was the matter, but her mistress was fainted away in her chair.

She was not fallen upon the ground, because it being a great easy chair, she sunk a little back against the side of the chair, and help coming immediately in, they kept her up; but it was not till a great while after, that she recovered enough to be sensible of anything.

Her husband ran immediately to the parlour door, and opening it, went into the garden, but there was nothing; and after that he ran to another door that opened from the house into the garden, and then to two other doors which opened out of his garden, one into the stable-yard, and another into the field beyond the garden, but found them all fast shut and barred; but on one side was his gardener, and a boy, drawing the rolling-stone: he asked them if anybody else had been in the garden, but they both constantly affirmed nobody had been there; and they were both rolling a gravel-walk near the house.

Upon this he comes back into the room, sits him down again, and said not one word for a good while; the woman and servants being busy all the while, and in a hurry, endeavouring to recover his wife.

After some time she recovered so far as to speak, and the first words she said, were:

"L—d bless me! what was it?"

"Nay," says her husband, "it was Alexander, to be sure."

With that she fell into a fit, and screamed and shrieked out again most terribly.

Her husband not thinking that would have affected her, did what he could to persuade her out of it again; but that would not do, and they were obliged to carry her to bed, and get some help to her; but she continued very ill for several days after.

However, this put an end for some considerable time to her solicitations about his disinheriting her son-in-law.

But time, that hardens the mind in cases of a worse nature, wore this off also by degrees, and she began to revive the old cause again, though not at first so eagerly as before.

Nay, he used her a little hardly upon it too, and if ever they had any words about it he would bid her hold her tongue, or that if she talked any more upon that subject, he would call Alexander again to open the casement.

This aggravated things much; and though it terrified her a great while, yet at length she was so exasperated, that she told him she believed he dealt with the devil, and that he had sold himself to the devil only to be able to fright his wife.

He jested with her, and told her any man would be beholden to the devil to hush a noisy woman, and that he was very glad he had found the way to do it, whatever it cost him.

She was so exasperated at this, that she threatened him if he played any more of his hellish arts with her she would have him indicted for a wizard, and having a familiar; and she could prove it, she said, plain enough, for that he had raised the devil on purpose to fright his wife.

The fray parted that night with ill words and ill nature enough, but he little thought she intended as she said, and the next day he had forgot it all, and was as good-humoured as if nothing had happened.

But he found his wife chagrined and disturbed very much, full of resentment, and threatening him with what she resolved to do.

However, he little thought she intended him the mischief she had in her head, offering to talk friendly to her; but she rejected it with scorn, and told him she would be as good as her word, for she would not live with a man that should bring the devil into the room as often as he thought fit, to murder his wife.

He strove to pacify her by fair words, but she told him she was in earnest with him: and, in a word, she was in earnest; for she goes away to a justice, and making an affidavit that her husband had a familiar spirit, and that she went in danger of her life, she obtained a warrant for him to be apprehended.

In short, she brought home the warrant, showed it him, and told him she had not given it into the hands of an officer, because he should have the liberty to go voluntarily before the justice of the peace, and if he thought fit to let her know when he would be ready, she would be so too, and would get some of her own friends to go along with her.

He was surprised at this, for he little thought she had been in earnest with him, and endeavoured to pacify her by all the ways possible; but she found she had frighted him heartily, and so indeed she had, for though the thing had nothing in it of guilt, yet he found it might expose him very much, and being loath to have such a thing brought upon the stage against him, he used all the entreaties with her that he was able, and begged her not to do it.

But the more he humbled himself the more she triumphed over him; and carrying things to an unsufferable height of insolence, she told him at last, she would make him do justice, as she called it; that she was sure she could have him punished if he continued obstinate, and she would not be exposed to witchcraft and sorcery; for she did not know to what length he might carry it.

To bring the story to a conclusion; she got the better of him to such a degree, that he offered to refer the thing to indifferent persons, friends on both sides; and they met several times, but could bring it to no conclusion. His friends said there was nothing in it, and they would not have him comply with anything upon the pretence of it; that he called for his son, and somebody opened the casement and cried, "Here"; that there was not the least evidence of witchcraft in that, and insisted that she could make nothing of it.

Her friends carried it high, instructed by her: she offered to swear that he had threatened her before with his son's ghost; that now he visibly raised a spectre; for that calling upon his son, who was dead to be sure, the ghost immediately appeared; that he could not have called up the devil thus to personate his son, if he had not dealt with the devil himself, and had a familiar spirit, and that this was of dangerous consequence to her.

Upon the whole, the man wanted courage to stand it, and was afraid of being exposed; so that he was grievously perplexed, and knew not what to do.

When she found him humbled as much as she could desire, she told him, if he would do her justice, as she called it (that is to say, settle his estate upon her son), she would put it up, on condition that he should promise to fright her no more with raising the devil.

That part of the proposal exasperated him again, and he upbraided her with the slander of it, and told her he defied her, and she might do her worst.

Thus it broke off all treaty, and she began to threaten him again; however, at length she brought him to comply, and he gives a writing under his hand to her, some of her friends being by, promising that he would comply if his son did not arrive, or send an account of himself, within four months.

She was satisfied with this, and they were all made friends again, and accordingly he gave the writing; but when he delivered it to her in presence of her two arbitrators, he took the liberty to say to her, with a grave and solemn kind of speech:

"Look you," says he, "you have worried me into this agreement by your fiery temper, and I have signed it against justice, conscience, and reason; but depend upon it, I shall never perform it."

One of the arbitrators said, "Why, sir, this is doing nothing; for if you resolve not to perform it, what signifies the writing? why do you promise what you do not intend shall be done? This will but kindle a new flame to begin with, when the time fixed expires."

"Why," says he, "I am satisfied in my mind that my son is alive."

"Come, come," says his wife, speaking to the gentleman that had argued with her husband, "let him sign the agreement, and let me alone to make him perform the conditions."

"Well," says her husband, "you shall have the writing, and you shall be let alone; but I am satisfied you will never ask me to perform it; and yet I am no wizard," adds he, "as you have wickedly suggested."

She replied, that she would prove that he dealt with the devil, for that he raised an evil spirit by only calling his son by his name; and so began to tell the story of the hand and the casement.

"Come," says the man to the gentleman that was her friend, "give me the pen; I never dealt with but one devil in my life, and there it sits," turning to his wife; "and now I have made an agreement with her that none but the devil would desire any man to sign, and I will sign it; I say, give me the pen, but she nor all the devils in hell will ever be able to get it executed; remember I say so."

She began to open at him, and so a new flame would have been kindled, but the gentlemen moderated between them, and her husband setting his hand to the writing put an end to the fray at that time.

At the end of four months she challenged the performance, and a day was appointed, and her two friends that had been the arbitrators were invited to dinner upon this occasion, believing that her husband would have executed the deeds; and accordingly the writings were brought all forth, engrossed, and read over; and some old writings, which at her marriage were signed by her trustees, in order to her quitting some part of the estate to her son, were also brought to be cancelled: the husband being brought over, by fair means or foul, I know not whether, to be in a humour, for peace' sake, to execute the deeds, and disinherit his son; alleging that, indeed, if he was dead it was no wrong to him, and if he was alive, he was very unkind and undutiful to his father, in not letting him hear from him in all that time.

Besides, it was urged that if he should at any time afterwards appear to be alive, his father (who had very much increased, it seems, in his wealth) was able to give him another fortune, and to make him a just satisfaction for the loss he should sustain by the paternal estate.

Upon these considerations, I say, they had brought over the poor low-spirited husband to be almost willing to comply; or, at least, willing or unwilling, it was to be done, and, as above, they met accordingly.

When they had discoursed upon all the particulars, and, as above, the new deeds were read over, she or her husband took the old writings up to cancel them; I think the story says it was the wife, not her husband, that was just going to tear off the seal, when on a sudden they heard a rushing noise in the parlour where they sat, as if somebody had come in at the door of the room which opened from the hall, and went through the room towards the garden door, which was shut.

They were all surprised at it, for it was very distinct, but they saw nothing. The woman turned pale, and was in a terrible fright; however, as nothing was seen, she recovered a little, but began to ruffle her husband again.

"What," says she, "have you laid your plot to bring up more devils again?"

The man sat composed, though he was under no little surprise too.

One of her gentlemen said to him, "What is the meaning of all this?"

"I protest, sir," says he, "I know no more of it than you do."

"What can it be then?" said the other gentleman.

"I cannot conceive," says he, "for I am utterly unacquainted with such things."

"Have you heard nothing from your son?" says the gentleman.

"Not one word," says the father; "no, not the least word these five years."

"Have you wrote nothing to him," says the gentleman, "about this transaction?"

"Not a word," says he; "for I know not where to direct a letter to him."

"Sir," says the gentleman, "I have heard much of apparitions, but I never saw any in my life, nor did I ever believe there was anything of reality in them; and, indeed, I saw nothing now; but the passing of some body, or spirit, or something, across the room just now, is plain; I heard it distinctly. I believe there is some unseen thing in the room, as much as if I saw it."

"Nay," says the other arbitrator, "I felt the wind of it as it passed by me. Pray," adds he, turning to the husband, "do you see nothing yourself?"

"No, upon my word," says he, "not the least appearance in the world."

"I have been told," says the first arbitrator, "and have read, that an apparition may be seen by some people and be invisible to others, though all in the same room together."

However, the husband solemnly protested to them all that he saw nothing.

"Pray, sir," says the first arbitrator, "have you seen anything at any other time, or heard any voices or noises, or had any dreams about this matter?"

"Indeed," says he, "I have several times dreamed my son is alive, and that I had spoken with him; and once that I asked him why he was so undutiful, and slighted me so, as not to let me hear of him in so many years, seeing he knew it was in my power to disinherit him."

"Well, sir, and what answer did he give?"

"I never dreamed so far on as to have him answer; it always waked me."

"And what do you think of it yourself," says the arbitrator; "do you think he's dead?"

"No, indeed," says the father, "I do believe in my conscience he's alive, as much as I believe I am alive myself; and I am going to do as wicked a thing of its kind as ever any man did."

"Truly," says the second arbitrator, "it begins to shock me, I don't know what to say to it; I don't care to meddle any more with it, I don't like driving men to act against their consciences."

With this the wife, who, as I said, having a little recovered her spirits, and especially encouraged because she saw nothing, started up: "What's all this discourse to the purpose," says she; "is it not all agreed already? what do we come here for?"

"Nay," says the first arbitrator, "I think we meet now not to inquire into why it is done, but to execute things according to agreement, and what are we frighted at?"

"I'm not frighted," says the wife, "not I; come," says she to her husband, haughtily, "sign the deed; I'll cancel the old writings if forty devils were in the room;" and with that she takes up one of the deeds, and went to tear off the seal.

That moment the same casement flew open again, though it was fast in the inside, just as it was before; and the shadow of a body was seen, as standing in the garden without, and the head reaching up to the casement, the face looking into the room, and staring directly at the woman with a stern and an angry countenance: "Hold," said the spectre, as if speaking to the woman, and immediately clapped the casement to again, and vanished.

It is impossible to describe here the consternation this second apparition put the whole company into; the wife, who was so bold just before, that she would do it though forty devils were in the room, screamed out like a woman in fits, and let the writing fall out of her hands: the two arbitrators were exceedingly terrified, but not so much as the rest; but one of them took up the award which they had signed, in which they awarded the husband to execute the deed to dispose of the estate from the son.

"I dare say," said he, "be the spirit a good spirit or a bad, it will not be against cancelling this;" so he tore his name out of the award, and so did the other, by his example, and both of them got up from their seats, and said they would have no more to do in it.

But that which was most unexpected of all was that the man himself was so frighted, that he fainted away; notwithstanding it was, as it might be said, in his favour.

This put an end to the whole affair at that time; and, as I understand by the sequel, it did so for ever.

The story has many particulars more in it, too long to trouble you with: but two particulars, which are to the purpose, I must not omit, viz.:

1.   That in about four or five months more after this second apparition, the man's son arrived from the East Indies, whither he had gone four years before in a Portuguese ship from Lisbon.

2.   That upon being particularly inquired of about these things, and especially whether he had any knowledge of them, or any apparition to him, or voices, or other intimation as to what was doing in England, relating to him; he affirmed constantly that he had not, except that once he dreamed his father had written him an angry letter, threatening him that if he did not come home he would disinherit him, and leave him not one shilling.   But he added, that he never did receive any such letter from his father in his life, or from any one else.

❋ ❋ ❋

RICHARD STEELE
(1672-1729)

STEELE was the son of a Dublin attorney.   He was sent to the Charterhouse School where his friendship with Addison began.   He then went to Oxford, but left, before taking a degree, to join the Horse Guards.   In 1709 he laid the foundations of his fame by starting the *Tatler*, in which he had the assistance of Addison.   The *Tatler* was followed by the *Spectator*, which proved to be a still greater success.   This was in turn succeeded by the *Guardian*; and it is on his essays and delightful stories in these three periodicals, so typical a literary feature of the age, that Steele's fame rests.

TOM VARNISH
(From *The Tatler*)

BECAUSE I have a professed aversion to long beginnings of stories, I will go into this at once, by telling you, that there dwells near the Royal Exchange as happy a couple as ever entered into wedlock. These live in that mutual confidence of each other, which renders the satisfaction of marriage even greater than those of friendship, and makes wife and husband the dearest appellations of human life.   Mr. Balance is a merchant of good consideration, and understands the world, not from speculation, but practice.   His wife is the daughter of an honest house, ever bred in a family-way; and has, from a natural good understanding, and great innocence, a freedom which men of sense know to be the certain sign of virtue, and fools take to be an encouragement to vice.

Tom Varnish, a young gentleman of the Middle-Temple, by the

bounty of a good father, who was so obliging as to die, and leave him, in his twenty-fourth year, besides a good estate, a large sum which lay in the hands of Mr. Balance, had by *this means* an intimacy at his house; and being one of those hard students who read plays for the improvement in the law, took his rules of life from thence. Upon mature deliberation, he conceived it very proper, that he, as a man of wit and pleasure of the town, should have an intrigue with *his merchant's* wife. He no sooner thought of this adventure, but he began it by an amorous epistle to the lady, and a faithful promise to wait upon her at a certain hour the next evening, when he knew her husband was to be absent.

The letter was no sooner received, but it was communicated to the husband, and produced no other effect in him, than that he joined with his wife to raise all the mirth they could out of this fantastical piece of gallantry. They were so little concerned at this dangerous man of mode, that they plotted ways to perplex him without hurting him. Varnish comes exactly at his hour; and the lady's well-acted confusion at his entrance gave him opportunity to repeat some couplets very fit for the occasion with very much grace and spirit. His theatrical manner of making love was interrupted by an alarm of the husband's coming; and the wife, in a personated terror, beseeched him, "if he had any value for the honour of a woman that loved him, he would jump out of the window." He did so, and fell upon feather-beds placed there on purpose to receive him.

It is not to be conceived how great the joy of an amorous man is, when he has suffered for his mistress, and is never the worse for it. Varnish the next day writ a most elegant billet, wherein he said all that imagination could form upon the occasion. He violently protested, "going out of the window was no way terrible, but as it was going from her;" with several other kind expressions, which procured him a second assignation. Upon his second visit, he was conveyed by a faithful maid into her bed chamber, and left there to expect the arrival of her mistress. But the wench, according to her instructions, ran in again to him, and locked the door after her to keep out her master. She had just time enough to convey the lover into a chest before she admitted the husband and his wife into the room.

You may be sure that trunk was absolutely necessary to be opened; but upon her husband's ordering it, she assured him, "she had taken all the care imaginable in packing up the things with her own hands, and he might send the trunk abroad as soon as he thought fit." The easy husband believed his wife, and the good couple went to bed; Varnish having the happiness to pass the night in the mistress's bedchamber without molestation. The morning arose, but our lover was not well situated to observe her blushes; so that all we know of his sentiments on this occasion is, that he heard Balance ask for the key, and say, "he would himself go with this chest, and have it opened before the captain of the ship, for the greater safety of so valuable a lading."

The goods were hoisted away; and Mr. Balance, marching by his chest with great care and diligence, omitting nothing that might give his passenger perplexity. But, to consummate all, he delivered the chest, with strict charge, "in case they were in danger of being taken, to throw it overboard, for there were letters in it, the matter of which might be of great service to the enemy."

❊ ❊ ❊

SIR WALTER SCOTT
(1771-1832)

SIR WALTER, born in Edinburgh, suffered from a severe fever in early childhood and, as a result, became permanently lame. While he studied for the Bar, to which he was called in 1792, he had a predilection for literature which was fed by insatiable reading of ballads and romances. In 1805 he produced his first great original work, *The Lay of the Last Minstrel*. It was so well received that he definitely decided on a literary career. Thereafter his novels followed one another regularly. In 1806 he formed a partnership with the Ballantynes which ultimately involved him in liabilities amounting to £130,000. In trying to pay off his obligations, he literally worked himself to death.

Wandering Willie's Tale, first published in *Redgauntlet* in 1824, was the first short story of importance that the famous novelist wrote. While some critics have called it "the finest short story in the language," it is scarcely surpassed as a weird tale.

WANDERING WILLIE'S TALE
(From *Redgauntlet*)

YE maun have heard of Sir Robert Redgauntlet of that ilk, who lived in these parts before the dear years. The country will lang mind him; and our fathers used to draw breath thick if ever they heard him named. He was out wi' the Hielandmen in Montrose's time; and again he was in the hills wi' Glencairn in the saxteen hundred and fifty-twa; and sae when King Charles the Second came in, wha was in sic favour as the laird of Redgauntlet? He was knighted at Lonon Court, wi' the king's ain sword; and being a red-hot prelatist, he came down here, rampauging like a lion, with commissions of lieutenancy (and of lunacy, for what I ken), to put down a' the Whigs and Covenanters in the country. Wild wark they made of it; for the Whigs were as dour as the Cavaliers were fierce, and it was which should first tire the other. Redgauntlet was aye for the strong hand; and his name is kend as wide in the country as Claverhouse's or Tam Dalyell's. Glen, nor dargle, nor mountain, nor cave could hide the puir hill-folk when Redgauntlet was out with bugle and bloodhound after them, as if they had been sae mony deer. And, troth, when they fand them, they didna make muckle mair ceremony than a Hielandman wi' a roe-buck. It was just, "Will ye tak' the test?" If not—"Make ready—present—fire!" and there lay the recusant.

Far and wide was Sir Robert hated and feared. Men thought he had a direct compact with Satan; that he was proof against steel and that bullets happed aff his buff-coat like hailstanes from a hearth; that he had a mear that would turn a hare on the side of Carrifra-gauns;[1] and muckle to the same purpose, of whilk mair anon. The best blessing they wared on him was, "Deil scowp wi' Redgauntlet!" He wasna a bad master to his ain folk, though, and was weel aneugh liked by his tenants; and as for the lackeys and troopers that rade out wi' him to the persecutions, as the Whigs caa'd those killing-times, they wad hae drunken themsells blind to his health at ony time.

Now you are to ken that my gudesire lived on Redgauntlet's grund —they ca' the place Primrose Knowe. We had lived on the grund, and under the Redgauntlets, since the riding-days, and lang before. It was a pleasant bit; and I think the air is callerer and fresher there than ony-where else in the country. It 's a' deserted now; and I sat on the broken door-cheek three days since, and was glad I couldna see the pligt the place was in—but that 's a' wide o' the mark. There dwelt my gude-sire, Steenie Steenson; a rambling, rattling chiel' he had been in his young days, and could play weel on the pipes; he was famous at "hoop-ers and girders," a' Cumberland couldna touch him at "Jockie Lattin," and he had the finest finger for the back-lint between Berwick and Car-lisle. The like o' Steenie wasna the sort that they made Whigs o'. And so he became a Tory, as they ca' it, which we now ca' Jacobites, just out of a kind of needcessity, that he might belang to some side or other. He had nae ill-will to the Whig bodies, and liked little to see the blude rin, though, being obliged to follow Sir Robert in hunting and hoisting, watching and warding, he saw muckle mischief, and maybe did some that he couldna avoid.

Now Steenie was a kind of favourite with his master, and kend a' the folk about the castle, and was often sent for to play the pipes when they were at their merriment. Auld Dougal MacCallum, the butler, that had followed Sir Robert through gude and ill, thick and thin, pool and stream, was specially fond of the pipes, and aye gae my gudesire

[1] A precipitous side of a mountain in Moffatdale.

his gude wurd wi' the laird; for Dougal could turn his master round his finger.

Weel, round came the Revolution, and it had like to hae broken the hearts baith of Dougal and his master. But the change was not a'the-gether sae great as they feared and other folk thought for. The Whigs made an unco crawing what they wad do with their auld enemies, and in special wi' Sir Robert Redgauntlet. But there were owermony great folks dipped in the same doings to make a spick-and-span new warld. So parliament passed it a' ower easy; and Sir Robert, bating that he was held to hunting foxes instead of Covenanters, remained just the man he was.[1] His revel was as loud, and his hall as weel lighted, as ever it had been, though maybe he lacked the fines of the nonconformists, that used to come to stock his larder and cellar; for it is certain he began to be keener about the rents than his tenants used to find him before, and they behooved to be prompt to the rent-day, or else the laird wasna pleased. And he was sic an awsome body that naebody cared to anger him; for the oaths he swore, and the rage that he used to get into, and the looks that he put on made men sometimes think him a devil incarnate.

Weel, my gudesire was nae manager—no that he was a very great misguider—but he hadna the saving gift, and he got twa terms' rent in arrear. He got the first brash at Whitsunday put ower wi' fair word and piping; but when Martinmas came there was a summons from the grund officer to come wi' the rent on a day preceese, or else Steenie be-hooved to flit. Sair wark he had to get the siller; but he was weel freended, and at last he got the haill scraped thegether—a thousand merks. The maist of it was from a neighbour they caa'd Laurie Lapraik —a sly tod. Laurie had wealth o' gear, could hunt wit' the hound and rin wi' the hare, and be Whig or Tory, saunt or sinner, as the wind stood. He was a professor in this Revolution warld, but he liked an orra sough of this warld, and a tune on the pipes, weel aneaugh at a by-time; and, bune a', he thought he had gude security for the siller he len my gudesire ower the stocking at Primrose Knowe.

Away trots my gudesire to Redgauntlet Castle wi' a heavy purse and a light heart, glad to be out of the laird's danger. Weel, the first thing he learned at the castle was that Sir Robert had fretted himsell into a fit of the gout because he did no appear before twelve o'clock. It wasna a'thegether for sake of the money, Dougal thought, but because he didna

---

[1] The caution and moderation of King William III., and his principles of unlimited toleration, deprived the Cameronians of the opportunity they ardently desired, to retaliate the injuries which they had received during the reign of prelacy, and purify the land, as they called it, from the pollution of blood. They esteemed the Revolution, therefore, only a half-measure, which neither compre-hended the rebuilding the kirk in its full splendour, nor the revenge of the death of the saints on their persecutors.

like to part wi' my gudesire aff the grund. Dougal was glad to see
Steenie, and brought him into the great oak parlour; and there sat the
laird his leesome lane, excepting that he had beside him a great, ill-
favoured jackanape that was a special pet of his. A cankered beast it
was, and mony an ill-natured trick it played; ill to please it was, and
easily angered—ran about the haill castle, chattering and rowling, and
pinching and biting folk, specially before ill weather, or disturbance in
the state. Sir Robert caa'd it Major Weir, after the warlock that was
burnt [1] and few folk liked either the name or the conditions of the
creature—they thought there was something in it by ordinar—and my
gudesire was not just easy in mind when the door shut on him, and he
saw himsell in the room wi' naebody but the laird, Dougal MacCallum,
and the major—a thing that hadna chanced to him before.

Sir Robert sat, or, I should say, lay, in a great arm-chair, wi' his
grand velvet gown, and his feet on a cradle; for he had baith gout and
gravel, and his face looked as gash and ghastly as Satan's. Major Weir
sat opposite to him, in a red-laced coat, and the laird's wig on his head;
and aye as Sir Robert girned wi' pain, the jackanape girned too, like a
sheep's head between a pair of tangs—an ill-faur'd, fearsome couple
they were. The laird's buff-coat was hung on a pin behind him, and his
broadsword and his pistols within reach; for he keepit up the auld fashion
of having the weapons ready, and a horse saddled day and night, just as
he used to do when he was able to loup on horseback, and sway after ony
of the hill-folk he could get speerings of. Some said it was for fear
of the Whigs taking vengeance, but I judge it was just his auld custom
—he wasna gine nor fear onything. The rental-book, wi' its black
cover and brass clasps, was lying beside him; and a book of sculduddery
sangs was put betwixt the leaves, to keep it open at the place where it
bore evidence against the goodman of Primrose Knowe, as behind the
hand with his mails and duties. Sir Robert gave my gudesire a look, as
if he would have withered his heart in his bosom. Ye maun ken he
had a way of bending his brows that men saw the visible mark of a
horseshoe in his forehead, deep-tinted, as if it had been stamped there.

"Are ye come light-handed, ye son of a toom whistle?" said Sir
Robert. "Zounds! if you are——"

My gudesire, with as gue a countenance as he could put on, made a
leg, and placed the bag of money on the table wi' a dash, like a man
that does something clever. The laird drew it to him hastily. "Is it all
here, Steenie, man?"

"Your honour will find it right," said my gudesire.

"Here, Dougal," said the laird, "gie Steenie a tass of brandy, till
I count the siller and write the receipt."

But they werena weel out of the room when Sir Robert gied a yelloch

---

[1] A celebrated wizard, executed at Edinburgh for sorcery and other crimes.

that garr'd the castle rock. Back ran Dougal; in flew the liverymen; yell on yell gied the laird, ilk ane mair awfu' than the ither. My gudesire knew not whether to stand or flee, but he ventured back into the parlour, where a' was gaun hirdie-girdie—naebody to say "come in" or "gae out." Terribly the laird roared for cauld water to his feet, and wine to cool his throat; and "Hell, hell, hell, and its flames," was aye the word in his mouth. They brought him water, and when they plunged his swoln feet into the tub, he cried out it was burning; and folks say that it *did* bubble and sparkle like a seething cauldron. He flung the cup at Dougal's head and said he had given him blood instead of Burgundy; and sure, aneugh, the lass washed clotted blood aff the carpet the neist day. The jackanape they caa'd Major Weir, it jibbered and cried as if it was mocking its master. My gudesire's head was like to turn; he forgot baith siller and receipt, and downstairs he banged; but, as he ran, the shrieks came fainter and fainter; there was a deep-drawn shivering groan, and word gaed through the castle that the laird was dead.

Weel, away came my gudesire wi' his finger in his mouth, and his best hope was that Dougal had seen the money-bag and heard the laird speak of writing the receipt. The young laird, now Sir John, came from Edinburgh to see things put to rights. Sir John and his father never 'greed weel. Sir John had been bred an advocate, and afterward sat in the last Scots Parliament and voted for the Union, having gotten, it was thought, a rug of the compensations—if his father could have come out of his grave he would have brained him for it on his awn hearthstane. Some thought it was easier counting with the auld rough knight than the fair-spoken young ane—but mair of that anon.

Dougal MacCallum, poor body, neither grat nor graned, but gaed about the house looking like a corpse, but directing, as was his duty, a' the order of the grand funeral. Now Dougal looked aye waur and waur when night was coming, and was aye the last to gang to his bed, whilk was in a little round just opposite the chamber of dais, whilk his master occupied when he was living, and where he new lay in state, as they caa'd it, weeladay! The night before the funeral Dougal could keep his awn counsel nae longer; he came doun wi' his proud spirit, and fairly asked auld Hutcheon to sit in his room with him for an hour. When they were in the round, Dougal took a tass of brandy to himsell, and gave another to Hutcheon, and wished him all health and lang life, and said that, for himsell, he wasna lang for this world; for that every night since Sir Robert's death his silver call had sounded from the state chamber just as it used to do at nights in his lifetime to call Dougal to help to turn him in his bed. Dougal said that, being alone with the dead on that floor of the tower (for naebody cared to wake Sir Robert Redgauntlet like another corpse), he had never daured to answer the call, but that now his conscience checked him for neglecting his duty; for, "though death breaks service," said MacCallum, "it shall never weak my service to Sir Robert; and I will answer his next whistle, so be you will stand by me, Hutcheon."

Hutcheon had nae will to the wark, but he had stood by Dougal in battle and broil, and he wad not fail him at this pinch; so doun the carles sat ower a stoup of brandy, and Hutcheon, who was something of a clerk, would have read a chapter of the Bible; but Dougal would hear naething but a blaud of Davie Lindsay, whilk was the waur preparation.

When midnight came, and the house was quiet as the grave, sure enough the silver whistle sounded as sharp and shrill as if Sir Robert was blowing it; and up got the two auld serving-men, and tottered into the room where the dead man lay. Hutcheon saw aneugh at the first glance; for there were torches in the room, which showed him the foul fiend, in his ain shape, sitting on the laird's coffin? Ower he couped as if he had been dead. He could not tell how lang he lay in a trance at the door, but when he gathered himsell he cried on his neighbour, and getting nae answer raised the house, when Dougal was found lying dead within twa steps of the bed where his master's coffin was placed. As for the whistle, it was gane anes and aye; but mony a time was it heard at the top of the house on the bartizan, and amang the auld chimneys and turrets where the howlets have their nests. Sir John hushed the matter up, and the funeral passed over without mair bogie wark.

But when a' was ower, and the laird was beginning to settle his affairs, every tenant was called up for his arrears, and my gudesire for the full sum that stood against him in the rental-book. Weel, away he trots to the castle to tell his story, and there he is introduced to Sir John, sitting in his father's chair, in deep mourning, with weepers and hanging cravat, and a small walking-rapier by his side, instead of the auld broadsword that had a hundredweight of steel about it, what with blade, chape, and basket-hilt. I have heard their communings so often tauld ower that I almost think I was there mysell, though I couldna be born at the time. [In fact, Alan, my companion, mimicked, with a good deal of humour, the flattering, conciliating tone of the tenant's address and the hypocritical melancholy of the laird's reply. His grandfather, he said, had, while he spoke, his eye fixed on the rental-book, as if it were a mastiff-dog that he was afraid would spring up and bite him.]

"I wuss ye joy, sir, of the head seat and white loaf and the brid lairdship. Your father was a kind man to freends and followers; muckle grace to you, Sir John, to fill his shoon—his boots, I suld say, for he seldom wore shoon, unless it were muils when he had the gout."

"Ay, Steenie," quoth the laird, sighing deeply, and putting his napkin to his een, "his was a sudden call, and he will be missed in the country no time to set his house in order—weel prepared Godward, no doubt, which is the root of the matter; but he left us behind a tangled hesp to wind, Steenie. Hem! hem! We maun go to business, Steenie; much to do, and little time to do it in."

Here he opened the fatal volume. I have heard of a thing they call Doomsday-book—I am clear it has been a rental of back-ganging tenants.

"Stephen," said Sir John, still in the same soft, sleekit tone of voice —"Stephen Stevenson, or Steenson, ye are down here for a year's rent behind the hand—due at last term."

Stephen. Please your honour, Sir John, I paid it to your father.

Sir John. Ye took a receipt, then, doubtless, Stephen, and can produce it?

Stephen. Indeed, I hadnae time, and it like your honour; for nae sooner had I set doun the siller, and just as his honour, Sir Robert, that 's gaen, drew it till him to count it and write out the receipt, he was ta'en wi' the pains that removed him.

"That was unlucky," said Sir John, after a pause. "But ye maybe paid it in the presence of somebody. I want but a *talis qualis* evidence, Stephen. I would go ower-strictly to work with no poor man."

Stephen. Troth, Sir John, there was naebody in the room but Dougal MacCallum, the butler. But, as your honour kens, he has e'en followed his auld master.

"Very unlucky again, Stephen," said Sir John, without altering his voice a single note. "The man to whom ye paid the money is dead, and the man who witnessed the payment is dead too; and the siller which should have been to the fore, is neither seen nor heard tell of in the repositories. How am I to believe a' this?"

Stephen. I dinna ken, your honour; but there is a bit memorandum note of the very coins, for, God help me! I had to borrow out of twenty purses; and I am sure that ilka man there set down will take his grit oath for what purpose I borrowed the money.

Sir John. I have little doubt ye *borrowed* the money, Steenie. It is the *payment* that I want to have proof of.

Stephen. The siller maun be about the house, Sir John. And since your honour never got it, and his honour that was canna have ta'en it wi' him, maybe some of the family may hae seen it.

Sir John. We will examine the servants, Stephen; that is but reasonable.

But lackey and lass, and page and groom, all denied stoutly that they had even seen such a bag of money as my gudesire described. What saw waur, he had unluckily not mentioned to any living soul of them his purpose of paying his rent. Ae quean had noticed something under his arm, but she took it for the pipes.

Sir John Redgauntlet ordered the servants out of the room and then said to my gudesire: "Now, Steenie, ye see ye have fair play; and, as I have little doubt ye ken better where to find the siller than ony other body, I beg in fair terms, and for your own sake, that you will end this fasherie; for, Stephen, ye maun pay or flit."

"The Lord forgie your opinion," said Stephen, driven almost to his wit's end—"I am an honest man."

"So am I, Stephen," said his honour; "and so are all the folks in this house, I hope. But if there be a knave among us, it must be he that tells the story he cannot prove." He paused, and then added, mair sternly: "If I understand your trick, sir, you want to take advantage of some malicious reports concerning things in this family, and particularly respecting my father's sudden death, thereby to cheat me out of the money, and perhaps take away my character by insinuating that I have received the rent I am demanding. Where do you suppose this money to be? I insist upon knowing."

My gudesire saw everything look so muckle against him that he grew nearly desperate. However, he shifted from one foot to another, looked to every corner of the room, and made no answer.

"Speak out, sirrah," said the laird, assuming a look of his father's, a very particular ane, which he had when he was angry—it seemed as if the wrinkles of his frown made that selfsame fearful shape of a horse's shoe in the middle of his brow; "speak out, sir! I *will* know your thoughts; do you suppose that I have this money?"

"Far be it frae me to say so," said Stephen.

"Do you charge any of my people with having taken it?"

"I wad be laith to charge them that may be innocent," said my gudesire; "and if there be any one that is guilty, I have nae proof."

"Somewhere the money must be, if there is a word of truth in your story," said Sir John; "I ask where you think it is—and demand a correct answer!"

"In hell, if you *will* have my thoughts of it," said my gudesire, driven to extremity—"in hell! with your father, his jackanape, and his silver whistle."

Down the stairs he ran (for the parlour was nae place for him after such a word) and he heard the laird swearing blood and wounds behind him, as fast as ever did Sir Robert, and roaring for the bailie and the baron-officer.

Away rode my gudesire to his chief creditor (him they caa'd Laurie Lapraik), to try if he could make onything out of him; but when he tauld his story, he got but the worst word in his wame—thief, beggar, and dyvour were the saftest terms; and to the hoot of these hard terms,

Laurie brought up the auld story of dipping his hand in the blood of God's saunts, just as if a tenant could have helped riding with the laird, and that a laird like Sir Robert Redgauntlet. My gudesire was, by this time, far beyond the bounds of patience, and, while he and Laurie were at deil speed the liars, he was wanchancie aneugh to abuse Lapraik's doctrine as weel as the man, and said things that garr'd folks' flesh grue that heard them—he wasna just himsell, and he had lived wi' a wild set in his day.

At last they parted, and my gudesire was to ride hame through the wood of Pitmurkie, that is a' fou of black firs, as they say. I ken the wood, but the firs may be black or white for what I can tell. At the entry of the wood there is a wild common, and on the edge of the common a little lonely change-house, that was keepit then by an hostler wife—they suld hae caa'd her Tibbie Faw—and there puir Steenie cried for a mutchkin of brandy, for he had had no refreshment the haill day. Tibbie was earnest wi' him to take a bite of meat, but he couldna think o' 't, nor would he take his foot out of the stirrup, and took off the brandy wholely at twa draughts, and named a toast at each. The first was, the memory of Sir Robert Redgauntlet, and may he never lie quiet in his grave till he had righted his poor bond-tenant; and the second was, a health to Man's Enemy, if he would but get him back the pock of siller, or tell him what came o' 't, for he saw the haill world was like to regard him as a thief and a cheat, and he took that waur than even the ruin of his house and hauld.

On he rode, little caring where. It was a dark night turned, and the trees made it yet darker, and he let the beast take its ain road through the wood; when all of a sudden, from tired and wearied that it was before, the nag began to spring and flee and stend, that my gudesire could hardly keep the saddle. Upon the whilk, a horseman, suddenly riding up beside him, said: "That 's a mettle beast of yours, freend; will you sell him?" So saying, he touched the horse's neck with his riding-wand, and it fell into its auld heigh-ho of a stumbling trot. "But his spunk 's soon out of him, I think," continued the stranger, "and that is like mony a man's courage, that thinks he wad do great things."

My gudesire scarce listened to this, but spurred his horse, with: "Gude-e'en to you, freend."

But it 's like the stranger was ane that dosna lightly yield his point; for, ride as Steenie liked, he was aye beside him at the selfsame pace. At last my gudesire, Steenie Steenson, grew half angry, and, to say the truth, half feard.

"What is that you want with me, freend?" he said. "If ye be a robber, I have nae money; if ye be a leal man, wanting company, I have nae heart to mirth or speaking; and if ye want to ken the road, I scarce ken it mysell."

"If you will tell me your grief," said the stranger, "I am one that, though I have been sair miscaa'd in the world, am the only hand for helping my freends."

So my gudesire, to ease his ain heart, mair than from any hope of help, told him the story from beginning to end.

"It 's a hard pinch," said the stranger; "but I think I can help you."

"If you could lend the money, sir, and take a lang day—Iken nae other help on earth," said my gudesire.

"But there may be some under the earth," said the stranger. "Come, I'll be frank wi' you; I could lend you the money on bond, but you would maybe scruple my terms. Now I can tell you that your auld laird is disturbed in his grave by your curses and the wailing of your family, and if ye daur venture to go to see him, he will give you the receipt."

My gudesire's hair stood on end at this proposal, but he thought his companion might be some humoursome chield that was trying to frighten him, and might end with lending him the money. Besides, he was bauld wi' brandy, and desperate wi' distress; and he said he had enough courage to go to the gate of hell, and a step farther, for that receipt.

The stranger laughed.

Weel, they rode on through the thickest of the wood, when, all of a sudden, the horse stopped at the door of a great house; and, but that he knew the place was ten miles off, my father would have thought he was at Redgauntlet Castle. They rode into the outer courtyard, through the muckle faulding yetts, and aneath the auld portcullis; and the whole front of the house was lighted, and there were pipes and fiddles, and as much dancing and deray within as used to be at Sir Robert's house at Pace and Yule, and such high seasons. They lap off, and my gudesire, as seemed to him, fastened his horse to the very ring he had tied him to that morning when he gaed to wait on the young Sir John.

"God!" said my gudesire, "if Sir Robert's death be but a dream!"

He knocked at the ha' door just as he was wont, and his auld acquaintance, Dougal MacCallum—just after his wont, too—came to open the door, and said: "Piper Steenie, are ye there, lad? Sir Robert has been crying for you."

My gudesire was like a man in a dream—he looked for the stranger, but he was gane for the time. At last he just tried to say: "Ha! Dougal Driveower, are you living? I thought he had been dead."

"Never fash yoursell wi' me," said Dougal, "but look to yoursell; and see ye tak' naething frae onybody here, neither meat, drink, or siller, except the receipt that is your ain."

So saying, he led the way out through halls and trances that were weel kend to my gudesire, and into the auld oak parlour; and there was as much singing of profane sangs, and birling of red wine, and blasphemy and sculduddery as had ever been in Redgauntlet Castle when it was at the blythest.

But Lord take us in keeping! what a set of ghastly revellers there were that sat around that table! My gudesire kend mony that had long before gane to their place, for often had he piped to the most part in the hall of Redgauntlet. There was the fierce Middleton, and the dissolute Rothes, and the crafty Lauderdale; and Dalyell, with his bald head and a beard to his girdle; and Earlshall, with Cameron's blude on his hand; and wild Bonshaw, that tied blessed Mr. Cargill's limbs till the blude sprung; and Dumbarton Douglas, the twice-turned traitor baith to country and king. There was the Bludy Advocate MacKenyie, who, for his worldly wit and wisdom, had been to the rest as a god. And there was Claverhouse, as beautiful as when he lived, with his long, dark, curled locks streaming down over his laced buff-coat, and with his left hand always on his right spule-blade, to hide the wound that the silver bullet had made. He sat apart from them all, and looked at them with a melancholy, haughty countenance; while the rest hallooed and sang and laughed, that the room rang. But their smiles were fearfully contorted from time to time; and their laughter passed into such wild sounds as made my gudesire's very nails grow blue, and chilled the marrow in his banes.

They that waited at the table were just the wicked serving-men and troopers that had done their work and cruel bidding on earth. There was the Lang Lad of the Nethertown, that helped to take Argyle; and the bishop's summoner, that they called the Deil's Rattlebag; and the wicked guardsmen in their laced coats; and the savage Highland Amorites, that shed blood like water; and mony a proud serving-man, haughty of heart and bloody of hand, cringing to the rich, and making them wickeder than they would be; grinding the poor to powder when the rich had broken them to fragments. And mony, mony mair were coming and ganging, a' as busy in their vocation as if they had been really alive.

Sir Robert Redgauntlet, in the midst of a' this fearful riot, cried, wi' a voice like thunder, on Steenie Piper to come to the board-head where he was sitting, his legs stretched out before him, and swathed up with flannel, with his holster pistols aside him, while the great broadsword rested against his chair, just as my gudesire had seen him the last time upon earth; the very cushion for the jackanape was close to him; but the creature itsell was not there—it wasna its hour, it 's likely; for he heard them say, as he came forward: "Is not the major come yet?" And another answered: "The jackanape will be here betimes the morn." And when my gudesire came forward, Sir Robert, or his ghaist, or the deevil in his likeness, said: "Weel, piper, hae ye settled wi' my son for the year's rent?"

With much ado my father gat breath to say that Sir John would not settle without his honour's receipt.

"Ye shall hae that for a tune of the pipes, Steenie," said the appearance of Sir Robert—"play us up Weel Hoddled, Luckie."

Now this was a tune my gudesire learned frae a warlock, that heard it when they were worshipping Satan at their meetings; and my gudesire had sometimes played it at the ranting suppers in Redgauntlet Castle, but never very willingly; and now he grew cauld at the very name of it, and said, for excuse, he hadna his pipes wi' him.

"MacCallum, ye limb of Beelzebub," said the fearfu' Sir Robert, "bring Steenie the pipes that I am keeping for him!"

MacCallum brought a pair of pipes might have served the piper of Donald of the Isles. But he gave my gudesire a nudge as he offered them; and looking secretly and closely, Steenie saw that the chanter was of steel, and heated to a white heat; so he had fair warning not to trust his fingers with it. So he excused himsell again, and said he was faint and frightened, and had not wind aneugh to fill the bag.

"Then ye maun eat and drink, Steenie," said the figure; "for we do little else here; and it 's speaking between a fou man and a fasting." Now these were the very words that the bloody Earl of Douglas said to keep the king's messenger in hand while he cut the head off MacLellan of Bombie, at the Threave Castle; and that put Steenie mair and mair on his guard. So he spoke up like a man, and said he came neither to eat nor drink, nor make minstrelsy; but simply for his ain—to ken what was come o' the money he had paid, and to get a discharge for it; and he was so stout-hearted by this time that he charged Sir Robert for conscience's sake (he had no power to say the holy name), and as he hoped for peace and rest, to spread no snares for him, but just to give him his ain.

The appearance gnashed its teeth and laughed, but it took from a large pocket-book the receipt, and handed it to Steenie. "There is your receipt, ye pitiful cur; and for the money, my dog-whelp of a son may go look for it in the Cat's Cradle."

My gudesire uttered mony thanks, and was about to retire, when Sir Robert roared aloud: "Stop, though, thou sack-doudling son of a —! I am not done with thee. HERE we do nothing for nothing; and you must return on this very day twelvemonth to pay your master the homage that you owe me for my protection."

My father's tongue was loosed of a suddenty, and he said aloud: "I refer myself to God's pleasure, and not to yours."

He had no sooner uttered the word than all was dark around him; and he sank on the earth with such a sudden shock that he lost both breath and sense.

How lang Steenie lay there he could not tell; but when he came to himself he was lying in the auld kirkyard of Redgauntlet parochine, just at the door of the family aisle, and the scutcheon of the auld knight, Sir Robert, hanging over his head. There was a deep morning fog on grass and gravestane around him, and his horse was feeding quietly beside the minister's twa cows. Steenie would have thought the whole was a dream, but he had the receipt in his hand fairly written and signed by the auld laird; only the last letters of his name were a little disorderly, written like one seized with sudden pain.

Sorely troubled in his mind, he left that dreary place, rode through the mist to Redgauntlet Castle, and with much ado he got speech of the laird.

"Well, you dyvour bankrupt," was the first word, "have you brought me my rent?"

"No," answered my gudesire, "I have not; but I have brought your honour Sir Robert's receipt for it."

"How, sirrah? Sir Robert's receipt! You told me he had not given you one."

"Will your honour please to see if that bit line is right?"

Sir John looked at every line, and at every letter, with much attention; and at last at the date, which my gudesire had not observed—— "From my appointed place," he read, "this twenty-fifth of November."

"What! That is yesterday! Villain, thou must have gone to hell for this!"

"I got it from your honour's father; whether he be in heaven or hell, I know not," said Steenie.

"I will debate you for a warlock to the Privy Council!" said Sir John. "I will send you to your master, the devil, with the help of a tar-barrel and a torch!"

"I intend to debate mysell to the Presbytery," said Steenie, "and tell them all I have seen last night, whilk are things fitter for them to judge of than a borrel man like me."

Sir John paused, composed himsell, and desired to hear the full history; and my gudesire told it him from point to point, as I have told you—neither more nor less.

Sir John was silent again for a long time, and at last he said, very composedly: "Steenie, this story of yours concerns the honour of many a noble family besides mine; and if it be a leasing-making, to keep yourself out of my danger, the least you can expect is to have a red-hot iron driven through your tongue, and that will be as bad as scaulding your fingers wi' a red-hot chanter. But yet it may be true, Steenie; and if the money cast up, I shall not know what to think of it. But where shall we find the Cat's Cradle? There are cats enough about the old house, but I think they kitten without the ceremony of bed or cradle."

"We were best ask Hutcheon," said my gudesire; "he kens a' the odd corners about as weel as—another serving-man that is now gane, and that I wad not like to name."

Aweel, Hutcheon, when he was asked, told them that a ruinous turret lang disused, next to the clock-house, only accessible by a ladder, for the opening was on the outside, above the battlements, was called of old the Cat's Cradle.

"There will I go immediately," said Sir John; and he took—with what purpose Heaven kens—one of his father's pistols from the hall-table, where they had lain since the night he died, and hastened to the battlements.

It was a dangerous place to climb, for the ladder was auld and frail, and wanted ane or two rounds. However, up got Sir John, and entered at the turret door, where his body stopped the only little light that was in the bit turret. Something flees at him wi' a vengeance, maist dang him back ower—bang! gaed the knight's pistol, and Hutcheon, that held the ladder, and my gudesire, that stood beside him, hears a loud skelloch. A minute after, Sir John flings the body of the jackanape down to them, and cries that the siller is fund, and that they should come up and help him. And there was the bag of siller sure aneugh, and mony orra thing besides, that had been missing for mony a day. And Sir John, when he had riped the turret weel, led my gudesire into the dining-parlour, and took him by the hand, and spoke kindly to him, and said he was sorry he should have doubted his word, and that he would hereafter be a good master to him, to make amends.

"And now, Steenie," said Sir John, "although this vision of yours tends, on the whole, to my father's credit as an honest man, that he should, even after his death, desire to see justice done to a poor man like you, yet you are sensible that ill-dispositioned men might make bad constructions upon it concerning his soul's health. So, I think, we had better lay the haill dirdum on that ill-deedie creature, Major Weir, and say naething about your dream in the wood of Pitmurkie. You had taen ower-muckle brandy to be very certain about onything; and, Steenie, this receipt"—his hand shook while he held it out—"it 's but a queer kind of document, and we will do best I think, to put it quietly in the fire."

"Od, but for as queer as it is, it 's a' the voucher I have for my rent," said my gudesire, who was afraid, it may be, of losing the benefit of Sir Robert's discharge.

"I will bear the contents to your credit in the rental-book, and give you a discharge under my own hand," said Sir John, "and that on the spot. And, Steenie, if you can hold your tongue about this matter, you shall sit, from this time downward, at an easier rent."

"Mony thanks to your honour," said Steenie, who saw easily in what corner the wind was; "doubtless I will be conformable to all your honour's commands; only I would willingly speak wi' some powerful minister on the subject, for I do not like the sort of soumons of appointment whilk your honour's father——"

"Do not call the phantom my father!" said Sir John, interrupting him.

"Well then, the thing that was so like him," said my gudesire; "he spoke of my coming back to see him this time twelvemonth, and it's a weight on my conscience."

"Aweel then," said Sir John, "if you be so much distressed in mind, you may speak to our minister of the parish; he is a douce man, regards the honour of our family, and the mair that he may look for some patronage from me."

Wi' that, my father readily agreed that the receipt should be burned; and the laird threw it into the chimney with his ain hand. Burn it would not for them, though; but away it flew up the lum, wi' a lang train of sparks at its tail, and a hissing noise like a squib.

My gudesire gaed down to the manse, and the minister, when he had heard the story, said it was his real opinion that, though my gudesire had gane very far in tampering with dangerous matters, yet as he had refused the devil's arles (for such was the offer of meat and drink), and had refused to do homage by piping at his bidding, he hoped that, if he held a circumspect walk hereafter, Satan could take little advantage by what was come and gane. And, indeed, my gudesire, of his ain accord, lang forswore baith the pipes and the brandy—it was not even till the year was out, and the fatal day past, that he would so much as take the fiddle or drink usquebaugh or tippenny.

Sir John made up his story about the jackanape as he liked himsell; and some believe till this day there was no more in the matter than the filching nature of the brute. Indeed, ye'll no hinder some to thread that it was nane o' the auld Enemy that Dougal and Hutcheon saw in the laird's room, but only that wanchancie creature the major, capering on the coffin; and that, as to the blawing on the laird's whistle that was heard after he was dead, the filthy brute could do that as weel as the laird himsell, if not better. But Heaven kens the truth, whilk first came out by the minister's wife, after Sir John and her ain gudeman were baith in the moulds. And then my gudesire, wha was failed in his limbs, but not in his judgment or memory—at least nothing to speak of —was obliged to tell the real narrative to his freends, for the credit of his good name. He might else have been charged for a warlock.

SAMUEL LOVER
(1797-1868)

SAMUEL LOVER, born in Dublin, was a painter of portraits, chiefly minatures. He produced a number of songs, some of which attained great popularity. He also wrote some novels, the best known of which is *Handy Andy*, and a number or stories dealing with Irish life. *Paddy at Sea* appeared in *Miscellaneous Stories and Sketches*, published by Constable, 1899.

PADDY AT SEA

IT has been the fashion to consider the Irishman rather as a soldier than a sailor, and yet the sea seems to offer something congenial to the Hibernia spirit.   It's dark depths—its flashes of light—its terrible energy—its sportive spray—its striking alterations of frowning storm and smiling calm—reflect the Irishman so vividly, that one would think it his peculiar element.

Many, however, have denied this, and have even gone so far as to say that the Irish make bad sailors, though one of England's greatest admirals, Nelson's co-mate, the noble Collingwood, bears direct testimony to the contrary.   In one of his letters to an officer who superintended the manning of his ships he says—"Do not send me any lubbers; but, if you can, get me some more of those Irish lads you sent me—they were all fine fellows, and are now top-ment, every one of them."

The Irish have a right by national descent to be good sailors. The Phœnicians, I need not say, were the great seamen of antiquity, and that the Irish may claim them as progenitors is a fact that has been long established.   The Irish buildings, arms, and language are all among its clearest evidences.

Pat's fitness for the sea might further be illustrated by the well-known skill and courage of the numerous fishermen and pilots who toil around his rocky shores, and pursue their avocations in the most tempestuous and dangerous weather.   I am tempted, however, at this moment, rather to fall in with the popular notion, and recount the experience of an honest Irishman, whose sympathies, as will be seen, lay more with the land than with the water, and whose extreme innocence of the latter, resembled that of a peasant who was observed crossing a ferry constantly, without any apparent object, and on being asked the reason, said he was shortly going to emigrate, and so took the ferry every morning "just to practise the saysikness."

Jimmy Hoy was a County Cork boy, who made one in the great exodus that was occasioned by the famine. Jimmy was not ashamed of his name—he boasted that it was "always ould and respectable;" that there "was cows in the family wanst;" and that "a pig was niver a stranger to them, nor a rasher of bacon at Aisther." Misfortune, however, had ground them down, as it had done a thousand others, to indigence, leaving at last only Jimmy and his old mother in existence; and when he found that existence was daily a harder thing to support, he turned his face to the West, and induced his mother, whom he loved with true Irish warmth, to accompany him. Accordingly, selling off all they possessed, and making the best of their way to Cork, where a fleet of emigrant ships was loading, it so happened that in the hurry and excitement of the time, and amidst the crowd of people they encountered, they unluckily got separated, and went on board of different vessels— an error that Jimmy only discovered when his own had hoisted anchor and was standing out to sea. From this point it will be best to allow our friend to speak for himself.

"So I scrambled, you see, on boord, and the minit my fut was under me—'Is my mother here?' says I. With that a scowlin' fellow that was haulin' in a rope that samed to have no end to it, turns to me and tells me I might go to—well, I won't say where. 'Not before you, sir,' says I; 'after you is manners,' making him a bow; and so I cries out and again, 'Plase, is my mother here aboord of ye?' and then as no one chose to answer me I ran about to look for her, on all the flures they call the decks, though the people stood as thick as a drove of cattle in an alley, and scrouging and roaring like that same, and I'd to squaze myself betwixt 'em from one flure to another; but not a squint of her could I ketch, sir, nor of any one as know'd her,—and so at last, when I kem back again, and was tearin' round the upper flure, plump I runs into the stomach of a grand burly man at the back, with a red face and a big nose, and a gowld band about his cap—and who should he be but the capt'n.

"'Who the d—l are you?' says he, pumping up all the breath I had left him.

"'I axes your honour's pardon,' says I; 'my name is Jimmy Hoy, and I was looking for my mother.'

"'And did you take me for your mother, you *omadhaun?*' says he.

"'Oh, not a bit,' says I, 'sir; for if I had, you'd have found it out —you'd have got a hug that would have set you scraming. And so now, perhaps, you'll tell me, sir, if my mother is aboord of ye?'

"'How should I know?' he roars out, for now his breath was coming back, and he was lookin' mighty fierce. 'And what brings you here at all, you lubberly son of a sea-calf?'

"'Sure, sir,' says I, 'I—I'm going to Ameriky; and as to my father, you're mistaken—he was no say baste at all, but Dennis Hoy, a County Cork man, and——'

" 'I don't remember you,' says he; 'you hav'n't paid your passage.'

" 'Axing your pardon,' says I; 'but I have, tho'. I paid it an hour ago, on shore, sir.'

" 'But you didn't pay it to me,' says he.

" 'Why, of coorse not,' says I, 'sir. You wouldn't have me pay it twice, would you?'

" 'Well, if you hav'n't paid it to me,' says he, 'you hav'n't paid it at all; so hand out your money, if you're going to make the voyage in this ship.'

" 'By my faith, sir,' I said, 'I can't,—and, saving your presence, if I could I wouldn't, seein' I've done that same already. But, sure, I don't want to be intruding; if I've got into the wrong ship you've only got to stop her till you put me aboord of the right one.'

" 'Well, that's a capital joke,' says he.

" 'Oh, it's not joking that I am,' says I, 'for I'm only axin' you what's fair, sir—for then, you see, I'd find my mother, and my mind would be at aise.'

" 'You and your mother may go to Chiny,' the capt'n bellows out —growing as red as any turkey-cock, and stamping his fut upon the flure till you'd have thought he'd drive it through it.

" 'Axin' your pardon again,' says I, 'sir, we're going to Ameriky— and as for Chiny, all I know about it is what I've seen upon a plate, and——'

" 'Howld your jaw,' says he, 'you vagabone, and pay your passige money at wanst.'

" 'I paid it wanst,' says I, 'sir, and I'd want a pocket as big as your ship to go on paying it for iver.'

" 'You swindlin' Irish scamp!' says he, 'don't provoke me, or I will be the death of you;' and then all of a sudden he got quiet—oh, so terrible quiet, sir, and with such a hard look about his eyes that, to say the truth, he frekened me. 'See now, my buck,' says he,—'since you can't pay your passige, you shall work your passage.'

" 'Work it, sir?' says I. 'Oh, I would, and willin',—if I only knowed the way.'

" 'Oh,' says he, with a wicked wink at me, 'we'll soon tache you that; we've a turn here for instructin' people that want to get their voyage for nothin'.' And with that he put his hand to the side of his mouth and give a whistle that would split a flag, and up runs to him a hairy villin that was enough to scare a herd of oxen if he'd come upon 'em onawares.

" 'Tare-all,' says he, 'just take this chap in hand and tache him how to work his passige. Don't spare him—do you hear now?'

" 'Aye, aye, sir,' growled out Tare-all, giving me a nod, and howlding up his finger as much as to say—'You'll come this way.'

"And so after him I wint, sir; and sad enough, as you may suppose —not thinking of myself, but what had become of my poor owld mother. After him I wint, to learn how I was to work my passige over—and by my troth, sir, it was the hardest thing I'd ever had to larn as yet.

"Were you ever aboord a ship, sir?—Oh, then sure it must have bothered you to hear the puzzlin' names they've got there. Don't they always make a woman of her? A ship's a 'she,' sir, you will remimber—and don't they talk about her *waist* to you, and, by my faith, it's not a small one—and tell you sometimes 'she's in stays,' too, tho' I can't say I ever seen 'em. Though, to be sure, they say besides that she's often mighty hard to manage—and that's like a woman sartainly.

"Then see the names they give to a rope, sir. First it is a hawser; then it's a painter—though what it paints I never knowed, sir; then it's a rattlin,—but that it's always doin'; and then it's the shrouds,—which manes, I suppose, that the poor passengers always get into them when the ship is going to the bottom. At the same time they're always agraaable to tache you what it's made of—they'll give you a taste of a rope's end a good deal sooner than a glass of whisky. And what is it like? perhaps you'll ask. Work your passige out to Ameriky and you'll learn it fast enough. Then they're so ignorant they don't know their right hand from their left. It's all starboord or larboord with them, though, by my throth, as every night I'd got to slape upon the flure, I found it mighty hard boord.

"The sailors, you see, are snug enough. They've got what they call their hammicks—little beds tied up to hooks that they swing about in at their aise; and it was after I'd been looking at them for a night or two in the deepest admiration, that I says to myself, says I, 'Why shouldn't I be making a little hammick for myself, to take a swing in like the rest, and not be lying here on the bare boords like a dumb baste in an outhouse?' And so the next day, looking round me, what should I see but a hape of canvas that no one seemed to care about; so I cut out of it a yard or two just to make the bed I wanted, and that done, says I, 'Jimmy Hoy, you'll slape to-night as snug as a cat in a blanket, anyhow,'—but I didn't for all that.

"I hadn't turned in half an hour when one of the crew crapes up to me—Bob Hobbs, sir, was his name,—and says he to me, 'Jimmy Hoy,' says he, 'it's mortial tired I am with my day's work, and the night before; not a wink of slape I've had,' says he, 'for this blessed eight-and-forty hours, so be a good fellow, Jimmy, now, and take my dooty for to-night.' Well, not liking to be ill-natured, though I didn't care much for the fellow, I tould him that I would, and so I slips out of my new bed, and mighty quick, sir, he slips into it, and up I goes on deck to take his place on the look-out.

"And thin ther kem on such a night, sir,—oh, murther! you'd have thought the divil himself was out at say, and was taking his divarshun —blowing, hailin', and rainin' for six mortial hours and more—and pitchin' the oushen up into the sky as if he was makin' haycocks. I thought the poor ship would have gone crazy. She jumped and rowled about as if her thratement was past endoorin'. Sure, if I had bargained for a bad night I couldn't have got a betther. Well, sir, the mornin' kem at last, and found me as well pickled as any herrin' in Cork harbour, and I was crawlin' off to my hammick, just to get a little slape and dry myself, when up comes the capt'n in a tearin' rage, and says he—

"'You're a pretty blackguard, ain't you now?'

"'Not to my knowledge, sir,' says I.

"'Your knowledge, indeed, you vagabone!'

"'Why, what is it I done?' says I.

"'Done?' says he, 'you villin—when you're upsettin' the ship's discipline. You took Bob Hobb's watch last night.'

"'Tuk what?' says I. 'His watch, sir. Oh, murther, capt'n!' says I, 'would you rob a poor boy of his charakther?'

"'I say you did, you rascal,' says he.

"'But I didn't, sir,' says I. 'I never took Bob Hobbs's watch, nor the watch of any other man—or woman ayther. I would scorn the dirty action—for I was rared in honest principles, and 'twas considered in my schoolin'. More be token, I couldn't, for Bob Hobbs told me himself that he had pawned his watch in Cork before he ever kem aboord.'

"'You stupid rascal!' he cried out, 'don't you know the manin' of what I say to you? but I'll make you understand me presently—if you've got no brains you've got a back.'

"And what do you think he meant by that, sir? The ould tiger was goin' to flog me—but, luckily for me, you see, the storm was gettin' worse. One of the sails was split in halves, and another was torn away entirely; so the capt'n, divil thank him! had to think about the ship, and not to be indulgin' his dirty vingeance upon me. So he roars out mighty loud, 'Set the storm jib there!' and half the crew run up the riggin' as quick as a crowd of monkeys, when—whisteroo!—would you belave it, sir! by the book in my pocket, if that same jib wasn't the very piece of canvas that I cut the two yards out of, jist to make myself a bed,—and the minit the capt'n spied it he roars out again like thunder, 'Who the d—l cut that out?'

"''Twas I, sir,' says I, 'but I only tuk two yards of it.'

"'Give him a dozen,' says the capt'n.

" 'Thank you, sir,' says I, 'but the two is quite enough for me.'

"And what do you think the villin meant by givin' me a dozen?—it was lashes that he meant, sir. Not contint with the rope's end I'd had already—though there was no end to it at all—he towld the hands to lay howld on me, and tie me to the mast,—but before the miscreant could plaze himself there kem a thunderin' crack right overhead, and down kemp hapes of sticks and canvas—and the capt'n bellows out agin, 'Clare the wrack! clare the wrack!—we'll sarve this lubber out directly.'

"Well, I was willin' to wait, sir—and sure they'd enough to do. I thought at first it was all over with us, and the ship would be capsizin'—and they had scarcely got her to rights a bit, and my mind was getting aisy, when I h'ard a voice callin' in the distance, Jip a Hoy! Jim a Hoy!' and I was lost in wonder entirely—'for who knows me,' says I, 'or cares for me, in the middle of the great Atlantic oushen? It is guardian angels that's taking pity on me, and coming here to have me from a lashing?' So I tried hard to loose myself, and looking round what did I see but a ship sailing towards us, and the voice that know'd me kem'd from that, and I h'ard it cry again—'Jip a Hoy! Jim a Hoy!' 'Here I am,' says I; "here's the man you're wantin'.'

" 'Howld your jaw!' says the capt'n.

" 'Why, isn't it me they're spakin' to?' says I, 'and isn't it civil in me to answer 'em? Is my mother got aboord of ye?'

" 'Bad luck to you and your mother! will you be quiet?' says the capt'n.

" 'No, I won't,' says I. 'Why wouldn't I answer when I'm spoke to?' And with that the voice kem again—'Jip a Hoy! Jim a Hoy!' 'Here I am,' says I agin—'any news, plaze, of my mother?'

"And with that the capt'n took a spakin' trumpet just to put me down, sir—to kape me from bein' h'ard; oh, I could see that plain enough—so I roared out louder than ever, 'Here's the man you're wantin';' but the trumpet gave him the advantage of me. I couldn't make out what he said at first, it was such a bellowing he kep up; but at last I h'ard him roar, 'Carried away fore-yard.'

" 'Don't be tellin' lies of me,' says I; "it's only two yards that I tuk. Just now you said I tuk a watch, and now it's four yards I've been staling. Oh, capt'n, but it's cruel of you to ruin my charakter as you've doing, and in hearin' of the ship too—and my mother perhaps aboord of her.'

"And then the voice kem from the ship agin—'Where are ye bound to?'

" 'I am bound to the mast,' says I, 'and the capt'n is going to murther me.'

" 'Will you howld your tongue, you rascal?' says the capt'n, looking pistols at me. 'No, I won't,' says I; 'I'll expose you to the whole world for the shameful way you're trating me.'

"Well, we soon lost sight of the ship; but the storm was as bad as iver, and only one good kem of it—they were too busy with the danger to be amusin' themselves with me. So I got myself loose at last,—and then seeing what a way they were in, I hadn't the heart to desart them, notwithstandin' my bad usage. 'No,' says I, 'I'll be ginerous, and stand by them like a man.' So I goes up to the capt'n, and overlookin' all he'd done, says I to him, quite kindly, 'Capt'n, is there anything I can do for you?'

" 'Kape out of my way, you vagabone, or I shall be tempted to do for you!' says he. And with that he made a kick at me as bad as a horse stung in a sandpit; but I made allowance for the throuble he was in, and didn't mind his timper.

"All this time I h'ard the sailors saying something about the anchor, and at last the capt'n was struck with a notion, and shouts out to them about me, 'Where's the best bower?'

" 'Here he is, sir,' says I, running up to him again, and making a low bow at the same time. 'I'm the best bower on boord, sir, for my mother, when I was at school, paid tuppence a week extra to have me taught manners.'

" 'I wish your neck was broke,' said he, 'you vagabone!' making another terrible kick at me in return for all my kindness to him; and then up kem the bos'n, and the capt'n says to him, says he, 'Have you let go now?'

" 'Aye, aye, sir,' answers Hairy-face,—and I may just make the remark that's all he ever did answer, the whole way acrost the oushen.

" 'Then, I think,' says the capt'n, 'we may depind on the best bower.'

" 'Oh! you may do that,' says I, 'sir; you may depind on me with sartainty.'

" 'Take that fellow out of my sight,' said he, 'if you don't want me to murder him;' so at that I walks away with Hairy-face to the other end of the ship, where I hear the sailors saying 'the anchor was coming home,' and that the capt'n ought to know it.

" 'He ought, you say,' says I; 'then of coorse I'll go and tell, if it's only to show him I bear no malice, and I'm still willin' to be useful.' Upon which I runs back to him, and says I, 'Capt'n, the anchor's coming home.'

" 'Thunder and ouns!' says he.

"Don't be angry, capt'n,' says I,—'small blame to it for comin' home on such a night as this. Who'd stay out, sir, that could help it?'

"Upon which Hairy-face runs up, and the capt'n then cries out to him, 'Is this thrue I hear—is the anchor coming home?'

" 'Aye, aye, sir,' growls out Hairy-face.

" 'Then we must cut and run,' says he; 'but we must try and save the anchor, so throw over the buoy.'

"Well, now, I must just stop to tell you that of all the mischievous little blackguards that ever deserved drowning, the cabin-boy was him, sir. And so, still wishing to be useful, notwithstandin' all their bad thratement of me, I ran off to ketch the villin; but the little vaga-bone was so nimble I couldn't at all lay howld of him; howsomedever, under the sarcumstances, I did the best I could, and then I ran back to the capt'n.

" 'Is the buoy overboard?' says he.

" 'Faith, then, I am sorry to say,' says I, 'capt'n, the boy's not over-board, for the young d——l run so fast I couldn't clap a hand on him, but the next best thing to be done I did. I threw over the black cook—and that will lighten the ship beautifully.'

" 'Threw overboard the cook, you murderin' villin!' roared the capt'n. 'You've saved me the job of doing it; you'll be hanged, thank heaven, at last.'

"But hanged I wasn't, I beg to say, for, in the confusion of the night it was a big tar barrel I threw overboard instid of the black cook, that same being much of his own size and colour.

"Well, to make a long story short, sir, in spite of the storm and all our danger, we got to Ameriky at last, when the capt'n felt so happy that he gave up his anymosity and the vingeance he vowed ag'inst me, and only laughed at the mistakes I'd made in turnin' my hand to the say service. And, what's more, when we reached New York, sir, who should I find but my ould mother, that had got in a week before me in the ship I ought to have come in, and that had had no storm at all —but mine's the bad luck of the Hoys, sir. And so, when I was on dhry land agin, I took a solemn oath, sir, that I'd niver work my passige any more across the Atlantic; and, by my sowl, if you're a wise man I think you'll do the same."

✳ ✳ ✳

ELIZABETH C. GASKELL
(1810-1865)

ELIZABETH C. GASKELL was born in London. After her marriage to William Gaskell, a Unitarian minister, she went to live in Manchester where her literary career began. After the loss of their only son—they had seven children—her husband, it is said, in order to distract her from her sorrow, urged her to write a long piece of fiction. And thus, *Mary Barton*, which laid the foundation of Mrs. Gaskell's literary career, was produced. Like all her work, this novel, depicting the life of the working classes, is written with simplicity and profound feeling. *Cranford*, which is now a recognized classic, was Mrs. Gaskell's finest contribution to English literature. Besides her novels, Mrs. Gaskell wrote some lovely stories, of which *The Half-Brothers* is an excellent example.

THE HALF-BROTHERS

MY mother was twice married. She never spoke of her first husband, and it is only from other people that I have learnt what little I know about him. I believe she was scarcely seventeen when she was married to him: and he was barely one-and-twenty. He rented a small farm up in Cumberland, somewhere towards the sea-coast; but he was perhaps too young and inexperienced to have the charge of land and cattle; anyhow, his affairs did not prosper, and he fell into ill health, and died of consumption before they had been three years man and wife, leaving my mother a young widow of twenty, with a little child only just able to walk, and the farm on her hands for four years more by the lease, with half the stock on it dead, or sold off one by one to pay the more pressing debts, and with no money to purchase more, or even to buy the provisions needed for the small consumption of every day. There was another child coming, too; and sad and sorry, I believe, she was to think of it. A dreary winter she must have had in her lonesome dwelling with never another near it for miles around; her sister came to bear her company, and they two planned and plotted how to make every penny they could raise go as far as possible. I can't tell you how it happened that my little sister, whom I never saw, came to sicken and die; but, as if my poor mother's cup was not full enough, only a fortnight before Gregory was born the little girl took ill of scarlet fever, and in a week she lay dead. My mother was, I believe, just stunned with this last blow. My aunt has told me that she did not cry; Aunt Fanny would have been thankful if she had; but she sat holding the poor wee lassie's hand, and looking in her pretty, pale, dead face, without so much as shedding a tear. And it was all the same, when they had to take her away to be buried. She just kissed the child, and sat her down in the window-seat to watch the little black train of people (neighbours—my aunt, and one far-off cousin, who were all the friends they could muster) go winding away amongst the snow, which had fallen thinly over the country the night before. When my aunt came back from the funeral, she found my mother in the same place, and as dry-eyed as ever. So she continued until after Gregory was born; and, somehow, his coming seemed to loosen the tears, and she cried day and night, till my aunt and the other watcher looked at each other in dismay, and would fain have stopped her if they had but known how. But she bade them let her alone, and not be over-anxious, for every drop she shed eased her brain, which had been in a terrible state before for want of the power to cry. She seemed after that to think of nothing but her new little baby; she had hardly appeared to remember either her husband or her little daughter that lay dead in Brigham churchyard—at least so Aunt Fanny said; but she was a great talker, and my mother was very silent by nature, and I think Aunt Fanny may have been mistaken in believing that my mother never thought of her husband and child just because she never spoke about them. Aunt Fanny was older than my mother, and had a way of treating her like a child; but, for all that, she was a kind, warm-hearted creature, who thought more of her sister's welfare than she did of her own; and it was on her bit of money that they principally lived, and on what the two could earn by working for the great Glasgow sewing merchants. But by-and-by my mother's eyesight began to fail. It was not that she was exactly blind, for she could see well enough to guide herself about the house, and to do a good deal of domestic work; but she could no longer do fine sewing and earn money. It must have been with the heavy crying she had had in her day, for she was but a young creature at this time, and as pretty a young woman, I have heard people say, as any on the country side. She took it sadly to heart that she could no longer gain anything towards the keep of herself and her child. My Aunt Fanny would fain have persuaded her that she had enough to do in managing their cottage and minding Gregory; but my mother knew that they were pinched, and that Aunt Fanny herself had not as much to eat, even of the commonest kind of food, as she could have done with; and as for Gregory, he was not a strong lad, and needed, not more food—for he always had enough, whoever went short—but better nourishment, and more flesh meat. One day—it was Aunt Fanny who told me all this about my poor mother, long after her death—as the sisters were sitting together, Aunt Fanny working, and my mother hushing Gregory to sleep, William Preston, who was afterwards my father, came in. He was reckoned an old bachelor; I suppose he was long past forty, and he was one of the wealthiest farmers thereabouts, and had known my grandfather well, and my mother and my aunt in their more prosperous days. He sat down, and began to twirl his hat by way of being agreeable; my Aunt Fanny talked, and he listened and looked at my mother. But he said very little, either on that visit, or on many another that he paid before he spoke out what had been the real purpose of his calling so often all along, and from the very first time he came to their house. One Sunday, however, my Aunt Fanny stayed away from church, and took care of the child, and my mother went alone. When she came back, she ran straight upstairs, without going into the kitchen to look at Gregory or speak any word to her sister, and Aunt Fanny heard her cry as if her heart was breaking; so she went up and scolded her right well through the bolted door, till at last she got her to open it. And then she threw herself on my aunt's neck, and told her that William Preston had asked her to marry him, and had promised to take good charge of her boy, and to let him want for nothing, neither in the way of keep nor of education, and that she had consented. Aunt Fanny was a good deal shocked at this; for, as I have said, she had often thought that my mother had forgotten her first husband very quickly, and now here was proof positive of it, if she could so soon think of marrying again. Besides, as Aunt Fanny used to say, she herself would have been a far more suitable match for a man of William Preston's age than Helen, who, though she was a widow, had not seen her four-and-twentieth summer. However, as Aunt Fanny said, they had not asked her advice; and there was much to be said on the other side of the question. Helen's eyesight would never be good for much again, and as William Preston's wife she would never need to do anything, if she chose to sit with her hands before her; and a boy was a great charge to a widowed mother; and now there would be a decent steady man to see after him. So, by-and-by, Aunt Fanny seemed to take a brighter view of the marriage than did my mother herself, who hardly ever looked up, and never smiled after the day when she promised William Preston to be his wife. But much as she had loved Gregory before, she seemed to love him more now. She was continually talking to him when they were alone, though he was far too young to understand her moaning words, or give her any comfort, except by his caresses.

At last William Preston and she were wed; and she went to be mistress of a well-stocked house, not above half-an-hour's walk from where Aunt Fanny lived. I believe she did all that she could to please my father; and a more dutiful wife, I have heard him himself say, could never have been. But she did not love him, and he soon found it out. She loved Gregory, and she did not love him. Perhaps, love would have come in time, if he had been patient enough to wait; but it just turned him sour to see how her eye brightened and her colour came at the sight of that little child, while for him who had given her so much she had only gentle words as cold as ice. He got to taunt her with the difference in her manner, as if that would bring love; and he took a positive dislike to Gregory,—he was so jealous of the ready love that always gushed out like a spring of fresh water when he came near. He wanted her to love him more, and perhaps that was all well and good, but he wanted her to love her child less, and that was an evil wish. One day, he gave way to his temper, and cursed and swore at Gregory, who had got into some mischief, as children will; my mother made some excuse for him; my father said it was hard enough to have to keep another man's child, without having it perpetually held up in its naughtiness by his wife, who ought to be always in the same mind as he was; and so from little they got to more; and the end of it was, that my mother took to her bed before her time, and I was born that very day. My father was glad, and proud, and sorry, all in a breath; glad and proud that a son was born to him; and sorry for his poor wife's state, and to think how his angry words had brought it on. But he was a man who liked better to be angry than sorry, so he soon found out that it was all Gregory's fault, and owed him an additional grudge for having hastened my birth. He had another grudge against him before long. My mother began to sink the day after I was born. My father sent to Carlisle for doctors, and would have coined his heart's blood into gold to save her, if that could have been; but it could not. My Aunt Fanny used to say sometimes, that she thought that Helen did not wish to live, and so just let herself die away without trying to take hold on life; but when I questioned her, she owned that my mother did all the doctors bade her do, with the same sort of uncomplaining patience with which she had acted through life. One of her last requests was to have Gregory laid in her bed by my side, and then she made him take hold of my little hand. Her husband came in while she was looking at us so, and when he bent tenderly over her to ask her how she felt now, and seemed to gaze on us two little half-brothers, with a grave sort of kindliness, she looked up in his face and smiled, almost her first smile at him; and such a sweet smile! as more besides Aunt Fanny have said. In an hour she was dead. Aunt Fanny came to live with us. It was the best thing that could be done. My father would have been glad to return to his old mode of bachelor life, but what could he do with two little children? He needed a woman to take care of him, and who so fitting as his wife's elder sister? So she had the charge of me from my birth; and for a time I was weakly, as was but natural, and she was always beside me, night and day watching over me, and my father nearly as anxious as she. For his land had come down from father to son for more than three hundred years, and he would have cared for me merely as his flesh and blood that was to inherit the land after him. But he needed something to love, for all that, to most people, he was a stern, hard man, and he took to me as, I fancy, he had taken to no human being before—as he might have taken to my mother, if she had had no former life for him to be jealous of. I loved him back again right heartily. I loved all around me, I believe, for everybody was kind to me. After a time, I overcame my original weakliness of constitution, and was just a bonny, strong-looking lad whom every passer-by noticed, when my father took me with him to the nearest town.

At home I was the darling of my aunt, the tenderly-beloved of my father, the pet and plaything of the old domestics, the "young master" of the farm-labourers, before whom I played many a lordly antic, assuming a sort of authority which sat oddly enough, I doubt not, on such a baby as I was.

Gregory was three years older than I. Aunt Fanny was always kind to him in deed and in action, but she did not often think about him, she had fallen so completely into the habit of being engrossed by me, from the fact of my having come into her charge as a delicate baby. My father never got over his grudging dislike to his step-son, who had so innocently wrestled with him for the possession of my mother's heart. I mistrust me, too, that my father always considered him as the cause of my mother's death and my early delicacy; and utterly unreasonable as this may seem, I believe my father rather cherished his feeling of alienation to my brother as a duty, than strove to repress it. Yet not for the world would my father have grudged him anything that money could purchase. That was, as it were, in the bond when he had wedded my mother. Gregory was lumpish and loutish, awkward and ungainly, marring whatever he meddled in, and many a hard word and sharp scolding did he get from the people about the farm, who hardly waited till my father's back was turned before they rated the step-son. I am ashamed—my heart is sore to think how I fell into the fashion of the family, and slighted my poor orphan step-brother. I don't think I ever scouted him, or was wilfully ill-natured to him; but the habit of being considered in all things, and being treated as something uncommon and superior, made me insolent in my prosperity, and I exacted more than Gregory was always willing to grant, and then, irritated, I sometimes repeated the disparaging words I had heard others use with regard to him, without fully understanding their meaning. Whether he did or not I cannot tell. I am afraid he did. He used to turn silent and quiet—sullen and sulky, my father thought it: stupid Aunt Fanny used to call it. But every one said he was stupid and dull, and this stupidity and dulness grew upon him. He would sit without speaking a word, sometimes, for hours; then my father would bid him rise and do some piece of work, may be, about the farm. And he would take three or four tellings before he would go. When we were sent to school, it was all the same. He could never be made to remember his lessons; the schoolmaster grew weary of scolding and flogging, and at last advised my father just to take him away, and set him to some farm-work that might not be above his comprehension. I think he was more gloomy and stupid than ever after this, yet he was not a cross lad; he was patient and good-natured, and would try to do a kind turn for any one, even if they had been scolding or cuffing him not a minute before. But very often his attempts at kindness ended in some mischief to the very people he was trying to serve, owing to his awkward, ungainly ways. I suppose I was a clever lad; at any rate, I always got plenty of praise; and was, as we called it, the cock of the school. The schoolmaster said I could learn anything I chose, but my father, who had no great learning himself, saw little use in much for me, and took me away betimes, and kept me with him about the farm. Gregory was made into a kind of shepherd, receiving his training under old Adam, who was nearly past his work. I think old Adam was almost the first person who had a good opinion of Gregory. He stood to it that my brother had good parts, though he did not rightly know how to bring them out; and, for knowing the bearings of the Fells, he said he had never seen a lad like him. My father would try to bring Adam round to speak of Gregory's faults and shortcomings; but, instead of that, he would praise him twice as much, as soon as he found out what was my father's object.

One winter-time, when I was about sixteen, and Gregory nineteen, I was sent by my father on an errand to a place about seven miles distant by the road, but only about four by the Fells. He bade me return by the road whichever way I took in going, for the evenings closed in early, and were often thick and misty; besides which, old Adam, now paralytic and bed-ridden, foretold a downfall of snow before long. I soon got to my journey's end, and soon had done my business; earlier by an hour, I thought, than my father had expected, so I took the decision of the way by which I would return into my own hands, and set off back again over the Fells, just as the first shades of evening began to fall. It looked dark and gloomy enough; but everything was so still that I thought I should have plenty of time to get home before the snow came down. Off I set at a pretty quick pace. But night came on quicker. The right path was clear enough in the day-time, although at several points two or three exactly similar diverged from the same place; but when there was a good light, the traveller was guided by the sight of distant objects—a piece of rock,—a fall in the ground—which were quite invisible to me now. I plucked up a brave heart, however, and took what seemed to me the right road. It was wrong, nevertheless, and led me whither I knew not, but to some wild boggy moor where the solitude seemed painful, intense, as if never footfall of man had come thither to break the silence. I tried to shout—with the dimmest possible hope of being heard—rather to reassure myself by the sound of my own voice; but my voice came husky and short, and yet it dismayed me; it seemed so weird and strange, in that noiseless expanse of black darkness. Suddenly the air was filled thick with dusky flakes, my face and hands were wet with snow. It cut me off from the slightest knowledge of where I was, for I lost every idea of the direction from which I had come, so that I could even retrace my steps; it hemmed me in, thicker, thicker, with a darkness that might be felt. The boggy soil on which I stood quaked under me if I remained long in one place, and yet I dared not move far. All my youthful hardiness seemed to leave me at once. I was on the point of crying, and only very shame seemed to keep it down. To save myself from shedding tears, I shouted—terrible, wild shouts for bare life they were. I turned sick as I paused to listen; no answering sound came but the unfeeling echoes. Only the noiseless, pitiless snow kept falling thicker, thicker—faster, faster! I was growing numb and sleepy. I tried to move about, but I dared not go far, for fear of the precipices which, I knew, abounded in certain places on the Fells. Now and then, I stood still and shouted again; but my voice was getting choked with tears, as I thought of the desolate helpless death I was to die, and how little they at home, sitting round the warm, red, bright fire, wotted what was become of me,—and how my poor father would grieve for me—it would surely kill him—it would break his heart, poor old man! Aunt Fanny too—was this to be the end of all her cares for me? I began to review my life in a strange kind of vivid dream, in which the various scenes of my few boyish years passed before me like visions. In a pang of agony, caused by such remembrance of my short life, I gathered up my strength and called out once more, a long, despairing, wailing cry, to which I had no hope of obtaining any answer, save from the echoes around, dulled as the sound might be by the thickened air. To my surprise I heard a cry—almost as long, as wild as mine—so wild, that it seemed unearthly, and I almost thought it must be the voice of some of the mocking spirits of the Fells, about whom I had heard so many tales. My heart suddenly began to beat fast and loud. I could not reply for a minute or two. I nearly fancied I had lost the power of utterance. Just at this moment a dog barked. Was it Lassie's bark—my brother's collie?—an ugly enough brute, with a white, ill-looking face, that my father always kicked whenever he saw it, partly for its own demerits, partly because it belonged to my brother. On such occasions, Gregory would whistle Lassie away, and go off and sit with her in some outhouse. My father had once or twice been ashamed of himself, when the poor collie had yowled out with the suddenness of the pain, and had relieved himself of his self-reproach by blaming my brother, who, he said, had no notion of training a dog, and was enough to ruin any collie in Christendom with his stupid way of allowing them to lie by the kitchen fire. To all which Gregory would answer nothing, nor even seem to hear, but go on looking absent and moody.

Yes! there again! It was Lassie's bark! Now or never! I lifted up my voice and shouted "Lassie! Lassie! For God's sake, Lassie!" Another moment, and the great white-faced Lassie was curving and gambolling with delight round my feet and legs, looking, however, up in my face with her intelligent, apprehensive eyes, as if fearing lest I might greet her with a blow, as I had done oftentimes before. But I cried with gladness, as I stooped down and patted her. My mind was sharing in my body's weakness, and I could not reason, but I knew that help was at hand. A grey figure came more and more distinctly out of the thick, close-pressing darkness. It was Gregory wrapped in his maud.

"Oh, Gregory!" said I, and I fell upon his neck, unable to speak another word. He never spoke much, and made me no answer for some little time. Then he told me we must move, we must walk for the dear life—we must find our road home, if possible; but we must move, or we should be frozen to death.

"Don't you know the way home?" asked I.

"I thought I did when I set out, but I am doubtful now. The snow blinds me, and I am feared that in moving about just now, I have lost the right gait homewards."

He had his shepherd's staff with him, and by dint of plunging it before us at every step we took—clinging close to each other, we went on safely enough, as far as not falling down any of the steep rocks, but it was slow, dreary work. My brother, I saw, was more guided by Lassie and the way she took than anything else, trusting to her instinct. It was too dark to see far before us; but he called her back continually, and noted from what quarter she returned, and shaped our slow steps accordingly. But the tedious motion scarcely kept my very blood from freezing. Every bone, every fibre in my body seemed first to ache, and then to swell, and then to turn numb with the intense cold. My brother bore it better than I, from having been more out upon the hills. He did not speak, except to call Lassie. I strove to be brave, and not complain; but now I felt the deadly fatal sleep stealing over me.

"I can go no farther," I said, in a drowsy tone. I remember I suddenly became dogged and resolved. Sleep I would, were it only for five minutes. If death were to be the consequence, sleep I would. Gregory stood still. I suppose, he recognised the peculiar phase of suffering to which I had been brought by the cold.

"It is of no use," said he, as if to himself. "We are no nearer home than we were when we started, as far as I can tell. Our only chance is in Lassie. Here! roll thee in my maud, lad, and lay thee down on this sheltered side of this bit of rock. Creep close under it, lad, and I'll lie by thee, and strive to keep the warmth in us. Stay! hast gotten aught about thee they'll know at home?"

I felt him unkind thus to keep me from slumber, but on his repeating the question, I pulled out my pocket-handkerchief, of some showy pattern, which Aunt Fanny had hemmed for me—Gregory took it, and tied it round Lassie's neck.

"Hie thee, Lassie, hie thee home!" And the white-faced ill-favoured brute was off like a shot in the darkness. Now I might lie down—now I might sleep. In my drowsy stupour, I felt that I was being tenderly covered up by my brother; but what with I neither knew nor cared—I was too dull, too selfish, too numb to think and reason, or I might have known that in that bleak bare place there was naught to wrap me in, save what was taken off another. I was glad enough when he ceased his cares and lay down by me. I took his hand.

"Thou canst not remember, lad, how we lay together thus by our dying mother. She put thy small, wee hand in mine—I reckon she sees us now; and belike we shall soon be with her. Anyhow, God's will be done."

"Dear Gregory," I muttered, and crept nearer to him for warmth. He was talking still, and again about our mother, when I fell asleep. In an instant—or so it seemed—there were many voices about me—many faces hovering round me—the sweet luxury of warmth was stealing into every part of me. I was in my own little bed at home. I am thankful to say, my first word was "Gregory?"

A look passed from one to another—my father's stern old face strove in vain to keep its sternness; his mouth quivered, his eyes filled with unwonted tears.

"I would have given him half my land—I would have blessed him as my son,—Oh God! I would have knelt at his feet, and asked him to forgive my hardness of heart."

I heard no more. A whirl came through my brain, catching me back to death.

I came slowly to my consciousness, weeks afterwards. My father's hair was white when I recovered, and his hands shook as he looked into my face.

We spoke no more of Gregory. We could not speak of him; but he was strangely in our thoughts. Lassie came and went with never a word of blame; nay, my father would try to stroke her, but she shrank away; and he, as if reproved by the poor dumb beast, would sigh, and be silent and abstracted for a time.

Aunt Fanny—always a talker—told me all. How, on that fatal night, my father, irritated by my prolonged absence, and probably more anxious than he cared to show, had been fierce and imperious, even beyond his wont, to Gregory; had upbraided him with his father's poverty, his own stupidity which made his services good for nothing—for so, in spite of the old shepherd, my father always chose to consider them. At last, Gregory had risen up, and whistled Lassie out with him—poor Lassie, crouching underneath his chair for fear of a kick or a blow. Some time before, there had been some talk between my father and my aunt respecting my return; and when Aunt Fanny told me all this, she said she fancied that Gregory might have noticed the coming storm, and gone out silently to meet me. Three hours afterwards, when all were running about in wild alarm, not knowing whither to go in search of me—not even missing Gregory, or heeding his absence, poor fellow—poor, poor fellow!—Lassie came home, with my handkerchief tied round her neck. They knew and understood, and the whole strength of the farm was turned out to follow her, with wraps, and blankets, and brandy, and everything that could be thought of. I lay in chilly sleep, but still alive, beneath the rock that Lassie guided them to. I was covered over with my brother's plaid, and his thick shepherd's coat was carefully wrapped round my feet. He was in his shirt-sleeves—his arm thrown over me—a quiet smile (he had hardly ever smiled in life) upon his still, cold face.

My father's last words were, "God forgive me my hardness of heart towards the fatherless child!"

And what marked the depth of his feeling of repentance, perhaps more than all, considering the passionate love he bore my mother, was this; we found a paper of directions after his death, in which he desired that he might lie at the foot of the grave, in which, by his desire, poor Gregory had been laid with OUR MOTHER.

❊   ❊   ❊

CHARLES DICKENS
(1812-1870)

DICKENS, born at Landport, near Portsmouth, where his father was a clerk in the Navy Pay-Office, was brought up amid great hardships which furnished him material for some of his famous novels. While acting as a parliamentary reporter, he began writing a series of papers which were later collected as the *Sketches by Boz*. These were followed by *Pickwick Papers*, which at first appeared in monthly parts and took the country by storm. Thenceforward, Dickens continued as a literary success. He had an extraordinary power of invention, a boundless flow of animal spirits, a marvellous keenness of observation, a genial humour and a generous amount of pathos which at times was a little excessive.

THE CONVICT'S RETURN
(From the *Pickwick Papers*)

WHEN I first settled in this village," said the old gentleman, "which is now just five-and-twenty years ago, the most notorious person among my parishioners was a man of the name of Edmunds, who leased a small farm near this spot. He was a morose, savage-hearted, bad man: idle and dissolute in his habits; cruel and ferocious in his disposition. Beyond the few lazy and reckless vagabonds with whom he sauntered away his time in the fields, or sotted in the ale-house, he had not a single friend or acquaintance; no one cared to speak to the man whom many feared, and every one detested—and Edmunds was shunned by all.

"This man had a wife and one son, who, when I first came here, was about twelve years old. Of the acuteness of that woman's sufferings, of the gentle and enduring manner in which she bore them, of the agony of solicitude with which she reared that boy, no one can form an adequate conception. Heaven forgive me the supposition, if it be an uncharitable one, but I do firmly and in my soul believe, that the man systematically tried for many years to break her heart; but she bore it all for her child's sake, and, however strange it may seem to many, for his father's too; for brute as he was and cruelly as he had treated her, she had loved him once; and the recollection of what he had been to her awakened feelings of forbearance and meekness under suffering in her bosom, to which all God's creatures, but women, are strangers.

"They were poor—they could not be otherwise when the man pursued such courses; but the woman's unceasing and unwearied exertions, early and late, morning, noon and night, kept them above actual want. Those exertions were but ill repaid. People who passed the spot in the evening—sometimes at a late hour of the night—reported that they had heard the moans and sobs of a woman in distress, and the sound of blows: and more than once, when it was past midnight, the boy knocked softly at the door of a neighbour's house, whither he had been sent, to escape the drunken fury of his unnatural father.

"During the whole of this time, and when the poor creature often bore about her marks of ill-usage and violence which she could not wholly conceal, she was a constant attendant at our little church. Regularly every Sunday, morning and afternoon, she occupied the same seat with the boy at her side; and though they were poorly dressed—much more so than many of their neighbours who were in a lower station—they were always neat and clean. Every one had a friendly nod and a kind word for "poor Mrs. Edmunds;" and sometimes, when she stopped to exchange a few words with a neighbour at the conclusion of the service in the little row of elm trees which leads to the church porch, or lingered behind to gaze with a mother's pride and fondness upon her healthy boy, as he sported before her with some little companions, her care-worn face would lighten up with an expression of heartfelt gratitude; and she would look, if not cheerful and happy, at least tranquil and contented.

"Five or six years passed away; the boy had become a robust and well-grown youth. The time that had strengthened the child's slight frame and knit his weak limbs into the strength of manhood had bowed his mother's form, and enfeebled her steps; but the arm that should have supported her was no longer locked in hers; the face that should have cheered her, no more looked upon her own. She occupied her old seat, but there was a vacant one beside her. The Bible was kept as carefully as ever, the places were found and folded down as they used to be: but there was no one to read it with her; and the tears fell thick and fast upon the book, and blotted the words from her eyes. Neighbours were as kind as they were wont to be of old, but she shunned their greetings with averted head. There was no lingering among the old elm trees now—no cheering anticipations of happiness yet in store. The desolate woman drew her bonnet closer over her face, and walked hurriedly away.

"Shall I tell you, that the young man, who, looking back to the earliest of his childhood's days to which memory and consciousness extended, and carrying his recollection down to that moment, could remember nothing which was not in some way connected with a long series of voluntary privations suffered by his mother for his sake, with ill-usage, and insult, and violence, and all endured for him;—shall I tell you, that he, with a reckless disregard of her breaking heart, and a sullen wilful forgetfulness of all she had done and borne for him, had linked himself with depraved and abandoned men, and was madly pursuing a headlong career, which must bring death to him, and shame to her? Alas for human nature! You have anticipated it long since.

"The measure of the unhappy woman's misery and misfortune was about to be completed. Numerous offences had been committed in the neighbourhod; the perpetrators remained undiscovered, and their boldness increased. A robbery of a daring and aggravated nature occasioned a vigilance of pursuit, and a strictness of search, they had not calculated on. Young Edmunds was suspected with three companions. He was apprehended—committed—tried—condemned—to die.

"The wild and piercing shriek from a woman's voice, which resounded through the court when the solemn sentence was pronounced, rings in my ears at this moment. That cry struck a terror to the culprit's heart, which trial, condemnation—the approach of death itself, had failed to awaken. The lips which had been compressed in dogged sullenness throughout, quivered and parted involuntarily; the face turned ashy pale as the cold perspiration broke forth from every pore; the sturdy limbs of the felon trembled, and he staggered in the dock.

"In the first transports of her mental anguish, the suffering mother threw herself upon her knees at my feet, and fervently besought the Almighty Being who had hitherto supported her in all her troubles, to release her from a world of woe and misery, and to spare the life of her only child. A burst of grief, and a violent struggle, such as I hope I may never have to witness again, succeeded. I knew that her heart was breaking from that hour: but I never once heard complaint or murmur escape her lips.

"It was a piteous spectacle to see that woman in the prison yard from day to day, eagerly and fervently attempting, by affection and entreaty, to soften the hard heart of her obdurate son. It was in vain. He remained obstinate, and unmoved. Not even the unlooked-for commutation of his sentence to transportation for fourteen years, softened for an instant the sullen hardihood of his demeanour.

"But the spirit of resignation and endurance that had so long upheld her, was unable to contend against bodily weakness and infirmity. She fell sick. She dragged her tottering limbs from the bed to visit her son once more, but her strength failed her and she sunk powerless on the ground.

"And now the boasted coldness and indifference of the young man were tested indeed; and the retribution that fell heavily upon him, nearly drove him mad. A day passed away and his mother was not there: another flew by, and she came not near him; a third evening arrived, and yet he had not seen her; and in four-and-twenty hours he was to be separated from her—perhaps for ever. Oh! how the long-forgotten thoughts of former days rushed upon his mind, as he almost ran up and down the narrow yard—as if intelligence would arrive the sooner for his hurrying—and how bitterly a sense of his helplessness and desolation rushed upon him, when he heard the truth! His mother, the only parent he had ever known, lay ill—it might be dying—within one mile of the ground he stood on; were he free and unfettered, a few minutes would place him by her side. He rushed to the gate, and grasping the iron rails with the energy of desperation, shook it till it rang again, and threw himself against the thick wall as if to force a passage through the stone; but the strong building mocked his feeble efforts, and he beat his hands together and wept like a child.

"I bore the mother's forgiveness and blessing to her son in prison; and I carried his solemn assurance of repentance, and his fervent supplication for pardon, to her sick bed. I heard, with pity and compassion, the repentant man devise a thousand little plans for her comfort and support when he returned; but I knew that many months before he could reach his place of destination, his mother would be no longer of this world.

"He was removed by night. A few weeks afterwards the poor woman's soul took its flight, I confidently hope, and solemnly believe, to a place of eternal happiness and rest. I performed the burial service over her remains. She lies in our little churchyard. There is no stone at her grave's head. Her sorrows were known to man: her virtues to God.

"It had been arranged previously to the convict's departure, that he should write to his mother as soon as he could obtain permission, and that the letter should be addressed to me. The father had positively refused to see his son from the moment of his apprehension, and it was a matter of indifference to him whether he lived or died. Many years passed over without any intelligence of him; and when more than half his term of transportation had expired, and I had received no letter, I concluded him to be dead, as indeed, I almost hoped he might be.

"Edmunds, however, had been sent a considerable distance up the country on his arrival at the settlement; and to this circumstance, perhaps, may be attributed the fact, that though several letters were despatched, none of them ever reached my hands. He remained in expiration of the term, steadily adhering to his old resolution and the pledge he gave his mother, he made his way back to England amidst innumerable difficulties, and returned, on foot, to his native place.

"On a fine Sunday evening, in the month of August, John Edmunds set foot in the village he had left with shame and disgrace seventeen years before. His nearest way lay through the churchyard. The man's heart swelled as he crossed the stile. The tall old elms, through whose branches the declining sun cast here and there a rich ray of light upon the shady path, awakened the associations of his earliest days. He pictured himself as he was then, clinging to his mother's hand, and walking peacefully to church. He remembered how he used to look up into her pale face; and how her eyes would sometimes fill with tears as she gazed upon his features—tears which fell hot upon his forehead as she stooped to kiss him, and made him weep too, although he little knew then what bitter tears hers were. He thought how often he had run merrily down that path with some childish playfellow, looking back, ever and again, to catch his mother's smile, or hear her gentle voice; and then a veil seemed lifted from his memory, and words of kindness unrequited, and warnings despised, and promises broken, thronged upon his recollection till his heart failed him, and he could bear it no longer.

"He entered the church. The evening service was concluded and the congregation had dispersed, but it was not yet closed. His steps echoed through the low building with a hollow sound, and he almost feared to be alone, it was so still and quiet. He looked round him. Nothing was changed. The place seemed smaller than it used to be, but there were the old monuments on which he had gazed with childish awe a thousand times; the little pulpit with its faded cushion; the Communion-table before which he had so often repeated the Commandments he had reverenced as a child, and forgotten as a man. He approached the old seat; it looked cold and desolate. The cushion had been removed, and the Bible was not there. Perhaps his mother now occupied a poorer seat, or possibly she had grown infirm and could not reach the church alone. He dared not think of what he feared. A cold feeling crept over him, and he trembled violently as he turned away.

"An old man entered the porch just as he reached it. Edmunds started back, for he knew him well; many a time he had watched him digging graves in the churchyard. What would he say to the returned convict?

"The old man raised his eyes to the stranger's face, bid him 'good-evening,' and walked slowly on. He had forgotten him.

"He walked down the hill, and through the village. The weather was warm, and the people were sitting at their doors, or strolling in their little gardens as he passed, enjoying the serenity of the evening, and rest from labour. Many a look was turned towards him, and many a doubtful glance he cast on either side to see whether any knew and shunned him. There were strange faces in almost every house; in some he recognised the burly form of some old schoolfellow—a boy when he last saw him—surrounded by a troop of merry children; in others he saw, seated in an easy chair at a cottage door, a feeble and infirm old man, whom he only remembered as a hale and hearty labourer. But they had all forgotten him, and he passed on unknown.

"The last soft light of the setting sun had fallen on the earth, casting a rich glow on the yellow corn sheaves, and lengthening the shadows of the orchard trees, and he stood before the old house—the home of his infancy—to which his heart had yearned with an intensity of affection not to be described, through long and weary years of captivity and sorrow. The paling was low, though he well remembered the time when it had seemed a high wall to him; and he looked over into the old garden. There were more seeds and gayer flowers than there used to be, but there were the old trees still—the very tree, under which he had lain a thousand times when tired of playing in the sun, and felt the soft mild sleep of happy boyhood steal gently upon him. There were voices within the house. He listened, but they fell strangely upon his ear; he knew them not. They were merry too; and he well knew that his poor old mother could not be cheerful, and he away. The door opened, and a group of little children bounded out, shouting and romping. The father, with a little boy in his arms, appeared at the door, and they crowded round him, clapping their tiny hands, and dragging him out, to join their joyous sports. The convict thought on the many times he had shrunk from his father's sight in that very place. He remembered how often he had buried his trembling head beneath the bed-clothes, and heard the harsh word, and the hard stripe, and his mother's wailing; and though the man sobbed aloud with agony of mind, as he left the spot, his fist was clenched, and his teeth were set, in fierce and deadly passion.

"And such was the return to which he had looked through the weary perspective of many years, and for which he had undergone so much suffering! No face of welcome, no look of forgiveness, no house to receive, no hand to help him—and this too in the old village. What was this loneliness in the wild thick woods, where man was never seen, to his!

"He felt that in the distant land of his bondage and infamy, he had thought of his native place as it was when he left it; not as it would be when he returned. The sad reality struck coldly at his heart, and his spirit sank within him. He had not courage to make inquiries, or to present himself to the only person who was likely to receive him with kindness and compassion. He walked slowly on; and shunning the road side like a guilty man, turned into a meadow he well remembered: and covering his face with his hands, threw himself upon the grass.

"He had not observed that a man was lying on the bank beside him; his garments rustled as he turned round to steal a look at the new-comer; and Edmunds raised his head.

"The man had moved into a sitting posture. His body was much bent, and his face was wrinkled and yellow. His dress denoted him an inmate of the work-house: he had the appearance of being very old, but it looked more the effect of dissipation or disease, than length of years. He was staring hard at the stranger, and though his eyes were lustreless and heavy at first, they appeared to glow with an unnatural and alarmed expression after they had been fixed upon him for a short time, until they seemed to be staring from their sockets. Edmunds gradually raised himself to his knees, and looked more and more earnestly upon the old man's face. They gazed upon each other in silence.

"The old man was ghastly pale. He shuddered and tottered to his feet. Edmunds sprang to his. He stepped back a pace or two. Edmunds advanced.

"'Let me hear you speak,' said the convict, in a thick broken voice.

"'Stand off!' cried the old man, with a dreadful oath. The convict drew closer to him.

"'Stand off!' shrieked the old man. Furious with terror he raised his stick, and struck Edmunds a heavy blow across the face.

"'Father—devil!' murmured the convict, between his set teeth. He rushed wildly forward, and clenched the old man by the throat—but he was his father; and his arm fell powerless by his side.

"The old man uttered a loud yell which rang through the lonely fields like the howl of an evil spirit. His face turned black: the gore rushed from his mouth and nose, and dyed the grass a deep dark red, as he staggered and fell. He had ruptured a blood-vessel: and he was a dead man before his son could raise him.

*   *   *

"In that corner of the churchyard," said the old gentleman, after a silence of a few moments, "in that corner of the churchyard of which I have before spoken, there lies buried a man, who was in my employment for three years after this event: and who was truly contrite, penitent, and humbled, if ever man was. No one save myself knew in that man's lifetime who he was, or whence he came:—it was John Edmunds the returned convict."

WILKIE COLLINS
(1824–1889)

COLLINS, born in London, studied for the Bar, but relinquished law for literature. His first novel, *Antonina*, was a historical romance, but he soon discovered that his true field was the novel of modern life. Among his numerous novels, *The Woman in White* (1860), and *The Moonstone* (1868), stand out pre-eminent. He wrote some masterly tales among which *Blow up with the Brig!* is an interesting example. The story is reprinted from the volume *After Dark*, first published in 1856.

"BLOW UP WITH THE BRIG!"
A Sailor's Story

I HAVE got an alarming confession to make. I am haunted by a Ghost.

If you were to guess for a hundred years, you would never guess what my ghost is. I shall make you laugh to begin with—and afterward I shall make your flesh creep. My Ghost is the ghost of a Bedroom Candlestick.

Yes, a bedroom candlestick and candle, or a flat candlestick and candle—put it which way you like—that is what haunts me. I wish it was something pleasanter and more out of the common way; a beautiful lady, or a mine of gold and silver, or a cellar of wine and a coach and horses, and such like. But, being what it is, I must take it for what it is, and make the best of it; and I shall thank you kindly if you will help me out by doing the same.

I am not a scholar myself, but I make bold to believe that the haunting of any man with any thing under the sun begins with the frightening of him. At any rate, the haunting of me with a bedroom candlestick and candle began with the frightening of me with a bedroom candlestick and candle—the frightening of me half out of my life; and, for the time being, the frightening of me altogether out of my wits. That is not a very pleasant thing to confess before stating the particulars; but perhaps you will be the readier to believe that I am not a downright coward, because you find me bold enough to make a clean breast of it already, to my own great disadvantage so far.

Here are the particulars, as well as I can put them:

I was apprenticed to the sea when I was about as tall as my own walking-stick; and I made good enough use of my time to be fit for a mate's berth at the age of twenty-five years.

It was in the year eighteen hundred and eighteen, or nineteen, I am not quite certain which, that I reached the before-mentioned age of twenty-five. You will please to excuse my memory not being very good for dates, names, numbers, places, and such like. No fear, though, about the particulars I have undertaken to tell you of; I have got them all shipshape in my recollection; I can see them, at this moment, as clear as noonday in my own mind. But there is a mist over what went before, and, for the matter of that, a mist likewise over much that came after—and it's not very likely to lift at my time of life, is it?

Well, in eighteen hundred and eighteen, or nineteen, when there was peace in our part of the world—and not before it was wanted, you will say—there was fighting, of a certain scampering, scrambling kind, going on in that old battle-field which we sea-faring men know by the name of the Spanish Main.

The possessions that belonged to the Spaniards in South America had broken into open mutiny and declared for themselves years before. There was plenty of bloodshed between the new Government and the old; but the new had got the best of it, for the most part, under one General Bolivar—a famous man in his time, though he seems to have dropped out of people's memories now. Englishmen and Irishmen with a turn for fighting, and nothing particular to do at home, joined the general as volunteers; and some of our merchants here found it a good venture to send supplies across the ocean to the popular side. There was risk enough, of course, in doing this; but where one speculation of the kind succeeded, it made up for two, at the least, that failed. And that's the true principle of trade, wherever I have met with it, all the world over.

Among the Englishmen who were concerned in this Spanish-American business, I, your humble servant, happened, in a small way, to be one.

I was then mate of a brig belonging to a certain firm in the City, which drove a sort of general trade, mostly in queer out-of-the-way places, as far from home as possible; and which freighted the brig, in the year I am speaking of, with a cargo of gunpowder for General Bolivar and his volunteers. Nobody knew anything about our instructions, when we sailed, except the captain; and he didn't half seem to like them. I can't rightly say how many barrels of powder we had on board, or how much each barrel held—I only know we had no other cargo. The name of the brig was the *Good Intent*—a queer name enough, you will tell me, for a vessel laden with gunpowder, and sent to help a revolution. And as far as this particular voyage was concerned, so it was. I mean that for a joke, and I hope you will encourage me by laughing at it.

The *Good Intent* was the craziest tub of a vessel I ever went to sea in, and the worst found in all respects. She was two hundred and thirty, or two hundred and eighty tons burden, I forget which; and she had a crew of eight, all told—nothing like as many as we ought by rights to have had to work the brig. However, we were well and honestly paid our wages; and we had to set that against the chance of foundering at sea, and, on this occasion, likewise the chance of being blown up into the bargain.

In consideration of the nature of our cargo, we were harassed with new regulations, which we didn't at all like, relative to smoking our pipes and lighting our lanterns; and, as usual in such cases, the captain, who made the regulations, preached what he didn't practise. Not a man of us was allowed to have a bit of lighted candle in his hand when he went below—except the skipper; and he used his light, when he turned in, or when he looked over his charts on the cabin table, just as usual.

This light was a common kitchen candle or "dip," and it stood in an old battered flat candlestick, with all the japan worn and melted off, and all the tin showing through. It would have been more seaman-like and suitable in every respect if he had had a lamp or a lantern; but he stuck to his old candlestick; and that same old candlestick has ever afterward stuck to *me*. That's another joke, if you please, and a better one than the first, in my opinion.

Well (I said "well" before, but it's a word that helps a man on like), we sailed in the brig, and shaped our course, first, for the Virgin Islands, in the West Indies; and, after sighting them, we made for the Leeward Islands next, and then stood on due south, till the lookout at the masthead hailed the deck and said he saw land. That land was the coast of South America. We had had a wonderful voyage so far. We had lost none of our spars or sails, and not a man of us had been harassed to death at the pumps. It wasn't often the *Good Intent* made such a voyage as that, I can tell you.

I was sent aloft to make sure about the land, and I did make sure of it.

When I reported the same to the skipper, he went below, and had a look at his letter of instructions and the chart. When he came on deck again, he altered our course a trifle to the eastward—I forget the point on the compass, but that don't matter. What I do remember is, that it was dark before we closed in with the land. We kept the lead going, and hove the brig to in from four to five fathoms water, or it might be six— I can't say for certain. I kept a sharp eye to the drift of the vessel, none of us knowing how the currents ran on that coast. We all wondered why the skipper didn't anchor; but he said No, he must first show a light at the foretopmast-head, and wait for an answering light on shore. We did wait, and nothing of the sort appeared. It was starlight and calm. What little wind there was came in puffs off the land. I suppose we waited, drifting a little to the westward, as I made it out, best part of an hour before anything happened—and then, instead of seeing the light on shore, we saw a boat coming toward us, rowed by two men only.

We hailed them, and they answered "Friends!" and hailed us by our name. They came on board. One of them was an Irishman, and the other was a coffee-coloured native pilot, who jabbered a little English.

The Irishman handed a note to our skipper, who showed it to me. It informed us that the part of the coast we were off was not oversafe for discharging our cargo, seeing that spies of the enemy (that is to say, of the old Government) had been taken and shot in the neighbourhood the day before. We might trust the brig to the native pilot; and he had his instructions to take us to another part of the coast. The note was signed by the proper parties; so we let the Irishman go back alone in the boat, and allowed the pilot to exercise his lawful authority over the brig. He kept us stretching off from the land till noon the next day—his instructions, seemingly, ordering him to keep up well out of sight of the shore. We only altered our course in the afternoon, so as to close in with the land again a little before midnight.

This same pilot was about as ill-looking a vagabond as ever I saw; a skinny, cowardly, quarrelsome mongrel, who swore at the men in the vilest broken English, till they were every one of them ready to pitch him overboard. The skipper kept them quiet, and I kept them quiet; for the pilot being given us by our instructions, we were bound to make the best of him. Near night-fall, however, with the best will in the world to avoid it, I was unlucky enough to quarrel with him.

He wanted to go below with his pipe, and I stopped him, of course because it was contrary to orders. Upon that he tried to hustle by me, and I put him away with my hand. I never meant to push him down; but somehow I did. He picked himself up as quick as lightning, and pulled out his knife. I snatched it out of his hand, slapped his murderous face for him, and threw his weapon overboard. He gave me one ugly look and walked aft. I didn't think much of the look then, but I remembered it a little too well afterward.

We were close in with the land again, just as the wind failed us, between eleven and twelve that night, and dropped our anchor by the pilot's directions.

It was pitch-dark, and a dead, airless calm. The skipper was on deck with two of our best men for watch. The rest were below, except the pilot, who coiled himself up, more like a snake than a man, on the forecastle. It was not my watch till four in the morning. But I didn't like the look of the night, or the pilot, or the state of things generally, and shook myself down on deck to get my nap there, and be ready for anything at a moment's notice. The last I remember was the skipper whispering to me that he didn't like the look of things either, and that he would go below and consult his instructions again. That is the last I remember before the slow, heavy, regular roll of the old brig on the groundswell rocked me off to sleep.

I was awoke by a scuffle on the forecastle and a gag in my mouth.

There was a man on my breast and a man on my legs, and I was bound and and foot in half a minute.

The brig was in the hands of the Spaniards. They were swarming ll over her. I heard six heavy splashes in the water, one after another. saw the captain stabbed to the heart as he came running up the com- anion, and I heard a seventh splash in the water. Except myself, every oul of us on board had been murdered and thrown into the sea. Why was left, I couldn't think, till I saw the pilot stoop over me with a antern and look, to make sure of who I was. There was a devilish grin n his face, and he nodded his head at me, as much as to say, *You* were ne man who hustled me down and slapped my face, and I mean to play ne game of cat and mouse with you in return for it!

I could neither move nor speak, but I could see the Spaniards take off ne main hatch and rig the purchases for getting up the cargo. A quarter f an hour afterward I heard the sweeps of a schooner, or other small essel, in the water. The strange craft was laid alongside of us, and the paniards set to work to discharge our cargo into her. They all worked ard except the pilot; and he came from time to time, with his lantern, have another look at me, and to grin and nod always in the same evilish way. I am old enough now not to be ashamed of confessing the uth, and I don't mind acknowledging that the pilot frightened me.

The fright, and the bonds, and the gag, and the not being able to ir hand or foot, had pretty nigh worn me out by the time the Spaniards ave over work. This was just as the dawn broke. They had shifted good part of our cargo on board their vessel, but nothing like all of , and they were sharp enough to be off with what they had got before aylight.

I need hardly say that I had made up my mind by this time to the orst I could think of. The pilot, it was clear enough, was one of the ies of the enemy, who had wormed himself into the confidence of our onsignees without being suspected. He, or more likely his employers, ad got knowledge enough of us to suspect what our cargo was; we had een anchored for the night in the safest berth for them to surprise us in; nd we had paid the penalty of having a small crew, and consequently an sufficient watch. All this was clear enough—but what did the pilot ean to do with *me?*

On the word of a man, it makes my flesh creep now, only to tell you hat he did with me.

After all the rest of them were out of the brig, except the pilot and vo Spanish seamen, these last took me up, bound and gagged as I was, wered me into the hold of the vessel, and laid me along on the floor, shing me to it with ropes' ends, so that I could just turn from one side the other, but could not roll myself fairly over, so as to change my ace. They then left me. Both of them were the worse for liquor;

but the devil of a pilot was sober—mind that!—as sober as I am at the present moment.

I lay in the dark for a little while, with my heart thumping as if it was going to jump out of me. I lay about five minutes or so when the pilot came down into the hold alone.

He had the captain's cursed flat candlestick and a carpenter's awl in one hand, and a long thin twist of cotton-yarn, well oiled, in the other. He put the candlestick, with a new "dip" candle lighted in it, down on the floor about two feet from my face, and close against the side of the vessel. The light was feeble enough; but it was sufficient to show a dozen barrels of gunpowder or more left all round me in the hold of the brig. I began to suspect what he was after the moment I noticed the barrels. The horrors laid hold of me from head to foot, and the sweat poured off my face like water.

I saw him go next to one of the barrels of powder standing against the side of the vessel in a line with the candle, and about three feet, or rather better, away from it. He bored a hole in the side of the barrel with his awl, and the horrid powder came trickling out, as black as hell, and dripped into the hollow of his hand, which he held to catch it. When he had got a good handful, he stopped up the hole by jamming one end of his oiled twist of cotton-yarn fast into it, and he then rubbed the powder into the whole length of the yarn till he had blackened every hair-breadth of it.

The next thing he did—as true as I sit here, as true as the heaven above us all—the next thing he did was to carry the free end of his long, lean, black, frightful slow-match to the lighted candle alongside my face. He tied it (the bloody-minded villain!) in several folds round the tallow dip, about a third of the distance down, measuring from the flame of the wick to the lip of the candlestick. He did that; he looked to see that my lashings were all safe; and then he put his face close to mine, and whispered in my ear, "Blow up with the brig!"

He was on deck again the moment after, and he and the two others shoved the hatch on over me. At the farthest end from where I lay they had not fitted it down quite true, and I saw a blink of daylight glimmering in when I looked in that direction. I heard the sweeps of the schooner fall into the water—splash! splash! fainter and fainter, as they swept the vessel out in the dead calm, to be ready for the wind in the offing. Fainter and fainter, splash, splash! for a quarter of an hour or more.

While those receding sounds were in my ears, my eyes were fixed on the candle.

It had been freshly lighted. If left to itself, it would burn for between six and seven hours. The slow-match was twisted round it about a third of the way down, and therefore the flame would be about two hours reaching it. There I lay, gagged, bound, lashed to the floor; seeing

my own life burning down with the candle by my side—there I lay, alone
on the sea, doomed to be blown to atoms, and to see that doom drawing on,
nearer and nearer with every fresh second of time, through nigh on two
hours to come; powerless to help myself, and speechless to call for help to
others. The wonder to me is that I didn't cheat the flame, the slow-
match, and the powder, and die of the horror of my situation before my
first half-hour was out in the hold of the brig.

I can't exactly say how long I kept the command of my senses after
I had ceased to hear the splash of the schooner's sweeps in the water. I
can trace back everything I did and everything I thought, up to a certain
point; but, once past that, I get all abroad, and lose myself in my memory
now, much as I lost myself in my own feelings at the time.

The moment the hatch was covered over me, I began, as every other
man would have begun in my place, with a frantic effort to free my
hands. In the mad panic I was in, I cut my flesh with the lashings as if
they had been knife-blades, but I never stirred them. There was less
chance still of freeing my legs, or of tearing myself from the fastenings
that held me to the floor. I gave in when I was all but suffocated for
want of breath. The gag, you will please to remember, was a terrible
enemy to me; I could only breathe freely through my nose—and that is
but a poor vent when a man is straining his strength as far as ever it will
go.

I gave in and lay quiet, and got my breath again, my eyes glaring and
straining at the candle all the time.

While I was staring at it, the notion struck me of trying to blow out
the flame by pumping a long breath at it suddenly through my nostrils. It
was too high above me, and too far away from me, to be reached in that
fashion. I tried, and tried, and tried; and then I gave in again, and lay
quiet again, always with my eyes glaring at the candle, and the candle
glaring at *me*. The splash of the schooner's sweeps was very faint by this
time. I could only just hear them in the morning stillness. Splash!
splash!—fainter and fainter—splash! splash!

Without exactly feeling my mind going, I began to feel it getting
queer as early as this. The snuff of the candle was growing taller and
taller, and the length of tallow between the flame and the slow-match,
which was the length of my life, was getting shorter and shorter. I calculated that I had rather less than an hour and a half to live.

An hour and a half! Was there a chance in that time of a boat pulling off to the brig from shore? Whether the land near which the vessel
was anchored was in possession of our side, or in possession of the enemy's
side, I made out that they must, sooner or later, send to hail the brig
merely because she was a stranger in those parts. The question for *me*
was, how soon? The sun had not risen yet, as I could tell by looking
through the chink in the hatch. There was no coast village near us, as

we all knew, before the brig was seized, by seeing no lights on shore
There was no wind, as I could tell by listening, to bring any strange vessel near. If I had had six hours to live, there might have been a chance
for me, reckoning from sunrise to noon. But with an hour and a half
which had dwindled to an hour and a quarter by this time—or, in other
words, with the earliness of the morning, the uninhabited coast, and the
dead calm all against me—there was not the ghost of a chance. As I
felt that, I had another struggle—the last—with my bonds, and only cut
myself the deeper for my pains.

I gave in once more, and lay quiet, and listened for the splash of the
sweeps.

Gone! Not a sound could I hear but the blowing of a fish now and
then on the surface of the sea, and the creak of the brig's crazy old spars
as she rolled gently from side to side with the little swell there was on
the quiet water.

An hour and a quarter. The wick grew terribly as the quarter slipped
away, and the charred top of it began to thicken and spread out mushroom-
shape. It would fall off soon. Would it fall off red-hot, and would the
swing of the brig cant it over the side of the candle and let it down on
the slow-match? If it would, I had about ten minutes to live instead of
an hour.

This discovery set my mind for a minute on a new tack altogether
I began to ponder with myself what sort of a death blowing up might be
Painful! Well, it would be, surely, too sudden for that. Perhaps just
one crash inside me, or outside me, or both; and nothing more! Perhaps
not even a crash; that and death and the scattering of this living body
of mine into millions of fiery sparks, might all happen in the same instant!
I couldn't make it out; I couldn't settle how it would be. The minute
of calmness in my mind left it before I had half done thinking; and I
got all abroad again.

When I came back to my thoughts, or when they came back to me (I
can't say which), the wick was awfully tall, the flame was burning with
a smoke above it, the charred top was broad and red, and heavily spreading
out to its fall.

My despair and horror at seeing it took me in a new way, which was
good and right, at any rate, for my poor soul. I tried to pray—in my own
heart, you will understand, for the gag put all lip-praying out of my
power. I tried, but the candle seemed to burn it up in me. I struggled
hard to force my eyes from the slow, murdering flame, and to look up
through the chink in the hatch at the blessed daylight. I tried once, tried
twice; and gave it up. I next tried only to shut my eyes, and keep them
shut—once—twice—and the second time I did it. "God bless old mother
and sister Lizzie; God keep them both, and forgive *me*." That was
all I had time to say, in my own heart, before my eyes opened again, in

spite of me, and the flame of the candle flew into them, flew all over me, and burned up the rest of my thoughts in an instant.

I couldn't hear the fish blowing now; I couldn't hear the creak of the spars; I couldn't think; I couldn't feel the sweat of my own death agony on my face—I could only look at the heavy, charred top of the wick. It swelled, tottered, bent over to one side, dropped—red-hot at the moment of its fall—black and harmless, even before the swing of the brig had canted it over into the bottom of the candlestick.

I caught myself laughing.

Yes! laughing at the safe fall of the bit of wick. But for the gag, I should have screamed with laughing. As it was, I shook with it inside me—shook till the blood was in my head, and I was all but suffocated for want of breath. I had just sense enough left to feel that my own horrid laughter at that awful moment was a sign of my brain going at last. I had just sense enough left to make another struggle before my mind broke loose like a frightened horse, and ran away with me.

One comforting look at the blink of daylight through the hatch was what I tried for once more. The fight to force my eyes from the candle and to get that one look at the daylight was the hardest I had had yet; and I lost the fight. The flame had hold of my eyes as fast as the lashings had hold of my hands. I couldn't look away from it. I couldn't even shut my eyes, when I tried that next, for the second time. There was the wick growing tall once more. There was the space of un-burned candle between the light and the slow-match shortened to an inch or less.

How much life did that inch leave me? Three-quarters of an hour? Half an hour? Fifty minutes? Twenty minutes? Steady! an inch of tallow-candle would burn longer than twenty minutes. An inch of tallow! the notion of a man's body and soul being kept together by an inch of tallow! Wonderful! Why, the greatest king that sits on a throne can't keep a man's body and soul together; and here's an inch of tallow that can do what the king can't! There's something to tell mother when I get home which will surprise her more than all the rest of my voyages put together. I laughed inwardly again at the thought of that, and shook and swelled and suffocated myself, till the light of the candle leaped in through my eyes, and licked up the laughter, and burned it out of me, and made me all empty and cold and quiet once more.

Mother and Lizzie. I don't know when they came back; but they did come back—not, as it seemed to me, into my mind this time, but right down bodily before me, in the hold of the brig.

Yes: sure enough, there was Lizzie, just as light-hearted as usual, laughing at me. Laughing? Well, why not? Who is to blame Lizzie for thinking I'm lying on my back, drunk in the cellar, with the beer-barrels all round me? Steady! she's crying now—spinning round and round in a fiery mist, wringing her hands, screeching out for help—fainter and fainter, like the splash of the schooner's sweeps. Gone—burned up in the fiery mist! Mist? fire? no; neither one nor the other. It's mother makes the light—mother knitting, with ten flaming points at the ends of her fingers and thumbs, and slow-matches hanging in bunches all round her face instead of her own grey hair. Mother in her old arm-chair, and the pilot's long skinny hands hanging over the back of the chair, dripping with gunpowder. No! no gunpowder, no chair, no mother—nothing but the pilot's face, shining red-hot, like a sun, in the fiery mist; turning upside down in the fiery mist; running backward and forward along the slow-match, in the fiery mist; spinning millions of miles in a minute, in the fiery mist—spinning itself smaller and smaller into one tiny point, and that point darting on a sudden straight into my head—and then, all fire and all mist—no hearing, no seeing, no thinking, no feeling—the brig, the sea, my own self, the whole world, all gone together!

After what I've just told you, I know nothing and remember nothing, till I woke up (as it seemed to me) in a comfortable bed, with two rough-and-ready men like myself sitting on each side of my pillow, and a gentleman standing watching me at the foot of the bed. It was about seven in the morning. My sleep (or what seemed like my sleep to me) had lasted better than eight months—I was among my own countrymen in the island of Trinidad—the men at each side of my pillow were my keepers, turn and turn about—and the gentleman standing at the foot of the bed was the doctor. What I said and did in those eight months, I never have known, and never shall. I woke out of it as if it had been one long sleep—that's all I know.

It was another two months or more before the doctor thought it safe to answer the questions I asked him.

The brig had been anchored, just as I had supposed, off a part of the coast which was lonely enough to make the Spaniards pretty sure of no interruption, so long as they managed their murderous work quietly under cover of night.

My life had not been saved from the shore, but from the sea. An American vessel, becalmed in the offing, had made out the brig as the sun rose; and the captain having his time on his hands in consequence of the calm, and seeing a vessel anchored where no vessel had any reason to be, had manned one of his boats and sent his mate with it, to look a little closer into the matter, and bring back a report of what he saw.

What he saw, when he and his men found the brig deserted and boarded her, was a gleam of candle-light through the chink in the hatchway. The flame was within about a thread's breadth of the slow-match when he lowered himself into the hold; and if he had not had the sense and coolness to cut the match in two with his knife before he touched the candle, he and his men might have been blown up along with the brig as well as me. The match caught, and turned into sputtering red fire, in the very act of putting the candle out; and if the communication with the powder-barrel had not been cut off, the Lord only knows what might have happened.

What became of the Spanish schooner and the pilot, I have never heard from that day to this.

As for the brig, the Yankees took her, as they took me, to Trinidad, and claimed their salvage, and got it, I hope, for their own sakes. I was landed just in the same state as when they rescued me from the brig— that is to say, clean out of my senses. But please to remember, it was a long time ago; and, take my word for it, I was discharged cured, as I have told you. Bless your hearts, I'm all right now, as you may see. I'm a little shaken by telling the story, as is only natural—a little shaken, my good friends, that's all.

❋ ❋ ❋

ROBERT LOUIS STEVENSON
(1850-1894)

STEVENSON, born in Edinburgh, was destined for the engineering profession which had been followed by his family for two previous generations. Having neither the inclination nor the strength, he turned to law and was called to the Bar in 1875. He never practised, however, but began writing. His poor health compelled him to travel about, seeking a desirable climate, and he finally settled in Samoa where he died. His novels are distinguished by a singularly fascinating style, graceful and subtle. Some of his short stories are veritable masterpieces, and *Markheim* is remarkable for "its economy of means and its precision of effect." "The duality of man's nature and the alternation of good and evil," which is the theme of this story, was a subject that had interested Stevenson. *Markheim* first appeared in Unwin's Annual, 1885, and was republished in 1887, in *The Merry Men.*

MARKHEIM

"YES," said the dealer, "our windfalls are of various kinds. Some customers are ignorant, and then I touch a dividend on my superior knowledge. Some are dishonest," and here he held up the candle, so that the light fell strongly on his visitor, "and in that case," he continued, "I profit by my virtue."

Markheim had but just entered from the daylight streets, and his eyes had not yet grown familiar with the mingled shine and darkness in the shop. At these pointed words, and before the near presence of the flame, he blinked painfully and looked aside.

The dealer chuckled. "You come to me on Christmas day," he resumed, "when you know that I am alone in my house, put up my shutters, and make a point of refusing business. Well, you will have to pay for that; you will have to pay for my loss of time, when I should be balancing my books; you will have to pay, besides, for a kind of manner that I remark in you to-day very strongly. I am the essence of discretion, and ask no awkward questions; but when a customer cannot look me in the eye, he has to pay for it." The dealer once more chuckled; and then, changing to his usual business voice, though still with a note of irony, "You can give, as usual, a clear account of how you came into the possession of the object?" he continued. "Still your uncle's cabinet? A remarkable collector, sir!"

And the little pale, round-shouldered dealer stood almost on tiptoe, looking over the top of his gold spectacles, and nodding his head with every mark of disbelief. Markheim returned his gaze with one of infinite pity, and a touch of horror.

"This time," said he, "you are in error. I have not come to sell, but to buy. I have no curios to dispose of; my uncle's cabinet is bare to the wainscot; even were it still intact, I have done well on the Stock Exchange, and should more likely add to it than otherwise, and my errand to-day is simplicity itself. I seek a Christmas present for a lady," he continued, waxing more fluent as he struck into the speech he had prepared; "and certainly I owe you every excuse for thus disturbing you upon so small a matter. But the thing was neglected yesterday; I must produce my little compliment at dinner; and, as you very well know, a rich marriage is not a thing to be neglected."

There followed a pause, during which the dealer seemed to weigh his statement incredulously. The ticking of many clocks among the curious lumber of the shop, and the faint rushing of the cabs in a near thoroughfare, filled up the interval of silence.

"Well, sir," said the dealer, "be it so. You are an old customer after all; and if, as you say, you have the chance of a good marriage, far be it from me to be an obstacle. Here is a nice thing for a lady now," he went on, "this hand-glass—fifteenth century, warranted; comes from a good collection, too; but I reserve the name, in the interests of my customer, who was, just like yourself, my dear sir, the nephew and sole heir of a remarkable collector."

The dealer, while he thus ran on in his dry and biting voice, had stooped to take the object from its place; and, as he had done so, a shock had passed through Markheim, a start both of hand and foot, a sudden leap of many tumultuous passions to the face. It passed as swiftly as it

ame, and left no trace beyond a certain trembling of the hand that now
eceived the glass.

"A glass," he said hoarsely, and then paused, and repeated it more
learly. "A glass? For Christmas? Surely not?"

"And why not?" cried the dealer. "Why not a glass?"

Markheim was looking upon him with an indefinable expression.
You ask me why not?" he said. "Why, look here—look in it—look at
ourself! Do you like to see it? No! nor I—nor any man."

The little man had jumped back when Markheim had so suddenly
onfronted him with the mirror; but now, perceiving there was nothing
orse on hand, he chuckled. "Your future lady, sir, must be pretty hard
avoured," said he.

"I ask you," said Markheim, "for a Christmas present, and you give
ae this—this damned reminder of years, and sins and follies—this hand-
onscience! Did you mean it? Had you a thought in your mind? Tell
ae. It will be better for you if you do. Come, tell me about yourself.
hazard a guess now, that you are in secret a very charitable man?"

The dealer looked closely at his companion. It was very odd, Mark-
eim did not appear to be laughing; there was something in his face like
n eager sparkle of hope, but nothing of mirth.

"What are you driving at?" the dealer asked.

"Not charitable?" returned the other, gloomily. "Not charitable; not
ous; not scrupulous; unloving, unbeloved; a hand to get money, a safe
▸ keep it. Is that all? Dear God, man, is that all?"

"I will tell you what it is," began the dealer, with some sharpness,
id then broke off again into a chuckle. "But I see this is a love-match
f yours, and you have been drinking the lady's health."

"Ah!" cried Markheim, with a strange curiosity. "Ah, have you
en in love? Tell me about that."

"I!" cried the dealer. "I in love! I never had the time, nor have I
ae time to-day for all this nonsense. Will you take the glass?"

"Where is the hurry?" returned Markheim. "It is very pleasant to
and here talking; and life is so short and insecure that I would not hurry
vay from any pleasure—no, not even from so mild a one as this. We
ould rather cling, cling to what little we can get, like a man at a cliff's
lge. Every second is a cliff, if you think upon it—a cliff a mile high—
gh enough, if we fall, to dash us out of every feature of humanity.
ence it is best to talk pleasantly. Let us talk of each other; why should
e wear this mask? Let us be confidential. Who knows, we might be-
me friends?"

"I have just one word to say to you," said the dealer. "Either make
ur purchase, or walk out of my shop."

"True, true," said Markheim. "Enough fooling. To business.
ow me something else."

The dealer stooped once more, this time to replace the glass upon th
shelf, his thin blond hair falling over his eyes as he did so. Markhein
moved a little nearer, with one hand in the pocket of his greatcoat; he
drew himself up and filled his lungs; at the same time many differen
emotions were depicted together on his face—terror, horror, and resolve
fascination and a physical repulsion; and through a haggard lift of hi
upper lip, his teeth looked out.

"This, perhaps, may suit," observed the dealer; and then, as he bega
to rearise, Markheim bounded from behind upon his victim. The long
skewerlike dagger flashed and fell. The dealer struggled like a hen
striking his temple on the shelf, and then tumbed on the floor in a heap

Time had some score of small voices in that shop, some stately an
slow as was becoming to their great age; others garrulous and hurried
All these told out the seconds in an intricate chorus of tickings. The
the passage of a lad's feet, heavily running on the pavement, broke i
upon these smaller voices and startled Markheim into the consciousness o
his surroundings. He looked about him awfully. The candle stood o
the counter, its flame solemnly wagging in a draught; and by that incon
siderable movement, the whole room was filled with noiseless bustle an
kept heaving like a sea: the tall shadows nodding, the gross blots of dark
ness swelling and dwindling as with respiration, the faces of the portrait
and the china gods changing and wavering like images in water. Th
inner door stood ajar, and peered into that leaguer of shadows with a lon
slit of daylight like a pointing finger.

From these fear-stricken rovings, Markheim's eyes returned to th
body of his victim, where it lay both humped and sprawling, incredibl
small and strangely meaner than in life. In these poor, miserly clothes
in that ungainly attitude, the dealer lay like so much sawdust. Markhein
had feared to see it, and, lo! it was nothing. And yet, as he gazed, thi
bundle of old clothes and pool of blood began to find eloquent voices
There it must lie; there was none to work the cunning hinges or direc
the miracle of locomotion—there it must lie till it was found. Found
ay, and then? Then would this dead flesh lift up a cry that would rin
over England, and fill the world with the echoes of pursuit. Ay, dead o
not, this was still the enemy. "Time was that when the brains were out,"
he thought; and the first word struck into his mind. Time, now that th
deed was accomplished—time, which had closed for the victim, had be
come instant and momentous for the slayer.

The thought was yet in his mind, when, first one and then another
with every variety of pace and voice—one deep as the bell from a cathe
dral turret, another ringing on its treble notes the prelude of a waltz—
the clocks began to strike the hour of three in the afternoon.

The sudden outbreak of so many tongues in that dumb chamber stag
gered him. He began to bestir himself, going to and fro with the candle

beleaguered by moving shadows, and startled to the soul by chance reflections. In many rich mirrors, some of home designs, some from Venice
or Amsterdam, he saw his face repeated and repeated, as it were an army
of spies; his own eyes met and detected him; and the sound of his own
steps, lightly as they fell, vexed the surrounding quiet. And still as he
continued to fill his pockets, his mind accused him, with a sickening itera-
tion, of the thousand faults of his design. He should have chosen a more
quiet hour; he should have prepared an alibi; he should not have used a
knife; he should have been more cautions, and only bound and gagged
the dealer, and not killed him; he should have been more bold, and killed
the servant also; he should have done all things otherwise; poignant regrets, weary, incessant toiling of the mind to change what was unchange-
able, to plan what was now useless, to be the architect of the irrevocable
past. Meanwhile, and behind all this activity, brute terrors, like the
scurrying of rats in a deserted attic, filled the more remote chambers of
his brain with riot; the hand of the constable would fall heavy on his
shoulder, and his nerves would jerk like a hooked fish; or he beheld, in
galloping defile, the dock, the prison, the gallows, and the black coffin.

Terror of the people in the street sat down before his mind like a
besieging army. It was impossible, he thought, but that some rumour of
the struggle must have reached their ears and set on edge their curiosity;
and now, in all the neighbouring houses, he divined them sitting motionless and with uplifted ear—solitary people, condemned to spend Christmas
dwelling alone on memories of the past, and now startingly recalled from
that tender exercise; happy family parties, struck into silence round the
table, the mother still with raised finger: every degree and age and
humour, but all, by their own hearths, prying and hearkening and weaving the rope that was to hang him. Sometimes it seemed to him he could
not move too softly; the clink of the tall Bohemian goblets rang out
loudly like a bell; and alarmed by the bigness of the ticking, he was
tempted to stop the clocks. And then, again, with a swift transition of
his terrors, the very silence of the place appeared a source of peril, and a
thing to strike and freeze the passer-by; and he would step more boldly,
and bustle aloud among the contents of the shop, and imitate, with elaborate bravado, the movements of a busy man at ease in his own house.

But he was now so pulled about by different alarms that, while one
portion of his mind was still alert and cunning, another trembled on the
brink of lunacy. One hallucination in particular took a strong hold on his
credulity. The neighbour hearkening with white face beside his window, the passer-by arrested by a horrible surmise on the pavement—these
could at worst suspect, they could not know; through the brick walls and
shuttered windows only sounds could penetrate. But here, within the
house, was he alone? He knew he was; he had watched the servant set
forth sweet-hearting, in her poor best, "out for the day" written in every

ribbon and smile. Yes, he was alone, of course; and yet, in the bulk of empty house about him, he could surely hear a stir of delicate footing— he was surely conscious, inexplicably conscious of some presence. Ay, surely; to every room and corner of the house his imagination followed it; and now it was a faceless thing, and yet had eyes to see with; and again it was a shadow of himself; and yet again behold the image of the dead dealer, reinspired with cunning and hatred.

At times, with a strong effort, he would glance at the open door which still seemed to repel his eyes. The house was tall, the skylight small and dirty, the day blind with fog; and the light that filtered down to the ground story was exceedingly faint, and showed dimly on the threshold of the shop. And yet, in that strip of doubtful brightness, did there not hang wavering a shadow?

Suddenly, from the street outside, a very jovial gentleman began to beat with a staff on the shop-door, accompanying his blows with shouts and railleries in which the dealer was continually called upon by name. Markheim, smitten into ice, glanced at the dead man. But no! he lay quite still; he was fled away far beyond ear-shot of these blows and shout- ings; he was sunk beneath seas of silence; and his name, which would once have caught his notice above the howling of a storm, had become an empty sound. And presently the jovial gentleman desisted from his knocking and departed.

Here was a broad hint to hurry what remained to be done, to get forth from this accusing neighbourhood, to plunge into a path of London multi- tudes, and to reach, on the other side of day, that haven of safety and apparent innocence—his bed. One visitor had come: at any moment another might follow and be more obstinate. To have done the deed, and yet not to reap the profit, would be too abhorrent a failure. The money, that was now Markheim's concern; and as a means to that, the keys.

He glanced over his shoulder at the open door, where the shadow was still lingering and shivering; and with no conscious repugnance of the mind, yet with a tremour of the belly, he drew near the body of his victim. The human character had quite departed. Like a suit half-stuffed with bran, the limbs lay scattered, the trunk doubled, on the floor; and yet the thing repelled him. Although so dingy and inconsiderable to the eye, he feared it might have more significance to the touch. He took the body by the shoulders, and turned it on its back. It was strangely light and supple, and the limbs, as if they had been broken, fell into the oddest postures. The face was robbed of all expression; but it was as pale as wax, and shockingly smeared with blood about one temple. That was, for Markheim, the one displeasing circumstance. It carried him back upon the instant, to a certain fair day in a fishers' village: a grey day, a piping wind, a crowd upon the street, the blare of brasses, the booming of drums, the nasal voice of a ballad-singer; and a boy going to and fro buried over head in the crowd and divided between interest and fear, until, coming out upon the chief place of concourse, he beheld a booth and a great screen with pictures, dismally designed, garishly coloured: Brownrigg with her apprentice; the Mannings with their murdered guest; Weare in the death-grip of Thurtell; and a score besides of famous crimes. The thing was as clear as an illusion; he was once again that little boy; he was looking once again, and with the same sense of physical revolt, at these vile pictures; he was still stunned by the thumping of the drums. A bar of that day's music returned upon his memory; and at that, for the first time, a qualm came over him, a breath of nausea, a sudden weakness of the joints, which he must instantly resist and conquer.

He judged it more prudent to confront than to flee from these considerations; looking the more hardily in the dead face, bending his mind to realise the nature and greatness of his crime. So little a while ago that face had moved with every change of sentiment, that pale mouth had spoken, that body had been all on fire with governable energies; and now, and by his act, that piece of life had been arrested, as the horologist, with interjected finger, arrests the beating of the clock. So he reasoned in vain; he could rise to no more remorseful consciousness; the same heart which had shuddered before the painted effigies of crime, looked on its reality unmoved. At best, he felt a gleam of pity for one who had been endowed in vain with all those faculties that can make the world a garden of enchantment, one who had never lived and who was now dead. But of penitence, no, not a tremor.

With that, shaking himself clear of these considerations, he found the keys and advanced towards the open door of the shop. Outside, it had begun to rain smartly; and the sound of the shower upon the roof had banished silence. Like some dripping cavern, the chambers of the house were haunted by an incessant echoing, which filled the ear and mingled with the ticking of the clocks. And, as Markheim approached the door, he seemed to hear, in answer to his own cautious tread, the steps of another foot withdrawing up the stair. The shadow still palpitated loosely on the threshold. He threw a ton's weight of resolve upon his muscles, and drew back the door.

The faint, foggy daylight glimmered dimly on the bare floor and stairs; on the bright suit of armour posted, halbert in hand, upon the landing; and on the dark wood-carvings, and framed pictures that hung against the yellow panels of the wainscot. So loud was the beating of the rain through all the house that, in Markheim's ears, it began to be distinguished into many different sounds. Footsteps and sighs, the tread of regiments marching in the distance, the chink of money in the counting, and the creaking of doors held stealthily ajar, appeared to mingle with the patter of the drops upon the cupola and the gushing of the water in the pipes. The sense that he was not alone grew upon him to the verge of madness. On every side he was haunted and begirt by presences. He heard them moving in the upper chambers; from the shop, he heard the dead man getting to his legs; and as he began with a great effort to mount the stairs, feet fled quietly before him and followed stealthily behind. If he were but deaf, he thought, how tranquilly he would possess his soul! And then again, and hearkening with ever fresh attention, he blessed himself for that unresting sense which held the outposts and stood a trusty sentinel upon his life. His head turned continually on his neck; his eyes, which seemed starting from their orbits, scouted on every side, and on every side were half-rewarded as with the tail of something nameless vanishing. The four-and-twenty steps to the first floor were four-and-twenty agonies.

On that first story, the doors stood ajar, three of them like three ambushes, shaking his nerves like the throats of cannon. He could never again, he felt, be sufficiently immured and fortified from men's observing eyes; he longed to be home, girt in by walls, buried among bedclothes, and invisible to all but God. And at that thought he wondered a little, recollecting tales of other murderers and the fear they were said to entertain of heavenly avengers. It was not so, at least, with him. He feared the laws of nature, lest, in their callous and immutable procedure, they should preserve some damning evidence of his crime. He feared tenfold more, with a slavish, superstitious terror, some scission in the continuity of man's experience, some wilful illegality of nature. He played a game of skill, depending on the rules, calculating consequence from cause; and what if nature, as the defeated tyrant overthrew the chess-board, should break the mould of their succession? The like had befallen Napoleon (so writers said) when the winter changed the time of its appearance. The like might befall Markheim: the solid walls might become transparent and reveal his doings like those of bees in a glass hive; the stout planks might yield under his foot like quicksands and detain him in their clutch; ay, and there were soberer accidents that might destroy him: if, for instance, the house should fall and imprison him beside the body of his victim; or the house next door should fly on fire, and the firemen invade him from all sides. These things he feared; and, in a sense, these things might be called the hands of God reached forth against sin. But about God himself he was at ease; his act was doubtless exceptional, but so were his excuses, which God knew; it was there, and not among men, that he felt sure of justice.

When he had got safe into the drawing-room, and shut the door behind him, he was aware of a respite from alarms. The room was quite dismantled, uncarpeted besides, and strewn with packing-cases and incongruous furniture; several great pier-glasses, in which he beheld himself at various angles, like an actor on a stage; many pictures, framed and unframed, standing, with their faces to the wall; a fine Sheraton sideboard, a cabinet of marquetry, and a great old bed, with tapestry hangings. The windows opened to the floor; but by great good fortune the lower part of the shutters had been closed, and this concealed him from the neighbours. Here, then, Markheim drew in a packing-case before the cabinet, and began to search among the keys. It was a long business, for there were many; and it was irksome, besides; for, after all, there might be nothing in the cabinet, and time was on the wing. But the closeness of the occupation sobered him. With the tail of his eye he saw the door— even glanced at it from time to time directly, like a besieged commander pleased to verify the good estate of his defences. But in truth he was at peace. The rain falling in the street sounded natural and pleasant. Presently, on the other side, the notes of a piano were wakened to the music of a hymn, and the voices of many children took up the air and words. How stately, how comfortable was the melody! How fresh the youthful voices! Markheim gave ear to it smilingly, as he sorted out the keys; and his mind was thronged with answerable ideals and images; church-going children and the pealing of the high organ; children afield, bathers by the brookside, ramblers on the brambly common, kite-flyers in the windy and cloud-navigated sky; and then, at another cadence of the hymn, back again to church, and the somnolence of summer Sundays, and the high genteel voice of the parson (which he smiled a little to recall) and the painted Jacobean tombs, and the dim lettering of the Ten Commandments in the chancel.

And as he sat thus, at once busy and absent, he was startled to his feet. A flash of ice, a flash of fire, a bursting gush of blood, went over him, and then he stood transfixed and thrilling. A step mounted the stair slowly and steadily, and presently a hand was laid upon the knob, and the lock clicked, and the door opened.

Fear held Markheim in a vice. What to expect he knew not, whether the dead man walking, or the official ministers of human justice, or some chance witness blindly stumbling in to consign him to the gallows. But when a face was thrust into the aperture, glanced round the room, looked at him, nodded and smiled as if in friendly recognition, and then withdrew again, and the door closed behind it, his fear broke loose from his control in a hoarse cry. At the sound of this the visitant returned.

"Did you call me?" he asked, pleasantly, and with that he entered the room and closed the door behind him.

Markheim stood and gazed at him with all his eyes. Perhaps there was a film upon his sight, but the outlines of the newcomer seemed to change and waver like those of the idols in the wavering candle-light of the shop; and at times he thought he knew him; and at times he thought he bore a likeness to himself; and always, like a lump of living terror, there lay in his bosom the conviction that this thing was not of the earth and not of God.

And yet the creature had a strange air of the commonplace, as he stood looking on Markheim with a smile; and when he added: "You are looking for the money, I believe?" it was in the tones of every-day politeness.

Markheim made no answer.

"I should warn you," resumed the other, "that the maid has left her sweetheart earlier than usual and will soon be here. If Mr. Markheim be found in this house, I need not describe to him the consequences."

"You know me?" cried the murderer.

The visitor smiled. "You have long been a favourite of mine," he said; "and I have long observed and often sought to help you."

"What are you?" cried Markheim: "the devil?"

"What I may be," returned the other, "cannot affect the service I propose to render you."

"It can," cried Markheim; "it does! Be helped by you? No, never; not by you! You do not know me yet; thank God, you do not know me!"

"I know you," replied the visitant, with a sort of kind severity or rather firmnes. "I know you to the soul."

"Know me!" cried Markheim. "Who can do so? My life is but a travesty and slander on myself. I have lived to belie my nature. All men do; all men are better than this disguise that grows about and stifles them. You see each dragged away by life, like one whom bravos have seized and muffled in a cloak. If they had their own control—if you could see their faces, they would be altogether different, they would shine out for heroes and saints! I am worse than most; myself is more overlaid; my excuse is known to me and God. But, had I the time, I could disclose myself."

"To me?" inquired the visitant.

"To you before all," returned the murderer. "I supposed you were intelligent. I thought—since you exist—you would prove a reader of the heart. And yet you would propose to judge me by my acts! Think of it; my acts! I was born and I have lived in a land of giants; giants have dragged me by the wrists since I was born out of my mother—the giants of circumstance. And you would judge me by my acts! But can you not look within? Can you not understand that evil is hateful to me? Can you not see within me the clear writing of conscience, never blurred by any willful sophistry, although too often disregarded? Can you not read me for a thing that surely must be common as humanity—the unwilling sinner?"

"All this is very feelingly expressed," was the reply, "but it regards me not. These points of consistency are beyond my province, and I care not in the least by what compulsion you may have been dragged away, so as you are but carried in the right direction. But time flies;

the servant delays, looking in the faces of the crowd and at the pictures on the hoardings, but still she keeps moving nearer; and remember, it is as if the gallows itself were striding towards you through the Christmas streets! Shall I help you; I, who know all? Shall I tell you where to find the money?"

"For what price?" asked Markheim.

"I offer you the service for a Christmas gift," returned the other.

Markheim could not refrain from smiling with a kind of bitter triumph. "No," said he, "I will take nothing at your hands; if I were dying of thirst, and it was your hand that put the pitcher to my lips, I should find the courage to refuse. It may be credulous, but I will do nothing to commit myself to evil."

"I have no objection to a death-bed repentance," observed the visitant.

"Because you disbelieve their efficacy!" Markheim cried.

"I do not say so," returned the other; "but I look on these things from a different side, and when the life is done my interest falls. The man has lived to serve me, to spread black looks under colour of religion, or to sow tares in the wheat-field, as you do, in a course of weak compliance with desire. Now that he draws so near to his deliverance, he can add but one act of service—to repent, to die smiling, and thus to build up in confidence and hope the more timorous of my surviving followers. I am not so hard a master. Try me. Accept my help. Please yourself in life as you have done hitherto; please yourself more amply, spread your elbows at the board; and when the night begins to fall and the curtains to be drawn, I tell you, for your greater comfort, that you will find it even easy to compound your quarrel with your conscience, and to make a truckling peace with God. I came but now from such a death-bed, and the room was full of sincere mourners, listening to the man's last words: and when I looked into that face, which had been set as a flint against mercy, I found it smiling with hope."

"And do you, then, suppose me such a creature?" asked Markheim. "Do you think I have no more generous aspirations than to sin, and sin, and sin, and, at last, sneak into heaven? My heart rises at the thought. Is this, then, your experience of mankind? or is it because you find me with red hands that you presume such baseness? and is this crime of murder indeed so impious as to dry up the very springs of good?"

"Murder is to me no special category," replied the other. "All sins are murder, even as all life is war. I behold your race, like starving mariners on a raft, plucking crusts out of the hands of famine and feeding on each other's lives. I follow sins beyond the moment of their acting; I find in all that the last consequence is death; and to my eyes, the pretty maid who thwarts her mother with such taking graces on a question of a ball, drips no less visibly with human gore than such a murderer as yourself. Do I say that I follow sins? I follow virtues also; they differ not by the thickness of a nail, they are both scythes for the reaping angel of Death. Evil, for which I live, consists not in action, but in character. The bad man is dear to me; not the bad act, whose fruits, if we could follow them far enough down the hurtling cataract of the ages, might yet be found more blessed than those of the rarest virtues. And it is not because you have killed a dealer, but because you are Markheim, that I offered to forward your escape."

"I will lay my heart open to you," answered Markheim. "This crime on which you find me is my last. On my way to it I have learned many lessons; itself is a lesson, a momentous lesson. Hitherto I have been driven with revolt to what I would not; I was a bond-slave to poverty, driven and scourged. There are robust virtues that can stand in these temptations; mine was not so; I had a thirst of pleasure. But to-day, and out of this deed, I pluck both warning and riches—both the power and a fresh resolve to be myself. I become in all things a free actor in the world; I begin to see myself all changed, these hands the agents of good, this heart at peace. Something comes over me out of the past; something of what I have dreamed on Sabbath evenings to the sound of the church organ, of what I forecast when I shed tears over noble books, or talked, an innocent child, with my mother. There lie my life; I have wandered a few years, but now I see once more my city of destination."

"You are to use this money on the Stock Exchange, I think?" remarked the visitor; "and there, if I mistake not, you have already lost some thousands?"

"Ah," said Markheim, "but this time I have a sure thing."

"This time, again, you will lose," replied the visitor quietly.

"Ah, but I keep back the half!" cried Markheim.

"That also you will lose," said the other.

The sweat started upon Markheim's brow. "Well, then, what matter?" he exclaimed. "Say it be lost, say I am plunged again in poverty, shall one part of me, and that the worse, continue until the end to override the better? Evil and good run strong in me, haling me both ways. I do not love the one thing, I love all. I can conceive great deeds, renunciations, martyrdoms; and though I be fallen to such a crime as murder, pity is no stranger to my thoughts. I pity the poor; who knows their trials better than myself? I pity and help them; I prize love, I love honest laughter; there is no good thing nor true thing on earth but I love it from my heart. And are my vices only to direct my life, and my virtues to lie without effect, like some passive lumber of the mind? Not so; good, also, is a spring of acts."

But the visitant raised his finger. "For six-and-thirty years that you have been in this world," said he, "through many changes of fortune and varieties of humour, I have watched you steadily fall. Fifteen years ago you would have started at a theft. Three years back you would have blenched at the name of murder. Is there any crime, is there any cruelty or meanness, from which you still recoil?—five years from now I shall detect you in the fact! Downward, downward, lies your way; nor can anything but death avail to stop you."

"It is true," Markheim said huskily, "I have in some degree complied with evil. But it is so with all: the very saints, in the mere exercise of living, grow less dainty, and take on the tone of their surroundings."

"I will propound to you one simple question," said the other; "and as you answer, I shall read to you your moral horoscope. You have grown in many things more lax; possibly you do right to be so; and at any account, it is the same with all men. But granting that, are you in any one particular, however trifling, more difficult to please with your own conduct, or do you go in all things with a looser rein?"

"In any one?" repeated Markheim, with an anguish of consideration. "No," he added, with despair, "in none! I have gone down in all."

"Then," said the visitor, "content yourself with what you are, for you will never change; and the words of your part on this stage are irrevocably written down."

Markheim stood for a long while silent, and indeed it was the visitor who first broke the silence. "That being so," he said, "shall I show you the money?"

"And grace?" cried Markheim.

"Have you not tried it?" returned the other. "Two or three years ago, did I not see you on the platform of revival meetings, and was not your voice the loudest in the hymn?"

"It is true," said Markheim; "and I see clearly what remains for me by way of duty. I thank you for these lessons from my soul; my eyes are opened, and I behold myself at last for what I am."

At this moment, the sharp note of the door-bell rang through the house; and the visitant, as though this were some concerted signal for which he had been waiting, changed at once in his demeanour.

"The maid!" he cried. "She has returned, as I forewarned you, and there is now before you one more difficult passage. Her master, you must say, is ill; you must let her in, with an assured but rather serious countenance—no smiles, no overacting, and I promise you success! Once the girl within, and the door closed, the same dexterity that has already rid you of the dealer will relieve you of this last danger in your path. Thenceforward you have the whole evening—the whole night, if needful—to ransack the treasures of the house and to make good your safety. This is help that comes to you with the mask of danger. Up!"

he cried: "up, friend; your life hangs trembling in the scales: up, and act!"

Markheim steadily regarded his counsellor. "If I be condemned to evil acts," he said, "there is still one door of freedom open—I can cease from action. If my life be an ill thing, I can lay it down. Though I be, as you say truly, at the beck of every small temptation, I can yet, by one decisive gesture, place myself beyond the reach of all. My love of good is damned to barrenness; it may, and let it be! But I have still my hatred of evil; and from that, to your galling disappointment, you shall see that I can draw both energy and courage."

The features of the visitor began to undergo a wonderful and lovely change: they brightened and softened with a tender triumph; and, even as they brightened, faded and dislimned. But Markheim did not pause to watch or understand the transformation. He opened the door and went down-stairs very slowly, thinking to himself. His past went soberly before him; he beheld it as it was, ugly and strenuous like a dream, random as chance-medley—a scene of defeat. Life, as he thus reviewed it, tempted him no longer; but on the farther side he perceived a quiet haven for his bark. He paused in the passage, and looked into the shop, where the candle still burned by the dead body. It was strangely silent. Thoughts of the dealer swarmed into his mind, as he stood gazing. And then the bell once more broke out into impatient clamour.

He confronted the maid upon the threshold with something like a smile.

"You had better go for the police," said he: "I have killed your master."

✳ ✳ ✳

GEORGE MOORE
(1852-   )

MOORE was born in County Mayo, Ireland, and was educated largely by himself. He went abroad to live in Paris, about 1872, for the purpose of studying painting; but falling under the influence of Zola, Huysmans, and the Goncourts, he pursued literature, and wrote several successful novels. His short stories appeared in a volume, *Untilled Fields*, 1903, from which *The Clerk's Quest* is reprinted, by permission of the publishers, Brentano's, Inc.

THE CLERK'S QUEST

FOR thirty years Edward Dempsey had worked low down in the list of clerks in the firm of Quin and Wee. He did his work so well that he seemed born to do it, and it was felt that any change in which Dempsey was concerned would be unlucky. Managers had looked at Dempsey doubtingly and had left him in his habits. New partners had come into the business, but Dempsey showed no sign of interest. He was interested only in his desk. There it was by the dim window, there were his pens, there was his penwiper, there was the ruler, there was the blotting-pad. Dempsey was always the first to arrive and the last to leave. Once in thirty years of service he had accepted a holiday. It had been a topic of conversation all the morning, and the clerks tittered when he came into the bank in the afternoon saying he had been looking into the shop windows all the morning, and had come down to the bank to see how they were getting on.

An obscure, clandestine, taciturn little man, occupying in life only the space necessary to bend over a desk, and whose conical head leaned to one side as if in token of his humility.

It seemed that Dempsey had no other ambition than to be allowed to stagnate at a desk to the end of his life, and this modest ambition would have been realised had it not been for a slight accident—the single accident that had found its way into Dempsey's well-ordered and closely guarded life. One summer's day, the heat of the areas arose and filled the open window, and Dempsey's somnolescent senses were moved by a soft and suave perfume. At first he was puzzled to say whence it came; then he perceived that it had come from the bundle of cheques which he held in his hand; and then that the odoriferous paper was a pale pink cheque in the middle of the bundle. He had hardly seen a flower for thirty years, and could not determine whether the odour was that of mignonette, or honeysuckle, or violet. But at that moment the cheques were called for; he handed them to his superior, and with cool hand and clear brain continued to make entries in the ledger until the bank closed.

But that night, just as he was falling asleep, a remembrance of the insinuating perfume returned to him. He wondered whose cheque it was, and regretted not having looked at the signature, and many times during the succeeding weeks he paused as he was making entries in the ledger to think if the haunting perfume were rose, lavender, or mignonette. It was not the scent of rose, he was sure of that. And a vague swaying of hope began. Dreams that had died or had never been born floated up like things from the depths of the sea, and many old things that he had dreamed about or had never dreamed at all drifted about.

Out of the depths of life a hope that he had never known, or that the severe rule of his daily life had checked long ago, began its struggle for life; and when the same sweet odour came again—he knew now it was the scent of heliotrope—his heart was lifted and he was overcome in a sweet possessive trouble. He sought for the cheque amid the bundle of cheques and, finding it, he pressed the paper to his face. The cheque was written in a thin, feminine handwriting, and was signed "Henrietta Brown," and the name and handwriting were pregnant with occult significances in Dempsey's disturbed mind. His hand paused amid the entries, and he grew suddenly aware of some dim, shadowy form, gracile and sweet-smelling as the spring—moist shadow of wandering cloud, emanation of earth, or woman herself? Dempsey pondered, and his absent-mindedness was noticed, and occasioned comment among the clerks.

For the first time in his life he was glad when the office hours were over. He wanted to be alone, he wanted to think, he felt he must abandon himself to the new influence that had so suddenly and unexpectedly entered his life. Henrietta Brown! the name persisted in his mind like a half-forgotten, half-remembered tune; and in his efforts to realise her beauty he stopped before the photographic displays in the shop windows; but none of the famous or the infamous celebrities there helped him in the least. He could only realise Henrietta Brown by turning his thoughts from without and seeking the intimate sense of her perfumed cheques. The end of every month brought a cheque from Henrietta Brown, and for a few moments the clerk was transported and lived beyond himself.

An idea had fixed itself in his mind. He knew not if Henrietta Brown was young or old, pretty or ugly, married or single; the perfume and the name were sufficient, and could no longer be separated from the idea, now forcing its way through the fissures in the failing brain of this poor little bachelor clerk—that idea of light and love and grace so inherent in man, but which rigorous circumstance had compelled Dempsey to banish from his life.

Dempsey had had a mother to support for many years, and had found it impossible to economise. But since her death he had laid by about one hundred and fifty pounds. He thought of this money with awe, and awed by his good fortune he wondered how much more he might save before he was forced to leave his employment; and to have touched a penny of his savings would have seemed to him a sin near to sacrilege. Yet he did not hesitate for a single moment to send Henrietta Brown, whose address he had been able to obtain through the bank books, a diamond brooch which had cost twenty pounds. He omitted to say whence it had come, and for days he lived in a warm wonderment satisfied in the thought that she was wearing something that he had seen and touched.

His ideal was now by him and always, and its dominion was so complete that he neglected his duties at the bank, and was censured by the amazed manager. The change of his condition was so obvious that it became the subject for gossip, and jokes were now beginning to pass into serious conjecturing. Dempsey took no notice, and his plans matured amid jokes and theories. The desire to write and reveal himself to his beloved had become imperative; and after some very slight hesitation—for he was moved more by instinct that by reason—he wrote a letter urging the fatality of the circumstances that separated them, and explaining rather than excusing this revelation of his identity. His letter was full of deference, but at the same time it left no doubt as to the nature of his attachments and hopes. The answer to this letter was a polite note begging him not to persist in this correspondence, and warning him that if he did it would become necessary to write to the manager of the bank. But the return of his brooch did not dissuade Dempsey from the pursuit of his ideal; and as time went by it became more and more impossible for him to refrain from writing love letters, and sending occasional presents of jewellery. When the letters and the jewellery were returned to him he put them away carelessly, and he bought the first sparkle of diamonds that caught his fancy, and forwarded ring, bracelet, and ear-ring, with whatever word of rapturous love that came up in his mind.

One day he was called into the manager's room, severely reprimanded, and eventually pardoned in consideration of his long and faithful service. But the reprimands of his employers were of no use and he continued to write to Henrietta Brown, growing more and more careless of his secret. He dropped brooches about the office, and his letters. At last the story was whispered from desk to desk. Dempsey's dismissal was the only course open to the firm; and it was with much regret that the partners told their old servant that his services were no longer required.

To their surprise Dempsey seemed quite unaffected by his dismissal; he even seemed relieved, and left the bank smiling, thinking of Henrietta, bestowing no thought on his want of means. He did not even think of providing himself with money by the sale of some of the jewellery he had about him, nor of his going to his lodging and packing up his clothes, he did not think how he should get to Edinburgh—it was there that she lived. He thought of her even to the exclusion of the simplest means of reaching her, and was content to walk about the streets in happy mood, waiting for glimpses of some evanescent phantom at the wood's edge wearing a star on her forehead, or catching sight in the wood's depths of a glistening shoulder and feet flying towards the reeds. Full of happy aspiration he wandered seeking the country through the many straggling villages that hang like children round the skirts of Dublin, and was passing through one of these at nightfall, and, feeling tired, he turned into the bar of an inn, and asked for bread and cheese.

"Come a long way, governor?" said one of two rough fellows.

"I am going a long way," replied Dempsey; "I am going north—very far north."

"And what may yer be going north for, if I may make bold to ask?"

"I am going to the lady I love, and I am taking her beautiful presents of jewellery."

The two rough fellows exchanged glances; and it is easy to imagine how Dempsey was induced to let them have his diamonds, so that inquiries might be made of a friend round the corner regarding their value. After waiting a little while, Dempsey paid for his bread and cheese, and went in search of the thieves. But the face of Henrietta Brown obliterated all remembrance of thieves and diamonds, and he wandered for a few days, sustained by his dream and the crusts that his appearance drew from the pitiful. At last he even neglected to ask for a crust, and, foodless, followed the beckoning vision, from sunrise to sundown.

It was a soft, quiet summer's night when Dempsey lay down to sleep for the last time. He was very tired, he had been wandering all day, and threw himself on the grass by the roadside. He lay there looking up at the stars, thinking of Henrietta, knowing that everything was slipping away, and he passing into a diviner sense. Henrietta seemed to be coming nearer to him and revealing herself more clearly; and when the word of death was in his throat, and his eyes opened for the last time, it seemed to him that one of the stars came down from the sky and laid its bright face upon his shoulder.

❊   ❊   ❊

OSCAR WILDE
(1854-1900)

WILDE was born in Dublin, and was educated at Trinity College, Dublin, later attending Oxford, where he inaugurated the "æsthetic" movement. He wrote poetry, plays and fiction; and all of his work is characterised by a brilliant and subtle style. Although he is best remembered for *The Picture of Dorian Gray*, and his supremely witty plays, his short stories are, nevertheless, an important part of his work.

THE SPHINX WITHOUT A SECRET

ONE afternoon I was sitting outside the Café de la Paix, watching the splendour and shabbiness of Parisian life, and wondering over my vermouth at the strange panorama of pride and poverty that was passing before me, when I heard some one call my name. I turned round, and saw Lord Murchison. We had not met since we had been at college together, nearly ten years before, so I was delighted to come across him again, and we shook hands warmly. At Oxford we had been great friends. I had liked him immensely, he was so handsome, so high-spirited, and so honourable. We used to say of him that he would be the best of fellows, if he did not always speak the truth, but I think we really admired him all the more for his frankness. I found him a good deal changed. He looked anxious and puzzled, and seemed to be in doubt about something. I felt it could not be modern scepticism, for Murchison was the stoutest of Tories, and believed in the Pentateuch as firmly as he believed in the House of Peers; so I concluded that it was a woman, and asked him if he was married yet.

"I don't understand women well enough," he answered.

"My dear Gerald," I said, "women are meant to be loved, not to be understood."

"I cannot love where I cannot trust," he replied.

"I believe you have a mystery in your life, Gerald," I exclaimed; "tell me about it."

"Let us go for a drive," he answered, "it is too crowded here. No, not a yellow carriage, any other colour—there, that dark green one will do;" and in a few moments we were trotting down the boulevard in the direction of the Madeleine.

"Where shall we go to?" I said.

"Oh, anywhere you like!" he answered—"to the restaurant in the Bois; we will dine there, and you shall tell me all about yourself."

"I want to hear about you first," I said, "tell me your mystery."

He took from his pocket a little silver-clasped morocco case, and handed it to me. I opened it. Inside there was the photograph of a woman. She was tall and slight, and strangely picturesque with her large vague eyes and loosened hair. She looked like a clairvoyante, and was wrapped in rich furs.

"What do you think of that face?" he said; "is it truthful?"

I examined it carefully. It seemed to me the face of some one who had a secret, but whether that secret was good or evil I could not say. Its beauty was a beauty moulded out of many mysteries—the beauty, in fact, which is psychological, not plastic—and the faint smile that just played across the lips was far too subtle to be really sweet.

"Well," he cried impatiently, "what do you say?"

"She is the Gioconda in sables," I answered. "Let me know all about her."

"Not now," he said; "after dinner," and began to talk of other things.

When the waiter brought us our coffee and cigarettes I reminded Gerald of his promise. He arose from his seat, walked two or three times up and down the room, and, sinking into an armchair, told me the following story:

"One evening," he said, "I was walking down Bond street above five o'clock. There was a terrific crush of carriages, and the traffic was almost stopped. Close to the pavement was standing a little yellow brougham, which, for some reason or other, attracted my attention. As I passed by there looked out from it the face I showed you this afternoon. It fascinated me immediately. All that night I kept thinking of it, and all the next day. I wandered up and down that wretched Row, peering into every carriage, and waiting for the yellow brougham; but I could not find *ma belle inconnue*, and at last I began to think she was merely a dream. About a week afterwards I was dining with Madame de Rastail. Dinner was for eight o'clock, but at half-past eight we were still waiting in the drawing-room. Finally the servant threw open the door, and announced Lady Alroy. It was the woman I had been looking for. She came in very slowly, looking like a moonbeam in grey lace, and, to my intense delight, I was asked to take her in to dinner. After we had sat down, I remarked quite innocently: 'I think I caught sight of you in Bond Street some time ago, Lady Alroy.' She grew very pale, and said to me in a low voice: 'Pray do not talk so loud; you may be overheard.' I felt miserable at having made such a bad beginning, and plunged recklessly into the subject of the French plays. She spoke very little, always in the same low musical voice, and seemed as if she was afraid of some one listening. I fell passionately, stupidly in love, and the indefinable atmosphere of mystery that surrounded her excited my most ardent curiosity. When she was going away, which she did very soon after dinner, I asked her if I might call and see her. She hesitated for a moment, glanced round to see if any one was near us, and then said: 'Yes, to-morrow at a quarter to five.' I begged Madame de Rastail to tell me about her: but all that I could learn was that she was a widow with a beautiful house in Park Lane, and as some scientific bore began a dissertation on widows, as exemplifying the survival of the matrimonially fittest, I left and went home.

"The next day I arrived at Park Lane punctual to the moment, but was told by the butler that Lady Alroy had just gone out. I went down to the club quite unhappy and very much puzzled, and after long consideration wrote her a letter, asking if I might be allowed to try my chance some other afternoon. I had no answer for several days, but at last I got a little note saying she would be at home on Sunday at four, and with this extraordinary postscript: 'Please do not write me here again; I will explain when I see you.' On Sunday she received me, and was perfectly charming; but when I was going away she begged of me, if I ever had occasion to write to her again, to address my letter to Mrs. Knox, care of Whittaker's Library, Green Street.' 'There are reasons,' she said, 'why I cannot receive letters in my own house.'

"All through the season I saw a great deal of her, and the atmosphere of mystery never left her. Sometimes I thought that she was in the power of some man, but she looked so unapproachable that I could not believe it. It was really very difficult for me to come to any conclusion, for she was like one of those strange crystals that one sees in museums, which are at one moment clear, and at another clouded. At last I determined to ask her to be my wife; I was sick and tired of the incessant secrecy that she imposed on all my visits, and on the few letters I sent her. I wrote to her at the library to ask her if she could see me the following Monday at six. She answered yes, and I was in the seventh heaven of delight. I was infatuated with her; in spite of the mystery, I thought then—in consequence of it, I see now. No; it was the woman herself I loved. The mystery troubled me, maddened me. Why did chance put me in its track?"

"You discovered it, then?" I cried.

"I fear so," he answered. "You can judge for yourself.

"When Monday came round I went to lunch with my uncle, and about four o'clock found myself in the Marylebone Road. My uncle, you know, lives in Regent's Park. I wanted to get to Piccadilly, and took a short cut through a lot of shabby little streets. Suddenly, I saw in front of me Lady Alroy, deeply veiled and walking very fast. On coming to the last house in the street, she went up the steps, took out a latch-key and let herself in. 'Here is the mystery,' I said to myself; and I hurried on and examined the house. It seemed a sort of place for letting lodgings. On the doorstep lay her handkerchief, which she had dropped. I picked it up and put it in my pocket. Then I began to consider what I should do. I came to the conclusion that I had no right to spy on her, and I drove down to the club. At six I called to see her. She was lying on a sofa, in a tea-gown of silver tissue looped up by some strange moonstones, that she always wore. She was looking quite lovely. 'I am so glad to see you,' she said; 'I have not been out all day.' I stared at her in amazement, and pulling the handkerchief out of my pocket, handed it to her. 'You dropped this in Cumnor Street this afternoon, Lady Alroy,' I said very calmly. She looked at me in terror, but made no attempt to take the handkerchief. 'What were you doing there?' I asked. 'What right have you to question me?' she answered. 'The right of a man who loves you,' I replied; 'I came here to ask you to be my wife.' She hid her face in her hands, and burst into floods of tears. 'You must tell me,' I continued. She stood up, and looking me straight in the face, said: 'Lord Murchison, there is nothing to tell you.' 'You went to meet some one,' I cried; 'this is your mystery.' She grew dreadfully white, and said, 'I went to meet no one.' 'Can't you tell the truth?' I exclaimed. 'I have told it,' she replied. I was mad, frantic; I don't know what I said, but I said terrible things to her. Finally I rushed out of the house. She wrote me a letter the next day; I sent it back unopened, and started for Norway with Alan Colville. After a month I came back, and the first thing I saw in 'The Morning Post' was the death of Lady Alroy. She had caught a chill at the Opera, and had died in five days of congestion of the lungs. I shut myself up and saw no one. I had loved her so much, I had loved her so madly. Good God! how I had loved that woman!"

"You went to the street, to the house in it?" I said.

"Yes," he answered.

"One day I went to Cumnor Street. I could not help it; I was tortured with doubt. I knocked at the door, and a respectable-looking woman opened it to me. I asked her if she had any rooms to let. 'Well, sir,' she replied, 'the drawing-rooms are supposed to be let; but I have not seen the lady for three months, and as rent is owing on them, you can have them.' 'Is this the lady?' I said, showing the photograph. 'That's her, sure enough,' she exclaimed; 'and when is she coming back, sir?' 'The lady is dead,' I replied. 'Oh, sir, I hope not!' said the woman; 'she was my best lodger. She paid me three guineas a week merely to sit in my drawing-rooms now and then.' 'She met some one here?' I said; but the woman assured me that it was not so, that she always came alone, and saw no one. 'What on earth did she do here?' I cried. 'She simply sat in the drawing-room, sir, reading books, and sometimes had tea,' the woman answered. I did not know what to say, so I gave her a sovereign and went away. Now, what do you think it all meant? You don't believe the woman was telling the truth?"

"I do."

"Then why did Lady Alroy go there?"

"My dear Gerald," I answered, "Lady Alroy was simply a woman with a mania for mystery. She took these rooms for the pleasure of going there with her veil down, and imagining herself a heroine. She had a passion for secrecy, but she herself was merely a Sphinx without a secret."

"Do you really think so?"

"I am sure of it," I replied.

He took out the morocco case, opened it, and looked at the photograph. "I wonder?" he said at last.

JOSEPH CONRAD
(1857-1924)

ALTHOUGH Conrad was born in Ukraine, of Polish parentage, and studied at Cracow, he became one of the foremost contemporary English writers. He began his English career by shipping as a British seaman; and it was while in the marine service that he began his first novel, *Almayer's Folly*. This was followed by other novels and short stories which soon brought him recognition. His prose is lucid and vigorous and his narratives possess an elemental grandeur that betoken a profound philosophy.

Il Conde is reprinted, by permission of the publishers, from *A Set of Six*, copyright, 1908, 1915, by Doubleday, Page and Company.

IL CONDE
"Vedi Napoli e poi mori."

THE first time we got into conversation was in the National Museum in Naples, in the rooms on the ground floor containing the famous collection of bronzes from Herculaneum and Pompeii: that marvellous legacy of antique art whose delicate perfection has been preserved for us by the catastrophic fury of a volcano.

He addressed me first, over the celebrated Resting Hermes which we had been looking at side by side. He said the right things about that wholly admirable piece. Nothing profound. His taste was natural rather than cultivated. He had obviously seen many fine things in his life and appreciated them: but he had no jargon of a dilettante or the connoisseur. A hateful tribe. He spoke like a fairly intelligent man of the world, a perfectly unaffected gentleman.

We had known each other by sight for some few days past. Staying in the same hotel—good, but not extravagantly up to date—I had noticed him in the vestibule going in and out. I judged he was an old and valued client. The bow of the hotel-keeper was cordial in its deference, and he acknowledged it with familiar courtesy. For the servants he was *Il Conde*. There was some squabble over a man's parasol—yellow silk with white lining sort of thing—the waiters had discovered abandoned outside the dining-room door. Our gold-laced door-keeper recognised it and I heard him directing one of the lift boys to run after *Il Conde* with it. Perhaps he was the only Count staying in the hotel, or perhaps he had the distinction of being *the* Count *par excellence*, conferred upon him because of his tried fidelity to the house.

Having conversed at the Museo—(and by the by he had expressed his dislike of the busts and statues of Roman emperors in the gallery of marbles: their faces were too vigorous, too pronounced for him)—having conversed already in the morning I did .not think I was intruding when in the evening, finding the dining-room very full, I proposed to share his little table. Judging by the quiet urbanity of his consent he did not think so either. His smile was very attractive.

He dined in an evening waistcoat and a "smoking" (he called it so) with a black tie. All this of very good cut, not new—just as these things should be. He was, morning or evening, very correct in his dress. I have no doubt that his whole existence had been correct, well ordered and conventional, undisturbed by startling events. His white hair brushed upwards off a lofty forehead gave him the air of an idealist, of an imaginative man. His white moustache, heavy but carefully trimmed and arranged, was not unpleasantly tinted a golden yellow in the middle. The faint scent of some very good perfume, and of good cigars (that last an odour quite remarkable to come upon in Italy) reached me across the table. It was in his eyes that his age showed most. They were a little weary with creased eyelids. He must have been sixty or a couple of years more. And he was communicative. I would not go so far as to call it garrulous—but distinctly communicative.

He had tried various climates, of Abbazia, of the Riviera, of other places, too, he told me, but the only one which suited him was the climate of the Gulf of Naples. The ancient Romans, who, he pointed out to me, were men expert in the art of living, knew very well what they were doing when they built their villas on these shores, in Baia, in Vico, in Capri. They came down to this seaside in search of health, bringing with them their trains of mimes and flute-players to amuse their leisure. He thought it extremely probable that the Romans of the higher classes were specially predisposed to painful rheumatic affections.

This was the only personal opinion I heard him express. It was based on no special erudition. He knew no more of the Romans than an average informed man of the world is expected to know. He argued from personal experience. He had suffered himself from a painful and dangerous rheumatic affection till he found relief in this particular spot of Southern Europe.

This was three years ago, and ever since he had taken up his quarters on the shores of the gulf, either in one of the hotels in Sorrento or hiring a small villa in Capri. He had a piano, a few books: picked up transient acquaintances of a day, week, or month in the stream of travellers from all Europe. One can imagine him going out for his walks in the streets and lanes, becoming known to beggars, shopkeepers, children, country people; talking amiably over the walls to the contadini—and coming back to his rooms or his villa to sit before the piano, with his white hair brushed up and his thick orderly moustache, "to make a little music for myself." And, of course, for a change there was Naples near by—life, movement, animation, opera. A little amusement, as he said, is necessary for health. Mimes and flute-players, in fact. Only unlike the magnates of ancient Rome, he had no affairs of the city to call him away from these moderate delights. He had no affairs at all. Probably he had never had any grave affairs to attend to in his life. It was a kindly existence, with its joys and sorrows regulated by the course of Nature—marriages, births, deaths —ruled by the prescribed usages of good society and protected by the State.

He was a widower; but in the months of July and August he ventured to cross the Alps for six weeks on a visit to his married daughter. He told me her name. It was that of a very aristocratic family. She had a castle —in Bohemia, I think. This is as near as I ever came to ascertaining his nationality. His own name, strangely enough, he never mentioned. Perhaps he thought I had seen it on the published list. Truth to say, I never looked. At any rate, he was a good European—he spoke four languages to my certain knowledge—and a man of fortune. Not of great fortune evidently and appropriately. I imagine that to be extremely rich would have appeared to him improper, *outré*—too blatant altogether. And obviously, too, the fortune was not of his making. The making of a fortune cannot be achieved without some roughness. It is a matter of temperament. His nature was too kindly for strife. In the course of conversation he mentioned his estate quite by the way, in reference to that painful and alarming rheumatic affection. One year, staying incautiously beyond the Alps as late as the middle of September, he had been laid up for three months in that lonely country house with no one but his valet and the caretaking couple to attend to him. Because, as he expressed it, he "kept no establishment there." He had only gone for a couple of days to confer with his land agent. He promised himself never to be so imprudent in the future. The first weeks of September would find him on the shores of his beloved gulf.

Sometimes in travelling one comes upon such lonely men, whose only business is to wait for the unavoidable. Deaths and marriages have made a solitude round them, and one really cannot blame their endeavours to make the waiting as easy as possible. As he remarked to me, "At my time of life freedom from physical pain is a very important matter."

It must not be imagined that he was a wearisome hypochondriac. He was really much too well-bred to be a nuisance. He had an eye for the small weaknesses of humanity. But it was a good-natured eye. He made a restful, easy, pleasant companion for the hours between dinner and bed-time. We spent three evenings together, and then I had to leave Naples in a hurry to look after a friend who had fallen seriously ill in Taormina. Having nothing to do, *Il Conde* came to see me off at the station. I was somewhat upset, and his idleness was always ready to take a kindly form. He was by no means an indolent man.

He went along the train peering into the carriages for a good seat for me, and then remained talking cheerily from below. He declared he would miss me that evening very much and announced his intention of going after dinner to listen to the band in the public garden, the Villa Nazionale. He would amuse himself by hearing excellent music and looking at the best society. There would be a lot of people, as usual.

I seem to see him yet—his raised face with a friendly smile under the thick moustaches, and his kind, fatigued eyes. As the train began to move, he addressed me in two languages: first in French, saying, *"Bon voyage"*; then, in his very good, somewhat emphatic English, encouragingly, because he could see my concern: "All will—be—well—yet!"

My friend's illness having taken a decidedly favourable turn, I returned to Naples on the tenth day. I cannot say I had given much thought to *Il Conde* during my absence, but entering the dining-room I looked for him in his habitual place. I had an idea he might have gone back to Sorrento to his piano and his books and his fishing. He was great friends with all the boatmen, and fished a good deal with lines from a boat. But I made out his white head in the crowd of heads, and even from a distance noticed something unusual in his attitude. Instead of sitting erect, gazing all round with alert urbanity, he drooped over his plate. I stood opposite him for some time before he looked up, a little wildly, if such a strong word can be used in connection with his correct appearance.

"Ah, my dear sir! Is it you?" he greeted me. "I hope all is well."

He was very nice about my friend. Indeed, he was always nice, with the niceness of people whose hearts are genuinely humane. But this time it cost him an effort. His attempts at general conversation broke down into dulness. It occurred to me he might have been indisposed. But before I could frame the inquiry he muttered:

"You find me here very sad."

"I am sorry for that," I said. "You haven't had bad news, I hope?"

It was very kind of me to take an interest. No. It was not that. No bad news, thank God. And he became very still as if holding his breath. Then, leaning forward a little, and in an odd tone of awed embarrassment, he took me into his confidence.

"The truth is that I have had a very—a very—how shall I say?— abominable adventure happen to me."

The energy of the epithet was sufficiently startling in that man of moderate feelings and toned-down vocabulary. The word unpleasant I should have thought would have fitted amply the worst experience likely to befall a man of his stamp. And an adventure, too. Incredible! But it is in human nature to believe the worst; and I confess I eyed him stealthily, wondering what he had been up to. In a moment, however, my unworthy suspicions vanished. There was a fundamental refinement of nature about the man which made me dismiss all idea of some more or less disreputable scrape.

"It is very serious. Very serious." He went on, nervously. "I will tell you after dinner, if you will allow me."

I expressed my perfect acquiescence by a little bow, nothing more. I wished him to understand that I was not likely to hold him to that offer, if he thought better of it later on. We talked of indifferent things, but with a sense of difficulty quite unlike our former easy, gossipy intercourse. The hand raising a piece of bread to his lips, I noticed, trembled slightly. This symptom, in regard to my reading of the man, was no less than startling.

In the smoking-room he did not hang back at all. Directly we had taken our usual seats he leaned sideways over the arm of his chair and looked straight into my eyes earnestly.

"You remember," he began, "that day you went away? I told you then I would go to the Villa Nazionale to hear some music in the evening."

I remembered. His handsome old face, so fresh for his age, unmarked by any trying experience, appeared haggard for an instant. It was like the passing of a shadow. Returning his steadfast gaze, I took a sip of my black coffee. He was systematically minute in his narrative, simply in order, I think, not to let his excitement get the better of him.

After leaving the railway station, he had an ice, and read the paper in a café. Then he went back to the hotel, dressed for dinner, and dined with a good appetite. After dinner he lingered in the hall (there were chairs and tables there) smoking his cigar; talked to the little girl of the Primo Tenore of the San Carlo theatre, and exchanged a few words with that "amiable lady," the wife of the Primo Tenore. There was no performance that evening, and these people were going to the Villa also. They went out of the hotel. Very well.

At the moment of following their example—it was half-past nine already—he remembered he had a rather large sum of money in his pocket-book. He entered, therefore, the office and deposited the greater part of it with the book-keeper of the hotel. This done, he took a carozella and drove to the seashore. He got out of the cab and entered the Villa on foot from the Largo di Vittoria end.

He stared at me very hard. And I understood then how really impressionable he was. Every small fact and event of that evening stood out in his memory as if endowed with mystic significance. If he did not mention to me the colour of the pony which drew the carozella, and the aspect of the man who drove, it was a mere oversight arising from his agitation, which he repressed manfully.

He had then entered the Villa Nazionale from the Largo di Vittoria end. The Villa Nazionale is a public pleasure-ground laid out in grass plots, bushes, and flower-beds between the houses of the Riviera di Chiaja and the waters of the bay. Alleys of trees, more or less parallel, stretch

its whole length—which is considerable. On the Riviera di Chiaja side
the electric tramcars run close to the railings. Between the garden and the
sea is the fashionable drive, a broad road bordered by a low wall, beyond
which the Mediterranean splashes with gentle murmurs when the weather
is fine.

As life goes on late at night in Naples, the broad drive was all astir
with a brilliant swarm of carriage lamps moving in pairs, some creeping
slowly, others running rapidly under the thin, motionless line of electric
lamps defining the shore. And a brilliant swarm of stars hung above the
land humming with voices, piled up with houses, glittering with lights—
and over the silent flat shadows of the sea.

The gardens themselves are not very well lit. Our friend went forward in the warm gloom, his eyes fixed upon a distant luminous region
extending nearly across the whole width of the Villa, as if the air had
glowed there with its own cold, bluish, and dazzling light. This magic
spot, behind the black trunks of trees and masses of inky foliage, breathed
out sweet sounds mingled with bursts of brassy roar, sudden clashes of
metal, and grave, vibrating thuds.

As he walked on, all these noises combined together into a piece of
elaborate music whose harmonious phrases came persuasively through a
great disorderly murmur of voices and shuffling of feet on the gravel of
that open space. An enormous crowd immersed in the electric light, as if
in a bath of some radiant and tenuous fluid shed upon their heads by
luminous globes, drifted in its hundreds round the band. Hundreds more
sat on chairs in more or less concentric circles, receiving unflinchingly the
great waves of sonority that ebbed out into the darkness. The Count
penetrated the throng, drifted with it in tranquil enjoyment, listening and
looking at the faces. All people of good society: mothers with their
daughters, parents and children, young men and young women all talking,
smiling, nodding to each other. Very many pretty faces, and very many
pretty toilettes. There was, of course, a quantity of diverse types: showy
old fellows with white moustaches, fat men, thin men, officers in uniform; but what predominated, he told me, was the South Italian type of
young man, with a colourless, clear complexion, red lips, jet-black little
moustache and liquid black eyes so wonderfully effective in leering or
scowling.

Withdrawing from the throng, the Count shared a little table in
front of the café with a young man of just such a type. Our friend had
some lemonade. The young man was sitting moodily before an empty
glass. He looked up once, and then looked down again. He also tilted
his hat forward. Like this——

The Count made the gesture of a man pulling his hat down over his
brow, and went on:

"I think to myself: he is sad; something is wrong with him; young men have their troubles. I take no notice of him, of course. I pay for my lemonade, and go away."

Strolling about in the neighbourhood of the band, the Count thinks he saw twice that young man wandering alone in the crowd. Once their eyes met. It must have been the same young man, but there were so many there of that type that he could not be certain. Moreover, he was not very much concerned except in so far that he had been struck by the marked, peevish discontent of that face.

Presently, tired of the feeling of confinement one experiences in a crowd, the Count edged away from the band. An alley, very sombre by contrast, presented itself invitingly with its promise of solitude and coolness. He entered it, walking slowly on till the sound of the orchestra became distinctly deadened. Then he walked back and turned about once more. He did this several times before he noticed that there was somebody occupying one of the benches.

The spot being midway between two lamp-posts the light was faint.

The man lolled back in the corner of the seat, his legs stretched out, his arms folded and his head drooping on his breast. He never stirred, as though he had fallen asleep there, but when the Count passed by next time he had changed his attitude. He sat leaning forward. His elbows were propped on his knees, and his hands were rolling a cigarette. He never looked up from that occupation.

The Count continued his stroll away from the band. He returned slowly, he said. I can imagine him enjoying to the full, but with his usual tranquillity, the balminess of this southern night and the sounds of music softened delightfully by the distance.

Presently, he approached for the third time the man on the garden seat, still leaning forward with his elbows on his knees. It was a dejected pose. In the semi-obscurity of the alley his high shirt collar and his cuffs made small patches of vivid whiteness. The Count said that he had noticed him getting up brusquely as if to walk away, but almost before he was aware of it the man stood before him asking in a low, gentle tone whether the signore would have the kindness to oblige him with a light.

The Count answered this request by a polite "Certainly," and dropped his hands with the intention of exploring both pockets of his trousers for the matches.

"I dropped my hands," he said, "but I never put them in my pockets. I felt a pressure there——"

He put the tip of his finger on a spot close under his breastbone, the very spot of the human body where a Japanese gentleman begins the operations of the Hari-kari, which is a form of suicide following upon dishonour, upon an intolerable outrage to the delicacy of one's feelings.

"I glance down," the Count continued in an awe-struck voice, "and what do I see? A knife! A long knife——"

"You don't mean to say," I exclaimed, amazed, "that you have been held up like this in the Villa at half-past ten o'clock, within a stone's throw of a thousand people!"

He nodded several times, staring at me with all his might.

"The clarionet," he declared, solemnly, "was finishing his solo, and I assure you I could hear every note. Then the band crashed *fortissimo*, and that creature rolled its eyes and gnashed its teeth hissing at me with the greatest ferocity, 'Be silent! No noise or——' "

I could not get over my astonishment.

"What sort of knife was it?" I asked, stupidly.

"A long blade. A stiletto—perhaps a kitchen knife. A long narrow blade. It gleamed. And his eyes gleamed. His white teeth, too. I could see them. He was very ferocious. I thought to myself: 'If I hit him he will kill me.' How could I fight with him? He had the knife and I had nothing. I am nearly seventy, you know, and that was a young man. I seemed even to recognise him. The moody young man of the café. The young man I met in the crowd. But I could not tell. There are so many like him in this country."

The distress of that moment was reflected in his face. I should think that physically he must have been paralysed by surprise. His thoughts, however, remained extremely active. They ranged over every alarming possibility. The idea of setting up a vigorous shouting for help occurred to him, too. But he did nothing of the kind, and the reason why he re-frained gave me a good opinion of his mental self-possession. He saw in a flash that nothing prevented the other from shouting, too.

"That young man might in an instant have thrown away his knife and pretended I was the aggressor. Why not? He might have said I attacked him. Why not? It was one incredible story against another! He might have said anything—bring some dishonouring charge against me —what do I know? By his dress he was no common robber. He seemed to belong to the better classes. What could I say? He was an Italian— I am a foreigner. Of course, I have my passport, and there is our con-sul—but to be arrested, dragged at night to the police office like a criminal!"

He shuddered. It was in his character to shrink from scandal, much more than from mere death. And certainly for many people this would have always remained—considering certain peculiarities of Neapolitan manners—a deucedly queer story. The Count was no fool. His belief in the respectable placidity of life having received this rude shock, he thought that now anything might happen. But also a notion came into his head that this young man was perhaps merely an infuriated lunatic.

This was for me the first hint of his attitude towards this adventure. In his exaggerated delicacy of sentiment he felt that nobody's self-esteem need be affected by what a madman may choose to do to one. It became apparent, however, that the Count was to be denied that consolation. He enlarged upon the abominably savage way in which that young man rolled his glistening eyes and gnashed his white teeth. The band was going now through a slow movement of solemn braying by all the trombones, with deliberately repeated bangs of the big drum.

"But what did you do?" I asked, greatly excited.

"Nothing," answered the Count. "I let my hands hang down very still. I told him quietly I did not intend making a noise. He snarled like a dog, then said in an ordinary voice:

"'Vostro portofolio.'"

"So I naturally," continued the Count—and from this point acted the whole thing in pantomime. Holding me with his eyes, he went through all the motions of reaching into his inside breast pocket, taking out a pocket-book, and handing it over. But that young man, still bearing steadily on the knife, refused to touch it.

He directed the Count to take the money out himself, received it into his left hand, motioned the pocketbook to be returned to the pocket, all this being done to the sweet thrilling of flutes and clarionets sustained by the emotional drone of the hautboys. And the "young man," as the Count called him, said: "This seems very little."

"It was, indeed, only 340 or 360 lire," the Count pursued. "I had left my money in the hotel, as you know. I told him this was all I had on me. He shook his head impatiently and said:

"'Vostro orologio.'"

The Count gave me the dumb show of pulling out his watch, detaching it. But, as it happened, the valuable gold half-chronometer he possessed had been left at a watch-maker's for cleaning. He wore that evening (on a leather guard) the Waterbury fifty-franc thing he used to take with him on his fishing expeditions. Perceiving the nature of this booty, the well-dressed robber made a contemptuous clicking sound with his tongue like this, "Tse-Ah!" and waved it away hastily. Then, as the Count was returning the disdained object to his pocket, he demanded with a threateningly increased pressure of the knife on the epigastrium, by way of reminder:

"'Vostri anelli.'"

"One of the rings," went on the Count, "was given me many years ago by my wife; the other is the signet ring of my father. I said, 'No. That you shall not have!'"

Here the Count reproduced the gesture corresponding to that declaration by clapping one hand upon the other, and pressing both thus against his chest. It was touching in its resignation. "That you shall not have," he repeated, firmly, and closed his eyes, fully expecting—I don't know whether I am right in recording that such an unpleasant word had passed his lips—fully expecting to feel himself being—I really hesitate to say

—being disembowelled by the push of the long, sharp blade resting murderously against the pit of his stomach—the very seat, in all human beings, of anguishing sensations.

Great waves of harmony went on flowing from the band.

Suddenly the Count felt the nightmarish pressure removed from the sensitive spot. He opened his eyes. He was alone. He had heard noth-ing. It is probable that "the young man" had departed, with light steps, some time before, but the sense of the horrid pressure had lingered even after the knife had gone. A feeling of weakness came over him. He had just time to stagger to the garden seat. He felt as though he had held his breath for a long time. He sat all in a heap, panting with the shock of the reaction.

The band was executing, with immense bravura, the complicated finale. It ended with a tremendous crash. He heard it unreal and re-mote, as if his ears had been stopped, and then the hard clapping of a thousand, more or less, pairs of hands, like a sudden hail-shower passing away. The profound silence which succeeded recalled him to himself.

A tramcar resembling a long glass box wherein people sat with their heads strongly lighted, ran along swiftly within sixty yards of the spot where he had been robbed. Then another rustled by, and yet another going the other way. The audience about the band had broken up, and were entering the alley in small conversing groups. The Count sat up straight and tried to think calmly of what had happened to him. The vile-ness of it took his breath away again. As far as I can make it out he was disgusted with himself. I do not mean to say with his behaviour. Indeed, if his pantomimic rendering of it for my information was to be trusted, it was simply perfect. No, it was not that. He was not ashamed. He was shocked at being the selected victim, not of robbery so much as of contempt. His tranquillity had been wantonly desecrated. His lifelong, kindly nicety of outlook had been defaced.

Nevertheless, at that stage, before the iron had time to sink deep, he was able to argue himself into comparative equanimity. As his agi-tation calmed down somewhat, he became aware that he was frightfully hungry. Yes, hungry. The sheer emotion had made him simply rave-nous. He left the seat and, after walking for some time, found him-self outside the gardens and before an arrested tramcar, without know-ing very well how he came there. He got in as if in a dream, by a sort of instinct. Fortunately he found in his trouser pocket a copper to satisfy the conductor. Then the car stopped, and as everybody was getting out he got out, too. He recognised the Piazza San Ferdinando, but appar-ently it did not occur to him to take a cab and drive to the hotel. He remained in distress on the Piazza like a lost dog, thinking vaguely of the best way of getting something to eat at once.

Suddenly he remembered his twenty-franc piece. He explained to me that he had had that piece of French gold for something like three years. He used to carry it about with him as a sort of reserve in case of accident. Anybody is liable to have his pocket picked—a quite different thing from a brazen and insulting robbery.

The monumental arch of the Galleria Umberto faced him at the top of a noble flight of stairs. He climbed these without loss of time, and directed his steps towards the Café Umberto. All the tables outside were occupied by a lot of people who were drinking. But as he wanted something to eat, he went inside into the café, which is divided into aisles by square pillars set all round with long looking-glasses. The Count sat down on a red plush bench against one of these pillars, waiting for his risotto. And his mind reverted to his abominable adventure.

He thought of the moody, well-dressed young man, with whom he had exchanged glances in the crowd around the bandstand, and who, he felt confident, was the robber. Would he recognise him again? Doubt-less. But he did not want ever to see him again. The best thing was to forget this humiliating episode.

The Count looked round anxiously for the coming of his risotto, and, behold! to the left against the wall—there sat the young man. He was alone at a table, with a bottle of some sort of wine or syrup and a carafe of iced water before him. The smooth olive cheeks, the red lips, the little jet-black moustache turned up gallantly, the fine black eyes a little heavy and shaded by long eyelashes, that peculiar expression of cruel discontent to be seen only in the busts of some Roman emperors —it was he, no doubt at all. But that was a type. The Count looked away hastily. The young officer over there reading a paper was like that, too. Same type. Two young men farther away playing draughts also resembled——

The Count lowered his head with the fear in his heart of being ever-lastingly haunted by the vision of that young man. He began to eat his risotto. Presently he heard the young man on his left call the waiter in a bad-tempered tone.

At the call, not only his own waiter, but two other idle waiters be-longing to a quite different row of tables, rushed towards him with obsequious alacrity, which is not the general characteristic of the waiters in the Café Umberto. The young man muttered something and one of the waiters walking rapidly to the nearest door called out into the Gal-leria: "Pasquale! O! Pasquale!"

Everybody knows Pasquale, the shabby old fellow who, shuffling be-tween the tables, offers for sale cigars, cigarettes, picture postcards, and matches to the clients of the café. He is in many respects an engaging scoundrel. The Count saw the grey-haired, unshaven ruffian enter the café, the glass case hanging from his neck by a leather strap, and, at a word from the waiter, make his shuffling way with a sudden spurt to the young man's table. The young man was in need of a cigar with which Pasquale served him fawningly. The old pedlar was going out, when the Count, on a sudden impulse, beckoned to him.

Pasquale approached, the smile of deferential recognition combining oddly with the cynical searching expression of his eyes. Leaning his case on the table, he lifted the glass lid without a word. The Count took a box of cigarettes and urged by a fearful curiosity, asked as casually as he could—

"Tell me, Pasquale, who is that young signore sitting over there?"

The other bent over his box confidentially.

"That, *Signor Conde*," he said, beginning to rearrange his wares busily and without looking up, "that is a young *Cavaliere* of a very good family from Bari. He studies in the University here, and is the chief, *capo*, of an association of young men—of very nice young men."

He paused, and then, with mingled discretion and pride of knowledge, murmured the explanatory word "Camorra" and shut down the lid. "A very powerful Camorra," he breathed out. "The professors themselves respect it greatly . . . *una lira e cinquanti centesimi, Signor Conde*."

Our friend paid with the gold piece. While Pasquale was making up the change, he observed that the young man, of whom he had heard so much in a few words, was watching the transaction covertly. After the old vagabond had withdrawn with a bow, the Count settled with the waiter and sat still. A numbness, he told me, had come over him.

The young man paid, too, got up and crossed over, apparently for the purpose of looking at himself in the mirror set in the pillar nearest to the Count's seat. He was dressed all in black with a dark green bow tie. The Count looked round, and was startled by meeting a vicious glance out of the corners of the other's eyes. The young *Cavaliere* from Bari (according to Pasquale; but Pasquale is, of course, an accomplished liar) went on arranging his tie, settling his hat before the glass, and meantime he spoke just loud enough to be heard by the Count. He spoke through his teeth with the most insulting venom of contempt and gazing straight into the mirror.

"Ah! So you had some gold on you—you old liar—you old *birba*—you *furfante*! But you are not done with me yet."

The fiendishness of his expression vanished like lightning and he lounged out of the café with a moody, impassive face.

The poor Count, after telling me this last episode, fell back trembling in his chair. His forehead broke into perspiration. There was a wanton insolence in the spirit of this outrage which appalled even me. What it was to the Count's delicacy I won't attempt to guess. I am sure that if he had been not too refined to do such a blatantly vulgar thing as dying from apoplexy in a café, he would have had a fatal stroke there and then. All irony apart, my difficulty was to keep him from seeing the full extent of my commiseration. He shrank from every excessive sentiment, and my commiseration was practically unbounded. It did not surprise me to hear that he had been in bed a week. He had got up to make his arrangements for leaving Southern Italy for good and all.

And the man was convinced that he could not live through a whole year in any other climate!

No argument of mine had any effect. It was not timidity, though he did say to me once: "You do not know what a Camorra is, my dear sir. I am a marked man." He was not afraid of what could be done to him. His delicate conception of his dignity was defiled by a degrading experience. He couldn't stand that. No Japanese gentleman, outraged in his exaggerated sense of honour, could have gone about his preparations for Hari-kari with greater resolution. To go home really amounted to suicide for the poor Count.

There is a saying of Neapolitan patriotism, intended for the information of foreigners, I presume: "See Naples and then die." *Vedi Napoli e poi mori*. It is a saying of excessive vanity, and everything excessive was abhorrent to the nice moderation of the poor Count. Yet, as I was seeing him off at the railway station, I thought he was behaving with singular fidelity to its conceited spirit. *Vedi Napoli!* . . . He had seen it! He had seen it with startling thoroughness—and now he was going to his grave. He was going to it by the *train de luxe* of the International Sleeping Car Company, *via* Trieste and Vienna. As the four long, sombre coaches pulled out of the station I raised my hat with the solemn feeling of paying the last tribute of respect to a funeral *cortège*. *Il Conde's* profile, much aged already, glided away from me in stony immobility, behind the lighted pane of glass—*Vedi Napoli e poi mori!*

* * *

H. G. WELLS
(1866-   )

WELLS, born at Bromley, Kent, is one of the most influential contemporary novelists of England. He has utilised his earlier scientific training in the plots of many of his books, and his liberal political and sociological views find expression in much of his writing. *Thirty Strange Stories* was one of Wells's first books (1897), and *The Stolen Bacillus* was one of this delightfully fantastic collection.

The *Stolen Bacillus* is reprinted from *Thirty Strange Stories*, by permission of the publishers, Harper & Brothers.

THE STOLEN BACILLUS

"THIS again," said the Bacteriologist, slipping a glass slide under the microscope, "is a preparation of the celebrated Bacillus of cholera—the cholera germ."

The pale-faced man peered down the microscope. He was evidently not accustomed to that kind of thing, and held a limp white hand over his disengaged eye. "I see very little," he said.

"Touch this screw," said the Bacteriologist; "perhaps the microscope is out of focus for you. Eyes vary so much. Just the fraction of a turn this way or that."

"Ah! now I see," said the visitor. "Not so very much to see, after all. Little streaks and shreds of pink. And yet those little particles, those mere atomies, might multiply and devastate a city! Wonderful!"

He stood up, and releasing the glass slip from the microscope, held it in his hand towards the window. "Scarcely visible," he said, scrutinising the preparation. He hesitated. "Are these—alive? Are they dangerous now?"

"Those have been stained and killed," said the Bacteriologist. "I wish, for my own part, we could kill and stain every one of them in the universe."

"I suppose," the pale man said with a slight smile, "that you scarcely care to have such things about you in the living—in the active state?"

"On the contrary, we are obliged to," said the Bacteriologist. "Here, for instance—" He walked across the room and took up one of several sealed tubes. "Here is the living thing. This is a cultivation of the actual living disease bacteria." He hesitated. "Bottled cholera, so to speak."

A slight gleam of satisfaction appeared momentarily in the face of the pale man. "It's a deadly thing to have in your possession," he said, devouring the little tube with his eyes. The Bacteriologist watched the morbid pleasure in his visitor's expression. This man, who had visited him that afternoon with a note of introduction from an old friend, interested him from the very contrast of their dispositions. The lank black hair and deep grey eyes, the haggard expression and nervous manner, the fitful yet keen interest of his visitor were a novel change from the phlegmatic deliberations of the ordinary scientific worker with whom the Bacteriologist chiefly associated. It was perhaps natural, with a hearer evidently so impressionable to the lethal nature of his topic, to take the most effective aspect of the matter.

He held the tube in his hand thoughtfully. "Yes, here is the pestilence imprisoned. Only break such a little tube as this into a supply of drinking-water, say to these minute particles of life that one must needs stain and examine with the highest powers of the microscope even to see, and that one can neither smell nor taste—say to them, 'Go forth, increase and multiply, and replenish the cisterns,' and Death—mysterious, untraceable Death, Death swift and terrible, Death full of pain and indignity—would be released upon this city, and go hither and thither seeking his victims. Here he would take the husband from the wife, here the child from its mother, here the statesman from his duty, and here the toiler from his trouble. He would follow the water-mains, creeping along streets, picking out and punishing a house here and a house there where they did not boil their drinking-water, creeping into the wells of the mineral-water makers, getting washed into salad, and lying dormant in ices. He would wait ready to be drunk in the horse-troughs, and by unwary children in the public fountains. He would soak into the soil, to reappear in springs and wells at a thousand unexpected places. Once start him at the water-supply, and before we could ring him in and catch him again he would have decimated the metropolis."

He stopped abruptly. He had been told rhetoric was his weakness. "But he is quite safe here, you know—quite safe."

The pale-faced man nodded. His eyes shone. He cleared his throat. "These Anarchist—rascals," said he, "are fools, blind fools—to use bombs when this kind of think is attainable. I think——"

A gentle rap, a mere light touch of the finger-nails was heard at the door. The Bacteriologist opened it. "Just a minute, dear," whispered his wife.

When he re-entered the laboratory his visitor was looking at his watch. "I had no idea I had wasted an hour of your time," he said. "Twelve minutes to four. I ought to have left here by half-past three. But your things were really too interesting. No, positively, I cannot stop a moment longer. I have an engagement at four."

He passed out of the room reiterating his thanks, and the Bacteriologist accompanied him to the door, and then returned thoughfully along the passage to his laboratory. He was musing on the ethnology of his visitor. Certainly the man was not a Teutonic type nor a common Latin one. "A morbid product, anyhow, I am afraid," said the Bacteriologist to himself. "How he gloated on those cultivations of disease-germs!" A disturbing thought struck him. He turned to the bench by the vapour-bath, and then very quickly to his writing-table. Then he felt hastily in his pockets, and then he rushed to the door. "I may have put it down on the hall table," he said.

"Minnie!" he shouted hoarsely in the hall.

"Yes, dear," came a remote voice.

"Had I anything in my hand when I spoke to you, dear, just now?"
Pause.

"Nothing, dear, because I remember——"

"Blue ruin!" cried the Bacteriologist, and incontinently ran to the front door and down the steps of his house to the street.

Minnie, hearing the door slam violently, ran in alarm to the window. Down the street a slender man was getting into a cab. The Bacteriologist, hatless, and in his carpet slippers, was running and gesticulating wildly towards this group. One slipper came off, but he did not wait for it. "He has gone *mad!*" said Minnie; "it's that horrid science of his;" and, opening the window, would have called after him. The slender man, suddenly glancing round, seemed struck with the same idea of mental disorder. He pointed hastily to the Bacteriologist, said something to the cabman, the apron of the cab slammed, the whip swished, the horse's feet clattered, and in a moment cab, and Bacteriologist hotly in pursuit, had receded up the vista of the roadway and disappeared round the corner.

Minnie remained straining out of the window for a minute. Then she drew her head back into the room again. She was dumbfounded. "Of course he is eccentric," she meditated. "But running about London—in the height of the season, too—in his socks!" A happy thought struck her. She hastily put her bonnet on, seized his shoes, went into the hall, took down his hat and light overcoat from the pegs, emerged upon the doorstep, and hailed a cab that opportunely crawled by. "Drive me up the road and round Havelock Crescent, and see if we can find a gentleman running about in a velveteen coat and no hat."

"Velveteen coat, ma'am, and no 'at. Very good, ma'am." And the cabman whipped up at once in the most matter-of-fact way, as if he drove to this address every day in his life.

Some few minutes later the little group of cabmen and loafers that collects round the cabmen's shelter at Haverstock Hill were startled by the passing of a cab with a ginger-coloured screw of a horse, driven furiously.

They were silent as it went by, and then as it receded—"That's 'Arry 'Icks. Wot's *he* got?" said the stout gentleman known as Old Tootles.

"He's a-using his whip, he is, *to* rights," said the ostler boy.

"Hullo!" said poor old Tommy Byles; "here's another bloomin' loonattic. Blowed if there ain't."

"It's old George," said Old Tootles, "and he's drivin' a loonattic, *as* you say. Ain't he a-clawin' out of the keb? Wonder if he's after 'Arry 'Icks?"

The group round the cabmen's shelter became animated. Chorus: "Go it, George!" "It's a race." "You'll ketch 'em!" "Whip up!" "She's a goer, she is!" said the ostler boy.

"Strike me giddy!" cried Old Tootles. "Here! *I'm* a-goin' to begin in a minute. Here's another comin'. If all the kebs in Hampstead ain't gone mad this morning!"

"It's a fieldmale this time," said the ostler boy.

"She's a followin' *him*," said Old Tootles. "Usually the other way about."

"What's she got in her 'and?"

"Looks like a 'igh 'at."

"What a bloomin' lark it is! Three to one on old George," said the ostler boy. "Nexst!"

Minnie went by in a perfect roar of applause. She did not like it, but she felt that she was doing her duty, and whirled on down Haverstock Hill and Camden Town High Street, with her eyes ever intent on the animated back view of old George, who was driving her vagrant husband so incomprehensibly away from her.

The man in the foremost cab sat crouched in the corner, his arms tightly folded, and the little tube that contained such vast possibilities of destruction gripped in his hand. His mood was a singular mixture of fear and exultation. Chiefly he was afraid of being caught before he could accomplish his purpose, but behind this was a vaguer but larger fear of the awfulness of his crime. But his exultation far exceeded his fear. No Anarchist before him had ever approached this conception of his. Ravachol, Vaillant, all those distinguished persons whose fame he had envied, dwindled into insignificance beside him. He had only to make sure of the water-supply, and break the little tube into a reservoir. How brilliantly he had planned it, forged the letter of introduction and got into the laboratory, and how brilliantly he had seized his opportunity! The world should hear of him at last. All those people who had sneered at him, neglected him, preferred other people to him, found his company undesirable, should consider him at last. Death, death, death! They had always treated him as a man of no importance. All the world had been in a conspiracy to keep him under. He would teach them yet what it is to isolate a man. What was this familiar street? Great Saint Andrew's Street, of course! How fared the chase? He craned out of the cab. The Bacteriologist was scarcely fifty yards behind. That was bad. He would be caught and stopped yet. He felt in his pocket for money, and found half-a-sovereign. This he thrust up through the trap in the top of the cab into the man's face. "More," he shouted, "if only we get away."

The money was snatched out of his hand. "Right you are," said the cabman, and the trap slammed, and the lash lay along the glistening side of the horse. The cab swayed, and the Anarchist, half-standing under the trap, put the hand containing the little glass tube upon the apron to preserve his balance. He felt the brittle thing crack, and the broken half of it rang upon the floor of the cab. He fell back into the seat with a curse, and stared dismally at the two or three drops of moisture on the apron.

He shuddered.

"Well! I suppose I shall be the first. *Phew!* Anyhow, I shall be a Martyr. That's something. But it is a filthy death, nevertheless. I wonder if it hurts as much as they say."

Presently a thought occurred to him—he groped between his feet. A little drop was still in the broken end of the tube, and he drank that to make sure. It was better to make sure. At any rate, he would not fail.

Then it dawned upon him that there was no further need to escape the Bacteriologist. In Wellington Street he told the cabman to stop, and got out. He slipped on the step, and his head felt queer. It was rapid stuff, this cholera poison. He waved his cabman out of existence, so to speak, and stood on the pavement with his arms folded upon his breast awaiting the arrival of the Bacteriologist. There was something tragic in his pose. The sense of imminent death gave him a certain dignity. He greeted his pursuer with a defiant laugh.

"Vive l'Anarchie! You are too late, my friend. I have drunk it. The cholera is abroad!"

The Bacteriologist from his cab beamed curiously at him through his spectacles. "You have drunk it! An Anarchist! I see now." He was about to say something more, and then checked himself. A smile hung in the corner of his mouth. He opened the apron of his cab as if to descend, at which the Anarchist waved him a dramatic farewell and strode off towards Waterloo Bridge, carefully jostling his infected body against as many people as possible. The Bacteriologist was so preoccupied with the vision of him that he scarcely manifested the slightest surprise at the appearance of Minnie upon the pavement with his hat and shoes and overcoat. "Very good of you to bring my things," he said, and remained lost in contemplation of the receding figure of the Anarchist.

"You had better get in," he said, still staring. Minnie felt absolutely convinced now that he was mad, and directed the cabman home on her own responsibility. "Put on my shoes? Certainly, dear," said he, as the cab began to turn, and hid the strutting black figure, now small in the distance, from his eyes. Then suddenly something grotesque struck him, and he laughed. Then he remarked, "It is really very serious, though.

"You see, that man came to my house to see me, and he is an Anarchist. No—don't faint, or I cannot possibly tell you the rest. And I wanted to astonish him, not knowing he was an Anarchist, and took up a cultivation of that new species of Bacterium I was telling you of, that infest, and I think cause, the blue patches upon various monkeys;

and, like a fool, I said it was Asiatic cholera. And he ran away with it to poison the water of London, and he certainly might have made things look blue for this civilised city. And now he has swallowed it. Of course I cannot say what will happen, but you know it turned that kitten blue, and the three puppies—in patches, and the sparrow—bright blue. But the bother is I shall have all the trouble and expense of preparing some more.

"Put on my coat on this hot day! Why? Because we might meet Mrs. Jabber. My dear, Mrs. Jabber is not a draught. But why should I wear a coat on a hot day because of Mrs. ——. Oh, *very* well."

✳ ✳ ✳

ARNOLD BENNETT
(1867-   )

BORN in the district of Shelton, a part of the "Five Towns" he deals with in some of his novels, Bennett was educated there for the law, and entered the offices of a local solicitor. He soon abandoned this career and entered the field of journalism in London. His reputation was definitely established with *The Old Wives' Tale* (1908), a novel in the manner of the best French realists. Since then Bennett has been steadily producing novels, plays and short stories. *Tales of the Five Towns* (1905) is one of his best collections of short stories.

Mary with the High Hand which appears in *Tales of the Five Towns* is published by Chatto and Windus, London. It is reprinted here by kind permission of the publisher and the author's representatives, James B. Pinker & Sons.

MARY WITH THE HIGH HAND

IN the front-bedroom of Edward Beechinor's small house in Trafalgar Road the two primary social forces of action and reaction—those forces which under a thousand names and disguises have alternately ruled the world since the invention of politics—were pitted against each other in a struggle rendered futile by the equality of the combatants. Edward Beechinor had his money, his superior age, and the possible advantage of being a dying man; Mark Beechinor had his youth and his devotion to an ideal. Near the window, aloof and apart, stood the strange, silent girl whose aroused individuality was to intervene with such effectiveness on behalf of one of the antagonists. It was early dusk on an autumn day.

"Tell me what it is you want, Edward," said Mark quietly. "Let us come to the point."

"Aye," said the sufferer, lifting his pale hand from the counterpane, "I'll tell thee."

He moistened his lips as if in preparation, and pushed back a tuft of spare grey hair, damp with sweat.

The physical and moral contrast between these two brothers was complete. Edward was forty-nine, a small, thin, stunted man, with a look of narrow cunning, of petty shrewdness working without imagination. He had been clerk to Lawyer Ford for thirty-five years, and had also furtively practised for himself. During this period his mode of life had never varied, save once, and that only a year ago. At the age of fourteen he sat in a grimy room with an old man on one side of him, a copying-press on the other, and a law-stationer's almanac in front, and he earned half a crown a week. At the age of forty-eight he still sat in the same grimy room (of which the ceiling had meanwhile been whitened three times), with the same copying-press and the almanac of the same law-stationers, and he earned thirty shillings a week. But now he, Edward Beechinor, was the old man, and the indispensable lad of fourteen, who had once been himself, was another lad, perhaps thirtieth of the dynasty of office-boys. Throughout this interminable and sterile desert of time he had drawn the same deeds, issued the same writs, written the same letters, kept the same accounts, lied the same lies, and thought the same thoughts. He had learnt nothing except craft, and forgotten nothing except happiness. He had never married, never loved, never been a rake, nor deviated from respectability. He was a success because he had conceived an object, and by sheer persistence attained it. In the eyes of Bursley people he was a very decent fellow, a steady fellow, a confirmed bachelor, a close un, a knowing customer, a curmudgeon, an excellent clerk, a narrow-minded ass, a good Wesleyan, a thrifty individual, and an intelligent burgess—according to the point of view. The lifelong operation of rigorous habit had sunk him into a groove as deep as the cañon of some American river. His ideas on every subject were eternally and immutably fixed, and, without being altogether aware of it, he was part of the solid foundation of England's greatness. In 1892, when the whole of the Five Towns was agitated by the great probate case of Wilbraham v. Wilbraham, in which Mr. Ford acted for the defendants, Beechinor, then aged forty-eight, was torn from his stool and sent out to Rio de Janeiro as part of a commission to take the evidence of an important witness who had declined all offers to come home.

The old clerk was full of pride and self-importance at being thus selected, but secretly he shrank from the journey, the mere idea of which filled him with vague apprehension and alarm. His nature had lost all its adaptability; he trembled like a young girl at the prospect of new experiences. On the return voyage the vessel was quarantined at Liverpool for a fortnight, and Beechinor had an attack of fever. Eight months afterwards he was ill again. Beechinor went to bed for the last time, cursing Providence, Wilbraham *v.* Wilbraham, and Rio.

Mark Beechinor was thirty, just nineteen years younger than his brother. Tall, uncouth, big-boned, he had a rather ferocious and forbidding aspect; yet all women seemed to like him, despite the fact that he seldom could open his mouth to them. There must have been something in his wild and liquid dark eyes which mutely appealed for their protective sympathy, something about him of shy and wistful romance that atoned for the huge awkwardness of this taciturn elephant. Mark was at present the manager of a small china manufactory at Longshaw, the farthest of the Five Towns in Staffordshire, and five miles from Bursley. He was an exceptionally clever potter, but he never made money. He had the dreamy temperament of the inventor. He was a man of ideas, the kind of man who is capable of forgetting that he has not had his dinner, and who can live apparently content amid the grossest domestic neglect. He had once spoilt a hundred and fifty pounds' worth of ware by firing it in a new kiln of his own contrivance; it cost him three years of atrocious parsimony to pay for the ware and the building of the kiln. He was impulsively and recklessly charitable, and his Saturday afternoons and Sundays were chiefly devoted to the passionate propagandism of the theories of liberty, equality, and fraternity.

"Is it true as thou'rt for marrying Sammy Mellor's daughter over at Hanbridge?" Edward Beechinor asked, in the feeble, tremulous voice of one agonised by continual pain.

Among relatives and acquaintances he commonly spoke the Five Towns dialect, reserving the other English for official use.

Mark stood at the foot of the bed, leaning with his elbows on the brass rail. Like most men, he always felt extremely nervous and foolish in a sick-room, and the delicacy of this question, so bluntly put, added to his embarrassment. He looked round timidly in the direction of the girl at the window; her back was towards him.

"It's possible," he replied. "I haven't asked her yet."

"Her'll have no money?"

"No."

"Thou'lt want some brass to set up with. Look thee here, Mark; I made my will seven years ago i' thy favour."

"Thank ye," said Mark gratefully.

"But that," the dying man continued with a frown—"that was afore thou'dst taken up with these socialistic doctrines o' thine. I've heard as thou'rt going to be th' secretary o' the Hanbridge Labour Church, as they call it."

Hanbridge is the metropolis of the Five Towns, and its Labour Church is the most audacious and influential of all the local activities, half secret, but relentlessly determined, whose aim is to establish the new democratic heaven and the new democratic earth by means of a gradual and bloodless revolution. Edward Beechinor uttered its abhorred name with a bitter and scornful hatred characteristic of the Toryism of a man who, having climbed high up out of the crowd, fiercely resents any widening or smoothing of the difficult path which he himself has conquered.

"They've asked me to take the post," Mark answered.

"What's the wages?" the older man asked, with exasperated sarcasm.

"Nothing."

"Mark, lad," the other said, softening, "I'm worth seven hundred pounds and this freehold house. What dost think o' that?"

Even in that moment, with the world and its riches slipping away from his dying grasp, the contemplation of this great achievement of thrift filled Edward Beechinor with a sublime satisfaction. That sum of seven hundred pounds, which many men would dissipate in a single night, and forget the next morning that they had done so, seemed vast and almost incredible to him.

"I know you've always been very careful," said Mark politely.

"Give up this old Labour Church"—again old Beechinor laid a withering emphasis on the phrase—"give up this Labour Church, and it's all thine—house and all."

Mark shook his head.

"Think twice," the sick man ordered angrily. "I tell thee thou'rt standing to lose every shilling."

"I must manage without it, then."

A silence fell.

Each brother was absolutely immovable in his decision, and the other knew it. Edward might have said: "I am a dying man; give up this thing to oblige me." And Mark could have pleaded: "At such a moment I would do anything to oblige you—except this, and this I really can't do. Forgive me." Such amenities would possibly have eased the cord which was about to snap; but the idea of regarding Edward's condition as a factor in the case did not suggest itself favourably to the grim Beechinor stock, so stern, harsh, and rude. The sick man wiped from his sunken features the sweat which continually gathered there. Then he turned upon his side with a grunt.

"Thou must fetch th' lawyer," he said at length, "for I'll cut thee off."

It was a strange request—like ordering a condemned man to go out and search for his executioner; but Mark answered with perfect naturalness:

"Yes. Mr. Ford, I suppose?"

"Ford? No! Dost think I want *him* meddling i' my affairs? Go to young Baines up th' road. Tell him to come at once. He's sure to be at home, as it's Saturday night."

"Very well."

Mark turned to leave the room.

"And, young un, I've done with thee. Never pass my door again till thou know'st I'm i' my coffin. Understand?"

Mark hesitated a moment, and then went out, quietly closing the door. No sooner had he done so than the girl, hitherto so passive at the window, flew after him.

There are some women whose calm, enigmatic faces seem always to suggest the infinite. It is given to few to know them, so rare as they are, and their lives usually so withdrawn; but sometimes they pass in the street, or sit like sphinxes in the church or the theatre, and then the memory of their features, persistently recurring, troubles us for days. They are peculiar to no class, these women; you may find them in a print gown or in diamonds. Often they have thin, rather long lips and deep rounded chins; but it is the fine upward curve of the nostrils and the fall of the eyelids which most surely mark them. Their glances and their faint smiles are beneficent, yet with a subtle shade of half-malicious superiority. When they look at you from under those apparently fatigued eyelids, you feel that they have an inward and concealed existence far beyond the ordinary—that they are aware of many things which you can never know. It is as though their souls, during former incarnations, had trafficked with the secret forces of nature, and so acquired a mysterious and nameless quality above all the transient attributes of beauty, wit, and talent. They exist: that is enough; that is their genius. Whether they control, or are at the mercy of, those secret forces; whether they have in fact learnt, but may not speak, the true answer to the eternal Why; whether they are not perhaps a riddle even to their own simple selves: these are points which can never be decided.

Everyone who knew Mary Beechinor, in her cousin's home, or at chapel, or in Titus Price's earthenware manufactory, where she worked, said or thought that "there was something about her . . ." and left the phrase unachieved. She was twenty-five, and she had lived under the same roof with Edward Beechinor for seven years, since the sudden death of her parents. The arrangement then made was that Edward should keep her, while she conducted his household. She had insisted on permission to follow her own occupation, and in order that she might be at liberty to do so she personally paid eighteenpence a week to a little girl who came in to perform sundry necessary duties every day at noon. Mary Beechinor was a paintress by trade. As a class the paintresses of the Five Towns are somewhat similar to the more famous mill-girls of Lancashire and Yorkshire—fiercely independent by reason of good wages earned, loving finery and brilliant colours, loud-tongued and aggressive, perhaps, and for the rest neither more nor less kindly, passionate, faithful, than any other Saxon women anywhere. The paintresses, however, have some slight advantage over the mill-girls in the outward reticences of demeanour, due no doubt to the fact that their ancient craft demands a higher skill, and is pursued under more humane and tranquil conditions. Mary Beechinor worked in the "band-and-line" department of the painting-shop at Price's. You may have observed the geometrical exactitude of the broad and thin coloured lines round the edges of a common cup and saucer, and speculated upon the means by which it was arrived at. A girl drew those lines, a girl with a hand as sure as Giotto's, and no better tools than a couple of brushes and a small revolving table called a whirler. Forty-eight hours a week Mary Beechinor sat before her whirler. Actuating the treadle, she placed a piece of ware on the flying disc, and with a single unerring flip of the finger pushed it precisely to the centre; then she held the full brush firmly against the ware, and in three seconds the band encircled it truly; another brush taken up, and the line below the band also stood complete. And this process was repeated, with miraculous swiftness, hour after hour, week after week, year after year. Mary could decorate over thirty dozen cups and saucers in a day, at three halfpence the dozen. "Doesn't she ever do anything else?" some visitor might curiously inquire, whom Titus Price was showing over his ramshackle manufactory. "No, always the same thing," Titus would answer, made proud for the moment of this phenomenon of stupendous monotony. "I wonder how she can stand it—she has a refined face," the visitor might remark; and Mary Beechinor was left alone again. The idea that her work was monotonous probably never occurred to the girl. It was her work—as natural as sleep, or the knitting which she always did in the dinner-hour. The calm and silent regularity of it had become part of her, deepening her original quiescence, and setting its seal upon her inmost spirit. She was not in the fellowship of the other girls in the painting-shop. She seldom joined their more boisterous diversions, nor talked their talk, and she never manœuvred for their men. But they liked her, and their attitude showed a certain respect, forced from them by they knew not what. The powers in the office spoke of Mary Beechinor as "a very superior girl."

She ran downstairs after Mark, and he waited in the narrow hall, where there was scarcely room for two people to pass. Mark looked at her inquiringly. Rather thin, and by no means tall, she seemed the merest morsel by his side. She was wearing her second-best crimson merino frock, partly to receive the doctor and partly because it was Saturday night; over this a plain bibless apron. Her cold grey eyes faintly sparkled in anger above the cheeks white with watching, and the dropped corners of her mouth showed a contemptuous indignation. Mary Beechinor was ominously roused from the accustomed calm of years. Yet Mark at first had no suspicion that she was disturbed. To him that pale and inviolate face, even while it cast a spell over him, gave no sign of the fires within.

She took him by the coat-sleeve and silently directed him into the gloomy little parlour crowded with mahogany and horsehair furniture, white antimacassars wax flowers under glass, and ponderous gilt-clasped Bibles.

"It's a cruel shame!" she whispered, as though afraid of being overheard by the dying man upstairs.

"Do you think I ought to have given way?" he questioned, reddening.

"You mistake me," she said quickly; and with a sudden movement she went up to him and put her hand on his shoulder. The caress, so innocent, unpremeditated, and instinctive, ran through him like a voltaic shock. These two were almost strangers; they had scarcely met till within the past week, Mark being seldom in Bursley. "You mistake me—it is a shame of *him!* I'm fearfully angry."

"Angry?" he repeated, astonished.

"Yes, angry." She walked to the window, and, twitching at the blindcord, gazed into the dim street. It was beginning to grow dark. "Shall you fetch the lawyer? I shouldn't if I were you. *I* won't."

"I must fetch him," Mark said.

She turned round and admired him. "What *will* he do with his precious money?" she murmured.

"Leave it to you, probably."

"Not he. I wouldn't touch it—not now; it's yours by rights. Perhaps you don't know that when I came here it was distinctly understood I wasn't to expect anything under his will. Besides, I have my own money. . . . Oh dear! If he wasn't in such pain, wouldn't I talk to him—for the first and last time in my life!"

"You must please not say a word to him. I don't really want the money."

"But you ought to have it. If he takes it away from you he's *unjust.*"

"What did the doctor say this afternoon?" asked Mark, wishing to change the subject.

"He said the crisis would come on Monday, and when it did Edward would be dead all in a minute. He said it would be just like taking prussic acid."

"Not earlier than Monday?"

"He said he thought Monday."

"Of course I shall take no notice of what Edward said to me—I shall call to-morrow morning—and stay. Perhaps he won't mind seeing me. And then you can tell me what happens to-night."

"I'm sure I shall send that lawyer man about his business," she threatened.

"Look here," said Mark timorously as he was leaving the house, "I've told you I don't want the money—I would give it away to some charity; but do you think I ought to pretend to yield, just to humour him, and let him die quiet and peaceful? I shouldn't like him to die hating——"

"Never—never!" she exclaimed.

"What have you and Mark been talking about?" asked Edward Beechinor apprehensively as Mary re-entered the bedroom.

"Nothing," she replied with a grave and soothing kindliness of tone.

"Because, miss, if you think——"

"You must have your medicine now, Edward."

But before giving the patient his medicine she peeped through the curtain and watched Mark's figure till it disappeared up the hill towards Bleakridge. He, on his part, walked with her image always in front of him. He thought hers was the strongest, most righteous soul he had ever encountered; it seemed as if she had a perfect passion for truth and justice. And a week ago he had deemed her a capable girl, certainly —but lackadaisical!

The clock had struck ten before Mr. Baines, the solicitor, knocked at the door. Mary hesitated, and then took him upstairs in silence while he suavely explained to her why he had been unable to come earlier. This lawyer was a young Scotsman who had descended upon the town from nowhere, bought a small decayed practice, and within two years had transformed it into a large and flourishing business by one of those feats of energy, audacity, and tact, combined, of which some Scotsmen seem to possess the secret.

"Here is Mr. Baines, Edward," Mary said quietly; and then, having rearranged the sick man's pillow, she vanished out of the room and went into the kitchen.

The gas-jet there showed only a point of blue, but she did not turn it up. Dragging an old oak rush-seated rocking-chair near to the range, where a scrap of fire still glowed, she rocked herself gently in the darkness.

After about half an hour Mr. Baines's voice sounded at the head of the stairs:

"Miss Beechinor, will ye kindly step up? We shall want some asseestance."

She obeyed, but not instantly.

In the bedroom Mr. Baines, a fountain-pen between his fine white teeth, was putting some coal on the fire. He stood up as she entered.

"Mr. Beechinor is about to make a new will," he said, without removing the pen from his mouth, "and ye will kindly witness it."

The small room appeared to be full of Baines—he was so large and fleshy and assertive. The furniture, even the chest of drawers, was dwarfed into toy-furniture, and Beechinor, slight and shrunken-up, seemed like a cadaverous manikin in the bed.

"Now, Mr. Beechinor." Dusting his hands, the lawyer took a newly-written document from the dressing-table, and, spreading it on the lid of a cardboard box, held it before the dying man. "Here's the pen. There! I'll help ye to hold it."

Beechinor clutched the pen. His wrinkled and yellow face, flushed in irregular patches as though the cheeks had been badly rouged, was covered with perspiration, and each difficult movement, even to the slightest lifting of the head, showed extreme exhaustion. He cast at Mary a long sinister glance of mistrust and apprehension.

"What is there in this will?"

Mr. Baines looked sharply up at the girl, who now stood at the side of the bed opposite him. Mechanically she smoothed the tumbled bedclothes.

"That's nowt to do wi' thee, lass," said Beechinor resentfully.

"It isn't necessary that a witness to a will should be aware of its contents," said Baines. "In fact, it's quite unusual."

"I sign nothing in the dark," she said, smiling. Through their half-closed lids her eyes glimmered at Baines.

"Ha! Legal caution acquired from your cousin, I presume." Baines smiled at her. "But let me assure ye, Miss Beechinor, this is a mere matter of form. A will must be signed in the presence of two witnesses, both present at the same time; and there's only yeself and me for it."

Mary looked at the dying man, whose features were writhed in pain, and shook her head.

"Tell her," he murmured with bitter despair, and sank down into the pillows, dropping the fountain-pen, which had left a stain of ink on the sheet before Baines could pick it up.

"Well, then, Miss Beechinor, if ye must know," Baines began with sarcasm, "the will is as follows: The testator—that's Mr. Beechinor—leaves twenty guineas to his brother Mark to show that he bears him no ill-will and forgives him. The rest of his estate is to be realised, and the proceeds given to the North Staffordshire Infirmary, to found a bed, which is to be called the Beechinor bed. If there is any surplus, it is to go to the Law Clerk's Provident Society. That is all."

"I shall have nothing to do with it," Mary said coldly.

"Young lady, we don't want ye to have anything to do with it. We only desire ye to witness the signature."

"I won't witness the signature, and I won't see it signed."

"Damn thee, Mary! thou'rt a wicked wench," Beechinor whispered in hoarse, feeble tones. He saw himself robbed of the legitimate fruit of all those interminable years of toilsome thrift. This girl by a trick would prevent him from disposing of his own. He, Edward Beechinor, shrewd and wealthy, was being treated like a child. He was too weak to rave, but from his aggrieved and furious heart he piled silent curses on her. "Go, fetch another witness," he added to the lawyer.

"Wait a moment," said Baines. "Miss Beechinor, do ye mean to say that ye will cross the solemn wish of a dying man?"

"I mean to say I won't help a dying man to commit a crime."

"A crime?"

"Yes," she answered, "a crime. Seven years ago Mr. Beechinor willed everything to his brother Mark, and Mark ought to have everything. Mark is his only brother—his only relation except me. And Edward knows it isn't me wants any of his money. North Staffordshire Infirmary indeed! It's a crime! . . . What business have *you*," she went on to Edward Beechinor, "to punish Mark just because his politics aren't——"

"That's beside the point," the lawyer interrupted. "A testator has a perfect right to leave his property as he chooses, without giving reasons. Now, Miss Beechinor, I must ask ye to be judeecious."

Mary shut her lips.

"Her 'll never do it. I tell thee, fetch another witness."

The old man sprang up in a sort of frenzy as he uttered the words, and then fell back in a brief swoon.

Mary wiped his brow, and pushed away the wet and matted hair. Presently he opened his eyes, moaning. Mr. Baines folded up the will, put it in his pocket, and left the room with quick steps. Mary heard him open the front-door and then return to the foot of the stairs.

"Miss Beechinor," he called, "I'll speak with ye a moment."

She went down.

"Do you mind coming into the kitchen?" she said, preceding him and turning up the gas; "there's no light in the front-room."

He leaned up against the high mantelpiece; his frock-coat hung to the level of the oven-knob. She had one hand on the white deal table. Between them a tortoiseshell cat purred on the red-tiled floor.

"Ye're doing a verra serious thing, Miss Beechinor. As Mr. Beechinor's solicitor, I should just like to be acquaint with the real reasons for this conduct."

"I've told you." She had a slightly quizzical look.

"Now, as to Mark," the lawyer continued blandly, "Mr. Beechinor explained the whole circumstances to me. Mark as good as defied his brother."

"That's nothing to do with it."

"By the way, it appears that Mark is practically engaged to be married. May I ask if the lady is yeself?"

She hesitated.

"If so," he proceeded, "I may tell ye informally that I admire the pluck of ye. But, nevertheless, that will has got to be executed."

"The young lady is a Miss Mellor of Hanbridge."

"I'm going to fetch my clerk," he said shortly. "I can see ye're an obstinate and unfathomable woman. I'll be back in half an hour."

When he had departed she bolted the front-door top and bottom, and went upstairs to the dying man.

Nearly an hour elapsed before she heard a knock. Mr. Baines had had to arouse his clerk from sleep. Instead of going down to the front-door, Mary threw up the bedroom window and looked out. It was a mild but starless night. Trafalgar Road was silent save for the steam-car, which, with its load of revellers returning from Hanbridge—that centre of gaiety—slipped rumbling down the hill towards Bursley.

"What do you want—disturbing a respectable house at this time of night?" she called in a loud whisper when the car had passed. "The door's bolted, and I can't come down. You must come in the morning."

"Miss Beechinor, ye will let us in—I charge ye."

"It's useless, Mr. Baines."

"I'll break the door down. I'm a strong man, and a determined. Ye are carrying things too far."

In another moment the two men heard the creak of the bolts. Mary stood before them, vaguely discernible, but a forbidding figure.

"If you must—come upstairs," she said coldly.

"Stay here in the passage, Arthur," said Mr. Baines; "I'll call ye when I want ye," and he followed Mary up the stairs.

Edward Beechinor lay on his back, and his sunken eyes stared glassily at the ceiling. The skin of his emaciated face, stretched tightly over the protruding bones, had lost all its crimson, and was green, white, yellow. The mouth was wide open. His drawn features wore a terribly sardonic look—a purely physical effect of the disease; but it seemed to the two spectators that this mean and disappointed slave of a miserly habit had by one superb imaginative effort realised the full vanity of all human wishes and pretensions.

"Ye can go; I shan't want ye," said Mr. Baines, returning to the clerk.

The lawyer never spoke of that night's business. Why should he? To what end? Mark Beechinor, under the old will, inherited the seven hundred pounds and the house. Miss Mellor of Hanbridge is still Miss Mellor, her hand not having been formally sought. But Mark, secretary of the Labour Church, is married. Miss Mellor, with a quite pardonable air of tolerant superiority, refers to his wife as "a strange, timid little creature—she couldn't say Bo to a goose."

* * *

JOHN GALSWORTHY
(1867-   )

GALSWORTHY, born in Surrey, was educated at Harrow and Oxford. He studied law, was admitted to the Bar, but after a limited practice, devoted himself to literature. He has written many plays, novels and short stories, the last being recently collected into a volume, *Caravan* (1925). Galsworthy is a sincere and profound artist with a liberal and humane attitude toward social problems.

Quality is reprinted, by permission of the publishers, from *The Inn of Tranquillity*, copyright, 1912, by Charles Scribner's Sons.

QUALITY

I KNEW him from the days of my extreme youth, because he made my father's boots; inhabiting with his elder brother two little shops let into one, in a small by-street—now no more, but then most fashionably placed in the West End.

That tenement had a certain quiet distinction; there was no sign upon its face that he made for any of the Royal Family—merely his own German name of Gessler Brothers; and in the window a few pairs of boots. I remember that it always troubled me to account for those unvarying boots in the window, for he made only what was ordered, reaching nothing down, and it seemed so inconceivable that what he made could ever have failed to fit. Had he bought them to put there? That, too, seemed inconceivable. He would never have tolerated in his house leather on which he had not worked himself. Besides, they were too beautiful—the pair of pumps, so inexpressibly slim; the patent leathers with cloth tops, making water come into one's mouth; the tall brown riding boots with marvellous sooty glow, as if, though new, they had been worn a hundred years. Those pairs could only have been made by one who saw before him the Soul of Boot—so truly were they prototypes incarnating the very spirit of all foot-gear. These thoughts, of course, came to me later, though even when I was promoted to him, at the age of perhaps fourteen, some inkling haunted me of the dignity of himself and brother. For to make boots—such boots as he made—seemed to me then, and still seems to me, mysterious and wonderful.

I remember well my shy remark, one day, while stretching out to him my youthful foot:

"Isn't it awfully hard to do, Mr. Gessler?"

And his answer, given with a sudden smile from out of the sardonic redness of his beard: "Id is an Ardt!"

Himself, he was as little as if made from leather, with his yellow crinkly face, and crinkly reddish hair and beard, and neat folds slanting down his cheeks to the corners of his mouth, and his guttural and one-toned voice; for leather is a sardonic substance, and stiff and slow of purpose. And that was the character of his face, save that his eyes, which were grey-blue, had in them the simple gravity of one secretly possessed by the Ideal. His elder brother was so very like him—though watery, paler in every way, with a great industry—that sometimes in early days I was not quite sure of him until the interview was over. Then I knew that it was he, if the words, "I will ask my brudder," had not been spoken; and that, if they had, it was his elder brother.

When one grew old and wild and ran up bills, one somehow never ran them up with Gessler Brothers. It would not have seemed becoming to go in there and stretch out one's foot to that blue iron-spectacled glance, owing him for more than—say—two pairs, just the comfortable reassurance that one was still his client.

For it was not possible to go to him very often—his boots lasted terribly, having something beyond the temporary—some, as it were, essence of boot stitched into them.

One went in, not as into most shops, in the mood of: "Please serve me, and let me go!" but restfully, as one enters a church; and, sitting on the single wooden chair, waited—for there was never anybody there. Soon, over the top edge of that sort of well—rather dark, as smelling soothingly of leather—which formed the shop, there would be seen his face, or that of his elder brother, peering down. A guttural sound, and the tip-tap of bast slippers beating the narrow wooden stairs, and he would stand before one without coat, a little bent, in leather apron, with sleeves turned back, blinking—as if awakened from some dream of boots, or like an owl surprised in daylight and annoyed at this interruption.

And I would say: "How do you do, Mr. Gessler? Could you make me a pair of Russia leather boots?"

Without a word he would leave me, retiring whence he came, or into the other portion of the shop, and I would continue to rest in the wooden chair, inhaling the incense of his trade. Soon he would come back, holding in his thin, veined hand a piece of gold-brown leather. With eyes fixed on it, he would remark: "What a beaudiful biece!" When

I, too, had admired it, he would speak again. "When do you wand dem?" And I would answer: "Oh! As soon as you conveniently can." And he would say: To-morrow fordnight?" Or if he were his elder brother: "I will ask my brudder!"

Then I would murmur: "Thank you! Good morning, Mr. Gessler." "Goot morning!" he would reply, still looking at the leather in his hand. And as I moved to the door, I would hear the tip-tap of his bast slippers restoring him, up the stairs, to his dream of boots. But if it were some new kind of foot-gear that he had not yet made me, then indeed he would observe ceremony—divesting me of my boot and holding it long in his hand, looking at it with eyes at once critical and loving, as if recalling the glow with which he had created it, and rebuking the way in which one had disorganised this masterpiece. Then, placing my foot on a thin piece of paper, he would two or three times tickle the outer edges with a pencil and pass his nervous fingers over my toes, feeling himself into the heart of my requirements.

I cannot forget that day on which I had occasion to say to him: "Mr. Gessler, that last pair of town walking-boots creaked, you know."

He looked at me for a time without replying, as if expecting me to withdraw or qualify the statement, then said:

"Id shouldn't 'ave greaked."

"It did, I'm afraid."

"You goddem wed before dey found demselves?"

"I don't think so."

At that he lowered his eyes, as if hunting for memory of those boots, and I felt sorry I had mentioned this grave thing.

"Zend dem back!" he said; "I will look at dem."

A feeling of compassion for my creaking boots surged up in me, so well could I imagine the sorrowful long curiosity of regard which he would bend on them.

"Zome boods," he said slowly, "are bad from birdt. If I can do noding wid dem, I dake dem off your bill."

Once (once only) I went absent-mindedly into his shop in a pair of boots bought in an emergency at some large firm's. He took my order without showing me any leather, and I could feel his eyes penetrating the inferior integument of my foot. At last he said:

"Dose are nod my boods."

The tone was not one of anger, nor of sorrow, not even of contempt, but there was in it something quiet that froze the blood. He put his hand down and pressed a finger on the place where the left boot, endeavoring to be fashionable, was not quite comfortable.

"Id 'urds you dere," he said. "Dose big virms 'ave no self-respect. Drash!" And then as if something had given way within him, he spoke long and bitterly. It was the only time I ever heard him discuss the conditions and hardships of the trade.

"Dey get id all," he said, "dey get id by adverdisement, nod by work. Dey dake it away from us, who lofe our boods. Id gomes to this— bresently I haf no work. Every year id gets less—you will see." And looking at his lined face I saw things I had never noticed before, bitter things and bitter struggle—and what a lot of grey hairs there seemed suddenly in his red beard!

As best I could, I explained the circumstances of the purchase of those ill-omened boots. But his face and voice made so deep impression that during the next few minutes I ordered many pairs. Nemesis fell! They lasted more terribly than ever. And I was not able conscientiously to go to him for nearly two years.

When at last I went I was surprised to find that outside one of the two little windows of his shop another name was painted, also that of a boot-maker—making, of course, for the Royal Family. The old familiar boots, no longer in dignified isolation, were huddled in the single window. Inside, the now contracted well of the one little shop was more scented and darker than ever. And it was longer than usual, too, before a face peered down, and the tip-tap of the bast slippers began. At last he stood before me, and, gazing through those rusty iron spectacles, said:

"Mr. ——, isn'd id?"

"Ah! Mr. Gessler," I stammered, "but your boots are really *too* good, you know! See, these are quite decent still!" And I stretched out to him my foot. He looked at it.

"Yes," he said, "beople do nod wand good boods, id seems."

To get away from his reproachful eyes and voice I hastily remarked: "What have you done to your shop?"

He answered quietly: "Id was too exbensive. Do you wand some boods?"

I ordered three pairs, though I had only wanted two, and quickly left. I had, I do not know quite what feeling of being part, in his mind, of a conspiracy against him; or not perhaps so much against him as against his idea of boot. One does not, I suppose, care to feel like that; for it was again many months before my next visit to his shop, paid, I remember, with the feeling: "Oh, well, I can't leave the old boy—so here goes! Perhaps it will be his elder brother!"

For his elder brother, I knew, had not character enough to reproach me, even dumbly.

And, to my relief, in the shop there did appear to be his elder brother, handling a piece of leather.

"Well, Mr. Gessler," I said, "how are you?"

He came close and peered at me.

"I am breddy well," he said slowly: "but my elder brudder is dead."

And I saw that it was indeed himself—but how aged and wan! And never before had I heard him mention his brother. Much shocked, I murmured: "Oh! I am sorry!"

"Yes," he answered, "he was a good man, he made a good bood; but he is dead." And he touched the top of his head, where the hair had suddenly gone as thin as it had been on that of his poor brother, to indicate, I suppose, the cause of death. "He could nod ged over losing de oder shop. Do you wand any boods?" And he held up the leather in his hand: "Id's a beaudiful biece."

I ordered several pairs. It was very long before they came—but they were better than ever. One simply could not wear them out. And soon after that I went abroad.

It was over a year before I was again in London. And the first shop I went to was my old friend's. I had left a man of sixty, I came back to one of seventy-five, pinched and worn and tremulous, who genuinely, this time, did not at first know me.

"Oh! Mr. Gessler," I said, sick at heart; "how splendid your boots are! See, I've been wearing this pair nearly all the time I've been abroad; and they're not half worn out, are they?"

He looked long at my boots—a pair of Russia leather, and his face seemed to regain steadiness. Putting his hand on my instep, he said: "Do dey vid you here? I 'ad drouble wid dat bair, I remember."

I assured him that they had fitted beautifully.

"Do you wand any boods?" he said. "I can make dem quickly; id is a slack dime."

I answered: "Please, please! I want boots all round—every kind!"

"I will make a vresh model. Your foot must be bigger." And with utter slowness, he traced round my foot, and felt my toes, only once looking up to say:

"Did I dell you my brudder was dead?"

To watch him was painful, so feeble had he grown; I was glad to get away.

I had given those boots up, when one evening they came. Opening the parcel, I set the four pairs out in a row. Then one by one I tried them on. There was no doubt about it. In shape and fit, in finish and quality of leather, they were the best he had ever made me. And in the mouth of one of the Town walking-boots I found his bill. The amount was the same as usual, but it gave me quite a shock. He had never before sent it till quarter day. I flew down-stairs, and wrote a cheque, and posted it at once with my own hand.

A week later, passing the little street, I thought I would go in and tell him how splendidly the new boots fitted. But when I came to where his shop had been, his name was gone. Still there, in the window, were the slim pumps, the patent leathers with cloth tops, the sooty riding boots.

I went in, very much disturbed. In the two little shops—again made into one—was a young man with an English face.

"Mr. Gessler in?" I said.

He gave me a strange, ingratiating look.

"No, sir," he said, "no. But we can attend to anything with pleasure. We've taken the shop over. You've seen our name, no doubt, next door. We make for some very good people."

"Yes, yes," I said; "but Mr. Gessler?"

"Oh!" he answered; "dead."

"Dead! But I received these boots from him last Wednesday week."

"Ah!" he said, "a shockin' go. Poor old man starved 'imself."

"Good God!"

"Slow starvation, the doctor called it! You see he went to work in such a way! Would keep the shop on; wouldn't have a soul touch his boots except himself. When he got an order, it took him such a time. People won't wait. He lost everybody. And there he'd sit, goin' on and on—I will say that for him—not a man in London made a better boot! But look at the competition! He never advertised! Would 'ave the best leather, too, and do it all 'imself. Well, there it is. What could you expect with his ideas?"

"But starvation——!"

"That may be a bit flowery, as the sayin' is—but I know myself he was sittin' over his boots day and night, to the very last. You see I used to watch him. Never gave himself time to eat; never had a penny in the house. All went in rent and leather. How he lived so long I don't know. He regular let his fire go out. He was a character. But he made good boots."

"Yes," I said, "he made good boots."

And I turned and went out quickly, for I did not want that youth to know that I could hardly see.

* * *

D. H. LAWRENCE
(1885-   )

LAWRENCE, born at Eastwood, Nottinghamshire, was educated at the University College, Nottingham. By the time his third novel had been published (*Sons and Lovers*, 1913) it "became evident that a writer of great force and originality was rising in the younger generation." His later work shows a marked influence of psychoanalysis, and concerns itself with a frank study of sex problems.

Two Blue Birds is reprinted from the *Dial Magazine*, by permission of the editor and arrangement with the author.

TWO BLUE BIRDS

THERE was a woman who loved her husband, but she could not live with him. The husband, on his side, was sincerely attached to his wife, yet he could not live with her. They were both under forty, both handsome, and both attractive. They had the most sincere regard for one another, and felt, in some odd way, eternally married to one another. They knew each other more intimately than they knew anybody else, they felt more known to one another than to any other person.

Yet they could not live together. Usually, they kept a thousand miles apart, geographically. But when he sat in the greyness of England, at the back of his mind, with a certain grim fidelity, he was aware of his wife, her strange yearning to be loyal and faithful, having her gallant affairs away in the sun, in the south. And she, as she drank her cocktail on the terrace over the sea, and turned her grey, sardonic eyes on the heavy, dark face of her admirer, whom she really liked quite a lot, she was actually preoccupied with the clear-cut features of her handsome young husband, thinking of how he would be asking his secretary to do something for him; asking in that good-natured, confident voice of a man who knows that his request will be only too gladly fulfilled.

The secretary, of course, adored him. She was *very* competent, quite young, and quite good-looking. She adored him. But then all his servants always did; particularly his women-servants. His men-servants were likely to swindle him.

When a man has an adoring secretary, and you are the man's wife, what are you to do? Not that there was anything "wrong"—if you know what I mean!—between them. Nothing you could call adultery, to come down to brass tacks. No, no! They were just the young master and his secretary. He dictated to her, she slaved for him and adored him, and the whole thing went on wheels.

He didn't "adore" her. A man doesn't need to adore his secretary. But he depended on her. "I simply rely on Miss Wrexall." Whereas he could never rely on his wife. The only thing he knew finally about *her* was that she didn't intend to be relied on.

So they remained friends, in the awful unspoken intimacy of the once married. Usually each year they went away together for a holiday, and if they had not been man and wife, they would have found a great deal of fun and stimulation in one another. The fact that they were married, had been married for the last dozen years, and couldn't live together for the last three or four, spoilt them for one another. Each had a private feeling of bitterness about the other.

However, they were awfully kind. He was the soul of generosity, and held her in real tender esteem, no matter how many gallant affairs she had. Her gallant affairs were part of her modern necessity. "After all, I've got to *live*. I can't turn into a pillar of salt in five minutes, just because you and I can't live together! It takes years for a woman like me to turn into a pillar of salt. At least I hope so!"

"Quite!" he replied. "Quite! By all means put them in pickle, make pickled cucumbers of them, before you crystallise out. That's my advice."

He was like that; so awfully clever and enigmatic. She could more or less fathom the idea of the pickled cucumbers, but the "crystal-lising out," what did that signify?

And did he mean to suggest that he himself had been well pickled, and that further immersion was for him unnecessary, would spoil his flavour? Was that what he meant? And herself, was she the brine and the vale of tears?

You never knew how catty a man was being, when he was really clever and enigmatic, withal a bit whimsical. He was adorably whim-sical, with a twist of his flexible, vain mouth, that had a long upper lip, so fraught with vanity! But then a handsome, clear-cut, histrionic young man like that, how could he help being vain? The women made him so.

Ah, the women! How nice men would be if there were no other women!

And how nice the women would be if there were no other men! That's the best of a secretary. She may have a husband, but a husband is the mere shred of a man, compared to a boss, a chief, a man who dictates to you and whose words you faithfully write down and then transcribe. Imagine a wife writing down anything her husband said to her!—But a secretary! Every *and* and *but* of his she preserves for ever. What are candied violets in comparison!

Now it is all very well having gallant affairs under the southern sun, when you know there is a husband whom you adore dictating to a secretary whom you are too scornful to hate yet whom you rather despise, though you allow she has her good points, away north in the place you ought to regard as home. A gallant affair isn't much good when you've got a bit of grit in your eye. Or something at the back of your mind.

What's to be done? The husband, of course, did not send his wife away.

"You've got your secretary and your work," she said. "There's no room for me."

"There's a bedroom and a sitting-room exclusively for you," he replied. "And a garden and half a motor-car. But please yourself entirely. Do what gives you most pleasure."

"In that case," she said, "I'll just go south for the winter."

"Yes, do!" he said. "You always enjoy it."

"I always do," she replied.

They parted with a certain relentlessness that had a touch of wistful sentiment behind it. Off she went to her gallant affairs, that were like the curate's egg, palatable in parts. And he settled down to work. He said he hated working, but he never did anything else. Ten or eleven hours a day. That's what it is to be your own master!

So the winter wore away, and it was spring, when the swallows homeward fly: or northward, in this case. This winter, one of a series similar, had been rather hard to get through. The bit of grit in the gallant lady's eye had worked deeper in, the more she blinked. Dark faces might be dark, and icy cocktails might lend a glow, she blinked her hardest, to blink that bit of grit away, without success. Under the spicy balls of the mimosa she thought of that husband of hers, in his library, and of that neat, competent but *common* little secretary of his, for ever taking down what he said!

"How a man can *stand* it! how *she* can stand it, common little thing as she is, I don't know!" the wife cried to herself.

She meant this dictating business, this ten hours a day intercourse *à deux*, with nothing but a pencil between them: and a flow of words.

What was to be done? Matters, instead of improving, had grown worse. The little secretary had brought her mother and sister into the establishment. The mother was a sort of cook-housekeeper, the sister was a sort of upper maid: she did the fine laundry, and looked after "his" clothes, and valeted him beautifully. It was really an excellent arrangement. The old mother was a splendid plain cook, the sister was all that could be desired as a *valet-de-chambre*, a fine laundress, an upper parlour-maid, and a table-waiter. And all economical to a degree. They knew his affairs by heart. His secretary flew to town when a creditor became dangerous, and she *always* smoothed over the financial crisis.

"He," of course, had debts, and he was working to pay them off. And if he had been a fairy prince who could call the ants to help him, he would not have been more wonderful than in securing this secretary and her family. They took hardly any wages. And they seemed to perform the miracle of loaves and fishes daily.

"She," of course, the wife who loved her husband, but helped him into debt, and she still was an expensive item. Yet when she appeared at her "home," the secretarial family received her with most elaborate attentions and deference. The knight returning from the Crusades, didn't create a greater stir. She felt like Queen Elizabeth at Kenilworth, a sovereign paying a visit to her faithful subjects. But perhaps there lurked always this hair in her coup: Won't they be glad to be rid of me again!

But they protested No! No! They had been waiting and hoping and praying she would come. They had been pining for her to be there, in charge: the mistress, "his wife". Ah, "his" wife!

"His" wife! His halo was like a bucket over her head.

The cook-mother was "of the people," so it was the upper-maid daughter who came for orders.

"What will you order for to-morrow's lunch and dinner, Mrs. Gee?"

"Well, what do you usually have?"

"Oh, we want *you* to say."

"No, what do you *usually* have?"

"We don't have anything fixed. Mother goes out and chooses the best she can find, that is nice and fresh. But she thought you would tell her now what to get."

"Oh, I don't know! I'm not very good at that sort of thing. Ask her to go on just the same; I'm sure she knows best."

"Perhaps you'd like to suggest a sweet?"

"No, I don't care for sweets—and you know Mr. Gee doesn't. So don't make one for me."

Could anything be more impossible! They had the house spotless and running like a dream: how could an incompetent and extravagant wife dare to interfere, when she saw their amazing and almost inspired economy! But they ran the place on simply nothing! simply marvellous people! And the way they strewed palm-branches under her feet!

But that only made her feel ridiculous, as if she were the ass, and the Crucifixion was next week.

"Don't you think the family manage very well?" he asked her tentatively.

"Awfully well! Almost romantically well!" she replied. "But I suppose you're perfectly happy?"

"I'm perfectly comfortable," he replied.

"I can see you are," she replied. "Amazingly so! I never knew such comfort! Are you sure it isn't bad for you?"

She eyed him stealthily. He looked very well, and extremely handsome, in his histrionic way. He was shockingly well-dressed and valeted. And he had that air of easy *aplomb* and good-humour which is so becoming to a man, and which he only acquires when he is cock of his own little walk, made much of by his own hens.

"No!" he said, taking his pipe from his mouth and smiling whim‹ sically round at her. "Do I look as if it were bad for me?"

"No, you don't," she replied promptly: thinking, naturally, as a woman is supposed to think nowadays, of his health and comfort, the foundation, apparently, of all happiness.

Then, of course, away she went on the backwash.

"Perhaps for your work, though, it's not so good as it is for *you*," she said, in a rather small voice. She knew he couldn't bear it if she mocked at his work for one moment. And he knew that rather small voice of hers.

"In what way?" he said, bristles rising.

"Oh, I don't know," she answered indifferently. "Perhaps it's not good for a man's work if he is too comfortable."

"I don't know about *that!*" he said, taking a dramatic turn round the library and drawing at his pipe. "Considering I work, actually, by the clock, for twelve hours a day, and for ten hours when it's a short day, I don't think you can say I am deteriorating from easy comfort."

"No, I suppose not," she admitted.

Yet she did think it, nevertheless. His comfortableness didn't consist so much in good food and a soft bed, as in having nobody, absolutely nobody and nothing to contradict him. "I do like to think he's got nothing to aggravate him," the secretary had said to the wife.

"Nothing to aggravate him"!—what a position for a man! Fostered by women who would let nothing "aggravate" him. If anything would aggravate his wounded vanity, this would!

So thought the wife. But what was to be done about it? In the silence of midnight she heard his voice in the distance, dictating away, like the voice of God to Samuel, alone and monotone, and she imagined the little figure of the secretary busily scribbling shorthand. Then in the sunny hours of morning, while he was still in bed—he never rose till noon—from another distance came that sharp insect-noise of the typewriter, like some immense grasshopper chirping and rattling. It was the secretary, poor thing, typing out his notes.

That girl—she was only twenty-eight—really slaved herself to skin and bone. She was small and neat, but she was actually worn out. She did far more work than he did, for she had not only to take down all those words he uttered, she had to type them out, make three copies, while he was still resting.

"What on earth she gets out of it," thought the wife, "I don't know. She's simply worn to the bone: for a very poor salary, and he's never kissed her, and never will, if I know anything about him."

Whether his never kissing her—the secretary, that is—made it worse or better, the wife did not decide. He never kissed anybody. Whether she herself—the wife, that is—wanted to be kissed by him, even that she was not clear about. She rather thought she didn't. What on earth did she want then? She was his wife. What on earth did she want of him?

She certainly didn't want to take him down in shorthand, and type out again all those words. And she didn't really want him to kiss her: she knew him too well. Yes, she knew him too well. If you know a man too well, you don't want him to kiss you.

What then? What did she want? Why had she such an extraordinary hang-over about him? Just because she was his wife? Why did she rather "enjoy" other men—and she was relentless about enjoyment—without ever taking them seriously? And why must she take him so damn seriously, when she never really "enjoyed" him?

Of course she *had* had good times with him, in the past, before—ah! before a thousand things, all amounting really to nothing. But she enjoyed him no more. She never even enjoyed being with him. There was a silent ceaseless tension between them, that never broke, even when they were a thousand miles apart.

Awful! That's what you call being married! What's to be done about it? Ridiculous, to know it all and not do anything about it!

She came back once more, and there she was, in her own house, a sort of super-guest, even to him. And the secretarial family devoting their lives to him.

Devoting their lives to him! But actually! Three women pouring out their lives for him day and night! And what did they get in return? Not one kiss! Very little money, because they knew all about his debts, and had made it their life-business to get them paid off! No expectations! Twelve hours' work a day! Comparative isolation, for he saw nobody!

And beyond that?—nothing! Perhaps a sense of uplift and importance because they saw his name and photograph in the newspapers sometimes. But would anybody believe that it was good enough?

Yet they adored it! They seemed to get a deep satisfaction out of it, like people with a mission. Extraordinary!

Well, if they did, let them. They were of course rather common, "of the people," there might be a sort of glamour in it for them.

But it was bad for him. No doubt about it. His work was getting diffuse and poor in quality—and what wonder! His whole tone was going down—becoming commoner. Of course it was bad for him.

Being his wife, she felt she ought to do something to save him. But how could she? That perfectly devoted, marvellous secretarial family, how could she make an attack on them? Yet she'd love to sweep them into oblivion. Of course they were bad for him: ruining his work, ruining his reputation as a writer, ruining his life. Ruining him with their slavish service.

Of course she ought to make an onslaught on them! But how *could* she! Such devotion! And what had she herself to offer in their place? Certainly not slavish devotion to him, nor to his flow of words! Certainly not!

She imagined him stripped once more naked of secretary and secretarily family, and she shuddered. It was like throwing the naked baby in the dust-bin. Couldn't do that!

Yet something must be done. She felt it. She was almost tempted to get into debt for another thousand pounds, and send in the bill, or have it sent to him, as usual.

But no! Something more drastic!

Something more drastic, or perhaps more gentle. She wavered between the two. And wavering, she first did nothing, came to no decision, dragged vacantly on from day to day, waiting for sufficient energy to take her departure once more.

It was spring! What a fool she had been to come up in spring! And she was forty! What an idiot of a woman to go and be forty!

She went down the garden in the warm afternoon, when birds were whistling loudly from the cover, the sky being low and warm, and she had nothing to do. The garden was full of flowers: he loved them for their theatrical display. Lilac and snowball bushes, and laburnum and red may, tulips and anemonies and coloured daisies. Lots of flowers! Borders of forget-me-nots! Bachelor's buttons! What absurd names flowers had! She would have called them blue dots and yellow blobs and white frills. Not so much sentiment, after all!

There is a certain nonsense, something showy and stagey about spring, with its pushing leaves and chorus-girl flowers, unless you have something corresponding inside you. Which she hadn't.

Oh, heaven! Beyond the hedge she heard a voice: a steady, rather theatrical voice. Oh, heaven!—he was dictating to his secretary in the garden. Good God, was there nowhere to get away from it! She looked around: there was indeed plenty of escape. But what was the good of escaping? He would go on and on. She went quietly towards the hedge, and listened.

He was dictating a magazine article about the modern novel. "What the modern novel lacks is architecture"—Good God! Architecture! He might just as well say: What the modern novel lacks is whale-bone, or a teaspoon, or a tooth stopped.

Yet the secretary took it down, took it down, took it down! No, this could not go on! It was more than flesh and blood could bear.

She went quietly along the hedge, somewhat wolf-like in her prowl, a broad, strong woman in an expensive mustard-coloured silk jersey and cream-coloured pleated skirt. Her legs were long and shapely, and her shoes were expensive.

With a curious wolf-like stealth she turned the hedge and looked across at the small, shaded lawn where the daisies grew impertinently. "He" was reclining in a coloured hammock under the pink-flowering horse-chestnut tree, dressed in white serge with a fine yellow-coloured linen shirt. His elegant hand dropped over the side of the hammock and beat a sort of vague rhythm to his words. At a little wicker table the little secretary, in a green knitted frock, bent her dark head over her note-book, and diligently made those awful shorthand marks. He was not difficult to take down, as he dictated slowly, and kept a sort of rhythm, beating time with his dangling hand.

"In every novel there must be one outstanding character with which we always sympathise—with *whom* we always sympathise—even though we recognise its—even when we are most aware of the human frailties—"

Every man his own hero, thought the wife grimly, forgetting that every woman is intensely her own heroine.

But what did startle her was a blue bird dashing about near the feet of the absorbed, shorthand-scribbling little secretary. At least it was a blue-tit, blue with grey and some yellow. But to the wife it seemed blue, that juicy spring day, in the translucent afternoon. The blue bird, fluttering round the pretty but rather *common* little feet of the little secretary.

The blue bird! The blue bird of happiness! Well I'm blest!— thought the wife. Well I'm blest!

And as she was being blest, appeared another blue bird, that is, another blue-tit, and began to wrestle with the first blue-tit. A couple of blue birds of happiness, having a fight over it! Well I'm blest!

She was more or less out of sight of the human preoccupied pair. But "he" was disturbed by the fighting blue birds, whose little feathers began to float loose.

"Get out!" he said to them mildly, waving a dark-yellow handkerchief at them. "Fight your little fight, and settle your private affairs elsewhere, my dear little gentlemen."

The little secretary looked up quickly, for she had already begun to write it down. He smiled at her his twisted whimsical smile.

"No, don't take that down," he said affectionately. "Did you see those two tits laying into one another?"

"No!" said the little secretary, gazing brightly round, her eyes half blinded with work.

But she saw the queer, powerful, elegant, wolf-like figure of the wife, behind her, and terror came into her eyes.

"I did!" said the wife, stepping forward with those curious, shapely, she-wolf legs of hers, under the very short skirt.

"Aren't they extraordinarily vicious little beasts?" said he.

"Extraordinarily!" she re-echoed, stooping and picking up a little breast-feather. "Extraordinarily! See how the feathers fly!"

And she got the feather on the tip of her finger, and looked at it. Then she looked at the secretary, then she looked at him. She had a queer, were-wolf expression between her brows.

"I think," he began, "these are the loveliest afternoons, when there's no direct sun, but all the sounds and the colours and the scents are sort of dissolved, don't you know, in the air, and the whole thing is steeped, steeped in spring. It's like being on the inside, you know how I mean, like being inside the egg and just ready to chip the shell."

"Quite like that!" she assented, without conviction.

There was a little pause. The secretary said nothing. They were waiting for the wife to depart again.

"I suppose," said the latter, "you're awfully busy, as usual?"

"Just about the same," he said, pursing his mouth deprecatingly.

Again the blank pause, in which he waited for her to go away again.

"I know I'm interrupting you," she said.

"As a matter of fact," he said, "I was just watching those two blue-tits."

"Pair of little demons!" said the wife, blowing away the yellow feather from her finger-tip.

"Absolutely!" he said.

"Well, I'd better go, and let you get on with your work," she said.

"No hurry!" he said, with benevolent nonchalance. "As a matter of fact, I don't think it's a great success, working out of doors."

"What made you try it?" said the wife. "You know you never could do it."

"Miss Wrexall suggested it might make a change. But I don't think it altogether helps, do you, Miss Wrexall?"

"I'm sorry," said the little secretary.

"Why should you be sorry?" said the wife, looking down at her as a wolf might look down half benignly at a little black-and-tan mongrel. "You only suggested it for his good, I'm sure!"

"I thought the air might be good for him," the secretary admitted.

"Why do people like you never think about yourselves?" the wife asked.

The secretary looked her in the eye.

"I suppose we do, in a different way," she said.

"A *very* different way!" said the wife ironically. "Why don't you make *him* think about *you*?" she added, slowly, with a sort of drawl. "On a soft spring afternoon like this, you ought to have him dictating poems to you, about the blue birds of happiness fluttering round your dainty little feet. I know *I* would, if I were his secretary."

There was a dead pause. The wife stood immobile and statuesque, in an attitude characteristic of her, half turning back to the little secretary, half averted. She half turned her back on everything.

The secretary looked at him.

"As a matter of fact," he said, "I was doing an article on the Future of the Novel."

"I know that," said the wife. "That's what's so awful! Why not something lively in the life of the novelist?"

There was a prolonged silence, in which he looked pained, and somewhat remote, statuesque. The little secretary hung her head. The wife sauntered slowly away.

"Just where were we, Miss Wrexall?" came the sound of his voice.

The little secretary started. She was feeling profoundly indignant. Their beautiful relationship, his and hers, to be so insulted!

But soon she was veering downstream on the flow of his words, too busy to have any feelings, except one of elation at being so busy.

Tea-time came: the sister brought out the tea-tray into the garden. And immediately, the wife appeared. She had changed, and was wearing a chicory-blue dress of fine cloth. The little secretary had gathered up her papers and was departing, on rather high heels.

"Don't go, Miss Wrexall," said the wife.

The little secretary stopped short, then hesitated.

"Mother will be expecting me," she said.

"Tell her you're not coming. And ask your sister to bring another up. I want you to have tea with us."

Miss Wrexall looked at the man, who was reared on one elbow in the hammock, and was looking enigmatical, Hamletish.

He glanced at her quickly, then pursed his mouth in a boyish negligence.

"Yes, stay and have tea with us for once," he said. "I see strawberries, and I know you're the bird for them."

She glanced at him, smiled wanly, and hurried away to tell her mother. She even stayed long enough to slip on a silk dress.

"Why, how smart you are!" said the wife, when the little secretary reappeared on the lawn, in chicory-blue silk.

"Oh, don't look at my dress, compared to yours!" said Miss Wrexall. They were of the same colour, indeed!

"At least you earned yours, which is more than I did mine," said the wife, as she poured tea. "You like it strong?"

She looked with her heavy eyes at the smallish, birdy, blue-clad, overworked young woman, and her eyes seemed to speak many inexplicable dark volumes.

"Oh, as it comes, thank you," said Miss Wrexall, learning nervously forward.

"It's coming pretty black, if you want to ruin your digestion," said the wife.

"Oh, I'll have some water in it, then."

"Better, I should say."

"How'd the work go?—all right?" asked the wife, as they drank tea, and the two women looked at each other's blue dresses.

"Oh!" he said. "As well as you can expect. It was a piece of pure flummery. But it's what they want. Awful rot, wasn't it, Miss Wrexall?"

Miss Wrexall moved uneasily on her chair.

"It interested me," she said. "Though not so much as the novel."

"The novel? Which novel?" said the wife. "Is there another new one?"

Miss Wrexall looked at him. Not for worlds would she give away any of his literary activities.

"Oh, I was jut sketching out an idea to Miss Wrexall," he said.

"Tell us about it!" said the wife. "Miss Wrexall, you tell us what it's about."

She turned on her chair, and fixed the little secretary.

"I'm afraid—" Miss Wrexall squirmed—"I haven't got it very clearly myself, yet."

"Oh, go along! Tell us what you have got then!"

Miss Wrexall sat dumb and very vexed. She felt she was being baited. She looked at the blue pleatings of her skirt.

"I'm afraid I can't," she said.

"Why are you afraid you can't? You're so very competent. I'm sure you've got it all at your finger-ends. I expect you write a good deal of Mr. Gee's books for him, really. He gives you the hint, and you fill it all in. Isn't that how you do it?" She spoke ironically, and as if she were teasing a child. And then she glanced down at the fine pleatings of her own blue skirt, very fine and expensive.

"Of course you're not speaking seriously?" said Miss Wrexall, rising on her mettle.

"Of course I am! I've suspected for a long time—at least, for some time—that you write a good deal of Mr. Gee's books for him, from his hints."

It was said in a tone of raillery, but it was cruel.

"I should be terribly flattered," said Miss Wrexall, straightening herself, "if I didn't know you were only trying to make me feel fool."

"Make you feel a fool? My dear child!—why, nothing could be further from me! You're twice as clever, and a million times as competent as I am. Why, my dear child, I've the greatest admiration for you! I wouldn't do what you do, not for all the pearls in India. I *couldn't*, anyhow—"

Miss Wrexall closed up and was silent.

"Do you mean to say my books read as if—" he began, rearing up and speaking in a narrowed voice.

"I do!" said his wife. "*Just* as if Miss Wrexall had written them from your hints. I *honestly* thought she did—when you were too busy—"

"How very clever of you!" he said.

"Very!" she cried. "Especially if I was wrong!"

"Which you were," he said.

"How very extraordinary!" she cried. "Well, I am once more mistaken!"

There was a complete pause.

It was broken by Miss Wrexall, who was nervously twisting her fingers.

"You want to spoil what there is between me and him, I can see that," she said bitterly.

"My dear, but what *is* there between you and him?" said the wife.

"I was *happy* working with him, working for him! I was *happy* working for him!" cried Miss Wrexall, tears of indignant anger and chagrin in her eyes.

"My dear child!" cried the wife, with simulated excitement, "go *on* being happy working with him, go on being happy while you can! If it makes you happy, why then, enjoy it! Of course! Do you think I'd be so cruel as to want to take it away from you?—working with him? *I* can't do shorthand and typewriting and double-entrance bookkeeping, or whatever it's called. I tell you, I'm utterly incompetent. I never earn anything. I'm the parasite on the British oak, like the mistletoe. The blue bird doesn't flutter round my feet. Perhaps they're too big and trampling."

She looked down at her expensive shoes.

"If I *did* have a word of criticism to offer," she said, turning to her husband, "it would be to you, Cameron, for taking so much from her and giving her nothing."

"But he gives me everything, everything!" cried Miss Wrexall. "He gives me everything!"

"What do you mean by everything?" said the wife, turning on her sternly.

Miss Wrexall pulled up short. There was a snap in the air, and a change of currents.

"I mean nothing that *you* need begrudge me," said the little secretary rather haughtily. "I've never made myself cheap."

There was a blank pause.

"My God!" said the wife. "You don't call that being cheap? Why, I should say you got nothing out of him at all, you only give! And if you don't call that making yourself cheap—my God!"

"You see, we see things different," said the secretary.

"I should say we do!—*thank God!*" rejoined the wife.

"On whose behalf are you thanking God?" he asked sarcastically.

"Everybody's, I suppose! Yours, because you get everything for nothing, and Miss Wrexall's, because she seems to like it, and mine because I'm well out of it all."

"You *needn't* be out of it all," cried Miss Wrexall magnanimously, "if you didn't *put* yourself out of it all."

"Thank you, my dear, for your offer," said the wife, rising. "But I'm afraid no man can expect *two* blue birds of happiness to flutter round his feet; tearing out their little feathers!"

With which she walked away.

After a tense and desperate interim, Miss Wrexall cried:

"And *really*, need any woman be jealous of *me!*"

"Quite!" he said.

And that was all he did say.

❊   ❊   ❊

STACY AUMONIER
(1887-   )

AUMONIER, after completing his education at Cranleigh, began his career as a decorative designer and landscape painter. He began writing in 1913, since when he has contributed a number of short stories to most of the leading magazines of England and America.

Mrs. Beelbrow's Lions is reprinted by kind permission of the author and his representative, Curtis Brown, Ltd., from *Miss Bracegirdle and Others*, copyright, 1923, by Doubleday, Page & Company.

MRS. BEELBROW'S LIONS

MRS. POULTENEY-BEELBROW is the kind of a woman who drips with refinement. Everything else had been squeezed out of her. Even her hair, which once was red, has been dried to a rusty grey. Her narrow face is pinched and bloodless; the lines of her figure blurred by shapeless and colourless materials, as though she resented any suggestion of organic functioning as though blood itself were not quite "nice." The voice is high pitched, toneless, ice-cold. She speaks with dead monotony, without enthusiasm. And yet one can hardly describe Mrs. Beelbrow as a woman who has not had enthusiasms. Lions! —lions have been the determining passion of Mrs. Beelbrow's life. A life amidst lions can hardly be called an apathetic life, you might say.

I would like to have known Mrs. Beelbrow when she was quite young, although the condition is difficult to visualise. She is now—that quite indeterminate age which æsthetic women sometimes arrive at too soon and forsake too early. She might easily be in the early thirties; on the other hand, she might be in the late forties; even later, ever earlier—she is *so* refined, you see. You can imagine her doing nothing so vulgar as visiting the Royal Academy or reading a popular magazine. As for the cinema, or a revue—oh, my dear!

It is only her eyes which sometimes give you an inkling of a restless soul. They are almost green with a tiny grey pupil. She sometimes smiles with her lips, but never with her eyes, which are always roaming —searching—lions.

She was a Miss Poulteney (you know, the Hull shipping people), and she married Beelbrow the stockbroker. God knows why! You can seldom find Beelbrow. Sometimes you may observe him standing against the wall at one of those overpowering receptions she gives. He is tubby, genial and negative. He smiles at his wife—busily occupied with lions —and mutters:

"Wonderful woman, my wife—wonderful! um-m."

And then he retires to the refreshment-room and waits on people. Everyone will tell you that Mrs. Beelbrow was once a remarkably talented violinist, though we have never met anyone who has heard her play. She certainly knows something about music, and can talk shiveringly about every ancient and modern composer of note, in addition to many composers without note. But do not imagine that her discriminations are confined to music. She shivers about architecture, sculpture, painting, and literature. She dissects tone-poems, eulogises discords, subdivides futurism into seven distinct planes, considers Synge too sensational, professes a pallid admiration for Bach when performed in an empty church, is coldly contemptuous of the Renaissance, dislikes Dickens, Scott, Zola and Tolstoi (in spite of the latter being a Russian and a lion). By the way, everything Russian exercises a curious influence over her—Russian and Chinese. Things Japanese she condemns as *bourgeois*. She is enormously refined, a sybarite of æsthetic values. She has no children, but she keeps a marmoset, a Borzoi, five chows, two smoke-grey Persian cats, a parakeet, and some baby crocodiles in a sunk tank in the conservatory. The latter she keeps because they remind her of the slow movement of some sonata by Sibelius.

But it is of the lions she keeps that we would speak. They are not real lions, of course. Real lions are peculiarly commonplace—reminiscent of Landseer and the Zoological Gardens. Mrs. Beelbrow's lions roar in drawing-rooms and concert halls. They are most indigenous to the soil of Central or Eastern Europe. She imports them from Russia, Bohemia, Hungary, Austria, or Tcheko Slovakia. No other breeds are any good. Neither must they be popular in the generally accepted sense. If you say to Mrs. Beelbrow: "I heard Kreisler play the Bach *chachonne* very finely last night," she shivers and says: "Ah! but have you heard De Borch play the slow movement of the Sczhklski sonata?"

You weakly reply, "No." The name of De Borch seems familiar, but you had never heard of him as a violinist.

She leans backwards and regards you through half-closed eyes. Upon her face there creeps an expression of genuine sympathy. There is an almost imperceptible shrug of the shoulders, and she turns away. You mutter "Damn!" and also repair to the refreshment-room, where Mr. Beelbrow waits on you. (The refreshments are very good.) He says:

"Have you seen my wife? She's a wonderful woman—wonderful—um-m!"

We should mention that this "um-m" of Mr. Beelbrow is a curious kind of low hum that he affixes at the end of every statement. It seems to deliberately contradict just what he has said. It is like a genteel "I don't think!"

It is said that in the old days Mrs. Beelbrow used to make a hobby of genuine lions, famous opera singers and painters. There is a full length of her by Sargent in the billiard-room; a very good portrait, too, if somewhat merciless. It is characteristic of her that it should now be in the billiard-room—a room that is only used on the night of a great crush to deposit hats and coats that are crowded out of the cloak-room. Sargeant is *passé*. If you mention the portrait to her, she says:

"Ah! but have you seen the pastel of me by Splitz?"

The pastel by Splitz is in the place of honour in the drawing-room. You suspect that it is meant to be a woman by the puce-coloured drapery and what appears to be long hair—or is it a waterfall in the background? She says of it:

"It is wonderful! Splitz got into it the expression of all that I have yearned for and never achieved. You can feel the wave-lengths of my thoughts vibrating esoterically."

"Good luck to Splitz! I hope he got his cheque."

The day came when Mrs. Beelbrow tired of genuine lions.

They were a little disillusioning, too business-like, and too fond of being waited on by Mr. Beelbrow in the refreshment-room. And so she said:

"I will make my own lions."

She travelled abroad, taking with her the marmoset, two of the chows, one smoke-grey Persian cat, the parakeet, the crocodiles in a special tank, and Mr. Beelbrow. It was in Budapest that she discovered her first embryo lion. His name was Skrâtch. She heard him playing the fiddle in an obscure café. She went to hear him three nights running. On the third night she went up to him after the performance, and she said: "Come with me. I will make you a lion."

Now we are anxious to deal fairly by Skrâtch. He was young, talented, poor and hungry. He had the normal ambitions, desires, appetites, and the weaknesses of the normal young man. He had often dreamed of being a lion, and after one or two beers he frequently persuaded himself that the accomplishment was not impossible. Nevertheless, he had never been blind to its difficulties. And here was a woman who came to him and said, quite simply: "I will make you a lion," in the same way that she might have said, "I will cut you a liver-sausage sandwich."

How could you expect Skrâtch to take it?

When he arrived in London he impressed us as being quite a pleasant, amiable young man. He had a thin body, but rather puffy sallow cheeks, jet black hair, and brown eyes. He was obviously at first a little apprehensive, suspicious. The eyes seemed to say:

"Oh well, anyway, they can't eat me."

He lived at Mrs. Beelbrow's, and had what she called finishing lessons with a Polish professor. It was exactly a year before Skrâtch was launched into lionhood. During that time no one heard him play a note. And yet a most remarkable thing happened in connection with the launching. Months before Skrâtch appeared in public the newspapers were always containing paragraphs about "a remarkable young violinist shortly expected from Budapest. Said to be a second Ysaye." Mrs. Beelbrow's drawing-room was always crowded, but Skrâtch never played. He was introduced to all kinds of people, and whispered about. I remember meeting there the critics of the,—no, perhaps this kind of revelation is not quite fair. Anyway, when Skrâtch gave his first orchestral concert at the Queen's Hall the affair had been so cleverly prepared that the place was packed. The press reviews, when not eulogistic, were for the most part non-committal. Dogs are afraid to bark at a lion. It would be a terrible blunder to condemn a real lion. One must wait and see what the general verdict is.

There is no denying also that Skrâtch did play very well. He was what is known as a talented violinist. One may assert without fear of contradiction that there were at that time in London probably thirty or forty violinists (leaving out, of course, the few supreme artists) equally as talented as Skrâtch. But they had not the *flair* of lions. They just went on with their job, playing when an opportunity occurred, but for the most part teaching.

The following day an advertisement appeared in the papers announcing that "owing to the colossal success of Herr Skrâtch's concert, three more would follow on such-and-such dates." The advertisement must have been sent in before the colossally successful concert took place. From that day forward Skrâtch did indeed become a qualified lion. The more responsible papers certainly began to damn him with faint praise, and even to pull him to pieces. But if you assert a thing frequently enough, insistently enough, and in large enough type, people will come to accept it. He became a kind of papier-maché lion and it didn't do the boy any good. For two years the hoardings and the newspapers reeked with advertisements and notices about the "great violinist Skrâtch."

And then he began to develop in other ways. From a slim, nervous boy he rapidly became a robustious, self-assured, florid man. His body filled out, his cheeks reddened, his hair grew unmanageable. He adopted an eccentric mode of dress. And Mrs. Beelbrow? The affair reacted upon her just as one might expect. She became more precious, more aloof, more impossible. She floated around the drawing-room with her protégé with an air which implied:

"Look at me! I'm the woman who made a lion!"

She wore a tiger skin and left Mr. Beelbrow at home to look after the live stock.

And after the first flush of triumph and excitement, Skrâtch treated Mrs. Beelbrow with complete indifference and contempt. He left lighted cigar-ends on the lid of the grand piano, spilt wine on his bed-linen, walked about the house all day in a dressing-gown, threw his boots at the servants and snubbed visitors. He would get up from the table in the middle of a meal and walk out of the room without an apology. He was even rude to her in public, and she revelled in it. The ruder he was the more delighted she appeared. She would glance round the room proudly, as much as to say:

"There! Didn't I tell you I had made a lion!"

They went about everywhere together. They went to the opera, the theatre, to concerts and receptions, for motor rides in the country, and they were always alone. Mr. Beelbrow was very busy, you see, making money in the city. (He had to do that to pay for Herr Skrâtch's publicity campaign.)

Of course, people began to talk. They might have talked on much less evidence than they had. The thing was simply thrown at them. She glued herself to him, and he accepted her and what she gave him as only right and proper. Sometimes he would treat her with playful familiarity. He would put his arm round her shoulders and call her "ol gel!" All very well, but how old really was Mrs. Beelbrow? What was happening in the dark places of *her* heart? Of course, it couldn't go on forever. We all shook our heads and were very wise, and we were right. It went on for nine months, and then Mr. Beelbrow—no, Mr. Beelbrow did nothing. He just sat tight, helped people to hock-cup, and expatiated upon his wife's remarkable character and abilities. The disruption came from outside.

Another woman appeared on the scene. Her name was Fanny Friedlander. She was an accompanist. Now, if you had wanted to invent a complete antithesis to Mrs. Beelbrow, Fanny would have saved you the trouble. She was it. She was young, common, ignorant and frivolous; at the same time she had emotional warmth. There was something sympathetic and lovable about her. She was not exclusively a man-hunter. She liked to be petted and admired. When she accompanied she wore red carnations in her hair, and cast glad, furtive glances at the audience, and sometimes at the soloist, who, of course was Herr Skrâtch.

Herr Skrâtch was not the kind of gentleman to make any bones about such a position. He flirted with her outrageously, even on the platform. Whether Mrs. Beelbrow made any protest about this affair at its inception is not known. By the time the infatuation was apparent it was too late. Inflated by his meretricious successes, he was in no mood to brook interference. Mrs. Beelbrow's face expressed little. I really believe she was rather fascinated by the girl herself. She seemed to be watching, a little bewildered and uncertain how to act.

It ended in the three of them going about everywhere together, the usual unsatisfactory triangle. The fact that she had to play his accompaniments was sufficient excuse for Fanny Friedlander to go with him to concerts where he was playing, and to call at Mrs. Beelbrow's for rehearsals, but hardly an excuse for her to go to the opera, the theatre, and motor rides, or even to stop all the afternoon at Mrs. Beelbrow's and then stay on to dinner. It was surmised that Mrs. Beelbrow only tolerated it because she knew that if she turned the girl out, Skrâtch would have gone with her. She appeared to be content with the crumbs the younger woman left over. Ah! but only for the moment, we were convinced.

At that time, as if conscious of his delinquency, Herr Skrâtch was a little more polite to Mrs. Beelbrow; whilst the girl made no end of a fuss of her in a loud common way that must have jarred the good lady's sensibilities horribly. We waited to see what would happen next, what would be the next move of Mrs. Beelbrow to rid herself of this dangerous rival. To our surprise, a few weeks later the girl went there to live. She was actually living in the Beelbrow's house! Was there ever a queerer *ménage à quatre?* There was Mrs. Beelbrow the lion-hunter, badly mauled by one of her own lions, entertaining her most dangerous enemy. She must have shut her eyes to all kinds of things. Skrâtch was behaving abominably. The girl was not the kind you could trust anyway. There was Mr. Beelbrow, quite negative, merely earning the money to support the absurd drama.

"It's incredible," said Jimmy Beale, one night in the club, "that a woman as conceited as Mrs. Beelbrow is, could possibly put up with such a damned indignity. It's making her look the prize fool of London."

"Love is more powerful than a sense of dignity," remarked some sententious bore from the corner.

Love? Well, an unanalysable quantity. I was perhaps the only one fortunate enough to have the opportunity to judge of the *dénouement* by any practical evidence. And even then it was only a fluke, a glance. It occurred a few nights before Skrâtch disappeared. Some say he went back to the obscure café in Budapest, taking the girl with him. It is hardly likely in view of the handsome *dot* which someone presented to Fanny.

It was one of Mrs. Beelbrow's most overwhelming crushes. You could not hear yourself speak for the roar of lions. I was squeezed against the folding doors. Behind a palm in the corner was an empire mirror, tilted at an angle. It was about the only thing I could see. It gave me a good view of certain people a little farther down the room. The first person I saw was Mrs. Beelbrow, and as I glanced at her I saw an expression come over her face, an expression I can only describe as one of blind jealousy—a nasty, vindictive, dangerous look.

"Oh, ho!" I thought, and sought for the reflection of Fanny or Herr Skrâtch. But to my astonishment I realised very clearly that her glance was not directed at these two at all. She was looking at Mr. Beelbrow, whose wicked, malevolent little eyes were fixed on Fanny's. Skrâtch for the moment was occupied with some other woman.

You might imagine that the defection of Skrâtch would have broken Mrs. Beelbrow's heart for the business. But, oh, dear, no! don't you believe it. Whatever you may say or think about Mrs. Beelbrow, she has proved herself a true and indomitable lion-hunter. Only last Thursday, I was again in her crowded drawing-room. A little East-end Jewess was playing the piano quite nicely. Mrs. Beelbrow was standing by the folding-doors, her face set and taut. When the child had finished, she murmured:

"Ah, if Teresa Carreño could have heard that! Teresa never reached that velvety warmth in her mezzo passages. I believe the child must be the reincarnation of—who would it be, Liszt? No, someone more Southern, more Byzantine. I will make her a lion."

In the refreshment-room Mr. Beelbrow was ladling out hock-cup as usual. When I approached him he said:

"Halloa, old boy! Have some of this? Good! Have you seen my wife? She's a wonderful woman—wonderful—um-m."

KATHERINE MANSFIELD
(1890-1923)

MISS MANSFIELD was born and spent her early years in New
Zealand. She married J. Middleton Murry, with whom she had been
associated in the publication of *Rhythm*, a literary review. She
achieved fame with her collection of brilliant short stories entitled
Bliss (1920), which was followed by *The Garden Party* (1922).
Meantime she had contributed to the *Athenæum* which was edited
by her husband. *The Apple-Tree*, printed here by kind permission of
Mr. Murry, has never before appeared in any book.

THE APPLE-TREE

THERE were two orchards belonging to the old house. One, that
we called the "wild" orchard lay beyond the vegetable garden; it
was planted with bitter cherries and damsons and transparent yellow plums. For some reason it lay under a cloud; we never played there,
we did not even trouble to pick up the fallen fruit; and there, every
Monday morning, to the round open space in the middle, the servant girl
and the washerwoman carried the wet linen; grandmother's nightdresses,
father's striped shirts, the hired man's cotton trousers and the servant
girl's "dreadfully vulgar" salmon pink flannelette drawers jigged and
slapped in horrid familiarity.

But the other orchard, far away and hidden from the house, lay at
the foot of a little hill and stretched right over to the edge of the paddocks—to the clumps of wattles bobbing yellow in the bright and the
blue gums with their streaming sickle-shaped leaves. There, under the
fruit trees the grass grew so thick and coarse that it tangled and knotted
in your shoes as you walked, and even on the hottest day it was damp to
touch when you stooped and parted it this way and that looking for windfalls—the apples marked with a bird's beak, the big bruised pears, the
quinces, so good to eat with a pinch of salt, but so delicious to smell that
you could not bite for sniffing. . . .

One year the orchard had its Forbidden Tree. It was an apple discovered by father and a friend during an after-dinner prowl one Sunday
afternoon.

"Great Scott!" said the friend, lighting upon it with every appearance of admiring astonishment: "Isn't that a——?" And a rich, splendid name settled like an unknown bird upon the little tree.

"Yes, I believe it is," said father lightly. He knew nothing whatever
about the names of fruit trees.

"Great Scott!" said the friend again: "They're wonderful apples.

Nothing like 'em—and you're going to have a tip-top crop. Marvellous apples! You can't beat 'em!"

"No, they're very fine—very fine," said father carelessly, but looking upon the tree with new and lively interest.

"They're rare—they're very rare. Hardly ever see 'em in England nowadays," said the visitor and set a seal on father's delight. For father was a self-made man and the price he had to pay for everything was so huge and so painful that nothing rang so sweet to him as to hear his purchase praised. He was young and sensitive still. He still wondered whether in the deepest sense he got his money's worth. He still had hours when he walked up and down in the moonlight half deciding to "chuck this confounded rushing to the office every day—and clear out—clear out once and for all." And now to discover that he'd a valuable apple tree thrown in with the orchard—an apple tree that this Johnny from England positively envied.

"Don't touch that tree. Do you hear me, children!" said he bland and firm; and when the guest had gone, with quite another voice and manner:

"If I catch either of you touching those apples you shall not only go to bed—you shall each have a good sound whipping!" Which merely added to its magnificence.

Every Sunday morning after church father with Bogey and me tailing after walked through the flower garden, down the violet path, past the lace-bark tree, past the white rose and syringa bushes, and down the hill to the orchard. The apple tree—like the Virgin Mary—seemed to have been miraculously warned of its high honour, standing apart from its fellow, bending a little under its rich clusters, fluttering its polished leaves, important and exquisite before father's awful eye. His heart swelled to the sight—we knew his heart swelled. He put his hands behind his back and screwed up his eyes in the way he had. There it stood—the accidental thing—the thing that no one had been aware of when the hard bargain was driven. It hadn't been counted on, hadn't in a way been paid for. If the house had been burned to the ground at that time it would have meant less to him than the destruction of his tree. And how we played up to him, Bogey and I, Bogey with his scratched knees pressed together, his hands behind his back, too, and a round cap on his head with "H.M.S. Thunderbolt" printed across it.

The apples turned from pale green to yellow; then they had deep pink stripes painted on them, and then the pink melted all over the yellow, reddened, and spread into a fine clear crimson.

At last the day came when father took out of his waistcoat pocket a little pearl pen-knife. He reached up. Very slowly and very carefully he picked two apples growing on a bough.

"By Jove! They're warm," cried father in amazement. "They're wonderful apples! Tip-top! Marvellous!" he echoed. He rolled them over in his hands.

"Look at that!" he said. "Not a spot—not a blemish!" And he walked through the orchard with Bogey and me stumbling after, to a tree stump under the wattles. We sat, one on either side of father. He laid one apple down, opened the pearl pen-knife and neatly and beautifully cut the other in half.

"By Jove! Look at that!" he exclaimed.

"Father!" we cried, dutiful but really enthusiastic, too. For the lovely red colour had bitten right through the white flesh of the apple; it was pink to the shiny black pips lying so justly in their scaly pods. It looked as though the apple had been dipped in wine.

"Never seen *that* before," said father. "You won't find an apple like that in a hurry!" He put it to his nose and pronounced an unfamiliar word. "Bouquet! What a bouquet!" And then he handed to Bogey one half, to me the other.

"Don't *bolt* it!" said he. It was agony to give even so much away. I knew it, while I took mine humbly and humbly Bogey took his.

Then he divided the second with the same neat beautiful little cut of the pearl knife.

I kept my eyes on Bogey. Together we took a bite. Our mouths were full of a floury stuff, a hard, faintly bitter skin,—a horrible taste of something dry. . . .

"Well?" asked father, very jovial. He had cut his two halves into quarters and was taking out the little pods. "Well?"

Bogey and I stared at each other, chewing desperately. In that second of chewing and swallowing a long silent conversation passed between us—and a strange meaning smile. We swallowed. We edged near father, just touching him.

"Perfect!" we lied. "Perfect—father. Simply lovely!"

But it was no use. Father spat his out and never went near the apple tree again.

❊ ❊ ❊

ALDOUS LEONARD HUXLEY
(1894-   )

HUXLEY is one of the younger writers who has leaped into prominence with his short stories. He was educated at Eton and Balliol College, Oxford. He has to his credit several volumes of stories as well as a novel and a book of poems.

Hubert and Minnie is reprinted by kind permission of the author and his representatives, James B. Pinker and Son, Inc., from *Young Archimedes,* copyright, 1924, by George H. Doran Company.

HUBERT AND MINNIE

FOR Hubert Lapell this first love-affair was extremely important. "Important" was the word he had used himself when he was writing about it in his diary. It was an event in his life, a real event for a change. It marked, he felt, a genuine turning-point in his spiritual development.

"Voltaire," he wrote in his diary—and he wrote it a second time in one of his letters to Minnie—"Voltaire said that one died twice; once with the death of the whole body and once before, with the death of one's capacity to love. And in the same way one is born twice, the second time being on the occasion when one first falls in love. One is born, then, into a new world—a world of intenser feelings, heightened values, more penetrating insights." And so on.

In point of actual fact Hubert found this new world a little disappointing. The intenser feelings proved to be rather mild! not by any means up to literary standards.

> "I tell thee I am mad
> In Cressid's love. Thou answer'st: she is fair;
> Pour'st in the open ulcer of my heart
> Her eyes, her hair, her cheek, her gait, her voice. . . ."

No, it certainly wasn't quite that. In his diary, in his letters to Minnie, he painted, it is true, a series of brilliant and romantic landscapes of the new world. But they were composite imaginary landscapes in the manner of Salvator Rosa—richer, wilder, more picturesquely clear-obscure than the real thing. Hubert would seize with avidity on the least velleity of an unhappiness, a physical desire, a spiritual yearning, to work it up in his letters and journals into something substantially romantic. There were times, generally very late at night, when he succeeded in persuading himself that he was indeed the wildest, unhappiest, most passionate of lovers. But in the daytime he went about his business nourishing something like a grievance against love. The thing was a bit of a fraud; yes, really, he decided, rather a fraud. All the same, he supposed it was important.

For Minnie, however, love was no fraud at all. Almost from the first moment she had adored him. A common friend had brought him to one of her Wednesday evenings. "This is Mr. Lapell; but he's too young to be called anything but Hubert." That was how he had been introduced. And laughing, she had taken his hand and called him Hubert at once. He too had laughed, rather nervously. "My name's Minnie," she said. But he had been too shy to call her anything at all that evening. His brown hair was tufty and untidy, like a little boy's, and he had shy grey eyes that never looked at you for more than a glimpse at a time, but turned away almost at once, as though they were afraid. Quickly he glanced at you, eagerly—then away again; and his musical voice, with its sudden emphases, its quick modulations from high to low, seemed always to address itself to a ghost floating low down and a little to one side of the person to whom he was talking. Above the brows was a forehead beautifully domed, with a pensive wrinkle running up from between the eyes. In repose his full-lipped mouth pouted a little, as though he were expressing some chronic discontent with the world. And, of course, thought Minnie, the world wasn't beautiful enough for his idealism.

"But after all," he had said earnestly that first evening, "one has the world of thought to live in. That, at any rate, is simple and clear and beautiful. One can always live apart from the brutal scramble."

And from the depths of the arm-chair in which, fragile, tired, and in these rather "artistic" surroundings almost incongruously elegant, she was sitting, Helen Glamber laughed her clear little laugh. "I think, on the contrary," she said (Minnie remembered every incident of that first evening), "I think one ought to rush about and know thousands of people, and eat and drink enormously, and make love incessantly, and shout and laugh and knock people over the head." And having vented these Rabelaisian sentiments, Mrs. Glamber dropped back with a sigh of fatigue, covering her eyes with a thin white hand; for she had a splitting headache, and the light hurt her.

"Really!" Minnie protested, laughing. She would have felt rather shocked if any one else had said that; but Helen Glamber was allowed to say anything.

Hubert reaffirmed his quietism. Elegant, weary, infinitely fragile, Mrs. Glamber lay back in her arm-chair, listening. Or perhaps, under her covering hand, she was trying to go to sleep.

She had adored him at first sight. Now that she looked back she could see that it had been at first sight. Adored him protectively, maternally—for he was only twenty and very young, in spite of the wrinkle between his brows, and the long words, and the undergraduate's newly discovered knowledge; only twenty, and she was nearly twenty-nine. And she had fallen in love with his beauty, too. Ah, passionately.

Hubert, perceiving it later, was surprised and exceedingly flattered. This had never happened to him before. He enjoyed being worshipped, and since Minnie had fallen so violently in love with him, it seemed the most natural thing in the world for him to be in love with Minnie. True, if she had not started by adoring him, it would never have occurred to Hubert to fall in love with her. At their first meeting he had found her certainly very nice, but not particularly exciting. Afterwards, the manifest expression of her adoration had made him find her more interesting, and in the end he had fallen in love himself. But perhaps it was not to be wondered at if he found the process a little disappointing.

But still, he reflected on those secret occasions when he had to admit to himself that something was wrong with this passion, love without possession could never, surely, in the nature of things, be quite the genuine article. In his diary he recorded aptly those two quatrains of John Donne:

> "So must pure lovers' souls descend
> To affections and to faculties,
> Which sense may reach and apprehend,
> Else a great prince in prison lies.
>
> To our bodies turn we then, that so
> Weak men on love revealed may look;
> Love's mysteries in souls do grow,
> But yet the body is his book."

At their next meeting he recited them to Minnie. The conversation which followed, compounded as it was of philosophy and personal confidences, was exquisite. It really, Hubert felt, came up to literary standards.

The next morning Minnie rang up her friend Helen Glamber and asked if she might come to tea that afternoon. She had several things to talk to her about. Mrs. Glamber sighed as she hung up the receiver. "Minnie's coming to tea," she called, turning towards the open door.

From across the passage her husband's voice came back to her. "Good Lord!" it said in a tone of far-away horror, of absent-minded resignation; for John Glamber was deep in his work and there was only a little of him left, so to speak, above the surface to react to the bad news.

Helen Glamber sighed again, and propping herself more comfortably against her pillows she reached for her book. She knew that far-away voice and what it meant. It meant that he wouldn't answer if she went on with the conversation; only say "h'm" or "m'yes." And if she persisted after that, it meant that he'd say, plaintively, heartbreakingly, "Darling, you *must* let me get on with my work." And at that moment she would so much have liked to talk a little. Instead, she went on reading at the point where she had broken off to answer Minnie's telephone call.

"By this time the flames had enveloped the gynecæum. Nineteen times did the heroic Patriarch of Alexandria venture into the blazing fabric, from which he succeeded in rescuing all but two of its lovely occupants, twenty-seven in number, all of whom he caused to be transported at once to his own private apartments. . . ."

It was one of those instructive books John liked her to read. History, mystery, lesson, and law. But at the moment she didn't feel much like history. She felt like talking. And that was out of the question; absolutely out of it.

She put down her book and began to file her nails and think of poor Minnie. Yes, poor Minnie. Why was it that one couldn't help saying Good Lord! heartfeltly, when one heard she was coming to tea? And why did one never have the heart to refuse to let her come to tea? She was pathetic, but pathetic in such a boring way. There are some people you like being kind to, people you want to help and befriend. People that look at you with the eyes of sick monkeys. Your heart breaks when you see them. But poor Minnie had none of the charms of a sick monkey. She was just a great big healthy young woman of twenty-eight who ought to have been married and the mother of children, and who wasn't. She would have made such a good wife, such an admirably solicitous and careful mother. But it just happened that none of the men she knew had ever wanted to marry her. And why should they want to? When she came into a room, the light seemed to grow perceptibly dimmer, the electric tension slackened off. She brought no life with her; she absorbed what there was, she was like so much blotting-paper. No wonder nobody wanted to marry her. And yet, of course, it was the only thing. Particularly as she was always falling in love herself. The only thing.

"John!" Mrs. Glamber suddenly called. "Is it really true about ferrets?"

"Ferrets?" the voice from across the passage repeated with a remote irritation. "Is what true about ferrets?"

"That the females die if they're not mated."

"How on earth should I know?"

"But you generally know everything."

"But, my darling, really. . . ." The voice was plaintive, full of reproach.

Mrs. Glamber clapped her hand over her mouth and only took it off again to blow a kiss. "All right," she said very quickly. "All right. Really. I'm sorry. I won't do it again. Really." She blew another kiss towards the door.

"But ferrets . . ." repeated the voice.

"Sh—sh, sh—sh."

"Why ferrets?"

"Darling," said Mrs. Glamber almost sternly, "you really must go on with your work."

Minnie came to tea. She put the case—hypothetically at first, as though it were the case of a third person; then, gaining courage, she put it personally. It was her own case. Out of the depths of her untroubled, pagan innocence, Helen Glamber brutally advised her. "If you want to go to bed with the young man," she said, "go to bed with him. The thing has no importance in itself. At least not much. It's only important because it makes possible more secret confidences, because it strengthens affection, makes the man in a way dependent on you. And then, of course, it's the natural thing. I'm all for nature except when it comes to painting one's face. They say that ferrets . . ." But Minnie noticed that she never finished the sentence. Appalled and fascinated, shocked and yet convinced, she listened.

"My darling," said Mrs. Glamber that evening when her husband came home—for he hadn't been able to face Minnie; he had gone to the Club for tea—"who was it that invented religion, and sin, and all that? And why?"

John laughed. "It was invented by Adam," he said, "for various little transcendental reasons which you would probably find it difficult to appreciate. But also for the very practical purpose of keeping Eve in order."

"Well, if you call complicating people's lives keeping them in order, then I dare say you're right." Mrs. Glamber shook her head. "I find it all too obscure. At sixteen, yes. But one really ought to have grown out of that sort of thing by twenty. And at thirty—the woman's nearly thirty, you know—well, really . . ."

In the end, Minnie wrote to Hubert telling him that she had made up her mind. Hubert was staying in Hertfordshire with his friend Watchett. It was a big house, the food was good, one was very comfortable; and old Mr. Watchett, moreover, had a very sound library. In the impenetrable shade of the Wellingtonias Hubert and Ted Watchett played croquet and discussed the best methods of cultivating the Me. You could do a good deal, they decided, with art—books, you know, and pictures and music. "Listen to Stravinsky's *Sacre*," said Ted Watchett, "and you're for ever excused from going to Tibet or the Gold Coast or any of those awful places. And then there's Dostoievsky instead of murder, and D. H. Lawrence as a substitute for sex."

"All the same," said Hubert, "one must have a *certain* amount of actual non-imaginative experience." He spoke earnestly, abstractedly; but Minnie's letter was in his pocket. "*Gnosce teipsum.* You can't really know yourself without coming into collision with events, can you?"

Next day, Ted's cousin, Phœbe, arrived. She had red hair and a milky skin, and was more or less on the musical comedy stage. "One foot on and one foot off," she explained. "The splits." And there and then she did them, the splits, on the drawing-room carpet. "It's quite easy," she said, laughing, and jumped up again with an easy grace that fairly took one's breath away. Ted didn't like her. "Tiresome girl," he said. "So silly, too. Consciously silly, silly on purpose, which makes it worse." And, it was true, she did like boasting about the amount of champagne she could put away without getting buffy, and the number of times she had exceeded the generous allowance and been "blind to the world." She liked talking about her admirers in terms which might make you suppose that they were all her accepted lovers. But then she had the justification of her vitality and her shining red hair.

"Vitality," Hubert wrote in his diary (he contemplated a distant date, after, or preferably before, his death, when these confessions and aphorisms would be published), "vitality can make claims on the world almost as imperiously as can beauty. Sometimes beauty and vitality meet in one person."

It was Hubert who arranged that they should stay at the mill. One of his friends had once been there with a reading party, and found the place comfortable, secluded, and admirably quiet. Quiet, that is to say, with the special quietness peculiar to mills. For the silence there was not the silence of night on a mountain; it was a silence made of continuous thunder. At nine o'clock every morning the mill-wheel began to turn, and its roaring never stopped all day. For the first moments the noise was terrifying, was almost unbearable. Then, after a little, one grew accustomed to it. The thunder became, by reason of its very unintermittence, a perfect silence, wonderfully rich and profound.

At the back of the mill was a little garden hemmed in on three sides by the house, the outhouses, and a high brick wall, and open on the fourth towards the water. Looking over the parapet, Minnie watched it sliding past. It was like a brown snake with arrowy markings on its back; and it crawled, it glided, it slid along for ever. She sat there, waiting; her train, from London, had brought her here soon after lunch; Hubert, coming across country from the Watchetts, would hardly arrive before six. The water flowed beneath her eyes like time, like destiny, smoothly towards some new and violent event.

The immense noise that in this garden was silence enveloped her. Inured, her mind moved in it as though in its native element. From beyond the parapet came the coolness and the weedy smell of water. But if she turned back towards the garden, she breathed at once the hot perfume of sunlight beating on flowers and ripening fruit. In the afternoon sunlight all the world was ripe. The old red house lay there, ripe, like a dropped plum; the walls were riper than the fruits of the nectarine trees so tenderly and neatly crucified on their warm bricks. And that richer silence of unremitting thunder seemed, as it were, the powdery bloom on a day that had come to exquisite maturity and was hanging, round as a peach and juicy with life and happiness, waiting in the sunshine for the bite of eager teeth.

At the heart of this fruit-ripe world Minnie waited. The water flowed towards the wheel; smoothly, smoothly—then it fell, it broke itself to pieces on the turning wheel. And time was sliding onwards, quietly towards an event that would shatter all the smoothness of her life.

"If you really want to go to bed with the young man, go to bed with him." She could hear Helen's clear, shrill voice saying impossible, brutal things. If any one else had said them, she would have run out of the room. But in Helen's mouth they seemed, somehow, so simple, so innocuous, and so true. And yet all that other people had said or implied—at home, at school, among the people she was used to meeting—seemed equally true.

But then, of course, there was love. Hubert had written a Shakespearean sonnet which began:

> "Love hallows all whereon 'tis truly placed,
> Turns dross to gold with one touch of his dart,
> Makes matter mind, extremest passion chaste,
> And builds a temple in the lustful heart."

She thought that very beautiful. And very true. It seemed to throw a bridge between Helen and the other people. Love, true love, made all the difference. It justified. Love—how much, how much she loved.

Time passed and the light grew richer as the sun declined out of the height of the sky. The day grew more and more deliciously ripe, swelling with unheard-of sweetness. Over its sun-flushed cheeks the thundery silence of the mill-wheel spread the softest, peachiest of blooms. Minnie sat on the parapet, waiting. Sometimes she looked down at the sliding water, sometimes she turned her eyes towards the garden. Time flowed, but she was now no more afraid of that shattering event that thundered there, in the future. The ripe sweetness of the afternoon seemed to enter into her spirit, filling it to the brim. There was no more room for doubts, or fearful anticipations, or regrets. She was happy. Tenderly, with a tenderness she could not have expressed in words, only with the gentlest of light kisses, with fingers caressingly drawn through the ruffled hair, she thought of Hubert, her Hubert.

Hubert, Hubert. . . . And suddenly, startlingly, he was standing there at her side.

"Oh," she said, and for a moment she stared at him with round brown eyes, in which there was nothing but astonishment. Then the expression changed. "Hubert," she said softly.

Hubert took her hand and dropped it again; looked at her for an instant, then turned away. Leaning on the parapet, he stared down into the sliding water; his face was unsmiling. For a long time both were silent. Minnie remained where she was, sitting quite still, her eyes fixed on the young man's averted face. She was happy, happy, happy. The long day ripened and ripened, perfection after perfection.

"Minnie," said the young man suddenly, and with a loud abruptness, as though he had been a long time deciding himself to speak and had at last succeeded in bringing out the prepared and pent-up words, "I feel I've behaved very badly towards you. I never ought to have asked you to come here. It was wrong. I'm sorry."

"But I came because I wanted to," Minnie exclaimed.

Hubert glanced at her, then turned away his eyes and went on addressing a ghost that floated, it seemed, just above the face of the sliding water. "It was too much to ask. I shouldn't have done it. For a man it's different. But for a woman . . ."

"But, I tell you, I wanted to."

"It's too much."

"It's nothing," said Minnie, "because I love you." And leaning forward, she ran her fingers through his hair. Ah, tenderness that no words could express! "You silly boy," she whispered. "Did you think I didn't love you enough for that?"

Hubert did not look up. The water slid and slid away before his eyes; Minnie's fingers played in his hair, ran caressingly over the nape of his neck. He felt suddenly a positive hatred for this woman. Idiot! Why couldn't she take a hint? He didn't want her. And why on earth had he ever imagined that he did? All the way in the train he had been asking himself that question. Why? Why? And the question had asked itself still more urgently just now as, standing at the garden door, he had looked out between the apple tree and watched her, unobserved, through a long minute—watched her sitting there on the parapet, turning her vague brown eyes now at the water, now towards the garden, and smiling to herself with an expression that had seemed to him so dim and vacuous that he could almost have fancied her an imbecile.

And with Phœbe yesterday he had stood on the crest of the bare chalk down. Like a sea at their feet stretched the plain, and above the dim horizon towered toward heroic clouds. Fingers of the wind lifted the red locks of her hair. She stood as though poised, ready to leap off into the boisterous air. "How I should like to fly!" she said. "There's something particularly attractive about airmen, I always think." And she had gone running down the hill.

But Minnie, with her dull hair, her apple-red cheeks, and big, slow body, was like a peasant girl. How had he ever persuaded himself that he wanted her? And what made it much worse, of course, was that she adored him, embarrassingly, tiresomely, like a too affectionate spaniel that insists on tumbling about at your feet and licking your hand just when you want to sit quietly and concentrate on serious things.

Hubert moved away, out of reach of her caressing hand. He lifted towards her for a moment a pair of eyes that had become, as it were, opaque with a cold anger; then dropped them again.

"The sacrifice is too great," he said in a voice that sounded to him like somebody else's voice. He found it very difficult to say this sort of thing convincingly. "I can't ask it of you," the actor pursued. "I won't."

"But it isn't a sacrifice," Minnie protested. "It's a joy, it's happiness. Oh, can't you understand?"

Hubert did not answer. Motionless, his elbows on the parapet, he stared down into the water. Minnie looked at him, perplexed only, at first; but, all at once she was seized with a nameless agonising doubt that grew and grew within her, as the silence prolonged itself, like some dreadful cancer of the spirit, until it had eaten away all her happiness, until there was nothing left in her mind but doubt and apprehension.

"What is it?" she said at last. "Why are you so strange? What is it, Hubert? What is it?

Leaning anxiously forward, she laid her two hands on either side of his averted face and turned it towards her. Blank and opaque with anger were the eyes. "What is it?" she repeated. "Hubert, what is it?"

Hubert disengaged himself. "It's no good," he said in a smothered voice. "No good at all. It was a mistake. I'm sorry. I think I'd better go away. The trap's still at the door."

And without waiting for her to say anything, without explaining himself any further, he turned and walked quickly away, almost ran, towards the house. Well, thank goodness, he said to himself, he was out of that. He hadn't done it very well, or handsomely, or courageously; but, at any rate, he was out of it. Poor Minnie! He felt sorry for her; but after all, what could he do about it? Poor Minnie! Still, it rather flattered his vanity to think that she would be mourning over him. And in any case, he reassured his conscience, she couldn't really mind very much. But on the other hand, his vanity reminded him, she did adore him. Oh, she absolutely worshipped . . .

The door closed behind him. Minnie was alone again in the garden. Ripe, ripe it lay there in the late sunshine. Half of it was in shadow now; but the rest of it, in the coloured evening light, seemed to have come to the final and absolute perfection of maturity. Bloomy with thundery silence, the choicest fruit of all time hung there, deliciously sweet, sweet to the core; hung flushed and beautiful on the brink of darkness.

Minnie sat there quite still, wondering what had happened. Had he gone, had he really gone? The door closed behind him with a bang, and almost as though the sound were a signal prearranged, a man walked out from the mill on to the dam and closed the sluice. And all at once

the wheel was still.   Apocalyptically there was silence; the silence of
soundlessness took the place of that other silence that was uninterrupted
sound.   Gulfs opened endlessly out around her; she was alone.   Across
the void of soundlessness a belated bee trailed its thin buzzing; the spar-
rows chirped, and from across the water came the sound of voices and
far-away laughter.   And as though woken from a sleep, Minnie looked
up and listened, fearfully, turning her head from side to side.

GERMANY

Introduction

GERMAN literature does not begin to assume national importance until the turn of the twelfth century. Until then Germany had gone through a preparatory period, producing little of significance. The *Lay of Hildebrand* (c. 800) is the earliest extant fragment of a national saga, which we owe to the Saxon, or the Low German races, who alone seemed able to give literary expression to the memories handed down from the fifth century.

In the thirteenth century we see the rise of the Minnesingers, who, like the Provençal troubadours, developed their songs of love and chivalry, much more robust and sincere than the French sources on which they are based. During this period flourished the great triumvirate of Minnesingers, Wolfram von Eschenbach, Walther von der Vogelweide, and Gottfried von Strassburg. The first of these gave shape to the magnificent epic romance, *Parsifal;* the last of these wrote what may be safely considered as the greatest epic romance in Europe, *Tristan.* At the same time was compiled that "monument of mediæval German poetry," the Nibelungenlied.

By the middle of the fourteenth century, chivalry was rapidly declining. While the stories of knighthood and courtliness still appealed, they had to be adapted to the demands imposed by a rising middle-class. Artistic beauty was abandoned for a moral purpose with an occasional mingling of broad coarseness, as is to be found in a collection of stories *Till Eulenspiegel* (1515). The middle classes, composed of artisans and tradesmen, formed into gilds of *meistersingers* who, in a measure carried on the traditions of the earlier *minnesingers.* A most significant, if not entirely literary, event of this period was the Reformation which eventually lead Luther to translate the Bible into *Gemeindeutsch*, or common German. It is a classic, a literary monument in itself, and forms the backbone of German prose. The fiction of this period is negligible, and with the exception of the celebrated chapbook of *Doctor Johann Faust* and *Der Goldfaden* by Wickram, little need detain us.

The Renaissance, which had flourished so brilliantly elsewhere, left no impress on Germany being devastated by the Thirty Years' War, and the only noteworthy novel of the seventeenth century is the *Adventures of Simplicissimus,* by Grimmelshausen (1669), a picaresque novel describing the horrors of the war. The eighteenth century is the classical period in German literature. This was ushered in by Klopstock, Wieland and Herder, forerunners of Lessing, Goethe, and Schiller. The Romantic movement of the early nineteenth century following the death of Schiller (1805) produced, among others, Tieck, Hauff, Hoffmann and the Grimms.

After the July revolution, there arose a group of authors, known as "Young Germany." They sought to break with romanticism and introduced a note of naturalism. Auerbach achieved his fame by publishing his *Village Tales of the Black Forest* (1842). A more imposing figure is that of Keller, whose novels and stories have received international recognition. Spielhagen was quite in vogue in the eighties, and Heyse, a contemporary and one of the most versatile writers of the century, acquired distinction by virtue of his remarkable and justly praised novelettes and short stories.

Toward the last part of the nineteenth century prose became more realistic and short stories attained full development with writers like Schnitzler, Clara Viebig, Sudermann and others. Wassermann, Thomas Mann, and Kellermann are contemporary writers who are destined to influence the prose of modern Germany.

❋ ❋ ❋

EULENSPIEGEL, THE MERRY JESTER
(Anonymous: 1483)

THE delectable stories collected under this title relate the adventures of a real character who figures in Flemish, Dutch, German and Swiss chronicles. The hero wanders about the country, playing pranks upon the clergy and nobility who oppressed labourer and farmer.

The present version, translated by Thomas Roscoe, is reprinted from his *German Novelists*, London, no date. This is merely one incident in the life of *The Merry Jester*.

EULENSPIEGEL CARRIES OFF THE PARSON'S HORSE
(From *Eulenspiegel, the Merry Jester*)

IN the village of Rosseinberg there lived a curate who had a very pretty chambermaid, and a good horse which he highly prized. Now, the Duke of Brunswick had a great desire to purchase the said horse, and sent more than once to know whether the parson would be inclined to dispose of him, for he did not venture to seize him, because the parson held his living upon the territories of the councillors of Brunswick. Still the parson obstinately refused to make any bargain, which, coming to Howleglass's ears, he said to the duke, "Sir, how much will you give me if I deliver you the parson's horse, safe and sound, into your hands?"

Then the duke made answer: "I will give you my rich robe of red satin, and a grand mantle all embroidered with pearls." So forthwith Howleglass took leave of the duke, and not only set out to the village, but on his arrival walked straight into the parson's house; for though he was pretty well known there, he received an honest welcome, considering who and what manner of man he was.

After he had sojourned there about three days he pretended to fall sick, and took to his bed at which both the priest and his servant-maid were much vexed. In spite of this, however, Howleglass kept getting worse and worse, so that at last the priest inquired whether he would like to be confessed and receive the sacrament of holy Church, to which Howleglass expressed his readiness. Upon this the priest took his confession, and questioned him well, at the same time exhorting him to save his soul, by expressing the utmost contrition for his faults, doubting that he had passed off some notable tricks and impostures in his time.

Howleglass replied, "That there was only one sin which he did not like to confess, and that he would rather do it to another holy man than to him, for should he inform his then confessor, he might, perhaps, be very angry." But the good man said, "Friend, it is too far to send for another priest, and should you unluckily die in the meantime, we shall both of us become sinners in the sight of Heaven; so haste to inform me, and trust me it will not be too great for absolution. Whether it happens to displease me or not need not trouble you; we are forbidden to publish our confessions." "Well," said Howleglass, "I should like to confess it, though I fear it will greatly enrage you, for all it is no great offence and it concerns yourself." The parson now became more urgent than ever to learn what it was, and he said, "Whatever petty theft or grand larceny you may have committed, your confessor, who stands before you, will forgive you; he is too much a Christian to hate you."

"Yes," said Howleglass, "but I know too well that you will be greatly offended, but still I feel I am going so very fast that I have no time for demurring. The truth is, good sir, that I have five times fallen from the path of grace, owing to the temptations of your servant-maid." The parson bit his lips, and hastily granting him absolution, left the room and went to summon his chambermaid. At the mention of the charge she was justly indignant; but the priest said he had heard it from confession—from a dying sinner, and was therefore bound to believe it.

"I say no," cried the maid, "you are not!" "I say yes," retorted her master, "I am!" "No!" "Yes!" And the dialogue became so warm that the priest making use of his staff began to lay it about the poor girl's shoulders. The malicious rogue, hearing the uproar as he lay in bed, laughed wickedly in his sleeve at the idea of having deceived the priest, but he lay still until evening. Then getting up as if nothing had been the matter, he asked the parson "How much he had spent during his malady?" Both the master and his maid were heartily glad to see him upon his legs, and walking towards the door, rejoiced on any terms to be rid of him.

But as he went out, Howleglass said to the priest, "Sir, recollect that you have published my confession; I am going to Holnstadt, and I shall inform the bishop." The parson, hearing this, suddenly grew calm, and even supplicated Howleglass that he would not serve him such an ill turn. He declared he would go as far as twenty crowns to purchase his secrecy, if he would not breathe a syllable of what had passed. "No, no," replied Howleglass, "I would not accept a hundred to have my tongue tied; I shall inform the bishop as it behooves me to do." In great perplexity, the poor parson then brought the servant-maid to use her utmost influence, on any terms, to prevent so fatal a catastrophe. At last, when he saw the parson in tears, Howleglass said, "Well I will consent then to take your horse, and will say nothing; if not, I will keep no terms with you." The parson made several offers of money to bribe Howleglass from his cruel resolution, to which he would not listen, and he finally rode away on the parson's horse, which he presented to the Duke of Brunswick. For this feat he was mightily praised and recompensed; the duke gave him the fine robe, and on hearing further particulars bestowed upon him another. The parson was in despair at the loss of his steed, and again vented his anger upon the poor chambermaid, so that she was compelled to seek safety in flight.

In this cruel manner was the poor priest deprived of his horse, and his maid-servant together, Howleglass having so mischievously worked a complete revolution in her master's mind, thus leading him to hate and maltreat her whom he had so tenderly regarded before.

❋ ❋ ❋

CHAPBOOK OF DOCTOR FAUST
(Anonymous: 16th Century)

A UNIQUE book, and one that wielded an important influence over continental literature, was *The Chapbook of Doctor Faust*, the earliest edition of which appeared in Berlin about 1587. The book is a "curious patchwork of genuine folk-tales that were really current about Doctor Faust," a charlatan, who, it is presumed from certain documents, flourished in the late fifteenth century.

The present version, translated by Thomas Roscoe, is reprinted
from his *German Novelists*, London, no date. It is one of the episodes
that constitute the *Life of Doctor Faust*.

DOCTOR FAUST ARRANGES A MARRIAGE

(From *The Veritable History of Dr. Faust*)

AT the city of Wittenburg there resided a certain young student, of
a noble and ancient family, the initials of whose name were N. N.
Now, this young nobleman was deeply in love with a beautiful lady,
also of high birth, who happened to have a great number of other lovers.
Among these were many lords of the land, but to none of them would
that cruel lady grant any return of love; and to none did she show herself
so extremely averse as to this same young lord, who was well acquainted
with Doctor Faustus, having frequently eaten and drunk at his table.
Such, indeed, was the strength of his love, and so great was his disappointment, that he suddenly grew very ill, and pined himself away almost to
nothing. When Doctor Faustus perceived that this noble young gentleman was so sadly sickened as to be unable to help himself, he one day
asked his demon Mephistopheles what it was that could cause it, and what
he could be pining about. The demon then related to him the whole
affair, upon which the Doctor went to visit the poor young gentleman,
and acquainted him with the source of all his suffering, at which the
unhappy lover showed great surprise. But Doctor Faustus consoled him,
and said that he must not take it so much to heart, for that he would prove
his friend in the matter. Moreover, if he would trust in him, that proud
lady should fall to the share of no one but him, and accept his hand with
her own good will. And according as the Doctor promised, so it happened; for by force of enchantment he softened her heart, and made her
fall so desperately in love with this young nobleman, that she wished him
never to be out of her sight, and would pay no attention to anybody else.
Doctor Faustus informed the young gentleman that he ought to decorate
himself in the best style, and go to an assembly where the lady would be
present with other young women, all eager to dance, and that he would
accompany him. At the same time he gave him a ring, which he told
him he must slip upon her finger as he was dancing with her, upon feeling the touch of which she would be sure to love and be constant to him
and no one else; but that he would have no need to make any proposal or
talk of marriage, as she would be sure to introduce the subject herself.
Before they set off to the ball he sprinkled a few magical drops upon the
young man's features, which improved them and his whole appearance
very surprisingly. On their arrival he contrived it exactly as the Doctor
had directed him, and upon touching the ring as she was dancing with

him, the young lady suddenly felt her heart transfixed with Cupid's bolts, and she could not obtain a wink of sleep during the whole of that night. Early in the morning she sent a message for him, and declared the everlasting love and attachment which she felt for him, at the same time offering her hand if he would be her husband. He upon this revealed the passionate affection he had so long felt for her, and taking her at her word, the marriage was shortly afterwards solemnised, to the infinite contentment of both parties. The young nobleman showed great respect to the Doctor ever afterwards, and bestowed many presents upon him in consequence.

❊ ❊ ❊

JEAN PAUL RICHTER
(1763-1825)

ALTHOUGH Richter (born in Bavaria), was idolised during his lifetime by his many readers, and regarded very highly by critics, including Carlyle who wrote a brilliant essay about him, his fame rapidly declined until now he is hardly read. While his work was irregular in structure, he possessed an extraordinarily fertile imagination, and a power of suggesting profound thoughts by means of simple incidents. *The New-Year's Night of an Unhappy Man*, which appears in *The Death of an Angel*, show the grotesque quality which marked Richter's style. The present version, translated by A. Kenney, is reprinted by permission of the publishers from *The Death of an Angel*. Published by Black and Armstrong, London, 1839.

THE NEW-YEAR'S NIGHT OF AN UNHAPPY MAN

AN old man stood on the new-year's midnight at the window, and gazed with a look of long despair, upwards to the immovable everblooming heaven, and down upon the still, pure, white earth, on which no one was then so joyless and sleepless as he. For his grave stood near him; it was covered over only with the snow of age, not with the green of youth; and he brought nothing with him out of the whole rich life, nothing with him, but errors, sins and disease, a wasted body, a desolated soul, the breast full of poison, an old age full of remorse. The beautiful days of his youth turned round to-day, as spectres, and drew him back again to that bright morning on which his father first placed him at the cross-road of life, which, on the right hand, leads by the sun-path of Virtue into a wide peaceful land full of light and of harvests, and full of angels, and which, on the left hand, descends into the mole-ways of

Vice, into a black cavern full of down-dropping poison, full of aiming serpents, and of gloomy, sultry vapours.

Ah! the serpents hung about his breast, and the drops of poison on his tongue.—And he knew, now, where he was!

Frantic, and with unspeakable grief, he called upwards to Heaven: "Oh! give me back my youth again!"—O, Father! place me once more at the cross-path of life, that I may choose otherwise than I did."

But his father and his youth had long since passed away.

He saw fiery exhalations dancing on the marshes, and extinguishing themselves in the churchyard, and he said: "These are the days of my folly!"—He saw a star fly from heaven, and, in falling, glimmer and dissolve upon the earth. "That am I!" said his bleeding heart, and the serpent-teeth of remorse dug therein further in its wounds.

His flaming fancy showed him sleepwalkers slinking away on the house-tops; and a windmill raised up its arms threateningly to destroy him; and a mask that remained behind in the empty charnel-house, assumed by degrees his own features.

In the midst of this paroxysm, suddenly the music for the new-year flowed down from the steeple, like distant church-anthems. He became more gently moved.—He looked round on the horizon and upon the wide world, and thought on the friends of his youth, who, better and more happy than he, were now instructors of the earth, fathers of happy children, and blest men—and he exclaimed: "Oh! I also might have slumbered, like you, this new-year's night with dry eyes, had I chosen it— Ah! I might have been happy, beloved parents! had I fulfilled your new-year's wishes and instructions."

In feverish recollection of the period of his youth, it appeared to him as if the mask with his features raised itself up in the charnel-house—at length, through the superstition, which, on the new-year's night, beholds spirits and futurity, it grew to a living youth in the position of the beautiful boy of the Capitol, pulling out a thorn; and his former blooming figure was bitterly placed as a phantasma before him.

He could behold it no longer—he covered his eyes.—A thousand, hot, draining tears streamed into the snow.—He, now, only softly sighed, inconsolably and unconsciously: "Only come again, youth! come again!"

And it came again, for he had only dreamed so fearfully on the new-year's night.—He was still a youth.—His errors alone had been no dream; but he thanked God, that, still young, he could turn round in the foul ways of Vice, and fall back on the sun-path which conducts into the pure land of harvests.

Turn with him, youthful reader, if thou standest on his path of error: This frightful dream will, in future, become thy judge; but shouldst thou one day call out, full of anguish: "Come again, beautiful youth!"—it would not come again.

HEINRICH ZSCHOKKE
(1771-1848)

ZSCHOKKE, born at Magdeburg, was educated at his native monasterial school. He continued his education at the University of Frankfort-on-the-Oder; and, when the Prussian Government declined to make him a professor, he settled in Switzerland. Here he began his literary career, receiving local recognition. His reputation rests on his tales written in a charming and lucid style. *The Broken Pitcher* is one of his most delightful stories.

The present version is reprinted from *Tales* by Heinrich Zschokke, translated by Parke Godwin, and published by G. P. Putnam's Sons, New York, no date.

THE BROKEN PITCHER

NAPOULE, it is true, is only a very little place on the Bay of Cannes; yet it is pretty well known through all Provence. It lies in the shade of lofty evergreen palms and darker orange-trees; but that alone would not make it renowned. Still they say that there are grown the most luscious grapes, the sweetest roses, and the handsomest girls. I don't know but it is so; in the meantime I believe it most readily. Pity that Napoule is so small, and cannot produce more luscious grapes, fragrant roses, and handsome maidens; especially as we might then have some of them transplanted to our own country.

As ever since the foundation of Napoule all the Napoulese women have been beauties, so the little Marietta was a wonder of wonders, as the chronicles of the place declare. She was called the *little* Marietta; yet she was not smaller than a girl of seventeen or thereabouts ought to be, seeing that her forehead just reached up to the lips of a grown man.

The chronicles aforesaid had very good ground for speaking of Marietta. I, had I stood in the shoes of the chronicler, would have done the same. For Marietta, who until lately had lived with her mother Manon at Avignon, when she came back to her birthplace quite upset the whole village. Verily, not the houses but the people and their heads; and not the heads of all the people, but of those particularly whose heads and hearts are always in great danger, when in the neighbourhood of two bright eyes. I know very well that such a position is no joke.

Mother Manon would have done much better if she had remained at Avignon. But she had been left a small inheritance, by which she received at Napoule an estate consisting of some vine-hills, and a house that lay in the shadow of a rock, between certain olive trees and African acacias. This is a kind of thing which no unprovided widow ever rejects;

and, accordingly, in her own estimation she was as rich and happy as though she were the Countess of Provence or something like it.

So much the worse was it for the good people of Napoule. They never suspected their misfortune, not having read in Homer how a single pretty woman had filled all Greece and Lesser Asia with discord and war.

Marietta had scarcely been fourteen days in the house, between the olive trees and the African acacias, before every young man of Napoule knew that she lived there, and that there lived not in all Provence a more charming girl than the one in that house.

Went she through the village, sweeping lightly along like a dressed-up angel, her frock, with its pale-green bodice, and orange leaves and rose-buds upon the bosom of it, fluttering in the breeze, and flowers and ribbons waving about the straw bonnet which shaded her beautiful features,—yes, then the grave old men spake out, and the young ones were struck dumb. And everywhere, to the right and left, little windows and doors were opened with a "good-morning," or a "good-evening, Marietta," as it might be, while she nodded to the right and left with a pleasant smile.

If Marietta walked into the church, all hearts (that is, of the young people) forgot Heaven; all eyes turned from the Saints, and the worshipping finger wandered idly among the pearls of the rosary. This must certainly have provoked much sorrow, at least among the more devout.

The maidens of Napoule particularly became very pious about this time, for they, most of all, took the matter to heart. And they were not to be blamed for it; for since the advent of Marietta, more than one prospective groom had become cold, and more than one worshipper of some beloved one, quite inconstant. There were bickerings and reproaches on all sides, many tears, pertinent lectures, and even rejections. The talk was no longer of marriages, but of separations. They began to return their pledges of truth, rings, ribbons, etc. The old persons took part with their children; criminations and strife spread from house to house; it was most deplorable.

Marietta is the cause of all, said the pious maidens, first; then, the mothers said it; next the fathers took it up; and finally, all—even the young men. But Marietta, shielded by modesty and innocence, like the petals of the rose-bud in its dark-green calix, did not suspect the mischief of which she was the occasion, and continued courteous to everybody. This touched the young men, who said: "why condemn the pure and harmless child—she is not guilty?" Then the fathers said the same thing; then the mothers took it up; and finally, all—even the pious maidens. For, let who would talk with Marietta, she was sure to gain their esteem. So before half a year had passed, everybody had spoken to her, and everybody loved her. But she did not suspect that she was the object of such general regard, as she had not before suspected that she was the object of dislike. Does the violet, hidden in the down-trodden grass, think how sweet it is?

Now, every one wished to make amends for the injustice they had done Marietta. Sympathy deepened the tenderness of their attachment. Marietta found herself greeted everywhere in a more friendly way than ever; she was more cordially welcomed; more heartily invited to the rural sports and dances.

All men, however, are not endowed with tender sympathy; but some have hearts hardened like Pharaoh's. This arises, no doubt, from that natural depravity which has come upon men in consequence of the fall of Adam, or because, at their baptism, the devil is not brought sufficiently under subjection.

A remarkable example of this hardness of heart was given by one Colin, the richest farmer and proprietor in Napoule, whose vineyards and olive gardens, whose lemon and orange trees could hardly be counted in a day. One thing particularly demonstrates the perverseness of his disposition; he was twenty-seven years old, and had never asked for what purpose girls had been created!

True, all the people, especially damsels of a certain age, willingly forgave him this sin, and looked upon him as one of the best young men under the sun. His fine figure, his fresh unembarrassed manner, his look, his laugh, enabled him to gain the favourable opinion of the aforesaid people, who would have forgiven him, had there been occasion, any one of the deadly sins. But the decision of such judges is not always to be trusted.

While both old and young at Napoule had become reconciled to the innocent Marietta, and proffered their sympathies to her, Colin was the only one who had no pity upon the poor child. If Marietta was talked of, he became as dumb as a fish. If he met her in the street, he would turn red and white with anger, and cast sidelong glances at her of the most malicious kind.

If, at evening, the young people met upon the seashore near the old castle ruins, for sprightly pastimes, or rural dances, or to sing catches, Colin was the merriest among them. But as soon as Marietta arrived the rascally fellow was silent, and all the gold in the world couldn't make him sing. What a pity, when he had such a fine voice! Everybody listened to it so willingly, and its store of songs was endless.

All the maidens looked kindly upon Colin, and he was friendly with all of them. He had, as we have said, a roguish glance, which the lasses feared and loved; and it was so sweet, they would like to have had it painted. But, as might naturally be expected, the offended Marietta did not look graciously upon him, and in that she was perfectly right. Whether he smiled or not it was all the same to her. As to his roguish glance, why she would never hear it mentioned; and therein too she was perfectly right. When he told a tale (and he knew thousands), and everybody listened, she nudged her neighbour, or perhaps threw tufts of grass at Peter or Paul, and laughed and chattered and did not listen to Colin at all. This behaviour quite provoked the proud fellow, so that he would break off in the middle of his story, and stalk sullenly away.

Revenge is sweet. The daughter of mother Manon well knew how to triumph. Yet Marietta was a right good child and quite too tender-hearted. If Colin was silent, it gave her pain. If he was downcast, she laughed no more. If he went away, she did not stay long behind; but hurried to her home, and wept tears of repentance, more beautiful than those of the Magdalen, although she had not sinned like the Magdalen.

Father Jerome, the pastor of Napoule, was an old man of seventy, who possessed all the virtues of a saint, and only one failing; which was, that by reason of his advanced years, he was hard of hearing. But, on that very account, his homilies were more acceptable to the children of his baptism and blessing. True, he preached only of two subjects, as if they comprehended the whole of religion. It was either, "Little children, love one another," or it was, "Mysterious are the ways of Providence." And truly there is so much Faith, Love, and Hope in these, that one might at a pinch be saved by them. The little children loved one another most obediently, and trusted in the ways of Providence. Only Colin, with his flinty heart, would know nothing of either; for even when he professed to be friendly, he entertained the deepest malice.

The Napoulese went to the annual market or fair of the city of Vence. It was truly a joyful time, and though they had but little gold to buy with, there were many goods to look at. Now Marietta and mother Manon went to the Fair with the rest, and Colin was also there. He bought a great many curiosities and trifles for his friends—but he would not spend a farthing for Marietta. And yet he was always at her elbow, though he did not speak to her, nor she to him. It was easy to see that he was brooding over some scheme of wickedness.

Mother Manon stood gazing before a shop, when she suddenly exclaimed: "Oh! Marietta, see that beautiful pitcher! A queen would not be ashamed to raise it to her lips. Only see; the edge is of dazzling gold, and the flowers upon it could not bloom more beautifully in the garden, although they are only painted. And in the midst of this Paradise! pray see, Marietta, how the apples are smiling on the trees. They are verily tempting. And Adam cannot withstand it, as the enchanting Eve offers him one for food! And do see, how the little frisking lamb skips around the old tiger, and the snow-white dove with its golden throat stands there before the vulture, as if she would caress him!"

Marietta could not satisfy herself with looking. "Had I such a pitcher, mother!" said she, "it is far too beautiful to drink out of; I would place my flowers in it and constantly peep into Paradise. We are at the fair in Vence, but when I look on the pitcher I feel as if I were in Paradise."

So spoke Marietta, and called all her companions to the spot, to share her admiration of the pitcher; but the young men soon joined the maidens, until at length almost half the inhabitants of Napoule were assembled before the wonderfully beautiful pitcher. But miraculously beautiful was it mainly from its inestimable, translucent porcelain, with gilded handles and glowing colours. They asked the merchant timidly: "Sir, what is the price of it?" And he answered: "Among friends, it is worth a hundred livres." Then they all became silent, and went away in despair. When the Napoulese were all gone from the front of the shop, Colin came there by stealth, threw the merchant a hundred livres upon the counter, had the pitcher put in a box well-packed with cotton, and then carried it off. What evil plans he had in view no one would have surmised.

Near Napoule, on his way home, it being already dusk, he met old Jacques, the Justice's servant, returning from the fields. Jacques was a very good man, but excessively stupid.

"I will give thee money enough to get something to drink, Jacques," said Colin, "if thou wilt bear this box to Manon's house, and leave it there; and if any one should see thee, and inquire from whom the box came, say, 'A stranger gave it to me.' But never disclose my name, or I will always detest thee."

Jacques promised this, took the drink-money, and the box, and went with it towards the little dwelling, between the olive trees and the African acacias.

Before he arrived there, he encountered his master, Justice Hautmartin, who asked: "Jacques, what art thou carrying?"

"A box for mother Manon. But, sir, I cannot say from whom it comes."

"Why not?"

"Because Mr. Colin would always detest me."

"It is well that thou canst keep a secret. But it is already late; give me the box, for I am going to-morrow to see Mrs. Manon; I will deliver it to her, and not betray that it came from Colin. It will save thee a walk, and furnish me a good excuse for calling on the old lady."

Jacques gave the box to his master, whom he was accustomed to obey explicitly in all things. The Justice bore it into his chamber, and examined it by the light with some curiosity. On the lid was neatly written with red chalk: "For the lovely and dear Marietta." But Herr Hautmartin well knew that this was some of Colin's mischief, and that some knavish trick lurked under the whole. He therefore opened the box carefully, for fear that a mouse or rat should be concealed within. When he beheld the wondrous pitcher, which he had seen at Vence, he was dreadfully shocked, for Herr Hautmartin was a skilful casuist, and knew that the inventions and devices of the human heart are evil from our youth upward. He saw at once, that Colin designed this pitcher as a means of bringing misfortune upon Marietta: perhaps to give out, when it should be in her possession, that it was the present of some successful lover in the town, or the like, so that all decent people would thereafter keep aloof from Marietta. Therefore Herr Hautmartin resolved, in order to prevent any evil reports, to profess himself the giver. Moreover, he loved Marietta, and would gladly have seen her observe more strictly towards himself the sayings of the grey-headed priest Jerome, "Little children, love one another." In truth, Herr Hautmartin was a little child of fifty years old, and Marietta did not think the saying applied particularly to him. Mother Manon, on the contrary, thought that the Justice was a clever little child; he had gold and a high reputation, from one end of Napoule to the other. And when the Justice spoke of marriage, and Marietta ran away in affright, mother Manon remained sitting, and had no fear for the tall, staid gentleman. It must also be confessed, that there were no faults in his person. And although Colin might be the handsomest man in the village, yet the Justice far surpassed him in two things, namely: in the number of his years, and in a very, very huge nose. Yes, this unique nose, which always went before the Justice like a herald, to proclaim his approach, was a real elephant among human noses.

With this proboscis, his good purpose, and the pitcher, the Justice went the following morning to the house between the olive trees and the African acacias.

"For the beautiful Marietta," said he, "I hold nothing too costly. Yesterday you admired the pitcher at Vence: to-day, allow me, lovely Marietta, to lay it and my devoted heart at your feet."

Manon and Marietta were transported beyond measure when they beheld the pitcher. Manon's eyes glistened with delight; but Marietta turned and said: "I can neither take your heart nor your pitcher."

Then mother Manon was angry, and cried out: "But I accept both heart and pitcher. Oh, thou little fool, how long wilt thou despise thy good fortune! For whom dost thou tarry? Will a count of Provence make thee his bride, that thou scornst the Justice of Napoule? I know better how to look after thy interests. Herr Hautmartin, I deem it an honour to call you my son-in-law."

Then Marietta went out and wept bitterly, and hated the beautiful pitcher with all her heart.

But the Justice, drawing the palm of his flabby hand over his nose, spoke thus judiciously:

"Mother Manon, hurry nothing. The dove will at length, when it learns to know me better, give way. I am not impetuous. I have some skill among women, and before a quarter of a year passes by, I will insinuate myself into Marietta's good graces."

"Thy nose is too large for that," whispered Marietta, who listened outside the door and laughed to herself. In fact, the quarter of the year passed by, and Herr Hautmartin had not yet pierced her heart even with the tip of his nose.

During this quarter of a year Marietta had other affairs to attend to. The pitcher gave her much vexation and trouble, and something else besides.

For a fortnight nothing else was talked of in Napoule, and every one said, it is a present from the Justice, and the marriage is already agreed upon. Marietta solemnly declared to all her companions, that she would rather plunge to the bottom of the sea than marry the Justice, but the maidens continued to banter her all the more, saying: "Oh, how blissful it must be to repose in the shadow of his nose!" This was her first vexation.

Then mother Manon had the cruelty to force Marietta to rinse out the pitcher every morning at the spring under the rock and to fill it with fresh flowers. She hoped by this to accustom Marietta to the pitcher and heart of the giver. But Marietta continued to hate both the gift and the giver, and her work at the spring became an actual punishment. Second vexation.

Then, when in the morning, she came to the spring, twice every week she found on the rock, immediately over it, some most beautiful flowers, handsomely arranged, all ready for the decoration of the pitcher. And on the flower stalks a strip of paper was always tied, on which was written, DEAR MARIETTA. Now no one need expect to impose upon little Marietta, as if magicians and fairies were still in the world. Consequently, she knew that both the flowers and papers must have come from Herr Hautmartin. Marietta, indeed, would not smell them, because the living breath from out the Justice's nose had perfumed them. Nevertheless, she took the flowers, because they were finer than wild flowers, and tore the slip of paper into a thousand pieces, which she strewed upon the spot where the flowers usually lay. But this did not vex Justice Hautmartin, whose love was unparalleled in its kind, as his nose was in its kind. Third vexation.

At length it came out in conversation with Herr Hautmartin, that he was not the giver of the beautiful flowers. Then, who could it be? Marietta was utterly astounded at the unexpected discovery. Thenceforth she took the flowers from the rock more kindly; but further, Marietta was,—what maidens are not wont to be,—very inquisitive. She conjectured first this and then that young man in Napoule. Yet her conjectures were in vain. She looked and listened far into the night; she rose earlier than usual. But she looked and listened in vain. And still twice a week in the morning the miraculous flowers lay upon the rock, and upon the strip of paper wound round them she always read the silent sigh, DEAR MARIETTA! Such an incident would have made even the most indifferent inquisitive. But curiosity at length became a burning pain. Fourth vexation.

Now Father Jerome, on Sunday, had again preached from the text: "Mysterious are the dispensations of Providence." And little Marietta thought, if Providence would only dispense that I might at length find out who is the flower dispenser. Father Jerome was never wrong.

On a summer night, when it was far too warm for rest, Marietta awoke very early, and could not resume her sleep. Therefore she sprang joyously from her couch as the first streaks of dawn flashed against the window of her little chamber, over the waves of the sea and the Lerinian Isles, dressed herself, and went out to wash her forehead, breast, and arms in the cool spring. She took her hat with her, intending to take a walk by the seashore, as she knew of a retired place for bathing.

In order to reach this retired spot, it was necessary to pass over the rocks behind the house, and thence down through the orange and palm trees. On this occasion Marietta could not pass through them; for, under the youngest and most slender of the palms, lay a tall young man, in profound sleep—near him a nosegay of most splendid flowers. A white paper lay thereon, from which, probably, a sigh was again breathing. How could Marietta get by there?

She stood still, trembling with fright. She would go home again. Hardly had she retreated a couple of steps, as she looked again at the sleeper, and remained motionless. Yet the distance prevented her from recognising his face. Now the mystery was to be solved, or never. She tripped lightly nearer to the palms—but he seemed to stir—then she ran again towards the cottage. His movements were but the fearful imaginings of Marietta—now she returned again on her way towards the palms —but his sleep might perhaps be only dissembled—swiftly she ran towards the cottage—but who would flee for a mere probability? She trod more boldly the path towards the palms.

With these fluctuations of her timid and joyous spirit, between fright and curiosity, with these to and fro trippings between the house and the palmtrees, she at length nearly approached the sleeper; at the same time curiosity became more powerful than fear.

"What is he to me? My way leads me directly past him. Whether he sleeps or wake, I will go straight on." So thought Manon's daughter. But she passed not by, but stood looking directly in the face of the flowergiver, in order to be certain who it was. Besides, he slept as if it were the first time in a month. And who was it? Now, who else should it be, but the arch, wicked Colin?

So it was *he* who had annoyed the gentle maiden, and given her so much trouble with Herr Hautmartin, because he bore a grudge against her; he had been the one who had teased her with flowers, in order to torture her curiosity. Wherefore? He hated Marietta. He behaved himself always most shamefully towards the poor child. He avoided her when he could; and when he could not, he grieved the good-natured little one. With all the other maidens of Napoule he was more chatty, friendly, courteous, than towards Marietta. Consider—he had never once asked her to dance, and yet she danced bewitchingly.

Now there he lay, surprised, taken in the act. Revenge swelled in Marietta's bosom. What disgrace could she subject him to? She took the nosegay, unloosed it, strewed his present over the sleeper in scorn. But the paper, on which again appeared the sigh, "Dear Marietta," she retained, and thrust quickly into her bosom. She wished to preserve this proof of his handwriting. Marietta was sly. Now she would go away. But her revenge was not yet satisfied. She could not leave the place without returning Colin's ill-will. She took the violet-colored silken ribbon from her hat, and threw it lightly around the sleeper's arm and around the tree, and with three knots tied Colin fast. Now when he awoke, how astonished he would be! How his curiosity would torment him to ascertain who had played him this trick! That he could not possibly discover. So much the better; it served him right.

Marietta had only been too lenient towards him. She seemed to regret her work when she had finished it. Her bosom throbbed impetuously. Indeed, I believe that a little tear filled her eye, as she compassionately gazed upon the guilty one. Slowly she retreated to the orange grove by the rocks—she looked around often—slowly ascended the rocks, looking down among the palm trees as she ascended. Then she hastened to mother Manon, who was calling her.

That very day Colin practised new mischief. What did he? He wished to shame the poor Marietta publicly. Ah! she never thought that every one in Napoule knew her violet-coloured ribbon! Colin remembered it but too well. Proudly he bound it around his hat, and exhibited it to the gaze of all the world as a conquest. And male and female cried out: "He has received it from Marietta!" And all the maidens said angrily: "The reprobate!" And all the young men who liked to see Marietta, cried out; "The reprobate!"

'How! mother Manon?'" shrieked the Justice Hautmartin, when he came to her house, and he shrieked so loudly, that it re-echoed wonderfully through his nose. "How! do you suffer this? my betrothed presents the young proprietor Colin with her hat band! It is high time that we celebrate our nuptials. When that is over, then I'll have a right to speak."

"You have a right!" answered mother Manon; "if things are so, the marriage must take place forthwith. When that is done, all will go right."

"But, mother Manon, Marietta always refuses to give me her consent."

"Prepare the marriage feast."

"But she will not even look kindly at me; and when I seat myself at her side, the little savage jumps up and runs away."

"Justice, only prepare the marriage feast."

"But if Marietta resists——"

"We will take her by surprise. We will go to Father Jerome on Monday morning early, and he shall quietly celebrate the marriage. This we can easily accomplish with him. I am her mother. You the first Judicial person in Napoule. He must obey. Marietta need know nothing about it. Early on Monday morning I will send her to Father Jerome all alone, with a message, so that she will suspect nothing. Then the Priest shall speak earnestly to her. Half an hour afterwards we two will come. Then swiftly to the altar. And even if Marietta should then say no, what consequence is it? The old Priest can hear nothing. But till then, mum to Marietta and all Napoule."

So the secret remained with the two. Marietta dreamed not of the good-luck which was in store for her. She thought only of Colin's wickedness, which had made her the common talk of the whole place. Oh! how she repented her heedlessness about the ribbon; and yet in her heart she forgave the reprobate his crime. Marietta was far too good. She told her mother, she told all her playmates: "Colin has found my lost hatband. I never gave it to him. He only wishes to vex me with it. You all know that Colin was always ill-disposed towards me, and always sought to mortify me!"

Ah! the poor child! she knew not what new abomination the malicious fellow was again contriving.

Early in the morning Marietta went to the spring with the pitcher. There were no flowers yet on the rock. It was still quite too early; for the sun had scarcely risen from the sea.

Footsteps were heard. Colin came in sight, the flowers in his hand. Marietta became very red. Colin stammered out: "good morning, Marietta," but the greeting came not from his heart; he could hardly bring it over his lips.

"Why dost thou wear my ribbon so publicly, Colin?" said Marietta, and placed the pitcher upon the rock. "I did not give it thee."

"Thou didst not give it to me, dear Marietta?" asked he, and inward rage made him deadly pale.

Marietta was ashamed of the falsehood, drooped her eyelids, and said, after a while: "Well, I did give it to thee, yet thou shouldst not have worn it so openly. Give it me back again."

Slowly he untied it; his anger was so great that he could not prevent the tears from filling his eyes, nor the sighs from escaping his breast. "Dear Marietta, leave thy ribbon with me," said he softly.

"No," answered she.

Then his suppressed passion changed into desperation. Sighing, he looked toward Heaven, then sadly on Marietta, who, silent and abashed, stood by the spring with downcast eyes.

He wound the violet-coloured ribbon around the stalks of the flowers, said, "There, take them all," and threw the flowers so spitefully against the magnificent pitcher upon the rock, that it was thrown down and dashed to pieces. Maliciously he fled away.

Mother Manon, lurking behind the window, had seen and heard all. When the pitcher broke, hearing and sight left her. She was scarcely able to speak for very horror. And as she pushed with all her strength against the narrow window, to shout after the guilty one, it gave way, and with one crash fell to the earth and was shattered in pieces.

So much ill-luck would have discomposed any other woman. But Manon soon recovered herself. "How lucky that I was a witness to this roguery!" exclaimed she; "he must to the Justice. He shall replace both pitcher and window-sash with his gold. It will give a rich dowry to Marietta." But when Marietta brought in the fragments of the shattered pitcher, when Manon saw the Paradise lost, the good man Adam without a head, and of Eve not a solitary limb remaining, the serpent unhurt, triumphing, the tiger safe, but the little lamb gone even to the very tail, as if the tiger had swallowed it, then mother Manon screamed forth curses against Colin, and said: "One can easily see that this *fall* came from the hand of the Devil."

She took the pitcher in one hand, Marietta in the other, and went about nine o'clock to where Herr Hautmartin was wont to sit in judgment. She there made a great outcry, and showed the broken pitcher and the Paradise lost. Marietta wept bitterly.

The Justice, when he saw the broken pitcher, and his beautiful bride in tears, flew into so violent a rage towards Colin that his nose was as violet-coloured as Marietta's well-known hat-band. He immediately despatched his bailiffs to bring the criminal before him.

Colin came overwhelmed with grief. Mother Manon now repeated her complaint with great eloquence, before justice, bailiffs, and scribes. But Colin listened not. He stepped to Marietta and whispered to her: "Forgive me, dear Marietta, as I forgive thee. I broke thy pitcher unintentionally; but thou, thou hast broken my heart!"

"What whispering is that?" cried Herr Hautmartin, with magisterial authority. "Hearken to this accusation, and defend yourself." "I have nought to defend. I broke the pitcher against my will," said Colin.

"That I verily believe," said Marietta, sobbing, "I am as guilty as he; for I offended and angered him,—then he threw the ribbon and flowers to me. He could not help it."

"Well, I should like to know!" cried mother Manon. "Do you intend to defend him? Mr. Justice, pronounce his sentence. He has broken the pitcher, and he does not deny it; and I, on his account, the window—will he deny that? Let us see."

"Since you cannot deny it, Mr. Colin," said the Justice, "you must pay three hundred livres for the pitcher, for it is worth that; and then for——"

"No," interrupted Colin, "it is not worth so much. I bought it at Vence at the Fair, for Marietta, for one hundred livres."

"You bought it, sir brazen face?" shrieked the Justice, and his whole face became like Marietta's hat-band. He could not or would not say more, for he dreaded a disagreeable investigation of the matter.

But Colin was vexed at the imputation, and said: "I sent this pitcher on the evening of the Fair, by your own servant, to Marietta. There stands Jacques in the door. He is a witness. Speak, Jacques, did I not give thee the box to carry to Mrs. Manon?"

Herr Hautmartin wished to interrupt this conversation by speaking loudly. But the simple Jacques said: "Only recollect, Herr Justice, you took away Colin's box from me, and carried what was in it to Frau Manon. The box lies even now, there under the papers."

Then the bailiffs were ordered to remove the simpleton; and Colin was also directed to retire, until he should be sent for again.

"Very well, Mr. Justice," interposed Colin, "but this business shall be your last in Napoule. I know this, that you would ingratiate yourself with Frau Manon and Marietta by means of my property. When you want me you will have to ride to Grasse to the Governor's." With that, Colin departed.

Herr Hautmartin was quite puzzled with this affair, and in his confusion knew not what he was about. Mrs. Manon shook her head. The affair was dark and mysterious to her. "Who will now pay me for the broken pitcher?" she asked.

"To me," said Marietta, with glowing, brightened countenance, "*to me* it is already paid for."

Colin rode that same day to the Governor, at Grasse, and came back early the next morning. But Mr. Hautmartin only laughed at him, and removed all mother Manon's suspicions, by swearing he would let his nose be cut off if Colin did not pay three hundred livres for the broken pitcher. He also went with mother Manon to talk with Father Jerome about the marriage, and impressed upon him the necessity of earnestly setting before Marietta her duty, as an obedient daughter, of not opposing the will of her mother in her marriage. This the pious old man promised, although he understood not the half of what they shouted in his ear.

Marietta took the broken pitcher into her bed-chamber, and now truly loved it; and it was as if Paradise were planted in her bosom, since it had been destroyed on the pitcher.

When Monday morning came, mother Manon said to her daughter: "Dress yourself handsomely, and carry this myrtle wreath to Father Jerome; he wants it for a bride." Marietta dressed herself in her Sunday clothes, took the myrtle wreath unsuspiciously, and carried it to Father Jerome.

On the way Colin met her, and greeted her joyfully, though timidly; and when she told him where she was taking the wreath, Colin said: "I am going the same way, for I am carrying the money for the Church's tenths to the Priest." And as they went on, he took her hand silently, and both trembled, as if they designed some great crime against each other.

"Hast thou forgiven me?" whispered Colin, anxiously. "Ah! Marietta, what have I done to thee, that thou art so cruel towards me?"

She could only say: "Be quiet, Colin, you shall have the ribbon again; and I will preserve the pitcher, since it came from you! Did it really come from you?"

"Ah! Marietta, canst thou doubt it? All I have I would gladly give thee. Wilt thou, hereafter, be as kind to me as thou art to others?"

She replied not. But as she entered the parsonage, she looked aside at him, and when she saw his fine eyes filled with tears, she whispered softly: "Dear Colin!" Then he bent down and kissed her hand. With this, the door of a chamber opened, and Father Jerome, with venerable aspect, stood before them. The young couple had nearly fallen from giddiness, and they held fast to each other. I know not whether this was the effect of the hand-kissing, or the awe they felt for the sage.

Marietta handed him the myrtle wreath. He laid it upon her head and said: "Little children, love one another," and then urged the good maiden, in the most touching and pathetic manner, to love Colin. For the old gentleman, from his hardness of hearing, had either mistaken the name of the bridegroom, or from want of memory, forgotten it and thought Colin must be the bridegroom.

Then Marietta's heart softened under the exhortation of the venerable Father, and with tears and sobs she exclaimed: "Ah! I have loved him for a long time, but he hates me!"

"I hate thee, Marietta?" cried Colin, "my soul has lived only in thee, since thou camest to Napoule. Oh! Marietta, how could I hope and believe that thou didst love me? Does not all Napoule worship thee?"

"Why, then, dost thou avoid me, Colin, and prefer all my companions before me?"

"Oh! Marietta, I feared and trembled with love and anxiety when I beheld thee; I had not the courage to approach thee; and when I was away from thee, I was most miserable."

As they talked thus with each other, the good Father thought they were quarrelling; and he threw his arms around them, brought them together, and said, imploringly: "Little children, little children, love one another."

Then Marietta sank on Colin's breast, and Colin threw his arms around her, and both faces beamed with rapture. They forgot the priest, the whole world. Colin's lips hung upon Marietta's sweet mouth. It was, indeed, only a kiss, but a kiss of sweetest self-forgetfulness. Each was sunk into the other. Both had so completely lost their recollection that, unwittingly, they followed the delighted Father Jerome into the church and before the altar.

"Marietta!" sighed he.

"Colin!" sighed she.

In the church there were many devout worshippers; but they witnessed Colin's and Marietta's marriage with amazement. Many ran out before the close of the ceremony, to spread the news in every direction throughout Napoule: "Colin and Marietta are married!"

When the solemnisation was over, Father Jerome honestly rejoiced that he had succeeded so well, and that such little opposition had been made by the parties. He led them into the parsonage.

Then mother Manon arrived, breathless; she had waited at home a long time for the bridegroom. He had not arrived. At the last stroke of the clock she grew anxious, and went to Herr Hautmartin's. There a new surprise awaited her. She learned that the Governor, together with the officers of the Viguerie, had appeared, and taken possession of the accounts, chests, and papers of the Justice, and, at the same time, arrested Herr Hautmartin.

"This surely is the work of that wicked Colin," thought she, and hurried to the parsonage, in order to apologise to Father Jerome for delaying the marriage. The good grey-headed old man advanced towards her, proud of his work, and leading by the hand the newly-married pair.

Now mother Manon lost her wits and her speech in good earnest when she learned what had happened. But Colin had more thoughts and powers of speech than in his whole previous life. He told of his love and the broken pitcher, the falsehood of the Justice, and how he had unmasked this unjust magistrate in the Viguerie at Grasse. Then he besought mother Manon's blessing, since all this had happened without any fault on the part of Marietta or himself.

Father Jerome, who, for a long while, could not make out what had happened, when he received a full explanation of the marriage through mistake, piously folded his hands and exclaimed, with uplifted eyes: "Wonderful are the dispensations of Providence!" Colin and Marietta kissed his hands; mother Manon, through sheer veneration of Heaven, gave the young couple her blessing, but remarked, incidentally, that her head seemed turned round.

Frau Manon herself was pleased with her son-in-law when she came to know the full extent of his property, and especially when she found that Herr Hautmartin and his nose had been taken as prisoner to Grasse.

"But am I then really a wife?" asked Marietta, "and really Colin's wife?"

Mother Manon nodded her head, and Marietta hung upon Colin's arm. Thus they went to Colin's farm, to his dwelling-house, through the garden.

"Look at the flowers, Marietta," said Colin, "how carefully I cultivated them for your pitcher?"

Colin, who had not expected so pleasant an event, now prepared a wedding feast on the spur of the occasion. Two days was it continued. All Napoule was feasted. Who shall describe Colin's rapture and extravagance?

The broken pitcher is preserved in the family to the present day, as a memorial and sacred relic.

❋ ❋ ❋

JOHANN LUDWIG TIECK
(1773-1853)

ALTHOUGH Tieck can boast of little originality or genius, he nevertheless wrote a number of excellent stories that won him a great deal of popularity in his day. With Novalis and the Schlegel brothers he was the leader of the Romantic school. Some of his best work was collected in three volumes under the title *Phantasus*. *The Friends*, a charming and delicate story full of a mystic quality that was characteristic of Tieck, appeared in that collection.

The present version, anonymously translated, is reprinted from *Tales from Phantasus*, published by James Burns, London, 1845.

THE FRIENDS

IT was a beautiful spring morning, when Lewis Wandel went out to visit a sick friend, in a village some miles distant from his dwelling. This friend had written to him to say that he was lying dangerously ill, and would gladly see him and speak to him once more.

The cheerful sunshine now sparkled in the bright green bushes; the birds twittered and leapt to and fro on the branches; the larks sang merrily above the thin fleeting clouds; sweet scents rose from the fresh meadows, and the fruit-trees of the garden were white and gay in blossom.

Lewis's eye roamed intoxicate around him; his soul seemed to expand;

but he thought of his invalid friend, and he bent forward in silent dejection. Nature had decked herself all in vain, so serenely and so brightly; his fancy could only picture to him the sick bed and his suffering brother.

"How song is sounding from every bough!" cried he; "the notes of the birds mingle in sweet unison with the whisper of the leaves; and yet in the distance, through all the charm of the concert, come the sighs of the sick one."

Whilst he thus communed, a troop of gaily-clad peasant girls issued from the village; they all gave him a friendly salutation, and told him that they were on their merry way to a wedding; that work was over for that day, and had to give place to festivity. He listened to their tale, and still their merriment rang in the distance on his ear; still he caught the sound of their songs, and became more and more sorrowful. In the wood he took his seat on a dismantled tree, drew the oft-read letter from his pocket, and ran through it once more:—

"My very dear friend,—I cannot tell why you have so utterly forgotten me, that I receive no news from you. I am not surprised that men forsake me; but it heartily pains me to think that you too care nothing about me. I am dangerously ill; a fever saps my strength: if you delay visiting me any longer, I cannot promise you that you will see me again. All nature revives, and feels fresh and strong; I alone sink lower in languor; the returning warmth cannot animate me; I see not the green fields, nothing but the tree that rustles before my window, and sings death-songs to my thoughts; my bosom is pent, my breathing is hard; and often I think the walls of my room will press closer together and crush me. The rest of you in the world are holding the most beautiful festival of life, whilst I must languish in the dwelling of sickness. Gladly would I dispense with spring, if I could but see your dear face once more: but you that are in health never earnestly think what it really is to be ill, and how dear to us then, in our helplessness, the visit of a friend is: you do not know how to prize those precious minutes of consolation, because the whole world receives you in the warmth and the fervour of its friendship. Ah! if you did but know, as I do, how terrible is death, and how still more terrible it is to be ill,—O Lewis, how would you hasten then to behold once more this frail form, that you have hitherto called your friend, and that by and by will be so ruthlessly dismembered! If I were well, I would haste to meet you, or fancy that you may perhaps be ill at this moment. If I never see you again—farewell."

What a painful impression did the suffering depicted in this letter make upon Lewis's heart, amid the liveliness of Nature, as she lay in brilliancy before him! He melted into tears, and rested his head on his hand.—"Carol now, ye foresters," thought he; "for ye know no lamentation; ye lead a buoyant poetic existence, and for this are those swift pinions granted you; oh, how happy are ye, that ye need not mourn: warm summer calls you, and ye wish for nothing more; ye dance forth to meet it, and when winter is advancing, ye are gone! O light-winged merry forest-life, how do I envy thee! Why are so many heavy cares burdened upon poor man's heart? Why may he not love without purchasing his love by wailing—his happiness by misery? Life purls on like a fleeting rivulet beneath his feet, and quenches not his thirst, his fervid longing."

He became more and more absorbed in thought, and at last he rose and pursued his way through the thick forest. "If I could but help him," cried he; "if Nature could but supply me with a means of saving him; but as it is, I feel nothing but my own impotency, and the pain of losing my friend. In my childhood I used to believe in enchantment and its supernatural aids; would I now could hope in them as happily as then!"

He quickened his steps; and involuntarily all the remembrances of the earliest years of his childhood crowded back upon him: he followed those forms of loveliness, and was soon entangled in such a labyrinth as not to notice the objects that surrounded him. He had forgotten that it was spring—that his friend was ill: he hearkened to the wondrous melodies, which came borne, as if from distant shores, upon his ear: all that was most strange united itself to what was most ordinary: his whole soul was transmuted. From the far vista of memory, from the abyss of the past, all those forms were summoned forth that ever had enraptured or tormented him; all those dubious phantoms were aroused, that flutter formlessly about us, and gather in dizzy hum around our heads. Puppets, the toys of childhood, and spectres, danced along before him, and so mantled over the green turf, that he could not see a single flower at his feet. First love encircled him with its twilight morning gleam, and let down its sparkling rainbow over the mead: his earliest sorrows glided past him in review, and threatened to greet him in the same guise at the end of his pilgrimage. Lewis sought to arrest all these changeful feelings, and to retain a consciousness of self amid the magic of enjoyment,—but in vain. Like enigmatic books, with figures grotesquely gay, that open for a moment and in a moment are closed, so unstably and fleetingly all floated before his soul.

The wood opened, and in the open country on one side lay some old ruins, encompassed with watch-towers and ramparts. Lewis was astonished at having advanced so quickly amid his dreams. He emerged from his melancholy, as he did from the shades of the wood; for often the pictures within us are but the reflection of outward objects. Now rose on him, like the morning sun, the memory of his first poetical enjoyments, of his earliest appreciations of that luscious harmony which many a human ear never inhales.

"How incomprehensibly," said he, "did those things commingle then,

which seemed to me eternally parted by such vast chasms; my most unde-
fined presentiments assumed a form and outline, and gleamed on me in
the shape of a thousand subordinate phantoms, which till then I had never
descried! So names were found me for things that I had long wished to
speak of: I became recipient of earth's fairest treasures, which my yearning heart had so long sought for in vain: and how much have I to thank
thee for since then, divine power of fancy and of poetry! How hast thou
smoothed for me the path of life, that erst appeared so rough and perplexed! Ever hast thou revealed to me new sources of enjoyment and
happiness, so that no arid desert presents itself to me now: every stream of
sweet voluptuous inspiration hath wound its way through my earth-born
heart: I have become intoxicate with bliss, and have communed with beings of heaven."

The sun sank below the horizon, and Lewis was astonished that it was
already evening. He was insensible of fatigue, and was still far from
the point which he had wished to reach before night: he stood still, without being able to understand how the crimson of evening could be so early
mantling the clouds; how the shadows of everything were so long, while
the nightingale warbled her song of wail in the thicket. He looked
around him: the old ruins lay far in the background, clad in blushing
splendour; and he doubted whether he had not strayed from the direct
and well-known road.

Now he remembered a phantasy of his early childhood, that till that
moment had never recurred to him: it was a female form of awe, that
glided before him over the lonely fields: she never looked round, yet he
was compelled, against his will, to follow her, and to be drawn on into
unknown scenes, without in the least being able to extricate himself from
her power. A slight thrill of fear came over him, and yet he found it
impossible to obtain a more distinct recollection of that figure, or to usher
back his mind into the frame, in which this image had first appeared to
him. He sought to individualise all these singular sensations, when, looking round by chance, he really found himself on a spot which, often as
he had been that way, he had never seen before.

"Am I spell-bound?" cried he; "or have my dreams and fancies
crazed me? Is it the wonderful effect of solitude that makes me irrecog-
nisable to myself; or do spirits and genii hover round me and hold my
senses in thrall? Sooth, if I cannot enfranchise myself from myself, I
will await that woman-phantom that floated before me in every lonely
place in my childhood."

He endeavoured to rid himself of every kind of phantasy, in order to
get into the right road again; but his recollections became more and more
perplexed; the flowers at his feet grew larger, the red glow of evening
more brilliant, and wondrously shaped clouds hung drooping on the earth,
like the curtains of some mystic scene that was soon to unfold itself. A

ringing murmur arose from the high grass, and the blades bowed to one another, as if in friendly converse; while a light warm spring rain dropped pattering amongst them, as if to wake every slumbering harmony in wood, and bush, and flower. Now all was rife with song and sound; a thousand sweet voices held promiscuous parley; song entwined itself in song, and tone in tone; while in the waning crimson of eve lay countless blue butterflies rocking, with its radiance sparkling from their wavy wings. Lewis fancied himself in a dream, when the heavy dark-red clouds suddenly rose again, and a vast prospect opened on him in unfathomable distance. In the sunshine lay a gorgeous plain, sparkling with verdant forests and dewy underwood. In its centre glittered a palace of a myriad hues, as if composed all of undulating rainbows and gold and jewels: a passing stream reflected its various brilliancy, and a soft crimson æther environed this hall of enchantment; strange birds, he had never seen before, flew about, sportively flapping each other with their red and green wings: larger nightingales warbled their clear notes to the echoing landscape: lambent flames shot through the green grass, flickering here and there, and then darting in coils round the mansion. Lewis drew nearer, and heard ravishing voices sing the following words: —

> Traveller from earth below,
> Wend thee not farther,
> In our hall's magic glow
> Bide with us rather.
> Hast thou with longing scann'd
> Joy's distant morrow,
> Cast away sorrow,
> And enter the wish'd-for land.

Without further scruple, Lewis stepped to the shining threshold, and lingering but a moment ere he set his foot on the polished stone, he entered. The gates closed after him.

"Hitherward! hitherward!" cried invisible lips, as from the inmost recesses of the palace; and with loudly throbbing heart he followed the voices. All his cares, all his olden remembrances were cast away: his inmost bosom rang with the songs that outwardly encompassed him: his every regret was stilled: his every conscious and unconscious wish was satisfied. The summoning voices grew so loud, that the whole building re-echoed them, and still he could not find their origin, though he long seemed to have been standing in the central hall of the palace.

At length a ruddy-cheeked boy stepped up to him, and saluted the stranger guest: he led him through magnificent chambers, full of splendour and melody, and at last entered the garden, where Lewis, as he said, was expected. Entranced he followed his guide, and the most delicious fragrance from a thousand flowers floated forth to meet him. Broad shady walks received them. Lewis's dizzy gaze could scarcely gain the tops of the high immemorial trees: bright-coloured birds sat perched upon the branches: children were playing on guitars in the shade, and they and the birds sang to the music. Fountains shot up, with the clear red of morning, sparkling upon them: the flowers were as high as shrubs, and parted spontaneously as the wanderer pressed through them. He had never before felt the hallowed sensations that then enkindled in him; never had such pure heavenly enjoyment been revealed to him: he was over-happy.

But bells of silver sound rang through the trees, and their tops were bowed: the birds and children with the guitars were hushed: the rose-buds unfolded: and the boy now conducted the stranger into the midst of a brilliant assembly.

Lovely dames of lofty form were seated on beautiful banks of turf, in earnest conference. They were above the usual height of the human race, and their more than earthly beauty had at the same time something of awe in it, from which the heart shrunk back in alarm. Lewis dared not interrupt their conversation: it seemed as if he were among the god-like forms of Homer's song, where every thought must be excluded that formed the converse of mortals. Odd little spirits stood round, as ready ministers, waiting attentively for the wink of the moment that should summon them from their posture of quietude: they fixed their glances on the stranger, and then looked jeeringly and significantly at each other. At last the beautiful women ceased speaking, and beckoned Lewis to approach; he was still standing with an embarrassed air, and drew near to them with trembling.

"Be not alarmed," said the fairest of them all; "you are welcome to us here, and we have long been expecting you: long have you wished to be in our abode,—are you satisfied now?"

"Oh, how unspeakably happy I am!" exclaimed Lewis; "all my dearest dreams have met with their fulfilment, all my most daring wishes are gratified now: yes, I am, I live among them. How it has happened so, I cannot comprehend: sufficient for me, that it is so. Why should I raise a new wail over this enigma, ere my olden lamentations are scarcely at an end?"

"Is this life," asked the lady, "very different from your former one?"

"My former life," said Lewis, "I can scarcely remember. But has, then, this golden state of existence fallen to my lot? this beautiful state, after which my every sense and prescience so ardently aspired; to which every wish wandered, that I could conceive in fancy, or realise in my inmost thought; though its image, veiled in mist, seemed ever strange in me—and is it, then, mine at last? have I, then, achieved this new existence, and does it hold me in its embrace? Oh, pardon me, I know not what I say in my delirium of ecstasy, and might well weigh my words more carefully in such an assemblage."

The lady sighed; and in a moment every minister was in motion; there was a stirring among the trees, everywhere a running to and fro, and speedily a banquet was placed before Lewis of fair fruits and fragrant wines. He sat down again, and music rose anew on the air. Rows of beautiful boys and girls sped round him, intertwined in the dance, while uncouth little cobolds lent life to the scene, and excited loud laughter by their ludicrous gambols. Lewis noted every sound and every gesture: he seemed newly-born since his initiation into this joyous existence. "Why," thought he, "are those hopes and reveries of ours so often laughed at, that pass into fulfilment sooner than ever had been expected? Where, then, is that border-mark between truth and error which mortals are ever ready with such temerity to set up? Oh, I ought in my former life to have wandered oftener from the way, and then perhaps I should have ripened all the earlier for this happy transmutation."

The dance died away; the sun sank to rest; the august dames arose; Lewis too left his seat, and accompanied them on their walk through the quiet garden. The nightingales were complaining in a softened tone, and a wondrous moon rose above the horizon. The blossoms opened to its silver radiance, and every leaf kindled in its gleam; the wide avenues became of a glow, casting shadows of a singular green; red clouds slumbered on the green grass of the fields: the fountains turned to gold, and played high in the clear air of heaven.

"Now you will wish to sleep," said the loveliest of the ladies, and shewed the enraptured wanderer a shadowy bower, strewed with soft turf and yielding cushions. Then they left him, and he was alone.

He sat down and watched the magic twilight glimmering through the thickly-woven foliage. "How strange is this!" said he to himself; "perhaps I am now only asleep, and I may dream that I am sleeping a second time, and may have a dream in my dream; and so it may go on for ever, and no human power ever be able to awake me. No! unbeliever that I am! it is beautiful reality that animates me now, and my former state perhaps was but the dream of gloom." He lay down, and light breezes played round him. Perfume was wafted on the air, and little birds sang lulling songs. In his dreams he fancied the garden all around him changed: the tall trees withered away; the golden moon fallen from the sky, leaving a dismal gap behind her; instead of the watery jet from the fountains, little genii gushed out, caracolling over each in the air, and assuming the strangest attitudes. Notes of woe supplanted the sweetness of song, and every trace of that happy abode had vanished. Lewis awoke amid impressions of fear, and chid himself for still feeding his fancy in the perverse manner of the habitants of earth, who mingle all received images in rude disorder, and present them again in this garb in a dream. A lovely morning broke over the scene, and the ladies saluted him again. He spoke to them more intrepidly, and was to-day more inclined to cheerfulness, as the surrounding world had less power to astonish him. He contemplated the garden of the palace, and fed upon the magnificence and the wonders that he met there. Thus he lived many days happily, in the belief that his felicity was incapable of increase.

But sometimes the crowing of a cock seemed to sound in the vicinity; and then the whole edifice would tremble, and his companions turn pale: this generally happened of an evening, and soon afterwards they retired to rest. Then often there would come a thought of earth into Lewis's soul; then he would often lean out of the windows of the glittering palace to arrest and fix these fleeting remembrances, and to get a glimpse of the high road again, which, as he thought, must pass that way. In this sort of mood, he was one afternoon alone, musing within himself why it was just as impossible for him then to recall a distinct remembrance of the world, as formerly it had been to feel a presage of this poetic place of sojourn,—when all at once a post-horn seemed to sound in the distance, and the rattle of carriage-wheels to make themselves heard. "How strangely," said he to himself, "does a faint gleam, a slight reminiscence of earth, break upon my delight—rendering me melancholy and dejected! Then, do I lack anything here? Is my happiness still incomplete?"

The beautiful women returned. "What do you wish for?" said they, in a tone of concern; "you seem sad."

"You will laugh," replied Lewis; "yet grant me one favour more. In that other life I had a friend, whom I now but faintly remember: he is ill, I think; restore him by your skill."

"Your wish is already gratified," said they.

"But," said Lewis, "vouchsafe me two questions."

"Speak!"

"Does no gleam of love fall on this wondrous world? Does no friendship perambulate these bowers? I thought the morning blush of springlove would be eternal here, which in that other life is too prone to be extinguished, and which men afterwards speak of as of a fable. To confess to you the truth, I feel an unspeakable yearning after those sensations."

"Then you long for earth again?"

"Oh, never!" cried Lewis; "for in that cold earth I used to sigh for friendship and for love, and they came not near me. The longing for those feelings had to supply the place of those feelings themselves; and for that reason I turned my aspirations hitherward, and hoped here to find every thing in the most beautiful harmony."

"Fool!" said the venerable woman: "so on earth you sighed for earth, and knew not what you did in wishing to be here; you have overshot your desires, and substituted phantasies for the sensations of mortals."

"Then who are ye?" cried Lewis, astounded.

"We are the old fairies," said she, "of whom you surely must have heard long ago. If you ardently long for earth, you will return thither again. Our kingdom flourishes when mortals are shrouded in night; but their day is *our* night. Our sway is of ancient date, and will long endure. It abides invisibly among men—to your eye alone has it been revealed." She turned away, and Lewis remembered that it was the same form which had resistlessly dragged him after it in his youth, and of which he felt a secret dread. He followed now also, crying, "No, I will not go back to earth! I will stay here!" "So then," said he to himself, "I devined this lofty being even in my childhood! And so the solution of many a riddle, which we are too idle to investigate, may be within ourselves."

He went on much further than usual, till the fairy garden was soon left far behind him. He stood on a romantic mountain-range, where the ivy clambered in wild tresses up the rocks; cliff was piled on cliff, and awe and grandeur seemed to hold universal sway. Then there came a wandering stranger to him, who accosted him kindly, and addressed him thus:—"Glad I am, after all, to see you again."

"I know you not," said Lewis.

"That may well be," replied the other; "but once you thought you knew me well. I am your late sick friend."

"Impossible! you are quite a stranger to me!"

"Only," said the stranger, "because to-day you see me for the first time in my true form: till now you only found in me a reflection of yourself. You are right too in remaining here; for there is no love, no friendship—not here, I mean, where all illusion vanishes."

Lewis sat down and wept.

"What ails you?" said the stranger.

"That it is you—you who were the friend of my youth: is not that mournful enough? Oh, come back with me to our dear, dear earth, where we shall know each other once more under illusive forms—where there exists the superstition of friendship! What am I doing here?"

"What will that avail?" answered the stranger. "You will want to be back again; earth is not bright enough for you: the flowers are too small for you, the song too suppressed. Colour there, cannot emerge so brilliantly from the shade; flowers there are of small comfort, and so prone to fade; the little birds think of their death, and sing in modest constraint: but here every thing is on a scale of grandeur."

"Oh, I will be contented!" cried Lewis, as the tears gushed profusely from his eyes. "Do but come back with me, and be my friend once more; let us leave this desert, this glittery misery!"

Thus saying, he opened his eyes, for some one was shaking him roughly. Over him leant the friendly but pale face of his once sick friend. "But are you dead?" cried Lewis.

"Recovered am I, wicked sleeper," he replied. "Is it thus you visit your sick friend? Come along with me; my carriage is waiting there, and a thunder-storm is rising."

Lewis rose: in his sleep he had glided off the trunk of the tree; his friend's letter lay open beside him. "So am I really on the earth again?" he exclaimed with joy; "really? and is this no new dream?"

"You will not escape from earth," answered his friend with a smile; and both were locked in heart-felt embraces.

"How happy I am," said Lewis, "that I have you once more, that I feel as I used to do, and that you are well again!"

"Suddenly," replied his friend, "I felt ill; and as suddenly I was well again. So I wished to go to you, and do away with the alarm that my letter must have caused you; and here, half-way, I find you asleep."

"I do not deserve your love at all," said Lewis.

"Why?"

"Because I just now doubted of your friendship."

"But only in sleep."

"It would be strange enough though," said Lewis, "if there really were such things as fairies."

"There are such, of a certainty," replied the other; "but it is all a fable, that their whole pleasure is to make men happy. They plant those wishes in our bosoms which we ourselves do not know of; those over-wrought pretensions—that super-human covetousness of super-human gifts; so that in our desponding delirium we afterwards despise the beautiful earth with all its glorious stores."

Lewis answered with a pressure of the hand

※ ※ ※

JACOB GRIMM
(1785-1863)

WILHELM GRIMM
(1786-1859)

THE BROTHERS GRIMM, who passed the whole of their lives together, are the founders of the science of folk-lore. Both very excellent scholars, they were interested in their national poetry in all of its phases. At the same time they went about collecting all the popular tales they could, and finally published them between 1812 and 1815 in a collection called *Children's and Household Stories*. This has made the name of the brothers Grimm famous throughout the civilised world. *Rumpelstiltskin* is taken from this delightful collection.

The present version, anonymously translated, is reprinted from an undated English edition of *Children's and Household Stories*.

RUMPELSTILTSKIN

THERE was once a poor Miller who had a beautiful daughter, and one day, having to go to speak with the King, he said, in order to make himself appear of consequence, that he had a daughter who could spin straw into gold. The King was very fond of gold, and thought to himself, "That is an art which would please me very well"; so he said to the Miller, "If your daughter is so very clever, bring her to the castle in the morning, and I will put her to the proof."

As soon as she arrived the King led her into a chamber which was full of straw, and, giving her a wheel and a reel, he said, "Now set yourself to work, and if you have not spun this straw into gold by an early hour to-morrow, you must die." With these words he shut the room door, and left the maiden alone.

There she sat for a long time, thinking how to save her life, for she did not know how to spin straw into gold; and her trouble increased more and more, till at last she began to weep. All at once the door opened and in stepped a little man, who said, "Good evening, fair maiden; why do you weep so sore?"

"Ah," she replied, "I must spin this straw into gold, and I am sure I do not know how."

The little man asked, "What will you give me if I spin it for you?"

"My necklace," said the maiden.

The Dwarf took it, placed himself in front of the wheel, and whirr, whirr, whirr, three times round, and the bobbin was full. Then he set up another, and whirr, whirr, whirr, thrice round again, and a second bobbin was full; and so he went on all night long, until all the straw was spun, and the bobbins were full of gold.

At sunrise the King came, and he was very much astonished to see the gold. The sight of it gladdened him, but did not make his heart less covetous. He caused the maiden to be led into another room, still larger, full of straw; and then he bade her spin it into gold during the night if she valued her life. The maiden was again quite at a loss what to do; but while she cried the door opened suddenly, as before, and the Dwarf appeared and asked her what she would give him in return for his assistance. "The ring off my finger," she replied. The little man took the ring and began to spin at once, and by the morning all the straw was changed to glistening gold.

The King was rejoiced above measure at the sight of this, but still he was not satisfied. So leading the maiden into another still larger room, full of straw as the others, he said, "This you must spin during the night; but if you accomplish it you shall be my bride. "For," thought he to himself, "a richer wife you cannot have in all the world."

When the maiden was left alone, the Dwarf once again appeared, and asked, for the third time, "What will you give me to do this for you?"

"I have nothing left that I can give you," replied the maiden.

"Then promise me your first-born child if you become Queen," said he.

The Miller's daughter thought, "Who can tell if that will ever happen?" and, not knowing how else to help herself out of her trouble, she promised the Dwarf what he asked; and he immediately set about and finished the spinning.

When morning came, and the King found all he had wished for done, he kept his promise, and the Miller's fair daughter became Queen.

About a year after the marriage, when she had ceased to think about the little Dwarf, she brought a fine child into the world; and, suddenly, soon after its birth, the little man appeared and demanded what she had promised. The frightened Queen offered him all the riches of the kingdom if he would leave her her child; but the Dwarf answered, "No; something human is dearer to me than all the wealth of the world."

The Queen began to weep and groan so much that the Dwarf had pity on her, and said, "I will leave you three days to think; if in that time you discover my name you shall keep your child."

All night long the Queen racked her brains for all the names she could think of, and sent a messenger through the country to collect far and wide any new names. The following morning came the Dwarf, and she began with "Caspar," "Melchior," "Balthasar," and all the odd names she knew; but at each the little man exclaimed, "That is not my name."

The second day the Queen inquired of all her people for uncommon and curious names, and called the Dwarf "Ribs-of-Beef," "Sheepshank," "Whalebone"; but at each he said, "This is not my name."

The third day the messenger came back and said, "I have not found a single name; but as I came to a high mountain near the edge of a forest where foxes and hares say good-night to each other, I saw there a little house, and before the door a fire was burning, and round this fire a very curious little man was dancing on one leg, and shouting,

"'To-day I stew, and then I bake,
To-morrow I the Queen's child take;
For she little thinks, or I much mistake,
That my name is Rumpelstiltskin!"

When the Queen heard this she was very glad, for now she knew the name. Soon after came the Dwarf, and asked, "Now, my lady Queen, what is my name?"

"First she said, "Are you called Conrade?"

"No."

"Are you called Hal?"

"No."

"Are you called Rumpelstiltskin?"

"A witch has told you! A witch has told you!" shrieked the little man, and stamped his right foot so hard in the ground with rage that he could not draw it out again. Then he took hold of his left leg with both his hands, and pulled away so hard that his right came off in the struggle, and he hopped away howling terribly. And from that day to this the Queen has heard no more of her troublesome visitor.

❋ ❋ ❋

GOTTFRIED KELLER

(1819-1890)

KELLER, born at Zürich, was first apprenticed to a landscape painter, and subsequently spent two years in Munich learning to paint. His inclinations prompted him to desert painting for literature, and his first work was a collection of poetry. He next wrote his important novel, *Der grüne Heinrich*, which displayed a great deal of power and originality. He returned to his native city where, in 1872, he published his beautiful series of stories, *Seven Legends*. Keller ranks highly among German novelists. *The Virgin and the Nun* is one of the charming and quaintly humorous stories in *Seven Legends*.

The present version, translated by Martin Wyness, is reprinted, from *Seven Legends*, by permission of the publishers, Gowans & Gray, Glasgow, 1911.

THE VIRGIN AND THE NUN

O that I had wings like a dove: for then would I
flee away, and be at rest.   Psalm LV. 6.

A CONVENT lay on a mountain overlooking a wide prospect
and its wall gleamed across the land. Within, it was full of
women, beautiful and unbeautiful, who all served the Lord and
his Virgin Mother after a strict rule.

The most beautiful of the nuns was called Beatrix, and was sacristan
of the convent. Of tall and commanding presence, she went about her
duties with stately carriage, saw to choir and altar, looked after the
sacristy, and rang the bell before the first flush of dawn and when the
evening-star arose.

Yet amid it all she cast many a tear-dimmed glance at the busy
loom of the blue distance. There she saw weapons glancing, heard the
horn of the hunters in the woods, and the clear shout of men, and her
breast filled with longing for the world.

At last she could control her desire no longer, and one clear, moonlit
night in June she rose, dressed herself and put on stout new shoes, and
went to the altar, equipped for a journey. "I have served thee faithfully
these many years," she said to the Virgin Mary, "but now take the keys
thyself; for I can endure the heat in my heart no longer!" With that
she laid her bundle of keys upon the altar, and went forth from the
convent. She made her way down amid the solitude of the mountain
and wandered on until she came to a cross-road in an oak-forest, where
uncertain which way to take, she sat down by the side of a spring, which
was provided with a stone basin and a bench for the benefit of wayfarers. Until the sun rose, she sat there, and was drenched with the
falling dew.

Then the sun came over the tops of the trees, and the first rays which
shot through the forest-road fell on a glittering knight who came riding
in full armour all alone. The nun stared with all her lovely eyes, and did
not lose an inch of the manly apparition; but she kept so still that the
knight would never have seen her had not the murmur of the fountain
caught his ear and guided his eyes. He at once turned aside to the
spring, dismounted from his horse and let it drink, while he greeted the
nun respectfully. He was a crusader who, after long absence, was
making his way home alone, for he had lost all his men.

In spite of his respectfulness, he never once removed his eyes from
the charms of Beatrix, who held hers just as steady, and gazed as fixedly
as ever on the warrior; for he was no inconsiderable part of that world
for which she had longed so in secret. But suddenly she cast down her

eyes and felt bashful. At last the knight asked her which way she was going, and whether he could be of any service to her. The full tones of his voice startled her; she looked at him once more, and, fascinated by his glances, acknowledged that she had run away from the convent to see the world, but that she was frightened already and did not know which way to turn.

At that the knight, who had all his wits about him, laughed heartily, and offered to conduct the lady so far on the right way, if she would trust herself to him. His castle, he added, was not more than a day's journey from where they were; and there, if she chose, she could make her preparations in security, and after more mature reflection could proceed on her way into the fair, wide world.

Without replying, but yet without opposition, she allowed herself, trembling somewhat nevertheless, to be lifted up on horseback. The knight swung himself up after her, and, with the rosy-blushing nun before him, trotted joyously through woods and meadows.

For two or three hundred lengths, she held herself erect and gazed straight before her, her hands clasped over her bosom. But soon she had laid her head back on his breast, and submitted to the kisses which the stalwart lord imprinted thereon. And by another three hundred lengths she was returning them as fervidly as if she had never rung a convent-bell. In such circumstances, they saw nothing of the bright landscape through which they journeyed. The nun, who once had longed to see the wide world, now shut her eyes to it, and confined herself to that portion of it which the horse could carry on its back.

The knight Wonnebold also scarcely gave a thought to his father's castle, until its towers glittered before him in the moonlight. But all was silent without the castle, and even more silent within, while never a light was to be seen. Wonnebold's father and mother were dead and all the menials departed, save an ancient castellan, who after long knocking made his appearance with a lantern, and almost died for joy when he saw the knight standing at the painfully-opened door. In spite of his solitude and his years the old man had maintained the interior of the castle in habitable condition, and especially had kept the knight's chamber in constant readiness, so that he might be able to go to rest the moment he should return from his travels. So Beatrix rested with him and appeased her longing.

Neither had any thought now of separating from the other. Wonnebold opened his mother's chests. Beatrix clad herself in her rich garments and adorned herself with her jewels, and so they lived for the moment splendidly and in joy, except that the lady remained without rights or title, and was regarded by her lover as his chattel; she desired nothing better for the meantime.

But one day a stranger baron and his train turned into the castle, which by this time was again staffed with servants, and great cheer was made in his honour. At length the men fell to dicing, at which the master of the house had such constant good luck that, flushed with good fortune and confidence, he risked his dearest possession, as he called it, to wit the fair Beatrix as she stood, with the costly jewels she was wearing, against an old, melancholy mountain-keep which his opponent laughingly staked.

Beatrix, who had looked on at the game well contented, now turned pale, and with good reason; for the throw which ensued left the presumptuous one in the lurch, and made the baron the winner.

He wasted no time, but at once took his leave with his fair prize and his attendants. Beatrix barely found time to appropriate the unlucky dice and hide them in her bosom, and then with streaming eyes followed the unfeeling winner.

After the little cavalcade had ridden some miles they reached a pleasant grove of young beeches, through which a clear brook flowed. Like a light-green silken tent, the tender foliage waved aloft, supported on the slender silvery stems, between which the spacious summer landscape was seen in glimpses. Here the baron meant to rest with his booty. He ordered his people to go a little farther ahead, while he got down in the pleasant greenwood with Beatrix, and made to draw her to his side with caresses.

At that she drew herself up proudly, and darting a flaming glance upon him exclaimed that he had won her person, but not her heart, which was not to be won against an old ruin. If she were a man, he would set something worth while against it. If he would stake his life, he might cast for her heart, which should be pledged to him for ever and be his own if he won; but if she won, his life should be in her hand, and she should be absolute mistress of her own person once again.

She said this with great gravity; but all the time looked at him with such a strange expression that his heart began to thump, and he regarded her in bewilderment. She seemed to become more and more beautiful as she continued in a softer voice, and with a searching look, "Who would choose to woo a woman when she returns not his wooing, and has received no proof of his courage? Give me your sword, take these dice, and risk it; then we may be united as two true lovers!" At the same time she pressed into his hand the ivory dice warm from her bosom. Bewitched, he gave her his sword and sword-belt, and forthwith threw eleven at one throw.

Next Beatrix took the dice, rattled them vigorously in her hollowed hands with a secret sigh to the Holy Mary the Mother of God, and threw twelve, so that she won.

"I make you a present of your life!" she said, bowed gravely to the baron, picked up her skirts and put the sword under her arm, and rapidly took her departure in the direction whence she had come. As soon as she was out of view of the still quite nonplussed and bewildered baron, she slyly proceeded no farther, but fetched a circuit about the grove, walked quietly back into it, and hid herself not fifty paces from the disappointed lover behind the beach-stems, which at that distance grew sufficiently closely to hide the prudent lady, if need were. She kept quite still; only a sunbeam fell upon a noble gem at her neck, so that it flashed through the grove unknown to her. The baron indeed saw the gleam, and stared at it a moment in his bewilderment. But he took it for a shining dewdrop on a tree-leaf, and never gave it a second thought.

At last he recovered from his stupefaction, and blew lustily upon his hunting-horn. When his people came, he sprang upon his horse and pursued after the eloping lady to secure her again. It was the best part of an hour before the riders returned, and despondently and slowly made their way through the beech-trees, this time without halting. When the lurking Beatrix saw the coast clear, she rose and hastened home without sparing her shoes.

During all this time Wonnebold had passed a very bad day, racked by remorse and anger; and, as he understood that he had disgraced himself in the eyes of his love, whom he had gambled away so lightly, he began to realise how highly he had unconsciously esteemed her, and how difficult it was to live without her. So, when she unexpectedly stood before him, without ever waiting to utter his surprise, he opened his arms to her, and she hastened into them without complaint or reproach. He laughed loudly as she related her stratagem, and he began to ponder over her fidelity; for the baron was a very comely and pretty fellow.

Accordingly, to guard against all future mischances, he made the fair Beatrix his lawful wedded wife in presence of all his peers and vassals, so that henceforth she ranked as a knight's lady and took her place among her equals at chase, feast and dance, as well as in the cottages of their dependents and in the family seat at church.

The years passed with their changes, and in the course of twelve fruitful harvests she bore her husband eight sons, who grew up like young stags.

When the eldest was eighteen years old, she rose one autumn night from her Wonnebold's side unperceived by him, laid all her worldly array carefully in the same chests from which it had once been taken, closed them, and laid the keys at the sleeper's side. Then she went barefooted to the bedside of her sons, and kissed them lightly one after the other. Last of all, she went again to her husband's bed, kissed him too, and then shore the long hair from her head, once more put on the dark nun's frock, which she had preserved carefully, and so left the castle by stealth, and made her way amid the raging wind of the autumn night and the falling leaves back to that convent from which she had once run away. Indefatigably she passed the beads of her rosary through her fingers, and as she prayed she thought over the life which she had enjoyed.

So she went on her pilgrimage uncomplaining, until she stood again before the convent-door. When she knocked, the door-keeper, who had aged somewhat, opened and greeted her by name as indifferently as if she had only been absent half an hour. Beatrix went past her into the church, and fell on her knees before the altar of the Holy Virgin, who began to speak and said, "Thou has stayed away rather long, my daughter. I have seen to thy duties as sacristan all the time; but now I am very glad that thou art returned and canst take back thy keys!"

The image leaned down, and handed the keys to Beatrix, who was both alarmed and delighted at the great miracle. Forthwith she set about her duties, saw to this and that, and when the bell rang for dinner she went to table. Many of the nuns had grown old, others were dead, young ones were newly come, and another abbess sat at the head of the table; but no one suspected what had happened to Beatrix, who took her accustomed seat; for Mary had filled her place in the nun's own form.

But another day, when some ten years had passed, the nuns were to celebrate a great festival, and agreed that each of them should bring the Mother of God the finest present she could devise. So one embroidered a rich church-banner, another an altar-cloth, and another a vestment. One composed a Latin hymn, and another set it to music. A third wrote and illuminated a prayer-book. Whoever could do nothing else stitched a new shirt for the Christ-child, and sister cook made him a dish of fritters. Only Beatrix had prepared nothing, for she was rather weary of life, and she lived with her thoughts more in the past than in the present.

When the feast-day came, and she had no gift to dedicate, the other nuns were surprised and reproached her so that she sat humbly aside as all the pretty things were being borne in festal procession and laid before the altar of the church, which was adorned with flowers, while the bells rang out and the incense-clouds rose on high.

Just as the nuns were proceeding to sing and play right skilfully, a grey-headed knight passed by on his way, with eight armed youths as lovely as pictures, all mounted on proud steeds and attended by a like number of tall esquires. It was Wonnebold with his sons, whom he was taking to the Imperial army.

Perceiving that high Mass was being celebrated in God's house, he called to his sons to dismount, and entered the church with them to offer a devout prayer to the Holy Virgin. Every one was lost in admiration at the noble spectacle, as the iron greybeard knelt with the eight youthful warriors, who looked like so many mail-clad angels; and the nuns were so put off their music that for a moment it ceased altogether. But Beatrix recognised them all for her children, from her husband, gave an exclamation and hastened to them, and, recalling herself to their memory, disclosed her secret, and declared the great miracle which she had experienced.

Then all were forced to admit that she had brought the Virgin the richest gift of the day. That it was accepted was testified by eight wreaths of fresh oak-leaves which suddenly appeared on the young men's heads, placed there by the invisible hand of the Queen of Heaven.

❀ ❀ ❀

HERMANN SUDERMANN
(1857-   )

SUDERMANN was born in East Prussia, and after an education at the Königsberg and Berlin Universities, became a journalist. He edited a journal for a year and subsequently devoted his time to literature. He has written a number of plays and novels, the former of which inaugurated a new period in the history of the German stage. He has also contributed several volumes of short stories, foremost of these being the volume entitled *The Indian Lily*.

The Victim is reprinted by permission of the publisher, from *The Indian Lily and Other Stories*, translated by Ludwig Lewisohn and published by B. W. Huebsch, copyright, 1911.

THE VICTIM

MADAME NELSON, the beautiful American, had come to us from Paris, equipped with a phenomenal voice and solid Italian technique. She had immediately sung her way into the hearts of Berlin music-lovers, provided that you care to call a mixture of snobbishness, sophisticated impressionableness and goose-like imitativeness—heart. She had, therefore, been acquired by one of our most distinguished opera houses at a large salary and with long leaves of absence. I use the plural of opera house in order that no one may try to scent out the facts.

Now we had her, more especially our world of Lotharios had her. Not the younger sons of high finance, who make the boudoirs unsafe with their tall collars and short breeches; nor the bearers of ancient names who, having hung up their uniforms in the evening, assume monocle and bracelet and drag these through second and third-class drawing-rooms. No, she belonged to those worthy men of middle age, who have their palaces in the west end, whose wives one treats with infinite respect, and to whose evenings one gives a final touch of elegance by singing two or three songs for nothing.

Then she committed her first folly. She went travelling with an Italian tenor. "For purposes of art," was the official version. But the time for the trip—the end of August—had been unfortunately chosen. And, as she returned ornamented with scratches administered by the tenor's pursuing wife—no one believed her.

Next winter she ruined a counsellor of a legation and magnate's son so thoroughly that he decamped to an unfrequented equatorial region, leaving behind him numerous promissory notes of questionable value.

This poor fellow was revenged the following winter by a dark-haired Roumanian fiddler, who beat her and forced her to carry her jewels to a pawn-shop, where they were redeemed at half price by their original donour and used to adorn the plump, firm body of a stupid little ballet dancer.

Of course her social position was now forfeited. But then Berlin forgets so rapidly. She became proper again and returned to her earlier inclinations for gentlemen of middle life with extensive palaces and extensive wives. So there were quite a few houses—none of the strictest tone, of course—that were very glad to welcome the radiant blonde with her famous name and fragrant and modest gowns—from Paquin at ten thousand francs apiece.

At the same time she developed a remarkable business instinct. Her connections with the stock exchange permitted her to speculate without the slightest risk. For what gallant broker would let a lovely woman lose? Thus she laid the foundation of a goodly fortune, which was made to assume stately proportions by a tour through the United States, and was given a last touch of solidity by a successful speculation in Dresden real estate.

Furthermore, it would be unjust to conceal the fact that her most recent admirer, the wool manufacturer Wormser, had a considerable share in this hurtling rise of her fortunes.

Wormser guarded his good repute carefully. He insisted that his illegitimate inclinations never lack the stamp of highest elegance. He desired that they be given the greatest possible publicity at race-meets and first nights. He didn't care if people spoke with a degree of rancour if only he was connected with the temporary lady of his heart.

Now, to be sure, there was a Mrs. Wormser. She came of a good Frankfort family. Dowry: a million and a half. She was modern to the very tips of her nervous, restless fingers.

This lady was inspired by such lofty social ideals that she would have considered an inelegant *liaison* on her husband's part an insult no

only offered to good taste in general, but to her own in particular. Such
an one she would never have forgiven. On the other hand, she approved of Madame Nelson thoroughly. She considered her the most
costly and striking addition to her household. Quite figuratively, of
course. Everything was arranged with the utmost propriety. At great
charity festivals the two ladies exchanged a friendly glance, and they
saw to it that their gowns were never made after the same model.

Then it happened that the house of Wormser was shaken. It wasn't
a serious breakdown, but among the good things that had to be thrown
overboard belonged—at the demand of the helping Frankforters—
Madame Nelson.

And so she waited, like a virgin, for love, like a man in the weather
bureau, for a given star. She felt that her star was yet to rise.

This was the situation when, one day, Herr von Karlstadt had himself presented to her. He was a captain of industry; international reputation; ennobled; the not undistinguished son of a great father. He
had not hitherto been found in the market of love, but it was said of
him that notable women had committed follies for his sake.

All in all, he was a man who commanded the general interest in
quite a different measure from Wormser.

But artistic successes had raised Madame Nelson's name once more,
too, and when news of the accomplished fact circulated, society found
it hard to decide as to which of the two lent the other a more brilliant
light, or which was the more to be envied.

However that was, history was richer by a famous pair of lovers.

But just as there had been a Mrs. Wormser, so there was a Mrs. von
Karlstadt.

And it is this lady of whom I wish to speak.

Mentally as well as physically Mara von Karlstadt did not belong
to that class of persons which imperatively commands the attention of
the public.

She was sensitive to the point of madness, a little sensuous, something of an enthusiast, coquettish only in so far as good taste demanded
it, and hopelessly in love with her husband. She was in love with him
to the extent that she regarded the conquests which occasionally came to
him, spoiled as he was, as the inevitable consequences of her fortunate
choice. They inspired her with a certain woeful anger and also with
a degree of pride.

The daughter of a great land owner in South Germany, she had
been brought up in seclusion, and had learned only very gradually how
to glide unconcernedly through the drawing-rooms. A tense smile
upon her lips, which many took for irony, was only a remnant of her
old diffidence. Delicate, dark in colouring with a fine cameo-like profile, smooth hair and a tawny look in her nearsighted eyes—thus she

glided about in society, and few but friends of the house took any notice
of her.

And this woman who found her most genuine satisfaction in the
peacefulness of life, who was satisfied if she could slip into her carriage at midnight without the annoyance of one searching glance, of
one inquiring word, saw herself suddenly and without suspecting the
reason, become the centre of a secret and almost insulting curiosity. She
felt a whispering behind her in society, she saw from her box the lenses
of many opera glasses pointing her way.

The conversation of her friends began to team with hints, and into
the tone of the men whom she knew there crept a kind of tender compassion which pained her even though she knew not how to interpret
it.

For the present no change was to be noted in the demeanour of her
husband. His club and his business had always kept him away from
home a good deal, and if a few extra hours of absence were now added
it was easy to account for these in harmless ways, or rather, not to account for them at all, since no one made any inquiry.

Then, however, anonymous letters began to come—thick, fragrant
ones with stamped coronets, and thin ones on ruled paper with the smudge
of soiled fingers.

She burned the first batch; the second batch she handed to her
husband.

The latter, who was not far from forty, and who had trained himself to an attitude of imperious brusqueness, straightened up, knotted his
bushy Bismarck moustache, and said:

"Well, suppose it is true. What have you to lose?"

She did not burst into tears of despair; she did not indulge in fits of
rage, she didn't even leave the room with quiet dignity; her soul seemed
neither wounded nor broken. She was not even affrighted. She only
thought: "I have forgiven him so much; why not forgive him this
too?"

And as she had shared him before without feeling herself degraded,
so she would try to share him again.

But she soon discovered that this logic of the heart would prove wanting in this instance.

In former cases she had concealed his weakness under a veil of care
and considerateness. The fear of discovery had made a conscious but
silent accessory of her. When it was all over she breathed deep relief
at the thought: "I am the only one who even suspected."

This time all the world seemed invited to witness the spectacle.

For now she understood all that in recent days had tortured her like
an unexplained blot, an alien daub in the face which every one sees but
he whom it disfigures. Now she knew what the smiling hints of

her friends and the consoling desires of men had meant. Now she recognised the reason why she was wounded by the attention of all.

She was "the wife of the man whom Madame Nelson . . ."

And so torturing a shame came upon her as though she herself were the cause of the disgrace with which the world seemed to overwhelm her.

This feeling had not come upon her suddenly. At first a stabbing curiosity had awakened in her a self-torturing expectation, not without its element of morbid attraction. Daily she asked herself: "What will develop to-day?"

With quivering nerves and cramped heart, she entered evening after evening, for the season was at its height, the halls of strangers on her husband's arm.

And it was always the same thing. The same glances that passed from her to him and from him to her, the same compassionate sarcasm upon averted faces, the same hypocritical delicacy in conversation, the same sudden silence as soon as she turned to any group of people to listen —the same cruel pillory for her, evening after evening, night after night.

And if all this had not been, she would have felt it just the same.

And in these drawing-rooms, there were so many women whose husbands' affairs were the talk of the town. Even her predecessor, Mrs. Wormser, had passed over the expensive immorality of her husband with a self-sufficing smile and a condescending jest, and the world had bowed down to her respectfully, as it always does when scenting a temperament that it is powerless to wound.

Why had this martyrdom come to her, of all people?

Thus, half against her own will, she began to hide, to refuse this or that invitation, and to spend the free evenings in the nursery, watching over the sleep of her boys and weaving dreams of a new happiness. The illness of her older child gave her an excuse for withdrawing from society altogether and her husband did not restrain her.

It had never come to an explanation between them, and as he was always considerate, even tender, and as sharp speeches were not native to her temper, the peace of the home was not disturbed.

Soon it seemed to her, too, as though the rude inquisitiveness of the world was slowly passing away. Either one had abandoned the critical condition of her wedded happiness for more vivid topics, or else she had become accustomed to the state of affairs.

She took up a more social life, and the shame which she had felt in appearing publicly with her husband gradually died out.

What did not die out, however, was a keen desire to know the nature and appearance of the woman in whose hands lay her own destiny. How did she administer the dear possession that fate had put in her power? And when and how would she give it back?

She threw aside the last remnant of reserve and questioned friends. Then, when she was met by a smile of compassionate ignorance, she asked women. These were more ready to report. But she would not and could not believe what she was told. He had surely not degraded himself into being one of a succession of moneyed rakes. It was clear to her that, in order to soothe her grief, people slandered the woman and him with her.

In order to watch her secretly, she veiled heavily and drove to the theatre where Madame Nelson was singing. Shadowlike, cowered in the depths of a box which she had rented under an assumed name and followed with a kind of pained voluptuousness the ecstasies of love which the other woman, fully conscious of the victorious loveliness of her body, unfolded for the benefit of the breathless crowd.

With such an abandoned raising of her radiant arms, she threw herself upon *his* breast; with that curve of her modelled limbs, she lay before *his* knees.

And in her awakened a reverent, renouncing envy of a being who had so much to give, beside whom she was but a dim and poor shadow, weary, with motherhood, corroded with grief.

At the same time there appeared a California mine owner, a multimillionaire, with whom her husband had manifold business dealings. He introduced his daughters into society and himself gave a number of luxurious dinners at which he tried to assemble guests of the most exclusive character.

Just as they were about to enter a carriage to drive to the "Bristol," to one of these dinners, a message came which forced Herr von Karlstadt to take an immediate trip to his factories. He begged his wife to go instead, and she did not refuse.

The company was almost complete and the daughter of the mine owner was doing the honours of the occasion with appropriate grace when the doors of the reception room opened for the last time and through the open doorway floated—rather than walked—Madame Nelson.

The petrified little group turned its glance of inquisitive horror upon Mrs. von Karlstadt, while the mine owner's daughter adjusted the necessary introductions with a grand air.

Should she go or not? No one was to be found who would offer her his arm. Her feet were paralysed. And she remained.

The company sat down at table. And since fate, in such cases, never does its work by halves, it came to pass that Madame Nelson was assigned to a seat immediately opposite her.

The people present seemed grateful to her that they had not been forced to witness a scene, and overwhelmed her with delicate signs of this gratitude. Slowly her self-control returned to her. She even dared to look about her observantly, and, behold, Madame Nelson appealed to her.

Her French was faultless, her manners equally so, and when the Californian drew her into the conversation, she practised the delicate art of modest considerateness to the extent of talking past Mrs. von Karlstadt in such a way that those who did not know were not enlightened and those who knew felt their anxiety depart.

In order to thank her for this alleviation of a fatally painful situation, Mrs. von Karlstadt occasionally turned perceptibly toward the singer. For this Madame Nelson was grateful in her turn. Thus their glances began to meet in friendly fashion, their voices to cross, the atmosphere became less constrained from minute to minute, and when the meal was over the astonished assembly had come to the conclusion that Mrs. von Karlstadt was ignorant of the true state of affairs.

The news of this peculiar meeting spread like a conflagration. Her women friends hastened to congratulate her on her strength of mind; her male friends praised her loftiness of spirit. She went through the degradation which she had suffered as though it were a triumph. Only her husband went about for a time with an evil conscience and a frowning forehead.

Months went by. The quietness of summer intervened, but the memory of that evening rankled in her and blinded her soul. Slowly the thought arose in her which was really grounded in vanity, she looked, in its execution, like suffering love—the thought that she would legitimise her husband's irregularity in the face of society.

Hence when the season began again she wrote a letter to Madame Nelson in which she invited her, in a most cordial way, to sing at an approaching function in her home. She proffered this request, not only in admiration of the singer's gifts, but also, as she put it, "to render nugatory a persistent and disagreeable rumour."

Madame Nelson, to whom this chance of repairing her fair fame was very welcome, had no indiscretion to assent, and even to accept the condition of entire secrecy in regard to the affair.

The chronicler may pass over the painful evening in question with suitable delicacy of touch. Nothing obvious or crass took place. Madame Nelson sang three enchanting songs, accompanied by a first-rate pianist. A friend of the house of whom the hostess had requested this favour took Madame Nelson to the *buffet*. A number of guileless individuals surrounded that lady with helpful adoration. An ecstatic mood prevailed. The one regrettable feature of the occasion was that the host had to withdraw—as quietly as possible, of course—on account of a splitting headache.

Berlin society, which felt wounded in the innermost depth of its ethics, never forgave the Karlstadts for this evening. I believe that in certain circles the event is still remembered, although years have now passed.

Its immediate result, however, was a breach between man and wife. Mara went to the Riviera, where she remained until spring.

An apparent reconciliation was then patched up, but its validity was purely external.

Socially, too, things readjusted themselves, although people continued to speak of the Karlstadt house with a smile that asked for indulgence.

Mara felt this acutely, and while her husband appeared oftener and more openly with his mistress, she withdrew into the silence of her inner chambers.

Then she took a lover.

Or, rather, she was taken by him.

A lonely evening. . . . A fire in the chimney. . . . A friend who came in by accident. . . . The same friend who had taken care of Madame Nelson for her on that memorable evening. . . . The fall of snow without. . . . A burst of confidence. . . . A sob. . . . A nestling against the caressing hand. . . . It was done. . . .

Months passed. She experienced not one hour of intoxication, not one of that inner absolution which love brings. It was moral slackness and weariness that made her yield again. . . .

Then the consequences appeared.

Of course, the child could not, must not, be born. And it was not born.

One can imagine the horror of that tragic time; the criminal flame of sleepless nights, the blood-charged atmosphere of guilty despair; the moans of agony that had to be throttled behind closed doors.

What remained to her was lasting invalidism.

The way from her bed to an invalid's chair was long and hard.

Time passed. Improvements came and gave place to lapses in her condition. Trips to watering-places alternated with visits to sanitariums.

In those places sat the pallid, anæmic women who had been tortured and ruined by their own or alien guilt. There they sat and engaged in wretched flirtations with flighty neurasthenics.

And gradually things went from bad to worse. The physicians shrugged their friendly shoulders.

And then it happened that Madame Nelson felt the inner necessity of running away with a handsome young tutor. She did this less out of passion than to convince the world—after having thoroughly fleeced it— of the unselfishness of her feelings. For it was her ambition to be counted among the great lovers of all time.

One evening von Karlstadt entered the sick chamber of his wife, sat down beside her bed and silently took her hand.

She was aware of everything, and asked with a gentle smile upon her white lips:

"Be frank with me: did you love her, at least?"

He laughed merrily. "What should have made me love this—business lady?"

They looked at each other long. Upon her face death had set its seal. His hair was grey, his self-respect broken, his human worth squandered. . . .

And then, suddenly, they clung to each other, and leaned their foreheads against each other, and wept.

❊ ❊ ❊

ARTHUR SCHNITZLER

(1862-   )

SCHNITZLER, born at Vienna, took a medical degree and, for a time, followed the practice of medicine. He turned to literature in the nineties and soon created for himself a distinguished position in Austrian literature. He has been equally successful in drama and fiction. His stories are graceful, brilliant and finished. Schnitzler won the Grillparzer prize in 1908.

Flowers, tender and wistful, is one of Schnitzler's exquisite tales. It is used in this collection by kind permission of the author and his representatives, Curtis Brown, Ltd.

FLOWERS

I WANDERED about the streets the whole afternoon, while the snow fell slowly, in large flakes—and now I am at home, my lamp is burning, my cigar is lighted and my books lie close by; in fact, I have everything that affords true comfort. Yet all is in vain; I can think of but one thing.

But had she not been dead for a long time as far as I was concerned?—yes, dead; or, as I thought with the childish pathos of the deceived, "worse than dead?" And now that I know that she is not "worse than dead," but simply dead, like the many others who lie out there, under the ground, forever—in spring, in the hot summer, and when the snow falls, as today—without any hope of ever returning—since that time I know that she did not die a moment sooner for me than she did for the rest of the world. Sorrow?—no. It is only the general horror that we all feel when something that once belonged to us, and whose entire being is still clear in our minds, sinks into the grave.

It was very sad when I discovered that she was deceiving me;—but there was so much else with it!—the fury and sudden hatred, and the horror of existence, and—ah, yes—the wounded vanity;—the sorrow only came later! But then there was the consolation that she also must be suffering.—I have them all yet, I can reread them at any time, those dozens of letters which sob, pray, and beseech forgiveness!—And I can still see her before me, in her dark dress and small straw hat, standing at the street corner in the twilight as I stepped out of the gate—looking after me.—And I still think of the last meeting when she stood in front of me with her large, beautiful eyes, set in that round, childlike face that now had become pale and wan.—I did not give her my hand when she left me;—when she left me for the last time.—And I watched her go down the street from my window and then she disappeared—forever. Now she can never return. . . .

My knowing it at all is due to an accident. I could have been unaware of it for weeks and months. I happened to meet her uncle one morning. I had not seen him for at least a year, as he does not come to Vienna very often. In fact, I had only met him two or three times before this. Our first meeting was three years ago at a bowling party. She and her mother were there also.—And then the following summer: I was in the Prater with a few friends. Her uncle was sitting at the next table with some gentlemen. They were all gay, and he drank to my health. And before he left he came up to me and told me confidentially that his niece was madly in love with me!—And in my half-giddiness it seemed very foolish and queer that the old gentleman should tell such a thing here, midst the music of the cymbals and violins—to me, who knew it so well, and on whose lips still clung the impression of her last kiss. And now, this morning! I almost walked past him. I asked for his niece, more out of politeness than interest. I knew nothing more about her; her letters had stopped coming a long time ago; only flowers she sent me, regularly. Recollections of our happiest days! Once a month they came; no card: just silent, humble flowers.—And when I asked the old gentleman he was all astonishment. "You don't know that the poor girl died a week ago?" It was a terrible shock!—Then he told me more. She was ill for a long while, but was in bed hardly a week. And her illness? "Melancholia—anæmia.—The doctors themselves were not quite sure."

I remained a long while on the spot where the old gentleman had left me;—I was enervated, as if I had just gone through some great trouble.—And now it seems to me as if today marks the termination of a part of my life. Why—why? It was simply something external. I had no more feeling for her; in fact, I seldom thought of her any more. But now that I have written this all down I feel better; I am more composed—I am beginning to appreciate the coziness of my home.

——It is foolish and tormenting to think of it any more.——There are certainly others today who have a great deal more to mourn about than I.

I have taken a walk. It is a serene winter's day. The sky looks so grey, so cold, so far away.——And I am very calm. The old gentleman whom I met yesterday—it seems as if it had been weeks ago. And when I think of her I can see her in a peculiarly sharp and finished outline; only one thing is lacking: the anger which always associated itself with my thoughts of her. The real appreciation that she is no more on earth, that she is lying in a coffin, that she has been buried, I have not—I feel no sorrow. The world seemed calmer to me today. I once knew for just one moment that there is neither happiness nor sorrow; no, there are only the grimaces of joy and sadness; we laugh and we weep and we invite our soul to be present. I could sit down now and read deep, serious books, and should soon be able to penetrate into all of their learning. Or, I could stand in front of old pictures, which heretofore have meant nothing to me, and now appreciate their true beauty.——And when I think of certain dear friends who have died, my heart does not feel as sad as it used to—death has become something friendly; it stalks among us but does not want to harm us.

Snow, high, white snow on all the streets. Little Gretel came to me and suggested that we ought to take a sleigh ride. And we drove out into the country, over the smooth road, the sleigh bells ringing and the blue-grey sky above us. Gretel rested against my shoulder and looked out upon the long road with happy eyes. We came to an inn that we knew well from the summer. The oven was all aglow, and it was so hot that we had to move the table away, as Gretel's left ear and cheek became fire red. I had to kiss the paler cheek. Afterwards, the return home in the twilight! Gretel sat very close to me and held both of my hands in hers.——Then she said: "At last I have you again." She had thus, without racking her brain, struck the right note to make me happy. But perhaps it was the biting, clear air that unchained my thoughts, for I feel freer and more contented than I have in the last few days.

A short while ago again, as I lay dozing on my couch, a strange thought came to my mind. I appeared hard and cold to myself. As one who, without tears, in fact, without any emotion, stands at the grave in which he has buried a dear one. As one who has grown so hard that he cannot reconcile the horror of death.——Yes, irreconcilable, that is it.

Gone, quite gone! Life, happiness, and a little love drives all that foolishness away. I go again among people. I like them; they are harmless, they chatter about all sorts of jolly things. And Gretel is a dear, kind creature; and she is prettiest when she stands at my window and the sunbeams shine on her golden hair.

Something strange happened today.——It is the day on which she always sent me flowers. And the flowers came again as—as if nothing had changed. They came with the first mail, in a long, narrow white box. It was quite early, and I was still sleepy. And only when I was actually opening the box did I gain full consciousness. Then I almost had a shock. And there lay, daintily tied with a golden string, violets and pinks.—They lay as in a coffin. And as I took the flowers in my hand a shudder went through my heart.—But I understand how it is that they came again today. When she felt her illness, perchance even when she felt death approaching, she gave her usual order to the florist so that I would not miss her attention. Certainly, that is the explanation; as something quite natural, as something touching perhaps. —And still as I held them in my hands, these flowers, and they seemed to nod and tremble, then, in spite of reason and will power, I looked upon them as something ghostly, as if they had come from her, as if they were her greeting—as if she wanted always, even now that she was dead, to tell me of her love—of her tardy faithfulness. Ah, we do not understand death, we will never understand it; and a person is dead only after all that have known him have also passed away. To-day I grasped the flowers differently than usual, as if I might injure them were I to hold them too tight—as if their souls might begin to sob softly. And as they now stand in front of me on my desk, in a narrow, light-green vase, they seem to nod their heads in mournful gratitude. The full pain of a useless yearning spreads over me from them, and I believe that they could tell me something if we could only understand the language of *all* living things—not only of the things that talk.

I do not want to let myself be fooled. They are only flowers. They are a message from the past. They are no call, surely no call from the grave. They are simply flowers, and some florist tied them together mechanically, put a bit of cotton around them, then laid them in the white box, and mailed it.—And now that they are here, why do I think about them?

I spend many hours in the open air and take long, lonely walks. When I am among people I do not feel compatible with them. And I notice it when the sweet, blonde girl sits in my room, chattering away about all sorts of things—I don't know about what. When she is gone, in a moment it is as if she were miles away from me, as if the flood of people had engulfed her and left no traces behind. I should hardly be surprised if she did not come again.

The flowers are in the tall, green vase; their stems are in the water and their scent fills the room. They still retain their odour—in spite of the fact that I have had them a week and that they are already fading. And I believe all sorts of nonsense that I used to laugh at: I believe in the possibility of conversing with things in nature—I believe that one can communicate with clouds and springs; and I am waiting fur these flowers to begin to talk. But no, I feel sure that they are always speaking—even now—they are forever crying out; and I can almost understand them.

How glad I am that the winter is over! Already the breath of spring throbs in the air. I am not living any differently than before, still I sometimes feel as if the boundaries of my existence are expanding. Yesterday seems far off, and the happenings of a few days past are like vague dreams. It is still the same when Gretel leaves me, especially when I have not seen her for several days; then our friendship appears like an affair of the past ages. She always comes, from afar, from so far away!—But when she begins to chatter it is like olden times again, and I then have a clear consciousness of the present. And then her words are almost too loud and the colours seem too harsh. Yet as soon as she leaves me all is gone; there are no after-pictures or gradual, fading recollections.—And then I am alone with my flowers. They are now quite faded, quite faded. They have no more perfume. Gretel had not noticed them at all; but today she saw them and it seemed as if she wanted to question me, but then she suddenly appeared to have a secret horror for them;—she stopped speaking altogether and soon left me.

The petals are slowly falling off. I never touch them; anyway, if I did they would crumble. It makes me very sad to see them faded. I do not know why I have not the courage to make an end of all this nonsense. The faded flowers make me ill. I cannot stand them and I rush out. Once in the street, I feel that I have to hurry back to them, to care for them. And then I find them in the same green vase where I left them, tired and sad. Last evening I wept before them, as one weeps at a grave. Yet I never gave a thought to the sender of them. Perhaps I am wrong, yet it seems as if Gretel feels that there is something strange in my room. She does not laugh any more. She does not speak so loud, with that clear, lively voice to which I am accustomed. And I do not receive her as I used to. Then there is the fear that she will question me; and I realise what torture those questions would be.

She frequently brings her sewing, and if I am still at my books she sits quietly at the table and sews or crochets; and she waits patiently until I have finished and put my books away and come up to her and take her sewing out of her hands. Then I remove the green shade from the lamp so that a mellow light floods the room. I do not like dark corners.

Spring! My window is wide open. Late last evening Gretel and I looked out on to the street. The air was warm and balmy. And when I looked at the corner, where the street lamp spreads a weak light, I suddenly saw a shadow. I saw it and I did not—I know that I did not see it—I closed my eyes and I could suddenly see through my eyelids. There stood the miserable creature, in the pale lamp light, and I saw her face very clearly, as if the yellow sunshine were on it, and I saw in the pale, emaciated face those wounded eyes. Then I walked slowly away from the window and sat down at my desk; the candle spluttered in the breeze. And I remained motionless, for I knew that the poor creature was standing at the corner, waiting; and if I had dared to touch the faded flowers I would have taken them out of the vase and brought them to her. Thus I thought, and sincerely thought; yet I knew all the while that it was foolish. Now Gretel also left the window and came over to the back of my chair where she remained a moment to touch my hair with her lips. Then she went and left me alone.

I stared at the flowers. There are hardly any more. Mostly bare stems, dry and pitiful. They make me ill and drive me mad. And it must be evident; otherwise Gretel would have asked me; but she feels it, too. Now she had fled as if there were ghosts in my room.

Ghosts!—They are, they are!—Dead things playing with life! And if faded flowers smell mouldy it is only the remembrance of the time when they were in bloom. And the dead return as long as we do not forget them. What difference does it make if they cannot speak now; —I can hear them! She does not appear any more, yet I can see her! And the spring outside, and the sunshine on my rug, and the perfume of the lilacs in the park, and the people who pass below and do not interest me, are they life? If I pull down the curtains, the sun is dead. I do not care to know about all these people, and they are dead. I close my window, and the perfume of the lilacs is gone and spring is dead. I am more powerful than the sun, the people, and the spring. But more powerful than I is remembrance, for that comes when it wills and from it there is no escape. And these dry stems are more powerful than the perfume of the lilacs and the spring.

I was pondering over these pages when Gretel entered. She had never come so early. I was surprised, astonished. She remained a moment on the threshold, and I gazed at her without greeting her. Then she smiled and approached me. In her hand she carried a bouquet of fresh flowers. Then, without speaking, she laid them on my desk. In the next moment, she seized the withered stems in the green vase. It seemed as if someone had grasped my heart;—but I could not utter a sound. And when I wanted to rise and take her by the arm, she smiled at me. Holding the faded flowers high above her, she hurried to the window and threw them out into the street. I felt I wanted to throw myself after them; but Gretel stood at the sill, facing me. And on her head was the sunshine, the bright sunshine. And the aroma of lilacs came in through the window. And I looked at the empty, green vase on my desk;—I am not sure, yet I think I felt freer,—

yes, freer. Then Gretel approached me, picked up her bouquet, and held in front of my face cool, white lilacs. Such a healthy, fresh perfume—so soft, so cool; I wanted to bury my face in them. Laughing, white, beautiful flowers—and I felt that the spectre was gone. Gretel stood behind me and ran her hands through my hair. "You silly boy," she said. Did she know what she had done? I grasped her hands and kissed her.

In the evening we went out into the open, into the spring. We have just returned! I have lighted my candle. We took a long walk, and Gretel is so tired that she has fallen asleep in the chair. She is very beautiful when she smiles thus in her sleep.

Before me, in the narrow, green vase are the lilacs. Down on the street—no, no, they are not there any longer. Already the wind has blown them away with the rest of the dust.

❊ ❊ ❊

JACOB WASSERMANN
(1873-   )

WASSERMANN, born in Bavaria, wandered about in his youth, and finally settled in Austria where he began to write. He says of himself that his literary career began "when realism and naturalism were rampant," although he has not identified himself with any school. He has written a number of successful novels and was first made known to the English-speaking world through his *World's Illusion*. *The Beast* is a powerful story and typifies Wassermann's philosophy.

The present version translated for this collection is taken from *Der Geist des Pilgers*, published by the Rikola Verlag, Vienna, 1923. It is used here by permission of the author and his representatives, Curtis Brown, Ltd.

THE BEAST

IN one of the former capitals of central Germany great labour riots, which the citizens still recall with horror, broke out in the wake of the revolution. Thousands of striking labourers gathered in mobs and marched, on that misty February morning, towards the busy streets of the inner city. The jeering rabble, usually idle all the time, joined them, and the deploying police was soon no longer able to cope with the threatening throng. The iron shutters rattled down over the displays in the shop-windows; cafés and restaurants were locked in panicky haste; house doors were slammed to, and curious and terrified faces appeared at the windows when the wild shouting and whistling of the approaching masses became audible. These broke their way like an unstemmed flood; stones were hurled at the houses and smashed the windows. Here and there a shot was fired. The constabulary force saw itself reduced to take measures of defense and prepared to resist the mob with sabres and clubs. Turmoil and bitterness grew with each passing moment. The shouts and yells sounded more and more horrible. Bare arms and grimly threatening fists were stretched forth; eyes burned with rapacious and vindictive hatred. Women goaded on the men; ragged children filled the air with ear-splitting screams; and the slightest provocation, perhaps an irritating word, and murder and plundering would have been inevitable.

At that moment, there drove across a public square which the most advanced of the throng had just reached, a rather huge wagon resembling a furniture van, but which instead of side-walls had loose brown canvas hangings, and these showed the coat-of-arms of the royal family which had till recently ruled over the country. The sight of the hated emblems whipped the anger of the rioters into fury. In an instant the wagon was surrounded; the efforts of the police to break through the human ring were futile. The driver had pulled up the two horses, which, on being reined in so abruptly, trembled violently. A man jumped from the running-board at the rear of the wagon, unslung a rifle from his shoulder and cocked the trigger. This was the signal for the attack. A well-aimed blow knocked him down; thirty or forty arms reached for the cloth decorated with the escutcheon. The coachman's vehement, threatening gesticulation remained unnoticed; a word which he hurled at them was drowned in the turmoil and the protecting cover fell away in shreds from the frame-work. No sooner had this happened, when all, even the boldest of them, were seized with the utmost horror. The whistling, screaming, howling subsided as if by command, and they who beheld the sight, subdued by their horror-stricken silence those in the rear who, only dimly conscious of something ominous, stared with frightened, reluctant glances at the necks in front of them.

On the wagon was a Nubian lion from the royal zoological gardens. Owing to the high cost of feeding and maintaining him and also because of a certain aversion against such playthings of their erstwhile lords, the new government had decided to sell the beast to a foreign country. And thus, on that very morning the lion had been sent to the railroad station to be forwarded to his new destination.

As the canvas-wall slipped down from the frame, the lion roused himself and then surveyed the thousands of people, so steadily, with an expression of awe-inspiring majesty, until no sound could be heard from them, not a breath was audible. In his flashing eyes was reflected the picture of an alien world. But what was the nature of that world out there? A world as hard and cold as stone, a world with no heaven or horizon, one of mysterious sounds and offensive odours. Did he have an inkling of the wild passions which burst forth from despair and misery, he, who knew neither despair nor misery, and of passions only the elemental, natural ones of his superior kind? Did he actually take in those disturbed, ugly faces before him, or was it only a partial aspect or some impression of a detail that reached him: grinning teeth, distorted forhead, protuding chin; the violent wrath in the glance, the soulless glance of Megæra, the sullen sneer of the emaciated?

But those out there felt, with almost religious awe, something entirely unknown to him. In the dirty holes where they lived and brooded their evil; where their sick ones were lying and their children were born, and where they gave way to gloomy thoughts over the injustice which was their heritage of an evil order. On all their ways and journeys and in all the dreams of their servile imaginations they never had a vision which reminded them so much of what lay beyond their world, of the greatness and might of Nature. An undefinable horror took possession of their gloom-enveloped souls. They trembled, their muscles became limp, and they bowed their heads and cast down their eyes; their closely knitted ranks broke and gaps opened here and there. This enabled the policemen to arrest several dangerous ringleaders, and for the time being the rebellion was nipped in the bud.

❊ ❊ ❊

THOMAS MANN

(1875-)

THOMAS MANN, born at Lubeck, went to Munich where he found employment in a fire insurance company. He abandoned this work, and took to writing, at the same time attending courses at the Munich University. He is best known to English and American readers through translations of *Buddenbrooks* and *The Magic Mountain*, both excellent novels. His work includes some dramas and two volumes of short stories.

A Railway Accident, from the second volume of Mann's collected stories, appears here for the first time in English. It was translated for this anthology by Winifred Katzin, and is printed by kind permission of the author and his publisher, Alfred A. Knopf.

A RAILWAY ACCIDENT

A STORY? But I don't know one to tell you. Very well, here's something.

One day, it's a good two years now, I was in a railway accident. Every detail of it stands out clearly still in my mind.

It was nothing first-rate, with the whole train telescoping and "bodies mutilated beyond recognition" and so forth—nothing like that. Still, it was an authentic wreck with all the proper paraphernalia, and it occurred at night into the bargain. It is not exactly an universal experience, so I shall tell you about it.

I was on my way to Dresden at the time, having been bidden thither by the friends of literature. One of those artist-cum-virtuoso tours which I have no objection to making every now and then. One puts on a grand air, and takes the stage, and displays one's person before the acclaiming multitude. One is not for nothing a subject of Wilhelm II. Moreover, Dresden is a lovely place (particularly the Zwingen), and I meant to spend the following fortnight or ten days up at the "Weisser Hirsch" to take a little cure, and if, thanks to the "treatments," the spirit should possess me, then to work. With this end in view, I had put my manuscript at the bottom of my trunk, with material for notes, a most imposing bundle wrapped up in brown paper and tied with a stout cord of the Bavarian colours.

I like to travel in comfort, especially when I am being paid for by somebody else. I therefore had reserved a sleeping-birth and a first-class compartment the day before, and felt that all my preparations were safely made. I was nevertheless in a state of feverish excitement as I always am at such times, for to me a trip spells adventure, and I never shall manage to acquire a correct nonchalance towards this matter of transportation. I am well aware that the night train leaves the Munich terminal, according to its regular routine, every night and arrives every morning at Dresden. But the moment I travel along with it and consign to it my own paltry destiny, this fact becomes immensely important. I suddenly cannot rid myself of the illusion that it is leaving to-day for me, and me alone, and this foolish fancy naturally leads to a feeling of profound and silent excitement which does not leave me until every circumstance of the departure is over; the packing of the trunk, the drive to the station with the trunk on top of the cab, the arrival there, the registration of luggage. Only then do I know that everything is safe and provided for. This is naturally followed by an agreeable sense of relaxation; the mind turns to new things; the vast unknown is thrown open through a pane of glass, and joyous anticipation fills the soul.

And so it was on this occasion. I had handsomely rewarded the porter for carrying my hand-baggage, so handsomely indeed that he had tipped his cap and wished me a pleasant journey. I stood at a window in the corridor of the sleeping-car, with my evening cigar, and watched the hubbub on the platform. There was a whirring and trundling, a scurrying up and down, leavetaking, sing-song cries of the newsboys and refreshment-vendors, and great electric moons glowing above it all, in the mist of an October evening. Two powerful men were dragging a hand-car laden with heavy luggage down the whole length of the train to the front, where the luggage-car was. I recognised my own trunk by certain special marks upon it. There it went, merely one of many, and in the bottom of it lay the precious great bundle of papers. "Don't worry," I thought to myself; "it's in safe hands!" See that conductor, with his military leather belt and cross-strap, his impressive sergeant-major moustachios and his dour, watchful eye. See how roughly he talks to the old woman with the threadbare black shawl over her head, just because she almost got into a second-class compartment. He is the State, our Father, law and safety. One would prefer to have little to do with him; he is severe; also his manners leave much to be desired. Put your trust, in him, however, and your trunk will be looked after as though it lay in Abraham's bosom.

A gentleman is strolling about the platform. He wears spats and a light overcoat of yellow; he has a dog by a leash. I never saw a finer little dog than that, sturdy, sleek, muscular, with a black-spotted coat, as well cared-for and amusing as those little dogs one sometimes sees in the circus who entertain the audience by rushing, with all the force of their little bodies, round and round the ring. He has a silver collar round his neck, and his leash is of a plait of coloured leather. But nobody could wonder at that after seeing his master, the gentleman with spats, for he is undoubtedly some nobleman. He wears a monocle which accentuates his features without distorting them. His moustache twists proudly upward, lending the corners of his mouth, and his chin as well, a supercilious and arrogant air. He asks a question of the military-looking conductor, and that ordinary mortal, who apparently knows by instinct that he is in a Presence, answers him at the salute. The gentleman then proceeds, gratified at having created an impression. He walks in his spats, very certain of himself; he has a cold face; his eyes regard things and people with sharpness. He is not affected with traveller's fever, that is clear to see; to him, so ordinary a matter as departing on a journey is no adventure. He is at home in life, and has no fear of its institutions and power; of the power he is himself a part. He is, in a word, a gentleman. I cannot take my eyes off him.

At what seems to him to be the correct moment, he steps in (the conductor had just turned his back). He passes me in the corridor, and although he bumps into me, he does not say "Beg pardon!" A gentleman! But this is a mere nothing compared with the next thing. Without the flicker of an eyelash, the gentleman takes his dog with him into the sleeping-car! Undoubtedly forbidden. Imagine *my* ever daring to take a dog into a sleeping-car! He does so on the strength of being a lord of life, and closes the door behind him.

A whistle blows, the engine replies. Slowly the train begins to move.

I remained a while longer at the window, looking at the crowd on the platform, still waving. I saw the iron bridge; lights swung in the air and passed by. . . . I went inside.

The sleeping car was not very full; there was an empty berth next to mine which had not been prepared for anyone, so I decided to install myself comfortably there for an hour's quiet reading. I brought my book and settled down. The couch was upholstered in some kind of silk material, salmon-coloured. A small collapsible table held an ashtray. The light was good. I read and smoked.

The conductor of the sleeping-cars comes in and asks me in a business-like manner for my ticket which I put into his grimy hand. He speaks politely, but with a purely professional politeness. He dispenses with the "good-night" greeting as from one human being to another, and moves on to knock on the door of the next compartment. That he should have forborne to do, however, for the gentleman with the spats was in there, and whether it was because the gentleman did not wish to show his dog or that he had already retired, I do not know. At all events, he flew into a terrible rage at anybody's having dared to disturb him. Yes, above the rumbling of the train, I could hear the imperial and elemental outbreak of his wrath through the thin partition. "What do you want?" he shouted; "leave me in peace, Affenschwanz!" He used the epithet "Affenschwanz"—a gentleman's epithet—the epithet of a horseman and a cavalier, heartening to hear. But the conductor of the sleeping-cars began to argue that he really needed the gentleman's ticket, and as I went out into the corridor in order to follow the episode at close range, I saw, at last, the gentleman's door jerked slightly ajar, and the ticket fly into the conductor's face; hard and with violence, into his face. He caught it in both hands, and although the edge of it had struck him in the eye and brought tears, he clicked his heels together and said "Thank you, sir," and touched his cap. Staggered, I returned to my book.

Smoking another cigar, I debated what might be done about it, and decided that nothing could be of any use. So I continued to smoke to the movement of the train, reading and very much at peace, and full of thoughts. Time passed. It was ten o'clock or half-past, or even later.

The other occupants of the sleeping-car had all gone to bed, and at last I decided to do likewise.

I got up and went into my compartment. It was a really luxurious little bedroom, with embossed leather upholstery, hooks for clothes and a nickel washbowl. The lower berth had been made up with snowy sheets, and the quilt thrown back invitingly. "O blessed modern age!" I think. One lies in this bed as in one's own bed at home; it shakes a little beneath one all night, and as a result, one is in Dresden in the morning. I reached for my grip in the net, to get my washing-materials. I had it at arm's length over my head. At that moment the wreck occurred. I remember it as though it had happened to-day.

There was a crash . . . but the word "crash" conveys little. It was a crash that one knew instantly to betoken dreadful events; a terrific, tearing crash, and of such violence that my grip flew out of my hands, I had no idea where to, and I myself was flung against the wall, striking my shoulder painfully. There was no time to think about anything, however. What followed was a frightful swaying of the coach, and while that lasted, one had no time to be afraid. Coaches always sway, passing over switches or turning abrupt curves; that one knows. But this was a kind of swaying which did not permit one to stand on one's feet; one was hurled from wall to wall, at every second expecting the coach to capsize. I seized upon a simple thought, but with great concentration and excluded every other thought from my mind. It was this: "Something is wrong, something is very wrong, something is all wrong." Literally! Besides this, there was one other: "stop! stop! stop!" Because I knew that if the train would only stop, much would be gained. And lo, at my unuttered inward command, the train did stop.

Until then, a silence of death had reigned in the sleeping-car. Now the terror broke loose. The high-pitched shrieking of women mingled with the men's muffled cries of alarm. In the next compartment to mine I heard someone call, "Help!"; it was unmistakably the voice which a little while before had uttered the epithet, the voice of the gentleman with the spats, but fear had given it a different timbre. "Help," he shouted, and as I stepped out into the corridor where the passengers were assembling, he burst out of his compartment in a silk dressing gown and stood there staring wildly about him. "Great God," he said. "God Almighty!" And as though thoroughly to abase himself, and so perhaps avert destruction from himself, he said imploringly, "Dear God!" But the next moment he changed his mind in favour of saving himself. He flung himself upon the little case fastened to the wall, in which an axe and saw are kept against all contingencies, smashed the glass with his bare fist and after all left the tools behind for he was not able immediately to reach them; breathing wildly he fought a way for himself through the gathering crowd of passengers making the half-dressed ladies shriek again and jumped for safety.

All this was the work of a moment. For the first time then I discovered my own fear, a certain feeling of weakness in the back, a momentary inability to swallow. The grimy handed conductor of the sleeping car had now rushed up with bloodshot eyes and everyone crowded round him. The ladies, their arms and shoulders bare, stood wringing their hands.

The train had gone off the track, the man informed them. Which, as it turned out later, was not the case. But look at the man; this circumstance has made him talk at last. He has abandoned his professional manner, the great event has undone his tongue! He spoke of his wife, familiarly, "I told my wife this was going to happen. 'Wife,' I said, 'I've got a feeling something's going to happen to-day!'" Well, something has certainly happened. Yes, we all agreed with him. Smoke was now coming into the coach, thick smoke, no one knew from where, and we all preferred to go out into the night.

This could only be done by jumping down from the footboard onto the track, which was no small distance. For there was no platform available, and our sleeping car was tilted considerably over on the other side, besides. But the ladies who had hurriedly covered their nakedness, jumped down in despair and soon we were all standing on the track between the rails.

The darkness was almost complete; one could see, however, that nothing was wrong with the hind coaches though they too stood lopsided. But in front—ten or twenty paces ahead!—not for nothing had the shock occurred with that terrific noise of tearing and cracking. What had been the train was now a chaos of debris—going nearer one could see how much of it there was as the little lanterns in the conductor's hands played over it.

That was where the news was coming from; excited people came away with reports of the situation. We were near a little station not far from Regensburg, and on account of a defective rail the express had switched onto a wrong track and run full steam into a freight train standing in the station, thrown it out of the station, smashed its rear end to bits and suffered considerable damage itself. The great engine built by Maffei of Munich had vanished; it had been demolished. Price, seventy thousand marks. And in the front coaches which lay almost prostrate on their sides the seats had almost met in the middle. No, thank the Lord, there were no lost lives to mourn over. There was talk of an old woman who had been "pulled from under" but no one had seen her. Still the passengers had all been badly shaken, children had been buried under luggage, the fright had been intense. The luggage car had been destroyed. What was that about the luggage car? It had been destroyed. There I stood. . . .

A railway official, hatless, rushes up. He is the station master. Wildly in a voice that whines he orders the passengers about so as to keep discipline and get them back into the coaches and off the tracks. But nobody pays any attention to him since he has neither cap nor a manner. He is to be pitied, that man. He will most likely be held responsible for the whole thing; perhaps this was the end of his career. His life might be shattered. It would not have been tactful to ask him about trunks.

Another official now approaches, limping, and I recognise him by the sergeant major moustachios. It is the guard, the vigilant and unmannerly guard of last night, the State, our Father. He hobbles along bent double holding his knee with his hand; nothing concerns him now but his knees. "Oh, oh," he says, "Oh!" "Why, what's this? What is the matter?" "Oh, sir, I was caught between them and got it in the chest. I only escaped over the roof. Oh! Oh!"—This escape over the roof had a smack of telling the newspapers. Most certainly the man would not have habitually used the word escape; he had probably not experienced an accident so much as the newspaper report of an accident. But what help was all that to me; he was in no position to tell me what had happened to my manuscript. At that moment came a young person from the wreckage, fresh, important and excited; him I asked after the heavy luggage. "Yes, my dear sir, but nobody knows what it looks like over there!" And his tone implied that I ought to be very glad to have escaped sound of body and limb. "Everything is in hopeless confusion. Ladies' shoes . . ." he said with an annihilating gesture, his nose curled up. "It'll turn up when they begin clearing up. Ladies' shoes. . . ."

There I stood, all alone by myself; I stood in the darkness between the railway tracks and racked my heart. Clearing up! They were contemplating clearing up with my manuscript. Destroyed then, torn to shreds, most likely squashed into nothing. What was I to do if that was the way of it? I had no copy of the part that had been already set down on paper so beautifully pieced and welded together, that already had life and sound—to say nothing of the notes and sketches, the whole thing the labour of years of accumulation, acquired by listening, a mine of material which I had made my own through searching and experience. What was I to do? I searched my mind and realised I would have to begin it all over again from the very beginning. Yes, with the patience of a dumb animal, with the tenacity of a profound realisation of a life whose marvellous and complex operations of small ingenuity and toil have been destroyed, after a moment of confusion and despair I should start all over again from the very beginning and perhaps this time it would go a little more easily. . . .

Meanwhile the fire brigade had arrived with torches which threw a glow of red over the wreckage and when I went forward to look at the baggage car, it turned out it was almost untouched and nothing was missing from the trunks. The goods and merchandise which had lain scattered about had come from the freight train, an inextricable conglomeration of debris, a sea of debris that strewed the ground far and wide. I felt better then and joined the people who stood there, gossiping together and making friends on the strength of the accident, exchanging tall yarns and being very important. What seemed very certain was that the engine driver had acted very bravely and averted a terrible disaster by using the emergency brakes in the nick of time. Otherwise, they said, there would undoubtedly have been a telescoping of the whole train which would have gone over the steep slope of the railway banks on the left. All praise to the engine driver! But he was nowhere to be seen. No one had set eyes on him yet his fame had gone the whole length of the train and we all praised him, though absent. "That man," said one man, pointing with outstretched hand into the night at large, "that man saved all our lives." And everyone nodded assent.

But our train was standing on a track which it had no business to be standing on, therefore it had to be safely backed up so that another would not drive into its rear. The firemen therefore took their places on the last coach with their burning pitch torches and with them went the excited young man who had been so greatly distressed over the ladies' shoes. He had seized a torch too and was swinging it like a signal though there was not a train in sight in all the world.

And little by little something like order was restored to things, and the State, our Father once more regained authority and calm. Telegrams had been sent and all necessary steps taken; an emergency train from Regensburg steamed cautiously into the station and great gas lanterns with reflectors were installed about the wreckage. Quarters were assigned to us passengers, and we had to wait in the little station house until our further disposal was provided for. Loaded down with our hand luggage, some of us with bandaged heads, we passed through a lane of curious natives into the little waiting room, where we perched ourselves as best we might. And at the end of an hour we were piled helterskelter into an extra train.

I had a first class ticket (because they were paying my expenses) but it helped me not at all for everyone preferred first class, so that those sections were even more crowded than the rest. Just as I found a small place, however, whom should I see facing me, squeezed into a corner? The gentleman with the spats and the cavalier epithets, my hero. His little dog was not with him; it had been taken away. In spite of all his gentleman's prerogatives, he sits now in a dark cage immediately behind the engine, glaring. The gentleman also has a yellow ticket which is of no use to him; he growls and tries to protest against communism, against the great levelling of classes before the majesty of disaster. He is answered by a common man who says righteously, "Think yourself glad ye got a seat!" And with a sour smile the gentleman resigns himself to the lunatic situation.

And who should come in next, assisted by two firemen, a little old lady, a little grandmother with a torn shawl over her head, the one who almost got into a second class coach in Munich. "Is this first class?" she keeps asking. "Is this really first class?" and when she is assured that it is and they make a place for her to sit down, she sinks with a "glory-be-to-God" into the plush cushions as if she had just been saved from death.

In Hof it was five o'clock and daylight. Breakfast; then an express took me along with it and brought me and my stuff into Dresden three hours late.

Well, that was the train accident I went through. Once in a life time it has to happen and though the logicians may object I have good reason to believe that nothing like it will happen soon again to me.

THE UNITED STATES

Introduction

DESCENDED from English fiction, the American story has a long line of immediate ancestors and, since the English language is itself descended from a Teutonic branch intermarried with French, therefore a lineage derived from earliest Germanic and Latin narrative.

Development of the form began somewhat over a hundred years ago in the tales of William Austin, Washington Irving, and Nathaniel Hawthorne. It remained for Edgar Allan Poe to express his observations on its characteristics, whether found in *Blackwood's* or *The Boston Token*, and to train it as a distinctly American growth.

Hawthorne had discovered its cultural susceptibility and had produced in *Twice Told Tales* (1837 and 1842) a flowering of New England soil. In reviewing Hawthorne's collections, Poe insisted upon the advantage over the novel the tale gained by totality; he observed the wisdom of seeking a single effect; he declared that originality as a trait in fiction is worth all the rest, that novelty of tone is no less commendable than novelty of matter, that every word should tell; he implied the power of restraint and suggestion; he affirmed that a work of art should be judged not by its magnitude but by its impression. Not all the qualities enumerated exist in Poe's own tales which are remarkable, however, for simplicity, unity, and directness.

In 1884 Poe's theories were exploited and enlarged by Brander Matthews in his *Philosophy of the Short Story*, the first critically scientific treatise after Poe's reviews. Thereafter, story makers worked with greater consciousness. Yet for a dozen years after Poe's death little of worth was produced; among the rare exceptions were a few stories of Fitz-James O'Brien. Then came the Civil War and its aftermath of journals offering new markets, new possibilities.

Before Poe's death (1849) were born Bret Harte, Frank Stockton, Henry James, Ambrose Bierce, William Dean Howells, Thomas Bailey Aldrich, and Mark Twain; just after, Charles Egbert Craddock (Miss Murfree), Henry Cuyler Bunner, and Thomas Nelson Page. Of these Bret Harte emphasised the elements of humour and locality for the far West as Dickens had emphasised them for London. A nation of local colourists carried on the movement so thoroughly as to draw from Henry Van Dyke in a lecture at Columbia University (about 1908) the statement that not a square mile of the United States had been left unrepresented. *The Luck of Roaring Camp* appeared in 1884, as did also Charles Egbert Craddock's *In the Tennessee Mountains*. Thomas Nelson Page wrote of "Ole Virginia", George W. Cable of Creole New Orleans, Sarah Orne Jewett and Mary Wilkins of rural New England, Hamlin Garland of the Mid-West, Jack London of Alaska. Humour, which made its advent with Mark Twain, continues to be a distinguishing feature of fiction in the United States; witness Booth Tarkington, Irvin Cobb, and Ring Lardner.

Frank Stockton and Thomas Bailey Aldrich bent the American story in another direction, that of the trick or surprise ending. Surprise is an old method of enforcing climax. Any one who has sung *Baby Lon* knows that English folk who listened to ballad makers five hundred years ago enjoyed surprise endings, any one who has heard with King Shahriyar the fabrications of Scheherazade knows the Arabians appreciated them even earlier, any one who has read Mary Austin's Indian legends knows that surprise is an essential of American aboriginal literature. But to the delight of readers, surprise was discovered anew in the second half of the Nineteenth Century. O. Henry (1862-1910) became the master of surprise climaxes which, joined to his Arabian Nights symmetry of plot, are largely responsible for his vogue.

Meanwhile William Dean Howells had added to the realistic qualities of brief narrative, a realism that Hamlin Garland portraying the West in pioneer days intensified in what he termed veritism. Meanwhile too Henry James had published before 1880, tales that influenced the more serious fictionists, notably Edith Wharton. To these two authors, Henry James and Edith Wharton, credit is due for deepening and enriching short story literature.

Although Harte, Aldrich, Stockton, and James diversified the type form, yet since 1890 most writers have been guided by the dicta of Poe, recalled and expanded by Brander Matthews. As Mr. Matthews himself said later, many now have got the seed. This truth accounts for the number of authors acceptable to current magazines—which the invention of the gasoline engine and its advertisement have greatly multiplied—for the journalistic prominence of the short story, and for the architecture which demands brevity, unity of tone and action, simple complication of plot, and effective climax. Among the moderns who uphold artistic traditions the foremost is Wilbur Daniel Steele.

New leaders, most of them too recent for contemporary estimate, began to publish about the time of the death of O. Henry (1910). Rebelling against the conventionality of literary moulds, they seek an artlessness which is yet the acme of art. They learn from the Russians, available in translations since 1915 as never before, much as their predecessors in the final quarter of the Nineteenth Century learned through

Matthews and Bunner from the French. Chief among them is Sherwood Anderson, who has already gained international respect.

❊ ❊ ❊

WILLIAM AUSTIN
(1778-1841)

BORN at Lunenburg, Massachusetts, 1778, graduated at Harvard in 1798, William Austin was a distinguished member of the Boston bar who also published a number of short stories. While in England in 1802-03 he met William Godwin, "Peter Pindar," and lawyers prominent in affairs of the day. His stories are the forerunners of Hawthorne in subject matter and treatment, lying in the twilight region between the supernatural and the real. Readers who desire a conclusive ending of the story here presented are referred to Hawthorne's *A Virtuoso's Collection* (*Mosses from an Old Manse*), where Peter Rugg is fixed for all time as doorkeeper to the museum owned by the Wandering Jew. *Peter Rugg* was first published in 1824 in the *New England Galaxy*. It is slightly condensed by the present editor.

PETER RUGG, THE MISSING MAN

FROM *Jonathan Dunwell of New York, to Mr. Herman Krauff.*
Sir,—Agreeably to my promise, I now relate to you all the particulars of the lost man and child which I have been able to collect. It is entirely owing to the humane interest you seemed to take in the report, that I have pursued the inquiry to the following result.

You may remember that business called me to Boston in the summer of 1820. I sailed in the packet to Providence, and when I arrived there I learned that every seat in the stage was engaged. I was thus obliged either to wait a few hours or accept a seat with the driver, who civilly offered me that accommodation. Accordingly, I took my seat by his side, and soon found him intelligent and communicative. When we had travelled about ten miles, the horses suddenly threw their ears on their necks, as flat as a hare's. Said the driver, "Have you a surtout with you?"

"No," said I; "why do you ask?"

"You will want one soon," said he. "Do you observe the ears of all the horses?"

"Yes; and was just about to ask the reason."

"They see the storm-breeder, and we shall see him soon."

At this moment there was not a cloud visible in the firmament. Soon after, a small speck appeared in the road.

"There," said my companion, "comes the storm-breeder. He always leaves a Scotch mist behind him. By many a wet jacket do I remember him. I suppose the poor fellow suffers much himself,—much more than is known to the world."

Presently a man with a child beside him, with a large black horse, and a weather-beaten chair, once built for a chaise-body, passed in great haste, apparently at the rate of twelve miles an hour. He seemed to grasp the reins of his horse with firmness, and appeared to anticipate his speed. He seemed dejected, and looked anxiously at the passengers, particularly at the stage-driver and myself. In a moment after he passed us, the horses' ears were up, and bent themselves forward so they nearly met.

"Who is that man?" said I; "he seems in great trouble."

"Nobody knows who he is, but his person and the child are familiar to me. I have met him more than a hundred times, and have been so often asked the way to Boston by that man, even when he was travelling directly from that town, that of late I have refused any communication with him; and that is the reason he gave me such a fixed look."

"But does he never stop anywhere?"

"I have never known him to stop anywhere longer than to inquire the way to Boston; and let him be where he may, he will tell you he cannot stay a moment, for he must reach Boston that night."

We were now ascending a high hill in Walpole; and as we had a fair view of the heavens, I was rather disposed to jeer the driver for thinking of his surtout; not a cloud as big as a marble could be discerned.

"Do you look," said he, "in the direction whence the man came. The storm never meets him; it follows him."

We presently approached another hill; and when at the height, the driver pointed out in an eastern direction a little black speck about as big as a hat. "There," said he, "is the seed-storm. We may possibly reach Polley's before it reaches us, but the wanderer and his child will go to Providence through rain, thunder, and lightning."

And now the horses hastened with increased speed. The little black cloud came on rolling over the turnpike; after it had spread itself to a great bulk it suddenly became more limited in circumference, grew more compact, dark, and consolidated. And now the successive flashes of chained lightning caused the whole cloud to appear like a sort of irregular net-work, and displayed a thousand fantastic images. The driver bespoke my attention to a remarkable configuration in the cloud. He said every flash of lightning near its centre discovered to him, distinctly, the form of a man sitting in an open carriage drawn by a black horse. But in truth I saw no such thing; the man's fancy was doubtless at fault.

In the meantime the distant thunder gave notice of a shower at hand; and just as we reached Polley's tavern the rain poured down in torrents. It was soon over, the cloud passing in the direction of the turnpike toward

Providence. In a few moments after, a respectable-looking man in a chaise stopped at the door. The man and child in the chair having excited some little sympathy among the passengers, the gentleman was asked if he had observed them. He said he had met them; that the man seemed bewildered, and inquired the way to Boston; that he was driving at great speed, as though he expected to outstrip the tempest; that the moment he had passed him, a thunder-clap broke directly over the man's head, and seemed to envelop both man and child, horse and carriage. "I stopped," said the gentleman, "supposing the lightning had struck him, but the horse only seemed to loom up and increase his speed; and as well as I could judge, he travelled just as fast as the thunder-cloud."

While this man was speaking, a pedlar with a cart of tin merchandise came up, all dripping; and on being questioned, he said he had met that man and carriage, within a fortnight, in four different States; that at each time he had inquired the way to Boston; and that a thunder-shower like the present had each time deluged his wagon and his wares, setting his tin pots afloat, so that he had determined to get a marine insurance for the future. But that which excited his surprise most was the strange conduct of his horse, for long before he could distinguish the man in the chair, his own horse stood still in the road, and flung back his ears. "In short," said the pedlar, "I wish never to see that man and horse again; they do not look to me as though they belonged to this world."

This was all I could learn at that time; and the occurrence soon after would have become with me, like one of those things which had never happened, had I not, as I stood recently on the door-step of Bennett's hotel in Hartford, heard a man say, "There goes Peter Rugg and his child! He looks wet and weary, and farther from Boston than ever." I was satisfied it was the same man I had seen more than three years before; for whoever has once seen Peter Rugg can never after be deceived as to his identity.

"Peter Rugg!" said I; "and who is Peter Rugg?"

"That," said the stranger, "is more than any one can tell exactly. He is a famous traveller, held in light esteem by all innholders, for he never stops to eat, drink, or sleep. I wonder why the government does not employ him to carry the mail."

"Ay," said a by-stander, "that is a thought bright only on one side; how long would it take in that case to send a letter to Boston, for Peter has already, to my knowledge, been more than twenty years travelling to that place."

"But," said I, "does the man never stop anywhere; does he never converse with any one? I saw the same man more than three years since, near Providence, and I heard a strange story about him. Pray, sir, give me some account of this man."

"Sir," said the stranger, "those who know the most respecting that man, say the least. I have heard it asserted that Heaven sometimes sets a mark on a man, either for judgment or a trial. Under which Peter Rugg now labours, I cannot say; therefore I am rather inclined to pity than to judge."

"You speak like a humane man," said I; "and if you have known him so long, I pray you will give me some account of him. Has his appearance much altered in that time?"

"Why, yes. He looks as though he never ate, drank, or slept; and his child looks older than himself, and he looks like time broken off from eternity, and anxious to gain a resting-place."

"And how does his horse look?" said I.

"As for his horse, he looks fatter and gayer, and shows more animation and courage than he did twenty years ago. The last time Rugg spoke to me he inquired how far it was to Boston. I told him just one hundred miles.

"'Why,' said he, 'how can you deceive me so? It is cruel to mislead a traveller. I have lost my way; pray direct me the nearest way to Boston.'

"I repeated, it was one hundred miles.

"'How can you say so?' said he; 'I was told last evening it was but fifty, and I have travelled all night.'

"'But,' said I, 'you are now travelling from Boston. You must turn back.'

"'Alas,' said he, 'it is all turn back! Boston shifts with the wind, and plays all around the compass. One man tells me it is to the east, another to the west; and the guide-posts too, they all point the wrong way.'

"'But will you not stop and rest?' said I; 'you seem wet and weary.'

"'Yes,' said he, 'it has been foul weather since I left home.'

"'Stop, then, and refresh yourself.'

"'I must not stop; I must reach home to-night, if possible: though I think you must be mistaken in the distance to Boston.'

"He then gave the reins to his horse, which he restrained with difficulty, and disappeared in a moment. A few days afterward I met the man a little this side of Claremont,* winding along the hills in Unity, at the rate, I believe, of twelve miles an hour."

"Is Peter Rugg his real name?"

"I know not, but presume he will not deny his name; you can ask him,—for see, he has turned his horse, and is passing this way."

In a moment a dark-coloured high-spirited horse approached, and would have passed without stopping, but I had resolved to speak to the man. Accordingly I stepped into the street; and as the horse approached, I made a feint of stopping him. The man immediately reined in his

* In New Hampshire.

horse. "Sir," said I, "may I be so bold as to inquire if you are not Mr. Rugg? for I think I have seen you before."

"My name is Peter Rugg," said he. "I have unfortunately lost my way; I am wet and weary, and will take it kindly of you to direct me to Boston."

"You live in Boston, do you; and in what street?"

"In Middle Street."

"When did you leave Boston?"

"I cannot tell precisely; it seems a considerable time."

"But how did you and your child become so wet? It has not rained here to-day."

"It has just rained a heavy shower up the river. But I shall not reach Boston to-night if I tarry. Would you advise me to take the old road or the turnpike?"

"Why, the old road is one hundred and seventeen miles, and the turnpike is ninety-seven."

"How can you say so? You impose on me; it is wrong to trifle with a traveller; you know it is but forty miles from Newburyport to Boston."

"But this is not Newburyport; this is Hartford."

"Do not deceive me, sir. Is not this town Newburyport, and the river that I have been following the Merrimack?"

"No, sir; this is Hartford, and the river the Connecticut."

He wrung his hands and looked incredulous. "Have the rivers, too, changed their courses, as the cities have changed places? But see! the clouds are gathering in the south, and we shall have a rainy night. Ah, that fatal oath!"

He would tarry no longer; his impatient horse leaped off, his hand flanks rising like wings; he seemed to devour all before him, and to scorn all behind.

I had now, as I thought, discovered a clew to the history of Peter Rugg; and I determined, the next time my business called me to Boston, to make further inquiry. Soon after, I was enabled to collect the following particulars from Mrs. Croft, an aged lady in Middle Street, who has resided in Boston during the last twenty years. Her narration is as follows:

Just at twilight last summer a person stopped at the door of the late Mrs. Rugg. Mrs. Croft on coming to the door perceived a stranger with a child by his side, in an old weather-beaten carriage, with a black horse. The stranger asked for Mrs. Rugg, and was informed that Mrs. Rugg had died at a good old age, more than twenty years before that time.

The stranger replied, "How can you deceive me so? Do ask Mrs. Rugg to step to the door."

"Sir, I assure you Mrs. Rugg has not lived here these twenty years; no one lives here but myself, and my name is Betsey Croft."

The stranger paused, looked up and down the street, and said, "Though the paint is rather faded, this looks like my house."

"Yes," said the child, "that is the stone before the door that I used to sit on to eat my bread and milk."

"But," said the stranger, "it seems to be on the wrong side of the street. Indeed, everything here seems to be misplaced. The streets are all changed, the people are all changed, the town seems changed, and what is strangest of all, Catherine Rugg has deserted her husband and child. Pray," continued the stranger, "has John Foy come home from sea? He went a long voyage; he is my kinsman. If I could see him, he could give me some account of Mrs. Rugg."

"Sir," said Mrs. Croft, "I never heard of John Foy. Where did he live?"

"Just above here, in Orange-tree Lane."

"There is no such place in this neighbourhood."

"What do you tell me! Are the streets gone? Orange-tree Lane is at the head of Hanover Street, near Pemberton's Hill."

"There is no such lane now."

"Madam, you cannot be serious! But you doubtless know my brother, William Rugg. He lives in Royal Exchange Lane, near King Street."

"I know of no such lane; and I am sure there is no such street as King Street in this town."

"No such street as King Street! Why, woman, you mock me! You may as well tell me there is no King George. However, madam, you see I am wet and weary, I must find a resting-place. I will go to Hart's tavern, near the market."

"Which market, sir? for you seem perplexed; we have several markets."

"You know there is but one market near the town dock."

"Oh, the old market; but no such person has kept there these twenty years."

Here the stranger seemed disconcerted, and uttered to himself quite audibly: "Strange mistake; how much this looks like the town of Boston! It certainly has a great resemblance to it; but I perceive my mistake now. Some other Mrs. Rugg, some other Middle Street.—Then," said he, "madam, can you direct me to Boston?"

"Why, this is Boston, the city of Boston; I know of no other Boston."

"City of Boston it may be; but it is not the Boston where I live. I recollect now, I came over a bridge instead of a ferry. Pray, what bridge is that I just came over?"

"It is Charles River Bridge."

"I perceive my mistake: there is a ferry between Boston and Charlestown; there is no bridge. Ah, I perceive my mistake. If I were in Boston my horse would carry me directly to my own door. But my horse shows by his impatience that he is in a strange place. Absurd, that I should have mistaken this place for the old town of Boston! It is a much finer city than the town of Boston. I fancy Boston must lie at a distance from this city, as the good woman seems ignorant of it."

At these words his horse began to chafe, and strike the pavement with his forefeet. The stranger seemed a little bewildered, and said, "No home to-night;" and giving the reins to his horse, passed up the street, and I saw no more of him.

It was evident that the generation to which Peter Rugg belonged had passed away.

This was all the account of Peter Rugg I could obtain from Mrs. Croft; but she directed me to an elderly man, Mr. James Felt, who lived near her, and who had kept a record of the principal occurrences for the last fifty years. At my request she sent for him; and after I had related to him the object of my inquiry, Mr. Felt told me he had known Rugg in his youth, and that his disappearance had caused some surprise; but as it sometimes happens that men run away,—sometimes to be rid of others, and sometimes to be rid of themselves,—and Rugg took his child with him, and his own horse and chair, and as it did not appear that any creditors made a stir, the occurrence soon mingled itself in the stream of oblivion; and Rugg and his child, horse, and chair were soon completely forgotten.

"It is true," said Mr. Felt, "sundry stories grew out of Rugg's affair, whether true or false I cannot tell; but stranger things have happened in my day, without even a newspaper notice."

"Sir," said I, "Peter Rugg is now living. I have lately seen Peter Rugg and his child, horse, and chair; therefore I pray you to relate to me all you know or ever heard of him."

"Why, my friend," said James Felt, "that Peter Rugg is now a living man, I will not deny; but that you have seen Peter Rugg and his child, is impossible, if you mean a small child; for Jenny Rugg, if living, must be at least—let me see—Boston massacre, 1770—Jenny Rugg was about ten years old. Why, sir, Jenny Rugg, if living, must be more than sixty years of age. That Peter Rugg is living is highly probable, as he was only ten years older than myself, and I was only eighty last March; and I am as likely to live twenty years longer as any man."

Here I perceived that Mr. Felt was in his dotage, and I despaired of gaining any intelligence from him.

I took my leave of Mrs. Croft, and proceeded to my lodgings at the Marlborough Hotel.

"If Peter Rugg," thought I, "has been travelling since the Boston massacre, there is no reason why he should not travel to the end of time."

In the course of the evening, I related my adventure in Middle Street.

"Ha!" said one of the company, smiling, "do you really think you have seen Peter Rugg? I have heard my grandfather speak of him, as though he seriously believed his own story."

"Sir," said I, "pray let us compare your grandfather's story of Mr. Rugg with my own."

"Peter Rugg, sir,—if my grandfather was worthy of credit,—once lived in Middle Street, in this city. He was a man in comfortable circumstances, had a wife and one daughter, and was generally esteemed for his sober life and manners. But, unhappily, his temper, at times, was altogether ungovernable, and then his language was terrible. In these fits of passion, if a door stood in his way, he would never do less than kick a panel through. He would sometimes throw his heels over his head, and come down on his feet, uttering oaths in a circle; and thus in a rage, he was the first who performed a somerset, and did what others have since learned to do for merriment and money. Once Rugg was seen to bite a tenpenny nail in halves. In those days, everybody, both men and boys, wore wigs; and Peter, at these moments of violent passion, would become so profane that his wig would rise up from his head. Some said it was on account of his terrible language; others accounted for it in a more philosophical way, and said it was caused by the expansion of his scalp, as violent passion, we know, will swell the veins and expand the head. While these fits were on him, Rugg had no respect for heaven or earth. Except this infirmity, all agreed that Rugg was a good sort of man; for when his fits were over, nobody was so ready to commend a placid temper as Peter.

"One morning, late in autumn, Rugg, in his own chair, with a fine large bay horse, took his daughter and proceeded to Concord. On his return a violent storm overtook him. At dark he stopped at Menotomy, now West Cambridge, at the door of a Mr. Cutter, a friend of his, who urged him to tarry the night. On Rugg's declining to stop, Mr. Cutter urged him vehemently. 'Why, Mr. Rugg,' said Cutter, 'the storm is overwhelming you. The night is exceedingly dark. Your little daughter will perish. You are in an open chair, and the tempest is increasing.' *Let the storm increase*,' said Rugg, with a fearful oath, '*I will see home to-night, in spite of the last tempest, or may I never see home!*' At these words he gave his whip to his high-spirited horse and disappeared in a moment. But Peter Rugg did not reach home that night, nor the next; nor, when he became a missing man, could he ever be traced beyond Mr. Cutter's, in Menotomy.

"For a long time after, on every dark and stormy night the wife of Peter Rugg would fancy she heard the crack of a whip, and the fleet tread of a horse, and the rattling of a carriage passing her door. The neighbours, too, heard the same noises, and some said they knew it was Rugg's horse; the tread on the pavement was perfectly familiar to them. This occurred so repeatedly that at length the neighbours watched with lanterns, and saw the real Peter Rugg, with his own horse and chair and the child sitting beside him, pass directly before his own door, his head turned toward his house, and himself making every effort to stop his horse, but in vain.

"The next day the friends of Mrs. Rugg exerted themselves to find her husband and child. They inquired at every public house and stable in town; but it did not appear that Rugg made any stay in Boston. No one, after Rugg had passed his own door, could give any account of him, though it was asserted by some that the clatter of Rugg's horse and carriage over the pavements shook the houses on both sides of the streets. And this is credible, if indeed Rugg's horse and carriage did pass on that night; for at this day, in many of the streets, a loaded truck or team in passing will shake the houses like an earthquake. However, Rugg's neighbours never afterward watched. Some of them treated it all as a delusion, and thought no more of it. Others of a different opinion shook their heads and said nothing.

"Thus Rugg and his child, horse, and chair were soon forgotten; and probably many in the neighbourhood never heard a word on the subject.

"There was indeed a rumour that Rugg was seen afterward in Connecticut, between Suffield and Hartford, passing through the country at headlong speed. This gave occasion to Rugg's friends to make further inquiry; but the more they inquired, the more they were baffled. If they heard of Rugg one day in Connecticut, the next they heard of him winding round the hills in New Hampshire; and soon after a man in a chair, with a small child, exactly answering the description of Peter Rugg, would be seen in Rhode Island inquiring the way to Boston.

"But that which chiefly gave a colour of mystery to the story of Peter Rugg was the affair at Charlestown bridge. The toll-gatherer asserted that sometimes, on the darkest and most stormy nights, when no object could be discerned, about the time when Rugg was missing, a horse and wheel-carriage, with a noise equal to a troop, would at midnight, in utter contempt of the rates of toll, pass over the bridge. This occurred so frequently that the toll-gatherer resolved to attempt a discovery. Soon after, at the usual time, apparently the same horse and carriage approached the bridge from Charlestown square. The toll-gatherer, prepared, took his stand as near the middle of the bridge as he dared, with a large three-legged stool in hand; as the appearance passed, he threw the stool at the horse, but heard nothing except the stool skipping across the bridge. The toll-gatherer asserted that the stool went directly through the body of the horse, and he persisted in that belief ever after. Whether Rugg ever passed the bridge again, the toll-gatherer would never tell; and when questioned, seemed anxious to waive the subject. And thus Peter Rugg and his child, horse, and carriage, remain a mystery to this day."

This, sir, is all that I could learn of Peter Rugg in Boston.

FURTHER ACCOUNT OF PETER RUGG

By Jonathan Dunwell

In the autumn of 1825, I attended the races at Richmond in Virginia.   As two new horses of great promise were run, the race-ground was never better attended, nor was expectation ever more deeply excited. The partisans of Dart and Lightning, the two race-horses, were equally anxious and equally dubious of the result.   To an indifferent spectator, it was impossible to perceive any difference.   They were equally beautiful to behold, alike in colour and height, and as they stood side by side they measured from heel to forefeet within half an inch of each other.   The eyes of each were full, prominent, and resolute; and when at times they regarded each other, they assumed a lofty demeanour, seemed to shorten their necks, project their eyes, and rest their bodies equally on their four hoofs.   They certainly showed signs of intelligence, and displayed a courtesy to each unusual even with statesmen.

It was now nearly twelve o'clock, the hour of expectation, doubt, and anxiety.   The riders mounted their horses; and so trim, light, and airy they sat on the animals as to seem a part of them.   The spectators had taken their places, and as many thousand breathing statues were there as spectators.   All eyes were turned to Dart and Lightning and their two fairy riders.   There was nothing to disturb this calm except a busy woodpecker on a neighbouring tree.   The signal was given, and Dart and Lightning answered it with ready intelligence.   At first they proceed at a slow trot, then they quicken to a canter, and then a gallop; presently they sweep the plain.   Both horses lay themselves flat on the ground, their riders bending forward and resting their chins between their horses' ears.

While these horses, side by side, thus appeared, flying without wings, flat as a hare, and neither gaining on the other, all eyes were diverted to a new spectacle.   Directly in the rear of Dart and Lightning, a majestic black horse of unusual size, drawing an old weather-beaten chair, strode over the plain; and although he appeared to make no effort, for he maintained a steady trot, before Dart and Lightning approached the goal the black horse and chair had overtaken the racers, who threw back their ears, and suddenly stopped in their course.   Thus neither Dart nor Lightning carried away the purse.

The spectators now were exceedingly curious to learn whence came the black horse and chair.   With many it was the opinion that nobody was in the vehicle.   Indeed, this began to be the prevalent opinion; for those at a short distance, so fleet was the black horse, could not easily discern who, if anybody, was in the carriage.   But both riders, very near to whom the black horse passed, agreed in this particular,—that a sad-looking man and a little girl were in the chair.   When they stated this I was

satisfied that the man was Peter Rugg. But what caused no little surprise, John Spring, one of the riders (he who rode Lightning) asserted
that no earthly horse without breaking his trot could, in a carriage, outstrip
his race-horse; and he persisted, with some passion, that it was not a horse,
but a large black ox. "What a great black ox can do," said John, "I cannot pretend to say; but no race-horse, not even flying Childers, could out-
trot Lightning in a fair race."

This opinion of John Spring excited no little merriment, for it was
obvious to every one that it was a powerful black horse that interrupted
the race; but John Spring, jealous of Lightning's reputation as a horse,
would rather have it thought that any other beast, even an ox, had been
the victor. However, the "horse-laugh" at John Spring's expense was
soon suppressed; for as soon as Dart and Lightning began to breathe more
freely, it was observed that both of them walked deliberately to the track
of the race-ground, and putting their heads to the earth, suddenly raised
them again and began to snort. They repeated this till John Spring said,
—"These horses have discovered something strange; they suspect foul
play. Let me go and talk with Lightning."

He went up to Lightning and took hold of his mane; and Lightning
put his nose toward the ground and smelt of the earth without touching
it, then reared his head very high, and snorted so loudly that the sound
echoed from the next hill. Dart did the same. John Spring stooped
down to examine the spot where Lightning had smelled. In a moment he
raised himself up, and the countenance of the man was changed. His
strength failed him, and he sidled against Lightning.

At length John Spring recovered from his stupor and exclaimed, "It
was an ox! I told you it was an ox. No real horse ever yet beat
Lightning."

And now, on a close inspection of the black horse's tracks, it was
evident to every one that the forefeet of the black horse were cloven.
Notwithstanding these appearances, to me it was evident that the strange
horse was in reality a horse. Yet when the people left the race-ground, I
presume one-half of all those present would have testified that a large
black ox had distanced two of the fleetest coursers that ever trod the
Virginia turf.

While I was proceeding to my lodgings, pondering on the events of
the day, a stranger rode up to me, and accosted me thus,—"I think your
name is Dunwell, sir."

"Yes, sir," I replied.

"Did I not see you a year or two since in Boston, at the Marlborough
Hotel?"

"Very likely, sir, for I was there."

"And you heard a story about one Peter Rugg?"

"I recollect it all," said I.

"The account you heard in Boston must be true, for here he was to-day. The man has found his way to Virginia, and for aught that appears, has been to Cape Horn. I have seen him before to-day, but never saw him travel with such fearful velocity. Pray, sir, where does Peter Rugg spend his winters, for I have seen him only in summer, and always in foul weather, except this time."

I replied, "No one knows where Peter Rugg spends his winters; where or when he eats, drinks, sleeps, or lodges. He seems to have an indistinct idea of day and night, time and space, storm and sunshine. His only object is Boston. It appears to me that Rugg's horse has some control of the chair; and that Rugg himself is, in some sort, under the control of his horse."

I then inquired of the stranger where he first saw the man and horse. "Why, sir," said he, "in the summer of 1824, I travelled to the North for my health; and soon after I saw you at the Marlborough Hotel I returned homeward to Virginia, and if my memory is correct, I saw this man and horse in every State between here and Massachusetts. Sometimes he would meet me, but oftener overtake me. He spoke but once, and that once was in Delaware. On his approach he checked his horse with some difficulty. A more beautiful horse I never saw. When he approached mine he reined in his neck, bent his ears forward until they met, and looked my horse full in the face. My horse immediately withered into half a horse, his hide curling up like a piece of burnt leather; spell-bound, he was fixed to the earth as though a nail had been driven through each hoof.

" 'Sir,' said Rugg, 'perhaps you are travelling to Boston; and if so, I should be happy to accompany you, for I have lost my way, and I must reach home to-night. See how sleepy this little girl looks; poor thing, she is a picture of patience.'

" 'Sir,' said I, 'it is impossible for you to reach home to-night, for you are in Concord, in the county of Sussex, which is in the State of Delaware.'

" 'What do you mean,' said he, 'by the State of Delaware? If I were in Concord, that is only twenty miles from Boston, and my horse Lightfoot could carry me to Charlestown ferry in less than two hours. You mistake, sir; you are a stranger here; this town is nothing like Concord. I am well acquainted with Concord. I went to Concord when I left Boston.'

" 'But,' said I, 'you are in Concord, in the State of Delaware.'

" 'What do you mean by State?' said Rugg.

" 'Why, one of the United States.'

" 'States!' said he, in a low voice; 'the man is a wag, and would persuade me I am in Holland.' Then, raising his voice, he said, 'You seem, sir, to be a gentleman, and I entreat you to mislead me not: tell me, quickly, for pity's sake, the right road to Boston, for you see my horse will swallow his bits; he has eaten nothing since I left Concord.'

" 'Sir,' said I, 'this town is Concord,—Concord in Delaware, not Concord in Massachusetts; and you are now five hundred miles from Boston.'

"Rugg looked at me for a moment, more in sorrow than resentment, and then repeated, 'Five hundred miles! Unhappy man, who would have thought him deranged; but nothing in this world is so deceitful as appearances. Five hundred miles! This beats Connecticut River.'

"What he meant by Connecticut River, I know not; his horse broke away, and Rugg disappeared in a moment."

I explained to the stranger the meaning of Rugg's expression, "Connecticut River," and the incident respecting him that occurred at Hartford, as I stood on the door-stone of Mr. Bennett's excellent hotel.

Soon after, I saw Rugg again, at the toll-gate on the turnpike between Alexandria and Middleburgh. While I was paying the toll, I observed to the toll-gatherer, that the drought was more severe in his vicinity than farther south.

"Yes," said he, "the drought is excessive; but if I had not heard yesterday, by a traveller, that the man with the black horse was seen in Kentucky a day or two since, I should be sure of a shower in a few minutes."

I looked all around the horizon, and could not discern a cloud that could hold a pint of water.

"Look, sir," said the toll-gatherer, "you perceive to the eastward, just above that hill, a small black cloud not bigger than a blackberry, and while I am speaking it is doubling and trebling itself, and rolling up the turnpike steadily, as if its sole design was to deluge some object."

"True," said I, "I do perceive it; but what connection is there between a thunder-cloud and a man and horse?"

"More than you imagine, or I can tell you. I know that cloud; I have seen it several times before, and can testify to its identity. You will soon see a man and black horse under it."

While he was speaking, we began to hear the distant thunder, and soon the chain-lightning performed all the figures of a country-dance. About a mile distant we saw the man and black horse under the cloud; but before he arrived at the toll-gate, the thunder-cloud had spent itself, and not even a sprinkle fell near us.

As the man, whom I instantly knew to be Rugg, attempted to pass, the toll-gatherer swung the gate across the road, seized Rugg's horse by the reins, and demanded two dollars.

Feeling some little regard for Rugg, I interfered, and began to question the toll-gatherer, and requested him not to be wroth with the man. The toll-gatherer replied that he had just cause, for the man had run his toll ten times, and moreover that the horse had discharged a cannon-ball at him, to the great danger of his life; that the man had always before approached so rapidly that he was too quick for the rusty hinges of the toll-gate, "but now I will have my full satisfaction."

Rugg looked wistfully at me, and said, "I entreat you, sir, to delay me not; I have found at length the direct road to Boston, and shall not reach home before night if you detain me. You see I am dripping wet, and ought to change my clothes."

The toll-gatherer then demanded why he had run his toll so many times.

"Toll! Why," said Rugg, "do you demand toll? There is no toll to pay on the king's highway."

"King's highway! Do you not perceive this is a turnpike?"

"Turnpike! There are no turnpikes in Massachusetts."

"That may be, but we have several in Virginia."

"Virginia! Do you pretend I am in Virginia?"

Rugg then, appealing to me, asked how far it was to Boston.

Said I, "Mr. Rugg, I perceive you are bewildered, and am sorry to see you so far from home; you are, indeed, in Virginia."

"You know me, then sir, it seems; and you say I am in Virginia. Give me leave to tell you, sir, that you are the most impudent man alive; for I was never forty miles from Boston, and I never saw a Virginian in my life. This beats Delaware!"

"Your toll, sir, your toll!"

"I will not pay you a penny," said Rugg; "you are both of you highway robbers. There are no turnpikes in this country. Take toll on the king's highway!" Then in a low tone, he said, "Here is evidently a conspiracy against me; alas, I shall never see Boston! The highways refuse me a passage, the rivers change their courses, and there is no faith in the compass."

But Rugg's horse had no idea of stopping more than one minute; for in the midst of this altercation, the horse, whose nose was resting on the upper bar of the turnpike-gate, seized it between his teeth, lifted it gently off its staples, and trotted off with it. The toll-gatherer, confounded, strained his eyes after his gate.

"Let him go," said I, "the horse will soon drop your gate, and you will get it again."

I then questioned the toll-gatherer respecting his knowledge of this man; and he related the following particulars:

"The first time," said he, "that man ever passed this toll-gate was in the year 1806, at the moment of the great eclipse. I thought the horse was frightened at the sudden darkness, and concluded he had run away with the man. But within a few days after, the same man and horse repassed with equal speed, without the least respect to the toll-gate or to me, except by a vacant stare. Some few years afterward, during the late war, I saw the same man approaching again, and I resolved to check his career. Accordingly I stepped into the middle of the road, and stretched wide both my arms, and cried, 'Stop, sir, on your peril!' At this the man said, 'Now, Lightfoot, confound the robber!' at the same time he gave the whip liberally to the flank of his horse, which bounded off with such force that it appeared to me two such horses, give them a place to stand, would overcome any check man could devise. An ammunition wagon which had just passed on to Baltimore had dropped an eighteen pounder in the road; this unlucky ball lay in the way of the horse's heels, and the beast, with the sagacity of a demon, clinched it with one of his heels and hurled it behind him. I feel dizzy in relating the fact, but so nearly did the ball pass my head, that the wind thereof blew off my hat; and the ball embedded itself in that gate-post, as you may see if you will cast your eye on the post. I have permitted it to remain there in memory of the occurrence,—as the people of Boston, I am told, preserve the eighteen-pounder which is now to be seen half embedded in Brattle Street Church."

I then took leave of the toll-gatherer, and promised him if I saw or heard of his gate I would send him notice.

A strong inclination had possessed me to arrest Rugg and search his pockets, thinking great discoveries might be made in the examination; but what I saw and heard that day convinced me that no human force could detain Peter Rugg against his consent. I therefore determined if I ever saw Rugg again to treat him in the gentlest manner.

In pursuing my way to New York, I entered on the turnpike in Trenton; and when I arrived at New Brunswick, I perceived the road was newly macadamised. The small stones had just been laid thereon. As I passed this piece of road, I observed that, at regular distances of about eight feet, the stones were entirely displaced from spots as large as the circumference of a half-bushel measure. This singular appearance induced me to inquire the cause of it at the turnpike-gate.

"Sir," said the toll-gatherer, "I wonder not at the question, but I am unable to give you a satisfactory answer. Indeed, sir, I believe I am bewitched, and that the turnpike is under a spell of enchantment; for what appeared to me last night cannot be a real transaction, otherwise a turnpike-gate is a useless thing."

"I do not believe in witchcraft or enchantment," said I; "and if you will relate circumstantially what happened last night, I will endeavour to account for it by natural means."

"You may recollect the night was uncommonly dark. Well, sir, just after I had closed the gates for the night, down the turnpike, as far as my eye could reach, I beheld what at first appeared to be two armies engaged. The report of the musketry, and the flashes of their firelocks, were incessant and continuous. As this strange spectacle approached me with the fury of a tornado, the noise increased; and the appearance rolled on in one compact body over the surface of the ground. The most splendid fireworks rose out of the earth and encircled this moving spectacle. You would have thought all the stars of heaven had met in merriment on the turnpike. In the midst of this luminous configuration sat a man in a miserable-looking chair, drawn by a black horse. The turnpike-gate ought, by the laws of Nature and the laws of the State, to have made a wreck of the whole, and dissolved the enchantment; but no, the horse without an effort passed over the gate, and drew the man and chair horizontally after him without touching the bar. This is what I call enchantment. What think you, sir?"

"My friend," said I, "you have grossly magnified a natural occurrence. The man was Peter Rugg, on his way to Boston. It is true, his horse travelled with unequalled speed, but as he reared high his forefeet, he could not help displacing the thousand small stones on which he trod, which flying in all directions struck one another, and resounded and scintillated. The top bar of your gate is not more than two feet from the ground, and Rugg's horse at every vault could easily lift the carriage over that gate."

This satisfied Mr. McDoubt, and I pursued my journey homeward to New York.

Little did I expect to see or hear anything further of Mr. Rugg, for he was now more than twelve hours in advance of me. I could hear nothing of him on my way to Elizabethtown, and therefore concluded that during the past night he had turned off from the turnpike and pursued a westerly direction; but just before I arrived at Powles's Hook, I observed a considerable collection of passengers in the ferry-boat, all standing motionless, and steadily looking at the same object. One of the ferry-men, Mr. Hardy, who knew me well, observing my approach delayed a minute, in order to afford me a passage, and coming up, said, "Mr. Dunwell, we have a curiosity on board that would puzzle Dr. Mitchell."

"Some strange fish, I suppose, has found its way into the Hudson."

"No," said he, "it is a man who looks as if he had lain hidden in the ark, and had just now ventured out. He has a little girl with him, the counterpart of himself, and the finest horse you ever saw, harnessed to the queerest-looking carriage that ever was made."

"Ah, Mr. Hardy," said I, "you have, indeed, hooked a prize; no one before you could ever detain Peter Rugg long enough to examine him."

"Do you know the man?" said Mr. Hardy.

"No, nobody knows him, but everybody has seen him. Detain him as long as possible; delay the boat under any pretence, cut the gear of the horse, do anything to detain him."

As I entered the ferry-boat, I was struck at the spectacle before me. There, indeed, sat Peter Rugg and Jenny Rugg in the chair, and there stood the black horse, all as quiet as lambs, surrounded by more than fifty men and women, who seemed to have lost all their senses but one. Not a motion, not a breath, not a nestle. They were all eye. Rugg appeared to them to be a man not of this world; and they appeared to Rugg a strange generation of men. Rugg spoke not, and they spoke not: nor was I disposed to disturb the calm, satisfied to reconnoitre Rugg in a state of rest. Presently, Rugg observed in a low voice, addressed to nobody, "A new contrivance, horses instead of oars; Boston folks are full of notions."

It was plain that Rugg was of Dutch extraction. He had on three pairs of small-clothes, called in former days of simplicity breeches, not much the worse for wear; but time had proved the fabric, and shrunk one more than another, so that they showed at the knees their different qualities and colours. His several waistcoats, the flaps of which rested on his knees, made him appear rather corpulent. His capacious drab coat would supply the stuff for half a dozen modern ones; the sleeves were like meal bags, in the cuffs of which you might nurse a child to sleep. His hat, probably once black, now of a tan colour, was neither round nor crooked. This dress gave the rotund face of Rugg an antiquated dignity. The man, though deeply sunburned, did not appear to be more than thirty years of age. He had lost his sad and anxious look, was quite composed, and seemed happy. The chair in which Rugg sat was very capacious, evidently made for service, and calculated to last for ages; the timber would supply material for three modern carriages. The horse, too, was an object of curiosity; his majestic height, his natural mane and tail, gave him a commanding appearance, and his large open nostrils indicated inexhaustible wind. It was quite apparent that the hoofs of his forefeet had been split, probably on some newly macadamised road, and were now growing together again; so that John Spring was not altogether in the wrong.

How long this dumb scene would otherwise have continued I cannot tell. Rugg discovered no sign of impatience. But Rugg's horse having been quiet more than five minutes, had no idea of standing idle; he began to whinny, and in a moment after, with his right forefoot he started a plank. Said Rugg, "My horse is impatient, he sees the North End. You must be quick, or he will be ungovernable."

At these words, the horse raised his left forefoot; and when he laid it down every inch of the ferry-boat trembled. Two men immediately seized Rugg's horse by the nostrils. The horse nodded, and both of them were in the Hudson. While we were fishing up the men, the horse was perfectly quiet.

"Fret not the horse," said Rugg, "and he will do no harm. He is only anxious, like myself, to arrive at yonder beautiful shore; he sees the North Church, and smells his own stable."

"Sir," said I to Rugg, practising a little deception, "pray tell me, for

I am a stranger here, what river is this, and what city is that opposite, for you seem to be an inhabitant of it?"

"This river, sir, is called Mystic River, and this is Winnisimmet ferry, —we have retained the Indian names,—and that town is Boston. You must, indeed, be a stranger in these parts, not to know that yonder is Boston, the capital of the New England provinces."

"Pray, sir, how long have you been absent from Boston?"

"Why, that I cannot exactly tell. I lately went with this little girl of mine to Concord, to see my friends; and I am ashamed to tell you, in returning lost the way, and have been travelling ever since. No one would direct me right. It is cruel to mislead a traveller. My horse, Lightfoot, has boxed the compass; and it seems to me he has boxed it back again. But, sir, you perceive my horse is uneasy; Lightfoot, as yet, has only given a hint and a nod. I cannot be answerable for his heels."

At these words Lightfoot reared his long tail, and snapped it as you would a whiplash. The Hudson reverberated with the sound. Instantly the six horses began to move the boat. The Hudson was a sea of glass, smooth as oil, not a ripple. The horses, from a smart trot, soon pressed into a gallop; water now ran over the gunwhale; the ferry-boat was soon buried in an ocean of foam, and the noise of the spray was like the roaring of many waters. When we arrived at New York, you might see the beautiful white wake of the ferry-boat across the Hudson.

Though Rugg refused to pay toll at turnpikes, when Mr. Hardy reached his hand for the ferriage, Rugg readily put his hand into one of his many pockets, took out a piece of silver, and handed it to Hardy.

"What is this?" said Mr. Hardy.

"It is thirty shillings," said Rugg.

"It might once have been thirty shillings, old tenor," said Mr. Hardy, "but it is not at present."

"The money is good English coin," said Rugg; "my grandfather brought a bag of them from England, and had them hot from the mint."

Hearing this, I approached near to Rugg, and asked permission to see the coin. It was a half-crown, coined by the English Parliament, dated in the year 1649. On one side, "The Commonwealth of England," and St. George's cross encircled with a wreath of laurel. On the other, "God with us," and a harp and St. George's cross united. I winked at Mr. Hardy, and pronounced it good current money; and said slowly, "I will not permit the gentleman to be imposed on, for I will exchange the money myself."

On this, Rugg spoke,—"Please to give me your name, sir."

"My name is Dunwell, sir," I replied.

"Mr. Dunwell," said Rugg, "you are the only honest man I have seen since I left Boston. As you are a stranger here, my house is your home; Dame Rugg will be happy to see her husband's friend. Step into my chair, sir, there is room enough; move a little, Jenny, for the gentleman, and we will be in Middle Street in a minute."

Accordingly I took a seat by Peter Rugg.

"Were you never in Boston before?" said Rugg.

"No," said I.

"Well, you will now see the queen of New England, a town second only to Philadelphia, in all North America."

"You forget New York," said I.

"Poh, New York is nothing; though I never was there. I am told you might put all New York in our mill-pond. No, sir, New York I assure you, is but a sorry affair; no more to be compared with Boston than a wigwam with a palace."

As Rugg's horse turned into Pearl Street, I looked Rugg as fully in the face as good manners would allow, and said, "Sir, if this is Boston, I acknowledge New York is not worthy to be one of its suburbs."

Before we had proceeded far in Pearl Street, Rugg's countenance changed: his nerves began to twitch; his eyes trembled in their sockets; he was evidently bewildered. "What is the matter, Mr. Rugg? you seem disturbed."

"This surpasses all human comprehension; if you know, sir, where we are, I beseech you to tell me."

"If this place," I replied, "is not Boston, it must be New York."

"No, sir, it is not Boston; nor can it be New York. How could I be in New York, which is nearly two hundred miles from Boston?"

By this time we had passed into Broadway, and then Rugg, in truth, discovered a chaotic mind. "There is no such place as this in North America. This is all the effect of enchantment; this is a grand delusion, nothing real. Here is seemingly a great city, magnificent houses, shops and goods, men and women innumerable, and as busy as in real life, all sprung up in one night from the wilderness; or what is more probable, some tremendous convulsion of Nature has thrown London or Amsterdam on the shores of New England. Or, possibly, I may be dreaming, though the night seems rather long; but before now I have sailed in one night to Amsterdam, bought goods of Vandogger, and returned to Boston before morning."

At this moment a hue-and-cry was heard, "Stop the madmen, they will endanger the lives of thousands!" In vain hundreds attempted to stop Rugg's horse. Lightfoot interfered with nothing; his course was straight as a shooting-star. But on my part, fearful that before night I should find myself behind the Alleghanies, I addressed Mr. Rugg in a tone of entreaty, and requested him to restrain the horse and permit me to alight.

"My friend," said he, "we shall be in Boston before dark, and Dame Rugg will be most exceedingly glad to see us."

"Mr. Rugg," said I, "you must excuse me. Pray look to the west; see that thunder-cloud swelling with rage, as if in pursuit of us."

"Ah," said Rugg, "it is in vain to attempt to escape. I know that cloud; it is collecting new wrath to spend on my head." Then checking his horse, he permitted me to descend, saying, "Farewell, Mr. Dunwell, I shall be happy to see you in Boston; I live in Middle Street."

It is uncertain in what direction Mr. Rugg pursued his course, after he disappeared in Broadway; but one thing is sufficiently known to everybody, —that in the course of two months after he was seen in New York, he found his way most opportunely to Boston.

It seems the estate of Peter Rugg had recently fallen to the Commonwealth of Massachusetts for want of heirs; and the Legislature had ordered the solicitor-general to advertise and sell it at public auction. Happening to be in Boston at the time, and observing his advertisement, which described a considerable extent of land, I felt a kindly curiosity to see the spot where Rugg once lived. Taking the advertisement in my hand, I wandered a little way down Middle Street, and without asking a question of any one, when I came to a certain spot I said to myself, "This is Rugg's estate; I will proceed no farther. This must be the spot; it is a counterpart of Peter Rugg." The premises, indeed, looked as if they had fulfilled a sad prophecy. Fronting on Middle Street, they extended in the rear to Ann Street, and embraced about half an acre of land. It was not uncommon in former times to have half an acre for a house-lot; for an acre of land then, in many parts of Boston, was not more valuable than a foot in some places at present. The old mansion-house had become a powder-post, and been blown away. One other building, uninhabited, stood ominous, courting dilapidation. The street had been so much raised that the bed-chamber had descended to the kitchen and was level with the street. The house seemed conscious of its fate; and as though tired of standing there, the front was fast retreating from the rear, and waiting the next south wind to project itself into the street. "The hand of destiny," said I, "has pressed heavy on this spot; still heavier on the former owners. Strange that so large a lot of land as this should want an heir! Yet Peter Rugg, at this day, might pass by his own door-stone, and ask, 'Who once lived here?'"

The auctioneer, appointed by the solicitor to sell this estate, was a man of eloquence, as many of the auctioneers of Boston are. The occasion seemed to warrant, and his duty urged, him to make a display. He addressed his audience as follows,—

"The estate, gentlemen, which we offer you this day, was once the property of a family now extinct. For that reason it has escheated to the Commonwealth. Lest any one of you should be deterred from bidding on so large an estate as this for fear of a disputed title, I am authorised by the solicitor-general to proclaim that the purchaser shall have the best of all titles,—a warranty-deed from the Commonwealth. I state this, gentlemen, because I know there is an idle rumour in this vicinity, that one Peter Rugg, the original owner of this estate, is still living. This rumour, gentlemen, has no foundation, and can have no foundation in the nature of things. It originated about two years since, from the incredible story of one Jonathan Dunwell, of New York. Mrs. Croft, indeed, whose husband I see present, and whose mouth waters for this estate, has countenanced this fiction. But, gentlemen, was it ever known that any estate, especially an estate of this value, lay unclaimed for nearly half a century, if any heir, ever so remote, were existing? For, gentlemen, all agree that old Peter Rugg, if living, would be at least one hundred years of age. It is said that he and his daughter, with a horse and chaise, were missed more than half a century ago; and because they never returned home, forsooth, they must be now living, and will some day come and claim this great estate. Such logic, gentlemen, never led to a good investment. Let not this idle story cross the noble purpose of consigning these ruins to the genius of architecture. A man's money, if not employed, serves only to disturb his rest. Look, then, to the prospect before you. Here is half an acre of land,—more than twenty thousand square feet,—a corner lot, with wonderful capabilities; none of your contracted lots of forty feet by fifty, where, in dog-days, you can breathe only through your scuttles. On the contrary, an architect cannot contemplate this lot of land without rapture, for here is room enough for his genius to shame the temple of Solomon. Then the prospect—how commanding! To the east, so near to the Atlantic that Neptune, freighted with the select treasures of the whole earth, can knock at your door with his trident. From the west, the produce of the river of Paradise—the Connecticut—will soon, by the blessings, of steam, railways, and canals, pass under your windows; and thus, on this spot, Neptune shall marry Ceres, and Pomona from Roxbury, and Flora from Cambridge, shall dance at the wedding.

"Gentlemen of science, men of taste, ye of the literary emporium,—to you this is holy ground. . . . One whom all the world knows was born in Middle Street, directly opposite to this lot. Ere long there will arise in full view of the edifice to be erected here, a monument, the wonder and veneration of the world. A column shall spring to the clouds; and on that column will be engraven one word,—a name of one who, when living, was the patron of the poor, the delight of the cottage, and the admiration of kings. Need I tell you his name? He fixed the thunder and guided the lightning.

"Men of the North End! Need I appeal to your patriotism in order to enhance the value of this lot? There, around that corner, lived James Otis; here, Samuel Adams; there, Joseph Warren; and around that other corner, Josiah Quincy. Here was the birthplace of Freedom; here Liberty was born, and nursed, and grew to manhood. Here is the nursery of

American Independence; here began the emancipation of the world; a thousand generations hence millions of men will cross the Atlantic just to look at the North End of Boston. Your fathers—what do I say— yourselves,—yes, this moment, I behold several attending this auction who lent a hand to rock the cradle of Independence.

"Men of speculation,—you, I know, will give me both of your ears when I tell you the city of Boston must have a piece of this estate in order to widen Ann Street. Do you all hear me? I say the city must have a large piece of this land in order to widen Ann Street. What a chance! The city scorns to take a man's land for nothing. If it seizes your property, it is generous beyond the dreams of avarice. The only oppression is, you are in danger of being smothered under a load of wealth. Bid, then, liberally, and do not let the name of Rugg damp your ardour. How much will you give per foot for this estate?"

Thus spoke the auctioneer, and gracefully waved his ivory hammer. From fifty to seventy-five cents per foot were offered in a few moments. The bidding laboured from seventy-five to ninety. At length one dollar was offered. The auctioneer seemed satisfied; and looking at his watch, said he would knock off the estate in five minutes, if no one offered more.

There was a deep silence during this short period. While the hammer was suspended, a strange rumbling noise arrested the attention of every one. As the sound approached nearer, some exclaimed, "The buildings in the new market are falling in promiscuous ruins." Others said, "No, it is an earthquake; we perceive the earth tremble." Others said, "Not so; the sound proceeds from Hanover Street, and approaches nearer;" and this proved true, for presently Peter Rugg was in the midst of us.

"Alas, Jenny," said Peter, "I am ruined; our house has been burned, and here are all our neighbours around the ruins. Heaven grant your mother, Dame Rugg, is safe."

"They don't look like our neighbours," said Jenny; "but sure enough our house is burned, and nothing left but the door-stone and an old cedar post. Do ask where mother is."

In the meantime more than a thousand men had surrounded Rugg and his horse and chair. Yet neither Rugg, personally, nor his horse and carriage, attracted more attention than the auctioneer. The confident look and searching eyes of Rugg carried more conviction to every one present that the estate was his, than could any parchment or paper with signature and seal. The impression which the auctioneer had just made on the company was effaced in a moment; and although the latter words of the auctioneer were, "Fear not Peter Rugg," the moment the auctioneer met the eye of Rugg his occupation was gone; his arm fell down to his hips, his late lively hammer hung heavy in his hand, and the auction was forgotten. The black horse, too, gave his evidence. He knew his journey was ended; for he stretched himself into a horse and a half, rested his head over the cedar post, and whinnied thrice, causing his harness to tremble from headstall to crupper.

Rugg then stood upright in his chair, and asked with some authority, "Who has demolished my house in my absence, for I see no signs of a conflagration? I demand by what accident this has happened, and wherefore this collection of strange people has assembled before my doorstep. I thought I knew every man in Boston, but you appear to me a new generation of men. Yet I am familiar with many of the countenances here present, and I can call some of you by name; but in truth I do not recollect that before this moment I ever saw any one of you. There, I am certain, is a Winslow, and here a Sargent; there stands a Sewall, and next to him a Dudley. Will none of you speak to me,—or is this all a delusion? I see, indeed, many forms of men, and no want of eyes, but of motion, speech, and hearing, you seem to be destitute. Strange! Will no one inform me who has demolished my house?"

Then spake a voice from the crowd, but whence it came I could not discern: "There is nothing strange here but yourself, Mr. Rugg. Time, which destroys and renews all things, has dilapidated your house, and placed us here. You have suffered many years under an illusion. The tempest which you profanely defied at Menotomy has at length subsided; but you will never see home, for your house and wife and neighbours have all disappeared. Your estate, indeed, remains, but no home. You were cut off from the last age, and you can never be fitted to the present. Your home is gone, and you can never have another home in this world."

❋ ❋ ❋

WASHINGTON IRVING
(1783-1859)

WASHINGTON IRVING, first American story writer to win world fame, was born in New York, April 3, 1783. When twenty-one, he went to Europe and remained two years. In 1809 he produced the *Knickerbocker History of New York*. After the War of 1812 he returned to Europe (1815), where he lived until 1832. *The Sketch Book* (1819), *Bracebridge Hall* (1822), and *Tales of a Traveller* (1824) were published during his residence in England. In 1826 he went to Spain as attache of the American legation, his stay of three years resulting incidentally in his *Life of Columbus* and *The Alhambra*. After three more years in England he returned to America, settled at Sunnyside, and continued to write, notably his biographies of Goldsmith and Washington. From 1842 to 1846 he was Minister to Spain. He died September 28, 1859, and was buried in Sleepy Hollow.

The Stout Gentleman is reprinted from *Bracebridge Hall*.

THE STOUT GENTLEMAN:

A Stage Coach Romance

"I'll cross it, though it blast me!"
——HAMLET.

IT was a rainy Sunday, in the gloomy month of November. I had been detained, in the course of a journey, by a slight indisposition, from which I was recovering: but I was still feverish, and was obliged to keep within doors all day, in an inn of the small town of Derby. A wet Sunday in a country inn! whoever has had the luck to experience one can alone judge of my situation. The rain pattered against the casements; the bells tolled for church with a melancholy sound. I went to the windows in quest of something to amuse the eye; but it seemed as if I had been placed completely out of the reach of all amusement. The windows of my bedroom looked out among tiled roofs and stacks of chimneys, while those of my sitting-room commanded a full view of the stable-yard. I know of nothing more calculated to make a man sick of this world than a stable-yard on a rainy day. The place was littered with wet straw that had been kicked about by travellers and stable-boys. In one corner was a stagnant pool of water, surrounding an island of muck; there were several half-drowned fowls crowded miserably together under a cart, among which was a miserable, crest-fallen cock, drenched out of all life and spirit: his drooping tail matted, as it were, into a single feather, along which the water trickled from his back; near the cart was a half-dozing cow, chewing the cud, and standing patiently to be rained on, with wreaths of vapor rising from her reeking hide; a wall-eyed horse, tired of the loneliness of the stable, was poking his spectral head out of a window, with the rain dropping on it from the eaves; an unhappy cur, chained to a doghouse hard by, uttered something every now and then, between a bark and a yelp; a drab of a kitchen wench tramped backwards and forwards through the yard in pattens, looking as sulky as the weather itself; everything, in short, was comfortless and forlorn, excepting a crew of hard-drinking ducks, assembled like boon companions round a puddle, and making a riotous noise over their liquor.

I was lonely and listless, and wanted amusement. My room soon became insupportable. I abandoned it, and sought what is technically called the travellers'-room. This is a public room set apart at most inns for the accommodation of a class of wayfarers, called travellers, or riders: a kind of commercial knights errant, who are incessantly scouring the kingdom in gigs, on horseback, or by coach. They are the only successors that I know of, at the present day, to the knights errant of yore. They lead the same kind of roving adventurous life, only changing the lance for a driving-whip, the buckler for a pattern-card, and the coat of mail for an upper Benjamin. Instead of vindicating the charms of peerless beauty, they rove about, spreading the fame and standing of some substantial tradesman, or manufacturer, and are ready at any time to bargain in his name; it being the fashion nowadays to trade, instead of fight, with one another. As the room of the hostel, in the good old fighting times, would be hung round at night with the armour of way-worn warriors, such as coats of mail, falchions, and yawning helmets; so the travellers' room is garnished with the harnessing of their successors, with box coats, whips of all kinds, spurs, gaiters, and oil-cloth covered hats.

I was in hopes of finding some of these worthies to talk with, but was disappointed. There were, indeed, two or three in the room; but I could make nothing of them. One was just finishing breakfast, quarreling with his bread and butter, and huffing the waiter; another buttoned on a pair of gaiters, with many execrations at Boots for not having cleaned his shoes well; a third sat drumming on the table with his fingers and looking at the rain as it streamed down the window-glass: they all appeared infected by the weather, and disappeared, one after the other, without exchanging a word.

I sauntered to the window and stood gazing at the people, picking their way to church, with petticoats hoisted midleg high, and dripping umbrellas. The bell ceased to toll, and the streets became silent. I then amused myself with watching the daughters of a tradesman opposite; who being confined to the house for fear of wetting their Sunday finery, played off their charms at the front windows, to fascinate the chance tenants of the inn. They at length were summoned away by a vigilant vinegar-faced mother, and I had nothing further from without to amuse me.

What was I to do to pass away the long-lived day? I was sadly nervous and lonely; and everything about an inn seems calculated to make a dull day ten times duller. Old newspapers, smelling of beer and tobacco smoke, and which I had already read half a dozen times. Good for nothing books, that were worse than rainy weather. I bored myself to death with an old copy of the *Lady's Magazine*. I read all the commonplace names of ambitious travellers scrawled on the panes of glass; the eternal families of the Smiths, and the Browns, and the Jacksons, and the Johnsons, and all the other sons; and I deciphered several scraps of fatiguing inn-window poetry, which I have met with in all parts of the world.

The day continued lowering and gloomy; the slovenly, ragged, spongy clouds drifted heavily along; there was no variety even in the rain; it was one dull, continued, monotonous patter—patter—patter, excepting that now and then I was enlivened by the idea of a brisk shower, from the rattling of the drops upon a passing umbrella.

It was quite *refreshing* (if I may be allowed a hackneyed phrase of the day) when, in the course of the morning, a horn blew, and a stage coach whirled through the street, with outside passengers stuck all over it, cowering under cotton umbrellas, and seethed together, and reeking with the steams of wet box-coats and upper Benjamins.

The sound brought out from their lurking-places a crew of vagabond boys, and vagabond dogs, and the carroty-headed hostler, and that non-descript animal yelped Boots, and all the other vagabond race that infest the purlieus of an inn; but the bustle was transient, the coach again whirled on its way; and boy and dog, hostler and Boots, all slunk back again to their holes; the street again became silent, and the rain continued to rain on. In fact, there was no hope of its clearing up, the barometer pointed to rainy weather; mine hostess's tortoise-shell cat sat by the fire washing her face, and rubbing her paws over her ears; and, on referring to the Almanack, I found a direful prediction stretching from the top of the page to the bottom through the whole month, "expect—much—rain—about—this—time!"

I was dreadfully hipped. The hours seemed as if they would never creep by. The very ticking of the clock became irksome. At length the stillness of the house was interrupted by the ringing of a bell. Shortly after, I heard the voice of a waiter at the bar; "The Stout Gentleman in No. 13 wants his breakfast. Tea and bread and butter, with ham and eggs; the eggs not to be too much done."

In such a situation as mine every incident is of importance. Here was a subject of speculation presented to my mind, and ample exercise for my imagination. I am prone to paint pictures to myself, and on this occasion I had some materials to work upon. Had the guest upstairs been mentioned as Mr. Smith, or Mr. Brown, or Mr. Jackson, or Mr. Johnson, or merely as "the gentleman in No. 13," it would have been a perfect blank to me. I should have thought nothing of it; but "The Stout Gentleman!"—the very name had in it something of the picturesque. It at once gave the size; it embodied the personage to my mind's eye, and my fancy did the rest.

He was stout, or, as some term it, lusty; in all probability, therefore, he was advanced in life, some people expanding as they grow old. By his breakfasting rather late, and in his own room, he must be a man accustomed to live at his ease, and above the necessity of early rising; no doubt a round, rosy, lusty old gentleman.

There was another violent ringing. The Stout Gentleman was impatient for his breakfast. He was evidently a man of importance; "well to do in the world;" accustomed to be promptly waited upon; of a keen appetite, and a little cross when hungry; "perhaps," thought I, "he may be some London Alderman; or who knows but he may be a member of Parliament?"

The breakfast was sent up, and there was a short interval of silence; he was, doubtless, making the tea. Presently, there was a violent ringing; and before it could be answered, another ringing still more violent. "Bless me! what a choleric old gentleman!" The waiter came down in a huff. The butter was rancid, the eggs were over-done, the ham was too salt:—the stout gentleman was evidently nice in his eating; one of those who eat and growl, and keep the waiter on the trot, and live in a state militant with the household.

The hostess got into a fume. I should observe that she was a brisk, coquettish woman; a little of a shrew, and something of a slammerkin, but very pretty withal: with a nincompoop for a husband, as shrews are apt to have. She rated the servants roundly for their negligence in sending up so bad a breakfast, but said not a word against the Stout Gentleman; by which I clearly perceived he must be a man of consequence, intitled to make a noise and to give trouble at a country inn. Other eggs, and ham, and bread and butter were sent up. They appeared to be more graciously received; at least there was no further complaint.

I had not made many turns about the travellers'-room, when there was another ringing. Shortly afterwards there was a stir and an inquest about the house. The Stout Gentleman wanted the *Times* or *The Chronicle* newspaper. I set him down, therefore, for a whig; or, rather, from his being so absolute and lordly where he had a chance, I suspected him of being a radical. Hunt, I had heard, was a large man; "who knows," thought I, "but it is Hunt himself?"

My curiosity began to be awakened. I inquired of the waiter who was this Stout Gentleman that was making all this stir; but I could get no information; nobody seemed to know him. The landlords of bustling inns seldom trouble their heads about the names or occupations of their transient guests. The colour of a coat, the shape or size of the person, is enough to suggest a travelling name. It is either the tall gentleman, or the short gentleman, or the gentleman in black, or the gentleman in snuff-colour; or, as in the present instance, the stout gentleman. A designation of the kind once hit on answers every purpose, and saves all further inquiry.

Rain—rain—rain! pitiless, ceaseless rain! No such thing as putting a foot out of doors, and no occupation nor amusement within. By and by I heard some one walking overhead. It was in the Stout Gentleman's room. He evidently was a large man by the heaviness of his tread; and an old man from his wearing such creaking soles. "He is doubtless," thought I, "some rich old square-toes of regular habits, and is now taking exercise after breakfast."

I now read all the advertisements of coaches and hotels that were stuck about the mantelpiece. The *Lady's Magazine* had become an abomination to me; it was as tedious as the day itself. I wandered out, not knowing what to do, and ascended again to my room. I had not been there long, when there was a squall from a neighbouring bedroom. A door opened and slammed violently; a chambermaid, that I had remarked for having a ruddy, good-humoured face, went down stairs in a violent flurry. The Stout Gentleman had been rude to her!

This sent a whole host of my deductions to the deuce in a moment. This unknown personage could not be an old gentleman; for old gentlemen are not apt to be so obstreperous to chamber-maids. He could not be a young gentleman; for young gentlemen are not apt to inspire such indignation. He must be a middle-aged man, and confounded ugly into the bargain, or the girl would not have taken the matter in such terrible dudgeon. I confess I was sorely puzzled.

In a few minutes I heard the voice of my landlady. I caught a glance of her as she came tramping up stairs; her face glowing, her cap flaring, her tongue wagging the whole way. "She'd have no such doings in her house, she'd warrant! If gentlemen did spend money freely, it was no rule. She'd have no servant maids of hers treated in that way, when they were about their work, that's what she wouldn't!"

As I hate squabbles, particularly with women, and above all with pretty women, I slunk back into my room, and partly closed the door; but my curiosity was too much excited not to listen. The landlady marched intrepidly to the enemy's citadel, and entered it with a storm; the door closed after her. I heard her voice in high, windy clamour for a moment or two. Then it gradually subsided, like a gust of wind in a garret; then there was a laugh; then I heard nothing more. .

After a little my landlady came out with an odd smile on her face, adjusting her cap, which was a little on one side. As she went down stairs I heard the landlord ask her what was the matter; she said, "Nothing at all, only the girl's a fool."—I was more than ever perplexed what to make of this unaccountable personage, who could put a good-natured chambermaid in a passion, and send away a termagant landlady in smiles. He could not be so old, nor cross, nor ugly either.

I had to go to work at his picture again, and to paint him entirely different. I now set him down for one of those stout gentlemen that are frequently met with swaggering about the doors of country inns. Moist, merry fellows, in Belcher handkerchiefs, whose bulk is a little assisted by malt-liquors. Men who have seen the world, and been sworn at Highgate; who are used to tavern life; up to all the tricks of tapsters, and knowing in the ways of sinful publicans. Free-livers on a small scale; who are prodigal within the compass of a guinea; who call all the waiters by name, touzle the maids, gossip with the landlady at the bar, and prose over a pint of port, or a glass of negus, after dinner.

The morning wore away in forming of these and similar surmises. As fast as I wove one system of belief, some movement of the unknown

would completely overturn it, and throw all my thoughts again into confusion. Such are the solitary operations of a feverish mind. I was, as
I have said, extremely nervous; and the continual meditation on the concerns of this invisible personage began to have its effect:—I was getting a
fit of the fidgets.

Dinner-time came. I hoped the Stout Gentleman might dine in the
travellers'-room, and that I might at length get a view of his person; but
no—he had dinner served in his own room. What could be the meaning of this solitude and mystery? He could not be a radical; there was
something too aristocratical in thus keeping himself apart from the rest of
the world, and condemning himself to his own dull company throughout
a rainy day. And then, too, he lived too well for a discontented politician.
He seemed to expatiate on a variety of dishes, and to sit over his wine like
a jolly friend of good-living. Indeed, my doubts on this head were soon
at an end; for he could not have finished his first bottle before I could
faintly hear him humming a tune; and on listening, I found it to be "God
Save the King." 'Twas plain, then, he was no radical, but a faithful subject; one that grew loyal over his bottle, and was ready to stand by king
and constitution, when he could stand by nothing else. But who could he
be! My conjectures began to run wild. Was he not some personage of
distinction travelling incog.? "God knows!" said I, at my wit's end; "it
may be one of the royal family, for aught I know, for they are all stout
gentlemen!"

The weather continued rainy. The mysterious unknown kept his
room, and as far as I could judge, his chair, for I did not hear him move.
In the meantime, as the day advanced, the travellers'-room began to be
frequented. Some, who had just arrived, came in buttoned up in box-
coats; others came home who had been dispersed about the town. Some
took their dinners, and some their tea. Had I been in a different mood,
I should have found entertainment in studying this peculiar class of men.
There were two especially, who were regular wags of the road, and versed
in all the standing jokes of travellers. They had a thousand sly things to
say to the waiting-maid, whom they called Louisa, and Ethelinda, and a
dozen other fine names, changing the name every time, and chuckling
amazingly at their own waggery. My mind, however, had become completely engrossed by the Stout Gentleman. He had kept my fancy in chase
during a long day, and it was not now to be diverted from the scent.

The evening gradually wore away. The travellers read the papers
two or three times over. Some drew round the fire and told long stories
about their horses, about their adventures, their over-turns, and breakings-
down. They discussed the credits of different merchants and different
inns; and the two wags told several choice anecdotes of pretty chamber-
maids, and kind landladies. All this passed as they were quietly taking
what they called their night-caps, that is to say, strong glasses of brandy

and water and sugar, or some other mixture of the kind; after which they one after another rang for "Boots" and the chambermaid, and walked off to bed in old shoes cut down into marvellously uncomfortable slippers.

There was only one man left; a short-legged, long-bodied, plethoric fellow, with a very large, sandy head. He sat by himself, with a glass of port wine negus, and a spoon; sipping and stirring, and meditating and sipping, until nothing was left but the spoon. He gradually fell asleep bolt upright in his chair, with the empty glass standing before him; and the candle seemed to fall asleep too, for the wick grew long, and black, and cabbaged at the end, and dimmed the little light that remained in the chamber. The gloom that now prevailed was contagious. Around hung the shapeless, and almost spectral, box-coats of departed travellers, long since buried in deep sleep. I only heard the ticking of the clock, with the deep-drawn breathings of the sleeping toper, and the drippings of the rain, drop—drop—drop, from the eaves of the house. The church bells chimed midnight. All at once the Stout Gentleman began to walk overhead, pacing slowly backwards and forwards. There was something extremely awful in all this, especially to one in my state of nerves. These ghastly great coats, these guttural breathings, and the creaking footsteps of this mysterious being. His steps grew fainter and fainter, and at length died away. I could bear it no longer. I was wound up to the desperation of a hero of romance. "Be he who or what he may," said I to myself, "I'll have a sight of him!" I seized a chamber candle, and hurried up to number 13. The door stood ajar. I hesitated—I entered; the room was deserted. There stood a large, broad-bottomed elbow-chair at a table, on which was an empty tumbler, and a *Times* newspaper, and the room smelt powerfully of Stilton cheese.

The mysterious stranger had evidently but just retired. I turned off, sorely disappointed, to my room, which had been changed to the front of the house. As I went along the corridor, I saw a large pair of boots, with dirty, waxed tops, standing at the door of a bed-chamber. They doubtless belonged to the unknown; but it would not do to disturb so redoubtable a personage in his den; he might discharge a pistol, or something worse, at my head. I went to bed, therefore, and lay awake half the night in a terribly nervous state; and even when I fell asleep, I was still haunted in my dreams by the idea of the Stout Gentleman and his wax-topped boots.

I slept rather late the next morning, and was awakened by some stir and bustle in the house, which I could not at first comprehend; until getting more awake, I found there was a mail-coach starting from the door. Suddenly there was a cry from below, "The gentleman has forgotten his umbrella! look for the gentleman's umbrella in No. 13!" I heard an immediate scampering of a chambermaid along the passage, and a shrill reply as she ran, "Here it is! here's the gentleman's umbrella!"

The mysterious stranger was then on the point of setting off. This was the only chance I should ever have of knowing him. I sprang out of bed, scrambled to the window, snatched aside the curtains, and just caught a glimpse of the rear of a person getting in at the coach-door. The skirts of a brown coat parted behind, and gave me a full view of the broad disk of a pair of drab breeches. The door closed—"all right!" was the word —the coach whirled off:—and that was all I ever saw of the Stout Gentleman!

❊ ❊ ❊

NATHANIEL HAWTHORNE
(1804-1864)

NATHANIEL HAWTHORNE, regarded by many the most accomplished artist in fiction America has produced, is best known for *The Scarlet Letter* (1850). Born July 4, 1804, in Salem, Massachusetts, he lived there and at Sebago Lake, Maine, until he went to Bowdoin College (1821-1825). In 1837 and 1842 he published two collections of *Twice-Told Tales*, followed by *Mosses from an Old Manse*, all of which stamp him the artistic representative of Puritan New England. From 1846 to 1849 he was surveyor of the port of Salem, but on losing his job again took up his pen and wrote the masterpiece whose immediate and lasting popularity is surpassed only by *Uncle Tom's Cabin*. Besides *A Wonder Book* and *Tanglewood Tales*, in which he retold Greek myths, he published *The House of the Seven Gables* (1851) and *The Blithedale Romance* (1852). Appointed by President Franklin Pierce as Consul to Liverpool, he remained there four years after which he spent some time in Rome where he gathered material for the second greatest of his romances, *The Marble Faun*. In 1860 he came home and settled at Concord. He died May 18, 1864, and was buried at (Concord) Sleepy Hollow.

Rappaccini's Daughter, perhaps the finest of his short stories, was written in 1844 and published in *Mosses from an Old Manse* (1846).

RAPPACCINI'S DAUGHTER
(From the Writings of Aubépine)

WE do not remember to have seen any translated specimens of the productions of M. de L'Aubépine—a fact the less to be wondered at, as his very name is unknown to many of his own countrymen as well as to the student of foreign literature. As a writer, he seems to occupy an unfortunate position between the Transcendentalists (who, under one name or another, have their share in all the current literature of the world) and the great body of pen-and-ink men who address the intellect and sympathies of the multitude. If not too refined, at all events too remote, too shadowy, and unsubstantial in his modes of development to suit the taste of the latter class, and yet too popular to satisfy the spiritual or metaphysical requisitions of the former, he must necessarily find himself without an audience, except here and there an individual or possibly an isolated clique. His writings, to do them justice, are not altogether destitute of fancy and originality; they might have won him greater reputation but for an inveterate love of allegory, which is apt to invest his plots and characters with the aspect of scenery and people in the clouds, and to steal away the human warmth out of his conceptions. His fictions are sometimes historical, sometimes of the present day, and sometimes, so far as can be discovered, have little or no reference either to time or space. In any case, he generally contents himself with a very slight embroidery of outward manners—the faintest possible counterfeit of real life—and endeavours to create an interest by some less obvious peculiarity of the subject. Occasionally a breath of Nature, a raindrop of pathos and tenderness, or a gleam of humour, will find its way into the midst of his fantastic imagery, and make us feel as if, after all, we were yet within the limits of our native earth. We will only add to this very cursory notice that M. de L'Aubépine's productions, if the reader chance to take them in precisely the proper point of view, may amuse a leisure hour as well as those of a brighter man; if otherwise, they can hardly fail to look excessively like nonsense.

Our author is voluminous; he continues to write and publish with as much praiseworthy and indefatigable prolixity as if his efforts were crowned with the brilliant success that so justly attends those of Eugène Sue. His first appearance was by a collection of stories in a long series of volumes entitled "Contes deux fois racontés." The titles of some of the more recent works (we quote from memory) are as follows: "Le Voyage Céleste à Chemin de Fer," 3 tom., 1838; "Le nouveau Père Adam et la nouvelle Mère Eve," 2 tom., 1839; "Roderic; ou le Serpent à l'estomac," 2 tom., 1840; "Le Culte du Feu," a folio volume of ponderous research into the religion and ritual of the old Persian Ghebers, published in 1841; "La Soirée du Château en Espagne," 1 tom., 8vo., 1842; and "L'Artiste du Beau; ou le Papillon Mécanique," 5 tom., 4to, 1843. Our somewhat wearisome perusal of this startling catalogue of volumes has left behind it a certain personal affection and sympathy, though by no means admiration, for M. de L'Aubépine; and we would fain do the little in our power towards introducing him favourably to the American public. The ensuing tale is a translation of his "Beatrice; ou la Belle Empoisonneuse," recently published in "La Revue Anti-Aristocratique." This journal, edited by the Comte de Bearhaven, has for some years past led the defence of liberal principles and popular rights with a faithfulness and ability worthy of all praise.

A young man, named Giovanni Guasconti, came, very long ago, from the more southern region of Italy, to pursue his studies at the University of Padua. Giovanni, who had but a scanty supply of gold ducats in his pocket, took lodgings in a high and gloomy chamber of an old edifice which looked not unworthy to have been the palace of a Paduan noble, and which, in fact, exhibited over its entrance the armorial bearings of a family long since extinct. The young stranger, who was not unstudied in the great poem of his country, recollected that one of the ancestors of this family, and perhaps an occupant of this very mansion, had been pictured by Dante as a partaker of the immortal agonies of his Inferno. These reminiscences and associations, together with the tendency to heartbreak natural to a young man for the first time out of his native sphere, caused Giovanni to sigh heavily as he looked around the desolate and ill-furnished apartment.

"Holy Virgin, signor!" cried old Dame Lisabetta, who, won by the youth's remarkable beauty of person, was kindly endeavouring to give the chamber a habitable air, "what a sign was that to come out of a young man's heart! Do you find this old mansion gloomy? For the love of Heaven, then, put your head out of the window, and you will see as bright sunshine as you have left in Naples."

Guasconti mechanically did as the old woman advised, but could not quite agree with her that the Paduan sunshine was as cheerful as that of southern Italy. Such as it was, however, it fell upon a garden beneath the window and expended its fostering influences on a variety of plants, which seemed to have been cultivated with exceeding care.

"Does this garden belong to the house?" asked Giovanni.

"Heaven forbid, signor, unless it were fruitful of better pot herbs than any that grow there now," answered old Lisabetta. "No; that garden is cultivated by the own hands of Signor Giacomo Rappaccini, the famous doctor, who, I warrant him, has been heard of as far as Naples. It is said that he distils these plants into medicines that are as potent as a charm. Oftentimes you may see the signor doctor at work, and perchance the signora, his daughter, too, gathering the strange flowers that grow in the garden."

The old woman had now done what she could for the aspect of the chamber; and, commending the young man to the protection of the saints, took her departure.

Giovanni still found no better occupation than to look down into the garden beneath his window. From its appearance, he judged it to be one of those botanic gardens which were of earlier date in Padua than elsewhere in Italy or in the world. Or, not improbably, it might once have been the pleasure-place of an opulent family; for there was the ruin of a marble fountain in the centre, sculptured with rare art, but so woefully shattered that it was impossible to trace the original design from the chaos of remaining fragments. The water, however, continued to gush and sparkle into the sunbeams as cheerfully as ever. A little gurgling sound ascended to the young man's window, and made him feel as if the fountain were an immortal spirit that sung its song unceasingly and without heeding the vicissitudes around it, while one century imbodied it in marble and another scattered the perishable garniture on the soil. All about the pool into which the water subsided grew various plants, that seemed to require a plentiful supply of moisture for the nourishment of gigantic leaves, and, in some instances, flowers gorgeously magnificent. There was one shrub in particular, set in a marble vase in the midst of the pool, that bore a profusion of purple blossoms, each of which had the lustre and richness of a gem; and the whole together made a show so resplendent that it seemed enough to illuminate the garden, even had there been no sunshine. Every portion of the soil was peopled with plants and herbs, which, if less beautiful, still bore tokens of assiduous care, as if all had their individual virtues, known to the scientific mind that fostered them. Some were placed in urns, rich with old carving, and others in common garden pots; some crept serpent-like along the ground or climbed on high, using whatever means of ascent was offered them. One plant had wreathed itself round a statue of Vertumnus, which was thus quite veiled and shrouded in a drapery of hanging foliage, so happily arranged that it might have served a sculptor for a study.

While Giovanni stood at the window he heard a rustling behind a screen of leaves, and became aware that a person was at work in the garden. His figure soon emerged into view, and showed itself to be that of no common labourer, but a tall, emaciated, sallow, and sickly-looking man, dressed in a scholar's garb of black. He was beyond the middle term of life, with grey hair, a thin, grey beard, and a face singularly marked with intellect and cultivation, but which could never, even in his more youthful days, have expressed much warmth of heart.

Nothing could exceed the intentness with which this scientific gardener examined every shrub which grew in his path: it seemed as if he was looking into their inmost nature, making observations in regard to their creative essence, and discovering why one leaf grew in this shape and another in that, and wherefore such and such flowers differed among themselves in hue and perfume. Nevertheless, in spite of this deep intelligence on his part, there was no approach to intimacy between himself and these vegetable existences. On the contrary, he avoided their actual touch or the direct inhaling of their odours with a caution that impressed Giovanni most disagreeably; for the man's demeanour was that of one walking among malignant influences, such as savage beasts, or deadly snakes, or evil spirits, which, should he allow them one moment of license, would wreak upon him some terrible fatality. It was strangely frightful to the young man's imagination to see this air of insecurity in a person cultivating a garden, that most simple and innocent of human toils, and which had been alike the joy and labour of the unfallen parents of the race. Was this garden, then, the Eden of the present world? And this man, with such a perception of harm in what his own hands caused to grow—was he the Adam?

The distrustful gardener, while plucking away the dead leaves or pruning the too luxuriant growth of the shrubs, defended his hands with a pair of thick gloves. Nor were these his only armour. When, in his walk through the garden, he came to the magnificent plant that hung its purple gems beside the marble fountain, he placed a kind of mask over his mouth and nostrils, as if all this beauty did but conceal a deadlier malice; but, finding his task still too dangerous, he drew back, removed the mask, and called loudly, but in the infirm voice of a person affected with inward disease—

"Beatrice! Beatrice!"

"Here am I, my father. What would you?" cried a rich and youthful voice from the window of the opposite house—a voice as rich as a tropical sunset, and which made Giovanni, though he knew not why, think of deep hues of purple or crimson and of perfumes heavily delectable. "Are you in the garden?"

"Yes, Beatrice," answered the gardener, "and I need your help."

Soon there emerged from under a sculptured portal the figure of a young girl, arrayed with as much richness of taste as the most splendid of the flowers, beautiful as the day, and with a bloom so deep and vivid that one shade more would have been too much. She looked redundant with life, health, and energy; all of which attributes were bound down and compressed, as it were, and girdled tensely, in their luxuriance, by her virgin zone. Yet Giovanni's fancy must have grown morbid while he looked down into the garden; for the impression which the fair stranger made upon him was as if here were another flower, the human sister of those vegetable ones, as beautiful as they, more beautiful than the richest of them, but still to be touched only with a glove, nor to be approached without a mask. As Beatrice came down the garden path, it was observable that she handled and inhaled the odour of several of the plants which her father had most sedulously avoided.

"Here, Beatrice," said the latter, "see how many needful offices require to be done to our chief treasure. Yet, shattered as I am, my life might pay the penalty of approaching it so closely as circumstances demand. Henceforth, I fear, this plant must be consigned to your sole charge."

"And gladly will I undertake it," cried again the rich tones of the young lady, as she bent towards the magnificent plant and opened her arms as if to embrace it. "Yes, my sister, my splendour, it shall be Beatrice's task to nurse and serve thee; and thou shalt reward her with thy kisses and perfumed breath, which to her is as the breath of life."

Then, with all the tenderness in her manner that was so strikingly expressed in her words, she busied herself with such attentions as the plant seemed to require; and Giovanni, at his lofty window, rubbed his eyes and always doubted whether it were a girl tending her favourite flower, or one sister performing the duties of affection to another. The scene soon terminated. Whether Dr. Rappaccini had finished his labours in the garden, or that his watchful eye had caught the stranger's face, he now took his daughter's arm and retired. Night was already closing in; oppressive exhalations seemed to proceed from the plants and steal upward past the open window; and Giovanni, closing the lattice, went to his couch and dreamed of a rich flower and beautiful girl. Flower and maiden were different, and yet the same, and fraught with some strange peril in either shape.

But there is an influence in the light of morning that tends to rectify whatever errors of fancy, or even of judgment, we may have incurred during the sun's decline, or among the shadows of the night, or in the less wholesome glow of moonshine. Giovanni's first movement, on starting from sleep, was to throw open the window and gaze down into the garden which his dreams had made so fertile of mysteries. He was surprised and a little ashamed to find how real and matter-of-fact an affair it proved to be, in the first rays of the sun which gilded the dew-drops that hung upon leaf and blossom, and, while giving a brighter beauty to each rare flower, brought everything within the limits of ordinary experience. The young man rejoiced that, in the heart of the barren city, he had the privilege of overlooking this spot of lovely and luxuriant vegetation. It would serve, he said to himself, as a symbolic language to keep him in communion with Nature. Neither the sickly and thoughtworn Dr. Giacomo Rappaccini, it is true, nor his brilliant daughter, were now visible; so that Giovanni could not determine how much of the singularity which he attributed to both was due to their own qualities and now much to his wonder-working fancy; but he was inclined to take a most rational view of the whole matter.

In the course of the day he paid his respects to Signor Pietro Baglioni, professor of medicine in the university, a physician of eminent repute, to whom Giovanni had brought a letter of introduction. The professor was an elderly personage, apparently of genial nature, and habits that might almost be called jovial. He kept the young man to dinner, and made himself very agreeable by the freedom and liveliness of his conversation, especially when warmed by a flask or two of Tuscan wine. Giovanni, conceiving that men of science, inhabitants of the same city, must needs be on familiar terms with one another, took an opportunity to mention the name of Dr. Rappaccini. But the professor did not respond with so much cordiality as he had anticipated.

"Ill would it become a teacher of the divine art of medicine," said

Professor Pietro Baglioni, in answer to a question of Giovanni, "to with-
hold due and well-considered praise of a physician so eminently skilled as
Rappaccini; but, on the other hand, I should answer it but scantily to my
conscience were I to permit a worthy youth like yourself, Signor Giovanni,
the son of an ancient friend, to imbibe erroneous ideas respecting a man
who might hereafter chance to hold your life and death in his hands. The
truth is, our worshipful Dr. Rappaccini has as much science as any member of the faculty—with perhaps one single exception—in Padua, or all
Italy; but there are certain grave objections to his professional character."

"And what are they?" asked the young man.

"Has my friend Giovanni any disease of body or heart, that he is so
inquisitive about physicians?" said the professor, with a smile. "But as for
Rappaccini, it is said of him—and I, who know the man well, can answer
for its truth—that he cares infinitely more for science than for mankind.
His patients are interesting to him only as subjects for some new experiment. He would sacrifice human life, his own among the rest, or whatever else was dearest to him, for the sake of adding so much as a grain of
mustard seed to the great heap of his accumulated knowledge."

"Methinks he is an awful man indeed," remarked Guasconti, mentally recalling the cold and purely intellectual aspect of Rappaccini.
"And yet, worshipful professor, is it not a noble spirit? Are there many
men capable of so spiritual a love of science?"

"God forbid," answered the professor, somewhat testily; "at least,
unless they take sounder views of the healing art than those adopted by
Rappaccini. It is his theory that all medicinal virtues are comprised
within those substances which we term vegetable poisons. These he cul-
tivates with his own hands, and is said even to have produced new varieties
of poison, more horribly deleterious than Nature, without the assistance
of this learned person, would ever have plagued the world withal. That
the signor doctor does less mischief than might be expected with such
dangerous substances is undeniable. Now and then, it must be owned, he
has effected, or seemed to effect, a marvellous cure; but, to tell you my
private mind, Signor Giovanni, he should receive little credit for such
instances of success—they being probably the work of chance—but should
be held strictly accountable for his failures, which may justly be considered
his own work."

The youth might have taken Baglioni's opinions with many grains of
allowance had he known that there was a professional warfare of long
continuance between him and Dr. Rappaccini, in which the latter was
generally thought to have gained the advantage. If the reader be inclined
to judge for himself, we refer him to certain black-letter tracts on both
sides, preserved in the medical department of the University of Padua.

"I know not, most learned professor," returned Giovanni, after musing on what had been said of Rappaccini's exclusive zeal for science—"I

know not how dearly this physician may love his art; but surely there is one object more dear to him. He has a daughter."

"Aha!" cried the professor, with a laugh. "So now our friend Giovanni's secret is out. You have heard of this daughter, whom all the young men in Padua are wild about, though not half a dozen have ever had the good hap to see her face. I know little of the Signora Beatrice save that Rappaccini is said to have instructed her deeply in his science, and that, young and beautiful as fame reports her, she is already qualified to fill a professor's chair. Perchance her father destines her for mine! Other absurd rumours there be, not worth talking about or listening to. So now, Signor Giovanni, drink off your glass of lachryma."

Guasconti returned to his lodgings somewhat heated with the wine he had quaffed, and which caused his brain to swim with strange fantasies in reference to Dr. Rappaccini and the beautiful Beatrice. On his way, happening to pass by a florist's, he bought a fresh bouquet of flowers.

Ascending to his chamber, he seated himself near the window, but within the shadow thrown by the depth of the wall, so that he could look down into the garden with little risk of being discovered. All beneath his eye was a solitude. The strange plants were basking in the sunshine, and now and then nodding gently to one another, as if in acknowledgment of sympathy and kindred. In the midst, by the shattered fountain, grew the magnificent shrub, with its purple gems clustering all over it; they glowed in the air, and gleamed back again out of the depths of the pool, which thus seemed to overflow with coloured radiance from the rich reflection that was steeped in it. At first, as we have said, the garden was a solitude. Soon, however—as Giovanni had half hoped, half feared, would be the case—a figure appeared beneath the antique sculptured portal, and came down between the rows of plants, inhaling their various perfumes as if she were one of those beings of old classic fable that lived upon sweet odours. On again beholding Beatrice, the young man was even startled to perceive how much her beauty exceeded his recollection of it; so brilliant, so vivid, was its character, that she glowed amid the sunlight, and, as Giovanni whispered to himself, positively illuminated the more shadowy intervals of the garden path. Her face being now more revealed than on the former occasion, he was struck by its expression of simplicity and sweetness—qualities that had not entered into his idea of her character, and which made him ask anew what manner of mortal she might be. Nor did he fail again to observe, or imagine, an analogy between the beautiful girl and the gorgeous shrub that hung its gemlike flowers over the fountain—a resemblance which Beatrice seemed to have indulged a fantastic humour in heightening, both by the arrangement of her dress and the selection of its hues.

Approaching the shrub, she threw open her arms, as with a passionate ardour, and drew its branches into an intimate embrace—so intimate that her features were hidden in its leafy bosom and her glistening ringlets all intermingled with the flowers.

"Give me thy breath, my sister," exclaimed Beatrice; "for I am faint with common air. And give me this flower of time, which I separate with gentlest fingers from the stem and place it close beside my heart."

With these words the beautiful daughter of Rappaccini plucked one of the richest blossoms of the shrub, and was about to fasten it in her bosom. But now, unless Giovanni's draughts of wine had bewildered his senses, a singular incident occurred. A small orange-coloured reptile, of the lizard or chameleon species, chanced to be creeping along the path, just at the feet of Beatrice. It appeared to Giovanni—but, at the distance from which he gazed, he could scarcely have seen anything so minute— it appeared to him, however, that a drop or two of moisture from the broken stem of the flower descended upon the lizard's head. For an instant the reptile contorted itself violently, and then lay motionless in the sunshine. Beatrice observed this remarkable phenomenon, and crossed herself, sadly, but without surprise; nor did she therefore hestitate to arrange the fatal flower in her bosom. There it blushed, and almost glimmered with the dazzling effect of a precious stone, adding to her dress and aspect the one appropriate charm which nothing else in the world could have supplied. But Giovanni, out of the shadow of his window, bent forward and shrank back, and murmured and trembled.

"Am I awake? Have I my senses?" said he to himself. "What is this being? Beautiful shall I call her, or inexpressibly terrible?"

Beatrice now strayed carelessly through the garden, approaching closer beneath Giovanni's window, so that he was compelled to thrust his head quite out of its concealment in order to gratify the intense and painful curiosity which she excited. At this moment there came a beautiful insect over the garden wall; it had, perhaps, wandered through the city, and found no flowers or verdure among those antique haunts of men until the heavy perfumes of Dr. Rappaccini's shrubs had lured it from afar. Without alighting on the flowers, this winged brightness seemed to be attracted by Beatrice, and lingered in the air and fluttered about her head. Now, here it could not be but that Giovanni Guasconti's eyes deceived him. Be that as it might, he fancied that, while Beatrice was gazing at the insect with childish delight, it grew faint and fell at her feet; its bright wings shivered; it was dead—from no cause that he could discern, unless it were the atmosphere of her breath. Again Beatrice crossed herself and sighed heavily as she bent over the dead insect.

An impulsive movement of Giovanni drew her eyes to the window. There she beheld the beautiful head of the young man—rather a Grecian than an Italian head, with fair, regular features, and a glistening of gold among his ringlets—gazing down upon her like a being that hovered in mid air. Scarcely knowing what he did, Giovanni threw down the bouquet which he had hitherto held in his hand.

"Signora," said he, "there are pure and healthful flowers. Wear them for the sake of Giovanni Guasconti."

"Thanks, signor," replied Beatrice, with her rich voice, that came forth as it were like a gush of music, and with a mirthful expression half childish and half womanlike. "I accept your gift, and would fain recompense it with this precious purple flower; but if I toss it into the air it will not reach you. So Signor Guasconti must even content himself with my thanks."

She lifted the bouquet from the ground, and then, as if inwardly ashamed at having stepped aside from her maidenly reserve to respond to a stranger's greeting, passed swiftly homeward through the garden. But few as the moments were, it seemed to Giovanni, when she was on the point of vanishing beneath the sculptured portal, that his beautiful bouquet was already beginning to wither in her grasp. It was an idle thought; there could be no possibility of distinguishing a faded flower from a fresh one at so great a distance.

For many days after this incident the young man avoided the window that looked into Dr. Rappaccini's garden, as if something ugly and monstrous would have blasted his eyesight had he been betrayed into a glance. He felt conscious of having put himself, to a certain extent, within the influence of an unintelligible power by the communication which he had opened with Beatrice. The wisest course would have been, if his heart were in any real danger, to quit his lodgings and Padua itself at once; the next wiser, to have accustomed himself, as far as possible, to the familiar and daylight view of Beatrice—thus bringing her rigidly and systematically within the limits of ordinary experience. Least of all, while avoiding her sight, ought Giovanni to have remained so near this extraordinary being that the proximity and possibility even of intercourse should give a kind of substance and realty to the wild vagaries which his imagination ran riot continually in producing. Guasconti had not a deep heart —or, at all events, its depths were not sounded now; but he had a quick fancy and an ardent southern temperament, which rose every instant to a higher fever pitch. Whether or no Beatrice possessed those terrible attributes, that fatal breath, the affinity with those so beautiful and deadly flowers which were indicated by what Giovanni had witnessed, she had at least instilled a fierce and subtle poison into his system. It was not love, although her rich beauty was a madness to him; nor horror, even while he fancied her spirit to be imbued with the same baleful essence that seemed to pervade her physical frame; but a wild offspring of both love and horror that had each parent in it, and burned like one and shivered like the other. Giovanni knew not what to dread; still less did he know what to hope; yet hope and dread kept a continual warfare in his breast, alternately vanquishing one another and starting up afresh to renew the contest. Blessed are all simple emotions, be they dark or bright! It is the lurid intermixture of the two that produces the illuminating blaze of the infernal regions.

Sometimes he endeavored to assuage the fever of his spirit by a rapid walk through the streets of Padua or beyond its gates: his footsteps kept time with the throbbings of his brain, so that the walk was apt to accelerate itself to a race. One day he found himself arrested; his arm was seized by a portly personage, who had turned back on recognising the young man and expended much breath in overtaking him.

"Signor Giovanni! Stay, my young friend!" cried he. "Have you forgotten me? That might well be the case if I were as much altered as yourself."

It was Baglioni, whom Giovanni had avoided ever since their first meeting, from a doubt that the professor's sagacity would look too deeply into his secrets. Endeavouring to recover himself, he stared forth wildly from his inner world into the outer one and spoke like a man in a dream.

"Yes; I am Giovanni Guasconti. You are Professor Pietro Baglioni. Now let me pass!"

"Not yet, not yet, Signor Giovanni Guasconti," said the professor, smiling, but at the same time scrutinising the youth with an earnest glance. "What! did I grow up side by side with your father? and shall his son pass me like a stranger in these old streets of Padua? Stand still, Signor Giovanni; for we must have a word or two before we part."

"Speedily, then, most worshipful professor, speedily," said Giovanni with feverish impatience. "Does not your worship see that I am in haste?"

Now, while he was speaking there came a man in black along the street, stooping and moving feebly like a person in inferior health. His face was all overspread with a most sickly and sallow hue, but yet so pervaded with an expression of piercing and active intellect that an observer might easily have overlooked the merely physical attributes and have seen only this wonderful energy. As he passed, this person exchanged a cold and distant salutation with Baglioni, but fixed his eyes upon Giovanni with an intentness that seemed to bring out whatever was within him worthy of notice. Nevertheless, there was a peculiar quietness in the look, as if taking merely a speculative, not a human, interest in the young man.

"It is Dr. Rappaccini!" whispered the professor when the stranger had passed. "Has he ever seen your face before?"

"Not that I know," answered Giovanni, starting at the name.

"He *has* seen you! he must have seen you!" said Baglioni, hastily. "For some purpose or other, this man of science is making a study of you. I know that look of his! It is the same that coldly illuminate his face as he bends over a bird, a mouse, or a butterfly, which, in pursuance of some experiment, he has killed by the perfume of a flower; a look as deep as Nature itself, but without Nature's warmth of love. Signor Giovanni, I will stake my life upon it, you are the subject of one of Rappaccini's experiments!"

"Will you make a fool of me?" cried Giovanni, passionately. "*That*, signor professor, were an untoward experiment."

"Patience! patience!" replied the imperturbable professor. "I tell thee, my poor Giovanni, that Rappaccini has a scientific interest in thee. Thou hast fallen into fearful hands! And the Signora Beatrice—what part does she act in this mystery?"

But Guasconti, finding Baglioni's pertinacity intolerable, here broke away, and was gone before the professor could again seize his arm. He looked after the young man intently and shook his head.

"This must not be," said Baglioni to himself. "The youth is the son of my old friend, and shall not come to any harm from which the arcana of medical science can preserve him. Besides, it is too insufferable an impertinence in Rappaccini, thus to snatch the lad out of my own hands, as I may say, and make use of him for his infernal experiments. This daughter of his! It shall be looked to. Perchance, most learned Rappaccini, I may foil you where you little dream of it!"

Meanwhile Giovanni had pursued a circuitous route, and at length found himself at the door of his lodgings. As he crossed the threshold he was met by old Lisabetta, who smirked and smiled, and was evidently desirous to attract his attention; vainly, however, as the ebullition of his feelings had momentarily subsided into a cold and dull vacuity. He turned his eyes full upon the withered face that was puckering itself into a smile, but seemed to behold it not. The old dame, therefore, laid her grasp upon his cloak.

"Signor! signor!" whispered she, still with a smile over the whole breadth of her visage, so that it looked not unlike a grotesque carving in wood, darkened by centuries. "Listen, signor! There is a private entrance into the garden!"

"What do you say!" exclaimed Giovanni, turning quickly about, as if an inanimate thing should start into feverish life. "A private entrance into Dr. Rappaccini's garden?"

"Hush! hush! not so loud!" whispered Lisabetta, putting her hand over his mouth. "Yes; into the worshipful doctor's garden, where you may see all his fine shrubbery. Many a young man in Padua would give gold to be admitted among those flowers."

Giovanni put a piece of gold into her hand.

"Show me the way," said he.

A surmise, probably excited by his conversation with Baglioni, crossed his mind, that this interposition of old Lisabetta might perchance be connected with the intrigue, whatever were its nature, in which the professor seemed to suppose that Dr. Rappaccini was involving him. But such a suspicion, though it disturbed Giovanni, was inadequate to restrain him. The instant that he was aware of the possibility of approaching Beatrice, it seemed an absolute necessity of his existence to do so. It mattered not whether she were angel or demon; he was irrevocably within her sphere, and must obey the law that whirled him onward, in ever-lessening circles, towards a result which he did not attempt to foreshadow; and yet, strange to say, there came across him a sudden doubt whether this intense interest on his part were not delusory; whether it were really of so deep and positive a nature as to justify him in now thrusting himself into an incalculable position; whether it were not merely the fantasy of a young man's brain, only slightly or not at all connected with his heart.

He paused, hesitated, turned half about, but again went on. His withered guide led him along several obscure passages, and finally undid a door, through which, as it was opened, there came the sight and sound of rustling leaves, with the broken sunshine glimmering among them. Giovanni stepped forth, and, forcing himself through the entanglement of a shrub that wreathed its tendrils over the hidden entrance, stood beneath his own window in the open area of Dr. Rappaccini's garden.

How often is it the case that, when impossibilities have come to pass and dreams have condensed their misty substance into tangible realities, we find ourselves calm, and even coldly self-possessed, amid circumstances which it would have been a delirium of joy or agony to anticipate! Fate delights to thwart us thus. Passion will choose his own time to rush upon the scene, and lingers sluggishly behind when an appropriate adjustment of events would seem to summon his appearance. So was it now with Giovanni. Day after day his pulses had throbbed with feverish blood at the improbable idea of an interview with Beatrice, and of standing with her, face to face, in this very garden, basking in the Oriental sunshine of her beauty, and snatching from her full gaze the mystery which he deemed the riddle of his own existence. But now there was a singular and untimely equanimity within his breast. He threw a glance around the garden to discover if Beatrice or her father were present, and, perceiving that he was alone, began a critical observation of the plants.

The aspect of one and all of them dissatisfied him; their gorgeousness seemed fierce, passionate, and even unnatural. There was hardly an individual shrub which a wanderer, straying by himself through a forest, would not have been startled to find growing wild, as if an unearthly face had glared at him out of the thicket. Several also would have shocked a delicate instinct by an appearance of artificialness indicating that there had been such commixture, and, as it were, adultery, of various vegetable species, that the production was no longer of God's making, but the monstrous offspring of man's depraved fancy, glowing with only an evil mockery of beauty. They were probably the result of experiment, which in one or two cases had succeeded in mingling plants individually lovely into a compound possessing the questionable and ominous character that distinguished the whole growth of the garden. In fine, Giovanni recognised but two or three plants in the collection, and those of a kind that he well knew to be poisonous. While busy with these contemplations he heard the rustling of a silken garment, and, turning, beheld Beatrice emerging from beneath the sculptured portal.

Giovanni had not considered with himself what should be his deportment; whether he should apologise for his intrusion into the garden, or assume that he was there with the privity at least, if not by the desire, of Dr. Rappaccini or his daughter; but Beatrice's manner placed him at his ease, though leaving him still in doubt by what agency he had gained admittance. She came lightly along the path and met him near the broken fountain. There was surprise in her face, but brightened by a simple and kind expression of pleasure.

"You are a connoisseur in flowers, signor," said Beatrice, with a smile, alluding to the bouquet which he had flung her from the window. "It is no marvel, therefore, if the sight of my father's rare collection has tempted you to take a nearer view. If he were here, he could tell you many strange and interesting facts as to the nature and habits of these shrubs; for he has spent a lifetime in such studies, and this garden is his world."

"And yourself, lady," observed Giovanni, "if fame says true—you likewise are deeply skilled in the virtues indicated by these rich blossoms and these spicy perfumes. Would you deign to be my instructress, I should prove an apter scholar than if taught by Signor Rappaccini himself."

"Are there such idle rumours?" asked Beatrice, with the music of a pleasant laugh. "Do people say that I am skilled in my father's science of plants? What a jest is there! No; though I have grown up among these flowers, I know no more of them than their hues and perfumes; and sometimes methinks I would fain rid myself of even that small knowledge. There are many flowers here, and those not the least brilliant, that shock and offend me when they meet my eye. But pray, signor, do not believe these stories about my science. Believe nothing of me save what you see with your own eyes."

"And must I believe all that I have seen with my own eyes!" asked Giovanni, pointedly, while the recollection of former scenes made him shrink. "No, signora; you demand too little of me. Bid me believe nothing save what comes from your own lips."

It would appear that Beatrice understood him. There came a deep flush to her cheek; but she looked full into Giovanni's eyes, and responded to his gaze of uneasy suspicion with a queenlike haughtiness.

"I do so bid you, signor," she replied. "Forget whatever you may have fancied in regard to me. If true to the outward senses, still it may be false in its essence; but the words of Beatrice Rappaccini's lips are true from the depths of the heart outward. Those you may believe."

A fervour glowed in her whole aspect and beamed upon Giovanni's consciousness like the light of truth itself; but while she spoke there was a fragrance in the atmosphere around her, rich and delightful, though evanescent, yet which the young man, from an indefinable reluctance, scarcely dared to draw into his lungs. It might be the odour of the flowers. Could it be Beatrice's breath which thus embalmed her words with a strange richness, as if by steeping them in her heart? A faintness passed like a shadow over Giovanni and flitted away; he seemed to gaze through the beautiful girl's eyes into her transparent soul, and felt no more doubt or fear.

The tinge of passion that had coloured Beatrice's manner vanished; she became gay, and appeared to derive a pure delight from her communion with the youth not unlike what the maiden of a lonely island might have felt conversing with a voyager from the civilised world. Evidently her experience of life had been confined within the limits of that garden. She talked now about matters as simple as the daylight or summer clouds, and now asked questions in reference to the city, or Giovanni's distant home, his friends, his mother, and his sisters—questions indicating such seclusion, and such lack of familiarity with modes and forms, that Giovanni responded as if to an infant. Her spirit gushed out before him like a fresh rill that was just catching its first glimpse of the sunlight and wondering at the reflections of earth and sky which were flung into its bosom. There came thoughts, too, from a deep source, and fantasies of a gemlike brilliancy, as if diamonds and rubies sparkled upward among the bubbles of the fountain. Ever and anon there gleamed across the young man's mind a sense of wonder that he should be walking side by side with the being who had so wrought upon his imagination, whom he had idealised in such hues of terror, in whom he had positively witnessed such manifestations of dreadful attributes—that he should be conversing with Beatrice like a brother, and should find her so human and so maidenlike. But such reflections were only momentary; the effect of her character was too real not to make itself familiar at once.

In this free intercourse they had strayed through the garden, and now, after many turns among its avenues, were come to the shattered fountain, beside which grew the magnificent shrub, with its treasury of glowing blossoms. A fragrance was diffused from it which Giovanni recognised as identical with that which he had attributed to Beatrice's breath, but incomparably more powerful. As her eyes fell upon it, Giovanni beheld her press her hand to her bosom as if her heart were throbbing suddenly and painfully.

"For the first time in my life," murmured she, addressing the shrub, "I had forgotten thee."

"I remember, signora," said Giovanni, "that you once promised to reward me with one of these living gems for the bouquet which I had the happy boldness to fling to your feet. Permit me now to pluck it as a memorial of this interview."

He made a step towards the shrub with extended hand; but Beatrice darted forward, uttering a shriek that went through his heart like a dagger. She caught his hand and drew it back with the whole force of her slender figure. Giovanni felt her touch thrilling through his fibres.

"Touch it not!" exclaimed she, in a voice of agony. "Not for thy life! It is fatal!"

Then, hiding her face, she fled from him and vanished beneath the sculptured portal. As Giovanni followed her with his eyes, he beheld the emaciated figure and pale intelligence of Dr. Rappaccini, who had been watching the scene, he knew not how long, within the shadow of the entrance.

No sooner was Guasconti alone in his chamber than the image of Beatrice came back to his passionate musings, invested with all the witchery that had been gathering around it ever since his first glimpse of her, and now likewise imbued with a tender warmth of girlish womanhood. She was human; her nature was endowed with all gentle and feminine qualities; she was worthiest to be worshipped; she was capable, surely on her part, of the height and heroism of love. Those tokens which he had hitherto considered as proofs of a frightful peculiarity in her physical and moral system were now either forgotten, or, by the subtle sophistry of passion, transmitted into a golden crown of enchantment, rendering Beatrice the more admirable by so much as she was the more unique. Whatever had looked ugly was now beautiful; or, if incapable of such a change, it stole away and hid itself among those shapeless half ideas which throng the dim region beyond the daylight of our perfect consciousness. Thus did he spend the night, nor fell asleep until the dawn had begun to awake the slumbering flowers in Dr. Rappaccini's garden, whither Giovanni's dreams doubtless led him. Up rose the sun in his due season, and, flinging his beams upon the young man's eyelids, awoke him to a sense of pain. When thoroughly aroused, he became sensible of a burning and tingling agony in his hand—in his right hand—the very hand which Beatrice had grasped in her own when he was on the point of plucking one of the gemlike flowers. On the back of that hand there was now a purple print like that of four small fingers, and the likeness of a slender thumb upon his wrist.

Oh, how stubbornly does love—or even that cunning semblance of love which flourishes in the imagination, but strikes no depth of root into the heart—how stubbornly does it hold its faith until the moment comes when it is doomed to vanish into thin mist! Giovanni wrapped a handkerchief about his hand and wondered what evil thing had stung him, and soon forgot his pain in a reverie of Beatrice.

After the first interview, a second was in the inevitable course of what we call fate. A third; a fourth and a meeting with Beatrice in the garden was no longer an incident in Giovanni's daily life, but the whole space in which he might be said to live; for the anticipation and memory of that ecstatic hour made up the remainder. Nor was it otherwise with the daughter of Rappaccini. She watched for the youth's appearance, and flew to his side with confidence as unreserved as if they had been playmates from early infancy—as if they were such playmates still. If, by any unwonted chance, he failed to come at the appointed moment, she stood beneath the window and sent up the rich sweetness of her tones to float around him in his chamber and echo and reverberate throughout his heart: "Giovanni! Giovanni! Why tarriest thou? Come down!" And down he hastened into that Eden of poisonous flowers.

But, with all this intimate familiarity, there was still a reserve in Beatrice's demeanour, so rigidly and invariably sustained that the idea of infringing it scarcely occurred to his imagination. By all appreciable signs, they loved; they had looked love with eyes that conveyed the holy secret from the depths of one soul into the depths of the other, as if it were too sacred to be whispered by the way; they had even spoken love in those gushes of passion when their spirits darted forth in articulated breath like tongues of long-hidden flame; and yet there had been no seal of lips, no clasp of hands, nor any slightest caress such as love claims and hallows. He had never touched one of the gleaming ringlets of her hair; her garment—so marked was the physical barrier between them —had never been waved against him by a breeze. On the few occasions when Giovanni had seemed tempted to overstep the limit, Beatrice grew so sad, so stern, and withal wore such a look of desolate separation, shuddering at itself, that not a spoken word was requisite to repel him. At such times he was startled at the horrible suspicions that rose, monster-like, out of the caverns of his heart and stared him in the face; his love grew thin and faint as the morning mist, his doubts alone had substance. But, when Beatrice's face brightened again after the momentary shadow, she was transformed at once from the mysterious, questionable being whom he had watched with so much awe and horror; she was now the beautiful and unsophisticated girl whom he felt that his spirit knew with a certainty beyond all other knowledge.

A considerable time had now passed since Giovanni's last meeting with Baglioni. One morning, however, he was disagreeably surprised by a visit from the professor, whom he had scarcely thought of for whole weeks, and would willingly have forgotten still longer. Given up as he had long been to a pervading excitement, he could tolerate no companions except upon condition of their perfect sympathy with his present state of feeling. Such sympathy was not to be expected from Professor Baglioni.

The visitor chatted carelessly for a few moment about the gossip of the city and the university, and then took up another topic.

"I have been reading an old classic author lately," said he, "and met with a story that strangely interested me. Possibly you may remember it. It is of an Indian prince, who sent a beautiful woman as a present to Alexander the Great. She was as lovely as the dawn and gorgeous as the sunset; but what especially distinguished her was a certain rich perfume in her breath—richer than a garden of Persian roses. Alexander, as was natural to a youthful conquerer, fell in love at first sight with this magnificent stranger; but a certain sage physician, happening to be present, discovered a terrible secret in regard to her."

"And what was that?" asked Giovanni, turning his eyes downward to avoid those of the professor.

"That this lovely woman," continued Baglioni, with emphasis, "had been nourished with poisons from her birth upward, until her whole nature was so imbued with them that she herself had become the deadliest poison in existence. Poison was her element of life. With that rich perfume of her breath she blasted the very air. Her love would have been poison—her embrace death. Is not this a marvellous tale?"

"A childish fable," answered Giovanni, nervously starting from his chair. "I marvel how your worship finds time to read such nonsense among your graver studies."

"By the by," said the professor, looking uneasily about him, "what singular fragrance is this in your apartment? Is it the perfume of your gloves? It is faint but delicious; and yet, after all, by no means agreeable. Were I to breathe it long, methinks it would make me ill. It is like the breath of a flower; but I see no flowers in the chamber."

"Nor are there any," replied Giovanni, who had turned pale as the professor spoke; "nor, I think, is there any fragrance except in your worship's imagination. Odours, being a sort of element combined of the sensual and the spiritual, are apt to deceive us in this manner. The recollection of a perfume, the bare idea of it, may easily be mistaken for a present reality."

"Ay; but my sober imagination does not often play such tricks," said Baglioni; "and, were I to fancy any kind of odour, it would be that of some vile apothecary drug, wherewith my fingers are likely enough to be imbued. Our worshipful friend Rappaccini, as I have heard, tinctures his medicaments with odours richer than those of Araby. Doubtless, likewise, the fair and learned Signora Beatrice would minister to her patients with draughts as sweet as a maiden's breath; but woe to him that sips them!"

Giovanni's face evinced many contending emotions. The tone in which the professor alluded to the pure and lovely daughter of Rappaccini was a torture to his soul; and yet the intimation of a view of her character, opposite to his own, gave instantaneous distinctness to a thousand dim suspicions, which now grinned at him like so many demons. But he strove hard to quell them and to respond to Baglioni with a true lover's perfect faith.

"Signor professor," said he, "you were my father's friend; perchance, too, it is your purpose to act a friendly part towards his son. I would fain feel nothing towards you save respect and deference; but I pray you to observe, signor, that there is one subject on which we must not speak. You know not the Signora Beatrice. You cannot, therefore, estimate the wrong—the blasphemy, I may even say—that is offered to her character by a light or injurious word."

"Giovanni! my poor Giovanni!" answered the professor, with a calm expression of pity, "I know this wretched girl far better than yourself. You shall hear the truth in respect to the poisoner Rappaccini and his poisonous daughter; yes, poisonous as she is beautiful. Listen; for, even should you do violence to my grey hairs, it shall not silence me. That old fable of the Indian woman has become a truth by the deep and deadly science of Rappaccini and in the person of the lovely Beatrice."

Giovanni groaned and hid his face.

"Her father," continued Baglioni, "was not restrained by natural affection from offering up his child in this horrible manner as the victim of his insane zeal for science; for, let us do him justice, he is as true a man of science as ever distilled his own heart in an alembic. What, then, will be your fate? Beyond a doubt you are selected as the material of some new experiment. Perhaps the result is to be death; perhaps a fate more awful still. Rappaccini, with what he calls the interest of science before his eyes, will hesitate at nothing."

"It is a dream," muttered Giovanni to himself; "surely it is a dream."

"But," resumed the professor, "be of good cheer, son of my friend. It is not yet too late for the rescue. Possibly we may even succeed in bringing back this miserable child within the limits of ordinary nature, from which her father's madness has estranged her. Behold this little silver vase! It was wrought by the hands of the renowned Benvenuto Cellini, and is well worthy to be a love gift to the fairest dame in Italy. But its contents are invaluable. One little sip of this antidote would have rendered the most virulent poisons of the Borgias innocuous. Doubt not that it will be as efficacious against those of Rappaccini. Bestow the vase, and the precious liquid within it, on your Beatrice, and hopefully await the result."

Baglioni laid a small, exquisitely wrought silver vial on the table and withdrew, leaving what he had said to produce its effect upon the young man's mind.

"We will thwart Rappaccini yet," thought he, chuckling to himself, as he descended the stairs; "but, let us confess the truth of him, he is a wonderful man—a wonderful man indeed; a vile empiric, however, in his practice, and therefore not to be tolerated by those .who respect the good old rules of the medical profession."

Throughout Giovanni's whole acquaintance with Beatrice, he had occasionally, as we have said, been haunted by dark surmises as to her character; yet so thoroughly had she made herself felt by him as a simple, natural, most affectionate, and guileless creature, that the image now held up by Professor Baglioni looked as strange and incredible as if it were not in accordance with his own original conception. True, there were ugly recollections connected with his first glimpses of the beautiful girl; he could not quite forget the bouquet that withered in her grasp, and the insect that perished amid the sunny air, by no ostensible agency save the fragrance of her breath. These incidents, however, dissolving in the pure light of her character, had no longer the efficacy of facts, but were acknowledged as mistaken fantasies, by whatever testimony of the senses they might appear to be substantiated. There is something truer and more real than what we can see with the eyes and touch with the finger. On such bitter evidence had Giovanni founded his confidence in Beatrice, though rather by the necessary force of her high attributes than by any deep and generous faith on his part. But now his spirit was incapable of sustaining itself at the height to which the early enthusiasm of passion had exacted it; he fell down, grovelling among earthly doubts, and defiled therewith the pure whiteness of Beatrice's image. Not that he gave her up; he did but distrust. He resolved to institute some decisive test that should satisfy him, once for all, whether there were those dreadful peculiarities in her physical nature which could not be supposed to exist without some corresponding monstrosity of soul. His eyes, gazing down afar, might have deceived him as to the lizard, the insect, and the flowers; but if he could witness, at the distance of a few paces, the sudden blight of one fresh and healthful flower in Beatrice's hand, there would be room for no further question. With this idea he hastened to the florist's and purchased a bouquet that was still gemmed with the morning dew-drops.

It was now the customary hour of his daily interview with Beatrice. Before descending into the garden, Giovanni failed not to look at his figure in the mirror—a vanity to be expected in a beautiful young man, yet, as displaying itself at that troubled and feverish moment, the

token of a certain shallowness of feeling and insincerity of character.
He did gaze, however, and said to himself that his features had never
before possessed so rich a grace, nor his eyes such vivacity, nor his cheeks
so warm a hue of super-abundant life.

"At least," thought he, "her poison has not yet insinuated itself into
my system. I am no flower to perish in her grasp."

With that thought he turned his eyes on the bouquet, which he had
never once laid aside from his hand. A thrill of indefinable horror shot
through his frame on perceiving that those dewy flowers were already
beginning to droop; they wore the aspect of things that had been fresh
and lovely yesterday. Giovanni grew white as marble, and stood motionless before the mirror, staring at his own reflection there as at the
likeness of something frightful. He remembered Baglioni's remark about
the fragrance that seemed to pervade the chamber. It must have been
the poison in his breath! Then he shuddered—shuddered at himself.
Recovering from his stupor, he began to watch with curious eye a spider
that was busily at work hanging its web from the antique cornice of
the apartment, crossing and recrossing the artful system of interwoven
lines—as vigorous and active a spider as ever dangled from an old ceiling. Giovanni bent towards the insect, and emitted a deep, long breath.
The spider suddenly ceased its toil; the web vibrated with a tremor
originating in the body of the small artisan. Again Giovanni sent forth
a breath, deeper, longer, and imbued with a venomous feeling out of
his heart: he knew not whether he were wicked, or only desperate.
The spider made a convulsive gripe with his limbs and hung dead across
the window.

"Accursed! accursed!" muttered Giovanni, addressing himself.
"Hast thou grown so poisonous that this deadly insect perished by thy
breath?"

At that moment a rich, sweet voice came floating up from the garden.
"Giovanni! Giovanni! It is past the hour? Why tarriest thou?
Come down!"

"Yes," muttered Giovanni again. "She is the only being whom my
breath may not slay! Would that it might!"

He rushed down, and in an instant was standing before the bright
and loving eyes of Beatrice. A moment ago his wrath and despair had
been so fierce that he could have desired nothing so much as to wither
her by a glance; but with her actual presence there came influences which
had too real an existence to be at once shaken off; recollections of the
delicate and benign power of her feminine nature, which had so often
enveloped him in a religious calm; recollections of many a holy and
passionate outgush of her heart, when the pure fountain had been un-
sealed from its depths and made visible in its transparency to his mental
eye; recollections which, had Giovanni known how to estimate them,

would have assured him that all this ugly mystery was but an earthly illusion, and that, whatever mist of evil might seem to have gathered over her, the real Beatrice was a heavenly angel. Incapable as he was of such high faith, still her presence had not utterly lost its magic. Giovanni's rage was quelled into an aspect of sullen insensibility. Beatrice, with a quick spiritual sense, immediately felt that there was a gulf of blackness between them which neither her nor she could pass. They walked on together, sad and silent, and came thus to the marble fountain and to its pool of water on the ground, in the midst of which grew the shrub that bore gem-like blossoms. Giovanni was affrighted at the eager enjoyment—the appetite, as it were—with which he found himself inhaling the fragrance of the flowers.

"Beatrice," asked he, abruptly, "whence came this shrub?"

"My father created it," answered she, with simplicity.

"Created it! created it!" repeated Giovanni. "What mean you, Beatrice?"

"He is a man fearfully acquainted with the secrets of Nature," replied Beatrice; "and, at the hour when I first drew breath, this plant sprang from the soil, the offspring of his science, of his intellect, while I was but his earthly child. Approach it not!" continued she, observing with terror that Giovanni was drawing nearer to the shrub. "It has qualities that you little dream of. But I, dearest Giovanni— I grew up and blossomed with the plant and was nourished with its breath. It was my sister, and I loved it with a human affection; for, alas!—has thou not suspected it?—there was an awful doom."

Here Giovanni frowned so darkly upon her that Beatrice paused and trembled. But her faith in his tenderness reassured her, and made her blush that she had doubted for an instant.

"There was an awful doom," she continued, "the effect of my father's fatal love of science, which estranged me from all society of my kind. Until Heaven sent thee, dearest Giovanni, oh, how lonely was thy poor Beatrice!"

"Was it a hard doom?" asked Giovanni, fixing his eyes upon her.

"Only of late have I known how hard it was," answered she, tenderly. "Oh, yes; but my heart was torpid, and therefore quiet."

Giovanni's rage broke forth from his sullen gloom like a lightning flash out of a dark cloud.

"Accursed one!" cried he, with venemous scorn and anger. "And, finding thy solitude wearisome, thou has severed me likewise from all the warmth of life and enticed me into thy region of unspeakable horror!"

"Giovanni!" exclaimed Beatrice, turning her large bright eyes upon his face. The force of his words had not found its way into her mind; she was merely thunderstruck.

"Yes, poisonous thing!" repeated Giovanni, beside himself with passion. "Thou hast done it! Thou hast blasted me! Thou hast filled my veins with poison! Thou hast made me as hateful, as ugly, as loathsome and deadly a creature as thyself—a world's wonder of hideous monstrosity! Now, if our breath be happily as fatal to ourselves as to all others, let us join our lips in one kiss of unutterable hatred, and so die!"

"What has befallen me?" murmured Beatrice, with a low moan out of her heart. "Holy Virgin, pity me, a poor heart-broken child!"

"Thou—dost thou pray?" cried Giovanni, still with the same fiendish scorn. "Thy very prayers, as they come from thy lips, taint the atmosphere with death. Yes, yes; let us pray! Let us to church and dip our fingers in the holy water at the portal! They that come after us will perish as by a pestilence! Let us sign crosses in the air! It will be scattering curses abroad in the likeness of holy symbols!"

"Giovanni," said Beatrice, calmly, for her grief was beyond passion, "why dost thou join thyself with me thus in those terrible words? I, it is true, am the horrible thing thou namest me. But thou—what hast thou to do, save with one other shudder at my hideous misery to go forth out of the garden and mingle with thy race, and forget that there ever crawled on earth such a monster as poor Beatrice?"

"Does thou pretend ignorance?" asked Giovanni, scowling upon her. "Behold! this power have I gained from the pure daughter of Rappaccini."

There was a swarm of summer insects flitting through the air in search of the food promised by the flower odours of the fatal garden. They circled round Giovanni's head, and were evidently attracted towards him by the same influence which had drawn them for an instant within the sphere of several of the shrubs. He sent forth a breath among them, and smiled bitterly at Beatrice as at least a score of the insects fell dead upon the ground.

"I see it! I see it!" shrieked Beatrice. "It is my father's fatal science! No, no, Giovanni; it was not I! Never! Never! I dreamed only to love thee and be with thee a little time, and so let thee pass away, leaving but thine image in mine heart; for, Giovanni, believe it, though my body be nourished with poison, my spirit is God's creature, and craves love as its daily food. But my father—he has united us in this fearful sympathy. Yes; spurn me, tread upon me, kill me! Oh, what is death after such words as thine? But it was not I. Not for a world of bliss would I have done it."

Giovanni's passion had exhausted itself in its outburst from his lips. There now came across him a sense, mournful, and not without tenderness, of the intimate and peculiar relationship between Beatrice and himself. They stood, as it were, in an utter solitude, which would be made none the less solitary by the densest throng of human life. Ought not, then, the desert of humanity around them to press this insulated pair closer together? If they should be cruel to one another, who was there to be kind to them? Besides, thought Giovanni, might there not still be a hope of his returning within the limits of ordinary nature, and leading Beatrice, the redeemed Beatrice, by the hand? Oh, weak, and selfish, and unworthy spirit, that could dream of an earthly union and earthly happiness as possible, after such deep love had been so biiterly wronged as was Beatrice's love by Giovanni's blighting words! No, no; there could be no such hope. She must pass heavily, with that broken heart, across the borders of Time—she must bathe her hurts in some fount of paradise, and forget her grief in the light of immortality, and *there* be well.

But Giovanni did not know it.

"Dear Beatrice," said he, approaching her, while she shrank away as always at his approach, but now with a different impulse, "dearest Beatrice, our fate is not yet so desperate. Behold! there is a medicine, potent, as a wise physician has assured me, and almost divine in its efficacy. It is composed of ingredients the most opposite to those by which thy awful father has brought this calamity upon thee and me. It is distilled of blessed herbs. Shall we not quaff it together, and thus be purified from evil?"

"Give it me!" said Beatrice, extending her hand to receive the little silver vial which Giovanni took from his bosom. She added, with a peculiar emphasis, "I will drink; but do thou await the result."

She put Baglioni's antidote to her lips; and, at the same moment, the figure of Rappaccini emerged from the portal and came slowly towards the marble fountain. As he drew near, the pale man of science seemed to gaze with a triumphant expression at the beautiful youth and maiden, as might an artist who should spend his life in achieving a picture or a group of statuary and finally be satisfied with his success. He paused; his bent form grew erect with conscious power; he spread out his hands over them in the attitude of a father imploring a blessing upon his children; but those were the same hands that had thrown poison into the stream of their lives. Giovanni trembled. Beatrice shuddered nervously, and pressed her hand upon her heart.

"My daughter," said Rappaccini, "thou art no longer lonely in the world. Pluck one of those precious gems from thy sister shrub and bid thy bridegroom wear it in his bosom. It will not harm him now. My science and the sympathy between thee and him have so wrought within his system that he now stands apart from common men, as thou dost, daughter of my pride and triumph, from ordinary women. Pass on, then, through the world, most dear to one another and dreadful to all besides!"

"My father," said Beatrice, feebly—and still as she spoke she kept her hand upon her heart—"wherefore didst thou inflict this miserable doom upon thy child?"

"Miserable!" exclaimed Rappaccini. "What mean you, foolish girl? Dost thou deem it misery to be endowed with marvellous gifts against which no power nor strength could avail an enemy—misery, to be able to quell the mightiest with a breath—misery, to be as terrible as thou art beautiful? Wouldst thou, then, have preferred the condition of a weak woman, exposed to all evil and capable of none?"

"I would fain have been loved, not feared," murmured Beatrice, sinking down upon the ground. "But now it matters not. I am going, father, where the evil which thou hast striven to mingle with my being will pass away like a dream—like the fragrance of these poisonous flowers, which will no longer taint my breath among the flowers of Eden. Farewell, Giovanni! Thy words of hatred are like lead within my heart; but they, too, will fall away as I ascend. Oh, was there not, from the first, more poison in thy nature than in mine?"

To Beatrice—so radically had her earthly part been wrought upon by Rappaccini's skill—as poison had been life, so the powerful antidote was death; and thus the poor victim of man's ingenuity and of thwarted nature, and of the fatality that attends all such efforts of perverted wisdom perished there, at the feet of her father and Giovanni. Just at that moment Professor Pietro Baglioni looked forth from the window, and called loudly, in a tone of triumph mixed with horror, to the thunderstricken man of science—

"Rappaccini! Rappaccini! and is *this* the upshot of your experiment!"

✳ ✳ ✳

EDGAR ALLAN POE
(1809-1849)

EDGAR POE was born in Boston, January 19, 1809. At the age of three years he was taken into the home of John Allan, Richmond, Virginia, with whose family he spent the years 1815-1820 in England. After a year in the University of Virginia and brief periods in the army and at West Point, he found himself at the age of twenty-two homeless, penniless but, conscious of his high destiny, bent on achieving a name in literature. The remaining eighteen years of his life he passed in Philadelphia, Richmond and New York. Ill, poverty-stricken, a victim to drink and to opium, he wrote criticism, poems and stories now recognised as works of the first—if not the only—great genius in American letters. Much of his writing was done in connection with his editorship of *The Southern Literary Messenger* and *Graham's Magazine*. He died in Baltimore, 1849, never having relinquished his hope of founding a great national publication.

The Cask of Amontillado was first published in *Godey's Lady's Book*, 1846.

THE CASK OF AMONTILLADO
(ROME)

THE thousand injuries of Fortunato I had borne as best I could; but when he ventured upon insult, I vowed revenge. You, who so well know the nature of my soul, will not suppose, however, that I gave utterance to a threat. *At length* I would be avenged; this was a point definitely settled—but the very definitiveness with which it was resolved precluded the idea of risk. I must not only punish, but punish with impunity. A wrong is unredressed when retribution overtakes its redresser. It is equally unredressed when the avenger fails to make himself felt as such to him who has done the wrong.

It must be understood that neither by word nor deed had I given Fortunato cause to doubt my good-will. I continued, as was my wont, to smile in his face, and he did not perceive that my smile *now* was at the thought of his immolation.

He had a weak point—this Fortunato—although in other regards he was a man to be respected and even feared. He prided himself on his connoisseurship in wine. Few Italians have the true virtuoso spirit. For the most part their enthusiasm is adopted to suit the time and opportunity—to practise imposture upon the British and Austrian millionaires. In painting and gemmary, Fortunato, like his countrymen, was a quack —but in the matter of old wines he was sincere. In this respect I did not differ from him materially: I was skilful in the Italian vintages myself, and bought largely whenever I could.

It was about dusk, one evening during the supreme madness of the carnival season, that I encountered my friend. He accosted me with excessive warmth, for he had been drinking much. The man wore motley. He had on a tight-fitting parti-striped dress, and his head was surmounted by the conical cap and bells. I was so pleased to see him that I thought I should never have done wringing his hand.

I said to him: "My dear Fortunato, you are luckily met. How remarkably well you are looking today! But I have received a pipe of what passes for Amontillado, and I have my doubts."

"How?" said he. "Amontillado? A pipe? Impossible! And in the middle of the carnival?"

"I have my doubts," I replied; "and I was silly enough to pay the full Amontillado price without consulting you in the matter. You were not to be found, and I was fearful of losing a bargain."

"Amontillado!"

"I have my doubts."

"Amontillado!"

"And I must satisfy them."

"Amontillado!"

"As you are engaged, I am on my way to Luchesi. If anyone has a critical turn, it is he. He will tell me——"

"Luchesi cannot tell Amontillado from Sherry."

"And yet some fools will have it that his taste is a match for your own."

"Come, let us go."

"Whither?"

"To your vaults."

"My friend, no; I will not impose upon your good nature. I perceive you have an engagement. Luchesi——"

"I have no engagement;—come."

"My friend, no. It is not the engagement, but the severe cold with which I perceive you are afflicted. The vaults are insufferably damp. They are encrusted with nitre."

"Let us go, nevertheless. The cold is merely nothing. Amontillado! You have been imposed upon. And as for Luchesi, he cannot distinguish Sherry from Amontillado."

Thus speaking, Fortunato possessed himself of my arm; and putting on a mask of black silk and drawing a *roquelaure* closely about my person, I suffered him to hurry me to my palazzo.

There were no attendants at home; they had absconded to make merry in honour of the time. I had told them that I should not return until the morning, and had given them explicit orders not to stir from the house. These orders were sufficient, I well knew, to insure their immediate disappearance, one and all, as soon as my back was turned.

I took from their sconces two flambeaux, and giving one to Fortunato, bowed him through several suites of rooms to the archway that led into the vaults. I passed down a long and winding staircase, requesting him to be cautious as he followed. We came at length to the foot of the descent, and stood together on the damp ground of the catacombs of the Montresors.

The gait of my friend was unsteady, and the bells upon his cap jingled as he strode.

"The pipe," he said.

"It is farther on," said I; "but observe the white web-work which gleams from these cavern walls."

He turned towards me, and looked into my eyes with two filmy orbs that distilled the rheum of intoxication.

"Nitre?" he asked, at length.

"Nitre," I replied. "How long have you had that cough?"

"Ugh! ugh! ugh!—ugh! ugh! ugh!—ugh! ugh! ugh!—ugh! ugh! ugh!—ugh! ugh! ugh!"

My poor friend found it impossible to reply for many minutes.

"It is nothing," he said, at last.

"Come," I said, with decision, "we will go back; your health is precious. You are rich, respected, admired, beloved; you are happy, as once I was. You are a man to be missed. For me it is no matter. We will go back; you will be ill, and I cannot be responsible. Besides, there is Luchesi——"

"Enough," he said; "the cough is a mere nothing; it will not kill me. I shall not die of a cough."

"True—true," I replied; "and, indeed, I had no intention of alarming you unnecessarily—but you should use all proper caution. A draught of this Medoc will defend us from the damps."

Here I knocked off the neck of a bottle which I drew from a long row of its fellows that lay upon the mould.

"Drink," I said, presenting him the wine.

He raised it to his lips with a leer. He paused and nodded to me familiarly, while his bells jingled.

"I drink," he said, "to the buried that repose around us."

"And I to your long life."

He again took my arm, and we proceeded.

"These vaults," he said, "are extensive."

"The Montresors," I replied, "were a great and numerous family."

"I forget your arms."

"A huge human foot d'or, in a field azure; the foot crushes a serpent rampant whose fangs are imbedded in the heel."

"And the motto?"

"Nemo me impune lacessit."

"Good!" he said.

The wine sparkled in his eyes and the bells jingled. My own fancy grew warm with the Medoc. We had passed through long walls of piled skeletons, with casks and puncheons intermingling, into the inmost recesses of the catacombs. I paused again, and this time I made bold to seize Fortunato by an arm above the elbow.

"The nitre!" I said; "see, it increases. It hangs like moss upon the vaults. We are below the river's bed. The drops of moisture trickle among the bones. Come, we will go back ere it is too late. Your cough——"

"It is nothing," he said; "let us go on. But first, another draught of the Medoc."

I broke and reached him a flagon of De Grâve. He emptied it at a breath. His eyes flashed with a fierce light. He laughed and threw the bottle upwards with a gesticulation I did not understand.

I looked at him in surprise. He repeated the movement—a grotesque one.

"You do not comprehend?" he said.

"Not, I," I replied.

"Then you are not of the brotherhood."

"How?"

"You are not of the masons."

"Yes, yes," I said; "yes, yes."

"You? Impossible! A mason?"

"A mason," I replied.

"A sign," he said, "a sign."

"It is this," I answered, producing from beneath the folds of my *roquelaure* a trowel.

"You jest," he exclaimed, recoiling a few paces. "But let us proceed to the Amontillado."

"Be it so," I said, replacing the tool beneath the cloak and again offering him my arm. He leaned upon it heavily. We continued our route in search of the Amontillado. We passed through a range of low arches, descended, passed on, and descending again, arrived at a deep crypt, in which the foulness of the air caused our flambeaux rather to glow than flame.

At the most remote end of the crypt there appeared another less spacious. Its walls had been lined with human remains, piled to the vault overhead, in the fashion of the great catacombs of Paris. Three sides of this interior crypt were still ornamented in this manner. From the fourth side the bones had been thrown down, and lay promiscuously upon the earth, forming at one point a mound of some size. Within the wall thus exposed by the displacing of the bones, we perceived a still interior crypt or recess, in depth about four feet, in width three, in height six or seven. It seemed to have been constructed for no especial use within itself, but formed merely the interval between two of the colossal supports of the roof of the catacombs, and was backed by one of their circumscribing walls of solid granite.

It was in vain that Fortunato, uplifting his dull torch, endeavoured to pry into the depth of the recess. Its termination the feeble light did not enable us to see.

"Proceed," I said; "herein is the Amontillado. As for Luchesi——"

"He is an ignoramus," interrupted my friend, as he stepped unsteadily forward, while I followed immediately at his heels. In an instant he had reached the extremity of the niche, and finding his progress arrested by the rock, stood stupidly bewildered. A moment more and I had fettered him to the granite. In its surface were two iron staples, distant from each other about two feet, horizontally. From one of these depended a short chain, from the other a padlock. Throwing the links about his waist, it was but the work of a few seconds to secure it. He was too much astounded to resist. Withdrawing the key I stepped back from the recess.

"Pass your hand," I said, "over the wall; you cannot help feeling the nitre. Indeed, it is *very* damp. Once more let me *implore* you to return. No? Then I must positively leave you. But I must first render you all the little attentions in my power."

"The Amontillado!" ejaculated my friend, not yet recovered from his astonishment.

"True," I replied; "the Amontillado."

As I said these words I busied myself among the pile of bones of which I have before spoken. Throwing them aside, I soon uncovered a quantity of building stone and mortar. With these materials and with the aid of my trowel, I began vigorously to wall up the entrance of the niche.

I had scarcely laid the first tier of the masonry when I discovered that the intoxication of Fortunato had in a great measure worn off. The earliest indication I had of this was a low moaning cry from the depth of the recess. It was *not* the cry of a drunken man. There was then a long and obstinate silence. I laid the second tier and the third, and the fourth; and then I heard the furious vibrations of the chain. The noise lasted for several minutes, during which, that I might hearken to it with the more satisfaction, I ceased my labours and sat down upon the bones. When at last the clanking subsided, I resumed the trowel, and finished without interruption the fifth, the sixth, and the seventh tier. The wall was now nearly upon a level with my breast. I again paused, and holding the flambeaux over the mason-work, threw a few feeble rays upon the figure within.

A succession of loud and shrill screams, busting suddenly from the throat of the chained form, seemed to thrust me violently back. For a brief moment I hesitated, I trembled. Unsheathing my rapier, I began to grope with it about the recess; but the thought of an instant reassured me. I placed my hand upon the solid fabric of the catacombs, and felt satisfied. I reapproached the wall; I replied to the yells of him who clamoured. I re-echoed, I aided, I surpassed them in volume and in strength. I did this, and the clamourer grew still.

It was now midnight, and my task was drawing to a close. I had completed the eighth, the ninth and the tenth tier. I had finished a portion of the last and the eleventh; there remained but a single stone to be fitted and plastered in. I struggled with its weight; I placed it partially in its destined position. But now there came from out the niche a low laugh that erected the hairs upon my head. It was succeeded by a sad voice, which I had difficulty in recognising as that of the noble Fortunato. The voice said—

"Ha! ha! ha!—he! he! he!—a very good joke, indeed—an excellent jest. We will have many a rich laugh about it at the palazzo—he! he! he!—over our wine—he! he! he!"

"The Amontillado!" I said.

"He! he! he!—he! he! he!—A very good joke indeed—an excellent jest. Will not they be awaiting us at the palazzo, the Lady Fortunato and the rest? Let us be gone."

"Yes," I said, "let us be gone."

"For the love of God, Montresor!"

"Yes," I said, "for the love of God!"

But to these words I hearkened in vain for a reply. I grew impatient. I called aloud—

"Fortunato!"

No answer. I called again—

"Fortunato!"

No answer still. I thrust a torch through the remaining aperture and let it fall within. There came forth in return only a jingling of the bells. My heart grew sick; on account of the dampness of the catacombs. I hastened to make an end of my labour. I forced the last stone into its position; I plastered it up. Against the new masonry I re-erected the old rampart of bones. For the half of a century no mortal has disturbed them. *In pace requiescat!*

❋ ❋ ❋

FITZ-JAMES O'BRIEN
(1828?-1862)

FITZ-JAMES O'BRIEN, born in Ireland, about 1828, received his education at Dublin University. Having squandered his patrimony in London, he emigrated to New York in 1852. Among the Bohemian spirits of the city his wit and joviality gave him popularity; among the writers, his gifts brought him high esteem. Plays, poems, criticisms, and stories flowed from his pen for a decade. On the declaration of Civil War, he obtained a commission, fought, and was fatally wounded February 26, 1862 (died, April 6, 1862).

O'Brien has been compared to Poe in his search for the rich and strange and in adapting to fiction new discoveries in the world of fact. His originality, his brilliant style, and his realistic handling of the supernatural are found at their best in *What Was It?* This story was first published in *Harper's*, March, 1859.

WHAT WAS IT?

IT is, I confess, with considerable diffidence that I approach the strange narrative which I am about to relate. The events which I purpose detailing are of so extraordinary a character that I am quite prepared to meet with an unusual amount of incredulity and scorn. I accept all such beforehand. I have, I trust, the literary courage to face unbelief. I have, after mature consideration, resolved to narrate, in as simple and straightforward a manner as I can compass, some facts that passed under my observation, in the month of July last, and which, in the annals of the mysteries of physical science, are wholly unparalleled.

I live at No. — Twenty-sixth Street, in New York. The house is in some respects a curious one. It has enjoyed for the last two years the reputation of being haunted. It is a large and stately residence, surrounded by what was once a garden, but which is now only a green enclosure used for bleaching clothes. The dry basin of what has been a fountain, and a few fruit trees ragged and unpruned, indicate that this spot in past days was a pleasant, shady retreat, filled with fruits and flowers and the sweet murmur of waters.

The house is very spacious. A hall of noble size leads to a large spiral staircase winding through its centre, while the various apartments are of imposing dimensions. It was built some fifteen or twenty years since by Mr. A——, the well-known New York merchant, who five years ago threw the commercial world into convulsions by a stupendous bank fraud. Mr. A——, as every one knows, escaped to Europe, and died not long after, of a broken heart. Almost immediately after the news of his decease reached this country and was verified, the report spread in Twenty-sixth Street that No. — was haunted. Legal measures had dispossessed the widow of its former owner, and it was inhabited merely by a caretaker and his wife, placed there by the house agent into whose hands it had passed for the purposes of renting or sale. These people declared that they were troubled with unnatural noises. Doors were opened without any visible agency. The remnants of furniture scattered through the various rooms were, during the night, piled one upon the other by unknown hands. Invisible feet passed up and down the stairs in broad daylight, accompanied by the rustle of unseen silk dresses, and the gliding of viewless hands along the massive balusters. The caretaker and his wife declared they would live there no longer. The house agent laughed, dismissed them, and put others in their place. The noises and supernatural manifestations continued. The neighbourhood caught up the story, and the house remained untenanted for three years. Several persons negotiated for it; but, somehow, always before the bargain was closed they heard the unpleasant rumours and declined to treat any further.

It was in this state of things that my landlady, who at that time kept a boarding-house in Bleecker Street, and who wished to move further up town, conceived the bold idea of renting No. —— Twenty-sixth Street. Happening to have in her house rather a plucky and philosophical set of boarders, she laid her scheme before us, stating candidly everything she had heard respecting the ghostly qualities of the establishment to which she wished to remove us. With the exception of two timid persons,— a sea-captain and a returned Californian, who immediately gave notice that they would leave,—all of Mrs. Moffat's guests declared that they would accompany her in her chivalric incursion into the abode of spirits.

Our removal was effected in the month of May, and we were charmed with our new residence. The portion of Twenty-sixth Street where our house is situated, between Seventh and Eighth avenues, is one of the pleasantest localities in New York. The gardens back of the houses, running down nearly to the Hudson, form, in the summer time, a perfect avenue of verdure. The air is pure and invigorating, sweeping, as it does, straight across the river from the Weehawken heights, and even the ragged garden which surrounded the house, although displaying on washing days rather too much clothesline, still gave us a piece of greensward to look at, and a cool retreat in the summer evenings, where we smoked our cigars in the dusk, and watched the fireflies flashing their dark lanterns in the long grass.

Of course we had no sooner established ourselves at No. —— than we began to expect ghosts. We absolutely awaited their advent with eagerness. Our dinner conversation was supernatural. One of the boarders, who had purchased Mrs. Crowe's "Night Side of Nature" for his own private delectation, was regarded as a public enemy by the entire household for not having bought twenty copies. The man led a life of supreme wretchedness while he was reading this volume. A system of espionage was established, of which he was the victim. If he incautiously laid the book down for an instant and left the room, it was immediately seized and read aloud in secret places to a select few. I found myself a person of immense importance, it having leaked out that I was tolerably well versed in the history of supernaturalism, and had once written a story the foundation of which was a ghost. If a table or a wainscot panel happened to warp when we were assembled in the large drawing-room, there was an instant silence, and every one was prepared for an immediate clanking of chains and a spectral form.

After a month of psychological excitement, it was with the utmost dissatisfaction that we were forced to acknowledge that nothing in the remotest degree approaching the supernatural had manifested itself. Once the black butler asseverated that his candle had been blown out by some invisible agency while he was undressing himself for the night; but as I had more than once discovered this coloured gentleman in a condition when one candle must have appeared to him like two, I thought it possible that, by going a step further in his potations, he might have reversed this phenomenon, and seen no candle at all where he ought to have beheld one.

Things were in this state when an accident took place so awful and inexplicable in its character that my reason fairly reels at the bare memory of the occurrence. It was the tenth of July. After dinner was over I repaired, with my friend Dr. Hammond, to the garden to smoke my evening pipe. Independent of certain mental sympathies which existed between the Doctor and myself, we were linked together by a vice. We both smoked opium. We knew each other's secret, and respected it. We enjoyed together that wonderful expansion of thought, that marvellous intensifying of the perceptive faculties, that boundless feeling of existence when we seem to have points of contact with the whole universe,—in short, that unimaginable spiritual bliss, which I would not surrender for a throne, and which I hope you, reader, will never—never taste.

Those hours of opium happiness which the Doctor and I spent together in secret were regulated with a scientific accuracy. We did not blindly smoke the drug of paradise, and leave our dreams to chance. While smoking, we carefully steered our conversation through the brightest and calmest channels of thought. We talked of the East, and endeavoured to recall the magical panorama of its glowing scenery. We criticised the most sensuous poets,—those who painted life ruddy with health, brimming with passion, happy in the possession of youth and strength and beauty. If we talked of Shakespeare's "Tempest," we lingered over Ariel, and avoided Caliban. Like the Guebers, we turned our faces to the East, and saw only the sunny side of the world.

This skilful colouring of our train of thought produced in our subsequent visions a corresponding tone. The splendours of Arabian fairyland dyed our dreams. We paced the narrow strip of grass with the tread and port of kings. The song of the *rana arborea,* while he clung to the bark of the ragged plum-tree, sounded like the strains of divine musicians. Houses, walls, and streets melted like rain clouds, and vistas of unimaginable glory stretched away before us. It was a rapturous companionship. We enjoyed the vast delight more perfectly because, even in our most ecstatic moments, we were conscious of each other's presence. Our pleasures, while individual, were still twin, vibrating and moving in musical accord.

On the evening in question, the tenth of July, the Doctor and myself drifted into an unusually metaphysical mood. We lit our large meerschaums, filled with fine Turkish tobacco, in the core of which burned a little black nut of opium, that, like the nut in the fairy tale, held within its narrow limits wonders beyond the reach of kings; we paced to and fro, conversing. A strange perversity dominated the currents of our thought. They would *not* flow through the sun-lit channels into which we strove to divert them. For some unaccountable reason, they constantly diverged into dark and lonesome beds, where a continual gloom brooded. It was in vain that, after our old fashion, we flung ourselves on the shores of the East, and talked of its gay bazaars, of the splendours of the time of Haroun, of harems and golden palaces. Black afreets continually arose from the depths of our talk, and expanded, like the one the fisherman released from the copper vessel, until they blotted everything bright from our vision. Insensibly, we yielded to the occult force that swayed us, and indulged in gloomy speculation. We had talked some time upon the proneness of the human mind to mysticism, and the almost universal love of the terrible, when Hammond suddenly said to me, "What do you consider to be the greatest element of terror?"

The question puzzled me. That many things were terrible, I knew. Stumbling over a corpse in the dark; beholding, as I once did, a woman floating down a deep and rapid river, with wildly lifted arms, and awful, upturned face, uttering, as she drifted, shrieks that rent one's heart while we, spectators, stood frozen at a window which overhung the river at a height of sixty feet, unable to make the slightest effort to save her, but dumbly watching her last supreme agony and her disappearance. A shattered wreck, with no life visible, encountered floating listlessly on the ocean is a terrible object, for it suggests a huge terror, the proportions of which are veiled. But it now struck me, for the first time, that there must be one great and ruling embodiment of fear,—a King of Terrors, to which all others must succumb. What might it be? To what train of circumstances would it owe its existence?

"I confess, Hammond," I replied to my friend, "I never considered the subject before. That there must be one Something more terrible than any other thing, I feel. I cannot attempt, however, even the most vague definition."

"I am somewhat like you, Harry," he answered. "I feel my capacity to experience a terror greater than anything yet conceived by the human mind;—something combining in fearful and unnatural amalgamation hitherto supposed incompatible elements. The calling of the voices in Brockden Brown's novel of 'Wieland' is awful; so is the picture of the Dweller of the Threshold, in Bulwer's 'Zanoni'; but," he added, shaking his head gloomily, "there is something more horrible still than those."

"Look here, Hammond," I rejoined, "let us drop this kind of talk, for Heaven's sake! We shall suffer for it, depend on it."

"I don't know what's the matter with me tonight," he replied, "but my brain is running upon all sorts of weird and awful thoughts. I feel as if I could write a story like Hoffman, tonight, if I were only master of a literary style."

"Well, if we are going to be Hoffmanesque in our talk, I'm off to bed. Opium and nightmares should never be brought together. How sultry it is! Good night, Hammond."

"Good night, Harry. Pleasant dreams to you."

"To you, gloomy wretch, afreets, ghouls, and enchanters."

We parted, and each sought his respective chamber. I undressed quickly and got into bed, taking with me, according to my usual custom, a book, over which I generally read myself to sleep. I opened the volume as soon as I had laid my head upon the pillow, and instantly flung it to the other side of the room. It was Goudon's "History of Monsters,"—a curious French work, which I had lately imported from Paris, but which, in the state of mind I had then reached, was anything but an agreeable companion. I resolved to go to sleep at once; so, turning down my gas until nothing but a little blue point of light glimmered on the top of the tube, I composed myself to rest.

The room was in total darkness. The atom of gas that still remained alight did not illuminate a distance of three inches round the burner. I desperately drew my arm across my eyes, as if to shut out even the darkness, and tried to think of nothing. It was in vain. The confounded themes touched on by Hammond in the garden kept obtruding themselves on my brain. I battled against them. I erected ramparts of would-be blankness of intellect to keep them out. They still crowded upon me. While I was lying still as a corpse, hoping that by a perfect physical inaction I should hasten mental repose, an awful incident occurred. A Something dropped, as it seemed, from the ceiling, plumb upon my chest, and the next instant I felt two bony hands encircling my throat, endeavoring to choke me.

I am no coward, and am possessed of considerable physical strength. The suddenness of the attack, instead of stunning me, strung every nerve to its highest tension. My body acted from instinct, before my brain had time to realise the terrors of my position. In an instant I wound two muscular arms around the creature, and squeezed it, with all the strength of despair, against my chest. In a few seconds the bony hands that had fastened on my throat loosened their hold, and I was free to breathe once more. Then commenced a struggle of awful intensity. Immersed in the most profound darkness, totally ignorant of the nature of the Thing by which I was so suddenly attacked, finding my grasp slipping every moment, by reason, it seemed to me, of the entire nakedness of my assailant, bitten with sharp teeth in the shoulder, neck, and chest, having every moment to protect my throat against a pair of sinewy, agile hands, which my utmost efforts could not confine, —these were a combination of circumstances to combat which required all the strength, skill, and courage that I possessed.

At last, after a silent, deadly, exhausting struggle, I got my assailant under by a series of incredible efforts of strength. Once pinned, with my knee on what I made out to be its chest, I knew that I was victor. I rested for a moment to breathe. I heard the creature beneath me panting in the darkness, and felt the violent throbbing of a heart. It was apparently as exhausted as I was; that was one comfort. At this moment I remembered that I usually placed under my pillow, before going to bed, a large yellow silk pocket handkerchief. I felt for it instantly; it was there. In a few seconds more I had, after a fashion, pinioned the creature's arms.

I now felt tolerably secure. There was nothing more to be done but to turn on the gas, and, having first seen what my midnight assailant was like, arouse the household. I will confess to being actuated by a certain pride in not giving the alarm before; I wished to make the capture alone and unaided.

Never losing my hold for an instant, I slipped from the bed to the floor, dragging my captive with me. I had but a few steps to make to reach the gas-burner; these I made with the greatest caution, holding the creature in a grip like a vice. At last I got within arm's length of the tiny speck of blue light which told we where the gas-burner lay. Quick as lightning I released my grasp with one hand and let on the full flood of light. Then I turned to look at my captive.

I cannot even attempt to give any definition of my sensations the instant after I turned on the gas. I suppose I must have shrieked with terror, for in less than a minute afterward my room was crowded with the inmates of the house. I shudder now as I think of that awful moment. *I saw nothing!* Yes; I had one arm firmly clasped round a breathing, panting, corporeal shape, my other hand gripped with all its strength a throat as warm, as apparently fleshy, as my own; and yet, with this living substance in my grasp, with its body pressed against my own, and all in the bright glare of a large jet of gas, I absolutely beheld nothing! Not even an outline,—a vapour!

I do not, even at this hour, realise the situation in which I found myself. I cannot recall the astounding incident thoroughly. Imagination in vain tries to compass the awful paradox.

It breathed. I felt its warm breath upon my cheek. It struggled fiercely. It had hands. They clutched me. Its skin was smooth, like my own. There it lay, pressed close up against me, solid as stone,—and yet utterly invisible!

I wonder that I did not faint or go mad on the instant. Some wonderful instinct must have sustained me; for, absolutely, in place of loosening my hold on the terrible Enigma, I seemed to gain an additional strength in my moment of horror, and tightened my grasp with such wonderful force that I felt the creature shivering with agony.

Just then Hammond entered my room at the head of the household. As soon as he beheld my face—which, I suppose, must have been an awful sight to look at—he hastened forward, crying, "Great heaven, Harry! what has happened?"

"Hammond! Hammond!" I cried, "come here. Oh, this is awful! I have been attacked in bed by something or other, which I have hold of; but I can't see it,—I can't see it!"

Hammond, doubtless struck by the unfeigned horror expressed in my countenance, made one or two steps forward with an anxious yet puzzled expression. A very audible titter burst from the remainder of my visitors. This suppressed laughter made me furious. To laugh at a human being in my position! It was the worst species of cruelty. *Now,* I can understand why the appearance of a man struggling violently, as it would seem, with an airy nothing, and calling for assistance against a vision, should have appeared ludicrous. *Then,* so great was my rage against the mocking crowd that had I the power I would have stricken them dead where they stood.

"Hammond! Hammond!" I cried again, despairingly, "for God's sake come to me. I can't hold the—the thing but a short while longer. It is overpowering me. Help me! Help me!"

"Harry," whispered Hammond, approaching me, "you have been smoking too much opium."

"I swear to you, Hammond, that this is no vision," I answered, in the same low tone. "Don't you see how it shakes my whole frame with its struggles? If you don't believe me, convince yourself. Feel it,—touch it."

Hammond advanced and laid his hand in the spot I indicated. A wild cry of horror burst from him. He had felt it!

In a moment he had discovered somewhere in my room a long piece of cord, and was the next instant winding it and knotting it about the body of the unseen being that I clasped in my arms.

"Harry," he said, in a hoarse, agitated voice, for, though he preserved his presence of mind, he was deeply moved, "Harry, it's all safe now. You may let go, old fellow, if you're tired. The Thing can't move."

I was utterly exhausted, and I gladly loosed my hold.

Hammond stood holding the ends of the cord that bound the Invisible, twisted round his hand, while before him, self-supporting as it were, he beheld a rope laced and interlaced, and stretching tightly around a vacant space. I never saw a man look so thoroughly stricken with awe. Nevertheless his face expressed all the courage and determination which I knew him to possess. His lips, although white, were set firmly, and one could perceive at a glance that, although stricken with fear, he was not daunted.

The confusion that ensued among the guests of the house who were witnesses of this extraordinary scene between Hammond and myself,—who beheld the pantomime of binding this struggling Something,—who beheld me almost sinking from physical exhaustion when my task of jailer was over,—the confusion and terror that took possession of the bystanders, when they saw all this, was beyond description. The weaker ones fled from the apartment. The few who remained clustered near the door and could not be induced to approach Hammond and his Charge. Still incredulity broke out through their terror. They had not the courage to satisfy themselves, and yet they doubted. It was in vain that I begged of some of the men to come near and convince themselves by touch of the existence in that room of a living being which was invisible. They were incredulous, but did not dare to undeceive themselves. How could a solid, living, breathing body be invisible, they asked. My reply was this. I gave a sign to Hammond, and both of us—conquering our fearful repugnance to touch the invisible creature—lifted it from the ground, manacled as it was, and took it to my bed. Its weight was about that of a boy of fourteen.

"Now, my friends," I said, as Hammond and myself held the creature suspended over the bed, "I can give you self-evident proof that here is a solid, ponderable body, which, nevertheless, you cannot see. Be good enough to watch the surface of the bed attentively."

I was astonished at my own courage in treating this strange event so calmly; but I had recovered from my first terror, and felt a sort of scientific pride in the affair, which dominated every other feeling.

The eyes of the bystanders were immediately fixed on my bed. At a given signal Hammond and I let the creature fall. There was a dull sound of a heavy body alighting on a soft mass. The timbers of the bed creaked. A deep impression marked itself distinctly on the pillow, and on the bed itself. The crowd who witnessed this gave a low cry, and rushed from the room. Hammond and I were left alone with our Mystery.

We remained silent for some time, listening to the low, irregular breathing of the creature on the bed, and watching the rustle of the bedclothes as it impotently struggled to free itself from confinement. Then Hammond spoke.

"Harry, this is awful."

"Ay, awful."

"But not unaccountable."

"Not unaccountable! What do you mean? Such a thing has never occurred since the birth of the world. I know not what to think, Hammond. God grant that I am not mad, and that this is not an insane fantasy!"

"Let us reason a little, Harry. Here is a solid body which we touch, but which we cannot see. The fact is so unusual that it strikes us with terror. Is there no parallel, though, for such a phenomenon? Take a piece of pure glass. It is tangible and transparent. A certain chemical coarseness is all that prevents its being so entirely transparent as to be totally invisible. It is not *theoretically impossible*, mind you, to make a glass which shall not reflect a single ray of light,—a glass so pure and homogeneous in its atoms that the rays from the sun will pass through it as they do through the air, refracted but not reflected. We do not see the air, and yet we feel it."

"That's all very well, Hammond, but these are inanimate substances. Glass does not breathe, air does not breathe. *This* thing has a heart that palpitates,—a will that moves it,—lungs that play, and inspire and respire."

"You forget the phenomena of which we have so often heard of late," answered the Doctor, gravely. "At the meetings called 'spirit circles,' invisible hands have been thrust into the hands of those persons round the table,—warm, fleshly hands that seemed to pulsate with mortal life."

"What? Do you think, then, that this thing is——"

"I don't know what it is," was the solemn reply; "but please the gods I will, with your assistance, thoroughly investigate it."

We watched together, smoking many pipes, all night long, by the bed-side of the unearthly being that tossed and panted until it was apparently wearied out. Then we learned by the low, regular breathing that it slept.

The next morning the house was all astir. The boarders congregated on the landing outside my room, and Hammond and myself were lions. We had to answer a thousand questions as to the state of our extraordinary prisoner, for as yet not one person in the house except ourselves could be induced to set foot in the apartment.

The creature was awake. This was evidenced by the convulsive manner in which the bedclothes were moved in its efforts to escape. There was something truly terrible in beholding, as it were, those second-hand indications of the terrible writhings and agonised struggles for liberty which themselves were invisible.

Hammond and myself had racked our brains during the long night to discover some means by which we might realise the shape and general appearance of the Enigma. As well as we could make out by passing our hands over the creature's form, its outlines and lineaments were human. There was a mouth; a round, smooth head without hair; a nose, which, however, was little elevated above the cheeks; and its hands and feet felt like those of a boy. At first we thought of placing the being on a smooth surface and tracing its outlines with chalk, as shoemakers trace the outline of the foot. This plan was given up as being of no value. Such an outline would give not the slightest idea of its conformation.

A happy thought struck me. We would take a cast of it in plaster of Paris. This would give us the solid figure, and satisfy all our wishes. But how to do it? The movements of the creature would disturb the setting of the plastic covering, and distort the mould. Another thought. Why not give it chloroform? It had respiratory organs,—that was evident by its breathing. Once reduced to a state of insensibility, we could do with it what we would. Doctor X—— was sent for; and after the worthy physician had recovered from the first shock of amazement, he proceeded to administer the chloroform. In three minutes afterward we were enabled to remove the fetters from the creature's body, and a modeller was busily engaged in covering the invisible form with the moist clay. In five minutes more we had a mould, and before evening a rough facsimile of the Mystery. It was shaped like a man,—distorted, uncouth, and horrible, but still a man. It was small, not over four feet and some inches in height, and its limbs revealed a muscular development that was unparalleled. Its face surpassed in hideousness anything I had ever seen, Gustave Doré, or Callot, or Tony Johannot, never conceived anything so horrible. There is a face in one of the latter's illustrations to *Un Voyage où il vous plaira*, which somewhat approaches the countenance of this creature, but does not equal it. It was the physiognomy of what I should fancy a ghoul might be. It looked as if it was capable of feeding on human flesh.

Having satisfied our curiosity, and bound every one in the house to secrecy, it became a question what was to be done with our Enigma? It was impossible that we should keep such a horror in our house; it was equally impossible that such an awful being should be let loose upon the world. I confess that I would have gladly voted for the creature's destruction. But who would shoulder the responsibility? Who would undertake the execution of this horrible semblance of a human being? Day after day this question was deliberated gravely. The boarders all left the house. Mrs. Moffat was in despair, and threatened Hammond and myself with all sorts of legal penalties if we did not remove the Horror. Our answer was, "We will go if you like, but we decline taking this creature with us. Remove it yourself if you please. It appeared in your house. On you the responsibility rests." To this there was, of course, no answer. Mrs. Moffat could not obtain for love or money a person who would even approach the Mystery.

The most singular part of the affair was that we were entirely ignorant of what the creature habitually fed on. Everything in the way of nutriment that we could think of was placed before it, but was never touched. It was awful to stand by, day after day, and see the clothes toss, and hear the hard breathing, and know that it was starving.

Ten, twelve days, a fortnight passed, and it still lived. The pulsations of the heart, however, were daily growing fainter, and had now nearly ceased. It was evident that the creature was dying for want of sustenance. While this terrible life-struggle was going on, I felt miserable. I could not sleep. Horrible as the creature was, it was pitiful to think of the pangs it was suffering.

At last it died. Hammond and I found it cold and stiff one morning in the bed. The heart had ceased to beat, the lungs to inspire. We hastened to bury it in the garden. It was a strange funeral, the dropping of that viewless corpse into the damp hole. The cast of its form I gave to Doctor X——, who keeps it in his museum in Tenth Street.

As I am on the eve of a long journey from which I may not return, I have drawn up this narrative of an event the most singular that has ever come to my knowledge.

❋ ❋ ❋

FRANK R. STOCKTON
(1834-1902)

DESTINED to become the best-known "trick" story writer of his day, Stockton was born in Philadelphia, 1834. He was thirty-eight years of age before he published his first short story for adults. About that time (1872) he moved to New York, where, while holding editorial positions, he produced a number of novels and briefer tales, the most famous of which is *The Lady or the Tiger*. His chief characteristic is a sly humor, which plays with impossible situations and pleasantly beguiles the reader into a momentary acceptance of his "facts." The climax of his whimsicality not infrequently results in a surprise ending.

A Tale of Negative Gravity, first published in the *Century Magazine* (Vol. 29, page 135), is chosen to illustrate best his peculiar individuality. It is here reprinted by special arrangement with and permission of the publishers from the first edition of *The Christmas Wreck and Other Stories*, Charles Scribner's Sons, New York City, copyright, 1886.

A TALE OF NEGATIVE GRAVITY

MY wife and I were staying at a small town in northern Italy; and on a certain pleasant afternoon in spring we had taken a walk of six or seven miles to see the sun set behind some low mountains to the west of the town. Most of our walk had been along a hard, smooth highway, and then we turned into a series of narrower roads, sometimes bordered by walls, and sometimes by light fences of reed, or cane. Nearing the mountain, to a low spur of which we intended to ascend, we easily scaled a wall about four feet high, and found ourselves upon pasture land, which led, sometimes by gradual ascents, and sometimes by bits of rough climbing, to the spot we wished to reach. We were afraid we were a little late, and therefore hurried on, running up the grassy hills, and bounding briskly over the rough and rocky places. I carried a knapsack strapped firmly to my shoulders, and under my wife's arm was a large, soft basket of a kind much used by tourists. Her arm was passed through the handles, and around the bottom of the basket, which she pressed closely to her side. This was the way she always carried it. The basket contained two bottles of wine, one sweet for my wife, and another a little acid for myself. Sweet wines give me a headache.

When we reached the grassy bluff, well known thereabouts to lovers of sunset views, I stepped immediately to the edge to gaze upon the scene, but my wife sat down to take a sip of wine, for she was very thirsty; and then, leaving her basket, she came to my side. The scene was indeed one of great beauty. Beneath us stretched a wide valley of many shades of green, with a little river running through it, and red-tiled houses here and there. Beyond rose a range of mountains, pink, pale-green, and purple where their tips caught the reflection of the setting sun, and of a rich grey-green in shadows. Beyond all was the blue Italian sky, illumined by an especially fine sunset.

My wife and I are Americans, and at the time of this story were middle-aged people and very fond of seeing in each other's company whatever there was of interest or beauty around us. We had a son about twenty-two years old, of whom we were also very fond, but he was not with us, being at that time a student in Germany. Although we had good health, we were not very robust people, and, under ordinary circumstances, not much given to long country tramps. I was of medium size, without much muscular development, while my wife was quite stout, and growing stouter.

The reader may, perhaps, be somewhat surprised that a middle-aged couple, not very strong, or very good walkers, the lady loaded with a basket containing two bottles of wine and a metal drinking-cup, and the gentleman carrying a heavy knapsack, filled with all sorts of odds and ends, strapped to his shoulders, should set off on a seven-mile walk, jump over a wall, run up a hill-side, and yet feel in very good trim to enjoy a sunset view. This peculiar state of things I will proceed to explain.

I had been a professional man, but some years before had retired upon a very comfortable income. I had always been very fond of scientific pursuits, and now made these the occupation and pleasure of much of my leisure time. Our home was in a small town; and in a corner of my grounds I built a laboratory, where I carried on my work and my experiments. I had long been anxious to discover the means, not only of producing, but of retaining and controlling, a natural force, really the same as centrifugal force, but which I called negative gravity. This name I adopted because it indicated better than any other the action of the force in question, as I produced it. Positive gravity attracts everything toward the centre of the earth. Negative gravity, therefore, would be that power which repels everything from the centre of the earth, just as the negative pole of a magnet repels the needle, while the positive pole attracts it. My object was, in fact, to store centrifugal force and to render it constant, controllable, and available for use. The advantages of such a discovery could scarcely be described. In a word, it would lighten the burdens of the world.

I will not touch upon the labours and disappointments of several years. It is enough to say that at last I discovered a method of producing, storing, and controlling negative gravity.

The mechanism of my invention was rather complicated, but the method of operating it was very simple. A strong metallic case, about eight inches long, and half as wide, contained the machinery for producing the force; and this was put into action by means of the pressure of a screw worked from the outside. As soon as this pressure was produced, negative gravity began to be evolved and stored, and the greater the pressure the greater the force. As the screw was moved outward, and the pressure diminished, the force decreased, and when the screw was withdrawn to its fullest extent, the action of negative gravity entirely ceased. Thus this force could be produced or dissipated at will to such degrees as might be desired, and its action, so long as the requisite pressure was maintained, was constant.

When this little apparatus worked to my satisfaction I called my wife into my laboratory and explained to her my invention and its value. She had known that I had been at work with an important object, but I had never told her what it was. I had said that if I succeeded I would tell her all, but if I failed she need not be troubled with the matter at all. Being a very sensible woman, this satisfied her perfectly. Now I explained everything to her, the construction of the machine, and the wonderful uses to which this invention could be applied. I told her that it could diminish, or entirely dissipate, the weight of objects of any kind. A heavily loaded wagon, with two of these instruments fastened to its sides, and each screwed to a proper force, would be so lifted and supported that it would press upon the ground as lightly as an empty cart, and a small horse could draw it with ease. A bale of cotton, with one of these machines attached, could be handled and carried by a boy. A car, with a number of these machines, could be made to rise in the air like a balloon. Everything, in fact, that was heavy could be made light; and as a great part of labour, all over the world, is caused by the attraction of gravitation, so this repellent force, wherever applied, would make weight less and work easier. I told her of many, many ways in which the invention might be used, and would have told her of many more if she had not suddenly burst into tears.

"The world has gained something wonderful," she exclaimed, between her sobs, "but I have lost a husband!"

"What do you mean by that?" I asked, in surprise.

"I haven't minded it so far," she said, "because it gave you something to do, and it pleased you, and it never interfered with our home pleasures and our home life. But now that is all over. You will never be your own master again. It will succeed, I am sure, and you may make a great deal of money, but we don't need money. What we need is the happiness which we have always had until now. Now there will be companies, and patents, and lawsuits, and experiments, and people calling you a humbug, and other people saying they discovered it long ago, and all sorts of persons coming to see you, and you'll be obliged to go to all sorts of places, and you will be an altered man, and we shall never be happy again. Millions of money will not repay us for the happiness we have lost."

These words of my wife struck me with much force. Before I had called her my mind had begun to be filled and perplexed with ideas of what I ought to do now that the great invention was perfected. Until now the matter had not troubled me at all. Sometimes I had gone backward and sometimes forward, but, on the whole, I had always felt encouraged. I had taken great pleasure in the work, but I had never allowed myself to be too much absorbed by it. But now everything was different. I began to feel that it was due to myself and to my fellow-beings, that I should properly put this invention before the world. And how should I set about it? What steps should I take? I must make no mistakes. When the matter should become known hundreds of scientific people might set themselves to work; how could I tell but that they might discover other methods of producing the same effect. I must guard myself against a great many things. I must get patents in all parts of the world. Already, as I have said, my mind began to be troubled and perplexed with these things. A turmoil of this sort did not suit my age or disposition. I could not but agree with my wife that the joys of a quiet and contented life were now about to be broken into.

"My dear," said I, "I believe, with you, that the thing will do us more harm than good. If it were not for depriving the world of the invention I would throw the whole thing to the winds. And yet," I added, regretfully, "I had expected a great deal of personal gratification from the use of this invention."

"Now, listen," said my wife, eagerly, "don't you think it would be best to do this: use the thing as much as you please for your own amusement and satisfaction, but let the world wait. It has waited a long time, and let it wait a little longer. When we are dead let Herbert have the invention. He will then be old enough to judge for himself whether it will be better to take advantage of it for his own profit, or simply to give it to the public for nothing. It would be cheating him if we were to do the latter, but it would also be doing him a great wrong if we were, at his age, to load him with such a heavy responsibility. Besides, if he took it up, you could not help going into it, too."

I took my wife's advice. I wrote a careful and complete account of the invention, and, sealing it up, I gave it to my lawyers to be handed to my son after my death. If he died first, I would make other arrangements. Then I determined to get all the good and fun out of the thing that was possible without telling any one anything about it. Even Herbert, who was away from home, was not to be told of the invention.

The first thing I did was to buy a strong leathern knapsack, and inside of this I fastened my little machine, with a screw so arranged that it could be worked from the outside. Strapping this firmly to my shoulders, my wife gently turned the screw at the back until the upward tendency of the knapsack began to lift and sustain me. When I felt myself so gently supported and upheld that I seemed to weigh about thirty or forty pounds, I would set out for a walk. The knapsack did not raise me from the ground, but it gave me a very buoyant step. It was no labour at all to walk; it was a delight, an ecstasy. With the strength of a man and the weight of a child, I gaily strode along. The first day I walked half a dozen miles at a very brisk pace, and came back without feeling in the least degree tired. These walks now became one of the greatest joys of my life. When nobody was looking, I would bound over a fence, sometimes just touching it with one hand, and sometimes not touching it at all. I delighted in rough places. I sprang over streams. I jumped and I ran. I felt like Mercury himself.

I now set about making another machine, so that my wife could accompany me in my walks; but when it was finished she positively refused to use it. "I can't wear a knapsack," she said, "and there is no other good way of fastening it to me. Besides, everybody about here knows I am no walker, and it would only set them talking."

I occasionally made use of this second machine, but I will only give one instance of its application. Some repairs were needed to the foundation-walls of my barn, and a two-horse wagon, loaded with building-stone, had been brought into my yard and left there. In the evening, when the men had gone away, I took my two machines and fastened them with strong chains, one on each side of the loaded wagon. Then, gradually turning the screws, the wagon was so lifted that its weight became very greatly diminished. We had an old donkey which used to belong to Herbert, and which was now occasionally used with a small cart to bring packages from the station. I went into the barn and put the harness on the little fellow, and, bringing him out to the wagon, I attached him to it. In this position he looked very funny, with a long pole sticking out in front of him and the great wagon behind him. When all was ready, I touched him up; and, to my great delight, he moved off with the two-horse load of stone as easily as if he were drawing his own cart. I led him out into the public road, along which he proceeded without difficulty. He was an opinionated little beast, and sometimes stopped, not liking the peculiar manner in which he was harnessed; but a touch of the switch made him move on, and I soon turned him and brought the wagon back into the yard. This determined the success of my invention in one of its most important uses, and with a satisfied heart I put the donkey into the stable and went into the house.

Our trip to Europe was made a few months after this, and was mainly on our son Herbert's account. He, poor fellow, was in great trouble, and so, therefore, were we. He had become engaged, with our full consent, to a young lady in our town, the daughter of a gentleman whom we esteemed very highly. Herbert was young to be engaged to be married, but as we felt that he would never find a girl to make him so good a wife, we were entirely satisfied, especially as it was agreed on all hands that the marriage was not to take place for some time. It seemed to us that in marrying Janet Gilbert, Herbert would secure for himself, in the very beginning of his career, the most important element of a happy life. But suddenly, without any reason that seemed to us justifiable, Mr. Gilbert, the only surviving parent of Janet, broke off the match; and he and his daughter soon after left the town for a trip to the West.

This blow nearly broke poor Herbert's heart. He gave up his professional studies and came home to us, and for a time we thought he would be seriously ill. Then we took him to Europe, and after a Continental tour of a month or two we left him, at his own request, in Göttingen, where he thought it would do him good to go to work again. Then we went down to the little town in Italy where my story first finds us. My wife had suffered much in mind and body on her son's account, and for this reason I was anxious that she should take outdoor exercise, and enjoy as much as possible the bracing air of the country. I had brought with me both my little machines. One was still in my knapsack, and the other I had fastened to the inside of an enormous family trunk. As one is obliged to pay for nearly every pound of his baggage on the Continent, this saved me a great deal of money. Everything heavy was packed into this great trunk,—books, papers, the bronze, iron, and marble relics we had picked up, and all the articles that usually weigh down a tourist's baggage. I screwed up the negative gravity apparatus until the trunk could be handled with great ease by an ordinary porter. I could have made it weigh nothing at all, but this, of course, I did not wish to do. The lightness of my baggage, however, had occasioned some comment, and

I had overheard remarks which were not altogether complimentary about people travelling around with empty trunks; but this only amused me.

Desirous that my wife should have the advantage of negative gravity while taking our walks, I had removed the machine from the trunk and fastened it inside of the basket, which she could carry under her arm. This assisted her wonderfully. When one arm was tired she put the basket under the other, and thus, with one hand on my arm, she could easily keep up with the free and buoyant steps my knapsack enabled me to take. She did not object to long tramps here, because nobody knew that she was not a walker, and she always carried some wine or other refreshment in the basket, not only because it was pleasant to have with us, but because it seemed ridiculous to go about carrying an empty basket.

There were English-speaking people stopping at the hotel where we were, but they seemed more fond of driving than walking, and none of them offered to accompany us on our rambles, for which we were very glad. There was one man there, however, who was a great walker. He was an Englishman, a member of an Alpine Club, and generally went about dressed in a knickerbocker suit, with grey woollen stockings covering an enormous pair of calves. One evening this gentleman was talking to me and some others about the ascent of the Matterhorn, and I took occasion to deliver in pretty strong language my opinion upon such exploits. I declared them to be useless, foolhardy, and, if the climber had any one who loved him, wicked.

"Even if the weather should permit a view," I said, "what is that compared to the terrible risk to life? Under certain circumstances," I added (thinking of a kind of waistcoat I had some idea of making, which, set about with little negative gravity machines, all connected with a conveniently handled screw, would enable the wearer at times to dispense with his weight altogether), "such ascents might be divested of danger, and be quite admissible; but ordinarily they should be frowned upon by the intelligent public."

The Alpine Club man looked at me, especially regarding my somewhat slight figure and thinnish legs.

"It's all very well for you to talk that way," he said, "because it is easy to see that you are not up to that sort of thing."

"In conversations of this kind," I replied, "I never make personal allusions; but since you have chosen to do so, I feel inclined to invite you to walk with me to-morrow to the top of the mountain to the north of this town."

"I'll do it," he said, "at any time you choose to name." And as I left the room soon afterward I heard him laugh.

The next afternoon, about two o'clock, the Alpine Club man and myself set out for the mountain.

"What have you got in your knapsack?" he said.

"A hammer to use if I come across geological specimens, a field-glass, a flask of wine, and some other things."

"I wouldn't carry any weight, if I were you," he said.

"Oh, I don't mind it," I answered, and off we started.

The mountain to which we were bound was about two miles from the town. Its nearest side was steep, and in places almost precipitous, but it sloped away more gradually toward the north, and up that side a road led by devious windings to a village near the summit. It was not a very high mountain, but it would do for an afternoon's climb.

"I suppose you want to go up by the road," said my companion.

"Oh, no," I answered, "we won't go so far around as that. There is a path up this side, along which I have seen men driving their goats. I prefer to take that."

"All right, if you say so," he answered, with a smile; "but you'll find it pretty tough."

After a time he remarked:

"I wouldn't walk so fast, if I were you."

"Oh, I like to step along briskly," I said. And briskly on we went.

My wife had screwed up the machine in the knapsack more than usual, and walking seemed scarcely any effort at all. I carried a long alpenstock, and when we reached the mountain and began the ascent, I found that with the help of this and my knapsack I could go uphill at a wonderful rate. My companion had taken the lead, so as to show me how to climb. Making a *detour* over some rocks, I quickly passed him and went ahead. After that it was impossible for him to keep up with me. I ran up steep places, I cut off the windings of the path by lightly clambering over rocks, and even when I followed the beaten track my step was as rapid as if I had been walking on level ground.

"Look here!" shouted the Alpine Club man from below, "you'll kill yourself if you go at that rate! That's no way to climb mountains."

"It's my way!" I cried. And on I skipped.

Twenty minutes after I arrived at the summit, my companion joined me, puffing, and wiping his red face with his handkerchief.

"Confound it!" he cried, "I never came up a mountain so fast in my life."

"You need not have hurried," I said, coolly.

"I was afraid something would happen to you," he growled, "and I wanted to stop you. I never saw a person climb in such an utterly absurd way."

"I don't see why you should call it absurd," I said, smiling with an air of superiority. "I arrived here in a perfectly comfortable condition, neither heated nor wearied."

He made no answer, but walked off to a little distance, fanning himself with his hat and growling words which I did not catch. After a time I proposed to descend.

"You must be careful as you go down," he said. "It is much more dangerous to go down steep places than to climb up."

"I am always prudent," I answered, and started in advance. I found the descent of the mountain much more pleasant than the ascent. It was positively exhilarating. I jumped from rocks and bluffs eight and ten feet in height, and touched the ground as gently as if I had stepped down but two feet. I ran down steep paths, and, with the aid of my alpenstock, stopped myself in an instant. I was careful to avoid dangerous places, but the runs and jumps I made were such as no man had ever made before upon that mountainside. Once only I heard my companion's voice.

"You'll break your —— neck!" he yelled.

"Never fear!" I called back, and soon left him far above.

When I reached the bottom I would have waited for him, but my activity had warmed me up, and as a cool evening breeze was beginning to blow I thought it better not to stop and take cold. Half an hour after my arrival at the hotel I came down to the court, cool, fresh, and dressed for dinner, and just in time to meet the Alpine man as he entered, hot, dusty, and growling.

"Excuse me for not waiting for you," I said; but without stopping to hear my reason, he muttered something about waiting in a place where no one would care to stay and passed into the house.

There was no doubt that what I had done gratified my pique and tickled my vanity.

"I think now," I said, when I related the matter to my wife, "that he will scarcely say that I am not up to that sort of thing."

"I am not sure," she answered, "that it was exactly fair. He did not know how you were assisted."

"It was fair enough," I said. "He is enabled to climb well by the inherited vigour of his constitution and by his training. He did not tell me what methods of exercise he used to get those great muscles upon his legs. I am enabled to climb by the exercise of my intellect. My method is my business and his method is his business. It is all perfectly fair."

Still she persisted:

"He *thought* that you climbed with your legs, and not with your head."

And now, after this long digression, necessary to explain how a middle-aged couple of slight pedestrian ability, and loaded with a heavy knapsack and basket, should have started out on a rough walk and climb, fourteen miles in all, we will return to ourselves, standing on the little bluff and gazing out upon the sunset view. When the sky began to fade a little we turned from it and prepared to go back to the town.

"Where is the basket?" I said.

"I left it right here," answered my wife. "I unscrewed the machine and it lay perfectly flat."

"Did you afterward take out the bottles?" I asked, seeing them lying on the grass.

"Yes, I believe I did. I had to take out yours in order to get at mine."

"Then," said I, after looking all about the grassy patch on which we stood, "I am afraid you did not entirely unscrew the instrument, and that when the weight of the bottles was removed the basket gently rose into the air."

"It may be so," she said, lugubriously. "The basket was behind me as I drank my wine."

"I believe that is just what has happened," I said. "Look up there! I vow that is our basket!"

I pulled out my field-glass and directed it at a little speck high above our heads. It was the basket floating high in the air. I gave the glass to my wife to look, but she did not want to use it.

"What shall I do?" she cried. "I can't walk home without that basket. It's perfectly dreadful!" And she looked as if she was going to cry.

"Do not distress yourself," I said, although I was a good deal disturbed myself. "We shall get home very well. You shall put your hand on my shoulder, while I put my arm around you. Then you can screw up my machine a good deal higher, and it will support us both. In this way I am sure that we shall get on very well."

We carried out this plan, and managed to walk on with moderate comfort. To be sure, with the knapsack pulling me upward, and the weight of my wife pulling me down, the straps hurt me somewhat, which they had not done before. We did not spring lightly over the wall into the road, but, still clinging to each other, we clambered awkwardly over it. The road for the most part declined gently toward the town, and with moderate ease we made our way along it. But we walked much more slowly than we had done before, and it was quite dark when we reached our hotel. If it had not been for the light inside the court it would have been difficult for us to find it. A travelling-carriage was standing before the entrance, and against the light. It was necessary to pass around it, and my wife went first. I attempted to follow her, but, strange to say, there was nothing under my feet. I stepped vigorously, but only wagged my legs in the air. To my horror I found that I was rising in the air! I soon saw, by the light below me, that I was some fifteen feet from the ground. The carriage drove away, and in the darkness I was not noticed. Of course I knew what had happened. The instrument in my knapsack had been screwed up to such an intensity, in order to support both myself and my wife, that when her weight was removed the force of the negative gravity was sufficient to raise me from the ground. But I was glad to find that when I had risen to the height I have mentioned I did not go up any higher, but hung in the air, about on a level with the second tier of windows of the hotel.

I now began to try to reach the screw in my knapsack in order to reduce the force of the negative gravity; but, do what I would, I could not get my hand to it. The machine in the knapsack had been placed so as to support me in a well-balanced and comfortable way; and in doing this it had been impossible to set the screw so that I could reach it. But in a temporary arrangement of the kind this had not been considered necessary, as my wife always turned the screw for me until sufficient lifting-power had been attained. I had intended, as I have said before, to construct a negative gravity waistcoat, in which the screw should be in front, and entirely under the wearer's control; but this was a thing of the future.

When I found that I could not turn the screw I began to be much alarmed. Here I was, dangling in the air, without any means of reaching the ground. I could not expect my wife to return to look for me, as she would naturally suppose I had stopped to speak to some one. I thought of loosening myself from the knapsack, but this would not do, for I should fall heavily, and either kill myself or break some of my bones. I did not dare to call for assistance, for if any of the simple-minded inhabitants of the town had discovered me floating in the air they would have taken me for a demon, and would probably have shot at me. A moderate breeze was blowing, and it wafted me gently down the street. If it had blown me against a tree I would have seized it, and have endeavoured, so to speak, to climb down it; but there were no trees. There was a dim street lamp here and there, but reflectors above them threw their light upon the pavement, and none up to me. On many accounts I was glad that the night was so dark, for, much as I desired to get down, I wanted no one to see me in my strange position, which, to any one but myself and wife, would be utterly unaccountable. If I could rise as high as the roofs I might get on one of them, and, tearing off an armful of tiles, so load myself that I would be heavy enough to descend. But I did not rise to the eaves of any of the houses. If there had been a telegraph-pole, or anything of the kind that I could have clung to, I would have taken off the knapsack, and would have endeavoured to scramble down as well as I could. But there was nothing I could cling to. Even the water-spouts, if I could have reached the face of the houses, were imbedded in the walls. At an open window, near which I was slowly blown, I saw two little boys going to bed by the light of a dim candle. I was dreadfully afraid that they would see me and raise an alarm. I actually came so near to the window that I threw out one foot and pushed against the wall with such force that I went nearly across the street. I thought I caught sight of a frightened look on the face of one of the boys; but of this I am not sure, and I heard no cries. I still floated, dangling, down the street. What was to be done? Should I call out? In that case, if I were not shot or stoned, my strange predicament, and the secret of my invention, would be exposed to the world. If I did not do this, I must either let myself drop and be killed or mangled, or hang there and die. When, during the course of the night, the air became more rarefied, I might rise higher and higher, perhaps to an altitude of one or two hundred feet. It would then be impossible for the people to reach me and get me down, even if they were convinced that I was not a demon. I should then expire, and when the birds of the air had eaten all of me that they could devour, I should forever hang above the unlucky town, a dangling skeleton, with a knapsack on its back.

Such thoughts were not re-assuring, and I determined that if I could find no means of getting down without assistance, I would call out and run all risks; but so long as I could endure the tension of the straps I would hold out and hope for a tree or a pole. Perhaps it might rain, and my wet clothes would then become so heavy that I would descend as low as the top of a lamp-post.

As this thought was passing through my mind I saw a spark of light upon the street approaching me. I rightly imagined that it came from a tobacco-pipe, and presently I heard a voice. It was that of the Alpine Club man. Of all people in the world I did not want him to discover me, and I hung as motionless as possible. The man was speaking to another person who was walking with him.

"He is crazy beyond a doubt," said the Alpine man. "Nobody but a maniac could have gone up and down that mountain as he did! He hasn't any muscles, and one need only look at him to know that he couldn't do any climbing in a natural way. It is only the excitement of insanity that gives him strength."

The two now stopped almost under me, and the speaker continued:

"Such things are very common with maniacs. At times they acquire an unnatural strength which is perfectly wonderful. I have seen a little fellow struggle and fight so that four strong men could not hold him."

Then the other person spoke:

"I am afraid what you say is too true," he remarked. "Indeed, I have known it for some time."

At these words my breath almost stopped. It was the voice of Mr. Gilbert, my townsman, and the father of Janet. It must have been he who had arrived in the travelling-carriage. He was acquainted with the Alpine Club man, and they were talking of me. Proper or improper, I listened with all my ears.

"It is a very sad case," Mr. Gilbert continued. "My daughter was engaged to marry his son, but I broke off the match. I could not have her marry the son of a lunatic, and there could be no doubt of his condition. He has been seen—a man of his age, and the head of a family—load himself up with a heavy knapsack, which there was no earthly necessity for him to carry, and go skipping along the road for miles, vaulting over fences and jumping over rocks and ditches like a young calf or a colt. I myself saw a most heart-rending instance of how a kindly man's nature can be changed by the derangement of his intellect. I was at some distance from his house, but I plainly saw him harness a little donkey which he owns to a large two-horse waggon loaded with stone, and beat and lash the poor little beast until it drew the heavy load some distance along the public road. I would have remonstrated with him on this horrible cruelty, but he had the waggon back in his yard before I could reach him."

"Oh, there can be no doubt of his insanity," said the Alpine Club man, "and he oughtn't to be allowed to travel about in this way. Some day he will pitch his wife over a precipice just for the fun of seeing her shoot through the air."

"I am sorry he is here," said Mr. Gilbert, "for it would be very painful to meet him. My daughter and I will retire very soon, and go away as early to-morrow morning as possible, so as to avoid seeing him."

And then they walked back to the hotel.

For a few moments I hung, utterly forgetful of my condition, and absorbed in the consideration of these revelations. One idea now filled my mind. Everything must be explained to Mr. Gilbert, even if it should be necessary to have him called to me, and for me to speak to him from the upper air.

Just then I saw something white approaching me along the road. My eyes had become accustomed to the darkness, and I perceived that it was an upturned face. I recognised the hurried gait, the form; it was my wife. As she came near me I called her name, and in the same breath entreated her not to scream. It must have been an effort for her to restrain herself, but she did it.

"You must help me to get down," I said, "without anybody seeing us."

"What shall I do?" she whispered.

"Try to catch hold of this string."

Taking a piece of twine from my pocket, I lowered one end to her. But it was too short; she could not reach it. I then tied my handkerchief to it, but still it was not long enough.

"I can get more string, or handkerchiefs," she whispered, hurriedly.

"No," I said; "you could not get them up to me. But, leaning against the hotel wall, on this side, in the corner, just inside of the garden gate, are some fishing-poles. I have seen them there every day. You can easily find them in the dark. Go, please, and bring me one of those."

The hotel was not far away, and in a few minutes my wife returned with a fishing-pole. She stood on tip-toe, and reached it high in air;

but all she could do was to strike my feet and legs with it. My most frantic exertions did not enable me to get my hands low enough to touch it.

"Wait a minute," she said; and the rod was withdrawn.

I knew what she was doing. There was a hook and line attached to the pole, and with womanly dexterity she was fastening the hook to the extreme end of the rod. Soon she reached up, and gently struck at my legs. After a few attempts the hook caught in my trousers, a little below my right knee. Then there was a slight pull, a long scratch down my leg, and the hook was stopped by the top of my boot. Then came a steady downward pull, and I felt myself descending. Gently and firmly the rod was drawn down; carefully the lower end was kept free from the ground; and in a few moments my ankle was seized with a vigorous grasp. Then some one seemed to climb up me, my feet touched the ground, an arm was thrown around my neck, the hand of another arm was busy at the back of my knapsack, and I soon stood firmly in the road, entirely divested of negative gravity.

"Oh, that I should have forgotten," sobbed my wife, "and that I should have dropped your arms, and let you go up into the air! At first I thought that you had stopped below, and it was only a little while ago that the truth flashed upon me. Then I rushed out and began looking up for you. I knew that you had wax matches in your pocket, and hoped that you would keep on striking them, so that you would be seen."

"But I did not wish to be seen," I said, as we hurried to the hotel; "and I can never be sufficiently thankful that it was you who found me and brought me down. Do you know that it is Mr. Gilbert and his daughter who have just arrived? I must see him instantly. I will explain it all to you when I come upstairs."

I took off my knapsack and gave it to my wife, who carried it to our room, while I went to look for Mr. Gilbert. Fortunately I found him just as he was about to go up to his chamber. He took my offered hand, but looked at me sadly and gravely.

"Mr. Gilbert," I said, "I must speak to you in private. Let us step into this room. There is no one here."

"My friend," said Mr. Gilbert, "it will be much better to avoid discussing this subject. It is very painful to both of us, and no good can come from talking of it."

"You cannot now comprehend what it is I want to say to you," I replied. "Come in here, and in a few minutes you will be very glad that you listened to me."

My manner was so earnest and impressive that Mr. Gilbert was constrained to follow me, and we went into a small room called the smoking-room, but in which people seldom smoked, and closed the door. I immediately began my statement. I told my old friend that I had discovered, by means that I need not explain at present, that he had considered me crazy, and that now the most important object of my life was to set myself right in his eyes. I thereupon gave him the whole history of my invention, and explained the reason of the actions that had appeared to him those of a lunatic. I said nothing about the little incident of that evening. That was a mere accident, and I did not care now to speak of it.

Mr. Gilbert listened to me very attentively.

"Your wife is here?" he asked, when I had finished.

"Yes," I said; "and she will corroborate my story in every item, and no one could ever suspect her of being crazy. I will go and bring her to you."

In a few minutes my wife was in the room, had shaken hands with Mr. Gilbert, and had been told of my suspected madness. She turned pale, but smiled.

"He did act like a crazy man," she said, "but I never supposed that anybody would think him one." And tears came into her eyes.

"And now, my dear," said I, "perhaps you will tell Mr. Gilbert how I did all this."

And then she told him the story that I had told.

Mr. Gilbert looked from the one to the other of us with a troubled air.

"Of course I do not doubt either of you, or rather I do not doubt that you believe what you say. All would be right if I could bring myself to credit that such a force as that you speak of can possibly exist."

"That is a matter," said I, "which I can easily prove to you by actual demonstration. If you can wait a short time, until my wife and I have had something to eat,—for I am nearly famished, and I am sure she must be,—I will set your mind at rest upon that point."

"I will wait here," said Mr. Gilbert, "and smoke a cigar. Don't hurry yourselves. I shall be glad to have some time to think about what you have told me."

When we had finished the dinner, which had been set aside for us, I went upstairs and got my knapsack, and we both joined Mr. Gilbert in the smoking-room. I showed him the little machine, and explained, very briefly, the principle of its construction. I did not give any practical demonstration of its action, because there were people walking about the corridor who might at any moment come into the room; but, looking out of the window, I saw that the night was much clearer. The wind had dissipated the clouds, and the stars were shining brightly.

"If you will come up the street with me," said I to Mr. Gilbert, "I will show you how this thing works."

"That is just what I want to see," he answered.

"I will go with you," said my wife, throwing a shawl over her head. And we started up the street.

When we were outside the little town I found the starlight was quite sufficient for my purpose. The white roadway, the low walls, and objects about us, could easily be distinguished.

"Now," said I to Mr. Gilbert, "I want to put this knapsack on you, and let you see how it feels, and how it will help you to walk." To this he assented with some eagerness, and I strapped it firmly on him. "I will now turn this screw," said I, "until you shall become lighter and lighter."

"Be very careful not to turn it too much," said my wife earnestly.

"Oh, you may depend on me for that," said I, turning the screw very gradually.

Mr. Gilbert was a stout man, and I was obliged to give the screw a good many turns.

"There seems to be considerable hoist in it," he said directly. And then I put my arms around him, and found that I could raise him from the ground. "Are you lifting me?" he exclaimed in surprise.

"Yes; I did it with ease," I answered.

"Upon—my—word!" ejaculated Mr. Gilbert.

I then gave the screw a half turn more, and told him to walk and run. He started off, at first slowly, then he made long strides, then he began to run, and then to skip and jump. It had been many years since Mr. Gilbert had skipped and jumped. No one was in sight, and he was free to gambol as much as he pleased. "Could you give it another turn?" said he, bounding up to me. "I want to try that wall." I put on a little more negative gravity, and he vaulted over a five-foot wall with great ease. In an instant he had leaped back into the road, and in two bounds was at my side. "I came down as light as a cat," he said. "There was never anything like it." And away he went up the road, taking steps at least eight feet long, leaving my wife and me laughing heartily at the preternatural agility of our stout friend. In a few minutes he was with us again. "Take it off," he said. "If I wear it any longer I shall want one myself, and then I shall be taken for a crazy man, and perhaps clapped into an asylum."

"Now," said I, as I turned back the screw before unstrapping the knapsack, "do you understand how I took long walks, and leaped and jumped; how I ran uphill and downhill, and how the little donkey drew the loaded wagon?"

"I understand it all," cried he. "I take back all I ever said or thought about you, my friend."

"And Herbert may marry Janet?" cried my wife.

"*May* marry her!" cried Mr. Gilbert. "Indeed he *shall* marry her, if I have anything to say about it! My poor girl has been drooping ever since I told her it could not be."

My wife rushed at him, but whether she embraced him or only shook his hands I cannot say; for I had the knapsack in one hand, and was rubbing my eyes with the other.

"But, my dear fellow," said Mr. Gilbert directly, "if you still consider it to your interest to keep your invention a secret, I wish you had never made it. No one having a machine like that can help using it, and it is often quite as bad to be considered a maniac as to be one."

"My friend," I cried, with some excitement, "I have made up my mind on this subject. The little machine in this knapsack, which is the only one I now possess, has been a great pleasure to me. But I now know it has also been of the greatest injury indirectly to me and mine, not to mention some direct inconvenience and danger, which I will speak of another time. The secret lies with us three, and we will keep it. But the invention itself is too full of temptation and danger for any of us."

As I said this I held the knapsack with one hand while I quickly turned the screw with the other. In a few moments it was high above my head, while I with difficulty held it down by the straps. "Look!" I cried. And then I released my hold, and the knapsack shot into the air and disappeared into the upper gloom.

I was about to make a remark, but had no chance, for my wife threw herself upon my bosom, sobbing with joy.

"Oh, I am so glad—so glad!" she said. "And you will never make another?"

"Never another!" I answered.

"And now let us hurry in and see Janet," said my wife.

"You don't know how heavy and clumsy I feel," said Mr. Gilbert, striving to keep up with us as we walked back. "If I had worn that thing much longer, I should never have been willing to take it off!"

Janet had retired, but my wife went up to her room. "I think she has felt it as much as our boy," she said, when she rejoined me. "But I tell you, my dear, I left a very happy girl in that little bed-chamber over the garden."

And there were three very happy elderly people talking together until quite late that evening. "I shall write to Herbert to-night," I said, when we separated, "and tell him to meet us all in Geneva. It will do the young man no harm if we interrupt his studies just now."

"You must let me add a postscript to the letter," said Mr. Gilbert, "and I am sure it will require no knapsack with a screw in the back to bring him quickly to us."

And it did not.

There is a wonderful pleasure in tripping over the earth like a winged Mercury, and in feeling one's self relieved of much of that attraction of gravitation which drags us down to earth, and gradually makes the movement of our bodies but weariness and labour. But this pleasure is not to be compared, I think, to that given by the buoyancy and lightness of two young and loving hearts, reunited after a separation which they had supposed would last for ever.

What became of the basket and the knapsack, or whether they ever met in upper air, I do not know. If they but float away and stay away from ken of mortal man, I shall be satisfied.

And whether or not the world will ever know more of the power of negative gravity depends entirely upon the disposition of my son Herbert, when—after a good many years, I hope—he shall open the packet my lawyers have in keeping.

[NOTE.—It would be quite useless for any one to interview my wife on this subject, for she has entirely forgotten how my machine was made. And as for Mr. Gilbert, he never knew.]

※ ※ ※

MARK TWAIN (SAMUEL L. CLEMENS)
(1835-1910)

THE first and greatest humorist in American literature was born November 30, 1835, at Florida, Missouri. He became a Mississippi River pilot and loved to hear on a dark night the pleasant sound that meant safe water—mark twain. He first used it as a *nom de plume* in 1863, since when it has proved the greatest of all pen names. After the Civil War and prospecting in California, Mark Twain turned definitely to writing. In the *Saturday Press* (New York), November 18, 1865, appeared *Jim Smiley and His Jumping Frog*, a story that set in motion the author's fame. (The tale was given the new title when published in his first collection: *The Celebrated Jumping Frog of Calaveras County, and Other Sketches.*) Many sketches, novels, and dramas followed, including *Innocents Abroad*, *A Connecticut Yankee at King Arthur's Court*, *Tom Sawyer*, *Huckleberry Finn* and *Saint Joan*. Mark Twain was a great traveller, having early visited Russia, Syria, and Spain before establishing his home in New York. Later he visited England, Scotland, Italy, Bermuda, and went on a lecturing tour around the world. On June 26, 1907, he was honoured at Oxford with the degree of Litt.D. He died April 21, 1910, at Stormfield, Redding, Connecticut.

The Celebrated Jumping Frog of Calaveras County is reprinted by arrangement with and permission of Harper and Brothers, New York City.

THE CELEBRATED JUMPING FROG OF CALAVERAS COUNTY

IN compliance with the request of a friend of mine, who wrote me from the East, I called on good-natured, garrulous old Simon Wheeler, and inquired after my friend's friend, *Leonidas W*. Smiley, as requested to do, and I hereunto append the result. I have a lurking suspicion that *Leonidas W*. Smiley is a myth; that my friend never knew such a personage; and that he only conjectured that, if I asked old Wheeler about him, it would remind him of his infamous *Jim* Smiley, and he would go to work and bore me nearly to death with some infernal reminiscence of him as long and tedious as it should be useless to me. If that was the design, it certainly succeeded.

I found Simon Wheeler dozing comfortably by the bar-room stove of the old, dilapidated tavern in the ancient mining camp of Angel's, and I noticed that he was fat and bald-headed, and had an expression of winning gentleness and simplicity upon his tranquil countenance. He roused up and gave me good-day. I told him a friend of mine had commissioned me to make some inquiries about a cherished companion of his boyhood named *Leonidas W*. Smiley—*Rev. Leonidas W*. Smiley—a young minister of the Gospel, who he had heard was at one time a resident of Angel's Camp. I added, that, if Mr. Wheeler could tell me anything about this Rev. Leonidas W. Smiley, I would feel under many obligations to him.

Simon Wheeler backed me into a corner and blockaded me there with his chair, and then sat me down and reeled off the monotonous narrative which follows this paragraph. He never smiled, he never frowned, he never changed his voice from the gentle-flowing key to which he tuned the initial sentence, he never betrayed the slightest suspicion of enthusiasm; but all through the interminable narrative there ran a vein of impressive earnestness and sincerity, which showed me plainly that, so far from his imagining that there was anything ridiculous or funny about his story, he regarded it as a really important matter, and admitted its two heroes as men of transcendent genius in *finesse*. To me, the spectacle of a man drifting serenely along through such a queer yarn without ever smiling, was exquisitely absurd. As I said before, I asked him to tell me what he knew of Rev. Leonidas W. Smiley, and he replied as follows. I let him go on in his own way, and never interrupted him once:

There was a feller here once by the name of *Jim* Smiley, in the winter of '49—or maybe it was the spring of '50—I don't recollect exactly, somehow, though what makes me think it was one or the other is because I remember the big flume wasn't finished when he first came to the camp; but anyway, he was the curiousest man about always betting on anything that turned up you ever see, if he could get anybody to bet on the other side; and if he couldn't, he'd change sides. Any way what suited the other man would suit him—any way just so's he got a bet, *he* was satisfied. But still he was lucky, uncommon lucky—he most always come out winner. He was always ready and laying for a chance; there couldn't be no solit'ry thing mentioned but that feller'd offer to bet on it, and take any side you please, as I was just telling you. If there was a horse-race, you'd find him flush, or you'd find him busted at the end of it; if there was a dog-fight, he'd bet on it; if there was a cat-fight, he'd bet on it; if there was a chicken-fight, he'd bet on it; why, if there was two birds setting on a fence, he would bet you which one would fly first; or if there was a camp-meeting, he would be there reg'lar, to be on Parson Walker, which he judged to be the best exhorter about here, and so he was, too, and a good man. If he even seen a straddle-bug start to go anywheres, he would bet you how long it would take him to get wherever he was going to, and if you took him up, he would foller that straddle-bug to Mexico but what he would find out where he was bound for and how long he was on the road. Lots of the boys here has seen that Smiley, and can tell you about him. Why, it never made no difference to *him*—he would bet on *any*thing—the dangdest feller. Parson Walker's wife laid very sick once, for a good while, and it seemed as if they warn't going to save her; but one morning he came in, and Smiley asked how she was, and he said she was considerable better—thank the Lord for his inf'nit mercy—and coming on so smart that, with the blessing of Prov'dence, she'd get well yet; and Smiley, before he thought, says, "Well, I'll risk two-and-a-half that she don't, anyway."

Thish-yer Smiley had a mare—the boys called her the fifteen-minute nag, but that was only in fun, you know, because, of course, she was faster than that—and he used to win money on that horse, for all she was so slow and always had the asthma, or the distemper, or the consumption, or something of that kind. They used to give her two or three hundred yards start, and then pass her under way, but always at the fag-end of the race she'd get excited and desperate-like, and come cavorting and straddling up, and scattering her legs around limber, sometimes in the air, and sometimes out to one side amongst the fences, and kicking up m-o-r-e dust, and raising m-o-r-e racket with her coughing and sneezing and blowing her nose—and always fetch up at the stand just about a neck ahead, as near as you could cipher it down.

And he had a little small bull pup, that to look at him you'd think he wan't worth a cent but to set around and look ornery and lay for a chance to steal something. But as soon as money was up on him, he was a different dog; his under-jaw'd begin to stick out like the fo'castle of a steam-boat, and his teeth would uncover, and shine savage like the furnaces. And a dog might tackle him, and bully-rag him, and bite him, and throw him over his shoulder two or three times, and Andrew Jackson —which was the name of the pup—Andrew Jackson would never let on but what *he* was satisfied, and hadn't expected nothing else—and the bets being doubled and doubled on the other side all the time, till the money was all up, and then all of a sudden he would grab that other dog jest by the j'int of his hind leg and freeze to it—not claw, you understand, but only jest grip and hang on till they throwed up the sponge, if it was a year. Smiley always come out winner on that pup, till he harnessed a dog once that didn't have no hind legs, because they'd been sawed off by a circular saw, and when the thing had gone along far enough, and the money was all up, and he come to make a snatch for his pet holt, he saw in a minute how he'd been imposed on, and how the other dog had him in the door, so to speak, and he 'peared surprised, and then he looked sorter discouraged-like, and didn't try no more to win the fight, and so he got shucked out bad. He give Smiley a look, as much to say his heart was broke and it was *his* fault for putting up a dog that hadn't no hind legs for him to take holt of, which was his main dependence in a fight, and then he limped off a piece and laid down and died. It was a good pup, was that Andrew Jackson, and would have made a name for hisself if he'd lived, for the stuff was in him, and he had genius—I know it, because he hadn't no opportunities to speak of, and it don't stand to reason that a dog could make such a fight as he could under them circumstances, if he hadn't no talent. It always makes me feel sorry when I think of that last fight of his'n, and the way it turned out.

Well, thish-yer Smiley had rat-tarriers, and chicken-cocks, and torn-cats, and all them kind of things, till you couldn't rest, and you couldn't fetch nothing for him to bet on but he'd match you. He ketched a frog one day, and took him home, and said he cal'klated to edercate him; and so he never done nothing for these three months but set in his back yard and learn that frog to jump. And you bet you he *did* learn him, too. He'd give him a little punch behind, and the next minute you'd see that frog whirling in the air like a doughnut—see him turn one summerset, or maybe a couple, if he got a good start, and come down flat-footed and all right, like a cat. He got him up so in the matter of catching flies, and kept him in practice so constant, that he'd nail a fly every time as far as he could see him. Smiley said all a frog wanted was education, and he could do most anything—and I believe him. Why, I've seen him set Dan'l Webster down here on this floor—Dan'l Webster was the name of the frog—and sing out, "Flies, Dan'l, flies!" and quicker'n you could wink, he'd spring straight up, and snake a fly off'n the counter there, and flop down on the floor again as solid as a gob of mud, and fall to scratching the side of his head with his hind foot as indifferent as if he hadn't no idea he's been doin' any more'n any frog might do. You never see a frog so modest and straight-for'ard as he was, for all he was so gifted.

And when it come to fair and square jumping on the dead level, he could get over more ground at one straddle than any animal of his breed you ever see. Jumping on a dead level was his strong suit, you understand; and when it come to that, Smiley, would ante up money on him as long as he had a red. Smiley was monstrous proud of his frog, and well he might be, for fellers that had travelled and been everywhere all said he laid over any frog that ever *they* see.

Well, Smiley kept the beast in a little lattice box, and he used to fetch him downtown sometimes and lay for a bet. One day a feller—a stranger in the camp, he was—come across him with his box, and says:

"What might it be that you've got in the box?"

And Smiley says, sorter indifferent like, "It might be a parrot, or it might be a canary, maybe, but it ain't—it's only just a frog."

An' the feller took it, and looked at it careful, and turned it round this way and that, and says, "H'm—so 'tis. Well, what's *he* good for?"

"Well," Smiley says, easy and careless, "he's good enough for *one* thing, I should judge—he can outjump any frog in Calaveras county."

The feller took the box again, and took another long, particular look, and give it back to Smiley, and says, very deliberate, "Well, I don't see no p'ints about that frog that's any better'n any other frog."

"Maybe you don't," Smiley says. "Maybe you understand frogs, and maybe you don't understand 'em; maybe you've had experience, and maybe you ain't only a amature, as it were. Anyways, I've got *my* opinion, and I'll risk forty dollars that he can outjump any frog in Calaveras county."

And the feller studied a minute, and then says, kinder sad like, "Well, I'm only a stranger here, and I ain't got no frog; but if I had a frog, I'd bet you."

And then Smiley says, "That's all right—that's all right—if you'll hold my box a minute, I'll go and get you a frog." And so the feller took the box, and put up his forty dollars along with Smiley's, and set down to wait.

So he set there a good while thinking and thinking to hisself, and then he got the frog out and pried his mouth open and took a teaspoon and filled him full of quail shot—filled him pretty near up to his chin—and set him on the floor. Smiley he went to the swamp and slopped around in the mud for a long time, and finally he ketched a frog, and fetched him in, and give him to this feller, and says:

"Now, if you're ready, set him alongside of Dan'l, with his forepaws just even with Dan'l, and I'll give the word." Then he says, "One-two-three-jump!" and him and the feller touched up the frogs from behind, and the new frog hopped off, but Dan'l give a heave, and hysted up his shoulders—so—like a Frenchman, but it wasn't no use—he couldn't budge; he was planted as solid as an anvil, and he couldn't no more stir than if he was anchored out. Smiley was a good deal surprised, and he was disgusted too, but he didn't have no idea what the matter was, of course.

The feller took the money and started away; and when he was going out at the door, he sorter jerked his thumb over his shoulder—this way at Dan'l, and says again, very deliberate, "Well *I* don't see no p'ints about that frog that's any better'n any other frog."

Smiley he stood scratching his head and looking down at Dan'l a long time, and at last he says, "I do wonder what in the nation that frog throw'd off for—I wonder if there ain't something the matter with him— he 'pears to look mighty baggy, somehow. And he ketched Dan'l by the nap of the neck, and lifted him up and says, "Why, blame my cats, if he don't weight five pounds!" and turned him upside down, and he belched out a double handful of shot. And then he see how it was, and he was the maddest man—he set the frog down and took out after that feller, but he never ketched him. And—

(Here Simon Wheeler heard his name called from the front yard, and got up to see what was wanted.) And turning to me as he moved away, he said: "Just set where you are, stranger, and rest easy—I ain't going to be gone a second."

But, by your leave, I did not think that a continuation of the history of the enterprising vagabond *Jim* Smiley would be likely to afford me much information concerning the Rev. *Leonidas W.* Smiley, and so I started away.

At the door I met the sociable Wheeler returning, and he buttonholed me and recommenced:

"Well, thish-yer Smiley had a yeller one-eyed cow that didn't have no tail, only jest a short stump like a bannanner, and—"

"Oh, hang Smiley and his afflicted cow!" I muttered, good-naturedly, and bidding the old gentleman good-day, I departed.

❋ ❋ ❋

FRANCIS BRET HARTE
(1839-1902)

THOUGH a New Yorker by birth (Albany, August 25, 1839), and an English resident the last third of his life, Bret Harte is associated with the western United States. Following the adventurers of '49, he had a varied experience in the new country, at length settling in San Francisco. Editor of *The Overland Monthly* (1868), he contributed to his second number *The Luck of Roaring Camp*, a story whose instant popularity turned his fortunes. In 1871 he came to New York, but he continued to write of western scenes and characters. In 1878 he accepted the consulate at Crefeld, whence he went to England (1879), where he lived until May 5, 1902. He lies buried in Camberley, Surrey. As he was influenced by Dickens he, in turn, influenced the early work of Kipling. First of the local colourists, a humourist, an impressionist, he was adapted to the medium of the short story and one of the first to mould its form and style. From 1867 to 1902 he published more than twenty volumes of sketches and tales.

The Postmistress of Laurel Run is from *Colonel Starbottle's Client* (1892) and is reprinted by permission of Houghton Mifflin and Company, Boston, Massachusetts.

THE POSTMISTRESS OF LAUREL RUN

THE mail stage had just passed Laurel Run,—so rapidly that the whirling cloud of dust dragged with it down the steep grade from the summit hung over the level long after the stage had vanished, and then, drifting away, slowly sifted a red precipitate over the hot platform of the Laurel Run post-office.

Out of this cloud presently emerged the neat figure of the postmistress with the mail-bag which had been dexterously flung at her feet from the top of the passing vehicle. A dozen loungers eagerly stretched out their hands to assist her, but the warning: "It's again the rules, boys, for any but her to touch it," from a bystander, and a coquettish shake of the head from the postmistress herself—much more effective than any official interdict—withheld them. The bag was not heavy,—Laurel Run was too recent a settlement to have attracted much correspondence,—and the young woman, having pounced upon her prey with a certain feline instinct, dragged it, not without difficulty, behind the partitioned inclosure in the office, and locked the door. Her pretty face, momentarily visible through the window, was slightly flushed with the exertion, and the loose ends of her fair hair, wet with perspiration, curled themselves over her forehead into tantalising little rings. But the window shutter was quickly closed, and this momentary but charming vision withdrawn from the waiting public.

"Guv'ment oughter have more sense than to make a woman pick mail-bags outer the road," said Jo Simmons sympathetically. "'Tain't in her day's work anyhow; Guv'ment oughter hand 'em over to her like a lady; it's rich enough and ugly enough."

"'Tain't Guv'ment; it's that stage company's airs and graces," interrupted a newcomer. "They think it mighty fine to go beltin' by, makin' everybody take their dust, just because *stoppin'* ain't in their contract. Why, if that expressman who chucked down the bag had any feelin's for a lady"—but he stopped here at the amused faces of his auditors.

"Guess you don't know much o' that expressman's feelin's, stranger," said Simmons grimly. "Why, you oughter see him just nussin' that bag like a baby as he comes tearin' down the grade, and then rise up and sorter heave it to Mrs. Baker ez if it was a five-dollar bokay! His feelin's for her! Why, he's give himself so dead away to her that we're looking for him to forget what he's doin' next, and just come sailin' down hisself at her feet."

Meanwhile, on the other side of the partition, Mrs. Baker had brushed the red dust from the padlocked bag, and removed what seemed to be a supplementary package attached to it by a wire. Opening it she found a handsome scent-bottle, evidently a superadded gift from the devoted expressman. This she put aside with a slight smile and the murmured word, "Foolishness." But when she had unlocked the bag, even its sacred interior was also profaned by a covert parcel from the adjacent post-master at Burnt Ridge, containing a gold "specimen" brooch and some circus tickets. It was laid aside with the other. This also was vanity and —presumably—vexation of spirit.

There were seventeen letters in all, of which five were for herself— and yet the proportion was small that morning. Two of them were marked "Official Business," and were promptly put by with feminine discernment; but in another compartment than that holding the presents. Then the shutter was opened, and the task of delivery commenced.

It was accompanied with a social peculiarity that had in time become a habit of Laurel Run. As the young woman delivered the letters, in turn, to the men who were patiently drawn up in Indian file, she made that simple act a medium of privileged but limited conversation on special or general topics,—gay or serious as the case might be, or the temperament of the man suggested. That it was almost always of a complimentary character on their part may be readily imagined; but it was invariably characterised by an element of refined restraint, and, whether from some implied understanding or individual sense of honour, it never passed the bounds of conventionality or a certain delicacy of respect. The delivery was consequently more or less protracted, but when each man had exchanged his three or four minutes' conversation with the fair postmistress, —a conversation at times impeded by bashfulness or timidity, on his part solely, or restricted often to vague smiling,—he resignedly made way for the next. It was a formal levee, mitigated by the informality of rustic tact, great good-humour, and infinite patience, and would have been amusing had it not always been terribly in earnest and at times touching. For it was peculiar to the place and the epoch, and indeed implied the whole history of Mrs. Baker.

She was the wife of John Baker, foreman of "The Last Chance," now for a year lying dead under half a mile of crushed and beaten-in tunnel at Burnt Ridge. There had been a sudden outcry from the depths at high hot noontide one day, and John had rushed from his cabin—his young, foolish, flirting wife clinging to him—to answer that despairing cry of his imprisoned men. There was one exit that he alone knew which might be yet held open, among falling walls and tottering timbers, long enough to set them free. For one moment only the strong man hesitated between her entreating arms and his brothers' despairing cry. But she rose suddenly with a pale face, and said, "Go, John; I will wait for you here." He went, the men were freed—but she had waited for him ever since!

Yet in the shock of the calamity and in the after struggles of that poverty which had come to the ruined camp, she had scarcely changed. But the men had. Although she was to all appearances the same giddy, pretty Betsy Baker, who had been so disturbing to the younger members, they seemed to be no longer disturbed by her. A certain subdued awe and respect, as if the martyred spirit of John Baker still held his arm around her, appeared to have come upon them all. They held their breath as this pretty woman, whose brief mourning had not seemed to affect her cheerfulness or even playfulness of spirit, passed before them. But she stood by her cabin and the camp—the only woman in a settlement of forty men—during the darkest hours of their fortune. Helping them to wash and cook, and ministering to their domestic needs, the sanctity of her cabin was, however, always kept as inviolable as if it had been *his* tomb. No one exactly knew why, for it was only a tacit instinct; but even one or two who had not scrupled to pay court to Betsy Baker during John Baker's life, shrank from even a suggestion of familiarity towards the woman who had said that she would "wait for him there."

When brighter days came and the settlement had increased by one or two families, and laggard capital had been hurried up to relieve the still beleaguered and locked-up wealth of Burnt Ridge, the needs of the community and the claims of the widow of John Baker were so well told in political quarters that the post-office of Laurel Run was created expressly for her. Every man participated in the building of the pretty yet substantial edifice—the only public building of Laurel Run—that stood in the dust of the great highway, half a mile from the settlement. There she was installed for certain hours of the day, for she could not be prevailed upon to abandon John's cabin, and here, with all the added respect due to a public functionary, she was secure in her privacy.

But the blind devotion of Laurel Run to John Baker's relict did not stop here. In its zeal to assure the Government authorities of the necessity for a post-office, and to secure a permanent competency to the postmistress, there was much embarrassing extravagance. During the first week the sale of stamps at Laurel Run post-office was unprecedented in the annals of the Department. Fancy prices were given for the first issue; then they were bought wildly, recklessly, unprofitably, and on all occasions. Complimentary congratulation at the little window invariably ended with "and a dollar's worth of stamps, Mrs. Baker." It was felt to be supremely delicate to buy only the highest priced stamps, without reference to their adequacy; then mere *quantity* was sought; then outgoing letters were all over-paid and stamped in outrageous proportion to their weight and even size. The imbecility of this, and its probable effect on the reputation of Laurel Run at the General Post-office, being pointed out by Mrs. Baker, stamps were adopted as local currency, and even for decorative purposes on mirrors and the walls of cabins. Everybody wrote letters, with the result, however, that those *sent* were ludicrously and suspiciously in excess of those received. To obviate this, select parties made forced journeys to Hickory Hill, the next post-office, with letters and circulars addressed to themselves at Laurel Run. How long the extravagance would have continued is not known, but it was not until it was rumoured that, in consequence of this excessive flow of business, the Department had concluded that a post*master* would be better fitted for the place that it abated, and a compromise was effected with the General Office by a permanent salary to the postmistress.

Such was the history of Mrs. Baker, who had just finished her afternoon levee, nodded a smiling "good-bye" to her last customer, and closed her shutter again. Then she took up her own letters, but, before reading them, glanced, with a pretty impatience, at the two official envelopes addressed to herself, which she had shelved. They were generally a "lot of new rules," or notifications, or "absurd" questions which had nothing to do with Laurel Run and only bothered her and "made her head ache," and she had usually referred them to her admiring neighbour at Hickory Hill for explanation, who had generally returned them to her with the brief indorsement, "Purp stuff, don't bother," or, "Hog wash, let it slide." She remembered now that he had not returned the last two. With knitted brows and a slight pout she put aside her private correspondence and tore open the first one. It referred with official curtness to an unanswered communication of the previous week, and was "compelled to remind her of rule 47." Again those horrid rules! She opened the other; the frown deepened on her brow, and became fixed.

It was a summary of certain valuable money letters that had miscarried on the route, and of which they had given her previous information. For a moment her cheeks blazed. How dare they; what did they mean! Her waybills and register were always right; she knew the names of every man, woman, and child in her district; no such names as those borne by the missing letters had ever existed at Laurel Run; no such addresses had ever been sent from Laurel Run post-office. It was a mean insinuation! She would send in her resignation at once! She would get "the boys" to write an insulting letter to Senator Slocumb,—Mrs. Baker had the feminine idea of Government as a purely personal institution,—and she would find out who it was that had put them up to this prying, crawling impudence! It was probably that wall-eyed old wife of the postmaster at Heavy Tree Crossing, who was jealous of her. "Remind her of their previous unanswered communication," indeed! Where was that communication, anyway? She remembered she had sent it to her admirer at Hickory Hill. Odd that he hadn't answered it. Of course, he knew about this meanness—could he, too, have dared to suspect her! The thought turned her crimson again. He, Stanton Green, was an old "Laurel Runner," a friend of John's, a little "triflin' " and "presoomin'," but still an old loyal pioneer of the camp! "Why hadn't he spoke up?"

There was the soft, muffled fall of a horse's hoof in the thick dust of the highway, the jingle of dismounting spurs, and a firm tread on the platform. No doubt one of the boys returning for a few supplemental remarks under the feeble pretence of forgotten stamps. It had been done before, and she had resented it as "cayotin' round;" but now she was eager to pour out her wrongs to the first comer. She had her hand impulsively on the door of the partition, when she stopped with a new sense of her impaired dignity. Could she confess this to her worshippers? But here the door opened in her very face, and a stranger entered.

He was a man of fifty, compactly and strongly built. A squarely-cut goatee, slightly streaked with grey, fell straight from his thin-lipped but handsome mouth; his eyes were dark, humorous, yet searching. But the distinctive quality that struck Mrs. Baker was the blending of urban ease with frontier frankness. He was evidently a man who had seen cities and knew countries as well. And while he was dressed with the comfortable simplicity of a Californian mounted traveller, her inexperienced but feminine eye detected the keynote of his respectability in the carefully-tied bow of his cravat. The Sierrean throat was apt to be open, free, and unfettered.

"Good-morning, Mrs. Baker," he said, pleasantly, with his hat already in his hand. "I'm Harry Home, of San Francisco." As he spoke his eye swept approvingly over the neat inclosure, the primly-tied papers, and well-kept pigeon-holes; the pot of flowers on her desk; her china-silk mantle, and killing little chip hat and ribbons hanging against the wall; thence to her own pink, flushed face, bright blue eyes, tendriled clinging hair, and then—fell upon the leathern mail-bag still lying across the table. Here it became fixed on the unfortunate wire of the amorous expressman that yet remained hanging from the brass wards of the lock, and he reached his hand toward it.

But little Mrs. Baker was before him, and had seized it in her arms. She had been too preoccupied and bewildered to resent his first intrusion behind the partition, but this last familiarity with her sacred official property—albeit empty—capped the climax of her wrongs.

"How dare you touch it!" she said indignantly. "How dare you come in here! Who are you, anyway? Go outside, at once!"

The stranger fell back with an amused, deprecatory gesture, and a long silent laugh. "I'm afraid you don't know me, after all!" he said pleasantly. "I'm Harry Home, the Department Agent from the San Francisco office. My note of advice, No. 201, with my name on the envelope, seems to have miscarried too."

Even in her fright and astonishment it flashed upon Mrs. Baker that she had sent that notice, too, to Hickory Hill. But with it all the feminine secretive instinct within her was now thoroughly aroused, and she kept silent.

"I ought to have explained," he went on smilingly; "but you are quite right, Mrs. Baker," he added, nodding towards the bag. "As far as you knew, I had no business to go near it. Glad to see you know how to defend Uncle Sam's property so well. I was only a bit puzzled to know" (pointing to the wire) "if that thing was on the bag when it was delivered to you?"

Mrs. Baker saw no reason to conceal the truth. After all, this official was a man like the others, and it was just as well that he should understand her power. "It's only the expressman's foolishness," she said, with a slightly coquettish toss of her head. "He thinks it smart to tie some nonsense on that bag with the wire when he flings it down."

Mr. Home, with his eyes on her pretty face, seemed to think it a not inhuman or unpardonable folly. "As long as he doesn't meddle with the inside of the bag, I suppose you must put up with it," he said laughingly. A dreadful recollection, that the Hickory Hill postmaster had used the inside of the bag to convey *his* foolishness, came across her. It would never do to confess it now. Her face must have shown some agitation, for the official resumed with a half-paternal, half-reassuring air: "But enough of this. Now, Mrs. Baker, to come to my business here. Briefly, then, it doesn't concern you in the least, except so far as it may relieve you and some others, whom the Department knows equally well, from a certain responsibility, and, perhaps, anxiety. We are pretty well posted down there in all that concerns Laurel Run, and I think" (with a slight bow) "we've known all about you and John Baker. My only business here is to take your place to-night in receiving the "Omnibus Way Bag," that you know arrives here at 9.30, doesn't it?"

"Yes, sir," said Mrs. Baker hurriedly; "but it never has anything for us, except"——(she caught herself up quickly, with a stammer, as she remembered the sighing Green's occasional offerings) "except a notification from Hickory Hill post-office. It leaves there," she went on with an affectation of precision, "at half past eight exactly, and it's about an hour's run——seven miles by road."

"Exactly," said Mr. Home. "Well, *I* will receive the bag, open it, and dispatch it again. You can, if you choose, take a holiday."

"But," said Mrs. Baker, as she remembered that Laurel Run always made a point of attending her evening levee on account of the superior leisure it offered, "there are the people who come for letters, you know."

"I thought you said there were no letters at that time," said Mr. Home quickly.

"No—but—but"—(with a slight hysterical stammer) "the boys come all the same."

"Oh!" said Mr. Home dryly.

"And—O Lord!"— But here the spectacle of the possible discomfiture of Laurel Run at meeting the bearded face of Mr. Home, instead of her own smooth cheeks, at the window, combined with her nervous excitement, overcame her so that, throwing her little frilled apron over her head, she gave way to a paroxysm of hysterical laughter. Mr. Home waited with amused toleration for it to stop, and, when she had recovered, resumed. "Now, I should like to refer an instant to my first communication to you. Have you got it handy?"

Mrs. Baker's face fell. "No; I sent it over to Mr. Green, of Hickory Hill, for information."

"What!"

Terrified at the sudden seriousness of the man's voice, she managed to gasp out, however, that, after her usual habit, she had not opened the official letters, but had sent them to her more experienced colleague for advice and information; that she never could understand them herself,— they made her head ache, and interfered with her other duties,—but he understood them, and sent her word what to do. Remembering also his usual style of indorsement, she grew red again.

"And what did he say?"

"Nothing; he didn't return them."

"Naturally," said Mr. Home, with a peculiar expression. After a few moments' silent stroking of his beard, he suddenly faced the frightened woman.

"You oblige me, Mrs. Baker, to speak more frankly to you than I had intended. You have—unwittingly, I believe—given information to a man whom the Government suspects of peculation. You have, without knowing it, warned the postmaster at Hickory Hill that he is suspected; and, as you might have frustrated our plans for tracing a series of embezzlements to their proper source, you will see that you might have also done great wrong to yourself as his only neighbour and the next responsible person. In plain words, we have traced the disappearance of money letters to a point when it lies between these two offices. Now, I have not the least hesitation in telling you that we do not suspect Laurel Run, and never have suspected it. Even the result of your thoughtless act, although it warned him, confirms our suspicion of his guilt. As to the warning, it has failed, or he has grown reckless, for another letter has been missed since. To-night, however, will settle all doubt in the matter. When I open that bag in this office to-night, and do not find a certain decoy letter in it, which was last checked at Heavy Tree Crossing, I shall know that it remains in Green's possession at Hickory Hill."

She was sitting back in her chair, white and breathless. He glanced at her kindly, and then took up his hat. "Come, Mrs. Baker, don't let this worry you. As I told you at first, *you* have nothing to fear. Even your thoughtlessness and ignorance of rules have contributed to show your own innocence. Nobody will ever be the wiser for this; we do not advertise our affairs in the Department. Not a soul but yourself knows the real cause of my visit here. I will leave you here alone for a while, so as to divert any suspicion. You will come, as usual, this evening, and be seen by your friends; I will only be here when the bag arrives, to open it. Good-bye, Mrs. Baker; it's a nasty bit of business, but it's all in the day's work. I've seen worse, and, thank God, you're out of it."

She heard his footsteps retreat into the outer office and die out of the platform; the jingle of his spurs, and the hollow beat of his horse's hoofs that seemed to find a dull echo in her own heart, and she was alone.

The room was very hot and very quiet; she could hear the warping and creaking of the shingles under the relaxing of the nearly level sunbeams. The office clock struck seven. In the breathless silence that followed, a woodpecker took up his interrupted work on the roof, and seemed to beat out monotonously on her ear the last words of the stranger: Stanton Green—a thief! Stanton Green, one of the "boys" John had helped out of the falling tunnel! Stanton Green, whose old mother in the States still wrote letters to him at Laurel Run, in a few hours to be a disgraced and ruined man forever! She remembered now, as a thoughtless woman remembers, tales of his extravagance and fast living, of which she had taken no heed, and, with a sense of shame, of presents sent her, that she now clearly saw must have been far beyond his means. What would the boys say? What would John have said? Ah! what would John have *done!*

She started suddenly to her feet, white and cold as on that day that she had parted from John Baker before the tunnel. She put on her hat and mantle, and going to that little iron safe that stood in the corner, unlocked it and took out its entire contents of gold and silver. She had reached the door when another idea seized her, and opening her desk she collected her stamps to the last sheet, and hurriedly rolled them up under her cape. Then with a glance at the clock, and a rapid survey of the road from the platform, she slipped from it, and seemed to be swallowed up in the waiting woods beyond.

Once within the friendly shadows of the long belt of pines, Mrs. Baker kept them until she had left the limited settlement of Laurel Run far to the right, and came upon an open slope of Burnt Ridge, where she knew Jo Simmons' mustang, Blue Lightning, would be quietly feeding. She had often ridden him before, and when she had detached the fifty-foot reata from his head-stall, he permitted her the further recognised familiarity of twining her fingers in his bluish mane and climbing on his back. The tool-shed of Burnt Ridge Tunnel, where Jo's saddle and bridle always hung, was but a canter farther on. She reached it unperceived, and—another trick of the old days—quickly extemporised a side-saddle from Simmons' Mexican tree, with its high cantle and horn bow, and the aid of a blanket. Then leaping to her seat, she rapidly threw off her mantle, tied it by its sleeves around her waist, tucked it under one knee, and let it fall over her horse's flanks. By this time Blue Lightning was also struck with a flash of equine recollection and pricked up his ears. Mrs. Baker uttered a little chirping cry which he remembered, and the next moment they were both careering over the Ridge.

The trail that she had taken, though precipitate, difficult, and dangerous in places, was a clear gain of two miles on the stage road. There was less chance of her being followed or meeting any one. The greater cañons were already in shadow; the pines on the farther ridges were separating their masses, and showing individual silhouettes against the sky, but the air was still warm, and the cool breath of night, as she well knew it, had not yet begun to flow down the mountain. The lower range of Burnt Ridge was still uneclipsed by the creeping shadow of the mountain ahead of her. Without a watch, but with this familiar and slowly changing dial spread out before her, she knew the time to a minute. Heavy Tree Hill, a lesser height in the distance, was already wiped out by that shadowy index finger—half past seven! The stage would be at Hickory Hill just before half past eight; she ought to anticipate it, if possible,—it would stay ten minutes to change horses,—she *must* arrive before it left!

There was a good two-mile level before the rise of the next range. Now, Blue Lightning! all you know! And that was much,—for with the little chip hat and fluttering ribbons well bent down over the bluish mane, and the streaming gauze of her mantle almost level with the horse's back, she swept down across the long tableland ilke a skimming blue-jay. A few more bird-like dips up and down the undulations, and then came the long, cruel ascent of the Divide.

Acrid with perspiration, caking with dust, slithering in the slippery, impalpable powder of the road, groggily staggering in a red dusty dream, coughing, snorting, head-tossing; becoming suddenly dejected, with slouching haunch and limp legs on easy slopes, or wildly spasmodic and agile on sharp acclivities, Blue Lightning began to have ideas and recollections! Ah! she was a devil for a lark—this lightly-clinging, caressing, blarneying, cooing creature—up there! He remembered her now

Ha! very well then. Hoop-la! And suddenly leaping out like a rabbit, bucking, trotting hard, ambling lightly, "loping" on three legs and re-creating himself,—as only a California mustang could,—the invincible Blue Lightning at last stood triumphantly upon the summit. The eve-ning star had just pricked itself through the golden mist of the horizon line,—eight o'clock! She could do it now! But here, suddenly, her first hesitation seized her. She knew her horse, she knew the trail, she knew herself,—but did she know *the man* to whom she was riding? A cold chill crept over her, and then she shivered in a sudden blast; it was Night at last swooping down from the now invisible Sierras, and possess-ing all it touched. But it was only one long descent to Hickory Hill now, and she swept down securely on its wings. Half-past eight! The lights of the settlement were just ahead of her—but so, too, were the two lamps of the waiting stage before the post-office and hotel.

Happily the lounging crowd were gathered around the hotel, and she slipped into the post-office from the rear, unperceived. As she stepped behind the partition, its only occupant—a good-looking young fellow with a reddish moustache—turned towards her with a flush of delighted surprise. But it changed at the sight of the white, determined face and the brilliant eyes that had never looked once towards him, but were fixed upon a large bag, whose yawning mouth was still open and propped up beside his desk.

"Where is the through money letter that came in that bag?" she said quickly.

"What—do—you—mean?" he stammered, with a face that had suddenly grown whiter than her own.

"I mean that it's a *decoy*, checked at Heavy Tree Crossing, and that Mr. Home, of San Francisco, is now waiting at my office to know if you have taken it!"

The laugh and lie that he had at first tried to summon to mouth and lips never reached them. For, under the spell of her rigid, truthful face, he turned almost mechanically to his desk, and took out a package.

"Good God! you've opened it already!" she cried, pointing to the broken seal.

The expression on her face, more than anything she had said, con-vinced him that she knew all. He stammered under the new alarm that her despairing tone suggested. "Yes!—I was owing some bills— the collector was waiting here for the money, and I took something from the packet. But I was going to make it up by next mail—I swear it."

"How much have you taken?"

"Only a trifle. I"—

"How much?"

"A hundred dollars!"

She dragged the money she had brought from Laurel Run from her pocket, and counting out the sum, replaced it in the open package. He ran quickly to get the sealing-wax, but she motioned him away as she dropped the package back into the mail-bag. "No; as long as the money is found in the bag the package may have been broken *accidentally*. Now burst open one or two of those other packages a little—so;" she took out a packet of letters and bruised their official wrappings under her little foot until the tape fastening was loosened. "Now give me something heavy." She caught up a brass two-pound weight, and in the same feverish but collected haste wrapped it in paper, sealed it, stamped it, and, addressing it in a large printed hand to herself at Laurel Hill, dropped it in the bag. Then she closed it and locked it; he would have assisted her, but she again waved him away. "Send for the expressman, and keep yourself out of the way for a moment," she said curtly.

An attitude of weak admiration and foolish passion had taken the place of his former tremulous fear. He obeyed excitedly, but without a word. Mrs. Baker wiped her moist forehead and parched lips, and shook out her skirt. Well might the young expressman start at the unexpected revelation of those sparkling eyes and that demurely smiling mouth at the little window.

"Mrs. Baker!"

She put her finger quickly to her lips, and threw a word of unutterable and enigmatical meaning into her mischievous face.

"There's a big San Francisco swell takin' my place at Laurel to-night, Charley."

"Yes, ma'am."

"And it's a pity that the Omnibus Way Bag happened to get such a shaking up and banging round already, coming here."

"Eh?"

"I say," continued Mrs. Baker, with great gravity and dancing eyes, "that it would be just *awful* if that keerful city clerk found things kinder mixed up inside when he comes to open it. I wouldn't give him trouble for the world, Charley."

"No, ma'am, it ain't like you."

"So you'll be particularly careful on *my* account."

"Mrs. Baker," said Charley, with infinite gravity, "if that bag *should* tumble off a dozen times between this and Laurel Hill, I'd hop down and pick it up myself."

"Thank you! shake!"

They shook hands gravely across the window-ledge.

"And you ain't going down with us, Mrs. Baker?"

"Of course not; it wouldn't do,—for *I ain't here*,—don't you see?"

"Of course!"

She handed him the bag through the door. He took it carefully, b in spite of his great precaution fell over it twice on his way to the road, where from certain exclamations and shouts it seemed that a like miserable mischance attended its elevation to the boot. Then Mrs. Baker came back into the office, and, as the wheels rolled away, threw herself into a chair, and inconsistently gave way for the first time to an outburst of tears. Then her hand was grasped suddenly and she found Green on his knees before her. She started to her feet.

"Don't move," he said, with weak hysteric passion, "but listen to me, for God's sake! I am ruined, I know, even though you have just saved me from detection and disgrace. I have been mad!—a fool, to do what I have done, I know, but you do not know all—you do not know why I did it—you cannot think of the temptation that has driven me to it. Listen, Mrs. Baker. I have been striving to get money, honestly, dishonestly—any way, to look well in *your* eyes—to make myself worthy of you—to make myself rich, and to be able to offer you a home and take you away from Laurel Run. It was all for *you*, it was all for love of *you*, Betsy, my darling. Listen to me!"

In the fury, outraged sensibility, indignation, and infinite disgust that filled her little body at that moment, she should have been large, imperious, goddess-like, and commanding. But God is at times ironical with suffering womanhood. She could only writhe her hand from his grasp with childish contortions; she could only glare at him with eyes that were prettily and piquantly brilliant; she could only slap at his detaining hand with a plump and velvety palm, and when she found her voice it was high falsetto. And all she could say was, "Leave me be, looney, or I'll scream!"

He rose, with a weak, confused laugh, half of miserable affectation and half of real anger and shame.

"What did you come riding over here for, then? What did you take all this risk for? Why did you rush over here to share my disgrace—for *you* are as much mixed up with this now as *I* am—if you didn't calculate to share *everything else* with me? What did you come here for, then, if not for *me*?"

"What did *I* come here for?" said Mrs. Baker, with every drop of red blood gone from her cheek and trembling limp. "What—did—I—come here for? Well!—I came here for *John Baker's* sake! John Baker, who stood between you and death at Burnt Ridge, as I stand between you and damnation at Laurel Run, Mr. Green! Yes, John Baker, lying under half of Burnt Ridge, but more to me this day than any living man crawling over it—in—in"—oh, fatal climax—"in a month o' Sundays! What did I come here for? I came here as John Baker's livin' wife to carry on dead John Baker's work. Yes, dirty work this time, may be, Mr. Green! but his work and for *him* only—precious! That's what I came here for; that's what I *live* for; that's what I'm waiting for—to be up to *him* and his work always! That's me—Betsy Baker!"

She walked up and down rapidly, tying her chip hat under her chin again. Then she stopped, and taking her chamois purse from her pocket, laid it sharply on the desk.

"Stanton Green, don't be a fool! Rise up out of this, and be a man again. Take enough out o' that bag to pay what you owe Gov'ment, send in your resignation, and keep the rest to start you in an honest life elsewhere. But light out o' Hickory Hill afore this time to-morrow."

She pulled her mantle from the wall and opened the door.

"You are going?" he said bitterly.

"Yes." Either she could not hold seriousness long in her capricious little fancy, or, with feminine tact, she sought to make the parting less difficult for him, for she broke into a dazzling smile. "Yes, I'm goin' to run Blue Lightning agin Charley and that way bag back to Laurel Run, and break the record."

It is said that she did! Perhaps owing to the fact that the grade of the return journey to Laurel Run was in her favour, and that she could avoid the long, circuitous ascent to the summit taken by the stage, or that, owing to the extraordinary difficulties in the carriage of the way bag,—which had to be twice rescued from under the wheels of the stage, —she entered the Laurel Run post-office as the coach leaders came trotting up the hill. Mr. Home was already on the platform.

"You'll have to ballast your next way bag, boss," said Charley, gravely, as it escaped his clutches once more in the dust of the road, "or you'll have to make a new contract with the company. We've lost ten minutes in five miles over that bucking thing."

Home did not reply, but quickly dragged his prize into the office, scarcely noticing Mrs. Baker, who stood beside him pale and breathless. As the bolt of the bag was drawn, revealing its chaotic interior, Mrs. Baker gave a little sigh. Home glanced quickly at her, emptied the bag upon the floor, and picked up the broken and half-filled money parcel. Then he collected the scattered coins and counted them. "It's all right, Mrs. Baker," he said gravely. "*He's* safe this time."

"I'm so glad!" said little Mrs. Baker, with a hypocritical gasp.

"So am I," returned Home, with increasing gravity, as he took the coin, "for, from all I have gathered this afternoon, it seems he was an old pioneer of Laurel Run, a friend of your husband's, and, I think, more fool than knave!" He was silent for a moment, clicking the coins against each other; then he said carelessly: "Did he get quite away, Mrs. Baker?"

"I'm sure I don't know what you're talking about," said Mrs. Baker, with a lofty air of dignity, but a somewhat debasing colour. "I don't see why *I* should know anything about it, or why he should go away at all."

"Well," said Mr. Home, laying his hand gently on the widow's shoulder, "well, you see, it might have occurred to his friends that the *coins were marked!* That is, no doubt, the reason why he would take their good advice and go. But, as I said before, Mrs. Baker, *you*'re all right, whatever happens—the Government stands by *you!*"

⁂

AMBROSE BIERCE
(1842-1914?)

A NATIVE of Ohio, Ambrose Bierce served with distinction throughout the Civil War. From California, where he began (1866) his career as journalist, he went to London and edited *The Lantern*. In 1876 he was back in California, editing *The Argonaut* and contributing to *The Overland Monthly*. Most of his short stories were written in the eighties. They are usually episodic tales of horror or the supernatural, treated in a coldly intellectual way which, joined to their gruesomeness, prevented ready editorial acceptance. His first collection, *In the Midst of Life*, did not find publication until 1891; *Can Such Things Be?* not until 1893. Though many volumes followed, these contain his best work. After some years in Washington, D. C., Bierce became interested in the cause of Villa and disappeared in Mexico. Rumours of his survival to the present (1927) are unsubstantiated.

An Occurrence at Owl Creek Bridge, published in the collection of 1891, is here included by special arrangement with A. and C. Boni, New York City.

AN OCCURRENCE AT OWL CREEK BRIDGE

I.

A MAN stood upon a railroad bridge in northern Alabama, looking down into the swift water twenty feet below. The man's hands were behind his back, the wrists bound with a cord. A rope closely encircled his neck. It was attached to a stout cross-timber above his head and the slack fell to the level of his knees. Some loose boards laid upon the sleepers supporting the metals of the railway supplied a footing for him and his executioners—two private soldiers of the Federal Army, directed by a sergeant who in civil life may have been a deputy sheriff. At a short remove upon the same temporary platform was an officer in the uniform of his rank, armed. He was a captain. A sentinel at each end of the bridge stood with his rifle in the position known as "support," that is to say, vertical in front of the left shoulder, the hammer resting on the forearm thrown straight across the chest— a formal and unnatural position, enforcing an erect carriage of the body. It did not appear to be the duty of these two men to know what was occurring at the centre of the bridge; they merely blockaded the two ends of the foot planking that traversed it.

Beyond one of the sentinels nobody was in sight; the railroad ran straight away into a forest for a hundred yards, then, curving, was lost to view. Doubtless there was an outpost farther along. The other bank of the stream was open ground—a gentle acclivity topped with a stockade of vertical tree trunks, loopholed for rifles, with a single embrasure through which protruded the muzzle of a brass cannon commanding the bridge. Midway of the slope between bridge and fort were the spectators—a single company of infantry in line, at "parade rest," the butts of the rifles on the ground, the barrels inclining slightly backward against the right shoulder, the hands crossed upon the stock. A lieutenant stood at the right of the line, the point of his sword upon the ground, his left hand resting upon his right. Excepting the group of four at the centre of the bridge, not a man moved. The company faced the bridge, staring stonily, motionless. The sentinels, facing the banks of the stream, might have been statues to adorn the bridge. The captain stood with folded arms, silent, observing the work of his subordinates, but making no sign. Death is a dignitary who when he comes announced is to be received with formal manifestations of respect, even by those most familiar with him. In the code of military etiquette silence and fixity are forms of deference.

The man who was engaged in being hanged was apparently about thirty-five years of age. He was a civilian, if one might judge from his habit, which was that of a planter. His features were good—a straight nose, firm mouth, broad forehead, from which his long dark hair was combed straight back, falling behind his ears to the collar of his well-fitting frock-coat. He wore a moustache and pointed beard, but no whiskers; his eyes were large and dark grey, and had a kindly expression which one would hardly have expected in one whose neck was in the hemp. Evidently this was no vulgar assassin. The liberal military code makes provision for hanging many kinds of persons, and gentlemen are not excluded.

The preparations being complete, the two private soldiers stepped aside and each drew away the plank upon which he had been standing. The sergeant turned to the captain, saluted and placed himself immediately behind that officer, who in turn moved apart one pace. These movements left the condemned man and the sergeant standing on the two ends of the same plank, which spanned three of the cross-ties of the bridge. The end upon which the civilian stood almost, but not quite, reached a fourth. This plank had been held in place by the weight of the captain; it was now held by that of the sergeant. At a signal from the former the latter would step aside, the plank would tilt and the condemned man go down between two ties. The arrangement commended itself to his judgment as simple and effective. His face had not been covered nor his eyes bandaged. He looked a moment at his "unsteadfast footing," then let his gaze wander to the swirling water of the stream racing madly beneath his feet. A piece of dancing driftwood caught his attention and his eyes followed it down the current. How slowly it appeared to move! What a sluggish stream!

He closed his eyes in order to fix his last thoughts upon his wife and children. The water, touched to gold by the early sun, the brooding mists under the banks at some distance down the stream, the fort, the soldiers, the piece of drift—all had distracted him. And now he became conscious of a new disturbance. Striking through the thought of his dear ones was a sound which he could neither ignore nor understand, a sharp, distinct, metallic percussion like the stroke of a blacksmith's hammer upon the anvil; it had the same ringing quality. He wondered what it was, and whether immeasurably distant or near by— it seemed both. Its recurrence was regular, but as slow as the tolling of a death knell. He awaited each stroke with impatience and—he knew not why—apprehension. The intervals of silence grew progressively longer; the delays became maddening. With their greater infrequency the sounds increased in strength and sharpness. They hurt his ear like the thrust of a knife; he feared he would shriek. What he heard was the ticking of his watch.

He unclosed his eyes and saw again the water below him. "If I could free my hands," he thought, "I might throw off the noose and spring into the stream. By diving I could evade the bullets and, swimming vigorously, reach the bank, take to the woods and get away home. My home, thank God, is as yet outside their lines; my wife and little ones are still beyond the invader's farthest advance."

As these thoughts, which have here to be set down in words, were flashed into the doomed man's brain rather than evolved from it, the captain nodded to the sergeant. The sergeant stepped aside.

II.

Peyton Farquhar was a well-to-do planter, of an old and highly respected Alabama family. Being a slave owner and, like other slave owners, a politician, he was naturally an original secessionist and ardently devoted to the Southern cause. Circumstances of an imperious nature, which it is unnecessary to relate here, had prevented him from taking

service with the gallant army that had fought the disastrous campaigns ending with the fall of Corinth, and he chafed under the inglori-
ous restraint, longing for the release of his energies, the larger life of
the soldier, the opportunity for distinction. That opportunity, he felt,
would come, as it comes to all in war time. Meanwhile he did what
he could. No service was too humble for him to perform in aid of
the South, no adventure too perilous for him to undertake if consistent
with the character of a civilian who was at heart a soldier, and who in
good faith and without too much qualification assented to at least a part
of the frankly villainous dictum that all is fair in love and war.

One evening while Farquhar and his wife were sitting on a rustic
bench near the entrance to his grounds, a grey-clad soldier rode up to
the gate and asked for a drink of water. Mrs. Farquhar was only too
happy to serve him with her own white hands. While she was fetching the water her husband approached the dusty horseman and inquired
eagerly for news from the front.

"The Yanks are repairing the railroads," said the man, "and are
getting ready for another advance. They have reached the Owl Creek
bridge, put it in order and built a stockade on the north bank. The
commandant has issued an order, which is posted everywhere, declaring
that any civilian caught interfering with the railroad, its bridges, tun-
nels or trains will be summarily hanged. I saw the order."

"How far is it to the Owl Creek bridge?" Farquhar asked.

"About thirty miles."

"Is there no force on this side the creek?"

"Only a picket post half a mile out, on the railroad, and a single
sentinel at this end of the bridge."

"Suppose a man—a civilian and student of hanging—should elude
the picket post and perhaps get the better of the sentinel," said Farquhar,
smiling, "what could he accomplish?"

The soldier reflected. "I was there a month ago," he replied. "I
observed that the flood of last winter had lodged a great quantity of
driftwood against the wooden pier at this end of the bridge. It is
now dry and would burn like tow."

The lady had now brought the water, which the soldier drank. He
thanked her ceremoniously, bowed to her husband and rode away. An
hour later, after nightfall, he repassed the plantation, going northward
in the direction from which he had come. He was a Federal scout.

·III·

As Peyton Farquhar fell straight downward through the bridge he
lost consciousness and was as one already dead. From this state he was
awakened—ages later, it seemed to him—by the pain of a sharp pressure upon his throat, followed by a sense of suffocation. Keen, poignant

agonies seemed to shoot from his neck downward through every fibre of his body and limbs. These pains appeared to flash along well-defined lines of ramification and to beat with an inconceivably rapid periodicity. They seemed like streams of pulsating fire heating him to an intolerable temperature. As to his head, he was conscious of nothing but a feeling of fulness—of congestion. These sensations were unaccompanied by thought. The intellectual part of his nature was already effaced; he had power only to feel, and feeling was torment. He was conscious of motion. Encompassed in a luminous cloud, of which he was now merely the fiery heart, without material substance, he swung through un-thinkable arcs of oscillation, like a vast pendulum. Then all at once, with terrible suddenness, the light about him shot upward with the noise of a loud plash; a frightful roaring was in his ears, and all was cold and dark. The power of thought was restored; he knew that the rope had broken and he had fallen into the stream. There was no additional strangulation; the noose about his neck was already suffocating him and kept the water from his lungs. To die of hanging at the bottom of a river!—the idea seemed to him ludicrous. He opened his eyes in the darkness and saw above him a gleam of light, but how distant, how in-accessible! He was still sinking, for the light became fainter and fainter until it was a mere glimmer. Then it began to grow and brighten, and he knew that he was rising toward the surface—knew it with reluctance, for he was now very comfortable. "To be hanged and drowned," he thought, "that is not so bad; but I do not wish to be shot. No; I will not be shot; that is not fair."

He was not conscious of an effort, but a sharp pain in his wrist ap-prised him that he was trying to free his hands. He gave the struggle his attention, as an idler might observe the feat of a juggler, without interest in the outcome. What splendid effort! What magnificent, what superhuman strength! Ah, that was a fine endeavor! Bravo! The cord fell away; his arms parted and floated upward, the hands dimly seen on each side in the growing light. He watched them with a new interest as first one and then the other pounced upon the noose at his neck. They tore it away and thrust it fiercely aside, its undulations resembling those of a water-snake. "Put it back, put it back!" He thought he shouted these words to his hands, for the undoing of the noose had been succeeded by the direst pang that he had yet experienced. His neck ached horribly; his brain was on fire; his heart, which had been fluttering faintly, gave a great leap, trying to force itself out at his mouth. His whole body was racked and wrenched with an insupport-able anguish! But his disobedient hands gave no heed to the command. They beat the water vigorously with quick, downward strokes, forcing him to the surface. He felt his head emerge; his eyes were blinded by the sunlight; his chest expanded convulsively, and with a supreme and crowning agony his lungs engulfed a great draught of air, which instantly he expelled in a shriek!

He was now in full possession of his physical senses. They were indeed, preternaturally keen and alert. Something in the awful disturbance of his organic system had so exalted and refined them that they made record of things never before perceived. He felt the ripples upon his face and heard their separate sounds as they struck. He looked at the forest on the bank of the stream, saw the individual trees, the leaves and the veining of each leaf—saw the very insects upon them; the locusts, the brilliant-bodied flies, the gray spiders stretching their webs from twig to twig. He noted the prismatic colours in all the dewdrops upon a million blades of grass. The humming of the gnats that danced above the eddies of the stream, the beating of the dragon-flies' wings, the strokes of the water-spiders' legs, like oars which had lifted their boat—all these made audible music. A fish slid along beneath his eyes and he heard the rush of its body parting the water.

He had come to the surface facing down the stream; in a moment the visible world seemed to wheel slowly round, himself the pivotal point, and he saw the bridge, the fort, the soldiers upon the bridge, the captain, the sergeant, the two privates, his executioners. They were in silhouette against the blue sky. They shouted and gesticulated, pointing at him. The captain had drawn his pistol, but did not fire; the others were unarmed. Their movements were grotesque and horrible, their forms gigantic.

Suddenly he heard a sharp report and something struck the water smartly within a few inches of his head; spattering his face with spray. He heard a second report, and saw one of the sentinels with his rifle at his shoulder, a light cloud of blue smoke rising from the muzzle. The man in the water saw the eye of the man on the bridge gazing into his own through the sights of the rifle. He observed that it was a grey eye and remembered having read that grey eyes were keenest, and that all famous marksmen had them. Nevertheless, this one had missed.

A counter-swirl had caught Farquhar and turned him half round; he was again looking into the forest on the bank opposite the fort. The sound of a clear, high voice in a monotonous singsong now rang out behind him, and came across the water with a distinctness that pierced and subdued all other sounds, even the beating of the ripples in his ears. Although no soldier, he had frequented camps enough to know the dread significance of that deliberate, drawling, aspirated chant; the lieutenant on shore was taking a part in the morning's work. How coldly and pitilessly—with what an even, calm intonation, presaging and enforcing tranquillity in the men—with what accurately measured intervals fell those cruel words:

"Attention, company! . . . Shoulder arms! . . . Ready! . . . Aim! . . . Fire!"

Farquhar dived—dived as deeply as he could. The water roared in his ears like the voice of Niagara, yet he heard the dulled thunder of the volley and, rising again toward the surface, met shining bits of metal, singularly flattened, oscillating slowly downward. Some of them touched him on the face and hands, then fell away, continuing their descent. One lodged between his collar and neck; it was uncomfortably warm and he snatched it out.

As he rose to the surface, gasping for breath, he saw that he had been a long time under water, he was perceptibly farther down stream —nearer to safety. The soldiers had almost finished reloading; the metal ramrods flashed all at once in the sunshine as they were drawn from the barrels, turned in the air, and thrust into their sockets. The two sentinels fired again, independently and ineffectually.

The hunted man saw all this over his shoulder; he was now swimming vigorously with the current. His brain was as energetic as his arms and legs; he thought with the rapidity of lightning.

"The officer," he reasoned, "will not make that martinet's error a second time. It is as easy to dodge a volley as a single shot. He has probably already given the command to fire at will. God help me, I cannot dodge them all!"

An appalling plash within two yards of him was followed by a loud, rushing sound, *diminuendo*, which seemed to travel back through the air to the fort and died in an explosion which stirred the very river to its deeps! A rising sheet of water curved over him, fell down upon him, blinded him, strangled him! The cannon had taken a hand in the game. As he shook his head free from the commotion of the smitten water he heard the deflected shot humming through the air ahead, and in an instant it was cracking and smashing the branches in the forest beyond.

"They will not do that again," he thought, "the next time they will use a charge of grape. I must keep my eye upon the gun; the smoke will apprise me—the report arrives too late; it lags behind the missile. That is a good gun."

Suddenly he felt himself whirled round and round—spinning like a top. The water, the banks, the forests, the now distant bridge, fort and men—all were commingled and blurred. Objects were represented by their colours only; circular horizontal streaks of colour—that was all he saw. He had been caught in the vortex and was being whirled on with a velocity of advance and gyration that made him giddy and sick. In a few moments he was flung upon the gravel at the foot of the left bank of the stream—the southern bank—and behind a projecting point which concealed him from his enemies. The sudden arrest of his motion, the abrasion of one of his hands on the gravel, restored him, and he wept with delight. He dug his fingers into the sand, threw it over himself in handfuls and audibly blessed it. It looked like diamonds, rubies, emeralds; he could think of nothing beautiful which it did not resemble. The trees upon the bank were giant garden plants; he noted a definite order in their arrangement, inhaled the fragrance of their blooms. A strange, roseate light shone through the spaces among their trunks and the wind made in their branches the music of aeolian harps. He had no wish to perfect his escape—was content to remain in that enchanting spot until retaken.

A whiz and rattle of grapeshot among the branches high above his head roused him from his dream. The baffled cannoneer had fired him a random farewell. He sprang to his feet, rushed up the sloping bank, and plunged into the forest.

All that day he travelled, laying his course by the rounding sun. The forest seemed interminable; nowhere did he discover a break in it, not even a woodman's road. He had not known that he lived in so wild a region. There was something uncanny in the revelation.

By nightfall he was fatigued, footsore, famishing. The thought of his wife and children urged him on. At last he found a road which led him in what he knew to be the right direction. It was as wide and straight as a city street, yet it seemed untravelled. No fields bordered it, no dwelling anywhere. Not so much as the barking of a dog suggested human habitation. The black bodies of the trees formed a straight wall on both sides, terminating on the horizon in a point, like a diagram in a lesson in perspective. Overhead, as he looked up through this rift in the wood, shone great golden stars looking unfamiliar and grouped in strange constellations. He was sure they were arranged in some order which had a secret and malign significance. The wood on either side was full of singular noises, among which—once, twice, and again—he distinctly heard whispers in an unknown tongue.

His neck was in pain and lifting his hand to it he found it horribly swollen. He knew that it had a circle of black where the rope had bruised it. His eyes felt congested; he could no longer close them. His tongue was swollen with thirst; he relieved its fever by thrusting it forward from between his teeth into the cold air. How softly the turf had carpeted the untravelled avenue—he could no longer feel the roadway beneath his feet!

Doubtless, despite his suffering, he had fallen asleep while walking, for now he sees another scene—perhaps he has merely recovered from a delirium. He stands at the gate of his own home. All is as he left it, and all bright and beautiful in the morning sunshine. He must have travelled the entire night. As he pushes open the gate and passes up the wide white walk, he sees a flutter of female garments: his wife, looking fresh and cool and sweet, steps down from the veranda to meet him. At the bottom of the steps she stands waiting, with a smile of ineffable joy, an attitude of matchless grace and dignity. Ah, how beautiful she is! He springs forward with extended arms. As he is about to clasp her he feels a stunning blow upon the back of the neck; a blinding white light blazes all about him with a sound like the shock of a cannon— then all is darkness and silence!

Peyton Farquhar was dead; his body, with a broken neck, swung gently from side to side beneath the timbers of the Owl Creek bridge.

❋   ❋   ❋

HENRY CUYLER BUNNER
(1855-1896)

A NEW YORKER, born in 1855, Bunner was editor of *Puck* from 1877 to the time of his death, nineteen years later. His stories were brief and humorous, as his magazine demanded. He collaborated with Brander Matthews in *Studies in Story Telling* (1884), the two authors sharing an interest in form, technique, brilliance of execution, and appreciation of the French masters. His *Short Sixes: Stories to be Told While the Candle Burns* (1890) was succeeded by four collections, most of which are perhaps over-journalistic, all of which are novel and scintillant.

Zenobia's Infidelity is reprinted from *Short Sixes*, copyright 1890, 1896, by Alice L. Bunner, by special arrangement with and permission of the publishers, Charles Scribner's Sons, New York City.

ZENOBIA'S INFIDELITY

D R. TIBBITT stood on the porch of Mrs. Pennypepper's boarding-house, and looked up and down the deserted Main Street of Sagawaug with a contented smile, the while he buttoned his driving-gloves. The little Doctor had good cause to be content with himself and with everything else—with his growing practice, with his comfortable boarding-house, with his own good-looks, with his neat attire, and with the world in general. He could not but be content with Sagawaug, for there never was a prettier country town. The Doctor looked across the street and picked out the very house that he proposed to buy when the one remaining desire of his soul was gratified. It was a house with a hip-roof and with a long garden running down to the river.

There was no one in the house to-day, but there was no one in any of the houses. Not even a pair of round bare arms was visible among the clothes that waved in the August breeze in every back-yard. It was Circus Day in Sagawaug.

The Doctor was climbing into his gig when a yell started him. A freckled boy with saucer eyes dashed around the corner.

"Doctor!" he gasped, "come quick! The circus got a-fire an' the trick elephant's most roasted!"

"Don't be silly, Johnny," said the Doctor, reprovingly.

"Hope to die—Honest Injun—cross my breast!" said the boy. The Doctor knew the sacredness of this juvenile oath.

"Get in here with me," he said, "and if I find you're trying to be funny, I'll drop you in the river."

As they drove toward the outskirts of the town, Johnny told his tale.

"Now," he began, "the folks was all out of the tent after the show was over, and one of the circus men, he went to the oil-barrel in the green wagon with Dan'l in the Lion's Den onto the outside of it, an' he took in a candle an' left it there, and fust thing the barrel busted, an' he wasn't hurted a bit, but the trick elephant she was burned awful, an' the ring-tailed baboon, he was so scared he had a fit. Say, did you know baboons had fits?"

When they reached the circus-grounds, they found a crowd around a small side-show tent. A strong odour of burnt leather confirmed Johnny's story. Dr. Tibbitt pushed his way through the throng, and gazed upon the huge beast, lying on her side on the grass, her broad shoulder charred and quivering. Her bulk expanded and contracted with spasms of agony, and from time to time she uttered a moaning sound. On her head was a structure of red cloth, about the size of a bushel-basket, apparently intended to look like a British soldier's forage-cap. This was secured by a strap that went under her chin—if an elephant has a chin. This scarlet cheese-box every now and then slipped down over her eye, and the faithful animal patiently, in all her anguish, adjusted it with her prehensile trunk.

By her side stood her keeper and the proprietor of the show, a large man with a dyed moustache, a wrinkled face, and hair oiled and frizzed. These two bewailed their loss alternately.

"The boss elephant in the business!" cried the showman. "Barnum never had no trick elephant like Zenobia. And them lynes and Dan'l was painted in new before I took the road this season. Oh, there's been a hoodoo on me since I showed ag'inst the Sunday-school picnic!"

"That there elephant's been like my own child," groaned the keeper, "or my wife, I may say. I've slep' alongside of her every night for fourteen damn years."

The Doctor had been carefully examining his patient.

"If there is any analogy—" he began.

"Neuralogy!" snorted the indignant showman; "'t ain't neuralogy, you jay pill-box, she's *cooked!*"

"If there is any analogy," repeated Dr. Tibbitt, flushing a little, "between her case and that of a human being, I think I can save your elephant. Get me a barrel of linseed oil, and drive these people away."

The Doctor's orders were obeyed with eager submission. He took off his coat, and went to work. He had never doctored an elephant, and the job interested him. At the end of an hour, Zenobia's sufferings were somewhat alleviated. She lay on her side, chained tightly to the ground, and swaddled in bandages. Her groans had ceased.

"I'll call to-morrow at noon," said the Doctor. "Good gracious, what's that?" Zenobia's trunk was playing around his waistband.

"She wants to shake hands with you," her keeper explained. "She's a lady, she is, and she knows you done her good."

"I'd rather not have anything of the sort," said the Doctor, decisively.

When Dr. Tibbitt called at twelve on the morrow, he found Zenobia's tent neatly roped in, an amphitheatre of circus-benches constructed around her, and this amphitheatre packed with people.

"Got a quarter apiece from them jays," whispered the showman, "jest to see you dress them wownds." Subsequently the showman relieved his mind to a casual acquaintance. "He's got a heart like a gun-flint, that doctor," he said; "made me turn out every one of them jays and give 'em their money back before he'd lay a hand to Zenobia."

But if the Doctor suppressed the clinic, neither he nor the showman suffered. From dawn till dusk people came from miles around to stare a quarter's worth at the burnt elephant. Once in a while, as a rare treat, the keeper lifted a corner of her bandages, and revealed the seared flesh. The show went off in a day or two, leaving Zenobia to recover at leisure; and as it wandered westward, it did an increased business simply because it had had a burnt trick elephant. Such, dear friends, is the human mind.

The Doctor fared even better. The fame of his new case spread far and wide. People seemed to think that if he could cure an elephant he could cure anything. He was called into consultation in neighbouring towns. Women in robust health imagined ailments, so as to send for him and ask him shuddering questions about "that *wretched* animal." The trustees of the orphan-asylum made him staff-physician—in this case the Doctor thought he could trace a connection of ideas, in which children and a circus were naturally associated. And the local newspaper called him a *savant*.

He called every day upon Zenobia, who greeted him with trumpetings of joyful welcome. She also desired to shake hands with him, and her keeper had to sit on her head and hold her trunk to repress the familiarity. In two weeks she was cured, except for extensive and permanent scars, and she waited only for a favorable opportunity to rejoin the circus.

The Doctor had got his fee in advance.

Upon a sunny afternoon in the last of August, Dr. Tibbitt jogged slowly toward Sagawaug in his neat little gig. He had been to Pelion, the next town, to call upon Miss Minetta Bunker, the young lady whom he desired to install in the house with the garden running down to the river. He had found her starting out for a drive in Tom Matson's dog-cart. Now, the Doctor feared no foe, in medicine or in love; but when a young woman is inscrutable as to the state of her affections, when the richest young man in the country is devoting himself to her, and when the young lady's mother is backing the rich man, a young country doctor may well feel perplexed and anxious over his chance of the prize.

The Doctor was so troubled, indeed, that he paid no heed to a heavy, repeated thud behind him, on the macadamised road. His gentle little mare heard it, though, and began to curvet and prance. The Doctor was pulling her in, and calming her with a "Soo—Soo—down, girl, down!" when he interrupted himself to shout:

"Great Cæsar! get off me!"

Something like a yard of rubber hose had come in through the side of the buggy, and was rubbing itself against his face. He looked around, and the cold sweat stood out on him as he saw Zenobia, her chain dragging from her hind-foot, her red cap a-cock on her head, trotting along by the side of his vehicle, snorting with joy, and evidently bent on lavishing her pliant, serpentine, but leathery caresses upon his person.

His fear vanished in a moment. The animal's intentions were certainly pacific, to put it mildly. He reflected that if he could keep his horse ahead of her, he could toll her around the block and back toward her tent. He had hardly guessed as yet the depth of the impression which he had made upon Zenobia's heart, which must have been a large organ, if the size of her ears was any indication—according to the popular theory.

He was on the very edge of the town, and his road took him by a house where he had a new and highly valued patient, the young wife of old Deacon Burgee. Her malady being of a nature that permitted it, Mrs. Burgee was in the habit of sitting at her window when the Doctor made his rounds, and indicating the satisfactory state of her health by a bow and a smile. On this occasion she fled from the window with a shriek. Her mother, a formidable old lady under a red false-front, came to the window, shrieked likewise, and slammed down the sash.

The Doctor tolled his elephant around the block without further misadventure, and they started up the road toward Zenobia's tent, Zenobia caressing her benefactor while shudders of antipathy ran over his frame. In a few minutes the keeper hove in sight. Zenobia saw him first, blew a shrill blast on her trumpet, close to the Doctor's ear, bolted through a snake fence, lumbered across a turnip-field, and disappeared in a patch of woods, leaving the Doctor to quiet his excited horse and to face the keeper, who advanced with rage in his eye.

"What do you mean, you cuss," he began, "weaning a man's elephant's affections away from him? You ain't got no more morals than a Turk, you ain't. That elephant an' me has been side-partners for fourteen years, an' here you come between us."

"I don't want your confounded elephant," roared the Doctor; "why don't you keep it chained up?"

"She busted her chain to git after you," replied the keeper. "Oh, I seen you two lally-gaggin' all along the road. I knowed you wa'n't no good the first time I set eyes on yer, a-sayin' hoodoo words over the poor dumb beast."

The Doctor resolved to banish "analogy" from his vocabulary.

The next morning, about four o'clock, Dr. Tibbitt awoke with a troubled mind. He had driven home after midnight from a late call, and he had had an uneasy fancy that he saw a great shadowy bulk ambling along in the mist-hid fields by the roadside. He jumped out of bed and went to the window. Below him, completely covering Mrs. Penny-pepper's nasturtium bed, her prehensile trunk ravaging the early chrysanthemums, stood Zenobia, swaying to and fro, the dew glistening on her seamed sides beneath the early morning sunlight. The Doctor hastily dressed himself and slipped downstairs and out, to meet this Frankenstein's-monster of affection.

There was but one thing to do. Zenobia would follow him wherever he went—she rushed madly through Mrs. Pennypepper's roses to greet him—and his only course was to lead her out of the town before people began to get up, and to detain her in some remote meadow until he could get her keeper to come for her and secure her by force or stratagem. He set off by the least frequented streets, and he experienced a pang of horror as he remembered that his way led him past the house of his one professional rival in Sagawaug. Suppose Dr. Pettengill should be coming home or going out as he passed!

He did not meet Dr. Pettengill. He did meet Deacon Burgee, who stared at him with more of rage than of amazement in his wrinkled countenance. The Deacon was carrying a large bundle of embroidered linen and flannel, that must have been tied up in a hurry.

"Good morning, Deacon," the Doctor hailed him, with as much ease of manner as he could assume. "How's Mrs. Burgee?"

"She's doin' fust rate, no thanks to no circus doctors!" snorted the Deacon. "An' if you want to know anything further concernin' her health, you ask Dr. Pettengill. *He's* got more sense than to go trailin' around the streets with a par-boiled elephant behind him, a-frightening women-folks a hull month afore the'r time."

"Why, Deacon!" cried the Doctor, "what—what is it?"

"It's a boy," responded the Deacon, sternly; "and it's God's own mercy that 't wa'n't born with a trunk and a tail."

The Doctor found a secluded pasture, near the woods that encircled the town, and there he sat him down, in the corner of a snake-fence, to wait until some farmer or market-gardener should pass by, to carry his message to the keeper. He had another message to send too. He had several cases that must be attended to at once. Unless he could get away from his pachydermatous familiar, Pettengill must care for his cases that morning. It was hard—but what was he to do?

Zenobia stood by his side, dividing her attention between the caresses she bestowed on him and the care she was obliged to take of her red cap, which was not tightly strapped on, and slipped in various directions at every movement of her gigantic head. She was unmistakably happy. From time to time she trumpeted cheerily. She plucked up tufts of grass, and offered them to the Doctor. He refused them, and she ate them herself. Once he took a daisy from her, absent-mindedly, and she was so greatly pleased that she smashed his hat in her endeavors to pet him. The Doctor was a kind-hearted man. He had to admit that Zenobia meant well. He patted her trunk, and made matters worse. Her elephantine ecstasy came near being the death of him.

Still the farmer came not, nor the market-gardener. Dr. Tibbitt began to believe that he had chosen a meadow that was *too* secluded. At last two boys appeared. After they had stared at him and at Zenobia for half-an-hour, one of them agreed to produce Dr. Pettengill and Zenobia's keeper for fifty cents. Dr. Pettengill was the first to arrive. He refused to come nearer than the furthest limit of the pasture.

"Hello, Doctor," he called out, "hear you've been seeing elephants. Want me to take your cases? Guess I can. Got a half-hour free. Brought some bromide down for you, if you'd like to try it."

To judge from his face, Zenobia was invisible. But his presence alarmed that sensitive animal. She crowded up close to the fence, and every time she flicked her skin to shake off the flies she endangered the equilibrium of the Doctor, who was sitting on the top rail, for dignity's sake. He shouted his directions to his colleague, who shouted back professional criticisms.

"Salicylate of soda for that old woman? What's the matter with salicylate of cinchonidia? Don't want to kill her before you get out of this swamp, do you?"

Dr. Tibbitt was not a profane man; but at this moment he could not restrain himself.

"*Damn you!*" he said, with such a vigour that the elephant gave a convulsive start. The Doctor felt his seat depart from under him—he was going—going into space for a brief moment, and then he scrambled up out of the soft mud of the cow-wallow back of the fence on which he had been sitting. Zenobia had backed against the fence.

The keeper arrived soon after. He had only reached the meadow when Zenobia lifted her trunk in the air, emitted a mirthful toot, and struck out for the woods with the picturesque and cumbersome gallop of a mastodon pup.

"Dern *you*," said the keeper to Dr. Tibbitt, who was trying to fasten his collar, which had broken loose in his fall; "if the boys was here, and I hollered 'Hey, Rube!' there wouldn't be enough left of yer to spread a plaster fer a baby's bile!"

The Doctor made himself look as decent as the situation allowed, and then he marched toward the town with the light of a firm resolve illuminating his face. The literature of his childhood had come to his aid. He remembered the unkind tailor who pricked the elephant's trunk. It seemed to him that the tailor was a rather good fellow.

"If that elephant's disease is gratitude," thought the Doctor, "I'll give her an antidote."

He went to the drug-store, and, as he went, he pulled out a blank pad and wrote down a prescription, from mere force of habit. It read thus:

PESSELS & MORTON,

Druggists,

Commercial Block, Main Street, Sagawaug.

Prescriptions Carefully Compounded.

℞

                         Calcium sul ʒij

                         Calcis chl ʒxvj

                         Capsicum pulv ʒi

                         M et ft. Bol.

                         Sig. Take at once.

                                   Tibbitt.

When the druggist looked at it, he was taken short of breath. "What's this?" he asked—"a bombshell?"

"Put it up," said the Doctor, "and don't talk so much." He lingered nervously on the druggist's steps, looking up and down the street. He had sent a boy to order the stable-man to harness his gig. By-and-by, the druggist put his head out of the door.

"I've got some asafœtida pills," he said, "that are kind o' tired, and half a pound of whale-oil soap, that's higher'n Haman——"

"Put 'em in!" said the Doctor, grimly, as he saw Zenobia coming in sight far down the street.

She came up while the Doctor was waiting for the bolus. Twenty-three boys were watching them, although it was only seven o'clock in the morning.

"Down, Zenobia!" said the Doctor, thoughtlessly, as he might have addressed a dog. He was talking with the druggist, and Zenobia was patting his ear with her trunk. Zenobia sank to her knees. The Doctor did not notice her. She folded her trunk about him, lifted him to her back, rose, with a heave and a sway, to her feet, and started up the road. The boys cheered. The Doctor got off on the end of an elm-branch. His descent was watched from nineteen second-story windows.

His gig came to meet him at last, and he entered it and drove rapidly out of town, with Zenobia trotting contentedly behind him. As soon as he had passed Deacon Burgee's house, he drew rein, and Zenobia approached, while his perspiring mare stood on her hind-legs.

"Zenobia—pill!" said the Doctor.

As she had often done in her late illness, Zenobia opened her mouth at the word of command, and swallowed the infernal bolus. Then they started up again, and the Doctor headed for Zenobia's tent.

But Zenobia's pace was sluggish. She had been dodging about the woods for two nights, and she was tired. When the Doctor whipped up, she seized the buggy by any convenient projection, and held it back. This damaged the buggy and frightened the horse; but it accomplished Zenobia's end. It was eleven o'clock before Jake Bumgardner's "Half-Way-House" loomed up white, afar down the dusty road, and the Doctor knew that his round-about way had at length brought him near to the field where the circus-tent had been pitched.

He drove on with a lighter heart in his bosom. He had not heard Zenobia behind him, for some time. He did not know what had become of her, or what she was doing, but he learned later.

The Doctor had compounded a pill well calculated to upset Zenobia's stomach. That it would likewise give her a consuming thirst he had not considered. But chemistry was doing its duty without regard to him. A thirst like a furnace burned within Zenobia. Capsicum and chloride of lime were doing their work. She gasped and groaned. She searched for water. She filled her trunk at a wayside trough and poured the contents into her mouth. Then she sucked up a puddle or two. Then she came to Bumgardner's, where a dozen kegs of lager-beer and a keg of what passed at Bumgardner's for gin stood on the side-walk. Zenobia's circus experience had taught her what a water-barrel meant. She applied her knowledge. With her forefoot she deftly staved in the head of one keg after another, and with her trunk she drew up the beer and the gin, and delivered them to her stomach. If you think her taste at fault, remember the bolus.

Bumgardner rushed out and assailed her with a bung-starter. She turned upon him and squirted lager-beer over him until he was covered with an iridescent lather of foam from head to foot. Then she fin-ished the kegs and went on her way, to overtake the Doctor.

The Doctor was speeding his mare merrily along, grateful for even a momentary relief from Zenobia's attentions, when, at one and the same time, he heard a heavy, uncertain, thumping on the road behind him, and the quick patter of a trotter's hoofs on the road ahead of him. He glanced behind him first, and saw Zenobia. She swayed from side to side, more than was her wont. Her red cap was far down over her left eye. Her aspect was rakish, and her gait was unsteady. The Doctor did not know it, but Zenobia was drunk.

Zenobia was sick, but intoxication dominated her sickness. Even sulphide of calcium withdrew courteously before the might of beer and gin. Rocking from side to side, reeling across the road and back, trum-peting in imbecile inexpressive tones, Zenobia advanced.

The Doctor looked forward. Tom Matson sat in his dog-cart, with Miss Bunker by his side. His horse had caught sight of Zenobia, and he was rearing high in air, and whinnying in terror. Before Tom could pull him down, he made a sudden break, overturned the dog-cart, and flung Tom and Miss Minetta Bunker on a bank by the side of the road. It was a soft bank, well grown with mint and stinging-nettles, just above a creek. Tom had scarce landed before he was up and off, running hard across the fields.

Miss Minetta rose and looked at him with fire in her eyes.

"Well!" she said aloud: "I'd like Mother to see you *now!*"

The Doctor had jumped out of his gig and let his little mare go galloping up the road. He had his arm about Miss Minetta's waist when he turned to face his familiar demon—which may have accounted for the pluck in his face.

But Zenobia was a hundred yards down the road, and she was utterly incapable of getting any further. She trumpeted once or twice, then she wavered like a reed in the wind; her legs weakened under her, and she sank on her side. Her red cap had slipped down, and she picked it up with her trunk, broke its band in a reckless swing that resembled the wave of jovial farewell, gave one titanic hiccup, and fell asleep by the road-side.

An hour later, Dr. Tibbitt was driving toward Pelion, with Miss Bunker by his side. His horse had been stopped at the toll-gate. He was driving with one hand. Perhaps he needed the other to show how they could have a summer-house in the garden that ran down to the river.

But it was evening when Zenobia awoke to find her keeper sitting on her head. He jabbed a cotton-hook firmly and decisively into her ear, and led her homeward down the road lit by the golden sunset. That was the end of Zenobia's infidelity.

❧ ❧ ❧

HAMLIN GARLAND
(1860-   )

HAMLIN GARLAND, born in West Salem, Wisconsin, moved to Iowa when he was nine, a little later to Minnesota, "the middle border," and when he was twenty to South Dakota. Of New England ancestry, he came East to study. While teaching in Boston, he began to write and to do for the West what Miss Wilkins was doing for New England, Howells for America. Since *Main Travelled Roads* (1891) Mr. Garland has been chief interpreter of the Middle Border in the Nineteenth Century. With hardy realism (veritism is his word) he depicts the hardships rather than the happiness of pioneer days, in such collections as the one mentioned, or *Prairie Folks* (1892-1898), or *They of the High Trails* (1916). He has written a number of Indian stories, besides a semi-historic trilogy of the Middle Border. He lives in New York City.

Drifting Crane is reprinted from *Prairie Folks* by permission of and arrangement with the author.

DRIFTING CRANE

THE people of Boomtown invariably spoke of Henry Wilson as the oldest settler in the Jim Valley, as he was of Buster County; but the Eastern man, with his ideas of an "old settler," was surprised as he met the short, silent, middle-aged man, who was very loath to tell anything about himself, and about whom many strange and thrilling stories were told by good story-tellers. In 1879 he was the only settler in the upper part of the valley, living alone on the banks of the Elm, a slow, tortuous stream pulsing lazily down the valley, too small to be called a river and too long to be called a creek. For two years, it is said, Wilson had only the company of his cattle, especially during the winter-time, and now and then a visit from an Indian, or a trapper after mink and musk-rats.

Between his ranch and the settlements in Eastern Dakota there was the wedge-shaped reservation known as the Sisseton Indian Reserve, on which were stationed the customary agency and company of soldiers. But, of course, at that time the Indians were not restricted closely to the bounds of the reserve, but ranged freely over the vast and beautiful prairie lying between the coteaux or ranges of low hills which mark out "the Jim Valley." The valley was unsurveyed for the most part, and the Indians naturally felt a sort of proprietorship in it, and when Wilson drove his cattle down into the valley and squatted, the chief, Drifting Crane, welcomed him, as a host might, to an abundant feast whose hospitality was presumed upon, but who felt the need of sustaining his reputation as a host, and submitted graciously.

The Indians during the first summer got to know Wilson, and liked him for his silence, his courage, his generosity; but the older men pondered upon the matter a great deal and watched with grave faces to see him ploughing up the sod for his garden. There was something strange in this solitary man thus deserting his kindred, coming here to live alone with his cattle; they could not understand it. What they said in those pathetic, dimly lighted lodges will never be known; but when winter came, and the newcomer did not drive his cattle back over the hills as they thought he would, then the old chieftains took long counsel upon it. Night after night they smoked upon it, and at last Drifting Crane said to two of his young men: "Go ask this cattleman why he remains in the cold and snow with his cattle. Ask him why he does not drive his cattle home."

This was in March, and one evening a couple of days later, as Wilson was about re-entering his shanty at the close of his day's work, he was confronted by two stalwart Indians, who greeted him pleasantly.

"How d'e do? How d'e do?" he said in reply. "Come in. Come in and take a snack."

The Indians entered and sat silently while he put some food on the table. They hardly spoke till after they had eaten. The Indian is always hungry, for the reason that his food supply is insufficient and his clothing poor. When they sat on the cracker-boxes and soap-boxes which served as seats, they spoke. They told him of the chieftain's message. They said they had come to assist him in driving his cattle back across the hills; that he must go.

To all this talk in the Indian's epigrammatic way, and in the dialect which has never been written, the rancher replied almost as briefly: "You go back and tell Drifting Crane that I like this place; that I'm here to stay; that I don't want any help to drive my cattle. I'm on the lands of the Great Father at Washington, and Drifting Crane ain't got any say about it. Now that sizes the whole thing up. I ain't got anything against you nor against him, but I'm a settler; that's my constitution; and now I'm settled I'm going to stay."

While the Indians discussed his words between themselves he made a bed of blankets on the floor and said: "I never turn anybody out. A white man is just as good as an Indian as long as he behaves himself as well. You can bunk here."

The Indians didn't understand his words fully, but they did understand his gesture, and they smiled and accepted the courtesy, so like their own rude hospitality. Then they all smoked a pipe of tobacco in silence, and at last Wilson turned in and went serenely off to sleep, hearing the mutter of the Indians lying before the fire.

In the morning he gave them as good a breakfast as he had—bacon and potatoes, with coffee and crackers. Then he shook hands, saying: "Come again. I ain't got anything against you. You've done y'r duty. Now go back and tell your chief what I've said. I'm at home every day. Good day."

The Indians smiled kindly, and drawing their blankets over their arms, went away toward the east.

During April and May two or three reconnoitring parties of landhunters drifted over the hills and found him out. He was glad to see them, for, to tell the truth, the solitude of his life was telling on him. The winter had been severe, and he had hardly caught a glimpse of a white face during the three midwinter months, and his provisions were scanty.

These parties brought great news. One of them was the advance surveying party for a great Northern railroad, and they said a line of road was to be surveyed during the summer if their report was favourable.

"Well, what d'ye think of it?" Wilson asked, with a smile.

"Think! It's immense!" said a small man in the party, whom the rest called Judge Balser. "Why, they'll be a town of four thousand inhabitants in this valley before snow flies. We'll send the surveyors right over the divide next month."

They sent some papers to Wilson a few weeks later, which he devoured as a hungry dog might devour a plate of bacon. The papers were full of the wonderful resources of the Jim Valley. It spoke of the nutritious grasses for stock. It spoke of the successful venture of the lonely settler Wilson, how his stock fattened upon the winter grasses without shelter, etc., what vegetables he grew, etc., etc.

Wilson was reading this paper for the sixth time one evening in May. He had laid off his boots, his pipe was freshly filled, and he sat in the doorway in vast content, unmindful of the glory of colour that filled the western sky, and the superb evening chorus of the prairie-chickens, holding conventions on every hillock. He felt something touch him on the shoulder, and looked up to see a tall Indian gazing down upon him with a look of strange pride and gravity. Wilson sprang to his feet and held out his hand.

"Drifting Crane, how d'e do?"

The Indian bowed, but did not take the settler's hand. Drifting Crane would have been called old if he had been a white man, and there was a look of age in the fixed lines of his powerful, strongly modelled face, but no suspicion of weakness in the splendid poise of his broad, muscular body. There was a smileless gravity about his lips and eyes which was very impressive.

"I'm glad to see you. Come in and get something to eat," said Wilson, after a moment's pause.

The chief entered the cabin and took a seat near the door. He took a cup of milk and some meat and bread silently, and ate while listening to the talk of the settler.

"I don't brag on my biscuits, chief, but they *eat*, if a man is hungry enough. An' the milk's all right. I suppose you've come to see why I ain't moseying back over the divide?"

The chief, after a long pause, began to speak in a low, slow voice, as if choosing his words. He spoke in broken English, of course, but his speech was very direct and plain, and had none of those absurd figures of rhetoric which romancers invariably put into the mouths of Indians. His voice was almost lion-like in its depth, and yet was not unpleasant. It was easy to see that he was a chief by virtue of his own personality.

"Cattleman, my young men brought me bad message from you. They brought your words to me, saying he will not go away."

"That's about the way the thing stands," replied Wilson, in response to the question that was in the old chief's steady eyes. "I'm here to stay. This ain't your land. This is Uncle Sam's land, and part of it'll be mine as soon as the surveyors come to measure it off."

"Who gave it away?" asked the chief. "My people were cheated out of it. They didn't know what they were doing."

"I can't help that. That's for Congress to say. That's the business of the Great Father at Washington." Wilson's voice changed. He knew and liked the chief; he didn't want to offend him. "They ain't no use making a fuss, chief. You won't gain anything."

There was a look of deep sorrow in the old man's face. At last he spoke again: "The cattleman is welcome; but he must go, because whenever one white man goes and calls it good, the others come. Drifting Crane has seen it far in the east, twice. The white men come thick as the grass. They tear up the sod. They build houses. They scare the buffalo away. They spoil my young men with whisky. Already they begin to climb the eastern hills. Soon they will fill the valley, and Drifting Crane and his people will be surrounded. The sod will all be black."

"I hope you're right," was the rancher's grim reply.

"But they will not come if the cattleman go back to say the water is not good. There is no grass, and the Indians own the land."

Wilson smiled at the childish faith of the chief. "Won't do, chief —won't do. That won't do any good. I might as well stay."

The chief rose. He was touched by the settler's laugh; his eyes flashed; his voice took on a sterner note. "The white man *must* go!"

Wilson rose also. He was not a large man, but he was a very resolute one. "I shan't go!" he said, through his clinched teeth. Each man understood the tones of the other perfectly.

It was a thrilling, a significant scene. It was in absolute truth the meeting of the modern vidette of civilisation with one of the rearguard of retreating barbarism. Each man was a type; each was wrong, and each was right. The Indian as true and noble from the barbaric point of view as the white man. He was a warrior and hunter—made so by circumstances over which he had no control. Guiltless as the panther, because war to a savage is the necessity of life.

The settler represented the unflagging energy and fearless heart of the American pioneer. Narrow-minded, partly brutalised by hard labour and a lonely life, yet an admirable figure for all that. As he looked into the Indian's face he seemed to grow in height. He felt behind him all the weight of the millions of westward-moving settlers; he stood the representative of an unborn State. He took down a rifle from the wall—the magazine rifle, most modern of guns; he patted the stock, pulled the crank, throwing a shell into view.

"You know this thing, chief?"

The Indian nodded slightly.

"Well, I'll go when—this—is—empty."

"But my young men are many."

"So are the white men—my brothers."

The chief's head dropped forward. Wilson, ashamed of his boasting, put the rifle back on the wall.

"I'm not here to fight. You can kill me any time. You could 'a' killed me to-night, but it wouldn't do any good. It 'ud only make it worse for you. Why, they'll be a town in here bigger'n all your tribe before two grass from now. It ain't no use, Drifting Crane; it's *got* to be. You an' I can't help n'r hinder it. I know just how you feel about it, but I tell yeh it ain't no use to fight."

Drifting Crane turned his head and gazed out on the western sky, still red with the light of the fallen sun. His face was rigid as bronze, but there was a dreaming, prophetic look in his eyes. A lump came into the settler's throat; for the first time in his life he got a glimpse of the infinite despair of the Indian. He forgot that Drifting Crane was the representative of a "vagabond race;" he saw in him, or rather *felt* in him, something almost magnetic. He was a *man*, and a man of sorrows. The settler's voice was husky when he spoke again, and his lips trembled.

"Chief, I'd go to-morrow if it 'ud do any good, but it won't— not a particle. You know that, when you stop to think a minute. What good did it do to massa*cree* all them settlers at New Ulm? What good will it do to murder me and a hundred others? Not a bit. A thousand others would take our places. So I might just as well stay, and we might just as well keep good friends. Killin' is out o' fashion; don't do any good."

There was a twitching about the stern mouth of the Indian chief. He understood all too well the irresistible logic of the pioneer. He kept his martial attitude, but his broad chest heaved painfully and his eyes grew dim. At last he said: "Good-bye. Cattleman right; Drifting Crane wrong. Shake hands. Good-bye." He turned and strode away.

The rancher watched him till he mounted his pony, picketed down by the river; watched him as, with drooping head and rein flung loose upon the neck of his horse, he rode away into the dusk, hungry, weary and despairing, to face his problem alone. Again, for the thousandth time, the impotence of the Indian's arm and the hopelessness of his fate were shown as perfectly as if two armies had met and soaked the beautiful prairie sod with blood.

"This is all wrong," muttered the settler. "There's land enough for us all, or ought to be. I don't understand—— Well, I'll leave it to Uncle Sam anyway." He ended with a sigh.

❊ ❊ ❊

MARY WILKINS FREEMAN
(1862-   )

INHERITOR of Salem traditions, Mary Wilkins grew up in Randolph, Massachusetts. The deaths of her sister, mother and father left her alone and, without special training, to make her living. She turned to the short story, believing it to be a simple form she could handle more easily than the novel. Even her initial ventures were of a pattern so excellent, a treatment so economic as to beguile the unwary into phrases about French influence. Though Miss Wilkins's preference lay in the realms of the mystical and allegorical (see *The Wind in the Rosebush*, 1903), it gave way to her recognition of demand for the actual and the necessity of meeting it. She wrote, therefore, tales pathetic or pleasant of "down East" folk, tales that establish her place in literature by her record of life in the years when she was part of that life. Her first two collections, *A Humble Romance* (1887) and *A New England Nun* (1891) have not been surpassed by her later work which, however, maintains her high level in craftsmanship and continues her interest in humanity. That interest was transferred, to some extent, from New England to New Jersey when (1902) she married Dr. Charles Freeman.

A New England Nun, already a classic, is here reprinted by kind permission of the publishers from *A New England Nun and Other Stories*. Copyright, 1891, by Harper & Brothers; copyright, 1919, by Mary E. Wilkins Freeman.

A NEW ENGLAND NUN

IT was late in the afternoon, and the light was waning. There was a difference in the look of the tree shadows out in the yard. Somewhere in the distance cows were lowing and a little bell was tinkling; now and then a farm-wagon tilted by, and the dust flew; some blue-shirted labourers with shovels over their shoulders plodded past; little swarms of flies were dancing up and down before the people's faces in the soft air. There seemed to be a gentle stir arising over everything for the mere sake of subsidence—a very premonition of rest and hush and night.

This soft diurnal commotion was over Louisa Ellis also. She had been peacefully sewing at her sitting-room window all the afternoon. Now she quilted her needle carefully into her work, which she folded precisely, and laid in a basket with her thimble and thread and scissors. Louisa Ellis could not remember that ever in her life she had mislaid one of these little feminine appurtenances, which had become, from long use and constant association, a very part of her personality.

Louisa tied a green apron round her waist, and got out a flat straw hat with a green ribbon. Then she went into the garden with a little blue crockery bowl, to pick some currants for her tea. After the currants were picked she sat on the back door-step and stemmed them, collecting the stems carefully in her apron, and afterwards throwing them into the hen-coop. She looked sharply at the grass beside the step to see if any had fallen there.

Louisa was slow and still in her movements; it took her a long time to prepare her tea; but when ready it was set forth with as much grace as if she had been a veritable guest to her own self. The little square table stood exactly in the centre of the kitchen, and was covered with a starched linen cloth whose border pattern of flowers glistened. Louisa had a damask napkin on her tea-tray, where were arranged a cut-glass tumbler full of teaspoons, a silver cream-pitcher, a china sugar-bowl, and one pink china cup and saucer. Louisa used china every day—something which none of her neighbours did. They whispered about it among themselves. Their daily tables were laid with common crockery, their sets of best china stayed in the parlor closet, and Louisa Ellis was no richer nor better bred than they. Still she would use the china. She had for her supper a glass dish full of sugared currants, a plate of little cakes, and one of light white biscuits. Also a leaf or two of lettuce which she cut up daintily. Louisa was very fond of lettuce, which she raised to perfection in her little garden. She ate quite heartily, though in a delicate, pecking way; it seemed almost surprising that any considerable bulk of the food should vanish.

After tea she filled a plate with nicely baked thin corn-cakes, and carried them out into the back yard.

"Cæsar!" she called. "Cæsar! Cæsar!"

There was a little rush, and the clank of a chain, and a large yellow-and-white dog appeared at the door of his tiny hut, which was half hidden among the tall grasses and flowers. Louisa patted him and gave him the corn-cakes. Then she returned to the house and washed the tea-things, polishing the china carefully. The twilight had deepened; the chorus of the frogs floated in at the open window wonderfully loud and shrill, and once in a while a long sharp drone from a tree-toad pierced it. Louisa took off her green gingham apron, disclosing a shorter one of pink and white print. She lighted her lamp, and sat down again with her sewing.

In about half an hour Joe Dagget came. She heard his heavy step on the walk, and rose and took off her pink-and-white apron. Under that was still another—white linen with a little cambric edging on the bottom; that was Louisa's company apron. She never wore it without her calico sewing apron over it unless she had a guest. She had barely folded the pink and white one with methodical haste and laid it in a table-drawer when the door opened and Joe Dagget entered.

He seemed to fill up the whole room. A little yellow canary that had been asleep in his green cage at the south window woke up and fluttered wildly, beating his little yellow wings against the wires. He always did so when Joe Dagget came into the room.

"Good-evening," said Louisa. She extended her hand with a kind of solemn cordiality.

"Good-evening, Louisa," returned the man, in a loud voice.

She placed a chair for him, and they sat facing each other, with the table between them. He sat bolt-upright, toeing out his heavy feet squarely, glancing with a good-humoured uneasiness around the room. She sat gently erect, folding her slender hands in her white-linen lap.

"Been a pleasant day," remarked Dagget.

"Real pleasant," Louisa assented, softly. "Have you been haying?" she asked, after a little while.

"Yes, I've been haying all day, down in the ten-acre lot. Pretty hot work."

"It must be."

"Yes, it's pretty hot work in the sun."

"Is your mother well to-day?"

"Yes, mother's pretty well."

"I suppose Lily Dyer's with her now?"

Dagget coloured. "Yes, she's with her," he answered, slowly.

He was not very young, but there was a boyish look about his large face. Louisa was not quite as old as he, her face was fairer and smoother, but she gave people the impression of being older.

"I suppose she's a good deal of help to your mother," she said, further.

"I guess she is; I don't know how mother'd get along without her," said Dagget, with a sort of embarrassed warmth.

"She looks like a real capable girl. She's pretty-looking, too," remarked Louisa.

"Yes, she is pretty fair looking."

Presently Dagget began fingering the books on the table. There was a square red autograph album, and a Young Lady's Gift-Book which had belonged to Louisa's mother. He took them up one after the other and opened them; then laid them down again, the album on the Gift-Book.

Louisa kept eyeing them with mild uneasiness. Finally she rose and changed the position of the books, putting the album underneath. That was the way they had been arranged in the first place.

Dagget gave an awkward little laugh. "Now what difference did it make which book was on top?" said he.

Louisa looked at him with a deprecating smile. "I always keep them that way," murmured she.

"You do beat everything," said Dagget, trying to laugh again. His large face was flushed.

He remained about an hour longer, then rose to take leave. Going out, he stumbled over a rug, and trying to recover himself, hit Louisa's work-basket on the table, and knocked it on the floor.

He looked at Louisa, then at the rolling spools; he ducked himself awkwardly toward them, but she stopped him. "Never mind," said she; "I'll pick them up after you're gone."

She spoke with a mild stiffness. Either she was a little disturbed, or his nervousness affected her, and made her seem constrained in her effort to reassure him.

When Joe Dagget was outside he drew in the sweet evening air with a sigh, and felt much as an innocent and perfectly well-intentioned bear might after his exit from a china shop.

Louisa, on her part, felt much as the kind-hearted, long-suffering owner of the china shop might have done after the exit of the bear.

She tied on the pink, then the green apron, picked up all the scattered treasures and replaced them in her work-basket, and straightened the rug. Then she set the lamp on the floor, and began sharply examining the carpet. She even rubbed her fingers over it, and looked at them.

"He's tracked in a good deal of dust," she murmured. "I thought he must have."

Louisa got a dust-pan and brush, and swept Joe Dagget's track carefully.

If he could have known it, it would have increased his perplexity and uneasiness, although it would not have disturbed his loyalty in the least. He came twice a week to see Louisa Ellis, and every time, sitting there in her delicately sweet room, he felt as if surrounded by a hedge of lace. He was afraid to stir lest he should put a clumsy foot or hand through the fairy web, and he had always the consciousness that Louisa was watching fearfully lest he should.

Still the lace and Louisa commanded perforce his perfect respect and patience and loyalty. They were to be married in a month, after a singular courtship which had lasted for a matter of fifteen years. For fourteen out of the fifteen years the two had not once seen each other, and they had seldom exchanged letters. Joe had been all those years in Australia, where he had gone to make his fortune, and where he had stayed until he made it. He would have stayed fifty years if it had taken so long, and come home feeble and tottering, or never come home at all, to marry Louisa.

But the fortune had been made in the fourteen years, and he had come home now to marry the woman who had been patiently and unquestioningly waiting for him all that time.

Shortly after they were engaged he had announced to Louisa his determination to strike out into new fields, and secure a competency before they should be married. She had listened and assented with the sweet serenity which never failed her, not even when her lover set forth on that long and uncertain journey. Joe, buoyed up as he was by his sturdy determination, broke down a little at the last, but Louisa kissed him with a mild blush, and said good-bye.

"It won't be for long," poor Joe had said, huskily; but it was for fourteen years.

In that length of time much had happened. Louisa's mother and brother had died, and she was all alone in the world. But greatest happening of all—a subtle happening which both were too simple to understand —Louisa's feet had turned into a path, smooth maybe under a calm, serene sky, but so straight and unswerving that it could only meet a check at her grave, and so narrow that there was no room for any one at her side.

Louisa's first emotion when Joe Dagget came home (he had not apprised her of his coming) was consternation, although she would not admit it to herself, and he never dreamed of it. Fifteen years ago she had been in love with him—at least she considered herself to be. Just at that time, gently acquiescing with and falling into the natural drift of girlhood, she had seen marriage ahead as a reasonable feature and a probable desirability of life. She had listened with calm docility to her mother's views upon the subject. Her mother was remarkable for her cool sense and sweet, even temperament. She talked wisely to her daughter when Joe Dagget presented himself, and Louisa accepted him with no hesitation. He was the first lover she had ever had.

She had been faithful to him all these years. She had never dreamed of the possibility of marrying any one else. Her life, especially for the last seven years, had been full of a pleasant peace, she had never felt discontented nor impatient over her lover's absence; still she had always looked forward to his return and their marriage as the inevitable conclusion of things. However, she had fallen into a way of placing it so far in the future that it was almost equal to placing it over the boundaries of another life.

When Joe came she had been expecting him, and expecting to be married for fourteen years, but she was as much surprised and taken aback as if she had never thought of it.

Joe's consternation came later. He eyed Louisa with an instant confirmation of his old admiration. She had changed but little. She still kept her pretty manner and soft grace, and was, he considered, every whit as attractive as ever. As for himself, his stunt was done; he had turned his face away from fortune-seeking, and the old winds of romance whistled as loud and sweet as ever through his ears. All the song which he had been wont to hear in them was Louisa; he had for a long time a loyal belief that he heard it still, but finally it seemed to him that although the winds sang always that one song, it had another name. But for Louisa the wind had never more than murmured; now it had gone down, and everything was still. She listened for a little while with half-wistful attention; then she turned quietly away and went to work on her wedding clothes.

Joe had made some extensive and quite magnificent alterations in his house. It was the old homestead; the newly-married couple would live there, for Joe could not desert his mother, who refused to leave her old home. So Louisa must leave hers. Every morning, rising and going about among her neat maidenly possessions, she felt as one looking her last upon the faces of dear friends. It was true that in a measure she could take them with her, but robbed of their old environments, they would appear in such new guises that they would almost cease to be themselves. Then there were some peculiar features of her happy solitary life which she would probably be obliged to relinquish altogether. Sterner tasks than these graceful but half-needless ones would probably devolve upon her. There would be a large house to care for; there would be company to entertain; there would be Joe's rigorous and feeble old mother to wait upon; and it would be contrary to all thrifty village traditions for her to keep more than one servant. Louisa had a little still, and she used to occupy herself pleasantly in summer weather with distilling the sweet and aromatic essences from roses and peppermint and spearmint. By-and-by her still must be laid away. Her store of essences was already considerable, and there would be no time for her to distil for the mere pleasure of it. Then Joe's mother would think it foolishness; she had already hinted her opinion in the matter. Louisa dearly loved to sew a linen seam, not always for use, but for the simple, mild pleasure which she took in it. She would have been loath to confess how more than once she had ripped a seam for the mere delight of sewing it together again. Sitting at her window during long sweet afternoons, drawing her needle gently through the dainty fabric, she was peace itself. But there was small chance of such foolish comfort in the future. Joe's mother, domineering, shrewd old matron that she was even in her old age, and very likely even Joe himself, with his honest masculine rudeness, would laugh and frown down all these pretty but senseless old maiden ways.

Louisa had almost the enthusiasm of an artist over the mere order and cleanliness of her solitary home. She had throbs of genuine triumph at the sight of the window-panes which she had polished until they shone like jewels. She gloated gently over her orderly bureau-drawers, with their exquisitely folded contents redolent with lavender and sweet clover and very purity. Could she be sure of the endurance of even this? She had visions, so startling that she half repudiated them as indelicate, of coarse masculine belongings strewn about in endless litter; of dust and disorder arising necessarily from a coarse masculine presence in the midst of all this delicate harmony.

Among her forebodings of disturbance, not the least was with regard to Cæsar. Cæsar was a veritable hermit of a dog. For the greater part of his life he had dwelt in his secluded hut, shut out from the society of his kind and all innocent canine joys. Never had Cæsar since his early youth watched at a woodchuck's hole; never had he known the delights of a stray bone at a neighbour's kitchen door. And it was all on account of a sin committed when hardly out of his puppyhood. No one knew the possible depth of remorse of which this mild-visaged, altogether innocent-looking old dog might be capable; but whether or not he had encountered remorse, he had encountered a full measure of righteous retribution. Old Cæsar seldom lifted up his voice in a growl or a bark; he was fat and sleepy; there were yellow rings which looked like spectacles around his dim old eyes; but there was a neighbour who bore on his hand the imprint of several of Cæsar's sharp white youthful teeth, and for that he had lived at the end of a chain, all alone in a little hut, for fourteen years. The neighbour, who was choleric and smarting with the pain of his wound, had demanded either Cæsar's death or complete ostracism. So Louisa's brother, to whom the dog had belonged, had built him his little kennel and tied him up. It was now fourteen years since, in a flood of youthful spirits, he had inflicted that memorable bite, and with the exception of short excursions, always at the end of the chain, under the strict guardianship of his master or Louisa, the old dog had remained a close prisoner. It is doubtful if, with his limited ambition, he took much pride in the fact, but it is certain that he was possessed of considerable cheap fame. He was regarded by all the children in the village and by many adults as a very monster of ferocity. St. George's dragon could hardly have surpassed in evil repute Louisa Ellis's old yellow dog. Mothers charged their children with solemn emphasis not to go too near to him, and the children listened and believed greedily, with a fascinated appetite for terror, and ran by Louisa's house stealthily, with many sidelong and backward glances at the terrible dog. If perchance he sounded a hoarse bark, there was a panic. Wayfarers chancing into Louisa's yard eyed him with respect, and inquired if the chain were stout. Cæsar at large might have seemed a very ordinary dog, and excited no comment whatever; chained, his reputation overshadowed him, so that he lost his own proper outlines and looked darkly vague and enormous. Joe Dagget, however, with his good-humoured sense and shrewdness, saw him as he was. He strode valiantly up to him and patted him on the head, in spite of Louisa's soft clamour of warning, and even attempted to set him loose. Louisa grew so alarmed that he desisted, but kept announcing his opinion in the matter quite forcibly at intervals. "There ain't a better-natured dog in town," he would say, "and it's downright cruel to keep him tied up there. Some day I'm going to take him out."

Louisa had very little hope that he would not, one of these days, when their interests and possessions should be more completely fused in one. She pictured to herself Cæsar on the rampage through the quiet and unguarded village. She saw innocent children bleeding in his path. She was herself very fond of the old dog, because he had belonged to her dead brother, and he was always very gentle with her; still she had great faith in his ferocity. She always warned people not to go too near him. She fed him on ascetic fare of corn-mush and cakes, and never fired his dangerous temper with heating and sanguinary diet of flesh and bones. Louisa looked at the old dog munching his simple fare, and thought of her approaching marriage and trembled. Still no anticipation of disorder and confusion in lieu of sweet peace and harmony, no forebodings of Cæsar on the rampage, no wild fluttering of her little yellow canary, were sufficient to turn her a hairs'-breadth. Joe Dagget had been fond of her and working for her all these years. It was not for her, whatever came to pass, to prove untrue and break his heart. She put the exquisite little stitches into her wedding-garments, and the time went on until it was only a week before her wedding-day. It was a Tuesday evening, and the wedding was to be a week from Wednesday.

There was a full moon that night. About nine o'clock Louisa strolled down the road a little way. There were harvest-fields on either hand, bordered by low stone walls. Luxuriant clumps of bushes grew beside the wall, and trees—wild cherry and old apple-trees—at intervals. Presently Louisa sat down on the wall and looked about her with mildly sorrowful reflectiveness. Tall shrubs of blueberry and meadow-sweet, all woven together and tangled with blackberry vines and horsebriers, shut her in on either side. She had a little clear space between them. Opposite her, on the other side of the road, was a spreading tree; the moon shone between its boughs, and the leaves twinkled like silver. The road was bespread with a beautiful shifting dapple of silver and shadow; the air was full of a mysterious sweetness. "I wonder if it's wild grapes?" murmured Louisa. She sat there some time. She was just thinking of rising, when she heard footsteps and low voices, and remained quiet. It was a lonely place, and she felt a little timid. She thought she would keep still in the shadow and let the persons, whoever they might be, pass her.

But just before they reached her the voices ceased, and the footsteps. She understood that their owners had also found seats upon the stone wall. She was wondering if she could not steal away unobserved, when the voice broke the stillness. It was Joe Dagget's. She sat still and listened.

The voice was announced by a loud sigh, which was as familiar as itself. "Well," said Dagget, "you've made up your mind, then, I suppose?"

"Yes," returned another voice; "I'm going day after to-morrow."

"That's Lily Dyer," thought Louisa to herself. The voice embodied itself in her mind. She saw a girl tall and full-figured, with a firm, fair face, looking fairer and firmer in the moonlight, her strong yellow hair braided in a close knot. A girl full of a calm rustic strength and bloom, with a masterful way which might have beseemed a princess. Lily Dyer was a favourite with the village folk; she had just the qualities to arouse the admiration. She was good and handsome and smart. Louisa had often heard her praises sounded.

"Well," said Joe Dagget, "I ain't got a word to say."

"I don't know what you could say," returned Lily Dyer.

"Not a word to say," repeated Joe, drawing out the words heavily. Then there was a silence. "I ain't sorry," he began at last, "that that happened yesterday—that we kind of let on how we felt to each other. I guess it's just as well we knew. Of course I can't do anything any different. I'm going right on an' get married next week. I ain't going back on a woman that's waited for me fourteen years, an' break her heart."

"If you should jilt her to-morrow, I wouldn't have you," spoke up the girl, with sudden vehemence.

"Well, I ain't going to give you the chance," said he; "but I don't believe you would, either."

"You'd see I wouldn't. Honour's honour, an' right's right. An' I'd never think anything of any man that went against 'em for me or any other girl; you'd find that out, Joe Dagget."

"Well, you'll find out fast enough that I ain't going against 'em for you or any other girl," returned he. Their voices sounded almost as if they were angry with each other. Louisa was listening eagerly.

"I'm sorry you feel as if you must go away," said Joe, "but I don't know but it's best."

"Of course it's best. I hope you and I have got common-sense."

"Well, I suppose you're right." Suddenly Joe's voice got an undertone of tenderness. "Say, Lily," said he, "I'll get along well enough myself, but I can't bear to think— You don't suppose you're going to fret much over it?"

"I guess you'll find out I sha'n't fret much over a married man."

"Well, I hope you won't—I hope you won't, Lily. God knows I do. And—I hope—one of these days—you'll—come across somebody else——"

"I don't see any reason why I shouldn't." Suddenly her tone changed. She spoke in a sweet, clear voice, so loud that she could have been heard across the street.

"No, Joe Dagget," said she, "I'll never marry any other man as long as I live. I've got good sense, an' I ain't going to break my heart nor make a fool of myself; but I'm never going to be married, you can be sure of that. I ain't that sort of a girl to feel this way twice."

Louisa heard an exclamation and a soft commotion behind the bushes; then Lily spoke again—the voice sounded as if she had risen. "This must be put a stop to," said she. "We've stayed here long enough. I'm going home."

Louisa sat there in a daze, listening to their retreating steps. After a while she got up and slunk softly home herself. The next day she did her housework methodically; that was as much a matter of course as breathing; but she did not sew on her wedding-clothes. She sat at her window and meditated. In the evening Joe came. Louisa Ellis had never known that she had any diplomacy in her, but when she came to look for it that night she found it, although meek of its kind, among her little feminine weapons. Even now she could hardly believe that she had heard aright, and that she would not do Joe a terrible injury should she break her troth-plight. She wanted to sound him without betraying too soon her own inclinations in the matter. She did it successfully, and they finally came to an understanding; but it was a difficult thing, for he was as afraid of betraying himself as she.

She never mentioned Lily Dyer. She simply said that while she had no cause of complaint against him, she had lived so long in one way that she shrank from making a change.

"Well, I never shrank, Louisa," said Dagget. "I'm going to be honest enough to say that I think maybe it's better this way; but if you'd wanted to keep on, I'd have stuck to you till my dying day. I hope you know that."

"Yes, I do," said she.

That night she and Joe parted more tenderly than they had done for a long time. Standing in the door, holding each other's hands, a last great wave of regretful memory swept over them.

"Well, this ain't the way we've thought it was all going to end, is it, Louisa?" said Joe.

She shook her head. There was a little quiver on her placid face.

"You let me know if there's ever anything I can do for you," said he. "I ain't ever going to forget you, Louisa." Then he kissed her, and went down the path.

Louisa, all alone by herself that night, wept a little, she hardly knew why; but the next morning, on waking, she felt like a queen who, after fearing lest her domain be wrested away from her, sees it firmly insured in her possession.

Now the tall weeds and grasses might cluster around Cæsar's little hermit hut, the snow might fall on its roof year in and year out, but he never would go on a rampage through the unguarded village. Now the little canary might turn itself into a peaceful yellow ball night after night, and have no need to wake and flutter with wild terror against its bars. Louisa could sew linen seams, and distil roses, and dust and polish and fold away in lavender, as long as she listed. That afternoon she sat with her needle-work at the window, and felt fairly steeped in peace. Lily Dyer, tall and erect and blooming, went past; but she felt no qualm. If Louisa Ellis had sold her birthright she did not know it, the taste of the pottage was só delicious, and had been her sole satisfaction for so long. Serenity and placid narrowness had become to her as the birthright itself. She gazed ahead through a long reach of future days strung together like pearls in a rosary, every one like the others, and all smooth and flawless and innocent, and her heart went up in thankfulness. Outside was the fervid summer afternoon; the air was filled with the sounds of the busy harvest of men and birds and bees; there were halloos, metallic clatterings, sweet calls, and long hummings. Louisa sat, prayerfully numbering her days, like an uncloistered nun.

O. HENRY
(1862-1910)

AT GREENSBORO, North Carolina, in 1862, was born William Sidney Porter, later to be known as O. Henry. At the age of nineteen he went to Texas, where he tried various occupations. In 1898 he was convicted of embezzling, nearly four years earlier, funds from the Bank at Austin and was sentenced to the Federal prison at Columbus, Ohio. Three years in the penitentiary developed in Sidney Porter what proved to be the greatest single influence the short story received in the first quarter of the Twentieth Century. In 1901, released on good conduct before the expiration of his term, he came to New York. Exploiting the four million, rather than the four hundred, he popularised democracy in fiction. In 1903 he began to write for the *New York World*, producing a story a week for nearly three years. He is a master of the concise, of humorous twists of phraseology, and of the surprise ending. Less than a year before his death (July, 1910) he published in *Hampton's Magazine* (November, 1909) *A Municipal Report*, frequently praised as his best narrative. It is here reprinted from *Strictly Business*, by special arrangement with the publishers, Doubleday, Page and Company, Garden City, New York.

A MUNICIPAL REPORT

> The cities are full of pride
> Challenging each to each—
> This from her mountainside,
> That from her burthened beach.
>
> —R. KIPLING.

Fancy a novel about Chicago or Buffalo, let us say, or Nashville, Tennessee! There are just three big cities in the United States that are "story cities"— New York, of course, New Orleans, and, best of the lot, San Francisco.—FRANK NORRIS.

EAST is East, and West is San Francisco, according to Californians. Californians are a race of people; they are not merely inhabitants of a State. They are the Southerners of the West. Now, Chicagoans are no less loyal to their city; but when you ask them why, they stammer and speak of lake fish and the new Odd Fellows Building. But Californians go into detail.

Of course they have, in the climate, an argument that is good for half an hour while you are thinking of your coal bills and heavy underwear. But as soon as they come to mistake your silence for conviction, madness comes upon them, and they picture the city of the Golden Gate as the Bagdad of the New World. So far, as a matter of opinion, no refutation is necessary. But, dear cousins all (from Adam and Eve descended), it is a rash one who will lay his finger on the map and say: "In this town there can be no romance—what could happen here?" Yes, it is a bold and a rash deed to challenge in one sentence history, romance, and Rand and McNally.

NASHVILLE—A city, port of delivery, and the capital of the State of Tennessee, is on the Cumberland River and on the N. C. & St. L. and the L. & N. railroads. This city is regarded as the most important educational centre in the South.

I stepped off the train at 8 P. M. Having searched the thesaurus in vain for adjectives, I must, as a substitution, hie me to comparison in the form of a recipe.

Take of London fog 30 parts; malaria 10 parts; gas leaks 20 parts; dewdrops gathered in a brick yard at sunrise, 25 parts; odour of honeysuckle 15 parts. Mix.

The mixture will give you an approximate conception of a Nashville drizzle. It is not so fragrant as a moth-ball nor as thick as pea-soup; but 'tis enough—'twill serve.

I went to a hotel in a tumbril. It required strong self-suppression for me to keep from climbing to the top of it and giving an imitation of Sidney Carton. The vehicle was drawn by beasts of a bygone era and driven by something dark and emancipated.

I was sleepy and tired, so when I got to the hotel I hurriedly paid it the fifty cents it demanded (with approximate lagnappe, I assure you). I knew its habits; and I did not want to hear it prate about its old "marster" or anything that happened "befo' de wah."

The hotel was one of the kind described as "renovated." That means $20,000 worth of new marble pillars, tiling, electric lights and brass cuspidors in the lobby, and a new L. & N. time table and a lithograph of Lookout Mountain in each one of the great rooms above. The management was without reproach, the attention full of exquisite Southern courtesy, the service as slow as the progress of a snail and as good-humoured as Rip Van Winkle. The food was worth travelling a thousand miles for. There is no other hotel in the world where you can get such chicken livers *en brochette*.

At dinner I asked a Negro waiter if there was anything doing in town. He pondered gravely for a minute, and then replied: "Well, boss, I don't really reckon there's anything at all doin' after sundown."

Sundown had been accomplished; it had been drowned in the drizzle long before. So that spectacle was denied me. But I went forth upon the streets in the drizzle to see what might be there.

It is built on undulating grounds; and the streets are lighted by electricity at a cost of $32,470 per annum.

As I left the hotel there was a race riot. Down upon me charged a company of freedmen, or Arabs, or Zulus, armed with—no, I saw with relief that they were not rifles, but whips. And I saw dimly a caravan of black, clumsy vehicles; and at the reassuring shouts, "Kyar you anywhere in the town, boss, fuh fifty cents," I reasoned that I was merely a "fare" instead of a victim.

I walked through long streets, all leading uphill. I wondered how those streets ever came down again. Perhaps they didn't until they were "graded." On a few of the "main streets" I saw lights in stores here and there; saw street cars go by conveying worthy burghers hither and yon; saw people pass engaged in the art of conversation, and heard a burst of semi-lively laughter issuing from a soda-water and ice-cream parlor. The streets other than "main" seemed to have enticed upon their borders houses consecrated to peace and domesticity. In many of them lights shone behind discreetly drawn window shades; in a few pianos tinkled orderly and irreproachable music. There was, indeed, little "doing." I wished I had come before sundown. So I returned to my hotel.

In November, 1864, the Confederate General Hood advanced against Nashville, where he shut up a National force under General Thomas. The latter then sallied forth and defeated the Confederates in a terrible conflict.

All my life I have heard of, admired, and witnessed the fine marksmanship of the South in its peaceful conflicts in the tobacco-chewing regions. But in my hotel a surprise awaited me. There were twelve bright, new, imposing, capacious brass cuspidors in the great lobby, tall enough to be called urns and so wide-mouthed that the crack pitcher of a lady baseball team should have been able to throw a ball into one of them at five paces distant. But, although a terrible battle had raged and was still raging, the enemy had not suffered. Bright, new, imposing, capacious, untouched, they stood. But, shades of Jefferson Brick! the tile floor—the beautiful tile floor! I could not avoid thinking of the battle of Nashville, and trying to draw, as is my foolish habit, some deductions about hereditary marksmanship.

Here I first saw Major (by misplaced courtesy) Wentworth Caswell. I knew him for a type the moment my eyes suffered from the sight of him. A rat has no geographical habitat. My old friend, A. Tennyson, said, as he so well said almost everything:

Prophet, curse me the blabbing lip,
And curse me the British vermin, the rat.

Let us regard the word "British" as interchangeable *ad lib*. A rat is a rat.

This man was hunting about the hotel lobby like a starved dog that had forgotten where he had buried a bone. He had a face of great acreage, red, pulpy, and with a kind of sleepy massiveness like that of Buddha. He possessed one single virtue—he was very smoothly shaven. The mark of the beast is not indelible upon a man until he goes about with a stubble. I think that if he had not used his razor that day I would have repulsed his advances, and the criminal calendar of the world would have been spared the addition of one murder.

I happened to be standing within five feet of a cuspidor when Major Caswell opened fire upon it. I had been observant enough to perceive that the attacking force was using Gatlings instead of squirrel rifles; so I sidestepped so promptly that the major seized the opportunity to apologise to a noncombatant. He had the blabbing lip. In four minutes he had become my friend and had dragged me to the bar.

I desire to interpolate here that I am a Southerner. But I am not one by profession or trade. I eschew the string tie, the slouch hat, the Prince Albert, the number of bales of cotton destroyed by Sherman, and plug chewing. When the orchestra plays Dixie I do not cheer. I slide a little lower on the leather-cornered seat and, well, order another Wurzburger and wish that Longstreet had—but what's the use?

Major Caswell banged the bar with his fist, and the first gun at Fort Sumter re-echoed. When he fired the last one at Appomattox I began to hope. But then he began on family trees, and demonstrated that Adam was only a third cousin of a collateral branch of the Caswell family. Genealogy disposed of, he took up, to my distaste, his private family matters. He spoke of his wife, traced her descent back to Eve, and profanely denied any possible rumour that she may have had relations in the land of Nod.

By this time I began to suspect that he was trying to obscure by noise the fact that he had ordered the drinks, on the chance that I would be bewildered into paying for them. But when they were down he crashed a silver dollar loudly upon the bar. Then, of course, another serving was obligatory. And when I had paid for that I took leave of him brusquely; for I wanted no more of him. But before I had obtained my release he had prated loudly of an income that his wife received, and showed a handful of silver money.

When I got my key at the desk the clerk said to me courteously: "If that man Caswell has annoyed you, and if you would like to make a complaint, we will have him ejected. He is a nuisance, a loafer, and

GREAT STORIES OF ALL NATIONS

without any known means of support, although he seems to have some money most of the time. But we don't seem to be able to hit upon any means of throwing him out legally."

"Why, no," said I, after some reflection; "I don't see my way clear to making a complaint. But I would like to place myself on record as asserting that I do not care for his company. Your town," I continued, "seems to be a quiet one. What manner of entertainment, adventure, or excitement have you to offer to the stranger within your gates?"

"Well, sir," said the clerk, "there will be a show here next Thursday. It is—I'll look it up and have the announcement sent up to your room with the ice water. Good night."

After I went up to my room I looked out the window. It was only about ten o'clock, but I looked upon a silent town. The drizzle continued, spangled with dim lights, as far apart as currants in a cake sold at the Ladies' Exchange.

"A quiet place," I said to myself, as my first shoe struck the ceiling of the occupant of the room beneath mine.

"Nothing of the life here that gives colour and variety to the cities in the East and West. Just a good, ordinary, humdrum, business town."

Nashville occupies a foremost place among the manufacturing centres of the country. It is the fifth boot and shoe market in the United States, the largest candy and cracker manufacturing city in the South, and does an enormous wholesale drygoods, grocery, and drug business.

I must tell you how I came to be in Nashville, and I assure you the digression brings as much tedium to me as it does to you. I was travelling elsewhere on my own business, but I had a commission from a Northern literary magazine to stop over there and establish a personal connection between the publication and one of its contributors, Azalea Adair.

Adair (there was no clue to the personality except the handwriting) had sent in some essays (lost art!) and poems that had made the editors swear approvingly over their one o'clock luncheon. So they had commissioned me to round up said Adair and corner by contract his or her output at two cents a word before some other publisher offered her ten or twenty.

At nine o'clock the next morning, after my chicken livers *en brochette* (try them if you can find that hotel), I strayed out into the drizzle, which was still on for an unlimited run. At the first corner I came upon Uncle Cæsar. He was a stalwart Negro, older than the pyramids, with grey wool, and a face that reminded me of Brutus, and a second afterwards of the late King Cettiwayo. He wore the most remarkable coat that I ever had seen or expect to see. It reached to his ankles and had once been a Confederate grey in colours. But rain and sun and age had so variegated it that Joseph's coat, beside it, would have faded to a pale monochrome. I must linger with that coat, for it has to do with the story—the story that is so long in coming, because you can hardly expect anything to happen in Nashville.

Once it must have been the military coat of an officer. The cape of it had vanished, but all adown its front it had been frogged and tasselled magnificently. But now the frogs and tassels were gone. In their stead had been patiently stitched (I surmised by some surviving "black mammy") new frogs made of cunningly twisted common hempen twine. This twine was frayed and disheveled. It must have been added to the coat as a substitute for vanished splendours, with tasteless but painstaking devotion, for it followed faithfully the curves of the long missing frogs. And, to complete the comedy and pathos of the garment, all its buttons were gone save one. The second button from the top alone remained. The coat was fastened by other twine strings tied through the buttonholes and other holes rudely pierced in the opposite side. There was never such a weird garment so fantastically bedecked and of so many mottled hues. The lone button was the size of a half-dollar, made of yellow horn and sewed on with coarse twine.

This Negro stood by a carriage so old that Ham himself might have started a hack line with it after he left the ark with the two animals hitched to it. As I approached he threw open the door, drew out a feather duster, waved it without using it, and said in deep, rumbling tones:

"Step right in, suh; ain't a speck of dust in it—jus' got back from a funeral, suh."

I inferred that on such gala occasions carriages were given an extra cleaning. I looked up and down the street and perceived that there was little choice among the vehicles for hire that lined the curb. I looked in my memorandum book for the address of Azalea Adair.

"I want to go to 861 Jessamine Street," I said, and was about to step into the hack. But for an instant the thick, long, gorilla-like arm of the old Negro barred me. On his massive and saturnine face a look of sudden suspicion and enmity flashed for a moment. Then, with quickly returning conviction, he asked blandishingly: "What are you gwine there for, boss?"

"What is that to you?" I asked, a little sharply.

"Nothin', suh, jus' nothin'. Only it's a lonesome kind of part of town and few folks ever has business out there. Step right in. The seats is clean—jes' got back from a funeral, suh."

A mile and a half it must have been to our journey's end. I could hear nothing but the fearful rattle of the ancient hack over the uneven brick paving; I could smell nothing but the drizzle, now further flavoured with coal smoke and something like a mixture of tar and oleander blossoms. All I could see through the streaming windows were two rows of dim houses.

The city has an area of 10 square miles; 181 miles of streets, of which 137 miles are paved; a system of waterworks that cost $2,000,000, with 77 miles of mains.

Eight-sixty-one Jessamine Street was a decayed mansion. Thirty yards back from the street it stood, outmerged in a splendid grove of trees and untrimmed shrubbery. A row of box bushes overflowed and almost hid the paling fence from sight; the gate was kept closed by a rope noose that encircled the gate post and the first paling of the gate. But when you got inside you saw that 861 was a shell, a shadow, a ghost of former grandeur and excellence. But in the story, I have not yet got inside.

When the hack had ceased from rattling and the weary quadrupeds came to a rest I handed my jehu his fifty cents with an additional quarter, feeling a glow of conscious generosity, as I did so. He refused it.

"It's two dollars, suh," he said.

"How's that?" I asked. "I plainly heard you call out at the hotel: 'Fifty cents to any part of the town.'"

"It's two dollars, suh," he repeated obstinately. "It's a long ways from the hotel."

"It is within the city limits and well within them," I argued. "Don't think that you have picked up a greenhorn Yankee. Do you see those hills over there?" I went on, pointing toward the east (I could not see them, myself, for the drizzle); "well, I was born and raised on their other side. You old fool nigger, can't you tell people from other people when you see 'em?"

The grim face of King Cettiwayo softened. "Is you from the South, suh? I reckon it was them shoes of yourn fooled me. They is somethin' sharp in the toes for a Southern gen'l'man to wear."

"Then the charge is fifty cents, I suppose?" said I inexorably.

His former expression, a mingling of cupidity and hostility, returned, remained ten seconds, and vanished.

"Boss," he said, "fifty cents is right; but I *needs* two dollars, suh; I'm *obleeged* to have two dollars. I ain't *demandin'* it now, suh; after I knows whar you's from; I'm jus' sayin' that I *has* to have two dollars to-night, and business is mighty po'."

Peace and confidence settled upon his heavy features. He had been luckier than he had hoped. Instead of having picked up a greenhorn, ignorant of rates, he had come upon an inheritance.

"You confounded old rascal," I said, reaching down into my pocket "you ought to be turned over to the police."

For the first time I saw him smile. He knew; *he knew*; HE KNEW.

I gave him two one-dollar bills. As I handed them over I noticed that one of them had seen parlous times. Its upper right-hand corner was missing, and it had been torn through in the middle, but joined again. A strip of blue tissue paper, pasted over the split, preserved its negotiability.

Enough of the African bandit for the present: I left him happy, lifted the rope and opened the creaky gate.

The house, as I said, was a shell. A paint brush had not touched it in twenty years. I could not see why a strong wind should not have bowled it over like a house of cards until I looked again at the trees that hugged it close—the trees that saw the battle of Nashville and still drew their protecting branches around it against storm and enemy and cold.

Azalea Adair, fifty years old, white-haired, a descendant of the cavaliers, as thin and frail as the house she lived in, robed in the cheapest and cleanest dress I ever saw, with an air as simple as a queen's, received me.

The reception room seemed a mile square, because there was nothing in it except some rows of books, on unpainted white-pine bookshelves, a cracked marble-top table, a rag rug, a hairless horsehair sofa and two or three chairs. Yes, there was a picture on the wall, a coloured crayon drawing of a cluster of pansies. I looked around for the portrait of Andrew Jackson and the pine-cone hanging basket but they were not there.

Azalea Adair and I had conversation, a little of which will be repeated to you. She was a product of the old South, gently nurtured in the sheltered life. Her learning was not broad, but was deep and of splendid originality in its somewhat narrow scope. She had been educated at home, and her knowledge of the world was derived from inference and by inspiration. Of such is the precious, small group of essayists made. While she talked to me I kept brushing my fingers, trying, unconsciously, to rid them guiltily of the absent dust from the half-calf backs of Lamb, Chaucer, Hazlitt, Marcus Aurelius, Montaigne and Hood. She was exquisite, she was a valuable discovery. Nearly everybody nowadays knows too much—oh, so much too much—of real life.

I could perceive clearly that Azalea Adair was very poor. A house and a dress she had, not much else, I fancied. So, divided between my duty to the magazine and my loyalty to the poets and essayists who fought Thomas in the valley of the Cumberland, I listened to her voice, which was like a harpsichord's, and found that I could not speak of contracts. In the presence of the nine Muses and the three Graces one hesitated to lower the topic to two cents. There would have to be another colloquy after I had regained my commercialism. But I spoke of my mission, and three o'clock of the next afternoon was set for the discussion of the business proposition.

"Your town," I said, as I began to make ready to depart (which is the time for smooth generalities), "seems to be a quiet, sedate place. A home town, I should say, where few things out of the ordinary ever happen."

It carries on an extensive trade in stoves and hollow ware with the West and South, and its flouring mills have a daily capacity of more than 2,000 barrels.

Azalea Adair seemed to reflect.

"I have never thought of it that way," she said, with a kind of sincere intensity that seemed to belong to her. "Isn't it in the still, quiet places that things do happen? I fancy that when God began to create the earth on the first Monday morning one could have leaned out one's window and heard the drops of mud splashing from His trowel as He built up the everlasting hills. What did the noisiest project in the world —I mean the building of the tower of Babel—result in finally? A page and a half of Esperanto in the *North American Review*."

"Of course," said I platitudinously, "human nature is the same everywhere; but there is more colour—er—more drama and movement and—er—romance in some cities than in others."

"On the surface," said Azalea Adair. "I have travelled many times around the world in a golden airship wafted on two wings—print and dreams. I have seen (on one of my imaginary tours) the Sultan of Turkey bowstring with his own hands one of his wives who had uncovered her face in public. I have seen a man in Nashville tear up his theatre tickets because his wife was going out with her face covered—with rice powder. In San Francisco's Chinatown I saw the slave girl Sing Yee dipped slowly, inch by inch, in boiling almond oil to make her swear she would never see her American lover again. She gave in when the boiling oil had reached three inches above her knee. At a euchre party in East Nashville the other night I saw Kitty Morgan cut dead by seven of her schoolmates and lifelong friends because she had married a house painter. The boiling oil was sizzling as high as her heart; but I wish you could have seen the fine little smile that she carried from table to table. Oh, yes, it is a humdrum town. Just a few miles of red brick houses and mud and stores and lumber yards."

Some one knocked hollowly at the back of the house. Azalea Adair breathed a soft apology and went to investigate the sound. She came back in three minutes with brightened eyes, a faint flush on her cheeks, and ten years lifted from her shoulders.

"You must have a cup of tea before you go," she said, "and a sugar cake."

She reached and shook a little iron bell. In shuffled a small Negro girl about twelve, barefoot, not very tidy, glowering at me with thumb in mouth and bulging eyes.

Azalea Adair opened a tiny, worn purse and drew out a dollar bill, a dollar bill with the upper right-hand corner missing, torn in two pieces and pasted together again with a strip of blue tissue paper. It was one of the bills I had given the piratical Negro—there was no doubt of it.

"Go up to Mr. Baker's store on the corner, Impy," she said, handing the girl the dollar bill, "and get a quarter of a pound of tea—the kind he always sends me—and ten cents worth of sugar cakes. Now, hurry. The supply of tea in the house happens to be exhausted," she explained to me.

Impy left by the back way. Before the scrape of her hard, bare feet had died away on the back porch, a wild shriek—I was sure it was hers—filled the hollow house. Then the deep, gruff tones of an angry man's voice mingled with the girl's further squeals and unintelligible words.

Azalea Adair rose without surprise or emotion and disappeared. For two minutes I heard the hoarse rumble of the man's voice; then something like an oath and a slight scuffle, and she returned calmly to her chair.

"This is a roomy house," she said, "and I have a tenant for part of it. I am sorry to have to rescind my invitation to tea. It was impossible to get the kind I always use at the store. Perhaps tomorrow Mr. Baker will be able to supply me."

I was sure that Impy had not had time to leave the house. I inquired concerning street-car lines and took my leave. After I was well on my way I remembered that I had not learned Azalea Adair's name. But to-morrow would do.

That same day I started in on the course of iniquity that this uneventful city forced upon me. I was in the town only two days, but in that time I managed to lie shamelessly by telegraph, and to be an accomplice—after the fact, if that is the correct legal term—to a murder.

As I rounded the corner nearest my hotel the Afrite coachman of the polychromatic, nonpareil coat seized me, swung open the dungeony door of his peripatetic sarcophagus, flirted his feather duster and began his ritual: "Step right in, boss. Carriage is clean—jus' got back from a funeral. Fifty cents to any——"

And then he knew me and grinned broadly. " 'Scuse me, boss; you is de gen'l'man what rid out with me dis mawnin'. Thank you kindly, suh."

"I am going out to 861 again to-morrow afternoon at three," said I, "and if you will be here, I'll let you drive me. So you know Miss Adair?" I concluded, thinking of my dollar bill.

"I belonged to her father, Judge Adair, suh," he replied.

"I judge that she is pretty poor," I said. "She hasn't much money to speak of, has she?"

For an instant I looked again at the fierce countenance of King Cettiwayo, and then he changed back to an extortionate old Negro hack driver.

"She ain't gwine to starve, suh," he said slowly. "She has reso'ces, suh; she has reso'ces."

"I shall pay you fifty cents for the trip," said I.

"Dat is puffeckly correct, suh," he answered humbly. "I jus' *had* to have dat two dollars dis mawnin', boss."

I went to the hotel and lied by electricity. I wired the magazine: "A. Adair holds out for eight cents a word."

The answer that came back was: "Give it to her quick, you duffer."

Just before dinner "Major" Wentworth Caswell bore down upon me with the greetings of a long-lost friend. I have seen few men whom I have so instantaneously hated, and of whom it was so difficult to be rid. I was standing at the bar when he invaded me; therefore I could not wave the white ribbon in his face. I would have paid gladly for the drinks, hoping, thereby, to escape another; but he was one of those despicable, roaring, advertising bibbers who must have brass bands and fireworks attend upon every cent that they waste in their follies.

With an air of producing millions he drew two one-dollar bills from a pocket and dashed one of them upon the bar. I looked once more at the dollar bill with the upper right-hand corner missing, torn through the middle, and patched with a strip of blue tissue paper. It was my dollar bill again. It could have been no other.

I went up to my room. The drizzle and the monotony of a dreary, eventless Southern town had made me tired and listless. I remember that just before I went to bed I mentally disposed of the mysterious dollar bill (which might have formed the clue to a tremendously fine detective story of San Francisco) by saying to myself sleepily: "Seems as if a lot of people here own stock in the Hack-Driver's Trust. Pays dividends promptly, too. Wonder if——" Then I fell asleep.

King Cettiwayo was at his post the next day, and rattled my bones over the stones out to 861. He was to wait and rattle me back again when I was ready.

Azalea Adair looked paler and cleaner and frailer than she had looked on the day before. After she had signed the contract at eight cents per word she grew still paler and began to slip out of her chair. Without much trouble I managed to get her up on the antediluvian horsehair sofa and then I ran out to the sidewalk and yelled to the coffee-coloured Pirate to bring a doctor. With a wisdom that I had not suspected in him, he abandoned his team and struck off up the street afoot, realising the value of speed. In ten minutes he returned with a grave, grey-haired and capable man of medicine. In a few words (worth much less than eight cents each) I explained to him my presence in the hollow house of mystery. He bowed with stately understanding, and turned to the old Negro.

"Uncle Cæsar," he said calmly, "run up to my house and ask Miss Lucy to give you a cream pitcher full of fresh milk and half a tumbler of port wine. And hurry back. Don't drive—run. I want you to get back sometime this week."

It occurred to me that Dr. Merriman also felt a distrust as to the speeding powers of the land-pirate's steeds. After Uncle Cæsar was gone, lumberingly, but swiftly, up the street, the doctor looked me over with great politeness and as much careful calculation until he had decided that I might do.

"It is only a case of insufficient nutrition," he said. "In other words, the result of poverty, pride, and starvation. Mrs. Caswell has many devoted friends who would be glad to aid her, but she will accept nothing except from that old Negro, Uncle Cæsar, who was once owned by her family."

"Mrs. Caswell!" said I, in surprise. And then I looked at the contract and saw that she had signed it, "Azalea Adair Caswell."

"I thought she was Miss Adair," I said.

"Married to a drunken, worthless loafer, sir," said the doctor. "It is said that he robs her even of the small sums that her old servant contributes toward her support."

When the milk and wine had been brought the doctor soon revived Azalea Adair. She sat up and talked of the beauty of the autumn leaves that were then in season, and their height of colour. She referred lightly to her fainting seizure as the outcome of an old palpitation of the heart. Impy fanned her as she lay on the sofa. The doctor was due elsewhere, and I followed him to the door. I told him that it was within my power and intentions to make a reasonable advance of money to Azalea Adair on future contributions to the magazine, and he seemed pleased.

"By the way," he said, "perhaps you would like to know that you have had royalty for a coachman. Old Cæsar's grandfather was a king in Congo. Cæsar himself has royal ways, as you may have observed."

As the doctor was moving off I heard Uncle Cæsar's voice inside: "Did he git bofe of dem two dollars from you, Mis' Zalea?"

"Yes, Cæsar," I heard Azalea Adair answer weakly. And then I went in and concluded business negotiations with our contributor. I assumed the responsibility of advancing fifty dollars, putting it as a necessary formality in binding our bargain. And then Uncle Cæsar drove me back to the hotel.

Here ends all of the story as far as I can testify as a witness. The rest must be only bare statements of facts.

At about six o'clock I went out for a stroll. Uncle Cæsar was at his corner. He threw open the door of his carriage, flourished his duster and began his depressing formula: "Step right in, suh. Fifty cents to anywhere in the city—hack's puffickly clean, suh—jus' got back from a funeral——"

And then he recognised me. I think his eyesight was getting bad. His coat had taken on a few more faded shades of colour, the twine strings were more frayed and ragged, the last remaining button—the button of yellow horn—was gone. A motley descendant of kings was Uncle Cæsar!

About two hours later I saw an excited crowd besieging the front of a drug store. In a desert where nothing happens this was manna; so I edged my way inside. On an extemporised couch of empty boxes and chairs was stretched the mortal corporeality of Major Wentworth Caswell. A doctor was testing him for the immortal ingredient. His decision was that it was conspicuous by its absence.

The erstwhile Major had been found dead on a dark street and brought by curious and ennuied citizens to the drug store. The late human being had been engaged in terrific battle—the details showed that. Loafer and reprobate though he had been, he had been also a warrior. But he had lost. His hands were yet clinched so tightly that his fingers would not be opened. The gentle citizens who had known him stood about and searched their vocabularies to find some good words, if it were possible, to speak of him. One kind-looking man said, after much thought: "When 'Cas' was about fo'teen he was one of the best spellers in school."

While I stood there the fingers of the right hand of "the man that was", which hung down the side of a white pine box, relaxed, and dropped something at my feet. I covered it with one foot quietly, and a little later on I picked it up and pocketed it. I reasoned that in his last struggle his hand must have seized that object unwittingly and held it in a death grip.

At the hotel that night the main topic of conversation, with the possible exceptions of politics and prohibition, was the demise of Major Caswell. I heard one man say to a group of listeners:

"In my opinion, gentlemen, Caswell was murdered by some of these no-account niggers for his money. He had fifty dollars this afternoon, which he showed to several gentlemen in the hotel. When he was found the money was not on his person."

I left the city the next morning at nine, and as the train was crossing the bridge over the Cumberland River I took out of my pocket a yellow horn overcoat button the size of a fifty-cent piece, with frayed ends of coarse twine hanging from it, and cast it out of the window into the slow, muddy waters below.

I wonder what's doing in Buffalo!

EDITH WHARTON
(1862-   )

EDITH NEWBOLD JONES, who was born in New York, was married (1885) to Edward Wharton, of Boston. For the past fifteen years or so she has resided in France. Of aristocratic tradition and lineage, a student of books and of people, a lover of art, Mrs. Wharton finds her subjects in the topmost of the intellectual and social strata. In 1899 she produced *The Greater Inclination,* the first of the many volumes that form the long and honorable line of her literary children down to *Twilight Sleep* (1927). She has been successful with the novel and the short story, and in all has reflected sincerely that phase of the passing show which claimed her attention —whether the study of evolution, the social life of New York, the supernatural, or the Great War. She has much in common with Henry James and holds, as he holds, a secure place in American letters.

The Debt, first published in *Scribner's Magazine*—volume 46, p. 165—is here reprinted by special arrangement with the publishers, from *Tales of Men and Ghosts,* copyright, 1910, by Charles Scribner's Sons, New York City.

THE DEBT

I

YOU remember—it's not so long ago—the talk there was about Dredge's "Arrival of the Fittest"? The talk has subsided, but the book of course remains: stands up, in fact, as the tallest thing of its kind since—well, I'd almost said since "The Origin of Species."

I'm not wrong, at any rate, in calling it the most important contribution yet made to the development of the Darwinian theory, or rather to the solution of the awkward problem about which that theory has had to make such a circuit. Dredge's hypothesis will be contested, may one day be disproved; but at least it has swept out of the way all previous conjectures, including of course Lanfear's great attempt; and for our generation of scientific investigators it will serve as the first safe bridge across a murderous black whirlpool.

It's all very interesting—there are few things more stirring to the imagination than that projection of the new hypothesis, light as a cobweb and strong as steel, across the intellectual abyss; but, for an idle observer of human motives, the other, the personal, side of Dredge's case is even more interesting and arresting.

Personal side? You didn't know there was one? Pictured him simply as a thinking machine, a highly specialised instrument of precision, the result of a long series of "adaptations," as his own jargon would put it? Well, I don't wonder—if you've met him. He does give the impression of being something out of his own laboratory: a delicate instrument that reveals wonders to the initiated, but is useless in an ordinary hand.

In his youth it was just the other way. I knew him twenty years ago, as an awkward lad whom young Archie Lanfear had picked up at college, and brought home for a visit. I happened to be staying at the Lanfears' when the boys arrived, and I shall never forget Dredge's first appearance on the scene. You know the Lanfears always lived very simply. That summer they had gone to Buzzard's Bay, in order that Professor Lanfear should be near the Biological Station at Woods' Holl, and they were picnicking in a kind of sketchy bungalow without any attempt at luxury. But Galen Dredge couldn't have been more awe-struck if he'd been suddenly plunged into a Fifth Avenue ball-room. He nearly knocked his head against the low doorway, and in dodging this peril trod heavily on Mabel Lanfear's foot, and became hopelessly entangled in her mother's draperies—though how he managed it I never knew, for Mrs. Lanfear's dowdy muslins ran to no excess of train.

When the Professor himself came in it was ten times worse, and I saw then that Dredge's emotion was a tribute to the great man's presence. That made the boy interesting, and I began to watch. Archie, always enthusiastic but vague, had said: "Oh, he's a tremendous chap—you'll see—" but I hadn't expected to see quite so early. Lanfear's vision, of course, was sharper than mine; and the next morning he had carried Dredge off to the Biological Station. That was the way it began.

Dredge is the son of a Baptist minister. He comes from East Lethe, New York State, and was working his way through college—waiting at White Mountain hotels in summer—when Archie Lanfear ran across him. There were eight children in the family, and the mother was an invalid. Dredge never had a penny from his father after he was fourteen; but his mother wanted him to be a scholar, and "kept at him," as he put it, in the hope of his going back to "teach school" at East Lethe. He developed slowly, as the scientific mind generally does, and was still adrift about himself and his tendencies when Archie took him down to Buzzard's Bay. But he had read Lanfear's "Utility and Variation," and had always been a patient and curious observer of nature. And his first meeting with Lanfear explained him to himself. It didn't, however, enable him to explain himself to others, and for a long time he remained, to all but Lanfear, an object of incredulity and conjecture.

"Why my husband wants him about——" poor Mrs. Lanfear, the kindest of women, privately lamented to her friends; for Dredge, at that time—they kept him all summer at the bungalow—had one of the most encumbering personalities you can imagine. He was as inexpressive as he is today, and yet oddly obtrusive: one of those uncomfortable presences whose silence is an interruption.

The poor Lanfears almost died of him that summer, and the pity of it was that he never suspected it, but continued to lavish on them a floundering devotion as inconvenient as the endearments of a dripping dog. He was full of all sorts of raw enthusiasms, which he forced on any one who would listen when his first shyness had worn off. You can't see him spouting sentimental poetry, can you? Yet I've known him to petrify a whole group of Mrs. Lanfear's callers by suddenly discharging on them, in the strident drawl of his state, "Barbara Frietchie" or "The Queen of the May." His taste in literature was uniformly bad, but very definite, and far more dogmatic than his views on biological questions. In his scientific judgments he showed, even then, a temperance remarkable in one so young; but in literature he was a furious propagandist, aggressive, disputatious, and extremely sensitive to adverse opinion.

Lanfear, of course, had been struck from the first by his gift of observation, and by the fact that his eagerness to learn was offset by his reluctance to conclude. I remember Lanfear's telling me that he had never known a lad of Dredge's age who gave such promise of uniting an aptitude for general ideas with the plodding patience of the observer. Of course when Lanfear talked like that of a young biologist his fate was sealed. There could be no question of Dredge's going back to "teach school" at East Lethe. He must take a course in biology at Columbia, spend his vacations at the Wood's Holl laboratory, and then, if possible, go to Germany for a year or two.

All this meant his virtual adoption by the Lanfears. Most of Lanfear's fortune went in helping young students to a start, and he devoted a liberal subsidy to Dredge.

"Dredge will be my biggest dividend—you'll see!" he used to say, in the chrysalis days when poor Galen was known to the world of science only as a slouching presence in Mrs. Lanfear's drawing-room. And Dredge, it must be said, took his obligations simply, with the dignity, and quiet consciousness of his own worth, which in such cases saves the beneficiary from abjectness. He seemed to trust himself as fully as Lanfear trusted him.

The comic part of it was that his only idea of making what is known as "a return" was to devote himself to the Professor's family. When I hear pretty women lamenting that they can't coax Professor Dredge out of his laboratory I remember Mabel Lanfear's cry to me: "If Galen would only keep away!" When Mabel fell on the ice and broke her leg, Galen walked seven miles in a blizzard to get a surgeon; but if he did her this service one day in the year, he bored her by being in the way for the other three hundred and sixty-four. One would have imagined at that time that he thought his perpetual presence the greatest gift he could bestow; for, except on the occasion of his fetching the surgeon, I don't remember his taking any other way of expressing his gratitude.

In love with Mabel? Not a bit! But the queer thing was that he did have a passion in those days—a blind hopeless passion for Mrs. Lanfear! Yes: I know what I'm saying. I mean Mrs. Lanfear, the Professor's wife, poor Mrs. Lanfear, with her tight hair and her loose shape, her blameless brow and earnest eye-glasses, and her perpetual air of mild misapprehension. I can see Dredge cowering, long and many-jointed, in a small drawing-room chair, one square-toed shoe coiled round an exposed ankle, his knees clasped in a knot of knuckles, and his spectacles perpetually seeking Mrs. Lanfear's eye-glasses. I never knew if the poor lady was aware of the sentiment she inspired, but her children observed it, and it provoked them to irreverent mirth. Galen was the predestined butt of Mabel and Archie; and secure in their mother's obtuseness, and in her worshipper's timidity, they allowed themselves a latitude of banter that sometimes made their audience shiver. Dredge meanwhile was going on obstinately with his work. Now and then he had fits of idleness, when he lapsed into a state of sulky inertia from which even Lanfear's remonstrances could not rouse him. Once, just before an examination, he suddenly went off to the Maine woods for two weeks, came back, and failed to pass. I don't know if his benefactor ever lost hope; but at times his confidence must have been sorely strained. The queer part of it was that when Dredge emerged from these eclipses he seemed keener and more active than ever. His slowly growing intelligence probably needed its periodical pauses of assimilation; and Lanfear was wonderfully patient.

At last Dredge finished his course and went to Germany; and when he came back he was a new man—was, in fact, the Dredge we all know. He seemed to have shed his encumbering personality, and have come to life as a disembodied intelligence. His fidelity to the Lanfears was unchanged; but he showed it negatively, by his discretions and abstentions. I have an idea that Mabel was less disposed to laugh at him, might even have been induced to softer sentiments; but I doubt if Dredge even noticed the change. As for his ex-goddess, he seemed to regard her as a motherly household divinity, the guardian genius of the darning needle; but on Professor Lanfear he looked with a deepening reverence. If the rest of the family had diminished in his eyes, its head had grown even greater.

II

From that day Dredge's progress continued steadily. If not always perceptible to the untrained eye, in Lanfear's sight it never flagged, and the great man began to associate Dredge with his work, and to lean on him more and more. Lanfear's health was already failing, and in my confidential talks with him I saw how he counted on Dredge to continue and develop his teachings. If he did not describe the young man as his predestined Huxley, it was because any such comparison between himself and his great predecessors would have been distasteful to him; but he evidently felt that it would be Dredge's part to reveal him to posterity. And the young man seemed at that time to take the same view. When he was not busy about Lanfear's work he was recording their conversations with the diligence of a biographer and the accuracy of a naturalist. Any attempt to question Lanfear's theories or to minimise his achievement, roused in his disciple the only flashes of wrath I have ever seen a scientific discussion provoke in him. In defending his master he became almost as intemperate as in the early period of his literary passions.

Such filial devotion must have been all the more precious to Lanfear because, about that time, it became evident that Archie would never carry on his father's work. He had begun brilliantly, you may remember, by a little paper on Limulus Polyphemus that attracted a good deal of notice when it appeared; but gradually his zoological ardour yielded to a passion for the violin, which was followed by a plunge into physics. At present, after a side-glance at the drama, I understand he's devoting what is left of his father's money to archæological explorations in Asia Minor.

"Archie's got a delightful little mind," Lanfear used to say to me, rather wistfully, "but it's just a highly polished surface held up to the show as it passes. Dredge's mind takes in only a bit at a time, but the bit stays, and other bits are joined to it, in a hard mosaic of fact, of which imagination weaves the pattern. I saw just how it would be years ago, when my boy used to take my meaning in a flash, and answer me with clever objections, while Galen disappeared into one of his fathomless silences, and then came to the surface like a dripping retriever, a long way beyond Archie's objections, and with an answer to them in his mouth."

It was about this time that the crowning satisfaction of Lanfear's career came to him: I mean, of course, John Weyman's gift to Columbia of the Lanfear Laboratory, and the founding, in connection with it, of a chair of Experimental Evolution. Weyman had always taken an interest in Lanfear's work, but no one had supposed that his interest would express itself so magnificently. The honour came to Lanfear at a time when he was fighting an accumulation of troubles: failing health, the money difficulties resulting from his irrepressible generosity, his disappointment about Archie's career, and perhaps also the persistent attacks of the new school of German zoologists.

"If I hadn't Galen I should feel the game was up," he said to me once, in a fit of half-real, half-mocking despondency. "But he'll do what I haven't time to do myself, and what my boy can't do for me."

That meant that he would answer the critics, and triumphantly reaffirm Lanfear's theory, which had been rudely shaken, but not dislodged.

"A scientific hypothesis lasts till there's something else to put in its place. People who want to get across a river will use the old bridge till the new one's built. And I don't see any one who's particularly anxious, in this case, to take a contract for the new one," Lanfear ended; and I remember answering with a laugh: "Not while Horatius Dredge holds the other."

It was generally known that Lanfear had not long to live, and the laboratory was hardly opened before the question of his successor in the chair of Experimental Evolution began to be a matter of public discussion. It was conceded that whoever followed him ought to be a man of achieved reputation, some one carrying, as the French say, a considerable "baggage." At the same time, even Lanfear's critics felt that he should be succeeded by a man who held his views and would continue his teaching. This was not in itself a difficulty, for German criticism had so far been mainly negative, and there were plenty of good men who, while they questioned the permanent validity of Lanfear's conclusions, were yet ready to accept them for their provisional usefulness. And then there was the added inducement of the Laboratory! The Columbia Professor of Experimental Evolution has at his disposal the most complete instrument of biological research that modern ingenuity has yet produced; and it's not only in theology or politics *que Paris vaut bien une messe!* There was no trouble about finding a candidate; but the whole thing turned on Lanfear's decision, since it was tacitly understood that, by Weyman's wish, he was to select his successor. And what a cry there was when he selected Galen Dredge!

Not in the scientific world, though. The specialists were beginning to know about Dredge. His remarkable paper on Sexual Dimorphism had been translated into several languages, and a furious polemic had broken out over it. When a young fellow can get the big men fighting over him his future is pretty well assured. But Dredge was only thirty-four, and some people seemed to feel that there was a kind of deflected nepotism in Lanfear's choice.

"If he could choose Dredge he might as well have chosen his own son," I've heard it said; and the irony was that Archie—will you believe it?—actually thought so himself! But Lanfear had Weyman behind him, and when the end came the Faculty at once appointed Galen Dredge to the chair of Experimental Evolution.

For the first two years things went quietly, along accustomed lines. Dredge simply continued the course which Lanfear's death had interrupted. He lectured well even then, with a persuasive simplicity surprising in the inarticulate creature one knew him for. But haven't you noticed that certain personalities reveal themselves only in the more impersonal relations of life? It's as if they woke only to collective contacts, and the single consciousness were an unmeaning fragment to them.

If there was anything to criticise in that first part of the course, it was the avoidance of general ideas, of those brilliant rockets of conjecture that Lanfear's students were used to seeing him fling across the darkness. I remember once saying this to Archie, who, having forgotten his absurd disappointment, had returned to his old allegiance to Dredge.

"Oh, that's Galen all over. He doesn't want to jump into the ring till he has a big swishing knock-down argument in his fist. He'll wait twenty years if he has to. That's his strength: he's never afraid to wait."

I thought this shrewd of Archie, as well as generous; and I saw the wisdom of Dredge's course. As Lanfear himself had said, his theory was safe enough till somebody found a more attractive one; and before that day Dredge would probably have accumulated sufficient proof to crystallise the fluid hypothesis.

III

The third winter I was off collecting in Central America, and didn't get back till Dredge's course had been going for a couple of months. The very day I turned up in town Archie Lanfear descended on me with a summons from his mother. I was wanted at once at a family council.

I found the Lanfear ladies in a state of explosive distress, which Archie's own indignation hardly made more intelligible. But gradually I put together their fragmentary charges, and learned that Dredge's lectures were turning into an organised assault on his master's doctrine.

"It amounts to just this," Archie said, controlling his women with the masterful gesture of the weak man. "Galen has simply turned round and betrayed my father."

"Just for a handful of silver he left us," Mabel sobbed in parenthesis, while Mrs. Lanfear tearfully cited Hamlet.

Archie silenced them again. "The ugly part of it is that he must have had this up his sleeve for years. He must have known when he was asked to succeed my father what use he meant to make of his opportunity. What he's doing isn't the result of a hasty conclusion: it means years of work and preparation."

Archie broke off to explain himself. He had returned from Europe the week before, and had learned on arriving that Dredge's lectures were stirring the world of science as nothing had stirred it since Lanfear's "Utility and Variation." And the incredible affront was that they owed their success to the fact of being an attempted refutation of Lanfear's great work.

I own that I was staggered: the case looked ugly, as Archie said. And there was a veil of reticence, of secrecy, about Dredge, that always kept his conduct in a half-light of uncertainty. Of some men one would have said off-hand: "It's impossible!" But one couldn't affirm it of him.

Archie hadn't seen him as yet; and Mrs. Lanfear had sent for me because she wished me to be present at the interview between the two men. The Lanfear ladies had a touching belief in Archie's violence: they

thought his as terrible as a natural force. My own idea was that if there
were any broken bones they wouldn't be Dredge's; but I was too curious
as to the outcome not to be glad to offer my services as moderator.

First, however, I wanted to hear one of the lectures; and I went the
next afternoon. The hall was jammed, and I saw, as soon as Dredge
appeared, what increased security and ease the sympathy of his audience
had given him. He had been clear the year before, now he was also
eloquent. The lecture was a remarkable effort: you'll find the gist of it
in Chapter VII. of *The Arrival of the Fittest*. Archie sat at my side in
a white rage; he was too intelligent not to measure the extent of the disaster. And I was almost as indignant as he when we went to see Dredge
the next day.

I saw at a glance that the latter suspected nothing; and it was characteristic of him that he began by questioning me about my finds, and only
afterward turned to reproach Archie for having been back a week without
letting him know.

"You know I'm up to my neck in this job. Why in the world didn't
you hunt me up before this?"

The question was exasperating, and I could understand Archie's stammer of wrath.

"Hunt you up? Hunt you up? What the deuce are you made of, to
ask me such a question instead of wondering why I'm here now?"

Dredge bent his slow calm scrutiny on his friend's agitated face; then
he turned to me.

"What's the matter?" he said simply.

"The matter?" shrieked Archie, his fist hovering excitedly above the
desk by which he stood; but Dredge, with unwonted quickness, caught the
fist as it descended.

"Careful—I've got a Kallima in that jar there." He pushed a chair
forward, and added quietly: "Sit down."

Archie, ignoring the gesture, towered pale and avenging in his place;
and Dredge, after a moment, took the chair himself.

"The matter?" Archie reiterated. "Are you so lost to all sense of
decency and honour that you can put that question in good faith? Don't
you really know what's the matter?"

Dredge smiled slowly. "There are so few things one really knows."

"Oh, damn your scientific hair-splitting! Don't you know you're
insulting my father's memory?"

Dredge thoughtfully turned his spectacles from one of us to the
other.

"Oh, that's it, is it? Then you'd better sit down. If you don't see
at once it'll take some time to make you."

Archie burst into an ironic laugh.

"I rather think it will!" he retorted.

"Sit down, Archie," I said, setting the example; and he obeyed, with a gesture that made his consent a protest.

Dredge seemed to notice nothing beyond the fact that his visitors were seated. He reached for his pipe, and filled it with the care which the habit of delicate manipulations gave to all the motions of his long knotty hands.

"It's about the lectures?" he said.

Archie's answer was a deep scornful breath.

"You've only been back a week, so you've only heard one, I suppose?"

"It was not necessary to hear even that one. You must know the talk they're making. If notoriety is what you're after——"

"Well, I'm not sorry to make a noise," said Dredge, putting a match to his pipe.

Archie bounded in his chair. "There's no easier way of doing it than to attack a man who can't answer you!"

Dredge raised a sobering hand. "Hold on. Perhaps you and I don't mean the same thing. Tell me first what's in your mind."

The question steadied Archie, who turned on Dredge a countenance really eloquent with filial indignation.

"It's an odd question for you to ask; it makes me wonder what's in yours. Not much thought of my father, at any rate, or you couldn't stand in his place and use the chance he's given you to push yourself at his expense."

Dredge received this in silence, puffing slowly at his pipe.

"Is that the way it strikes you?" he asked at length.

"God! It's the way it would strike most men."

He turned to me. "You too?"

"I can see how Archie feels," I said.

"That I am attacking his father's memory to glorify myself?"

"Well, not precisely: I think what he really feels is that, if your convictions didn't permit you to continue his father's teaching, you might perhaps have done better to sever your connection with the Lanfear lectureship."

"Then you and he regard the Lanfear lectureship as having been founded to perpetuate a dogma, not to try and get at the truth?"

"Certainly not," Archie broke in. "But there's a question of taste, of delicacy, involved in the case that can't be decided on abstract principles. We know as well as you that my father meant the laboratory and the lectureship to serve the ends of science, at whatever cost to his own special convictions; what we feel—and you don't seem to—is that you're the last man to put them to that particular use; and I don't want to remind you why."

A slight redness rose through Dredge's sallow skin. "You needn't," he said. "It's because he pulled me out of my hole, woke me up, made me, shoved me off from the shore. Because he saved me ten or twenty years of muddled effort, and put me where I am at an age when my best working years are still ahead of me. Every one knows that's what your father did for me, but I'm the only person who knows the time and trouble it took."

It was well said, and I glanced quickly at Archie, who was never closed to generous emotions.

"Well, then——?" he said, flushing also.

"Well, then," Dredge continued, his voice deepening and losing its nasal edge, "I had to pay him back, didn't I?"

The sudden drop flung Archie back on his prepared attitude of irony. "It would be the natural inference——with most men."

"Just so. And I'm not so very different. I knew your father wanted a successor——some one who'd try and tie up the loose ends. And I took the lectureship with that object."

"And you're using it to tear the whole fabric to pieces!"

Dredge paused to re-light his pipe. "Looks that way," he conceded. "This year anyhow."

"This year——?" Archie echoed.

"Yes. When I took up the job I saw it just as your father left it. Or rather, I didn't see any other way of going on with it. The change came gradually, as I worked."

"Gradually? So that you had time to look round you, to know where you were, to see that you were fatally committed to undoing the work he had done?"

"Oh, yes——I had time," Dredge conceded.

"And yet you kept the chair and went on with the course?"

Dredge refilled his pipe, and then turned in his seat so that he looked squarely at Archie.

"What would your father have done in my place?" he asked.

"In your place——?"

"Yes: supposing he'd found out the things I've found out in the last year or two. You'll see what they are, and how much they count, if you'll run over the report of the lectures. If your father'd been alive he might have come across the same facts just as easily."

There was a silence which Archie at last broke by saying: "But he didn't, and you did. There's the difference."

"The difference? What difference? Would your father have suppressed the facts if he'd found them? It's you who insult his memory by implying it! And if I'd brought them to him, would he have used his hold over me to get me to suppress them?"

"Certainly not. But can't you see it's his death that makes the difference? He's not here to defend his case."

Dredge laughed, but not unkindly. "My dear Archie, your father wasn't one of the kind who bother to defend their case. Men like him are the masters, not the servants, of their theories. They respect an idea only as long as it's of use to them; when its usefulness ends they chuck it out. And that's what your father would have done."

Archie reddened. "Don't you assume a good deal in taking it for granted that he would have had to do so in this particular case?"

Dredge reflected. "Yes: I was going too far. Each of us can only answer for himself. But to my mind your father's theory is refuted."

"And you don't hesitate to be the man to do it?"

"Should I have been of any use if I had? And did your father ever ask anything of me but to be of as much use as I could?"

It was Archie's turn to reflect. "No. That was what he always wanted, of course."

"That's the way I've always felt. The first day he took me away from East Lethe I knew the debt I was piling up against him, and I never had any doubt as to how I'd pay it, or how he'd want it paid. He didn't pick me out and train me for any object but to carry on the light. Do you suppose he'd have wanted me to snuff it out because it happened to light up a fact he didn't fancy? I'm using his oil to feed my torch with: yes, but it isn't really his torch or mine, or his oil or mine: they belong to each of us till we drop and hand them on."

Archie turned a sobered glance on him. "I see your point. But if the job had to be done I don't see that you need have done it from his chair."

"There's where we differ. If I did it at all I had to do it in the best way, and with all the authority his backing gave me. If I owe your father anything, I owe him that. It would have made him sick to see the job badly done. And don't you see the way to honour him, and show what he's done for science, was to spare no advantage in my attack on him—that I'm proving the strength of his position by the desperateness of my assault?" Dredge paused and squared his lounging shoulders. "After all," he added, "he's not down yet, and if I leave him standing I guess it'll be some time before anybody else cares to tackle him."

There was a silence between the two men; then Dredge continued in a lighter tone: "There's one thing, though, that we're both in danger of forgetting: and that is how little, in the long run, it all counts either way." He smiled a little at Archie's indignant gesture.

"The most we can any of us do—even by such a magnificent effort as your father's—is to turn the great marching army a hair's breadth nearer what seems to us the right direction; if one of us drops out, here and there, the loss of headway's hardly perceptible. And that's what I'm coming to now."

He rose from his seat, and walked across to the hearth; then, cautiously resting his shoulder-blades against the mantel-shelf jammed with miscellaneous specimens, he bent his musing spectacles on Archie.

"Your father would have understood why I've done what I'm doing; but that's no reason why the rest of you should. And I rather think it's the rest of you who've suffered most from me. He always knew what I was there for, and that must have been some comfort even when I was most in the way; but I was just an ordinary nuisance to you and your mother and Mabel. You were all too kind to let me see it at the time, but I've seen it since, and it makes me feel that, after all, the settling of this matter lies with you. If it hurts you to have me go on with my examination of your father's theory, I'm ready to drop the lectures tomorrow, and trust to the Lanfear Laboratory to breed up a young chap who'll knock us both out in time. You've only got to say the word."

There was a pause while Dredge turned and laid his extinguished pipe carefully between a jar of embryo sea-urchins and a colony of regenerating planarians.

Then Archie rose and held out his hand.

"No," he said simply; "go on."

❉ ❉ ❉

MARY HUNTER AUSTIN
(1868——)

A NATIVE of Illinois, Mary Hunter was married (1891) to Stafford Austin of California. For some years, she has lived in Santa Fé, New Mexico. From the outset of her career she has been interested in the American Indian and his setting and has written a number of books about him, culminating in *The American Rhythm* (1923). Thoroughly familiar with certain tribes of the aborigines, she has transferred through her genius to others not so familiar the Red Man's art of story telling. "Your American aboriginal has," she says, "an acute sense of design, and his short story patterns all have a firm outline and a remarkably compact content, never without the little sting near the end by which the story implants its virus often so deftly that, though you feel the sting, you are not always aware until after reflection just what the biting point of the story is."

Papago Wedding, which received from the O. Henry Memorial Committee the special one hundred dollar prize for the best very brief story of 1925, is here reprinted by special permission of the author.

PAPAGO WEDDING

THERE was a Papago woman out of Pantak who had a marriage paper from a white man after she had borne him five children, and the man himself was in love with another woman. This Shuler was the first to raise cotton for selling in the Gila Valley—but the Pimas and Papagoes had raised it long before that—and the girl went with him willingly. As to the writing of marriage, it was not then understood that the white man is not master of his heart, but is mastered by it, so that if it is not fixed in writing it becomes unstable like water and is puddled in the lowest place. The Sisters at San Xavier del Bac had taught her to clean and cook. Shuler called her Susie, which was nearest to her Papago name, and was fond of the children. He sent them to school as they came along, and had carpets in the house.

In all things Susie was a good wife to him, though she had no writing of marriage and she never wore a hat. This was a mistake which she learned from the sisters. They, being holy women, had no notion of the brujeria which is worked in the heart of the white man by a hat. Into the presence of their God also, without that which passes for a hat, they do not go. Even after her children were old enough to notice it, Susie went about the country with a handkerchief tied over her hair, which was long and smooth on either side of her face, like the shut wings of a raven.

By the time Susie's children were as tall as their mother, there were many white ranchers in the Gila country, with their white wives, who are like Papago women in this, that if they see a man upstanding and prosperous, they think only that he might make some woman happy, and if they have a cousin or a friend, that she should be the woman. Also the white ones think it so shameful for a man to take a woman to his house without a writing that they have no scruple to take him away from her. At Rinconada there was a woman with large breasts, surpassing well looking, and with many hats. She had no husband and was new to the country, and when Shuler drove her about to look at it, she wore each time a different hat.

This the Papagoes observed, and, not having visited Susie when she was happy with her man, they went now in numbers, and by this Susie understood that it was in their hearts that she might have need of them. For it was well known that the white woman had told Shuler that it was a shame for him to have his children going about with a Papago woman who had only a handkerchief to cover her head. She said it was keeping Shuler back from being the principal man among the cotton grow-ers of Gila Valley, to have in his house a woman who would come there without a writing. And when the other white women heard that she had said that, they said the same thing. Shuler said, "My God, this is the truth, I know it," and the woman said that she would go to Susie and tell her that she ought to go back to her own people and not be a shame to her children and Shuler. There was a man from Pantak on the road, who saw them go, and turned in his tracks and went back, in case Susie should need him, for the Papagoes, when it is their kin against whom there is brujeria made, have in-knowing hearts. Susie sat in the best room with the woman and was polite. "If you want Shuler," she said, "you can have him, but I stay with my children." The white woman grew red in the face and went out to Shuler in the field where he was pretending to look after something, and they went away together.

After that Shuler would not go to the ranch except of necessity. He went around talking to his white friends. "My God," he kept saying, "what can I do, with my children in the hands of that Papago?" Then he sent a lawyer to Susie to say that if she would go away and not shame his children with a mother who had no marriage writing and no hat, he would give her money, so much every month. But the children all came in the room and stood by her, and Susie said, "What I want with money when I got my children and this good ranch?" Then Shuler said "My God!" again, and "What can I do?"

The lawyer said he could tell the Judge that Susie was not a proper person to have care of his children, and the Judge would take them away from Susie and give them to Shuler. But when the day came for Susie to come into court, it was seen that though she had a handkerchief on her hair, her dress was good, and the fringe of her shawl was long and fine. All the five children came also, with new clothes, well looking. "My God!" said Shuler, "I must get those kids away from that Papago and into the hands of a white woman." But the white people who had come to see the children taken away saw that although the five looked like Shuler, they had their mouths shut like Papagoes; so they waited to see how things turned out.

Shuler's lawyer makes a long speech about how Shuler loves his children, and how sorry he is in his heart to see them growing up like Papagoes, and water is coming out of Shuler's eyes. Then the Judge asks Susie if she has anything to say why her children shall not be taken away.

"You want to take these children away and giff them to Shuler?" Susie asks him. "What for you giff them to Shuler?" says Susie, and the white people are listening. She says, "Shuler's not the father of them. Thees children all got different fathers," says Susie. "Shuler——"

Then she makes a sign with her hand. I tell you if a woman makes that sign to a Papago he could laugh himself dead but he would not laugh off that. Some of the white people who have been in the country a long time know that sign and they begin to laugh.

Shuler's lawyer jumps up. . . . "Your Honour, I object——"

The Judge waves his hand. "I warn you the Court cannot go behind the testimony of the mother in such a case. . . ."

By this time everybody is laughing, so that they do not hear what the lawyer says. Shuler is trying to get out of the side door, and the Judge is shaking hands with Susie.

"You tell Shuler," she says, "if he wants people to think hees the father of thees children he better giff me a writing. Then maybe I think so myself."

"I will," said the Judge, and maybe two, three days after that he takes Shuler out to the ranch and makes the marriage writing. Then all the children come around Susie and say, "Now, Mother, you will have to wear a hat." Susie, she says, "Go, children, and ask your father." But it is not known to the Papagoes what happened after that.

* * *

(NEWTON) BOOTH TARKINGTON
(1869-   )

A SON of Indianapolis, Indiana, Booth Tarkington was educated at Princeton, and has since received the degree of Litt.D. from his alma mater and from Columbia University. A term in the legislature led to his writing *The Gentleman from Indiana* (1899), through which he sprang into a popularity that has never waned. He cares little for form; he relies greatly on the charm and power of immediate expression—though he writes an all but perfect short story or novel—and how well his reliance is justified is evidenced by his large number of readers. His stories of politics (for example, *In the Arena*, 1905) and of society (see *The Conquest of Canaan*, also 1905) mirror American life truly for the periods represented. Studies in small boy psychology (*Penrod*, 1914; *Penrod and Sam*, 1916), studies of adolescence (*Seventeen*, 1916) and of women (*Women*, 1926) have exercised his talents of late. *The Plutocrat* (1927) presents humorously the American man of wealth abroad. Through all his work this same leaven of humour ferments yeastily, entertainingly.

The One Hundred Dollar Bill, which first appeared in *McCall's Magazine* January, 1923, is here reprinted by special arrangement with and permission of the author's publishers, Doubleday, Page an Company, Garden City, New York.

THE ONE HUNDRED DOLLAR BILL

THE new one hundred dollar bill, clean and green, freshening the heart with the colour of springtime, slid over the glass of the teller's counter and passed under his grille to a fat hand, dingy on the knuckles, but brightened by a flawed diamond. This interesting hand was a part of one of those men who seem to have too much fattened muscle for their clothes; his shoulders distended his overcoat; his calves strained the sprightly checked cloth, a little soiled, of his trousers; his short neck bulged above the glossy collar. His hat, round and black as a pot and appropriately small, he wore slightly obliqued, while under its curled brim his small eyes twinkled surreptitiously between those upper and nether puffs of flesh that mark the too faithful practitioner of unhallowed gaieties. Such was the first individual owner of the new one hundred dollar bill, and he at once did what might have been expected of him.

Moving away from the teller's grille, he made a cylindrical packet of bills smaller in value—"ones" and "fives"—then placed round them, as a wrapper, the beautiful one hundred dollar bill, snapped a rubber band over it; and the desired inference was plain; a roll all of hundred dollar bills, inside as well as outside. Something more was plain, too: obviously the man's small head had a sportive plan in it, for the twinkle between his eye puffs hinted of liquor in the offing and lively women impressed by a show of masterly riches. Here, in brief, was a man who meant to make a night of it, who would feast, dazzle, compel deference and be loved. For money gives power, and power is loved; no doubt he would be loved. He was happy, and went out of the bank believing that money is made for joy.

So little should we be certain of our happiness in this world. The splendid one hundred dollar bill was taken from him untimely, before nightfall that very evening. At the corner of two busy streets he parted with it to the law, though in a mood of excruciating reluctance and only after a cold-blooded threatening on the part of the lawyer. This latter walked away thoughtfully with the one hundred dollar bill, not now quite so clean, in his pocket.

Collinson was the lawyer's name, and in years he was only twenty-eight, but already of the slightly harried appearance that marks the young husband who begins to suspect that the better part of his life was his bachelorhood. His dark, ready-made clothes, his twice soled shoes, and his hair, which was too long for a neat and businesslike aspect, were symptoms of necessary economy; but he did not wear the eager look of a man who saves to "get on for himself." Collinson's look was that of an employed man who only deepens his rut with his pacing of it.

An employed man he was, indeed; a lawyer without much hope of ever seeing his name on the door or on the letters of the firm that employed him, and his most important work was the collection of small debts. This one hundred dollar bill now in his pocket was such a collection, small to the firm and the client, though of a noble size to himself and the long-pursued debtor from whom he had just collected it.

The banks were closed; so was the office, for it was six o'clock and Collinson was on his way home when by chance he encountered the debtor; there was nothing to do but to keep the bill overnight. This was no hardship, however, as he had a faint pleasure in the unfamiliar experience of walking home with such a thing in his pocket; and he felt a little important by proxy when he thought of it.

Upon the city the November evening had come down dark and moist. Lighted windows and street lamps appeared and disappeared in the altering thicknesses of fog, but at intervals, as Collinson walked on northward, he passed a small shop, or a cluster of shops, where the light was close to him and bright, and at one of these oases of illumination he lingered a moment, with a thought to buy a toy in the window for his three-year-old little girl. The toy was a gaily coloured acrobatic monkey that willingly climbed up and down a string, and he knew that the "baby," as he and his wife still called their child, would scream with delight at the sight of it. He hesitated, staring into the window rather longingly, and wondering if he ought to make such a purchase. He had twelve dollars of his own in his pocket, but the toy was marked "35 cents," and he decided he could not afford it. So he sighed and went on, turning presently into a darker street.

When he reached home, the baby was crying over some inward perplexity not to be explained; and his wife, pretty and a little frowzy, was as usual, and as he had expected. That is to say, he found her irritated by cooking, bored by the baby, and puzzled by the dull life she led. Other women, it appeared, had happy and luxurious homes, and during the malnutritious dinner she had prepared she mentioned many such women by name, laying particular stress upon the achievements of their husbands. Why should she ("alone," as she put it) lead the life she did in one room and kitchenette, without even being able to afford to go to the movies more than once or twice a month? Mrs. Theodore Thompson's husband had bought a perfectly beautiful little sedan automobile; he gave his wife everything she wanted. Mrs. Will Gregory had merely mentioned that her old Hudson seal coat was wearing a little, and her husband had instantly said: "What'll a new one come to, girlie? Four or five hundred? Run and get it!" Why were other women's husbands like that—and why, oh, why—was hers like *this*?

"My goodness!" he said. "You talk as if I had sedans and sealskin coats and theatre tickets *on* me! Well, I haven't; that's all!"

"Then go out and get 'em!" she said fiercely. "Go out and get 'em!"

"What with?" he inquired. "I have twelve dollars in my pocket, and a balance of seventeen dollars at the bank; that's twenty-nine. I get twenty-five from the office day after to-morrow—Saturday; that makes fifty-four; but we have to pay forty-five for rent on Monday; so that'll leave us nine dollars. Shall I buy you a sedan with a sealskin coat on Tuesday, out of the nine?"

Mrs. Collinson began to 'weep a little. "The old, old story!" she said. "Six long, long years it's been going on now! I ask you how much you've got, and you say, 'nine dollars,' or 'seven dollars,' or 'four dollars,' and once it was sixty-five cents! Sixty-five cents; that's what we had to live on! Sixty-five *cents!*"

"Oh hush!" he said wearily.

"Hadn't you better hush a little yourself?" she retorted. "You come home with twelve dollars in your pocket and tell your wife to hush! That's nice? Why can't you do what decent men do?"

"What's that?"

"Why, give their wives something to live for. What do you give me, I'd like to know! Look at the clothes I wear, please!"

"Well, it's your own fault," he muttered.

"What did you say! Did you say it's my fault I wear clothes any women I know wouldn't be *seen* in?"

"Yes, I did. If you hadn't made me get you that platinum ring——"

"What!" she cried, and flourished her hand at him across the table. "Look at it! It's platinum, yes; but look at the stone in it, about the size of a pinhead, so's I'm ashamed to wear it when any of my friends see me! A hundred and sixteen dollars is what this magnificent ring cost you, and how long did I have to beg before I got even that little out of you? And it's the best thing I own and the only thing I ever did get out of you!"

"Oh, Lordy!" he moaned.

"I wish you'd seen Charlie Loomis looking at this ring to-day," she said, with a desolate laugh. "He happened to notice it, and I saw him keep glancing at it, and I wish you'd seen Charlie Loomis's expression!"

Collinson's own expression became noticeable upon her introduction of this name; he stared at her gravely until he completed the mastication of one of the indigestibles she had set before him; then he put down his fork and said:

"So you saw Charlie Loomis again to-day. Where?"

"Oh, my!" she sighed. "Have we got to go over all that again?"

"Over all what?"

"Over all the fuss you made the last time I mentioned Charlie's name.

I thought we settled it you were going to be a little more sensible about him."

"Yes," Collinson returned. "*I* was going to be more sensible about him, because you were going to be more sensible about him. Wasn't that the agreement?"

She gave him a hard glance, tossed her head so that the curls of her bobbed hair fluttered prettily, and with satiric mimicry repeated his question. "Agreement! Wasn't that the agreement! Oh, my, but you do make me tired, talking about 'agreements'! As if it was a crime my going to a vaudeville matinee with a man kind enough to notice that my husband never takes me anywhere!"

"Did you go to a vaudeville with him to-day?"

"No, I didn't!" she said. "I was talking about the time when you made such a fuss. I didn't go anywhere with him to-day."

"I'm glad to hear it," Collinson said. "I wouldn't have stood for it."

"Oh, you wouldn't?" she cried, and added a shrill laugh as further comment. "You 'wouldn't have stood for it'!"

"Never mind," he returned doggedly. "We went over all that the last time, and you understand me. I'll have no more foolishness about Charlie Loomis."

"How nice of you! He's a friend of yours; you go with him yourself; but your wife mustn't even look at him, just because he happens to be the one man that amuses her a little. That's fine!"

"Never mind," Collinson said again. "You say you saw him to-day. I want to know where."

"Suppose I don't choose to tell you."

"You'd better tell me, I think."

"Do you? I've got to answer for every minute of my day, have I?"

"I want to know where you saw Charlie Loomis."

She tossed her curls again, and laughed. "Isn't it funny!" she said. "Just because I like a man, he's the one person I can't have anything to do with! Just because he's kind and jolly and amusing, and I like his jokes and his thoughtfulness toward a woman when he's with her, I'm not to be allowed to see him at all! But my *husband*—oh, that's entirely different! *He* can go out with Charlie whenever he likes and have a good time, while I stay home and wash the dishes! Oh, it's a lovely life!"

"Where did you see him to-day?"

Instead of answering his question, she looked at him plaintively and allowed tears to shine along her lower eyelids. "Why do you treat me like this?" she asked in a feeble voice. "Why can't I have a man friend if I want to? I do like Charlie Loomis. I do like him——"

"Yes! That's what I noticed!"

"Well, but what's the good of always insulting me about him? He has time on his hands of afternoons, and so have I. Our janitor's wife is crazy about the baby and just adores to have me leave her in their flat—the longer the better. Why shouldn't I go to a matinee or a picture show sometimes with Charlie? Why should I just have to sit around instead of going out and having a nice time, when he wants me to?"

"I want to know where you saw him to-day!"

Mrs. Collinson jumped up. "You make me sick!" she said, and began to clear away the dishes.

"I want to know where——"

"Oh, hush up!" she cried. "He came here to leave a note for you."

"Oh," said her husband. "I beg your pardon. That's different."

"How sweet of you!"

"Where's the note, please?"

She took it from her pocket and tossed it to him. "So long as it's a note for *you* it's all right, of course," she said. "I wonder what you'd do if he'd written one to me!"

"Never mind," said Collinson, and read the note.

Dear Collie: Dave and Smithie and Old Bill and Sammy Hoag and maybe Steinie and Sol are coming over to the shack about eight-thirty. Home brew and the old pastime. *You* know! Don't fail.

CHARLIE.

"You've read this, of course," Collinson said. "The envelope wasn't sealed."

"I have not," his wife returned, covering the prevarication with a cold dignity. "I'm not in the habit of reading other people's correspondence, thank you! I suppose you think I do so because you'd never hesitate to read any note *I* got; but I don't do everything you do, you see!"

"Well, you can read it now," he said, and gave her the note.

Her eyes swept the writing briefly, and she made a sound of wonderment, as if amazed to find herself so true a prophet. "And the words weren't more than out of my mouth. *You* can go and have a grand party right in his flat, while your wife stays home and gets the baby to bed and washes the dishes!"

"I'm not going."

"Oh, no!" she said mockingly. "I suppose not. I see you missing one of Charlie's stag parties!"

"I'll miss this one."

But it was not to Mrs. Collinson's purpose that he should miss the party; she wished him to be as intimate as possible with the debonair Charlie Loomis; and so, after carrying some dishes into the kitchenette in meditative silence, she reappeared with a changed manner. She went to her husband, gave him a shy little pat on the shoulder and laughed good-naturedly. "Of course you'll go," she said. "I do think you're silly about me never going out with him when it would give me a little inno-cent pleasure and when you're not home to take me, yourself; but I wasn't really in such terrible earnest, all I said. You work hard the whole time, honey, and the only pleasure you ever do have, it's when you get a chance to go to one of these little penny-ante stag parties. You haven't been to one for ever so long, and you never stay after twelve; it's really all right with me. I want you to go."

"Oh, no," said Collinson. "It's only penny-ante, but I couldn't af-ford to lose anything at all."

"If you did lose, it'd only be a few cents," she said. "What's the difference, if it gives you a little fun? You'll work all the better if you go out and enjoy yourself once in a while."

"Well, if you really look at it that way, I'll go."

"That's right, dear," she said, smiling. "Better put on a fresh col-lar and your other suit, hadn't you?"

"I suppose so," he assented, and began to make the changes she sug-gested.

When he had completed his toilet, it was time for him to go. She came in from the kitchenette, kissed him, and then looked up into his eyes, letting him see a fond and brightly amiable expression.

"There, honey," she said. "Run along and have a nice time. Then maybe you'll be a little more sensible about some of *my* little pleasures."

He held the one hundred dollar bill folded in his hand, meaning to leave it with her, but as she spoke a sudden recurrence of suspicion made him forget his purpose. "Look here," he said. "I'm not making any bargain with you. You talk as if you thought I was going to let you run around to vaudevilles with Charlie because you let me go to this party. Is that your idea?"

It was, indeed, precisely Mrs. Collinson's idea, and she was instantly angered enough to admit it in her retort. "Oh, aren't you *mean!*" she cried. "I might know better than to look for any fairness in a man like you!"

"See here——"

"Oh, hush up!" she said. "Shame on you! Go on to your party!" With that she put both hands upon his breast, and pushed him toward the door.

"I won't go. I'll stay here."

"You will, too, go!" she cried, shrewishly. "I don't want to look at you around here all evening. It'd make me sick to look at a man with-out an ounce of fairness in his whole mean little body!"

"All right," said Collinson, violently, "I *will* go!"

"Yes! Get out of my sight!"

And he did, taking the one hundred dollar bill with him, to the penny-ante poker party.

The gay Mr. Charlie Loomis called his apartment "the shack" in jocular depreciation of its beauty and luxury, but he regarded it as a perfect thing, and in one way it was: for it was perfectly in the family likeness of a thousand such "shacks." It had a ceiling with false beams, walls of green burlap, spotted with coloured "coaching prints," brown shelves supporting pewter plates and mugs, "mission" chairs, a leather couch with violent cushions, silver-framed photographs of lady friends and officer friends, a drop light of pink-shot imitation alabaster, a papier-maché skull tobacco jar among moving-picture magazines on the round card table; and, of course, the final Charlie Loomis touch—a Japanese man-servant.

The master of all this was one of those neat, stoutish young men with fat, round heads, sleek, fair hair, immaculate, pale complexions, and infirm little pink mouths—in fact, he was of the type that may suggest to the student of resemblances a fastidious and excessively clean white pig with transparent ears. Nevertheless, Charlie Loomis was of a free-handed habit in some matters, being particularly indulgent to pretty women and their children. He spoke of the latter as "the kiddies," of course, and liked to call their mothers "kiddo," or "girlie." One of his greatest pleasures was to tell a woman that she was "the dearest, bravest little girlie in the world." Naturally he was a welcome guest in many households, and would often bring a really magnificent toy to the child of some friend whose wife he was courting. Moreover, at thirty-three he had already done well enough in business to take things easily, and he liked to give these little card parties, not for gain, but for pastime. He was cautious and disliked high stakes in a game of chance.

"I don't consider it hospitality to have any man go out o' my shack sore," he was wont to say. "Myself, I'm a bachelor and got no obligations; I'll shoot any man that can afford it for anything he wants to. Trouble is, you never can tell when a man can't afford it or what harm his losin' might mean to the little girlie at home and the kiddies. No, boys, penny-ante and ten-cent limit is the highest we go in this ole shack. Penny-ante and a few steins of the ole home-brew that hasn't got a divorce in a barrel of it!"

Penny-ante and the ole home-brew had been in festal operation for half an hour when the morose Collinson arrived this evening. Mr. Loomis and his guests sat about the round table under the alabaster drop light; their coats were off; cigars were worn at the deliberative poker angle; colourful chips and cards glistened on the cloth; one of the players wore a green shade over his eyes; and all in all, here was a little poker party for a lithograph.

"Ole Collie, b'gosh!" Mr. Loomis shouted, humorously. "Here's your vacant cheer; stack all stuck out for you 'n' ever'thin'! Set daown, neighbour, an' Smithie'll deal you in, next hand. What made you so late? Helpin' the little girl at home get the kiddy to bed? That's a great kiddy of yours, Collie."

Collinson took the chair that had been left for him, counted his chips and then as the playing of a "hand" still preoccupied three of the company, he picked up a silver dollar that lay upon the table near him. "What's this?" he asked. "A side bet? Or did somebody just leave it here for me?"

"Yes; for you to look at," Mr. Loomis explained. "It's Smithie's."

"What's wrong with it?"

"Nothin'. Smithie was just showin' it to us. Look at it."

Collinson turned the coin over and saw a tiny inscription that had been lined into the silver with a point of steel. "Luck," he read—"Luck hurry back to me!" Then he spoke to the owner of this marked dollar. "I suppose you put that on there, Smithie, to help make sure of getting our money to-night."

But Smithie shook his head, which was a large, gaunt head, as it happened—a head fronted with a sallow face shaped much like a coffin, but inconsistently genial in expression. "No," he said. "It just came in over my counter this afternoon, and I noticed it when I was checkin' up the day's cash. Funny, ain't it: 'Luck hurry back to me!'"

"Who do you suppose marked that on it?" Collinson said thoughtfully.

"Golly!" his host exclaimed. "It won't do you much good to wonder about that!"

Collinson frowned, continuing to stare at the marked dollar. "I guess not, but really I should like to know."

"I would, too," Smithie said. "I been thinkin' about it. Might 'a' been somebody in Seattle or somebody in Ipswich, Mass., or New Orleans or St. Paul. How you goin' to tell? It's funny how some people like to believe luck depends on some little thing like that."

"Yes, it is," Collinson assented, still brooding over the coin.

The philosophic Smithie extended his arm across the table collecting the cards to deal them, for the "hand" was finished. "Yes, sir, it's funny," he repeated. "Nobody knows exactly what luck is, but the way I guess it out, it lays in a man's believin' he's in luck, and some little object like this makes him kind of concentrate his mind on thinkin' he's going to be lucky, because of course you often know you're goin' to win, and then you do win. You don't win when you want to win, or when you need to; you win when you believe you'll win. I don't know who it was that said, 'Money's the root of all evil'; but I guess he didn't have too much sense! I suppose if some man killed some other man for a dollar, the poor fish that said that would let the man out and send the dollar to the chair——"

But here this garrulous and discursive guest was interrupted by immoderate protests from several of his colleagues. "Cut it out!" "My Lord!" "Do something!" "Smithie! Are you ever goin' to deal?"

"I'm going to shuffle first," he responded, suiting the action to the word, though with deliberation, and at the same time continuing his discourse. "It's a mighty interesting thing, a piece o' money. You take this dollar, now: Who's it belonged to? Where's it been? What different kind o' funny things has it been spent for sometimes? What funny kind of secrets do you suppose it could 'a' heard if it had ears? Good people have had it and bad people have had it. Why, a dollar could tell more about the human race—why, it could tell all about it!"

"I guess it couldn't tell all about the way you're dealin' those cards," said the man with the green shade. "You're mixin' things all up."

"I'll straighten 'em all out then," said Smithie cheerfully. "They say, 'Money talks.' Golly! If it could talk, what couldn't it tell? Nobody'd be safe. I got this dollar now, but who's it goin' to belong to next, and what'll he do with it? And then after that! Why, for years and years and years, it'll go on from one pocket to another, in a millionaire's house one day, in some burglar's flat the next, maybe, and in one person's hand money'll do good, likely, and in another's it'll do harm. We all want money; but some say it's a bad thing, like that dummy I was talkin' about. Lordy! Goodness or badness, I'll take all anybody——"

He was interrupted again, and with increased vehemence. Collinson, who sat next to him, complied with the demand to "ante up," then placed the dollar near his little cylinder of chips, and looked at his cards. They proved unencouraging, and he turned to his neighbour. "I'd sort of like to have that marked dollar, Smithie," he said. "I'll give you a paper dollar and a nickel for it."

But Smithie laughed, shook his head and slid the coin over toward his own chips. "No, sir. I'm goin' to keep it—a while, anyway."

"So you do think it'll bring you luck, after all!"

"No. But I'll hold on to it for this evening, anyhow."

"Not if we clean you out, you won't," said Charlie Loomis. "You know the rules o' the old shack: only cash goes in this game; no I. O. U. stuff ever went here or ever will. Tell you what I'll do, though, before you lose it: I'll give you a dollar and a quarter for your ole silver dollar, Smithie."

"Oh, you want it, too, do you? I guess I can spot what sort of luck you want it for, Charlie."

"Well, Mr. Bones, what sort of luck do I want it for?"

"You win, Smithie," one of the other players said. "We all know what sort o' luck ole Charlie wants your dollar for: he wants it for luck with the dames."

"Well, I might," Charlie admitted not displeased. "I haven't been so lucky that way lately—not so dog-gone lucky!"

All of his guests, except one, laughed at this, but Collinson frowned, still staring at the marked dollar. For a reason he could not have put into words just then, it began to seem almost vitally important to him to own this coin if he could, and to prevent Charlie Loomis from getting possession of it. The jibe, "He wants it for luck with the dames," rankled in Collinson's mind: somehow it seemed to refer to his wife.

"I'll tell you what I'll do, Smithie," he said. "I'll bet two dollars against that dollar of yours that I hold a higher hand next deal than you do."

"Here! Here!" Charlie remonstrated. "Shack rules! Ten-cent limit."

"That's only for the game," Collinson said, turning upon his host with a sudden sharpness. "This is an outside bet between Smithie and me. Will you do it, Smithie? Where's your sporting spirit?"

So liberal a proposal at once roused the spirit to which it appealed. "Well, I might, if some o' the others'll come in too, and make it really worth my while."

"I'm in," the host responded with prompt inconsistency; and others of the party, it appeared, were desirous of owning the talisman. They laughed and said it was "crazy stuff," yet they all "came in," and, for the first time in the history of this "shack," what Mr. Loomis called "real money," was seen upon the table as a stake. It was won, and the silver dollar with it, by the largest and oldest of the gamesters, a fat man with a walrus moustache that inevitably made him known in this circle as "Old Bill." He smiled condescendingly, and would have put the dollar in his pocket with the "real money," but Mr. Loomis protested.

"Here! What you doin'?" he shouted, catching Old Bill by the arm. "Put that dollar back on the table!"

"What for?"

"What for? Why, we're goin' to play for it again. Here's two dollars against it I beat you on the next hand."

"No," said Old Bill calmly. "It's worth more than two dollars to me. It's worth five."

"Well, five then," his host returned. "I want that dollar!"

"So do I," said Collinson. "I'll put in five dollars if you do."

"Anybody else in?" Old Bill inquired, dropping the coin on the table; and all of the others again "came in." Old Bill won again; but once more Charlie Loomis prevented him from putting the silver dollar in his pocket.

"Come on now!" Mr. Loomis exclaimed. "Anybody else but me in this for five dollars next time?"

"I am," said Collinson, swallowing with a dry throat; and he set forth all that remained to him of his twelve dollars. In return he received a pair of deuces, and the jubilant Charlie won.

He was vainglorious in his triumph. "Didn't that little luck piece just keep on tryin' to find the right man?" he cried, and read the inscription loudly. "'Luck hurry back to me!' Righto! You're home where you belong, girlie! Now we'll settle down to our reg'lar little game again."

"Oh, no," said Old Bill. "You wouldn't let me keep it. Put it out there and play for it again."

"I won't. She's mine now."

"I want my luck piece back myself," said Smithie. "Put it out and play for it. You made Old Bill."

"I won't do it."

"Yes, you will," Collinson said, and he spoke without geniality. "You put it out there."

"Oh, yes, I will," Mr. Loomis returned mockingly. "I will for ten dollars."

"Not I," said Old Bill. "Five is foolish enough!" And Smithie agreed with him. "Nor me!"

"All right, then. If you're afraid of ten, I keep it. I thought the ten'd scare you."

"Put that dollar on the table," Collinson said. "I'll put ten against it."

There was a little commotion among these mild gamesters; and someone said: "You're crazy, Collie. What do you want to do that for?"

"I don't care," said Collinson. "That dollar's already cost me enough, and I'm going after it."

"Well, you see, I want it, too," Charlie Loomis retorted cheerfully; and he appealed to the others. "I'm not askin' him to put up ten against it, am I?"

"Maybe not," Old Bill assented. "But how long is this goin' to keep on? It's already balled our game all up, and if we keep on foolin' with these side bets, why, what's the use?"

"My goodness!" the host exclaimed. "I'm not pushin' this thing, am I? I don't want to risk my good old luck piece, do I? It's Collie that's crazy to go on, ain't it?" He laughed. "He hasn't showed his money yet, though, I notice, and this old shack is run on strickly cash principles. I don't believe he's got ten dollars more on him!"

"Oh, yes, I have."

"Let's see it, then!"

Collinson's nostrils distended a little, but he said nothing, fumbled in his pocket, and then tossed the one hundred dollar bill, rather crumpled, upon the table.

"Great heavens!" shouted Old Bill. "Call the doctor; I'm all of a swoon!"

"Look at what's spilled over our nice clean table!" another said, in an awed voice. "Did you claim he didn't have ten on him, Charlie?"

"Well, it's nice to look at," Smithie observed. "But I'm with Old Bill. How long are you two goin' to keep this thing goin'? If Collie wins the luck piece I suppose Charlie'll bet him fifteen against it, and then——"

"No, I won't," Charlie interrupted. "Ten's the limit."

"Goin' to keep on bettin' ten against it all night?"

"No," said Charlie. "I tell you what I'll do with you, Collinson; we both of us seem kind o' set on this luck piece, and you're already out some on it. I'll give you a square chance at it and at catchin' even. It's twenty minutes after nine. I'll keep on these side bets with you till ten o'clock, but when my clock hits ten, we're through, and the one that's got it then keeps it, and no more foolin'. You want to do that, or quit now? I'm game either way."

"Go ahead and deal," said Collinson. "Whichever one of us has it at ten o'clock, it's his, and we quit."

But when the little clock on Charlie's green painted mantelshelf struck ten, the luck piece was Charlie's and with it an overwhelming lien on the one hundred dollar bill. He put both in his pocket. "Remember this ain't my fault; it was you that insisted," he said, and handed Collinson four five-dollar bills as change.

Old Bill, platonically interested, discovered that his cigar was sparkless, applied a match, and casually set forth his opinion. "Well, I guess that was about as poor a way of spendin' eighty dollars as I ever saw, but it all goes to show there's truth in the old motto that anything at all can happen in any poker game! That was a mighty nice hundred dollar bill you had on you, Collie; but it's like what Smithie said: a piece o' money goes hoppin' around from one person to another—it don't care!—and yours has gone and hopped to Charlie. The question is: Who's it goin' to hop to next?" He paused to laugh, glanced over the cards that had been dealt him, and concluded: "My guess is 't some good-lookin' woman'll prob'ly get a pretty fair chunk o' that hundred dollar bill out o' Charlie. Well, let's settle down to the old army game."

They settled down to it, and by twelve o'clock (the invariable closing hour of these pastimes in the old shack) Collinson had lost four dollars and thirty cents more. He was commiserated by his fellow gamesters as they put on their coats and overcoats, preparing to leave the hot little rooms. They shook their heads, laughed ruefully in sympathy, and told him he oughtn't to carry hundred dollar bills upon his person when he went out among friends. Old Bill made what is sometimes called an unfortunate remark.

"Don't worry about Collie," he said, jocosely. "That hundred dollar bill prob'ly belonged to some rich client of his."

"What!" Collinson said, staring.

"Never mind, Collie; I wasn't in earnest," the joker explained. "Of course I didn't mean it."

"Well, you oughtn't to say it," Collinson protested. "People say a thing like that about a man in a joking way, but other people hear it sometimes and don't know they're joking, and a story gets started."

"My goodness, but you're serious!" Old Bill exclaimed. "You look like you had a misery in your chest, as the rubes say; and I don't blame you! Get on out in the fresh night air and you'll feel better."

He was mistaken, however; the night air failed to improve Collinson's spirits as he walked home alone through the dark and chilly streets. There was, indeed, a misery in his chest, where stirred a sensation vaguely nauseating; his hands were tremulous and his knees infirm as he walked. In his mind was a confusion of pictures and sounds, echoes from Charlie Loomis' shack; he could not clear his mind's eye of the one hundred dollar bill; and its likeness, as it lay crumpled on the green cloth under the drop light, haunted and hurt him as a face in a coffin haunts and hurts the new mourner.

It seemed to Collinson then that money was the root of all evil and the root of all good, the root and branch of all life, indeed. With money, his wife would have been amiable, not needing gay bachelors to take her to vaudevilles. Her need of money was the true foundation of the jealousy that had sent him out morose and reckless to-night; of the jealousy that had made it seem, when he gambled with Charlie Loomis for the luck dollar, as though they really gambled for luck with her.

It still seemed to him that they had gambled for luck with her, and Charlie had won it. But as Collinson plodded homeward in the chilly midnight, his shoulders sagging and his head drooping, he began to wonder how he could have risked money that belonged to another man. What on earth had made him do what he had done? Was it the mood his wife had set him in as he went out that evening? No; he had gone out feeling like that often enough, and nothing had happened.

Something had brought this trouble on him, he thought; for it appeared to Collinson that he had been an automaton, having nothing to do with his own actions. He must bear the responsibility for them; but he had not willed them. If the one hundred dollar bill had not happened to be in his pocket—That was it! And at the thought he mumbled desolately to himself: "I'd been all right if it hadn't been for that." If the one hundred dollar bill had not happened to be in his pocket, he'd have been "all right." The one hundred dollar bill had done this to him. And Smithie's romancing again came back to him: "In one person's hands money'll do good, likely; in another's it'll do harm." It was the money that did harm or good, not the person; and the money in his hands had done this harm to himself.

He had to deliver a hundred dollars at the office in the morning, somehow; for he dared not take the risk of the client's meeting the debtor.

There was a balance of seventen dollars in his bank, and he could pawn his watch for twenty-five, as he knew well enough, by experience. That would leave fifty-eight dollars to be paid, and there was only one way to get it. His wife would have to let him pawn her ring. She'd have to!

Without any difficulty he could guess what she would say and do when he told her of his necessity: and he knew that never in her life would she forego the advantage over him she would gain from it. He knew, too, what stipulations she would make, and he had to face the fact that he was in no position to reject them. The one hundred dollar bill had cost him the last vestiges of mastery in his own house; and Charlie Loomis had really won not only the bill and the luck, but the privilege of taking Collinson's wife to vaudevilles. And it all came back to the same conclusion: The one hundred dollar bill had done it to him. "What kind of a thing is this life?" Collinson mumbled to himself, finding matters wholly perplexing in a world made into tragedy at the caprice of a little oblong slip of paper.

Then, as he went on his way to wake his wife and face her with the soothing proposal to pawn her ring early the next morning, something happened to Collinson. Of itself the thing that happened was nothing, but he was aware of his folly as if it stood upon a mountain top against the sun—and so he gathered knowledge of himself and a little of the wisdom that is called better than happiness.

His way was now the same as upon the latter stretch of his walk home from the office that evening. The smoke fog had cleared and the air was clean with a night wind that moved briskly from the west; in all the long street there was only one window lighted, but it was sharply outlined now, and fell as a bright rhomboid upon the pavement before Collinson. When he came to it he paused, at the hint of an inward impulse he did not think to trace; and, frowning, he perceived that this was the same shop window that had detained him on his homeward way, when he had thought of buying a toy for the baby.

The toy was still there in the bright window: the gay little acrobatic monkey that would climb up or down a red string as the string slacked or straightened; but Collinson's eye fixed itself upon the card marked with the price "35 cents."

He stared and stared. "Thirty-five cents!" he said to himself. "Thirty-five cents!"

Then suddenly he burst into loud and prolonged laughter.

The sound was startling in the quiet night, and roused the interest of a meditative policeman who stood in the darkened doorway of the next shop. He stepped out, not unfriendly.

"What you havin' such a good time over, this hour o' the night?" he inquired. "What's all the joke?"

Collinson pointed to the window. "It's that monkey on the string," he said. "Something about it struck me as mighty funny!"

So, with a better spirit, he turned away, still laughing, and went home to face his wife.

※ ※ ※

MELVILLE DAVISSON POST
(1871-   )

BORN in West Virginia, April 19, 1871, Melville Davisson Post served through the law his apprenticeship to the short story. Interest in crime and criminals led him to create the characters Randolph Mason, Uncle Abner, Monsieur Jonquelle, the sleuth of St. James's Square, and Walker of the Secret Service, for whom he constructed many excellent tales of mystery. Among the moderns Mr. Post is a conservative, holding the belief that plot—in the best sense—is essential to the very nature of the term, short story. A logician to the ultimate, he exemplifies the working of law and order in tales carefully planned, carefully built. Since *The Strange Schemes of Randolph Mason* (1896), he has published over a dozen volumes, now and then sounding a deeper note as in *The Mountain School Teacher* (1922).

The Doomdorf Mystery, one of his best tales, appeared in *The Saturday Evening Post* (1914), in *Uncle Abner* (1918) and has been reprinted a number of times. It is here reproduced by special arrangement with and permission of the author and his publishers, D. Appleton and Company, New York City.

THE DOOMDORF MYSTERY

THE pioneer was not the only man in the great mountains behind Virginia. Strange aliens drifted in after the Colonial wars. All foreign armies are sprinkled with a cockle of adventurers that take root and remain. They were with Braddock and La Salle, and they rode north out of Mexico after her many empires went to pieces.

I think Doomdorf crossed the seas with Iturbide when that ill-starred adventurer returned to be shot against a wall; but there was no

Southern blood in him. He came from some European race remote and barbaric. The evidences were all about him. He was a huge figure of a man with a black spade beard, broad, thick hands, and square, flat fingers.

He had found a wedge of land between the Crown's grant to Daniel Davisson and a Washington survey. It was an uncovered triangle not worth the running of the lines; and so, no doubt, was left out, a sheer rock standing up out of the river for a base, and a peak of the mountain rising northward behind it for an apex.

Doomdorf squatted on the rock. He must have brought a belt of gold pieces when he took to his horse, for he hired old Robert Steuart's slaves and built a stone house on the rock, and he brought the furnishings overland from a frigate in the Chesapeake; and then in the handfuls of earth, wherever a root would hold, he planted the mountain behind with peach trees. The gold gave out; but the devil is fertile in resources. Doomdorf built a log still and turned the first fruits of the garden into a hell-brew. The idle and the vicious came with their stone jugs, and violence and riot flowed out.

The government of Virginia was remote and its arm short and feeble; but the men who held the lands west of the mountains against the savages under grants from George, and after that held them against George himself, were efficient and expeditious. They had long patience, but when that failed they went up from their fields and drove the thing before them out of the land, like a scourge of God.

There came a day when my Uncle Abner and Squire Randolph rode through the gap of the mountains to have the thing out with Doomdorf. The work of his brew, which had the odours of Eden and the impulses of the devil in it, could be borne no longer. The drunken negroes had shot old Duncan's cattle and burned his haystacks, and the land was on its feet.

They rode alone, but they were worth an army of little men. Randolph was vain and pompous and given over to extravagance of words, but he was a gentleman beneath it, and fear was an alien and a stranger to him. And Abner was the right hand of the land.

It was a day in early summer and the sun lay hot. They crossed through the broken spine of the mountains and trailed along the river in the shade of the great chestnut trees. The road was only a path and the horses went one before the other. It left the river when the rock began to rise and, making a detour through the grove of peach trees, reached the house on the mountain side. Randolph and Abner got down, unsaddled their horses and turned them out to graze, for their business with Doomdorf would not be over in an hour. Then they took a steep path that brought them out on the mountain side of the house.

A man sat on a big red-roan horse in the paved court before the door. He was a gaunt old man. He sat bare-headed, the palms of his hands resting on the pommel of his saddle, his chin sunk in his black stock, his face in retrospection, the wind moving gently his great shock of voluminous white hair. Under him the huge red horse stood with his legs spread out like a horse of stone.

There was no sound. The door to the house was closed; insects moved in the sun; a shadow crept out from the motionless figure, and swarms of yellow butterflies maneuvered like an army.

Abner and Randolph stopped. They knew the tragic figure—a circuit rider of the hills who preached the invective of Isaiah as though he were the mouthpiece of a militant and avenging overlord; as though the government of Virginia were the awful theocracy of the Book of Kings. The horse was dripping with sweat and the man bore the dust and the evidences of a journey on him.

"Bronson," said Abner, "where is Doomdorf?"

The old man lifted his head and looked down at Abner over the pommel of the saddle.

" 'Surely,' " he said, " 'he covereth his feet in his summer chamber.' "

Abner went over and knocked on the closed door, and presently the white, frightened face of a woman looked out at him. She was a little faded woman, with fair hair, a broad foreign face, but with the delicate evidences of gentle blood.

Abner repeated his question.

"Where is Doomdorf?"

"Oh, sir," she answered with a queer lisping accent, "he went to lie down in his south room after his midday meal, as his custom is; and I went to the orchard to gather any fruit that might be ripened." She hesitated and her voice lisped into a whisper: "He is not come out and I cannot wake him."

The two men followed her through the hall and up the stairway to the door.

"It is always bolted," she said, "when he goes to lie down." And she knocked feebly with the tips of her fingers.

There was no answer and Randolph rattled the doorknob.

"Come out, Doomdorf!" he called in his big, bellowing voice.

There was only silence and the echoes of the words among the rafters. Then Randolph set his shoulder to the door and burst it open.

They went in. The room was flooded with sun from the tall south windows. Doomdorf lay on a couch in a little offset of the room, a great scarlet patch on his bosom and a pool of scarlet on the floor.

The woman stood for a moment staring; then she cried out:

"At last I have killed him!" And she ran like a frightened hare.

The two men closed the door and went over to the couch. Doomdorf had been shot to death. There was a great ragged hole in his waist-coat. They began to look about for the weapon with which the deed had been accomplished, and in a moment found it—a fowling piece lying in two dogwood forks against the wall. The gun had just been fired; there was a freshly exploded paper cap under the hammer.

There was little else in the room—a loom—woven red carpet on the floor; wooden shutters flung back from the windows; a great oak table, and on it a big, round, glass water bottle, filled to its glass stopper with raw liquor from the still. The stuff was limpid and clear as spring water; and, but for its pungent odour, one would have taken it for God's brew instead of Doomdorf's. The sun lay on it and against the wall where hung the weapon that had ejected the dead man out of life.

"Abner," said Randolph, "this is murder! The woman took that gun down from the wall and shot Doomdorf while he slept."

Abner was standing by the table, his fingers round his chin.

"Randolph," he replied, "what brought Bronson here?"

"The same outrages that brought us," said Randolph. "The mad old circuit rider has been preaching a crusade against Doomdorf far and wide in the hills."

Abner answered, without taking his fingers from about his chin:

"You think this woman killed Doomdorf? Well, let us go and ask Bronson who killed him."

They closed the door, leaving the dead man on his couch, and went down into the court.

The old circuit rider had put away his horse and got an ax. He had taken off his coat and pushed his shirtsleeves up over his long elbows. He was on his way to the still to destroy the barrels of liquor. He stopped when the two men came out, and Abner called to him.

"Bronson," he said, "who killed Doomdorf?"

"I killed him," replied the old man, and went on toward the still.

Randolph swore under his breath. "By the Almighty," he said, "everybody couldn't killed him!"

"Who can tell how many had a hand in it?" replied Abner.

"Two have confessed!" cried Randolph. "Was there perhaps a third? Did you kill him, Abner? And I too? Man, the thing is impossible!"

"The impossible," replied Abner, "looks here like the truth. Come with me, Randolph, and I will show you a thing more impossible than this."

They returned through the house and up the stairs to the room. Abner closed the door behind them.

"Look at this bolt," he said; "it is on the inside and not connected with the lock. How did the one who killed Doomdorf get into this room, since the door was bolted?"

"Through the windows," replied Randolph.

There were but two windows, facing the south, through which the sun entered. Abner led Randolph to them.

"Look!" he said. "The wall of the house is plumb with the sheer face of the rock. It is a hundred feet to the river and the rock is as smooth as a sheet of glass. But that is not all. Look at these window frames; they are cemented into their casement with dust and they are bound along their edges with cobwebs. These windows have not been opened. How did the assassin enter?"

"The answer is evident," said Randolph: "The one who killed Doomdorf hid in the room until he was asleep; then he shot him and went out."

"The explanation is excellent but for one thing," replied Abner: "How did the assassin bolt the door behind him on the inside of this room after he had gone out?"

Randolph flung out his arms with a hopeless gesture.

"Who knows?" he cried. "Maybe Doomdorf killed himself."

Abner laughed.

"And after firing a handful of shot into his heart he got up and put the gun back carefully into the forks against the wall!"

"Well," cried Randolph, "there is one open road out of this mystery. Bronson and this woman say they killed Doomdorf, and if they killed him they surely know how they did it. Let us go down and ask them."

"In the law court," replied Abner; "that procedure would be considered sound sense; but we are in God's court and things are managed there in a somewhat stranger way. Before we go let us find out, if we can, at what hour it was that Doomdorf died."

He went over and took a big silver watch out of the dead man's pocket. It was broken by a shot and the hands lay at one hour after noon. He stood for a moment fingering his chin.

"At one o'clock," he said, "Bronson, I think, was on the road to this place, and the woman was on the mountain among the peach trees."

Randolph threw back his shoulders.

"Why waste time in speculation about it, Abner?" he said. "We know who did this thing. Let us go and get the story of it out of their own mouths. Doomdorf died by the hand of either Bronson or this woman."

"I could better believe it," replied Abner, "but for the running of a certain awful law."

"What law?" said Randolph. "Is it a statute of Virginia?"

"It is a statute," replied Abner, "of an authority somewhat higher. Mark the language of it: 'He that killeth with the sword must be killed with the sword.'"

He came over and took Randolph by the arm.

"Must! Randolph, did you mark particularly the word 'must'? It is a mandatory law. There is no room in it for the vicissitudes or chance or fortune. There is no way round that word. Thus, we reap what we sow and nothing else; thus, we receive what we give and nothing else. It is the weapon in our hands that finally destroys us. You are looking at it now." And he turned him about so that the table and the weapon and the dead man were before him. " 'He that killeth with the sword must be killed with the sword.' And now," he said, "let us go and try the method of the law courts. Your faith is in the wisdom of their ways."

They found the old circuit rider at work in the still, staving in Doomdorf's liquor casks, splitting the oak heads with his ax.

"Bronson," said Randolph, "how did you kill Doomdorf?"

The old man stopped and stood leaning on his ax.

"I killed him," replied the old man, "as Elijah killed the captains of Ahaziah and their fifties. But not by the hand of any man did I pray the Lord God to destroy Doomdorf, but with fire from heaven to destroy him."

He stood up and extended his arms.

"His hands were full of blood," he said. "With his abomination from these groves of Baal he stirred up the people to contention, to strife and murder. The widow and the orphan cried to heaven against him. 'I will surely hear their cry,' is the promise written in the Book. The land was weary of him; and I prayed the Lord God to destroy him with fire from heaven, as he destroyed the Princes of Gomorrah in their palaces!"

Randolph made a gesture as of one who dismisses the impossible, but Abner's face took on a deep, strange look.

"With fire from heaven!" he repeated slowly to himself. Then he asked a question. "A little while ago," he said, "when we came, I asked you where Doomdorf was, and you answered me in the language of the third chapter of the Book of Judges. Why did you answer me like that, Bronson?—'Surely he covereth his feet in his summer chamber.' "

"The woman told me that he had not come down from the room where he had gone up to sleep," replied the old man, "and that the door was locked. And then I knew that he was dead in his summer chamber like Eglon, King of Moab."

He extended his arm toward the south.

"I came here from the Great Valley," he said, "to cut down these groves of Baal and to empty out this abomination; but I did not know that the Lord had heard my prayer and visited His wrath on Doomdorf until I was come up into these mountains to his door. When the woman spoke I knew it." And he went away to his horse, leaving the ax among the ruined barrels.

Randolph interrupted.

"Come Abner," he said, "this is wasted time. Bronson did not kill Doomdorf."

Abner answered slowly in his deep, level voice:

"Do you realise, Randolph, how Doomdorf died?"

"Not by fire from heaven, at any rate," said Randolph.

"Randolph," replied Abner, "are you sure?"

"Abner," cried Randolph, "you are pleased to jest, but I am in deadly earnest. A crime has been done here against the state. I am an officer of justice and I propose to discover the assassin if I can."

He walked away toward the house and Abner followed, his hands behind him and his great shoulders thrown loosely forward, with a grim smile about his mouth.

"It is no use to talk with the mad old preacher," Randolph went on. "Let him empty out the liquor and ride away. I won't issue a warrant against him. Prayer may be a handy implement to do a murder with, Abner, but it is not a deadly weapon under the statutes of Virginia. Doomdorf was dead when old Bronson got here with his Scriptural jargon. This woman killed Doomdorf. I shall put her to an inquisition."

"As you like," replied Abner. "Your faith remains in the methods of the law courts."

"Do you know of any better methods?" said Randolph.

"Perhaps," replied Abner, "when you have finished."

Night had entered the valley. The two men went into the house and set about preparing the corpse for burial. They got candles, and made a coffin, and put Doomdorf in it, and straightened out his limbs, and folded his arm across his shot-out heart. Then they set the coffin on benches in the hall.

They kindled a fire in the dining room and sat down before it, with the door open and the red fire-light shining through on the dead man's narrow, everlasting house. The woman had put some cold meat, a golden cheese and a loaf on the table. They did not see her, but they heard her moving about the house; and finally, on the gravel court outside, her step and the whinny of a horse. Then she came in, dressed as for a journey. Randolph sprang up.

"Where are you going?" he said.

"To the sea and a ship," replied the woman. Then she indicated the hall with a gesture. "He is dead and I am free."

There was a sudden illumination in her face. Randolph took a step toward her. His voice was big and harsh.

"Who killed Doomdorf?" he cried.

"I killed him," replied the woman. "It was fair!"

"Fair!" echoed the justice. "What do you mean by that?"

The woman shrugged her shoulders and put out her hands with a foreign gesture.

"I remember an old, old man sitting against a sunny wall, and a little girl, and one who came and talked a long time with the old man, while the little girl plucked yellow flowers out of the grass and put them into her hair. Then finally the stranger gave the old man a gold chain and took the little girl away." She flung out her hands. "Oh, it was fair to kill him!" She looked up with a queer pathetic smile.

"The old man will be gone by now," she said; "but I shall perhaps find the wall there, with the sun on it, and the yellow flowers in the grass. And now, may I go?"

It is a law of the story-teller's art that he does not tell a story. It is the listener who tells it. The story-teller does but provide him with the stimuli.

Randolph got up and walked about the floor. He was a justice of the peace in a day when that office was filled only by the landed gentry, after the English fashion; and the obligations of the law were strong on him. If he should take liberties with the letter of it, how could the weak and evil be made to hold it in respect? Here was this woman before him a confessed assassin. Could he let her go?

Abner sat unmoving by the hearth, his elbow on the arm of his chair, his palm propping up his jaw, his face clouded in deep lines. Randolph was consumed with vanity and the weakness of ostentation, but he shouldered his duties for himself. Presently he stopped and looked at the woman, wan, faded like some prisoner of legend escaped out of fabled dungeons into the sun.

The firelight flickered past her to the box on the benches in the hall, and the vast, inscrutable justice of heaven entered and overcame him.

"Yes," he said. "Go! There is no jury in Virginia that would hold a woman for shooting a beast like that." And he thrust out his arm, with the fingers extended toward the dead man.

The woman made a little awkward curtsy.

"I thank you, sir." Then she hesitated and lisped, "But I have not shoot him."

"Not shoot him!" cried Randolph. "Why, the man's heart is riddled!"

"Yes, sir," she said simply, like a child. "I kill him, but have not shoot him."

Randolph took two long strides toward the woman.

"Not shoot him!" he repeated. "How then in the name of heaven, did you kill Doomdorf?" And his big voice filled the empty places of the room.

"I will show you, sir," she said.

She turned and went away into the house. Presently she returned with something folded up in a linen towel. She put it on the table between the loaf of bread and the yellow cheese.

Randolph stood over the table, and the woman's deft fingers undid the towel from round its deadly contents; and presently the thing lay there uncovered.

It was a little crude model of a human figure done in wax with a needle thrust through the bosom.

Randolph stood up with a great intake of the breath.

"Magic! By the eternal!"

"Yes, sir," the woman explained, in her voice and manner of a child. "I have try to kill him many times—oh, very many times!—with witch words which I have remember; but always they fail. Then, at last, I make him in wax, and I put a needle through his heart; and I kill him very quickly."

It was as clear as daylight, even to Randolph, that the woman was innocent. Her little harmless magic was the pathetic effort of a child to kill a dragon. He hesitated a moment before he spoke, and then he decided like the gentleman he was. If it helped the child to believe that her enchanted straw had slain the monster—well, he would let her believe it.

"And now, sir, may I go?"

Randolph looked at the woman in a sort of wonder.

"Are you not afraid," he said, "of the night and the mountains, and the long road?"

"Oh, no, sir," she replied simply. "The good God will be everywhere now."

It was an awful commentary on the dead man—that this strange half-child believed that all the evil in the world had gone out with him; that now that he was dead, the sunlight of heaven would fill every nook and corner.

It was not a faith that either of the two men wished to shatter, and they let her go. It would be daylight presently and the road through the mountains to the Chesapeake was open.

Randolph came back to the fireside after he had helped her into the saddle, and sat down. He tapped on the hearth for some time idly with the iron poker; and then finally he spoke.

"This is the strangest thing that ever happened," he said. "Here's a mad old preacher who thinks that he killed Doomdorf with fire from Heaven, like Elijah the Tishbite; and here is a simple child of a woman who thinks she killed him with a piece of magic of the Middle Ages— each as innocent of his death as I am. And yet, by the eternal, the beast is dead!"

He drummed on the hearth with the poker, lifting it up and letting it drop through the hollow of his fingers.

"Somebody shot Doomdorf. But who? And how did he get into and out of that shut-up room? The assassin that killed Doomdorf must have gotten into the room to kill him. Now, how did he get in?" He spoke as to himself, but my uncle sitting across the hearth replied:

"Through the window."

"Through the window!" echoed Randolph. "Why, man, you yourself showed me that the window had not been opened, and the precipice below it a fly could hardly climb. Do you tell me now that the window was opened?"

"No," said Abner, "it was never opened."

Randolph got on his feet.

"Abner," he cried, "are you saying that the one who killed Doomdorf climbed the sheer wall and got in through a closed window, without disturbing the dust or the cobwebs on the window frame?"

My uncle looked Randolph in the face.

"The murderer of Doomdorf did even more," he said. "That assassin not only climbed the face of that precipice and got in through the closed window, but he shot Doomdorf to death and got out again through the closed window without leaving a single track or trace behind, and without disturbing a grain of dust or a thread of a cobweb."

Randolph swore a great oath.

"The thing is impossible!" he cried. "Men are not killed to-day in Virginia by black art or a curse of God."

"By black art, no," replied Abner; "but by the curse of God, yes. I think they are."

Randolph drove his clenched right hand into the palm of his left.

"By the eternal!" he cried. "I would like to see the assassin who could do a murder like this, whether he be an imp from the pit or an angel out of Heaven."

"Very well," replied Abner, undisturbed. "When he comes back to-morrow I will show you the assassin who killed Doomdorf.

When day broke they dug a grave and buried the dead man against the mountain among his peach trees. It was noon when that work was ended. Abner threw down his spade and looked up at the sun.

"Randolph," he said, "let us go and lay an ambush for this assassin. He is on the way here."

And it was a strange ambush that he laid. When they were come again into the chamber where Doomdorf died he bolted the door; then he loaded the fowling piece and put it carefully back on its rack against the wall. After that he did another curious thing. He took the blood-stained coat, which they had stripped off the dead man when they had prepared his body for the earth, put a pillow in it and laid it on the couch precisely where Doomdorf had slept. And while he did these things Randolph stood in wonder and Abner talked:

"Look you, Randolph. . . . We will trick the murderer. . . . We will catch him in the act."

Then he went over and took the puzzled justice by the arm.

"Watch!" he said. "The assassin is coming along the wall!"

But Randolph heard nothing, saw nothing. Only the sun entered. Abner's hand tightened on his arm.

"It is here! Look!" And he pointed to the wall.

Randolph, following the extended finger, saw a tiny brilliant disk of light moving slowly up along the wall toward the lock of the fowling piece. Abner's hand became a vise and his voice ran as over metal.

"'He that killeth with the sword must be killed with the sword.' It is the water bottle, full of Doomdorf's liquor, focusing the sun. . . . And look, Randolph, how Bronson's prayer was answered!"

The tiny disk of light travelled on the plate of the lock.

"It is fire from Heaven!"

The words rang above the roar of the fowling piece, and Randolph saw the dead man's coat leap up on the couch, riddled by the shot. The gun, in its natural position on the rack, pointed to the couch standing at the end of the chamber, beyond the offset of the wall, and the focused sun had exploded the percussion cap.

Randolph made a great gesture, with his arm extended.

"It is a world," he said, "filled with the mysterious joinder of accident!"

"It is a world," replied Abner, "filled with the mysterous justice of God!"

❋ ❋ ❋

SHERWOOD ANDERSON
(1876-   )

AMONG the first to break away from the short story form preferred in America since the time of Poe is Sherwood Anderson. His first book, *Windy MacPherson's Son* (1916), has been followed annually by a novel or a collection of stories which, like those of Theodore Dreiser, are notable, negatively, for their no-form, for their non-dependence on the usual architecture; positively, for their success in catching the essence of life and crystallising it in a mood or a picture. From Ohio, the State of his birth (September 13, 1876), Mr. Anderson moved to Chicago, then to New York, and is now settled in Virginia. His first story, *The Rabbit Pen*, published in 1914, initiated a constantly growing popularity which, on the appearance of his *Triumph of the Egg* (1921), approached international fame.

Death in the Woods, first published in *The American Mercury,*
September, 1926, won an O. Henry Memorial Prize as one of the
two best stories of the year. It is here reprinted by special permission of the author and his agent, O. K. Liveright, New York City.

DEATH IN THE WOODS

I

SHE was an old woman and lived on a farm near the town in
which I lived. All country and small-town people have seen such
old women, but no one knows much about them. Such an old
woman comes into town driving an old worn-out horse or she comes
afoot carrying a basket. She may own a few hens and have eggs to
sell. She brings them in a basket and takes them to a grocer. There
she trades them in. She gets some salt pork and some beans. Then she
gets a pound or two of sugar and some flour.

Afterward she goes to the butcher's and asks for some dog meat.
She may spend ten or fifteen cents, but when she does she asks for something. In my day the butchers gave liver to anyone who wanted to
carry it away. In our family we were always having it. Once one of
my brothers got a whole cow's liver at the slaughter-house near the fair-
ground. We had it until we were sick of it. It never cost a cent. I
have hated the thought of it ever since.

The old farm woman got some liver and a soup bone. She never
visited with anyone, and as soon as she got what she wanted she lit out
for home. It made quite a load for such an old body. No one gave
her a lift. People drive right down a road and never notice an old
woman like that.

There was such an old woman used to come into town past our house
one summer and fall when I was sick with what was called inflamma-
tory rheumatism. She went home later carrying a heavy pack on her
back. Two or three large gaunt-looking dogs followed at her heels.

The old woman was nothing special. She was one of the nameless
ones that hardly anyone knows, but she got into my thoughts. I have
just suddenly now, after all these years, remembered her and what happened. It is a story. Her name was, I think, Grimes, and she lived
with her husband and son in a small unpainted house on the bank of a
small creek four miles from town.

The husband and son were a tough lot. Although the son was but
twenty-one, he had already served a term in jail. It was whispered
about that the woman's husband stole horses and ran them off to some
other county. Now and then, when a horse turned up missing, the man

had also disappeared. No one ever caught him. Once, when I was loafing at Tom Whitehead's livery barn, the man came there and sat on the bench in front. Two or three other men were there, but no one spoke to him. He sat for a few minutes and then got up and went away. When he was leaving he turned around and stared at the men. There was a look of defiance in his eyes. "Well, I have tried to be friendly. You don't want to talk to me. It has been so wherever I have gone in this town. If, some day, one of your fine horses turns up missing, well, then what?" He did not say anything actually. "I'd like to bust one of you on the jaw," was about what his eyes said. I remember how the look in his eyes made me shiver.

The old man belonged to a family that had had money once. His name was Grimes, Jake Grimes. It all comes back clearly now. His father, John Grimes, had owned a sawmill when the country was new and had made money. Then he got to drinking and running after women. When he died, there wasn't much left.

Jake blew in the rest. Pretty soon there wasn't any more lumber to cut and his land was nearly all gone.

He got his wife off a German farmer, for whom he went to work one June day in the wheat harvest. She was a young thing then and scared to death. You see, the farmer was up to something with the girl —she was, I think, a bound girl, and his wife had her suspicions. She took it out on the girl when the man wasn't around. Then, when the wife had to go off to town for supplies, the farmer got after her. She told young Jake that nothing really ever happened, but he didn't know whether to believe it or not.

He got her pretty easy himself, the first time he was out with her. He wouldn't have married her if the German farmer hadn't tried to tell him where to get off. He got her to go riding with him in his buggy one night when he was threshing on the place, and then he came for her the next Sunday night.

She managed to get out of the house without her employer's seeing, but when she was getting into the buggy he showed up. It was almost dark, and he just popped up suddenly at the horse's head. He grabbed the horse by the bridle and Jake got out his buggy whip.

They had it out all right! The German was a tough one. Maybe he didn't care whether his wife knew or not. Jake hit him over the face and shoulders with the buggy whip, but the horse got to acting up and he had to get out.

Then the two men went for it. The girl didn't see it. The horse started to run away and went nearly a mile down the road before the girl got him stopped. Then she managed to tie him to a tree beside the road. (I wonder how I know all this. It must have stuck in my mind from the small-town tales when I was a boy.) Jake found her there after he got through with the German. She was huddled up in the buggy seat, crying, scared to death. She told Jake a lot of stuff, how the German had tried to get her, how he chased her once into the barn, how another time, when they happened to be alone in the barn together, he tore her dress open clear down the front. The German, she said, might have got her that time if he hadn't heard his old woman drive in at the gate. She had been off to town for supplies. Well, she would be putting the horse in the barn. The German managed to sneak off to the fields without his wife seeing. He told the girl he would kill her if she told. What could she do? She told a lie about ripping her dress in the barn when she was feeding the stock. I remember now that she was a bound girl and did not know where her father and mother were. Maybe she did not have any father. You know what I mean.

II

She married Jake and had a son and daughter but the daughter died.

Then she settled down to feed stock. That was her job. At the German's place she had cooked the food for the German and his wife. The wife was a strong woman with big hips and worked most of the time in the fields with her husband. She fed them and fed the cows in the barn, fed the pigs, the horses, and the chickens. Every moment of every day as a young girl was spent feeding something.

Then she married Jake Grimes and he had to be fed. She was a slight thing, and when she had been married for three or four years, and after the two children were born, her slender shoulders became stooped.

Jake always had a lot of big dogs around the house, that stood near the unused sawmill near the creek. He was always trading horses when he wasn't stealing something, and had a lot of poor bony ones about. Also, he kept three or four pigs and a cow. They were all pastured in the few acres left of the Grimes place and Jake did little.

He went into debt for a threshing outfit and ran it for several years, but it did not pay. People did not trust him. They were afraid he would steal the grain at night. He had to go a long way off to get work, and it cost too much to get there. In the winter he hunted and cut a little firewood, to be sold in some near-by town. When the boy grew up he was just like his father. They got drunk together. If there wasn't anything to eat in the house when they came home the old man gave his old woman a cut over the head. She had a few chickens of her own and had to kill one of them in a hurry. When they were all killed she wouldn't have any eggs to sell when she went to town, and then what would she do?

She had to scheme all her life about gettings things fed, getting the pigs fed so they would grow fat and could be butchered in the fall. When they were butchered her husband took most of the meat off to town and sold it. If he did not do it first the boy did. They fought sometimes and when they fought the old woman stood aside trembling.

She had got the habit of silence anyway—that was fixed. Sometimes, when she began to look old—she wasn't forty yet—and when the husband and son were both off, trading horses or drinking or hunting or stealing, she went around the house and the barnyard muttering to herself.

How was she going to get everything fed?—that was her problem. The dogs had to be fed. There wasn't any hay in the barn for the cow and the horses. If she didn't feed the chickens how could they lay eggs? Without eggs to sell how could she get things in town, things she had to have to keep the life of the farm going? Thank heaven, she did not have to feed her husband—in a certain way. That hadn't lasted long after their marriage and after the babies came. Where he went on his long trips she did not know. Sometimes he was gone from home for weeks, and after the boy grew up they went off together.

They left everything at home for her to manage and she had no money. She knew no one. No one ever talked to her in town. When it was winter she had to gather sticks of wood for her fire, had to try to keep the stock fed with very little grain.

The stock in the barn cried to her hungrily, the dogs followed her about. In the winter the hens laid few enough eggs. They huddled in the corners of the barn and she kept watching them. If a hen lays an egg in the barn in the winter and you do not find it, it freezes and breaks.

One day in winter the old woman went off to town with a few eggs and the dogs followed her. She did not get started until nearly three o'clock and the snow was heavy. She hadn't been feeling very well for several days and so she went muttering along, scantily clad, her shoulders stooped. She had an old grain bag in which she carried her eggs, tucked away down in the bottom. There weren't many of them, but in winter the price of eggs is up. She would get a little meat for the eggs, some salt pork, a little sugar, and some coffee, perhaps. It might be the butcher would give her a piece of liver.

When she got to town and was trading in her eggs the dogs lay by the door outside. She did pretty well, got the things she needed, more than she had hoped. Then she went to the butcher and he gave her some liver and some dog meat.

It was the first time anyone had spoken to her in a friendly way for a long time. The butcher was alone in his shop when she went in and was annoyed by the thought of such a sick-looking old woman out on such a day. It was bitter cold and the snow, that had let up during the afternoon, was falling again. The butcher said something about her husband and her son, swore at them, and the old woman stared at him, a look of mild surprise in her eyes as he talked. He said that if either the husband or the son were going to get any of the liver or the heavy bones with scraps of meat hanging to them that he had put into the grain bag, he'd see him starve first.

Starve him, eh? Well, things had to be fed. Men had to be fed, and the horses that weren't any good but maybe could be traded off, and the poor thin cow that hadn't given any milk for three months.

Horses, cows, pigs, dogs, men.

III

The old woman had to get back before darkness came if she could. The dogs followed at her heels, sniffing at the heavy grain bag she had fastened on her back. When she got to the edge of town she stopped by a fence and tied the bag on her back with a piece of rope she had carried in her dress pocket for just that purpose. That was an easier way to carry it. Her arms ached. It was hard when she had to crawl over fences, and once she fell over and landed in the snow. The dogs went frisking about. She had to struggle to get to her feet again, but she made it. The point of climbing over the fences was that there was a short cut over a hill and through a wood. She might have gone around by the road, but it was a mile farther that way. She was afraid she couldn't make it. And then, besides, the stock had to be fed. There was a little hay left, a little corn. Perhaps her husband and son would bring some home when they came. They had driven off in the only buggy the Grimes family had, a rickety thing, a rickety horse hitched to the buggy, two other rickety horses led by halters. They were going to trade horses, get a little money if they could. They might come home drunk. It would be well to have something in the house when they came back.

The son had an affair on with a woman at the county seat, fifteen miles away. She was a bad woman, a tough one. Once, in the summer, the son had brought her to the house. Both she and the son had been drinking. Jake Grimes was away and the son and his woman ordered the old woman about like a servant. She didn't mind much; she was used to it. Whatever happened, she never said anything. That was her way of getting along. She had managed that way when she was a young girl at the German's and ever since she had married Jake. That time her son brought his woman to the house they stayed all night, sleeping together just as though they were married. It hadn't shocked the old woman, not much. She had got past being shocked early in life.

With the pack on her back she went painfully along across an open field, wading in the deep snow, and got into the woods.

There was a path, but it was hard to follow. Just beyond the top of the hill, where the wood was thickest, there was a small clearing. Had someone once thought of building a house there? The clearing was as large as a building lot in town, large enough for a house and a garden. The path ran along the side of the clearing and when she got there the old woman sat down to rest at the foot of a tree.

It was a foolish thing to do. When she got herself placed, the pack against the tree's trunk, it was nice, but what about getting up again? She worried about that for a moment and then quietly closed her eyes.

She must have slept for a time. When you are about so cold you can't get any colder. The afternoon grew a little warmer and the snow came thicker than ever. Then after a time the weather cleared. The moon even came out.

There were four Grimes dogs that had followed Mrs. Grimes into town, all tall gaunt fellows. Such men as Jake Grimes and his son always keep just such dogs. They kick and abuse them, but they stay. The Grimes dogs, in order to keep from starving, had to do a lot of foraging for themselves, and they had been at it while the old woman slept with her back to the tree at the side of the clearing. They had been chasing rabbits in the woods and in adjoining fields, and in their ranging had picked up three other farm dogs.

After a time all the dogs came back to the clearing. They were excited about something. Such nights, cold and clear and with a moon, do things to dogs. It may be that some old instinct, come down from the time when they were wolves and ranged the woods in packs on winter nights, comes back into them.

The dogs in the clearing, before the old woman, had caught two or three rabbits and their immediate hunger had been satisfied. They began to play, running in circles in the clearing. Round and round they ran, each dog's nose at the tail of the next dog. In the clearing, under the snow-laden trees and under the wintry moon they made a strange picture, running thus silently, in a circle their running had beaten in the soft snow. The dogs made no sound. They ran around and around in the circle.

It may have been that the old woman saw them doing that before she died. She may have awakened once or twice and looked at the strange sight with dim old eyes.

She wouldn't be very cold now, just drowsy. Life hangs on a long time. Perhaps the old woman was out of her head. She may have dreamed of her girlhood, at the German's, and before that, when she was a child and before her mother lit out and left her.

Her dreams couldn't have been very pleasant. Not many pleasant things had happened to her. Now and then one of the Grimes dogs left the running circle and came to stand before her. The dog thrust his face close to her face. His red tongue was hanging out.

The running of the dogs may have been a kind of death ceremony. It may have been that the primitive instinct of the wolf, having been aroused in the dogs by the night and the running, made them somehow afraid.

"Now we are no longer wolves. We are dogs, the servants of men. Keep alive, man! When man dies we become wolves again."

When one of the dogs came to where the old woman sat with her back against the tree and thrust his nose close to her face he seemed satisfied and went back to run with the back. All the Grimes dogs did it at some time during the evening, before she died. I knew all about it afterward, when I grew to be a man, because once in a wood on another winter night I saw a pack of dogs act just like that. The dogs were waiting for me to die as they had waited for the old woman that night when I was a child, but when it happened to me I was a young man and had no intention whatever of dying.

The old woman died softly and quietly. When she was dead and when one of the Grimes dogs had come to her and had found her dead all the dogs stopped running.

They gathered about her.

Well, she was dead now. She had fed the Grimes dogs when she was alive, what about now?

There was the pack on her back, the grain bag containing the piece of salt pork, the liver the butcher had given her, the dog meat, the soup bones. The butcher in town, having been suddenly overcome with a feeling of pity, had loaded her grain bag heavily. It had been a big haul for the old woman.

A big haul for the dogs now.

IV

One of the Grimes dogs sprang suddenly out from among the others and began worrying the pack on the old woman's back. Had the dogs really been wolves that one would have been the leader of the pack. What he did, all the others did.

All of them sank their teeth into the grain bag the old woman had fastened with ropes to her back.

They dragged the old woman's body out into the open clearing. The worn-out dress was quickly torn from her shoulders. When she was found, a day or two later, the dress had been torn from her body clear to the hips but the dogs had not touched her body. They had got the meat out of the grain bag, that was all. Her body was frozen stiff when it was found and the shoulders were so narrow and the body so slight that in death it looked like the body of some charming young girl.

Such things happened in towns of the Middle West, on farms near town, when I was a boy. A hunter out after rabbits found the old woman's body and did not touch it. Something, the beaten round path in the little snow-covered clearing, the silence of the place, the place where the dogs had worried the body trying to pull the grain bag away or tear it open—something startled the man and he hurried off to town.

I was in Main Street with one of my brothers, who was taking the afternoon papers to the stores. It was almost night.

The hunter came into a grocery and told his story. Then he went to a hardware shop and into a drug store. Men began to gather on the sidewalks. Then they started out along the road to the place in the wood.

My brother should have gone on about his business of distributing papers, but he didn't. Everyone was going to the woods. The undertaker went and the town marshal. Several men got on a dray and rode out to where the path left the road and went into the woods, but the horses weren't very sharply shod and slid about on the slippery roads. They made no better time than those of us who walked.

The town marshal was a large man whose leg had been injured in the Civil War. He carried a heavy cane and limped rapidly along the road. My brother and I followed at his heels, and as we went other men and boys joined the crowd.

It had grown dark by the time we got to where the old woman had left the road, but the moon had come out. The marshal was thinking there might have been a murder. He kept asking the hunter questions. The hunter went along with his gun across his shoulder, a dog following at his heels. It isn't often a rabbit hunter has a chance to be so conspicuous. He was taking full advantage of it, leading the procession with the town marshal. "I didn't see any wounds. She was a beautiful young girl. Her face was buried in the snow. No, I didn't know her." As a matter of fact, the hunter had not looked closely at the body. He had been frightened. She might have been murdered and someone might spring out from behind a tree and murder him too. In a woods, in the late afternoon, when the trees are all bare and there is white snow on the ground, when all is silent, something creepy steals over the mind and body. If something strange or uncanny has happened in the neighbourhood, all you think about is getting away from there as fast as you can.

The crowd of men and boys had got to where the old woman crossed the field and went, following the marshal and the hunter up the slight incline and into the woods.

My brother and I were silent. He had his bundle of papers in a bag slung across his shoulder. When he got back to town he would have to go on distributing his papers before he went home to supper. If I went along, as he had no doubt already determined I should, we would both be late. Either Mother or our younger sister would have to warm our supper.

Well, we would have something to tell. A boy did not get such a chance very often. It was lucky we just happened to go into the grocery when the hunter came in. The hunter was a country fellow. Neither of us had ever seen him before.

Now the crowd of men and boys had got to the clearing. Darkness comes quickly on such winter nights, but the full moon made everything clear. My brother and I stood near the trees beneath which the old woman had died.

She did not look old, lying there frozen in that light. One of the men turned her over in the snow and I saw everything. My body trembled with some strange mystical feeling, and so did my brother's. It might have been the cold.

Neither of us had ever seen a woman's body before. It may have been the snow, clinging to the frozen flesh, that made it look so white and lovely, so like marble. No woman had come with the party from town, but one of the men, he was the town blacksmith, took off his overcoat and spread it over her. Then he gathered her into his arms and started off to town, all the others following silently. At that time no one knew who she was.

v

I had seen everything, had seen the oval in the snow, like a miniature race track, where the dogs had run, had seen how the men were mystified, had seen the white, bare, young-looking shoulders, had heard the whispered comments of the men.

The men were simply mystified. They took the body to the undertaker's, and when the blacksmith, the hunter, the marshal, and several others had got inside, they closed the door. If Father had been there, perhaps he could have got in, but we boys couldn't.

I went with my brother to distribute the rest of his papers, and when we got home it was my brother who told the story.

I kept silent and went to bed early. It may have been I was not satisfied with the way he told it.

Later, in the town, I must have heard other fragments of the old woman's story. She was recognised the next day and there was an investigation.

The husband and son were found somewhere and brought to town, and there was an attempt to connect them with the woman's death, but it did not work. They had perfect enough alibis.

However, the town was against them. They had to get out. Where they went, I never heard.

I remember only the picture there in the forest, the men standing about, the naked, girlish-looking figure, face down in the snow, the tracks made by the running dogs, and the clear, cold winter sky above. White fragments of clouds were drifting across the sky. They went racing across the little open space among the trees.

The scene in the forest had become for me, without my knowing it, the foundation for the real story I am now trying to tell. The fragments, you see, had to be picked up slowly, long afterward.

Things happened. When I was a young man I worked on the farm of a German. The hired girl was afraid of her employer. The farmer's wife hated her.

I saw things at that place. Once, later, I had a half-uncanny, mystical sort of adventure with dogs in a forest on a clear, moonlit winter night. When I was a schoolboy, and on a summer day, I went with a boy friend out along a creek some miles from town and came to the house where the old woman had lived. No one had lived in the house since her death. The doors were broken from the hinges, the window lights were all broken. As the boy and I stood in the road outside, two dogs, just roving farm dogs, no doubt, came running around the corner of the house. The dogs were tall, gaunt fellows and came down to the fence and glared through at us, standing in the road.

The whole thing, the story of the old woman's death, was to me, as I grew older, like music heard from far off. The notes had to be picked up slowly one at a time. Something had to be understood.

The woman who died was one destined to feed animal life. Anyway, that is all she ever did. She was feeding animal life before she was born, as a child, as a young woman working on the farm of the German, after she married, when she grew old, and when she died. She fed animal life in cows, in chickens, in pigs, in horses, in dogs, in men. Her daughter had died in childhood, and with her one son she had no articulate relations. On the night when she died she was hurrying homeward, bearing on her body food for animal life.

She died in the clearing in the woods, and even after her death continued feeding animal life.

You see it is likely that, when my brother told the story, that night when we got home and my mother and sister sat listening, I did not think he got the point. He was too young and so was I. A thing so complete has its own beauty.

I shall not try to emphasise the point. I am only explaining why I was dissatisfied then, and have been ever since. I speak of that only that you may understand why I have been impelled to try to tell the simple story over again.

WILBUR DANIEL STEELE
(1886-   )

BY CHANCE, Wilbur Daniel Steele was born in Greensboro, North Carolina, the son of a Methodist educator, Wilbur Fletcher Steele. Wilbur Daniel took his A.B. degree from the University of Denver, where his father had become Professor of Biblical Science, then studied fine arts at Julian's in Paris (1908-1909) and in the Art Students' League, New York (1909-1910). Now about the age of twenty-four he put aside the brush for the pen, and since 1914 has published steadily, with annual representation in most anthologies. His sense of form is responsible for his apparently intuitive knowledge of structure, his cosmopolitan life—he is a globe wanderer—for his awareness of the fresh and novel, and his creative energy for the vitality of his stories. Of America's contemporary greatest, he has received three prizes from the O. Henry Memorial Commission. The first was awarded to *For They Know Not What They Do*, as one of the two best stories of the year (1919); the second was conferred upon him as the story writer of most distinction in 1919, 1920, 1921; the third was awarded *Bubbles* (*Harper's Magazine*, August) as best of the year 1926. *The Man Who Saw through Heaven* (*Harper's*, September) and *Blue Murder* (*Harper's*, October) were barred from the 1925 prizes, through Mr. Steele's being temporarily *hors concours*. *Blue Murder* is characteristic of Mr. Steele's genius and is presented here with grateful thanks to the author for the privilege of reprint.

BLUE MURDER

AT Mill Crossing it was already past sunset. The rays, redder for what autumn leaves were left, still laid fire along the woods crowning the stony slopes of Jim Bluedge's pastures; but then the line of the dusk began and from that level it filled the valley, washing with transparent blue the buildings scattered about the bridge, Jim's house and horse-sheds and hay-barns, Frank's store, and Camden's blacksmith shop.

The mill had been gone fifty years, but the falls which had turned its wheel still poured in the bottom of the valley, and when the wind came from the Footstool way their mist wet the smithy, built of the old stone on the old foundations, and their pouring drowned the clink of Camden's hammer.

Just now they couldn't drown Camden's hammer, for he wasn't in the smithy; he was at his brother's farm. Standing inside the smaller of the horse paddocks behind the sheds he drove in stakes, one after another, cut green from saplings, and so disposed as to cover the more glaring of the weaknesses in the five-foot fence. From time to time, when one was done and another to do, he rested the head of his sledge in the pocket of his leather apron (he was never without it; it was as though it had grown on him, lumpy with odds and ends of his trade—bolts and nails and rusty pliers and old horseshoes) and, standing so, he mopped the sweat from his face and looked up at the mountain.

Of the three brothers he was the dumb one. He seldom had anything to say. It was providential (folks said) that of the three enterprises at the Crossing one was a smithy; for while he was a strong, big, hungry-muscled fellow, he never would have had the shrewdness to run the store or the farm. He was better at pounding—pounding while the fire reddened and the sparks flew, and thinking, and letting other people wonder what he was thinking of.

Blossom Bluedge, his brother's wife, sat perched on the top bar of the paddock gate, holding her skirts around her ankles with a trifle too much care to be quite unconscious, and watched him work. When he looked at the mountain he was looking at the mares, half a mile up the slope, grazing in a line as straight as soldiers, their heads all one way. But Blossom thought it was the receding light he was thinking of, and her own sense of misgiving returned and deepened.

"You'd have thought Jim would be home before this, wouldn't you, Cam?"

Her brother-in-law said nothing.

"Cam, look at me!"

It was nervousness, but it wasn't all nervousness—she was the prettiest girl in the valley; a small part of it was mingled coquetry and pique.

The smith began to drive another stake, swinging the hammer from high overhead, his muscles playing in fine big rhythmical convulsions under the skin of his arms and chest, covered with short blond down. Studying him cornerwise, Blossom muttered, "Well, don't look at me, then!"

He was too dumb for any use. He was as dumb as this: when all three of the Bluedge boys were after her a year ago, Frank, the storekeeper, had brought her candy: chocolates wrapped in silver foil in a two-pound Boston box. Jim had laid before her the Bluedge farm and with it the dominance of the valley. And Camden! To the daughter of Ed Beck, the apple grower, Camden had brought a box of apples!—and been bewildered, too, when, for all she could help it, she had had to clap a hand over her mouth and run into the house to have her giggle.

A little more than just bewildered, perhaps. Had she, or any of them, ever speculated about that? . . . He had been dumb enough before; but that was when he had started being as dumb as he was now.

Well, if he wanted to be dumb let him be dumb. Pouting her pretty lips and arching her fine brows, she forgot the unimaginative fellow and turned to the ridge again. And now, seeing the sun was quite gone, all the day's vague worries and dreads—held off by this and that—could not be held off longer. For weeks there had been so much talk, so much gossip and speculation and doubt.

"Camden," she reverted suddenly. "Tell me one thing, did you hear——"

She stopped there. Some people were coming into the kitchen yard, dark forms in the growing darkness. Most of them lingered at the porch, sitting on the steps and lighting their pipes. The one that came out was Frank, the second of her brothers-in-law. She was glad. Frank wasn't like Camden, he would talk. Turning and taking care of her skirts, she gave him a bright and sisterly smile.

"Well, Frankie, what's the crowd?"

Far from avoiding the smile, as Camden's habit was, the storekeeper returned it with a brotherly wink for good measure. "Oh, they're tired of waiting down the road, so they come up here to see the grand arrival." He was something of a man of the world; in his calling he had acquired a fine turn for skepticism. "Don't want to miss being on hand to see what flaws they can pick in 'Jim's five hundred dollars' wuth of expiriment.' "

"Frank, ain't you the least bit worried over Jim? So late?"

"Don't see why."

"All the same, I wish either you or Cam could've gone with him."

"Don't see why. Had all the men from Perry's stable there in Twinshead to help him get the animal off the freight, and he took an extra rope and the log chain and the heavy waggon, so I guess no matter how wild and woolly the devil is he'll scarcely be climbing in over the tailboard. Besides, them Western horses ain't such a big breed, even a stallion."

"All the same—(look the other way, Frankie)——" Flipping her ankles over the rail, Blossom jumped down beside him. "Listen, Frank, tell me something, did you hear—did you hear the reason Jim's getting him cheap was because he killed a man out West there, what's-its-name, Wyoming?"

Frank was taking off his sleeve protectors, the pins in his mouth. It was Camden, at the bars, speaking in his sudden deep rough way, "Who the hell told you that?"

Frank got the pins out of his mouth. "I guess what it is, Blossie, what's mixed you up is his having that name 'Blue Murder.' "

"No, sir! I got some sense and some ears. You don't go fooling me."

Frank laughed indulgently and struck her shoulder with a light hand. "Don't you worry. Between two horsemen like Jim and Cam——"

"Don't Cam me! He's none of my horse. I told Jim once——"

Breaking off, Camden hoisted his weight over the fence and stood outside, his feet spread and his hammer in both hands, an attitude that would have looked a little ludicrous had any one been watching him.

Jim had arrived. With a clatter of hoofs and a rattle of wheels he was in the yard and come to a standstill, calling aloud as he threw the lines over the team, "Well, friends, here we are."

The curious began to edge around, closing a cautious circle. The dusk had deepened so that it was hard to make anything at any distance of Jim's "expiriment" but a blurry silhouette anchored at the wagon's tail. The farmer put an end to it, crying from his eminence, "Now, now, clear out and don't worry him; give him some peace tonight, for Lord's sake! Git!" He jumped to the ground and began to whack his arms, chilled with driving, only to have them pinioned by Blossom's without warning.

"Oh, Jim, I'm so glad you come. I been so worried; gi' me a kiss!"

The farmer reddened, eyeing the cloud of witnesses. He felt awkward and wished she could have waited. "Get along, didn't I tell you fellows?" he cried with a trace of the Bluedge temper. "Go wait in the kitchen then: I'll tell you all about everything soon's I come in. . . . Well, now—wife——"

"What's the matter?" she laughed, an eye over her shoulder. "Nobody's looking that matters. I'm sure Frank don't mind. And as for Camden——"

Camden wasn't looking at them. Still standing with his hammer two-fisted and his legs spread, his chin down and his thoughts to himself (the dumbhead) he was looking at Blue Murder, staring at the other dumbhead, which, raised high on the motionless column of the stallion's neck, seemed hearkening with an exile's doubt to the sounds of this new universe, tasting with wide nostrils the taint in the wind of equine strangers, and studying with eyes accustomed to far horizons these dark pastures that went up in the air.

Whatever the smith's cogitations, presently he let the hammer down and said aloud, "So you're him, eh?"

Jim had put Blossom aside, saying, "Got supper ready? I'm hungry!" Excited by the act of kissing and the sense of witnesses to it, she fussed her hair and started kitchenward as he turned to his brothers.

"Well, what do you make of him?"

"Five hundred dollars," said Frank. "However, it's your money."

Camden was shorter. "Better put him in."

"All right; let them bars down while I and Frank lead him around."

"No, thanks!" The storekeeper kept his hands in his pockets. "I just cleaned up, thanks. Cam's the boy for horses."

"He's none o' my horses!" Camden wet his lips, shook his shoulders, and scowled. "Be damned, no!" He never had the right words, and it made him mad. Hadn't he told Jim from the beginning that he washed his hands of this fool Agricultural College squandering, "and a man-killer to the bargain?"

"Unless," Frank put in shyly, "unless Cam's scared."

"Oh, is Cam scared?"

"Scared?" And still, to the brothers' enduring wonder, the big dense fellow would rise to that boyhood bait. "Scared? The hell I'm scared of any horse ever wore a shoe! Come on, I'll show you! I'll show you!"

"Well, be gentle with him, boys; he may be brittle." As Frank sauntered off around the shed he whistled the latest tune.

In the warmth and light of the kitchen he began to fool with his pretty sister-in-law, feigning princely impatience and growling with a wink at the assembled neighbours, "When do we eat?"

But she protested, "Land, I had everything ready since five, ain't I? And now, if it ain't you, it's them to wait for. I declare for men!"

At last one of the gossips got in a word.

"What you make of Jim's purchase, Frank?"

"Well, it's Jim's money, Darred. If I had the running of his farm——" Frank began drawing up chairs noisily, leaving it at that.

Darred persisted. "Don't look to me much like an animal for women and children to handle, not yet awhile."

"Cowboys han'les 'em, Pa." That was Darred's ten-year-old, big-eyed.

Blossom put the kettle back, protesting, "Leave off, or you'll get me worried to death; all your talk. . . . I declare, where are those bad boys?" Opening the door she called into the dark, "Jim! Cam! Land's sake!"

Subdued by distance and the intervening shreds, she could hear them at their business—sounds muffled and fragmentary, soft thunder of hoofs, snorts, puffings, and the short words of men in action: "Aw, leave him be in the paddock tonight." . . . "With them mares there, you damn fool?" . . . "Damn fool, eh? Try getting him in at that door and see who's the damn fool!" . . . "Come on, don't be so scared." . . . "Scared eh? Scared?" . . .

Why was it she always felt that curious tightening of all her powers of attention when Camden Bluedge spoke? Probably because he spoke so rarely, and then so roughly, as if his own thickness made him mad. Never mind.

"Last call for supper in the dining car, boys!" she called, and closed the door. Turning back to the stove she was about to replace the tea water for the third time when, straightening up, she said, "What's that?"

No one else had heard anything. They looked at one another.

"Frank, go—go see what—go tell the boys to come in."

Frank hesitated, feeling foolish, then went to the door.

Then everyone in the room was out of his chair.

There were three sounds. The first was human and incoherent. The second was incoherent, too, but it wasn't human. The third was a crash, a ripping and splintering of wood.

When they got to the paddock they found Camden crawling from beneath the wreckage of the fence where a gap was opened on the pasture side. He must have received a blow on the head, for he seemed dazed. He didn't seem to know they were there. At a precarious balance—one hand at the back of his neck—he stood facing up the hill, gaping after the diminuendo of floundering hoofs, invisible above.

So seconds passed. Again the beast gave tongue, a high wild horning note, and on the black of the stony hill to the right of it a faint shower of sparks blew like fireflies where the herding mares wheeled. It seemed to awaken the dazed smith. He opened his mouth. "Almighty God!" Swinging, he flung his arms toward the shed. "There! There!"

At last someone brought a lantern. They found Jim Bluedge lying on his back in the corner of the paddock near the door to the shed. In the lantern light, and still better in the kitchen when they had carried him in, they read the record of the thing which Camden, dumb in good earnest now, seemed unable to tell them with anything but his strange, unfocussed stare.

The bloody offence to the skull would have been enough to kill the man, but it was the second, full on the chest above the heart, that told the tale. On the caved grating of the ribs, already turning blue under the yellowish down, the iron shoe had left its mark, and when, laying back the rag of shirt, they saw that the toe of the shoe was upward and the cutting caulk-ends down they knew all they wanted to know of that swift, black, crushing episode.

No outlash here of heels in fright. Here was a forefoot. An attack aimed and frontal; an onslaught reared, erect; beast turned biped; red eyes mad to white eyes aghast. . . . And only afterward, when it was done, the blood-fright that serves the horses for conscience; the blind rush across the enclosure; the fence gone down. . . .

No one had much to say. No one seemed to know what to do.

As for Camden, he was no help. He simply stood propped on top of his legs where someone had left him. From the instant when with his "Almighty God!" he had been brought back to memory, instead of easing its hold as the minutes passed, the event to which he remained the only living human witness seemed minute by minute to tighten its grip. It set its sweat-beaded stamp on his face, distorted his eyes, and tied his tongue. He was no good to any one.

As for Blossom, even now—perhaps more than ever now—her dependence on physical touch was the thing that ruled her. Down on her knees beside the lamp they had set on the floor, she plucked at one of the dead man's shoes monotonously, and as it were idly swaying the toe like an inverted pendulum from side to side. That was all. Not a word. And when Frank, the only one of the three with any sense, got her up finally and led her away to her room, she clung to him.

It was lucky that Frank was a man of affairs. His brother was dead, and frightfully dead, but there was tomorrow for grief. Just now there were many things to do. There were people to be gotten ridden of. With short words and angry gestures he cleared them out, all but Darred and a man named White, and to these he said, "Now, first thing, Jim can't stay here." He ran and got a blanket from a closet. "Give me a hand and we'll lay him in the icehouse overnight. Don't sound good, but it's best, poor fellow. Cam, come along!"

He waited a moment, and as he studied the wooden fool the blood poured back into his face. "Wake up, Cam! You great big scared stiff, you!"

Camden brought his eyes out of nothingness and looked at his brother. A twinge passed over his face, convulsing the mouth muscles. "Scared?"

"Yes, you're scared!" Frank's lip lifted, showing the tips of his teeth. "And I'll warrant you something: if you wasn't the scared stiff you was, this hellish damn thing wouldn't have happened, maybe. Scared! you a blacksmith! Scared of a horse!"

"Horse!" Again that convulsion of the mouth muscles, something between irony and an idiot craft. "Why don't you go catch 'im?"

"Hush it! Don't waste time by going loony now, for God's sake. Come!"

"My advice to anybody—" Camden looked crazier than ever, knotting his brows. "My advice to anybody is to let somebody else go catch that— that—" Opening the door he faced out into the night, his head sunk between his shoulders and the fingers working at the ends of his hanging arms; and before they knew it he began to swear. They could hardly hear because his teeth were locked and his breath soft. There were all the vile words he had ever heard in his life, curses and threats and abominations, vindictive, violent, obscene. He stopped only when at a sharp word from Frank he was made aware that Blossom had come back into the room. Even then he didn't seem to comprehend her return but stood blinking at her, and at the rifle she carried, with his distraught bloodshot eyes.

Frank comprehended. Hysteria had followed the girl's blankness. Stepping between her and the body on the floor, he spoke in a persuasive, unhurried way. "What you doing with that gun, Blossie? Now, now, you don't want that gun, you know you don't."

It worked. Her rigidity lessened appreciably. Confusion gained.

"Well, but— Or, Frank—well, but when we going to shoot him?"

"Yes, yes, Blossie—now, yes—only you best give me that gun; that's the girlie." When he had got the weapon he put an arm around her shoulders. "Yes, yes, course we're going to shoot him; what you think? Don't want an animal like that running round. Now first thing in the morning——"

Hysteria returned. With its strength she resisted his leading.

"No, now! Now! He's gone and killed Jim! Killed my husband! I won't have him left alive another minute! I won't! Now! No, sir, I'm going myself, I am! Frank, I am! Cam!"

At this name, appealed to in that queer screeching way, the man in the doorway shivered all over, wet his lips, and walked out into the dark.

"There, you see?" Frank was quick to capitalise anything. "Cam's gone to do it. Cam's gone, Blossie . . . Here, one of you—Darred, take this gun and run give it to Camden, that's the boy."

"You sure he'll kill him, Frank? You sure?"

"Sure as daylight. Now you come along back to your room like a good girl and get some rest. Come, I'll go with you."

When Frank returned to the kitchen ten minutes later, Darred was back.

"Well, now, let's get at it and carry out poor Jim, he can't lay here. . . . Where's Cam gone now, damn him!"

"Cam? Why, he's gone and went."

"Went where?"

"Up the pasture like you said."

"Like I——" Frank went an odd colour. He walked to the door. Between the light on the sill and the beginnings of the stars where the woods crowned the mountain was all one blackness. One stillness, too. He turned on Darred. "But, look, you never gave him that gun, even."

"He didn't want it."

"Lord's sake; what did he say?"

"Said nothing. He'd got the log chain out of the waggon and when I caught him he was up hunting his hammer in under that wreck at the fence. Once he found it he started off up. 'Cam,' says I, 'here's a gun; want it?' He seemed not to. Just went on walking on up."

"How'd he look?"

"Look same's you seen him looking. Sick."

"The damned fool!"

Poor dead Jim! Poor fool Camden! As the storekeeper went about his business and afterward when, the icehouse door closed on its tragic tenant and White and Darred had gone off home, he roamed the yard, driven here and there, soft-footed, waiting, hearkening—his mind was for a time not his own property but the plaything of thoughts diverse and wayward. Jim, his brother, so suddenly and so violently gone. The stallion. That beast that had kicked him to death. With anger and hate and pitiless impatience of time he thought of the morrow, when they would catch him, take their revenge with guns and clubs. Behind these speculations, covering the background of his consciousness and stringing his nerves to endless vigil, spread the wall of the mountain: silent from instant to instant but devising under its black silence (who-could-know-what instant to come), a neigh, a yell, a spark-line of iron hoofs on rolling flints, a groan. And still behind that and deeper into the borders of the unconscious, the storekeeper thought of the farm that had lost its master, the rich bottoms, the broad, well-stocked pastures, the fat barns, and the comfortable house whose chimneys and gable ends fell into changing shapes of perspective against the stars as he wandered here and there. . . .

Jim gone. . . . And Camden, at any moment. . . .

His face grew hot. An impulse carried him a dozen steps. "I ought to go up. Ought to take the gun and go up." But there shrewd sanity put on the brakes. "Where's the use? Couldn't find him in this dark. Besides, I oughtn't to leave Blossom here alone."

With that he went around toward the kitchen, thinking to go in. But the sight of the lantern, left burning out near the sheds, sent his ideas off on another course. At any rate, it would give his muscles and nerves something to work on. Taking the lantern and entering the paddock, he fell to patching the gap into the pasture, using broken boards from the wreck. As he worked his eyes chanced to fall on footprints in the dung-mixed earth—Camden's footprints, leading away beyond the little ring of light. And beside them, taking off from the landing-place of that prodigious leap, he discerned the trail of the stallion. After a moment he got down on his knees where the earth was softest, holding the lantern so that its light fell full.

He gave over his fence-building. Returning to the house his gait was no longer that of the roamer; his face, caught by the periodic flare of the swinging lantern, was the face of another man. In its expression there was a kind of fright and a kind of calculating eagerness. He looked at the clock on the kitchen shelf, shook it, and read it again. He went to the telephone and fumbled at the receiver. He waited till his hand quit shaking, then removed it from the hook.

"Listen, Darred," he said, when he had got the farmer at last, "get White and whatever others you can and come over first thing it's light. Come a-riding and bring your guns. No, Cam ain't back."

He heard Blossom calling. Outside her door he passed one hand down over his face, as he might have passed a wash-rag, to wipe off what was there. Then he went in.

"What's the matter with Blossie? Can't sleep?"

"No, I can't sleep. Can't think. Can't sleep. Oh, Frankie!"

He sat down beside the bed.

"Oh, Frankie, Frankie, hold my hand!"

She looked almost homely, her face bleached out and her hair in a mess on the pillow. But she would get over that. And the short sleeve of the nightgown on the arm he held was edged with pretty lace.

"Got your watch here?" he asked. She gave it to him from under the pillow. This, too, he shook as if he couldn't believe it was going.

Pretty Blossom Beck. Here, for a wonder, he sat in her bedroom and held her hand. One brother was dead and the other was on the mountain.

But little by little, as he sat and dreamed so, nightmare crept over his brain. He had to arouse and shake himself. He had to set his thoughts resolutely in other roads. . . . Perhaps there would be even the smithy. The smithy, the store, the farm. Complete. The farm, the farmhouse, the room in the farmhouse, the bed in the room, the wife in the bed. Complete beyond belief. If . . . Worth dodging horror for. If . . .

"Frank, has Cam come back?"

"Cam? Don't you worry about Cam. . . . Where's that watch again? . . ."

Far from rounding up their quarry in the early hours after dawn, it took the riders, five of them, till almost noon simply to make certain that he wasn't to be found—not in any of the pastures. Then, when they discovered the hole in the fence far up in the woods beyond the crest, where Blue Murder had led the mares in a break for the open country of hills and ravines to the south, they were only at the beginning.

The farmers had left their work undone at home and, as the afternoon lengthened and with it the shadows in the hollow places, they began to eye one another behind their leader's back. Yet they couldn't say it; there was something in the storekeeper's air to-day, something zealous and pitiless and fanatical, that shut them up and pulled them plodding on.

Frank did the trailing. Hopeless of getting anywhere before sundown in that unkempt wilderness of a hundred square miles of scrub, his companions slouched in their saddles and rode more and more mechanically, knee to knee, and it was he who made the casts to recover the lost trail and, dismounting to read the dust, cried back: "He's still with 'em," and with gestures of imperious excitement beckoned them on.

"Which you mean?" Darred asked him once. "Cam or the horse?"

Frank wheeled his beast and spurred back at the speaker. It was extraordinary. "You don't know what you're talking about!" he cried, with a causelessness and a disordered vehemence which set them first staring, then speculating. "Come on, you dumbheads; don't talk—ride!"

By the following day, when it was being told in all the farmhouses, the story might vary in details and more and more as the tellings multiplied, but in its fundamentals it remained the same. In one thing they certainly all agreed: they used the same expression—"It was like Frank was drove. Drove in a race against something, and no sparing the whip."

They were a good six miles to the south of the fence. Already the road back home would have to be followed three parts in the dark.

Darred was the spokesman. "Frank, I'm going to call it a day."

The others reined up with him but the man ahead rode on. He didn't seem to hear. Darred lifted his voice. "Come on, call it a day, Frank. To-morrow, maybe. But you see we've run it out and they're not here."

"Wait," said Frank over his shoulder, still riding on into the pocket.

White's mount—a mare—laid back her ears, shied, and stood trembling. After a moment she whinnied.

It was as if she had whinnied for a dozen. A crashing in the woods above them to the left and the avalanche came—down-streaming, erupting, wheeling, wheeling away with volleying snorts, a dark rout.

Darred, reining his horse, began to shout, "Here they go this way, Frank!" But Frank was yelling, "Up here, boys! This way, quick!"

It was the same note, excited, feverish, disordered, breaking like a child's. When they neared him they saw he was off his horse, rifle in hand, and down on his knees to study the ground where the woods began. By the time they reached his animal the impetuous fellow had started up into the cover, his voice trailing, "Come on; spread out and come on!"

One of the farmers got down. When he saw the other three keeping their saddles he swung up again.

White spoke this time. "Be darned if I do!" He lifted a protesting hail, "Come back here, Frank! You're crazy! It's getting dark!"

It was Frank's own fault. They told him plainly to come back and he wouldn't listen.

For a while they could hear his crackle in the mounting underbrush. Then that stopped, whether he had gone too far for their ears or whether he had come to a halt to give his own ears a chance. . . . Once, off to his right, a little higher up under the low ceiling of the trees that darkened moment by moment with the rush of night, they heard another movement, another restlessness of leaves and stones. Then that was still, and everything was still.

Darred ran a sleeve over his face and swung down. "God alive, boys!"

It was the silence. All agreed there—the silence and the deepening dusk.

The first they heard was the shot. No voice. Just the one report. Then after five breaths of another silence a crashing of growth, a charge in the darkness under the withered scrub, continuous and diminishing.

They shouted, "Frank!" No answer. They called, "Frank Bluedge!"

Now, since they had to, they did. Keeping contact by word, and guided partly by directional memory (and mostly in the end by luck), after a time they found the storekeeper in a brake of ferns, lying across his gun.

They got him down to the open, watching behind them all the while. Only then, by the flares of successive matches, under the noses of snorting horses, did they look for the damage done.

They remembered the stillness and the gloom; it must have been quite black in there. The attack had come from behind—equine and pantherine at once, and planned and cunning. A deliberate lunge with a forefoot again: the shoe which had crushed the backbone between the shoulder blades was a foreshoe, that much they saw by the match flares in the red wreck.

They took no longer getting home than they had to, but it was longer than they would have wished. With Frank across his own saddle, walking their horses and with one or another ahead to pick the road (it was going to rain, and even the stars were lost), they made no more than a creeping speed.

None of them had much to say on the journey. Finding the break in the boundary fence and feeling through the last of the woods, the lights of their farms began to show in the pool of blackness below, and Darred uttered a part of what had lain in the minds of them all during the return: "Well, that leaves Cam."

None followed it up. None cared to go any closer than he was to the real question. Something new, alien, menacing and pitiless had come into the valley of their lives with that beast they had never really seen; they felt its oppression, every one, and kept the real question back in their minds:

"Does it leave Cam?"

It answered itself. Camden was at home when they got there.

He had come in a little before them, empty-handed. Empty-headed, too. When Blossom, who had waited all day, part of the time with neighbour women who had come in and part of the time alone to the point of going mad—when she saw him coming down the pasture, his feet stumbling and his shoulders dejected, her first feeling was relief. Her first words, however, were, "Did you get him, Cam?" And all he would answer was, "Gi' me something to eat, can't you? Gi' me a few hours' sleep, can't you? Then wait!"

He looked as if he would need more than a few hours' sleep. Propped on his elbows over his plate it seemed as though his eyes would close before his mouth would open.

His skin was scored by thorns and his shirt was in ribbons under the straps of his iron-sagged apron, but it was not by these marks that his twenty-odd hours showed: it was by his face. While yet his eyes were open and his wits still half awake, his face surrendered. The flesh relaxed into lines of stupor, a putty-formed, putty-coloured mask of sleep.

Once he let himself be aroused. This was when, to an abstracted query as to Frank's whereabouts, Blossom told him Frank had been out with four others since dawn. He heaved clear of the table and opened his eyes at her showing the red around the rims.

He spoke with the thick tongue of a drunkard. "If anybody but me lays hand on the stallion I'll kill him. I'll wring his neck."

Then he relapsed into his stupidity, and not even the arrival of the party bringing his brother's body seemed able to shake him so far clear of it again.

At first, when they had laid Frank on the floor where on the night before they had laid Jim, he seemed hardly to comprehend.

"What's wrong with Frank?"

"Some more of Jim's 'expiriment.'"

"Frank see him? He's scared, Frank is. Look at his face there."

"He's dead, Cam."

"Dead, you say? Frank dead? Dead of fright, is that it?"

Even when, rolling the body over, they showed him what was what, he appeared incapable of comprehension, of amazement, of passion, or of any added grief. He looked at them all with a kind of befuddled protest. Returning to his chair and his plate, he grumbled, "Le' me eat first, can't you? Can't you gi' me a little time to sleep?"

"Well, you wouldn't do much to-night anyway, I guess." At White's words Blossom opened her mouth for the first time.

"No, nothing to-night, Cam. Cam! Camden! Say! Promise!"

"And then to-morrow, Cam, what we'll do is to get every last man in the valley, and we'll go at this right. We'll lay hand on that devil ———"

Camden swallowed his mouthful of cold steak with difficulty. His obsession touched, he showed them the rims of his eyes again.

"You do and I'll wring your necks. The man that touches that animal before I do gets his neck wrang. That's all you need to remember."

"Yes, yes—no—that is———" Poor Blossom. "Yes, Mr. White, thanks; no, Cam's not going out to-night. . . . No, Cam, nobody's going to interfere—nor nothing. Don't worry there. . . ."

Again poor Blossom! Disaster piled too swiftly on disaster; no discipline but instinct left. Caught in fire and flood and earthquake and not knowing what to come, and no creed but "save him who can!"—by hook or crook of wile or smile. With the valley of her life emptied out, and its emptiness repeopled monstrously and pressing down black on the roof under which (now that Frank was gone to the icehouse, too, and the farmers back home) one brother was left of three—she would tread softly, she would talk or she would be dumb, as her sidelong glimpses of the awake-asleep man's face above the table told her was the instant's need; or if he would eat, she would magic out of nothing something, anything; or if he would sleep, he could sleep, so long as he slept in that house where she could know he was sleeping.

Only one thing. If she could touch him. If she could touch and cling.

Lightning filled the windows. After a moment the thunder came avalanching down the pasture and brought up against the clapboards of the house. At this she was behind his chair. She put out a hand. She touched his shoulder. The shoulder was bare, the shirt ripped away; it was caked with sweat and with the blackening smears of scratches, but for all its exhaustion and dirt it was flesh alive—a living man to touch.

Camden blundered up. "What the hell!" He started off two steps and wheeled on her. "Why don't you get off to bed, for Goll sake!"

"Yes, Cam, yes—right off, yes."

"Well, I'm going, I can tell you. For Goll sake. I need some sleep!"

"Yes, that's right, yes, Cam, good-night, Cam—only—only you promise—promise you won't go out—nowheres."

"Go out? Not likely I won't! Not likely! Get along!"

It took her no time to get along then—quick and quiet as a mouse.

Camden lingered to stand at one of the windows where the lightning came again, throwing the black barns and paddocks at him from the white sweep of the pastures crowned by woods.

As it had taken her no time to go, it took Blossom no time to undress and get in bed. When Camden was on his way to his room he heard her calling, "Cam! Just a second, Cam!"

In the dark outside her door he drew one hand down over his face, wiping off whatever might be there. Then he entered.

"Yes? What?"

"Cam, set by me a minute, won't you? And Cam, oh, Cam, hold my hand."

As he slouched down, his fist enclosing her fingers, thoughts awakened and ran and fastened on things. They fastened, tentatively at first, upon the farm. Jim gone. Frank gone. The smithy, the store, and the farm. The whole of Mill Crossing. The trinity. The three in one. . . .

"Tight, Cam, for pity's sake! Hold it tight!"

His eyes, falling to his fist, strayed up along the arm it held. The sleeve, rumpled near the shoulder, was trimmed with pretty lace.

"Tighter, Cam!"

A box of apples. That memory hidden away in the cellar of his mind. Hidden away clamped down in the dark, till the noxious vapours, the murderous vapours of its rotting had filled the shut-up house he was. . . . A box of red apples for the apple-grower's girl . . . the girl who sniggered and ran away from him to laugh at him. . . .

And there, by the unfolding of a devious destiny, he sat in that girl's bedroom, holding that girl's hand. Jim who had got her, Frank who had wanted her lay side by side out there in the icehouse under the lightning. While he, the "dumb one"—the last to be thought of with anything but amusement and the last to be feared—his big hot fist inclosing her imprecating hand now, and his eyes on the pretty lace at her shoulder— He jumped up with a gulp and a clatter of iron.

"What the——" He flung her hand away. "What the hell!" He swallowed. "Damn you, Blossie Beck!" He stared at her with repugnance and mortal fright. "Why, you—you—you——"

He moderated his voice with an effort, wiping his brow, "Good night. You must excuse me, Blossie; I wasn't meaning—I mean—I hope you sleep good. I shall. . . . Good-night!"

In his own brain was the one word "Hurry!"

She lay and listened to his boots going along the hall and heard the closing of his door. She ought to have put out the lamp. But even with the shades drawn, the lightning around the edges of the window unnerved her; in the dark alone it would have been more than she could bear.

She lay so till she felt herself nearing exhaustion from the sustained rigidity of her limbs. Rain came and with the rain, wind. Around the eaves it neighed like wild stallions; down the chimneys it moaned like men.

Slipping out of bed and pulling on a bathrobe she ran from her room, barefooted, and along the hall to Camden's door.

"Cam!" she called. "Oh, Cam!" she begged. "Please, please!"

And now he wouldn't answer her.

New lightning, diffused through all the sky by the blown rain, ran at her along the corridor. She pushed the door open. The lamp was burning on the bureau but the room was empty and the bed untouched.

Taking the lamp she skittered down to the kitchen. No one there. . . .

"Hurry!"

Camden had reached the woods when the rain came. Lighting the lantern he had brought, he made his way on to the boundary fence. There, about a mile to the east of the path the others had taken that day, he pulled the rails down and tumbled the stones together in a pile. Then he proceeded another hundred yards, holding the lantern high and peering through the streaming crystals of the rain.

Blue Murder was there. Neither the chain nor the sapling had given way. The lantern and, better than the lantern, a globe of lightning, showed the tethered stallion glistening and quivering, his eyes all whites at the man's approach.

"Gentle, boy; steady, boy!" Talking all the while in the way he had with horses, Camden put a hand on the taut chain and bore with a gradually progressive weight, bringing the dark head nearer. "Steady, boy; gentle there, damn you; gentle!"

Was he afraid of horses? Who was it said he was afraid of horses?

The beast's head was against the man's chest, held there by an arm thrown over the bowed neck. As he smoothed the forehead and fingered the nose with false caresses, Camden's "horse talk" ran on—the cadence one thing, the words another.

"Steady, Goll damn you; you're going to get yours. Cheer up, cheer up, the worst is yet to come. Come now! Come easy! Come along!"

When he had unloosed the chain he felt for and found with his free hand his hammer hidden behind the tree. Throwing the lantern into the brush, where it flared for an instant before dying, he led the stallion back as far as the break he had made in the fence. Taking a turn with the chain around the animal's nose, like an improvised hackamore, he swung from the stone pile to the slippery back. A moment's shying, a sliding caracole of amazement and distrust, a crushing of knees, a lash of the chain-end, and that was all there was to that. Blue Murder had been ridden before. . . .

In the smithy, chambered in the roaring of the falls and the swish and shock of the storm, Camden sang as he pumped his bellows, filling the cave beneath the rafters with red. The air was nothing, the words were mumbo-jumbo, but they swelled his chest. His eyes, cast from time to time at his wheeling prisoner, had lost their look of helplessness and surly distraction.

Scared? He? No, no, no! Now that he wasn't any longer afraid of time, he wasn't afraid of anything on earth.

"Shy, you devil!" He wagged his exalted head. "Whicker, you hellion! Whicker all you want to, stud horse! To-morrow they're going to get you, the dumb fools! To-morrow they can have you. I got you to-night!"

He was more than other men; he was enormous. Fishing an iron shoe from that inseparable apron pocket of his, he thrust it into the coals and blew and blew. He tried it and it was burning red. He tried it again and it was searing white. Taking it out on the anvil he began to beat it, swinging his hammer one-handed, gigantic. So in the crimson light, irradiating iron sparks, he was at his greatest. Pounding, pounding. A man in the dark of night with a hammer about him can do wonders; with a horseshoe about him he can cover up a sin. And if the dark of night in a paddock won't hold it, then the dark of undergrowth on a mountainside will. . . .

Pounding, pounding; thinking, thinking, in a great halo of hot stars. Feeding his hungry, his insatiable muscles.

"Steady now, you blue bastard! Steady, boy!"

What he did not realise in his feverish exaltation was that his muscles were not insatiable. In the thirty-odd hours past they had had a feast spread before them and they had had their fill. . . . More than their fill.

As with the scorching iron in his tongs he approached the stallion, he had to step over the nail-box he had stepped over five thousand times in the routine of every day.

A box of apples, eh? Apples to snigger at, eh? But whose girl are you now? . . . Scared, eh?

His foot was heavier of a sudden than it should have been. This five thousand and first time, by the drag of the tenth of an inch, the heel caught the lip of the nail-box.

He tried to save himself from stumbling. At the same time, instinctively, he held the iron flame in his tongs away.

There was a scream out of a horse's throat; a whiff of hair and burnt flesh.

There was a lash of something in the red shadows. There was another sound and another wisp of stench. . . .

When, guided by the stallion's whinnying, they found the smith next day, they saw by the cant of his head that his neck was broken, and they perceived that he, too, had on him the mark of a shoe. It lay up one side of his throat and the broad of a cheek. It wasn't blue this time, however, it was red. It took them some instants in the sunshine pouring through the wide door to comprehend this phenomenon. It wasn't sunk in by a blow this time; it was burned in, a brand.

Darred called them to look at the stallion, chained behind the forge.

"Almighty God!" The words sounded funny in his mouth. They sounded the funnier in that they were the same ones the blundering smith had uttered when, staring uphill from his clever wreckage of the paddock fence, he had seen the mares striking sparks from the stones where the stallion struck none. And he, of all men, a smith!

"Almighty God!" called Darred. "What can you make of these here feet?"

One fore-hoof was freshly pared for shoeing; the other three hoofs were as virgin as any yearling's on the plains. Blue Murder had never been shod. . . .

RUSSIA

Introduction

ALTHOUGH the history of Russian literature may go back as far as the eleventh century, little of value was produced until the eighteenth. Sumarokov (1718-1777) was the first Russian to regard literature as a profession. He tried his hand at poetry, fables and dramas, and his writings influenced Russian literature up to Pushkin. Karamzin (1766-1826), who wrote a remarkable *History of the Russian Empire,* besides a number of novels and short stories, was largely responsible for purifying the language of its Church-Slavic structure.

Pushkin and Lermontov, both belonging to the romantic period of the nineteenth century, may be considered the founders of modern Russian literature. While they were great poets, they also wrote some short stories in the romantic tradition. It is interesting to know that they were romanticists even in life, for they were both killed in duels.

Gogol was the first master of fiction to turn to realism, and in his great novel, *Dead Souls*, he satirises all classes of Russian society. Gogol was followed by Turgenev, Dostoievsky and Tolstoy, the three masters of Russian fiction. Though they were great artists, their work, as well as that of other Russian authors, is essentially profound and purposeful, dealing with the problems of life, and is not concerned with "art for art's sake".

Chekhov, who contributed immensely to the fame of the Russian short story, is a phenomenon in Russian literature inasmuch as he is the only writer of importance with a real sense of humour. And even his humour is frequently sorrow-laden. Gorky is the best known Russian author living to-day, although in Gorky's judgment Bunin is more deserving of the honour.

In the first decade of the present century, a new movement came into prominence in Russian literature; namely, the Symbolist movement; and for a space it appeared as if it would usurp the position of the realists of the revolutionary school. Sologub and Bely are the outstanding leaders of the Symbolists.

ALEXANDER PUSHKIN
(1799-1837)

PUSHKIN is the first great figure in Russian literature. After graduating from the Lyceum at Tsarskoe Selo (1817), he gave himself up to the pleasures of society, though not deserting literature, for which he had conceived an early passion and which had been nurtured by his nurse. In 1820 he was banished to the Caucasus for writing and promoting liberal views, a most reprehensible crime in the eyes of the government. And thus the government proved to be, quite unconsciously, a blessing in disguise; for Pushkin, deprived of the deleterious influence of social life, devoted himself entirely to writing, and bequeathed to the world some lovely poetry, exquisite fairy tales and delightful stories. Pushkin met his death in a duel, a romantic end for a romantic character.

The Coffin-Maker, which appears in *The Prose Tales of Alexander Pushkin*, is translated by T. Keane. The volume was published in London, 1894.

THE COFFIN-MAKER

THE last of the effects of the coffin-maker, Adrian Prokhoroff, were placed upon the hearse, and a couple of sorry-looking jades dragged themselves along for the fourth time from Basmannaia to Nikitskaia, whither the coffin-maker was removing with all his household. After locking up the shop, he posted upon the door a placard announcing that the house was to be let or sold, and then made his way on foot to his new abode. On approaching the little yellow house, which had so long captivated his imagination, and which at last he had bought for a considerable sum, the old coffin-maker was astonished to find that his heart did not rejoice. When he crossed the unfamiliar threshold and found his new home in the greatest confusion, he sighed for his old hovel, where for eighteen years the strictest order had prevailed. He began to scold his two daughters and the servant for their slowness, and then set to work to help them himself. Order was soon established; the ark with the sacred images, the cupboard with the crockery, the table, the sofa, and the bed occupied the corners reserved for them in the back room; in the kitchen and parlour were placed the articles comprising the stock-in-trade of the master—coffins of all colours and of all sizes, together with cupboards containing mourning hats, cloaks and torches.

Over the door was placed a sign representing a fat Cupid with an inverted torch in his hand and bearing this inscription: "Plain and coloured coffins sold and lined here; coffins also let out on hire, and old ones repaired."

The girls retired to their bedroom; Adrian made a tour of inspection of his quarters, and then sat down by the window and ordered the tea-urn to be prepared.

The enlightened reader knows that Shakespeare and Walter Scott have both represented their grave-diggers as merry and facetious individuals, in order that the contrast might more forcibly strike our imagination. Out of respect for the truth, we cannot follow their example, and we are compelled to confess that the disposition of our coffin-maker was in perfect harmony with his gloomy occupation. Adrian Prokhoroff was usually gloomy and thoughtful. He rarely opened his mouth, except to scold his daughters when he found them standing idle and gazing out of the window at the passers by, or to demand for his wares an exorbitant price from those who had the misfortune—and sometimes the good fortune—to need them. Hence it was that Adrian, sitting near the window and drinking his seventh cup of tea, was immersed as usual in melancholy reflections. He thought of the pouring rain which, just a week before, had commenced to beat down during the funeral of the retired brigadier. Many of the cloaks had shrunk in consequence of the downpour, and many of the hats had been put quite out of shape. He foresaw unavoidable expenses, for his old stock of funeral dresses was in a pitiable condition. He hoped to compensate himself for his losses by the burial of old Trukhina, the shopkeeper's wife, who for more than a year had been upon the point of death. But Trukhina lay dying at Rasgouliai, and Prokhoroff was afraid that her heirs, in spite of their promise, would not take the trouble to send so far for him, but would make arrangements with the nearest undertaker.

These reflections were suddenly interrupted by three masonic knocks at the door.

"Who is there?" asked the coffin-maker.

The door opened, and a man, who at the first glance could be recognised as a German artisan, entered the room, and with a jovial air advanced towards the coffin-maker.

"Pardon me, respected neighbour," said he in that Russian dialect which to this day we cannot hear without a smile; "pardon me for disturbing you . . . I wish to make your acquaintance as soon as possible. I am a shoemaker, my name is Gottlieb Schultz, and I live across the street, in that little house just facing your windows. To-morrow I am going to celebrate my silver wedding, and I have come to invite you and your daughters to dine with us."

The invitation was cordially accepted. The coffin-maker asked the shoemaker to seat himself and take a cup of tea, and thanks to the open-hearted disposition of Gottlieb Schultz, they were soon engaged in friendly conversation.

"How is business with you?" asked Adrian.

"Just so so," replied Schultz; "I cannot complain. My wares are not like yours; the living can do without shoes, but the dead cannot do without coffins."

"Very true," observed Adrian; "but if a living person hasn't anything to buy shoes with, you cannot find fault with him, he goes about barefooted; but a dead beggar gets his coffin for nothing."

In this manner the conversation was carried on between them for some time; at last the shoemaker rose and took leave of the coffin-maker, renewing his invitation.

The next day, exactly at twelve o'clock, the coffin-maker and his daughters issued from the doorway of their newly-purchased residence, and directed their steps towards the abode of their neighbour. I will not stop to describe the Russian caftan of Adrian Prokhoroff, nor the European toilettes of Akoulina and Daria, deviating in this respect from the usual custom of modern novelists. But I do not think it superfluous to observe that they both had on the yellow cloaks and red shoes, which they were accustomed to don on solemn occasions only.

The shoemaker's little dwelling was filled with guests, consisting chiefly of German artisans with their wives and foremen. Of the Russian officials there was present but one, Yourko the Finn, a watchman, who, in spite of his humble calling, was the special object of the host's attention. For twenty-five years he had faithfully discharged the duties of postillion of Pogorelsky. The conflagration of 1812, which destroyed the ancient capital, destroyed also his little yellow watch-house. But immediately after the expulsion of the enemy, a new one appeared in its place, painted grey and with white Doric columns, and Yourko began again to pace to and fro before it, with his axe and grey coat of mail. He was known to the greater part of the Germans who lived near the Nikitskaia Gate, and some of them had even spent the night from Sunday to Monday beneath his roof.

Adrian immediately made himself acquainted with him, as with a man whom, sooner or later, he might have need of, and when the guests took their places at the table, they sat down beside each other. Herr Schultz and his wife and their daughter Lotchen, a young girl of seventeen, did the honours of the table and helped the cook to serve. The beer flowed in streams; Yourko ate like four, and Adrian in no way yielded to him; his daughters, however, stood upon their dignity. The conversation, which was carried on in German, gradually grew more and more boisterous. Suddenly the host requested a moment's attention, and uncorking a sealed bottle, he said with a loud voice in Russian:

"To the health of my good Louise!"

The champagne foamed. The host tenderly kissed the fresh face of his partner, and the guests drank noisily to the health of the good Louise.

"To the health of my amiable guests!" exclaimed the host, uncorking a second bottle; and the guests thanked him by draining their glasses once more.

Then followed a succession of toasts. The health of each individual guest was drunk; they drank to the health of Moscow and to quite a dozen little German towns; they drank to the health of all corporations in general and of each in particular; they drank to the health of the masters and foremen. Adrian drank with enthusiasm and became so merry that he proposed a facetious toast to himself. Suddenly one of the guests, a fat baker, raised his glass and exclaimed:

"To the health of those for whom we work, our customers!"

The proposal, like all the others, was joyously and unanimously received. The guests began to salute each other; the tailor bowed to the shoemaker, the shoemaker to the tailor, the baker to both, the whole company to the baker, and so on. In the midst of these mutual congratulations, Yourko exclaimed, turning to his neighbour:

"Come, little father! Drink to the health of your corpses!"

Everybody laughed, but the coffin-maker considered himself insulted, and frowned. Nobody noticed it, the guests continued to drink, and the bell had already rung for vespers when they rose from the table.

The guests dispersed at a late hour, the greater part of them in a very merry mood. The fat baker and the bookbinder, whose face seemed as if bound in red morocco, linked their arms in those of Yourko and conducted him back to his little watch-house, thus observing the proverb: "One good turn deserves another."

The coffin-maker returned home drunk and angry.

"Why is it," he exclaimed aloud, "why is it that my trade is not as honest as any other? Is a coffin-maker brother to the hangman? Why did those heathens laugh? Is a coffin-maker a buffoon? I wanted to invite them to my new dwelling and give them a feast, but now I'll do nothing of the kind. Instead of inviting them, I will invite those for whom I work: the orthodox dead."

"What is the matter, little father?" said the servant, who was engaged at that moment in taking off his boots: "Why do you talk such nonsense? Make the sign of the cross! Invite the dead to your new house! What folly!"

"Yes, by the Lord! I will invite them," continued Adrian. "And that, too, for to-morrow! . . . Do me the favour, my benefactors, to come and feast with me to-morrow evening; I will regale you with what God has sent me."

With these words the coffin-maker turned into bed and soon began to snore.

It was still when Adrian was awakened out of his sleep. Trukhina, the shopkeeper's wife, had died during the course of that very night, and a special messenger was sent off on horseback by her bailiff to carry the news to Adrian. The coffin-maker gave him ten copecks to buy brandy with, dressed himself as hastily as possible, took a droshky and set out for Rasgouliai. Before the door of the house in which the deceased lay, the police had already taken their stand, and the trades-people were passing backwards and forwards, like ravens that smell a dead body. The deceased lay upon a table, yellow as wax, but not yet disfigured by decomposition. Around her stood her relatives, neighbours and domestic servants. All the windows were open; tapers were burning; and the priests were reading the prayers for the dead. Adrian went up to the nephew of Trukhina, a young shopman in a fashionable surtout, and informed him that the coffin, wax candles, pall, and the other funeral accessories would be immediately delivered with all possible exactitude. The heir thanked him in an absent-minded manner, saying that he would not bargain about the price, but would rely upon him acting in everything according to his conscience. The coffin-maker, in accordance with his usual custom, vowed that he would not charge him too much, exchanged significant glances with the bailiff, and then departed to commence operations.

The whole day was spent in passing to and fro between Rasgouliai and the Kikitskaia Gate. Towards evening everything was finished, and he returned home on foot, after having dismissed his driver. It was a moonlight night. The coffin-maker reached the Nikitskaia Gate in safety. Near the Church of the Ascension he was hailed by our acquaintance Yourko, who, recognising the coffin-maker, wished him good-night. It was late. The coffin-maker was just approaching his house, when suddenly he fancied he saw some one approach his gate, open the wicket, and disappear within.

"What does that mean?" thought Adrian. "Who can be wanting me again? Can it be a thief come to rob me? Or have my foolish girls got lovers coming after them? It means no good, I fear!"

And the coffin-maker thought of calling his friend Yourko to his assistance. But at that moment, another person approached the wicket and was about to enter, but seeing the master of the house hastening towards him, he stopped and took off his three-cornered hat. His face seemed familiar to Adrian, but in his hurry he had not been able to examine it closely.

"You are favouring me with a visit," said Adrian, out of breath. "Walk in, I beg of you."

"Don't stand on ceremony, little father," replied the other, in a hollow voice; "you go first, and show your guests the way."

Adrian had no time to spend upon ceremony. The wicket was open; he ascended the steps followed by the other. Adrian thought he could hear people walking about in his rooms.

"What the devil does all this mean!" he thought to himself, and he hastened to enter. But the sight that met his eyes caused his legs to give way beneath him.

The room was full of corpses. The moon, shining through the windows, lit up their yellow and blue faces, sunken mouths, dim, half-closed eyes, and protruding noses. Adrian, with horror, recognised in them people that he himself had buried, and in the guest who entered with him, the brigadier who had been buried during the pouring rain. They all, men and women, surrounded the coffin-maker, with bowings and salutations, except one poor fellow lately buried gratis, who, conscious and ashamed of his rags, did not venture to approach, but meekly kept aloof in a corner. All the others were decently dressed; the female corpses in caps and ribbons, the officials in uniforms, but with their beards unshaven, the tradesmen in their holiday *caftans*.

"You see, Prokhoroff," said the brigadier in the name of all honourable company, "we have all risen in response to your invitation. Only those have stopped at home who were unable to come, who have crumbled to pieces and have nothing left but fleshless bones. But even of these there was one who hadn't the patience to remain behind—so much did he want to come and see you . . ."

At this moment a little skeleton pushed his way through the crowd and approached Adrian. His fleshless face smiled affably at the coffin-maker. Shreds of green and red cloth and rotten linen hung on him here and there as on a pole, and the bones of his feet rattled inside his big jack-boots, like pestles in mortars.

"You do not recognise me, Prokhoroff," said the skeleton.

"Don't you remember the retired sergeant of the guards, Peter Petrovitch Kourilkin, the same to whom, in the year 1799, you sold your first coffin, and that too, of deal instead of oak?"

With these words the corpse stretched out his bony arms towards him; but Adrian, collecting all his strength, shrieked and pushed him from him. Peter Petrovitch staggered, fell, and crumbled all to pieces. Among the corpses arose a murmur of indignation; all stood up for the honour of their companion, and they overwhelmed Adrian with such threats and imprecations, that the poor host, deafened by their shrieks and almost crushed to death, lost his presence of mind, fell upon the bones of the retired sergeant of the Guards, and swooned away.

For some time the sun had been shining upon the bed on which lay the coffin-maker. At last he opened his eyes and saw before him the servant attending to the tea-urn. With horror, Adrian recalled all the incidents of the previous day. Trukhina, the brigadier, and the sergeant, Kourilkin, rose vaguely before his imagination. He waited in silence for the servant to open the conversation and inform him of the events of the night.

"How you have slept, little father Adrian Prokhorovitch!" said Aksina, handing him his dressing-gown. "Your neighbour, the tailor, has been here, and the watchman also called to inform you that to-day is his nameday; but you were so sound asleep, that we did not wish to wake you."

"Did any one come for me from the late Trukhina?"

"The late? Is she dead then?"

"What a fool you are! Didn't you yourself help me yesterday to prepare the things for her funeral?"

"Have you taken leave of your senses, little father, or have you not yet recovered from the effects of yesterday's drinking-bout? What funeral was there yesterday? You spent the whole day feasting at the German's, and then came home drunk and threw yourself upon the bed, and have slept till this hour, when the bells have already rung for mass."

"Really!" said the coffin-maker greatly relieved.

"Yes indeed," replied the servant.

"Well, since that is the case, make the tea as quickly as possible and call my daughters."

❊ ❊ ❊

IVAN TURGENEV
(1818-1883)

TURGENEV, who had essentially a refined nature, was brought up on one of his father's estates in Orel where he witnessed the vicious effects of serfdom. He was educated at the St. Petersburg University, and completed his studies at Berlin. His attempts at poetry were abortive and he turned his efforts to prose. His publication of the *Memoirs of a Hunter* had a tremendous effect on the public that had never read such sympathetic stories about the serfs as were included in this volume. In 1852, for writing a eulogy on Gogol, he was banished to his estate. After his release, he went abroad and spent most of his remaining years in Paris where he wrote his remarkable novels and stories.

The Raspberry Water is taken from the collection of stories entitled the *Memoirs of a Hunter*. The present version is by Maxim Lieber.

THE RASPBERRY WATER

IN the month of August, the heat between noon and three o'clock is so intolerable that the most resolute hunter is constrained to forego his favourite sport. Even his dog, despite his devotion, begins to lick his spurs, that is to say, follows behind with hanging tongue and screwed up eyes. Should the master turn round to reproach him, he lifts his confused countenance and painfully wags his tail, but does not advance. I happened to be hunting on just such a day. For quite a space I resisted the temptation to abandon the hunt and stretch myself in some sheltering shade; for a long time my indefatigable dog continued to search among the thickets. But the heat became so stifling, that I was compelled to save the little strength remaining.

My only thought was to reach the shore of the Ista, a little river already familiar to my benevolent readers. I went down along the bank toward a spring well known throughout this district as The Raspberry Water. This spring gushes forth from a crevice in the bank, which time has little by little transformed into a small though deep ravine, and thence it tumbles into the river with a bubbling sound. Sturdy young oak bushes enhance the picturesque ravine, while around the spring gleams a short velvet moss. The sun's rays scarcely ever caress its cool and silver water.

On the grass I found a birch-bark dipper left there by some philanthropic muzhik. I quenched my thirst, stretched myself in the shade and let my eye leisurely explore the spot. Near the bay, formed at its slope by the flowing rapid I dominated, while recumbent like a rustic fluvial divinity, and which swarmed with frisking little fishes, two old men whom I had failed to notice before, sat with their backs toward the ravine. One of them, rather strong and tall, was dressed in a dark-green kaftan and a woollen cap; the other, wretchedly lean, wrapped up in a tattered jacket and bareheaded, was holding the pot of worms and from time to time would cover his grey head with his hand as if to ward off a sun stroke. I regarded the latter with some attention, and recognised in him Stepouchka from Shumikhino. You will, dear reader, permit me to introduce this man to you.

Several versts from my village lies the parish of Shumikhino lorded over by a stone church dedicated to Saints Kozma and Damian. Opposite this church had sprawled at one time a spacious manor-house, flanked by a number of structures,—offices, work-shops, stables, bath-houses, bowers, chambers for guests and servants, orangeries, swings and other more or less useful structures. This mansion had been inhabited by wealthy landed gentry. All went well with them until one morning a fire burned everything.

The masters moved away to suitable temporary quarters. The manor was deserted, and the ash heap became in the course of time a fair enough vegetable garden adorned with ruins, the relics of the former foundations. With several beams that had been rescued from the fire, a hut had hastily been constructed. This was covered with planks that had been bought about ten years ago for the purpose of erecting a pavilion in the Gothic style. Here lodged the gardener, Mitrofan, his wife, Aksinia, and their seven children. Mitrofan was charged with supplying vegetables for his master's table, one hundred and fifty versts distant; Aksinia was entrusted with the care of the Tyrolian cow, purchased dearly in Moscow, which being unfortunately sterile, gave no milk. Aksinia also had charge of a crested, smoke-coloured drake, the sole fowl of the "lord." Because of their extreme youth, no tasks were assigned to the children.

I happened, on two occasions, to pass the night with this gardener, and, incidentally, he used to sell me cucumbers which, God knows why, were distinguished, even in summer, by their size and their thick yellow skin. It was at his house that I first saw Stepouchka.

Every man has some kind of a position in society, some connection; every house-serf receives, if not wages, at least a few coins with which to satisfy his needs. Stepouchka received nothing, was not related to any one, and no one seemed to trouble about his existence. This man had not even a past; no one ever spoke to him; I truly believe he was not even included in the census. There were vague rumours abroad that, once upon a time, he had been valet, but one could explain neither whose son he was nor how he had come to be among the subjects of the lord of Shumikhino, nor, for that matter, how he had procured the jacket that had covered his shoulders from time immemorial. Where did he live? How did he live? No one knew, and, moreover, no one seemed to care.

There was the old centenarian, Trofimitch he was called, who knew the genealogy of all the serfs back to the fourth generation. All that he could recall was merely that Stepouchka had been born of a Turkish woman whom his late master, General Alexei Romanitch, had brought back with him.

Even on festival days, days of liberal good cheer when, according to the ancient Russian custom, they would eat buckwheat patties and quaff green vodka, Stepouchka did not appear at the large tables or the wine casks mounted on wooden horses; he did not dare salute the dispensers of good cheer, or kiss the master's hand while drinking, at one draught, to his health a bumper filled by the fat hand of the superintendent. He hoped for nothing and had nothing, except mayhap some kind soul, in passing, gave the poor devil the remainder of his unfinished patty. On Easter day every one exchanges embraces; and people would embrace him as well, for, after all, he was a human being. But he did not tuck up his greasy sleeve, he did not draw forth a red egg from his rear pocket; he did not present it, blinking and panting, to the young masters or the lady, their mistress.

In the summer he lived in a pen behind the chicken coop; in the winter, in the anteroom of the village bath-house. On extremely cold days he used to hoist himself into a hay loft. He got accustomed to being humiliated, even to receiving an occasional kick without so much as uttering a plaint. He had apparently never in all his life opened his mouth, neither to ask, nor to complain.

After the conflagration, this poor forsaken fellow took shelter with the gardener, Mitrofan, who did not say to him, "Live with me," but neither did he say, "Get along with you." Besides, to live with the gardener was well beyond Stepouchka's ambition: he hovered about the garden. He moved about without being seen or heard; he sneezed and coughed into his hand, and even then with an air of affright. Always careworn and silent he came and went, like an ant, seeking his food, merely his food.

Indeed, had not my Stepouchka been concerned about his nourishment from morning to night, he would have died of hunger. Bad business; not to know in the morning if you will eat by nightfall. One day he would be seen sitting against a paling devouring a large radish, sucking a carrot, or tearing into shreds a rotten head of cabbage. Then again he would be carrying a bucket of water, grumbling under his breath the while, light a fire beneath a pot, draw from next his chest an indescribable black morsel and throw it into the bowl. And again, in his little cubby hole, he would fidget about with a piece of wood, drive several nails into it and make himself a little shelf on which to deposit his bread, and he did all this with the greatest possible silence in secret. If you looked at him, he disappeared. Sometimes he would absent himself for a couple of days, and, of course, no one troubled about his absence; and then, all of a sudden, it transpired that he was back again, in the shelter of a paling, stealthily gathering some shavings under an old iron tripod.

His face is small, his eyes yellowish, his abundant hair grows down to his eyebrows and temples; he has a very pointed nose and very large ears, transparent like those of a bat; his beard has not been shaved for fifteen days, no more no less. This was the Stepouchka whom I encountered on the bank of the Ista, seated near another old fellow.

I accosted them, greeted them, and sat down beside them. In Stepouchka's companion I recognised a man also known to me. He was a freedman who had belonged to Count Peter Illitch. His name was Mikhailo Savelitch, nicknamed Tuman (The Fog). He lived with the consumptive burgher, the inn-keeper of Bolkhovo, where I often stopped. Those who travel along the Orel highway,—young officials and other idlers (merchants burdened with their feather-beds had not the time to tarry there) can still behold at a short distance from Troitski, an enormous, wooden, two-storied house or, at least, the skeleton of a house utterly abandoned, its roof caving in, its shutters barricaded, standing just on the edge of the road. At high noon, on a beautiful sun-flooded day, no sadder spectacle than this ruin can be imagined. Here in days gone by dwelt Count Peter Illitch, wealthy and great lord, in the manner of the last century, and famous for his hospitality. All the important people of Orel used to foregather here; to amuse themselves, to regale themselves, to dance to their heart's content to the deafening thunder of a private orchestra, the burst of rockets and Roman candles. It is probable that more than one old woman, in passing this deserted mansion, sighs reminiscently for those vanished days. There for many years the count had lead a joyous existence; there he had strolled with a radiant face, a smile on his lips amid the throng of convivial guests who worshipped him. Unfortunately, his wealth was exhausted at this stage of his life. Seeing himself totally ruined, he repaired to Petersburg to seek some employment, and,—he died in an hotel chamber before he had received a definite answer. Tuman, who had served him in his days of splendour, had received his emancipation papers during the count's lifetime. He was a man of seventy, still retaining his good appearance. He smiled almost continually, as only those of Queen Catherine's time smile; an honest smile. When speaking, he opened and closed his mouth slowly, he screwed up his eyes, his words had a nasal sound. He blew his nose, and took some snuff slowly and solemnly.

"Well, Mikhailo Savelitch," I asked, "hast thou caught some fish?"

"Please be so good as to look in the basket: two perch, five mullets. . . . Show them, Stepan."

Stepouchka held the basket for me.

"And how art thou, Stepan?" I asked him.

"E-e-eh- we-e-ll, quite well, little father," replied Stepouchka, stammering. Each word he uttered seemed to weigh a pud.

"And how is it with Mitrofan?"

"We- we-well, of—course, little father."

The poor fellow turned away.

"They don't bite at all," remarked Tuman. "It's too hot for fishing. All the fish have gone off now to sleep in the shade of the bushes. . . . Hey, Stepan, put a worm on the hook."

Stepan seized a worm in the pot, put it in the palm of his left hand, patted it, put it on the hook, spat on it and gave it to Tuman.

"Thanks, Stepan. And you, little father," he resumed turning to me, "are you hunting?"

"As you see."

"That's it. What sort of a dog have you there? Is he English or a Finland breed?" (The old fellow never lost an opportunity to show that he had seen a bit of the world.)

"I don't know of what breed he is, but he is a good dog."

"That's so. And you always hunt with dogs?"

"I have a couple of leashes."

Tuman smiled and nodded his head.

"Yes, that's the way of the world. There are those who love dogs, and others who wouldn't accept the best of them as a gift. I think, according to my judgment, that dogs, as well as horses, should be kept for show, for style, so to speak. The late Count, God rest his soul, was not, it's true, a sportsman by nature; but he kept dogs. And twice a year he made a show of going out on a grand hunt. The whippers-in would assemble in the courtyard, attired in gallon-trimmed scarlet kaftans, and blow their horns. His Illustriousness would appear, animated; the horse would be led up to his Illustriousness; his Illustriousness would mount assisted by the chief huntsman who placed his feet in the stirrups, doffed his cap and presented him with the reins on it. His Illustriousness would deign to crack his whip, the huntsmen would halloo at the dogs and, they were off. A groom follows the Count, leading a couple of favourite hounds on a leash. It's wonderful, you see. The groom is seated very high, very high on a Cossack saddle, his little eyes rolling and his cheeks rosy. There were many visitors present, that's understood. It was amusing, and just as it should be. . . . Ah, the Asiatic has escaped!" he added suddenly, drawing up his line.

"It appears that the Count, how would you say it, had a pretty lively time of it?" I remarked.

The old fellow spat on his bait and flung the line back.

"He was a real lord; everybody knew that. One may say that the best people of Petersburg came to visit him; they would wear the Order of St. Andrew, the highest in the Empire to sit at his table. And he certainly was a past master at the art of entertaining. He would summon me and say, 'Tuman, I must have some live sterlet to-morrow. Order them to be brought, do you hear?' 'I obey, your Highness.' From Paris he used to import embroidered kaftans, wigs, canes, perfumes, ladecolone, best quality, snuff boxes and large pictures, large, very large. Did he give any banqueta? Akh, God, Lord of my life! . . . What fire works and pleasure drives! Cannon would even be fired off. He had an orchestra of forty musicians for whom he got a German conductor. But he was such a conceited fellow. Fancy, he wanted to eat at his Highness' table, and he was so insistent, that his Highness told him to go packing. His Highness said, 'My musicians know their business without him.' There was nothing to say to that; the master was within his rights. They would start to dance, and dance till dawn, chiefly the lacossaize matradoura. . . . He . . . he . . . he! thou art caught, brother!" (He drew a little perch from the water.) "Here, take it, Stepan."

"He was a master, a real master," continued the old fellow, casting his line back again, "and a kind soul at that. He would thrash me a times, and the minute he turned his head away, he'd forgotten all abou it. One thing only, those mistresses he maintained, there you are, it wa those mistresses who ruined him; he took them chiefly from the lowe classes. And they had to have so much. They had to have, indeed, th most costly things in Europe. Hang it all, and why not follow pleasure? It's the only thing for a gentleman . . . but one should not go so far as to ruin oneself. Let me see, there was one in particular, Akulina was her name; she's dead now, may God rest her soul! She was one in a hundred. The daughter of the village policeman of Sitovo. . . . My what a wicked wench. She used to slap the Count, can you picture it? She had completely bewitched him, yes. I had a nephew whose brow she shaved. . . . He had spilled some chocolate on her new gown. And he was not the only one whose brow she shaved. . . . Nevertheless I say that those were good little times," added the old fellow, sighing deeply. He bowed his head and was silent.

"One can see that you had a severe master," I resumed after a pause.

"That was the taste and the custom of those times," replied Tuman, nodding his head.

"Things have changed now," I remarked, observing him attentively. He cast a sidelong glance at me.

"Yes, nowadays things are, fortunately, . . . better," he murmured, and he flung his line far out.

We were seated in the shade; but it was nonetheless stifling. The burning face sought the wind; but there was not even a breeze. The sun's rays darted pitilessly from a dark blue sky. Directly ahead of us, on the opposite shore, was a field of gleaming yellow oats, cut up with stalks of wormwood, and not a single ear of the grain stirred. A little lower, I saw a peasant's horse plunged to his knees in water, and swishing himself lazily with his wet tail. Now and then, some twenty paces from us, under the foliage of an overhanging bush, a large fish swam up, exhaled some air that mounted in bubbles to the surface, then gently sank to the bottom, leaving a faint swell in his wake. Grasshoppers were chirping in the rusty grass; the quails were crying lazily; the hawks hovered over the fields, and often stopped motionless with a swift fluttering of their wings and a spreading of their tails like a fan. We sat thus motionless, crushed by the oppressive heat. All of a sudden, behind us, in the ravine, we heard a noise. Someone was descending to the spring. I looked round and saw a peasant of some fifty odd years, dust-covered, his shirt coming over his trousers, wearing bark-slippers, his coat and birch-bark wallet over his shoulders. He crouched down at the spring, slaked his thirst, and then rose to his feet.

"Hey, Vlas!" cried Tuman, who recognised him at a first glance. "Good day, brother. Whence has God brought thee?"

"Good day, Mikhailo Savelitch," replied the peasant, approaching. "I come from afar."

"And where the devil hast thou been hiding?" asked Tuman.

"I've been to Moscow, to find the master."

"Why?"

"To petition him."

"Oh! . . . and what about?"

"That he might reduce my quit-rent, or put me on duty-service. . . . My son is dead, and I myself can't manage things now."

"Thy son is dead?"

"Dead. In Moscow. He was employed as a cabman, and I must admit that he paid my quit-rent for me."

"So thou art now on a quit-rent basis?"

"Yes."

"Well, and what about the master."

"The master? . . . Oh, he drove me off, saying, 'How darest thou come to me? Why dost thou think I have a superintendent? Thou art supposed to report to him first. . . . Thou speakest of duty-service. And where am I to transfer thee for duty-service? Hadst better pay up thine arrears.' He was very angry."

"And so thou hast returned?"

"Akh, yes! I should have liked, besides, to learn whether the deceased had by chance left any goods or money behind him; but I failed to get any information. I said to his employer: "I am Vlas, Philip's father;' and he said to me: 'How do I know that? And, moreover, thy son left nothing, nothing; he owes me money into the bargain.' After that I left."

The peasant delivered this tale with the air of one who might speak of someone else; but his little eyes swam with tears, and his lips quivered.

"Art thou going home now?"

"Where else should I be going? My woman is there whistling into her fist with hunger."

"Thou mightest . . ." suddenly stuttered Stepouchka,—then grew confused, stopped short, and began rummaging in the pot of worms.

"Art thou going to seek the superintendent?" Tuman asked, regarding Stepan with astonishment.

"Why should I seek him? Dost thou think I have anything with which to pay my arrears? . . . My boy was sick for about a year before he died, and he did not pay even his own quit-rent. Bah! Why should I worry? Thou canst ring blood from a stone. . . . Be as shrewd as you will, brother, it comes to the same thing. . . . Oh, well, my head is a sorry forfeit, and there's nothing else. . . . (The peasant broke into a singular laugh.) Let Kintilian Semionitch bother about it." And he laughed once again.

"Akh, brother Vlas, that's bad . . . bad, indeed," muttered Tuman.

"How is it bad? No. . . ." Vlas's voice broke; then he resumed: "My, what heat!" and he mopped his face with his sleeve.

"Who is your master?" I asked the peasant.

"Count——, Valerian Petrovitch."

"The son of Peter Illitch?"

"Yes, the son of Peter," replied Tuman. "The deceased Peter Illitch had during his lifetime detached from his estates Vlas's village and deeded it to his son."

"Is the Count well?"

"Yes, thank God," replied Vlas. "He is so handsome that you would not recognise him."

"You see, little father," continued Tuman, addressing me, "putting the peasant on quit-rent near Moscow might be satisfactory. But here?"

"At how much is the tax fixed?"

"At ninety-five rubles a household," murmured Vlas.

"Well, then, think of it, master. At Vlassovo there is very little ground, because it's all of the Count's forest."

"And it is rumoured that he has sold that," said the peasant.

"Well, you see how it is. . . . Stepan, let's have a worm! Say, hast thou fallen asleep? Stepan!"

Stepouchka started. The peasant sat down beside us. We were all pensive and silent. On the other shore, someone intoned a melancholy song. Our poor Vlas was disconsolate.

Half an hour later we parted company.

❊ ❊ ❊

FEODOR DOSTOIEVSKY
(1821-1881)

AFTER graduating from the School of Engineering in St. Petersburg in 1843, Dostoievsky received an appointment. This he soon resigned in order to devote himself to literature. *Poor People,* his first novel, appeared three years later and caused its author to be hailed as a "new Gogol." For supposed participation in a conspiracy he was sentenced to Siberia in 1849, whence he returned to Russia ten years later. He began a periodical in which he published two of his novels based on his Siberian experiences. While his work lacks the artistic perfection of Tolstoy or Turgenev, it is unsurpassed for profound psychological analysis and character study which, to a great extent, anticipated some of the modern scientific discoveries.

Dostoievsky wrote a number of excellent short stories, of which *The Beggar Boy at Christ's Christmas Tree* is a fine example. The present version is by Maxim Lieber.

THE BEGGAR BOY AT CHRIST'S CHRISTMAS TREE

I AM a novelist, and I believe I have made up this story. While I say "I believe," I am certain that I did make it up. But somehow I cannot help feeling that this really happened somewhere, and must have happened on a Christmas eve, in a large city, on a terribly frosty day.

I can see a boy, a little boy, some six years old, or less. This boy awoke that morning in a cold and clammy cellar. He wore some kind of a loose coat, and shivered with cold. His breath issued from his mouth like white steam, and, sitting on the edge of a box, he found it amusing to emit this steam and watch it disappear. But he was terribly hungry. Several times that morning he had gone up to the cot, where, on a mat not thicker than a pancake and with some kind of a bundle for a pillow, his sick mother was lying. How did she come here? She had possibly come with her boy from some provincial town and had suddenly fallen ill. The landlady, who let "corners" to lodgers, had been taken to the police station two days before; the lodgers had gone about their business and the only one left had been lying dead drunk for the last twenty-four hours, having thus anticipated the holiday. In another corner, groaning with rheumatism, lay an old woman of eighty, who had at one time been a children's nurse, but was now left to die alone. She was scolding and grumbling at the boy, so that he became afraid of going near her corner. He had found water to drink outside in the hall, but could not find a crust anywhere; and he tried a number of times to wake his mother. He began at last to fear the darkness; twilight had long set in, but no one made a light. Feeling his mother's face, he wondered why she did not move at all and was as cold as the wall. It was very cold here, he thought. He stood awhile, forgetting to remove his hand from the dead woman's shoulder, then he breathed on his small fingers to warm them, and, fumbling for his shabby cap on the cot, he softly groped his way out of the cellar. He would have gone sooner, but was scared of the big dog which had been howling all day outside a neighbour's door at the head of the stairs. Now the dog had left, and he went into the street.

Mercy, what a city! Never before had he seen anything like it. The town he had come from, the nights were always so pitch dark: just one lamp for the whole street. The little low, wooden houses were closed with shutters; the streets were deserted after dusk. People shut themselves up in the houses, and only packs of dogs, hundreds and thousands of them, barked and howled all night long. But he had been warm and had been given enough to eat, while there. . . . Lord! if he only *had* something to eat! And what a noise and bustle! What dazzling light, what crowds of people! . . . horses, carriages. . . . And the cold, the bitter cold! Frozen steam rose in clouds from the horses, out of their warmly-breathing mouths and nostrils; through the flaky snow is heard the clanking of their hoofs against the stones, and there is such a pushing, jostling. . . . And, oh, Lord! he does so crave a morsel to eat! . . . And his tiny fingers all at once begin to hurt him so. A policeman passed him, and turned away, to avoid seeing the boy.

And now another street. What a wide one! Here they will surely be run over! How these people run, and race and shout! And the light—so much light! And, oh! what is this? A huge window. And behind the glass—a tree, so tall,—reaching up to the ceiling. It is a Christmas tree, and on it ever so many little lights, gilt paper and apples, and little dolls and horses; and about the room children—so clean and well dressed,—running, playing, laughing, and eating and drinking things. Now one little girl begins to dance with a little boy,—such a pretty little girl! And you can hear music through the glass. And as the little boy in the street looks on in wonder, he too laughs, though his toes are beginning to ache, and his fingers are so red and stiff with cold that he cannot bend them, and it hurts to move them. Suddenly he remembered how they hurt him, and he began to cry, and ran on. But there again is another window, and behind it in the room another tree; there are tables laden with cakes,—all sorts of them—red, yellow, with almonds; and four richly dressed young ladies sit there and give the cakes away to all who come; and the door is opened incessantly and people enter from the street. The little boy stole up to the door, suddenly opened it and went in. Oh dear, how they shouted and waved him back with their hands! One lady went up to him hastily, slipped a copper into his hand, and herself opened the door for him. How frightened he was! He dropped the coin, which rolled, clinking, down the steps: he could not bend his rigid, red fingers to hold it. He ran away as fast as he could, with no idea of where he was running. He felt like crying, but he was too frightened, and could only run, and meantime breathe on his hands to warm them. He was miserable; he felt so strange, so alone and forlorn. Suddenly . . . oh Lord, what is this now? An admiring crowd stands before a window, and behind the pane are three dolls, dressed in red and green gowns, looking just as if they were alive! One is a little old man who sits there, playing on a very large fiddle, and the other two stand close by and play on small fiddles; they regard each other and nod their heads in time while their lips move; they are speaking but one cannot hear them through the glass. At first the boy thought they were really alive, and when he realised they were dolls, he laughed. Never had he seen such dolls and never thought there could be such! He wanted to cry, yet had to laugh,—the dolls were so very, very amusing! At this moment he felt that someone took hold of him from behind: a wicked, big boy who stood beside him, suddenly struck him on the head, snatched away his cap and tripped him. The little fellow stumbled to the ground, and people began to shout; numb with fright, he somehow picked himself up and ran, ran madly on, till, half unconsciously, he slipped into a gateway and found himself in a courtyard, where he cowered down behind a stack of wood. He felt safe there; it was dark, and "they" would not find him.

He sat huddled up and could not catch his breath from fright. Suddenly, quite suddenly, he felt comfortable; hands and feet ceased to ache, and grew as warm as if he were sitting on a stove. Then he shuddered and gave a start; why, he had almost fallen asleep! How nice it would be to sleep here. "I will rest here awhile, and go to look at the dolls again," thought the boy, smiling to himself, adding: "Just as though they are alive!" . . . Then it seemed to him that he heard his mother singing. "Mother, I am asleep; it is so nice to sleep here!"

"Come to my Christmas tree, little boy!" a gentle voice whispered near him.

At first he thought it was his mother; but it was not she. Who is it then that calls him? He cannot see; but someone is bending over him; embraces him in the dark. He puts forth his hands . . . and lo! what a flood of bright light! . . . And oh! what a tree! But no, it cannot be; he has never seen such trees. . . . *Where* is he, now? Shining radiance everywhere, and so many, many little dolls all around him. . . . But no! they are not dolls; these are all little boys and little girls, so pretty and bright, dancing, flying, and they crowd around him and kiss him, and, as he gazes, he sees his mother looking at him, laughing happily.

"Mamma, Mamma! Oh, how nice it is here!" he exclaims, and again kisses the children, and wants to tell them at once about the dolls behind the shop window. He asks them: "Who are you, little boys? Who are you, little girls?" He laughs and loves them all.

"This is Christ's Christmas tree," they answer. "On this day Christ always has a tree for such little children as have no tree of their own. . . ."

And he discovered that these boys and girls were all children like himself; that some had frozen to death in the baskets in which they had been deposited on doorsteps; others had died in wretched hovels, whither they had been sent from the Foundlings' Hospital; others again had starved to death at their mothers' dried-up breasts; had been suffocated in the foul air of third-class railroad carriages. And now, here they were all angels, Christ's guests, and He Himself was in their midst, extending His hands to them, blessing them and their poor, sinful mothers. . . . And the mothers stand there, a little apart, weeping; each one knows her little boy or girl; and the children fly up to them, and kiss them, and wipe away their tears with their tiny hands, and beg them not to weep, for they, the children, are so happy. . . .

And down below, on that Christmas morning, the porter found the body of a little boy who had hidden behind a stack of wood, and there frozen to death. His mother was also found. . . . She had died before him. They had met before God in heaven. . . .

Why in the world have I made up such a story, in this matter of fact diary of mine, which should treat only of real events? . . . But then, you see, I cannot help fancying that all this may have really happened,— I mean what took place in the basement and behind the woodstack. As to Christ's Christmas tree, I can't tell you whether or not it may have really happened. But it is a novelist's business to invent.

❋ ❋ ❋

LEO TOLSTOY
(1828-1910)

TOLSTOY began his literary career in the Caucasus where he was enrolled in the army. He took part in the Crimean War, after which he settled at St. Petersburg and wrote a number of stories that began to show his disillusionment with existing society. While he was writing his great novels and stories, he devoted himself to the education of the peasants. His fame as a writer is slightly overshadowed by his religious and social work to which he gave up the last thirty years of his life.

The Empty Drum, an anti-war story, is one of a number of folk-tales which Tolstoy adapted. The present version is by Maxim Lieber.

THE EMPTY DRUM

EMILYAN, who worked out as a day-labourer, was crossing the meadow one day on his way to work, when he nearly stepped on a frog that hopped right in front of him. He just managed to avoid it. Suddenly he heard someone calling to him from behind. He looked round and saw a lovely girl who said to him:

"Why don't you marry, Emilyan?"

"How can I marry, my pretty maid? I have nothing in this world, and no one would have me."

"Well, then," said the maid, "take me for a wife."

The girl appealed to Emilyan. "I should like to," said he, "but where could we live?"

"Why worry about that?" said the girl. "All one has to do is to work hard and sleep less, and one can find food and clothing anywhere."

"Very well, let us get married, then," said he. "Where shall we go?"

"Let us go to the city."

And Emilyan and the girl went to the city. She took him to a small cottage on the outskirts of the city, and they were married and began keeping house.

One day the king, coming through the city, passed by Emilyan's cottage. Emilyan's wife came out to look at him. When the king saw her he was surprised. "Where did such a beauty come from?" he thought. He stopped his carriage, called Emilyan's wife and questioned her, "Who are you?"

"The wife of the peasant Emilyan," said she.

"How did you, such a beautiful woman, come to marry a peasant? You ought to be a queen."

"Thank you for your compliment," said she, "but I am well content with my husband."

The king talked with her awhile, and then rode on. He arrived at his palace, but Emilyan's wife was on his mind. He was sleepless throughout the night, scheming how to get her for himself. He could think of no way of doing it, and therefore summoned his servants and asked them to plan some way.

The king's servants said, "Have Emilyan come here as a workman, and we will work him to death. His wife will be left a widow, and you will then be able to have her."

The king heeded their counsel. He sent for Emilyan to come as a workman and to live at the palace with his wife.

The messengers came to Emilyan with the king's command. His wife said, "Go and work there during the day, but come home to me at night."

Emilyan went, and when he reached the palace, the king's steward questioned him, "Why have you come alone without your wife?"

"Why should I have her with me? She has her own home."

At the palace they gave Emilyan more work than two could have completed, and he began without hope of finishing it. But when evening came, lo and behold! it was all done. The steward saw that he had finished, and gave him four times the amount for the next day. Emilyan went home, and found everything there neat and in order; the stove was heated, the meal was being prepared, and his wife was sitting by the table sewing and awaiting his return. She welcomed him, set the table, gave him his supper, and then began to ask him about his work.

"Well," said he, "it's not so good. They gave me more than my strength was equal to. They will kill me with work."

"Don't worry about your work," said she. "Don't look behind nor before you to see how much has been done or how much you have left to be done. Just keep right on working, and all will be well."

So Emilyan went to sleep. The next morning he went to work again and toiled on without ever turning round. And lo and behold! it was all done by the evening, and in the twilight he returned home for the night.

Ever they kept increasing his tasks, and he nevertheless managed to get through in time to go home for the night. After a week had thus passed, the king's servants saw they could not overcome him with rough work, and they began assigning him to work that necessitated skill; but this availed little more. Carpentry, masonry, or roofing—no matter what —Emilyan finished in time to go home to his wife for the night. And a second week passed.

Then the king summoned his servants and said, "Why should I feed you for doing nothing? Two weeks have passed and I fail to see what you have done. You were going to kill Emilyan with work, but from my windows I can see him going home every evening, singing cheerfully. Is it your purpose to ridicule me?"

The servants began to make excuses. "We tried our very best to tire him out," they said, "but he found nothing too difficult. No work seemed to tire him. Then we had him do things requiring skill, thinking he lacked the wit for it, but he accomplished everything. Whatever task he is put to, he does with little effort. Either he or his wife must know magic. We are tired with it all, and try to think of something he cannot do. We have determined to have him build a cathedral in one day. Will you send for Emilyan and command him to build a cathedral opposite the palace in a single day? And if he does not succeed, let his head be cut off in punishment."

The king sent for Emilyan. "Attend well my command," said he. "Build me a new cathedral on the square opposite my palace, and have it all done by to-morrow evening. If it is ready I will reward you, and if you fail your head will be cut off."

Emilyan heard the king's command, turned round and went home. "Well," thought he, "my end is near." He came to his wife and said, "Get ready, wife, we must escape from here, or I shall surely be lost."

"What makes you so frightened?" she asked, "and why must we run away?"

"How can I help being frightened?" said he. "The king has ordered me to-morrow to build a cathedral, all in a single day. If I fail he will have my head cut off. The only thing to be done is to fly while there is time."

But his wife would not hear of this. "The king has many soldiers. They will catch us anywhere. We can't escape from him, but must obey him as long as you have the strength."

"But how can I obey him when I lack the strength?"

"Listen, little father, don't be worried. Eat your supper now and go to bed. Get up a little earlier in the morning and all will be well."

And Emilyan went to sleep. His wife wakened him next day.

"Go quickly," said she, "and build your cathedral. Here are nails and a hammer. There is enough work for the day."

Emilyan went to the city, and when he arrived at the square, a large cathedral, almost finished, stood there. Emilyan started to work, and by evening he completed it.

The king awoke and looked out from his window, and saw the cathedral already built, with Emilyan driving in the last nails. And the king was not pleased to see the cathedral. He was angered not to be able to punish Emilyan and take away his wife. And he called his servants again. "Emilyan has finished his task, and there is nothing to punish him for. Even this," he said, "was easy for him. A craftier plan must be devised, or I will punish you as well as him."

And the king's servants suggested that he should order Emilyan to construct a river round the palace, and have ships sailing on it. The king summoned Emilyan and explained his new task.

"If," said he, "you are able to erect a cathedral in one night, you should also be able to do this. See to it that it is ready to-morrow, or else your head will be cut off."

Emilyan despaired more than ever, and returned, disconsolate, to his wife.

"Why are you so downcast?" said his wife. "Have you some new task to perform?"

Emilyan told her. "We must escape," said he.

But his wife said, "You can't escape from the soldiers; they will catch us wherever we be. There is nothing but to obey."

"But how can I obey?"

"Well, little father," said she, "don't be so gloomy. Eat your supper now and go to bed. Get up early, and all will get done betimes."

And Emilyan went to sleep. The next morning his wife wakened him.

"Go," said she, "to the city. All is ready. At the wharf you will find just one mound. Take your spade and level it."

When Emilyan reached the city, he saw a river encircling the palace, with ships sailing about. And when the king awoke, he saw Emilyan levelling the mound. He was surprised, but not overjoyed at the sight of the river or the ships. He was merely annoyed at not being able to punish Emilyan. "There is no task that he cannot do. What shall we set him next?" And he summoned his servants to take counsel.

"Plan some task," said he, "beyond Emilyan's power. For whatever you have thus far schemed, he has accomplished, and I cannot take his wife from him."

The king's servants pondered a long time, and at last conceived a plan. They came to the king and said, "Summon Emilyan and say to him: 'Go somewhere, you don't know where, and bring back something, you don't know what.' Now there will be no escape for him, for wherever he goes, you can say he went to the wrong place, and whatever he brings, you can say he brought back the wrong thing. Then you can have him beheaded and have his wife."

This pleased the king. "That," he said, "is a brilliant thought." And the king sent for Emilyan and said to him, "Go somewhere you don't know where, and bring back something you don't know what. If you fail, I will cut your head off."

Emilyan went to his wife and told her what the king had said. His wife thought a while.

"Well," said she, "they have taught the king how to trap you. We must act wisely." She sat down, cudgelled her brain, and then spoke to her husband. "You will have to go far, to our grandmother—the old peasant woman—and you must ask her help. She will give you something, and you will take it at once to the palace; I shall be there. I cannot escape them now. They will take me by force, but not for long. If you follow our little grandmother, you will quickly rescue me."

The wife prepared her husband for the journey. She gave him a wallet as well as a spindle. "Give her this. By this she will know you are my husband." And then she showed him the road.

Emilyan set out. He arrived beyond the city and saw some soldiers drilling. Emilyan stopped to watch them. When the drill was over, the soldiers sat down to rest. Emilyan drew near and asked, "Do you know, my brothers, the direction to 'somewhere I don't know where', and where I can find 'something I don't know what'?"

The soldiers listened in amazement. "Who sent you on this quest?" asked they.

"The king," he replied.

"From the day we became soldiers, we have ourselves gone 'we don't know where', and have sought 'we don't know what'. We surely cannot help you."

After he had rested a while, Emilyan continued on his way. He travelled on and on, and at last came to a forest where he found a hut. In the hut sat a little old woman—the old peasant woman—spinning flax and weeping. When the old woman saw Emilyan, she cried out to him, "What have you come for?"

Emilyan gave her the spindle and told her his wife had sent it. In answer to her questions, Emilyan began to tell her about his life: how he married the girl; how they had gone to live in the city; how he had drudged at the palace; how he had built the cathedral, and made a river with ships; and how the king had told him to go somewhere, he knew not where, and bring back something, he knew not what.

The little old woman heard his story, and then ceased weeping. She muttered to herself. Then she said to him, "Very well, my son, sit down and have something to eat."

Emilyan ate, and the little grandmother spoke to him. "Here is a little ball of thread; roll it before you, and follow it wherever it rolls. You will go far, till you get to the sea. There you will find a great city. You will enter the city and ask for a night's lodging at the last house. There you will find what you seek."

"But how shall I recognise it, granny?"

"When you see that which men obey sooner than father or mother, that will be it. Seize it and take it to the king. If the king will say it is not the right thing, answer him: 'If it is not the right thing, it must be broken'; then beat the thing and take it down to the river, smash it and pitch it into the water. Then you will recover your wife."

Emilyan said good-bye to the old woman, and rolled the little ball before him. It rolled on and on until it reached the sea, and by the sea was a great city, and at the end of the city was a large house. There Emilyan asked for shelter, and it was granted him. He went to sleep, and awoke early in the morning to hear a father calling his son and telling him to cut firewood. But the son would not obey. "It is too early," he said, "I have time enough." Then Emilyan heard the mother say, "Go, son your father's bones ache him; would you have him go? It is time to get up."

"There's time enough," the son muttered and went off to sleep again. Scarcely had he fallen asleep when there came a crashing noise in the street. The son jumped up, hastily put on his clothes and ran into the street. Emilyan jumped up also, and followed him to see what a son obeys more than his father or mother. He saw a man walking along the street carrying a round thing on which he beat with sticks. And *this* had made the thundering noise which the son had obeyed. Emilyan ran up closer and examined it; and saw it was round like a small tub, and skins were stretched over both ends. He asked what it was called.

"A drum," he was told.

Emilyan was astonished, and asked them to give him this object, but they refused. So Emilyan ceased asking, and walked along, following the drummer. He walked all day, and when the drummer lay down to sleep, Emilyan snatched the drum and ran off with it.

He ran and ran, and at last came back to his own city. He hoped to see his wife, but she was not at home. The day after he had gone away, they had taken her to the king. Emilyan went to the palace and told them to announce to the king that 'He, who went he knew not where, has returned, and brought back he knows not what.'

When they told the king, he asked Emilyan to return the next day.

But Emilyan insisted, "Tell the king I have come to-day, and have brought what he wanted. Let him come to me, or I will go to him."

The king came out. "Where have you been?" he asked.

"I don't know," Emilyan replied.

"What did you bring?"

Emilyan showed him the drum, but the king refused to look at it.

"That's not it."

"If it's not the right thing, it must be beaten," said Emilyan, "and the devil take it."

Emilyan came out of the palace and beat the drum, and as he did so, all the king's army ran to follow him, saluting Emilyan and awaiting his commands.

From the window the king began to shout to his army, forbidding them to follow Emilyan. But they did not heed the king and kept on following Emilyan.

When the king perceived this, he ordered Emilyan's wife returned to him, and asked Emilyan for the drum.

"I cannot do that," said Emilyan. "I must beat it, and then pitch the scraps into the river."

Emilyan went to the river, still carrying the drum and followed by the soldiers. At the bank of the river, Emilyan beat the drum into pieces and threw them into the water. And all the soldiers ran off in all directions. Then Emilyan took his wife and brought her home. And thenceforth the king ceased to worry him, and he lived happily ever after.

❋ ❋ ❋

ANTON CHEKHOV

(1860-1904)

CHEKHOV, the son of a former serf, was born in the city of Taganrog. After receiving his M.D. degree from the Moscow University, he began to contribute short stories to periodicals, and issued his first collected volume in 1887. This immediately established his reputation which grew, with each succeeding volume, until he became one of the world's greatest masters of the short story. His work is characterised by pathos, a profound sympathy for humanity, and, withal, a jovial scepticism of the philosopher.

The Darling is one of Chekhov's finest stories. The present translation is reprinted from *The Pagan* Magazine, Copyright, 1917, by permission of the publisher.

THE DARLING

OLINKA, daughter of a retired government-official, sat pensively on the porch facing the court-yard of her house. It was hot; the flies were an insistent nuisance, and she thought with pleasure of the approaching evening. Dark rain-clouds loomed up in the west, and a moist breeze blew, now and then.

In the middle of the yard stood Kukin, manager and owner of the Tivoli Pleasure-Garden, who lived as lodger in a wing of the house, and gazed at the sky.

"Rain again!" he exclaimed with vexation and disappointment in his tone; "day in and day out, nothing but rain, as if out of spite; it's enough to drive one to despair; it simply means ruin for me. Every day greater losses." He clapped his hands together in despair, and continued, turning to Olinka: "That's a life for you! . . . You see, Olga Semyonovna, that's our miserable life . . . it's enough to make one cry. A man gives up all his energy, labour, effort—suffers want, worries night and day trying to improve matters,—with what result? On the one hand, the public, stupid, barbarian; I give them the best operettas, féeries —the most accomplished singers—as though they appreciate, or understand, anything.—What they really want is a cheap circus—trash. . . . On the other hand there's the cursed weather. Rain almost every evening. . . . from the first days of May through the whole month of June— it's awful—. The people stay away.—But I have to pay for my lease just the same—and the artists—

On the morrow, toward evening, again clouds began to lower, and Kukin's bitter complaints were interspersed with almost hysterical laughter.

"Good, good! let it rain! Let the whole Tivoli be drowned in a flood! myself, included!—me and my cursed luck— Let 'em *sue* me— that's right! Let 'em send me to Siberia—yes, to the scaffold! Ha, ha, ha, ha!"—

The next day was identical with the foregoing ones.

Olinka would listen to Kukin in grave silence, and at times she was even on the verge of tears. She finished by loving him for his misfortunes.

Kukin was short, thin, yellow-visaged, with a piping little tenor voice. His face was nearly always a mask of despair. Nevertheless he wakened in Olinka a feeling of genuine, profound affection.

It was her nature to be always in love with someone or other. She could not live without loving. First it was her father; then an aunt who used to come to visit them occasionally. When she was in the High-school she was in love with her French-teacher. She was a quiet, good-hearted, girl, with soft gentle eyes. She was also quite robust. At sight of her plump rosy cheeks, and white neck, and her naïve, good-natured smile, men would say to themselves with a little grin, "Ah, yes, she's the goods!"

Other women could not help interrupting their conversation occasionally, and seize her hand, exclaiming fervidly, "*Du*-sheetsch-ka!" (darling-little-soul!).

The house in which she had lived from the day of her birth, belonged to her by right of inheritance, and was not far from the Tivoli-Garden. In the evening, and during the night, she could hear the music, and see the fireworks—it seemed to her as if Kukin was defying his ill-luck, and coming to close quarters with his inveterate enemy, the indifferent public. Her heart melted at the thought, and she could not sleep. When he returned home in the morning, she would tap on the window of her bedroom to attract his attention, and show him her smiling face through the curtains.

He proposed to her and she accepted him.

When her soft throat and well-rounded shoulders were close to him, he clapped his hands together gleefully and cried, "Dushitchka!"

He was happy. But on the day of the wedding, and later in the evening, it rained, and his face was eloquent with despair.

After the wedding they lived happily together. She acted as cashier in the box-office, and attended to the general management of the Garden. Her plump pink cheeks and naïve, amiable smile shone everywhere, —behind the glass-pane of the box-office, in the wings of the theatre, at the buffet.—She assured her friends that the stage was the most important, useful, and wonderful institution in society. "There is no enjoyment greater and more refined than the theatre; there can be no real education and culture without it", she would say. "But the public do not realise this", she would add; "all they want is cheap circuses. Yesterday we gave "Faust", and almost all the boxes were empty. But if Vanyichka had given some trashy operetta, believe me the theatre would have been packed. To-morrow we are going to produce Orfeo—you'll come, won't you?"

Thus, whatever her husband said of the theatre she repeated. Like him she detested the public for its ignorance, and its indifference to good art. At rehearsal she corrected the actors and made suggestions to the musicians. And when the newspapers gave an unfavourable criticism she actually wept, and went to the editors to plead for fairer treatment.

The actors were fond of her and called her "Dushitchka". If they cheated her out of little loans, occasionally, she did not complain to Kukin, but cried in secret.

In winter they were more prosperous. They leased the Municipal-Theatre for the season, and sub-leased it to stock-companies and other troupes. Olinka grew stouter and was radiant with happiness. But Kukin kept growing thinner and yellower, and complained of financial losses, though business was fairly good all winter. At night he coughed, and she gave him medicinal-tea mixed with raspberries; she also rubbed him with alcohol and wrapped him in soft shawls.

"Poor dear," she would murmur lovingly; "poor, dear, Vanyichka"—

While he was away in Moscow, organising a company for the summer-season, she felt very lonely; she sat at her window and looked out into the court-yard, or gazed at the stars.

Kukin was delayed in Moscow, and wrote her to prepare the Tivoli for the summer.

Late one evening she heard a knocking at the gate-wicket. The sleepy kitchen-maid went stumblingly to open it.

"I have a telegram for you; open!" a voice cried.

Olinka had received other telegrams from her husband, but this time she felt, for some inexplicable reason, almost palsied with nervousness. She opened the telegram with trembling hands, and read the following:

"Ivan Petrovitch died suddenly to-day! we await your wishes. Funeral takes place Tuesday."

"Oh Lord!" she cried, bursting into tears; "Vanyitchka! dear, dear Vanyitchka! —Why has such misfortune befallen me?!— Why did I ever come to love you?!—To whom have you left your Olinka! your poor unfortunate Olinka"—

Kukin was buried in Moscow on Tuesday. Olinka returned home the next day. No sooner did she enter her room than she threw herself on the bed and began to sob so violently that her neighbors heard her.

"Poor Duschitchka", they cried, crossing themselves; "Olga Duschitchka—how she takes on, poor thing"—

Three months later Olinka was on her way home from mass, in deep mourning. Besides her walked Vasilya Andreyitch, manager of Babakov's lumber-yard. He wore a straw hat, a white vest, and a gold chain, and looked more like a landed-proprietor than a merchant.

"Everything has its course, Olga Semyonovna", he was saying with dignified emotion; "if any of those who are dear to us pass away it is God's will; we must remember this and submit with resignation."

When they reached her house he took leave of her.

The rest of the day she was obsessed with the memory of his dignified voice, and she had scarcely closed her eyes when the vision of his black beard obtruded itself upon her.

He had made a deep impression on her, and she, evidently, had affected him likewise. Because, several days later, an elderly lady, a distant acquaintance of hers, came to have tea with Olinka; and no sooner were they both seated at the table than the visitor began to talk of Vasilya Andreyitch. She commended on his good-nature, and his strong stable qualities—the best woman in the world should deem herself lucky if she could marry such a man.

Three days later Andreyitch himself paid Olinka a visit. He stayed only a short while and spoke little, but Olinka, nevertheless, became so enamoured of him that she was feverish all night and could not sleep. In the morning she sent for the elderly lady.

They were presently engaged, and soon after, married.

After their marriage they lived happily. He sat, as usual, in his lumber-yard till noon. Then he would go away on business and she took his place in the office, making out bills and attending to customers.

"Lumber has risen twenty per cent this year", she would tell them; "you see, in former years we dealt with the owners of the town-forest, but now Vasyichka must go as far as Mohilev to buy timber. And the taxes we have to pay! Lord, Lord!" . . . and she would put her hands to her cheeks and slowly shake her head from side to side.

It seemed to her as if she had been in the lumber-business for years and years; that the most important factor in civilisation is the forest; her voice was touchingly intimate as she spoke of logs and beams, rafters and planks and shingles . . . Her very thoughts were the echo of her husband's. If he thought that it was too hot in the house—or that business was bad, she thought the same.

Andreyitch did not like to go out much and she was also in perfect accord with him on this point.

"You are always indoors", her friends would say to her; "you ought to go out once in a while, to the theatre, or circus."

"Vasya and I have no time for the theatre," she would answer with dignity. "We have too much to do to waste time on such frivolous nonsense. What do people find in theatres to amuse them, anyway?"

Every Saturday night they would go to mass, and to early morning mass, on holidays; on the way home they would walk placidly, with pious tranquil faces, while her satin dress rustled genteelly. At home they drank tea, with preserves, and dumplings. In the office the samovar was always prepared, and customers were invited to tea and crullers. Once a week the couple went to the Baths and walked home together, flushed, radiant.

"We have nothing to complain of, thank God," she would tell her acquaintances; "may Heaven be as kind to others as to us" . . . .

When her husband was away on business in some distant province she felt very lonesome. She could not sleep at night and even cried.

Occasionally an army-veterinary, Smernin by name, would come to visit her in the evening. He was a lodger in a wing of the house. He told her stories, or played cards with her; this diverted her.

Most interesting of all, were the stories of his private life. He was married and had a little son, but was divorced from his wife because she had deceived him. Now, he said, he detested her. He was sending her forty roubles a month for the child's bringing-up.

Olinka would sigh and shake her head at these tales, and she pitied Platonich.

"Heaven help you!" she would exclaim at parting, lighting him to the stairs with a candle. "Thank you for keeping me company. . . . May God and the Blessed Virgin keep you!"

She would utter these sentiments in a solemn tone, just like her husband's. When the door had already shut behind him she would call him back and say to him: "Do you know, Vladimir Platonitch, you ought to make up with your wife. You ought to forgive her for your son's sake. . . . You know, he is probably beginning to understand". . . .

When her husband returned from his trip, she told him in low tones about the veterinary and his unhappy married-life. Both sighed, shook their heads, and spoke of the little son who must be longing for his father. And moved by a strange sudden impulse arising from the same current of thought, they both kneeled down before the holy-image, and bowed to the ground in prayer that they might beget children.

And so they lived in serene peace, in love and accord, for six years. One winter-day Vasilya Andreyitch was drinking tea in his lumber-yard. He went out to wait on a customer, and thus caught a cold. He became ill, and although the best physicians were called in, he died in about four months.

And again Olinka was a widow.

"How hast thou left me!" she sobbed as he was buried; "how shall I live without thee, miserable me!—Good-people, take pity on one that is lone and forsaken". . . .

She put on mourning and resolved nevermore to wear hat or gloves. She seldom left the house, and then went only to the church and her husband's grave. Her life was almost monastic.

When the six months had passed she doffed her mourning and opened wide the window-shutters of her house. Occasionally she was seen marketing with her cook, but of her domestic existence little was known. They did notice, however, that she now sat in the garden, sometimes, drinking tea with the veterinary while the latter read the papers to her. And on happening to meet an acquaintance, once, she remarked to her: "In our town there is no veterinary supervision worth mentioning; that's why disease is so prevalent. You see, people get sick from bad milk— or catch diseases from infected cattle and horses. Yes, it's plain enough; domestic animals ought to be looked after quite as carefully as human beings."

She was repeating the veterinary's remarks, echoing, as was her nature, his thoughts and opinions. It was clear that she could not live without masculine friendship for even a year, and she now found her happiness in the wing of her house. Another would have been condemned for this, but of Olinka no one could think evil. For everything in her life was so simple and pure.

They tried to keep their union a secret, but did not succeed. For

Olinka could not keep secrets. When Platonitch's friends, army-men, came to visit him she would speak about the epidemic among horned-beasts, as she poured out the tea, and of conditions in the town-slaughter-houses.

On hearing her speak in this fashion Platonich felt greatly embarrassed. Even more so when his friends began to laugh. He seized her hands, in a rage, and muttered: "I told you—I've told you not to talk about things you don't know!"——

"But Valodytchka—then what shall I talk about?"

And, with her eyes full of tears, she put her arms around him, entreating him not to be angry with her.

And both of them were happy.

But her happiness did not endure. The veterinary left with his regiment and did not return, having been despatched to some distant far-Russian outpost.

Olinka was utterly forsaken. She became thin and ugly. Passers-by in the street no longer looked or smiled at her. Yes—her best years were behind her.

A new and strange life began for her, about which it is sad to think. Toward evening she would sit on the porch and fancy she was hearing the music in the Tivoli, and seeing the blazing sky-rockets. . . . But it excited no emotion in her. She would stare vacantly into the silent courtyard, thinking of nothing, wishing for nothing. At night she would go to sleep and dream only of the empty house and yard. She ate and drank mechanically. Worst of all she was now left opinionless. She observed everything around her without being able to make any comment or to form any opinion, and so could talk about nothing. What a terrible thing it must be to have no power of thinking out an opinion for one's self! . . . You see for instance, a bottle on a table . . . or the rain outside . . . or a peasant on his wagon—But why all these things, and what for—their meaning and significance,—not a trace of understanding, not a shadow of an opinion, for all the money in the world. When Kukin was alive, or Andreyitch, or the veterinary, it was different. But now her mind felt as empty as the court-yard, while her heart was overfilled with bitterness and sorrow.

The house grew blackened with the changing weather of years; the roof became rusty; the outhouse sunken-in; the whole courtyard over-run with weeds. Olinka herself grew old.

One hot July day, toward evening, someone knocked at the gate-wicket. As Olinka approached to open it she stopped, stupefied. Behind the wicket stood the veterinary, now gray, in civilian clothes.

"Darling mine!" she murmured with a quiver of joy. "From where has the Lord brought you?"

"I want to settle here for good," he answered; "I have resigned my commission, and have come here to lead an independent citizen's life, like other townspeople. It's time, too, for my son to go to the gymnasium,* he's grown up now—And do you know,—I have made up with my wife. . . .

"Where is she?" asked Olinka.

"She is with our son in a hotel, while I am looking around for an apartment."

"Why, my dear,—why not move into this house? I won't ask for any rent." . . . She grew very agitated and began to cry.

The very next day repairs were begun on the house; the walls were painted and whitewashed; Olinka, with arms akimbo, walked about busily overseeing all the activities. The old smile shone on her face, and she looked as though rejuvenated. Presently the veterinary's wife, a thin, plain, woman, with clipped hair and the look of a spoiled child, came. With her was Sascha, a boy of ten, small for his age, stout, with clear blue eyes and dimpled cheeks. No sooner had he entered the house than he began chasing the cat, and his merry laughter rang through the house. Olinka chatted with him, and gave him tea—her heart felt warm and pressed-together with joy, as if the lad were her own son, her own flesh and blood.

In the evening, as they sat in the dining-room, while he prepared his lessons, she looked at him and whispered pityingly: "Dove mine, pretty one, you are so smart, and white"——

He was studying aloud,—"An island is a body of land surrounded by water"——

"An island is a body of land surrounded by water"—she repeated after him. This was the first opinion she had uttered with decision after several years of silence and vacuity of thought.

At supper she gave evidence of her renewed mental activity by speaking to Sascha's parents about the difficulties children now experienced in the gymnasium, but that a classic training is nevertheless better than a technical or commercial one, because from the gymnasium paths are open to the professions of medicine, engineering, etc. So Sascha began to attend the gymnasium.

His mother went to visit her sister in Kharkoff but did not come back. His father rode off, somewhere, every day, and occasionally did not return for three days a time. It seemed to Olinka that they had abandoned the lad who must be dying of hunger. So she took him to her living-rooms and gave him one for his own use.

The boy is living with her now over half a year. She goes to his room every morning, and wakes him, calling: "Sascha! get up, darling, it is time for school."

He gets up, dresses, says his prayers, has his breakfast, and goes off

* Equivalent to upper-grade public- and high-school.

to school, knapsack on his shoulder. She follows quietly behind and calls "Sascha!" he turns around and she gives him a candy.

"Go home, auntie", he says—I know how to get to school myself" —She stops and follows him only with her eyes till he is lost in the shadow of the entrance to the school-building.

How she loves him!—She would give him her life—this stranger-lad, with his dimples and blue eyes—Why?—who knows?—

On her way home from market she meets an acquaintance, who greets her smilingly.

"How are you, Duschitchka Olga? how are things, dear?"

After a few words in answer—: "Studying in the gymnasium is very hard these days. Just think: yesterday, in the first class, they had to learn a whole fable by heart. And a Latin translation. And a problem in mathematics. How can a little fellow be expected to learn all that?"

And she continues to talk about the teachers, and lessons, and text-books, echoing Sascha in almost all his words.

Three o'clock they eat together. In the evening they do his lessons together. She puts him to bed, making the sign of the cross devoutly over him, and murmurs a prayer for the boy.

One day she suddenly hears a knock at the gate. She starts up in affright, thinking it may be a telegram from Kharkoff from Sascha's mother asking for the lad, perhaps . . . Oh God!—She is all a-tremble.

But it's only the veterinary—"Thank Heaven!" she murmurs.

❋ ❋ ❋

FEDOR SOLOGUB
(1863-   )

SOLOGUB, the greatest of Russian Symbolists, was born in St. Petersburg, the son of a tailor. On his father's death, his mother became a domestic servant, and Sologub received his education with the help of her employer. He got an appointment as schoolmaster and for twenty-five years followed the profession of pedagogy. His great novel, *The Little Demon*, appeared in 1907, after being hawked about for five years, and met with enormous success. He has also written a number of short stories among which *The White Dog* is a good example of his beautiful, poetic and mystic prose.

The present version, anonymously translated, is reprinted from *The Pagan* Magazine, Copyright, 1916, by permission of the publisher.

THE WHITE DOG

MARIA IVANOVNA has been working several years as pattern-maker in a ladies-tailoring establishment, where she had started as apprentice at an early age.

In the course of time she had become utterly weary of everything pertaining to her work, the patterns, the noise of the sewing-machines, the caprices of customers. . . . She was very irritable, and found fault with everybody. For the apprentices there was no respite from her scolding.

Now it was Tanyichka, the youngest of the working-girls, till recently an apprentice. Tanya did not answer, at first. Then in a gentle, placid voice that made everyone but Maria laugh, she said: "You are a perfect dog, Maria Ivanovna." The older girl, feeling shamefully affronted, exclaimed: "You're a dog yourself!"

Tanya kept on sewing. From time to time she stopped, and repeated calmly, "Yes, you are a dog; you're always barking; you have the muzzle of a dog, and the ears of a dog. Madam will chase you soon, you're such a mad cur, such a low beast."

Tanyichka was a plump, rosy, dainty miss, with a sweet innocent little face, in which cruel cunning was scarcely visible. She looked very naïve, and dressed like a simple apprentice. Her eyes shone bright from under her eyebrows, which arched prettily over her broad white forehead. Her dark chestnut hair was combed flat and smooth, and parted in the middle. Her voice was clear, sweet, seductive. From the distance one would have thought she was saying the most amiable things to Maria Ivanovna.

While the working-girls laughed, the apprentices only ventured to giggle, covering their mouths with their black aprons, and casting apprehensive glances at Maria, who was red with rage.

"You nasty little wretch!" she screamed, "I'll scratch your eyes out!"

Tanya in her bland voice replied: "Your paws aren't long enough. If you keep on barking and snapping, we'll have to muzzle you."

Maria was about to throw herself on the girl, when the mistress of the establishment, a large stout woman, entered, her skirts a-swish.

"Maria Ivanovna!" she exclaimed severely, "what is all this scandalous tumult about?"

"Will you permit her to call me a dog?" Maria answered in a voice trembling with anger.

"For no reason at all she started to yell at me," began Tanya plaintively; "she is forever scolding, no matter what I do."

The mistress looked at her harshly, and said: "Tanyichka, I know you. Do you mean to tell me you didn't begin it? Don't imagine that because you're a master-worker now you can run things here. If you don't put a stop to this fussing I'll tell your mother . . . she'll attend to you!"

Tanya flushed with vexation, but tried to preserve her air of gentle innocence. With perfect self-restraint she answered: "Forgive me, Erinna Petrovna; I'll never do it again. I always try not to provoke her, but she is so harsh. For the least little thing she is ready to pull my hair. I'm just as good a worker as she is. I'm not an errand-girl any more."

"Oh, getting quite important, I see," said the mistress ironically, approaching the girl. Two resounding slaps, accompanied by two exclamations of "Oh! Oh!" from Tanya, broke through the stillness of the room.

Almost sick with anger Maria wended her way homeward. Tanya had touched a very sore spot.

"So I'm a dog," she reflected. "Well, and if I am, is that any of her damned business? Do I study her to see whether she's a snake, or a fox, or anything? Do I sneak after her, and spy around, to see what sort of beast she is? To me she's Tatanya, that's all. There's plenty to be found wrong with everybody; a dog isn't the worst. . . .

It was a bright summer night. A cool, languid breeze stole across from the neighbouring fields to the peaceful streets of the town. The moon rose clear and full; such a moon as shines on wild desert-steppes whose inhabitants, their spirits oppressed with troubled memories of primeval days, howl and moan under its livid light. . . .

And with such a strangely troubled spirit, forgetful of her actual self, tortured with elemental longings, Maria choked back a savage cry that was struggling for utterance in her throat.

She began to undress, but stopped suddenly. What was the use? She knew well she would be unable to sleep.

She walked out of the room. In the corridor she felt the warm loose boards shaking and creaking, while little splinters and grains of sands tickled the soles of her feet.

On the piazza sat Granny Stepanita, a dark withered wrinkled little old woman. She was stooping forward, as if to bask in the light of the moon. Maria sat down on the steps near her, looking up at her sideways. She observed that the old woman's nose was long and curved, like the beak of a bird.

"An old crow," thought Maria, and smiled at the idea, while her eyes lighted up, and her heart felt less oppressed. The furrows of her wilted face vanished in the pale-green moonlight; she became young, nimble, merry, again, as in her girlhood days . . . before the moon's baleful power made her howl and moan at night under the windows of the bath-house. . . .

She moved closer to the old woman, and said gently:

"Granny Stepanita, I've been wanting to ask you a question for a long time."

The old woman turned toward Maria Ivanovna, and in a sharp, craving voice croaked: "Well, my pretty one, ask."

Maria laughed silently. A light breeze passed over her back, and she shivered. Again, in a low voice, she spoke to the old woman. "Granny, it seems to me . . . but I know it can't be true . . . how shall I say it? . . . Don't feel offended, please . . . I mean no harm". . . .

"Well, speak, little one; what is it?"

She looked at Maria with keen, piercing eyes and waited.

"I can't help fancying that you,—you won't feel offended, Granny? . . . you look like a crow."

The old woman turned away and nodded her head silently. She seemed to be recalling something; her head with its beak-like nose kept drooping forward and nodding. Maria thought she must be dozing, nodding, and dozing, and whispering ancient, very ancient, incantations.

In the courtyard it was still; neither dark nor light. Everything seemed as if under a spell, like a vision in a dream, yet too real to be only a dream. . . . Everything was permeated with a strange witchery that oppressed the soul with painful yearning. Countless odours, undistinguishable by day, became sharp and distinct, evoking vague memories of ages long past.

Scarcely audible was the murmur of Stepana. "Yes, a crow, but without wings. And though I caw and caw * no misfortune befalls anyone. I have the gift of prophecy, but they don't heed me. Only, when I see someone whom fate has doomed, I feel an irresistible desire to croak and caw". . . . She suddenly spread out her arms, and in a raucous voice screeched "Caw! Caw!"

Maria shivered.

"Granny, for whom are you cawing?" she asked.

"For you, my pretty one," she answered; "for you."

An uncanny fear settled on Maria, sitting there with the old woman. She got up and returned to her room.

Then she sat down near the window and listened. Two voices were audible from beyond the courtyard.

"She barks and barks," muttered a harsh bass-voice.

"Did you see her, uncle?" rejoined a sweet tenor.

Maria thought it must be the blonde, freckled, curly-haired young fellow who lives in the same house.

* A sign of ill-omen.

There was a pause. But presently the harsh bass again blurted out.

"Sure I saw her; a large white dog, near the bath-house, baying at the moon."

To Maria it sounded like the voice of a black-bearded, low-browed, pig-eyed, heavy-legged fellow.

"What does she bark for?" asked the sweet-voiced tenor.

"Not for any good that I can see," blurted out the other; "and where she comes from I don't know either."

"But what if she's a soul from Purgatory?" the younger one asked.

"You must never turn back," the older one said.

Maria didn't quite understand what he meant, but she listened no further. Human speech mattered little to her now. For the moon showered its light full on her face, calling to her cruelly, irresistibly, with its every beam. Her yearning became so oppressively painful that she could remain seated no longer. She got up and undressed quickly. White, stark-naked, she walked into the corridor and opened the door.

No one was about. She hurried across the courtyard, then through the garden, till she reached the bath-house. The sharp tingle of the cold night-air and the chill ground under her feet quickened her blood.

She lay down in the grass on her belly, raised herself on her elbows, and turned her face toward the pallid moon. Then she uttered a prolonged moaning howl.

"Listen, uncle! do you hear her baying?" exclaimed the fair-haired one, shivering with fear.

"Howling again, damn her!" muttered the harsh bass.

Both rose from the bench where they had been sitting, and walked through the courtyard and garden toward the bath-house. The black-bearded fellow, armed with a rifle, led the way. The other followed timorously, looking back over his shoulder ever and anon.

Near the bath-house a white dog-like form lay cowering, baying at the moon. Her black-crested head was tilted full toward the moon's witching light. Her hind-paws were drawn under her, while her fore-paws rested lightly on the ground.

In the fantastic pale-green moon-glow the dog looked enormous, monstrous, unearthly. The black shock of hair on the crown of her head wound sinuously down her back in an unbraided coil. Her tail was invisible, covered by her limbs, no doubt. From the distance her body looked curiously naked, dimly reflecting the livid moonlight. One could almost fancy it was a woman lying there, moaning and howling. The black-bearded fellow took aim; his companion crossed himself and murmured indistinctly.

There was a loud report. The dog sprang up on her hind paws, howling fearfully, and darted forward, the blood streaming over her naked body. . . . Not a dog but a woman. . . .

The two men, wild with terror, threw themselves on the ground, and began to howl. . . .

❋ ❋ ❋

MAXIM GORKY
(1868-   )

GORKY, despite a youth and young manhood spent in aimless wandering and constant deprivation, attained phenomenal celebrity as a writer before his thirtieth year. From the moment his first two volumes were issued (1898) until 1905 he "aroused, next to Tolstoy, the greatest public interest." While this interest has waned since 1917, principally because of his sympathies with the Soviet government, Gorky has, nevertheless, made important contributions of permanent value to Russian literature.

Her Lover, from *Best Russian Short Stories*, Boni & Liveright, is reprinted by permission of Maxim Gorky.

HER LOVER

AN acquaintance of mine once told me the following story.
When I was a student at Moscow I happened to live alongside one of those ladies whose repute is questionable. She was a Pole, and they called her Teresa. She was a tallish, powerfully-built brunette, with black, bushy eyebrows and a large coarse face as if carved out by a hatchet—the bestial gleam of her dark eyes, her thick bass voice, her cabman-like gait and her immense muscular vigour, worthy of a fishwife, inspired me with horror. I lived on the top flight and her garret was opposite to mine. I never left my door open when I knew her to be at home. But this, after all, was a very rare occurrence. Sometimes I chanced to meet her on the staircase or in the yard, and she would smile upon me with a smile which seemed to me to be sly and cynical. Occasionally, I saw her drunk, with bleary eyes, tousled hair, and a particularly hideous grin. On such occasions she would speak to me.

"How d'ye do, Mr. Student!" and her stupid laugh would still further intensify my loathing of her. I should have liked to have changed my quarters in order to have avoided such encounters and greetings; but my little chamber was a nice one, and there was such a wide view from the window, and it was always so quiet in the street below—so I endured.

And one morning I was sprawling on my couch, trying to find some sort of excuse for not attending my class, when the door opened, and the bass voice of Teresa the loathsome resounded from my threshold:

"Good health to you, Mr. Student!"

"What do you want?" I said. I saw that her face was confused and supplicatory. . . . It was a very unusual sort of face for her.

"Sir! I want to beg a favour of you. Will you grant it me?"

I lay there silent, and thought to myself:

"Gracious! . . . Courage, my boy!"

"I want to send a letter home, that's what it is," she said; her voice was beseeching, soft, timid.

"Deuce take you'" I thought; but up I jumped, sat down at my table, took a sheet of paper, and said: .

"Come here, sit down, and dictate!"

She came, sat down very gingerly on a chair, and looked at me with a guilty look.

"Well, to whom do you want to write?"

"To Boleslav Kashput, at the town of Svieptziana, on the Warsaw Road. . . ."

"Well, fire away!"

"My dear Boles . . . my darling . . . my faithful lover. May the Mother of God protect thee! Thou heart of gold, why hast thou not written for such a long time to thy sorrowing little dove, Teresa?"

I very nearly burst out laughing. "A sorrowing little dove!" more than five feet high, with fists a stone and more in weight, and as black a face as if the little dove had lived all its life in a chimney, and had never once washed itself! Restraining myself somehow, I asked:

"Who is this Bolest?"

"Boles, Mr. Student," she said, as if offended with me for blundering over the name, "he is Boles—my young man."

"Young man!"

"Why are you so surprised, sir? Cannot I, a girl, have a young man?"

She? A girl? Well!

"Oh, why not?" I said. "All things are possible. And has he been your young man long?"

"Six years."

"Oh, ho!" I thought. "Well, let us write your letter. . . ."

And I tell you plainly that I would willingly have changed places with this Boles if his fair correspondent had been not Teresa but something less than she.

"I thank you most heartily, sir, for your kind services," said Teresa to me, with a curtsey. "Perhaps I can show you some service, eh?"

"No, I most humbly thank you all the same."

"Perhaps, sir, your shirts or your trousers may want a little mending?"

I felt that this mastodon in petticoats had made me grow quite red with shame, and I told her pretty sharply that I had no need whatever of her services.

She departed.

A week or two passed away. It was evening. I was sitting at my window whistling and thinking of some expedient for enabling me to get away from myself. I was bored; the weather was dirty. I didn't want to got out, and out of sheer ennui I began a course of self-analysis and reflection. This also was dull enough work, but I didn't care about doing anything else. Then the door opened. Heaven be praised! Some one came in.

"Oh, Mr. Student, you have no pressing business, I hope?"

It was Teresa. Humph!

"No. What is it?"

"I was going to ask you, sir, to write me another letter."

"Very well! To Boles, eh?"

"No, this time it is from him."

"Wha-at?"

"Stupid that I am! It is not for me, Mr. Student, I beg your pardon. It is for a friend of mine, that is to say, not a friend but an acquaintance—a man acquaintance. He has a sweetheart just like me here, Teresa. That's how it is. Will you, write a letter to this Teresa?"

I looked at her—her face was troubled, her fingers were trembling. I was a bit fogged at first—and then I guessed how it was.

"Look here, my lady," I said, "there are no Boleses or Teresas at all, and you've been telling me a pack of lies. Don't you come sneaking about me any longer. I have no wish whatever to cultivate your acquaintance. Do you understand?"

And suddenly she grew strangely terrified and distraught; she began to shift from foot to foot without moving from the place, and spluttered comically, as if she wanted to say something and couldn't. I waited to see what would come of all this, and I saw and felt that, apparently, I had made a great mistake in suspecting her of wishing to draw me from the path of righteousness. It was evidently something very different.

"Mr. Student!" she began, and suddenly, waving her hand, she turned abruptly towards the door and went out. I remained with a very unpleasant feeling in my mind. I listened. Her door was flung violently to—plainly the poor wench was very angry. . . . I thought it over, and resolved to go to her, and, inviting her to come in here, write everything she wanted.

I entered her apartment. I looked round. She was sitting at the table, leaning on her elbows, with her head in her hands.

"Listen to me," I said.

Now, whenever I come to this point in my story, I always feel horribly awkward and idiotic. Well, well!

"Listen to me," I said.

She leaped from her seat, came towards me with flashing eyes, and laying her hands on my shoulders, began to whisper, or rather to hum in her peculiar bass voice:

"Look you, now! It's like this. There's no Boles at all, and there's no Teresa either. But what's that to you? Is it a hard thing for you to draw your pen over paper? Eh? Ah, and *you*, too! Still such a little fair-haired boy! There's nobody at all, neither Boles, nor Teresa, only me. There you have it, and much good may it do you!"

"Pardon me!" said I, altogether flabbergasted by such a reception, "what is it all about? There's no Boles, you say?"

"No. So it is."

"And no Teresa either?"

"And no Teresa. I'm Teresa."

I didn't understand it at all. I fixed my eyes upon her, and tried to make out which of us was taking leave of his or her senses. But she went again to the table, searched about for something, came back to me, and said in an offended tone:

"If it was so hard for you to write to Boles, look, there's your letter, take it! Others will write for me."

I looked. In her hand was my letter to Boles. Phew!

"Listen, Teresa! What is the meaning of all this? Why must you get others to write for you when I have already written it, and you haven't sent it?"

"Sent it where?"

"Why, to this—Boles."

"There's no such person."

I absolutely did not understand it. There was nothing for me but to spit and go. Then she explained.

"What is it?" she said, still offended. "There's no such person, I tell you," and she extended her arms as if she herself did not understand why there should be no such persons. "But I wanted him to be. . . . Am I then not a human creature like the rest of them? Yes, yes, I know, I know, of course. . . . Yet no harm was done to any one by my writing to him that I can see. . . ."

"Pardon me—to whom?"

"To Boles, of course."

"But he doesn't exist."

"Alas! alas! But what if he doesn't? He doesn't exist but he *might!* I write to him, and it looks as if he did exist. And Teresa—that's me, and he replies to me, and then I write to him again. . . ."

I understood at last. And I felt so sick, so miserable, so ashamed, somehow. Alongside of me, not three yards away, lived a human creature who had nobody in the world to treat her kindly, affectionately, and this human being had invented a friend for herself!

"Look, now! you wrote me a letter to Boles, and I gave it to some one else to read it to me; and when they read it to me I listened and fancied that Boles was there. And I asked you to write me a letter from Boles to Teresa—that is to me. When they write such a letter for me, and read it to me, I feel quite sure that Boles is there. And life grows easier for me in consequence."

"Deuce take you for a blockhead!" said I to myself when I heard this.

And from thenceforth, regularly, twice a week, I wrote a letter to Boles, and an answer from Boles to Teresa. I wrote those answers well. . . . She, of course, listened to them, and wept like anything, roared, I should say, with her bass voice. And in return for my thus moving her to tears by real letters from the imaginary Boles, she began to mend the holes I had in my socks, shirts, and other articles of clothing. Subsequently, about three months after this history began, they put her in prison for something or other. No doubt by this time she is dead.

My acquaintance shook the ash from his cigarette, looked pensively up at the sky, and thus concluded:

Well, well, the more a human creature has tasted of bitter things the more it hungers after the sweet things of life. And we, wrapped round in the rags of our virtues, and regarding others through the mist of our self-sufficiency, and persuaded of our universal impeccability, do not understand this.

And the whole thing turns out pretty stupidly—and very cruelly. The fallen classes, we say. And who are the fallen classes, I should like to know? They are, first of all, people with the same bones, flesh, and blood and nerves as ourselves. We have been told this day after day for ages. And we actually listen—and the devil only knows how hideous the whole thing is. Or are we completely depraved by the loud sermonising of humanism? In reality, we also are fallen folks, and, so far as I can see, very deeply fallen into the abyss of self-sufficiency and the conviction of our own superiority. But enough of this. It is all as old as the hills—so old that it is a shame to speak of it. Very old indeed—yes, that's what it is!

ALEXANDER KUPRIN

(1870-   )

KUPRIN began his literary career as a member of the Gorky (Knowledge) school, but he soon became sufficiently significant to assume individual importance. His early training was for the army, and, consequently, his earlier stories treat of military life. He achieved literary prominence with *The Duel*, a novel that appeared immediately after the Russo-Japanese war and was acclaimed by all anti-militarists.

Caprice is one of Kuprin's later stories. The present version, anonymously translated, is reprinted from *The Pagan* Magazine, Copyright, 1916, by permission of the publisher.

CAPRICE

WAVES of light, from three gas chandeliers ornamented with crystal prisms, flooded the theatre-hall of the University. The stage was decorated with flags, palms, and ferns. Near the proscenium stood a highly-polished grand-piano, with open top.

Although the hall seemed quite full, yet people kept streaming in through the entrance-doors. One's eyes grew dizzy watching the seated throng of bald heads, chevelures, black frock-coats, uniforms, ladies' bright dresses . . . slowly waving fans, slim white-gloved hands, agitated gestures . . . and coquettish, feminine, holiday-smiles. . . .

A handsome singer, with a self-assured, almost haughty air, climbed up on the stage and walked up to the proscenium. He wore a frock-coat, with a red gardenia in the lapel. His accompanist followed in his footsteps, unobserved, like a shadow.

The hall grew still. Several student-dandies with badges on their coat-fronts, evidently the arrangement committee, bustled about impatiently in the chill coat-room. They were anxiously awaiting the arrival of Henrietta Ducroix, prima-donna of the Parisian opera, who was a guest-singer in the city for the winter season. Although she had received the deputation of students with charming amiability, and assured them that she would deem it a great honour to sing at their entertainment, nevertheless, the number in which she was to appear had already begun, and she had not yet arrived. Was it possible that she had left them in the lurch? . . . This was the uneasy, though unspoken, thought that flitted through the minds of the half-frozen arrangement committee. They hurried incessantly to the window, pressing their faces against the panes, and staring into the darkness of the wintry night.

The grinding sound of an approaching carriage became audible, and two big carriage-lamps flashed by the window. The committee hurried to the doors, bumping and jostling one another in their eager haste.

It was indeed "the" Ducroix. She blew into the coat-room like a fragrant breeze, smiling to the students, and pointing significantly to her throat, which was wrapped in costly sables; the gesture meant that she wanted to explain why she was late, but could not speak,—the room was so chilly,—for fear of catching cold.

As the Ducroix number was long past, and the disappointed public had given up expecting her, her sudden appearance on the stage came as an overwhelming surprise. Hundreds of youthful throats, and twice as many strong palms, gave her such a long and deafening ovation, that even she, who was used to being idolised by the public, felt a flattered titillation.

She stood on the stage, bent slightly forward, her laughing black eyes slowly passing along the front rows of spectators. She wore a dress of shining white satin, the corsage suspended from her shoulders by narrow ribbons, showing her beautiful arms, her high full bosom,—cut quite low,—and her fair proud neck, looking as if chiselled from warm marble. . . .

Several times the applause subsided, but no sooner did she approach the piano, than a new wave of enthusiasm brought her back to the proscenium. Finally she made a pleading gesture, smiling bewitchingly, and motioned to the piano. The crying and applause gradually died down, while the whole hall gazed at her, fascinated. From the perfectly quiet, but living listening stillness issued the first notes of a Saint-Saens romance.

Alexei Sumiloff, a second-year medical student, stood near the stage leaning against a pillar, and listened to the singing with half-shut eyes. He loved music with a strange, profound, almost sickly passion, hearing it not only with his ears, but feeling it with all his nerves, with every fibre of his being. The sound of the beautiful voice penetrated into the depths of his soul, and reverberated with a sweet shiver through his whole body, so that for moments at a time it seemed to him the voice was singing within him, within his own heart. . . .

The shouting and clapping after every encore caused him almost physical pain. He looked at the audience with an expression of fear, pleading, and suffering.

The Ducroix began a new aria, and Alexei again lowered his eyes, abandoning himself utterly to the waves of glorious sound. He wished yearningly that the singing might never cease. . . .

They forced her to give almost a dozen encores, and let her go only when she put her hand to her throat, smiling sweetly, and shook her head in regretful protest.

Sumiloff heaved a deep, broken sigh, as if he had just awakened from a lovely day-dream.

As he was descending the stairs he felt a sudden tap on the shoulder. He turned around and saw the jurist-student Beeber, his former class-mate in the Gymnasium, the son of a well-known millionaire. Beeber was radiant with happy excitement. He put his arm around Sumiloff's waist and hugged him affectionately, whispering in his ear: "She has consented. The troikas will be here in a few minutes". . . .

"Who has consented?" asked Sumiloff.

"She . . . the Ducroix. . . . We've ordered supper in the European. . . . She refused, at first,—absolutely. . . . But she weakened, after a while. . . . The whole gang'll be there. . . . You're coming along, of course, aren't you?". . . .

"I? . . . No; I don't care to go". . . .

Sumiloff did not belong to Beeber's "crowd," which comprised the golden youth of the University, the sons of substantial proprietors, bankers, and merchants. Beeber was quite conscious of this, but he felt so elated that he wished to bestow his kindness on everybody. He therefore protested at Sumiloff's refusal.

"Oh, come, don't talk nonsense; you must come along. . . . What're your objections?" . . .

Sumiloff, with a rather embarrassed laugh, answered: "You see . . . well,—you know . . . my . . ."

"Oh, never mind! . . . You'll give me the details later. . . . All right, old boy, then you're with us". . . .

By this time the troikas had arrived. . . . The horses neighed and tossed their heads, causing the bells around their necks to jingle merrily. The students disposed themselves pell-mell in the troikas, their voices sounding rather shrill and strained through the frosty night-air.

Sumiloff sat next to Beeber. He was still under the influence of the music, his mind absorbed in a strange revery, while the troikas raced through the deserted streets. The whistling of the wind, the singing of the steel runners over the snow . . . the cries of the students, and the ceaseless jingle of the bells, blended in a wondrous harmony. . . . There were moments when he did not comprehend,—or forgot, rather, —what was happening to him, and where he was being taken.

* * *

At the supper-table all the students crowded around the Ducroix. They kept on kissing her hands, and paying her bold compliments in bad French. Her handsome, fascinating décolleté person intoxicated them more than the champagne . . . their eyes fairly gleamed with desire. . . . She was trying to answer them all at once . . . laughing uproariously as she leaned back on the satin-covered divan . .

slapping her young courtiers lightly on their too-free lips with her fan. . . .

Sumiloff was not used to wine . . . the two goblets he had drunk mounted to his head. He sat in a corner, shielding his eyes from the light of the candelabra, and looking at the Ducroix with enraptured eyes. Inwardly he wondered at the audacity of his colleagues in behaving so familiarly with the great singer . . . at the same time he felt vexed, envious . . . and even jealous. . . .

Sumiloff was by nature timid, and his upbringing in a genteel, conservative family, had increased his bashfulness. His intimate friends called him "young lady." He was indeed, in many ways, quite naïve and child-like, with rare purity of thought and feeling. . . .

"Who is the gentleman over there in the corner?" asked the Ducroix pointing to Alexei. "He seems to be afraid of us, like a mouse. . . . Perhaps the gentleman is a poet. . . . Listen, Mr. Poet. . . . Come here!" exclaimed the singer.

Sumiloff approached with an embarrassed air, and stopped in front of the singer. . . . He felt the blood rushing to his cheeks.

"Mon dieu! Your poet is quite a handsome fellow" . . . laughed the Ducroix. "He looks like a high-school miss. . . . My word! he is actually blushing. . . . How pretty!" . . .

She looked with genuine pleasure at his straight, slim, flexible figure . . . his clear, rosy face covered with a light down . . . his fair, soft hair falling in disorder over his forehead. . . . Suddenly seizing his hand, the singer forced him to sit down near her on the divan.

"Why didn't you want to come over to me?" she asked. "You are too proud. . . . Do you expect a woman to make overtures to you . . . ?"

Alexei was dumb. One of the students, who had never seen him in their company, said, with a malicious little laugh: "Madam, our colleague doesn't understand French". . . .

The remark affected Alexei like the lash of a whip. He turned around sharply, and gazing at the speaker, answered curtly, but in most elegant French, the French which was once the pride of the Russian nobility, and still remains such in some families . . . : "It is quite unnecessary, Monsieur, that you should speak for me, particularly as I have not the honor of being acquainted with you."

While he spoke his brows contracted and his blue eyes flashed.

"Bravo! bravo!" cried the singer, without letting his hand go. "What is your name, mon poète?"

Sumiloff, whose anger had subsided, became bashful again, and blushed as he answered: "Alexei."

"How? how? . . . Ale,—"

Sumiloff repeated the name.

"Oh, that's the same as Alexis. Well, Monsieur Alexis, as a punishment for keeping distant, you'll have to escort me home. I want to take a walk . . . otherwise I'll get up with a headache to-morrow."

The carriage stopped in front of a first-class hotel. Sumiloff assisted her from the carriage and began to take leave of her. She looked at him with a seductive expression of tenderness, and asked: "Won't you see my little den?"

"I should be . . . very . . . happy," he stammered nervously; "but I'm afraid . . . it's so late". . . .

"Come!" she answered. "I want to punish you completely. . . ."

* * *

While she was changing her clothes Alexei gazed about the room. He observed that she had furnished the commonplace apartment with an elegant coquettish chic which only a Parisienne is capable of. The air was scented with a subtle perfume which he had first perceived when he sat beside her in the carriage.

She re-appeared in a loose, white, gold-clasped peignoir. She sat down on a low Turkish divan, arranging the folds of her gown about her feet, and with an imperative gesture motioned Alexei to sit down next to her. He obeyed.

"Closer, closer . . . still closer . . . so! Now, then, let's have a little chat, Monsieur Alexei. In the first place, where did you gain such mastery of the French tongue? You express yourself like a Marquis". . . .

Sumiloff told her that he had had French governesses from his earliest childhood, and that French was the language most spoken in his family.

She then began to overwhelm him with numerous questions about his family, his studies, his friends. . . . He had scarcely time to answer any of them. Suddenly, in a low, soft voice, she asked: "Tell me . . . have you ever loved any woman. . . ."

"Yes. . . . When I was fourteen I was in love with my cousin". . . .

"No one else? . . ."

"No."

"On your word of honour?"

"On my word of honour."

"And you have never loved a woman . . . altogether . . . ?"

He understood, and while he fingered the fringes of the table-cloth nervously, whispered, "No . . . never". . . .

"Don't you love me?" she asked in the same faint whisper, bending so close to him that he felt the warmth of her cheeks. . . . "Look into a person's face when you're spoken to," she exclaimed with playful vexation, seizing his head in her hands and causing him to look into her eyes. . . . Her passionate glance frightened him, at first . . . then saddened him . . . and finally awoke the same passion in him. . . . He bent closer to her . . . her lips were moist, burning. . . .

* * *

"Is Madame Ducroix at home?"

"No."

"Are you sure? . . Perhaps she has returned by this time."

The fat, liveried footman, with his red, swollen, sleepy face rubbed his back against the door-jamb.

"What do you mean, am I sure . . . ? It's my business to know whether she's in or not. Why are you so all-fired anxious about her? . . . You've been running up here these last two weeks bothering me about her. . . . If I tell you she ain't home, she ain't home; that settles it. . . . She don't want to see you . . . d'you understand? . . . That's the whole story. . . ."

The whole story! . . . He felt his heart throbbing painfully, aching with vain longing . . . burning with anger. . . . Why had she done this to him? . . .

LEONID ANDREYEV
(1871-1919)

ANDREYEV, born at Orel of middle-class folk, received his preliminary education in his native city, later attending the University of St. Petersburg. At the end of his first term he attempted suicide for disappointed love, a fact worth remembering in considering Andreyev's work through which runs a current of fatalism and oppressive, horrifying pessimism. He represents the most tragic phase in the evolution of the Russian *Intelligentsia*, and therefore his best writing has a definite place in the nation's literature.

The Lie is a powerful story exemplifying Andreyev's morbidity. The present version is by Maxim Lieber.

THE LIE

I

YOU are lying! I know you are lying!"

"What are you shouting about? Need everyone hear us?"

Here she lied again, for I was not shouting. I was speaking in a quiet tone of voice. I was holding her hand and speaking gently and very quietly while this venomous word "lie" hissed like a snake.

"I love you," she continued, "and you should believe me. Doesn't this convince you?" And she kissed me. But when I wanted to hold her hand and press her close, she had already gone. She left the dark passage and I followed her into the room where a gay party was just ending. How did I know where it was? She had told me I might come there, and I did so, observing couples dancing all night long. No one approached me or addressed me; I was a stranger to all, and sat in a corner near the musicians. The mouth of a great brass trumpet was pointed straight toward me, and someone, concealed in it, kept roaring, and every so often would give a coarse jerky laugh: "Ho! ho! ho!"

From time to time a white, scented cloud came near me. It was she. I know not how she managed to caress me unobserved by others, but for one fleeting little second her shoulder pressed against mine; for one fleeting little second I would lower my eyes and see a white neck in a décolleté white dress. When I raised my eyes I beheld a profile so white, severe and truthful, that it resembled the face of a pensive angel perched on the tombstone of forgotten dead. I saw her eyes. They were large, greedy for light, beautiful and calm. Within their blue setting, the pupils sparkled darkly, and whenever I looked into them they were black and seemed to be unfathomably deep. Perhaps I looked at them for so short a space that my heart failed to beat, but never had I approached so terribly and profoundly the meaning of infinity, and never appreciated it so forcibly. With fear and pain I felt my very life being drawn into her eyes, until I became a stranger to myself, mute and desolate, almost dead. Then she would whirl away, snatching my life with her, and dance again with her tall, haughty, but handsome partner. I studied his every detail, the shape of his shoes, the width of his high shoulders, the even wave of his rebellious locks, while with his indifferent, unseeing glance he seemed to crush me against the wall, until I felt as flat and meaningless as the wall itself.

When they began to snuff the candles, I went up to her and said, "It's time to go. I'll see you home."

She registered surprise. "But I am going with him," and she pointed to the tall and handsome person, who did not even glance at us. She took me into the empty room and kissed me.

"You lie," I said very quietly.

"We shall meet to-morrow. You must come," she replied.

As I drove home, the green frosty morn broke over the high roofs. In the whole street there were only the two of us, the sledge-driver and I. He crouched forward, shielding his face from the wind, and I behind him huddled up as well, covering my face up to my eyes. The sledge-driver had his thoughts and I had mine; while there behind the thick walls thousands of people were sleeping, and they also had their dreams and thoughts. I thought of her and of how she had lied. I thought of death, and it appeared to me that these walls, catching the morning light, already gazed upon me dead; and for that reason they were so cold and upright. I do not know the sledge-driver's thoughts, nor do I know what those concealed by the walls were dreaming. But neither did they know my thoughts or dreams.

So we drove on through the long, straight streets, while the dawn rose over the roofs, and all around us was white and motionless. A sweet-scented cloud approached me and straight into my ear some invisible one laughed: "Ho! ho! ho!"

II

She had lied. She did not come, and I waited for her in vain. A grey, frozen semi-darkness settled down from the dark sky, and I knew not when the twilight merged into evening and when the evening turned into night. It seemed to me all one long night. I paced back and forth, with the same, even, monotonous steps of utter dejection. I went no closer to the tall house, where my beloved dwelt, nor to the glazed front door which reflected the yellow shade of its roof, but I walked up and down on the opposite side of the street, with the same regular strides—backwards and forwards, backwards and forwards. Going forward I never took my eye off the glazed door, and when turning back, I stopped often and turned my head, and then the snow pricked my face with its sharp needles. And those needles were so long, so sharp, so cold, that they penetrated to my very heart and pierced it with weariness and anger at my hopeless waiting. From the light north to the dark south the cold wind howled and whistled, played over the icy roofs, and racing down, lashed my face with sharp little snowflakes, and rattled the glass of the empty street lamps, in which the desolate yellow flame shivered with cold and bent before the wind. I felt sorry for the desolate flame that lived only by night, and I thought that, should I go away, all life would end in this street, and only the snowflakes would flurry through the empty space, and the yellow flame would continue to shiver and flicker in its solitude and cold.

I waited for her, but she did not come. And it seemed to me that the desolate flame and I were alike, except that my lamp was not empty, for people did occasionally appear in that space that I went on measuring with my steps. They grew up silently behind me, big and dark, passed me, and, suddenly, like grim phantoms, vanished round the corner of the white building. Then again they would emerge from round the corner, come up to me, and then slowly melt away in the vast distance mist-laden by the silently falling snow. Bundled up, formless and silent, they so resembled each other and myself, that it appeared as if scores of people were walking backwards and forwards, as I was, waiting, shivering and silent, and thinking their own enigmatic and melancholy thoughts.

I waited for her, but she did not come. I do not know why I did not cry out and weep for pain. I do not know why I laughed and was happy, and bent my fingers as if they were claws, and seemed to clutch in them that little venemous creature hissing like a snake,—the lie. It coiled round my arms and bit my heart until my head grew dizzy with its poison. Everything was a lie. The boundary disappeared between the time I had not yet been born and the time I began to live, and I thought that I had always been alive, or else never before. And always, before I lived and when I began to live, she had ruled over me. And it seemed strange that she had a name and a body, and that her existence had a beginning and an end. She had no name, she was always the one who lies, and always made you wait eternally and never came. I don't know why, but I laughed, and the sharp needles pierced my heart, and some invisible one laughed into my ear: "Ho! ho! ho!"

Opening my eyes, I glanced at the lighted windows of the big house, and they quietly spoke to me with their blue and red tongues: "She is deceiving you now. While you are wandering about, waiting and suffering, she, lovely, bright and treacherous, is in here listening to the whispers of the tall, handsome man who despises you. If you were to rush in and kill her, you would do a good deed, for you would kill a lie."

I tightly clenched the hand in which I held the knife, and, laughing, answered: "Yes, I will kill her."

But the windows regarded me mournfully and added sadly, "You will never slay her. Never! because the weapon in your hand is as much a lie as are her kisses."

The silent shadows had long ago disappeared, and I was left alone in that cold spot,—I and the desolate tongues of flame shivering with cold and despair. In the neighbouring church belfry the clock began to strike, and its melancholy, metallic sound quivered and sobbed, flying out into space and getting lost in furiously whirling snowflakes. I began to count the strokes and was seized by a fit of laughter: the clock struck fifteen! The belfry was old, and so was the clock, and although it showed the correct time, it struck haphazardly, occasionally so often, that the old bell-ringer had to climb up to stop the spasmodic strokes of the tongue with his hand. For whom did those quivering, melancholy sounds, embraced and strangled by the frosty darkness, tell a lie? So pitiful and grotesque was that useless lie.

With the last lying sounds of the clock the glazed door slammed, and the tall man came down the steps. I saw only his back, but I recognised it, for I had seen him only last evening, proud and contemptuous. I recognised his step, and it was lighter, more assured than last evening. I too had thus often left this house. He had that walk assumed by men who have just been kissed by the lying lips of a woman.

III

I threatened, I implored, I ground my teeth.

"Tell me the truth!"

But with a face as cold as snow, her eyebrows raised in surprise, her dark, unfathomable eyes shining mysterious and passionless, she assured me, "I am not lying to you."

She knew that I could not prove she lied, and that all my heavy, massive creation of torturing thoughts would be dissipated by one word from her,—one lying word. I waited for it, and it came from her lips, sparkling on the surface with the colours of truth, but dark in its depths: "I love you! Am I not all yours?"

We were far from the town, and the snowclad fields looked in through the dark windows. Above them was darkness, and around them was darkness, thick, motionless, silent, but the fields gleamed with their own latent light, like the face of a corpse in the dark. Just one candle threw its light over the well-heated room, and even on its reddish flame there appeared the pallid reflection of the dead fields.

"I want to know the truth, however sad it may be. Perhaps I shall die when I know it, but death is more welcome than life without truth. There is a lie in your kisses, falsehood in your eyes. Tell me the truth, and I will leave you forever," I said. But she was silent, and her coldly searching glance penetrated my heart, drew out my soul, and studied it with a strange curiosity. And I cried out, "Answer, or I will kill you!"

"Kill me," she calmly replied. "Sometimes life is so wearisome. But you can not get truth by threats."

And then I fell on my knees, clasped her hand, wept, and implored for pity and the truth.

"Poor fellow," said she, putting her hand on my head, "poor fellow!"

"Have pity," I prayed, "I yearn for the truth."

And as I looked at her smooth forehead, I thought that truth was there behind that slender partition. I madly wanted to break the skull to find the truth. And there behind a white bosom beat her heart, and I madly wanted to tear that bosom with my nails, to see, if only for once, an exposed human heart. And the pointed yellow flame of the candle, fast expiring, was motionless. The walls seemed to fall away into space in the growing darkness. It was so sad, so desolate, so frightful.

"Poor fellow," she said, "poor fellow!"

And the yellow flame of the candle flickered spasmodically, turned blue, and then went out. Darkness enveloped us. I could not see her face nor her eyes, for her arms had clasped my head, and I no longer felt the lie. I shut my eyes, and neither thought nor lived, but merely absorbed the touch of her hands, and it seemed to me true. And in the darkness her faint whisper sounded strange and fearsome: "Put your arms about me. I am afraid!"

Then again there was silence, and again the faint whisper filled with fear.

"You want the truth—but do I know it? Oh, how I wish I knew it. Protect me,—oh, I'm so frightened!"

I opened my eyes. The pale darkness of the room fled from the tall windows, gathered near the walls and hid itself in the corners, and silently there looked in through the windows some huge and deadly white thing. It seemed as if someone's dead eyes were searching for us, and enfolding us in their icy stare. Shivering we pressed close together, while she whispered, "Oh, I'm so frightened!"

IV

I killed her.

I killed her, and when she lay a flat and lifeless mass at the window, beyond which gleamed the white fields, I put my foot on her corpse and laughed. It was not the laugh of a madman; oh, no! I laughed because my breast heaved evenly and lightly, because within it reigned peace and happiness, and from my heart had fallen the worm that had been gnawing it. Bending down I looked into her dead eyes. Large eyes, greedy for light, they remained open, and resembled the eyes of a wax doll, round, dull eyes that seemed to be covered with mica. I could touch them with my fingers, open and shut them, and I was not afraid, because in those black unfathomable pupils there no longer lived the demon of lies and doubt, that so long had insatiably sucked my blood.

When they arrested me I laughed; and to those who seized me, this seemed terribly barbaric. They turned from me in disgust and drew back. Others, with imprecations on their lips, advanced straight towards me; but when they caught my joyful glance, their faces paled and their feet were rooted to the ground.

"Madman!" they exclaimed, and this word seemed to ease them, because it helped to solve the enigma,—how I, a lover, could kill my beloved, and yet laugh. Only one fat and jolly looking individual called me by another name. It came as a blow and darkened the light in my eyes.

"Poor man," he said compassionately, without anger, for he was fat and jolly. "Poor man!"

"Don't!" I cried out. "Don't call me that!"

I don't know why I flung at him. I certainly did not want to kill him, or even touch him, but all these frightened people who considered me a madman and a criminal became all the more alarmed, and screamed out so, that it made me laugh again.

When they led me out of the room where the corpse lay, I repeated loudly and obstinately, looking at the fat, jolly man, "I am happy, happy!"

And that was true.

V

Once, in my childhood, I saw a panther in the zoological gardens that struck my imagination and long held my thoughts. He was not like the other beasts who stupidly dozed or viciously gazed at the visitors. He walked about from corner to corner, in a straight line, with mathematical precision, each time turning at the same spot, each time brushing his sleek fur against the same bar of his cage. His sharp, voracious head was bent down, and his eyes looked straight before him, never once turning aside. The livelong day crowds chattered before his cage, but he kept pacing back and forth, never once so much as glancing at the spectators. A few in the crowd smiled, but most of them regarded seriously, even sadly this living picture of dull, dejected brooding, and departed with a sigh. And as they went away, they turned once more and glanced at him inquiringly, incomprehensibly, feeling there was something in common between their own human state and that of this imprisoned beast. And when, after I had grown up, people or books mentioned eternity, I recalled the panther, and I seemed to realise the significance of eternity and its tortures.

I became such a panther in my stone cage. I walked and thought. I walked in one line across my cage from corner to corner, and my thoughts travelled along one short line, so heavily that it seemed as if I were carrying not merely a head but a whole world on my shoulders. These thoughts consisted of but one word, but what a vast, what a torturing, what a destructive word!

"Lie!" was the word.

Again it darted forth hissing from all the corners, and coiled itself about my soul; but it had ceased to be a little snake, it had grown into a great, fierce, gleaming serpent, and it stung me and smothered me in its iron coils. And when I shrieked out with pain, as though my whole breast were swarming with reptiles, I could only utter that repulsive, hissing-like sound: "Lie!"

And as I walked with my thoughts, the smooth, grey asphalt of the floor changed before my eyes into a grey, transparent abyss. My feet ceased to feel the touch of the floor, and I imagined I was floating at an immeasurable height above the misty darkness. And when my bosom heaved forth its hissing groan, there, from below, from under that impenetrable shroud, there slowly rose a horrible echo, so slowly and feebly, as though it were travelling through a thousand years, and in each particle of fog had lost some of its strength. I understood that there, below, it was whistling like the wind that tears down trees, but it reached my ears in one short whispered word: "Lie!"

This mean whisper wrought me into a rage, and I stamped on the floor and screamed: "There is no lie! I've killed the lie!"

I purposely turned away, for I knew what it would answer, and slowly, from the bottomless abyss, came the reply: "Lie!"

As you see, I had made a terrible mistake. I had killed the woman, but had made the lie immortal. Don't kill a woman until by prayer, torture and fire you have torn the truth from her soul.

So I thought as I paced from corner to corner of my cell.

VI

Dark and dreadful is the place where she has carried the truth, and the lie—and there I am going. At the very throne of Satan I shall clutch her, and, falling on my knees, will weep and say, "Tell me the truth!"

But God! oh, God! This too is a lie. There is darkness there, and emptiness of the centuries, of infinity, but she is not there,—she is nowhere. But the lie has remained. It is immortal. I feel it in every atom of the air, and when I breathe, it enters my breast with hisses and tears it—tears it!

Oh! What madness it is for a man to seek the truth! What anguish!

Help! Save me!

POLAND

Introduction

NOT until comparatively modern times has there been any worthy prose contribution to Polish literature which, as regards poetry, has had a distinguished tradition going back to its golden age in the last part of the sixteenth century. Mickiewicz (1798-1855) the greatest poet of the romantic period, overshadowed all preceding poets in Poland. Krasiński, conceded to rank next in importance, wrote some short stories besides his famous poems and dramas.

Midway between romanticism and realism stands Vincent Pol (1807-1872), a curious mixture of poet prosateur and geographer. Kraszewski is a prolific writer of political and historical novels. Greater than Kraszewski in the field of the novel is Sienkiewicz, one of the few Polish novelists to have won a world reputation.

Eliza Orzeszkowa is one of the most popular of recent writers. Zeromski and Reymont, both distinguished novelists, died in 1925. Reymont won the Nobel Prize for literature just before his death. Of the many contemporary writers who have shown promise may be mentioned Mme. Rygier-Nalkowska and Gustav Danilowski, both followers of Zeromski whose work is coloured by a deep pessimism and "futility of individual effort"; and Waclaw Berent, a novelist of rare talent.

❊ ❊ ❊

ZYGMUNT KRASIŃSKI
(1812-1859)

KRASIŃSKY, born in Paris, is one of the most noted of modern Polish authors. His life was embittered by the fact that his father, at one time a general in Napoleon's army, had become unpopular among the Poles by his adherence to the Russian government. His best known work is *The Undivine Comedy*, a powerful and vigorous poem enveloped in mysticism, a quality that pervades most of his work and makes him the representative of nationalistic-mystic tendencies. In *A Legend* there is more hopefulness expressed—at least for the spiritual future of Poland—than Krasiński ordinarily manifested in his other work.

The present version, by Prof. Šarka Hrbkova, has been prepared for this volume.

A LEGEND

IT seemed to me that precisely during the vigil at the Birth of our Lord I emerged from the gates of Rome and walked along the Campanile. The pagan graves were warming themselves in the rays of the sun—it was early morn—and the sky as clear and the plain as sad as in ages past.

I walked all day long borne by the strength of the soul. The ancient aqueducts ran along beside me but I went on beyond. The ivy, as in the pictured models of the manger of Christ, rustled on the walls of the ancient ruins. Above me swept flocks of white birds—before me on the ground wriggled a glistening snake. The roar of the ocean began to call me!

And when I stood on the highest summit of the earth, when I beheld the sea the sun was already setting—and far out over the water stood a black blot like a living thing, constantly growing larger and flying landward towards me—until it increased to a huge size when the sun had faded completely and twilight had begun to descend.

It was a great black ship, without sails or masts—dashing the waves into foam with its timbers. From the centre of the ship a column of smoke belched forth gliding back into the infinite.

Ever more darkly—like an inky spectre it circled in the expanse with thunderous roar—when two night lights gleamed before it on the ocean and a voice sounded from the deck, "Is this the last night of the vigil of the Birth of our Lord?"

Alarmed in spirit I answered from my height, "It is true, to-day is the vigil." And at once the ship stopped at the very edge, the pale stream enveloped her, and slack and sparks were emitted from her sides. In the ruddy glow rapidly declining—for a moment the deck gleamed brightly. Figures stood there in crimson caps and white cloaks—I heard the jangling of chains.—It seemed to me that a heavy long bridge was lowered from the ship to the shore—and upon it in the darkness the figures came rushing out directing their steps toward me.

And when they were very close, they asked as with one voice, "Which way is the road that leads to Rome?" I answered, "There is no road. This is a wilderness." And they answered, "Then lead us." And when I hesitated, they again spoke in low, sad tones, "We are what is left of the Polish nobility, an angel appeared to us, an angel not unlike those whom our forefathers saw, for he had wings without brilliance and a mourning veil over his brow—but we know he was sent from heaven, and he it was who directed us hither. We have been sailing for a long time, the gales have been terrific and many difficulties have we had at sea but the will of the Lord shall be accomplished if to-day at midnight, we arrive at the basilica of St. Peter."

Thereupon I said to them, "Follow me, thou unhappy people." And I turned to go back from the shore of the ocean toward the city, trembling and praying as if I were crossing a cemetery and as if the dead were rising up and following me.

A wind arose and no more clouds were visible. Everywhere in the deep dark sky the stars were twinkling, while below was a vast black plain! Only now and then we passed dusky mounds or a pile of grey ruins or mayhap the gates of an aqueduct. In the distance one could hear the rustle of tall reeds—above at times sounded the shriek of a night bird, and near by, somewhere among the sunken graves came the murmurings from beneath the earth!

They strode along behind me—I could feel on my back their heavy breathing—I moved on swiftly for they were in haste—I could hear the plumes on their caps flutter in the breeze and the very folds of their capes puff up with the wind!

It seemed to me that I beheld a wandering light in the distance—and immediately a second and a third. When I advanced I beheld a great number of lights on the plain moving rapidly from all sides in one direction. And the sound of many voices began to hum in the wilderness.

When I came nearer I saw a great body of pilgrims passing over the Campanile with torches in their hands. The glow which they cast went with them between two solid walls of blackness but the light glistened on the tall crosses, pictures of saints and on the flags of various nations which fluttered in the breezes.

Into the very centre of the multitudes I lead my own group, and at that instant I beheld the melancholy features of those who followed me. A strange ecstasy was in their eyes but it was not the lustre of life. They carried swords on which they leaned as did the other pilgrims upon their staffs.

Hardly had I entered with them into the light of the torches when it seemed to me that the masses stood still asking, "Who are you and whence do you come?"

They paused and a strange smile passed over their lips while they answered as one, "Is there no longer anyone on this earth who recognises us?"

A low hum constantly growing in strength filled the air and it seemed to me that all the bands of pilgrims of a sudden cried out, "We know you—you are the last heroes of the earth."

Then they marched forward saying, "We saw an angel with a black band on his brow who commanded us to hasten to Rome. Tell us, did any of you also hear that voice?"

In the multitude a great tumult arose in answer, "Amen,—that same angel bade us leave our homes—his voice increased in the night about our heads and he gave us no peace. In these days, he said, Christ would be born for the last time at the grave of Peter and from that moment nothing shall be born nor nothing shall die on earth."

And the multitude became silent and stood as if startled by its own words.

The Poles were the first to move onward—throwing back their white capes over their shoulders—. From all sides of the Campanile a greater and greater mass of pilgrims crowded forward. Already we saw the battlements of the city—already we heard the harmony of the bells—sounding more clearly the nearer we came.

On the gates, on the towers, festoons of lights appeared and more loudly echoed the bells as one after another awoke to join the rest until soon all the church bells of Rome resounded.

It seemed to me that the night was transformed into white day. I did not in the least recognise the streets from which I had departed in the morning. There where once ruins projected frequented only by owls —baskets of blooming flowers and glowing lamps now swung. The Roman populace came forth in throngs shouting: "Let us rejoice—rejoice ye all, for today Christ is born to us."

And when they beheld the Polish nobles entering the gates and the stream of pilgrims behind them gaily springing forward they cried out: "Why are you so sad, you, our guests? If the long voyage has wearied you, moisten your lips with the juice of the orange. Remove your white caps and your black cloaks—behold, here are clusters of myrtle—here, camelias, we offer them to you to adorn your temples with garlands!"

But in silence and with furrowed brows, the Poles advanced through their midst and marching said to me, "Where is the basilica of Peter? We must hasten and our hearts are downcast. Is the midnight hour close in truth?"

I lead them across the Forum. It seemed to me that the Amphitheatre of Flavianus—recently empty, dark and ancient—stood now like a giant of resplendent light from its base to its massive shields gleaming with lamps so that every ivy leaf upon them could be plainly distinguished. Women and children in glistening garments promenaded through various portions of the structure and clapped their hands in welcome to us who approached.

Every arch in the Forum and every column glowed and blazed. At the summit a wall of golden flames, the Capitol, shone forth. The very stars in heaven had grown pallid before the great flood of brilliance.

The people continued to shout: "Hosanna, Hosanna!" And the pilgrims sang psalms of penitence. The masses perpetually surged hither and thither, sounding guitars, scattering flaring sparks in the air, and through the centre of all this sea we proceeded in garments of blackness, slowly, in sorrow of soul.

From every balcony, every roof, from the streets, violets and roses descended upon us.

Already the bell of the Capitol boomed far behind us, and before us in the wide space sounded the bell of St. Peter. At last it rang independently, more sonorously than all the rest.

We hastened in the direction of that voice, we crossed the bridge over the Tiber, the houses on its banks standing out like quiet conflagrations, the river like a ribbon of flame. The angel palace bristled with cannon, every instant one of them blazed forth and thundered.

We turned and entered the courtyard of St. Peter's. Its dome was hung with thousands of scarlet lamps, the cross at its summit like a diamond, the pillars at either side of the court as if of twisted fires. In the centre were two fountains like two flowing rainbows, and I beheld a vast mass of people waiting there. The doors of the cathedral stood open and within an infinitude of blazing brightness.

While it was possible the Poles and the other pilgrims advanced but at the steps and at the base of the portico, the throng closed up the way. Pausing therefore, they demanded a passageway, but ever more closely from the front, from the rear and from the sides, the crowds pressed in upon them.

Then the voices of the Romans arose: "Are we not the first, has not this church been our own for ages upon ages?" And among the pilgrims were heard other voices saying: "Up to this time the Polish nobles have lead the way for us, shall they be allowed to enter the holy place before us?"

And I looked and saw that the Poles had lifted their swords in token that they would defend themselves. With a pure fire their blades flashed in the clear air!

But at that instant on the battlements of the basilica high above the heads of the people appeared a figure in royal purple which spoke in thunderous tones: "Let pass those who for the Catholic faith ransomed another nation from death and later for that faith perished themselves. Give passageway to the dead, first of all!" And the cardinal extended his hand toward the right and toward the left as if he were dividing the multitude, and down below the masses did indeed separate and make way—which, seeing, he turned back into the building.

And together with the Poles I mounted the steps and advanced directly through the portico into the church and on up to the chief altar before the lamps which burn at the tomb of Peter. Here they paused, and removing their crimson caps, they unfastened their white capes and kneeling, worshipped, holding their unsheathed weapons in hand.

The snowy gleam of marble shone in the vast cathedral, the silvery transparent smoke of the incense rose to the arched dome and floated above us. On the mosaic floor lay scattered flowers and palms. From all the chapels echoed choirs of gentle joyful voices and off in the distance around the doors, the space began to fill. The pilgrims marched through that world of song and light just as they did through the city, dark and unrejoicing. A stream of Romans rolled into the basilica, noisily. And when each group had taken its place under its own banner, at its own altar, then the great expanse became silent again, as if it were a vast vacant space. The songs in the chapels were stilled and from the Vatican echoed the sounds of trumpets giving sign that the people were approaching.

Through the centre of the church proceeded all the friars and monks of Rome, the elders one after another, some in white robes, others in grey horse-hair cloth, with crucifixes in their hands. Then came the bishops wearing their mitres and silvery trains and after them the cardinals in splendid crimson, around them priests in dalmatics and troops of children in white garments, carrying wine, incense and wreaths.

And when the procession arrived at the main altar where the crowds separated forming a clear path between walls of living people who now suddenly fell to their knees, an aged grey-haired man walked slowly forward, wearing on his head a triple crown and a white vestment over his golden surplice.

At a great distance behind him remained the soldiers, attendants and the throne borne by priests. He stood alone in the centre of the throng and of the cathedral, alone he ascended the main altar. It seemed to me, that each step took an interminable length of time and that he never would come to us.

And as he thus advanced in the centre of those bowing before him touching their foreheads to the ground, he closed his eyes at times as if seeking relief from so many lights. Now and then he essayed to make but tremblingly left unfinished the sign of his blessing, until, pausing, he sighed and lifted up his hands to heaven, but he was unable to hold them upraised—they sank exhaustedly!

At his deep drawn sigh, the people lifted their heads. The sorrow of their father caused all to grow pale and then, I noted, that from the main altar one of the cardinals had turned away, the same one who had ordered that we should be admitted. With grave step, he descended towards the aged eldest of elders and extended his hand, turning shining eyes upon the grave of Peter. The aged man advanced a few steps but with lingering difficulty. The cardinal shook the rings of his long hair with a sidelong motion giving signal to those who had remained in the rear who at once hastened forward carrying the golden throne.

Then the father who is on earth grasped the arm of the throne with his pallid hand and seated himself. Quickly they lifted him up and the trumpets in the church again thundered forth. The cardinal walked along beside the throne. The people lifted themselves from the floor, the bell began to ring and twelve times the arched dome quivered. Around the main altar a cloud of incense arose and from it the pope ascended the steps as the cardinal announced: "Christ is born."

From amid the group of pilgrims at once a voice cried out mournfully: "Will not the words of the angel be borne out in truth that Christ is born for the last time?"

And the Roman people shout out angrily: "Who dares blaspheme in the church of Peter?"

One of the Polish nobles stepped forth crying: "They are not blaspheming. We do not fear you—they speak the truth—I myself and my brethren beheld the angel of sorrow."

The cardinal again like a prince of power waved his hand and said, "Peace unto the people of good will, pray ye now for the mass has begun —the time is short and today there must be prayers on earth as in heaven."

We all began to pray awaiting great things. And our holy father sat before us on the throne.

From the chapels again arose voices like angels' choirs, full of heavenly rapture. A portion of the night passed and white-robed priests came and offered their hands to our father. He descended from the throne and approached the altar taking the chalice in his hands, for the moment had come for the holy sacrifice. The cardinal poured wine into the chalice.

Just at the moment the chalice was being uplifted, when all had fallen to their knees, a voice from the air was heard which uttered, "I live!" And when, aquiver, we raised our heads, we beheld a large figure with head bent upon the central gate, slowly dissolving—ever becoming more misty—the hands bloody, the feet bleeding, but the figure itself of snowy whiteness—and—melting like snow—it vanished.

Then the cardinal, as the pope holding the chalice in his hands, still hesitated, himself uttered the words: "Ite, missa est!" and then he cried in a powerful voice, "The times are fulfilled" and rending the purple on his breast, he extended his hand toward the grave of Peter saying, "Awake and speak!"

From every lamp above the tomb a fiery tongue burst forth and a wreath of flames swung over the dark sepulcher. From the depths of that darkness, a body arose with hands upstretched to the dome, and standing buried in the tomb to its breast, it shrieked, "Woe!"

After this outcry it seemed to all of us that the vaulted arch of the dome cracked for the first time.

The cardinal then said, "Peter, do you recognise me?"

And the body answered, "Your head rested on the bosom of the Master at the last supper and you have never perished from the earth."

The cardinal responded, "Now it is commanded to me to linger among human beings and to embrace the earth and hold it to my bosom as the Master held mine that last night of His life on earth."

And the body replied, "Do as you have been commanded."

Then the cardinal again waved his hands as with the authority of a prince, and the body repeated: "Woe be unto me!" and fell with a terrible crash as into an abyss, back into its grave. Above, the vaulted arches began anew to shiver and break.

Horror overwhelmed us all. Only the Polish nobles gazed with dauntless eyes, leaning upon their swords.

The pope in his triple crown had knelt down on the steps of the altar and, as immovable as a statue, continued kneeling.

The cardinal spoke: "Go forth, all of you—you and you and you,—lest some of you perish beneath the ruins of these walls."

The people answered from all sides, "Lead us—you—under whose protection we have this day entered."

A cry of terror arose for the arches ever more thunderously burst into fissures, the pillars and columns all about shook and lamps were shattered and extinguished by a great wind.

Then spoke the cardinal, "Father—mine—do you wish to remain here?"

And the aged man lifting his hands to his crown, answered in a sorrowful voice: "I wish to die here—leave me, my son."

All the people heard these words, and shrieked, "Run—let us run away!"

And the Romans were the first to recover and began to flee.

And each troop or band moved from its altar with its banner and made haste to fly away.

Then the cardinal, kneeling at last, pressed his lips to the old man's brow and made the sign of a blessing around his crown like a garland of livid light in the air, then he descended and walked toward the gate of the church with a marvellous glow encircling his brow. The entire church was twisted and bent as a dying body in the last throes, but he, with uplifted hand, stayed the cracking, tumbling vault above the people and stood watching until the last one of them had gone.

And departing he said to the Polish nobles, "People, follow after me."

But these did not answer.

He turned his head back again and said, "Follow after me."

They did not move.

When he had reached the gate, driving the people before him like a shepherd, he beckoned them for the last time with his hand.

But they only lifted up their swords as if with their edges, they would hold up the falling walls and they cried out altogether. "We shall not desert that aged man—it is bitter, indeed, to die all alone—and who should die with him if not we?—Go you, all—we do not know how to run away."

The cardinal stopped on the very threshold and from a distance made to them the sign of his blessing and of the garland of livid light. In his eyes that moment a tear glistened as he said, "Yet a moment more and you perish."

But in that moment they were hastening to the main altar to offer a hand to the kneeling and dying. They advanced in their white caps and in the gleaming of their swords—and the four twisted columns of the altar snapped like a split tree and came crashing down—even the metal canopy dropped in ruins—the entire white cupola like a sinking world, fell to the ground.

And all the porticoes, even the palace of the Vatican and the colonnade in the court cracked and burst, falling into dust. Both of the fountains like two white doves, fell to the ground perishing. The populace rushed ever farther on like a sea forced from its shores and, it seemed that it was already morn, though the sun had not yet risen. But I seemed to see only the morning star above a pile of ruins, as high, as immense as had formerly been the basilica of Peter.

Upon this gigantic mountain the cardinal ascended and it seemed that I followed after him carried on by strength of soul.

When he had attained the summit, he seated himself there as on a throne and gazed at the world. His purple robes dropped from his body and he was transformed into a figure of white ensilvered by the mild glow. In his hands was a book and over it he bent his head reading attentively.

His face was entranced with an expression of love and fulness of peace.

I approached him and said just as the sun began to rise: "Sir, is it true that Christ was born for the last time yesterday in that church which to-day is no more?"

With a strange smile and without lifting his eyes from his book, he responded, "From the time of Christ none are born and none die on this earth."

Hearing this I lost my great fear and asked, "Sir, and those whom I led thither yesterday, shall they lie forever under those ruins,—all those dead around the aged dead man?"

And the white saint answered me, "Fear not for them. Because they performed the last service for him, God will reward them—for those who pass out of life are like those who are entering upon it, the dead just as the living are of God. Instead of loss—they gain—it will be better for them and for the sons of their sons."

And when I understood, I rejoiced and my soul awakened.

ELIZA ORZESZKOWA
(1843-1910)

ELIZA ORZESZKOWA and Marie Konopnicka are the leading Polish women writers of the modern period. Orzeszkowa occupied herself chiefly with the problems of women in her novels and shorter stories. Her zealous demand for educational opportunities for women is best worked out in her novels *Pan Grab* and *Memories of Vaclav and Marta*. She has espoused the cause of the proletariat and has particularly set forth the rights of the peasant class whose story she tells most appealingly in her popular novels *Among Peasants and Gentlemen, Cham, The Lowlands* and other less extensive works. She continues to have an ever widening circle of readers.

Do You Remember?, one of her lovely stories, appears here for the first time in English. It is translated for this volume by Prof. Šarka Hrbkova.

DO YOU REMEMBER?

HE was a highly esteemed man and had once regarded himself as fortunate. Even though he did not have very far to go to reach his fiftieth year, he had preserved his dark thick hair, his smooth skin, his easy polished movements. And because for thirty years he had followed a set purpose he had attained a high position and had everything that he desired.

"How far I have travelled!" he sometimes said to himself. "My mother did not rock me in a golden cradle. Father and mother! They were poor though not beggars! What a life they led!—Perpetual worry, trouble, toil! I couldn't live three years in that fashion! From such depths to rise as high as I have—it is art! I had to suffer it all, though, to reach this height—and it came to pass!—and how successfully! What is lacking?"—

But for the past two years or so he was less satisfied and gay. Something ailed him though he himself could not define it. He sought help of doctors, he visited mineral springs and health resorts, he tried the special baths, gymnastics—nothing relieved him. He felt neither pain nor weakness but something was wrong with him. Even his boon companions saw that there was something amiss. On his brow formerly so smooth, wrinkles appeared, at first as fine as a silk thread but constantly growing deeper—

"What has happened to him?" his friends asked.

"What is the matter with me?" he asked himself. And he answered his own query and that of his friends by saying, "How do I know? Either the world has changed or I have become stupid.   I myself do not know what ails me!"—

As customarily, he was again in the theatre to-day.   He saw all his friends and let himself be seen by all.   But to-day he felt disgusted with it all.   It was the Christmas season of gay festivities.   He jumped into the sleigh, wrapped himself up closely in his furs and cried, "Drive home!"

Swiftly and directly the black horse headed through the city square to the street.

Yawning, he entered his dwelling, and ordered his man servant to brew some tea.   Then he flung himself on a couch and sighed. Around him was expensive furniture, mirrors, carpets, everything elegant. But beside his valet, there was not a living soul in the house.   He was unmarried.

Walking about the brilliantly lighted room, his eyes gazed glassily, he gnawed the end of his moustache between his teeth and several times growled out: "The devil take such an existence?"   He was discontented with life.   After such struggles, in such a fine position, with honours and income—to be discontented with life?   Strange!

He stepped up to his writing desk and picked up in his soft white hand an unopened letter.   A new light suddenly came into his eyes, and he smiled.

"From Anulka!   On my soul, from Anulka!   She hasn't written for such a long time that I thought she never was going to write again. And now, she has thought to do it again—How glad I am!"

Anulka was his sister and lived in obscurity in their little native village.   For twenty years they had not seen each other.   She seldom wrote to him and he replied very briefly or not at all.   Months, even years passed in which his sister never came into his mind.   But now when he recognised her handwriting on the envelope, he felt glad, unutterably glad.   And when he was breaking open the letter a smile lit up his face and the wrinkles disappeared from his forehead.

The first half of the letter his eyes skimmed over rapidly but the latter portion he read more and more slowly, pausing over it at length.

"Do you remember"—wrote the proprietress of the little village estate—"how father used to have long talks in the evening with the tenant, and we, still little children, used to look out from the corner at the moving shadow of his long beard and what fun we got out of it? What trivial things used to suffice in those times for our happiness!   Do you remember the first time our parents took us to the hunter's lodge in the depths of the forest?   I often go there now.   Not a thing has changed there.   The same pine-trees, straight, slender, touching the sky just as in the old days, even the ferns grow as tall as those in which we got lost once upon a time. And when our parents after long searching found us, they forgot to be angry but instead, petted and hugged us close and because we were so tired out, they carried us in their arms to the huntsman's lodge. Do you remember that, Vladya? I wonder if you remember the rustling of the forest that we used to listen to for hours at a time when we went walking? And, since I'm talking about trees, do you remember those three old wide-spreading wild ash trees under which we usually ate our lunch and in the evening our bread with honey that you never could get enough of? I, in my stinginess, would exchange my share of the honey for the nuts that you brought from the hazel brush. Do you remember? Those wild ash trees are older and more branched out and they still stand where they always did, the honey is just the same, even the nuts still grow in the glade; only you, Vladya, are not here and you never will be, never——"

He read that far, then his eyes glanced up at the beginning of the letter and with a smile which at intervals waned and then brightened in his eyes and on his lips, he read that portion. Then he continued reading the latter part of the missive penned by the gentle soul of a woman.

"And do you remember our children's room? It was not large and had white walls and a window which looked out on the garden where mother used to plant various medicinal herbs which always had such a sweet fragrance? Do you remember how mother used to discuss at length with other women her troubles and woes or how she had doctored pale thin children with home remedies? In that same room my own children, Stach and Julka, have now grown up and now it is Julie's bedroom. The walls are still white and the window looks out on the garden in which I plant sweet-flag and mallow. Not long ago I found up in the attic your wooden pony which you got as a Christmas gift and I stood it up in a corner of the room. It is a memento of you—for perhaps you are living, not for us——"

His hands holding the letter dropped, his eyes fixed themselves on vacancy and he shook his head. Then he read further, "And do you remember the old nurse, Kacenka Holubova?—What many amusing and wise sayings and proverbs she uttered and her hands, black and rough, how tenderly they dressed and combed us. She had a heart of gold and she loved us very devotedly, that simple peasant woman. She brought up Stach and Julka, too, and she lived with us all her life in that very room in which, do you remember, the apples used to be put away for the winter,—the one whose window looked out on the birch grove. But—you surely don't know it—she is no longer among the living. She died a year ago and before her death kept speaking of you. A few minutes before dying, she said, Hasn't Vladya written? He has gone away from us! May God bless him!" We buried her in our cemetery just below the fir grove. But you will never see the grave of our faithful Holubova!——"

Again he dropped the letter to his knees and lost himself in thought. And anyone who knew him from the office, club or theatre, to have seen him now, would have been very much astonished. Stooping over, his head sunk on his chest, his eyes dull and fixed, his brow furrowed by numberless wrinkles, he looked aged, aged——

After a few moments, without finishing the reading of his letter, he himself sat writing: "I had forgotten everything, my Anulka, and yet I remember it all again. But man is such a strange creature that he does not understand himself. Now, however, it seems to me that I understand myself. While I was still going forward, I kept thinking; just this and this and then—but when I had reached my goal —Oh, it's a cruel joke—this living of ours! You toil, torture yourself, race like a madman, and when you have attained that which you sought, you see that in your hands you hold—nothing. If I had someone here, perhaps that 'nothing' would give me joy but as it is— everything has vanished and only emptiness remains. How good i seems to have you call me 'Vladya'! A fine Vladya, fat as a barrel and old—already so old!—but still Vladya. For twenty years now I have not spoken my mother tongue, the language of my father and mother. I've been a stranger to it all the time—until to-day—once more. Strange thing! While I was young everything pleased me, all was one to me. But now, when the blood in my veins has grown calmer, something else has happened! Do you know what? You are happier than I, Anulka! You have much: Stach and Julka, property, many kindly messages, cares, your own people. You love your herbs, your wild ashes, white walls, nuts, forests, your peasant women and their children—You are right, that forest rustled beautifully and th perfume of mother's sweet-flag stimulated the senses. And I wonder if you can still devour as many nuts as you used to? And the hazel brush,—haven't you cut it out yet? And what became of our dog Burk?—Make my reverent bow to the forests, the wild ashes, to m wooden horse and to the grave of old Holubova! Or else, do you know what? I will take a trip out to see you. I can't leave now, my work will not permit, but in the summer, God willing, I will come. Or else the devil take it, I'll fix things better—A year, two years and I'll take my leave of everything here and will return completely to you and to our own people."

A great tear dropped down on the next word and, spreading, made it illegible.

WLADYSLAW REYMONT
(1867-1925)

REYMONT, born in the county of Piotrkow, spent his youth in various occupations and wrote his first novel while he was in charge of a railway section. There followed a series of novels and a number of short stories, all displaying an artist with a keen sense of observation, a warm sympathy for the life of the peasant class with which his works mainly deal. His great epic tetralogy, *The Peasants*, was awarded the Noble prize for literature in 1924. *Twilight* is one of Reymont's finest stories.

The present version, anonymously translated, is reprinted from *The Pagan* magazine, copyright, 1916, by permission of the publisher.

TWILIGHT

SOKOL lay dying. He had been lying thus a long time. He had fallen sick, and was kicked about like a useless carcass. Good people said it would be wrong to kill him, even though his handsome hide would make such fine leather. Yes, good people let him die slowly, alone and forgotten. The same good souls rewarded him with a kick, occasionally, to remind him that he was dying too slowly. But they took no other notice of him. Once in a while the hunting-dogs, with whom he had been wont to leap in the chase, came to visit him. But dogs have ugly souls . . . (from too much contact with human beings.) And at every call of their masters they left Sokol precipitately. Only Lappa, an old blind Siberian-hound, stayed with him longer than the rest. He lay dozing under the feed-trough, oppressed with sorrow at the sight of Sokol, whose large, pleading, tearful eyes frightened him.

So the old horse was left to his solitary misery. The days kept him company . . . golden, rosy days, or grey and harsh and painful ones, filling the stall with their weeping. . . . They peered into his eyes, then silently departed, as if awe-stricken. . . .

But Sokol was afraid only of the nights, the short, fearful, silent, stifling nights of June. It was then that he felt he was surely dying. . . . And he became almost frantic with terror. He would tear at his halter, and beat with his hoofs against the wall . . . he wanted to escape . . . to run, and run. . . .

One day, as the sun was setting, he jumped up, stared at the flecks of light that filtered in through the cracks in the walls, and began to neigh long and plaintively. Not a single voice answered him from the close heavy stillness of the departing day. Swallows flitted by, and chirped from their nests, or darted like feathered arrows among the golden host of insects that buzzed in the sun's last rays. From the distant meadows was heard the sharp ringing and swishing of busy scythes. And from the fields of grain and flowers came a rustling, and humming, and whispering.

But about Sokol there was a deep, awful silence, that made him shiver. Sombre panic seized him; he began to tug frenziedly at his halter . . . it broke, and he fled into the yard.

The sun blinded him and a wild pain gnawed at his entrails. He lowered his head, and stood motionless, as if stunned. Little by little, however, he came to himself again; dim memories of fields, forests, meadows, floated through his brain. . . . There awoke in him a resistless desire to run . . . a longing to conquer vast distances . . . a craving thirst to live again. . . . He began to seek eagerly for an exit from the yard. It was a square yard, three sides of which were shut in by various buildings. He searched in vain. He tried again and again, though he could barely stand on his legs, though every movement caused him indescribable pain, though the blood kept flowing from his old sores. . . .

At last he struck a wooden fence from which he could see the manor-house. He gazed at the flower-covered lawn before it, where dogs were basking, at the house itself with its windows glittering golden in the sun, and began to neigh pleadingly, piteously. . . .

If anyone had come and said a kind word to him, or smoothed his coat caressingly, he would willingly have laid down and died. But all about was deserted, drowsy, still. . . .

In despair he began to bite the rails, and wrench the gate, leaning against it with all his weight. It burst open, and he walked into the garden. He approached the verandah, still neighing plaintively; but no one heard him. He stood thus a long time, gazing at the curtained windows, and even tried to climb up the steps. Then he walked all around the house.

Suddenly he seemed to forget everything. . . . He saw only visions of vast grain-fields, as limitless as the sea, stretching away to a distant, endlessly distant, horizon. Bewitched by these alluring fancies he began to stagger and stumble forward with all his waning might. . . .

Sokol shivered. His eyes grew glazed with suffering. He breathed heavily and nosed the damp grass to cool his heated nostrils. . . . He was very thirsty . . . but he kept staggering onward, impelled by his sombre panic and the resistless impulse to escape. As he stumbled among the stalks of wheat and corn his feet grew heavier and heavier. The furrows were like pit-falls; the grass entangled his feet and dragged him down. The bushes barred his path. The whole earth seemed to pull him eagerly toward itself. Often the grain hid the horizon from his gaze.

His poor dumb soul sank deeper and deeper into the darkness of terror. Recognising nothing, he kept staggering blindly forward as in a fog. A partridge, leading her brood, flew up suddenly between his legs, causing him to start in affright and remain motionless, without daring to stir. Crows that flew silently across the fields, stopped, on observing him, and sat down on a pear-tree, cawing and croaking evilly.

He dragged himself into the meadow, and sank exhausted to the ground. He stretched out his legs, looked up into the skyey wastes, and sighed piteously. The crows flew down from the trees and hopped along the ground nearer and nearer. The corn bent over and stared at him with its red poppy-eyes. Still nearer came the crows, sharpening their beaks in the hard grass-tufts. Some flew over him, cawing ravenously, lower and lower, till he saw their terrible round eyes, and half-open beaks. But he could not stir. He struck his paws into the ground and fancied he was up again, galloping across the field . . . in the chase . . . the hounds beside him barking . . . flying like the wind. . . .

His agony grew so intense that he gave one savage neigh and sprang to his feet. The crows flew away, screeching. . . .

But now he saw nothing . . . understood nothing. . . . Everything wavered about him . . . spun, tossed, crashed. . . . He felt himself sinking, as in a deep mire. . . . A cold shiver ran over his body, and he lay still. . . .

The sunk sank. Obliterating twilight covered everything with a silent mantle. The barking of a dog grew audible in the distance.

Lappa ran up to his friend, but Sokol did not recognise him. The old dog licked him, pawed at the ground, ran barking across the field hither and thither, calling for help, but no one came. . . .

The grass looked into Sokol's wide-open eyes. . . . The trees approached him, and reached out their sharp claw-like twigs to him. The birds grew still. Thousands of living things began to crawl over his body, to pinch, and claw, and rend his flesh. . . . The crows cawed frightfully.

Lappa, bristling with terror, moaned and howled weirdly. . . .

HUNGARY

Introduction

ALTHOUGH many branches of Hungarian literature go back to the sixteenth century, there is little evidence of noteworthy fiction until we reach the early nineteen hundreds. In the *Aurora*, a magazine founded by Alexander Kisfaludi, appeared the first prose of significance contributed by a group of writers whose vigorous work justified its recognition. In 1839, Jozsef Eötvös, a distinguished writer and statesman, edited the *Inundation Book*, a collection of narratives by the most celebrated authors of the period. *The Village Notary*, one of Eötvös' finest novels, is considered a Hungarian classic.

The most prolific and brilliant novelist of the nineteenth century is Maurus Jokai whose work has earned for him a wide reputation. An equally splendid novelist and short-story writer is Koloman Mikszath, whose originality, charm and freshness has assured him a permanent position in Hungarian letters. Among the many authors whom Mikszath influenced may be mentioned Etienne Barsony, a gifted writer of short stories.

The beginning of the twentieth century witnessed the introduction of new tendencies in Hungarian literature. Its effect was to create a modern school warring against the traditionalists who, inspired by a profound nationalism, are utterly opposed to cosmopolitan and radical ideas. The most important of the moderns is Andre Ady, a brilliant poet and novelist. Molnar and Biro are contemporary dramatists who have also written short stories.

✳ ✳ ✳

KAROLY KISFALUDI
(1788-1830)

KISFALUDI, born near Raab, achieved in his brief but colourful life lasting fame as a dramatist and short-story writer. He was "the founder of the school of Magyar humourists, and his comic types amuse and delight to this day. . . . Apart from his own works it is the supreme merit of Kisfaludi to have revived and nationalised the Magyar literature, giving it a range and scope undreamed of before his time."

The Assignation was probably inspired by one of the campaigns in which Kisfaludi served. The translation, by Mr. Joseph Szebenyei, was made for this volume.

THE ASSIGNATION

IT happened that my regiment had been stationed near Lake Como and it was from here that we went to meet the French in support of the threatened left wing of the Darvady brigade; and there it was that my friend the Major "bit the dust."

We had a lovely and lively time in the small town near Lake Como for several months, for the Italian women enjoyed the company of our Hussars and each and everyone of us could count our successes by the dozen among the passionate and lovely Signorinas. My friend the Major was perhaps the only exception as far as I knew. He was of the more serious-minded and melancholy type, who fell in love with women and wanted to marry them instead of having a gay time with one and then begin with the next one. The Major was made of different stuff. He fell in love with a young girl the second day we had spent there and he would stare up at her window at night while the rest of us had scattered all over the town to keep rendezvous and drink to the health of the most beautiful women in the world.

The Major was in love and no doubt his passion found proper response on the part of the lovely young lady. That we could hardly doubt, for the Major was the finest, the best looking and most companionable fellow amongst the score of officers. We also knew that the favour he had found with the object of his ideal was not shared at all by her honourable parents. Those were not the times for matrimonial affairs. A soldier was a roving vagabond and not destined for family life. Especially a foreign soldier, who might be in one country to-day and at the other end of the world to-morrow. One really could not blame the parents for not being enthusiastic over his suit.

Our morals, too, were rather of the loose sort, soldierly morals so to say, when love did not particularly demand the sanction of the church, at least not on the part of Hussars in a foreign land, even allowing for the fact that we had to deal with an allied nation. All is fair in war and love. We urged him to take what he could, and, I am reasonably certain, he would not have hesitated, had the girl not been exacting in the observance of etiquette and moral standards. But she was. It was of no avail to explain to her that love has its own rewards.

She insisted that he marry her and that she would be only too happy to become his wife. He would have done so, if even for a day, but the girl never had the chance to be alone with him long enough to consult a priest, let alone to get married in secret.

It was a hopeless case and the Major was dejected and more melancholy than ever. He never took part at our carousings and lively parties, he accepted no invitations from the many exclusive families whose homes we frequented, but spent most of his time at the Fiaria mansion under the chaperonage of the old lady, and he could not even hold his fair one's hand in secret, or whisper passionate words of love to her. Now and then only could they exchange a few words, when they chanced to dance together, or when the old lady's attention was called to something more important than the guarding of the girl's honour.

Several months passed and the Major had made no headway at all. The old people, however, noticed that the girl's infatuation had reached a dangerous point and they decided to act. In those days when parents decided to act, it always meant that they selected a suitable man, at least a man who suited them, and informed their obedient daughter of the fact. The girl cried and buried her face in the cushion, the usual procedure in cases of unhappy love. But that helped little and the preparations were going on briskly for the great day. The man she was to marry was a native countryman, a man of high position in society, a rich man with family connections and traditions. She hated the man and loved the Major even more passionately. She pleaded and wept in vain. What would become of the world if girls would be disobedient to their parents?

The day was appointed and the marriage feast was to take place within a few days after the announcement. The girl could not rebel openly. But she did rebel inwardly and to show her disdain and contempt for her future lord and master, she sent word to the Major, by a trusted servant girl, to visit her in her room the night before the marriage ceremony was to take place and that she would hang a white kerchief on her windowsill to indicate that all was well and he might climb through her window into her chamber.

"It is my desperation that drives me to this act," she wrote, "an act my maidenly sense of purity forbade to consider before. It is to you I want to offer myself, and to you only."

The day arrived, but the sun had not set. Soon after sunset, however, a messenger arrived from the General commanding the corps to say that the regiment would march immediately towards Genoa to support the left flank of the Darvady brigade against advancing cavalry. Immediately.

Just that day, just at that hour, when a hopeless dream, a burning desire was about to be consummated. Just that night, when the door of happiness would have opened, only to be closed again for ever after. To miss an assignation of this kind and to march to another of such a different nature, where they distribute everything but kisses and love.

But why immediately? Why not in the morning, or early after midnight? Is it so very urgent to meet the enemy, to kill and to be killed by cold steel? Couldn't it be postponed a day, a few hours? Couldn't the departure be postponed by preparations just for a few hours, on some pretext or other? What if the messenger had been delayed and delivered the order six hours later? Could not a messenger be delayed by enemy patrols, by bad roads, by detours he had to make? Who could ever blame him for being late at the appointment?

Passion and sense of duty and honour fought a violent battle within his soul. But just for a fleeting moment. It might cost the lives of many of his comrades, it might offer unlimited strategic advantages to the enemy, it might cost us the war. Obey! soldier, obey! There was no alternative. You have to march.

He gave orders; and when the first stars appeared in the sky, the regiment was in the saddle and riding through the town, the Major giving his orders to the subalterns. Larks were singing among the lilac bushes under his sweetheart's window as they neared the house. The bugle was silent as they passed the mansion. The Major feared lest it should frighten the lark away from under her windows. Why not let her enjoy that at least as long as she would be waiting in vain for the coming of her lover. There was the white kerchief sadly hanging from the windowsill, but even the breeze was absent and it dangled lifelessly, mournfully in the heat.

The regiment marched out of the sleeping town in silence.

"Forward, boys, let us hurry." From the top of a hill just outside the town he looked back and saw the white kerchief where the hot breeze stirred it somewhat more lively, and it waved like a farewell sigh.

The monotonous tramp of the horses was the only sound audible. The enemy was far off yet and soon the town lay far behind.

The Major did not miss his second assignation. He was there on the minute. And if he had dallied but half an hour, the left wing of the brigade would have been outflanked and disaster would have followed. It was a passionate rendezvous, as between sweethearts who have long been waiting to embrace. The Major reaped his reward by the victory of his men; but paid for it with his own life. He fell on the field of battle; but had saved his honour.

And in the town the kerchief was still dangling in the breeze when the Major's body was brought back for burial. And we, who knew of it, said to each other: "There, a girl's honour was also saved by a miracle."

MAURUS JOKAI
(1825-1904)

JOKAI, born at Rev-Komarom, at first studied law. His temperament was, however, hardly attuned to this profession, and he soon turned to literature. His talent was soon recognised and, after the appearance of *Working Days*, his first important romance, he was appointed editor of the most important Hungarian literary journal. He became politically involved in the revolution of 1848. As a result he was a political suspect for the next fourteen years of his life during which he produced his great romances besides innumerable short stories.

The Room With Forty-Eight Stars has been especially translated for this volume by Joseph Szebenyei.

THE ROOM WITH FORTY-EIGHT STARS

ON my arrival in Paris, as it befits an eighteen carat Hungarian gentleman, I proceeded to make preparations to be present at the Grand Opera. I bought a box: let the French see whom they have to deal with, let them know that a Magyar gentleman will sit in a box even if he is alone.

I was quite well aware of the fact, partly through my mirror and partly through the adoring glances of Budapest seamstresses, that I was a good looking fellow; I certainly made much of this fact. I swept the auditorium with my glasses in the firm belief, that every woman in every box would fall in love with me within an hour, and I was only sorry to note that those sitting just beneath or just above me were deprived of the pleasure of seeing me. But the thought comforted me, there are a great number of most beautiful French girls who will compensate me for this loss in quantity.

I need hardly say that my triumph was complete; that every lorgnet held by feminine hands was directed in the direction of my box; that Countesses and Princesses threw yearning and sighing glances toward me and that I had not missed a single occasion of returning their admiring glances and faint, secret smiles. There is no doubt about it that a Hungarian cavalier is a real one even in Paris and that no other could attract attention in such prolific manner. I don't deny that I thought of Attila, our noble ancestor, during this one hour with pity, for he vainly tried to conquer the white-limbed dames of foggy Lutetia, a feat that seemed so easy now to one of his descendants . . . but I am afraid I am trespassing the modest limits of boastfulness.

Let it suffice to say that one of the Princesses at the theatre was certainly caught in the net as tightly as could be wished for. She sa just opposite and was as beautiful as an angel; she almost seemed to be hovering in the air amidst her lace and silk and she was so bedecked with diamonds and precious stones as to give one the impression of gazing up, at the stars on a clear, brilliant night. I was certain she could not have been a poor devil, but a Goddess in disguise.

My fairy angel had not taken her eyes off from my box during the whole performance, and if you had asked her what was going on on the stage, I doubt if she could have told you. One need not have been too well versed in worldly matters or too sophisticated to understand the import of such bewildering behaviour on her part. I know. "Très humble serviteur, Madame," I said to myself, "I shall be there."

At the end of the performance I had hurried to the lobby where she had to pass. My little Goddess did not keep me waiting too long; she came almost immediately. Oh, from close range she was even more beautiful, more adorable and more charming; I am not in the habit of being swept into ecstasy over feminine beauty, for I know the effect of cosmetics upon feminine charms, I know exactly how much diamonds and Brussel lace enhance a woman's appearance, I can calculate with mathematical precision how glow added to glow may benefit a subject; I know what breeding and studied poise may add to the effect of a beautiful woman; still she was more angelic, more refined, more beautiful than any poet could imagine, let alone describe.

As she slipped past me, I felt a slight touch on my hand and when I recovered from my surprise, I found I had been holding a tiny card in my hand, rolled up and tied together with a precious ring. She had slipped it into my hand. But her blinding beauty and the touch of her hand had deprived me of my senses at that moment, so that I could not realise at first what had happened. There was a name on the visiting card: "Marchesa Barcheschi, Boulevard des Italiens" and underneath in pearly letters it said: "At 12 to-morrow."

The ring that inclosed the visiting card was a precious one, worth at least five hundred francs, according to the bijoutier I had consulted on the subject of its value.

That's what I call luck. It could have been no mean person who ties her love messages with a five hundred franc ring. She could have been no adventuress, but certainly a lady of high rank and I thought it was very nice of her to entrust such a precious piece of jewelry to a stranger she had never set eyes on before. She was not afraid that, instead of attending the rendezvous, he would visit the pawnshop with the pledge of love. She must surely have set me down as a Hungarian gentleman.

The adventure appeared to me most pleasing and satisfactory; I could hardly wait for twelve o'clock next morning. I put on my best morning suit and ordered a carriage to drive me to Boulevard des Italiens.

The driver knew the house well and drove up to it without hesitation. Who would not know where the Marchesa lived? But he could not drive in through the driveway, for he was just a hired man, and the rules are that only private equipages may drive into the garden alley leading up to the entrance. There were quite a number of these inside the garden roads.

Just let them be. They will have to wait in the ante-chambre when I present my card and the ring.

A tremendously huge doorkeeper came to meet me. He had a morose and murderous face, but as soon as he saw the ring, his dark features melted and a smile appeared on his face. He rank a bell and a footman, all gold and silver-braided, appeared, bowed deeply, handed me over to another lackey even more gorgeously decorated and he led me through a dozen wonderful corridors and apartments, salons, furnished in a princely style, so that their grandeur hurt the eye.

I have seen quite a number of lordly palaces, gorgeous mansions and what not, but I may say here and now that I have never set eyes on anything more luxurious, more brilliant in decorations, panels, pictures and wainscoting than I had found at this Marchesa's. My very eyesight was in acute danger through the brilliance of the place.

At last we entered a salon, something like an amphitheatre, the decoration and appointments of which surpassed anything I could imagine; marble statues, American flowers, silk tapestries and carpets a thousand years old, porcelain and silver mountings everywhere, paintings by great masters (at least I thought so) in golden frames. And just underneath the ceiling, there where forty-eight stars, one over each picture frame, about the size of my palm, with dark glass ornaments within them. It was a unique idea.

But I had very little time to examine these wonderful stars, for the door opened and my Goddess entered quite unceremoniously.

She was even more beautiful than last night at the Opera, if such a thing were possible. She had a babyish look in her eyes, modest and unassuming, a noble gait in her movements, large, lovely eyes and lips that were provocative to the highest degree. And she smiled. She smiled to please me and because she was pleased to see me. She came to meet me and offered her hand,—soft, lovely, velvety hands she had,— bade me sit down next to her on a silk tapestried sofa. She bashfully dropped her eyes and begged me not to misjudge her for her hasty act last night, but that she could not restrain herself in confessing her sentiments towards me. I dropped on my knees before her and confessed that I loved her. She became frightened at my passionate appeal and rose, then ran away to a distance and stared at me with her large innocent eyes in fright. I saw that I had begun rather more vehemently than I should have, so I decided to go easier and succeeded in persuading her to sit down again next to me and permit me to apologise for my vehemence, dictated by passionate love. She began to weep silently and told me that she had never met a man before who could have understood her. I swore that I shall be the one who will understand her and immediately I began to recite verses to her, and she wiped her tears and broke into a lovely smile. She had not left my tenderness unrewarded, for she bent forward and kissed my forehead in a motherly way, as I sat at her feet on a cushion; then I had pressed her white lily fingers to my heart and kissed her on the lips with such terrific passion that she almost lost her breath and looked at me reproachfully. She called me her "Little Romeo" and I called her my Juliette and thus we acted the first act of the *Romeo and Juliette,* where people only promise that they will love each other for ever after.

Then we said good-bye to each other, and as I was about to leave, my Goddess whispered in my ear:

"To-morrow at noon, come again."

She slipped away for fear of a parting kiss and waving her hand from the other end of the room she whispered:

"My Romeo."

"My Juliette, my heavenly Juliette," I stammered and left the place in a daze, not unlike a crazed Romeo.

I certainly lost my balance; I wanted to find out who she was and whence she came, who were her people, for it was certain she was no common person. She loved me passionately. I had never met such passion in a woman. It killed me, and altered my soul completely. And now I should have to wait a whole day to see her again. I should be counting the minutes until noon to-morrow. Would I be able to retain the little sense I had brought from home?

Towards evening, just to kill the time and in the hope that I might get a fleeting glimpse of her again, I turned my steps towards the Grand Opera House. On my way there I met Count Arthur, an old chum from home, who had been living several years in the French capital. We were very glad to have met and embraced heartily. After the first words of greeting we began to discuss spending the evening together. I proposed the opera.

"Oh, who goes to the opera these days?" he protested. "It's boring, stupid, where people sing and talk about love they don't feel and mimic things that are unreal, where even jealousy is sham and the actors lie to you at such lengths as their parts demand. You come along with me to a place where everything is real, love and jealousy and hatred, where at least one of the actors thinks he is playing at life and real things. One can see genuine plays there. We shall see Othello played tonight and have a fine time."

I let him take me wherever he willed. It cost a hundred francs to enter but what was that to me? We passed through several out of the way streets and entered a dark courtyard, where we ascended some back stairs and paid a hundred francs each at the box office. Then an usher pushed each of us into a tiny booth, so small in fact, that there was room only for a single person. It was dark inside with only a dark glass pane, large enough to place your eyes against it. I looked through the pane and to my shocking amazement I recognised the room I had visited earlier in the day, the Goddess on the sofa, seated next to an English-looking man, the pictures and the forty-eight stars behind each of which were a couple of peeping eyes. The girl was now performing *Othello* with the other fellow, the same as she had performed *Romeo* with me. The poor idiot behaved most queerly, but I must admit that my fairy love played her part just as well now as before, and she could cry or play the wild Desdemona just as she could impersonate innocent Juliette. She made him jealous. The poor fellow almost hanged himself and was on the verge of killing the lady in his jealousy. The comedy was really worth the hundred francs.

It may be imagined that I did not keep the next day's appointment with the Marchesa in the starry room. I was unwilling to act the second part of *Romeo and Juliette* to the peeping audience. On the contrary, I took the train and slipped out of Paris, lest someone should come to me and apologise for not applauding my brilliant acting of Romeo.

✷ ✷ ✷

KOLOMAN MIKSZATH
(1849-1910)

MIKSZATH is the most notable successor to Jokai. His stories are excellent studies of the peasant life in Hungary, of which he was a keen student. Through his work runs a delicious humour and a gentle satire with which he seems to castigate the practices of his countrymen.

The Grass of Lohina is just such a delightful story. The present version has been especially translated for this volume by Joseph Szebenyei.

THE GRASS OF LOHINA

I AM trying to visualise what the grass of Lohina looks like. The grass that grows on the pastures round the village of Lohina and of which they say that hidden among its million blades, there is the "grass of knowledge." Beautiful Slovak women search for it and hope to discover it again. Have they found it once already? Of course, they have. That's just it. Let me tell you about it.

The Lohina Justice of the Peace, Mr. Michael Szekula, found a missive tied to a piece of stone, near his broken window, that some scoundrel must have thrown. It said that unless the village minister would be expelled from the rectory, the Judge had better move his furniture and family out of the village, for the "red cock will alight on it within a week from today."

That bird had a very bad reputation among the Slovak villagers. Their houses were thatched with straw and cane and they needed but a tiny spark to bring ruin and devastation upon a whole community.

He had kept his promise. (Who would have thought it, who would have thought it?) The fire swept away one-third of the village on the exact date the missive had predicted. And before the cinders had been made properly harmless another missive arrived, this time at the house of the sacristan, Andeas Mirava, written in the same hand on the same kind of coarse, yellowish paper, tied round a stone with the same kind of thread as the first one.

The reverend gentleman was not spared any too well in this one either: That his grandfather was a Jew and that he himself was a papist; that he was not a decent man, nothing was sacred in his eyes; that he had married the young woman only in order to have her married sister in his house now and again. (That much was certainly true, that the minister's sister-in-law was staying just then at the rectory, but what of it?) Then the note told of the minister's various escapades in his bachelor days and these too were no less libelous. Of course, they were all inventions. Who ever heard of a bachelor minister patting the cheeks of his pretty servant girls? Libels, pure and unadulterated libels. And suppose they were true? Why tell the whole world?

The good people of Lohina cared very little about what was being said, though their neighbouring villagers had a lot to say about the minister and his doings.

"Why didn't you chase him away?"

"Because we did not believe in the threats of fire. A barking dog rarely bites."

When the second missive arrived the neighbouring villagers became sarcastic.

"You do believe now, don't you? Aren't you going to chase off the minister even now?"

"Why should we?" they answered. "We believe now that the red cock is coming, but we are prepared for it. We can move out of the village."

And they did. They settled down in tents just outside the village and waited for the fire to come. The houses, excepting a few brick buildings, had been standing deserted. The villagers took it rather jovially and their faces only became grave when the second date arrived and the village began to burn again. This time, there being no wind, only a few houses suffered, but what good did it do as long as the third missive was already in the hands of the richest man in the village threatening an even greater disaster unless the minister was removed.

The case began to assume a serious aspect. The county authorities would have to take the matter in hand. Take action speedily. Which means that the said authorities usually turn on their other side and sleep on. Still, something had to be done, and, consequently, the county Governor ordered Mr. Michael Sotony, the newly appointed County Judge, to investigate.

You must know that a County Judge in Hungary is the son of a rich man who has become desperately bored with gambling and squandering his all on women. Having arrived at this state of mind he accepts an appointment as a county official, usually a County Judge, on the principle that if God gives one a position, he will add a little brains as well to enable the delinquent to do justice to the office. Mr. Sotony was no exception to the rule. Still, feeling somewhat inexperienced in matters of criminal investigation, he called upon a friend, who had neither rich father nor position but brains, to accompany him to Lohina and assist him in unmasking the dangerous incendiary. This jobless but brainy person was Martin Teleskey and when he read the three anonymous missives he declared: "The Lohina case is as simple as can be. Child's play. I shall get the man."

They started for Lohina the next morning accompanied by the notary Hamar who, being very short sighted, was noted for erasing with his nose what he had written with his hand. They began with the minister. His name was Samuel Belinka, a handsome young man with a Roman nose and big blue eyes, the kind of minister the women of the congregation would vote for. He had been married two months previously. He said he had no enemies, none than he knew of. He suspected no one.

"But you see the notes reveal quite a number of things that only intimates could know of. Who were your servant girls?"

"One is still with us and two others who left live with their folks."

"Would either of the two have cause to hate you?"

"Absolutely not."

Teleskey evolved an idea. The minister gave no clue whatever to the identity of the criminal. He would have to be approached from a different direction.

"How many people do you think can write among the three hundred inhabitants of Lohina? Perhaps a hundred. We are going to get them all to write a few sentences and . . ."

"Brilliant idea. He can't escape us. The man must have been one of them. No stranger would bother about the minister."

The idea was communicated to the Justice of the Peace and the village teacher. They both agreed that it was the only way. They drove to the edge of the forest where the villagers set up their homes and the three hundred people flocked around them all eager to take the test.

It's no small matter when the county authorities arrive at a village. The honour of the community depends on the hospitality they can offer. I mean the quality of the food and wine. The village aldermen were already at work on proper arrangements. The finest cook was no doubt Mrs. Szekula and the finest looking girl to serve at the table was unquestionably Apolka, the Gypsy horse dealer's daughter, who moved like a young tiger and from whose hands any big, learned man would eat with greater appetite. Their eyes had to be fed as well and where could they find a person more apt to feed men's eyes than Apolka? Not in seven counties of the Carpathians.

By the time the Commission arrived at the scene the kettle was already steaming with the paprika-chicken, and Apolka was busy setting the table for the visitors and the head-men of the village.

Three other cross-legged tables were set up for the official investigation and soon the writing tests began. Long-haired old folk and worried young people came to the tables one by one and wrote dictated sentences with terrific effort and a generous amount of blots. It took a long time, for none of them were experts in the art. The strange thing about it was that the young people had all the same handwriting. Every handwriting resembled the writing on the threatening notes and this gave cause for no amount of confusion until it was discovered that they had learnt to write from the same teacher and as they had never practised it since they had left school, each one of the young people could have been accused with the crime on the basis of identical handwriting. It led to nowhere. The idea was good but availed little. There was not one individual character in the whole village as far as writing went.

There was a pause in the work of investigation and Judge Szekula took advantage of it to divert the attention of the gentlemen to more enjoyable channels:

"That's Apollonia there," he said pointing to the Gypsy girl. "She'll serve at the table. The best looking lassie we've got."

The three investigators looked and enjoyed the sight.

"Her father is a horse dealer," went on Mr. Szekula, "that is, he only sells them but doesn't do much buying, you see."

"I see," said Sotony, "he just gets them? Has he never been caught at it?"

"He's very clever at getting the papers to fit the animals. Otherwise he is quite respectable. Settled down these last ten years. No complaints against him, so why bother? He gets his horses from distant stables, sells them cheaply to our men, so why trouble?"

Half in a whisper the County Judge inquired:

"What is she like?"

"Good."

That meant everything. It conveyed all the discouragement any visitor could expect at Lohina. As much as to say: "Nothin' doin'."

Martin Teleskey, the special investigator, listened to their talk without saying a word. Then suddenly he rose and walked over to the girl who had been pealing potatoes under the oak-tree where the fire-place was set up. He talked to the girl for a few minutes, then returned to the Sotony table.

"Well, how did you like her?" asked the Justice of the Peace with no end of pride in his voice.

"Not bad. I talked to her in an official capacity, however."

They all laughed, for the term "official capacity" is regarded as rather elastic under the Carpathians.

"I've never seen so much fire in a pair of innocent eyes. She's just the kind I could go mad over if I were twenty years younger than I am," he remarked rather to himself; and the rest of the company gazed with dreamy eyes in the direction of the fire-place. "Like a young deer. There's rhythm in her body. "Gypsy," he concluded with a contemptuous shrug of his shoulder.

"What did you say to her in your official capacity?" asked Sotony in a sarcastic tone.

"I just wanted to ask her if she can knit."

They all smiled.

"She certainly can!" said the Justice of the Peace.

"I really need someone who can handle the knitting needles," went on Teleskey. "Will you please ask her to come here."

The notary was dispatched to fetch the girl. It was generally agreed that she would need a lot of coaxing, for girls of her kind hate to appear before an official body.

"The innocent little lamb," remarked Sotony ironically.

But she did not come without much coaxing. She walked somewhat falteringly, dropping her big, black eyes full of demonic fire, untying her embroidered apron as she approached and carrying it on her round arm leisurely, as ladies carry their cloaks. She wore her skirt long, not like the peasant women, and it reached even below her ankles; and her hair was done up round her head in two plaits unlike that of the peasant girls who wore it dangling down their backs in a single thick plait. Her slim, snake-like body wavered and reeled slightly as she came forward and she walked with the gait of a Princess, proud and

conscious of the eyes that rested upon her. The flush of embarrassment suffused her brown face to a dark red and on her marble forehead there sat a commanding wrinkle, lending a mannish character to
her oval face.

Sotony followed her every movement as she advanced and when she
arrived within a few feet he could not suppress an "Oh."

"I called you, Apolla, because I wanted to ask your assistance in a
little matter. Now don't get frightened," said Teleskey, in a fatherly
tone. "The notary here tells me that you are an expert with the
knitting needles."

"Yes, sir," she answered with a coquettish nod of her head.

"Have you got your needles here, my child?"

"No, they are at home."

"My man will go and fetch them then; you are busy around here,
I understand."

"No, no," she protested, "I'll get them myself. No one could find
them anyhow. Besides, we live at the end of the village; it isn't far."

"Didn't your people move out of the house?"

"Ours is of brick and shingled; it wouldn't burn."

Teleskey whispered to his notary:

"You accompany the girl. See that she doesn't talk to anyone on
the way about the needles."

When the girl departed they all wanted to know why Teleskey
wanted the knitting needles, but he would not reveal his secret to
them.

Apolka returned with the notary in about fifteen minutes, bringing
knitting needles and wondering what they were needed for. The onlookers were dispersed and the procedure began all over again.

"Just come a little closer, Apolka," said Teleskey in a serene and
officious tone. "Don't be frightened. Just sit down here opposite.
Why, you are the most important person here now."

With that he handed her the threads with which the missives had
been tied up in each case and requested her to knit them into a part of
a stocking, whatever large piece they would make. "It's wool alright,"
he said, and they had undoubtedly been plucked from a stocking. The
"kink" was still in them as they had been knitted once before.

The County Judge looked elated and they were all amazed at the
cleverness of the investigator.

Apolka reached out for the threads and her hand seemed to tremble
slightly. She started to work and the needles made fast progress, though
she dropped an eye now and again in her embarrassment as the observant
and admiring glances of the men followed the movements of her
slender fingers.

The official knitting was completed at last. It did look rather official, for it turned out to be a bad piece of work, still it gave evidence of having been taken from a yellowish-blue stocking.

Teleskey then asked how many women in the village wore stockings and who they were. The Justice of the Peace gave the list.

"The minister's wife and sister-in-law, the miller's wife and his three daughters, the Jewish shop-keeper's wife and mother, the tailor's wife and, of course, Apolka. That's about all. The others go barefooted as a rule."

"The notary will go and search their houses for a pair of stockings of this colour. And should he find a pair which show signs of having been threaded, he had better take that person in custody immediately. Someone is playing rather light-heartedly with his head," he added, for incendiarism is punishable by death.

Apolka walked off and began to set the table for lunch as if the affair concerned her little. The notary marched off to attend to his mission and the gentlemen settled down to await the outcome of the search, smoking and sipping from the glasses in front of them. Suddenly Teleskey jumped up and turned red with anger and indignation, waving a slip of yellowish paper in his hand.

"Just fancy, the scoundrel. He slipped a missive into my pocket. Well, I never. . . . Just read this."

He handed the paper to Sotony who could not help smiling as he read the epistle:

You stupid old goat, you had better stop this investigation, or your own house and barn will go the way Lohina went. We've got your number alright, so you'd do better if you'd call a stop.

It was in the same hand as the others and even the paper was of similar hue and fabric.

"It was slipped into my own pocket. Just fancy, the impudent rascal. He must be here in our midst. But who is he?"

"It must be the devil himself," suggested the Justice of Peace.

"Or a woman," added Sotony.

Apolka's soft girlish voice rang out from under the oak: "Dinner is ready."

They took their seats around the table and Apolka passed the food around, moving lightly and smiling at every move, parrying the flattering remarks she received from every person she served and grateful for the attention bestowed upon her by all and sundry.

The dinner was just over when the notary appeared with the report that no stocking of that colour and make was to be found in any of the houses visited. The investigation turned out to be a vain effort and Teleskey was on the point of giving up. Then suddenly someone suggested that it would be wise to go and see old man Hrobak, a sage and prophet who lived somewhere on a mountain-side, and ask him

what he thought of the affair. They all agreed to accept the suggestion in lieu of anything better, but the difficulty was that no one seemed
to know how to get to old man Hrobak's hut.

"I know where he lives," said Apolka, "and I can take you there
if you want me to."

She had roamed about for years in the Carpathians with her tribe
before her father had settled down in Lohina and the official men were
pleased to have her for a guide. Horses were saddled and they started
out, Apolka leading the way, sitting astride in the saddle and riding
up the winding road at a fast pace so that the men had a hard time to
keep up with her. Sotony followed close upon her tracks as the path
broadened so as to permit him to ride beside her; he looked at the girl
with hungry eyes and said:

"It's a pity, Apolka, that you should wither away in a place like
this. Among the wolves and the bears."

Apolka was a hard person with whom to begin a conversation. Her
answers were usually curt and sharp, though she could be lovely and
purring when it pleased her.

"I'd rather live among the bears and wolves. They have never yet
hurt me. But men did."

"If you'd be reasonable and smart, Apolka, you could have silk
gowns and a carriage and four."

"I don't want anything. It doesn't interest me."

"Are you going to be a nun?"

She bent her head over the horse's neck and looked at Sotony from
underneath her curved arm, smiling and coquettish:

"Perhaps worse than that even."

"There is something wrong with you, Apolka. I can read it in
your eyes. Something is gnawing away at the root of your heart."

She looked into the distance with dreamy eyes, but did not reply. She
drew up her horse,—by way of answer,—and permitted the others to
catch up with them. Sotony was annoyed. He said to himself: "Why
this would mean 'there's nothing doin'.' " He was not used to being
treated in this manner by Gypsy girls.

A plaintive song in detached shreds came to them from the north.

"We've just got to follow the sound of that song and we'll soon
reach old Hrobak's hut," she said.

Suddenly the song changed into a wailing cry and as they turned again,
they discerned a small hut standing on a slight clearing. It had but one
tiny window and it was roofed with cane. Broad cracks in the roof and
the walls suggested that the kitchen smoke had a fine time there; it could
escape anyway it pleased.

An old, wrinkled woman was sitting on a log in front of the hut.
She was weeping bitterly.

"What's the trouble, mother? Why are you crying?"

"My father beat me," she sobbed.

"Come on, now, stop that crying," said Apolka. "Do you remember me?"

"Of course I do. You are the daughter of the Gypsy horse thief."

An old man came out from the hut. He was white with age and moved but slowly. He was old Hrobak's son.

"We'd like to see your father," said Apolka. "How is he getting on?"

"Fine. I told this insolent daughter of mine to fetch him his milk, but she'd rather sit around and sing love songs. I gave her a slap or two, and now she's crying in the presence of strangers."

From all this you may surmise that Old Hrobak was a very old man indeed. He lay in a wicker chair, a few feet away under a pine tree.

Apolka seated herself on a log and Sotony took a seat next to her.

"Aren't you going to see the old man?" asked Teleskey.

"No. I know who is the fire-bug," he added softly.

The girl looked at him, pale and nervous.

"Who is it?"

"You. You set my heart on fire, though it was damp and never reacted to incendiarism before. I love you, Apolka."

She acted like a suffocating bird, shook her head, trembled all over and dropped her head. . . .

"I'll take you along with me, and will love you and care for you all my life," he went on, his eyes on fire and his cheeks burning with passion.

"No, no," she said and jumping up she ran towards the pine tree where the others had surrounded the withered old Hrobak. He had no hair on his head, no teeth in his mouth and looked a million years old, if one. He held a similarly withered pipe between his gums, but it had no tobacco in it. He just sucked it as a baby would suck a finger.

"You've come about that fire-bug matter, I suppose," he said in a babyish, shrill voice.

They related to him what had happened and told him of their investigation and its negative results. He was told of the writing test and the stocking incident, everything in fact.

"It was a good stroke," he harped, "but you must know that the needles have no tongues and the stocking has a beginning but has no end. Besides, it is a queer stuff to deal with. What else have you done?"

"We have spoken to the minister."

"Well, he ought to know. The fellow who gets hit with a stone ought to know where the missile came from. Still, you seem to be inexperienced children," continued the Slovak Methuselah, "and you ought to go back and tell the Governor to send shrewder men than you."

"Why do you say that, father?" asked Teleskey, pocketing the offence. "Did we make any mistake?"

"Of course, you did. You must have asked the minister who hates him most in the village. Why not ask him who loves him most? Now leave me, I am getting sleepy."

They looked at each other in amazement. Old Hrobak is right. The prophet of the mountains had opened their eyes.

Back they trotted, but not the way they came. Teleskey decided to have a look in at the neighbouring village and find out what they had to say, for the neighbours always know more than the villagers themselves.

They rode up to the village inn. There was quite a crowd there discussing the happenings in the burned village a mile away. They knew of the developments, for news travels fast in the Carpathians, especially when matters concerned the minister, who was young and handsome.

They had hardly settled down to a glass of wine when suddenly a young woman burst in, her eyes aflame, and she carried a basket of freshly cut grass on her back.

"Here I am," she shouted. "I can tell you all about it, if you want to know."

She gave Apolka a terrible look and pointing at her with a vicious finger she screamed:

"That girl is the owner of the yellowish blue stocking, if you want to know. She is the one who was jilted by the minister and she is the one who took him from me. So there you are. Just ask her to show you the stockings she wears. . . ."

She looked around triumphantly and drew back a step for effect. The investigating commission looked at her in amazement, then turned towards the accused Apolka. She looked there trembling and flushed. Without any prompting she came forward and raised her skirt as far as her knees. A pair of the most beautiful legs were revealed and a pair of pure white stockings, with not the slightest colouring on them, covered those shapely legs. When this was done, blushing and tears rolling down her cheeks, she recovered herself and with the innate passion and hatred of the Oriental race, she looked her accuser up and down and without saying a word, walked out of the place; turning back at the door and not being able to contain herself, she shouted:

"You were the minister's sweetheart. You are jealous."

They pronounced Apolka innocent and the accuser, having cast her eyes down in defeat, walked out after her with the grass of knowledge on her back and the contempt of the whole congregation at her heels.

Apolka triumphed, but Magdalena, the accuser, fainted as she stepped outside. (There's a God after all, who punishes the false.) It was a tremendous sensation and they talked of this scene there in the village inn for many a day thereafter.

It was getting dark. They decided to return to Lohina and come back the next day to interrogate Magdalena in detail.

"She's good material," said Teleskey; "she knows something, no doubt."

The wind was rather chilly and the frogs just began their nightly conference in the shallow ponds as they set out for the ride back over the mountain paths and along dangerous precipices.

This time Apolka rode behind the men and had not spoken ever since the terrible scene at the inn. Sotony stayed behind as they were riding up hill and spoke to the girl in a low tone:

"You see the trouble you were in, poor girl?"

She gave no answer, just shrugged her shoulder.

"You must get out of here. You can't stay with these people. You are suspected, as sure as I live."

"Why should they suspect me? What do they know about me?" She hissed.

Before Sotony could get hold of her, she slipped off her horse and lay there prone and fainting. Her horse walked on as if nothing had happened. Sotony sprang to her aid, while the others rode on unaware of the incident. It was dark and chilly up on the hills and the moon had not yet appeared. The girl had fainted and as he came up to her, he noticed that her leg was hurt in the fall and warm blood covered her ankle. He instinctively reached out to pull down her stocking and stop the flow of the blood. As he did so, he noticed that she had two pairs of stockings on. The top one was white and the lower one was the yellowish-blue. . . . He stared and paused. He pulled back the stockings and the girl came to just as he finished placing the garter in its place.

They sat there for a while silently. As she looked around and noticed the blood on her leg, she looked at the man and seemed suddenly to understand everything.

"Did you see it?" she asked.

"Yes. Is it true?"

"Yes. You can take me to the gallows. I am ready."

He did not answer. His heart was full of pity for the unfortunate young thing and he was wondering how it could be possible. At last he asked her:

"How did that girl know, Apolka? Did she have the grass of knowledge in her basket?"

Inexpressible hatred trembled on her lips as she said:

"Yes, the grass of knowledge, ha, ha, ha. She knows things without that. . . . She was his sweetheart first and he left her for me. She thinks that he is still coming to see me. She must have been peeping through my window this morning too, when I went home for the needles and saw me pull the white stockings over the others. I had no time to change, you see."

Sotony asked no more questions. There being only one horse, he picked her up and they rode on the one.

"Where should I take you?"

"Anywhere you like," said the girl, dropping her eyes bashfully.

"You know where I will take you? To my house. You'll sleep on silk cushions and wash with perfumed water. . . . Right?"

"Anywhere, I don't care. . . . Yes . . . I am going to sleep on silk cushions. . . ."

"Why be so depressed? You needn't worry. Nobody will ever know."

She turned her face to him and even smiled. He went on:

"We'll be happy there. I shall see you every day and we shall never speak of this ugly thing again. Give me a kiss, Apolka."

"Not now. . . . There. . . ."

They reached the Zeleno precipice.

"Be very careful here; it's a dangerous place," she cautioned him.

As he was about to shorten the reins, she suddenly slipped out of his embrace and threw herself into the darkness that hovered over the crevice and flew . . . flew . . . down into the bottomless abyss. . . . As if a stone were dropping down into the dark, unfathomable hell. . . .

The chasm swallowed her up mutely as if it had been waiting for her all that time. . . .

The Lohina firebug was never discovered . . . and they never suffered another fire; but the minister had to go, nevertheless.

❊ ❊ ❊

ETIENNE BÁRSONY
(1855-   )

BÁRSONY, a disciple of Mikszath, has written some notable stories about peasant and animal life. *The Dancing Bear* is one of his characteristic stories.

The present version, translated by Eugene Lucas, is reprinted from the Lock and Key Library, published by The Review of Reviews Co., copyright, 1909, by whose permission it is here used.

THE DANCING BEAR

FIFE and drum were heard from the big market-place. People went running towards it. In a village the slightest unusual bustle makes a riot. Everybody is curious to know the cause of the alarm, and whether the wheels of the world are running out of their orbit. In the middle of the great dusty market-place some stunted locust trees were hanging their faint, dried foliage, and from far off one could already see that underneath these miserable trees a tall, handsome, young man and a huge, plump, dark-brown, growling bear were hugging each other.

Joco, the bear-leader, was giving a performance. His voice rang like a bugle-horn, and, singing his melancholy songs, he from time to time interrupted himself and hurrahed, whereupon the bear began to spring and roar angrily. The two stamped their feet, holding close together, like two tipsy comrades. But the iron-weighted stick in the young man's hand made it evident that the gigantic beast was quite capable of causing trouble, and was only restrained from doing so because it had learnt from experience that the least outbreak never failed to bring down vengeance upon its back. The bear was a very powerful specimen from Bosnia, with thick brown fur and a head as broad as a bull's. When he lifted himself up on his hind legs he was half a head taller than Joco, his master.

The villagers stood round them with anxious delight, and animated the bear with shouts of "Jump, Ibrahim! Hop, Ibrahim!" but nobody ventured to go near. Joco was no stranger to these people. After every harvest he visited the rich villages of Bánát with his bear. They knew that he was a native of the frontier of Slavonia, and they were not particularly keen to know anything else about him. A man who leads such a vagrant life does not stay long in any one place, and has neither friends nor foes anywhere. They supposed that he spent part of the year in Bosnia, perhaps the winter, visiting, one after the other, the Servian monasteries. Now, in midsummer, when he was least to be expected, they suddenly hear his fife and drum.

Ibrahim, the big old bear, roused the whole village in less than a quarter of an hour with his far-reaching growls. The dogs crouched horror-struck, their hair standing on end, barking at him in fear and trembling.

When Joco stopped at some street corner, or in the market-place, and began to beat his rattling drum, the bear lifted himself with heavy groans on his hind legs, and then the great play began, the cruel amusement, the uncanny, fearful embracings which one could never be sure would not end fatally. For Joco is not satisfied to let Ibrahim jump and dance, but, whistling and singing, grasps the wild beast's skin, and squeezes his paws; and so the two dance together, the one roaring and groaning, the other singing with monotonous voice a melancholy song.

The company of soldiers stationed in the village was just returning from drill, and Captain Winter, Ritter von Wallishausen, turned in curiosity his horse's head towards the crowd, and made a sign to Lieutenant Vig to lead the men on. His fiery half-blood Graditz horse snuffed the digusting odour of the wild beast, and would go no nearer.

The Captain called a hussar from the last line that passed him, and confided the stubborn horse to his charge. Then he bent his steps towards the swaying crowd. The villagers opened out a way for him, and soon the Captain stood close behind the bear-leader. But before he could fix his eyes on Ibrahim they were taken captive by something else.

A few steps away from Joco a young girl sat upon the ground, gently stroking a light-coloured little bear. They were both so huddled up together that the villagers scarcely noticed them, and the Captain was therefore all the better able to observe the young woman, who appeared to be withdrawing herself as much as possible from public gaze. And really she seemed to be an admirable young creature. She was slight of build, perhaps not yet fully developed, with the early ripeness of the Eastern beauty expressed in face and figure—a black cherry, at sight of which the mouth of such a gourmand as the Ritter von Wallishausen would naturally water! Her fine face seemed meant only to be the setting of her two black eyes. She wore a shirt of coarse linen, a frock of many-coloured material, and a belt around her waist. Her beautifully formed bosom, covered only by the shirt, rose and fell in goddesslike shamelessness. A string of glass beads hung round her neck, and two long earrings tapped her cheeks at every movement. She made no effort to hide her bare feet, but now and then put back her untidy but beautiful black hair from her forehead and eyes; for it was so thick that if she did not do so she could not see.

The girl felt that the Captain's fiery gaze was meant for her and not for the little bear. She became embarrassed, and instinctively turned her head away. Just at this moment Joco turned round with Ibrahim. The tall Servian peasant let the whistle fall from his hand, and the wild dance came to an end. Ibrahim understood that the performance was over, and, putting down his front paws on the ground, licked, as he panted, the strong iron bars of his muzzle.

The Captain and Joco looked at each other. The powerful young bear-leader was as pale as death. He trembled as if something terrible had befallen him. Captain Winter looked at him searchingly. Where, he asked himself, had he met this man?

The villagers did not understand what was going on, and began to shout, "Zorka! Now, Zorka, it is your turn with Mariska." The cries of the villagers brought Joco to himself, and with a motion worthy of a player he roused the little bear to its feet. Then he made signs to the girl. Being too excited to blow his whistle, he started singing and beating the drum; but his voice trembled so much that by and by he left off singing and let the girl go through her performance alone.

Then the Captain saw something that wrought him up to ecstasy. Zorka was singing a sad Bosnian song in her tender, crooning voice, and dancing with graceful steps round the little bear, who, to tell the truth, also danced more lightly than the heavy Ibrahim, and was very amusing when he lifted his paw to his head as Hungarians do when they are in high spirits and break forth in hurrahs.

Captain Winter, however, saw nothing but the fair maid, whose pearly white teeth shone out from between her red lips. He felt he would like to slip a silk ribbon round her waist, which swayed as lightly as a reed waving to and fro in the wind, and lead her off as if she were a beautiful coloured butterfly.

Zorka grew tired of the sad, melancholy song, and began to dance wildly and passionately. Perhaps her natural feminine vanity was roused within her, and she wanted to show off at her best before the handsome soldier. Her eyes sparkled; a flush spread from time to time over her face; with her sweet voice she animated the little bear, crying, "Mariska, Mariska, jump!" But after a while she seemed to forget the growling little creature altogether, and went on dancing a kind of graceful fandango of her own invention. As she swayed, it seemed as if the motion and excitement caused every fibre of her body to flash out a sort of electric glow. By the time the girl flung herself, quite exhausted, in the dust at his feet, Captain Winter was absolutely beside himself. Such a morsel of heavenly daintiness did not often drop in his path now that he was fasting in this purgatory of a village. His stay there had been one long Lent, during which joys and pleasures had been rare indeed.

*   *   *

It began to grow dark. At the other end of the market-place several officers were on their way to supper at the village inn where they always messed. The Captain turned to the man and woman in possession of the bears and ordered them in no friendly tone to go with him to the inn as his guests. Joco bowed humbly like a culprit, and gloomily led on his comrade, Ibrahim. Zorka, on the contrary, looked gay as she walked along beside the light-coloured bear.

The Captain looked again and again at the bear-leader walking in front of him. "Where have I seen this fellow before?" he kept asking himself. His uncertainty did not last long. His face brightened. "Oh, yes; I remember!" he inwardly exclaimed. Now he felt sure that this black cherry of Bosnia, this girl with the waist of a dragon-fly, was his.

The inn, once a gentleman's country-house, was built of stone. The bears were lodged in a little room which used to serve the former owner of the house as pantry, and were chained to the strong iron lattice of the window. In one corner of this little room the landlord ordered one of his servants to make a good bed of straw. "The Captain will pay for it," he said.

When everything was ready in the little room, the Captain called Joco and took him there. He knew that what he was going to do was not chivalrous; but he had already worked himself up to a blaze of excitement over the game he meant to play, and this fellow was too stupid to understand what a hazardous piece of play it was. When they were alone he stood erect before the bear-leader and looked fixedly into his eyes.

"You are Joco Hics," he said; "two years ago you deserted from my regiment."

The strong, tall, young peasant began to tremble so that his knees knocked together, but could not answer a single word. Fritz Winter, Ritter von Wallishausen, whispered into Joco's ear, his speech agitated and stuttering: "You have a woman with you," he said, "who surely is not your wife. Set her free. I will buy her from you for any price you ask. You can go away with your bears and pluck yourself another such flower where you found this one."

Joco stood motionless for a while as if turned into stone. He did not tremble any longer: the crisis was over. He had only been frightened as long as he was uncertain whether or not he would be instantly hanged if he were found out.

"In all Bosnia," he answered gloomily, "there was only one such flower and that I stole."

Before a man who was willing to share his guilt, he dared acknowledge his crime. In truth, this man was no better than himself. He only wore finer clothes.

The Captain became impatient. "Are you going to give her up, or not?" he asked. "I do not want to harm you; but I could put you in prison and in chains, and what would become of your sweetheart then?"

Joco answered proudly: "She would cry her eyes out for me; otherwise she would not have run away from her rich father's house for my sake."

Ah! thought the Captain, if it were only that! By degrees I could win her to me.

But it was not advisable to make a fuss, whether for the sake of his position or because of his wife, who lived in town.

"Joco, I tell you what," said the Captain, suddenly becoming calm. "I am going away now for a short time. I shall be gone about an hour. By that time everybody will be in bed. The officers who sup with me, and the innkeeper and his servants, will all be sound asleep. I give you this time to think it over. When I come back you will either hold out your hand to be chained or to receive a pile of gold in it. In the meantime I shall lock you in there, because I know how very apt you are to disappear." He went out, and turned the key twice in the lock. Joco was left alone.

When the hour had expired Captain Winter noisily opened the door. His eyes sparkled from the strong wine he had taken during supper, as well as from the exquisite expectation which made his blood boil.

Joco stood smiling submissively before him. "I have thought it over, sir," he said. "I will speak with the little Zorka about it."

Ritter Winter now forgot that he was speaking with a deserter, whom it was his duty to arrest. He held out his hand joyfully to the Bosnian peasant, and said encouragingly: "Go speak with her; but make haste. Go instantly."

They crept together to the pantry where the girl slept near the chained bears. Joco opened the door without making a sound, and slipped in. It seemed to the Captain that he heard whispering inside. These few moments seemed an eternity to him. At last the bear-leader reappeared and, nodding to the Captain, said: "Sir, you are expected."

Captain Winter had undoubtedly taken too much wine. He staggered as he entered the pantry, the door of which the bear-leader shut and locked directly he had entered. He then listened with such an expression on his face as belongs only to a born bandit. Almost immediately a growling was heard, and directly afterwards some terrible swearing and a fall. The growling grew stronger and stronger. At last it ended in a wild roar. A desperate cry disturbed the stillness of the night: "Help! help!"

In the yard and round about it the dogs woke up, and with terrible yelping ran towards the pantry, where the roaring of the bear grew ever wilder and more powerful. The rattling of the chain and the cries of the girl mingled with Ibrahim's growling. The neighbours began to wake up. Human voices, confused questionings, were heard. The inn-keeper and his servants appeared on the scene in their night clothes, but, hearing the terrible roaring, fled again into security. The Captain's cries for help became weaker and weaker. And now Joco took his iron stake, which he always kept by him, opened the door, and at one bound was at the side of the wild beast. His voice sounded again like thunder, and the iron stick fell with a thud on the bear's back. Ibrahim had smelt blood. Beneath his paws a man's mangled body was writhing. The beast could hardly be made to let go his prey. In the light that came through the small window, Joco soon found the chain from which not long before he had freed Ibrahim, and with a swift turn he put the muzzle over the beast's jaws. It was done in a twinkling. During this time Zorka had been running up and down the empty yard, crying in vain for help. Nobody had dared come near.

The following day Captain Fritz Winter, Ritter von Wallishausen, was lying between burning wax candles upon his bier. Nobody could be made responsible for the terrible accident. Why did he go to the bears when he was not sober?

But that very day the siren of Bosnia danced her wild dance again in the next village, and with her sweet, melodious voice urged the light-coloured little bear: "Mariska, jump, jump!"

✳ ✳ ✳

LOUIS BIRO
(1880-   )

BIRO, though best known as a dramatist, has written some admirable short stories. He is of the moderns, and exceedingly cosmopolitan in his tendencies. *Darkening Shadows* is one of his early stories and displays that inimitable cynicism which is invariably found in contemporary Hungarian literature.

The present version, translated by L. Schwartz, is reprinted from *The Pagan* magazine, by permission of the publisher.

DARKENING SHADOWS

LINKED arm in arm, the director led him across the stage to Elizabeth Geltz, who stood in the farthest corner.

"Elizabeth, allow me to introduce Eugene Forgacs" . . .

The artist reached out her hand with a gentle smile. Forgacs bowed, greatly embarrassed.

Before leaving, the director whispered in his ear,—"Court her, for everything depends on her." Forgacs could find nothing to say to the great artist, who felt amused at his helplessness.

"Where have you been engaged till now?" she asked.

"In small cities, with travelling companies," replied the composer.

"Oh!—well, it will be different hereafter. You will be called to Budapest, Vienna, Paris, Berlin—everywhere!" . . .

"All depends on you!" cried Forgacs excitedly, repeating the director's words.

She became serious.

"I will sing my best. I always give my best to my art. And you have made my task easier, for your music is really beautiful."

Forgacs could no longer control his emotion.

"I never dreamed that my work would ever be performed. When I sent my score to the director, I felt sure it would be returned."

For a few moments they remained silent. Then she spoke again.

"How old are you?"

"Twenty-seven."

Her smile died out, giving way to an expression of pain.

"All right, then. . . . Excuse me now. . . . I have so much to do.
. . . Don't fail to come to our rehearsals" . . . .

Forgacs left; he felt very happy. And he did not fail to attend
the rehearsals, every one of them. It was a delight to him to hear
his own music, make new acquaintances, and drink in the first intoxicating breaths of his approaching fame. To Elizabeth his gratitude
was unbounded. He was sure she would bring him success. She encouraged him in the face of every new difficulty . . . introduced him
to prominent members of the musical profession and of the art-world
in general, and was most enthusiastic in her praise of his score of "The
Revolutionist."

Forgacs became deeply devoted to Elizabeth, who, as a singer, was
celebrated from St. Petersburg to London. It was gratitude mingled with
a feeling that filled his heart; he felt flattered that this singer, who was
honoured by all the great composers, should take such a keen interest in
his compositions.

After each rehearsal he kissed her hand reverently, too moved to utter
all he felt. Once, when he seemed rather discouraged, she tried to cheer
him, and gently stroked his hair.

Some minutes later he was on his way home in the company of Horn,
a journalist.

"My good friend Forgacs," the latter was saying, warningly, "watch
out!" . . .

"Why?"

"Mother 'Lizbeth will get you in her net. . . . You are still young
and inexperienced. You are just the kind she likes. To such as you
Grandma Elizabeth can still prove dangerous. Now, now, don't explain.
. . . I saw her caress your hair. . . . Be careful or you'll become a
laughing-stock!"

Forgacs was stupefied. He could hardly understand of whom Horn
spoke. "Mother Elizabeth." . . . "Grandma Elizabeth" . . . He felt
shocked, and pained, to the depth of his soul. Elizabeth had become the
loftiest ideal to him . . . the very perfection of womanhood. He murmured something expressive of his state of mind.

"You are surprised?" asked Horn. "Oh, I know how grateful you
feel toward her,—and she is worthy of it. But—good Heavens, man, she
is an old woman! . . . And she cannot make her peace with old age.
Her warm blood compels her to ensnare young men . . . mere
lads" . . .

Forgacs grew numb.

"How old *is* she?" he asked bitterly.

"How old? Hm. . . . Twenty years ago she was a celebrated artist. So she must be at least forty-eight, or fifty."

They parted. Forgacs groped his way, dazed. It occurred to him, suddenly, that he had only seen the woman on the darkened stage. She always took care that they should not meet elsewhere. He remembered her only by the splendid lines of her strong, slender figure. He had never thought of her looks, or age. To him she was perfection, and what he had just heard about her stabbed cruelly.

On the following day when Forgacs spoke to her, timidly, he avoided the singer's glance. They stood in the darkest corner of the stage. The composer could hardly see her face, and, as on former occasions, when the rehearsal was over, she dismissed him gently.

Within a week the first performance was given. Behind the scenes Forgacs fairly quivered. Elizabeth approached him and placed her hands on his shoulders. Her face was rouged and otherwise made-up.

"Courage!" she whispered to him.

The curtain went up. Forgacs trembled. Elizabeth Geltz began her aria. The composer listened intently. His trembling ceased.

"Wonderful! How she sings! . . . What an artist! And how beautiful she is!" . . .

A storm of applause. Forgacs felt his heart hammering furiously. The director approached him.

"Bravo! . . . A grand success! What this woman can accomplish! Unbelievable!" . . .

The curtain went down. Applause again. Called out to the footlights, Forgacs bowed right and left, confusedly. Called out again. And again.

Exalted with happiness he dashed to the artist's dressing-room. Elizabeth smiled at him.

"Didn't I tell you?"

As he bent down to kiss her hands, Forgacs' eyes filled with tears.

"Leave me now," she bade him; "I want to dress; but if you have no engagement, after the performance, come up to my apartment for a cup of tea."

Forgacs left. From all sides he was showered with congratulation. "Elizabeth Geltz is still the greatest in her art! Incomparable!"

After the second act, again thunders of applause. And the same after the third . . . long, sincere applause, presaging fame.

The director seized Forgacs by the arm.

"Come with us, if you have no other engagement, and spend half an hour at our table. Let us talk over your success, and let my friends celebrate with you."

Forgacs went along. He was hailed and flattered, and felt happy beyond his boldest dreams. At eleven o'clock he departed. Once alone, he remembered Elizabeth's invitation. The composer looked at his watch. Still not too late. He directed his steps toward her house, his heart still beating elatedly. He rang the bell and was admitted.

The artist came to the door to greet him. A flimsy gown of pale-blue clung to her form.

"I thought you wouldn't come."

"Oh, how could you think that! If you only knew how grateful I feel toward you. . . ."

The woman threw a sidelong glance at her visitor. For a moment she closed her eyes. Then, slowly lifting her long black eyelashes, she smiled at him warmly, alluringly. . . .

"Would you care for a cup of tea?"

"Yes."

"What will you do now?"

Forgacs began to unfold his plans, and became more and more confiding. He spoke of his dreams, which had now come true. Elizabeth sat in a softly lighted corner and listened with keen sympathy. Forgacs rose to put aside the empty cup.

"I'll take it from you," she said. "Won't you have another?"

"No, thank you."

The singer placed the cup on the table. Then she sat down beside him,—very close.

"Don't you want to leave Budapest?"

"Not just yet. I feel well and happy here. And grateful . . . ever so grateful to you."

She bent toward him, and caressed his hair. He saw her at close range . . . in the subdued light . . . but closer than ever before.

Her face was discreetly, artistically, rouged. But not even colour could hide the wrinkles and lines which had come to stay. Everywhere,—about her forehead, and mouth, and throat,—wrinkles . . . the skin flabby . . . old . . . pathetic . . . ugly. . . .

Every repulsive rumour he had ever heard about her flashed through his mind. She leaned still closer to him. Frightened, and sickened, Forgacs trembled an instant; then, involuntarily, with an expression of disgust, he drew back from her.

She noticed it. Her eyes opened wide, and her lips quivered. She stood up, and for an instant remained speechless. So she stood, gazing into space. Then, with a heroic gesture she threw her head back, and crossed the drawing-room to a large mirror that stood against the wall. The anguish and bitterness in her heart as she gazed into the glass! . . . Presently she sat down again. Drawing a handkerchief from her bosom she wiped the entire make-up from her features . . . the rouge from her cheeks, the charcoal from her eyebrows and lids . . . all of it, she wiped away, with slow and weary movements.

Forgacs stared at her, dumfounded. Once again she walked up to the mirror, and without turning around, murmured in an exhausted voice,

"Go. . . ."

Forgacs rose, crushed, while tears started to his eyes. Silently he stole out of the room, as if he were leaving a corpse behind. . . .

YIDDISH

Introduction

YIDDISH, sometimes designated as Hebrew, originally a dialect of Judæo-German, has, by necessity, developed to such an extent, that it has achieved the rank of a distinguished literature. Incidentally Yiddish authors, almost more than any other, have devoted themselves to the short story. This condition, imposed upon them because of the limited Jewish audience they could reach, compelled them to seek and find expression in periodicals and daily journals where they developed a form that is highly artistic.

Russian and Scandinavian literature has greatly influenced Yiddish writers, who are essentially emotional and readily respond to a spirit of melancholy. But, fortunately, their morbidity is tempered with a native humour. Sholom Aleichem is the most famous humourist Yiddish literature has produced, Isaac Loeb Peretz is the foremost representative of the Hassidist, or mystic movement, and Micah Joseph Berdychewski is the Nietzschean exponent. While there have been a good many original authors besides those mentioned above, the majority of story-writers have, allowing for slight deviation, been followers of either of these three.

In the past decade Yiddish literary activities have been gradually shifting from America and eastern Europe to Palestine, where an attempt is under way to revive the ancient Hebrew as opposed to Yiddish. In such an event Yiddish might eventually become extinct. Nevertheless, its contribution to world literature will have become a permanent fact.

❊ ❊ ❊

ISAAC LOEB PERETZ
(1851-1915)

PERETZ, born in Poland, studied law and practised for a short time before turning to literature. His first work was done in Hebrew, but anxious to reach a larger public, he soon began writing in Yiddish. Peretz is one of the most distinguished writers, his stories achieving a rare beauty and tenderness.

A Reincarnated Melody, translated by Joseph Kling, is reprinted from *The Pagan* magazine, by permission of the publisher.

A REINCARNATED MELODY

NINE or ten leagues before Berditchev, right beyond the forest, lies the town of Makhnovka. And in this town there were quite a few musicians; but the foremost among them was Reb Haïm'l.

Reb Haïm'l was a musician of rare attainments,—a pupil of the celebrated Pedhotzor of Berditchev.

He was not a creator of melodies, not a composer in other words. But when it came to performing a musical work, interpreting it, making its beauty manifest, endowing it with a heart almost,—*that* he could do; there lay his strength.

Reb Haïm'l was a slim dried-up figure of a Jew; but no sooner did he begin to play than he became transfigured. His ever-drooping lids slowly lifted, and from his deep soft eyes a spiritual radiance shone over his countenance. It seemed clear to us, then, that he is not really among his fellows, but that his hands play of their own accord, and that his soul is soaring far, far aloft in the Heaven of Song.

Sometimes his voice would join with the music of his violin. . . . And a voice he had! . . . clear,—so clear, and smooth, and full. . . .

If he hadn't been such an unassuming, pious Jew,—a simpleton, almost—Haïm'l would not have remained in Makhnovka to lead a miserable existence, with his wife and eight children. As likely as not he would have been singing in a theatre, or as chief-cantor in some world-renowned synagogue; that's the kind of men *Berditchev* sends out into the world.

But Reb Haïm'l sat at home, living on credit from the various food-shops, month after month, on the prospect of a profitable wedding among the town-gentry, that *must* take place sooner or later.

And sure enough, about this time a grand wedding did take place . . . at the house of Beril Katzner's widow.

Beril Katzner himself,—may the Lord be merciful to him!—was a terrible usurer, and a miser beyond belief. He grudged himself a mouthful of food, and would stoop to pick up the crumbs the children dropped at their meal. A cruel heart, he had, this Beril! Just before his death, almost with his last breath, he calls to his son and tells him to bring in the books (of accounts); points to the unpaid interest-accounts with a brown-bluish finger, and says: "See that these are paid! . . . And without delay . . . do you hear?" . . . Then he called his wife over and told her to put away the copper utensils hanging on the wall. "If I look away even for a moment, everything goes to the dogs!" . . . And with these words he expired.

But he did leave a fortune of half a million (rubles).

As I was telling you, the widow was marrying off a daughter, and she was rather in a hurry, because she was herself setting her cap for a second marriage. She felt greatly relieved, now that the burden of an unmarried daughter was off her hands.

Haïm'l also had a daughter to marry off . . . so the wedding meant almost as much to him as the advent of Messiah.

But, as if out of evil spite, the widow makes up her mind to have Pedhotzor come down from Berditchev! . . . The reason? Well, she's to have guests from Kiev, and they are folks who know what's what. So for their sake she wants a new El-Molo-Ra'h'mim (elegiac prayer-chant) before the canopy ceremony,—not the old threadbare one. Since she has gone to so much expense already, an additional item is of no great matter either way. At any rate, she would *show* those Kiev people. . . .

When Haïm'l heard this he nearly collapsed.

All the townsfolk, also, were stirred up over the news. Haïm'l was well liked. . . . And then, the sheer pity of it . . . such extreme poverty as his . . . they felt more than indignant. Well, there was much talk and discussion, and finally a compromise was reached, namely, that Haïm'l and his company were to play, after all, but that he was to go to Berditchev, at the expense of the bride's mother, and obtain a new prayer-chant from Pedhotzor.

Haïm'l did indeed receive a few rubles,—of which he left the greater part with his wife,—hired a wagon, and set out for Berditchev.

And here begins the story of the Reincarnated Melody.

* * *

You know the proverb: The poor man's luck is like his poverty. . . . Just because Haïm'l happened to be on his way to Berditchev along one road, Pedhotzor was leaving Berditchev along another road. . . . He had been invited to Tolna to a post-Sabbath feast.

You know, I dare say, that the Tolnan (Rabbi) esteemed Pedhotzor very highly. "The Sanctities of the Toirahz*," he was wont to say, "are hidden in his melodies. Only, it is a pity that he (Pedhotzor) himself is not cognizant of their existence."

In the meantime Haïm'l roamed about the streets of Berditchev like a poisoned animal. What was to be done? . . . Return home without the El-Molo-Ra'h'mim he dared not . . . how could he face the angry uproar? . . . Should he follow Pedhotzor to Tolna, or wait for his return? . . . But either of these was unfeasible, for he had only enough money left to return home. . . . The widow had given him a mere trifle, and he had left most of that at home.

So he was in utter despair . . . when quite by chance he happens across the following scene:

Fancy, on a bright sunny weekday a young woman in Sabbath and holiday attire,—or, as they say in those parts, decked out in honey and vinegar,—comes tripping along the street. . . . On her head she wears

* Scriptures.

a curious sort of bonnet, with long, long, gay-coloured ribbons . . . and in her hand she carries a large white silver plate. Following her is a company of musicians, playing lustily.

And she skips along, halting occasionally before a house or shop, and does a little dance. People come out . . . doors and windows open, and fill with curious spectators.

The music plays; the young woman dances . . . the ribbons flutter in the wind . . . the plate gleams and flashes . . . the onlookers cry Mozel tov! (Good luck!) and throw coins . . . the dancer catches them, flashing and ringing, in her plate, with rhythmic precision. . . .

What does it all mean?

Simply this: Berditchev, being a Jewish town, has Jewish customs; this is a custom of collecting money for a poor bride's dowry. Haïm'l knows of the existence of this custom. He knows that the women invent the dances, and that Pedhotzor himself composes the music for them; that's his contribution. People come to him and tell him about the bride, and her family, and her poverty. . . . He listens in silence, meditating . . . occasionally covering his face with his hands. . . . When they have finished, and all is still, Pedhotzor starts to hum the beginning of the composition he has improvised.

All this Haïm'l knows; then why does he stand there with mouth and ears agape?

Because never in all his life has he heard such a melody. . . . It echoes tears and laughter at the same time. It fills one with gladness and with sorrow . . . with heart-ache and heart-ease . . . all blended and commingled . . . the melody of an orphan's wedding!

Haïm'l leaped up . . . he had found his melody!

On the way from Berditchev the driver took on more passengers; Haïm'l did not object.

These people declared, later, that no sooner they entered the forest than Reb Haïm'l began to sing. It was the Pedhotzor tune he sang, but he made a new melody of it . . . the Mozel-tov of the charity-bride became transformed into a true El-Molo-Ra'h'mim. . . .

And in the midst of the quiet rustling of the trees arose a soft, a strong yet soft melody. . . . To the listeners it seemed that the melody was being taken up by an invisible chorus, and that their song was the soft rustling of the trees. . . .

Gentle and poignant was the sad melody . . . pleading mercy like one that is dying. . . . As it kept on it became more grief-filled . . . the pleading changed to broken cries . . . as of one who is striking his breast—"I-have-sinned"—on the Day-of-Atonement or during confession-before-Death.

Louder and deeper with sorrow his voice rose, now and then breaking, as if choked with tears . . . as if struck with anguish. . . . Then several deep sighs, and a sharp cry . . . now another . . . then silence! . . . the stillness of death. . . .

Again the melody rises up . . . this time passing to wild burning cries that soar and whirl and flutter . . . like a chorus of wails that rise to Heaven at a funeral. . . .

And in the midst of it all a pure child-voice comes floating in . . . a pale timid trembling child-voice. . . . And it is chanting Kadish (Prayer-for-the-dead).

The melody changes again . . . is filled, now, with meditative fancies . . . with a myriad of soothing whispers, consoling, gently-sweet . . . with such persuasive goodness and heart-touching faith, that one feels cheered again, and solaced . . . and craves again to live and hope. . . .

The passengers were in ecstasy.

"What *is* it?" they asked him.

"An El-Molo-Ra'h'mim for Reb Katzner's orphan-daughter."

"She hardly deserves it," they commented; "too wonderful a composition for such an occasion. . . . But the world will learn of it, soon enough, and take it from you. . . . And the Kiev-people will die of envy."

But the Kiev-people did not die of envy.

There was no real respectable Jewish wedding at the Katzners; and the El-Molo-Ra'h'mim fell flat. The Kiev-folk preferred to dance with the ladies. . . . What did they care about prayer-chants, and sermons? . . .

Besides, for whose benefit an El-Molo-Ra'h'mim? For the old dead miser? If the skinflint were alive the bride would no doubt be without a dowry; certainly without a trousseau; the whole wedding would have been so different. . . . If he could come back to life and see the bride's black silk dress, and her veil . . . the wines, and meats, and cakes under which the table creaked . . . he would surely suffer death again, and this time more painfully.

And what need of the whole marriage-ceremony anyhow? . . . Only an old foolish custom. . . .

"Faster!" cried the guests from Kiev to Haïm'l.

Poor man! . . . He stopped his little orchestra, and with beating heart continued to draw his bow across the violin. There were tears in the eyes of the plebeian element present. . . . Just then a Kiev-an cries out: "What's this?! a wedding or a funeral?" . . . But Haïm'l pretends not to hear and keeps on playing. Whereupon the Kiev-an begins to whistle.

And it cannot be denied that he whistles well. He has caught on to the melody, and whistles it perfectly. . . . Keeps on whistling faster, gayer, wilder . . . the same melody . . . the very same. . . .

The orchestra is quite still . . . it is a battle now, between the pious soulful violin and the licentious impudent whistler.

And the whistler conquers! . . . drowns out the voice of the fiddle! . . . It has ceased to lament . . . it moans, at first, then begins to laugh.

Suddenly Haïm'l pauses. . . . With tightened lips and blazing eyes he jumps to another string and begins to play faster, faster . . . to overtake the whistler. . . .

Oh no! . . . this is not playing, now, it is the very soul of the violin breaking into tortured screams that flare and whirl like a tempest. . . . And it seemed that everything about whirled in unison . . . the house, the orchestra, the bride in her chair, and Haïm'l himself with his fiddle. . . .

It was neither a gay ditty, nor a mournful El-Molo-Ra'h'mim, but a mad, mad dance . . . a wild, uncanny St. Vitus dance, it was,—Lord's mercy! . . .

And it keeps on unceasingly . . . till the string bursts. . . .

❋ ❋ ❋

SHOLOM ALEICHEM
(1859-1916)

SHOLOM RABINOVITZ, writing under the pseudonym of Sholom Aleichem, was born in Russia and spent the greater part of his life in Kiev. He tried his hand at every form of writing, but he will be best remembered for his short stories. These are for the most part related with humour, a humour that is, however, pregnant with the tragedy of his folk.

Eva is an excellent story and is representative of Sholom Aleichem. His description of Tevye is superb. Here is a character who attempts to be scholarly and profound in biblical lore, and succeeds in misquoting its literature. But he is exceptionally human. The present version, translated by Joseph Kling, is reprinted from *The Pagan* magazine, by permission of the publisher.

EVA

PRAISE be the Lord, our beneficent God!"; that is to say, the deeds of Heaven are most just. At any rate, it's our business to find them so. But if we don't it makes no difference anyway . . . we can't improve on them, can we? . . . Not a bit. Take me, for example. I've tried my level best, like a clever man, to make things go as they ought to.

With what success? . . . None,—none at all. So I have given up trying. "Tevye," I say to myself, "you're a fool! You can't reform the world. The Lord has laid upon us the 'burden and sorrow of bringing up children'; in other words, even though children are a source of tribulation, one mustn't complain.

Here you have my oldest daughter, Tzaitel, for example, who is head over heels in love with that tailor-fellow, Mottil Komzoil. Do I oppose her in any way? . . . Not in the least. Though I know well enough that he is only a simple fellow, scarcely able to read his prayers. But then,—not all of us can be educated, as you say. Besides, he is a perfectly honest fellow, and works hard to support himself and his family,—a considerable brood, as you may know. It goes without saying that they're having a pretty tough time of it. But not according to Tzaitel; she insists that everything is all right . . . couldn't be any better . . .except for the slight inconvenience of having very little to eat.

And so my "Chapter of Miseries" begins; in other words, let's call this, Trouble No. 1.

Now about my second daughter, Hodel, I needn't tell you anything . . . you know *her* story . . . she's gone,*—lost to me forever . . . God alone knows whether my eyes will ever behold her again,—unless it be in the World-to-come. I cannot mention her name without feeling as if my heart is dying within me. "Why not forget her, then?" you ask. Easily said. . . . But how is it possible to forget a living human being,—especially such a one as my daughter Hodel was. You ought to read the letter she writes me. . . . She is doing very well, she says; *he* is in prison and *she* works for a living; she does washing and reads books; sees him every week, and hopes that soon there will be a "fine mess" † here . . . "At last the sun will rise," she writes, "and the darkness will be dispelled." . . . Then he, and many others like him, will return home and begin the real work of pulling down and rebuilding our topsy-turvy world." . . . How does that strike you?

But wait! . . . Observe how the Lord of the World,—(who is indeed a "benign and merciful Lord," as you say)—deals with me. . . . "A little patient, Tevye," He says, "and I'll manage things so that you will forget all your troubles." And so indeed, I really did forget all my troubles. How? . . . Just listen. It's worth hearing. To no other but you would I tell the story, for the shame of it is even greater than the sorrow. . . . But as the Holy Script has it, "Shall I seek concealment from Abraham?"; in other words, from you I have no secrets. But one thing I must beg of you, and that is,—silence. Need I tell you why? . . . You understand . . . the pain of it is deep, but the shame,—the shame is even deeper. . . .

* Exiled with her lover to Siberia for revolutionary activities.
† A revolution.

Well then,—you remember the quotation in the Perek: "The Lord sought to bestow His fortune." . . . It applies to me in this way,— namely, that Providence, seeking to make manifest Its great beneficence, blesses me with seven children, all females,—daughters, I mean. . . . And all pretty . . . clever . . . charming . . . healthy . . . as hand- some and straight as young pine-trees. . . . Would to God that they were ugly frights instead! It might have been better for them, and healthier for me. For,—tell me, pray,—what is the good of a blooded horse if it's always stabled? What's the good of having handsome daugh- ters if one must bring them up in an out-of-the-way corner, without a soul knowing about them, except Anton Poperila, the village-elder; Hvedka Galagan, the village scribe, and worst of all, the village-priest,— may his memory be accursed! I cannot bear even the mention of his name. . . . Not because *I* am a Jew, and *he* a Christian priest. . . . On the contrary, he and I have known each other for I don't know how many years . . . by which I do not mean to say, of course, that we go to each other's parties, or that we celebrate each other's holidays. . . . Only,—just so. . . . "Good morning . . . how are you?" . . . a few words of conversation . . . and "Good-bye." . . . To enter into any discussion with him is not my particular delight. . . For, when I do permit myself a few random remarks, he immediately starts with a long chapter of arguments about *our* God, and *your* God, and the like. . . . I don't like to see him get the best of the argument, naturally, so I reply with a proverb, and add: "There is a passage in the Scripture,"——

"Oh, the Scriptures!" he interrupts, "I know the Scriptures as well as you do; and perhaps a little better, even." . . . And he begins to recite aloud certain portions of the Bible, with the Gentile pronunciation of course. . . . "Bereshet barah alakim" . . . In my turn, I interrupt, with the remark, "There's a certain Commentary,——"

"Oh, a Commentary! . . . That means Tal-mud, and Tal-mud I hate . . . Tal-mud is sheer falsehood." Which, of course, makes me quite angry, so that I begin to use rather violent language to him. . . . But do you suppose, for a moment, that he gets at all provoked? Not a bit. He only looks at me, laughs, and strokes his beard. . . . Be- lieve me, there is nothing more exasperating than to see a person whom you are abusing, and calling ugly names, look at you smilingly, without answering . . . you feel that you are bursting with rage, and he keeps on smiling. . . . I didn't understand then, as I do now, the meaning of that smile of his. . . .

Well,—one evening, as I am nearing home, after my day's journey, I encounter Hvedka the Scribe with my daughter Eva, the one next to Hodel, you know. No sooner does the gentleman see me than he lifts his cap to me, bows, and walks off.

"What was Hvedka doing here?" I ask Eva.

"Nothing," she answers.

"How do you mean, nothing?"

"We were just chatting," she says.

"Why,—what business have you with Hvedka?" I ask.

"Oh, we're old acquaintances," she replies.

"So? . . . I am happy to know it! . . . An admirable choice, I must say." . . .

"But you don't know him, father; why do you speak of him in that tone?" . . .

"Quite true,—I don't happen to know the gentleman's pedigree. . . . But it's quite evident that his ancestors must have been really *great* people. . . . His father, I dare say, was a shepherd, at least, if not a night-watchman, or just a plain drunkard." . . . To which she rejoins: "I don't know who and what his father was, and what's more, I don't care . . . to me all people are equally well-born. But what I do know is that Hvedka is an uncommon person."

"In what way, may I ask, is he an uncommon person?" I say.

"I would tell you, but I am sure you wouldn't understand . . . Hvedka is a second Gorky." . . .

"A second Gorky?" I exclaim,—"then, evidently, there must have been a first; may I know who he was?" . . .

"Gorky," she replies, "is one of the foremost men in the world."

"Indeed! . . . And where does he live, this great Master? . . . What's his business? . . . What sort of sermons does he preach?" . . .

"Gorky," she answers, "is a famous author . . . a writer . . . a man who writes books . . . and a fine, honest, noble man besides. He also is of common stock. . . . Studied by himself . . . not school-learned . . . here is his picture."

So saying, she takes a photograph out of her pocket, and shows it to me.

"So! . . . So this is the Great Reb Gorky! . . . I could swear that I've seen him somewhere in the neighbourhood . . . either loading bags into the cars at the railway-station, or dragging logs from the forest. . . ."

"Do you consider it a disgrace for a man to work for his living? . . . don't you yourself work hard for your living? . . . don't we all work? . . .

"Of course, of course . . . quite so. . . . It is even written plainly, in our sacred books: 'By the labour of thy hands shalt thou live,' or in other words, if you don't work you won't eat. Still I don't see what that has to do with Hvedka. . . . I'd feel much happier if you knew him more distantly. . . . You mustn't forget, 'Whence you come and whither you are bound'; in other words, who *you* are and who *he* is. . . ." To which she replies: "God created all men equal." . . .

"Certainly, certainly," I answer, "but remember that every creature seeks its own kind. As it is written: 'Each according to his donation.'" . . .

"It's remarkable," she says, "how you always manage to find quotations to suit your arguments. . . . Couldn't you manage to find a passage, somewhere, that explains how we ourselves have divided mankind into Jew and Gentile, master and servant, aristocrat and beggar . . . ?"

"Ta! ta! ta!" I exclaim; "you're driving recklessly into the seventh Heaven!" . . . And I try to make her understand that our present order of things has existed from the very beginning of the world. . . .

Whereupon she asks rather pertly: "But why should our present order of things *have been* such from the beginning of the world? . . ."

To which I rejoin: "Oh, now,—if you're going to begin asking questions, why this and why that, there'll be 'No end to speech,'—a story without end, in other words" . . .

"But if we are not to question, and to reason, why has God gifted us with intelligence?" she asks.

"It is a custom among our people," I answer, "that when a chicken begins to crow like a rooster, to take her to the Shoichet * . . . as it is stated in the Blessings: 'He giveth understanding to the rooster'" . . .

"Isn't it about time you stopped chattering out there!" exclaims Golda, my wife, through the window; "the milk-soup's been on the table now over an hour, and he keeps on saying grace." . . .

"Here we are! the second half of the program!" I remark. . . . "Not for nothing have our sages said, 'In seven things may'st thou know a fool'; the meaning of which is 'A woman's speech has no end.' We are discussing matters of deep moment and she breaks in with her milk-soup."

And she: "My soup is as much a matter of moment as all your grand discussions are."

"Congratulations!" I exclaim; "another philosopher in the family,— and hot from the oven, too! Not enough that our daughter has become 'enlightened,' but Tevye's wife also wants to fly through the chimney heavenward."

"Oh, is it flying to heaven you're talking about? . . . Then take my blessing, and fly in the other direction!"

How do you like that for an appetizer on an empty stomach? . . .

But to return to my story . . . thus passing from the "Prince to the Princess," as the saying is . . . I mean, to the priest,—may his name perish. . . .

One evening, as I am driving home with my empty dairy-jugs, and nearing the village, I meet the reverend gentleman in his handsome car-

* **Mosaic-ritual slaughterer.**

riage. His own holy self holds the reins while his well-kept beard streams in the wind.

"Well-met!" I say to myself, "it would make me just as happy to meet Beelzebub in person" . . .

"Good evening," he says to me, "don't you recognise me; or,—what is it?". . .

"You will grow rich soon," I answer, doffing my cap, and make as if to drive on.

"Hold on!" he exclaims, "stop a minute . . . what's your hurry? . . . I have something to tell you."

"Oh, with pleasure . . . if it's something good. But if it isn't, you may as well postpone it for another occasion."

"What do you mean by another occasion?" he asks.

"By another occasion, I mean when Messiah will come."

"But Messiah is already come, long since," he rejoins.

"I've heard that before, more than once. Tell us something new, little father."

"That's just what I mean to do," he says. "The fact is that I want to talk to you about yourself,—that is to say, about your daughter."

At the word "daughter" I feel a sudden tug at my heart. What has he to do with my daughter? . . . Aloud I say: "My daughters are not the kind that need other people's services; they can speak for themselves without any help."

"But it happens to be a matter about which your daughter cannot speak for herself. Someone must do it for her. It's a question of her future."

"How does my daughter's future concern any one?" I ask. "It seems to me, that if there is any question at all about my daughter's future she has a father to look after her, thank Heaven."

"True," he answers, "you are indeed her father, but you are blind to her welfare. . . . She craves to get into another sphere, and you do not, or will not understand her."

"Whether I do not, or will not, understand her is a matter which we may discuss another time. What I should like to know now is how her welfare concerns you." . . .

"It concerns me because she is at present under my care."

"What do you mean 'under your care'?" I ask.

"I mean that she is under my guardianship," he replies, and looks me straight in the face, while he strokes his handsome flowing beard.

His words naturally make me start. "What! you call yourself my daughter's guardian? . . . By what right?" And I feel a burning anger rising within me. He, on the other hand, answers nonchalantly, with a little smile: "Easy there, Tevel, don't get excited. Let's talk this over quietly. . . . I think you know, Tevel, that I am far from being your enemy, even though you're a Jew. You know how I esteem your brother-Jews, and how grieved I am at their stubbornness in not realising that we mean their good." . . .

"Don't talk to me now about friendship and esteem . . . your words are poison to me . . . they pierce my heart like deadly bullets. . . . If you are really my friend, as you say you are, I beg one favour of you: Leave my daughter alone!"

"Don't be foolish, Tevel; no harm will befall her. . . . In fact, she ought to be quite happy . . . her young man is a perfect jewel . . . would that my fortune were as bright."

"Amen," I answer with a feigned laugh. But inwardly I feel as if consumed by fire.

"And who," I say, "may the lucky man be,—if it is not indiscreet of me to ask . . . ?"

"I think you know him," he replies; "he is a very honest, well-behaved, young fellow; self-educated,—but a man of culture nevertheless; he is head over heels in love with your daughter, and wants to marry her, but cannot, because he is not a Jew." . . .

Hvedka! flashes through my mind. I feel utterly stunned; the blood rushes to my head, and a cold perspiration covers my body; I can scarcely keep my seat on the wagon. But I control myself. I mustn't let him see my agony. . . . No! . . . I'll see him hanged first!

So I take up the reins and make off, without as much as a "By-your-leave." . . .

When I reach home I find the house in a frightful mess. The children are crying . . . my Golda is more dead than alive. . . . I look around for Eva,—but she is nowhere to be seen. I know it is useless to ask where she is. . . . I feel the anguish of death, while a towering rage blazes up in me. And on whom do I vent my bitter anger? . . . On my wife and children,—poor innocents. . . . I am unable to remain still a moment . . . find no peace anywhere. . . . Presently I find myself on the way to the stall, with fodder for my horse. Unluckily for the beast, he has got himself into mischief by sticking his forepaws into the bin; so I seize a stick and belabour him cruelly. "Plague take you! stupid beast!" I cry. "So may you give up the ghost right now, if I have a single nibble of oats for you. Misery is all I possess . . . misery, and grief, and suffering." . . . In such language I address my nag. . . . But soon I come to myself. . . . "The poor beast is also one of God's creatures!" I say to myself. . . . "Why should I ill-treat him? . . . So I fill up his bin with chopped straw, promising him a bit of hay on the Sabbath.

Then I return to the house, and bury myself in a corner, to brood over my misfortune. . . . I think and think till my head almost bursts. . . . trying to figure out the full import of the passage: "How have I sinned and what is my transgression?" How have I, Tevye, fallen from grace more than other mortals, that I should be punished more cruelly than all men? . . . "Oh Lord of the World, Great God of Israel! . . . What am I that you keep me so constantly in mind and unfailingly bless me with new troubles and calamities?" . . .

As I lie brooding thus, I hear my Golda sighing brokenly, and her grief adds to my wretchedness.

"Golda," I call; "aren't you asleep?"

"No," she answers; "why do you ask?"

"Oh, just so. . . . It looks as though we're in a bad fix. . . . What, —what would you advise?" . . .

"What can I advise? . . . It's all so strange, so cruelly perplexing. . . . A girl gets up in the morning, looking well and strong, . . . dresses herself . . . then begins to embrace me, without rhyme or reason. . . . 'What ails you?' I ask her. No answer. Then she goes out to look after the cows. . . . An hour passes . . . two . . . three. . . . No sign of her. So I say to the children: 'Suppose you run over to the priest's' " . . .

"But how did you know she was at the priest's?"

"How did I know? . . . How shouldn't I know,—more's the pity! . . . Have I no eyes? . . . Am I not her mother?" . . .

"True . . . but since you *have* eyes and *are* her mother, why didn't you tell me anything about it all along? . . ."

"Tell *you?* . . . When are you home? . . . And if I *should* tell you, would you listen to me? . . . you have a quotation ready for everything I say. If only you succeed in silencing me with your quotations you're satisfied."

So my Golda speaks to me . . . and I,—I cannot say she is altogether wrong . . . how should she,—a woman,—understand the beauty of our wise and sacred writings? . . . And to hear her, in the dark, sighing and weeping, grieves me beyond measure. . . . So I say to her: "Golda," I say, "you are vexed because I have a habit of answering you with quotations. . . . I cannot help answering that with another quotation. It is written: 'Like a father's pity for his children'; in other words, a father loves his child. Why it is not written: 'Like a mother's pity for her children'? that is to say, a *mother* loves her child . . . ? Because a mother is not a father. A father knows how to reason with a child. . . . Wait till to-morrow morning . . . you'll see how I'll talk to her." . . .

"I hope you'll be able to see her and him too, . . . he's not really a bad man, even though he is a priest, . . . he is not without pity. . . . You'll fall at his feet and beseech him to have pity on us. . . ."

"What! to that limb of Satan! . . . I am to cringe before that heathen, curse his name! . . . Are you out of your senses? . . . Never shall the Evil One have that power. . . . No enemy of mine shall live to see me so humbled!"

"There,—you see? . . . didn't I tell you?"

"Well, what did you expect? . . . that I would let a woman lead me by the nose? . . . I'll let your woman's brains think for me?" . . . In such discussions we spent the night. . . .

No sooner did I hear the first cock-crow than I got up, recited my prayers, hitched up the wagon, and started out for the priest's house, . . . thus following a woman's advice after all. But what alternative had I? . . . Where else *could* I go? . . .

On reaching the court-yard of the priest's house, I am greeted cordially by his dogs, who seek to improve the appearance of my coat, and to taste the fleshy portion of my legs. . . . It's a lucky thing I brought my whip along so that I could make plain to them the meaning of "Not a dog shall open his mouth to bark," in other words, if a dog barks, let him know the reason why.

At the sound of their barking, the priest and his wife came running out, scattered the lively pack, after much ado, and invited me into the house. I was given a cordial welcome; my host even wanted to put up the samovar, but I objected. I let him know in a few words that I had something to say to him "under four eyes." . . . He guessed my meaning, and nodded to his wife to close the door,—on the outside.

I came straight to the point, without beating about the bush, by asking 'nim, first, whether he believes in God. . . . And second, whether he realises what it means to separate a loving father from his daughter. . . . And further to tell me what he considers a virtuous deed, and what an iniquity. . . . And one thing more: To tell me what he thinks of a man who steals into his neighbour's house and tries to turn things topsyturvy, furniture and all. . . .

He remained sitting, sort of stunned; then he says to me: "Tevel!" says he, "you're a clever fellow. . . . You ask me four questions at once, and want me to answer them all in the same breath. . . . Take your time, and I'll answer them one by one." . . .

"No, little father, you'll never answer them . . . and do you know why? . . . Because I know your arguments beforehand, by this time. . . . You better tell me this one thing: Is there any hope of my seeing my daughter again,—yes or no?"

At which he starts up and exclaims: "What do you mean by 'seeing her again'? . . . She is in no danger, . . . quite the contrary." . . .

"Oh, I know, I know. . . . You want to make her happy. . . . But that's not what I'm after. . . . I want to know where my daughter is, and whether I can see her or not."

"I'm sorry," he replies, "I will grant you everything but that."

"So! . . . that's different," I rejoin. . . . "Clear speech,—short, and to the point. Good-bye," I say, "and may Heaven repay you a hundredfold!"

When I reach home I find my Golda huddled up on the bed, exhausted with weeping.

"Get up, wife dear," I exclaim, "let us prepare to sit 'shiva,' as God has ordained. . . . 'The Lord giveth and the Lord taketh away.' . . . We are not the first nor the last. . . . Let us suppose we never had a daughter Eva, . . . or let us imagine that she, like Hodel, has gone away to the 'Dark Hills.' God is merciful and just; He knows what He does." . . .

In speeches of this nature, I give vent to the fulness of my heart, while tears choke me, . . . but Tevye is not a woman. . . . Tevye knows how to control himself. . . . Or can pretend to, at least. . . . For,—how is it possible to look indifferent, when one's shame is so great, and still more when one loses a daughter, . . . loses her utterly, as if she had died. . . . Such a daughter, . . . a jewel, . . . perhaps the most cherished of the family, maybe because in her childhood she was snatched from the very claws of death more than once, . . . nursed as one nurses a feeble chick. . . . Or it may be because she was so good and loving to us. . . .

In our holy books it is written: "Thou livest, willy-nilly," which means, no man willingly takes his own life. There is no wound so deep but that it will heal in time, and no sorrow so great but it will gradually be forgotten. I mean, not really *forgotten*, but as the sages have it: "A man may be compared to a cow." . . . A man must toil and drudge for his crust of bread. All of us took up our work again; my wife and children with the jugs, and I with my horse and wagon.

I made it a point of warning all of my household never to mention the name of Eva again. She is no more, . . . blotted out. . . .

One day, after I had finished with my customers at Boiberick, I betook myself home through the wood. . . . I let my nag amble leisurely along; he nibbles stealthily at the grass, here and there, along the roadside, while I fall to meditating on everything imaginable, . . . on life, and death, . . . this world and the world-to-come, . . . and what the word "world" really signifies, . . . and what our life stands for, . . . and the like, in order to dispel my obsession. . . . I mean the memory of my daughter Eva. . . . But as if out of spite her image keeps haunting me unceasingly. . . . I see her tall, and fresh, and fair, like a young pine. . . . Or as she used to be in her childhood, small, and feeble, and ailing. . . . Or as an infant on my arm, . . . her little head leaning on my shoulder. . . . And for the moment I forget her unspeakable conduct, and feel such a yearning, such a painful, gnawing, longing for her. . . .

But again I remind myself, . . . and a consuming rage possesses me, against him and her, . . . against the whole world,—myself in-

cluded. . . . I want to root her out of my heart, . . . blot her from
my memory . . . and cannot. . . . What better does she deserve? . . .
Have I been a faithful son of Israel all these years . . . toiling and
moiling to bring up my children in ways of righteousness, to see them fall
suddenly away from me, like leaves from a tree, carried away with the
smoke and wind? . . . Behold, a tree growing, in the forest. . . .
Comes a creature with an axe and chops off its branches one by one. . . .
What remains?—the pity of it!—A limbless, naked, blasted, trunk. . . .
Oh, thou son of Adam! Be merciful. . . . Aim thy axe at the root,
. . . let not the barren trunk stand leafless and withering in the
forest. . . .

And as I sit meditating thus, I observe that my horse has stopped. . . .
What can that mean? . . . I look up: Eva! . . . Yes. . . . Eva,
her very self! Not changed in the slightest . . . even the same
clothes. . . .

My first impulse is to jump off the wagon, seize her in my arms and
kiss her tenderly. . . . But then the thought flashes through my mind,
"Tevye! Do you mean to behave like a woman?" . . . And I pull the
reins, crying, "Get up there, you lazy carcass!" guiding him to the right.
I look around . . . she likewise has turned to the right, and motions
to me with her hand, as if to say: "Stop, stop! I want to speak to you."

I feel a sudden twinge, a tugging at my heart, while my limbs relax
nervelessly . . . a second more and I must leap off the wagon. . . .
But with a great effort I restrain myself, and make the horse turn to the
left. She keeps on after the wagon, and looks at me so strangely . . .
her face as pale as death. . . . What shall I do?—stand still, or go
ahead? . . . Before I can look around again she is at the horse's head,
her hand on the bridle. . . .

"Father!" she cries, "I will not let you stir from this spot, even though
it should cost me my life, till you have heard what I have to say to you.
. . . Listen to me, father dear, I implore you. . . ."

"Oh—ho!"—I say to myself, "so you mean to take me by force, do
you? . . . Nay, nay, daughter mine . . . evidently you don't know
your father yet," . . . and I begin to whip the horse with a will. He
obeys with alacrity, but keeps looking around.

"Stop that!" I exclaim; "keep your eyes where they belong, Mr. Wise-
acre." . . . And do you suppose that I myself am not dying to turn
around, to take a look, a single glance, at least, at the spot where she is
standing? . . .

But no! . . . Tevye is not a woman. . . . Tevye knows how to
contend with the Tempter. . . .

Well, to make a long story short,—(I don't want to take up too much
of your time)—what I suffered during that homeward journey ought to
atone for all my sins. . . . It was a foretaste of Gehenna, Inferno, and

all the other tortures described in our holy books. All the way home I seemed to hear her footsteps running after the wagon, and her voice calling to me pleadingly, "Father, father, dear . . . listen to me." . . .

And suddenly I ask myself, "Tevye, what makes you so cocksure of yourself? . . . How will it hurt you if you stop a moment and listen to her? . . . Perhaps she really has something of importance to tell you . . . who knows? . . . Maybe she regrets her action, and wants to return. . . . Or, she is under his heel, perhaps, and comes to you to rescue her from her misery?" . . .

Thus I reflect, and wonder, and speculate . . . maybe this, and maybe that. . . . And I torment myself, and call myself the worst names. . . . "What are you so excited about?" I ask myself. . . . Why do you fuss and fume in this fashion, you obstinate fool! . . . Turn about and call her back. . . . She is your daughter, after all . . . your own flesh and blood." . . .

And suddenly bizarre thoughts begin to pass through my head, such as,—"What constitutes a Jew, and what a non-Jew? . . . and why has God created Jews and Gentiles? . . . And since God *has* created Jews, why are they so unfriendly and antagonistic to one another?" . . . And I feel vexed with myself for not being book-learned enough to be able to answer all these perplexing questions. . . .

So to drive away my gloomy meditations, I begin to chant the evening-prayer: "Blessed is the man that dwelleth . . . etc.," loud and fervently, as the Lord has ordained. But what's the good of praying when, within me, I hear a different chant . . . "Eva . . . Ev-a . . . Eva." Eva." . . . The louder I pray, the stronger grows the inner chant. . . . The more I try to forget her the clearer her image becomes. . . . I can even hear her voice still calling to me: "Listen to me, father dear" . . . I put my hands to my ears that I may not hear . . . and shut my eyes that I may not see. . . . I recite my prayers without knowing what I'm saying . . . and I beat my breast penitently without knowing why . . . and I feel broken and desolate. . . .

I told no one about the incident of our meeting, said nothing about her to anybody. . . . I have made no inquiries about her, although I know well enough where she is, and where he is, and what they are doing. . . . But will people hear Tevye lament and complain? . . . Oh no! Tevye isn't that kind of a man.

I am curious to know whether all men are such crazy fools as I am,— or am I an exception . . . ? For example, it once happened,—but you won't laugh at me, will you?—once I put on my Sabbath-coat, and went to the railway-station, ready to take the train to *them* . . . (I know where they live.) I walked over to the ticket-agent and asked him for a ticket.

"Where to?" he asks.

"To Yehoopitz," I answer.

"There is no such town," he says.

"Well, that isn't my fault," I reply. . . . And return home, take off my Sabbath-coat, and go back to my work. . . . "Each to his work and to his labour," as the sages have it; in other words, the tailor to his shears, and the shoe-maker to his last. . . . See! you *are* laughing at me. . . . I am even sure you're saying to yourself: "This Tevye is a simple lunatic." . . . So I guess we'll say: "Till the chimes ring again"; I mean, enough for to-day! . . .

Good-bye now. . . . Live well, and write us a letter once in a while. . . . But I must remind you again,—not a syllable of this to anyone, I pray you; mum's the word. I mean, don't write a story about me . . . write about anyone else you like, but not about me. . . . Exit Tevye, for good and all." . . .

✳ ✳ ✳

JUDAH STEINBERG
(1863-1908)

STEINBERG, born in Bessarabia, began, after a short business career, teaching. In 1905 he removed to Odessa and became a correspondent for one of the New York Jewish dailies. He wrote several volumes of short stories and soon earned recognition as a distinguished writer of clear and fluent prose with rare ability to delineate characters.

A Livelihood is reprinted from the volume, *Yiddish Tales*, translated by Helena Frank, copyright, 1912, by the Jewish Publication Society of America, by whose permission it is here used.

A LIVELIHOOD

THE two young fellows Maxim Klopatzel and Israel Friedman were natives of the same town in New Bessarabia, and there was an old link existing between them: a mutual detestation inherited from their respective parents. Maxim's father was the chief Gentile of the town, for he rented the corn-fields of its richest inhabitant; and as the lawyer of the rich citizen was a Jew, little Maxim imagined, when his father came to lose his tenantry, that it was owing to the Jews. Little Struli * was the only Jewish boy he knew (the children were next door neighbours), and so a large share of their responsibility was laid on

* Diminutive of Israel.

Struli's shoulders. Later on, when Klopatzel, the father, had abandoned the plough and taken to trade, he and old Friedman frequently came in contact with each other as rivals.

They traded and traded, and competed one against the other, till they both became bankrupt, when each argued to himself that the other was at the bottom of his misfortune—and their children grew up in mutual hatred.

A little later still, Maxim put down to Struli's account part of the nails which were hammered into his Saviour, over at the other end of the town, by the well, where the Government and the Church had laid out money and set up a crucifix with a ladder, a hammer, and all other necessary implements.

And Struli, on his part, had an account to settle with Maxim respecting certain other nails driven in with hammers, and torn scrolls of the Law, and the history of the ten martyrs of the days of Titus, not to mention a few later ones.

Their hatred grew with them, its strength increased with theirs.

When Krushevan began to deal in anti-Semitism, Maxim learned that Christian children were carried off into the Shool, Struli's Shool, for the sake of their blood.

Thenceforth Maxim's hatred of Struli was mingled with fear. He was terrified when he passed the Shool at night, and he used to dream that Struli stood over him in a prayer robe, prepared to slaughter him with a ram's horn trumpet.

This because he had once passed the Shool early one Jewish New Year's Day, had peeped through the window, and seen the ram's horn blower standing in his white shroud, armed with the Shofar, and suddenly a heartrending voice broke out with Min ha-Mezar, and Maxim, taking his feet on his shoulders, had arrived home more dead than alive. There was very nearly a commotion. The priest wanted to persuade him that the Jews had tried to obtain his blood.

So the two children grew into youth as enemies. Their fathers died, and the increased difficulties of their position increased their enmity.

The same year saw them called to military service, from which they had both counted on exemption as the only sons of widowed mothers; only Israel's mother had lately died, bequeathing to the Czar all she had—a soldier; and Maxim's mother had united herself to a second provider—and there was an end of the two "only sons!"

Neither of them wished to serve; they were too intellectually capable, too far developed mentally, too intelligent, to be turned all at once into Russian soldiers, and too nicely brought up to March from Port Arthur to Mukden with only one change of shirt. They both cleared out, and stowed themselves away till they fell separately into the hands of the military.

They came together again under the fortress walls of Mukden.

They ate and hungered sullenly round the same cooking pot, received punches from the same officer, and had the same longing for the same home.

Israel had a habit of talking in his sleep, and, like a born Bessarabian, in his Yiddish mixed with a large portion of Roumanian words.

One night, lying in the barracks among the other soldiers, and sunk in sleep after a hard day, Struli began to talk sixteen to the dozen. He called out names, he quarrelled, begged pardon, made a fool of himself —all in his sleep.

It woke Maxim, who overheard the homelike names and phrases, the name of his native town.

He got up, made his way between the rows of sleepers, and sat down by Israel's pallet, and listened.

Next day Maxim managed to have a large helping of porridge, more than he could eat, and he found Israel, and set it before him.

"Maltzimesk!" said the other, thanking him in Roumanian, and a thrill of delight went through Maxim's frame.

The day following, Maxim was hit by a Japanese bullet, and there happened to be no one beside him at the moment.

The shock drove all the soldier-speech out of his head. "Help, I am killed!" he called out, and fell to the ground.

Struli was at his side like one sprung from the earth, he tore off his Four-Corners, and made his comrade a bandage.

The wound turned out to be slight, for the bullet had passed through, only grazing the flesh of the left arm. A few days later Maxim was back in the company.

"I wanted to see you again, Struli," he said, greeting his comrade in Roumanian.

A flash of brotherly affection and gratitude lighted Struli's Semitic eyes, and he took the other into his arms, and pressed him to his heart.

They felt themselves to be "countrymen," of one and the same native town.

Neither of them could have told exactly when their union of spirit had been accomplished, but each one knew that he thanked God for having brought him together with so near a compatriot in a strange land.

And when the battle of Mukden had made Maxim all but totally blind, and deprived Struli of one foot, they started for home together, according to the passage in the Midrash, "Two men with one pair of eyes and one pair of feet between them." Maxim carried on his shoulders a wooden box, which had now become a burden in common for them, and Struli limped a little in front of him, leaning lightly against his companion, so as to keep him in the smooth part of the road and out of other people's way.

Struli had become Maxim's eyes, and Maxim, Struli's feet; they were two men grown into one, and they provided for themselves out of one pocket, now empty of the last ruble.

They dragged themselves home. "A kasa, a kasa!" whispered Struli into Maxim's ear, and the other turned on him his two glazed eyes looking through a red haze, and set in swollen red lids.

A childlike smile played on his lips:

"A kasa, a kasa!" he repeated, also in a whisper.

Home appeared to their fancy as something holy, something consoling, something that could atone and compensate for all they had suffered and lost. They had seen such a home in their dreams.

But the nearer they came to it in reality, the more the dream faded. They remembered that they were returning as conquered soldiers and crippled men, that they had no near relations and but few friends, while the girls who had coquetted with Maxim before he left would never waste so much as a look on him now he was half-blind; and Struli's plans for marrying and emigrating to America were frustrated; a cripple would not be allowed to enter the country.

All their dreams and hopes finally dissipated, and there remained only one black care, one all-obscuring anxiety: how were they to earn a living?

They had been hoping all the while for a pension, but in their service book was written "on sick-leave." The Russo-Japanese war was distinguished by the fact that the greater number of wounded soldiers went home "on sick-leave," and the money assigned by the Government for their pension would not have been sufficient for even a hundredth part of the number of invalids.

Maxim showed a face with two wide open eyes, to which all the passers-by looked the same. He distinguished with difficulty between a man and a telegraph post, and wore a smile of mingled apprehension and confidence. The sound feet stepped hesitatingly, keeping behind Israel, and it was hard to say which steadied himself most against the other. Struli limped forward, and kept open eyes for two. Sometimes he would look round at the box on Maxim's shoulders, as though he felt its weight as much as Maxim.

Meantime the railway carriages had emptied and refilled, and the locomotive gave a great blast, received an answer from somewhere a long way off, a whistle for a whistle, and the train set off, slowly at first, and then gradually faster and faster, till all that remained of it were puffs of smoke hanging in the air without rhyme or reason.

The two felt more depressed than ever. "Something to eat? Where are we to get a bite?" was in their minds.

Suddenly Israel remembered with a start: this was the anniversary of his mother's death—if he could only say one Kaddish for her in a Klaus!

"Is it far from here to a Klaus?" he inquired of a passer-by.

"There is one a little way down that side-street," was the reply.

"Maxim!" he begged of the other, "come with me!"

"Where to?"

"To the synagogue."

Maxim shuddered from head to foot. His fear of a Jewish Shool had not left him, and a thousand foolish terrors darted through his head.

But his comrade's voice was so gentle, so childishly imploring, that he could not resist it, and he agreed to go with him into the Shool.

It was the time for Afternoon Prayer, the daylight and the dark held equal sway within the Klaus, the lamps before the platform increasing the former to the east and the latter to the west. Maxim and Israel stood in the western part, enveloped in shadow. The Cantor had just finished "Incense," and was entering upon Ashré, and the melancholy night chant of Minchah and Maariv gradually entranced Maxim's emotional Roumanian heart.

The low, sad murmur of the Cantor seemed to him like the distant surging of a sea, in which men were drowning by the hundreds and suffocating with the water. Then, the Ashré and the Kaddish ended, there was silence. The congregation stood up for the Eighteen Benedictions. Here and there you heard a half-stifled sigh. And now it seemed to Maxim that he was in the hospital at night, at the hour when the groans grow less frequent, and the sufferers fall one by one into a sweet sleep.

Tears started into his eyes without his knowing why. He was no longer afraid, but a sudden shyness had come over him, and he felt, as he watched Israel repeating the Kaddish, that the words, which he, Maxim, could not understand, were being addressed to someone unseen, and yet mysteriously present in the darkening Shool.

When the prayers were ended, one of the chief members of the congregation approached the "Manchurian," and gave Israel a coin into his hand.

Israel looked round—he did not understand at first what the donour meant by it.

Then it occurred to him—and the blood rushed to his face. He gave the coin to his companion, and explained in a half-sentence or two how they had come by it.

Once outside the Klaus, they both cried, after which they felt better.

"A livelihood!" the same thought struck them both.

"We can go into partnership!"

MICAH JOSEPH BERDYCZEWSKI
(1865-1921)

BERDYCZEWSKI, born in Russia, after completing his studies, devoted himself to the pursuit of literature. He brought to his work a mind steeped in Nietzschean philosophy which he had absorbed while living at Berlin. His heroes are gloomy, despondent, and delight in torturing themselves by self-analysis.

Military Service is reprinted from the volume, *Yiddish Tales*, translated by Helena Frank, copyright, 1912, by the Jewish Publication Society of America, by whose permission it is here used.

MILITARY SERVICE

THEY look as if they'd enough of me!"

So I think to myself, as I give a glance at my two great top-boots, my wide trousers, and my shabby green uniform, in which there is no whole part left.

I take a bit of looking-glass out of my box, and look at my reflection. Yes, the military cap on my head *is* a beauty, and no mistake, as big as Og, king of Bashan, and as bent and crushed as though it had been sat upon for years together.

Under the cap appears a small, washed-out face, yellow and weazened, with two large black eyes that look at me somewhat wildly.

I don't recognise myself; I remember me in a grey jacket, narrow, close-fitting trousers, a round hat, and a healthy complexion.

I can't make out where I got those big eyes, why they shine so, why my face should be yellow, and my nose pointed.

And yet I know that it is I myself, Chayyim Blumin, and no other; that I have been handed over for a soldier, and have to serve only two years and eight months, and not three years and eight months, because I have a certificate to the effect that I have been through the first four classes in a secondary school.

Though I know quite well that I am to serve only two years and eight months, I feel the same as though it were to be forever; I can't, somehow, believe that my time will some day expire, and I shall once more be free.

I have tried from the very beginning not to play any tricks, to do my duty and obey orders, so that they should not say, "A Jew won't work—a Jew is too lazy."

Even though I am let off manual labour, because I am on "privileged rights," still, if they tell me to go and clean the windows, or polish the flooring with sand, or clear away the snow from the door, I make no fuss and go. I wash and clean and polish, and try to do the work well, so that they should find no fault with me.

They haven't yet ordered me to carry pails of water.

Why should I not confess it? The idea of having to do that rather frightens me. When I look at the vessel in which the water is carried, my heart begins to flutter: the vessel is almost as big as I am, and I couldn't lift it even if it were empty.

I often think: What shall I do, if to-morrow, or the day after, they wake me at three o'clock in the morning and say coolly:

"Get up, Blumin, and go with Ossadtchok to fetch a pail of water!"

You ought to see my neighbour Ossadtchok! He looks as if he could squash me with one finger. It is as easy for him to carry a pail of water as to drink a glass of brandy. How can I compare myself with him?

I don't care if it makes my shoulder swell, if I could only carry the thing. I shouldn't mind about that. But God in Heaven knows the truth, that I won't be able to lift the pail off the ground, only they won't believe me, they will say:

"Look at the lazy Jew, pretending he is a poor creature that can't lift a pail!"

There—I mind that more than anything.

I don't suppose they *will* send me to fetch water, for, after all, I am on "privileged rights," but I can't sleep in peace: I dream all night that they are waking me at three o'clock, and I start up bathed in a cold sweat.

Drill does not begin before eight in the morning, but they wake us at six, so that we may have time to clean our rifles, polish our boots and leather girdle, brush our coat, and furbish the brass buttons with chalk, so that they should shine like mirrors.

I don't mind the getting up early, I am used to rising long before daylight, but I am always worrying lest something shouldn't be properly cleaned, and they should say that a Jew is so lazy, he doesn't care if his things are clean or not, that he's afraid of touching his rifle, and pay me other compliments of the kind.

I clean and polish and rub everything all I know, but my rifle always seems in worse condition than the other men's. I can't make it look the same as theirs, do what I will, and the head of my division, a corporal, shouts at me, calls me a greasy fellow, and says he'll have me up before the authorities because I don't take care of my arms.

But there is worse than the rifle, and that is the uniform. Mine is *years* old—I am sure it is older than I am. Every day little pieces fall out of it, and the buttons tear themselves out of the cloth, dragging bits of it after them.

I never had a needle in my hand in all my life before, and now I sit whole nights and patch and sew on buttons. And next morning, when the corporal takes hold of a button and gives a pull, to see if it's firmly sewn, a pang goes through my heart: the button is dragged out, and a piece of the uniform follows.

Another whole night's work for me!

After the inspection, they drive us out into the yard and teach us to stand: it must be done so that our stomachs fall in and our chests stick out. I am half as one ought to be, because my stomach is flat enough anyhow, only my chest is weak and narrow and also flat—flat as a board.

The corporal squeezes in my stomach with his knee, pulls me forward by the flaps of the coat, but it's no use. He loses his temper, and calls me greasy fellow, screams again that I am pretending, that I *won't* serve, and this makes my chest fall in more than ever.

I like the gymnastics.

In summer we go out early into the yard, which is very wide and covered with thick grass.

It smells delightfully, the sun warms us through, it feels so pleasant.

The breeze blows from the fields, I open my mouth and swallow the freshness, and however much I swallow, it's not enough, I should like to take in all the air there is. Then, perhaps, I should cough less, and grow a little stronger.

We throw off the old uniforms, and remain in our shirts, we run and leap and go through all sorts of performances with our hands and feet, and it's splendid! At home I never had so much as an idea of such fun.

At first I was very much afraid of jumping across the ditch, but I resolved once and for all—I've *got* to jump it. If the worst comes to the worst, I shall fall and bruise myself. Suppose I do? What then? Why do all the others jump it and don't care? One needn't be so very strong to jump!

And one day, before the gymnastics had begun, I left my comrades, took heart and a long run, and when I came to the ditch, I made a great bound, and, lo and behold, I was over on the other side! I couldn't believe my own eyes that I had done it so easily.

Ever since then I have jumped across ditches, and over mounds, and down from mounds, as well as any of them.

Only when it comes to climbing a ladder or swinging myself over a high bar, I know it spells misfortune for me.

I spring forward, and seize the first rung with my right hand, but I cannot reach the second with my left.

I stretch myself, and kick out with my feet, but I cannot reach any higher, not by so much as a vershok, and so there I hang and kick with my feet, till my right arm begins to tremble and hurt me. My head goes round, and I fall onto the grass. The corporal abuses me as usual, and the soldiers laugh.

I would give ten years of my life to be able to get higher, if only three or four rungs, but what can I do, if my arms won't serve me?

Sometimes I go out to the ladder by myself, while the soldiers are still asleep, and stand and look at it: perhaps I can think of a way to manage? But in vain. Thinking, you see, doesn't help you in these cases.

Sometimes they tell one of the soldiers to stand in the middle of the yard with his back to us, and we have to hop over him. He bends down a little, lowers his head, rests his hands on his knees, and we hop over him one at a time. One takes a good run, and when one comes to him, one places both hands on his shoulders, raises oneself into the air, and— over!

I know exactly how it ought to be done; I take the run all right, and plant my hands on his shoulders, only I can't raise myself into the air. And if I do lift myself up a little way, I remain sitting on the soldier's neck, and were it not for his seizing me by the feet, I should fall, and perhaps kill myself.

Then the corporal and another soldier take hold of me by the arms and legs, and throw me over the man's head, so that I may see there is nothing dreadful about it, as though I did not jump right over him because I was afraid, while it is that my arms are so weak, I cannot lean upon them and raise myself into the air.

But when I say so, they only laugh, and don't believe me. They say, "It won't help you; you will have to serve anyhow!"

When, on the other hand, it comes to "theory," the corporal is very pleased with me.

He says, that except himself no one knows "theory" as I do.

He never questions me now, only when one of the others doesn't know something, he turns to me:

"Well, Blumin, *you* tell me!"

I stand up without hurrying, and am about to answer, but he is apparently not pleased with my way of rising from my seat, and orders me to sit down again.

"When your superior speaks to you," says he, "you ought to jump up as though the seat were hot," and he looks at me angrily, as much as to say, "You may know theory, but you'll please to know your manners as well, and treat me with proper respect."

"Stand up again and answer!"

I start up as though I felt a prick from a needle, and answer the question as he likes it done: smartly, all in one breath, and word for word according to the book.

He, meanwhile, looks at the primer, to make sure I am not leaving anything out, but as he reads very slowly, he cannot catch me up, and when I have got to the end, he is still following with his finger and reading. And when he has finished, he gives me a pleased look, and says enthusiastically "Right!" and tells me to sit down again.

"Theory," he says, "that you *do* know!"

Well, begging his pardon, it isn't much to know. And yet there are soldiers who are four years over it, and don't know it then. For instance, take my comrade Ossadtchok; he says that, when it comes to "theory," he would rather go and hang or drown himself. He says, he would rather have to carry three pails of water than sit down to "theory."

I tell him, that if he would learn to read, he could study the whole thing by himself in a week; but he won't listen.

"Nobody," he says, "will ever ask *my* advice."

One thing always alarmed me very much: However was I to take part in the manœuvres?

I cannot lift a single pud (I myself only weigh two pud and thirty pounds), and if I walk three versts, my feet hurt, and my heart beats so violently that I think it's going to burst my side.

At the manœuvres I should have to carry as much as fifty pounds' weight, and perhaps more: a rifle, a cloak, a knapsack with linen, boots, a uniform, a tent, bread, and onions, and a few other little things, and should have to walk perhaps thirty to forty versts a day.

But when the day and the hour arrived, and the command was given "Forward, march!" when the band struck up, and two thousand men set their feet in motion, something seemed to draw me forward, and I went. At the beginning I found it hard, I felt weighted to the earth, my left shoulder hurt me so, I nearly fainted. But afterwards I got very hot, I began to breathe rapidly and deeply, my eyes were starting out of my head like two cupping-glasses, and I not only walked, I ran, so as not to fall behind—and so I ended by marching along with the rest, forty versts a day.

Only I did not sing on the march like the others. First, because I did not feel so very cheerful, and second, because I could not breathe properly, let alone sing.

At times I felt burning hot, but immediately afterwards I would grow light, and the marching was easy, I seemed to be carried along rather than to tread the earth, and it appeared to me as though another were marching in my place, only that my left shoulder ached, and I was hot.

I remember that once it rained a whole night long, it came down like a deluge, our tents were soaked through, and grew heavy. The mud was thick. At three o'clock in the morning an alarm was sounded, we were ordered to fold up our tents and take to the road again. So off we went.

It was dark and slippery. It poured with rain. I was continually stepping into a puddle, and getting my boot full of water. I shivered and shook, and my teeth chattered with cold. That is, I was cold one minute and hot the next. But the marching was no difficulty to me, I scarcely felt that I was on the march, and thought very little about it. Indeed, I don't know what I *was* thinking about, my mind was a blank.

We marched, turned back, and marched again. Then we halted for half an hour, and turned back again.

And this went on a whole night and a whole day.

Then it turned out that there had been a mistake: it was not we who ought to have marched, but another regiment, and we ought not to have moved from the spot. But there was no help for it then.

It was night. We had eaten nothing all day. The rain poured down, the mud was ankle-deep, there was no straw on which to pitch our tents, but we managed somehow. And so the days passed, each like the other. But I got through the manœuvres, and was none the worse.

Now I am already an old soldier; I have hardly another year and a half to serve—about sixteen months. I only hope I shall not be ill. It seems I got a bit of a chill at the manœuvres, I cough every morning, and sometimes I suffer with my feet. I shiver a little at night till I get warm, and then I am very hot, and I feel very comfortable lying abed. But I shall probably soon be all right again.

They say one may take a rest in the hospital, but I haven't been there yet, and don't want to go at all, especially now I am feeling better. The soldiers are sorry for me, and sometimes they do my work, but not just for love. I get three pounds of bread a day, and don't eat more than one pound. The rest I give to my comrade Ossadtchok. He eats it all, and his own as well, and then he could do with some more. In return for this he often cleans my rifle, and sometimes does other work for me, when he sees I have no strength left.

I am also teaching him and a few other soldiers to read and write, and they are very pleased.

My corporal also comes to me to be taught, but he never gives me a word of thanks.

The superior of the platoon, when he isn't drunk, and is in good humour, says "you" to me instead of "thou," and sometimes invites me to share his bed—I can breathe easier there, because there is more air, and I don't cough so much, either.

Only it sometimes happens that he comes back from town tipsy, and makes a great to-do: How do I, a common soldier, come to be sitting on his bed?

He orders me to get up and stand before him "at attention," and declares he will "have me up" for it.

When, however, he has sobered down, he turns kind again, and calls me to him; he likes to tell him "stories" out of books.

Sometimes the orderly calls me into the orderly-room, and gives me a report to draw up, or else a list or a calculation to make. He himself writes badly, and is very poor at figures.

I do everything he wants, and he is very glad of my help, only it wouldn't do for him to confess to it, and when I have finished, he always says to me:

"If the commanding officer is not satisfied, he will send you to fetch water."

I know it isn't true, first, because the commanding officer mustn't know that I write in the orderly-room, a Jew can't be an army secretary; secondly, because he is certain to be satisfied: he once gave me a note to write himself, and was very pleased with it.

"If you were not a Jew," he said to me then, "I should make a corporal of you."

Still, my corporal always repeats his threat about the water, so that I may preserve a proper respect for him, although I not only respect him, I tremble before his size. When *he* comes back tipsy from town, and finds me in the orderly-room, he commands me to drag his muddy boots off his feet, and I obey him and drag off his boots.

Sometimes I don't care, and other times it hurts my feelings.

❋ ❋ ❋

DAVID PINSKI
(1872-   )

PINSKI, born in Russia, has been residing in the United States for the past quarter century. Although he is generally known as a dramatist, he began his literary career as a writer of short stories. With him the story has acquired an exceptionally high artistic form. *The Black Cat* which is taken from his volume *Temptations* is an excellent psychological study of a man suffering from sexual obsession. Its treatment is exceedingly delicate.

The present version, which appears in *Temptations*, is translated by Isaac Goldberg and published by Brentano's, copyright, 1919. It is reprinted by permission of the publishers and that of the author.

THE BLACK CAT

IT has been raining for already two days,—a soft, leisurely drizzle, but an endless one. Often it increases in vehemence. It begins to patter upon my roof with rapid fury. Then it seems that at last it is over. Now the dense grey clouds will empty themselves and the downpour will cease. The great fury abates, the racket upon the roof becomes gradually quiet, yet the rain continues to fall, softly and leisurely. Often so softly that it seems to have stopped. Then I look out of the window with just a ray of hope that I shall see a clear sky. But by the wheels that roll incessantly across the pavement I recognise the eternal rain. The eternal rain. The eternal. . . .

I lower the shades and turn on the electric light. Let it be night. I'll seat myself upon the armchair before my desk and pursue my thoughts, and think and think of——

Of my fortune—or of my misfortune?

It has come upon me so suddenly that I don't know how to take it. The day before yesterday I was so happy, and to-day my heart is so heavy, so heavy. . . . I know that this is the effect of the ceaseless rain, —of the weeping, lamenting, grey, dark-grey outdoors. Still, I am so restless. My feeling comes from within,—comes over me from the depths of my heart and my soul. It seems to me that I *must* be moody, and I cannot understand how I could have been so high-spirited the day before yesterday. I am vexed that I can no longer be so merry.

So suddenly. So suddenly. . . .

Can it have happened only ten days ago?

Only ten days ago.

She brought me a manuscript, which I was to read and appraise for her.

Young—perhaps twenty, and maybe only eighteen.

And beautiful—beautiful? Yes, even strikingly beautiful. Scarcely had I opened the door and beheld her, when a strange sensation clutched at my heart.

Her eyes! Those deep, black eyes under the long black lashes! They pierced me at once. I could not tear myself away from them. And thus overwhelmed, only half conscious, I received the impression that those eyes were set in a rather long, dark-complexioned, youthful countenance, and that around a low, alluring forehead played several black curls mischievously, and that her whole figure was very svelte and supple,—almost that of a child.

And her voice! Like her eyes. Deep, and of a dark quality, and so warm. No sooner had she asked, "Does Mr. So-and-so live here, and are you not he?" than my eyes and my ears were so completely filled with her that I forgot I must not keep her standing at the door, and that I must invite her in.

She invited herself, however. She entered my room, far beyond the threshold, and I closed the door slowly, without removing my glance from her. And remained standing as if hypnotised, without knowing whether to make inquiry or to wait until she would tell me who she was and what she wished of me.

She laughed. Deep, warm, ringing laughter. Why did I not ask her to be seated?

Oh, yes. Pardon. And I, the father of a daughter almost as old as she, turned red with embarrassment, it seems. I hastened to fetch her a chair, but she had already chosen one and sat down.

She continues to speak, while I take my place in my armchair before the desk and gaze, gaze upon her, my ears thirstily and enchantedly drinking in the sound of her voice.

She tells me that she pictured me exactly as I am. She has read everything I have written. She knows all my writings well and has imagined a picture of me. And the picture is correct. But she did not think I possessed so many grey hairs. That makes no difference, however. For I am young. She is certain of that. But she still has no idea of how my voice sounds. She thus hints that I have said nothing as yet. And she laughs.

I join the laughter and am at a loss for words. I feel that I must say something *significant*,—that the maidenly vision with the beautiful childlike figure, who knows all my writings and has formed a perfect image of me, is now waiting for deep and notable words to issue from my lips. Nor do I desire to be insignificant. I don't care to utter plain, ordinary, pedestrian words. So I smile and wait for her to speak further.

She looks about the room, resting her glance for a moment upon the paintings that hang upon my walls. And soon she transfers her eyes once more to me. Sharp, penetrating glances, with a great question in them. And now there rises in her eyes a smile of subtle irony.

Because I do not inquire, she explains in her deep voice, she is compelled to speak for herself. Why does one come to a famous author? Naturally, she has for a long time desired to know me, but without a special reason she would never have dared to come. Now, however, she comes as to a doctor or a lawyer, on a professional visit, for an opinion and for counsel. She has written something and wishes to enjoy the criticism of an authority. Will I not take the trouble?

I reply politely, very politely: "Certainly, with the greatest of pleasure."

She laughs. Oh, she does not believe that her piece will afford me much pleasure. The very handwriting is impossible. Should I prefer, perhaps, to have her read it to me?

I desire to hear the sound of her voice. But if she reads she will look at the manuscript during the entire reading, and I'll be unable to see her eyes.

Then she adds, "But I read very badly. My reading is even worse than my handwriting." She laughs: she does not care to read, either. For if she reads it now, I'll express my opinion at once, and she will have to arise, say "Good day," and never call again. She would rather leave the manuscript with me, and then she will come,—yes, she will really *come* and hear the answer. She does not wish it by mail. She will certainly have a number of questions to ask. She would prefer to come,—and since, naturally, I shall not have read her manuscript through, she will have to call again and again. . . .

She deposits upon my desk a small manuscript. For the first time I see her hand. A wee little hand,—white, tender skin, through which the lines of the joints are visible.

I take the manuscript, glance at the title-page, peep at the beginning and at the middle, and feel her deep black eyes upon me. And as I raise my head I encounter her glances with the great question in them, and also the subtle irony.

Something taps at my window. And now it miaows. I know that a cat has taken refuge upon my window-sill from the endless downpour. I am certain of it, yet I arise from my chair and walk over to take a look. This furnishes some distraction from my thoughts. And an excuse for moving. My feet are like ice.

I raise the shade and shudder with fright. A large black cat is looking up at me from the outer darkness, with her burning, phosphorescent eyes. I hate a black cat. Not that I am superstitious, yet in my memory and my nerves there is a residue of everything that superstition has created concerning black cats. I rap at the window to drive her away. But she pays little heed to my rapping. She turns around, selects a comfortable spot and lies down. I am on the point of opening the window and thrusting her into the street below, but I don't care to touch her. I take pity on her, too. Outside the rain is still falling, falling. Let her lie and rest on a dry spot. Who cares?

I lower the shade and return to my writing table.

Just a moment to banish the black cat from my mind, and I'll pursue my thoughts anew.

Now then—of my fortune and misfortune. But did I not previously think: *or* my misfortune?

I answered her, Yes. She could leave the manuscript with me. I would read it over,—read it over very carefully, and tell her my opinion.

The whole truth?

Of course.

When would she come for the answer?

I'd tell her a few days later.

Why a few days later? Why not to-morrow? She would come to-morrow. The piece was such a short one. One could read it in less than half an hour.

So I yield to her. Very well. Let her come to-morrow.

My wife has meanwhile entered the room. I introduce her. My wife is affable and smiles, but *she* is sullen, curt and unbending.

She arises from her place. Now she will leave.

My wife laughs. "Am I driving you away?"

She, somewhat aloof, replies, No. She has simply been sitting long enough.

And on the threshold she asks, insinuatingly, "You will read my manuscript personally?"

For a second I am strongly impelled to return her manuscript, thus wreaking vengeance upon her for my wife.

But she has already closed the door and is gone, without having waited for a reply. Perhaps she had noticed the spark of displeasure that shone in my eyes.

"What sort of impudent cat is that?" asks my wife.

I burst into laughter.

The next day she did not come. Nor the day after. But on both days I *thought* that she had not come. I did not wish to give the matter thought, but it haunted me, made me uneasy. If she had promised to come, she should have kept her word.

I read her manuscript. A very wretched tale. It was supposed to depict the yearning of a solitary woman for an unknown man. But the words were weak and the colours false. And I could not get away from the idea that perhaps she had written them just to have a pretext for coming to me. "The impudent cat!"

On the third day she came. From the door she laughed to me with her deep, staccato laughter. "Kept you waiting?"

"Catch me telling you, you cat!"

I bid her enter the room. She advances to the centre, looks about, gazes toward the door by which my wife entered three days before, directs her deep look upon me, taking a chair, and speaks with her deep, velvety voice. "Have you read through my manuscript?"

I am about to tell her the truth, but I feel that I cannot dismiss her from me forever,—that I desire her to come to me again,—so I reply,

"I've read it, but not read it through. You will have to forgive me."

"Where did you leave off?"

Yes, where am I to tell her I left off?

"Perhaps you haven't even started to read it yet?" she suggests, seeing that no answer to her previous question is forthcoming.

I assure her that I really have read her tale, commencing to relate the contents, and betraying myself by disclosing a knowledge of the end.

"Then you've read it all!" she laughs.

"Yes," I confess. "But only superficially,—I merely thumbed the pages."

And she, with her deep voice, declares, "Oh, my little story isn't so deep that it requires a second reading. You may tell me your opinion. I will not cry if my little piece is valueless. I know myself that its worth is very small. And as to my coming to you again, you needn't worry. I have brought another manuscript that I wrote in the past two days."

Heavens, what is that? Fie! What a scare I got!

The black cat has sprung into the room.

I look at her in terror. And only gradually does my astonishment master my fear. How did she jump in? For the window is closed!

I go over to the window. The cat presses close to the wall underneath and gazes up at me, as if entreating me not to cast her out. I raise the shade. I examine the window. It is shut and fastened. I examine the panes. Ah, yes, down in the left-hand corner a small opening has been broken through. A small opening, forming together with the frame a triangle. And the glass bordering the hole glitters with many sharp, uneven, jagged edges.

When was the pane broken? How have I failed to notice it sooner? Why has nobody in the house noticed it?

And how has the cat crawled through? That large black cat through such a small aperture? She must have scratched her entire skin. I turn to look at her and am seized with murderous rage. I am about to kick her, and resolve to throw her back into the rain and the darkness. If only for the sake of the yellow canary that I have in a brass cage in another room. But I myself do not wish to do this. I don't care to touch the wet cat, and I feel sure that I'll stain my fingers with blood.

I summon the housemaid and order her to throw out the cat. She does not ask how the cat got in. She is certain that some one let the animal in and would like to know who could have been so careless. Her first thought and chief concern is the yellow songbird of whom the entire household is so fond. She seizes the cat and dashes out with it.

She opens the street-door and throws the animal out with a curse. I wish to learn whether her hands are smeared with blood, but she does not reappear. She has gone back to her work. I am content. For a long conversation would have ensued, and I desire to be alone and undisturbed. I'll find out later.

To resume.

She sat and spoke for a long time. She also arose from her place and approached me, so close that I could feel her breath and an odour of new-mown hay enveloped me; a warmth radiated from her, making me uncomfortably warm. Several times she placed her hand upon my hair, —my hair that was more grey than black—the impudent cat! How dare she! Suppose my wife should happen to come in and surprise us.

She noticed my furtive glances toward the door and laughed. She had seen my wife leave the house, she asserted. With a young girl. Was that my daughter? As she spoke she caressed my grey hair and looked at me with those deep eyes full of endearment and desire. And she added, with her velvety, resonant voice, "I detest authors' wives!"

And then: "An artist should not be married. He should be free —for all and each. . . ."

I maintained a significant silence. What should I say to her? I must be careful with this woman.

She took my hand and examined my fingers. She held them long and tenderly, fondling them with her own thin, warm fingers.

Then I had to discourse to her about my creative work, and the touch of her fingers was immensely pleasant, and I spoke with increasing warmth and friendliness, so that she might not release my hands.

All at once she leaned forward and kissed me upon the lips, as I was in the middle of a sentence,—in the very middle of a word.

Like a flash she disappeared from the room.

The cat! The cat has again sprung into the room. Naturally, through the same opening in the window-pane. I scold and curse. But this time I'll not summon the maid. I open the window, seize the cat by the neck and throw her into the street with all my strength. I do not see her fall, but I hear her strike the stony pavement far off. There, now she will hesitate long before she'll come. That is, if she is able to move at all.

I close the window and sigh with relief. But that hole must be stuffed. If it were not for the inclemency of the weather and the lateness of the hour, I would send for the glazier. But for the present it must be stuffed with something. I hunt about, find a newspaper and stop the hole.

Now I may calmly give myself once more over to my thoughts.

A kiss. A bound. Vanished——

She came the following day. With her deep eyes, her deep voice and her singing youth.

I feared her coming; I tried to hope that she would not come. No sooner had I caught sight of her than my heart began to pound excitedly.

She had again arrived just after my wife had left the house. Had she watched for her to leave? How long had she been lurking outside? I asked her and she laughed.

Oh, what was the difference! She had waited much longer before coming to me for the first time. The thought of using the manuscript as a pretext had been slow to suggest itself to her.

But—wouldn't I prefer to come to her? She had her own room. She might receive any one she pleased; she was perfectly free.

She said all this so simply. So sweetly, so innocently, so naturally, —with that deep velvety voice of hers, and her fathomless eyes and her intense youth.

I wanted to cry out, No! I felt with all my being that I should say No. But at the same time I knew that the struggle was in vain.

She had ignited something within me, and I was all aflame,—burning, burning.

She seized me in an embrace and pressed upon my lips a long, passionate kiss. Within me, my being shouted, sang and exulted.

I was young again! Young again! How we both rejoiced!

To-morrow I am supposed to visit her. Until to-day I longed for to-morrow to arrive. And now I am afraid of it. To-day I do not desire it. I tremble lest I go to her after all. Whither will this lead? Who is she? What is she? Why has she singled *me* out? I have grey hairs already and a grown-up daughter almost her age.

Isn't that the rustle of the paper with which I stuffed the broken pane?

Yes. Somebody's clawing and tearing at it.

Or perhaps it's the black cat again! I jump to my feet and run to the window. Yes. The black cat has pulled out the paper and has already thrust her head in through the opening.

No! This time you shall not crawl in! I place my hand upon her head and press, press with all my strength. Oh, surely I'll crush the feline life out of her! . . .

Yet. . . . Yet. . . . How strong she is! . . . She plants herself firmly upon her forepaws and gradually thrusts herself backward through the opening and from under my hand. And now she already has her forepaws on the outer side of the window. . . . I am seized with terror. . . . Hot and cold chills pass through me. . . . I begin to call for help. . . .

Fie, what an evil dream! How my heart throbs! I go to the window. Outside it is still raining; the night is black, and on the window ledge lies the black cat, peacefully coiled into a ball.

I place my hot forehead against the cool window-pane and am consumed by a passionate wish. May the *other one*, too, be only an evil dream! And I shudder.

Oh! Oh!

To-morrow—to-morrow—to-morrow! . . .

❀ ❀ ❀

SHOLOM ASCH
(1880-   )

SHOLOM ASCH, born in Poland, began, like many other Jewish authors, writing in Hebrew, but soon took to the more popular Yiddish. He is a versatile and gifted writer, having met with success as a dramatist as well as a short story writer. He is recognised as an exponent of realism, and much of his work is devoted to describing the patriarchal Jewish life in the Russian villages.

A Jewish Child is a lovely and poignant tale of a conflict between a whim and a precept of orthodox faith. The present version is reprinted from the volume, *Yiddish Tales*, translated by Helena Frank, copyright, 1912, by the Jewish Publication Society of America, by whose permission it is here used.

A JEWISH CHILD

THE mother came out of the bride's chamber, and cast a piercing look at her husband, who was sitting beside a finished meal, and was making pellets of bread crumbs previous to saying grace.

"You go and talk to her! I haven't a bit of strength left!"

"So, Rochel-Leon has brought up children, has she, and can't manage them! Why! People will be pointing at you and laughing—a ruin to your years!"

"To my years! A ruin to *yours*! *My* children, are they? Are they not yours, too? Couldn't you stay at home sometimes to care for them and help me to bring them up, instead of trapesing round—the black year knows where and with whom?"

"Rochel, Rochel, what has possessed you to start a quarrel with me now? The bridegroom's family will be arriving directly."

"And what do you expect me to do, Moishehle, eh?! For God's sake! Go in to her, we shall be made a laughing-stock."

The man rose from the table, and went into the next room to his daughter. The mother followed.

On the little sofa that stood by the window sat a girl about eighteen, her face hidden in her hands, her arms covered by her loose, thick, black hair. She was evidently crying, for her bosom rose and fell like a stormy sea. On the bed opposite lay the white silk wedding-dress, the Chuppeh-Kleid, with the black, silk Shool-Kleid, and the black stuff morning-dress, which the tailor who had undertaken the outfit had brought not long ago. By the door stood a woman with a black scarf round her head and holding boxes with wigs.

"Channehle! You are never going to do me this dishonour? to make me the talk of the town?" exclaimed the father. The bride was silent.

"Look at me, daughter of Moisheh Groiss! It's all very well for Genendel Freindel's daughter to wear a wig, but not for the daughter of Moisheh Groiss? Is that it?"

"And yet Genendel Freindel might very well think more of herself than you: she is more educated than you are, and has a larger dowry," put in the mother.

The bride made no reply.

"Daughter, think how much blood and treasure it has cost to help us to a bit of pleasure, and now you want to spoil it for us? Remember, for God's sake, what you are doing with yourself! We shall be excommunicated, the young man will run away home on foot!"

"Don't be foolish," said the mother who took a wig out of a box from the woman by the door, and approached her daughter. "Let us try on the wig, the hair is just the colour of yours," and she laid the strange hair on the girl's head.

The girl felt the weight, put up her fingers to her head, met among her own soft, cool, living locks, the strange, dead hair of the wig, stiff and cold, and it flashed through her, Who knows where the head to which this hair belonged is now? A shuddering enveloped her, and as though she had come in contact with something unclean, she snatched off the wig, threw it onto the floor and hastily left the room.

Father and mother stood and looked at each other in dismay.

The day after the marriage ceremony, the bridegroom's mother rose early, and, bearing large scissors, and the wig and a hood which she had brought from her home as a present for the bride, she went to dress the latter for the "breakfast."

But the groom's mother remained outside the room, because the bride had locked herself in, and would open her door to no one.

The groom's mother ran calling aloud for help to her husband, who, together with a dozen uncles and brothers-in-law, was still sleeping soundly after the evening's festivity. She then sought out the bride-groom, an eighteen-year-old boy with his mother's milk still on his lips, who, in a silk caftan and a fur cap, was moving about the room in bewildered fashion, his eyes on the ground, ashamed to look anyone in the face. In the end she fell back on the mother of the bride, and these two went in to her together, having forced open the door between them.

"Why did you lock yourself in, dear daughter. There is no need to be ashamed."

"Marriage is a Jewish institution!" said the groom's mother, and kissed her future daughter-in-law on both cheeks.

The girl made no reply.

"Your mother-in-law has brought you a wig and a hood for the procession to the Shool," said her own mother.

The band had already struck up the "Good Morning" in the next room.

"Come now, Kallehshi, Kalleh-leben, the guests are beginning to assemble."

The groom's mother took hold of the plaits in order to loosen them.

The bride bent her head away from her, and fell on her own mother's neck.

"I can't, Mame-leben! My heart won't let me, Mame-krön!"

She held her hair with both hands, to protect it from the other's scissors.

"For God's sake, my daughter, my life," begged the mother.

"In the other world you will be plunged for this into rivers of fire. The apostate who wears her own hair after marriage will have her locks torn out with red hot pincers," said the other with the scissors.

A cold shiver went through the girl at these words.

"Mother-life, mother-crown!" she pleaded.

Her hands sought her hair, and the black silky tresses fell through them in waves. Her hair, the hair which had grown with her growth, and lived with her life, was to be cut off, and she was never, never to have it again—she was to wear strange hair, hair that had grown on another person's head, and no one knows whether that other person was alive or lying in the earth this long time, and whether she might not come any night to one's bedside, and whine in a dead voice:

"Give me back my hair, give me back my hair!"

A frost seized the girl to the marrow, she shivered and shook.

Then she heard the squeak of scissors over her head, tore herself out of her mother's arms, made one snatch at the scissors, flung them across the room, and said in a scarcely human voice:

"My own hair! May God Himself punish me!"

That day the bridegroom's mother took herself off home again, together with the sweet-cakes and the geese which she had brought for the wedding breakfast for her own guests. She wanted to take the bridegroom as well, but the bride's mother said: "I will not give him back to you! He belongs to me already!"

The following Sabbath they led the bride in procession to the Shool wearing her own hair in the face of all the town, covered only by a large hood.

But may all the names she was called by the way find their only echo in some uninhabited wilderness.

A summer evening, a few weeks after the wedding: The young man had just returned from the Stübel, and went to his room. The wife was already asleep, and the soft light of the lamp fell on her pale face, showing here and there among the wealth of silky-black hair that bathed it. Her slender arms were flung round her head, as though she feared that someone might come by night to shear them off while she slept. He had come home excited and irritable: this was the fourth week of his married life, and they had not yet called him up to the Reading of the Law, the Chassidim pursued him, and to-day Chayyim Moisheh had blamed him in the presence of the whole congregation, and had shamed him, because *she,* his wife, went about in her own hair. "You're no better than a clay image," Reb Chayyim Moisheh had told him. "What do you mean by a woman's saying she won't? It is written: 'And he shall rule over thee.' "

And he had come home intending to go to her and say: "Woman, it is a precept in the Torah! If you persist in wearing your own hair, I may divorce you without returning the dowry," after which he would pack up his things and go home. But when he saw his little wife asleep in bed, and her pale face peeping out of the glory of her hair, he felt a great pity for her. He went up to the bed, and stood a long while looking at her, after which he called softly:

"Channehle . . . Channehle . . . Channehle. . . ."

She opened her eyes with a frightened start, and looked round in sleepy wonder:

"Nosson, did you call? What do you want?"

"Nothing, your cap has slipped off," he said, lifting up the white nightcap, which had fallen from her head.

She flung it on again, and wanted to turn towards the wall.

"Channehle, Channehle, I want to talk to you."

The words went to her heart. The whole time since their marriage he had, so to say, not spoken to her. During the day she saw nothing of him, for he spent it in the house-of-study or in the Stübel. When he came home to dinner, he sat down to the table in silence. When he wanted anything, he asked for it speaking into the air, and when really obliged to exchange a word with her, he did so with his eyes fixed on the ground, too shy to look her in the face. And now he said he wanted to talk to her, and in such a gentle voice, and they two alone together in their room!

"What do you want to say to me?" she asked softly.

"Channehle," he began, "please don't make a fool of me, and don't make a fool of yourself in people's eyes. Has not God decreed that we should belong together? You are my wife and I am your husband, and is it proper, and what does it look like, a married woman wearing her own hair?"

Sleep still half dimmed her eyes, and had altogether clouded her thought and will. She felt helpless, and her head fell lightly towards his breast.

"Child," he went on still more gently, "I know you are not so depraved as they say. I know you are a pious Jewish daughter, and His Blessed Name will help us, and we shall have pious Jewish children. Put away this nonsense! Why should the whole world be talking about you? Are we not man and wife? Is not your shame mine?"

It seemed to her as though *someone*, at once very far away and very near, had come and was talking to her. Nobody had ever yet spoken to her so gently and confidingly. And he was her husband, with whom she would live so long, so long, and there would be children, and she would look after the house!

She leant her head lightly against him.

"I know you are very sorry to lose your hair, the ornament of your girlhood. I saw you with it when I was a guest in your home. I knew that God gave you grace and loveliness, I know. It cuts me to the heart that your hair must be shorn off, but what is to be done? It is a rule, a law of our religion, and after all we are Jews. We might even, God forbid, have a child conceived to us in sin, may Heaven watch over and defend us."

She said nothing, but remained resting lightly in his arm, and his face lay in the stream of her silky-black hair with its cool odour. In that hair dwelt a soul, and he was conscious of it. He looked at her long and earnestly, and in his look was a prayer, a pleading with her for her own happiness, for her happiness and his.

"Shall I?" . . . he asked, more with his eyes than with his lips.

She said nothing, she only bent her head over his lap.

He went quickly to the drawer, and took out a pair of scissors.

She laid her head in his lap, and gave her hair as a ransom for their happiness, still half-asleep and dreaming. The scissors squeaked over her head, shearing off one lock after the other, and Channehle lay and dreamt through the night.

On waking next morning, she threw a look into the glass which hung opposite the bed. A shock went through her, she thought she had gone mad, and was in the asylum! On the table beside her lay her shorn hair, dead!

She hid her face in her hands, and the little room was filled with the sound of weeping!

❋ ❋ ❋

JOSEPH OPATOSHU
(1887-   )

OPATOSHU, born at Mlava, Poland, came to America in 1907. Here he continued his studies and graduated as a Civil Engineer. He had, nevertheless, strong literary leanings, and when, in 1910, his first stories began to appear he was encouraged to devote himself exclusively to literature. In 1912 he published his first novel, *A Romance of a Horse-thief*, which brought him into the first rank of the younger Yiddish writers. Since then he has published a number of novels, chiefly *Forest*, which has been translated into several European languages and been hailed as a masterpiece. He has also written many short stories of high artistic quality. He is one of the neo-romanticists who have broken with the school of Berdychewski.

Winter Wolves, translated by Joseph Kling, is reprinted from *The Pagan* magazine, by permission of the author and publisher.

WINTER WOLVES
I

NIGHT. . . .
    Solomon Krodnick * took out a loaded revolver from a chest, put several pairs of boots into a bag, and glanced at the clock on the wall.

"Hm . . . twelve . . . a whole hour yet," he said to himself.

He turned down the lamp and began to pace the room back and forth.

Solomon's wife, Tertza, was lying under a feather-bed, snoring. He looked at her, muttered contemptuously, and directed his gaze to his daughter Sarah,—a girl of about thirty—who was sleeping on a cot, and sighed deeply. . . . "She should be a mother by now," he said to himself. He felt that he was to blame, somehow, for her spinster-

* Horse-thief.

hood. Another man might well be a grandfather at his age . . . and he,——

"The old days are gone," he reflected. "How much easier life used to be! . . . Money was plentiful. . . . Matchmakers were constantly pestering me about her. . . . She had suitors by the score. . . . And I,—fool that I was, wasn't satisfied with any of them, but kept on choosing." . . .

The gander that slept under the stove suddenly awoke in his coop, and flapped his wings.

"Yes," meditated Solomon, "if this job goes through all right, with God's help, I'll buy Berka a team and marry her off to him at once. . . . It'll be a load off my head. The Lord knows she has little enough to gain by waiting." . . .

He pulled out a pouch of tobacco from his bosom, rolled a cigarette, and lit it with a live coal from the stove. He gave a few puffs, and glanced at the window. It was even darker outside than within. He could hear the whistling of the frosty wind, and shivered. The dusky shadows on the wall cast a gloom over him. He moved up closer to the stove and fell to musing again. . . .

"Zanvill must now be on his way to the wood. . . . If everything goes well they will cross the wood quickly, lead the two horses out of the stable, walk them to the hill, and then,—Crack! Away to Simon the horse-dealer! Over two hundred rubels in this stroke of business." . . . The mere thought of the money cheered him. He smiled, yawned, took a few gulps of whiskey from a pocket-flask, and began to chew a piece of dry cheese. The whistle of a night-watchman and the howling of a homeless dog broke through the stillness. He threw some dried turf into the stove and continued his meditations.

"But what if they catch us?" . . . His lean old body shivered. It isn't so long ago that he was caught with the Donn mares. . . . He recalls the rain of blows on his body, his slashed face, and streaming blood. . . . How they did beat him! He had been in bed several weeks, and served a year in prison besides.

He had at that time made up his mind to try some new business; after every "job" he swore it was the last. . . .

"A dog's life," he murmured. . . . "Past fifty . . . and what has my life been? Only fear and terror. . . . And money? . . . Not a cursed penny." . . .

He recalled how one Sabbath-afternoon he sat in the House-of-Prayer and listened to a preacher who was describing the World-to-come. . . . How, soon after death, the angel Hadommah comes to one's tomb, knocks three times, and asks the inmate's name. If he is a man of virtue he answers straightway, but if he is a man of sin he forgets it, and so becomes an eternal wanderer. . . .

Solomon tried to shake off the gloom that was settling on him. He thought of Simon the horse-dealer, and felt a sudden burning hatred against him. Thirty years ago they were both horse-thieves; to-day Solomon is still a hunted outcast, and Simon, a respected merchant, the head of the Old Synagogue. His daughters have dowries of thousands of rubels and his sons-in-law live with him at his expense. . . . While he, Solomon, lies awake nights racking his brains about getting money for Sarah's dowry, planning to steal horses,—for Simon's benefit.

He heaved a dull sigh, and glanced up again at the clock. . . . Well, time to be moving. . . .

He drew on a sheepskin jacket and tightened it about his body with a green belt, into which he stuck a pair of mittens. Then he threw the sack of boots over his shoulder, extinguished the lamp, and went out.

II

Zanvill strode along the highway with firm tread. The snow crunched and crackled under his feet; his face was frost-pinched and purple red. He wore a caracul-cap that reached below his ears, a sheepskin-jacket, and a pair of deep boots. His hands were stuck in his pockets and he whistled through his teeth.

He stood still. Before him lay snow-covered fields, stretching as far as the eye could see, gleaming like silver in the moonlight. They seemed to rise higher and higher till they reached the level of the hoary hill in the distance. The pine-wood looked like a great white cloud that moved nearer and nearer. He felt a close kinship to, a comradely familiarity with all the mighty forms of nature about him. He drew a long breath, the blood tingling through his strong body, and smiled like a happy boy. To give vent to his overflowing spirits he threw himself on his back in the snow, and spread out his arms cross-wise. He lay thus for several minutes, gazing up into the steel-blue, star-twinkling sky. Then he jumped up, and observing the curious impress of his body in the snow, burst into laughter. A metallic echo in the distance answered him.

He proceeded on his way to the wood. The old-man must be there by this time, he thought. It's really no job for a decent thief, to walk off with a few horses. Anybody can do that. What's the trick? You walk up to the stable; it's dark and no one can see you; you wrench off a board, crawl in, unlock the door, and lead the horses out.

But to break into a house where people are asleep, and rip open a safe,—that's a different matter. This horse-stealing business is all right for the old-man, but,—he shrugged his shoulders. Then he stopped, lighted a cigarette, and resumed his march.

His reflections gradually shape themselves into hazardous plans. . . .

In the Polish Church there is a Madonna of gold set with precious stones, it is said. He'll break in and steal it. For the money from its sale he'll buy long-maned Cossack horses and all sorts of weapons. Then he'll get together a gang of the right kind of fellows, and retreat into the forests of Radzenov. There they'll build a cave, not far from the Zholdevka,* so that if they are closely pursued they can jump in and swim across to Prussia. They will all live as free as the birds. They'll saddle their horses, take up their rifles, attack lordly manors, and hold up parties of merchants on their way to Warsaw. In a short time the whole neighborhood will be in awe of them. But the poor will have no reasons to fear. . . . In due time the people will come to him like tenants to their lord. . . . Then he'll choose a refined young girl with fiery black eyes and long black hair, and make her his queen. . . .

He increases his pace and is presently lost in the white distance. . . .

III

Beyond the town near the wood Solomon stopped, placed the bag on the ground, and waited, craning his long, scraggy neck to listen. Then he put two fingers into his mouth and emitted a shrill whistle. From the other end of the wood came an answering whistle.

"A fine lad," thought Solomon; "if only he weren't so wild, and would take a father's advice once in a while, I'd be provided for in my old age. But here he goes and gets tangled up with Gradool's widow, like a fool. If she were pretty, at least, it wouldn't be so bad. . . . But that such a handsome husky fellow should be running after a little creature without colour, figure, or looks . . . it's mortifying. The whole town is scandalised, and I haven't dared to show my face in the House-of-Prayer for the last six months."

Zanvill appeared at the edge of the wood and shouted, "Come, dad, it's late!"

Solomon seized the bag and hurried up to him.

"How about the horses?" asked Solomon.

"It's all right; they're asleep in the stable."

They walked on, faster and faster, looking like two wolves whom hunger has driven out of the forest into the high-road. The old man constantly felt his bosom and muttered to himself, "Roan . . . chestnut . . . bay . . . Simon   horse-dealer. . . . Cholera!" . . . Every now and then he plucked Zanvill by the sleeve. . . . "Wait! I hear someone." . . .

Zanville stopped, pricked up his ears, opened his eyes wide, and looked around, but saw no one. "The old man is losing his nerve," he smiled to himself, and strode on.

Solomon felt a shivering cold through all his body. It occurred to

* A stream.

him that Tertza must now be lying snugly under the warm feather-
bed.

"A dog's life," he muttered again; "about time I quit this beautiful
business."

They suddenly heard the barking of a dog.

"Oh the cursed beasts!" exclaimed Solomon; "the cholera destroy
them! Why did God ever create the curs?"

In the distance several scattered houses became visible. All was
still.

Zanvill took the bag and started for the village, when a shaggy black
hound suddenly sprang in his path, barking loud. Zanvill retreated;
the dog followed. Then he made a sudden turn and threw himself on
the animal. He caught him by the weasand with both hands and began
to strangle him. The dog did not struggle long; his eyes became glazed,
and his tongue lolled out. Zanvill flung the lifeless body aside and spat
out. He looked around for his father, but he was gone.

Zanvill found him under a hillock, his teeth chattering . . . the
sight of the dog being strangled had been too much for him.

They neared the house. Zanvill threw the bag over his shoulder
and deftly lifted the door off its hinges. A warm vapour struck his face.
He took out a bottle of whisky, drugged the horses, put boots on their
legs, and led them out quietly. Near the hillock Solomon joined him.
He took off the boots and put them back into the bag. Then they
mounted the horses and sped away into the silent night.

BELGIUM

Introduction

BELGIAN literature, properly speaking, is composed of three groups; namely, Flemish, Walloon and French, and since we treat Flemish or Dutch literature in the Holland section, we are here concerned with that part of Belgian literature written in French.

Many of the writers of the early part of the nineteenth century were followers of the French tradition, and with the exception of Charles de Coster (1827-1879), who wrote the brilliant and picturesque romance of *Tyl Ulenspiegel*, Belgium can not be said to have produced any striking or original literature.

The significant movement in Belgian literature dates, according to Sir Edmund Gosse, from the banquet given to Camille Lemonnier in 1883, by the younger generation of artists and men of letters as a protest against the official literature that had refused the quinquennial prize to Lemonnier for his *Un Mâle*. The young writers founded a review, *La Jeune Belgique*, and among its early contributors we find Georges Eekhoud (b. 1854), Georges Rodenbach (1855-1898) and Ivan Gilkin. This group, as well as that contributing to *L'Art Moderne*, edited by the able Edmont Picard, soon became so vigorous that they attracted recognition. The most famous of all modern Belgian writers is Maeterlink, and another great figure is Émile Verhaeren.

✻ ✻ ✻

CAMILLE LEMONNIER
(1844-1913)

LEMONNIER, born at Brussels, studied law and received an appointment in a government office. He resigned from his clerkship after three years and took to literature, writing art criticism at first. He wrote a number of novels and several volumes of short stories in which he displayed a capacity to portray peasant life about him. Lemonnier spent much of his time in Paris where he was one of the early contributors to the *Mercure de France*.

The Glass House is taken from his volume of short stories, *Poupées d'Amour*. It has been translated for this collection by Thurston Macauley.

THE GLASS HOUSE

"IS that you, my Jean?"

The carpet deadened his footsteps as he came into the room. He thought she was asleep over there by the half-opened window, the curtains of which were fluttering ever so lightly in the breeze. But Elise's keen ears were aware of the least sound.

"Your Jean himself. . . ."

And at that moment he moved forward towards the hands, so delicate and pale, that she stretched out before her, as if she might already feel his presence, in the gently stirred currents of air, before he reached her side. Her hands touched his clothes, then brushed his face which he leaned over her chair.

"Yes, it is you . . ." she murmured. "I always feel fortunate in seeing you with these hands, which take the place of my poor eyes. . . . Come nearer . . . how good you smell—sweet with the scent of this beautiful day!"

"Dear—my *dear!*"

He kissed the dark eyelids veiled in the faded whiteness of her face. She did not let him raise himself again, but held his head, with both hands, against her cheek, keeping that faithful kiss to her sightless eyes.

"Like that—oh, always! . . . The warmth of your lips seems to open my eyes again! Oh, my Jean that I lost, I can see you again!"

He made a scarcely perceptible motion of weariness.

"Now, Elise. . . ."

"True, I am also very exacting. Scold me! I could stay this way for hours, without thinking, feeling a delicious little shiver because I have you near me, close to me. . . . You must remember that I myself no longer see—I see only through you. . . . Sit there, my Jean. . . . You've been out quite a while. . . . You must have lots to tell me about. . . ."

He drew up a foot-stool and sat down, with her little hands entwined like rings around his fingers.

"The leaves are out on all the trees along the boulevards," he said. "I saw your friends, Jeanne and Emilienne. . . . They are always beautiful, too—like you, my Elise. . . ."

A smile brightened the heavy darkness of the blind woman.

"Tell me that again, dear. . . . It's so good to think the others haven't changed! . . . that everything around me is just as it was when I was there—when I wasn't groping in shadow! . . . And haven't you seen that woman again who was so interested in me and for whom I'm so often mistaken?"

"Madame Dulac? Oh, she's nothing like you! She's all grey—one of the homeliest women I've ever seen!"

"You see, her voice makes me uncomfortable. She has the voice of a person without a soul. And, still, her voice is musical—she has certain liquid notes like the singing of a warbler. . . . She seems to come here for something I don't know about. Forgive me, my dear Jean, if I make you listen to me too much. All my senses are eyes since I no longer see. . . . That woman appears to me as an ominous, black beauty. . . . And, then, I don't know why, I seem to feel that you are deceiving me a little."

"Nonsense! Only you are beautiful!"

"Oh, I'm so afraid! . . . Look—isn't there a wrinkle there in my cheeks? Haven't some white hairs appeared since yesterday? Oh, that I might always be what I seemed to you—still the pretty Elise you flattered so lovingly."

Again she lifted her pale hands, delicate and brilliant human orchids moved by mysterious life: her fingers always seemed to be weaving with some unseen silk, making lace out of threads of air. She drew Jean's face near hers, into the light that came from the windows. She looked at him with her sightless eyes as if she actually saw him, as if she wanted to read his mind in his eyes.

"No, no, Elise—not a wrinkle, not a white hair. . . . Your cheeks are always like roses—your dear, unwrinkled forehead like golden wheat of summer."

"And you, you also are beautiful, my Jean—you are always young and beautiful in my lifeless eyes. . . . I've never stopped seeing you as you were when I loved you before. . . . And, yet, sometimes it seems something has changed in you: when you tell me I am always as beautiful as of old your voice isn't quite the same."

Elise lost her sight ten years ago. Daylight gradually grew dim, finally going out altogether, veiling the delicate brilliancy of her eyes. She lived on the other side of a dark wall, bound to the world only by the tender affection of her husband, Jean, who became a living and tangible light that her hands felt gently. Like a rose, shedding petal after petal, her lovely face withered, wrinkles forming around the hideous wounds of the sockets. The vital strength thus drew the golden curls from her hair, which was now entirely white. She was no more than a faint ghost of the lovely Elise that was.

But a miracle of love made her believe she had still kept her youth. For ten years Jean religiously deluded her with the lie of her beauty perpetuated through the outrage of blindness. Thus was the illusion a brittle glass house for her, a fragile, enchanted palace where she continued to dwell as in a dream: her life stopped just at the time before daylight went out. This endlessly enlightened the images at the bottom of her mind, caressing the agony of her sightlessness. And, magician to the end of this fantastic world, which he created in a golden haze over the impenetrable gloom before her eyes, Jean, with a touching deceit, had thus persuaded her that nothing around her had changed, that the flowers on the ground were always in bloom, that the years spared the appearance of those she loved. Living amidst these fancies, Elise wore only light dresses and ribbons which appealed to her superannuated coquetterie (for she wished to be clad just as she had been at the time she last saw herself in the mirror) though which were in sharp contrast to the decline of her aging body.

But, one day, having fallen asleep listening to the street noises that came in on the light breeze through the window, as she didn't fancy going out and voluntarily prolonged her languishing ease in the armchair, she was awakened by a whispering at the end of the apartment. She recognised Jean's voice and another who was talking to him, somewhat ironically, was Madame Dulac, who had always made her so uneasy. She got up from her chair and, with hands outstretched before her, she walked silently over the carpet as far as the room from which the voices had come.

"You are beautiful!" said Jean. "For me you hold the beauty of desire and great delight. . . . See, I am at your knees! I've begun to live only since I've placed myself in your keeping!"

A flute-like laugh broke out.

"Don't you tell your poor wife the same thing? Doesn't she, with her hideous mask and white hair, also believe that she is the living beauty for you? Oh, my dear, all that's so ridiculous!"

They could see a slim shadow appear in the light of the doorway. "Jean! My Jean!"

The glass house was shattered—her heart broken. . . . Elise took one last step, whirled around and fell at the feet of her husband.

* * *

GEORGES RODENBACH
(1855-1898)

RODENBACH spent most of his years in Paris where he was intimate with Edmond de Goncourt. Some of his work is imitative of the French, but "the best part of his production is the outcome of a passionate idealism of the quiet Flemish towns in which he had passed his childhood."

The City Hunter is taken from his volume *Le Douet des Brumes*. It has been translated for this collection by Jacques Le Clercq.

THE CITY HUNTER

THE other day, I recognised the back of my friend X——. He was walking ahead of me down the avenue. One could tell he was happy from his jaunty gait and from the swift movements of his walking-stick. With the latter, he was describing arabesques in the air perhaps corresponding to the lines of his palm and including his destiny.

After a few moments, I noticed he was following a woman. What? X—— following a woman? A man of established position, a man distinguished, intelligent, popular, still handsome and quite able to win favours in the drawing-rooms of Society?

He had never been known to have a love-affair or even a flirtation. He was married, moreover, and people believed him to be utterly faithful to his wife.

Yet there he was, occupied in following a passer-by. I assured myself his case must be more complicated than appeared. Surely a man with a character as subtle as his could not be suspected of low vice or of an indescriminate sensuality?

At the end of the avenue, he came to a halt. He appeared to be abandoning his purpose. Of a sudden, he obliqued in my direction. We met almost face to face.

"Ha! Caught you this time!" I exclaimed. "So you follow women in the street, eh?"

"Certainly, I do. Indeed, that is the only reason for which I walk abroad."

Doubtless my expression betrayed a certain astonishment or an air of mistrust at the possibility of irony on his part. He considered it fitting to insist, as though his explanation were plausible and he must bring it forth immediately.

"Of course," he said. "Everybody goes hunting at this time of the year! I don't go out to the country; my field is here. The great capitals are forests. Woman is a rich and multiform game. I set forth every afternoon, I go a-hunting. I make sure my gloves, my hat, my entire costume are in order, precisely as a hunter makes sure of his rifles and dogs.

"And I savour the emotion, the delicious anguish of lying in wait, of watching, of pursuit, of bringing down my game—just as any hunter.

"And in the matter of game, there is a like variety. There are women who flutter through the streets with a whirring of birds' wings. There are women who pass by in the colourful dress of pheasants. There are women who surge and vanish amid the crowd like hares through the grasses. There are women who would charge, like a wild boar, at the first sign of approach.

"To pursue all this game! To follow all these women! And, like a good hunter, to load one's rifle properly; to vary one's ammunition; to select the proper projectile; to modify one's gunmanship. Small-shot or buck? Shall one riddle the bird or wing it? To accost a woman in one admirable phrase or rapidly to utter a few brief and deft words that close, torpid as a wing, over a voice about to protest?

"Thus a great presence of mind is required of the glance. To recognise a woman's particular quality instantly, just as one recognises the nature of game by the noise of its flight, though it be invisible, through the silence."

"And I used to think you were true to your wife!" I said, amused and more than a trifle astounded.

"I am," my friend replied, "absolutely. But this is another business. No true hunter ever eats the game he kills. He does not relish game, whether partridge or pheasant or venison or hare. As for me, I never possess the women I follow—those I hunt, if you prefer.

"Hunting is a cerebral pleasure, a nervous joy that proves quite sufficient in itself. All the delight of it consists in what comes before and after. To dress, to arm oneself, to set forth, to lie in ambush, to track one's game, to beat it, to force it out from under cover; to experience every little curiosity; to know the tactics of the sport, the watch, the emotion, the uncertainty of success, the passage of the bird within one's reach—a thing that will last but a second, yet everything depends upon it! Then afterwards, the satisfaction to one's vanity, the tally of those brought down, and the exaggerated account one gives of one's exploits to others. . . . Here are the secret delights of the chase; they are one and the same, whether you hunt woman or game. The actual moment of firing is but a detail. . . ."

"You are very clever," I observed to my friend. "But your cleverness and fantasy strike me as highly artificial!"

"Not at all," he protested. "They are the purest of reality. I do exactly as I told you. Unless I had discovered this sport, I would die of boredom as I walk the streets. This is my way of entertainment when out for a stroll. As I said, I go a-hunting! What tales, what wonderful tales of hunting I could tell!

"And the accidents, the hazards of pursuit, that delicious tang of petty danger when one forces one's game to its lair. This has more than once been my experience. Then the pursuit of a woman is an excitement, a fever; there comes a point when you can no longer stop! At such times, I have followed the women I was pursuing into houses where perhaps they lived, into hotels where they might be staying as visitors or whither they might be luring me, being agreeable.

"It requires a suppleness of skill, a subtlety of flair. To formulate a decision instantly, then to act! To follow, now close at hand, now at a wider interval, for a brief or lengthy period of time! To smile or to adopt a languid air! To appear a sentimentalist or a conqueror! To pursue a woman upstairs or to stand waiting under her window! There are women that must be accosted in unfrequented streets, others in the turmoil of the boulevard! One woman must be drawn into a passage, another into a cab!

"I have performed in this manner with nuances savant and efficacious. . . . A thousand subterfuges! And all this no further than to the limits of certitude, to that instant when the woman one has pursued acquiesces. An immediate docility, consent to an assignation in the future, or merely an amiable playfulness that yet foretells success in spite of appearances— these have been enough, in all manner of cases, to satisfy me.

"As soon as this occurred, I abandoned the sport. In other words, I fled from the conversation, the assignation of fulfilment, whatever the case might be. For these, in fine, were but three phases of success. Guarantee of success alone mattered to me; when I received it, it was enough. I have already told you no true hunter eats the game he kills. I, too, have no use for the woman I have brought down. . . ."

My friend grew silent. He gazed into the distance, levelling his grey eye, as though a new prey were about to arise. Because of what he had just told me, I noticed for the first time how grey his eyes were— theirs was the grey of steel, the grey of the barrel of a rifle. . . . At the same time, his nostrils twitched. His was the nose of a hunting-dog, picking up a scent. The whole train of the hunt was resumed in him. Women passed by in the distance, graceful, indeed, as birds in the colourful dress of pheasants—all game for the taking!

Yet my friend's story had troubled me and made me anxious on his account. What did this aimless excitement, this cerebral debauch purport? I veiled my impression of worry, yet I was able to convey a little of it to him.

"Have a care!" I said. "That pleasure may become a danger. There is a strange mania in all this, perhaps a touch of Sadism."

"In any case," he replied, "I am not the only one. The great capitals are filled with hunters like myself. Sometimes when I have been following a woman for a while, I notice there are four or five of us walking behind and around her. It is exactly like a beat! The bird flies between several guns. . . .

"Moreover, there are every sort of hunting and all kinds of taste! There are specialists, too! Some fancy only a certain species of women —blondes or brunettes, lithe women with a thinness as of shrubs, fat women with the flesh of noble animals. Others prefer women who are young but whose hair is grey. Women in mourning have their devotees, in public gardens where their black weeds blend so prettily with dead leaves. Some men lie in wait only for widows. . . . .

"These are the hunters who relish game that is already wounded. For here, too, is every variety of hunter. The man who pursues young virgins corresponds to the hunter who likes to go after wild duck only. The man who persists in tracking stern women corresponds to the hunter of wild boar. . . . ."

"And how many do you tally?" I asked my friend. "If there are so many hunters in the forests of large cities, the frail feminine game must succumb plentifully."

"Yes, statistics have been determined. Of the women accosted, the proportion that succumbs is one to four. In these figures, one must make generous allowance for women from the provinces and strangers, who are dazed by the fever of Paris, who wheel round and round in flight, who go blind and fall easily. And then, it all hinges on so little—one word, one particular moment, destiny, the skill of the hunter.

"Here, especially, the analogy of hunt is striking. A woman is like game—you miss her as easily as you catch her."

❋ ❋ ❋

EMILE VERHAEREN
(1855-1916)

VERHAEREN, born at Saint-Amand, near Antwerp, was educated at Ghent and, later, at the University of Louvain. In 1881 he was admitted to the bar at Brussels, but soon after turned completely to literature. He edited, in succession, *La Semaine* and *Le Type* until these were suppressed by the authorities, when he devoted himself to *La Jeune Belgique*. While Verhaeren is essentially a poet, he has written several plays and a few volumes of short stories.

The Horse Fair at Opdorp is translated by Keene Wallis and appears in the volume, *Five Tales by Emile Verhaeren*, published by Albert and Charles Boni, copyright, 1924, by whose permission it is here used.

THE HORSE FAIR AT OPDORP

EVERY year, in June, there is a spectacular horse fair—and sleek and well groomed are the exhibits—in the little village of Opdorp, on the boundary line between Flanders and Brabant.

Around a wide mall with smooth-shaven green grass and elm, ash, and willow trees, is the circle of houses—their walls like white coats, their roofs like red caps—and they gaze at each other with the bright eyes of their spotless windows. At one end of the oval stands the church with its steeple and glittering gold weathercock, and about the church lies the humble unfenced burying-ground.

The village is sleepy, sedate, unpretentious. Men go about their monotonous work unhurried, putting forth their leisurely hands as if to unravel the precious web of time without tangling it.

On week-days an aroma of butter and cheese streams out of the cellars. At night the herds of cows wind slowly home from the ponds and pastures. Behind them the drover whistles his tune. There is a loud mooing and lowing. A gate creaks open and shut. No other sign of animation save, on Sunday, the church bell promising a richer, better life. The people crowd to mass, vespers, and compline. On Monday the village relapses into tedium and pursues its regulated and monotonous round.

But the annual fair makes Opdorp famous. In the first grey of morning awkward foals are to be seen gangling into town at the heels of their mothers; then come formidable stallions led with a halter by peasant lads; then the work brutes, obstinate and powerful slaves which have survived God knows how many seed times, how many harvests, how many struggles through the thick Flemish gumbo.

They file along past the booths, and the jackpuddings frighten them with booings, thwack them on the rumps with lath swords, joke about their coarse breed and make merry over their woolly tails and their hoofs, big and round like immense mushrooms and looking the more cumbersome for their matted fetlocks. A battle rises between peasants and clowns. The former lash out their fists with right good will, the latter deftly skip away and counter with a mocking flick on the nose. There is deafening uproar within and without the placarded tents, and in the streets and lanes the mingled whinnying of the horse and the thud of the rattling gallop on the pavement. As soon as the trumpets, trombones, and bass drums make themselves heard the festival turns into an orgy. It is as if the entire village had been transformed into a gigantic wreath of clamour in which shrill squeals, insolent whistles, and yodeling catcalls represent the lurid flowers. Nevertheless, notwithstanding the fun and excitement, the fair is less and less frequented. People have a reason for staying away.

In their times the bishops of Ghent and Tournay sent their riding-masters to this fair, the abbots of Aberbode and Perck found here the choicest of their animals, and above all, the undertaker of the little city of Termonde, every five years, sent his handsomest hearse, drawn by four lean, seedy black mares, which after several years of hard service must be replaced that the pomp of a well-directed funeral might have nothing to fear from critics.

As soon as the coming of the hearse was heralded, the jackpuddings jumped back onto the stages and outdid themselves in follies. Four gilded skeletons hung at the sides of the vehicle; one clown reached out and chucked them under the chin, another thrust flowers between their flesh-less ribs. The musicians, with swelling cheeks, blew their most doleful funeral march. Excited monkeys frisked chattering up and down the standards of the booths. The snake-charmer, wrapping her boa con-strictor around her waist, seized the monster's head and turned it, with wide open jaws, toward the dark vehicle approaching.

The equipage proceeded slowly past the grotesque, cynical masquerade. The plumes and black hangings brushed the tawdry bunting and shamed the staggering posters and flaring streamers. The hearse was full of good-for-nothing boys and girls of the streets, dancing and pushing each other around the trestles which at other times served to sustain the coffin. In front of the church a couple of sextons were added to the retinue. And that the sacrilege might be complete, the dead lights burned ghastly and unnecessary.

The hearse stopped at the inn of the Three Kings. As soon as he had unhitched, the driver sold his horses, which looked at the knacker with furtive eyes. The hearse driver quickly bought four others without haggling over the price, because the undertaker of Termonde was rich.

And hardly was the landlady paid, a glass hastily emptied, the harness furbished up, the girths lengthened to fit the plump new animals, when the rejuvenated equipage set itself again in motion, the seats and running boards occupied by street boys and church wardens. It went back the way it had come, but this time the masqueraders ceased their buffoonery and stood respectfully as if awed by its now formidable appearance. Women could be seen crossing themselves. Death, which a moment ago had limped along forlorn and superannuated, now seemed to step forth trim and jaunty to combat.

It happened, it must have been twenty years ago—and since then the annual fair has been as if accursed—that the new horses were fiery and ungovernable and dashed through the village like a tornado. They darted around the booths and among the stands and further along on the high-way, they took fright at a wayside scarecrow and ran away. The people who had climbed into the hearse were panicstricken. A few, to avoid the danger, jumped off into the soft earth of the roadside embankments, others, huddling against each other, uttered such unearthly cries that people rushed out of the farmhouses wringing their hands and imploring heaven. In broad daylight, with flying curtains and pelting wheels, the hearse, a living black clatter, hurtled past. The lamps jostled their supports, the cross, jostled out of its standards, was shaken from right to left and from left to right, the silver fringe became entangled in the bushes, and black tatters were left hanging on the branches.

From the ramparts in Termonde the approaching whirlwind was observed. Great was the terror. Particular anxiety was felt for the church wardens, worthy dignitaries who were not nimble-footed enough to jump out.

The mad hearse traversed the entire city. There were shrieks and cries. The panic spread from house to house, from quarter to quarter. Women, stretching out their hands to aid their own imperiled boys and girls, were caught up and carried along on the dashboards. An old man was run over. The streets were rapidly emptied. Pale faces were pressed to the windowpanes. People ran along, breathless, behind the hearse. The bell-ringer in the main square thought to ring the alarm bell, but death ran too quickly and in its lightning flight soon struck the opposite end of the suburbs.

The mad horses, white with foaming sweat, bloody-muzzled, stopped for the first time at the wall of a cemetery. One of them fell down heavily. A little girl was killed. A church warden had his leg broken. All the others sustained some injury. Only the driver came off unhurt, without so much as a bruise, and as his horses, for their part, had recovered from their fright, he, in the end, laughed over the adventure.

But the townfolk could not so easily be reassured. What unhappy event was foreshadowed by this significant accident? Prayers and devotions were redoubled. To no avail.

During the interminable winter the city was devastated by an unknown fever, and the Scheldt overflowed three times. The streets through which the hearse had come were the most heavily smitten. The path of affliction extended straight back to Opdorp.

How quickly the neat little village lost its aspect of peace! Every day there was a death. This lasted for months and months until the cemetery had to be enlarged. Even today the recollection of this black event has not been dimmed: it is even said that in a few years the famous fair of Opdorp will have to be stricken out of the calendar.

HOLLAND

Introduction

PROSE fiction in Holland prospered poorly until the seventeenth century when Johann van Heemskerk published his *Batavian Arcadia* (1637), the first original Dutch romance. This was followed by *Mirandor* (1675), a very spirited romance in the manner of *Gil Blas*, written by Nikolaes Heinsius. More than a century elapsed before the revival of the novel form. In 1782 Elizabeth Wolff and Agatha Deken collaborated in the writing of *Sara Burgehar*, a splendid story which won immediate recognition.

In the nineteenth century we see a wider interest displayed in fiction. Justus van Maurik wrote some lovely stories of Amsterdam life. Arnold Buning won popularity with his *Marine Sketches*. Mention should be made of Douwes Dekker writing under the name of Multatuli, whose *Max Havelaar* has been accepted as a classic, even outside of Holland.

The best known of the modern writers is Louis Couperus, a fine poet and extremely sensitive artist. Frederick van Eeden, a delightful and subtle humourist, although less known, is an equally splendid novelist. Hermann Heijermans dominates modern drama. He has also written some delightful stories. A contemporary writer of great power is Styn Streuvels, a young baker by trade, whose peasant stories have achieved considerable success.

❋ ❋ ❋

FREDERIK WILLEM VAN EEDEN
(1860-   )

VAN EEDEN, born at Haarlem, studied medicine at the University of Amsterdam. In 1885 he identified himself with the literary group known as *de Nieuwe Gids* so designated from their periodical, in which van Eeden first published his famous novel *The Little Johannes*. He has also written a number of plays, and his *Studies* are gems of literary style.

Johannes Attends a Party is one episode in the highly satirical novel *The Little Johannes*. It has been translated by James Penninck especially for this collection.

JOHANNES ATTENDS A PARTY

WHILE Johannes stayed at the house, the day of the fearful evening-party drew near. By now he had become a little less bashful and he had confided his fears to others. A carriage drove him to the neighbouring town, where he was provided with suitable clothes for the coming festivities. But still his uneasiness was not appeased.

"Dear Lady," said Johannes that afternoon, when he was alone with his hostess and the children, "will you please tell the people that I really cannot play on any instrument. I would like nothing better than being an inconspicuous spectator."

"But, Johannes," spoke the lady of the house, "that would make it very unpleasant for me after all I told about you. They all expect something from you."

"But I don't know anything," replied Johannes nervously.

"He is telling stories, Mammy," interrupted Olga, "he can make sounds with castanets and imitate wild beasts."

"Oh yes, all sorts of wild beasts; so terribly real," affirmed Frieda.

"Is that true, Johannes? Well, now then."

It was true that Johannes, in order to amuse his little lady-friends, had imitated in their company all sorts of animal-sounds, like those of a horse, donkey, cow, dog, cat, pig, sheep and goat. He also was moderately clever in imitating the songs of birds to rouse the little girls to high admiration. And with one single instrument he really was proficient.

Every school- and street-boy in Holland carries during certain months of the year a pair of castanets in his pocket. So many a fall day, going slowly from the school to the house, Johannes had shortened the way with an incessant: "van-je-rik-ketik-ketik, van-je-rik-ketikketik, van-je-rik-ketikketik-tak-tak."

And now the little girls started to coax him, that he also should include Mammy in his audience. Whereupon he produced his castanets, which he himself had manufactured, and rattled cheerful tunes.

"That is fine," exclaimed the Countess, "you should dance and sing at the same time like the Spaniards."

He did not understand how to dance, stated Johannes, but singing, well, he would have a try at it.

So he sang several popular airs, like: "Oh, mother, the sailor", and "Sarah, watch your dress", accompanied by the rhythm of the castanets.

The children thought the performance beautiful.

Spurred on by their enthusiasm he commenced to improvise all kinds of follies. The girls applauded him and became increasingly jolly. Johannes postured before them and announced his recitation, as if facing a regular audience.

The Countess and the children sat in a row, and the latter's glee was uncontrolable.

Johannes announced sketches from the animal-world, and, with continuous clapper-accompaniment, he started to sing to the air of *The Carnival de Venise:*

> "A chicken arrived from Japan
> And solemnly assured a lame frog,
> That she never would wed the man,
> As he was too much of a hog."

The children howled with delight and stamped their feet as a sign of approval. "Some more, Jo, some more, Johannes. Come now."

"That's precious," cried the Countess, who now commenced to speak Dutch.

> "A grasshopper, in a voice very thin,
> To a chimpanzee cried on its way,
> Permit me to borrow your skin,
> I am due at a great bal-masqué."

"He shouldn't have done that. That's greedy. Some more, Jo," laughed the children.

> "A trout, who sat on a stoop,
> Inquired of his permanent guest,
> About hairs he found in his soup,
> Which certainly was a great pest."

"Ho, Ho," cried the lady, "be careful; that is a little too crude."

"Oh nay, Mammy, just funny," shouted Frieda and Olga together. "Go on, go on, he is a scream. Oh, don't stop, Jo."

But Johannes felt a trifle upset by the rebuke, resulting in the cessation of further animal-sketches.

In the evening the Countess and Johannes rode in a state-carriage to Lady Crimmetart.

The latter resided in a very beautiful manor-house, a castle in a magnificent park. From a distance Johannes saw all the brilliantly-lit windows and the string of carriages before the columns of the main entrance. A sort of canopy was stretched out in front, while a vividly-red carpet ran from the portico, affording protection to the guests, while they walked from their carriages to the splendid vestibule. A row of lackeys, twenty on each side, flanked the entrance. They looked very imposing, tall and heavily built, wearing trousers of yellow plush and red coats braided with gold stripes. Johannes was quite surprised to note that they all seemed very old, as their well-combed hair was pure white. However, that was caused by the sprinkling of white power and was part of the etiquette. Johannes felt very small and shabby when he stepped between the first of those liveried potentates.

Inside there was a sea of brilliant lights. Johannes became quite confused. He mounted the wide steps of a high, covered staircase of many-coloured marble. Vaguely he became aware of flowers, electric lamps, rich carpets, wide, glittering-white surfaces of gentlemen's dress-shirts bordered by evening-coats, ladies' bare necks covered with jewels and white furs. There was a subdued whispering of soft voices, rustling of silk dresses, the calling of names.

In the distance, at the head of the staircase, the high-bred features of Lady Crimmetart glimmered as a warning signal on a railroad track. All the guests advanced toward her, as their names were called. They received a handshake and bowed.

"What name, sir?" asked a giant lackey, obliquely bending over him. Johannes stammered something, but the Countess repeated it in a different form.

"Professor Johannes from Holland," he heard some one announce.

He bowed, received a hand, and saw the grin on the powdered face change into a sweetly artificial smile. Lady Crimmetart's neck and arms were of such a fatness and nudity, that Johannes became fairly scared and did not dare to look at them openly. A whole mass of precious stones were strewn over their surface. Large, flat, similarly-sized, squarely cut diamonds alternated with pear-shaped pearls. Three white ostrich feathers swayed in her coiffure. There were no animals around, but she carried a fan and a crutch-cane with golden knob.

"How are you?" asked a coarse voice. But, evidently, no answer was expected. Because, before Johannes could frame the reply that he felt fairly well, she was already grinning at some one else.

Next to her stood a short, compact gentleman with a glitteringly bald head, a red face with hard, sharp lines, and a large bulbous nose, just such a face as one will see cut out of the knobs of walking-canes and umbrellas. That was Lord Crimmetart, and he pressed Johannes's hand in a firm manner.

For about an hour or so Johannes, feeling deserted and lonesome, was lost in the moving crowd, till he nearly became nauseated by the subdued noise, the talk, the rustle of dresses, the glitter of lights and jewelry, and the glamour of silk garments, liveries, bare necks and expensive shirt-fronts, the heavy odours of perfume and flowers. It was so crowded, that, at times, he could not move at all, while the gentlemen and ladies spoke to him with their faces almost touching his own. How he longed for a quiet nook and an ordinary human being! Everybody was talking but himself. Nobody felt so forlorn as he. Moreover he couldn't understand what they all had to tell to each other. If he caught any stray conversation it always happened to be about the crowded hall and the animated party. But surely they did not come together just to talk about that. The feast of the elves in the rabbithole in the dunes seemed to Johannes far more enjoyable than the music that streamed from a strike-orchestra, hidden behind tall laurels. The latter affected Johannes with a painful desire, which made him sit down, unnoticed, letting the people shove past and by him, while he dreamily stared in front of him with brimming eyes at the thought of the stillness of the dunes and a murmuring sea on a moon-lit night.

"Professor Johannes, allow me to introduce to you Professor von Pennewitz," it suddenly boomed into his ears. Terrified he arose.

There stood Lady Crimmetart next to a little man with sparse, grey locks, which hung down on his coat collar. The sight of him did not at all fit in with Johannes's dream.

"This is a prodigy, Professor von Pennewitz, a young poet, who interprets his own compositions. Also a famous medium. No doubt you will have to discuss important matters with him."

The introduction having been accomplished, Lady Crimmetart disappeared again amidst her guests, leaving the two professors bowing to each other: Johannes confused and bashful, von Pennewitz continuing to bow, while rubbing his hands and elevating himself on his toes with a smiling face.

"Now the examination will commence," thought Johannes and he waited with the patience of a doomed man for the learned questions, by which this great man would expose him in all his ignorance.

"Eh, have you known the family for a long time?" asked von Pennewitz, frequently blowing between his half-opened lips, while rearranging his glasses with spread fingers, and, head lowered, leering at Johannes over the top of his spectacles.

"No, not at all," answered Johannes, shaking his head negatively.

"No?" questioned von Pennewitz, blithely rubbing his hands and rearing himself on his toes. Then, continuing in bad English: "Well, come on now; that gives me pleasure. Neither do I. Strange people, don't you think so, young man?"

Johannes, reviving a bit by having something in common, conceded the point after some hesitation.

"Do you also have such types in Holland? Surely on a more moderate scale, he—Ha, Ha, Ha. These here are immensely rich. Did you taste their champagne? No? Now then, you ought to make a trip to the sideboard. It is worth the trouble, I assure you."

Glad to have at least some one's company Johannes followed the little man, who guided him through the crowd.

At the sideboard they drank of the foaming wine.

"But, sir," remarked Johannes, "I heard that Lady Crimmetart is very clever."

"So, so," stated the professor, again glancing at Johannes over the top of his glasses, while nodding his head: "Yes, I won't say anything against that. She travelled quite a bit—papa kept a boarding-school —picked up a little of everything.—Nowadays one can gather a great deal from newspapers. Do you read newspapers, young man?"

"Not very much, sir," said Johannes.

"Good—be careful about it. Let me give you a bit of advice, which is double-plated. Don't read many newspapers and don't eat many oysters. Especially don't eat any oysters in Rome. I have recently left behind me a fatal case of oyster-poisoning—that of a student in Rome."

Johannes resolved then and there to eat anything in Rome rather than oysters.

"Is Lord Crimmetart also clever, professor?" queried Johannes.

"He possesses a sufficiency of shrewdness. To become a Lord and multi-millionaire by means of blood-purifying pills only, you will have to be quite a cunning rogue. Try it yourself sometimes— ha, ha, ha!"

At which the professor laughed heartily, blew through his fingers, sniffed, rattled with his false teeth and emptied his glass. When he regained his speech he was serious.

"But remember, young man, that you should not marry till the ship is in a safe harbour. There Crimmetart did a stupid thing. Now he could get one far prettier. He even could have had Countess Dolores, if he was so minded."

Johannes felt himself getting flushed and red in the face.

"I am staying at her house, sir," he interposed in a somewhat hurt tone.

"So, so, so," nodded the professor. "Now I didn't say anything bad about her, remember. A most charming woman. A perfect beauty. Is she your hostess? well, well, well."

"There is His Grace the Bishop," roared the deep voice of Lady Crimmetart in passing, while, greatly agitated, she pressed forward toward the entrance-hall.

Filled with curiosity Johannes looked for the white mitre and the gilt crosier. But all he saw was a tall, ordinary gentleman, clothed in black and wearing gaiters. His face was smoothly benevolent and wore an affected smile. In his hand he held a strangely-looking shovelhat, with sides turned up by little strings, as if to prevent them from falling over his face. Lady Crimmetart received him with as warm welcome as Aunt Serena bestowed on the dominie. Johannes wished he was still at Aunt Serena's.

"Sir," somebody spoke in his ear. "My lady wishes to know whether you have brought your instrument. If so, she would be pleased to have you commence."

Johannes gave a scared look. The questioner was a dignified gentleman with moustache brushed up, black satin knee breeches and a red dress-coat. Perhaps he was a master of ceremonies.

"I have no instrument," stammered Johannes, but he covertly touched the castanets in his pocket. "I can not do anything," he repeated, feeling very unhappy.

The elegant gentleman looked to right and left as if ascertaining whether he had made a mistake. He went away for a short time and returned with Countess Dolores.

"What seems to be the trouble now, dear Johannes? You should not leave us in the lurch."

"But, dear Lady, I really can't——"

The elegant gentleman regarded him very coolly and seriously, as if he had experienced such whims of progenies before this. Johannes's forehead became damp and sticky.

"Why surely, Johannes, you will have great success."

"What directions shall I give to the accompanist?" asked the stylish gentleman. Johannes did not understand the nature of the question, but the Countess framed a reply.

Soon he stood within a circle of guests, near a piano, while hundreds of eyes, with or without glasses, were focussed on him. Right in front of him, next to Lady Crimmetart, sat the Bishop, gazing at him doubtfully and severely with a hard, cold look in his light-coloured eyes.

The master of ceremonies called out loudly and impressively: "The Dutch National Hymn", which compelled Johannes to use his castanets and sing with all his power. In order to insure inspiration he gazed at the beautiful features with the nearsighted eyes of the Countess, assuring himself that he was singing for her pleasure only. He exerted himself to give his best, and, beginning with: "Oh, mother, the sailor" and "We are going to America" he ended with "The Chicken from Japan" and "The Tiger from Timbuktoo," running through his whole repertoire.

They listened and looked at him as if he were a rare insect, but nobody laughed. Neither the blue, bulging eyes of the hostess, nor the severe features of the Bishop, nor any of the other hundreds of pairs of eyes of the richly-clad and distinguished ladies and gentlemen, exhibited the slightest token of gay or even agreeable emotions. But after all that was not to be wondered at, as they didn't understand one word of the songs. But still it was not encouraging. After a while none of the guests looked at him any longer, while they commenced to talk and laugh amongst themselves. To his immense surprise there was some sort of applause at the end of his recital. Furthermore Countess Dolores came to him and pressed his hand, while showering congratulations on "his wonderful success". Lady Crimmetart also bellowed at him that it was tremendously interesting. A tall, thin young lady, clad in white satin, whose prominent collarbones were but partly hidden by a ten-string pearl collar, shook his hand fervently and gave him a most charming smile. She expressed herself to be very glad to have heard *The Carnival of Venice* in its original form by an inhabitant of the City itself.

"How extremely interesting, professor. . . . What is your name again? . . . to live in a City, which stands entirely in water, and where everybody walks around in wooden shoes."

"Was that altogether your own composition, Professor Johannes?" asked an ugly, good-natured, little lady in a simple, black dress. And several ladies of riper age requested the privilege to introduce themselves to him. He really felt somewhat better at all those marks of appreciation, although he somewhat doubted their genuine nature. However, when he approached a group of tall, broad-shouldered, young Britons with high collars, rosy close-shaved cheeks and neat, shiny, well-dressed, short-waving, blond hair, who, one hand in their pockets, stood drinking champagne, he heard expressions like: "Beastly", "Rotten" and "Humbug". He felt that all that was said within his hearing was for his benefit only. Shortly after it became clear to him what success really did mean in such a company.

A solidly-built young lady with very artistic coiffure and beautiful, white teeth, sang a German song, accompanied by the piano. She produced thrillers and vocal scales like a regular music box. First shaking her head to and fro she then threw it backwards, while she kept her mouth wide open. The sounds, which issued forth, pierced Johannes through marrow and bones. He found it most difficult to grasp the meaning of the words, as she used a fantastic sort of German, but, apparently, she became greatly excited over an unfaithful sweetheart, after which she died purely from an affection of the heart. After she had finished she sent a sweet smile to the audience and bowed repeatedly. A lively applause resounded, intermingled with "Bis" and "Encore", which had been entirely absent from Johannes's performance. So he would not join the present shouts of approbation.

Feeling downhearted he sought out Countess Dolores. She was the only source of confidence and consolation he knew of. He appealed to her for permission to go home, as he felt tired and out-of-place there.

Countess Dolores did not look very much pleased herself. She had derived no satisfaction from his entertainment. However, she said: "Cheer up, my boy, don't permit yourself to feel discouraged. You still possess other talents, do you not? Have you already spoken to Ranji-Banji-Sing?"

For some time Johannes had watched the tall Indian, when, with head held high and stately steps, he was treading through the colourful crowd.

He had wide nostrils, large, beautiful, slightly veiled eyes, a light-brown skin, splendid blue-black, waving hair and a thin beard. He carried his white turban and yellow-silk gown with ceremonious dignity. Whenever he was addressed he bowed gracefully and deeply, closed his eyes and smiled with great affability, while he placed his hands, with their pale nails and upward-inclined fingertips, on his breast.

Johannes had followed his movements with great intentness, as of one he felt greater attraction for than any of the others, and he had visioned deep-blue skies, stately elephants, rustling palms and pink-marbled palace-façades on the shores of holy rivers. However, he had not dared to address him on his own initiative.

But now the Countess and Johannes went in search of him, and found him near Lady Crimmetart and surrounded by various other ladies, to whom he, by turns, with laughing courtesy, granted interviews.

"Mr. Ranji-Banji-Sing," began Countess Dolores, "have you already made the acquaintance of Professor Johannes from Holland? He is a great medium and undoubtedly will be in sympathy with you."

The Indian again exhibited his white teeth, while he smiled courteously and shook hands. But Johannes felt that it was not well-meant.

"You surely are also a medium, Mr. Sing?" asked one of the ladies. "Such a great theosophist like you must be."

Ranji-Banji-Sing threw his head back with an appearance of disdain. He made a gesture of denial with his tightly-locked fingers. Smiling contemptuously he replied in broken English: "Theosophists no mediums . . . tricks are low . . . street-artists for money. Theosophists and Yogi know everything just as well, know much more, but make no show. That is low breeding . . . unworthiness."

The slim, brown hand swept before the nose of Johannes to and fro in a manner to indicate contempt, and the dark face of the Indian took on an expression as if he had to swallow something bitter.

That was a little too much for Johannes. He spoke spitefully, feeling himself misunderstood by the only one, whom he wished to impress favourably.

"I never do tricks, sir. I demonstrate nothing. I am no medium."

"Not professionally, not as a business-medium, of course," explained Countess Dolores, in order to save the situation.

"Then you don't show how to turn tables upside down, or produce writing on slates or cause a rain of flowers?" asked the Indian, while his features cleared instantly.

"No, sir, not at all," replied Johannes vehemently.

"If I had known that," shouted Lady Crimmetart, while her eyes seemed to threaten to leave their sockets.

"But Mr. Sing, couldn't you demonstrate something for us, just for once. Something wonderful: a flying tambourine or a violin which plays without human aid? Come on now, come on, while we ask you so very pleasantly and while I look at you with a regard full of admiration? Please. . . ." And she leered at Ranji-Banji-Sing in a manner that somehow failed to rouse Johannes's jealousy.

The theosophist bowed again, while a sweet smile played around his lips. He closed his eyes, and a frown appeared on his face, as if he felt compelled to give but a reluctant consent.

The guests now repaired to a ladies' boudoir, encased by glass walls, which, with its foreign plants, resembled a sort of conservatory. The place was bathed in soft light, creating a semi-darkness. They formed a circle around a table with the Indian in the centre. The Indian forthwith expelled Johannes from the circle with the words: "No sympathy . . . bad influence."

Slates, which Mr. Sing held underneath the table with one hand, commenced to receive messages. The scratching of the pencil could be heard distinctly, after which the slate was brought to light, revealing "sayings" in foreign languages, Latin and Sanskrit, which were translated by the Indian and proved to contain the spirit of wise and ennobling lessons in sentiment.

Suddenly Johannes had the misfortune to notice that the slate, upon which writing was supposed to appear mysteriously, was being exchanged by the Indian theosophist at a moment when he had diverted the attention of all present. And now Johannes added to his fateful observation the still worse imprudence by exclaiming loudly: "I have discovered the secret; he exchanges the slates under cover."

An all-around commotion followed immediately.

But Ranji-Banji-Sing, with the greatest calm, produced the exchanged slate, showing, with a triumphant smile, that it was clean of writing.

Johannes was dumbfounded; he knew for a certainty that he had witnessed a deception, and he could not forbear to call out: "I saw it anyhow."

"Shame on you," thundered the voice of Lady Crimmetart, while all the other ladies shouted indignantly: "Shame, shame."

Ranji-Banji-Sing retaliated with a scornful smile: "I have pity . . . Yogi knows no hate . . . but deplore miscreant. Bad Karma (spirit of Revelation). Unfortunate creature this."

That did not correspond with what Mr. Lieverlee had said, when he had praised Johannes's Karma.

But after this incident the Countess Dolores became convinced that she would derive no further pleasure from her protégé. So she and Johannes took their departure.

Good-naturedly she did not reproach him, but, on the contrary, consoled him with pleasant jokes.

In the hall of the Countess's residence Johannes noticed newspapers lying around. Contrary to the advice of Professor von Pennewitz he commenced to look them through. One news-item riveted his attention. The strike of the miners in Germany had been brought to an end, but the miners had lost the fight. The news disturbed him very much and he passed a sleepless night, which seemed never to end.

❋ ❋ ❋

LOUIS COUPERUS
(1863-1923)

COUPERUS, born at The Hague, spent his boyhood in the Dutch East Indies. His first novel, *Eline Vere*, published in 1889, was written under the influence of Tolstoy. He is best known to the English-speaking world through his series of *Books of the Small Souls*. He was a great traveller and scholar, employing his classic research in some of his historical romances.

About Myself and Others is one of the stories in the *Legends of the Blue Coast* and has been translated by James Penninck especially for this collection.

ABOUT MYSELF AND OTHERS
(From *Legends of the Blue Coast*)

THERE is nothing that amuses me as much as little, very little adventures. Sometimes life bores me terribly in the sense that often it does not afford me any amusement. I work much, read much, love my quarters, where I study and write. I often find life very dull, I mean lacking in interest, and am likely to exclaim: "My God, my God, how bored I feel!" I yawn, stretch out my arms in despair and go out. Sometimes I meet with a little, very little adventure, and that amuses me. Then I return home with a contented smile. I at once sit down to write, and surround myself with heavy books containing old history. I dote on little adventures. I am going to tell you about the little summer-adventure with my friend Louis.

One evening I sat on a bench in the Promenades des Anglais. That is the hour and place for little bits of adventures. Apparently nothing happens there, except that people pass by, sit down and dream. In reality numerous little adventures spring up. Are humorous novelettes woven there? Is there a development into a romance, and, very occasionally, into a tragedy? Have no fear. The case in which my friend Louis was involved is nothing else than a miniature comedy, a tiny farce.

Well, I am sitting on a bench; a young man seats himself next to me. He is a good-looking fellow, a bit of a dandy in a white suit of clothes with white shoes, altogether dressed in an elegant and very simple manner. There is an absence of loud colours and he looks decidedly distinguished. He has fine eyes with long lashes. Doffing his straw hat he exposes deep-black hair. Perhaps he is little over twenty.

He regards me in an ingratiating manner.

He opens the conversation with a: "Fine evening."

"Splendid," I retort.

"The evenings in Nice during August are delightful."

I agree with him. "But the City is not very lively," I add.

"Quite true, the City is quiet. However, there will be an improvement as soon as the season starts. Are you living here?"

"Yes, sir."

"Summers included?"

"I have just returned from a trip."

"Is that so? I myself have just arrived."

"Do you intend staying during the winter?"

"Yes, I live with my aunt, who is here for her health."

"At this time of the year? Is your aunt in Nice now?"

"Yes, sir, by her doctor's advice."

It occurs to me that it is rather strange to have doctors advise his aunt to come to Nice for her health during August. But my imagination is very flexible. And I imagine that his aunt might reason thus: "They are going to send me to Nice, because I cannot stand a rigorous climate, so I might as well go now and at once take my choice of vacant residences . . . because I abhor moving."

However I do not share her point-of-view. Within a short time I intend to leave this place and don't expect to see aunt's nephew again. But aunt's nephew is inclined to be companionable. Evidently I interest him.

"Are you from the South?" he asks.

"I? no."

"Then you are from the North, a Parisian?"

"Neither of the two, my dear sir. I am not a Frenchman."

"Oh, so. You have no strange accent at all."

"I have lived a long time in France."

"Are you perhaps a Russian?"

"No, I am a Belgian from Brussels."

"I am from Montpellier. Tout ce qu'il y a de plus Midi. Permit me to introduce myself. My name is de St. Gasc."

It occurs to me that it is a fine-sounding name.

"Greatly pleased," I counter courteously. "My name is de Cèze. May I make a guess at your first name?"

That amuses him, and in a jovial tone he gives his consent.

"Amédée," I guess.

"Amédée de St. Gasc."

"Oh, no," he protests with a coquettish gesture, holding both hands up in the air.

"Gaston . . . Hector . . . Adhémar."

"No, no, no!" he ejaculates, "my name is Louis."

"Your name is Louis? Well, that is curious. My name is also Louis."

"Oh, yes?"

"Louis de Cèze. It is a standing joke on the part of my friends to omit my family name. They always call me 'Louis the Sixteenth'."

He laughs as if pleased at the joke.

"Is your aunt also a de St. Gasc?"

"No," he says with a laugh, which seems very attractive.

And, after a slight pause, he adds:

"My aunt is Spanish, Madame Avelenada. My parents live in Montpellier. I have accompanied her to this place, because the doctors have advised Nice."

"In August," I supply inwardly.

"I am the favourite of my aunt, her pet child. A quiet existence, living with her. I don't know anybody here. During the afternoons I drive around with aunt. In the evenings she makes no demands on me. She is not very bothersome. Enfin, I am her pet relative, you know." He smiles at me very understandingly, saying: "I am very glad to have made your acquaintance. I hope we will remain friends. You might show me Nice and Monte Carlo. I love to play occasionally and take a chance with a couple of hundred-franc bills."

He is trying to tell me that he can afford to throw a couple of hundred-franc bills around . . . that a couple of hundred-franc bills means nothing to Louis de St. Gasc. Of course if one is the pet child of Madame Avelenada . . .

"We might go together to Monte Carlo," I suggest. "I just love gambling. But I can't afford to lose much."

"Oh, I will lend you the money," says my friend Louis.

"That's mighty fine."

"Well, I enjoy your company very much. May I call you by your first name?"

"Why, certainly."

"I am not in the habit of being familiar. But you seem to invite an exception."

"Where do you and your aunt live?"

"In the Villa Aubert, Boulevard Dubouchage. A very well furnished apartment. Aunt took her servants along. She is used to her cook. For dinner there will be partridges. Yes, yes, aunt is fond of a good table."

Partridges in August, I think. I simply dote on fowl. Why does not our cook give us game once in awhile?

"And tell me about yourself, Louis," says my friend Louis in a sort of sentimental way.

"Well, my name is Louis, just like yours. Louis de Cèze. And what else?"

He is leaning against the back of the bench in a graceful attitude, smilingly awaiting further confidences, while watching the ocean.

"I have no aunt who spoils me. I am all alone," I supply.

"Alone . . . ?"

"Yes, do you know where the Hotel Majestic is situated at Cimiez?"

"I have seen it."

"I am employed there as a cashier."

He gazed at me in some surprise.

"As a cashier?" he repeats.

"Yes," I said seriously. "That is quite a difficult position in such an immense hotel. It is not a bad place. My salary is one hundred and fifty francs a month."

"That is not much," he murmurs.

"I can live on it," I say modestly. "I have relations, I am of good family, but have run down a bit. What is there to tell . . . living expenses, women, debts, you understand. So I took the position. I have free living. A small room, near the servants' quarters in the attic. I receive my meals, not the menu of the dining-table, I assure you. No partridges, Mr. Louis."

He makes a wide gesture and murmurs something, as if trying to dismiss the subject, starting another lead:

"That is a splendid ring you wear."

"A souvenir," I explain. "I never would dispose of that."

"Do you like light-coloured cravats?"

"Yes, in the summer."

"I don't care for them. I always wear black neckties, they go well with a background of coloured shirts."

"You are very elegant," I remark.

"Oh, no," he parries the compliment, "you are elegant."

"Well," I come back, "the management demands that we are well dressed."

"An expensive hotel, is it not?"

"About twenty francs a day, room and meals. Running between twenty and thirty francs."

"Will you come with me to Monte Carlo some day?"

"If you will lend me some money . . . with pleasure. I cannot afford to play on my salary of one hundred and fifty francs."

"I will lend you some money. Will we go to-morrow?"

"Very well," I agree. "That suits me perfectly. To-morrow by the eleven o'clock train."

So we shake hands on it and say: "Au revoir".

I have not the slightest inclination to go with my friend Louis to Monte Carlo. The next morning at the appointed hour of eleven I call our cook, who I saw had just returned from the market, into my room.

"Madeleine, it is now open season, why don't you ever serve partridges? Are they very expensive?"

"Partridges? Monsieur, in August? I haven't seen any in the market."

"A friend of mine already had partridges. . . ."

"But, Monsieur, that is impossible. There are no partridges. Perhaps the gentleman received some from a friend. They are not for sale in the market. Monsieur will have to be patient for a little while."

That affords me consolation. I now feel sure that Louis de St. Gasc has eaten no more partridges than Louis de Cèze.

That same afternoon I go by a roundabout way through the Boulevard Dubouchage and ring the bell of the Villa Aubert.

I ask the caretaker: "Concierge, is a Mr. de St. Gasc living here?"

"What name, sir?"

"De St. Gasc."

"No, sir."

"Sorry, it must be a villa farther on."

That evening, as usual, I proceed to the Promenade des Anglais. Suddenly my friend Louis sits alongside of me.

"You broke your promise," he reproaches me in a gentle voice. "Why weren't you at the station for our trip to Monte Carlo?"

"It was impossible," I said seriously. "I was too busy with the hotel's finances. It is a very laborious occupation. Those ciphers make me dull."

"Poor fellow, what a job for 150 francs."

I make a gesture, which should indicate my resignation to the yoke with which Fate has burdened me.

Louis talks in order to soothen my rasped feelings. He talks very seriously . . . altogether a charming conversationalist. His discourse is of the sea, which supposedly foams with more effect over a real beach than it hurls itself against a stone ridge, which girdles the azure coastline. He tells me that he is passionately fond of horseback riding. On a horse, and then just roaming over long stretches of veldt. He is reminiscent about steeplechases, as he possesses many acquaintances of note, who own castles and hunting-preserves.

He talks vivaciously, and himself believes all he is telling. He gives me a description of his hunting-dress; how his new coat is lined, and of the cut of his new waistcoat. Quite different from the styles of last year. He mentions casually that he does not care for women, and then jumps suddenly to literature. He has read voluminously: Balzac, Flaubert, Zola, de Goncourt. . . . His literary taste is rather good.

"Do you like Zola?"

"Zola," I repeat. "Didn't he write 'Nana'?"

"Yes, didn't you read anything else from his pen?"

"No," I offer it as an excuse. "I don't read much. I am too busy with my ledgers."

"Have you read Goncourt?"

"Who is he?" I ask.

"A good author," he replies, regarding me with some slight pity.

Assured by this time that we have little in common in a literary sense, he makes a new start with the stage. But I haven't seen any of the latest plays, not even the Rafale of Bernstein. The pressing affairs of the hotel at Cimiez do not leave my evenings free, as happens in the case of the aunt's nephew, Louis de St. Gasc.

He does not find me very intelligent nor well-informed. But he can cover other fields of conversation, and, notwithstanding my limited range of bookreading, we get along quite well.

The day after to-morrow is the twenty-fifth he informs me with a smile. The twenty-fifth of August.

"That is so," I exclaim. "I came near forgetting."

The twenty-fifth of August is the anniversary of St. Louis of France. As I have a Catholic aunt—although she is not Spanish—and as said aunt never forgets me on the twenty-fifth of August, I remember the date instantly, far better than literary data.

"Then," rejoins Louis de St. Gasc, "you have no leanings toward St. Louis de Gonzague?"

"Why no," I reply, "wasn't he a Portugese? What have I to do with a Portugese for a patron? I am very fond of St. Louis of France, because he was a king, who travelled. . . ."

"Historically you seem to be well instructed," engagingly smiles my friend Louis. "Now to-morrow is our nameday. Do you know," he he moves up a little closer, "I would very much like to have a souvenir from you. A small affair to remember you by. I dote on small presents. You will let me have this small gold piece, won't you?"

"All right," I agree. "And what do I get from you?"

"Oh, whatever you like to have. I have it: a pin; do you care for pins? A jewelled stickpin for your scarf?"

"With pleasure," I state modestly, "but let it be of trifling value."

"Oh, yes," agrees Louis de St. Gasc, to whom bills of hundred francs are but slips of paper, not to overlook the wealthy aunt and the many acquaintances with castles and hunting-preserves. "Then I will give you the stickpin to-morrow. And when will you give me the little gold coin?"

"To-morrow," I promise, elated at the thought of so much affection for the approach of our nameday.

"What is it?" he asks, with a greedy look at the gold piece, while with deft fingers he rubs over its surface.

"A Roman coin," I answer. "Quite ancient, that is, if it is genuine."

"Then it might not be genuine?"

"There are so many imitations."

"But I will get it the day after to-morrow?"

"Of course."

"In the evening after to-morrow I will bring the scarfpin."

"Excellent. But make no extra expense for me."

"Oh, let me have my own way about it. I say, Louis, if I should . . . have to write you sometimes, should I address you at the Majestic?"

"Yes . . . but what would you write about?"

"Well" . . . nonchalantly . . . "I might have occasion. I would like to have your address." Then, "No General Delivery?"

"That is not necessary. Louis de Cèze, Majestic. Don't add "cashier" to my name."

"No . . . certainly not. I am sorry, but to-morrow I won't be able to see you. Aunt is going to have friends for dinner. Till the day after to-morrow then, hè? I with the stickpin."

"And I with the gold coin," I add dramatically.

A handshake, very intimate, and a separation for one whole day.

On the next afternoon I proceed to the Majestic.

I ask the porter: "Any letters for Mr. Louis de Cèze?"

The porter runs over the mail: "No, sir."

"Should any letters arrive for Mr. Louis de Cèze please forward them to this address."

I hand him my card and conduct a search in my pocket for a five-franc piece.

"Here is a letter," suddenly discovers the porter. . . . "Mr. Louis de Cèze, Hotel Majestic." His discovery saves the five-francs piece, for which I bless the gods. Thereafter I read the letter.

"My dear Louis."

"I must see you without fail to-morrow morning, the morning of our nameday. Something terrible has happened to me. Imagine, after I left you yesterday, I was held up by apaches, near my home in the Avenue

Dubouchage. It was very late, the street was deserted, and, of course, there was no policeman in sight. There were four of them; they have beaten me up and taken everything away from me, including some five hundred francs. I dragged myself home. I hardly dare to show my face to my aunt in the condition I am in. So I am going to stay in bed this morning and won't appear at dinner. But to-morrow morning I wish to see you. Not at my house though, as I must avoid to arouse any suspicion in my aunt. She is so shy and also ailing, and won't see anybody she does not know well. Therefore don't call at Villa Aubert, my dear fellow. But I must see you. Aunt is already angry with me, because I spend too much money. Should she hear of my experience she would be furious.

"Dear Louis, I am going to borrow some money on some jewellery of mine. I need two hundred francs. Couldn't you help me with two or three hundred francs? You would oblige me immensely. You will receive them back within a week, because I am going to write to Montpellier at once. I can count on your letting me have three hundred francs to-morrow morning, can't I? I am in great despair. Of course five hundred francs really mean nothing, but it just happens right after aunt had reproached me with spending too much money.

"My very dear Louis, you are my only hope.

"Your loyal friend,

"LOUIS DE ST. GASC."

"P.S.

"It also would give me pleasure to receive the little gold coin to-morrow morning for my nameday, my best friend. The scarfpin I shall buy as soon as I am out of my difficulties, as soon as I have received word from Montpellier."

To my own great chagrin I entirely forget to show myself in front of the Majestic with three hundred francs in my pocket and the little gold piece, detached from my watch chain in order to hand it to my friend Louis. It was all the fault of my Catholic (but not Spanish) aunt, who arrived to embrace me, bring me a bouquet of flowers and a little medal. A sweet woman indeed. Therefore it was evening before I met my friend de St. Gasc on the Promenade. He was already sitting there when I arrived.

He was decidedly angry.

But I also had many cares and seated myself next to him with a deep sigh. A few moments' silence, interrupted by my sighs deep down from the bottom of my stomach.

At last he condescended to open the conversation.

"Why didn't you come out of the hotel this morning for a few minutes? I have been waiting for you for fully one hour."

"Why?" I ask with eyes wide open and full of naïve surprise, "and where?"

"In front of the Majestic," he answers crossly. "In front of your hotel. Didn't you receive my letter?"

"A letter?" . . . still showing surprise and wide open eyes. . . . "No," I counter, "I haven't received any letter."

"You didn't receive any letter?"

"My dear chap, that's nothing to be wondered at. So many letters go astray. If I had known that you wished to see me . . . I myself am very much in need to talk to you, my good Louis. I am in a bad predicament. You must help me out, dear fellow, you must. Think of it: a shortage in the cash of the Majestic: nearly one thousand francs short. . . . How it happened . . . I don't know. I am honest . . . I am an honest man. Who stole it? I don't know. But I am responsible. That is the disgusting part of it. I might leave my little gold coin in pawn. If it is genuine I am certain to get a loan of one hundred francs on it. But what is one hundred francs? . . . My dear Louis, you must . . . do you hear, you *must* lend me nine hundred francs. Ask your aunt for them. Otherwise I am lost, dishonoured. I will lose my position and go to prison. Louis, my dearest Louis, help me, I implore you. What is nine hundred francs to you? I will write to my family. For the sake of the name, which I would stain, they undoubtedly will pay the money. Within a week, my dear Louis, you will have the money back again. My friend, my very best friend, my only friend, help me out!"

"I am sorry, my dear fellow" . . . this came in somewhat chilling tones . . . "but I just had written to you that I have been attacked by apaches."

"Attacked?"

"And robbed."

"Robbed?"

"Of five hundred francs."

"Louis, my dear friend Louis, what a terrible nameday for us. You know, I am going to denounce St. Louis of France. That settles him. Henceforth I take the Portugese: St. Louis de Gonzague."

"Then you are not in a position to help me?" asks Louis de St. Gasc.

"*I*, help *you*?" I question him in a dull voice and overcome by despair. "*I*? who must have at least nine hundred francs, and, even at that, only when my gold coin is genuine. *I*? help *you*? You must help ME. You must bleed your aunt."

"I am sorry" . . . by this time the voice has become icy . . . "but that is impossible. As far as I am concerned I am going to see an usurer. . . ."

"And I . . . I am going to commit suicide."

My friend Louis does not seem very much shocked by my decision.

He comes to his feet and stretches out his hand.

"I am going now, at once. I am going in search of an usurer. . . . No bad feelings, I hope, because I am not able to help you."

"Of course not," I assure him, pressing his hand.

The evenings on the Promenade des Anglais follow one after the other with the same beautiful environment, but they have lost their mutual resemblance.

Because my friend Louis is surely still engaged in the search for an usurer.

I have not seen him again.

❊ ❊ ❊

HERMAN HEIJERMANS
(1864-1924)

HEIJERMANS, whose name is chiefly connected with Dutch drama, was at one time connected with *De Telegraaf*, to which he contributed his clever sketches later collected in a volume and known as the "Falklands."

Chicken is one of the delightful stories in the book, and has been translated by James Penninck especially for this collection.

CHICKEN
(From *Samuel Falkland*)

I HAVE something extra, Lou."

"What is it?"

"Well, look in the kitchen cupboard."

Lou, who has just lit the lamp very carefully, because he did not want to break the chimney, which has been cracked for the last three months, is in no hurry. First he warms his big, ugly hands at the small stove.

"Go and see now."

"You tell me what it is."

"No, 'tis a surprise."

Finally he goes into the kitchen, lights a match and throws the light on the cupboard."

"What foolishness!" he exclaims.

"What?"

"What foolishness! How will you fry it?"

"In the milkpan."

"It is too large for that."

"I have measured it."

"But you don't know how to fry it."

"Yes, I do."

"You will make a mess of it."

But by now I am used to having my ability doubted. Starting with the day on which I wanted to experiment with omelets, that is to say a new sort of omelet, in which I had mixed a spoonful of pommerans-bitter with the beaten eggs, Lou's faith in me had vanished. And yet the omelet looked beautiful, reddish-brown, crusted here and there with small, black spots, and brass-coloured underneath. Lou claimed that it smelled of turpentine. Of course his jealousy prompted him to say so, because the idea had not occurred to him first. But, generally speaking, I would not recommend a pommerans-omelet. It seems to lie a little bit heavy on one's stomach.

"You will make a mess of it."

"Just wait a little." I am not going to let him know that I had an interview with the farmer at the front door. He asked me (that is, the farmer) one guilder and twenty-five cents. I got it for ninety, after some bargaining. The people across the street were looking so sharply at the chicken in my hand, that I felt ashamed to stand talking kitchen matters at the front door. After I had paid the price I continued the interview.

"Do you happen to know how to fry a chicken?" A wide grin spread over his freckled face, as if he felt sorry that he sold a chicken to one so ignorant of chickenlore for 35 cents under the price.

"Do you have to fry it yourself?"

"Yes, the housekeeper is going to get married to-day."

"Well, first boil it a little while. Then fry it richly in butter for about half an hour."

"Will it be well done by that time?"

"Sure, you can easily pull it apart."

"But is it a fresh chicken?" I asked, while I smelled the fowl.

"Do you think that I sell rotten stuff? You should not smell so much of the inside."

Lou stands there grinning at me, when I commence to saw the legs off with one of our wonderful knives, which remain sharp and never have seen a grindstone. I say that it is a fallacy that kitchen-knives should be sharpened. We have been cleaning ours in cold water for two years now. There is quite a fight between the sinews and the knife. But a Hollander, famed through his struggles with the watery element, is not to be downed by chicken legs. Pieps and Poel carry the feet in triumph to the garden.

"It does not fit in the milkpan."

"Now don't be conceited. You should put it in this way."

The chicken rests in the narrow steel pan (which won't hold two pints of milk) in a praying attitude, the flesh of the wings bulging upwards and the feet forced aside. Some water is poured into the pan with a handful of salt, and we both tend to our work again. Women make so much fuss over cooking, but it is easy to cook and study at the same time.

I am reading the *Worldpeace* by Couperus; a delicious book, which permits one to watch the chicken. Is it any wonder that women adore Couperus?

I am just immersed in the uproar, when Lou shouts from the other room.

"Say!"

"Yes?"

"We can have chicken soup from this."

"Why, no, you can't drink that dirty water."

"That's all you know. How do they make chicken soup at home?"

"That's so. But it will be pretty thin."

"If you let it draw long enough you will get excellent bouillon."

Chicken soup plus fried chicken for ninety cents is certainly cheap.

After a quarter of an hour the water is jumping around in such an alarming manner that I fear for the chicken as a unity. Lou arrives with two large soup plates. Carefully I drain the boiling bouillon into the plates, while holding the pan over the coalbox. The chicken seems to suffer from an overdose of emotions. I put a goodly-sized portion of butter into the pan and place a plate on top in order to "smother" the chicken. Then I taste the soup. "It is very good," says Lou, in the way he usually makes his remarks.

I drink the soup: one spoonful, two, three.

"It needs a little more salt," ventures Lou. We add some salt.

But then as, accidentally, I look up and notice Lou spooning with our soup, I get such a fit of laughter that I have great trouble to recover.

"Why are you laughing, you little idiot?"

I keep on laughing, and Lou's soup gets into the wrong channel.

There the two of us just stand bursting out laughing, holding the plates in our hands, till at last I throw my soup into the sink.

But Lou, who first declared the soup to be very good, feels in honour bound to take some more, till, after some five or six spoonsful, he is compelled to state that he can go no further.

Holding the *Worldpeace* in my lap I sit on guard near the frying chicken. The dogs, Pieps and Poel, who are aware that something important is taking place, rub themselves against my legs in an uneasy manner.

"It smells rattling good," says Lou.

An agreeable fried-chicken-smell, some sort of an aroma, which defies description, pervades the house. Strange that no musical composer ever derived inspiration from the sizzling of a frying chicken.

The bell rings. It is Lob.

"It smells good here," is his first remark.

"Chicken," says I.

"Take your coat off and stay for dinner."

"Now," says Lob. "With great pleasure."

"We start immediately. You like to have some soup in the meantime?"

Lou is becoming nervous.

"Bouillon? Yes, please."

"We intended to keep this for to-morrow. Each of us had one helping."

Lob commences to apply his spoon to his plate, which I keep out of reach of Lou. I am using the *Worldpeace* as a screen, while Lou has a hundred things to look after in the other room.

"Good soup, don't you think so?"

"Excellent," says the prospective apothecary courteously. After the fifth or sixth spoonful he commences to slow up. I am afraid to look at Lou.

"Does it taste right to you?"

"Oh, yes, it needs a little flavouring."

"Lou, give Lob some salt."

Lou brings the salt and Lob continues drinking, fearfully slow, freely perspiring, and with pauses between spoonsful.

"It is very warm here," he remarks.

In the other room Lou bursts out laughing. "It is nothing," he explains, "I am reading a joke."

Lob has finished. "One becomes heated drinking soup, hè?"

Now we lay the table. The chicken is transferred to a round plate. It shows one doubtful black spot, while the gravy is of a peculiar, black shade, like coalblack. Of course Lou is in charge of the carving.

"It is burned," he says.

"Don't bother with remarks, it looks splendid." The skin is blackened.

"The sauce is somewhat bitter," says Lob.

"Probably the cook has again added some pommerans," Lou insinuates.

I eat in silence and philosophise.

Chickens will not enter our house again.

Lob claims to have suffered a two days' illness, caused by our combination soup and fried chicken.

LATIN AMERICA

BRAZIL

MONTEIRO LOBATO
(1883-   )

MONTEIRO LOBATO was born in the environs of São Paulo, Brazil. He comes to writing through the accident of having written a vigorous letter in denunciation of the practice of clearing fields by fire; it was such an original document that it was featured on the first page of an important daily. Since then Lobato has become a leader in the new Brazilian literature. He has helped to shake native letters free of the strong French influence that was denationalising it, and has taken his characters and his style from his native land. He is the author of many short tales, edits the important review, *Revista do Brasil*, and heads a large publishing house that encourages Brazilian talent. *O Comprador de fazendas* comes from his collection, *Urupês*. *Brazilian Literature,* by Isaac Goldberg (A. A. Knopf, New York, 1922) has a special chapter on Lobato, pages 277-291.

THE FARM MAGNATE *

A WORSE farm than the Corn Stalk estate didn't exist. It had already ruined three owners, so that malicious gossip whispered: "It's a stalk, all right." Its latest proprietor, a certain David Moreira de Souza, had acquired it on the instalment plan, convinced that it was a bonanza; but there he was, too, dragging along under the burden of debt, scratching his head in despair.

The coffee-trees would be bare as sticks, year in, year out, either lashed by the hail or blighted by terrible frosts, and their yield never filled a good-sized basket.

The pasture grounds, sterile, and pasture indeed to all manner of plagues, were the camping ground of destructive ants who shared the field with deadly weeds, swarming with lice. Any beast that set foot there was soon a framework of ribs covered with vermin, a most pitiful sight to see.

* This authorised version was printed originally in *World Fiction,* January, 1923. (The magazine is extinct.) It now appears with revisions.

The underbrush which here replaced the native forests revealed, through the sparsity of the wild cane, the most exhausted of dry soil. On such soil as this the manioc waved thin little knotty branches, the sugar-cane grew no thicker than a reed, producing cane so wizened that they passed whole through the mill.

The horses were covered with lice. The pigs that escaped the pest competed in thinness with the cows of Pharaoh's dreams.

On every side the cutting-ant, day and night, mowed down the grass of the pasture-lands, so that in October the sky was clouded by winged ants at their aerial love-making.

The roads were left half laid, fences on the ground, farm-hands' quarters with shaky, leaky roofs—the prophecy of ugly rooms beneath. Even upon the manor-house the general decay had laid its hand, loosening sections of plaster, rotting the floors. Windows without panes, loose-jointed furniture, cracked walls. . . . It is doubtful that there was any-thing whole in the place.

Within this crumbling frame the owner, rendered prematurely old by his successive disappointments, and gnawed, moreover, by the voracious canker-worm of the recurring payments, would scratch the top of his grey head a hundred times a day.

His wife, poor Donna Izaura, with the strength of her maturity gone, had accumulated in her face all the spots and crow's feet that are the product of years of hard toil.

Zico, their eldest, had turned out a good-for-nothing, fond of rising at ten, primping until eleven, and spending the rest of the day in unsuc-cessful love-affairs.

In addition to this idler they had Zilda, then about eighteen—a nice enough girl, but sentimental beyond all reason and parental peace of mind. All she did was read love stories and build castles in the air.

The one way out of this situation was to sell the accursed farm. It was difficult, however, to get hold of a big enough fool. Several prospec-tive purchasers had already been decoyed there by artful advertisements; but they all turned up their noses scornfully and had not deigned to make an offer.

"I wouldn't have it as a gift," they grumbled to themselves.

Moreira's dizzy brain, after so much diligent scratching, suggested a wily plan: to set plants from the rich neighbouring soil in the fringes of the thickets and one or two of the other places where visitors might look. The rascal did even more. In a certain hollow he stuck a stick of garlic imported from red earth. And he manured the coffee-trees along the road enough to cover up the decrepitude of the others. Wherever a sunbeam plainly betrayed the sterility of the soil, there the old man would conceal the barrenness under a screen of rich sifted earth.

One day he received a letter from his agent announcing a new prospect. "Play up to this fellow," was the agent's advice, "for he'll fall. His name is Pedro Trancoso, and he's very rich, very young, very talkative, and wants to run a farm for the fun of it. Everything depends on how well you can take him in."

Moreira got ready for the job. First of all he notified all his hands to be at their posts and know what to say. He trained them to answer with consummate skill all the questions that visitors put, in such a way that the barren tracts were transformed into marvels of fertility. Prospective purchasers, inasmuch as they suspect the information furnished them by the proprietor, are in the habit of secretly questioning the help. Here, if this happened, and it always did happen, dialogues of this sort would take place:

"Does it ever freeze here?"

"A mite, and that only in bad years."

"Peas pretty good?"

"Holy Virgin! Only this year I planted five quarts and I gathered fifty bushels. You just ought to see them!"

"Are the cattle troubled with ticks?"

"Bah! One now and then. But there's no better place for breeding. No bad weeds in the pastures. It's a pity the poor owner hasn't the strength he needs, for this would be a model estate!"

The supernumeraries having been trained in their parts, at night, the family discussed the preparations for receiving their guest. The revival of their dying hopes filled everybody with happiness.

"Something tells me that this time the deal will go through," said the good-for-nothing son. And then he announced that he was going to need three *contos de reis* to set himself up in business.

"What business?" asked his father, astonished.

"A store, in Volta Redonda."

"Volta Redonda! I wondered how any sensible idea could find lodging in your windy garret. What are you going to do? Sell Tudinha's people on trust?"

The youth did not blush, but he said nothing; he had his reasons.

The wife wanted a house in the city; for a long time she had had an eye on one, on a certain street—a nice house for people in comfortable circumstances.

Zilda asked for a piano, and crates and more crates of novels.

That night they went to bed happy and early the next day they sent to the city for some delicacies for their guests—butter, cheese, cookies. There was some hesitancy about the butter.

"It's really not worth the trouble," grumbled the wife. "It means three thousand *reis*. I'd rather buy the piece of goods that I need so much with that money."

"We've got to do it, old girl. Sometimes a mere trifle will clinch a bargain. Butter is grease and grease oils the wheels."

The butter won out.

While they were waiting for these things, Donna Izaura got busy with the house, sweeping, dusting and arranging the guest room. She killed the fattest of the bony chickens and a lame little suckling pig. She was making dough for pastry when:

"Here he comes!" shouted Moreira from the window, where he had been posted since early morning, as nervous as he could be, sweeping the road with an old pair of binoculars. Without leaving his observation post he kept transmitting to his busied wife the details that he could make out.

"He's young. . . . Well dressed. . . . Panama hat. . . . He looks like Chico Canhambora. . . ."

At last the guest arrived, dismounted and presented his card. Pedro Trancoso de Carvalhaes Fagundes. Fine appearance. The air of one who has plenty of money. Younger and far more refined than any that had thus far visited the estate.

He told a number of tales with the ease of one who is absolutely at home in the world; he related his trip, the incidents on the way,—a tiny, long-tailed marmoset that he had seen hanging from a branch.

After the two men had gone into the sitting room, Zico, unable to restrain his curiosity, put his ear against the keyhole, from which strategic point he whispered to the women who were busy arranging the table whatever he managed to catch of the conversation. All at once, making a suggestive grimace, he called to his sister in a stage-whisper:

"He's a bachelor, Zilda!"

Without any pretence whatsoever the girl dropped her knives and forks and disappeared. A half an hour later she returned, wearing her best dress, and with two round red spots on her cheeks. Anybody who had gone into the farm chapel then would have noticed the absence of several petals from the red silk paper roses that adorned Saint Anthony, and a lighted candle at the feet of the image.

In the country, rouge and marriages spring alike from the oratory. . . .

Trancoso was going on at great length about various agricultural questions.

"Our native hogs? Pff! A backward stock, and wild to boot. I'm for Poland Chinas. Large Black isn't so bad, either. But the Polands beat them all!"

Moreira, who was innocent of all knowledge in the matter, and familiar with only his own famished pigs, who had neither name nor breed, unconsciously opened his mouth wide with astonishment.

"As far as cattle are concerned," continued Trancoso, "it's my opinion that all of the authorities, from Barreto to Prado, are dead wrong. I don't believe in either selection or cross-breeding. I'd like to see the finest breeds introduced at once—the Polled Angus, or Red Lincoln. We haven't any pastures, you say? Then let's make them. Let's plant alfalfa. Let's build silos. Assis Brasil once confessed to me . . ."

Assis Brasil! This fellow rubbed elbows with the authorities in agriculture! He was an intimate friend of them all—Prado, Barreto, Contrim. . . . And of ministers, as well! "I've already talked this over with Bezerra. . . ."

Never had the estate been honoured by so distinguished a gentleman —so high up in society and so widely travelled.

He spoke of Argentina and of Chicago as if he had returned from there but yesterday.

Moreira's mouth opened wider and wider until it reached the maximum degree of aperture permitted by the maxillary muscles. At this juncture a timid, feminine voice announced that lunch was ready.

Introductions followed. Zilda was the recipient of compliments such as she had never dreamed of, and they set her heart fluttering. Like praise was meted out to the chicken stew, the *tu'tu*, the pie and even the drinking water.

"Such pure, crystal-clear, absolutely drinkable water, Senhor Moreira, is worth the best of wines. Happy those who may quaff of it!"

The family exchanged glances. Never had it occurred to them that they had anything so precious in the house, and each one unwittingly sipped his liquid as though he were tasting the nectar for the first time. Zico even smacked his lips.

Donna Izaura was beside herself with joy. The eulogy of her cooking had won her heart. That praise more than compensated her for all her trouble.

"There, Zico," she whispered to her son, "see what an education means. That's what you call refinement!"

After the coffee, which was greeted with a "Delicious!" Senhor Moreira invited the young man for a ride on horseback.

"Impossible, my dear man. I never go riding right after eating. It gives me cephalalgia."

Zilda blushed. Zilda always blushed when she did not understand a word.

"We'll go out in the afternoon. I'm in no hurry. I'd prefer a nice walk through the apple orchard; it's good for the digestion."

As the two men sauntered off toward the orchard, Zilda and Zico made a dash for the dictionary.

"It isn't in the S's," said the boy.

"Try C," advised the girl.

After some difficulty they found the word.

"Headache—well, what do you think of that!   Such a simple thing!"

That afternoon, on their horseback ride, Trancoso admired every-thing that he laid eyes on, to the great amazement of the farmer, who heard his property praised for the first time.

Prospective purchasers, as a rule, ran down everything and had eyes only for the defects; in front of a hollow they exclaimed upon the dangers of sliding soil; they found the water either bad or insufficient; all they saw when they looked at an ox were the ticks.   Not so Tran-coso.   He praised things to the skies.   When they reached the camou-flaged spots, and Moreira pointed with a trembling finger to the plants, the youth went into ecstasies.

"The deuce!   This is extraordinary!"

It was before the garlic that his amazement reached its climax.

"This is simply marvellous!   Never did I imagine that I should find in these parts even the sign of such a plant!" he declared, plucking off a leaf which he put in his notebook as a souvenir.

In the house he took Donna Izaura into his confidence.

"Really, madam, the quality of this land far exceeds my expecta-tions.   Even garlic!   That's positively astounding!"

Donna Izaura lowered her eyes.

The next scene took place on the veranda.

It was night.   A night filled with the chirping of the crickets, the croaking of the frogs, the heavens star-studded and peace lying over all earth.

Trancoso, comfortably ensconced in a rocking-chair, transformed his after-dinner drowsiness into poetic languor.

"This chirping of the crickets—how enchanting!   I adore these starry nights, and this bucolic, rustic life—so healthy and happy!

"But it's very sad," ventured Zilda.

"Do you think so, really?   Would you rather have the strident song of the locust in the glaring sunlight?" he asked, mellowing his voice.   "It must be that some little cloud casts its shadow over your heart. . . ."

Moreira, seeing that the situation was becoming sentimental, and well aware that it might lead to matrimonial consequences, clapped his hand to his forehead and roared: "The devil!   I've forgotten all about . . ."   He did not say just what he had forgotten, nor was it necessary.   He hurried off, leaving the two alone.

The dialogue continued, with more honey and roses than before.

"You are a poet!" exclaimed Zilda, at one of his tenderest remarks.

"Who is not a poet beneath the stars of heaven and beside a star of the earth?"

"Ah me!" sighed the quivering lass.

Trancoso's bosom, too, heaved a sigh.   His eyes rose to a cloud that resembled the Milky Way, and his lips murmured, as if to himself, one of those commonplaces that conquer maidens:

"Love! . . . The Milky Way of Life! The perfume of roses, the mists of dawn! . . . To love, to listen to the stars. . . . Love ye, for only those who love understand the message of the stars!"

This was mere smugglers' slop. Nevertheless, to the inexperienced palate of the maiden, it tasted like Lachrymæ Christi. She felt the fumes rise to her head. She was eager to reciprocate. She rummaged among the rhetorical figures of her memory.

"What a pretty thing to put on a post-card!"

Coffee and cakes came to interrupt the budding idyll.

What a night was that! One would have said that the angel of happiness had spread his glittering wings over that sad household. Zilda beheld before her very eyes the realisation of all the passionate novels she had ever devoured. Donna Izaura had visions of marrying her off to a wealthy magnate. Moreira dreamed that his debts were all paid and that a handsome surplus jingled in his pockets. And Zico, picturing himself transformed into a merchant, spent the entire night in dreamland, selling goods on trust to Tudinha's people, until the man, won over by such magnanimity, conceded him his daughter.

Only Trancoso slept like a rock, unvisited by dream or nightmare. It's great to be rich!

The next day he visited the rest of the estate—the coffee plantation and the pastures; he informed himself about the methods of breeding and the modern improvements. And as the enthusiasm of the excellent young man continued, Moreira, who had decided the previous evening to ask forty *contos* for the "Corn Stalk," thought it would be a good idea to raise the price. After the scene of the garlic shoot, he made up his mind to ask forty-five; at the end of the examination of the cattle he had raised the figure to fifty; on the way back from the coffee plantation he went up to sixty. When at last the great question arrived, the old fellow replied in a firm voice:

"Seventy-five," and he awaited the answer, ready for a storm of objection.

To his surprise, however, Trancoso found the price reasonable.

"Why, that's not bad at all," he replied. "It's a lower figure than I had expected."

The old codger bit his lip and tried to remedy his error.

"Seventy-five, yes, but . . . not including the cattle."

"Oh, certainly," responded Trancoso.

". . . nor the pigs, either."

"Of course."

". . . nor the furniture."

"Quite natural."

The farmer gasped; there was nothing more to exclude. He called himself a stupid ass. Why hadn't he asked eighty?

His wife, apprised of the situation, called him an idiot.

"But, woman, even forty would have been a fortune!"

"Then eighty would have been twice as good. Don't make excuses. I never yet saw a Moreira who wasn't a blockhead. It's in the blood. You're not to blame."

For a moment they were both sullen, but the cloud of their ill-humour was dispelled by their eagerness to build castles in the air with this unexpected windfall.

Zico took advantage of the favourable gale to clinch the promise of the three *contos* that he needed for establishing his business.

Donna Izaura changed her mind about their new home. She had thought of another one now—on the street through which all the religious processions passed; Eusebio Leite's house.

"But that costs twelve *contos*," protested the husband.

"Yes, but it's much better than that other hovel. Well laid out. The only thing I don't like about it is the bedroom, so close to the roof. Too dark."

"We can put in a skylight."

"Then the garden needs repairs. Instead of the poultry-yard . . ."

Into the wee small hours, they were busy restoring the house, painting it, transforming it into the most delightful of city residences. As they were drowsily putting the finishing touches to the job, Zico knocked at the door.

"Three *contos* won't be enough, father; I must have five. I forgot to count the taxes, and the rent and other little things. . . ."

The father, between two yawns, generously conceded six.

And Zilda? She was sailing the high seas of a fairy-tale.

Let her sail on.

The day when the genial prospective purchaser had to leave came at last. Trancoso said his farewells. He was indeed sorry that he could not prolong so delightful a stay, but important matters demanded his presence elsewhere. The life of a capitalist is not so ideal as it seems. . . . The proposition was as good as settled; he would give his definite answer within a week.

So he left, taking with him a package of eggs—he liked the breed of hens they raised there very much. And a little sack of *carás*—a tidbit of which he was gluttonously fond.

He took, in addition, an excellent souvenir: Rosilho, Moreira's roan, the best horse on the farm. He had praised the animal so highly during their rides that the proprietor had felt in honour bound to refuse to sell; instead he presented the horse to him.

"You see," said Moreira, summing up the general opinion, "a

very wealthy young man; upright; as learned as a university graduate, and yet amiable, well-bred, not turning up his nose like the trash that has been coming here. Breeding will show!"

The old lady was most pleased by his lack of formality. To take eggs and *carás* away with him! How democratic!

They all agreed upon the fellow's merits, each praising him after his own fashion. And thus, even after he had left, the wealthy young man filled the thoughts of the household for a whole week.

But the week passed without bringing the eagerly awaited reply. Then another. And still another. Moreira, a little worried, wrote to him. No reply. He recalled a friend who lived in the same city, and sent him a letter requesting him to ask the capitalist for his definite decision. As for the price, he would come down a trifle. He would let the farm go at fifty-five, at fifty, even forty, including the cattle and the furniture.

His friend replied without delay. As the envelope was torn open, the four hearts beat violently; that paper contained their common fate.

The letter read:

"Dear Moreira:

"Either I am much mistaken or you have been taken in. There isn't any capitalist hereabouts by the name of Trancoso Carvalhaes. There is a Trancosinho, the son of Mrs. Veva, better known as Sacatrapos. He's a scamp who lives by his wits and deceives folks who don't know him. Not long ago he travelled through the state of Minas, from one farm to another, under various pretexts. At times he's a prospective purchaser; he spends a week at the home of the owner, wearing him out with walks and rides looking over the property. He eats and drinks of the very best, makes love to the servants, the daughter of the house, or whomever else he finds—he's a rare article!—and then, when everything is just about settled, he skips out. He's done this a hundred times, always changing the scene of his activities. The rascal likes a change of diet. As this is the only Trancoso around here, I won't bother transmitting your offer. Imagine that good-for-nothing buying a farm!"

Moreira collapsed into a chair, utterly crushed, the letter dropping from his fingers. Then the blood rushed to his face and his eyes blazed.

"The dirty dog!"

The four hopes of the household came tumbling down with a crash, amidst the tears of the daughter, the fury of the mother and the rage of the two men. Zico declared that he would set out at once in search of the rascal and smash his face for him.

"Patience, my boy. The world goes round. One fine day I'll come across the thief, and then I'll square accounts."

Poor air castles! The beautiful châteaux of Spain, reared during a month of miraculous wealth were transformed into gloomy, abandoned ruins. Donna Izaura mourned her cakes, her butter, her pullets. As for Zilda, the disaster was like a hurricane roaring through a flourishing garden. She took to bed with a fever. Her face grew thin. All the tragic passages of the novels she had devoured passed before her mind's eye; in every instance she was the victim. There were days when she thought of suicide. In the end she became accustomed to the idea and she continued to live. She thus had the opportunity of discovering that this business of dying for love occurs only in romantic fiction.

This is the end of the tale—for the parquet; for the gallery there is a little more. Orchestra patrons are accustomed to be content with a few clever, amusing touches in good taste. They come into the theatre after the play has begun, and leave before the epilogue. The gallery, however, wants the show complete, so that they may get their money's worth down to the last cent. In novels and tales they demand the definite solution of the plot. They want to know, and rightly, too, whether So-and-so died, whether the girl got married and lived happily ever after, whether the man sold the estate at last, and for how much.

A sound, human curiosity, worthy of all respect.

Did poor Moreira sell his farm?

It hurts me to confess that he didn't. And his failure to sell it came about in the most inconceivable manner that the devil ever concocted. The devil, of course. For who else is capable of snarling the thread of the skein with so many loops and blind knots just when the knitting is approaching its happy completion?

Fortune willed that that rascal, Trancosinho, should win fifty *contos* in the lottery. Don't laugh. Why shouldn't it have been Trancoso, since Luck is blind—and he had the right number in his pocket? He won the fifty *contos*—a sum which was the height of affluence for a pauper like him.

It took him weeks to get over his stupefaction. Then he decided to become a landed proprietor. He would stop gossip by realising a project that had never occurred to him in the wildest flights of his imagination: he would buy a farm.

He ran mentally over the list of all he had visited during the years of his wanderings, and finally settled upon the Corn Stalk. The determining factor was, above all, the recollection of the girl and the old lady's cakes. He planned to entrust the management to his father-in-law, and live a life of ease, lulled by Zilda's love and his mother-in-law's culinary accomplishments.

So he wrote to Moreira announcing his return for the purpose of closing the deal.

When that letter reached the Corn Stalk, there were roars of rage mingled with howls of vengeance.

"The day of reckoning has come!" cried the old man. "The scoundrel liked the feast and is coming back for more. But this time I'll spoil his appetite, see if I don't!" he concluded, rubbing his palms in foretaste of vengeance.

A flash of hope passed over Zilda's worn heart. The dark night in her soul was lighted by the moonbeam of a "Who can tell?" But she did not dare say a word for fear of her father and brother, who were plotting a terrible settlement. She hoped for a miracle. She lighted another candle to Saint Anthony.

The great day arrived. Trancoso burst in upon the estate mounted upon Rosilho, whom he set a-prancing. Moreira came out to welcome him, his arms behind his back. Before dropping his reins the amiable rogue burst into effusive greetings:

"My dear, dear Moreira! At last the day has come. I am ready to take over your estate at once."

Moreira was all a-quiver. He waited for the knave to dismount. No sooner had Trancoso released the reins and come toward him, all smiles, with open arms, than the old man drew from under his coat a cat-o'-nine-tails and fell upon him with ungodly zeal.

"So you want a farm, do you? Here, here's your farm. Thief!" and slash, slash fell the whip tails.

The poor young man, dazed by this unexpected attack, rushed to his horse and threw himself blindly on it, while Zico sailed into him with all the vigorous resentment of a brother-in-law-that-might-have-been.

Donna Izaura set the dogs upon him:

"Dig your teeth into him, Brinquinho! Chew him up, Joli!"

The ill-fated farm magnate, cornered like a fox, dug the spurs into his horse and fled beneath a shower of insults—and stones. As he cleared the gateway, he could make out, amidst the shouting, the shrieking taunts of the old lady:

"Cake-gobbler! Butter-glutton! You're welcome to them. This is your last trick, egg-robber, yam thief!"

And Zilda?

Behind the window, her eyes burned out with weeping, the sad lass saw the gallant cavalier of her golden dream disappear forever in clouds of dust.

And thus the unlucky Moreira lost the one good stroke of business that Fortune was ever to offer him: The double riddance of his daughter and of the Corn Stalk.

ARGENTINA

MANUEL UGARTE
(1878-   )

MANUEL UGARTE was born in Buenos Aires, Argentina. His literary maturity, however, is associated with long residence in Paris. He was one of the most productive of the Spanish-American modernists, having done much to acclimatise the French manner in the Spanish new world. He has done many things in most of the literary forms,—the short story, poetry, criticism, journalism. In 1900-1901 he visited the United States and Mexico, awakening suddenly to the danger of Yankee imperialism. He became at once a propagandist of this idea and has remained convinced of its truth. It is thoroughly presented in *The Destiny of a Continent* which, in a translation by Catherine Alison Phillips, edited with excellent taste by Professor J. Fred Rippy of the University of Chicago, was published by A. A. Knopf, New York, in 1925. Ugarte's new preface is dated July, 1923, from Nice. The story by which he is represented in this collection—*El Curandero*—comes from Ugarte's *Cuentos de la Pampa*, Tales of the Pampa, Paris, 1902.

THE HEALER

BENITO MARCAS lived on the outskirts of the town of Tapalque, in one of those wretched shanties, improvised out of débris and supported by tree-trunks, which in South America are the only dwelling of the Indian who has been conquered and manacled by civilisation.

On either side of the roads,—which the rain transforms into pools, thus allowing passage only on the side,—near the fields of prickly pear, may be seen from time to time the houses of the old frontier of the Pampa. In one corner of the hut, on a triangle of iron under which some stumps are crackling, is a smoking *olla* or a kettle boiling with water meant for *mate*. A few paces away, the runt of a horse with his bony flanks and protruding ribs. About him, attracted by the manure, a clutter of pecking hens that is dispersed only by a twitch of the beast, who is defending himself against the mosquitoes with a lash of his tail. Amid these surroundings, under the rays of a sun that bakes the plain, generally dozes a family in tatters. The men are almost always tall and strong, with a coppery complexion and proud eyes. They wear spurred boots, sashes, wide-brimmed sombreros and long knives in their belts. The women wear percale dresses and kerchiefs around their heads.

Often there are two or three barefooted children, playing or quarrelling. And the family groups, sunken in resignation, squat in a circle about the light, chat lazily and sip through metal tubes the fragrant juice of the *mate*.

Benito Marcas belonged to one of those families of docile Indians who were the first to yield to the white invasion. Of his native character he preserved only the ingeniousness that enabled him to measure distances with the unaided eye, to know men by their tracks, and to divine the virtues of plants.

He did not possess, like his neighbour Juan Pedrusco, that irritability which, despite the heel of tyranny, still survives in a few Indians as a relic of the free beast. Juan Pedrusco's character was suspicious and peevish; Benito Marcas's was frank and affable. Benito had surrendered to civilisation and was resigned to his rôle as member of a conquered race; Juan nursed his resentment.

When the rebellious tribes that were being harrassed by the army succeeded in reaching the settlement, sacking the churches and carrying off their booty in a wild dash across the Pampa, Juan Pedrusco's eyes shone with joy. Benito Marcas, on the other hand, looked upon the incursion with disapproval, and explained in his semi-Spanish jargon that such skirmishes were criminal, and that it was better to use a little judgment.

Both worked during the sheep-shearing season on one of the neighbouring estates. But during the idle months, while Pedrusco laboriously wove his sashes, Marcas wandered over the plain, collecting the mysterious roots that he alone could distinguish. From the trunks of trees or from the underbrush that grew on the edge of the swamps, he extracted certain medicinal qualities that, combined according to formulas inherited from his father, served to cure more than one ailment. People called him the healer, and he accepted the name. At that time there was only one doctor in Tapulque. And the countryfolk preferred the knowledge of the Indian to the drugs of the apothecary, perhaps because they imagined that the healer's curses were endowed with some strange powers of witchcraft.

The first thing that occurred to Juan Pedrusco, when his wife fell ill, was to go over to Benito's and explain the case to him. Not that the notion of meeting his neighbour was at all pleasant. Marcas, in his younger days, had courted Pedrusco's wife, and Pedrusco could not forget the adventure. She was, to be sure, at that time single; and truly enough she had dismissed her suitor and married Pedrusco; yet all this did not keep him from feeling a certain smart whenever he spoke the name of his rival. Marcas had afterward married another woman and time had buried the grudge. Only an illness, however, could bring Pedrusco to call upon Marcas.

After hesitating for a while he cracked his whip across his horse's flank and galloped off over the roads that had been made impassable by recent rains.

The points of the red kerchief that he wore on his neck floated in the sun like butterflies over the massive shoulders of the Indian. Under the wide-brimmed sombrero shone his prominent cheek-bones, his narrow forehead and those bestial, elusive eyes of his, which glittered with the fleeting flash of a concealed knife.

Arrived at Marcas's hut he dismounted with agility, threw the reins over the horse's neck and entered the yard. As nobody came out to receive him he knocked and pronounced the customary greeting: "Ave Maria. . . ."

A beautiful Indian maid appeared at the door and smiled welcome to the recent arrival.

Marcas followed immediately, in his affable way. He was a midget of a fellow, with a lugubrious expression,—one of the finer type of Indian who, with a little schooling, could have competed with the civilised white. His eyes were bright, his features regular, and the cut of his mouth bore a certain seal of distinction and aristocracy.

It was a glorious afternoon and the plains lay under the heavens in all their vastness, dotted here and there by a ramshackle dwelling, a group of animals or a horseman who broke the line of the horizon with his centaur-like silhouette. . . .

Marcas and Pedrusco squatted down before the fire where a kettle was boiling and drank a few bowls of *mate*.

They made a curious contrast. Each was about forty; but while Pedrusco had a common face, harsh features and the compact body of a primitive athlete, Marcas gave evidence of a more delicate, a more perfect nature, as if these two survivors of a vanished nation were prolonging, after the catastrophe, their ancient hierarchies.

Pedrusco accepted a cigarette and proceeded to explain the symptoms of the illness.

At first the trouble had been no more than a minor inflammation on the right arm, a slight stab on moving it, and at times a sharp, prolonged pain. But the sick woman was losing weight, she ran a temperature, and both sleep and appetite were gone. Her features were changing. Her arm was swollen; her skin had become drawn and shiny. Yesterday a sore had opened near her elbow. Now she was unable to do any work, or even to move.

Marcas seemed to be pondering the case. The affair was more serious than Pedrusco imagined. After a last drink of *mate*, which he sipped standing, he harnessed his horse and they were off.

Night was lowering over the Pampa, and under the cloudy sky reigned the silent solemnity of the South American twilight. The earth, here and there bathed in the blood-red gleams of the setting sun, melted at the horizon into the clouds. And the haze of early evening emphasised the sadness of the solitary trees, the humble huts, and the deserted roads, whence came like a foreboding the wild neighing of the horses.

Pedrusco's hut was not far from Marcas's, and they reached it before nightfall.

In a dim, ill-smelling chamber that served at the same time as a dining-room and sleeping-quarters were strewn the few pieces of furniture that comprised the belongings of the couple. The roof was so low that their heads almost touched it. The floor was of soft earth. The sick woman, a robust Indian, still young, whose contracted features revealed a savage energy despite the suffering she had gone through, was stretched out on a straw bed, wrapped in some old clothes. . . .

Marcas took the tallow candle from the table and brought it over to the bed. The black, loose hair of the woman took on a blue glint in this sudden light. With a brusque effort she sat up; and without raising her eyes to see who the newcomer was, without pronouncing a word, with an icy coldness she uncovered her free, bare arm where, at the elbow, an ulcer was festering.

Marcas kneeled down beside the bed, so as to see better. His bony fingers pressed the wound and a stream of yellow pus trickled out. . . . Then he leaned against her shoulder and the patient scarcely restrained a wail.

When they had come out into the plain, which was bathed in moonlight, Pedrusco was about to ask a question; but Marcas silenced him and took him farther from the house, so that the sick woman shouldn't hear. . . .

"It's a malignant tumour," he said, in a low voice.

And he explained the origin of those infections that attack the blood, and that a blow or some specially difficult work can bring to the surface. The trouble isn't in the skin, but in the hollow of the joint which at first becomes inflamed, then fills with water and at last develops ulcers. . . .

The Indian eyed the healer uneasily.

"But it will go away, of course . . . ." he said, as if all this explanation was so much idle talk.

"I don't know," answered Marcas, worried. "If the trouble is only in the arm . . . why, surely. . . . But if it's got a grip on the body itself . . ."

Pedrusco raised his eyes in surprise. What? Couldn't this little sore that was only the size of a finger-tip be healed? Wasn't there some concoction or plaster to fight it with?

In his primitive mind was born the idea of betrayal. A healer who had won fame throughout the region for his skill simply must know a way to cure such a minor ailment. He was assailed by the thought that Marcas wanted to avenge himself for his defeat in love.

Then he tried to insist, to corner his adversary and wring a promise. . . .

"But you surely will be able to cure her . . ." he said, seeking through the darkness the eyes of his former rival.

"I'll do all I can," answered the healer, mounting his horse in a single leap and preparing to leave.

"You mean you'll do whatever you please . . ." thought the Indian. His sudden suspicion had already become, for him, a reality.

Marcas, who was quick-witted, sensed the situation, and rode off full of bitterness. Pedrusco's wife, with whom he had had a passing love-affair more than fifteen years ago, was completely indifferent to him now. He was married and had two children; his life had taken an altogether different direction. He could scarcely recall, from the distant days of his youth, the transitory disappointment of a rejection that he had very soon forgotten, and that he had never lamented. But he was hurt by the idea that anybody could think him capable of such an infamy. . . .

Next morning, nevertheless, he knocked very early at the door of Pedrusco's cabin. He brought a number of herbs which, he thought, should produce a caustic effect. With a dignity full of reserve he arranged them and cooked them in a little stove. Then he bathed and bandaged the wound, recommended a few precautions, and was off, trying his best to evade his neighbour's questions and importunities.

For the next month he was there every morning at the same hour, and tried a number of concoctions, always with failure. The fistula kept growing; the patient became weaker and weaker, and her body seemed to be yielding to paralysis. In vain the healer summoned every resource he could think of. But his salves and plasters were merely soothing measures. His primitive medicine, based upon oral traditions and eked out by emollients, could wage no battle against a cancer that the best surgeon could not have conquered.

One morning as he was leaving the hut, Pedrusco stopped him and assailed him with brutal speech. What remedies were these that only made the patient worse? Did he imagine, maybe, that he could play like this with a person's life? He, Pedrusco, wasn't going to stand by idly. He loved that woman and he was going to defend her.

Marcas tried to explain the situation and to forestall Pedrusco's anger. He confessed that he was powerless before this incurable malady. He said that he had done everything possible. And, understanding the drama that was boiling in Pedrusco's heart, he made up his mind never to come back. From that day he avoided any encounter with the sick woman's husband, and resumed in solitude his poor, obscure existence as an intermediary between civilisation and barbarism.

A month had gone by, and the incident was still fresh in Marcas's mind.

One night, after he had gone to bed later than usual, he thought he heard a noise outside, near his shanty. The dog was barking strangely. It seemed that someone was trying to get into the place. . . .

Marcas warned his wife not to make a sound, seized his farmer's knife, and stood waiting in the darkness. . . .

There was a moment of silence, as if the marauder had hesitated an instant before the shut door.

The healer, without knowing why, suddenly felt that this was Pedrusco. out for revenge. He resigned himself to anything that might happen. There was no avenue of escape. The only way out was through the door, and behind the door lurked danger.

A vigorous hand tried to spring the lock, which resisted more than Marcas had hoped. When at last this obstacle yielded, and the door flew suddenly open, the two men met face to face, in the light of the selfsame moonbeams. . . .

Marcas would have wished to explain, to cry out the truth, which rose in his throat. But a single word stirred the ancient savage in his bosom. "Coward!" Pedrusco had hissed, seeing him hesitate.

And Marcas was unable to restrain himself. . . .

The two Indians clashed in a ferocious encounter that joined their bodies, merging them in a single instinctive clinch. Their arms struggled till they snapped, and Marcas, the weaker, fell. . . . Whereupon Pedrusco, who had managed to keep his feet, stabbed him three times.

Only a moan was heard . . . a single moan . . . and a vast silence descended over the solemnity of the plains. The icy, round moon shed a heavenly radiance over the sleeping earth. It was as though nothing had happened,—as if the scene had been a mere phantasm that had been routed by the triumphant light.

As Pedrusco was preparing for flight, a shot rang out from the inside of the hut. It was the wife of the victim, trying to avenge herself. But her hands had been clumsy and the assassin made his escape. The Indian woman, running in pursuit, could descry only the silhouette of a horseman vanishing into the night. It was the flight of barbarism over the endless plains, which lay in a silence as vast as eternity.

MEXICO

MANUEL GUTIÉRREZ-NÁJERA
(1859-1895)

GUTIÉRREZ-NÁJERA, considered one of the greatest of the Mexican poets, is also among the chief precursors of the modernist movement, which, with the publication of Dario's *Azul* in 1888, initiated a new period in Spanish literature on both sides of the ocean. A year before his death he founded, together with Carlos Díaz Dufóo, the important *Revista azul*. His poems and tales are rich in whimsy and pathos; his prose—in the original, of course, is far more revolutionary than his verse. The variant of the Rip Van Winkle legend by which he is here introduced is taken from *Cuentos color de humo* (Smoke-Coloured Tales). There is an extended study of Gutiérrez-Nájera in Isaac Goldberg's *Studies in Spanish-American Literature*, 1920, Brentano's, New York, pages 16-46.

RIP-RIP

I DIDN'T actually see what's related in this tale! I must have dreamt it.

What things the eyes behold when they are closed! It seems impossible that we should have so many people and so many things inside of us . . . for when the eyelids droop, one's glance, like a housewife shutting her balcony window, goes back into the house to see what's there. Very well, then; this house of mine, this house of Madame Glance that I possess, or that possesses me, is a palace, a farmhouse, a city, a world, a universe . . . but a universe in which present, past and future are eternally present. To judge from what I see when I'm asleep, I think to myself and even for you, my readers: Good Heavens! What sights the blind must behold! And those who are forever asleep, —what do they vision? Love, from what they say, is blind. And love is the one creature that sees God.

Whose is the legend of Rip-Rip? I understand that Washington Irving set it down and gave it literary form in one of his books. I know, too, that there's a comic opera by the same name and with the same plot. But I haven't read the tale of the North American novelist and historian, nor have I heard the opera. But I've seen Rip-Rip just the same.

If it weren't sinful, I'd suggest that Rip-Rip must have been the son of the monk Alpheus. This monk was a German,—a lumbering, phlegmatic fellow who was, I imagine, also somewhat deaf; he spent a hundred years, utterly unaware of their passage, listening to the singing of a bird. Rip-Rip was less of a northerner than Rip Van Winkle, and less fond of music; he was much more fond of his whisky. And he slept a great many years.

The Rip-Rip that I saw fell asleep, for some reason that I don't know, in some cave that he'd entered . . . who can tell why?

But he didn't sleep as long as the legendary Rip. I believe he slept for ten years . . . perhaps five . . . perhaps one; in any case, his slumber was rather short. He was a bad sleeper. But the fact is that he grew old while sleeping, for this happens often to those who sleep a great deal. And as Rip-Rip had no watch, and even if he had, would not have wound it every twenty-four hours; as the calendar hadn't been invented in his day; and as there are no mirrors in the woods, Rip-Rip couldn't very well have taken note of the hours, the days, the months that had passed during his slumber, nor could he discover that he had already become an old man. It's the usual case: a long time before a fellow knows that he's old, his friend have discovered it and tell him so.

Rip-Rip, still somewhat drowsy, and ashamed to have spent a whole night away from his household—he who was so faithful and practical a husband—said to himself, not without a start: "Let's be getting home!"

And off went Rip-Rip with his silver white beard (which he thought was very blond), making his way with painful effort through those almost inaccessible paths. His legs sagged beneath him. "It must be the effect of my sleep!" But no, it was the effect of old age, which is not the sum of years but the sum of slumbers!

As he clumped laboriously onward, Rip-Rip thought:

"My poor little wife! How alarmed she must be! I can't understand how it happened. I must have been ill . . . very ill. I left at daybreak . . . this very hour at dawn . . . so that I've spent the day and night away from home. But, what did I do? I don't go to the tavern; I'm not a drinker. . . . Doubtless my illness surprised me in the mountain and I fell unconscious in that cave. . . . She must have searched all over for me. . . . Naturally, since she loves me so and is kind-hearted. She can't have slept a wink. . . . She must be weeping her eyes out. . . . To think of her coming alone, at night, to this pathless, forsaken wood! Though, no . . . she can't have come alone. I'm well liked in the village, and have a lot of friends . . . especially John the miller. Surely, when the village saw her affliction, everybody must have turned out to help her look for me. . . . Especially John. But the baby? My little girl? Could they have taken the infant along, too? At such an hour? And in this cold? It's quite likely, for she's so fond of me, and she's so fond of her little daughter,—she's so fond of us both, that she wouldn't leave the child alone for anything in the world, and she wouldn't let anything in the world hold her back from hunting me out. What a crazy thing to have done! Will it harm her, I wonder? The important thing is that she . . . but, which is she? . . .

And Rip-Rip strode on his way . . . he could not run.

He reached the village at last. It was almost the same, and yet . . . it was not the same. The steeple of the parish-house seemed whiter; the alcade's home was surely higher; the main store seemed to have a different entrance, and the passing people wore other faces. Could he still be half asleep? Was he still sick?

The first friend he happened upon was the curate. It was he, surely, with his green umbrella and his high hat,—the highest hat in the place, —with his breviary that was always shut, and his frock coat, that was always a cassock.

"Good day, reverend father."

"Pardon me, my son."

"It wasn't my fault, father . . . I didn't go off on a drunk . . . and I haven't been up to any mischief. . . . My poor little wife. . . ."

"I begged your pardon, didn't I? Off with you, now, for we've too many beggars here as it is."

Beggars? What did the curate mean by that? He had never asked alms. He made no contributions to the church, for he had no money. He never attended the Lenten services because he was a hard-working man, from night to morn. But he went to seven o'clock mass on every feast day and confessed and took communion every year. There was no reason why the curate should treat him with such scant courtesy. None whatever!

He let the curate go without an answer, for he was sorely tempted to give him a drubbing . . . and he was the curate.

His step somewhat lighter now because of his anger, Rip-Rip continued on his way. Fortunately his house was nearby. . . . He could already see the light in its windows. . . . And as the door was farther off than the windows, he drew close to the nearest of the windows to call out to his wife, Luz: "Here I am! An end to your worrying!"

He had no need to cry out. The window was open: Luz was sewing peacefully, and, at the moment of Rip-Rip's arrival, John—John the miller—was kissing her on the lips.

"Will you be back soon, darling?"

Rip-Rip felt that everything about him was going red. The wretch! The wretch! . . . Trembling like a drunkard or like a decrepit old man, he entered the house. He was intent on murder, but he was so weak that no sooner had he made his way to the room in which they were speaking than he fell to the floor. He could not get up; he could not speak. But he could keep his eyes open, wide open, to see how his adulterous wife and his treacherous friend turned pale with horror.

And they both turned pale. A shriek from her—the same shriek that poor Rip-Rip had heard when a robber had been discovered entering the house—and then John's arms around him, but not to strangle him. Rather they were pitying, sustaining, and were lifting him from the floor.

Rip-Rip would have given his life,—indeed, his very soul,—to have been able to pronounce a single word, a blasphemy.

"He's not drunk, Luz; he's sick."

And Luz, though still afraid, approached the vagabond stranger.

"Poor old man! I wonder what's the matter with him. Perhaps he came to beg an alms and collapsed with hunger."

"But we might harm him if we gave him anything to eat now. I'll take him first to my bed."

"No, not to your bed, for the poor fellow's very filthy. I'll call the boy, and the three of us will manage to take him to the apothecary's."

At this moment the girl came in.

"Mamma! Mamma!"

"Don't be frightened, dear, it's a man."

"How ugly, mamma! He scares me! He looks just like the bogey-man!"

And Rip heard everything.

He saw, too; but he wasn't sure of what he saw. This little room was the very same . . . his own. He rested in that big chair of leather and cane every night when he came back weary from toil, after having sold his little crop of wheat to the mill where John was superintendent. These window curtains were his special luxury. He had bought them at the cost of much skimping and many a sacrifice. That was John, and she was Luz . . . but they weren't the same. And the infant was no longer a baby.

Had he died? Could he be crazy? But he felt that he was alive! He listened . . . he heard . . . as one hears in a nightmare.

They bore him to the apothecary's, and there they left him, for the little girl was afraid of him. Luz went off with John . . . and nobody seemed to find it at all strange that she took him by the arm, and that she left her husband behind, dying. He couldn't move, he couldn't cry out, and proclaim: "I'm Rip!"

At last, after several hours, perhaps several years, or maybe many centuries, he was able to speak it. But they did not recognise him, they would not acknowledge him!

"Poor fellow! He must be mad!" said the apothecary.

"We'd better take him to the alcalde, for the fellow may become violent," suggested another.

"Yes, that's so. We can tie him if he offers resistance."

And they were about to tie him. But grief and anger had restored Rip's powers. Like a mad dog he attacked his tormentors, and succeeded in freeing himself from their clutches. He broke into a run. He would dash to his house, he would kill! But the villagers pursued him and cornered him. It was a hunt, and he was the beast.

The instinct of self-preservation gained the ascendency over every other desire. His first thought was now to escape from the village, make for the mountains, go into hiding and return later, after nightfall, for vengeance and justice.

At last he left his pursuers behind. And there was Rip, raving in the hills like a hungry wolf! Yonder he crashed on through the thickest part of the woods! He was thirsty . . . thirsty as a conflagration must be. And he made straight for the brook . . . to drink, to plunge into the water and lash it with his arms . . . perhaps, perhaps to drown himself. He reached the stream and there, to the surface, rose death to receive him. Yes, for this was death in the shape of a man,—the image of that decrepit fellow who peered at him out of the crystalline waters! There could be no doubt of it. That livid spectre had come for him. It was not a creature of flesh and blood, certainly; it was no human being, for it moved at the same time that Rip did, and yet the movements did not disturb the water. It wasn't a corpse, for its hands and arms were wringing and twisting. And it wasn't Rip, no, not he! It was like one of his ancestors, who had come to take him off to his dead father. But—"how about my image?" queried Rip. "Why isn't my body reflected in this mirror? I look and shout, and yet the echo of the mountain doesn't repeat my voice but the voice of some stranger. How is that?"

And there went Rip to find himself in the bosom of the waves! And the old man, surely, took him off to his dead father, for Rip has never returned!

* * *

An extravagant dream, this; isn't it?

I saw Rip as a very poor man; I saw him wealthy. I saw him young, I saw him old; at times in a woodsman's hut, and at other times in a house whose windows were bright with white curtains; now he was seated in that big chair of cane and leather, now in a sofa of ebony and satin . . . he was not any particular man, he was many men . . . perhaps all mankind. I can't understand how Rip couldn't speak, nor how his wife and his friend failed to recognise him, despite the fact that he had grown so old. Nor why he preferred to escape from those who wished to tie him up as a madman. Nor do I know how many years he had been sleeping, or lying in a torpor in that cave.

How long did he sleep? How long does it take for those whom we love and by whom we are loved, to forget us? Is forgetting a crime? Are those who forget wicked? You've already seen how kind were Luz and Juan when they came to the assistance of poor Rip as he lay there dying. The girl, to be sure, was frightened; but we may hardly blame her; she had no remembrance of her father. They were all innocent; they were all good . . . and nevertheless, the spectacle is very maddening.

Jesus of Nazareth did very well to resurrect but a single being, and that one a man who had no wife, who had no children and who had only just died. It is best to heap plenty of earth upon the dead.

❋ ❋ ❋

SANTO DOMINGO

FABIO FIALLO

(1865-   )

FABIO FIALLO was born in Santo Domingo; he has served his country at home and abroad with a passionate belief in the integrity of the small nation. His first book, *Primavera sentimental*, a collection of poems, was published in Argentina; his second, *Cuentos frágiles*, appeared in New York (1908). The little piece by which he is represented here is the first of the Fragile Tales; like his poems, the *contes* are cut with cameo-like precision. Fiallo achieved his first important recognition from the pen of the great poet, Rubén Darío, of whom he afterwards became an intimate friend. He has pleaded the cause of Santo Domingo at Washington and is enshrined in the hearts of his countrymen both as poet and tribune. In his latest book, *La canción de una vida* (Madrid, 1926) he collects the poetry of a lifetime; a forthcoming volume will do the same service for his prose.

THE MARBLE BUST

MY jealousy? I really can't tell how it began. Tristan, the exquisite painter of flowers, the pleasant landscape artist, was in affection and intimacy a very brother to me. At my table his place was between Margaret and myself; whenever we went for a stroll in the country, she would give him her arm and have him recite dulcet, musical poems which I, quite charmed by his talent, applauded.

This gift of a fresh, rich improvisation which the painter pretended to disdain in favour of his floral canvases was perhaps the most powerful fascination that he exercised upon women. I knew this, and despite myself I'd think of it when I saw him hand in hand with Margarita running over the meadows, now in search of a nightingale's nest that was always far away, or again in quest of some wild flower which, when found, would be the inspiration for a respectful madrigal, but—ah!—a madrigal that was yet too tender and always heard with evident joy.

Moreover, back there in the parlour of our cottage someone kept me in a state of constant suspicion; not with his words, but with that malign expression of his, morning and night, whenever Margarita greeted me with a good-bye kiss or a kiss of welcome.

Now, wasn't it crazy to yield to the insidious suggestion of that marble bust which, on the gilt mirror table, sat smiling so mockingly and perversely? It was sheer madness, and yet how many times, on some silly pretext, I managed to dismiss Margarita and be left alone with that smiling, malicious, white face to question it impatiently: "What goes on here when I'm not around? . . . Tristan . . . eh? . . ." And the cursed bust would smile . . . smile. . . . . What despair! What rage!

One morning, as she offered me her lips before I left, Margarita announced that she, too, was going out.

The surprise awakened in me by this intention, which certainly was in no wise a strange one, did not pass unnoticed by Margarita's eyes. She looked at me in astonishment and asked the reason for my disturbance. I laughed loudly to ease her mind and throw her off the track, kissed her and left.

Once in the street I planned my strategy. It was seven-thirty by my watch; I'd go to the office and stay there till nine. An hour and a half was time enough for her to give her various orders to the maid and to primp up with her habitual coquetry.

An hour! That's a long time when jealousy is gnawing at your heart and accelerating its beat.

At last I could contain myself no longer, and several minutes before the hour set by my own plan, I took my hat and set off in the direction of our cottage.

By the time I was at the threshold I had almost repented. Wasn't this unworthy of me? What demonstrable cause did I have for such a procedure? Wasn't Margarita invariably as good and affectionate as she ever had been? Nevertheless I entered.

"Margarita?" . . .

The maid, surprised by my unexpected return, stammered a few words, while the marble bust smiled, smiled more perversely than ever.

"Oh, I know where to find her!"

On my way, I took counsel. I must be cautious lest the faithless woman and her accomplice escape.

When I reached Tristan's studio he rushed out to receive me.

"What's the matter? What ails you?" he asked, taking me by the arm and trying to seat me in the reception hall.

"What ails me? Come, and I'll tell you," I answered, as I tried to make my way to the adjacent room, which, I was now convinced, was at once an artist's studio and a Don Juan's bedchamber.

The curtain was drawn. Yet there was something that for a moment paralysed my heart. It was the scent that came from there. I knew that presence; it was the very same that she shed wherever she went. The perfume that came from the studio, entering my lungs and poisoning my soul, was the perfume, the odour of her person, her flesh, —Margarita's.

My eyes closed and I wavered. Tristan caught me firmly in his arms.

My weakness lasted less than a minute. At the very moment that I came to myself, a gust of air raised the bottom of the curtain for a second and I saw, on the carpet that covered the tiles of the studio, the white, naked foot of Margarita.

Ah, the faithless wretch! With a leap I fell into the room. . . .

When Tristan, amazed, reached my side, I was covering my face in shame with both hands. . . . What had created that perfume in the painter's studio was a huge basket of fresh cut flowers.

One of the flowers, a beautiful white lily, was lying on the carpet.

I've never cared to tell Margarita why, that selfsame morning, when I returned to our home of love, I found, broken into a thousand fragments on the floor, the marble bust; that bust which, on the gilt mirror table, sat smiling so mockingly, so perversely.

※ ※ ※

CHILE

ARMANDO ZEGRI
(1891-　　)

BORN in Punta Arenas, Chile, of Spanish and Arabian parents. After a journalistic career in Santiago, he made a tour of South America, lecturing on Latin-American literature. For the past few years he has resided in Paris and New York, as representative of a group of South American newspapers. He is known in Spain and

Spanish-speaking countries as an exponent of modern tendencies. His work is a conscious reaction against Latin lyricism, and is characterised by economy and discipline. His best known works are: *La Risa del Dragon*, an exotic poem in prose; *Minerva la de Glaucos Ojos*, a collection of tales, essays and criticism; and *El Ultimo Decadente*, a cerebral novel that has caused widespread comment. *Nights in Talca* is taken from *Memorias del Ultimo Decadente*, now in preparation.

NIGHTS IN TALCA

AFTER nine o'clock in the evening, Talca produces the impression of an abandoned town. The dust-covered streets remain dark and deserted. Where do the inhabitants conceal themselves? There are intervals of time when even the bark of a dog is unheard—the guardian dog of the gates of Latin-American towns.

In the square, only melancholy trees, only coaches and drowsy coachmen. Truly the atmosphere of a somnolent city!

At midnight a train arrives; the station is now filled with mingled voices, whistling, and the hard tread of horses. Then the grating sound of a hotel door, first opened and instantly closed. Nothing afterwards. Silence. Calm. The streets with their rows of irregular houses form absurd shapes in the darkness. Far off, in the background, the range of the Andes.

Talca has a volcano which flames in the night, when the town appears dead, like an ignis fatuus.

My memories of Talca are those of the night, because I knew the town most intimately then.

In the corner of my house, lived a widow with her only daughter. She was a mixed Indian, a superb type of woman. She had been married for seven years to a German merchant, rich, fair-complexioned, but neuresthenic. The result of the marriage was the daughter, a strange creature, an exotic bird enclosed in a provincial cage. My father had courted the widow, and took me with him on different occasions to visit her, so as to avoid gossip. They left us to our own resources, and so we naturally ended in taking a fancy to each other. She was the first love of my life—the first love of an adolescent which, while it endures, contains everything that is most beautiful, sacred, ideal and immutable in the universe . . . and which plays so little importance in our lives when it is ended.

I used to see her at night, and we would converse together for hours, holding each other's hand, beside an iron-barred window. The idyl lasted one whole summer. She would leave her bed to go to the window. She wore a long night-robe, and at that hour her hair always fell down her back. I would see her appear in the interior of the dark room, rhythmically advancing toward the window, smiling, and extending her hand to me. . . . The nights were warm and generally there was a moon in the clear sky. On moon-lit nights, the town lamp-lighters would extinguish the lamps, and the deserted streets would then be plunged into superb contrasts of light and shadow. The vision of my friend in the dark room with her white robe and flowing hair, slowly advancing so as not to make a stir and awaken the widow, suggested the image of Ophelia to me. All that we required to make the picture perfect was a fountain and anemones. The setting was pure and romantic, all except the direction our love was taking.

The widow undoubtedly judged the lad by the characteristics of the father, for after the first day of our meeting, she took the precaution of locking the door with a double-lock, and hiding it securely away until the next morning.

At about this time I was completing my secondary studies, and was preparing to enter the university. Several weeks before my final examinations, my father resolved to make a trip to the south. He would there seek a house in which to establish ourselves during my university years. My father was an energetic man, with the energy of a soldier, and a certain spirit of a nomad chief. I was accustomed to obey his commands instantly and without comment.

During the time my father was away, I lived with some relatives. I would go to bed early, at half past eight. But hours afterward, when the rest of the family was asleep, I would leave the room with extraordinary caution, pass to the yard, and from the yard to the street, by scaling a high wooden door. From midnight to four in the morning I spent beside the iron-barred window, kissing the hand of my sweetheart. I would return to my room in the same way as I had left it, and at eight o'clock, breakfast hour, would take my place with the other members of the family.

These escapades of mine were repeated, night after night, for a month. Nobody in the house suspected my adventures. On the contrary, they held a lofty idea of my seriousness and love of study. Meanwhile, the widow never forget to double-lock the door with her own hands, and to conceal the key.

To circumvent the fidelity of the jealous mother, Ophelia and I conceived a superb plan. A plan for the last night.

The examinations over, I was expected to leave for Concepcion, there to rejoin my father. On the day of departure, at four o'clock in the afternoon, I entered the coach that was crammed with packets, boxes and bags. The coach stopped at the door of the widow. I sprang out to bid good-bye. The widow came out to the door with her daughter;

and after embracing the both of them, I again entered the coach. Turning the corner, between the clouds of dust raised by the horses, I waved my sombrero to the eager handkerchief wavings of the two women.

Near the station, I ordered the coachman to stop at a hotel entrance. At the hotel I dispatched a telegram to my father to the effect that I had missed my train, and that I would take the first one next morning without fail. I shut myself up in my room, opened the valises, took out my best clothes and put them on. It was then five o'clock in the afternoon. I had seven hours yet to wait. Our rendezvous was fixed, as usual, for midnight. We assumed that the widow, believing me miles away, would not go to the trouble of double-locking the door. Meanwhile, anxious not to be recognised, I dared not issue into the street, or enter the bar-room, or the yard, or the hall, or the dining-room of the hotel. Nervously, distractedly, I paced up and down my room. I wished to read, but the letters on the pages of the book grew blurred, and from them issued a white form with hair streaming down her back. Finally, I decided to lie on the bed. I took my alarm clock, wound it, adjusted the hands of the dial for a quarter to twelve, and prepared myself, as best I could, for sleep.

I slept until the next day. I was wakened at ten minutes to eight, with just enough time to shut my bags and catch the train.

CZECHOSLOVAKIA

Introduction

WITH the exception of the excellent work of Bozena Nemcova, Czech prose of the first part of the nineteenth century can make no pretensions to great originality. She was one of the first to turn to the peasants and their land for her material, and was later to be followed by a number of women who contributed materially and artistically to the development of the Czech novel.

Madame Nemcova represented the romantic tendencies which were soon to be swept away by realism influenced by Heine and the Young German movement. Jan Neruda is one of the outstanding figures of this period best represented by its philosophic scepticism. A great novelist of this period was Karolina Svetla (1830-1899), a profound admirer of George Sand. Svatopluk Čech ranks high both as poet and novelist, and stands to the fore of the nationalist school.

Alois Jirasek (b. 1851) is the most popular novelist today, although the real value of his work is considerably overshadowed by his deep patriotism which has endeared him to the natives. A more vigorous and artistic writer is Karel Čapek, whose works have placed him in the forefront of Czech literature.

❋ ❋ ❋

JAN NERUDA
(1834-1891)

NERUDA, born at Prague, attended the school of St. Vít and the Malá Strana (Small Side) German school, later, studied the Czech language and literature at the academic gymnasium, and then took up law and philosophy, at the University. The publication of his poem, *Oběšenec* (The Hanged Man), started him on a newspaper and literary career and three years later his first book, *Hřbitovní Kvítí*, (Church Yard Blossoms) appeared, after which Neruda held a field of his own for his frank confessions tinged with an irony and a temperate, cold sort of scepticism unknown in youth. His second work *A Book of Verses* was received with far more favor, its numerous gems flashing their brilliance before a public which was now keener in appreciation. Some of the poems in this collection as his *Lines to My Mother* have become national lyrics and ballads.

The ability to see the individual and the different, as well as the skill to strike them off is best displayed by Neruda in his short genre sketches, arabesques and stories. There is a freedom and independence in his realism which makes his figures as clear cut as medallions. They are usually characters in his own intimately known Prague, some of them drawn exclusively from types known in his boyhood home, and others of the wider Prague in his *Pražské Obrázky* (Prague Pictures) and *Ruzni Lidé* (Various Sorts of People).

A Lodger for the Night appears here for the first time in English in a translation by Prof. Šarka B. Hrbkova prepared for this volume.

A LODGER FOR THE NIGHT

WE were playing at the game of "A Thousand and One Nights." That is to say, we were sitting in front of the coffee-house on Eskebia and were relating in turn what remarkable experiences we had had on our travels. The company was made up of the following: there were we two Czechs who had just arrived from the shores of the Red Sea, the landlord of the coffee-house who was a Pole, two acquaintances of the day, a Magyar and a German, then the bar maid, also a Czech, and a Prague native at that hailing from Small Side.

The Pole was a child of the Paris emigration. As a youth he had sailed to America, travelling its length from Canada to Patagonia and as a man settling down here in Cairo, never having set eyes on the homeland of the Poles. The Magyar was a Kuman. He had spent many years in the army and as a soldier he had also been in Prague. How he got to Cairo where he conducted a wine business, he would not reveal. The German was employed during the winter season with the Cairo theatre and now in the summer he gave music lessons.

The bar woman, happy because she could serve fellow countrymen, had sat for a long time at our table. The other guests had all left; it was considerably past midnight. The broad city square was silent. Only occasionally the far-off howling of dogs reached us. A few belated wayfarers hurried past.

The sky was dark green, the stars glimmered flutteringly as if they wanted to fly closer to earth. The tall palms spread their bushy crowns above us mutely and immovably. The air was mild and refreshing. Luxuriously we sat, sipped and told our tales.

Again it was the turn—the third time around—of the musician, the German, to relate something. We called him "the knight" on account of the chivalrous character of his first tale.

"Well, Sir Knight?"

"Just let me get my narghile started and I'll be ready! Shall it be something from Swabia, yes?

"So be it!"

And he began.

"I was travelling through Swabia on foot. With knapsack on my back, a stick in my hand, my pipe in my mouth, I journeyed merrily from town to town all alone. Wherever my fancy drew me, where the valley or mountain beckoned, I went. And I'd walk steadily each day until my eyes and heart became indifferent, my nerves lost perception and my head sank on my breast. Then I'd just stay and rest in the tavern of the nearest village.

I still had three days' journey to Augsburg which was my original goal, when I dropped into a little village. It was on the main highway and so the tavern was somewhat larger than the average. The wine was good, the food appetising and in the earlier part of the evening there were scarcely any guests. Not until much later did the "élite" arrive for a game of nine-pins and though I had been thoroughly weary before, I like to play nine-pins so I joined in a game with the company.

It was very late when I said good-night and asked the landlord to take me to my room. The rest went on playing. They had collected every candlestick in the place and had set them around in the bowling-alley.

"Don't you dare take any of our candles with you!" they warned me.

"No, I won't. The host will only light me up and will bring the candle right back with him. I'll go to sleep directly anyhow."

So the tavern-keeper led me to my bedroom. It was on the upper floor to which a pair of terribly rickety, wooden steps ascended.

"Here you have two beds," he said, when we entered a spacious chamber. "Lie down where you please."

I saw that the nearest bed was but three steps distant, that a chair stood beside it and so I immediately sent the tavern-keeper away with his candle.

I threw my knapsack on the floor, sat down on the edge of the bed and began to undress, laying my clothing on the chair. Right under the windows the nine-pins struck and fell clatteringly. I was fairly "greedy" for sleep, as the saying goes, and looked forward to the first delightful stretch and to the peaceful sensation which quickly permeates one's body. Involuntarily I was already picturing to myself how the noise from the bowling alley would gradually seem more and more distant and faint until it would utterly cease in an azure dream.

So—now only to draw back the feather-bed cover and stretch myself out! I was running my hand along the top of the cover to find the pillow when I leaped back affrighted. My breath suddenly stopped, instantly all my sleepiness fled. I wanted to shriek out but my throat was tightly drawn. I stood transfixed, my right hand reaching out into the darkness, the fingers being convulsively extended. I felt a cold, clammy, sticky dampness on my fingers . . . no, no, I was not mistaken . . . there in my bed lay a corpse, its mouth wide open, covered with foam, . . . I had just touched the protruding teeth. . . .

I leaped to the window and pushed it out together with the frame.

"Murder . . . murder!" I screamed. "Catch the landlord down there, . . . don't let him go . . . a murdered man lies in my bed! . . . Come up stairs at once, all of you!"

Down below I heard a confused tumult of voices. I saw lights flashing.

"My guest has gone crazy," shouted the tavern-keeper. "Come on, all of you . . . we may have to tie him down!"

The stairs outside creaked and swayed under the heavy, rapid footsteps. I never moved a single step from the window and kept my right hand extended with the moist fingers spread out.

The door opened and the first to enter was the tavern-keeper carrying a candle, all the others trooping behind him with lighted candles also.

"There . . . go there!" I shrieked frantically and pointed to the bed. Instead of looking at the bed they all stared at me. So I myself leaped to the bed and tore back the cover.

There lay a dead man, quite aged, fully dressed, his mouth open and covered with bloody foam.

The landlord approached calmly, held the candle close to the man's face and then said to his son, a burly young fellow, "Well, you would have had a mighty long walk . . . you see, I said to you. . . . 'Don't go after him, Vitus. Let him go.' You kept wanting to follow him up or the main road."

The others all stood around dumbly.

"But what is this? How did it happen?" I cried in a rage.

"Well, he came yesterday and went to bed. When he didn't show up this morning, we thought he ran off without paying his bill. And here, he's an honest man and we were wronging him. Vitus, you go and get the sexton and have him take the corpse to the vault. This gentleman will lie down in the other bed here . . . won't you, sir?"

* * *

SVATOPLUK ČECH
(1846-1908)

SVATOPLUK ČECH, the son of a government official, spent his youth travelling about and studied native customs and traditions. He began his literary career under a pseudonym after he had studied law.

Čech's title to superlative distinction in the field of poetry is earned through works which discuss broad humanitarian, religious and political questions with democratic solutions in each case. His most popular long poem, which has been dramatised as well as set to music in an opera of the same name, is "The Blacksmith of Lesetin," a story of the struggle of the Czechs to resist Germanisation.

"A Candidate for Immortality" is one of his longer prose works and his "Ikaros" and "The Hawk *versus* the Dove" are popular classics in nearly every Czech home library. In twelve rich and varied collections of short stories, Čech has shown himself a master of technique in this field of literary development. His best collections are *Humoresques, Arabesques, Tales, Humorous and Otherwise.*

The Apple-Tree was originally contributed by the translator, Prof. Šarka B. Hrbkova to the monthly publication *World Fiction* to which thanks are due for permission to reprint here.

THE APPLE-TREE

IN the register of legal cases tried by Dr. X, the rural district is very poorly represented. One wouldn't even distinguish anything rural about some of his country clients. For instance, Mr. Raubitschek, Mr. Abeles or Mr. Koretz visit the attorney and bring with them nothing distinctively bucolic except a huge, much handled, sweat-stained wallet with numerous compartments filled with notes of credit and drafts with many an awkward rustic signature in the angular German characters known as "Schvabach."

If these accordion-like receptacles of the Messrs. Raubitschek, Abeles and Koretz were able to produce music, they would doubtless play many a fine selection from the Czech countryside which would inspire the listener to tears rather than to laughter. But these gentlemen usually leave it to the bailiff's hireling in some country town to complete the silent tunes of their harmonicas by a short public performance on an old rumbling drum, preceding the forced sale.

As I have said, Dr. X has very few country cases. But to make up for the lack of many there is one which presents a picture of pastoral life with all its characteristics.

I am of the opinion that every attorney's office in the city has at least one such typical rural figure which at times refreshes with its zephyrs of old-fashioned simplicity the heavy air poisoned by the pestilential exhalations from the new fangled maladies of society.

I think that such cases are for the lawyer himself a necessary mental recreation. He has disposed of a long line of city clients who are hardened, distrustful and who, like an animal possessed as in Goethe's simile, whirl about perpetually in the empty circle of their own dry-as-dust affairs. His head is full of figures, merchandise, drafts, pensions, houses and similar things. Just then the door opens again and with a respectful "May God grant you good afternoon!" there enters the reception room a bulky figure squeezing with both hands a shaggy cap, in greatest embarrassment.

Involuntarily the face of the lawyers brightens.

"A right good welcome to you, my good man! Sit down, sit down! Well, have you had rain out your way, too? And what are you bringing us?"

And the "good man" tells his story in his simple "home grown" manner, interspersing his remarks with pithy phrases and many gestures. The lawyer smiles. He is amused by the history of the dispute which has as its stage a village green in the centre of thatched roofs covered with moss or a mass of rustling golden leaves; in short, a wide free region which he probably does not long for in his comfortable city room but to which at times he likes to fly in fancy from the piles of dusty documents and law books. He is amused by his country client's naïve confidence in his—the lawyer's—all powerfulness and utterly diabolical shrewdness. Finally there is a pleasant fascination even in the silent readiness with which a countryman of that sort before each interview draws out spontaneously an advance payment from some tattered little book or from the knotted corner of a handkerchief and in the willingness with which he later pays legal fees of whatever size.

In addition to these bright phases this country clientele also, to be sure, has some shady sides. Not among the last of these is the fact that such an individual usually smells of fur and in winter likes to sit close to the office stove where gradually like a snow man he thaws out into pools of dirty water.

In the case which I refer to, this rustic affair was reported in the register of Dr. X under the modest title of Matthew Prochazka. The matter first came to the office some three years ago and in a short time won all hearts. It began with a dispute whose subject was far more suitable for the background of a pastoral idyl or as material for a poem than as the object of a legal controversy.

It was an apple-tree. An apple-tree—of poetic association—as charming in May time when thousands of buzzing bees flit about its crown enveloped in fragrant white and rose blossoms as in the fall when its green branches bend beneath the sweet burden of blushing apples.

The thing happened this way. On the boundary line which divided the Prochazka farm from the field belonging to Barbara Vrchcabova stood a lone apple-tree in whose shadow in former years the owners of the two neighbouring properties used often at harvest time to sit at rest beside each other in perfect harmony. But one time Mrs. Vrchcabova had the tree, which was now quite old, garnered of its fruit—although, as later the alternate conflicting documents verified, this act gained for her not even a full basket of sourish apples—and a few days later Matthew

Prochazka preferred, through his legal representative, a two-page charge against her for trespass against property.

Since that time a great many other quarrels between the two neighbours had been added to the dispute over the apple-tree. They included controversies about the boundary line, the overhanging eaves, a stopped-up window, a protruding rafter and other illegal trespass *vi clam precario*, but the apple-tree still held the foreground and became for the office an inseparable symbol of the personality of Matthew Prochazka.

"Well, what about the apple-tree?" was the first question of the clerks whenever they magnanimously opened a conversation with him and the chief began each relation of the occurrences in a new quarrel of his country client with his rapacious neighbour by jabbing a dot in the centre of a sheet of paper with the words: "Here, then, stands the apple-tree—and here to the right, etc."

Many of the later altercations had long ago been concluded happily or unhappily, but the strife for the apple-tree dragged along endlessly like a coloured thread from a magician's mouth. I don't know the cause of its unnatural length, whether the contest slid over from the firm ground of possessed prosperity to the slippery arena of the question of ownership, or whether the progress of the law-suit was held back by some *probatio diabolica*—I cannot say, for I do not understand such things. But certain it is that Prochazka continued to ask at each visit. "And how far along are we, please, with the apple-tree?"

"It won't be long now and the preliminary evidence will all be in," answered the lawyer.

"Let it cost what it will—just see to it, Mr. Lawyer, that she has a big lot of expense!"

It was no wonder that good old Prochazka wished that every evil might befall his neighbour. Being a childless widower and proprietor of a fine estate, he might have enjoyed complete earthly bliss if an envious fate had not destined Mrs. Vrchcabova of all people to be his neighbour. It was she who most effectually embittered his life. On three sides her property encompassed his, not with the friendly embrace of neighbourly love, but like a ferocious beast thrusting out its deadly talons to seize its prey. The property line separating the two estates was not a peaceful insensible marking, but it gave evidence on every hand of being a boundary of furious attack and fierce defence. Every corner was a sharp tooth fastening itself into the neighbouring land; every boundary mark gnawed its way in like the root of a polyp through its innumerable suction organs. Every landmark on the two estates aroused the suspicion that year by year it was advancing and that, most assuredly, not by pin-head degrees as did the petrified shepherds in the old folk tales. Indeed, even the house belonging to Mrs. Vrchcabova with the attractive inn adjoining it seemed to be gradually moving forward into

Matthew Prochazka's lot, blinking more and more greedily through its several windows from day to day. In fact, the upper dormer appeared to grin mockingly and the shameless pumpkins in their impatience climbed over the fence into their neighbour's property.

To be sure, I don't know who was the lamb and who the wolf of it, after all, both were not wolves but certain it is that a faction in our office accepted Prochazka's version of the situation with a neutral smile. That smile did not vanish even when Prochazka, confirmed by solemn oath, vowed that his restless neighbour would finally drive him to sell his estate and emigrate somewhere into Russia or America, and when he swore that he had his fill up to the neck of law-suits, and that the woman was a fiend incarnate, that she had the premature death of her husband on her conscience, and that he could relate things about her that would make his listeners' hair stand on end.

In the meantime, one law-suit followed swift on the heels of the other. It was only a brief time ago that a certain impertinent rafter projecting a good nine inches over into the aerial property of Matthew Prochazka had been, by the court's findings, happily driven back into Barbara Vrchca-bova's roof and already Prochazka's legal representative was making preparations for a new action for trespass on property through the wilful pulling out of two stakes from a certain fence, beginning the *species facti* with the customary digging in of a point into the middle of the sheet of paper accompanied by the words, "Here, then, stands the apple-tree."

"Stood," Matthew Prochazka corrected him just as he had several times previously.

I must, to be sure, add the information that the unfortunate apple-tree did not even survive the end of the argument. One stormy night it passed from this earthly surface, having been shattered and set afire by lightning, concluding its career gloriously and beautifully like a splendid meteor. This, however, did not have the slightest effect on the further development of the law-suit which pursued its calm, regular way unconcernedly over the fallen, charred remains of the apple-tree. For the purpose of the court-action it still existed, flourished, bloomed, bore sourish apples—*quod non est in actis, non est in mundo!*

A few days after the drawing up of the documents in the new action involving the fence, Prochazka again visited the office.

"The complaint is already lodged," his legal friend greeted him. "Did you see to it that nothing was removed?"

"Both the stakes lie just where they fell on the ground."

"Good. The point is that the commission at its local investigation must find an undisturbed picture of the act of trespass."

"But there's another snag to it, Mr. Attorney."

"What sort of snag?"

"Through that opening in the fence—you understand—her chickens are flocking into my garden and are causing all kinds of damage. My poor dead wife used to like to keep chickens and I myself enjoy seeing a brood of fine golden goslings or speckled chicks cheeping around a bustling mother-hen. But Mrs. Vrchcabova even in that line passes all limits. Her yard is a regular garrison of poultry. It fairly swarms with roosters, chickens, ducks, turkeys, hens and cocks. She doesn't keep them for profit or for pleasure but, God knows, only to torture me from morning until night with their crowing, clucking, peeping and chattering, and to fly over the fence into my garden and cause destruction until my heart fairly aches. Even before this, it kept me busy driving away that motley flock, but since those two poles in the fence are missing, they nest in my garden as if they were at home. But I'm going to put an end to that sort of thing. I'm going to buy myself, you understand, a double barrelled gun and I'll shoot whatever runs through the fence, even if it's her finest turkey."

"You'd certainly not do yourself any good by that. I advise a different method. Just help yourself to several of her hens and other poultry as security for the damage you have suffered. It is a special kind of security—or pledge-right that the law in this instance provides."

A few days after this counsel Prochazka again entered the office in very apparent excitement.

"Well, did you capture the poultry?" asked the attorney.

"Yes, I did."

"And what was the result?"

"This!" Prochazka brushed away the dry yellow hair from his forehead and showed a blood clotted bruise and several good sized swellings.

"A fight, then?"

"And what a fight! She came over with her hired man and maid for the poultry. She called me a robber, thief, scoundrel. She snatched the chickens from my possession by force and when I rushed after her, she picked up one of those loose stakes and hit me on the head. I picked up the other stake and we would undoubtedly have broken them over each other's heads if the neighbours hadn't come between us."

"Well we'll teach her some manners. Tell the whole affair again in detail. We will prefer a court charge against her to-morrow for an offence against the security of honour. You will go personally to the county court to attend the trial. I will give you complete instructions as to your procedure. I would go with you but I can't on account of matters which are simply impossible of postponement."

After that interview Prochazka did not appear in the office for so long a time that it seemed strange to all of us. A week passed by, two, three weeks and the office painfully missed among its common frequenters the bulky figure of the sturdy countryman.

In the meantime, the long anticipated consummation was realised: the suit over the apple-tree was ended by a decision wholly in favor of Matthew Prochazka on every point at issue.

When the successful litigant after a considerable length of time again stepped into the office, the attorney triumphantly waved the decree before his eyes.

"We've won, friend, we've won!"

But to the attorney's great amazement, Prochazka's eyes glistened only for an instant and then immediately the expression of embarrassment with which he had entered again overspread his face.

"What makes you stand so unmovedly? What has happened to you? Did the trial at the county court for insult to your honour end unfavourably for you?"

"No!"

"Well, what then? Just read this splendid decision. Mrs. Vrchcabova must have turned every colour in the spectrum when she read it. Just glance at the huge costs and indemnities which she will have to pay you."

"It's too late now," stuttered Prochazka.

"Late? Why—late?" asked the advocate in astonishment.

"Because we're about half each other's now."

"You—and Mrs. Vrchcabova?"

"Yesterday we had our first banns announced from the pulpit."

"Impossible! You don't mean to say that you intend to marry Mrs. Vrchcabova? For heaven's sake, tell me, how did it happen?"

"It happened all right. This unusual history begins at the county court during the proceedings against her for assault upon my honour. When they called us into the courtroom, the judge was sitting at his desk writing with his back turned to us. You probably know him, Mr. Attorney, don't you?"

"I've seen him a good many times. He's one of those elderly judges who would serve himself and others best if he'd retire to his well-earned rest."

"To be sure, he is a very old man. His head is as white as milk. But his cheeks still glow with health. Well, then, he was sitting with his back to us and kept on writing. At the other desk sat a clerk with pen in hand arranging some papers in front of him. We sat silent for awhile. Then Mrs. Vrchcabova began. She opened all her flood gates. But I know how to do a little talking myself. She never in her life heard so much peppery truth as she listened to in that little space of time. I told her everything that was burdening my heart. I read her a complete register of her sins and I returned everyone of her insults with a generous supplement. She flew at me, wept, stamped her feet— in short, we created such a disturbance that the assistants in the adjoining rooms began to open the doors and the clerk looked anxiously in the direction of the judge. But the judge nodded his head and smiled but kept on writing. After I had eased my feelings properly and Mrs. Vrchcabova had become hoarse from shouting, he put his pen behind his ear, took a pinch of snuff and then turned to me.'

"'Well, did you tell each other everything?' he asked. 'I think it would be best now if you'd shake hands and go home. And it would be best if hereafter you'd live in harmony and neighbourly love at home and quit running here to us to the court with such matters. By this perpetual squabbling you don't serve either your honour or your pocketbooks.'"

"That's the way with those old men," bitterly commented the attorney. "They like to transform the judge's chair into a pulpit. Well, and how did the affair end? Did you govern yourself according to my instructions?"

"What was I to do?" answered Prochazka in a depressed voice. "The judge rebuked us so thoroughly and yet in such humorous fashion that at last we involuntarily shook hands half in laughter."

"So! Well, you messed things up beautifully!" cried the attorney striding violently back and forth in the room. "If that's the way you follow my advice, why do you come back to ask it at all? Why do you lodge complaints? What was the use of all those expenditures? To be sure, I forgot that now you belong to each other. No doubt the judge immediately performed the marriage ceremony, too?"

"Yes, more than halfway. When we offered our hands to each other, he suggested with a smile that we ought to clasp hands in a different place and in that way all the conflict over the fences and boundaries would be swept away at one stroke. He insisted that we were just made for each other anyway. After that each of us rode home by a different route. But the following Sunday I went to Mokrin to high mass and the Chaplain preached so beautifully about friendly harmony and love for one's neighbour; and all the time the sun shone through the high windows so cheerily down on the gilded pulpit, on the pictures and altar roses, on the schoolgirls at the railing and on the assembled parish that it all made my heart melt. And when later I made my way homeward through the field path and looked around over God's golden blessings, waving all about me, when I noted the flies buzzing merrily in the air and the little worms swarming in the grass, I couldn't help thinking of the advice of the old judge. And the further I walked the more forcefully the thought kept pressing in upon me that by marrying Mrs. Vrchcabova I could the most easily conclude the endless law-suits and secure the blessed peace for which I've yearned so long. I deliberated that after all she isn't an ugly looking woman, that she is a good housekeeper and that our lands adjoin. In this mood I walked as far as the inn on her place.

I stopped there perspiring and tired and gazed involuntarily at the inviting house with its walls covered with grapevines. I looked at her garden with its thicket of sunflowers, at the yard filled with many coloured poultry. That's the way my place used to look when my wife was living. Just then I saw my neighbour right before me in the open window watering the flowers. When I caught sight of her so suddenly before me, I reached for my cap without even thinking, and she at once called out with an agreeable smile, 'God's greetings to you, neighbour! Won't you come in and have a glass of ale?' And I involuntarily entered the inn and—and——"

"Well, and what are you coming to me for? Do you expect me to write up your marriage agreement?"

"Oh, I'll come here with my intended bride some day to settle all that. But today I have something different on my heart."

"Well, then—what is it?"

"We've taken counsel with each other already about certain matters touching on our future combined property. Her lands—you know— neighbour on the other side with the property of the cottager, Mares. He's a fellow who is as slick as the oiliest—you know—and he has a wedge of poppies there extending into her land and—you know—he is wearing a path right over the field——"

The face of his legal adviser broadened into frank laughter.

"Slower—old man," he said. "We'll have to write it all down in regular order. Just wait, we'll sharpen up a new pencil for that rascal, Mares. There! Well, then, here stands the—that is, stood the appletree and here—etc.——"

❊ ❊ ❊

KAREL ČAPEK
(1890-   )

ČAPEK, born at Svatonovice in Czechoslovakia, the son of a capable Czech physician, received a good education. He is the most widely known Czechoslovak dramatic writer of today. He has been on the staff of the *Národní Listy* (National Journal), an important Czech daily in Prague, and since 1919 has been an editorial writer on the *Lidové Noviny* (People's Journal). Two years ago he was called to the staff of the Prague Vinohrady Theatre as dramatic critic and adviser. In the philosophy expressed in his writings he says, in a personal letter to the translator of *The Island,* that he was most influenced by our own James and Dewey.

Čapek has written, either alone or in collaboration with his brother Joseph, six novels and collections of short stories, all of them abounding

in fresh and unique situations. His best known collection of short
stories from which the present one is selected is *Glowing Depths*,
the title responding to the fervidity and ardour not only of the
natures he depicts but of his own youth when he wrote the lurid tales.

The *Island*, which appears in *Glowing Depths*, is translated by
Prof. Šarka B. Hrbkova.

THE ISLAND

AT one time there lived in Lisbon a certain Dom Luiz de Faria
who later sailed away in order to see the world, and having visited
the greater part of it, died on an island as remote as one's imagination can picture. During his life in Lisbon he was a man full of wisdom and judgment. He lived as such men usually do, in a way to
gratify his own desires without doing harm to others, and he occupied
a position in affairs commensurate with his innate pride. But even that
life eventually bored him and became a burden to him. Therefore he
exchanged his property for money and sailed away on the first ship out
into the world.

On this ship he sailed first to Cadiz and then to Palermo, Constan-
tinople and Beiruth, to Palestine, Egypt and around Arabia clear up to
Ceylon. Then they sailed around lower India and the islands including Java whence they struck for the open sea again heading towards the
east and south. Sometimes they met fellow countrymen who were homeward bound and who wept with joy when they asked questions about their
native land.

In all the countries they visited Dom Luiz saw so many things that
were extraordinary and well-nigh marvellous, that he felt as if he had
forgotten all his former life.

While they sailed thus over the wide sea, the stormy season overtook
them and their boat tossed on the waves like a cork which has neither
a goal nor anchor. For three days the storm increased in violence. The
third night the ship struck a coral reef.

Dom Luiz during the terrific crash felt himself lifted to a great
height and then plunged down into the water. But the water hurled him
back and pitched him unconscious on a broken timber.

When he recovered consciousness, he realised that it was bright noon
and that he was drifting on a pile of shattered beams wholly alone on a
calm sea. At that instant he felt for the first time a real joy in being
alive.

He floated thus until evening and throughout the night and the entire
succeeding day, but not a glimpse of land did he have. Besides, the pile
of rafters on which he floated was becoming loosened by the action of
the water, and piece after piece detached itself, Dom Luiz vainly trying

to tie them together with strips of his own clothing. At last only three weak timbers remained to him and he sank back in weariness. With a feeling of being utterly forsaken, Dom Luiz made his adieu to life and resigned himself to the will of God.

The third day at dawn he saw that the waves were bearing him to a beautiful island of charming groves and green thickets which seemed to be floating on the bosom of the ocean.

Finally, covered with salt and foam he stepped out on the land. At that instant several savages emerged from the forest, but Dom Luiz gave utterance to an unfriendly shout for he was afraid of them. Then he knelt down to pray, sank to the earth and fell asleep on the shore of the ocean.

When the sun was setting, he was awakened by a great hunger. The sand all around him was marked by the prints of bare flat feet. Dom Luiz was much rejoiced for he realised that around him had walked and sat many savages who had discussed and wondered about him but had done him no injury. Forthwith he went to seek food but it had already grown dark. When he had passed to the other side of the cliff, he beheld the savages sitting in a circle eating their supper. He saw men, women and children in that circle, but he took a position at some distance, not being bold enough to go closer, as if he were a beggar from some far-off province.

A young female of the savage group arose from her place and brought him a flat basket full of fruit. Luiz flung himself upon the basket and devoured bananas, figs, both dried and fresh, other fruits and fresh clams, meat dried in the sun and sweet bread of a very different sort from ours. The girl also brought him a pitcher of spring water and, seating herself in a squat position, she watched him eat and drink. When Luiz had had his fill, he felt a great relief in his whole body and began to thank the girl aloud for her gifts and for the water, for her kind-heartedness and for the mercifulness of all the others. As he spoke thus, a deep gratitude like the sweet anguish of an overflowing heart grew in him and poured itself out in beautiful words which he had never before been able to utter so well. The savage girl sat in front of him and listened.

Dom Luiz felt that he must repeat his gratitude in a way to make her understand and so he thanked her as fervently as if he were praying. In the meantime the savages had all gone away into the forest and Luiz was afraid that he would remain alone in the unfamiliar place with this great joy in his heart. So he began to relate things to the girl to detain her—telling her where he came from, how the ship was wrecked and what sufferings he had endured on the sea. All the while the savage maid lay before him flat on her stomach and listened silently. Then Luiz observed that she had fallen asleep with her face on the earth.

Seating himself at some distance, he gazed at the heavenly stars and listened to the murmur of the sea until sleep overcame him.

When he awoke in the morning, he looked for the maid but she had vanished. Only the impression of her entire body—straight and long like a green twig—remained in the sand. And when Luiz stepped into the hollow, it was warm and sun-heated. Then he followed the shore-line to inspect the island. Sometimes he had to go through forests or underbrush; often he had to skirt swamps and climb over boulders. At times he met groups of savages but he was not afraid of them. He noted that the ocean was a more beautiful blue than anywhere else in the world and that there were blossoming trees and unusual loveliness of vegetation. Thus he journeyed all day long enjoying the beauty of the island which was the most pleasing of any he had ever seen. Even the natives, he observed, were far more handsome than other savage tribes.

The following day he continued his inspection, encircling the entire island which was of an undulating surface blessed with streams and flowering verdure, just as one would picture paradise. By evening he reached the spot on the shore where he had landed from the sea and there sat the young savage girl all alone braiding her hair. At her feet lay the timbers on which he had floated hither. The waves of the impassable sea splashed up as far as the rafters so that he could advance no farther. Here Dom Luiz seated himself beside her and gazed at the sweep of the water bearing off his thoughts wave on wave. After many hundreds of waves had thus come and gone, his heart overflowed with an immeasurable sorrow and he began to pour out his grief, telling how he had journeyed for two days making a complete circumference of the island but that nowhere had he found a city or a harbour or a human being resembling himself. He told how all his comrades had perished at sea and that he had been cast up on an island from which there was no return; that he was left alone among low savage beings who spoke another language in which it was impossible to distinguish words or sense. Thus he complained bitterly and the savage maid listened to him lying on the sand until she fell asleep as if rocked to slumber by the grievous lullaby of his tribulations. Then Luiz became silent and breathed softly.

In the morning they sat together on the rock overlooking the sea giving a view of the entire horizon. There Dom Luiz reviewed his whole life, the elegance and splendour of Lisbon, his love affair, his voyages and all that he had seen in the world and he closed his eyes to vision more clearly the beautiful scenes in his own life. When he again opened his eyes, he saw the savage girl sitting on her heels and looking before her with a somewhat unintelligent gaze. He saw that she was lovely, with a small body and slender limbs, as brown as the earth, and finely erect.

After that he sat often on the rock looking out for a possible passing

ship. He saw the sun rise up from the ocean and sink in its depths and
he became accustomed to this just as he did to all else. He learned day
by day more of the pleasant sweetness of the island and its climate. It
was like an isle of love. Sometimes the savages came to him and gazed
on him with respect as they squatted in a circle about him like penguins.
Among them were tattooed men and venerable ancients and these brought
him portions of food that he might live.

When the rainy season came, Dom Luiz took up his abode in the
young savage girl's hut. Thus he lived among the wild natives and
went naked just as they did but he felt scorn for them and did not learn
a single word of their language. He did not know what name they gave
to the island on which he lived, to the roof which covered his head or
to the woman who in the eyes of God was his only mate. Whenever
he returned to the hut, he found there food prepared for him, a couch
and the quiet embrace of his brown wife. Although he regarded her
as not really or wholly a human being, but rather more nearly like other
animals, nevertheless he treated her as if she understood him, telling her
everything in his own language and feeling fully satisfied because she
listened to him attentively. He narrated to her everything that occupied
his mind—events of his former life in Lisbon, things about his home,
details of his travels. At first it grieved him that the savage maiden
neither understood his words nor the significance of what he was saying
but he became accustomed even to that and continued to recount everything in the same phrases and also with variations and always afterward
he took her into his arms.

But in the course of time his narrations grew shorter and more interrupted. The adventures he had had slipped the memory of Dom Luiz
just as if they hadn't happened or as if nothing had ever happened. For
whole days he would lie on his couch lost in thought and silence. He
became accustomed to his new life and continued to sit on his rock but
he no longer kept a lookout for passing ships. Thus many years passed
and Luiz forgot about returning, forgot the past; even his own native
speech and his mind was as mute as his tongue. Always at night he returned to his hut but he never learned to know the natives any more intimately than he had the day he arrived on the island.

Once in the summer he was deep in the forest when such a strange
unrest overwhelmed him suddenly that he ran out of the wood to behold
out on the ocean a beautiful ship at anchor. With violently beating heart
he rushed to the shore to mount his boulder and when he reached it, he
saw on the beach a group of sailors and officers. He concealed himself
behind the rock like a savage and listened. Their words touched the
margin of his memory and he then realised that the newcomers were
speaking his native tongue. He rose then and tried to address them but
he only gave utterance to a loud shout. The new arrivals were fright-

ened and he gave a second outcry. They raised their carbines but in that instant his tongue became untangled and he cried out, "Seignors,—have mercy!" All of them cried out in joy and hastened forward to him. But Luiz was seized by a savage instinct to flee before them. They, however, had completely surrounded him and one after another embraced him and overwhelmed him with questions. Thus he stood in the midst of the group—naked and full of anguish, looking in every direction for a loophole of escape.

"Don't be afraid," an elderly officer said to him. "Just recall that you are a human being. Bring him meat and wine for he looks thin and miserable. And you—sit down here among us and rest while you get accustomed again to the speech of human beings instead of to screeches which no doubt apes employ as speech."

They brought Dom Luiz sweet wine, prepared meats and biscuits. He sat among them as if in a dream and ate and gradually began to feel his memory returning. The others also ate and drank and conversed merrily rejoicing that they had found a fellow countryman. When Luiz had partaken of some of the food, a delicious feeling of gratitude filled him just as that time when the savage maiden had fed him but in addition he now felt a joy in the beautiful speech which he heard and understood and in the companionable people who addressed him as a brother. The words now came to his tongue of themselves and he expressed his thanks to them as best he could.

"Rest a little longer," the old officer said to him, "and then you can tell us who you are and how you got here. Then the precious gift of language will return to you for there is nothing more beautiful than the power of speech which permits a man to talk, to relate his adventures and to pour out his feelings."

While he was speaking a young sailor tuned up and began softly to sing a song about a man who went away beyond the sea while his sweetheart implores the sea and the winds and the sky to restore him to her, the pleading grief of the maiden being expressed in the most touching words one could find anywhere. After him others sang or recited other poems of similar content, each of them a little sadder in strain. All the songs gave voice to the longing for a loved one they told of ships sailing to far distant lands and of the ever changeful sea. At the last everyone was filled with memories of home and of all whom they had left behind. Dom Luiz wept copious tears, painfully happy in the afflictions he had suffered and in their joyous solution, when after having become unused to civilised speech he now heard the beautiful music of poetry. He wept because it was all like a dream which he feared could not be real.

Finally the old officer arose and said, "Children, now we will inspect the island which we found here in the ocean and before the sun sets we will gather here to row back to the ship. At night we will lift anchor and under God's protection, we will sail back. You, my friend," he turned to Luiz, "if you have anything that is yours and that you want to take with you as a souvenir, bring it here and wait for us till just before sunset."

The sailors scattered over the island shore and Dom Luiz betook himself to the savage woman's hut. The farther he advanced the more he loitered, turning over in his mind just how he should tell the savage that he must go away and forsake her. He sat down on a stone and debated with himself for he could not run away without any show of gratitude when he had lived with her for ten years. He recalled all the things she had done for him, how she had provided his food and shelter and had served him with her body and by her labours. Then he entered her hut, sat down beside her and talked a great deal and very hurriedly as if thus he could the better convince her. He told her that they had come for him and that he must now sail away to attend to very necessary affairs of which he conjured up a great quantity. Then he took her in his arms and thanked her for everything that she had done for him and he promised her that he would soon return, accompanying his promises with solemn vows and protestations. When he had talked a long time, he noticed that she was listening to him without the faintest understanding or comprehension. This angered him and, losing his patience, he repeated all his arguments as emphatically as possible and he stamped his feet in his irritability. It suddenly occurred to him that the sailors were probably pushing off, not waiting for him, and he rushed out from the hut in the middle of his speech and hastened to the shore.

But as yet no one was there so he sat down to wait. But the thought worried him that in all likelihood the savage woman had not thoroughly understood what he had said to her about being compelled to go away. That seemed such a terrible thing to him that he suddenly started back on a run to explain everything to her once more. However, he did not step into her hut but looked through a crack to see what she was doing. He saw that she had gathered fresh grass to make a soft bed for him for the night; he saw her placing fruit for him to eat and he noted for the first time that she herself ate only the poorer specimens—those that were dwarfed or spotted and for him she selected the most beautiful—all the large and perfect samples of fruit. Then she sat down as immovable as a statue and waited for him. Of a sudden Dom Luis comprehended clearly that he must yet eat the fruit set out for him and lie down on the couch prepared so carefully and complete her expectations before he could depart.

Meantime the sun was setting and the sailors gathered on the shore to push off to the ship. Only Dom Luiz was missing and so they called out to him, "Seignor! Seignor!" When he did not come, they scattered in various directions on the edge of the forest to seek him, all the time continuing to call out to him.   Two of the seamen ran quite close to him, calling him all the while but he hid among the shrubbery, his heart pounding in his breast for fear they would find him.   Then all the voices died down, and the darkness came.   Splashing the oars, the seamen rowed to the vessel loudly lamenting the lost survivor of the wreck. Then absolute quiet ensued and Dom Luiz emerged from the underbrush and returned to the hut.   The savage woman sat there unmoved and patient.   Dom Luiz ate the fruit, lay down on the freshly made couch with her beside him.

When dawn was breaking Dom Luiz lay sleepless and gazed out through the door of the hut where beyond the trees of the forest could be seen the sunlit sea—that sea on which the beautiful ship was just sailing away from the island.   The savage woman lay beside him asleep but she was no longer attractive as in former years but ugly and terrible to look upon.   Tear after tear rolled down on her bosom while Dom Luiz, in a whisper, lest she might hear, repeated beautiful words, wonderful poems describing the sorrow of longing and of vain eternal yearning.

Then the ship disappeared beyond the horizon and Dom Luiz remained on the island but he never uttered a single word from that day during all the years that preceded his death.

BULGARIA

Introduction

ALTHOUGH Bulgarian literature holds forth promise, it has hitherto been too much under the influence of France and Russia to develop a marked national character. As literatures go, that of Bulgaria is comparatively young; its foundations having been laid by Ivan Vazoff (1850-1921), Bulgaria's most distinguished poet and novelist. Dimitr Ivanov, under the pen name of Elin-Pelin, has written several collections of short stories which depict native life. Among the important followers of Vazoff are Stoyan Michaelovsky (b. 1850), a dramatist of fine ability, and M. Gheorgieff, a writer of popular tales. Tedor Panov, himself a colourful individual, is the author of several novels and collections of short stories. Of the several women who have contributed to contemporary literature, Nadejda Stancioff, now Lady Muir, has achieved distinction with her short stories.

❋ ❋ ❋

TEDOR PANOV

(1885-)

PANOV, born at Sofia, left his country after a preliminary education and went to Russia to study law. While at the University, he participated in the Russian Revolution and was, consequently, dismissed from the University, imprisoned and sent to Siberia. In 1902 he served in the Macedonian rebellion against the Turks. Three years later he was again involved in the revolutionary movement in the Caucasus. In 1908 he was sent by several Russian newspapers to Persia to act as their correspondent. But things became too hot for him when he began attacking Russian diplomacy, and he was subsequently expelled, only to return secretly and join the Persian revolutionaries in their conflict for constitutional rights. This only enumerates a part of Panov's adventurous career during which he succeeded in writing a series of political tracts, four successful novels and a number of lovely stories. His works betray the poetic idealist and the philosophic cynic, qualities directly attributable to his rebellious and erratic life.

Happiness, here translated for the first time into English by Prof. Šarka B. Hrbkova, is printed by permission of the translator.

HAPPINESS

HE was young, slender and handsome.

What did he lack?

. . . Happiness. . . .

Always, relentlessly, everywhere, like a shadow, Longing followed him . . . intense Longing. If he kept vigil by day, his fervently beating heart was in its grip, and his gaze filled with Longing, wandered apace in unknown realms.

And what was it he longed for?

. . . Something . . . everything!

The nightingale sang impassioned notes, caressing a rose-bud. Its trilling—clear as the morning zephyr, was borne afar.

All else was silent, each listener held his breath. And the heavens and stars and even the moon, entranced, heard that song.

They listened and swooned for very rapture and love.

At intervals when the nightingale paused for a moment, a sigh of ecstasy and amorous Desire swept through the universe.

"A-a-h!" softly breathed the earth. And this "A-a-h!" was borne to the trees, to the grass, to the stars and to the moon, and a scarcely perceptible echo died in the summits of the distant mountains.

Everything sighed in dreamy enchantment. And in that sighing was hidden love-lorn yearning.

The nightingale sang on. . . . The rapturously sporific moon rays softly embraced the rose-bushes and the nightingale. And the stars listened to the song of love and with a tender smile encouraged the bird-poet: "Sing, beloved, sing!"

The nightingale immersed in his delicate trills was exhilarated with ardent love-fervour. And ever pressing his heart closer and closer to the rose-bud, he pleaded: "Open, sweet! . . . Let me just once inhale your virgin aroma! Let me sink my head among your scarlet petals! . . ."

Thus the nightingale pleaded, implored and made melody until late into the night. And then his ringing trills grew fainter. In his voice ever louder sobbed the unsatisfied desire until at last the singer became silent, sighing softly and deeply—"A-a-h!"

And in that sigh lingering long among the rose-bushes, wept Desire, vain ungratified Desire.——

The young man stood there long, listening to the nightingale's song, long after it ceased, suffering the burden of a sleepless night.

And what more?

The gnawing worm of Desire penetrated ever deeper into his soul and more firmly clutched his heart. . . .

In the shade of the age-old trees of the forest on the green grass he lay day and night. Outstretched, he gazed up into the clear sky.

A zephyr flitting in from somewhere stole among the twigs and hardly touching the leaves softly fluttered the tips of the grass-blades with a mild tender smile.

The giant trees and mighty branches stood silently unmoved. From them exhaled ancient repose for they were submerged in deep slumber and in their everlasting dreams were hidden great mysteries. Even the lighthearted breeze quietly gliding among them only fondled their leaves for it feared to disturb their sublime tranquillity.

And why did they sleep the deep sleep of the dead?

Mayhap in their charmed slumber the youth was to seek the solution of his Desire?

He listened to the roar of the mountain stream.

The stream flowed down from the summits of the mounts where everlasting snow rested in heavy layers. It blustered, fought with the boulders, carried down crags, scratched the breast of the steep mountain, gouged deeper and deeper and its foaming waves tore away rocks which crashed madly one upon the other.

Whither hastened that stream?

It knew not. . . .

From time immemorial it had flowed and rushed wildly on, itself never knowing whither. It will vanish perhaps in the sea or in a torrent or in the scattered sands. That the stream knows not.

And its roar and its fuming . . . are they not impotent fury against the Unknown? . . .

Desire!

The youth could not bear the straining load of Desire: it was too heavy for him!

And so he traversed the white world seeking his Happiness.

Many, many times the sun rose and sank. The days alternated with the nights and year flowed on into year.

And still the young man wandered over the earth!

He passed through villages—many villages. In one of them once on a time he found the peasants sleeping a deep sleep, wearied by their hard labour. Impenetrable darkness enwrapped the poor huts. Grave-like stillness. Silence to rouse dread. . . . So hushed that one could hardly hear the yelping of the dogs.

"Happiness! Where are you?" cried the youth.

No answer.

He approached the door of one of the cottages. His heart throbbed with anxious foreboding.

After a while he heard beyond the door a muffled moan and a deep despairing sigh.

That must be Happiness lamenting at this late hour in the blackness of the dismal hut!

The young man sadly walked away.

He crossed rivers, lakes and valleys and even ascended a high mountain.

There a shepherd was pasturing his flock. The thick short grass glistened with the early dew. The wind gently ruffled the wool of the sheep which shivered in the morning coolness and tried to warm themselves in the rays of the dawning sun.

The shepherd, a young man with a pouch on his back, sat on a rock and played a horn, gazing in revery off into the blue distance. The low tender tones as caressing as the first gleam of the sun, dreamy as the eyes of a maiden, flowed from his horn and united like that white mist over yonder on the mountains—and like it—crept softly over the grass, the cliffs and the forests.

The flock listened to the shepherd's song.

"Tell me, tell me, what it is you sing of?"

"Of what? Does the wind sing of anything? I sing because I cannot be without music . . . it is sad! . . . I sing of things that are not."

"Do you know Happiness, shepherd?"

"Happiness? I have never met it in our mountains. Here am only I and my sheep as you see. And a bit of snow and mist. . . . Happiness is surely not a wood-nymph—them I know—every one. . . . People say that off there—far—far—, do you see?—there is a beautiful city. Perhaps Happiness dwells there . . . I do not know . . . I have never yet been there. . . ."

The young man descended the mountain seized with greater longing than ever and set out toward the wonderful city.

The city was indeed wonderful—he had never seen the like. Great buildings, broad streets, merchant structures, theatres, gardens, palaces . . . and all bathed in a blinding, dazzling light. Wealth, splendour and gilded luxury gleamed everywhere.

He crossed one street and entered another. In front of a railing enclosing a rich park stood a small beggar lad shivering with cold and imploring alms with sorrowful voice.

The young man went on. . . .

He stopped to gaze through the window of a theatre. There the audience in an unending ecstasy applauded a young artiste whom they extolled as their goddess. With sweet graciousness she bowed and it seemed as if Happiness shone in her smile.

But in a few moments she entered her dressing room, sank wearriedly on a chair, wrung her hands despairingly and wept in grief.

The young man departed from the great city and did not even look back.

The mournful sobs of the little beggar and the hopeless weeping of the goddess adored by the populace drove him on and on.

For a long time he wandered over the earth. At last he paused in a mountain canyon where amid forbidding crags in a deep cave dwelt an ancient hermit. Far away from people and close to God. . . .

"Do you know, aged man, where it is that Happiness dwells?" he asked gently as he entered into the presence of the ancient sage.

The old man, buried in his parchments, was searching the wisdom of the ages. Long it was before he answered the vain question of the youthful earth-dweller. And when he raised his hoary head, he looked with dim gaze into the young man's eyes and a bitter smile appeared on his sunken face.

Was he thinking of his vanished youth?

"Happiness for you?" the wise man asked and Doubt trembled in his tones.

And he lost himself in thought. . . .

When he raised his head, he spoke harshly.

"Vanity, oh vanity! . . . There is no Happiness! All is a dream!" The young man sobbed.

"Why then do I need Life? Why do I suffer these tortures? What was the use of all my journeying?"

The old man's heart softened. He pitied the youthful dreamer.

"Don't weep! Here is the path you seek! Go! You are still young! No one has as yet returned. If you come back, you will bring Happiness to earth!"

And the young man went. Weariness, after his long journey, departed; for in his soul was born Hope to grow each day with Desire.

He strode up steep paths and mounted higher and higher. . . . Around him sharp grey cliffs glittered ominously in the last rays of the sinking sun. Above the heights Death hovered and fanned the air with her breath. Nothing here spoke of Life or Youth. Everything was silently portentous as if under the curse of impending doom.

In the path of the young man soon appeared a deep chasm. He paused some steps from it, amazed and awed in speechless reverence.

The chasm was caused by a great rift in the mountain yawning deep in the earth from its very summit to its uttermost base. It was not wide. From verge to verge it was possible to leap but with slight effort.

A heavy mist was rising from the depths and the roar and shriek of the underground streams resounded in muffled re-echoings from the lower distances, filling the air with terror and dread.

And one could hear how, far below the veil of darkness, the elements raged and seethed in horrid ravings.

All that did not, however, frighten the youth. . . .

On the opposite brink, on a grey moss-covered rock, leaning on her arm, lay a forest numph.

Her golden hair glittered ruddily in the sunset glow.

The youth noticed how, under the transparent skin, the blood coursed through her marble body. And her breasts heaved with undulating regularity. From her half-closed eyes mysterious, bewitching glances shot forth.

The youth stood transfixed in his place and appealingly extended his hand to her. He understood in one swift instant why the nightingale sang, whither the mountain stream hastened, why the ancient trees kept secret silence, and whither the tones of the shepherd's horn invited.

He knelt imploringly before her without turning his inspired eyes from her—from earthly Happiness!

Behind the forest nymph Death was hiding. Malevolently she showed her hacked teeth in a dreadful grimace and extended her keen scythe over the chasm. The last rays of the dying sun were resplendent in its gleaming blade and a dim reflection rested in the thick cloud arising out of the yawning chasm.

The forest nymph lay there and beckoned him on with her hand, lured him with her eyes and intoxicated him with the trembling of her virgin bosom.

Death laughed holding the scythe in her hands . . . and the scythe scintillated ever more brightly.

. . . Fool! . . . Whither are you rushing?

And the young man, so long in quest of Happiness, tortured by it, inspired by its beauty, measured the chasm with his eye and leaped . . . not into the embrace of the forest nymph but upon the scythe of Death.

And the people henceforth called it "The Chasm of Happiness."

JUGOSLAVIA

Introduction

THE literature of Jugoslavia, or Serbo-Croat literature, is a branch of the great Slavonic group. The development of the Serbian and Croatian was originally somewhat uneven, for the Croats, due to their dependence on Austria-Hungary, were not so influenced as the Serbs by the Russian language and culture.

Dositey Obradovich (1739-1811), Minister of Public Education at the first Serbian college at Belgrade, and Vuk Stefanovich Karajich (1787-1864) were responsible for many literary as well as linguistic reforms that stimulated an interest in the national traditions and folk-songs. Karajich, who collected a number of volumes of folk lore, created a source for subsequent writers and paved the way for a national literature.

Jugoslavian literature has reflected the tendencies of the French, German and Russian literatures; and since the beginning of the present century Romanticism has been superseded by realism. The drama and the novel have been rather slow in developing, but the short story has made determined progress, and many gifted writers have expressed themselves in this form. The outstanding Serbian short story writers are B. Stanković (b. 1876), Laza K. Lazarevich (1851-1890), and Milovan Glishich (1847-1908). A. G. Matoš (1873-1914) and Vladimir Tresčec (b. 1870) may be considered as the most important of the Croatian.

❊ ❊ ❊

MILOVAN GLISHICH
(1847-1908)

GLISHICH, born near Valjevo of an old peasant family, received his early schooling at this city, later attending the University of Belgrade. He was a correspondent during the Turco-Serbian war of 1876, subsequently a newspaper editor. His early work showed evidence of Romantic influence, which he later shook off and became one of the foremost representatives of realism. His stories depict rural life with all its simplicity and humour.

Vouya Goes A-wooing is typical of Glishich's stories. The present version, translated by Vaso Trivanovich, is here published for the first time in English.

VOUYA GOES A-WOOING

I

WHEN Almighty God created the village of Petnyiza, he endowed it with many generous gifts. He gave it that beautiful mountain Osoye and its caves and that worthy parson Micha. To the parson he gave a good and industrious wife, called Mary, and a house full of many good things. The house stood at the very foot of the mountain under the shade of a splendid tree. Early one morning the parson's nephew Vouya found himself sitting under this particular tree, armed with a thick needle and thread, anxious to add another patch to his badly torn coat before the parson left his bedchamber.

Vouya sits and darns, thanking the Lord for so many blessings and looking furtively towards the house, for he knows that either the parson or his wife will appear at any moment and send him on an early errand.

And there, the figure of the parson's wife appears in the doorway. She looks this way and that around the house and under the tree.

"Again I find you darning, my sorrow."

"Again, posha," * mumbles Vouya.

"Is it finished?"

"Two more stitches only."

"Eh, well, take this key, run to the church and bring the parson's habit and prayer book. He needs them. Hurry!"

Having said that, posha left the key on the little bench in front of the house and vanished behind the door.

Vouya finished the last stitch. Greatly pleased with his workmanship, he threw the coat round his shoulders, took the key and ran with great speed up through the orchard, scattering chickens and hens along the way.

Vouya was very obedient. He executed faithfully all the commands of the parson and his wife. He rang the bells in the church, lighted the candles and vigil lamps, handed the incense to the parson and even sang hymns when the need was urgent.

Nor was this all that Vouya could do. He knew how to bind books, and even to-day one could find in the church of Petnyiza a number of holy books bound by Vouya. He worked all day long like an ant. It is true he was somewhat clumsy, but still industrious.

And Vouya could not discuss anything intelligently. He stammered and mumbled, but could not converse. Occasionally, he would attempt to contribute something to the conversation, only to become confused like

* "Posha" diminutive of "popadija," parson's wife.

a chicken with its head off, say some nonsense to the amusement of his listeners, and then remain silent and ashamed.

Although Vouya was industrious and obedient, he could not, like other industrious people, get rid of his poverty. He went about in rags, his hair protruding through his cap, his coat covered with patches, his trousers in an even worse condition than his coat, his shoes never new.

Perhaps the reason for this dilapidated condition of his attire was his crazy habit of sleeping fully dressed. He liked to go to bed in his coat and trousers and with his cap on his head. Both the parson and parson's wife tried to break him of that habit. They advised him and scolded him, but to no avail. To all their remonstrances he would reply, "But it is warmer this way" or "Suppose, posha, you should need me some night to do an errand quickly, would there be time to dress?" And so on. But be that as it may, the truth was that some devil did not permit him to become a man!

"Ough, that boy is as slow as a snail!" exclaimed Parson Micha, pacing impatiently up and down in front of the house, waiting for Vouya to bring the habit and prayer book.

"He will be here shortly" said posha, and then added smiling, "I felt sorry for the poor boy when I saw him this morning sitting under the tree and darning his coat like an orphan."

"How can I help him, when some devil keeps him as he is?"

"He has no luck, the unfortunate one."

"No, he has not," affirmed the parson and then continued seriously, "To tell you the truth I often think and ponder trying to find some way of helping him. I see him, working like an ant, without getting anywhere, without a clean shirt on his back. I do not know what to do with him, unless—unless we find him a wife."

"Find him a wife!" exclaimed the parson's wife, laughing. "The Lord have mercy upon your soul."

"And why not? I mean it seriously. Who knows, perhaps a wife will make a man out of him."

"For Heaven's sake, parson, be reasonable! Just take a look at him!" said posha, pointing at Vouya who was seen running through the orchard. "Is there a girl that would consent to marry him?"

"Never mind his looks. A new suit, boots and hat will make a bridegroom out of him," answered the parson lowering his voice, and then whispered into his wife's ear, "Do think about it."

"Here are the things," mumbled Vouya, extending the habit and prayer book to the parson.

"Bring them along," said the parson. "You are going with me. Let us go. Good-bye, posha!"

And Parson Micha and Vouya went down to the village to read a prayer to some old woman.

II

One day after lunch, two beautifully saddled horses stood in front of the parson's house.

Parson Micha, his hands clasped behind his back, was pacing nervously up and down the yard. He wore his best suit, although the day was neither Sunday nor holiday. It was clear that the parson was on his way to visit some important friend.

"What is the matter with that fellow, posha? Is he ever coming out?"

"Just a moment, Micha," answered his wife from the house.

In a little while Vouya appeared on the doorstep.

Nobody would have recognised him.

Dressed in beautiful cloth trousers, a vest embroidered with gold, an overcoat, a new fez and boots on his feet—Vouya looked like a new man, even his face appeared changed, fairer and rosier.

"Let us go! Mount your horse!" said the parson to Vouya seriously and then smiled, looking at his wife who stood on the doorstep suppressing an almost unconquerable desire to laugh. He called her aside and asked, "Well, what do you think?"

"A different man."

"Didn't I tell you? That suit of my late nephew, the Lord have mercy upon his soul, fits him perfectly."

"Yes, the poor fellow was of the same build as Vouya."

"A different man, indeed," said the parson, looking at Vouya who was fussing round the travelling bags.

"Only, you know, I am afraid he will do something foolish," remarked the parson's wife very slowly.

"Don't worry! I know how to handle him. . . . And isn't Boshko going to be surprised to see us? His adopted daughter will be just the right kind of wife for Vouya."

"If you would only leave Boshko in peace. . . ."

"And why?"

"You could find him a girl here in the village. Boshko is a well-to-do man. His is a wealthy house."

"That makes no difference. Boshko will not tell me no. And besides, you know, it is better to find him a wife in some distant village. Here everybody knows Vouya."

Having said that, the parson walked towards the horses. Vouya was still fussing with his travelling bag.

"What? Haven't you mounted yet!?"

"Alright, parson, I am ready. Just a moment," mumbled Vouya, running around the horse looking for the best way of getting himself into the saddle.

The parson mounted his horse and shouted at Vouya impatiently, "Mount! Aren't you ever going to mount that horse?"

Vouya tried bravely; but that new suit seemed to be very much in his way. And the horse was restive. Finally with the help of the parson's wife he found himself astride the horse.

"Open the gate, posha!" exclaimed the parson, starting his horse and laughing at Vouya's clumsy horsemanship.

The parson's wife opened the gate and asked, "And when shall I expect you home, parson?"

"Tomorrow evening if we finish our work successfully. If we fail, then you may expect us earlier. . . . Good-bye!"

Restive horses covered the ground quickly, and in a moment the parson and Vouya found themselves on the broad road to Lajkovaz.

III

Only a moment, and the sun will sink behind the mountains.

The parson, riding well in front and singing a psalm, looked back at Vouya frequently and urged him to a faster pace.

"Hurry, Vouya! Faster. . . . It is getting late."

At the sound of the parson's voice Vouya jumped as if from a trance, touched the horse with the stirrup, bouncing violently in the saddle.

"Vouya, do you hear me?"

"Yes, parson. What is it, parson?" asked Vouya almost plaintively.

"You know what business is taking us to Boshko's?"

"I know," replied Vouya, blushing crimson.

"You see," continued the parson, "that is a wealthy house. You go there for the first time. Open your eyes wide and make me proud of you."

"Yes, parson. I shall, parson," Vouya assured him in a barely audible voice.

"Don't say anything stupid, if your head is dear to you."

"No, parson. I shall not, parson," stammered Vouya, reddening.

By that time they reached the gate of Boshko's house and halted the horses.

A terrible fear gripped Vouya's heart. He heard a fearful noise in his ears. The parson appeared to him—the good Lord have mercy upon us—like a different man, as if he were not his uncle, as if he had now for the first time set his eyes upon him.

"Hey, master!" shouted Parson Micha.

A dog barked, straining the chain which tied him to the house.

"Hey, master!" called the parson again.

The dog barked more furiously.

A girl appeared peeping through the door of the house and disappeared quickly. It was Stamena, Boshko's adopted daughter.

"Hey, master!" shouted the parson at the top of his voice.

The dog barked violently, pulling against the chain with such force that the noise was heard all the way down to the gate.

Then Boshko dropped in front of the house from somewhere and answered the call.

"Hey. . . . Who is calling? Who?"

"Come down here. . . . Hey. . . . Come down here!" shouted the parson.

Boshko ran down and, recognising the parson, opened the gate joyfully. The parson and Vouya dismounted. The parson shook hands cordially with Boshko and introduced his nephew. Then the three of them walked up to the house conversing pleasantly. The dog had not ceased barking.

Boshko called his wife and other members of the household and told them to take care of the guests.

In the twinkling of an eye both horses were tied to a plum tree behind the new house. Stamena brought out the chairs for the guests, kissed the parson's hand and ran back into the house. The mistress of the house also kissed the parson's hand and inquired about the health of his wife. Then came Boshko's two brothers, exchanged greetings with the parson, took their seats and opened up a conversation.

Vouya kept his seat silently without being conscious of what was transpiring around him.

The mistress of the house brought out a wooden jug of brandy and a glass. She served the guests and offered a drink to Vouya.

At that moment Vouya felt the chair tottering and slipping from under him. He swayed heavily to one side, almost tumbling over. The parson looked at him in wonder.

The first dusk began to envelop the earth. Boshko called upon his household to have dinner ready.

Everybody became very busy. Some members of the household disappeared in the house; some in the cellar; still others in the dairy-house. Boshko remained alone with his guests.

Parson Micha thought this a good moment to explain his mission. First, he mentioned how industrious Vouya was. He even knew a trade. And, then, the time had come for him to build his own nest. And so on—the parson enumerated all of Vouya's virtues, and then put it up to Boshko, "Well, what do you say? Are you willing to consider the matter?"

Boshko remained silent for a moment or two and then replied slowly. He believed that everything his old acquaintance and good friend, the parson, had said was true. He himself did not find fault with the young man. He was willing to accept him into the family, but there was Stamena. Of course, it was her affair.

The parson was pleased that Boshko had no objections, and he arranged with him to approach the girl in the morning.

Vouya listened to this conversation in silence, his agony breaking out in heavy beads of perspiration upon his forehead.

In the meantime the mistress of the house announced that dinner was ready. Boshko and his guests went into the house, where the entire household was assembled already, and took their places at the table.

The parson was happy. He joked with Boshko, teased the mistress of the house, and Stamena and Boshko's daughters-in-law.

Vouya remained silent. The host urged him to eat, but he touched nothing. He smiled without knowing what was funny. It seemed to him that the parson's *chita* * stood on Boshko's head; while the parson wore the headwear of the hostess. One moment he would see only women at the table; and then they would become transformed into priests. And even Stamena, the Lord have mercy upon her soul, appeared with a long beard. . . . That was funny, and he laughed.

The parson would now and then give him a black look.

"Well, brother, it is time to retire," said the parson to Boshko, after having eaten and drunk and joked and talked to his satisfaction.

"Alright, parson," answered Boshko and told Stamena to go and prepare the room for the guests.

Stamena lighted a torch on the fire that burned in the hearth and went into the adjoining building.

Vouya stretched himself a little, yawned once or twice, as a man who hears that it is time to retire, and then disappeared unobserved somewhere outside.

The parson and Boshko were deeply engaged in conversation and failed to see Vouya's disappearance.

Vouya went directly behind the house, where the horses still stood tied to the plum-tree.

Through the window of the adjoining house, the light of the torch illuminated the yard and the horses. Stamena could be seen making beds.

Vouya removed the travelling bag from his horse and disappeared in darkness. . . .

Stamena finished her work in the guest-room, took the torch, walked down the steps and started towards the house to tell her father that the room was ready for the guests.

On her way she met Vouya. He dropped from somewhere out of darkness and, seeing Stamena, asked without knowing why "Well, are we going to retire, my soul?"

Stamena screamed, dropped the torch and flew away.

Vouya went into the house and, with one foot over the doorstep, asked, "Well, parson, are we going to retire?"

* A sort of cap worn by priests.

If the house had fallen on the parson's head he would not have been more terrified than he was at the sight of Vouya.

The new suit was not there. Vouya wore the same old cap, the same worn-out coat, the same torn trousers. . . . His old suit in which he had spent so many days and nights, for, as we know, Vouya lived according to that saying "in what you walk in daytime in that you should sleep at night."

It seemed to the parson that some terrible evil spirit stood in Vouya's place on the doorstep.

"What has happened to you, unfortunate one?" the parson barely asked.

"Well, parson, I was afraid to soil it . . . you know that suit does not belong to me . . ." mumbled Vouya.

The parson stood petrified.

Boshko looked in consternation now at the parson and now at Vouya.

The mistress of the house appeared next and, seeing Vouya, jumped up startled and said "The room is ready."

"Eh, well, let us go to sleep," remarked Boshko to himself and went out silently.

The parson shook his head at Vouya ominously and left the house without saying "Good-night" to anybody. Vouya followed him slowly.

The mistress of the house escorted them with a torch to their sleeping quarters and returned to the house.

IV

"Is the parson up?" asked Boshko early next morning.

"Up and gone," replied his wife.

"Really?"

"Yes indeed. I arose before daybreak. The horses were missing. So I peeped into the guestroom. . . . The parson was not there . . . nor the other fellow. . . . They must have left early."

"Well, God's will," remarked Boshko smiling.

In the meantime the parson and Vouya were well on the way home.

The parson rode whistling. Vouya kept silence. The whole world seemed to him topsy-turvy . . . somehow strange. The road seemed to be full of holes, big, strange holes.

At an evil time, the parson turned around and said "And why did you expose me to such ridicule, for the love of mercy?"

"Well, parson. . . ." Vouya wanted to say something, but got no further.

"And where did you get those rags, the Lord have mercy upon your soul?"

"Well, I brought them along," whispered Vouya, "I put them in the bag."

"Thank God that the girl did not see you."

"She saw me!" exclaimed Vouya almost joyfully.

"In those rags?"

"Yes, sir, God is my witness."

"And?" asked the parson scowling.

"She just screamed and ran away."

"Ough!" exclaimed the parson and then shouted at Vouya: "Let that horse go! Look out! You will break your neck in that hole!"

Having said that, the parson struck the horse with the whip and angrily rode on.

In a little while the parson's home became visible.

Posha had risen early and was doing some work in front of the house. Seeing the parson and Vouya hurrying home, she clasped her hands and exclaimed to herself "What is this, God help us!"

She looked again more carefully, not believing her eyes.

By that time both horsemen reached the gate.

Posha ran and opened the door. Never before had she seen the parson so terrible. She did not dare to tell him "Welcome home!"

The parson dismounted, furious, threw the reins to Vouya and said curtly "Unsaddle the horses and take them to the orchard."

Vouya dismounted quickly and took down the bags and the rest.

"When did you leave Lajkovaz?" asked Posha.

"Before dawn!"

"If you had only listened to me. . . ."

"For Heaven's sake, Posha, keep quiet! I have got enough trouble anyhow!" said the parson and went into the house.

His wife followed him inside.

Vouya unsaddled the horses and drove them to the orchard. Then he went into his workshop and started to bind an old psalm-book.

That day he would not eat in the house. He excused himself that he was too busy, took some bread and ate outside.

From that time on Parson Micha never mentioned the subject of Vouya's marriage. He went to visit Boshko after Stamena's wedding.

Vouya remained unchanged. He sat under the tree in the morning darning his suit; rang the bells in the church; bound old books; occasionally sang hymns, and obeyed his parson.

Nobody remembers that he had ever married.

VLADIMIR TRESČEC
(1870-   )

TRESČEC, born at Topusko, Croatia, passed his primary, secondary and university studies in his native country and then took a postgraduate course in Vienna. He travelled much throughout Europe. In 1895 he accepted a government position in Bosnia and thence came to the Government in Croatia in 1907. Two years later he became the director of the Croatian National Theatre in Zagreb. Besides many of his original stories he translated several works of Daudet, Zola and Bourget. The present story, translated by Ivan Mladineo, is here published for the first time in English.

FERID

CAN you imagine a sea of rock? Wherever you cast your eye—rock! White, grey, naked rock, high up in the sky; the highest pile touching the azure is called Veleš. Below it, imagine, between the rocks, a lake, endlessly long, muddy, full of fruitful sand—it is called Blato.

In the midst of such scenery I became acquainted with Ferid Bey, while awaiting, behind a rock, the fall of wild ducks. I heard shots from his gun about two hundred paces away and when it became dark he appeared behind a rock by the light of a young moon; he seemed to me like a giant with a cannon on his shoulder.

His gun was actually longer than a meter and the barrel wider than a child's arm. I smiled to myself, I, the owner of a light Lancaster with double barrel. But when I saw Ferid carrying a bag full of ducks, I took my cap off to him and we became close friends. Because, you must know, on a hunt, friendships are formed most quickly, the heart being full to overflowing. That is the reason that hunting is not for ladies who wish to remain virtuous.

That autumn we found each other nearly every day at Blato, and just at that time, Herzeg-Bosnia was up in arms, due to the first military service draft.

—"You are a hero"—said Ferid to me,—"when you dare to be here alone."

I laughed aloud.

—"Is it heroism when one does not care for life? What do I care? Today I am and tomorrow I am not".—

—"Right", said Ferid, but I saw in his eyes that he was talking tactfully, not being of my mind.

Army officers and Ferid's friends wondered about our comradeship. Otherwise he never looked upon nor greeted any "Švabo" except himself. He was a proud Herzegovinian, accustomed to century-long liberty and lordliness.

My duties kept me from Ferid Bey a few days. The rebels again killed one of our lieutenants and four soldiers in the vicinity. Nearly the entire Mostar garrison was sent to apprehend the murderers.

One afternoon—after a hot July-like day in October—I came, with my men, upon a small village near Blagaj.

As I approached the first house, I noticed a large number of soldiers, a whole battalion. The Colonel, seeing me, cried, apparently happy!

—"We got one already!"—

I was quite glad and forgot all the hardships of the day: "There, we will avenge our comrades!"

—"There he is, now he will be shot!"—added my Colonel, well rounded and a red-faced brother Pole.

I looked there and saw Ferid Bey leaning against the wall and looking toward the sky.

—"Is it possible?"—against my will I exclaimed,—"Have you proof?"—

The Colonel smiled,—"There they are!"—the two men were sitting on a rock, with heads bent, circling with their eyes hither and thither. They were Ferid Bey's two land tenants, who brought the army to his village and told—same blood and same tongue!—that they had seen with their own eyes, Ferid Bey behind a rock, aiming at and killing our officer.

I was dazed. Fanatical, century-old hatreds of the land tenants against their Bey was well known to me so that I doubted the truthfulness of these "witnesses". I began to question these men, hoping that the officers might have misunderstood them. They repeated the same story, however. Before they were through with their story, something behind me roared:

—"You lie!"—

When I turned, Ferid Bey was still there, handcuffed, eyes turned up and head upright.

The witnesses laughed into his face. They already had the reward in their pockets.

Then I approached Ferid Bey.

—"Why don't you defend yourself, man?"—

Without even looking at me, he replied:

—"They do not even ask me, but only those bastards. . . ."

As he stood against the wall, erect, tall, quiet, he seemed to me like a hero, a martyr. I felt a chill through my heart. I turned again to the Colonel who in the meantime ordered the selection and placing of the firing squad.

"What day and at what time was officer Rančič killed?"

"The day before yesterday, Wednesday, before dark."

"Day before yesterday, Wednesday, afternoon, until night, Ferid Bey was hunting with me at Blato."

"What, is it possible?"—exclaimed the Colonel evidently disappointed.

"My officer's word is a guarantee for that!"

"And those witnesses?"

"Lying like dogs."

"To the gallows with them!"—

I untied Ferid Bey's arms. His body was shaking like a leaf in the wind, and he was unable to speak.

When, a little later, we had coffee together, Ferid told me solemnly: "Sir, brother, whatever you desire from me, it is yours!"

From that time on, we were very close friends. Ferid was dear to me from the first moment and now I was unable to escape the impression of this heroic figure, this ordinary, and at the same time, aristocratic spirit, and I asked myself:

"Haven't there remained here, on the shores of the River Neretva, other Roman relics besides the stone bridges?"—

How Ferid—a decade younger—did serve me and look after me! He did not permit me to carry the catch nor a gun, everything he would burden upon himself, and when I came to his home he was unable to seat me sufficiently high and soft, bringing out all the rugs and pillows he possessed—pouring coffee and lemonade into me and rolling cigars for me so that I very often became sick. Before me was no longer a great hero, but a small child, a tender sweetheart.

"If I could only satisfy you . . . if I could only know what you desire most!"—he would often sigh.

One day a thought, insane and insolent, struck my head. Was it excessive good humour or what? Was I unusually exhilarated? I do not recall now. When Ferid was accepting coffee from someone's hands through an unlocked door, I noticed through the opening something that looked like a dream about oriental odalisks, about Gruzian girls and I felt, as if struck by lightning, a big, enchanting eye. In a moment an idea had evolved in my head and I said:

"Here, Ferid, I wish something."

"Now, brother, be it what it may, it shall be!"

I hesitated for a moment and nearly was ashamed, but a desire for adventure was stronger than honesty.

"It is not right for your wife to conceal herself, when I am your brother! I would just like to see her once."

Ferid, who was pouring coffee for me from a small ibrik, paused for a moment. He looked into my eyes, seriously, calmly, and then asked with unusually soft voice:

"Do you really wish it?"

Inquisitive and frolicsome, I repeated:

"Yes, I do!"

He became silent, raised his hand to his head, pushed his fez on his neck and rubbed his head and face with his hand. Then he stooped before me, staring at the floor, then, suddenly, he turned away from me, but I jumped to see his face and I noticed two big tears which he quickly wiped away.

I saw, in those two tears, all the great torture this hero suffered. I was sorry and I said:

"For God's sake, pardon me, Ferid, I was not conscious that my request was something so great and difficult, I did not know, believe me! There, I am telling you: I refuse to see her, positively, so help me God! Please believe me! I did not consider it as something important, I was only joking."

As I was thus speaking, Ferid was weeping. Then he quieted himself and said:

"And your joke nearly cost Zadiha her head!"

"How, for heaven's sake? What had you intended to do?"

"For the second time you saved my head. . . . After your eyes would have looked at her, no other eye would have ever seen her alive but only the eye of this pistol."

At the same time he placed his hand on a beautiful, silver-mounted pistol, of Albanian make, took my hand and before I could understand what he wanted, he pressed it to his lips and forehead.

When I actually saved his life he failed to find a word of thanks, and now he kissed my hand.

Then, for the first time, I understood Hamlet's words, when he says, how great love cannot permit even a wind to caress the face of a sweetheart without envy.

✳ ✳ ✳

FRANCIS XAVIER MEŠKO
(1874-   )

BESIDE Ivan Cankar, Meško is the founder of the Slovene psychological novel. He is a very lyrical writer, a painter of sentimental moods. While there is usually not much plot in his stories, they abound in description of inner conflict, and a complex of depression pervades all his works.

The present story, translated by Helen P. Hlacha, is here published for the first time in English.

THE MAN WITH THE RAGGED SOUL

I

DUSK came early; it was already late autumn.
Lighting my lamp, I seated myself to the table to write. A time like this, full of melancholy peace, full of silent, dreaming secrets, is most agreeable for writing.

I had been working for some time when I heard footsteps and conversation out in the passageway. The aged servant with a candle in her hand opened the door saying:

"Over here! Come right in!"

Lifting the shade of my lamp, I saw a young man standing before the door which the old servant immediately closed behind her again, an unknown man with a waving chestnut beard and long curling hair. I looked at him in silence waiting for him to say what he wished, and thought to myself: "A labourer without employment. He's come for help. Had he but come sooner!"

He also studied me silently for some moments with large eyes, blue as two lakes.

"Pardon me, your reverence, for disturbing you at this late hour" he said after a moment and again bowed with a courtesy and elegance one would not have expected of an ordinary labourer. He spoke German with a foreign accent—I had heard travellers from Southern Germany and they spoke with a similar pronunciation. He spoke very hastily almost excitedly. "I came because I'd like to talk to you about various things."

"Won't you please sit down?"

I indicated a chair on the opposite side of the table. But he ignored my sign, as if he hadn't seen it; drawing closer a chair near my own, he seated himself right beside me.

I frankly acknowledge my heart was not quite at ease; I sat in the mute and unhearing night in an isolated, silent room with this unknown man, broad-shouldered and powerful, who might fell me with one swing of his large muscular hand which he held on the table, restlessly sliding it back and forth, or one blow of the stout stick he clutched in his other hand and upon which he leaned even while sitting, as if terribly tired, and as if it were pouring its strength into his veins to hold him upright.

"I'm on a journey and I've come to you"—he began and studied me yet more carefully and constrainedly as if he were analysing my eyes, trying to fathom the thoughts that were hiding behind them and gleaming there revealingly.

"Why is he looking at me so queerly? Has he really come for some special purpose, with dishonest intentions?" I pondered uneasily. Inwardly I raged at the old servant for having brought him up. But anger did not alter the situation. I was a prisoner. Therefore I returned in the friendliest way:

"I am very glad. What then is it you wish to talk over with me?"

"Do you know all the folks in the parish?"

"I'm here four years; I believe I'm pretty well acquainted."

"But do you know the Hubers down the valley?"

"Very little. Only that I've heard them spoken of."

"Don't you associate with them?"

"No. We don't have the opportunity to meet; they're Protestants."

Thumping his staff he leaned closer towards me.

"What of it? I thought that perhaps the daughter of the Hubers sometimes came to you."

"What for?"

"For some advice, let's say. Young girls need advice."

I wondered at the stranger's thoughts. Wondered also at the rapid, and in a way, almost mechanical completeness with which he spoke, as if he were rapidly reciting a learned speech.

"No, she has never come. I do not even know her."

"No? That's funny. I thought—oh, what was I going to say? See here, I'd like to know something about those Hubers from you."

"I'm sorry I have nothing to tell you about them. Don't you know them? It appears you're not from these parts."

"I know them, by God, I know them even too well." He chuckled distressfully and hatefully. He drew his right hand into a fist and laid it heavily upon the table like a ponderous ruddy mallet.

"Do I know them! When no one on earth has done me so much harm as those people."

I looked at him in astonishment. His restless eyes, fixed piercingly on me gleamed with an inner flame.

I began to feel not merely uncomfortable, but oppressed.

"I'll tell you frankly: I'm the Hubers' son."

A forceful silence fell. I stared at him and he at me. In a moment I recalled some talk about him that had been rumoured in the neighbourhood. That he had often been in jail, I had heard somewhere. When he had served in the army his intelligence had earned him a lieutenancy, but military life had been so severe that he had deserted during the third year. He had come home. The police were after him shortly. Seeing no other way of escape he had jumped, fully clothed, into the Drava and swum across. Despite that he had been caught. When the officers had raged at him for causing them such inconvenience and jumping in the river, he had coolly waved them off: "You should have done the same!" They had stuck him into a military uniform again. This had so offended him that he had immediately upon serving his time in the army, gone to

America. He was not driven there by greed and the desire for gold and wealth, as many others are; disgust with his homeland alone, had driven him there.

All this passed with lightning speed through my mind as I now faced him.

"You're Hubers' son?" I drawled slowly and deliberately, to break this uncomfortable silence which distressed and awed me.

"Yes. But I'm ashamed of it. Ashamed of my name, ashamed of my father."

His eyes flashed like lightning beneath his broad strong brow.

"Why, sir? I haven't as yet heard anything wrong about your father."

"No? He's a fiend! He's to blame for my misfortune. He had me placed under guardianship, he had me put into prison."

"Your father? It's hardly believable."

"Because you do not know him. You admitted you didn't know him. Then how can you defend him?"

"I'm not defending him. But it seems strange to me."

"Not to me. For I know him." He deliberated, brushing his hair from his forehead. "If I go home now I'll probably kill him."

I wanted to smile but I didn't succeed.

"You didn't believe it? Needn't. Even better if you don't." He deliberated again. "Perhaps I'd not really kill him. But I'll set their house afire. Let the whole rabble perish."

"You'll think that over well. After all, they're your people."

Silence overcame him; confusedly he bit his lips. He was filled with gloom as the sky before a most terrific storm.

"You are right. I probably will think it over. For I'd only be harming myself. I'd be stuck into that hole again."

"It's well that you realise that."

He nodded as if agreeing. He asked quietly: "But where shall I go? Where shall I turn to—where?"

"You can stop here somewhere for the night."

"Where?"

"Perhaps at the inn. The innkeeper is a Protestant."

"A Protestant?" It seemed as if this information aroused some sort of interest. However, after a moment he shook his head uninterestedly and almost involuntarily.

"That doesn't mean anything. An innkeeper is an innkeeper—they're all money hungry."

"Of course, money is not refused at any inn. If you perhaps just haven't any, at least permit me to offer you a trifle."

I figured out inwardly: "In this way I can most easily and pleasantly be rid of him."

However, I reckoned wrongly. My offer was not at all to his liking.
"Thanks. I'm no beggar."

"I know it. But I'm glad to help you from the bottom of my heart
if you wish."

He thought once more.

"I am quite pressed, it's true . . . but first chance, I'll return it."

"I thank you; it's not necessary."

"I don't want it that way, I've told you I'm not a beggar. I'll take
it as a loan and return it." He fell into deep thought again. "Perhaps
we will not see each other for a long time. In that case I'll tell my sister
to repay you."

"As you wish."

We rose to our feet.

"I have been disturbing you for a long time. Pardon me! But I
did not know to whom to turn. And I thought that here I'd be most
likely to learn something about those people. You say the innkeeper's a
Protestant. Perhaps he knows some more. Perhaps he'll tell me. If he
isn't a rascal, of course. Because whom can you or dare you trust these
days?"

I sighed in relief as I lighted his way down the stairs. In strange
contrast to his agitated, almost angry entrance on coming, he continually
and courteously repeated that I pardon him for visiting him so late at
such an inopportune hour.

"That's nothing. Good-bye."

II

Midsummer, nearing noon. I was returning from the parish annex.
I crossed the yard of my neighbour Luke below the church. When suddenly, out of the grass, beneath the wide spreading branches of an apple-
tree, there rose a young man with a waving golden beard and long hair
a shade darker.

I stared in some amazement, it was an exotic vision.

"Don't you know me any more?"

The first moment I was actually embarrassed. Presently it came to
me when and where I had already seen those large blue eyes, that waving,
almost wild beard.

"Of course I know you. It's long since we've seen each other."

"Long indeed. I've been roaming."

"And now you're home again?"

"Home?" His eyes which appeared even more restless, even more
shifting, darted a gleam of burning anger. "But I have no home." And
then, as if he felt he had not really told the truth and immediately felt
ashamed, just as a well-bred child feels shame, he admitted after a moment of calm, quietly and sadly: "It's true, I'm staying with those down

in the valley. However—is that my home? Where they all hate me?"

"Perhaps you just imagine that."

"Imagine? Judge for yourself. First of all I'll tell you of my father—although the name 'father'—that man is not worthy of it, excepting that he gave me life, not another thing, and even that life is damned. And this man, day before yesterday, kicked me in my stomach so that I fell to the floor."

"Perhaps you offended him?"

"I didn't. He came home drunk. But I'll tell you the truth, this is only the second time in my life that I have seen him drunk, many years ago and the day before yesterday. Both times he stormed against me and let me feel his hatred. For, they say, truth lies in wine. Full of this, the man showed his loathing for me."

"If a grey-haired man has become drunk, may it not have been in despair over you?" I silently thought to myself, and my heart felt heavy: But aloud I asked: "And what did you do?"

"What could I have done? Kept my mouth shut. I suffered in silence. And believe me, in my soul I smouldered like a volcano. I could have killed the old man with one blow. But what good would that do me? I'd harm myself, most of all."

"Of course. I'm glad you realise that. And he's your father."

"No, he is no longer my father."

He raised his stout stick as if he wanted to strike someone and beat him to the ground. I heard him grit his teeth.

"But your sister?" I tried to touch a tender chord to soften his anger. "Wasn't she attached to you?"

"Sister? She? She hates me more than any of the others do."

"But the last time you spoke of her with affection."

"Maybe. Strange moments sometimes come over a person, without any reason he becomes soft as a little girl. But I'll tell you the truth to-day: she's a cat, a tigress! She'd tear the heart out of my breast with pleasure."

I wondered to myself: "So he has really thrust them all from him, turned them all to enemies?"

"That's strange, I thought."

"I know. That I loved her, you wanted to say." He stopped as if someone had cut his voice off and fell into deep thought. He stared past me into the mute, empty and lifeless distance with those shifting, and at the same time, dreaming eyes. "Perhaps I do really like her. She'd probably really be the only one who'd sorrow for me if I were no longer. And I—yes, I would also sorrow for her."

"See, you have at least one dear soul in this world."

He struck the earth with his staff.

"What good does that do me? When my soul is ragged. They've torn it to shreds."

"Aren't you judging a bit too harshly, my dear sir?"

"Too harshly? Too harshly when they have proclaimed me—an idiot!"

He grasped his head with both hands.

"An idiot!—Ha, ha!"

"Is this possible? Poor fellow!"

"Not only possible, dear sir, but the truth, the naked, terrible truth. . . . I worked at the bee farm several days ago. I fixed this and that, cleaned up here and there, moved and changed old hives. When I found a paper from court. And what do you suppose it said?"

He fell silent and looked at me with glaring eyes. I kept still and waited.

"It was a summons for old man Huber, to come to court in the case of one Alois Huber, proclaimed idiot. And that was I!"

He stopped as if destroyed by the terrible weight of such an indictment and conviction. His broad, soldierly chest heaved rapidly and fully, he breathed aloud, almost with a rattle, like one heavily sick with pneumonia.

"And see, so they want to make me an idiot by force and trickery. Shall I still love them after this and not hate and curse them?"

"No, no. Your nearest ones, you must not and cannot."

He laughed sadly.

"I know; a curse always returns to the curser. I know. I don't care for those who profane and speak foully. See, now, with that innkeeper, the Protestant, there was almost a friendship. But a few days ago I heard him say a filthy English phrase. I don't know whether he really knows English or whether he picked that dirt up somewhere, and himself doesn't know what it means. But I ask you this: how can I be friends with a person who says such things?"

"That pleases me, Mr. Huber, I respect you for this already."

He waved his hand in protest.

"It's not necessary. And there's no reason. For I, too, have cursed already, cursed rottenly. In my wanderings, I was hungry and thirsty plenty of times, and I went begging. Necessity forced me or I'd have dropped in the middle of the street from hunger. And what did people do when I asked them for help in God's name? First of all they called me down, then threw me a pittance. They threw it to me like a dog. In my want and misery I thanked them graciously, these noble hearts, with words of gratitude but in my heart I cursed them into hell. I know it was ugly and mean. After all they were people who had never before seen me, who weren't under the slightest obligation to me. But those people down in the valley I ought to have full right there."

He raised his mighty powerful fist toward the heavens, and threateningly shook it.

"May the Almighty strike them, if there is one. And may he strike and shatter me. For what do I live and suffer?"

My heart felt shrunken. "Is the man raving?"

"But see, you've just condemned blasphemers," I tried to pacify him.

"I did. But now I don't care. When my soul is all ragged. What do I want here in this world?"

"Calm yourself, please."

"Calm myself? I would gladly, gladly, but how?"

He covered his eyes with his hands.

"What do you intend to do now? Where are you thinking of going?"

"Where? Who knows? The bird knows where to fly at eventide. I do not. I'll drift around in the world until I drop on the street or behind some wall."

I reached in my pocket.

"I'd like to give you a trifle for your journey, if I may."

"Don't reach for money. Let it be; I owe you a crown already. Don't think I've forgotten it. But I haven't it now. Pardon me!— No, put your money back in your pocket. How can money help me when my soul is all tattered?"

"I'd gladly give it to you. But if you do not wish it. Remain in good health and may you be happier when we meet again!"

"Are you going already? Are you in a hurry? Perhaps I may accompany you to the parish house?"

"If you please."

"Perhaps you have a nice book? Reading at times quiets and consoles me somewhat. In reading one forgets."

"I'll see. I hope there'll be something."

I searched and brought one out to the front of the house where he waited, sitting on a bench buried in deep thought.

"Thank you. I love books."

"That's nice—I do too. And it's just ringing noon. Wait a moment, I'll order you a little dinner."

"No thank you! I reckon, it's not my misfortune that I have eaten too little in life, too little rather than too much."

"Do you think so? Hardly!"

"Be it as it may. That's all without any meaning. And what good would it do me if I ate even so much and so well? If my soul is sick and all ragged?"

He rose and hastily said farewell.

I stared after him in deep thought as he crossed the courtyard with long resolute strides, with raised head, seemingly young, strong, healthy and blooming.   And yet—he had been a poor broken man, a man with a wounded heart and ragged soul. . . .

My heart grew heavy as he departed midst the cottages of the village. "Where does your path lie, you poor, lonely excommunicated man? Will we ever meet again—in what way?"

But the future is silent.

CHINA

Introduction

CHINESE literature is remarkable for its antiquity, variety of subject matter and treatment, for its ennobling sentiments and lofty ideals. But while it has achieved distinction in the realms of poetry and philosophy, fiction has been comparatively neglected; and as the Chinese did not regard this latter form of literature seriously, it was only cultivated by those who had failed in their higher studies. As a rule, fiction lacked all the fine qualities embodied in the other forms, and frequently descended to "depths of objectionable pornography."

But even Chinese make exceptions to their rules. They concede that a few books might well be studied, for one reason or another. One of these is the *San Kuo Chih*, a historical romance of the 13th century, so dashing and colourful that, according to Professor Giles, it at times welcomes comparison with the works of Scott. Another work is the *Marvellous Tales, Ancient and Modern*, a collection of stories by anonymous writers, dating from the 15th century. But the book that has continued to enjoy pre-eminence, with scholars as well as lay readers, is the *Liao-Chai-Chih-I*, or *Strange Stories from a Chinese Studio*. This collection of weird, fantastic tales was written in 1679 by P'u Sung-Ling.

❊　❊　❊

THE SACRIFICE OF YANG CHIAO-AI
(Anonymous: about 15th Century)

CHIN KU CH'I KUAN, translated into English as the *Marvellous Tales, Ancient and Modern*, an anonymous collection of short stories, is one of the outstanding contributions to the field of Chinese fiction. Vivid and picturesque, they present a remarkable picture of the quaint customs of mediæval Chinese life. Some of these are fascinating tales, possessing that charm and poetic flavour which is such an integral part of anything Chinese.

The Sacrifice of Yang Chiao-Ai is reprinted, with slight modifications, from the volume *The Restitution of the Bride and Other Stories*, translated by E. Butts Howell. It is published by T. Werner Laurie, Ltd., copyright, 1926, by whose permission it is here used.

THE SACRIFICE OF YANG CHIAO-AI

IN ancient days there lived in the State of Ch'i * a man named Kuan Chung and a man named Pao Shu. The two had been fast friends from childhood, and remained constant to one another through their poverty. Subsequently Pao Shu obtained the confidence of Duke Huan of the Ch'i State, and, after rising to great eminence, he recommended Kuan Chung to be prime minister. Kuan Chung thus became greater than his friend; but the two were constant in their desire to act in all things for the good of the State, and remained true to one another in the time of plenty as they had been in the days of their distress.

A saying of Kuan Chung has remained: "Three battles have I fought and each time have I been defeated, yet Pao Shu has never attributed to me lack of courage for he knows that I had an old mother. I have served thrice as minister and three times have I been dismissed, yet Pao Shu has never attributed to me lack of ability, for he knows that it was because I was unlucky. I have thrice asked advise of Pao Shu, yet he has never attributed to me a lack of intelligence, for he knows when a situation is a difficult one. I have often engaged in buying and selling with Pao Shu and have always taken the larger share of the profits. Yet he did not think that this was due to avarice, since he knew of my poverty. My father and my mother brought me up, but Pao Shu alone has understood me."

I wish now to tell of two friends who met together by chance but became sworn brothers. Each sacrificed his life for the other, thus leaving behind him a reputation like to endure for ten thousand years.

During the Period of Spring and Autumn,† there reigned in the State of Ch'u a king who held scholars in high esteem and regarded highly the path of virtue, encouraging the learned to remain near his person and attracting to himself all those of virtuous behaviour. And scholars of all districts, hearing of this correct attitude, left their homes and went in great numbers to dwell in the State of Ch'u.

* The Ch'i State embraced the larger portion of the present province of Shantung. It arose in 1122 B.C. and lasted until 412 B.C. Duke Huan lived from 684 B.C. to 642 B.C. An attempt was made on his life by the Kuan Chung mentioned here, who shot an arrow at him, but the shaft was arrested by the buckle of the Duke's girdle. When the Duke came into power he forgave his would-be assassin and, as here stated, made him his prime minister.

† The "Period of Spring and Autumn" was about the middle of the Chou dynasty, which lasted from 1122 to 255 B.C. There is a mistake here in the original, however, as the events recorded in this story—which is more or less historical—took place after the beginning of the Han dynasty, 206 B.C. The king of the Ch'u State mentioned here was named Liu Chiao and was the younger brother of Kao Tsu, the first Han emperor. See also Note 68. The Ch'u State comprised the present Hupei province.

Now in the far north-west, among the Mountains of Piled Rocks, there was a certain worthy named Tso Po-t'ao, whose parents had died while he was in infancy but who, applying himself to his studies with assiduity beyond the common, acquired learning sufficient to enable him to assist his generation and to bring comfort to the common people. And when this man was about forty years of age, he observed how all the petty rulers under heaven were constantly warring one upon another, and how those who practised charity to others were few, while those who followed violent ways were many. On this account he did not embark upon an official career, but later, when he heard that the King of Ch'u was an upright and virtuous person and was seeking for scholars and men of correct behaviour, he put his books into a bag, and, taking leave of his neighbours, set forth for the Ch'u State and came at length to the district of Yung. It was then the depth of winter and he was overtaken by a terrible storm of sleet and snow.

Nevertheless Tso Po-t'ao walked all day through the storm, his clothes wet through to the skin, and as dusk fell he came to a village where he hoped to find a resting-place for the night. Seeing, through a grove of bamboos, a light shining from some window, he made his way hastily towards it, and encountered a low fence surrounding a grass-thatched hut. He opened the gate of the fence and knocked upon the crazy door of the hut, which was at once thrown open, and a man came out to greet him. Tso stood under the eaves and made a hasty reverence.

"I am a man from the far north-west," he said, "and my name is Tso Po-t'ao. I am on a journey to the State of Ch'u and have been overtaken by this storm. I know not where to seek a lodging, and I would pray you to allow me to rest here for the night, faring forth again when daylight comes once more. Will you grant me this favour, sir?"

On hearing this request, the man hurriedly returned Po-t'ao's salutation and asked him to enter the hut, which, as Po-t'ao saw when he was within, contained no furniture at all except a large bed, on which was a heap of books. Since his host was thus evidently a scholar, Po-t'ao was about to prostrate himself when the other begged him not to do so but to rest until a fire had been kindled and then he could dry his garments and they could talk together. So saying, he lit a fire of dried bamboo sticks and Po-t'ao dried his clothes. The host then prepared a meal of food and wine, which he set before his guest, treating him with kindness and liberality; and Po-t'ao inquired the other's name.

"Your servant is called Yang Chiao-ai," was the answer. "In my early infancy, both my parents died and I live here alone. I was ever devoted to learning and I do not till the soil. To-day, by the luck of heaven, you have come here from afar and my only shame is that I have so poor an entertainment to offer you. I pray that you will forgive my shortcomings in this matter."

"In that I am blessed with shelter in the midst of yonder storm," replied Po-t'ao, "and that I receive food and wine in addition, I am your debtor to an extent that I shall never forget."

And that night the two lay upon the bed, head to foot and foot to head, and each in turn spoke out the learning that his breast contained and neither closed his eyes in sleep. Next day at dawn the storm blew as hard as ever, and Yang therefore retained Po-t'ao in his hut and placed before him all the food he had. They swore brothership together, and Yang kotowed first to Po-t'ao, for the latter was his senior by five years. Thus they dwelt together for three days, and at last the storm died down.

"You, my worthy brother, have talent enough to fit you to become prime minister to a king," said Po-t'ao, "and sufficient resolution to adjust all human affairs. Do you not intend to register your name as a prospective official? It would be pity indeed were you to grow old among the forests and the streams."

"It is not because I am unwilling to hold office," was the reply. "I have never met with any opportunity to rise."

"But," said Po-t'ao, "this ruler of Ch'u is a man of upright character, who is now begging scholars to enter his service. If such is your intention, why do you not journey to him now with me?"

"I ask nothing better than to obey you, sir," replied Yang Chiao-ai. And, putting together a few cash, he left his hut of reeds, and the two set forth together with their faces towards the south. But after they had journeyed for two days, the blizzard swept down upon them once more, and they stayed for shelter in an inn until their stock of cash was exhausted. Then, carrying their single bundle alternately, they started once more through the storm, which ceased not at all, the wind blowing harder and ever harder. At last the sleet turned to snow alone, and fell all day.

The two came at length to Ch'i Yang, where their way joined a road through the mountains of Liang. There they met a charcoal burner, who said: "This road has no habitation upon it for a hundred *li* and more. It is a wild and mountainous region before you, where tigers and packs of wolves roam abroad. You will be well advised not to go farther."

Po-t'ao and his friend consulted together.

"The old saying has it that in life and in death all things are settled by heaven's decree," said Yang. "Since we have come thus far, we had better go on without regret."

So on they went for one more day, and at night they sheltered in an ancient grave. But their clothes were thin and the bitter wind cut them to the very bones. Next day the snow fell thicker than ever and soon stood fully a foot deep all over the mountains. The cold was more than Po-t'ao could bear.

"There is no habitation of man in front of us for the next hundred *li*," he said. "Our stock of food will soon be at an end, and we are but ill-clad to resist the cold. If one of us goes on alone to Ch'u, he may arrive there; but if both of us go on we will both either freeze or starve to death. We shall thus perish like the grass on the hillside and no one will look after our bodies. What profit will there be in that? I will therefore now take off my clothes and will give them to you to wear over your own, my worthy brother, and you can take all the food with you likewise. Push on with all your strength and resolution, for I am indeed unable to move further. Better that I die in this place, and you can go on and see the king of Ch'u, who will certainly give you employment in the affairs of state. Then you can come again to this place and find my body and bury it. The delay will make no matter."

"What reason is there in such a plan?" cried Chiao-ai. "We two, though not born of the same parents, have an affection for one another which surpasses that of real brothers. How can I go on alone in order to gain advancement?" Thus he refused, and, supporting his friend, struggled on with him.

After another ten *li*, Po-t'ao said: "The snowstorm is more severe than ever; I am unable to move further. Let us find a resting-place by the wayside."

They saw hard by an old hollow mulberry tree, which afforded some slight shelter from the storm; but within the hollow there was room only for one man. Chiao-ai helped Po-t'ao inside, and Po-t'ao begged him to strike a spark with his flint and steel and kindle a fire of dry sticks to warm them somewhat. This he did, but when he returned after his quest for fuel he found Po-t'ao stripped naked and all his clothes lying in a heap on the ground.

"What is this, my brother?" asked Chiao-ai in alarm.

"There is no other course," was the answer. "Do not spoil your own chance, but put on my clothes over your own, and go forward with the food. As for me, I will wait here for death."

"No, no," cried Chiao-ai, embracing his friend and weeping bitterly. "Let us rather both die together, for how can we be parted?"

"If we both die here of cold and hunger," replied Po-t'ao, "our bones will bleach, and who will bury them?"

"True," answered Chiao-ai, "but if only one is to go on, let me be the one to remain. Put on my clothes; do you take the food and walk on, and I will die here!"

"I have ever suffered from sickness," said the other, "while you are much younger and much stronger than I. Moreover, my learning is not equal to yours, and I am therefore less fitted than you to survive. When you meet the King of Ch'u, he will certainly give you a post of importance. My death will matter little, so delay no longer but hurry away!"

"This day you are dying of hunger in a hollow mulberry tree," wailed

Chiao-ai, "and it is I alone who benefits. That stamps me as one without virtue. I cannot do this thing!"

"Since I entered your hut on that night, after I had left the Mountains of Piled Rocks," replied Po-t'ao, "I have regarded you as an old and tried friend. I know moreover that your learning is of no common order. I therefore beseech you to go forward. That I was caught in the storm that night was a sign of heaven's will that my end was near. If you stay here and die with me, it will be imputed to me as a crime."

So saying, Po-t'ao made as if to throw himself into the swollen river that flowed before them, but Chiao-ai embraced him, weeping and attempting to wrap the clothes again round him, and thrust him back into the hollow of the tree. Po-t'ao cast him off, and again Chiao-ai tried to protect him, but as he strove he saw a change come over his friend's body; he saw that his arms and legs became white and stiffened and that he could no longer speak. Po-t'ao motioned with his hand as if once more to bid him depart, and Chiao-ai for the last time attempted to envelop his friend in his garments. But the cold had pierced his marrow, his hands and his feet were frozen, and his breathing had almost ceased.

"If I stay here, too," thought Chiao-ai, "I shall undoubtedly die also, and when I am dead, who will bury my brother?" So he knelt down in the snow and kotowed, weeping, to the other. "Your virtueless younger brother will leave you," he cried. "I pray that your spirit will protect me. If I obtain even a small post, I will bury your body with all pomp."

Po-t'ao inclined his head slightly as if in reply, and a moment afterwards breathed his last.

Chiao-ai then put on the other's clothes and took the food. He cast one last look upon his friend's body and then left, weeping bitterly.

Chiao-ai arrived at length at the Ch'u State, half-frozen and half-starved. He entered an inn to rest, and next day went into the city, where he was told that the King of Ch'u was indeed inviting learned men to help him. He heard also how he could obtain an audience, for outside the palace gates a house of reception had been erected, and the King had ordered a high minister of state called P'ei Chung to meet and entertain all scholars who came. Chiao-ai accordingly made his way thither and happened to arrive just as the minister was alighting from his chariot. He went up, therefore, and saluted him, and the minister seeing that, though the clothes of Chiao-ai were ragged, his deportment was most dignified and correct, hastily returned the salutation and asked him whence he came.

"Your humble servant is named Yang Chiao-ai," was the reply, "a man from Yung Chou. Hearing that your honourable country had a need of scholars, I have come hither to offer my services."

So P'ei Chung invited him into the house of reception and caused food and wine to be laid before him, placing also a sleeping-room at his disposal. Next day P'ei Chung came again to visit him and to put to him certain questions upon literary matters to test his knowledge. These were answered as quickly as the flowing of water and P'ei Chung was greatly pleased. He repaired to the King's presence and reported the arrival of Chiao-ai, to whom the King gave immediate audience.

"How can my country become rich, and at the same time maintain an efficient army?" asked the King; and Chiao-ai gave a prompt answer under ten headings, all bearing upon the political difficulties existing at that time. The King was overjoyed at the reply and caused a feast to be prepared for Chiao-ai at the royal table. He then conferred upon him the title and standing of a vice-minister of state, and gave him a hundred taels of fine gold and a hundred rolls of brocaded satin. At this, Chiao-ai kotowed again, but as he did so his tears broke forth and he wept bitterly.

"Why, sir," asked the King, "do you weep?"

Then Chiao-ai related the story of how Tso Po-t'ao had given to him his clothes, his food, and his life.

The story cut the King to the heart, and all his ministers expressed their sorrow and admiration.

"And what, sir, is your desire in this matter?" asked the King.

"Your servant would crave leave to return to that place," replied Chiao-ai, "and bury the body of my friend. That done, I will come again and serve your majesty."

The King then conferred upon Tso Po-t'ao the posthumous rank of vice-minister, and granted a large sum for his funeral. Thus Chiao-ai took leave of the King and hastened back to the mountains of Liang, where he searched for and found the hollow mulberry tree and in it the body of Po-t'ao. And the body appeared the same as it had been in life.

Chiao-ai ordered his men to summon the headman of the nearest village. An auspicious site was selected—a terrace on the mountain side near to a reedy pond. In front there was a mountain torrent, behind was a high mass of rocks, and all round the mountains formed a half-circle. The protection of the favouring powers of nature was complete.*

---

* The orientation of tombs, houses, cities, etc., in China is regulated by the peculiar and obscure system known as "Feng Shui," which may be defined as the science of the Unseen World of Nature with special reference to the effect of the forces thereof upon human welfare. Any long description would be out of place here, but it may be said that the forces in question proceed from a proper combination of the "Yang" and the "Yin," the male and female elements from which the universe has been evolved.

In deciding upon the site of a grave, flowing water, hills and trees are important factors, and to this is due the fact that graves in China are often such pleasant places to visit, for the need for fuel which has deforested so large an area of the country, almost invariably respects the trees planted round a grave.

The attention paid to graves is not entirely prompted by a sense of duty, for it is generally held that due observance of ceremonial in this direction will be rewarded by an increased measure of prosperity for the living members of the family.

The body was then washed in water and fragrant essences, and was clad in the robes of a minister of state. The inner and outer coffins were prepared and the body placed therein and buried, a mound being raised over the spot. A wall was built to surround the place, trees were planted all round, and thirty paces from the tomb a temple for sacrifice was erected, and in it an effigy of Tso Po-t'ao was set up. Outside they raised a memorial archway of white stone, and, near by, a small house was built for a caretaker.

When all this was at last completed, a sacrifice was performed in the temple, and at the ceremonial mourning there was no one of the dwellers around who did not come to weep, all remaining until the sacrificial ceremony was at an end.

That night Chiao-ai sat up in the temple, and, with candles lighted around him, he sighed and meditated, sleeping not at all. Of a sudden he felt a breath of cold air blowing around him. The candles flickered and then shone bright again. He looked and saw the figure of a man standing in the shadows, as though in doubt whether to advance or retire, and a sound as of distant moaning was heard.

"Who is there?" asked Chiao-ai. "And what do you here in the dead of the night?"

No answer came, so Chiao-ai rose and stepped forward to look. To his great amazement he saw the figure of Po-t'ao standing before him.

"My elder brother," he said, "you have not long departed this life, and in that you come this night to see me there must be some special cause."

"That you have not forgotten me, brother," replied the shade, "I am indeed grateful. No sooner had you received your appointment than you came hither to bury my body. I, too, thanks to you, have been granted distinction and the burial rites appropriate thereto. All that has been of the best. But I grieve to say that my grave has been placed adjacent to that of Ching K'o,* a man who while on earth plotted to assassinate the King of Ch'in. His plot failed and he was decapitated; but Kao Chienli buried his body in this place, and now the spirit of Ching K'o is fierce and terrible. Each night he comes with a drawn sword and menaces me with curses. 'You are one who died of cold and hunger,' he cries. 'How dare you have your grave built on my land, thus spoiling the favouring influences of my own tomb? If you do not remove yourself, I will

---

* Ching K'o was an adventurer of the Yen State, who was persuaded by his prince to undertake the assassination of the King of Ch'in, who afterwards became the famous First Emperor, Shih Huang-ti of the Ch'in dynasty. Ching K'o was accordingly sent on a pretended mission to tender to the State of Ch'in the humble allegiance of the Yen State, carrying with him a rolled map of Yen in which a sword was concealed. Ching K'o obtained access to the sovereign, drew out his sword, and struck his blow. He only succeeded, however, in wounding his intended victim, whom he pursued down a passage, but the king drew his own sword as he ran and, turning suddenly, killed his assailant (227 B.C.).

break open your grave and take out the coffin, casting it in pieces to the void!' Thus am I threatened, and I have come specially to tell you, and to ask you to move my burial-place elsewhere, thereby averting this calamity which threatens me."

Chiao-ai was about to question the apparition further when again he felt the gust of cold air, and the figure vanished.

He found himself back in his seat in the sacrificial temple and thought at first that he must have been dreaming. But the spirit's words were very fresh in his memory.

When day came he summoned the headman of the village and asked him if there were any other tomb near by.

"Yes, indeed, sir," was the reply. "Yonder, where the pine trees are thickest, is the tomb of Ching K'o, and his temple stands in front of it."

"That one was executed for attempting the assassination of the King of Ch'in," said Chiao-ai. "Why, then, is he buried here?"

"Kao Chien-li was a man of this place," replied the headman, "and when he heard that his friend Ching K'o had met a violent end, his body being cast away outside the capital, he stole the body and brought it to this place, burying it here. Up to the present time the spirit of Ching K'o has caused the prayers of these country people to be answered, so that they built a temple here and now sacrifice threat four times a year so as to ensure good luck."

On hearing these words, Chiao-ai bethought him of his vision, and he with his attendants repaired to the temple of Ching K'o. He pointed at the effigy of Ching K'o which was within, and cursed him, saying: "You were but a rustic of the state of Yen, and you received protection and benefit at the hands of the Prince of Yen, namely, a remarkable concubine and valuable jewels for your own use. You had not the wit to devise a means of carrying out the mission entrusted to you, for, going to the Chin-state to assassinate the king thereof, you failed and met your own end, thus confounding the fortunes of the state of Yen. Then you came to this place and are now deceiving these rustics into doing sacrifice to you. My elder brother, Tso Po-t'ao, on the other hand, was one of the most noteworthy scholars of the age, a person of pure virtue and noble incorruptibility. How can you dare to attempt to drive him out? If you persist, I will pull down your temple and dig up your grave, and I will also put an end to these sacrifices which are performed in your honour."

His threat thus ended, he went across to the tomb of Tso Po-t'ao.

"If Ching K'o comes again to-night," he prayed, "appear to me once more and tell me of it." He then went over to the temple of Tso Po-t'ao and in the evening lit the candles and waited. At dead of night he saw the figure of his friend approaching and heard him moaning in dismay.

"Your action, my worthy younger brother," said the spirit, "has only succeeded in arousing still more the wrath of Ching K'o. He has now with him a large following of retainers, which he has acquired through the devotion of the rustics of this place, in that they have burned constantly in sacrifice the paper effigies of men.* So up! my worthy younger brother, and help me by making other effigies of dry grass stuffed into garments of terrifying colours. Let each one bear weapons in his hands and let all be burned before my tomb. Thus shall I obtain the protection of these effigies and Ching K'o will no longer have power to do me harm."

The apparition vanished and Chiao-ai spent the night in causing his retainers to make the necessary effigies, dressing them up in gaudy raiment, a sword and a pike being provided for each one. Thus many tens were made and they were all drawn up in line before the tomb and burned.

Chiao-ai then prayed, saying: "If there be a cessation of this trouble, my worthy elder brother, I beseech that you will appear again and tell me of it."

He returned to the temple, and the next night he heard the wind rise, and through the storm there was a sound as of the cries of men fighting in the distance. Chiao-ai arose and looked out from the window, and there he saw the figure of Po-t'ao hurrying towards him.

"The men that you burned," cried the spirit, "have proved to be of no worth! Ching K'o has the assistance of Kao Chien-li, and in a short while my body will be cast out of my tomb. Move my grave elsewhere, I beseech you, that this calamity may be avoided."

"But how can this man dare to act thus?" exclaimed Chiao-ai. "I must myself assist you in your fight against him."

"You are one who is still living," replied the spirit, "while we are shades. Although living men may have great valour and strength, yet a great gulf separates them from the land of the departed, and no human aid can avail in such a case. It is true that I have the assistance of the grass effigies that you gave me, but these, as it turns out, are unable to do anything but shout and cannot oppose spirits so powerful as those which compass my hurt."

"It is well," replied Chiao-ai. "Go now, and I will find a way when to-morrow's light comes."

Next morning Chiao-ai went again to the temple of Ching K'o and renewed his cursing. He smashed down the image and was about to fire

* Until as late as the Han dynasty, the practice of burying live people and animals with the bodies of kings and other powerful folk in China was wide-spread, the idea being, of course, that the unfortunates so treated should continue their services to their master after life. When this practice was discontinued, representative figures made of earthenware were first used, and, later, figures of paper or straw were made and burned at the grave.

That the need for such attentions to the dead is still felt is evidenced by the fact that to-day no elaborate funeral procession (in north China, at least) is complete without a paper motor-car—generally a faithful replica of a certain inexpensive but excellent American vehicle, with number complete—which is carried round with the other paper desiderata and burned at the grave side.

the temple when the elders of the village came and besought him vehemently not to do so.

"This is the place," they cried, "whither we all come to burn our incense. If we cause offence to the spirit of Ching K'o, a grave calamity will certainly overwhelm us."

And more and more of the villagers came, and supplicated with such intensity that Chiao-ai could not bring himself to oppose their wish. So he repaired again to the temple of Po-t'ao.

There he composed a memorial of thanks to the King of Ch'u.

"Tso Po-t'ao gave up his stock of food to Your servant," the memorial ran, "and Your servant was thus able to survive to have the honour of meeting Your Sacred Majesty. Your servant has received at Your Majesty's hands honours and rank sufficient for the needs of his whole life. And in a future reincarnation, Your servant's entire existence will be devoted to repaying the obligation."

Thus he wrote with all sincerity; and he handed the memorial to his followers, telling them to deliver it upon their return. Then he went again to the tomb of Tso Po-t'ao, and, prostrating himself, he wept for a long space. At last he rose, and, turning once more to his men, he spoke as follows:

"My elder brother is being oppressed by a terrible spirit, that of the infamous Ching K'o. He has therefore no rest in his tomb. This state of things is intolerable to me and I would have burned Ching K'o's temple and devastated his grave but that I would not willingly offend these country folk. It is better for me, therefore, to die and myself become a spirit, thus acquiring ability to give my strength in helping my brother to oppose the danger that threatens him. I charge you all, then, to bury my body here on the right hand of his tomb, and so, alive or dead, we shall bear each other company. His noble act of self-sacrifice in giving to me his stock of food will in this way also be repaid.

"Return therefore to the King of Ch'u and beseech him to follow my advice, and he will always be able to protect his country from the oppression of others."

Having spoken these words, Chiao-ai drew a knife from his girdle and plunged it deep into his own throat. Thus he fell and died.

His followers tried to raise him up, but his life was spent. They quickly prepared a coffin and placed his body, clad appropriately, within it, and Yang Chiao-ai was buried by the side of his friend Tso Po-t'ao.

That night, in the second watch, a terrible storm of wind and rain arose. Lightning and thunder clove the air and in the midst of the storm there were sounds as of men in the battlefield urging each other on to kill. Full ten *li* away could this be heard.

When dawn approached, all went out to see. They found that the grave of Ching K'o had been struck by a thunderbolt and split open, and that his white bones were scattered all round in front of the grave, while the pines and cypress-trees that before stood round had all been plucked out by the roots. As they gazed, the temple itself caught fire and was burned to the ground. The headman of the village was terrified at the sight, and one and all repaired to the tomb of Tso and Yang to burn incense and to prostrate themselves.

The retainers all returned to the land of Ch'u and reported these matters to the King, who was touched to the heart by the virtuous act of Chiao-ai. He sent a high official to the spot to raise a handsome temple to his memory and he promoted Chiao-ai to yet higher rank. He granted also for the temple a wooden tablet, on which was inscribed:

"In Commemoration of a Loyal Sacrifice,"

and he erected a monument in stone, on which were recorded the exploits of the two friends, while to this day incense is burned in their memory.

Thus the divinity of Ching K'o was from that time brought to naught, and the villagers performed their seasonal sacrifices instead to the holy pair, from whom they received a never-ending series of remarkable manifestations.

* * *

P'U SUNG-LING
(1622-1679?)

VERY little is known about P'u Sung-Ling, the author of *Liao Chai*, or *Strange Stories*, a book which has enjoyed immense popularity in China. He was born in the province of Shantung; and while he passed his examinations for his bachelor's degree, he nevertheless failed in his higher studies. It is to this failure that we owe the writing of his remarkable collection of stories, so interesting for the sidelights it throws on folk lore and Chinese life in general. Aside from this, the collection is "invaluable as the expression of the most masterly style of which his language is capable."

The Donkey's Revenge is one of the stories in the volume, *Strange Stories from a Chinese Studio*, translated by Herbert A. Giles, and published by Kelly and Walsh, Shanghai, by whose permission it is here reprinted.

THE DONKEY'S REVENGE
(From *Strange Stories from a Chinese Studio*)

CHUNG CH'ING-YÜ was a scholar of some reputation, who lived in Manchuria. When he went up for his master's degree, he heard that there was a Taoist priest at the capital who would tell people's fortunes, and was very anxious to see him; and at the conclusion of the second part of the examination,* he accidentally met him at Pao-t'u-ch'üan.† The priest was over sixty years of age, and had the usual white beard flowing down over his breast. Around him stood a perfect wall of people inquiring their future fortunes, and to each the old man made a brief reply: but when he saw Chung among the crowd, he was overjoyed, and, seizing him by the hand, said, "Sir, your virtuous intentions command my esteem." He then led him up behind a screen, and asked if he did not wish to know what was to come; and when Chung replied in the affirmative, the priest informed him that his prospects were bad. "You may succeed in passing this examination," continued he, "but on returning covered with honour to your home, I fear that your mother will be no longer there." Now Chung was a very filial son; and as soon as he heard these words, his tears began to flow, and he declared that he would go back without competing any further. The priest observed that if he let this chance slip, he could never hope for success; to which Chung replied that, on the other hand, if his mother were to die he could never hope to have her back again, and that even the rank of Viceroy would not repay him for her loss. "Well," said the priest, "you and I were connected in a former existence, and I must do my best to help you now." So he took out a pill which he gave to Chung, and told him that if he sent it post-haste by some one to his mother, it would prolong her life for seven days, and thus he would be able to see her once again after the examination was over. Chung took the pill, and went off in very low spirits; but he soon reflected that the span of human life is a matter of destiny, and that every day he could spend at home would be one more day devoted to the service of his mother. Accordingly, he got ready to start at once, and, hiring a donkey, actually set out on his way back. When he had gone about half-a-mile, the donkey turned round and ran home; and when he used his whip, the animal threw itself down on the ground. Chung got into a great perspiration, and his servant recommended him to remain where he was; but this he would not hear of, and hired another donkey, which served him exactly the same trick as the other one. The sun was now sinking behind the hills, and his servant advised his master to stay and

---

* The examination consists of three bouts of three days each, during which periods the candidates remain shut up in their examination cells day and night.
† The name of a place.

finish his examination while he himself went back home before him. Chung had no alternative but to assent, and the next day he hurried through with his papers, starting immediately afterwards, and not stopping at all on the way either to eat or to sleep. All night long he went on, and arrived to find his mother in a very critical state; however, when he gave her the pill she so far recovered that he was able to go in and see her. Grasping his hand, she begged him not to weep, telling him that she had just dreamt she had been down to the Infernal Regions, where the King of Hell had informed her with a gracious smile that her record was fairly clean, and that in view of the filial piety of her son she was to have twelve years more of life. Chung was rejoiced at this, and his mother was soon restored to her former health.

Before long the news arrived that Chung had passed his examination; upon which he bade adieu to his mother, and went off to the capital, where he bribed the eunuchs of the palace to communicate with his friend the Taoist priest. The latter was very much pleased, and came out to see him, whereupon Chung prostrated himself at his feet. "Ah," said the priest, "this success of yours, and the prolongation of your good mother's life, is all a reward for your virtuous conduct. What have I done in the matter?" Chung was very much astonished that the priest should already know what had happened; however, he now inquired as to his own future. "You will never rise to high rank," replied the priest, "but you will attain the years of an octogenarian. In a former state of existence you and I were once travelling together, when you threw a stone at a dog, and accidentally killed a frog. Now that frog has reappeared in life as a donkey, and according to all principles of destiny you ought to suffer for what you did; but your filial piety has touched the Gods, a protecting star-influence has passed into your nativity sheet, and you will come to no harm. On the other hand, there is your wife; in her former state she was not as virtuous as she might have been, and her punishment in this life was to be widowed quite young; you, however, have secured the prolongation of your own term of years, and therefore I fear that before long your wife will pay the penalty of death." Chung was much grieved at hearing this; but after a while he asked the priest where his second wife to be was living. "At Chung-chou," replied the latter; "she is now fourteen years old." The priest then bade him adieu, telling him that if any mischance should befall him he was to hurry off towards the south-east. About a year after this, Chung's wife did die; and his mother then desiring him to go and visit his uncle, who was a magistrate in Kiangsi, on which journey he would have to pass through Chung-chou, it seemed like a fulfilment of the old priest's prophecy. As he went along, he came to a village on the banks of a river, where a large crowd of people was gathered together round a theatrical performance which was going on there. Chung would have passed quietly by, had not a stray donkey followed so close behind him that he turned round and hit it over the ears. This startled the donkey so much that it ran off full gallop, and knocked a rich gentleman's child, who was sitting with its nurse on the bank, right into the water, before any one of the servants could lend a hand to save it. Immediately there was a great outcry against Chung, who gave his mule the rein and dashed away, mindful of the priest's warning, towards the south-east. After riding about seven miles, he reached a mountain village, where he saw an old man standing at the door of a house, and, jumping off his mule, made him a low bow. The old man asked him in, and inquired his name and whence he came; to which Chung replied by telling him the whole adventure. "Never fear," said the old man; "you can stay here, while I send out to learn the position of affairs." By the evening his messenger had returned, and then they knew for the first time that the child belonged to a wealthy family. The old man looked grave and said, "Had it been anybody else's child, I might have helped you; as it is I can do nothing." Chung was greatly alarmed at this; however, the old man told him to remain quietly there for the night, and see what turn matters might take. Chung was overwhelmed with anxiety, and did not sleep a wink; and next morning he heard that the constables were after him, and that it was death to any one who should conceal him. The old man changed countenance at this, and went inside, leaving Chung to his own reflections; but towards the middle of the night he came and knocked at Chung's door, and, sitting down, began to ask how old his wife was. Chung replied that he was a widower; at which the old man seemed rather pleased, and declared that in such case help would be forthcoming; "for," said he, "my sister's husband has taken the vows, and become a priest,* and my sister herself has died, leaving an orphan girl who has now no home; and if you would only marry her . . ." Chung was delighted, more especially as this would be both fulfilment of the Taoist priest's prophecy and a means of extricating himself from his present difficulty; at the same time, he declared he should be sorry to implicate his future father-in-law. "Never fear about that," replied the old man; "my sister's husband is pretty skilful in the black art. He has not mixed much with the world of late; but when you are married, you can discuss the matter with my niece." So Chung married the young lady, who was sixteen years of age, and very beautiful; but whenever he looked at her he took occasion to sigh. At last she said, "I may be ugly; but you needn't be in such a hurry to let me know it;" whereupon Chung begged

---

* This interesting ceremony is performed by placing little conical pastilles on a certain number of spots, varying from three to twelve, on the candidate's head. These are then lighted and allowed to burn down into the flesh, while the surrounding parts are vigorously rubbed by attendant priests in order to lessen the pain. The whole thing lasts about twenty minutes, and is always performed on the eve of Shâkyamuni Buddha's birthday. The above was well described by Mr. S. L. Baldwin in the *Foochow Herald*.

her pardon, and said he felt himself only too lucky to have met with such a divine creature; adding that he sighed because he feared some misfortune was coming on them which would separate them forever. He then told her his story, and the young lady was very angry that she should have been drawn into such a difficulty without a word of warning. Chung fell on his knees, and said he had already consulted with her uncle, who was unable himself to do anything, much as he wished it. He continued that he was aware of her power; and then, pointing out that his alliance was not altogether beneath her, made all kinds of promises if she would only help him out of his trouble. The young lady was no longer able to refuse, but informed him that to apply to her father would entail certain disagreeable consequences, as he had retired from the world, and did not any more recognise her as his daughter. That night they did not attempt to sleep, spending the interval in padding their knees with thick felt concealed beneath their clothes; and then they got into chairs and were carried off to the hills. After journeying some distance, they were compelled by the nature of the road to alight and walk; and it was only by a great effort that Chung succeeded at last in getting his wife to the top. At the door of the temple they sat down to rest, the powder and paint on the young lady's face having all mixed with the perspiration trickling down; but when Chung began to apologise for bringing her to this pass, she replied that it was a mere trifle compared with what was to come. By-and-by, they went inside; and threading their way to the wall behind, found the young lady's father sitting in contemplation,* his eyes closed, and a servant-boy standing by with a chowry.† Everything was beautifully clean and nice, but before the dais were sharp stones scattered about as thick as the stars in the sky. The young lady did not venture to select a favourable spot; she fell on her knees at once, and Chung did likewise behind her. Then her father opened his eyes, shutting them again almost instantaneously; whereupon the young lady said, "For a long time I have not paid my respects to you. I am now married, and I have brought my husband to see you." A long time passed away, and then her father opened his eyes and said, "You're giving a great deal of trouble," immediately relapsing into silence again. There the husband and wife remained until the stones seemed to pierce into their very bones; but after a while the father cried out, "Have you brought the donkey?" His daughter replied that they had not; whereupon they were told to go and fetch it at once, which they did, not knowing what the meaning of this order was. After a few more days' kneeling, they suddenly heard that the murderer of the child had been caught and beheaded, and were just congratulating each other on the success of their scheme, when a

---

* There is a room in most Buddhist temples specially devoted to this purpose.
† The Buddhist emblem of cleanliness; generally a yak's tail and commonly used as a fly-brush.

servant came in with a stick in his hand, the top of which had been chopped off. "This stick," said the servant, "died instead of you. Bury it reverently, that the wrong done to the tree may be somewhat atoned for.* Then Chung saw that at the place where the top of the stick had been chopped off there were traces of blood; he therefore buried it with the usual ceremony, and immediately set off with his wife, and returned to his own home.

---

* Tree-worship can hardly be said to exist in China at the present day; though at a comparatively recent epoch this phase of religious sentiment must have been widely spread.

JAPAN

Introduction

THE short story form in Japan has made great strides in the Taisho Era, an important period in the cultural history of the Japanese people. During this period Russian literature, particularly of the realist and symbolist schools, exercised a tremendous influence over the younger writers.

Mrs. Yayoi Nogami is, indisputably, the foremost novelist of Japan. Not since Murasaki Shikibu, the author of the celebrated *Genji Mono-gatari*, has there been as great a woman novelist.

Other recent writers who have contributed stories of an enduring value are Mori Ogwai, at one time an army surgeon general; Nagai Kafu, a very colorful and sombre artist, and Shimazaki Toson, an exceptional lyric writer. They have each written stories that possess ineffable charm and show the reader a tender picture of Japanese life which he but seldom gets.

❋ ❋ ❋

LAFCADIO HEARN
(1850-1904)

HEARN was born at Leucadia, one of the Greek Ionian Islands. Thrown on his own resources after a rather casual education, he came to America and began work on newspapers, finally conducting a literary column on the New Orleans *Times-Democrat*. In 1891 he went to Japan and here he first found himself. He fell completely under the spell of Japan and became a naturalised Japanese, assuming the name of Yakumo Koizumi. He wrote a number of books on Japan, mostly essays, stories and folk tales.

Of a Dancing Girl is a lovely story, as delicate as some Japanese print, executed in that crystalline style that stamps Hearn as a consummate artist. It appears in his *Glimpses of Unfamiliar Japan*, copyright, 1922, by Setsu Koizumi, and published by Houghton Mifflin Company. It is reprinted here by permission of the publishers.

OF A DANCING-GIRL

NOTHING is more silent than the beginning of a Japanese banquet; and no one, except a native, who observes the opening scene could possibly imagine the tumultuous ending.

The robed guests take their places, quite noiselessly and without speech, upon the kneeling-cushions. The lacquered services are laid upon the mattings before them by maidens whose bare feet make no sound. For a while there is only smiling and flitting, as in dreams. You are not likely to hear any voices from without, as a banqueting-house is usually secluded from the street by spacious gardens. At last the master of ceremonies, host or provider, breaks the hush with the consecrated formula: "*O-somatsu degozarimasu ga!—dōzo o-hashi!*" whereat all present bow silently, take up their hashi (chopsticks), and fall to. But hashi, deftly used, cannot be heard at all. The maidens pour warm saké into the cup of each guest without making the least sound; and it is not until several dishes have been emptied, and several cups of saké absorbed, that tongues are loosened.

Then, all at once, with a little burst of laughter, a number of young girls enter, make the customary prostration of greeting, glide into the open space between the ranks of the guests, and begin to serve the wine with a grace and dexterity of which no common maid is capable. They are pretty; they are clad in very costly robes of silk; they are girdled like queens; and the beautifully dressed hair of each is decked with mock flowers, with wonderful combs and pins, and with curious ornaments of gold. They greet the stranger as if they had always known him; they jest, laugh, and utter funny little cries. These are the geisha,* or dancing-girls, hired for the banquet.

Samisen † tinkle. The dancers withdraw to a clear space at the farther end of the banqueting-hall, always vast enough to admit of many more guests than ever assemble upon common occasions. Some form the orchestra, under the direction of a woman of uncertain age; there are several samisen, and a tiny drum played by a child. Others, singly or in pairs, perform the dance. It may be swift and merry, consisting wholly of graceful posturing,—two girls dancing together with such coincidence of step and gesture as only years of training could render possible. But more frequently it is rather like acting than like what we Occidentals call dancing,—acting accompanied with extraordinary waving of sleeves and fans, and with a play of eyes and features, sweet, subtle, subdued, wholly Oriental. There are more voluptuous dances known to Geisha, but upon ordinary occasions and before refined audiences they portray

---

* The Kyōto word is *maiko*.
† Guitars of three strings.

beautiful old Japanese traditions, like the legend of the fisher Urashima, beloved by the Sea God's daughter; and at intervals they sing ancient Chinese poems, expressing a natural emotion with delicious vividness by a few exquisite words. And always they pour the wine,—that warm, pale yellow, drowsy wine which fills the veins with soft contentment, making a faint sense of ecstasy, through which, as through some poppied sleep, the commonplace becomes wondrous and blissful, and the geisha Maids of Paradise, and the world much sweeter than, in the natural order of things, it could ever possibly be.

The banquet, at first so silent, slowly changes to a merry tumult. The company break ranks, form groups; and from group to group the girls pass, laughing, prattling,—still pouring saké into the cups which are being exchanged and emptied with low bows.* Men begin to sing old samurai songs, old Chinese poems. One or two even dance. A geisha tucks her robe well up to her knees; and the samisen strike up the quick melody, *"Kompira funé-funé."* As the music plays, she begins to run lightly and swiftly in a figure of 8, and a young man, carrying a saké bottle and cup, also runs in the same figure of 8. If the two meet on a line, the one through whose error the meeting happens must drink a cup of saké. The music becomes quicker and quicker and the runners run faster and faster, for they must keep time to the melody; and the geisha wins. In another part of the room, guests and geisha are playing ken. They sing as they play, facing each other, and clap their hands, and fling out their fingers at intervals with little cries; and the samisen keep time.

> *Choito,—don-don!*
>   *Otagaidané;*
> *Choito,—don-don!*
>   *Oidemashitané;*
> *Choito,—don-don!*
>   *Shimaimashitané.*

Now, to play ken with a geisha requires a perfectly cool head, a quick eye, and much practice. Having been trained from childhood to play all kinds of ken,—and there are many,—she generally loses only for politeness, when she loses at all. The signs of the most common ken are a Man, a Fox, and a Gun. If the geisha make the sign of the Gun, you must instantly, and in exact time to the music, make the sign of the Fox, who cannot use the Gun. For if you make the sign of the Man, then she will answer with the sign of the Fox, who can deceive the Man, and you lose. And if she make the sign of the Fox first, then you should make the sign of the Gun, by which the Fox can be killed. But all the while you must watch her bright eyes and supple hands. These are

---

* It is sometimes customary for guests to exchange cups, after duly rinsing them. It is always a compliment to ask for your friend's cup.

pretty; and if you suffer yourself, just for one fraction of a second, to think how pretty they are, you are bewitched and vanquished.

Notwithstanding all this apparent comradeship, a certain rigid decorum between guest and geisha is invariably preserved at a Japanese banquet. However flushed with wine a guest may have become, you will never see him attempt to caress a girl; he never forgets that she appears at the festivities only as a human flower, to be looked at, not to be touched. The familiarity which foreign tourists in Japan frequently permit themselves with geisha or with waiter-girls, though endured with smiling patience, is really much disliked, and considered by native observers an evidence of extreme vulgarity.

For a time the merriment grows; but as midnight draws near, the guests begin to slip away, one by one, unnoticed. Then the din gradually dies down, the music stops; and at last the geisha, having escorted the latest of the feasters to the door, with laughing cries of *Sayōnara*, can sit down alone to break their long fast in the deserted hall.

Such is the geisha's rôle. But what is the mystery of her? What are her thoughts, her emotions, her secret self? What is her veritable existence beyond the night circle of the banquet lights, far from the illusion formed around her by the mist of wine? Is she always as mischievous as she seems while her voice ripples out with mocking sweetness the words of the ancient song?

> *Kimi to neyaru ka, go sengoku toruka?*
> *Nanno gosengoku kimi to neyo?* *

Or might we think her capable of keeping that passionate promise she utters so deliciously?

> *Omae shindara tera ewa yaranu!*
> *Yaete konishite sake de nomu.* †

"Why, as for that," a friend tells me, "there was O-Kama of Ōsaka who realised the song only last year. For she, having collected from the funeral pile the ashes of her lover, mingled them with saké, and at a

---

* "Once more to rest beside her, or keep five thousand koku?
What care I for koku? Let me be with her!"

There lived in ancient times a hatamoto called Fuji-eda Geki, a vassal of the Shōgun. He had an income of five thousand koku of rice,—a great income in those days. But he fell in love with an inmate of the Yoshiwara, named Ayaginu, and wished to marry her. When his master bade the vassal choose between his fortune and his passion, the lovers fled secretly to a farmer's house, and there committed suicide together. And the above song was made about them. It is still sung.

† "Dear, shouldst thou die, grave shall hold thee never!
I thy body's ashes, mixed with wine, will drink."

banquet drank them, in the presence of many guests." In the presence of many guests! Alas for romance!

Always in the dwelling which a band of geisha occupy there is a strange image placed in the alcove. Sometimes it is of clay, rarely of gold, most commonly of porcelain. It is reverenced: offerings are made to it, sweetmeats and rice bread and wine; incense smoulders in front of it, and a lamp is burned before it. It is the image of a kitten erect, one paw outstretched as if inviting,—whence its name, "the Beckoning Kitten." * It is the *genius loci:* it brings good-fortune, the patronage of the rich, the favor of banquet-givers. Now, they who know the soul of the geisha aver that the semblance of the image is the semblance of herself,— playful and pretty, soft and young, lithe and caressing, and cruel as a devouring fire.

Worse, also, than this they have said of her: that in her shadow treads the God of Poverty, and that the Fox-women are her sisters; that she is the ruin of youth, the waster of fortunes, the destroyer of families; that she knows love only as the source of the follies which are her gain, and grows rich upon the substance of men whose graves she has made; that she is the most consummate of pretty hypocrites, the most dangerous of schemers, the most insatiable of mercenaries, the most pitiless of mistresses. This cannot all be true. Yet this much is true,—that, like the kitten, the geisha is by profession a creature of prey. There are many really lovable kittens. Even so there must be really delightful dancing-girls.

The geisha is only what she has been made in answer to foolish human desire for the illusion of love mixed with youth and grace, but without regrets or responsibilities: wherefore she has been taught, besides ken, to play at hearts. Now, the eternal law is that people may play with impunity at any game in this unhappy world except three, which are called Life, Love, and Death. Those the gods have reserved to themselves, because nobody else can learn to play them without doing mischief. Therefore, to play with a geisha any game much more serious than ken, or at least *go,* is displeasing to the gods.

The girl begins her career as a slave, a pretty child bought from miserably poor parents under a contract, according to which her services may be claimed by the purchasers for eighteen, twenty, or even twenty-five years. She is fed, clothed, and trained in a house occupied only by geisha; and she passes the rest of her childhood under severe discipline. She is taught etiquette, grace, polite speech; she has daily lessons in dancing; and she is obliged to learn by heart a multitude of songs with their airs. Also she must learn games, the service of banquets and weddings, the art of dressing and looking beautiful. Whatever physical gifts she may have are carefully cultivated. Afterwards she is taught to handle

* Maneki-Neko.

musical instruments: first, the little drum (*tsudzumi*), which cannot be sounded at all without considerable practice; then she learns to play the samisen a little, with a plectrum of tortoise-shell or ivory. At eight or nine years of age she attends banquets, chiefly as a drum-player. She is then the most charming little creature imaginable, and already knows how to fill your wine-cup exactly full, with a single toss of the bottle and without spilling a drop, between two taps of her drum.

Thereafter her discipline becomes more cruel. Her voice may be flexible enough, but lacks the requisite strength. In the iciest hours of winter nights, she must ascend to the roof of her dwelling-house, and there sing and play till the blood oozes from her fingers and the voice dies in her throat. The desired result is an atrocious cold. After a period of hoarse whispering, her voice changes its tone and strengthens. She is ready to become a public singer and dancer.

In this capacity she usually makes her first appearance at the age of twelve or thirteen. If pretty and skilful, her services will be much in demand, and her time paid for at the rate of twenty to twenty-five sen per hour. Then only do her purchasers begin to reimburse themselves for the time, expense, and trouble of her training; and they are not apt to be generous. For many years more all that she earns must pass into their hands. She can own nothing, not even her clothes.

At seventeen or eighteen she has made her artistic reputation. She has been at many hundreds of entertainments, and knows by sight all the important personages of her city, the character of each, the history of all. Her life has been chiefly a night life; rarely has she seen the sun rise since she became a dancer. She has learned to drink wine without ever losing her head, and to fast for seven or eight hours without ever feeling the worse. She has had many lovers. To a certain extent she is free to smile upon whom she pleases; but she has been well taught, above all else to use her power of charm for her own advantage. She hopes to find Somebody able and willing to buy her freedom,—which Somebody would almost certainly thereafter discover many new and excellent meanings in those Buddhist texts that tell about the foolishness of love and the impermanency of all human relationships.

At this point of her career we may leave the geisha: thereafter her story is apt to prove unpleasant, unless she die young. Should that happen, she will have the obsequies of her class, and her memory will be preserved by divers curious rites.

Some time, perhaps, while wandering through Japanese streets at night, you hear sounds of music, a tinkling of samisen floating through the great gateway of a Buddhist temple, together with shrill voices of singing-girls; which may seem to you a strange happening. And the deep court is thronged with people looking and listening. Then, making your way through the press to the temple steps, you see two geisha seated upon the matting within, playing and singing, and a third dancing before a little table. Upon the table is an ihai, or mortuary tablet; in front of the tablet burns a little lamp, and incense in a cup of bronze; a small repast has been placed there, fruits and dainties,—such a repast as, upon festival occasions, it is the custom to offer to the dead. You learn that the kaimyō upon the tablet is that of a geisha; and that the comrades of the dead girl assemble in the temple on certain days to gladden her spirit with songs and dances. Then whosoever pleases may attend the ceremony free of charge.

But the dancing-girls of ancient times were not as the geisha of today. Some of them were called shirabyōshi; and their hearts were not extremely hard. They were beautiful; they wore queerly shaped caps bedecked with gold; they were clad in splendid attire, and danced with swords in the dwellings of princes. And there is an old story about one of them which I think it worth while to tell.

I

It was formerly, and indeed still is, a custom with young Japanese artists to travel on foot through various parts of the empire, in order to see and sketch the most celebrated scenery as well as to study famous art objects preserved in Buddhist temples, many of which occupy sites of extraordinary picturesqueness. It is to such wanderings, chiefly, that we owe the existence of those beautiful books of landscape views and life studies which are now so curious and rare, and which teach better than aught else that only the Japanese can paint Japanese scenery. After you have become acquainted with their methods of interpreting their own nature, foreign attempts in the same line will seem to you strangely flat and soulless. The foreign artist will give you realistic reflections of what he sees; but he will give you nothing more. The Japanese artist gives you that which he feels,—the mood of a season, the precise sensation of an hour and place; his work is qualified by a power of suggestiveness rarely found in the art of the West. The Occidental painter renders minute detail; he satisfies the imagination he evokes. But his Oriental brother either suppresses or idealises detail,—steeps his distances in mist, bands his landscapes with cloud, makes of his experience a memory in which only the strange and the beautiful survive, with their sensations. He surpasses imagination, excites it, leaves it hungry with the hunger of charm perceived in glimpses only. Nevertheless, in such glimpses he is able to convey the feeling of a time, the character of a place, after a fashion that seems magical. He is a painter of recollections and of sensations rather than of clear-cut realities; and in this lies the secret of his amazing power,—a power not to be appreciated by those who have never witnessed the scenes of his inspiration. He is above all things impersonal. His human figures are devoid of all individuality; yet they have inimitable merit as types embodying the characteristics of a class: the childish curiosity of the peasant, the shyness of the maiden, the fascination of the jorō, the self-consciousness of the samurai, the funny, placid prettiness of the child, the resigned gentleness of age. Travel and observation were the influences which developed this art; it was never a growth of studios.

A great many years ago, a young art student was travelling on foot from Kyōto to Yedo, over the mountains. The roads then were few and bad, and travel was so difficult compared to what it is now that a proverb was current, *Kawai ko wa tabi wo sasé* (A pet child should be made to travel). But the land was what it is to-day. There were the same forests of cedar and of pine, the same groves of bamboo, the same peaked villages with roofs of thatch, the same terraced rice-fields dotted with the great yellow straw hats of peasants bending in the slime. From the wayside, the same statues of Jizō smiled upon the same pilgrim figures passing to the same temples; and then, as now, of summer days, one might see naked brown children laughing in all the shallow rivers, and all the rivers laughing to the sun.

The young art student, however, was no *kawai ko:* he had already travelled a great deal, was inured to hard fare and rough lodging, and accustomed to make the best of every situation. But upon this journey he found himself, one evening after sunset, in a region where it seemed possible to obtain neither fare nor lodging of any sort,—out of sight of cultivated land. While attempting a short cut over a range to reach some village, he had lost his way.

There was no moon, and pine shadows made blackness all around him. The district into which he had wandered seemed utterly wild; there were no sounds but the humming of the wind in the pine-needles, and an infinite tinkling of bell-insects. He stumbled on, hoping to gain some river bank, which he could follow to a settlement. At last a stream abruptly crossed his way; but it proved to be a swift torrent pouring into a gorge between precipices. Obliged to retrace his steps, he resolved to climb to the nearest summit, whence he might be able to discern some sign of human life; but on reaching it he could see about him only a heaping of hills.

He had almost resigned himself to passing the night under the stars, when he perceived, at some distance down the farther slope of the hill he had ascended, a single thin yellow ray of light, evidently issuing from some dwelling. He made his way towards it, and soon discerned a small cottage, apparently a peasant's home. The light he had seen still streamed from it, through a chink in the closed storm-doors. He hastened forward, and knocked at the entrance.

II

Not until he had knocked and called several times did he hear any stir within; then a woman's voice asked what was wanted. The voice was remarkably sweet, and the speech of the unseen questioner surprised him, for she spoke in the cultivated idiom of the capital. He responded that he was a student, who had lost his way in the mountains; that he wished, if possible, to obtain food and lodging for the night; and that if this could not be given, he would feel very grateful for information how to reach the nearest village,—adding that he had means enough to pay for the services of a guide. The voice, in return, asked several other questions, indicating extreme surprise that any one could have reached the dwelling from the direction he had taken. But his answers evidently allayed suspicion, for the inmate exclaimed: "I will come in a moment. It would be difficult for you to reach any village to-night; and the path is dangerous."

After a brief delay the storm-doors were pushed open, and a woman appeared with a paper lantern, which she so held as to illuminate the stranger's face, while her own remained in shadow. She scrutinised him in silence, then said briefly, "Wait; I will bring water." She fetched a wash-basin, set it upon the doorstep, and offered the guest a towel. He removed his sandals, washed from his feet the dust of travel, and was shown into a neat room which appeared to occupy the whole interior, except a small boarded space at the rear, used as a kitchen. A cotton zabuton was laid for him to kneel upon, and a brazier set before him.

It was only then that he had a good opportunity of observing his hostess, and he was startled by the delicacy and beauty of her features. She might have been three or four years older than he, but was still in the bloom of youth. Certainly she was not a peasant girl. In the same singularly sweet voice she said to him: "I am now alone, and I never receive guests here. But I am sure it would be dangerous for you to travel farther to-night. There are some peasants in the neighbourhood, but you cannot find your way to them in the dark without a guide. So I can let you stay here until morning. You will not be comfortable, but I can give you a bed. And I suppose you are hungry. There is only some shōjin-ryōri,*—not at all good, but you are welcome to it."

The traveller was quite hungry, and only too glad of the offer. The young woman kindled a little fire, prepared a few dishes in silence,— stewed leaves of na, some aburagé, some kampyō, and a bowl of coarse rice,—and quickly set the meal before him, apologising for its quality. But during his repast she spoke scarcely at all, and her reserved manner embarrassed him. As she answered the few questions he ventured upon

---

* Buddhist food, containing no animal substances. Some kinds of shōjin-ryōri are quite appetizing.

merely by a bow or by a solitary word, he soon refrained from attempting to press the conversation.

Meanwhile, he had observed that the small house was spotlessly clean, and the utensils in which his food was served were immaculate. The few cheap objects in the apartment were pretty. The fusuma of the oshiire and zendana * were of white paper only, but had been decorated with large Chinese characters exquisitely written, characters suggesting, according to the law of such decoration, the favourite themes of the poet and artist: Spring Flowers, Mountain and Sea, Summer Rain, Sky and Stars, Autumn Moon, River Water, Autumn Breeze. At one side of the apartment stood a kind of low altar, supporting a butsudan, whose tiny lacquered doors, left open, showed a mortuary tablet within, before which a lamp was burning between offerings of wild-flowers. And above this household shrine hung a picture of more than common merit, representing the Goddess of Mercy, wearing the moon for her aureole.

As the student ended his little meal the young woman observed: "I cannot offer you a good bed, and there is only a paper mosquito-curtain. The bed and the curtain are mine, but to-night I have many things to do, and shall have no time to sleep; therefore I beg you will try to rest, though I am not able to make you comfortable."

He then understood that she was, for some strange reason, entirely alone, and was voluntarily giving up her only bed to him upon a kindly pretext. He protested honestly against such an excess of hospitality, and assured her that he could sleep quite soundly anywhere on the floor, and did not care about the mosquitoes. But she replied, in the tone of an elder sister, that he must obey her wishes. She really had something to do, and she desired to be left by herself as soon as possible; therefore, understanding him to be a gentleman, she expected he would suffer her to arrange matters in her own way. To this he could offer no objection, as there was but one room. She spread the mattress on the floor, fetched a wooden pillow, suspended her paper mosquito-curtain, unfolded a large screen on the side of the bed toward the butsudan, and then bade him good-night in a manner that assured him she wished him to retire at once; which he did, not without some reluctance at the thought of all the trouble he had unintentionally caused her.

III

Unwilling as the young traveller felt to accept a kindness involving the sacrifice of another's repose, he found the bed more than comfortable. He was very tired, and had scarcely laid his head upon the wooden pillow before he forgot everything in sleep.

Yet only a little while seemed to have passed when he was awakened

---

* The term *oshiire* and *zendana* might be partly rendered by "wardrobe" and "cupboard." The *fusuma* are sliding screens serving as doors.

by a singular sound. It was certainly the sound of feet, but not of feet walking softly. It seemed rather the sound of feet in rapid motion, as of excitement. Then it occurred to him that robbers might have entered the house. As for himself, he had little to fear because he had little to lose. His anxiety was chiefly for the kind person who had granted him hospitality. Into each side of the paper mosquito-curtain a small square of brown netting had been fitted, like a little window, and through one of these he tried to look; but the high screen stood between him and whatever was going on. He thought of calling, but this impulse was checked by the reflection that in case of real danger it would be both useless and imprudent to announce his presence before understanding the situation. The sounds which had made him uneasy continued, and were more and more mysterious. He resolved to prepare for the worst, and to risk his life, if necessary, in order to defend his young hostess. Hastily girding up his robes, he slipped noiselessly from under the paper curtain, crept to the edge of the screen, and peeped. What he saw astonished him extremely.

Before her illuminated butsudan the young woman, magnificently attired, was dancing all alone. Her costume he recognised as that of a shirabyōshi, though much richer than any he had ever seen worn by a professional dancer. Marvellously enhanced by it, her beauty, in that lonely time and place, appeared almost supernatural; but what seemed to him even more wonderful was her dancing. For an instant he felt the tingling of a weird doubt. The superstitions of peasants, the legends of Fox-women, flashed before his imagination; but the sight of the Buddhist shrine, of the sacred picture, dissipated the fancy, and shamed him for the folly of it. At the same time he became conscious that he was watching something she had not wished him to see, and that it was his duty, as her guest, to return at once behind the screen; but the spectacle fascinated him. He felt, with not less pleasure than amazement, that he was looking upon the most accomplished dancer he had ever seen; and the more he watched, the more the witchery of her grace grew upon him. Suddenly she paused, panting, unfastened her girdle, turned in the act of doffing her upper robe, and started violently as her eyes encountered his own.

He tried at once to excuse himself to her. He said he had been suddenly awakened by the sound of quick feet, which sound had caused him some uneasiness, chiefly for her sake, because of the lateness of the hour and the lonesomeness of the place. Then he confessed his surprise at what he had seen, and spoke of the manner in which it had attracted him. "I beg you," he continued, "to forgive my curiosity, for I cannot help wondering who you are, and how you could have become so marvellous a dancer. All the dancers of Saikyō I have seen, yet I have never seen among the most celebrated of them a girl who could dance like you; and once I had begun to watch you, I could not take away my eyes."

At first she had seemed angry, but before he had ceased to speak her expression changed. She smiled, and seated herself before him. "No, I am not angry with you," she said. "I am only sorry that you should have watched me, for I am sure you must have thought me mad when you saw me dancing that way, all by myself; and now I must tell you the meaning of what you have seen."

So she related her story. Her name he remembered to have heard as a boy,—her professional name, the name of the most famous of shira-byōshi, the darling of the capital, who, in the zenith of her fame and beauty, had suddenly vanished from public life, none knew whither or why. She had fled from wealth and fortune with a youth who loved her. He was poor, but between them they possessed enough means to live simply and happily in the country. They built a little house in the mountains, and there for a number of years they existed only for each other. He adored her. One of his greatest pleasures was to see her dance. Each evening he would play some favourite melody, and she would dance for him. But one long cold winter he fell sick, and, in spite of her tender nursing, died. Since then she had lived alone with the memory of him, performing all those small rites of love and homage with which the dead are honoured. Daily before his tablet she placed the customary offerings, and nightly danced to please him, as of old. And this was the explanation of what the young traveller had seen. It was indeed rude, she continued, to have awakened her tired guest; but she had waited until she thought him soundly sleeping, and then she had tried to dance very, very lightly. So she hoped he would pardon her for having unintentionally disturbed him.

When she had told him all, she made ready a little tea, which they drank together; then she entreated him so plaintively to please her by trying to sleep again that he found himself obliged to go back, with many sincere apologies, under the paper mosquito-curtain.

He slept well and long; the sun was high before he woke. On rising, he found prepared for him a meal as simple as that of the evening before, and he felt hungry. Nevertheless he ate sparingly, fearing the young woman might have stinted herself in thus providing for him; and then he made ready to depart. But when he wanted to pay her for what he had received, and for all the trouble he had given her, she refused to take anything from him, saying: "What I had to give was not worth money, and what I did was done for kindness alone. So I pray that you will try to forget the discomfort you suffered here, and will remember only the good-will of one who had nothing to offer."

He still endeavoured to induce her to accept something; but at last, finding that his insistence only gave her pain, he took leave of her with such words as he could find to express his gratitude, and not without a secret regret, for her beauty and her gentleness had charmed him more than he would have liked to acknowledge to any but herself. She indicated to him the path to follow, and watched him descend the mountain until he had passed from sight. An hour later he found himself upon a highway with which he was familiar. Then a sudden remorse touched him: he had forgotten to tell her his name: For an instant he hesitated; then said to himself, "What matters it? I shall be always poor." And he went on.

IV

Many years passed by, and many fashions with them; and the painter became old. But ere becoming old he had become famous. Princes, charmed by the wonder of his work, had vied with one another in giving him patronage; so that he grew rich, and possessed a beautiful dwelling of his own in the City of the Emperors. Young artists from many provinces were his pupils, and lived with him, serving him in all things while receiving his instruction; and his name was known throughout the land.

Now, there came one day to his house an old woman, who asked to speak with him. The servants, seeing that she was meanly dressed and of miserable appearance, took her to be some common beggar, and questioned her roughly. But when she answered: "I can tell to no one except your master why I have come," they believed her mad, and deceived her, saying: "He is not now in Saikyō, nor do we know how soon he will return."

But the old woman came again and again,—day after day, and week after week,—each time being told something that was not true: "To-day he is ill," or, "To-day he is very busy," or, "To-day he has much company, and therefore cannot see you." Nevertheless she continued to come, always at the same hour each day, and always carrying a bundle wrapped in a ragged covering; and the servants at last thought it were best to speak to their master about her. So they said to him: "There is a very old woman, whom we take to be a beggar, at our lord's gate. More than fifty times she has come, asking to see our lord, and refusing to tell us why,—saying that she can tell her wishes only to our lord. And we have tried to discourage her, as she seemed to be mad; but she always comes. Therefore we have presumed to mention the matter to our lord, in order that we may learn what is to be done hereafter."

Then the Master answered sharply: "Why did none of you tell me of this before?" and went out himself to the gate, and spoke very kindly to the woman, remembering how he also had been poor. And he asked her if she desired alms of him.

But she answered that she had no need of money or of food, and only desired that he would paint for her a picture. He wondered at her wish, and bade her enter his house. So she entered into the vestibule, and, kneeling there, began to untie the knots of the bundle she had brought with her. When she had unwrapped it, the painter perceived curious rich quaint gar-

ments of silk broidered with designs in gold, yet much frayed and discoloured by wear and time,—the wreck of a wonderful costume of other
days, the attire of a shirabyōshi.

While the old woman unfolded the garments one by one, and tried to
smooth them with her trembling fingers, a memory stirred in the Master's
brain, thrilled dimly there a little space, then suddenly lighted up. In
that soft shock of recollection, he saw again the lonely mountain dwelling
in which he had received unremunerated hospitality,—the tiny room prepared for his rest, the paper mosquito-curtain, the faintly burning lamp
before the Buddhist shrine, the strange beauty of one dancing there alone
in the dead of the night. Then, to the astonishment of the aged visitor,
he, the favoured of princes, bowed low before her, and said: "Pardon
my rudeness in having forgotten your face for a moment; but it is more
than forty years since we last saw each other. Now I remember you well.
You received me once at your house. You gave up to me the only bed
you had. I saw you dance, and you told me all your story. You had been
a shirabyōshi, and I have not forgotten your name."

He uttered it. She, astonished and confused, could not at first reply
to him, for she was old and had suffered much, and her memory had
begun to fail. But he spoke more and more kindly to her, and reminded
her of many things which she had told him, and described to her the
house in which she had lived alone, so that at last she also remembered;
and she answered, with tears of pleasure: "Surely the Divine One who
looketh down above the sound of prayer has guided me. But when my
unworthy home was honoured by the visit of the august Master, I was not
as I now am. And it seems to me like a miracle of our Lord Buddha that
the Master should remember me."

Then she related the rest of her simple story. In the course of years,
she had become, through poverty, obliged to part with her little house;
and in her old age she had returned alone to the great city, in which her
name had long been forgotten. It had caused her much pain to lose her
home; but it grieved her still more that, in becoming weak and old, she
could no longer dance each evening before the butsudan, to please the
spirit of the dead whom she had loved. Therefore she wanted to have a
picture of herself painted, in the costume and the attitude of the dance,
that she might suspend it before the butsudan. For this she had prayed
earnestly to Kwannon. And she had sought out the Master because of his
fame as a painter, since she desired, for the sake of the dead, no common
work, but a picture painted with great skill; and she had brought her
dancing attire, hoping that the Master might be willing to paint her
therein.

He listened to all with a kindly smile, and answered her: "It will
be only a pleasure for me to paint the picture which you want. This day
I have something to finish which cannot be delayed. But if you will

come here to-morrow, I will paint you exactly as you wish, and as well as I am able."

But she said: "I have not yet told to the Master the thing which most troubles me. And it is this,—that I can offer in return for so great a favour nothing except these dancer's clothes; and they are of no value in themselves, though they were costly once. Still, I hoped the Master might be willing to take them, seeing they have become curious; for there are no more shirabyōshi, and the maiko of these times wear no such robes."

"Of that matter," the good painter exclaimed, "you must not think at all! No; I am glad to have this present chance of paying a small part of my old debt to you. So to-morrow I will paint you just as you wish."

She prostrated herself thrice before him, uttering thanks, and then said, "Let my lord pardon, though I have yet something more to say. For I do not wish that he should paint me as I now am, but only as I used to be when I was young, as my lord knew me."

He said: "I remember well. You were very beautiful."

Her wrinkled features lighted up with pleasure, as she bowed her thanks to him for those words. And she exclaimed: "Then indeed all that I had hoped and prayed for may be done! Since he thus remembers my poor youth, I beseech my lord to paint me, not as I now am, but as he saw me when I was not old and, as it has pleased him generously to say, not uncomely. O Master, make me young again! Make me seem beautiful that I may seem beautiful to the soul of him for whose sake I, the unworthy, beseech this! He will see the Master's work: he will forgive me that I can no longer dance."

Once more the Master bade her have no anxiety, and said: "Come to-morrow, and I will paint you. I will make a picture of you just as you were when I saw you, a young and beautiful shirabyōshi, and I will paint it as carefully and as skilfully as if I were painting the picture of the richest person in the land. Never doubt, but come."

V

So the aged dancer came at the appointed hour; and upon soft white silk the artist painted a picture of her. Yet not a picture of her as she seemed to the Master's pupils, but the memory of her as she had been in the days of her youth, bright-eyed as a bird, lithe as a bamboo, dazzling as a tennin * in her raiment of silk and gold. Under the magic of the Master's brush, the vanished grace returned, the faded beauty bloomed again. When the kakemono had been finished, and stamped with his seal, he mounted it richly upon silken cloth, and fixed to it rollers of cedar with ivory weights, and a silken cord by which to hang it; and he placed it in a little box of white wood, and so gave it to the shirabyōshi.

---

* *Tennin,* a "Sky-Maiden," a Buddhist angel.

And he would also have presented her with a gift of money. But though he pressed her earnestly, he could not persuade her to accept his help. "Nay," she made answer, with tears, "indeed I need nothing. The picture only I desired. For that I prayed; and now my prayer has been answered, and I know that I never can wish for anything more in this life, and that if I come to die thus desiring nothing, to enter upon the way of Buddha will not be difficult. One thought alone causes me sorrow,—that I have nothing to offer to the Master but this dancer's apparel, which is indeed of little worth, though I beseech him to accept it; and I will pray each day that his future life may be a life of happiness, because of the wondrous kindness which he has done me."

"Nay," protested the painter, smiling, "what is it that I have done? Truly nothing. As for the dancer's garments, I will accept them, if that can make you more happy. They will bring back pleasant memories of the night I passed in your home, when you gave up all your comforts for my unworthy sake, and yet would not suffer me to pay for that which I used; and for that kindness I hold myself to be still in your debt. But now tell me where you live, so that I may see the picture in its place." For he had resolved within himself to place her beyond the reach of want.

But she excused herself with humble words, and would not tell him, saying that her dwelling-place was too mean to be looked upon by such as he; and then, with many prostrations, she thanked him again and again, and went away with her treasure, weeping for joy.

Then the Master called to one of his pupils: "Go quickly after that woman, but so that she does not know herself followed, and bring me word where she lives." So the young man followed her, unperceived.

He remained long away, and when he returned he laughed in the manner of one obliged to say something which it is not pleasant to hear, and he said: "That woman, O Master, I followed out of the city to the dry bed of the river, near to the place where criminals are executed. There I saw a hut such as an Eta might dwell in, and that is where she lives. A forsaken and filthy place, O Master!"

"Nevertheless," the painter replied, "to-morrow you will take me to that forsaken and filthy place. What time I live she shall not suffer for food or clothing or comfort."

And as all wondered, he told them the story of the shirabyōshi, after which it did not seem to them that his words were strange.

VI

On the morning of the day following, an hour after sunrise, the Master and his pupil took their way to the dry bed of the river, beyond the verge of the city, to the place of outcasts.

The entrance of the little dwelling they found closed by a single shutter, upon which the Master tapped many times without evoking a response. Then, finding the shutter unfastened from within, he pushed it slightly aside, and called through the aperture. None replied, and he decided to enter. Simultaneously, with extraordinary vividness, there thrilled back to him the sensation of the very instant when, as a tired lad, he stood pleading for admission to the lonesome little cottage among the hills.

Entering alone softly, he perceived that the woman was lying there, wrapped in a single thin and tattered futon, seemingly asleep. On a rude shelf he recognised the butsudan of forty years before, with its tablet, and now, as then, a tiny lamp was burning in front of the kaimyō. The kakemono of the Goddess of Mercy with her lunar aureole was gone, but on the wall facing the shrine he beheld his own dainty gift suspended, and an ofuda beneath it,—an ofuda of Hito-koto-Kwannon,*—that Kwannon unto whom it is unlawful to pray more than once, as she answers but a single prayer. There was little else in the desolate dwelling; only the garments of a female pilgrim, and a mendicant's staff and bowl.

But the Master did not pause to look at these things, for he desired to awaken and to gladden the sleeper, and he called her name cheerily twice and thrice.

Then suddenly he saw that she was dead, and he wondered while he gazed upon her face, for it seemed less old. A vague sweetness, like a ghost of youth, had returned to it; the lines of sorrow had been softened, the wrinkles strangely smoothed, by the touch of a phantom Master mightier than he.

* * *

SHIMAZAKI TOSON
(1871-   )

SHIMAZAKI TOSON first achieved eminence as a lyric poet. He suffered, along with other writers, a period of disillusionment in consequence of the Russo-Japanese war. Thereafter Mr. Shimazaki turned to naturalism and produced some novels and short stories which have established him as an artist of great charm.

Tsugaru Strait, translated by Torao Taketomo, is reprinted by permission of the publisher from the volume, *Paulownia*, copyright, 1918, by Duffield & Co., New York.

* Her shrine is at Nara,—not far from the temple of the giant Buddha.

TSUGARU STRAIT

AS my wife is hard of hearing, she cannot understand what I say unless I speak close to her ear, in rather a loud voice.

Though the time to go on board the ship was approaching, she was still leaning on the window at the first floor of the inn, and would not even prepare to start. Vacantly she was contemplating the sight of the dark green sea, the seamews flying in groups, and the *Surugamaru*, the regular liner, which was about to start for Hakodate, ready to take us two on board. At such times, she is always weeping, calling to her mind our departed son. This I noticed by the sight of her back. I stroked her on the shoulder and urged her to start.

"Come. Get ready, get ready!"

The day was perfect for a voyage. It was the time when the regular steamship lines were interrupted by the rumour that the Russian ships from Vladivostock, which not long before had passed through Tsugaru Strait, were appearing now and then along the Pacific coast. During five or six days only was this line between Awomori and Hakodate in operation. As it was disappointing to my wife and myself to go home after having come so far, and as the Russian ships were said to be cruising on the open sea in the vicinity of Oshima and the Izu Islands—the very night before we had heard that the fleet of the enemy was sunk, the announcement of which some of the newspapers printed in an extra—we left the inn, not worrying about the ships, trusting somewhat to the truth of the statements in the extra.

There were soldiers in the streets in sober khaki-coloured summer uniform, watching us hurrying toward the pier. As my wife was walking in meditation, her slowness somewhat irritated me. She suddenly stopped and this is what she said:

"Ah! Ah! If only Ryunosuke were living I would bring him with us to a place like this and give him pleasure."

She sighed. Ryunosuke was the name of our son. I did not know what to do and, putting my mouth close to her ear, as if to scold her, I said:

"You will try me if you keep constantly calling him to mind!"

Instantly, my wife flushed.

"Oh! You are so cruel! I am living only because of the consolation of his memory. If you wish me not to speak of him, bid me die."

My wife is tiresome, for she is just a baby, and I am only a nurse who is taking care of this infant of forty years.

"Tut! tut! How could you say such a thing in the street? Look, everybody is turning and laughing at us."

I spoke thus, but the words were not heard by my wife. Ah!

Nothing is so hard to foresee as human life. We never expected such a sad end to our son, nor did we ever dream of going together for this journey. It was caused by chance. The daily accidents, who can understand them? It was unforeseen that we should pass a night at this far eastern port of Oshu. It was unforeseen that we should go aboard this ship. Above all, it was unforeseen that we should be crossing Tsugaru Strait.

It was not long before the boat started. She left the shore with the brave shouts of the boatmen, in the Nanbu accent. The sailors of the ship were leaning on the bulwark, looking down at the approaching boats filled with passengers. Unfortunately, the first and the second classes were both full on that day. Although I was somewhat fearful, on account of travelling with my wife, to take the third class and be treated like cargo, I concluded from experience that nothing is better than the deck in such fine weather. Instantly upon our arrival on the steamer, we took our places at the prow.

Meanwhile, upon the stroke of the bell announcing ten o'clock, the noisy sounds of the weighing anchor were heard. The steam whistle was blown as if to bid farewell, and it resounded through the sky overhanging the harbour. The ship began to sail.

The deck where we took our place was near to the mast, larger than one could reach around. When the cool wind blew from the southwest, sending the gay sunshine with the breezes, I felt at last somewhat revived. We spread the mat under the canvas shades and rested ourselves, leaning on some of the cargo. After a while I wanted to have a smoke, but, searching around my waist, I found there was no tobacco pouch. Then, gazing at my face, my wife said:

"You see? Surely you have left it again at the inn," and she smiled.

This was quite a surprise to me. I thought I was very composed, but, although I was constantly scolding my wife to brace her up, it was proved by this oversight that my own dejection was more than that of hers. "Now, then," I thought, "I myself must be somewhat queer," and I suddenly felt dispirited. The more I tried not to be overcome, the more my brain was oppressed with deep chagrin. No doubt I was becoming an idiot.

The ship sailed out from the gulf of Awomori, leaving behind the lighthouse of Hiradate, white in the distance; the sun was mounting higher in the sky. The dark blue waves of the Japan current rolled in from the Sea of Japan, broke resoundingly against the side of the ship, and sparkled in the sunshine. In the lazy hours of the voyage, people came and went on the deck, pausing to admire the view. I also leaned on the bulwark and listened to the sounds of the summer tides, filling my mind with the voice of the late July sea. Suddenly, my thoughts were possessed by my son. Bitter recollections gushed up in my heart. It may sound strange, coming from a parent's lips, but, although he was only a boy when he died, he was clever enough to understand the joy and sorrow of life; my Ryunosuke was not a boy to be beaten by his fellow students in any of his studies.

Observing the world, I notice that the present age, lacking in faith, does not keep the young mind in quietude. Such was the short life of my son. Such an insatiable spirit as his could not help investigating the meaning of life, from exploring all its works, its glories, and its decadences. Leaving the curious multitudes, who looked upon him as a great fool in his misconceptions, how did he feel when he retired from this life, silently, with unutterable sorrow in his mind?

The desperation of thought—if the word could be applied also to the life of this youth—this was certainly the transient but brave span of Ryunosuke. Pity that he was not a sage! He discovered that his learning made him ignorant. Alas! my son quit his studies and his studies quit him. At last he went to Nikkwo, and died by throwing himself into the fall of Kegon. I shall never forget that day when my son came home quite unexpectedly, and bade us farewell without telling us his intention, nor that evening when I gave him my last reproof. The next morning, and the second morning—there has been grief in every morning since that time. My wife became crazed, weeping and crying.

"It is your fault that you gave him such a reproof! Give me back my son alive, now, at once!"

It was inevitable. We were compelled to constrain her by force; we wrapped her in quilts, holding her; we scolded and cajoled her. But the strength of the crazed woman was almost more than ours. I myself did not eat nor sleep regularly for seven days. Indeed, the condition of my wife at that time was such that it would not have been impossible for her to have followed our son, to have thrown herself into the waterfall of Nikkwo mountain. When she became a bit calmer I thought of a plan, which was this journey. I hoped that her distressed mind might be cured by seeing some of the famous places. As she had exquisite taste, in spite of her appearance, I thought I might be able to buy some Obi, or sashes, if she cared for them. Inducing her to see the modern fashions, hoping to quiet her, we started out on this journey.

Alas, my son! After he had passed through the bitterest sufferings, at the moment he came to think about death, even he could hardly have dreamed of his father becoming an idiot, and his mother a lunatic, weeping during the day, thinking during the night, and roaming thus far to the northern sea. I, who am speaking this, am only a man who has spent a most ordinary but peaceful and quiet life in the country. How could I foresee that this peaceful life would change abruptly in its forty-third year? Seeking relief, we felt like wandering pilgrims. Inhaling the sea air of July, two fools were listening to the dreamy sounds of the waves, meditating upon the death of their only child.

Strange imaginings came into my mind. If the dead body should float up from the basin of that waterfall, and be borne away by the current, where would it go? Nowhere but into this ocean! Yes, yes, this restless place of wind and wave; this must be the grave of my son! Here Ryunosuke must be sleeping for ever and ever . . . thus, in fancy, I was indulging my thoughts when the bell of twelve o'clock resounded through the ship.

For lunch, a Bento in a square luncheon-box, was distributed to each of the passengers. We could not eat ours on account of the boiled cuttle-fish. But two young men, who came with their own luncheons, took their seat close to us, and began to eat with gusto. One of them looked as though he were accustomed to labour. He reminded me of "Ankosan," the young men who are said, after indulgence in wine and women, to draw the snow-sledges at such a place as Goryokaku.

The other boy looked two or three years younger than his friend, and seemed just about the age of my son. Apparently, he was a student, as was shown by his naïve appearance. And then, the youthfulness of the expression about his eyes when he looked at the sea through his spectacles, was singularly like that of Ryunosuke. There is such a thing as the "haunting resemblance of the stranger." However, I was quite surprised in my own mind, wondering whether it was possible for anyone else to see such a resemblance. How I gazed, rubbing my eyes, at the silhouette of the student!

As for my wife, I looked at her and saw she entertained the same feeling. When we looked at each other, we understood our mutual thought without a word. Ah! it is unreasonable that I should meet my dead son on this ship, and it was a trick of my imagination that caused me to think that only if I should address him, he would speak to me saying: "Father! Father!" and, taking my hand, would complain of the mysteries and fears and agonies of the other world. "Surely he is my son, my Ryunosuke." Such an absurd thought could only spring from the foolish heart of a parent. I do not know how often I repeated "Ryunosuke! Ryunosuke!" in my mind. I was tempted to cry out in a loud voice, and was astonished at my own absurdity.

At last I addressed the young man.

"Pardon me. Where do you come from?"

"I?" the student smiled. "I came from Goshu."

"Goshu? Then you came from a long way off!"

"Yes. I have an uncle in Sendai, and came up to ask his assistance, but as I found him absent, being called out for war . . . Anyway, I am going up to Hokkaido to try to find some work there. I have been told that there is profitable employment at Sapporo. If I cannot find work in Sapporo, I may go even to Asahigawa."

"Is that so? Young men ought to be that way. You do not need to worry. You will find plenty of work, if only you have a mind to do it."

Thus, comforting him, I recognised the simple, cheerful, and yet manly temperament of this student. Now and then the older companion glanced stealthily toward us with distrustful looks. I could not understand why this student had such a companion. I inquired of him, and was told that they became comrades by chance. They seemed not especially friends nor men from the same district; in other words, they were only fellow wanderers.

My wife took out some apples from her package. These were bought the evening before, at Awomori, from a basket when we were surrounded by the women who sell fruits. Ryunosuke was fond of things with a delicate flavour, which my wife seemed to remember. As if to give them to her son, she selected the alluring yellow apples from the green ones and recommended them to the two young men. I told the younger one in detail of the loss of my son and the reason of starting on this journey with my wife, who cannot hear well, and added:

"This also must be the work of fate, to meet you in this place. Please take one of them. Don't be ceremonious."

"Come, they are so kind. Let us accept them," said the companion, as he pushed forth impudently.

"Please do so," I urged them, offering my knife.

My wife was leaning on me like a child, and gazing at the hands of the student paring the apple. Tears of memory seemed to flow ceaselessly down her cheeks. Forgetting everything, even our bodies, we longed for the recalled face of our son whom we never expected to see in this world.

The student and his companion bit the apples like hungry animals, so that even the crunching sounded delicious, and ate them heartily with vigour and appetite.

"Sweet! Isn't it?" Whispering to his companion, the student smelled the flavour of the apple, squinting his eyes.

"Sweet!" The companion also tasted his eagerly.

By the time the one o'clock bell had rung, all of the passengers were tired of their journey; some of them were lying down with their packages as pillows, some were sleeping on the deck with their mouths open like fishes. The reports of the Russo-Japanese War, which were much discussed about the mast, had entirely ceased. There was nobody on this ship who did not desire speedily to reach Hakodate. The only passengers who wished to continue the journey as long as possible in this way were ourselves; that was because we knew there were only three hours more to be with this young man, and be reminded of Ryunosuke. After parting from him here, we were not sure that we should ever meet him again; nay, not only should we never see again our son, but we should probably never again in our lives see the face that resembled his.

"You are gazing at something, aren't you?"

The student stepped out and patted the shoulder of his companion. The companion turned to him.

"Look at that smoke."

"Smoke?"

'It is strange that smoke appears in this direction."

"Let me see! Where—no, there is no smoke, nothing like it."

"Why, can't you see it?"

Wondering at the conversation of these two men, I also left the side of the mast. Far off to the east of the Strait the dark "Father Tide"— on which groups of cuttle-fish are accustomed to ride down, that Kurile tide dipping the horizon,—shone white and yellow, under the rays of the sun. Groups of clouds were floating in the sky. The excessive heat of a mid-summer noon on the thirtieth of July, seemed to burn the sea. The sky above the horizon was a dark grey, mingled with purple. The air was hazy, but nothing like smoke was to be seen. Before I realised it, the captain, who, for some time had been reading "The Law of General Average," went up to the bridge, and was eagerly looking through the marine glass.

Suddenly, we felt uneasy. The ship had probably sailed at a fair speed since leaving Awomori. When she was sailing at full speed toward Cape Oma, which was on her starboard side, the cloud of smoke was seen exactly in that direction. After twenty minutes, a second smoke appeared, then a third. The Vladivostock fleet, which was said to have appeared along the coast of the Pacific Ocean, was slowly sailing from Cape Oma to Cape Tatsuhi. Approaching nearer, the ships became more distinct. When the three grey ships of the enemy, of portentous appearance, were seen approaching our defenceless vessel, sailors and passengers all stood up. The battle formation of the enemy was in single line. First came the *Rossia*, then the *Gronboi*—with the *Riurick* a little behind them.

Joyful or sad memories or imaginings were all blotted out by this unexpected view. Nobody remained in the dark cabin. Forgetting the vertigo, the nausea, and the sufferings of fatigue, the hundred and fifty passengers came out at once on deck. All those who have been standing at the stern passed through the kitchen and pressed toward the prow.

"Go down! Go down! Go down if you want to save your life!"

But the cries and scolding of the sailors could not control the confusion of the excited men, screaming women and children. The dreadful sound of the engine gave an added touch of gloom. As the enemy were known to be such vicious fighters that they sank even the sailing boat *Seishomaru* and robbed it of the money and cargo, all on board felt that there was no time for delay. They bared their feet, and tucked up their skirts, in order to be as prepared as possible.

"I will take charge of your wife."

The words of the student were hardly heard. Having already lost her colour, my wife stood shuddering, close to the student.

Death—we were face to face with that force! A group of sailors took off the duck rain-covers from the lifeboats to prepare them for lowering at any moment. As it was the captain's hope to be within the limit of the protection of the fort, if only the ship could run one hour more at full speed, the ship dashed along with all possible speed, nay, even with a desperate force rather than speed.

In this dangerous situation there appeared, suddenly, from the direction of Hakodate, our fleet running in the same direction as the Russian ships. The enemy also saw this fleet and, seeming to hesitate, stopped their advance. The fact is that it was the time when they took the last resolution to pass the Tsugaru Strait again. Sending up volumes of black smoke, they began all at once to flee like a flock of birds. With the exclamation of "Banzai! Banzai!" all the people on the deck shook their hats toward our fleet.

"Now, we are safe!"

Turning back to my wife, I sighed with relief.

"Safe!" I repeated. My wife was still leaning on the shoulder of the student.

As my wife and I, turning again to the thought of our son, settled down to spend the few remaining hours in conversation with the student, the mount Gagyu appeared to our view. We caught sight of the red cliff jutting into the sea, the rugged precipice from whose surface the reflection of the sun shone white on the sky of the port of Hakodate. A sea-gull flew near to the bulwark as if to congratulate us on our safe arrival.

We arrived at the entrance of the port at the appointed hour, four o'clock. Ah! How great the joy of the people when they saw the streets of Hakodate from the deck. The grey roofs of planed board on the slope of the mountain; the new ridge poles soaring among the houses built in Nanbu style of stone and sand; the landscape covered with the green leaves of Matsubuna and Itaya, from the high tower of the temple shining in sunlight to the custom house, hospital, and the buildings of many schools. This prospect of the port of New Japan extended before our eyes, exciting our interest.

The enormous group of people, gathered on the seashore, raised a wild shout of joy to welcome the safe arrival of the liner. The *Surugamaru* also made the air resound with whistles! Passing through the many sailing ships, steamboats, cargo-boats, sampans and lighters, the *Surugamaru* approached the pier,—looking like a scared water-bird, who had barely escaped from peril, and was hurrying to the shore, crying out to her friends. When the ship stopped, and seemed to sigh with relief, the waves lapped about her with whisperings.

Then the passengers jumped into the sampans and hastened to land on the pier. What a sight of madness! Persons landing, persons waiting to receive them, parents embracing their children, sisters their sisters, caressing and embracing! All the women wept for joy, which stirred the emotion of all onlookers.

At last the time came to part with the student. Full of regret, I was standing vacantly in the crowd, and forgot not only the clamouring hotel-runners, but everything, even to the package I placed on the ground and the bag I was carrying, wishing only to continue speaking with this young man. How I was moved at this unexpected intimacy and this parting, thinking over the events of the day's voyage!

Becoming conscious of the disappearance of his companion, we turned back and saw his arm firmly taken by a big policeman.

"There! pickpocket!" said those who gathered around us.

"Look! What are you thinking about? Don't you know you have been robbed?"

Being addressed by the policeman, I was aware for the first time that the package I had placed on the ground was gone.

"What! Impudent!" exclaimed the student excitedly. "I am not such a man as to commit lawlessness!"

"Don't be excited. Where did you come from? I myself did not see you break the law. But you are the companion of the man who did it, aren't you?"

As the policeman said this, I told him every fact I knew, and defended the student from the imputation of being a suspicious character. The policeman nodded at each of my words and, after he inquired of the student how he became a companion of such a scoundrel as the pickpocket, he made more inquiries and admonitions, and also advised me to appear against the thief in court.

"Wait a bit. I want to keep your name and address."

The policeman took out his note-book and gazed at the face of the student.

"What is your address?"

"Kusatsu town, Awata district, Omi county."

"Your name?"

"Nishihara Yasutaro."

"Your age?"

"Nineteen."

After this catechism, the student bade farewell to my wife and me, and started again on his wanderings. I looked at the appearance of his back as he disappeared, and could not help being again reminded of my departed Ryunosuke. My wife, weeping and scarcely able to stand, looked after him, leaning on my shoulder. Gazing this way and that, we continued to look until the straw summer hat, the student-like figure in the white cloth of Kasuri, disappeared amid the crowd, and at last faded away.

※   ※   ※

NAGAI KAFU
(1879-   )

MR. NAGAI KAFU spent most of his younger days in China, America and France. His translator tells us that when his two volumes of stories, written in America and France, were published, he appeared as a new star in the literary world of Japan.

The Bill-Collecting, translated by Torao Taketomo, is reprinted by permission of the publisher from the volume, *Paulownia*, copyright, 1918, by Duffield & Co., New York.

THE BILL-COLLECTING

I

INSTANTLY after she got up from the bed where she was sleeping with Omatsu, her companion, Oyo put on her narrow-sleeved Hanten as usual, and, wrapping her head with a towel in the manner of the "sister's cap," she began to sweep the parlour.

Oyo is the maidservant in Kinugawa, an assignation house.

As they had guests in the inner room of Yojohan, who had been lodging there since the evening before, Oyo wiped up every place with the dust cloth except that room, including the railings and stairways of the first floor. Coming down to the fireplace near the counter she found the mistress, with toothbrush in her mouth, already uncovering the charcoal fire of the previous evening. In contrast to the dark, humid interior where the odour of wine seemed to drift from somewhere, the winter sunshine glittering on the opposite side of the street and through the frosted-glass screen of the front lattice gate, looked quite warm and cheerful. As soon as the mistress saw Oyo, who was bidding her "Good-morning," she said all at once:

"Now, Oyo, I wish you would go directly after breakfast, as the place is far."

Being thus ordered, Oyo took up her chopsticks for breakfast, eating before Omatsu and Otetsu the cook. After having finished her toilet and changed her dress, and listening again to the instructions and messages from the mistress, she started. It was almost seven o'clock when she set out in the new wooden clogs that were given her by the regular geisha girls as a present at the end of the last year, and she heard the voice of the cook-supplier at the kitchen, the man who came to get the plates and bowls.

Oyo went out by the familiar short-cut through the lane between the houses of the geisha girls. Coming out into the open street of Ginza, which was filled with sunshine, she looked around her as though surprised at the new appearance of things. Her bosom pulsated to the sounds of trolleys passing by, and she not only felt that she had forgotten all the messages charged by the mistress, but even the route which she thought she had understood well when she left home. She became confused, so that the way seemed further than she had supposed.

It had been five years since Oyo entered service, in the autumn, at the age of fourteen, at Kinugawa, the assignation house. She had been at Hakone and at Enoshima, she knew Haneda and the shrine of Narita, but it was only as an attendant of the guests and geisha girls in the great carousels of many people that she went to these places. Once, though she was a woman, she had walked alone through the night with two or three hundred yen in cash in her sash. But it was not further than a few blocks where she went to an accustomed bank on behalf of the mistress. It was only once or twice in a year that she rode a really long distance by trolley, to visit her home at Minami-Senju for holiday.

To a woman of down-town who knows nothing about the suburbs of Tokyo, except Fukagawa, Shinagawa, and Asakusa, even to hear the name of Okubo in the uptown district where Oyo was going to-day to collect the bill, caused her to imagine a place where foxes and badgers live. As she also felt fearful that she might not be able to return home that day if she did not catch the trolley as soon as possible, she hurried to the square of Owaricho, not even stopping at the beautiful show windows of Matsuya, and Mikamiya and Tenshodo.

"Good-morning, Maid Oyo!"

Suddenly, being thus addressed from the crowd which was waiting for the trolley, Oyo turned back and saw an employed girl of Tamaomiya, who had her hair dressed in Hisashigami and wore the half-coat of Koki silk.

"Kimi chan. Going to temple?"

As is a habit of woman, Oyo looked at the hair and clothing of this geisha girl, which was not particularly unusual.

"No. I have a patient at home," Kimi chan, the employed girl, said apologetically, as though answering the question of the employer. "Where are you going?"

"To the place called Okubo. I was told to take the Shinjuku line. Is this the place to wait for it?"

"Shinjuku. . . . Then it is on the other side. You must take the car from the other side of the street."

"Oh!" Oyo cried, with such a loud voice that she surprised herself. And as if she could not hear the formal salutation of the employed girl, "Please keep me in mind again . . ." she crossed the square to the other side almost in rapture. Though it was a winter morning her forehead perspired. Having heaved a sigh of relief before the glass door of the Café Lion, Oyo turned back with a wonder-stricken look to the other side of the street where was the clock on the roof of the Hattori clock store, thinking that it was a marvellous thing that she was not killed in the midst of the square where so many trolleys are crossing. By that time the employed girl of Tamaomiya, almost crushed among the crowds on the conductor's platform, went away toward the Mihara bridge, and though many almost empty cars followed it, the only thing that passed the tracks where Oyo was waiting was a lumbering horse truck loaded with casks. The sidewalk near to the Café Lion was so filled with persons waiting for transfers that they overflowed on to the street pavement. Unconsciously, Oyo looked at the blue sky of winter, calling to mind the clock on the roof of Hattori's building, which pointed to half-past eleven. She became so impatient that she felt she could not wait any longer. The complaints of the persons who were waiting for transfers, speaking in loud voices, the breaking of the wires or the stoppage of the electric current, disturbed her as though it were the announcement of a fire burning her house. Exhausted by waiting, Oyo, like the others, leaned against the glass door of the Café and hung her head. Suddenly becoming conscious of a commotion, Oyo also ran in order not to be too late for the car, but, being only a helpless woman, she could hardly approach the first car. Even the next one she missed, for a big man of dark complexion, crossing in from the side, had pushed her away when her foot was already on the step. Moreover, her side lock of Ichogaeshi was rubbed up by the sleeve of the double manteau with great force.

"Now I won't mind what becomes of me. I will wait even half a day, or a day, as long as they want me to wait."

Oyo, who had already become desperate, purposely followed behind the crowd, to take the next approaching car.

When they came to Hibiya park, a seat was left, so Oyo could at last rest her tired back. Then the inside of the car was calmer and the streets outside opened out and became more quiet, and in the warmth of the inside of the car, with the sun shining on the back of her neck and shoulders, she nodded involuntarily with the light jolting of the car. The fatigue of the body, which has to work every night until one o'clock at the earliest, pressed on her eyelids all at once. As Oyo is the favourite servant of the mistress, raised by her from childhood, she must help her not only in the parlour of the guests, but also as chambermaid. To be made a companion in the late drinking of the guest in her busy time is bearable, but the most disgusting thing is the troublesome task of washing clean, in a hot-water cup, the whole set of artificial teeth of a guest nearly sixty years of age, every time after his meal.

In a short time there were indications of the stopping of the car and passengers coming and going. Oyo awakened all at once, surprised, and looked out of the window. She saw a leafy tree, a high bank and a low bridge on the waterless moat. The conductors, enough to frighten her, were assembled in front of the new house at the corner. Many empty cars were left as if they were to be given away. With this sight of unfamiliar streets, Oyo felt unutterable helplessness. She became anxious about the thing in her sash, fearing that it had been stolen in her absent-minded moments. Also she doubted whether this was the place to leave the car. Impatiently she moved a bit from the end and said:

"Please, what is this place?"

The high-boned, flat-faced, slant-eyed conductor, who seemed to perceive the embarrassed figure of Oyo by a glance, did not move from the platform. Shrugging his shoulders, as if cold, and turning his head to the other side, he pulled the bell so that Oyo, who had left her seat, was upset by the moving car and thrown with all the weight of her body on the lap of a man looking like a foreman of the labourers, who was sitting near to the entrance. Feeling abashed, Oyo tried to get up quickly; she noticed that a big arm, as heavy as iron, was laid on her back as if to embrace her body; she struggled with all her might.

"Ehe! he! he!"

With the vile, frightful laughter there was a smell of wine.

"How can I stand it when I am held fast by a girl!"

"What good luck to have!" chanted one of the group that was sitting on the other side, and they burst into laughter.

Oyo flushed like fire, and wished even to jump out of the moving car. After that she felt that all the eyes in the car were looking constantly at her. Even then, she had not gained her composure after the fright of the moment when she felt herself closely embraced by a labourer. All at once Oyo became conscious that no one in the car was dressed like her—in Meisen silk, with folds laid somewhat loose, grey Hawori with an embroidered crest on it, and an apron of Itoöri neatly tied. All the other women were in Hisashigami and in close folds, and most of the men passengers were soldiers. Her helplessness riding among these unknown people became more keen. Just at the time when she was about to ask the conductor, who came to inspect the transfer tickets, regarding the station before Shinjuku, her embarrassment and helplessness became all but overwhelming.

"This is the Awoyama line, Miss. If you wish to go to Shinjuku, there is no other way but to transfer at Awoyama Itchome, and again at

Shiocho." Throwing the transfer ticket on the lap of Oyo, the conductor hurried to fix the dislocated pole.

As she had understood that she could go all the way without transfering, Oyo, on hearing that she had to transfer not once but twice, felt as if she was thrown at last into the labyrinthine jungle of Yawata.

II

After going here and there, Oyo was able at last to realise that Tenmacho Nichome was the station before Shinjuku. How far would the trouble of the unknown route continue? Oyo regretted that she had come, and thought that she would never again go on an errand to an unknown place, no matter how she might be scolded. It is far better to stay at home with the sweeping, and to dry the bed-clothes or to wash the Yukata to offer to the guests. In this broad street, more bustling than she could have expected, she could not tell whether she had to turn to the right or to the left. Nevertheless, as she could not stand in the middle of the street, she was thinking about paying her own money secretly to ride in a Kuruma, when she saw a Kurumaya from the stand, and asked him how much she would have to pay to ride to Okubo.

"Give me fifty sen."

"Don't fool me."

Being much provoked, Oyo did not even turn to the Kurumaya, who called out something to her from her back, and walked aimlessly to a side street. Seeing a little girl with tucks at her shoulders in front of a tobacco shop, she asked in an almost weeping tone:

"Please, my girl, will you kindly let me know how to get to Yochomachi of Okubo?"

"Yochomachi?" said the girl cheerfully. "Go straight this way, and going down a slope you will find a policeman's post. . . . You had better ask at the policeman's post."

Oyo felt revived for the first time.

"Thank you ever so much."

Putting an overwhelming sentiment of thanks into these simple words, Oyo walked away, looking curiously at the sights on both sides of the somewhat narrow street. There was a European building for moving pictures on one side. From the lane near to the building a few geisha girls came out, laughing about something in loud voices. Looking at them, Oyo wondered: "Why are there geisha girls in such a place?" Suddenly she heard a tremendous noise. Before she could think what was the matter, she saw many soldiers on horseback riding from the open street to this narrow side street. There was the gate of a temple at one side of the beginning of the slope, and, taking advantage of an open place, Oyo was fortunate enough to get out of the way. She saw six or seven men employed on the telegraph wires, squatting on the earth, eating their luncheon. A bamboo ladder was leaned against a wire pole on the other side of the street.

"Hello! The beauty!"

Their teasing started Oyo running away in embarrassment.

"We are receiving an extraordinary Benten."

"Hey, my girl! May I offer you a glass?"

Some of them were looking intently at the folds of her skirts. They could not contain themselves any longer, when a sudden wind had brushed aside the skirts of her underclothes. All of them burst in at once.

"Luck to see!"

"It is worth two yen at Sinjuku!"

"The red clothes are said to keep long!" And they continued to say things which were unbearable to hear. But is not the procession of the soldiers endless, stirring up the sand on all sides? And how much Oyo wished to escape!

Oyo finally got away from the place and went down the slope, almost running, when she suddenly stumbled on a stone and hardly kept from falling. In front of it she saw something that looked like a squirming heap of rags, which said:

"Ladies and gentlemen, passing by, please, a penny . . ."

Two or three leper beggars, at whom one could not bear to look a second time, were making bows on the sand of the street. The town at the foot of the slope was visible, with the dirty roofs in confusion, at the bottom of the valley-like lowland. Oyo wondered without any reason whether the town over yonder was the outcasts' quarter.

Going down the slope and turning to the left as she was instructed by the girl of the tobacco shop she easily found a policeman's post. As a policeman who looked good-natured was standing in the middle of the street, she asked him her route.

"What number of Yochomachi is it?"

"It is number sixty-two. The house is Mr. Inuyama's."

"Number sixty-two—then you have to go straight along this way, and go up the slope before a big wine-shop."

"I see."

"And let me see, is it the third side street after you go straight up the slope? . . . You turn there to the left, where you will find number sixty-two."

"Much obliged to you."

Before she had gone less than half a block, she found a wine-shop that looked like the one she was told about, and also a slope, so she thought rest of the route was quite short. Feeling somewhat proud that she had come this far alone without the Kuruma or without going much out of the way, she forgot a while even the fatigue of her legs, but when she began to go up the slope, she had to meet another unexpected trouble.

Though the down-town district had had such continuous clear weather that it was annoyed by the dust, the up-town quarter of the city seemed to have had rain the night before and the street, which was not broad, was so deep in mud that Oyo could not even find the sidewalk. By the time she discovered that the mud was melting frost, which had not had time to dry, not only the toes of her new wooden clogs, but also her white socks newly washed, were all splashed with mud. On one side of the road was the bank covered with sepiaria and on the other side was a cryptomeria hedge, where, taking advantage of the fact that there were no passers-by, Oyo took out her pocket-papers and wiped, she knew not how often, the mud from the mat lining of her wooden clogs. As she glanced up she thought the third side street to which she had been directed by the policeman might be the corner she sought.

III

The mud of the melting frost became harder and harder. A big, masterless dog was roaming about with a menacing look. The rasping sounds of a violin were heard. The dreary sigh of the wind came from the trees near by. Far at the end of the side street the ground seemed to slope again, and, though the winter sunshine was falling gently on the roofs of the new houses and on the deep forest that covered the rears of all the houses, either side of the road was dark in shade, and all the houses were surrounded with fences of four-inch boards. Each had a small gate containing a slide-door, the faces of which were smeared with mud that had not been washed off, which seemed to have been placed there in mischief by the boys in the neighbourhood.

The number and name of the house, which Oyo found at last, after examining all the labels on the houses on both sides, was on the support of the small gate, where the mud was splashed thickest and dirtiest.

Inuyama Takemasa. . . .

Oyo looked at it again before she entered the gate. The gentleman called Mr. Inuyama was the most captious, unsympathetic and unreasonable among the numerous guests that came to Kinugawa. No matter how busy they were in attendance in the parlours, he would not be satisfied if he could not call up Oyo and all the other maids into his room. If the mistress did not come to salute him every time he came he would be angry and say: "You insult me," or "You treat me coldly." It was said that he gave up his membership in the parliament as it did not suit his dignity. His profession at present was that of a politician. He was fond of geishas as young as babies, and if the girls did not obey his will, he was so furious that nobody could touch him, and Oyo not only despised him more than any of the other guests, but also was afraid, without any reason, of his forbidding appearance and loud voice. He always wore European clothes and used to come in a Kuruma pulled by two drawers, saying that the lower class of people ride in the trolley. Once in a certain conversation, when the mistress had said to him that "in these days not only the expenses of your pleasure and the tips for geisha become dearer, but even your expense for Kuruma must be very considerable," he laughed:

"Mistress, the money is earned to spend. Ha! ha! ha! ha!"

But these prosperous days were no longer. When it was hardly December of that year, Mr. Inuyama suddenly stopped coming, and in spite of many letters he would not respond to the bill of two hundred yen of that month and the fifty-yen balance of the previous month. Kinugawa was obliged to talk it over with a geisha who first brought Mr. Inuyama after their meeting at a certain Matsumotoro, but, it was almost clear that she could not shake her sleeve when she had none, and so January passed in this way, and now it was February. The mistress sent Oyo to the mansion of Mr. Inuyama to reconnoitre.

Oyo had known numerous cases of this kind, not only of men like Mr. Inuyama, but also of many other guests. She thought this nothing more than the bad ways of people. She thought only that they will be enjoying themselves at some other house, if they do not come to hers, then, it will be good of them if they will be more considerate and pay the bill. The reason Oyo looked again at the label on the gate was the fact that the gate of his mansion was so dirty. But, to enter the gate was better than the annoyance of walking around aimlessly any longer in the frost-melting road, so she looked around from the porch with its dirty and broken paper-screen, wondering which was the servants' entrance.

On the right hand, beyond the bamboo fence, was visible the roof of a one-storied house looking cold under the garden trees. She got a glimpse of an old red blanket and a dirty cotton gown hung on a clothes-pole, through the crevices of the bamboo fence. On the left hand, further on, were one-storied houses with lattice gates, and another that looked like a rented house. Beside the wheel-well, where the plum-blossoms showed their buds, a fishmonger was cutting a salted salmon. Two maidservants in careless Hisashigami, who carried babies under quilted gowns and wore European aprons which had become grey, seemed to be at the height of their silly conversation with the fishmonger. As soon as they caught sight of Oyo, whose appearance was quite different, they sharpened their eyes, and, seeming rather to fear her, looked her over attentively from top to toe. The road from the well to the servants' entrance was spread with straw bags of charcoal, and the muddy water of the melting frost ran into the feet of people walking on them. Being in much perplexity Oyo could not move a step, and bending her waist, said:

"I beg your pardon."

Both of the maidservants stood wonder-stricken with open mouths.

"Is this Mr. Inuyama's house?"

Suddenly one of the maidservants began to grow uneasy, and, perceiving her manner, Oyo said:

"I came with a message from Kyobashi. Is the master at home?"

"He is absent."

Then the baby on her back began to cry.

Oyo, as she was ordered by the mistress, remembered how to proceed when she was told the master was absent, namely, to call madam to the servants' entrance and leave the word that she was the messenger from Mizuta, which was the name of her mistress. However, as Oyo was only eighteen or nineteen, she felt somewhat timid and stood on the walk, forgetting even that the water of the melting frost was overflowing on her polished wooden clogs. The baby on the back of the maidservant cried more and more.

"Chiyo! Chiyo!" Suddenly, a voice of woman, close to her ears, aroused her.

Being astonished, Oyo turned and saw at the broken paper-screens of the servants' entrance not farther than six inches, the big face of a woman, like a horse, with the eyes widely separated from each other. The careless Hisashigami could not be beaten by the maidservants. She was a big, clumsy madam in a dirty and creased Hifu.

Just then, the fishmonger came to offer three slices of the salted salmon to madam. Madam continued talking with the fishmonger, and Oyo, at last somewhat aroused and feeling at the same time a sense of deep disappointment, went out from the gate as if to escape. For she felt that her troubles in coming so far had been all in vain. She was exceedingly sorry for her mistress, as she had been entirely deceived by this humbug.

When Oyo rode again in the trolley she felt, at first, the fatigue of the vain effort and at the same time the fact that she was unbearably hungry, but being unable to do anything about it, she arrived at Ginza. The sun was already declining. Calling to her mind the clockstand of Hattori, which she saw when she was waiting for the car that morning, she looked up, and lo! was it not already near to four o'clock. Oyo felt her heart sinking with melancholy, picturing in her mind the flash of her mistress' eye, who never would say to her: "How early you are!" when she returned from the far-away errand. The electric lights were already lit in the shops. . . .

THE SCANDINAVIAN COUNTRIES

Introduction

SCANDINAVIAN literature traces its development to the Icelandic universified epics known as Sagas that grew up some thousand years ago when the recital of the heroic exploits of the great kings of Norway and Denmark was a welcome form of entertainment. Of the hundred and fifty odd sagas, about forty have been preserved in writing; and among these, one of the best is the *Heimskringla* by Snorri Sturluson who is also responsible for the *Prose Edda*. The novel and short story form as recognised to-day came into its own in the nineteenth century with the works of Jon Thoroddsen who wielded a great influence over his contemporaries. Gestur Palsson (1852-1891) was a most distinguished writer of stories that were widely imitated.

The Danish language was too closely identified with the Icelandic to allow for an impetus to a distinct literature, but the period of the Reformation first gave evidence of an original effort, and in Hedvig Holberg (1684-1754) we hail the founder of modern Danish literature. Holberg, a most brilliant dramatist, stands out in his period as impressively as Ohlenschlager (1779-1850), Denmark's greatest poet, does in his. Steen Blicher (1782-1848) achieved immense success with his short stories, and produced a masterpiece in his collection called *The Spinning Room*.

Hans Christian Andersen (1805-1875), famous the world over for his inimitable fairy tales, won his reputation with his first volume of *Fairy Tales* published in 1835. Meyer Goldschmidt (1819-1887), one of the writers that bridged the gap between Romanticism and Naturalism, found popularity with his delightful stories.

Jacobsen (1847-1885) who may be considered as Denmark's greatest prose artist was hailed by Brandes as the founder of the Naturalists. With the death of Jacobsen, Drachmann (1846-1908), a writer of freshness, vigour and originality came to the front. Among recent writers Herman Bang (1858-1912) has gradually developed a distinguished reputation, J. V. Jensen has produced some noteworthy stories, besides his well known novel, *The Long Journey*, and Pontoppidan, who won the Nobel Prize in 1917 has added to his list of significant novels and short stories.

The beginnings of Norwegian literature are to a great extent similar to that of Danish. The two events that led to the establishment of a Norwegian literature was the foundation of the University of Christiania in 1811, and the separation of Norway from Denmark in 1814. The name that stands out most prominently in the field of prose fiction in the last half of the nineteenth century is that of Björnson. Jonas Lie and Alexander Kielland, who owe much to his example, have contributed some excellent stories and Lie, in particular, enjoyed great popularity. Hans Kinck is an accomplished writer of peasant stories. His novels which have but recently been translated into German have created an unusual sensation, and he is admitted by all critics to be an author of rare gifts, especially at his best in short stories. A writer of first magnitude among contemporaries is Knut Hamsun. Johan Bojer, though recognised as a distinguished author in many countries, is not considered seriously by Norwegian critics.

There was little of any significant prose produced in Sweden before the eighteenth century. Jacob Henrik Mörk (1714-1763) was the first novelist of importance. His moral, long-winded romances resembled those of Richardson. Karl J. L. Almqvist (1793-1866) was the outstanding novelist of his period.

In the last quarter of the nineteenth century a violent controversy arose between the old and the new schools of literature, through which the latter came forth victoriously. The influences responsible for this situation were the Spencerian philosophy, the realism of Zola, the drama of Ibsen and Björnson and, to a great extent, the criticism of Brandes. The greatest name in recent Swedish literature is that of Strindberg, whose *Master Olaf* inaugurated the revolutionary movement. A remarkable novelist of recent times is Selma Lagerlöf who achieved a great success with *Gösta Berlings Saga*. Hjalmar Söderberg, a keenly ironic novelist, has been influenced by Anatole France. Sigfrid Siwertz has produced some distinguished novels displaying unusual skill in the treatment of his studies in degeneration.

※   ※   ※

ICELAND

THE STORY OF THE VOLSUNGS

(Anonymous, 12th Century)

THIS tale is one of the many thrilling episodes which, strung together, make up the *Volsunga Saga*. This is one of the most beautiful and highly finished of the many Icelandic sagas through which we learn of the hardy life pursued by the early Scandinavians.

The present version, translated by William Morris and Magnusson, is from *The Story of the Volsungs*, Camelot Series, London, no date.

THE BIRTH OF SINFJOTLI, THE SON OF SIGMUND

SO on a tide it befell as Signy sat in her bower, that there came to her a witch-wife exceeding cunning, and Signy talked with her in such wise, "Fain am I," say she, "that we should change semblances together."

She says, "Even as thou wilt then."

And so by her wiles she brought it about that they changed semblances, and now the witch-wife sits in Signy's place according to her rede, and goes to bed by the king that night, and he knows not that he has other than Signy beside him.

But the tale tells of Signy, that she fared to the earth-house of her brother, and prayed him give her harbouring for the night; "For I have gone astray abroad in the woods, and know not whither I am going."

So he said she might abide, and that he would not refuse harbour to one lone woman, deeming that she would scarce pay back his good cheer by tale-bearing: so she came into the house, and they sat down to meat, and his eyes were often on her, and a goodly and fair woman she seemed to him; but when they are full, then he says to her, that he is right fain that they should have but one bed that night; she nowise turned away therefrom, and so for three nights together he laid her in bed by him.

Thereafter she fared home, and found the witch-wife, and bade her change semblances again, and she did so.

Now as time wears, Signy brings forth a man-child, who was named Sinfjotli, and when he grew up he was both big and strong, and fair of face, and much like unto the kin of the Volsungs, and he was hardly yet ten winters old when she sent him to Sigmund's earth-house; but this trial she had made of her other sons or ever she had sent them to Sigmund, that she had sewed gloves on to their hands through flesh and skin, and they had borne it ill and cried out thereat; and this she now did to Sinfjotli, and he changed countenance in nowise thereat. Then she flayed off the kirtle so that the skin came off with the sleeves, and said that this would be torment enough for him; but he said—

"Full little would Volsung have felt such a smart as this."

So the lad came to Sigmund, and Sigmund bade him knead their meal up, while he goes to fetch firing; so he gave him the meal-sack, and then went after the wood, and by then he came back had Sinfjotli made an end of his baking. Then asked Sigmund if he had found nothing in the meal.

"I misdoubted me that there was something quick in the meal when I first fell to kneading of it, but I have kneaded it all up together, both the meal and that which was therein, whatsoever it was."

Then Sigmund laughed out, he said—

"Naught wilt thou eat of this bread to-night, for the most deadly of worms hast thou kneaded up therewith."

Now Sigmund was so mighty a man that he might eat venom and have no hurt therefrom; but Sinfjotli might abide whatso venom came on the outside of him, but might neither eat or drink thereof.

❊ ❊ ❊

DENMARK

HANS CHRISTIAN ANDERSEN
(1805-1875)

ANDERSEN, born at Odense, was the son of poor parents and had no educational opportunities at first. Later some friends came to his assistance and enabled him to attend the University. He attained immediate popularity with the publication of his first volume of fairy tales. Although he wrote plays, novels and books of travel, these never excelled the charming, delicately satiric and subtle prose of his tales which have increasingly captivated the world's reading public.

What the Old Man Does is Always Right is reprinted from an anonymously translated edition published in London, no date.

WHAT THE OLD MAN DOES IS ALWAYS RIGHT

I WILL tell you the story which was told to me when I was a little boy. Every time I thought of the story, it seemed to me to become more and more charming; for it is with stories as it is with many people—they become better as they grow older.

I take it for granted that you have been in the country, and seen a very old farmhouse with a thatched roof, and mosses and small plants growing wild upon the thatch. There is a stork's nest on the summit of the gable; for we can't do without the stork. The walls of the house are sloping, and the windows are low, and only one of the latter is made so that it will open. The baking-oven sticks out of the wall like a little fat body. The elder-tree hangs over the paling, and beneath its branches, at the foot of the paling, is a pool of water in which a few ducks are disporting themselves. There is a yard dog too, who barks at all comers.

Just such a farmhouse stood out in the country; and in this house dwelt an old couple—a peasant and his wife. Small as was their property, there was one article among it that they could do without—a horse, which made a living out of the grass it found by the side of the high-road. The old peasant rode into the town on this horse; and often his neighbours borrowed it of him, and rendered the old couple some service in return for the loan of it. But they thought it would be best if they sold the horse, or exchanged it for something that might be more useful to them. But what might this *something* be?

"You'll know that best, old man," said the wife. "It is fair-day to-day, so ride into town, and get rid of the horse for money, or make a good exchange: whichever you do will be right for me. Ride off to the fair."

And she fastened his neckerchief for him, for she could do that better than he could; and she tied it in a double bow, for she could do that very prettily. Then she brushed his hat round and round with the palm of her hand, and gave him a kiss. So he rode away upon the horse that was to be sold or to be bartered for something else. Yes, the old man knew what he was about.

The sun shone hotly down, and not a cloud was to be seen in the sky. The road was very dusty, for many people who were all bound for the fair were driving, or riding, or walking upon it. There was no shelter anywhere from the sunbeams.

Among the rest, a man was trudging along, and driving a cow to the fair. The cow was as beautiful a creature as any cow can be.

"She gives good milk, I'm sure," said the peasant. "That would be a very good exchange—the cow for the horse."

"Hallo, you there with the cow!" he said; "I tell you what—I fancy a horse costs more than a cow, but I don't care for that; a cow would be more useful to me. If you like, we'll exchange."

"To be sure I will," said the man; and they exchanged accordingly.

So that was settled, and the peasant might have turned back, for he had done the business he came to do; but as he had once made up his mind to go to the fair, he determined to proceed, merely to have a look at it; and so he went on to the town with his cow.

Leading the animal, he strode sturdily on; and after a short time he overtook a man who was driving a sheep. It was a good fat sheep, with a fine fleece on its back.

"I should like to have that fellow," said our peasant to himself. "He would find plenty of grass by our palings, and in the winter we could keep him in the room with us. Perhaps it would be more practical to have a sheep instead of a cow. Shall we exchange?"

The man with the sheep was quite ready, and the bargain was struck. So our peasant went on in the high-road with his sheep.

Soon he overtook another man, who came into the road from a field, carrying a great goose under his arm.

"That's a heavy thing you have there. It has plenty of feathers and plenty of fat, and would look well tied to a string, and paddling in the water at our place. That would be something for my old woman; she could make all kinds of profit out of it. How often she has said, 'If we only had a goose!' Now, perhaps she can have one; and, if possible, it shall be hers. Shall we exchange? I'll give you my sheep for your goose, and thank you into the bargain."

The other man had not the least objection; and accordingly they exchanged, and our peasant became the proprietor of the goose.

By this time he was very near the town. The crowd on the high-road became greater and greater; there was quite a crush of men and cattle. They walked in the road, and close by the palings; and at the barrier they even walked into the toll-man's potato-field, where his own fowl was strutting about with a string to its leg, lest it should take fright at the crowd, and stray away, and so be lost. This fowl had short tail-feathers, and winked with both its eyes, and looked very cunning. "Cluck, cluck!" said the fowl. What it thought when it said this I cannot tell you; but directly our good man saw it, he thought, "That's the finest fowl I've ever seen in my life! Why, it's finer than our parson's brood hen. On my word, I should like to have that fowl. A fowl can always find a grain or two, and can almost keep itself. I think it would be a good exchange if I could get that for my goose.

"Shall we exchange?" he asked the toll-taker.

"Exchange!" repeated the man; "well, that would not be a bad thing."

And so they exchanged; the toll-taker at the barrier kept the goose, and the peasant carried away the fowl.

Now he had done a good deal of business on his way to the fair, and he was hot and tired. He wanted something to eat, and a glass of brandy to drink; and soon he was in front of the inn. He was just about to step in, when the ostler came out, so they met at the door. The ostler was carrying a sack.

"What have you in that sack?" asked the peasant.

"Rotten apples," answered the ostler; "a whole sackful of them— enough to feed the pigs with."

"Why, that's terrible waste! I should like to take them to my old woman at home. Last year the old tree by the turf-hole only bore a single apple, and we kept it in the cupboard till it was quite rotten and spoiled. 'It was always property,' my old woman said; but here she could see a quantity of property—a whole sackful. Yes, I shall be glad to show them to her."

"What will you give me for the sackful?" asked the ostler.

"What will I give? I will give my fowl in exchange."

And he gave the fowl accordingly, and received the apples, which he carried into the guest-room. He leaned the sack carefully by the stove, and then went to the table. But the stove was hot: he had not thought of that. Many guests were present—horse-dealers, ox-herds, and two Englishmen—and the two Englishmen were so rich that their pockets bulged out with gold coins, and almost burst; and they could bet too, as you shall hear.

Hiss-s-s! hiss-s-s! What was that by the stove? The apples were beginning to roast!

"What is that?"

"Why, do you know——" said our peasant.

And he told the whole story of the horse that he had changed for a cow, and all the rest of it, down to the apples.

"Well," said one of the two Englishmen. "There will be a disturbance."

"What?—give me what?" said the peasant. "She will kiss me, and say, 'What the old man does is always right.'"

"Shall we wager?" said the Englishman. "We'll wager coined gold by the ton—a hundred pounds to the hundredweight!"

"A bushel will be enough," replied the peasant. "I can only set the bushel of apples against it; and I'll throw myself and my old woman into the bargain—and I fancy that's piling up the measure."

"Done—taken!"

And the bet was made. The host's carriage came up, and the Englishmen got in, and the peasant got in; away they went, and soon they stopped before the peasant's farm.

"Good evening, old woman."

"Good evening, old man."

"I've made the exchange."

"Yes, you understand what you're about," said the woman.

And she embraced him, and paid no attention to the stranger guests, nor did she notice the sack.

"I got a cow in exchange for the horse," said he.

"Heaven be thanked!" said she. "What glorious milk we shall now have, and butter and cheese on the table! That was a most capital exchange!"

"Yes, but I changed the cow for a sheep."

"Ah, that's better still!" cried the wife. "You always think of everything: we have just pasture enough for a sheep. Ewe's-milk and cheese, and woollen jackets and stockings! The cow cannot give those, and her hairs will only come off. How you think of everything!"

"But I changed away the sheep for a goose."

"Then this year we shall really have roast goose to eat, my dear old man. You are always thinking of something to give me pleasure. How charming that is! We can let the goose walk about with a string to her leg, and she'll grow fatter still before we roast her."

"But I gave away the goose for a fowl," said the man.

"A fowl? That *was* a good exchange!" replied the woman. "The fowl will lay eggs and hatch them, and we shall have chickens: we shall have a whole poultry-yard!   Oh, that's just what I was wishing for."

"Yes, but I exchanged the fowl for a sack of shrivelled apples."

"What!—I must positively kiss you for that," exclaimed the wife. "My dear, good husband!   Now I'll tell you something.   Do you know, you had hardly left me this morning before I began thinking how I could give you something very nice this evening.   I thought it should be pancakes with savoury herbs.   I had eggs, and bacon too; but I wanted herbs.   So I went over to the schoolmaster's—they have herbs there, I know—but the schoolmistress is a mean woman, though she looks so sweet.   I begged her to lend me a handful of herbs.   'Lend!' she answered me; 'nothing at all grows in our garden, not even a shrivelled apple.   I could not even lend you a shrivelled apple, my dear woman.'   But now *I* can lend *her*— ten, or a whole sackful.   That I'm very glad of; that makes me laugh!" And with that she gave him a sounding kiss.

"I like that!" exclaimed both the Englishmen together.   "Always going downhill, and always merry; that's worth the money."

So they paid a hundredweight of gold to the peasant, who was not scolded, but kissed.

Yes, it always pays, when the wife sees and always asserts that her husband knows best, and that whatever he does is right.

You see, that is my story.   I heard it when I was a child; and now you have heard it too, and know that "What the old man does is always right."

❊　❊　❊

JENS PETER JACOBSEN
(1847-1885)

ALTHOUGH his collected works represent a slender quantity, Jacobsen has exercised a far-reaching influence over recent Scandinavian literature.   Born in Jutland, he was equipped for a scientific career and, during a botanical expedition, contracted a pulmonary disease. This compelled him to abandon botany, and Jacobsen turned to literature.   Under the guidance of Dr. Brandes, who was impressed with his ability, Jacobsen began writing his masterpiece, *Marie Grubbe*.   He is also the author of several magnificent and highly imaginative short stories, of which *The Plague at Bergamo* is one of the best.

The present version appeared in the *American Scandinavian Review*, October, 1917, and is here reprinted by permission of the editor.

THE PLAGUE AT BERGAMO

OLD BERGAMO nestled on the summit of a little mountain, hedged around with walls and gates, and New Bergamo nestled at the foot of the mountain, open to the four winds of heaven.

One day the plague broke out down in the new town and spread frightfully; a great many people died, and the others fled across the plains to the four corners of the world. The citizens of Old Bergamo set fire to the forsaken town in order to purify the air, but it did no good; people began to die up there, too, at first one a day, then five, then ten, and finally twenty, and very many more as the plague reached its climax.

They could not flee as the inhabitants of the new town had done. There were a few who tried it, but they led the life of hunted animals, hiding in ditches and in underground channels, under hedges and in green fields; for the first refugees from the plague had carried it with them into the homes of the peasants, and now the latter stoned any stranger they met, hunted him off their land, or felled him to the ground, like a mad dog, without mercy or pity; for they thought it justifiable self-defence.

The people in Old Bergamo, therefore, were obliged to remain where they were, and day by day it grew hotter, and day by day the horrible disease clutched the town more fiercely. Fear grew to madness, and it seemed as if the earth had swallowed up what little order and good government there had once been, and brought forth evil instead.

When the plague first broke out, the people worked together in unity and concord; they took care that the bodies were decently buried, and saw to it that great bonfires were lighted every day on the market-places and squares in order that the wholesome smoke might blow through the streets. Juniper and vinegar were provided for the poor, and, above everything else, the people gathered early and late in the churches. Alone and in processions, they carried their prayers to God, and every evening, when the sun sank to rest, the bells of all churches called mournfully to heaven from a hundred swinging throats. Fasts were ordered, and the holy relics were shown each day on the altars.

Finally, one day, when they did not know what else to do, they proclaimed from the balcony of the town hall, amid the sound of trumpets and trombones, that the Holy Virgin should be the *podesta* or ruler of their town henceforth and in all eternity.

But it did no good, nothing did any good. When the people perceived this, and became gradually convinced that heaven could not or would not help, they did not simply fold their hands in their laps and say: "We are prepared for the worst." No, it seemed as if sin had developed from a secret, imperceptible disease into a horrible visible and raging plague, which worked hand in hand with the physical pestilence, and endeavoured

to murder the soul, as the other destroyed the body. Their proceedings
were so incredible, their wickedness so immense! The air was filled with
blasphemy and ungodliness, with the groans of gluttons and the howling
of drunkards, and the wildest night never covered more debauchery than
was displayed there in broad daylight.

"Let us eat to-day, for to-morrow we die!" It seemed as if they had
set these words to music, which was played by many different instruments
in a ceaseless, hellish concert. Ay, if every possible sin had not already
been discovered, they would surely have unearthed it now, for there was
no path which they, in their worthlessness, were not ready to follow. The
most unnatural vices flourished among them, and even the rare sins of
necromancy, magic, and exorcism were well known to them; for there
were many who expected from the powers in hell the protection Heaven
had not vouchsafed them.

Anything approaching compassion or readiness to help one another
disappeared from their characters; each thought only of himself. A sick
man was considered a common foe, and if some unfortunate happened to
fall in the street, exhausted with the first feverish dizziness of the plague,
no door was opened to him—no, they pricked him with their spears and
threw stones at him, forcing him to crawl out of the way of those who
were still sound.

Day by day the plague increased. The summer sun blazed down on
the town; no drop of rain fell; no breath of wind stirred. The corpses
rotting in the houses and the corpses carelessly buried bred a stench, which
permeated the motionless atmosphere of the streets and attracted swarms
and clouds of ravens and crows, until the walls and roofs were black with
them. Round about on the outside wall of the town were perched marvellous, large, foreign birds from far away, with beaks eager for spoil
and claws expectantly crooked; there they sat and looked down with their
calm, greedy eyes, as if waiting for the whole unfortunate town to be
turned into one single carrion-pit.

Eleven weeks had passed since the outbreak of the plague, when the
guards in the tower and others who were standing in high places saw a
strange procession cross the plains and turn into the streets of the new
town, passing between the stones discolored by smoke and the black heaps
of ashes. A crowd of people! At least six hundred men and women, old
and young, carrying great black crosses and broad red banners which
floated like fire and blood over their heads. They sang as they marched
forward, and the mournful tones of utter despair rose through the still,
sultry air.

Brown, gray, and black are their costumes, but they all have a red
mark on their breasts. As they come nearer, it is seen to be a cross; for
they are coming nearer. They press forward, up the steep path, walled
on either side, which leads to the old town. It seems like a sea of white

faces. They carry scourges in their hands. On their red flags a rain of fire is pictured, and among the fires the black crosses sway from side to side.

From the dense crowd there rises a smell of sweat, ashes, dust of highway, and old incense. They no longer sing, neither do they speak—nothing is heard but the tripping, pattering sound of their bare feet.

Face after face disappears in the shadow of the town gate, and emerges into the light on the other side with a dazed, tired expression and half-closed eyelids.

Then the song begins again—it is a Miserere. They grasp their scourges more tightly and step out more boldly, as if it were a war song. They seem to have come from a famished town, for their cheeks are hollow, their bones stand out, their lips are bloodless, and dark rings are under their eyes.

The inhabitants of Bergamo crowd around watching them with amazement and anxiety. Red and gluttonous faces contrast with pale countenances; sluggish glances exhausted by debauchery fall under the gaze of piercing, flaming eyes; mocking blasphemers stand arrested, open-mouthed at the sound of hymns.

All the scourges are stained with blood!

This procession made a strange impression on the townspeople, but it was not long before they shook themselves free of its influence. Some of them recognised a half-crazy shoemaker of Brescia among the crusaders, and immediately the whole troop became a laughing-stock. Anyway, it was something new, a distraction from the life of every day, and, because the strangers walked towards the cathedral, the people followed behind, just as they would have followed a band of jugglers or a tame bear.

As they pressed on, however, they grew angry. They felt sobered by the solemnity of these people, and understood very well that these shoemakers and tailors had come to convert them, to pray for them, and to speak words which they had no inclination to hear. Among the townspeople were two lean, grey-haired philosophers, who had made ungodliness a system; these two, out of the evil of their hearts, excited the passions of the mob, and as they neared the church, their behaviour grew more threatening at every step, their bursts of temper wilder. There was but little more needed to make them lay violent hands on these uninvited flagellants. But, when they were within a few yards of the church, the doors of a tavern were thrown open, and a whole troop of carousers tumbled out, one over the other. They placed themselves at the head of the procession and led the way forward, singing and bellowing, with jeers and mocking gestures—that is, all except one, who turned a somersault on the moss-grown steps of the church.

This created a pleasant diversion, so they all entered peacefully into the sanctuary.

It was indeed strange to be there again, to walk through the great cool church in an atmosphere where the odor of snuffed wax candles was still distinctly perceptible, to walk over the old sunken stones of the pavement, where the half-erased ornaments and bright shining inscriptions had often occupied their thoughts. And, while their half-curious and half-unwilling gaze sought rest in the gentle twilight under the vaulted roof, or fell on the subdued gleam of dusty gold and smoke-stained colors, or was lost in the shadows around the altar, there rose in their hearts a longing which could not be suppressed.

In the meantime, the drunkards from the tavern continued their noise and misconduct, even in front of the great altar, and one of them, a large and broad-shouldered butcher, took off his white apron and tied it around his neck, so that it hung down over his back like a surplice, and then, with the wildest words, full of wickedness and blasphemy, he conducted mass. An old, fat, little fellow, nimble and quick on his feet in spite of his flesh, with a face like a peeled gourd, was the priest's clerk, and made the responses in the most immoral manner imaginable; he kneeled down and courtesied, turning his back to the altar, rang the bell as he would have rung a jester's bell, and made wheels with the censer, while the other drunkards lay stretched full length on the steps, roaring with laughter and hiccoughing with drink.

Then the whole assembly laughed and mocked the strangers, calling on them to pay good attention and see if they could discover what the people of Bergamo thought of their God. For it was not so much because they wished to insult God that they made fun of the procession, but rather because they took pleasure in thinking that each blasphemous word must be a thorn in the hearts of these saints.

The saints kept together in the middle of the nave and groaned aloud with pain. Their hearts seethed with hate and thirst for revenge; they prayed God with eyes and hands raised to avenge Himself for all this mockery offered Him here in His own house. They would be willing— nay glad—to be destroyed with these audacious creatures, if He would but show His power. They would joyfully permit themselves to be crushed under His feet, if He would but triumph and cause horror, despair, and a too-late repentance to shriek from all these ungodly lips.

They began a Miserere, every note of which sounded like an echo of that rain of sulphur which overwhelmed Sodom, like an echo of the strength of Samson possessed when he tore down the pillars in the house of the Philistines. They prayed with songs and words; they bared their shoulders and prayed with their scourges. They knelt in rows one behind the other, uncovered to their waists, and flung the barbed and knotted ropes on bleeding backs. In rage and frenzy they beat themselves, until the blood flew from the stinging whips. Every blow was a sacrifice to God. If they could only beat harder, if they could only tear themselves into a thousand bloody shreds here in His sight! Their bodies, which had sinned against His commandments, should be punished, martyred, and annihilated, so that He might see how they hated them, so that He might see how they became dogs to please Him—less than dogs beneath His will —the lowest worms, eating the dust under His feet! And blow followed blow, until their arms dropped at their sides, or they fell writhing in convulsions. They lay there, row upon row of them, all with frenzied, sparkling eyes, with foam on their lips and blood dropping from their flesh.

Those who looked on suddenly felt their hearts beat and their cheeks burn while they breathed heavily. It seemed as if something cold had been drawn tightly around their heads, and their knees became weak. For this they understood; in their brains there was a tiny spot of frenzy which responded to this frenzy.

To feel oneself the slave of a powerful and harsh God, to fling oneself at His feet, to belong to Him utterly, not in quiet piety or in the inactivity of silent prayer, but in madness and in the intoxication of self-abasement, in blood and wailing, with scourges wet with blood—this they could understand. Even the butcher became silent, and the toothless philosophers bowed their grey heads to avoid those piercing eyes.

Finally the church grew still; nothing was heard but the surging of the crowd. Then one of the strangers, a young monk, rose and spoke. He was white as a shroud; his black eyes glowed like dying coals, and the lines about his mouth, sombre and hardened by pain, seemed like a carving in wood rather than the features of a human face.

He raised his thin, sickly hands to heaven in prayer, and the sleeves of his black robe slipped down from his lean, white arms.

Then he spoke.

He spoke of hell, of its being eternal, as heaven is eternal, of the solitary world of torture which every one of the damned must suffer and must fill with his shrieking, of the seas of sulphur which are there, of fields full of scorpions, of flames that wrap themselves about one like a garment, and of quiet, hard flames that bore into one like a spear twisted around in a wound.

It was quite still. Breathless, they listened to his words; for he spoke as if he had seen it with his own eyes, as they asked one another if he were not one of the damned sent to them out of the jaws of hell to bear witness before them.

Then he preached a long time about the law and about the severity of the law—that every jot and tittle in it must be fulfilled, and that every transgression of which they were guilty would be added to their account. " 'But Christ died for our sins,' you say; 'we are no longer subject to the law.' But I say unto you that hell will not be cheated out of a single one of you, and that not one single iron tooth on the torture wheel of hell will spare your flesh. You trust in Golgotha's cross. Come, come, come and look at it! I will lead you to His feet. It was, as you know, on a Friday that they pushed him out of their gates, and laid the heaviest end of the cross on His shoulders, and let Him carry it to a barren hill outside of the town, while crowds of them went along and raised so much dust with their feet that it lay like a red cloud over the spot. They tore His clothes off and uncovered Him, as the judges order a malefactor exposed, that all may see the flesh to be delivered to torture. They laid Him on the cross and stretched Him out, and drove an iron nail through each one of His quivering hands, and a nail through His crossed feet; with clubs they hit the nails straight on their heads. They raised the cross in a hole in the ground, but it would not stand firm and straight, and they shoved it back and forth, and drove in pegs and wedges all around, and those that did it pulled down the brims of their hats so that the blood of His hands might not fall in their eyes. And from above He looked down on the soldiers who drew lots for His torn raiment, and on the whole howling multitude for whom He suffered that they might be redeemed, and in the whole multitude there was not one compassionate eye. Those below looked up at Him who hung there, suffering and exhausted. They looked at the board above His head on which 'King of the Jews' was written, and mocked Him and called to Him: 'Thou that destroyest the temple, and buildest it in three days, save thyself. If thou be the Son of God come down from the cross.' Then the only begotten Son of God was wroth, and saw that they were not worth redemption, the hordes that fill the earth, and He tore His feet free over the head of the nail, and He clasped His hands about the nails in His hands and pulled them out so the arms of the cross bent like a bow, and sprang to the earth, and seized His garments so the dice rolled over the brow of Golgotha, and He threw it around Him in royal anger and ascended unto heaven. And the cross remained empty, and the great work of redemption was never fulfilled. There is no mediator between us and God; no Jesus died for us on the cross! *No Jesus died for us on the cross!*"

He was silent. As he uttered the last words, he bent forward over the crowd and seemed to hurl them at their heads. At that a wave of terror ran through the church and in the corners people began to sob.

Then the butcher pressed forward with hands raised threateningly, pale as a corpse, and shouted: "Monk, monk, nail Him again to the cross, nail Him!" Behind him, some one hissed hoarsely: "Yes, yes, crucify Him, crucify Him!" From every mouth the cry rang under the vaulted roof, threatening and commanding in a whirlwind of cries: "Crucify Him, crucify Him!"

Clear and loud came a single quivering voice: "Crucify Him!" But the monk looked down on the outstretched arms, on the distorted faces with dark openings between the shrieking lips, where the rows of teeth gleamed white as the teeth of enraged wild beasts, and in a moment of ecstasy he raised his arms to heaven and laughed. Then he stepped down. His people raised the banners with the rain of sulphur and their bare, black crosses, and crowded out of the church. Again they crossed the market-place and passed through the tower gate.

The people of Old Bergamo stared after them as they passed down the mountain. The steep path, walled on either side, was misty in the light of the sun which sank to rest beyond the plain, and the shadows of their great crosses, swaying from side to side in the crowd, were thrown, black and distinct, on the red walls of the town.

The song died in the distance. First one, then another banner, gleamed red in the smoke-stained desolation of the new town and disappeared in the sunset light of the plain.

✳ ✳ ✳

HERMANN JOACHIM BANG
(1858-1912)

AT the age of twenty, Bang published two volumes of critical essays, and in 1880 appeared his novel, *Families Without Hope*, which at once aroused attention. He subsequently produced several more novels and collections of short stories which placed him in the front rank of Scandinavian writers.

Irene Holm, translated by Jacob Wittmer Hartmann, appeared in the *Scandinavian American Review*, May, 1916, and is here reprinted by permission of the editor.

IRENE HOLM

I

IT was announced by the constable's son from the church steps after the services one Sunday that Miss Irene Holm, danseuse at the Royal Theatre, would begin her courses in etiquette, dancing, and gesture, in the inn, on the first of November, for children as well as for those more advanced—ladies and gentlemen—provided a sufficient number of applications be made. Price, five crowns for each child; reduction for several from the same family.

Seven applied, Jens Larsen furnishing the three at the reduced rate. Miss Irene Holm considered the number sufficient. She arrived at the inn one evening toward the end of October, her baggage an old champagne basket tied with a rope. She was small and worn, with a forty-year-old baby face under her fur cap, and old handkerchiefs tied about her wrists as a protection against rheumatism. She enunciated very distinctly and said, "Thank you so much—but I can do it myself," whenever any one offered to do anything for her and she looked quite helpless. She would have nothing but a cup of tea and then crept into her bed in the little chamber behind the public room, her teeth chattering whenever she thought of the possibility of ghosts.

The next day she appeared with her hair curled, and wearing a close-fitting coat edged with fur, on which the tooth of time had left a visible impress. She had to pay visits to her honored patrons, the parents of her pupils, she said. And might she ask the way? Mrs. Hendriksen went to the doorway and pointed over the flat fields. Miss Holm courtesied her thanks to the three doorsteps.

"Old thing," said Mrs. Hendriksen. She remained standing in the doorway and looked after Miss Holm, who was taking a roundabout way to Jens Larsen's house on the dike, to spare her footgear. Miss Holm was shod in goatskin boots and wore ribbed stockings.

When she had visited the parents—Jens Larsen paid nine crowns for his three—Miss Holm looked about for a room. She got a little white-washed chamber at the smith's, looking out upon the flat fields, and furnished with a bureau, a bed, and a chair. In the corner, between the bureau and the window, the champagne basket was set down. Miss Holm moved in. The morning was spent in making applications of curling pins, cold tea and warm slate pencils. When the curls were in order, she tidied the room, and in the afternoon she crocheted. She sat on the champagne basket in the corner and took advantage of the last vestige of daylight. The smith's wife came in and sat down on the wooden chair and talked, while Miss Holm listened, smiling graciously and nodding her curled head.

The woman spun out the story in the dark for an hour, until it was time for supper, but Miss Holm scarcely knew what she had said. Outside of dancing and gesture, and calculations as to her daily bread—a tedious, eternal calculation—the things of this world had much difficulty in forcing their way into Miss Holm's consciousness. She sat still on her basket with her hands in her lap and only looked fixedly at the line of light under the smith's door. She never went out, for she became home-sick as soon as she saw the desolate flat fields, and she was afraid of bulls and of runaway horses. Later in the evening, she would boil water in the tiled oven and eat supper. Then she would put up her curls in papers, and when she had undressed as far as her petticoats, she would practice her steps at the bedpost, moving her legs until it made her perspire.

The smith and his wife did not budge from the keyhole. They had a rear view of the leaps of the ballet; the curling-papers stood out from her head like quills upon the fretful porcupine. Miss Holm was so engrossed that she began to hum aloud as she moved up, down, up, down, in her exercises. The smith and his wife and the children were glued to the keyhole.

When Miss Holm had practiced the prescribed number of minutes, she crept into bed. After practicing she always thought of the time "when she was a student at the ballet-school," and suddenly she would laugh aloud, a carefree laugh, just as she lay there. She fell asleep, still thinking of the time—the happy time—the rehearsals, when they stuck each other's legs with pins . . . and screamed . . . the evenings in the dressing-rooms . . . what a bustle, all the voices . . . and the director's bell. . . . Miss Holm would still wake up at night, if she dreamt of having missed an entrance.

II

"Now—one—two—" Miss Holm raised her skirt and put out her foot . . . "toes out—one—two—three."

The seven had their toes turned inward—with their fingers in their mouths as they hopped about.

"Little Jens—toes out—one—two—three—make a bow—one—two —three—once more . . ."

Jens Larsen's three children made the bow with their tongues sticking rigidly out of their mouths.

"Little Marie to the right—one—two—three—." Marie went to the left. . . . "Do it over—one—two—three—"

Miss Holm jumped about as a kid, so that a goodly portion of her stockings was visible. The course was in full progress. They danced three times a week in the inn-room with two lamps that hung from the beams. The ancient dust arose in the old room under their stamping. The seven were as completely at sea as a school of fish. Miss Holm straightened their backs and curved their arms.

"One—two—three—clap hands."

"One—two—three—clap hands." The seven staggered as they did so and nearly lost their balance.

Miss Holm got dust in her throat through shouting. They were to dance a waltz, two by two, held each other at arm's length, awkwardly and nervously, as though turning in their sleep. Miss Holm talked and swung them around.

"Good—turn—four—five—good—turn—little Jette."

Miss Holm followed up Jens Larsen's middle child and little Jette and swung them around like a top.

"Good—good—little Jette."

Her eyes smarted with the dust. The seven continued hopping in the middle of the floor in the twilight.

When Miss Holm came home after the dancing lessons, she would tie a handkerchief around her curly head. She went about with a perpetual catarrh, and in unoccupied hours she sat with her nose over a bowl of boiling water to relieve it.

They had music for their lessons: Mr. Brodersen's violin. Miss Holm got two new pupils, advanced ones. They all kept moving to Tailor Brodersen's instrument and the dust rose in clouds and the tiled stove danced on its lion's claws. The number of visitors also increased; from the manse came the pastor's daughter and the young curate.

Miss Holm demonstrated under the two oil-lamps with her chest thrown out and her foot extended: "Move your legs, little children, move your legs, that's it . . ."

Miss Holm moved her legs and raised her skirt a little, for there were spectators.

Every week Miss Holm would send her crocheting to Copenhagen. The mail was delivered to the schoolmaster. Invariably she had either sealed or addressed improperly, and the schoolmaster had to do it over, while she stood by and looked on with the humility of a sixteen-year-old.

The newspapers, which the mail had brought, lay ready for distribution on one of the school desks, and one day she begged to be permitted to look at *Berling's*. She had looked at the pile for a week before she had picked up the courage to ask. After that she came every day, in the noon period—the teacher knew her soft knock, with one knuckle. "Come in, Miss; it is open," he would say.

She went into the schoolroom and took *Berling's* from the pile. She read the announcements of the theatres, the repertoire and the criticisms, of which she understood nothing, but it was about the people "down there." It took her a long time to get through a column, while her index finger followed gracefully along the lines. When she had finished reading, she crossed the passage and knocked as before.

"Well," said the teacher, "anything new in town?"

"At least it's about the people down there," she said. "The old conditions, you know."

"The poor little thing," said the teacher, looking out of the window after her. Miss Holm went home to her crocheting.

"The poor little thing, she's crazy about her dancing-master," he said.

A ballet by a new ballet-master was to be performed at the theatre. Miss Holm knew the list of characters by heart and also the names of all the solo dancers. "You see, we were at school together," she said, "all of us."

On the evening of the ballet she was feverish, as if it were she that was to dance. She lighted the two candles, gray with age, that stood on the dresser, one on each side of the plaster cast of Thorwaldsen's Christ, and she sat on her champagne basket and looked into the flame. But she could not bear being alone. All the old unrest of the theatre came over her. She went into the smith's rooms, where they were at supper, and sat down on a chair by the side of the huge old clock. She talked more in those few hours than all the rest of the year. It was all about theatres and premières, the great soloists, and the master-steps. She hummed and swayed with the upper part of her body as she sat. The smith enjoyed it so much that he began to growl out an ancient cavalry ditty, and he said: "Mother, we'll drink a punch on that—a real arrack!"

The punch was brewed, and the two candles from the bureau were put on the table and they drank and talked away, but in the midst of the merriment, Miss Holm suddenly grew still, great tears came into her eyes, and she rose and went to her room. In there she settled down on her basket, burst into tears, and sat for a long time before she undressed and went to bed. She went through no "steps" that night.

She was thinking of one thing: He had been at school with her. She lay still in her bed. Now and then she sighed in the dark, and her head moved uneasily on the pillow. In her ears sounded the voice of the ballet-master at school, angry and derisive, "Holm has no go. Holm has no go." He shouted it, and it echoed through the hall. How clearly she heard it—how clearly she saw the hall! The figurantes practiced in long rows, one step at a time. Tired, she leaned against the wall a moment and again the sharp voice of the ballet-master: "Holm, haven't you any ambition at all?"

She saw their room at home, her mother, sitting in the armchair complaining, and her sister working the busy sewing-machine near the lamp, and she heard her mother say in her asthmatic voice: "Did Anna Stein dance the solo?"

"Yes, mother."

"I suppose she had La Grande Napolitaine?"

"Yes, mother."

"And you two entered school at the same time," said her mother, looking over at her from behind the lamp.

"Yes, mother."

And she beheld Anna Stein in the embroidered skirt—with ribbons fluttering in her tambourine, a living and rejoicing vision in the radiance of the footlights, in her great solo. Suddenly she laid her head down in the pillows and sobbed, desperately and ceaselessly in her impotence and despair. It was morning before she fell asleep.

The ballet had been a success. Miss Holm read the criticism at the school. While she was reading, a few small old woman's tears fell on the copy of *Berling's*.

From her sister came letters. Letters of notes due and telling of sore distress. On those days Miss Holm forgot about her crocheting and would sit pressing her temples, the open letter in her lap. Finally she would make the rounds of "her" parents, and blushing and paling would beg half her pay in advance, and what she got she would send home.

The days passed. Miss Irene Holm went to her lessons and returned. She obtained new pupils, half a dozen young farm hands who had united for the purpose of dancing three evenings a week in Peter Madsen's big room near the woods. Miss Holm walked two miles through the winter darkness, as frightened as a hare, pursued by all the old ghost stories that had been current at the ballet school. She had to pass a pond surrounded by willows, stretching their great arms up in the darkness. She felt her heart as a cold stone in her breast.

They danced for three hours, and she gave the commands, swung them about and danced with the gentlemen pupils until her cheeks were a hectic red. When she had to go home, Peter Madsen's gate was locked, and the farmhand went out with her, carrying a light to open the gate. He held the lantern high in his hand for a moment as she walked out into the darkness, hearing his "good night" behind her, and the gate as it scraped over the stones and was locked. The first part of the way there were hedges with bushes that waved and nodded.

Spring was coming and Miss Irene Holm's course was drawing to a close. The party at Peter Madsen's wanted to have a final dance at the inn.

III

The affair was very fine with "Welcome" in transparencies over the door, and cold supper at two kroner per cover, and the curate and the pastor's daughter to grace the table. Miss Holm was dressed in barège with trimmings and Roman ribbons about her hair. Her fingers were covered with rings exchanged with her friends at the school. Between the dances she sprayed lavender water on the floor and threatened the ladies with the bottle. Miss Holm looked quite young again.

First they danced a quadrille. The parents and the old folks stood along the walls and in the doorways, each one looking after his own offspring, with an appearance of great awe. The young people whirled around in the quadrille with faces like masks, as cautious in their steps as if they were dancing on eggs. Miss Holm was all encouraging smiles and French endearments under her breath. The band consisted of Mr. Brodersen and his son. Mr. Brodersen, junior, was working the piano which the pastor had lent for the occasion.

When the round dance began, the tone of those present became less constrained. The men applied themselves to the punch in the middle room, and the gentlemen pupils asked Miss Holm to dance. She moved with her head on one side raising herself on her toes with her belated sixteen-year-old gracefulness. The other couples stopped dancing, and Miss Holm and her partner held the floor alone. The men came into the doorway of the little room and all were plunged in profound admiration of Miss Holm, who advanced her feet further beyond her petticoat and swayed with her hips. The pastor's daughter was so amused that she pinched the curate in the arm. After a mazurka, the schoolmaster shouted "Bravo" and all clapped their hands. Miss Holm made the ballet bow with two fingers on her heart. It was time for supper, and she arranged a Polonaise. All were in it; the women nudged each other with embarrassment and delight; the men said: "Well, old woman, I guess we'll try."

A couple began singing "The Country Soldier" and beating time to accompany the song. Miss Irene Holm sat with the schoolmaster under the bust of His Majesty the King. The general tone once more became solemn, after they had seated themselves, and only Miss Holm continued speaking, in the parlor manner, as the players do in a Scribe comedy. Gradually things became more gay. The men began to drink each other's health and to clink glasses across the table.

There was boisterous merriment at the table occupied by the young people, and it was some time before it was quiet enough for the schoolmaster to speak. He spoke of Miss Holm and of the nine muses. He spoke at length, while all along the table the others sat and looked down into their plates. Their faces assumed a solemn and tense expression, as when the parish clerk appeared in the choir-door at church, and they played with little pieces of bread. The speaker was approaching the subject of Freya and her two cats, and proposed a toast for the "Priestess of Art, Miss Irene Holm." Nine long hurrahs were shouted, and everyone wanted to drink with Miss Holm.

Miss Holm had not understood the speech and was much flattered. She rose and saluted with her glass, held aloft by her curved arm. The festive powder had all disappeared in the heat and the exertion, and she had dark red spots in her cheeks.

There was a great hullabaloo: the young people sang, the older folks drank to each other in private and rose from their places, slapped each other on the back and poked each other in the stomach, out on the floor. The women were becoming anxious lest their better halves should take too much. In the midst of the merry-making, Miss Holm, who had become very cheerful, could be heard laughing carelessly, as she had laughed thirty years before, at the dancing school.

Then the schoolmaster said: "Miss Holm really ought to dance." But she *had* danced!

"Yes, but for them all—a solo—that was the thing!"

Miss Holm had understood at once, and a bold wish flamed up within her: they would let her *dance*. But she began to laugh and said to Peter

Madsen's wife: "The organist wants me to dance,"—as if that were the most ridiculous thing in the world.

Those standing near heard it, and there was a general cry: "Yes— you must dance!"

Miss Holm was flushed up to her hair and said that "the festive atmosphere was almost too exalted."

"And besides there was no music."

"And you couldn't dance in long skirts."

A man shouted across the hall: "They can be raised!" and all laughed aloud and went on begging her.

"Yes, if the pastor's young lady will play a tarantella."

The pastor's young lady was surrounded. She was willing and would try. The schoolmaster rose and struck his glass. "Ladies and gentle- men," he said, "Miss Holm will honor us by dancing." They cried "Hurrah!" and began to get up from the tables. The curate was black and blue, so hard had the pastor's daughter pinched him.

Miss Holm and the latter went in to try the music. Miss Holm was feverish and went back and forth, stretching her limbs. She pointed to the board floor, with its hills and valleys, and said: "But one is not accus- tomed to dance in a circus!"

At last she said: "All right. The show can begin." She was quite hoarse with emotion. "I shall come in after the first ten beats," she said. "I'll give a signal." She went into the side-room to wait.

Her public entered and stood around in a semi-circle, whispering and curious. The schoolmaster took the candles from the table and set them up in the window-frame, as if for an illumination. Then a knock came at the side-room door.

The pastor's daughter began to play, and all looked toward the door. After the tenth beat it opened, and all clapped their hands. Miss Holm was dancing with her skirt tied up in a Roman scarf. It was "La Grande Napolitaine." She walked on her toes and made turns. The spectators looked at her feet and marveled, for their motion was as that of two drumsticks, and when she stood on one leg, the people clapped again.

She said "Faster!"—and began to whirl around. She smiled and beckoned and fanned and fanned. The upper part of her body, her arms, seemed to have more to do every moment; it became rather a mimic per- formance than a dance. She looked closely into the faces of the on- lookers—her mouth opened—smiled—showed all its teeth (some were awful),—she beckoned, acted,—she knew and felt nothing but her "solo." At last she was having her solo! This was no longer "La Napolitaine." It was Fenella, the kneeling Fenella, the beseeching Fenella, the tragic Fenella.

She knew not how she had got up nor how she had got out. She had only heard the music stop suddenly—and the *laughter*—laughter, while she suddenly noticed all the faces.   She rose, extended her arms once more, through force of habit—and made her courtesy, while they shouted. Within, in the side-room, she stood at the table a moment, it was dark to her, so absolutely void.   Then slowly, and with very stiff hands, she loosened the sash, and smoothed out the skirt, and went in quietly to where the clapping was still going on.

She courtesied, standing close to the piano, but did not raise her eyes from the floor.   They were in a hurry to begin dancing.   Miss Holm went around quietly saying "Good-bye," and the pupils pressed the money, wrapped in paper, into her hands.   Peter Madsen's wife helped her on with her things and at the last moment the pastor's daughter and the curate came and asked to be allowed to accompany her.

They walked along silently.   The pastor's daughter was absolutely unhappy, and wanted to make some apology, but did not know what to say, and the little danseuse continued walking with them, silent and pale.

Finally the curate spoke, tortured by the silence: "You see, Miss, those people have no appreciation of the tragic."

Miss Holm remained silent.   They had arrived at the smith's house, and she courtesied as she gave them her hand.   The pastor's daughter put her arms around her and kissed her: "Good-night, Miss," she said, and her voice was unsteady.   The curate and she waited in the road until they had seen the light in the danseuse's room.

Miss Holm took off the barège skirt and folded it up.   Then she un-wrapped her money and counted it and sewed it up in a little pocket in her petticoat.   She managed the needle very awkwardly as she sat thus by candle-light.

The next morning, her champagne basket was lifted into the mail-coach.   It was a rainy day, and Miss Holm crept in under a leaky umbrella; she drew up her legs under her, so that she presented a very Turkish appearance on her basket.   When they were ready to drive off, with the postman walking by the side of the coach—one passenger being all the poor nag could draw—the pastor's daughter came down from the parsonage, bareheaded.   She brought a white chip basket with her, saying: "You can't go off without provisions!"

She bent down under the umbrella and, taking Miss Holm's head in her hands, she kissed her twice.   The old danseuse burst into tears, caught the girl's hand and kissed it.   The pastor's daughter remained standing in the road and looked after the old umbrella, as long as she could still see it.

Miss Irene Holm had announced a spring course in "Modern Society Dancing" in a neighbouring town.   Six pupils had applied.   Thither she went—to continue what we are in the habit of calling Life.

*   *   *

NORWAY

BJÖRNSTJERNE BJÖRNSON
(1832-1910)

BJÖRNSON, one of the founders of modern Norwegian literature, developed an instinct for poetry early in his youth. He matriculated at the University of Christiania and soon began to work as a journalist and dramatic critic. In 1857 appeared *Synnove Solbakken*, the first of his peasant novels, which was shortly succeeded by a number of others. In the same year he was appointed director of the theatre at Bergen and began producing his social plays. Several years later, he collected and published a number of short stories some of which created a great sensation.

Fidelity was translated by R. B. Anderson, and published in the volume, *The Bridal March*, Boston, 1881.

FIDELITY

YONDER on the plains in my native parish, there dwelt a husband and wife with their six sons. They toiled faithfully on a very large but hitherto neglected gard, until an accidental wound from an axe ended the husband's days, and the wife was left alone with the hard work and the six children. She did not lose her courage, but led her eldest two sons forward to the side of the coffin, and made them promise her over their father's corpse to care for their little brothers and sisters, and to be a help to her as far as God gave them strength. They promised, and they kept their word until the youngest son was confirmed. Then they considered themselves released from their pledge; the eldest married the widow of a gardman, and the next to the eldest shortly afterward married her well-to-do sister.

The four brothers who remained at home were to have the entire management, after having until now been continually under control themselves. They did not feel much ambition for this; from childhood up they had been accustomed to keep together, either in couples or all four, and did so more than ever now that they must depend solely on one another for help. Not one of them would state his own opinion about anything until he felt sure of that of the others; indeed they were not certain of their own opinions until they had looked into one another's faces. Without having made any compact, there was still a mute agreement among them, that they would never separate as long as their mother lived.

She herself, however, preferred to have things somewhat differently arranged, and got the two who had already left home to agree with her. The gard had become a well-tilled piece of land; more help was needed, and so the mother proposed to pay the eldest two for their portion, and divide the gard among the four sons at home, in such a way that they would keep together in couples, each couple occupying half of the gard. There should be erected a new set of houses alongside of the old ones; two of the sons should take possession of them; the other two should remain with her. But of the couple that left home, one must marry; for they would need help about the house and the cattle; and the mother named the girl whom she would like to have for a daughter-in-law.

None of them had any objections to offer, but now the question arose, which two should move away, and of these two, which one should marry? The eldest of the four said that he was quite willing to leave home, but he would never marry; and each of the others in turn objected.

Finally they agreed with the mother that the girl should be allowed to decide the matter. And up at the summer stable one evening the mother asked her if she would be willing to come to the plains as a wife, and the girl proved to be quite willing. Well, then, which of the boys would she like to marry; for she could have whichever one she pleased. Why, she had not considered the matter. Then she must do so now, for it was left to her to decide. Well, then, she supposed it might be the eldest; but him, she was told, she could not have; he was not willing. Then the girl named the youngest. But the mother thought there would be something strange in that; "for he was the youngest."

"Then the next to the youngest!"

"Why not the next to the eldest?"

"To be sure, why not the next to the eldest?" replied the girl; for he was the one she had been thinking of the whole time, therefore had not dared name him.

Now the mother had judged, from the moment the eldest had refused, that this must be because he thought the next to the eldest and the girl had an eye on each other. So the next to the eldest married the girl, and the eldest moved with him into the new home. How the gard was now divided no outsider could learn, for the brothers worked together as they had done before, and they stored away their harvest, now in one barn, now in the other.

After a time the mother's health began to fail; she needed rest, consequently, help, and the sons agreed to engage permanently a girl who was in the habit of working here. The youngest brother was to ask the girl the next day they were gathering leaves; he knew her best. Now the youngest must for some time have had a secret liking for this girl; for when he came to speak to her he did it in such a singular manner that she thought he was asking her to marry him, and she said "Yes." The youth was frightened, and going at once to his brothers told them what a mistake had been made. They all four became very grave, and none of them dared utter the first word. But the next to the youngest could see that the youngest really cared for the girl, and that was the reason why he was so frightened. At the same time he saw clearly that it was his own lot to be a bachelor; for if the youngest should marry he could not. This seemed to him rather hard, for there was one of whom he himself had thought; but now nothing could come of that. It was *he*, then, who made the first remark, namely, that they would be surest of the girl if she should come to the gard as the wife of one of them. Always when one had spoken the others agreed, and the brothers now went to talk with their mother. But when they got home they found their mother ill in earnest; they must wait until she was well; and as she did not become well again, they once more held counsel together. In it the youngest proposed that as long as the mother lay in bed no change must be made, and this was agreed to; for the girl must have no more to care for than the mother. Thus it remained.

For sixteen years the mother lay in bed. For sixteen years the intended daughter-in-law waited on her patiently and without a murmur. For sixteen years the sons met every evening for devotions at her bedside, and on Sundays the eldest two also joined them. She often begged them in these peaceful hours to remember her who had tended her; they understood what she meant by this, and promised. During all these sixteen years she blessed her illness, because it had allowed her to taste a mother's joy to the last; she thanked them every time they gathered about her bedside,—and one day this was for the last time.

When she was dead her six sons met to bear her themselves to the grave. It was customary here for women as well as men to attend funerals, and this time the whole parish followed, men and women, all who were able to walk, even the children;—first the deacon, as leader of the singing, then the six sons with the coffin, and then a long train of people, all singing so that they were heard more than a mile away. And when the body was laid to rest, and the six sons had filled the grave, the whole procession repaired to the church, for there the youngest son was to be married; the brothers would have it so, because this funeral and wedding really belonged together. Here the priest, who was my now deceased father, spoke so eloquently of fidelity that I, who chanced to be present, thought when I came out of church that it was something that belonged with the mountains and the sea and the grandeur of the entire surrounding nature.

*   *   *

JONAS LIE
(1833-1908)

THE works of Jonas Lie occupy a prominent position in Norwegian literature. He spent his youth at Trömso, where his father had been appointed sheriff, gaining acquaintance with sea-faring life which he later described in his stories. In 1851 he went to the University of Christiania where Ibsen and Björnson were his fellow-students. He studied law and later practised at Kongsvinger. It was not until after some unfortunate business speculation that he decided to try his hand at literature. In 1890, with the publication of *The Visionary*, he sprang to sudden fame. Although he travelled extensively after this, it did not hinder him from producing novels and short stories. In 1874 appeared his first great novel, *The Pilot and His Wife*. This placed him at the head of Norwegian novelists, and assured him, with Björnson and Ibsen, a stipend from the government.

The Story of a Chicken, translated by Anders Orbeck, appeared in the *American Scandinavian Review*, November, 1925, and is here reprinted by permission of the editor.

THE STORY OF A CHICKEN

THERE was once an egg that rolled about uneasily in its nest. The mother hen had to keep constantly kicking it back into place. That must be an extraordinary bit of life within, she reflected.

No sooner had the chick broken forth into the world, and brushed away the bits of shell from her eyes, than she craned her neck and cackled and demanded to know the meaning of all this.

The mother flapped her wings in horror at such a presumptuous question, and had to reassure herself twice before she felt fully convinced that it wasn't a young cock.

She kept her eyes on her—couldn't do otherwise—all day long, to the neglect of the rest of her flock. The young thing went prancing about, stopped every once in a while, and put on an air of "well, did you ever!" And when the mother called her brood together at sunset, she grumbled merely and lagged behind. And when the mother ran after her and began pecking at her, she countered with angry cries of chi-chi-chi-chichi-che-e-p.

She couldn't see why she should necessarily have to go to roost and sleep just at night time. Why not as well in the day time?

Even before she had learned to cackle properly she craned her neck in indignation and eyed askance the maid who called "chick-chick-chick" to them and scattered corn and peas about. As if chickens lived for the sole purpose of getting out there in the yard! And she couldn't—peep-peep-peep-peep-peep—for the life of her see why the young should run about in nothing but yellow down while the elders wore black and brown and even mottled feathers.

Day by day, as she grew older, her cackling grew louder and clearer. And was there—peep-peep-peep-peep-peep—any sense in their going about bareheaded almost while the cock sported a red comb and other such things and was privileged to crow the loudest of any in the barnyard? And these—cock-a-doodle-doo—windbag young-cocks, who swagger about so pompously one might almost think they would crack, who begin to crow like lords and masters long before they have the slightest sign of a comb— really—one might almost ask if it were they who laid the eggs!

We'll just turn our backs on them and appear not to notice them, she clucked angrily to her sisters. Every one with an ounce of self-respect should feel it her bounden duty to start a demonstration and fly away the moment she but glimpsed the top of a cock's comb.

But gradually, as first one and then another of her sisters found themselves rudely awakened from sentimental clucks and came to realize that her prying into affairs and officious domination had somehow severed tender bonds, there developed among them a feeling of anger and resentment. If she but opened her bill to say something, they flew in upon her, pecked at her savagely, and plucked out her feathers. As a result she could hardly appear presentable—nay, dared hardly show herself any longer.

Then she sat down and moped.

And as she pondered and discovered things amiss here and there, she came gradually to entertain vague suspicions, and to wonder just how all this about eggs and chickens and hens really hung together. No matter how many eggs were laid or how many chickens were hatched, there were never any more chickens, whether old or young, in the barnyard than before. But every blessed morning madam came out and collected eggs by the score in her apron and carried them away.

Whereupon the poor distracted hens raced wildly about, seeking and seeking and grieving, grieving and seeking. Yet they forgot everything completely the moment they heard the cock call. And when morning came they sat there on their new eggs as unthinking and hopeful and blissful as ever.

It really wouldn't do any harm to look into things a bit, she thought, and see where all this led to. For the hens merely told her that things went according to natural law and order.

She hopped lightly over to the fence and peeped through the cracks. There was the hutch literally white with egg-shells that had been cast out! The sight depressed her, and she did nothing but grieve and ponder over it day and night. All this industrious hatching and laying and laying and hatching came to nothing then after all. The shells out there—bleached skeletons—represented for them the ultimate goal.

All their yearnings and desires and tender all-important clucks and ecstasies, all the maternal dignity which the hens prided themselves on and felt so sure of,—all this but led to the rubbish pile!

She stared and stared at the broken bits of shell, which looked to her like so many tomb-stones in a cemetery, until she was half stupefied. And overwhelmed she raised her voice and prophesied and cackled wildly about how terribly unthinking and ignorant and simple-minded they were who still clung to the old convention of laying eggs.

Whereupon the rest sputtered among themselves angrily and intimated that she knew not whereof she spoke. Did she know anything of a mother's joy as she sits brooding on her eggs, pondering the number of times the sun still must set before the young emerged, and whether they would be white or mottled or black or brown, or how many perhaps would be cocks and resemble their father?

And when they emerged yellow and awkward and funny and silly and stubborn and the mother had her hands full managing them as she wandered about, so weighted down with cares that her head all but swam, —then certainly she had other things to do than give herself up to extravagant notions! One who is fulfilling her natural function should not concern herself with idle speculation.

And whenever there was any danger, they concluded, such as a lurking cat or a circling hawk, there was of course the cock. Surely he was their natural protector at such times. But little did she comprehend, with all her super-wisdom and arrogance, how their hearts beat when the vigilant lord lifted up his voice and filled the air with his solicitous and reassuring cry.

She gave them up completely. Did they do anything but think about the cock eternally, dream about him, talk about him, day and night! Never a thought about anything else!

But she was destined to live through yet further revelations of the secret horrors of life. One day she had flown onto the roof of the henhouse and stood looking out over the fence. And lo,—there stood the cook on the kitchen stoop, knife in hand, beheading chicken after chicken, old and young, as fast as she could extract them from her apron, while the poor headless creatures flopped about on the ground and against the wall.

Now she knew full well what the world was like!

She screwed up her neck to say something: her voice was hoarse.

What was the good of sitting and brooding day in and day out on a batch of eggs, growing thin the while, anticipating with joy the first "peep-peep" of the young, or afterwards scratching around blissfully blind and happy, picking up kernels for them and then teaching them to pick for themselves, when there was no future in store for them anyway? It was merely to fatten them for the slaughter and the table,—in another moment they would feel the bloody knife!

She pondered and thought and reflected until her head ached at the thought of the terrible responsibility involved in the laying of eggs.

She visualised the inevitably bitter disappointment the mother hen must feel when her eggs are taken away from her, while they are still warm, almost as they are laid. And the horrible end, should any of the eggs hatch and the little chicks run about with the mother happy and trusting,—really, she couldn't bring herself to think about it. There was nothing to do but to keep them in ignorance of their fate and support them in this wilderness called life until that last terrifying hour.

And all the deception which thus crept into the mother love, which of all things in this world should be the purest and truest,—she fainted and fell off the roost.

She could see only one solution: the whole chicken race should out and out refuse to lay. Half beside herself she raced around in circles, plucked the pin feathers from her tail, and concluded that it was her mission to write and thus save the coming generations from all this nameless misery.

With these heavy thoughts she secluded herself in the shade of the bushes at the far end of the henyard right up against the fence. There she wandered in solitude and sought peace and comfort amid the deceptions and disappointments of life.

One night, after a vain effort to get sleep and rest, she went out long before sunup and paced back and forth by herself. To cool her hot feverish head now and then in the clammy mould or the dewy grass served somewhat to calm her.

As she squeezed through a little opening underneath the fence and emerged on the other side, the first glow of the morning sun met her full in the eyes.

And there, on the top of the rubbish heap with all those egg shells, stood a young cock, his neck craned full length, crowing lustily towards the rising sun.

Before she could fully grasp the situation or realise what had happened, she found herself out there with him. She stood motionless, eyeing his marvellously erect and stately form, his resplendent and iridescent feathery garb, his sparkling green wing feathers, his gracefully arched tail.

He promenaded majestically back and forth with a stately measured tread and legs high upraised. His comb a fiery red and his bill wide open, as if about to sound the war-trumpet, he hurled forth his fearless defiance aaginst every enemy that threatened the chicken-yard.

After each time he craned his neck and crew he glanced down at her, until finally, dizzy and helpless, intoxicated with all his glory, she felt almost as if she could give her life for him.

Nearer and nearer he came, strutting past her, the egg-shells crackling underneath his feet, chivalrous and gallant, the passion in his voice increasing with every crowing. His seductive cock-a-doodle-doo rang out over the whole yard, until she suddenly felt the rustle of feathers about her like a blustering storm, and delirious with delight she yielded and forgot everything in the ecstasy of the moment.

In the sweet confusion she realised that she had become his bride.

❊ ❊ ❊

ALEXANDER KIELLAND
(1849-1906)

KIELLAND, who came under the influence of Ibsen, was sufficiently original to develop into a prominent literary figure. To quote Havelock Ellis, in Kielland we have "a realistic novelist of most dainty and delicate art, beneath which may be heard the sombre undertone of his sympathy with the weak and oppressed." *At the Fair* is reprinted from *Tales from Two Countries* by Alexander Kielland, translated by William Archer, copyright, 1891, by Harper and Brothers, by whose permission it is here used.

AT THE FAIR

IT was by the merest chance that Monsieur and Madame Tousseau came to Saint-Germain-en-Laye in the early days of September.

Four weeks ago they had been married in Lyons, which was their home; but where they had passed these four weeks they really could not have told you. The time had gone hop-skip-and-jump; a couple of days had entirely slipped out of their reckoning, and, on the other hand, they remembered a little summer-house at Fontainebleau, where they had rested one evening, as clearly as if they had passed half their lives there.

Paris was, strictly speaking, the goal of their wedding-journey, and there they established themselves in a comfortable little *hôtel garni*. But the city was sultry and they could not rest; so they rambled about among the small towns in the neighbourhood, and found themselves, one Sunday at noon, in Saint-Germain.

"Monsieur and Madame have doubtless come to take part in the fête?" said the plump little landlady of the Hôtel Henri Quatre, as she ushered her guests up the steps.

The fête? They knew of no fête in the world except their own wedded happiness; but they did not say so to the landlady.

They soon learned that they had been lucky enough to drop into the very midst of the great and celebrated fair which is held every year, on the first Sunday of September, in the Forest of Saint-Germain.

The young couple were highly delighted with their good hap. It seemed as though Fortune followed at their heels, or rather ran ahead of them, to arrange surprises. After a delicious tête-à-tête dinner behind one of the clipped yew trees in the quaint garden, they took a carriage and drove off to the forest.

In the hotel garden, beside the little fountain in the middle of the lawn, sat a ragged condor which the landlord had bought to amuse his guests. It was attached to its perch by a good strong rope. But when the sun shone upon it with real warmth, it fell a-thinking of the snow-peaks of Peru, of mighty wing-strokes over the deep valleys—and then it forgot the rope.

Two vigorous strokes with its pinions would bring the rope up taut, and it would fall back upon the sward. There it would lie by the hour, then shake itself and clamber up to its little perch again.

When it turned its head to watch the happy pair, Madame Tousseau burst into a fit of laughter at its melancholy mien.

The afternoon sun glimmered through the dense foliage of the interminable straight-ruled avenue that skirts the terrace. The young wife's veil fluttered aloft as they sped through the air, and wound itself right round Monsieur's head. It took a long time to put it in order again, and Madame's hat had to be adjusted ever so often. Then came the relighting of Monsieur's cigar, and that, too, was quite a business; for Madame's fan would always give a suspicious little flirt every time the match was lighted; then a penalty had to be paid, and that, again, took time.

The aristocratic English family which was passing the summer at Saint-Germain was disturbed in its regulation walk by the passing of the gay little equipage. They raised their correct gray or blue eyes; there was neither contempt nor annoyance in their look—only the faintest shade of surprise. But the condor followed the carriage with its eyes, until it became a mere black speck at the vanishing-point of the straight-ruled interminable avenue.

"La joyeuse fête des Loges" is a genuine fair, with gingerbread cakes, sword-swallowers, and waffles piping hot. As the evening falls, coloured lamps and Chinese lanterns are lighted around the venerable oak which stands in the middle of the fairground, and boys climb about among its topmost branches with maroons and Bengal lights.

Gentlemen of an inventive turn of mind go about with lanterns on their hats, on their sticks, and wherever they can possibly hang; and the most inventive of all strolls around with his sweetheart under a great umbrella, with a lantern dangling from each rib.

On the outskirts, bonfires are lighted; fowls are roasted on spits, while potatoes are cut into slices and fried in dripping. Each aroma seems to have its amateurs, for there are always people crowding round; but the majority stroll up and down the long street of booths.

Monsieur and Madame Tousseau had plunged into all the fun of the fair. They had gambled in the most lucrative lottery in Europe, presided over by a man who excelled in dubious witticisms. They had seen the fattest goose in the world, and the celebrated flea "Bismarck," who could drive six horses. Furthermore, they had purchased gingerbread, shot at a target for clay pipes and soft-boiled eggs, and finally had danced a waltz in the spacious dancing-tent.

They had never had such fun in their lives. There were no great people there—at any great, none greater than themselves. As they did not know a soul, they smiled to every one, and when they met the same person twice they laughed and nodded to him.

They were charmed with everything. They stood outside the great circus and ballet marquees and laughed at the shouting buffoons. Scraggy mountebanks performed on trumpets, and young girls with well-floured shoulders smiled alluringly from the platforms.

Monsieur Tousseau's purse was never at rest, but they did not grow impatient of the perpetual claims upon it. On the contrary, they only laughed at the gigantic efforts these people would make to earn—perhaps half a franc, or a few centimes.

Suddenly they encountered a face they knew. It was a young American whom they had met at the hotel in Paris.

"Well, Monsieur Whitmore;" cried Madame Tousseau, gaily, "here at last you've found a place where you can't possibly help enjoying yourself."

"For my part," answered the American, slowly, "I find no enjoyment in seeing the people who haven't money making fools of themselves to please the people who have."

"Oh, you're incorrigible!" laughed the young wife. "But I must compliment you on the excellent French you are speaking to-day."

After exchanging a few more words, they lost each other in the crowd; Mr. Whitmore was going back to Paris immediately.

Madame Tousseau's compliment was quite sincere. As a rule the grave American talked deplorable French, but the answer he had made to Madame was almost correct. It seemed as though it had been well thought out in advance—as though a whole series of impressions had condensed themselves into these words. Perhaps that was why his answer sank so deep into the minds of Monsieur and Madame Tousseau.

Neither of them thought it a particularly brilliant remark; on the contrary, they agreed that it must be miserable to take so gloomy a view of things. But, nevertheless, his words left something rankling. They could not laugh so lightly as before, Madame felt tired, and they began to think of getting homewards.

Just as they turned to go down the long street of booths in order to find their carriage, they met a noisy crew coming upward.

"Let us take the other way," said Monsieur.

They passed between two booths, and emerged at the back of one of the rows. They stumbled over the tree-roots before their eyes got used to the uncertain light which fell in patches between the tents. A dog, which lay gnawing at something or other, rose with a snarl, and dragged its prey further into the darkness, among the trees.

On this side the booths were made up of old sails and all sorts of strange draperies. Here and there light shone through the openings, and at one place Madame distinguished a face she knew.

It was the man who had sold her that incomparable gingerbread— Monsieur had half of it still in his pocket.

But it was curious to see the gingerbread-man from this side. Here was something quite different from the smiling obsequiousness which had said so many pretty things to her pretty face, and had been so unwearied in belauding the gingerbread—which really was excellent.

Now he sat crouched together, eating some indescribable mess out of a checked pocket-handkerchief—eagerly, greedily, without looking up.

Further down they heard a muffled conversation. Madame was bent upon peeping in; Monsieur objected, but he had to give in.

An old mountebank sat counting a handful of coppers, grumbling and growling the while. A young girl stood before him, shivering and pleading for pardon; she was wrapped in a long water-proof.

The man swore, and stamped on the ground. Then she threw off the water-proof and stood half naked in a sort of ballet costume. Without saying a word, and without smoothing her hair or preening her finery, she mounted the little steps that led to the stage.

At that moment she turned and looked at her father. Her face had already put on the ballet-expression. The mouth remained fixed, but the eyes tried, for a second, to send him a beseeching smile. The mountebank shrugged his shoulders, and held out his hand with the coppers; the girl turned, ducked under the curtain, and was received with shouts and applause.

Beside the great oak-tree the lottery man was holding forth as fluently as ever. His witticisms, as the darkness thickened, grew less and less dubious. There was a different ring, too, in the laughter of the crowd; the men were noisier, the mountebanks leaner, the women more brazen, the music falser—so it seemed, at least, to Madame and Monsieur.

As they passed the dancing-tent the racket of a quadrille reached their ears. "Great heavens!—was it really there that we danced?" said Madame, and nestled closer to her husband.

They made their way through the rout as quickly as they could; they would soon reach their carriage, as it was just beyond the circus-marquee. It would be nice to rest and escape from all this hubbub.

The platform in front of the circus-marquee was now vacant. Inside in the dim and stifling rotunda, the performance was in full swing.

Only the old woman who sold the tickets sat asleep at her desk. And a little way off, in the light of her lamp, stood a tiny boy.

He was dresesd in tights, green on one side, red on the other; on his head he had a fool's cap with horns.

Close up to the platform stood a woman wrapped in a black shawl. She seemed to be talking to the boy.

He advanced his red leg and his green leg by turns, and drew them back again. At last he took three steps forward on his meagre shanks and held out his hand to the woman.

She took what he had in it, and disappeared into the darkness.

He stood motionless for a moment, then he muttered some words and burst into tears.

Presently he stopped, and said: "Maman m'a pris mon sou!"—and fell to weeping again.

He dried his eyes and left off for a time, but as often as he repeated to himself his sad little history—how his mother had taken his sou from him—he was seized with another and a bitterer fit of weeping.

He stooped and buried his face in the curtain. The stiff, wrinkly oil-painting must be hard and cold to cry into. The little body shrank together; he drew his green leg close up under him, and stood like a stork upon the red one.

No one on the other side of the curtain must hear that he was crying. Therefore he did not sob like a child, but fought as a man fights against a broken heart.

When the attack was over, he blew his nose with his fingers, and wiped them on his tights. With the dirty curtain he had dabbled the tears all over his face until it was streaked with black; and in this guise, and dry eyed, he gazed for a moment over the fair.

Then: "Maman m'a pris mon sou"—and he set off again.

The backsweep of the wave leaves the beach dry for an instant while the next wave is gathering. Thus sorrow swept in heavy surges over the little childish heart.

His dress was so ludicrous, his body so meagre, his weeping was so wofully bitter, and his suffering so great and man-like——

——But at home at the hotel—the Pavillon Henri Quatre, where the Queens of France condescended to be brought to bed—there the condor sat and slept upon its perch.

And it dreamed its dream—its only dream—its dream about the snow-peak of Peru and the mighty wing-strokes over the deep valleys; and then it forgot its rope.

It uplifted its ragged pinions vigorously, and struck two sturdy strokes. Then the rope drew taut, and it fell back where it was wont to fall—it wrenched its claw, and the dream vanished——

——Next morning the aristocratic English family was much concerned, and the landlord himself felt annoyed, for the condor lay dead upon the grass.

❋ ❋ ❋

SWEDEN

AUGUST STRINDBERG
(1849-1912)

BORN at Stockholm, Strindberg attended the University of Upsala. Poverty compelled him to drop his studies for a time and turn to the serious business of earning a living. With *Master Olaf* (1872) he began his varied career as playwright, novelist and story writer. This play marked the beginning of the new movement in Swedish literature, and, with the *Red Room*, a series of short stories, definitely established Strindberg as an important and original author.

A Funeral is reprinted from the volume, *The German Lieutenant and Other Stories*, published by T. Werner Laurie, Ltd., London, 1915.

A FUNERAL

THE cooper sat with the barber in the inn at Engsung and played a harmless game of lansquenet for a barrel of beer. It was one o'clock in the afternoon of a snowy November day. The tavern was quite empty, for most people were still at work. The flames burned brightly in the clay fire-place which stood on four wooden feet in a corner, and looked like a coffin; the fir twigs on the ground smelt pleasantly; the well-panelled walls kept out all draughts and looked warm; the bull-finch in his cage twittered now and then, and looked out of the window, but he had to put his head on one side to see if it was fine. But it was snowing outside. The innkeeper sat behind his counter and reckoned up chalk-strokes on a black slate; now and then he interjected a humorous remark or a bright idea which seemed to please the other two.

Then the great bell in the church began to toll with a dull and heavy sound, in keeping with the November day.

"What the devil is that cursed ringing for?" said the cooper, who felt too comfortable in life to enjoy being reminded of death.

"Another funeral," answered the innkeeper. "There is never anything else."

"Why the deuce do people want to have such a fuss made about them after they are dead," said the barber. "Trump that, Master Cooper!"

"So I did," said the cooper, and pocketed the trick in his leather apron.

Down the sloping road which led to the Nicholai Gate, a funeral procession wended its way. There was a simple, roughly planed coffin, thinly coated with black paint so that the knots in the wood showed through. A single wreath of whortleberries lay on the coffin lid. The undertaker's men who carried the bier looked indifferent and almost humiliated because they were carrying a bier without a cover and fringes.

Behind the coffin walked three women—the dead man's mother and her two daughters; they looked crushed with grief. When the funeral reached the gate of the churchyard, the priest met it and shook hands with the mourners; then the service began in the presence of some old women and apprentices who had joined the procession.

"I see now—it is the clerk, Hans Schönschreiber," said the innkeeper, who had gone to the window, from which he could overlook the churchyard.

"And none of his fellow-clerks follow him to the grave," said the cooper. "A bad lot, these clerks!"

"I know the poor fellow," said the barber. "He lived like a church mouse and died of hunger."

"And a little of pride," added the innkeeper.

"Not so little though," the cooper corrected him. "I knew his father; he was a clerk too. See now! these fellows who go in for reading and writing die before their time. They go without dinner and beg if necessary in order to look fine gentlemen; and yet a clerk is only a servant and can never be his own master, for only the King is his own master in this life."

"And why should it be more gentleman-like to write?" asked the barber. "Isn't it perhaps just as difficult to cut a courtier's and to make him look smart, or to let someone's blood when he is in danger of his life?"

"I would like to see the clerk who would take less than ten years to make a big beer barrel," said the cooper. "Why, one knows the fellows require two years to draw up their petitions and such-like."

"And what is the good of it all?" asked the innkeeper. "Can I scribble such letters as they do, but don't I keep my accounts right? See here I draw a crucifix on the slate—that means the sexton; here I scribble the figure of a barrel—that stands for the cooper; then in a twinkling,

however many strokes I have to make, I know exactly how much each
has drunk."

"Yes, but no one else except yourself can read it, Mr. Innkeeper,"
objected a young man who had hitherto sat silent in a corner.

"That is the best of it," answered the innkeeper, "that no one can
poke his nose into my accounts, and therefore I am just as good a clerk
as anyone."

The cooper and the barber grinned approval.

"I knew the dead man's father," resumed the innkeeper. "He was a
clerk too! And when he died I had to rub out many chalk-strokes which
made up his account, for he wanted to be a fine gentleman, you see. All
the inheritance he left to the son, who now lies with his nose pointing
upwards, was a mother and two sisters. The young fellow wanted to
be a tradesman in order to get food for four mouths, but his mother
would not consent; she said it was a shame to step downward when one
was above. And heavens, how the poor young fellow had to write! I
know exactly what went on. The three women lived in one room and
he in a rat-hole. All he could scrape together he had to give them; and
when he came from work to eat his dinner, they deafened him with complaints. There was no butter on the bread, no sugar on the cakes; the
elder sister wanted to have a new dress, and the younger a new mantle.
Then he had to write through the whole night, and how he wrote! At
last when his breast-bone stuck out like a hook and his face was as yellow
as a leather strap, one day he felt tired; he came to me and borrowed
a bottle of brandy. He was melancholy but also angry, for the elder
sister had said she wanted a velvet jacket such as she had seen in the German shop, and his mother said ladies of their class could not do with less.
The young fellow worked and slaved, but not with the same zest as
formerly. And fancy! when he came here and took a glass to ease his
chest, his conscience reproached him so much that he really believed he
was stealing. And he had other troubles, the poor young fellow. A
wooer came after the younger sister—a young pewterer from Peter
Apollo Street. But the sister said 'No!' and so did the mother, for he
was only a pewterer. Had he been a clerk, she would have said 'Yes' and
persuaded him that she loved him, and it is likely that she would really
have done so, for such is love!"

All laughed except the young man, who struck in, "Well, innkeeper,
but he loved her, although she was so poor, and he was well off; that
proves that love can be sincere, doesn't it?"

"Pooh!" said the innkeeper, who did not wish to be interrupted. "But
something else happened, and that finished him. He went and fell in
love. His mother and sister had not counted on that, but it was the law
of nature. And when he came and said that he thought of marrying, do
you know what they said?—'Have you the means to?' And the youth,

who was a little simple, considered and discovered that he had not means to establish a new family since he had one already, and so he did not marry; but he got engaged. And then there was a lot of trouble! His mother would not receive his fiancée, because her father could not write, and especially because she herself had been a dressmaker. It was still worse when the young man went in the evenings to her, and would not stay at home. A fine to-do there was! But still he went on working for his mother and sisters, and I know that in the evening he sat and wrote by his fiancée's side, while she sewed, only to save time and to be able to be near her. But his mother and sisters believed evil of the pair, and showed it too. It was one Sunday about dinner-time; he told me himself the young fellow, when he came here to get something for his chest, for now he coughed terribly. He had gone out with his fiancée to Brunkeberg, and as they were coming home over the North Bridge, whom did they meet but his mother and sisters? His fiancée wanted to turn back, but he held her arm firmly and drew her forward. But his mother remained standing by the bridge railings and looked into the water; the elder sister spat before her, and did the same, but the younger—she was a beauty! She stood still and stared at the young woman's woollen mantle and laughed, for she had one of English cloth—and just because of that, her brother's fiancée had to wear wool. Fancy the impudent hussy!"

"That was simply want of sense in the child," said the young man.

"Want of sense!" exclaimed the cooper indignantly. "Want of sense!" But he could not say any more.

The innkeeper took no notice of the interruption and continued: "It was a Christmas Eve, the last Christmas Eve on which he was alive. He came to me as usual to get something for his chest, which was very bad. 'A Merry Christmas, Hans!' I said. I sat where I am sitting now, and he sat just where you are sitting, young sir. "Are you bad?' I asked. 'Yes,' he answered, 'and your slate is full.' 'It doesn't matter,' I answered, 'we can write down the rest in the great book up there. A glass of hot *Schnapps* does one good on Christmas Eve.' He was coughing terribly, and so he took a drink. Then his tongue was loosened. He said how miserable and forlorn he felt this evening. He had just left his home. The Christmas table was laid. His mother and sisters were soft and mild, as one usually is on such an evening. They said nothing, they did not reproach him, but when he took his coat and was about to go out, his mother wept and said it was the first Christmas Eve that her son was absent. But do you think that she had so much heart as to say 'Go to her, bring her here, and let us be at peace like friends.' No! she only thought of herself, and so he went with an aching heart. Poor fellow! But hear what followed. Then he came to his fiancée. She was glad and happy to have him, and now she saw that he loved her better than anything else on earth. But the young man, whose heart was torn in two, was not so cheerful as she wished him to be, and then she was vexed with him, a little only of course. Then they talked about marriage, but he could not agree with her. No, he had duties towards his father's widow. But she quoted the priest who had said a man should leave father and mother and remain with his wife. He asked whether he had not left his mother and home this evening with a bleeding heart in order to be with her. She replied that she had already noticed, when he came, that he was depressed because he was going to spend the evening with her. He answered it was not that which depressed him, but his having to leave his old mother on Christmas Eve. Then she objected that he could not deny he had been depressed when he came to her—and so they went on arguing, you can imagine how!"

The cooper nodded intelligently.

"Well, it was a pleasant Christmas for him. Enough! The young fellow was torn in two, piece by piece; he never married. But now he lies at rest, if the coffin nails hold; but it was a sad business for him, poor devil, even if he was a fool. And God bless his soul! Hans Schönschreiber, if you have no greater list of debts than you had with me, they are easily settled!"

So saying, the innkeeper took his black slate from the counter, and with his elbow rubbed out a whole row of chalk-strokes which had been made under a hieroglyph which looked like a pen in an inkpot.

"See," said the barber, who had been looking through the window to hide his red eyes, "see, there she is!"

Outside in the churchyard the funeral service was at an end; the priest had pressed the hands of the mourners and was about to go; the sexton plied his spade in order to fill up the grave again, as a woman dressed in black pressed through the crowd, fell on her knees by the edge of the grave, and offered a silent prayer. Then she let fall a wreath of white roses into the grave, and a faint sobbing and whispering was audible as the rose leaves fell apart on the black coffin lid. Then she stood up to go, erect and proud, but did not at first notice in the crowd that her dead lover's mother was regarding her with wild and angry looks as though she saw her worst enemy, who had robbed her of her dearest. Then they stood for a moment opposite one another, revengeful and ready for battle; but suddenly their features assumed a milder expression, their pale faces twitched, and they fell in each other's arms and wept. They held each other in a long, convulsive embrace, and then departed side by side.

The innkeeper wept like a child without attempting to hide his emotion, the barber pressed his face against the window, and the cooper took the cards out of his pocket as though to arrange them; but the young man, his head propped in his hands, had placed himself against the wall in order to have a support, for he wept so that his whole body shook and his legs trembled.

The innkeeper first broke the silence. "Who will now help the poor family? The pewterer would be accepted now, were he to make another proposal."

"How do you know that, innkeeper?" asked the young man, much moved, as he stepped into the centre of the room.

"Well, I heard it yesterday when I was up there helping at the preparations for the funeral. But the pewterer will not have her now, as she would not have him then."

"Yes he will, innkeeper!" said the young man. "He will have her though she were ever so selfish and bad-tempered, poor, and wretched, for such is love!"

So saying, he left the astonished innkeeper and his friends.

"Deuce take me—that was he himself!" said the barber.

"Things do not always end so happily," remarked the cooper.

"How about the clerk?" objected the barber.

"No, they did not end well with him, but with the others, you know. They had, as it were, more right to live than he, the young one; for they were alive first, and he who first comes to the mill, grinds his corn first."

"The young fellow was stupid, that was the whole trouble," said the barber.

"Yes, yes," concluded the innkeeper. "He certainly was stupid, but it was fine of him anyhow."

In that they were all agreed.

* * *

SELMA LAGERLÖF

(1858-   )

SELMA LAGERLÖF, born on the ancestral estate of Warmland, taught for some time at Landskrona, devoting herself partly to writing. On achieving public recognition, she abandoned teaching and turned completely to literature, producing novels, short stories and delightful travel sketches. In 1909 she won the Nobel Prize for literature, and in 1914 was elected the first woman member of the Swedish Academy.

The Outlaws, translated by Grace Isabel Colbron, appeared in *Short Story Classics*, published by P. F. Collier & Son, copyright, 1907.

THE OUTLAWS

A PEASANT had killed a monk and fled to the woods. He became an outlaw, upon whose head a price was set. In the forest he met another fugitive, a young fisherman from one of the outermost islands, who had been accused of the theft of a herring net. The two became companions, cut themselves a home in a cave, laid their nets together, cooked their food, made their arrows, and held watch one for the other. The peasant could never leave the forest. But the fisherman, whose crime was less serious, would now and then take upon his back the game they had killed, and would creep down to the more isolated houses on the outskirts of the village. In return for milk, butter, arrow-heads, and clothing he would sell his game, the black mountain cock, the moor hen, with her shining feathers, the toothsome doe, and the long-eared hare.

The cave which was their home cut down deep into a mountain-side. The entrance was guarded by wide slabs of stone and ragged thornbushes. High up on the hillside there stood a giant pine, and the chimney of the fireplace nestled among its coiled roots. Thus the smoke could draw up through the heavy hanging branches and fade unseen into the air. To reach their cave the men had to wade through the stream that sprang out from the hill slope. No pursuer thought of seeking their trail in this merry brooklet. At first they were hunted as wild animals are. The peasants of the district gathered to pursue them as if for a baiting wolf or bear. The bowmen surrounded the wood while the spear carriers entered and left no thicket or ravine unsearched. The two outlaws cowered in their gloomy cave, panting in terror and listening breathlessly as the hunt passed on with noise and shouting over the mountain ranges.

For one long day the young fisherman lay motionless, but the murderer could stand it no longer, and went out into the open where he could see his enemy. They discovered him and set after him, but this was far more to his liking than lying quiet in impotent terror. He fled before his pursuers, leaped the streams, slid down the precipices, climbed up perpendicular walls of rock. All his remarkable strength and skill awoke to energy under the spur of danger. His body became as elastic as a steel spring, his foot held firm, his hand grasped sure, his eye and ear were doubly sharp. He knew the meaning of every murmur in the foliage; he could understand the warning in an upturned stone.

When he had clambered up the side of a precipice he would stop to look down on his pursuers, greeting them with loud songs of scorn. When their spears sang above him in the air, he would catch them and hurl them back. As he crashed his way through tangled underbrush something within him seemed to sing a wild song of rejoicing. A gaunt, bare hilltop stretched itself through the forest, and all alone upon its crest there stood a towering pine. The red brown trunk was bare, in the thick grown boughs at the top a hawk's nest rocked in the breeze. So daring had the fugitive grown that on another day he climbed to the nest while his pursuers sought him in the woody slopes below. He sat there and twisted the necks of the young hawks as the hunt raged far beneath him. The old birds flew screaming about him in anger. They swooped past his face, they struck at his eyes with their beaks, beat at him with their powerful wings, and clawed great scratches in his weather-hardened skin. He battled with them laughing. He stood up in the rocking nest as he lunged at the birds with his knife, and he lost all thought of danger and pursuit in the joy of battle. When recollection came again and he turned to look for his enemies, the hunt had gone off in another direction. Not one of the pursuers had thought of raising his eyes to the clouds to see the prey hanging there, doing schoolboy deeds of recklessness while his life hung in the balance. But the man trembled from head to foot when he saw that he was safe. He caught for a support with his shaking hands; he looked down giddily from the height to which he had climbed. Groaning in fear of a fall, afraid of the birds, afraid of the possibility of being seen, weakened through terror of everything and anything, he slid back down the tree trunk. He laid himself flat upon the earth and crawled over the loose stones until he reached the underbrush. There he hid among the tangled branches of the young pines, sinking down, weak and helpless, upon the soft moss. A single man might have captured him.

Tord was the name of the fisherman. He was but sixteen years old, but was strong and brave. He had now lived for a whole year in the wood.

The peasant's name was Berg, and they had called him "The Giant." He was handsome and well-built, the tallest and strongest man in the entire county. He was broad-shouldered and yet slender. His hands were delicate in shape, as if they had never known hard work, his hair was brown, his face soft-coloured. When he had lived for some time in the forest his look of strength was awe-inspiring. His eyes grew piercing under bushy brows wrinkled by great muscles over the forehead. His lips were more firmly set than before, his face more haggard, with deepened hollows at the temples, and his strongly marked cheek-bones stood out plainly. All the softer curves of his body disappeared, but the muscles grew strong as steel. His hair turned grey rapidly.

Tord had never seen any one so magnificent and so mighty before. In his imagination, his companion towered high as the forest, strong as the raging surf. He served him humbly, as he would have served a master, he revered him as he would have revered a god. It seemed quite natural that Tord should carry the hunting spear, that he should drag the game home, draw the water, and build the fire. Berg, the Giant, accepted all these services, but scarce threw the boy a friendly word. He looked upon him with contempt, as a common thief.

The outlaws did not live by pillage, but supported themselves by hunting and fishing. Had not Berg killed a holy man, the peasants would soon have tired of the pursuit and left them to themselves in the mountains. But they feared disaster for the villages if he who had laid hands upon a servant of God should go unpunished. When Tord took his game down into the valley they would offer him money and a pardon for himself if he would lead them to the cave of the Giant, that they might catch the latter in his sleep. But the boy refused, and if they followed him he would lead them astray until they gave up the pursuit.

Once Berg asked him whether the peasants had ever tried to persuade him to betrayal. When he learned what reward they had promised he said scornfully that Tord was a fool not to accept such offers. Tord looked at him with something in his eyes that Berg, the Giant, had never seen before. No beautiful woman whom he had loved in the days of his youth had ever looked at him like that; not even in the eyes of his own children, or of his wife, had he seen such affection. "You are my God, the ruler I have chosen of my own free will." This was what the eyes said. "You may scorn me, or beat me, if you will, but I shall still remain faithful."

From this on Berg gave more heed to the boy and saw that he was brave in action but shy in speech. Death seemed to have no terrors for him. He would deliberately choose for his path the fresh formed ice on the mountain pools, the treacherous surface of the morass in springtime. He seemed to delight in danger. It gave him some compensation for the wild ocean storms he could no longer go out to meet. He would tremble in the night darkness of the wood, however, and even by day the gloom of a thicket or a deeper shadow could frighten him. When Berg asked him about this he was silent in embarrassment.

Tord did not sleep in the bed by the hearth at the back of the cave, but every night, when Berg was asleep the boy would creep to the entrance and lie there on one of the broad stones. Berg discovered this, and although he guessed the reason he asked the boy about it. Tord would not answer. To avoid further questions he slept in the bed for two nights, then returned to his post at the door.

One night, when a snow-storm raged in the treetops, piling up drifts even in the heart of the thickets, the flakes swirled into the cave of the outlaws. Tord, lying by the entrance, awoke in the morning to find himself wrapped in a blanket of melting snow. A day or two later he fell ill. Sharp pains pierced his lungs when he tried to draw breath. He endured the pain as long as his strength would stand it, but one evening, when he stooped to blow up the fire, he fell down and could not rise again. Berg came to his side and told him to lie in the warm bed. Tord groaned in agony, but could not move. Berg put his arm under the boy's body and carried him to the bed. He had a feeling while doing it as if he were touching a clammy snake; he had a taste in his mouth as if he had eaten unclean horseflesh, so repulsive was it to him to touch the person of this common thief. Berg covered the sick boy with his own warm bear-skin rug and gave him water. This was all he could do, but the illness was not dangerous, and Tord recovered quickly. But now that Berg had had to do his companion's work for a few days, and had had to care for him, they seemed to have come nearer to one another. Tord dared to speak to Berg sometimes, as they sat together by the fire cutting their arrows.

"You come of good people, Berg," Tord said one evening. "Your relatives are the richest peasants in the valley. The men of your name have served kings and fought in their castles."

"They have more often fought with the rebels and done damage to the king's property," answered Berg.

"Your forefathers held great banquets at Christmas time. And you held banquets too, when you were at home in your house. Hundreds of men and women could find place on the benches in your great hall, the hall that was built in the days before St. Olaf came here to Viken for christening. Great silver urns were there, and mighty horns, filled with mead, went the rounds of your table."

Berg looked at the boy again. He sat on the edge of the bed with his head in his hands, pushing back the heavy tangled hair that hung over his eyes. His face had become pale and refined through his illness. His eyes still sparkled in fever. He smiled to himself at the pictures called up by his fancy—pictures of the great hall and of the silver urns, of the richly clad guests, and of Berg, the Giant, lording it in the place of honor. The peasant knew that even in the days of his glory no one had ever looked at him with eyes so shining in admiration, so glowing in reverence, as this boy did now, as he sat by the fire in his worn leather jacket. He was touched, and yet displeased. This common thief had no right to admire him.

"Were there no banquets in your home?" he asked.

Tord laughed: "Out there on the rocks where father and mother live? Father plunders the wrecks and mother is a witch. When the weather is stormy she rides out to meet the ships on a seal's back, and those who are washed overboard from the wrecks belong to her."

"What does she do with them?" asked Berg.

"Oh, a witch always needs corpses. She makes salves of them, or perhaps she eats them. On moonlit nights she sits out in the wildest surf and looks for the eyes and fingers of drowned children."

"That is horrible!" said Berg.

The boy answered with calm confidence: "It would be for others, but not for a witch. She can't help it."

This was an altogether new manner of looking at life for Berg. "Then thieves have to steal, as witches have to make magic?" he questioned sharply.

"Why, yes," answered the boy. "Every one has to do the thing he was born for." But a smile of shy cunning curled his lips, as he added: "There are thieves who have never stolen."

"What do you mean by that?" spoke Berg.

The boy still smiled his mysterious smile and seemed happy to have given his companion a riddle. "There are birds that do not fly; and there are thieves who have not stolen," he said.

Berg feigned stupidity, in order to trick the other's meaning: "How can any one be called a thief who has never stolen?" he said.

The boy's lips closed tight as if to hold back the words. "But if one has a father who steals—" he threw out after a short pause.

"A man may inherit house and money, but the name thief is given only to him who earns it."

Tord laughed gently. "But when one has a mother—and that mother comes and cries, and begs one to take upon one's self the father's crime—and then one can laugh at the hangman and run away into the woods. A man may be outlawed for the sake of a fish net he has never seen."

Berg beat his fist upon the stone table, in great anger. Here this strong, beautiful boy had thrown away his whole life for another. Neither love, nor riches, nor the respect of his fellow men could ever be his again. The sordid care for food and clothing was all that remained to him in life. And this fool had let him, Berg, despise an innocent man. He scolded sternly, but Tord was not frightened any more than a sick child is frightened at the scolding of his anxious mother.

. . . .

High up on one of the broad wooded hills there lay a black swampy lake. It was square in shape, and its banks were as straight, and their corners as sharp as if it had been the work of human hands. On three sides steep walls of rock rose up, with hardy mountain pines clinging to the stones, their roots as thick as a man's arm. At the surface of the lake, where the few strips of grass had been washed away, these naked roots twisted and coiled, rising out of the water like myriad snakes that had tried to escape from the waves, but had been turned to stone in their struggle. Or was it more like a mass of blackened skeletons of long-drowned giants which the lake was trying to throw off? The arms and legs were twisted in wild contortions, the long fingers grasped deep into the rocks, the mighty ribs formed arches that upheld ancient trees. But now and again these iron-hard arms, these steel fingers with which the climbing pines supported themselves, would loosen their hold, and then the strong north wind would hurl the tree from the ridge far out into the swamp. There it would lie, its crown burrowing deep in the muddy water. The fishes found good hiding places amid its twigs, while the roots rose up over the water like the arms of some hideous monster, giving the little lake a repulsive appearance.

The mountains sloped down on the fourth side of the little lake. A tiny rivulet foamed out here; but before the stream could find its path it twisted and turned among boulders and mounds of earth, forming a whole colony of islands, some of which scarce offered foothold, while others carried as many as twenty trees on their back.

Here, where the rocks were not high enough to shut out the sun, the lighter foliaged trees could grow. Here were the timid, grey-green alders, and the willows with their smooth leaves. Birches were here, as they always are wherever there is a chance to shut out the evergreens, and there were mountain ash and elder bushes, giving charm and fragrance to the place.

At the entrance to the lake there was a forest of rushes as high as a man's head, through which the sunlight fell as green upon the water as it falls on the moss in the true forest. There were little clearings among the reeds, little round ponds where the water lilies slumbered. The tall rushes looked down with gentle gravity upon these sensitive beauties, who closed their white leaves and their yellow hearts so quickly in their leather outer dress as soon as the sun withdrew his rays.

One sunny day the outlaws came to one of these little ponds to fish. They waded through the reeds to two high stones, and sat there throwing out their bait for the big green, gleaming pike that slumbered just below the surface of the water. These men, whose life was now passed entirely among the mountains and the woods, had come to be as completely under the control of the powers of nature as were the plants or the animals. When the sun shone they were open-hearted and merry, at evening they became silent, and the night, which seemed to them so all-powerful, robbed them of their strength. And now the green light that fell through the reeds and drew out from the water stripes of gold, brown, and black-green, smoothed them into a sort of magic mood. They were completely shut out from the outer world. The reeds swayed gently in the soft wind, the rushes murmured, and the long, ribbon-like leaves struck them lightly in the face. They sat on the grey stones in their grey leather garments, and the shaded tones of the leather melted into the shade of the stones. Each saw his comrade sitting opposite him as quietly as a stone statue. And among the reeds they saw giant fish swimming, gleaming and glittering in all colours of the rainbow. When the men threw out their lines and watched the rings on the water widen amid the reeds, it seemed to them that the motion grew and grew until they saw it was not they themselves alone that had occasioned it. A Nixie, half human, half fish, lay sleeping deep down in the water. She lay on her back, and the waves clung so closely to her body that the men had not seen her before. It was her breath that stirred the surface. But it did not seem to the watchers that there was anything strange in the fact that she lay there. And when she had disappeared in the next moment they did not know whether her appearance had been an illusion or not.

The green light pierced through their eyes into their brains like a mild intoxication. They saw visions among the reeds, visions which they would not tell even to each other. There was not much fishing done. The day was given up to dreams and visions.

A sound of oars came from among the reeds, and they started up out of their dreaming. In a few moments a heavy boat, hewn out of a tree trunk, came into sight, set in motion by oars not much broader than walking sticks. The oars were in the hands of a young girl who had been gathering water-lilies. She had long, dark brown braids of hair, and great dark eyes, but she was strangely pale, a pallor that was not grey, but softly pink tinted. Her cheeks were no deeper in colour than the rest of her face; her lips were scarce redder. She wore a bodice of white linen and a leather belt with a golden clasp. Her skirt was of blue with a broad red hem. She rowed past close by the outlaws without seeing them. They sat absolutely quiet, less from fear of discovery than from the desire to look at her undisturbed. When she had gone, the stone statues became men again and smiled:

"She was as white as the water-lilies," said one. "And her eyes were as dark as the water back there under the roots of the pines."

They were both so merry that they felt like laughing, like really laughing as they had never laughed in this swamp before, a laugh that would echo back from the wall of rock and loosen the roots of the pines.

"Did you think her beautiful?" asked the Giant.

"I do not know, she passed so quickly. Perhaps she was beautiful."

"You probably did not dare to look at her. Did you think she was the Nixie?"

And again they felt a strange desire to laugh.

While a child, Tord had once seen a drowned man. He had found the corpse on the beach in broad daylight, and it had not frightened him, but at night his dreams were terrifying. He had seemed to be looking out over an ocean, every wave of which threw a dead body at his feet. He saw all the rocks and islands covered with corpses of the drowned, the drowned that were dead and belonged to the sea, but that could move, and speak, and threaten him with their white stiffened fingers.

And so it was again. The girl whom he had seen in the reeds appeared to him in his dreams. He met her again down at the bottom of the swamp lake, where the light was greener even than in the reeds, and there he had time enough to see that she was beautiful. He dreamed that he sat on one of the great pine roots in the midst of the lake while the tree rocked up and down, now under, now over the surface of the water. Then he saw her on one of the smallest islands. She stood under the red mountain ash and laughed at him. In his very last dream it had gone so far that she had kissed him. But then it was morning, and he heard Berg rising, but he kept his eyes stubbornly closed that he might continue to dream. When he did awake he was dazed and giddy from what he had seen during the night. He thought much more about the girl than he had done the day before. Toward evening it occurred to him to ask Berg if he knew her name.

Berg looked at him sharply. "It is better for you to know it at once," he said. "It was Unn. We are related to each other."

And then Tord knew that it was this pale maiden who was the cause of Berg's wild hunted life in forest and mountain. He tried to search his memory for what he had heard about her.

Unn was the daughter of a free peasant. Her mother was dead, and she ruled in her father's household. This was to her taste, for she was independent by nature, and had no inclination to give herself to any husband. Unn and Berg were cousins, and the rumor had long gone about that Berg liked better to sit with Unn and her maids than to work at home in his own house. One Christmas, when the great banquet was to be given in Berg's hall, his wife had invited a monk from Draksmark, who, she hoped, would show Berg how wrong it was that he should neglect her for another. Berg and others besides him hated this monk because of his appearance. He was very stout and absolutely white. The ring of hair around his bald head, the brows above his moist eyes, the colour of his skin, of his hands, and of his garments, were all white. Many found him very repulsive to look at.

But the monk was fearless, and as he believed that his words would have greater weight if many heard them, he rose at the table before all the guests, and said: "Men call the cuckoo the vilest of birds because he brings up his young in the nest of others. But here sits a man who takes no care for his house and his children, and who seeks his pleasure with a strange woman. Him I will call the vilest of men." Unn rose in her place. "Berg, this is said to you and to me," she cried. "Never have I been so shamed, but my father is not here to protect me." She turned to go, but Berg hurried after her. "Stay where you are," she said. "I do not wish to see you again." He stopped her in the corridor, and asked her what he should do that she might stay with him. Her eyes glowed as she answered that he himself should know best what he must do. Then Berg went into the hall again and slew the monk.

Berg and Tord thought on awhile with the same thoughts, then Berg said: "You should have seen her when the white monk fell. My wife drew the children about her and cursed Unn. She turned the faces of the children toward her, that they might always remember the woman for whose sake their father had become a murderer. But Unn stood there so quiet and so beautiful that the men who saw her trembled. She thanked me for the deed, and prayed me to flee to the woods at once. She told me never to become a robber, and to use my knife only in some cause equally just."

"Your deed had ennobled her," said Tord.

And again Berg found himself astonished at the same thing that had before now surprised him in the boy. Tord was a heathen, or worse than a heathen; he never condemned that which was wrong. He seemed to know no sense of responsibility. What had to come, came. He knew of God, of Christ, and the Saints, but he knew them only by name, as one knows the names of the gods of other nations. The ghosts of the Scheeren Islands were his gods. His mother, learned in magic, had taught him to believe in the spirits of the dead. And then it was that Berg undertook a task which was as foolish as if he had woven a rope for his own neck. He opened the eyes of this ignorant boy to the power of God, the Lord of all justice, the avenger of wrong who condemned sinners to the pangs of hell everlasting. And he taught him to love Christ and His Mother, and all the saintly men and women who sit before the throne of God praying that His anger may be turned away from sinners. He taught him all that mankind has learned to do to soften the wrath of God. He told him of the long trains of pilgrims journeying to the holy places; he told him of those who scourged themselves in their remorse; and he told him of the pious monks who flee the joys of this world.

The longer he spoke the paler grew the boy and the keener his attention as his eyes widened at the visions. Berg would have stopped, but the torrent of his own thoughts carried him away. Night sank down upon them, the black forest night, where the scream of the owl shrills ghostly through the stillness. God came so near to them that the brightness of His throne dimmed the stars, and the angels of vengeance descended upon the mountain heights. And below them the flames of the underworld fluttered up to the outer curve of the earth and licked greedily at this last refuge of a race crushed by sin and woe.

Autumn came, and with it came storm. Tord went out alone into the woods to tend the traps and snares, while Berg remained at home to mend his clothes. The boy's path led him up a wooded height along which the falling leaves danced in circles in the gust. Again and again the feeling came to him that some one was walking behind him. He turned several times, then went on again when he had seen that it was only the wind and the leaves. He threatened the rustling circles with his fist, and kept on his way. But he had not silenced the sounds of his vision. At first it was the little dancing feet of elfin children; then it was the hissing of a great snake moving up behind him. Beside the snake there came a wolf, a tall, grey creature, waiting for the moment when the adder should strike at his feet to spring upon his back. Tord hastened his steps, but the visions hastened with him. When they seemed but two steps behind him, ready for the spring, he turned. There was nothing there, as he had known all the time. He sat down upon a stone to rest. The dried leaves played about his feet. The leaves of all the forest trees were there: the little yellow birch leaves, the red-tinged mountain ash leaves, the dried, black-brown foliage of the elm, the bright red aspen leaves, and the yellow-green fringes of the willows. Faded and crumpled, broken and scarred, they were but little like the soft, tender shoots of green that had unrolled from the buds a few months ago.

"Ye are sinners," said the boy. "All of us are sinners. Nothing is pure in the eyes of God. Ye have already been shrivelled up in the flame of His wrath."

Then he went on again, while the forest beneath him waved like a sea in storm, although it was still and calm on the path around him. But he heard something he had never heard before. The wood was full of voices. Now it was like a whispering, now a gentle plaint, now a loud threat, or a roaring curse. It laughed, and it moaned. It was as the voice of hundreds. This unknown something that threatened and excited, that whistled and hissed, a something that seemed to be, and yet was not, almost drove him mad. He shivered in deadly terror, as he had shivered before, the day that he lay on the floor of his cave, and heard his pursuers rage over him through the forest. He seemed to hear again the crashing of the branches, the heavy footsteps of the men, the clanking of their arms, and their wild, bloodthirsty shouts.

It was not alone the storm that roared about him. There was something else in it, something yet more terrible; there were voices he could not understand, sounds as of a strange speech. He had heard many a mightier storm than this roar through the rigging. But he had never heard the wind playing on a harp of so many strings. Every tree seemed to have its own voice, every ravine had another song, the loud echo from the rocky wall shouted back in its own voice. He knew all these tones, but there were other stranger noises with them. And it was these that awoke a storm of voices within his own brain.

He had always been afraid when alone in the darkness of the wood. He loved the open sea and the naked cliffs. Ghosts and spirits lurked here in the shadows of the trees.

Then suddenly he knew who was speaking to him in the storm. It was God, the Great Avenger, the Lord of all Justice. God pursued him because of his comrade. God demanded that he should give up the murderer of the monk to vengeance.

Tord began to speak aloud amid the storm. He told God what he wanted to do, but that he could not do it. He had wanted to speak to the Giant and to beg him make his peace with God. But he could not find the words; embarrassment tied his tongue. "When I learned that the world is ruled by a God of Justice," he cried, "I knew that he was a lost man. I have wept through the night for my friend. I know that God will find him no matter where he may hide. But I could not speak to him; I could not find the words because of my love for him. Do not ask that I shall speak to him. Do not ask that the ocean shall rise to the height of the mountains."

He was silent again, and the deep voice of the storm, which he knew for God's voice, was silent also. There was a sudden pause in the wind, a burst of sunshine, a sound as of oars, and the gentle rustling of stiff reeds. These soft tones brought up the memory of Unn.

Then the storm began again, and he heard steps behind him, and a breathless panting. He did not dare to turn this time, for he knew that it was the white monk. He came from the banquet in Berg's great hall, covered with blood, and with an open axe cut in his forehead. And he whispered: "Betray him. Give him up, that you may save his soul."

Tord began to run. All this terror grew and grew in him, and he tried to flee from it. But as he ran he heard behind him the deep, mighty voice, which he knew was the voice of God. It was God Himself pursuing him, demanding that he should give up the murderer. Berg's crime seemed more horrible to him than ever it had seemed before. A weaponless man had been murdered, a servant of God cut down by the steel. And the murderer still dared to live. He dared to enjoy the light of the sun and the fruits of the earth. Tord halted, clinched his fists, and shrieked a threat. Then, like a madman, he ran from the forest, the realm of terror, down into the valley.

.   .   .   .

When Tord entered the cave the outlaw sat upon the bench of stone, sewing. The fire gave but a pale light, and the work did not seem to progress satisfactorily. The boy's heart swelled in pity. This superb Giant seemed all at once so poor and so unhappy.

"What is the matter?" asked Berg. "Are you ill? Have you been afraid?"

Then for the first time Tord spoke of his fear. "It was so strange in the forest. I heard the voices of spirits and I saw ghosts. I saw white monks."

"Boy!"

"They sang to me all the way up the slope to the hilltop. I ran from them, but they ran after me, singing. Can I not lay the spirits? What have I to do with them? There are others to whom their appearance is more necessary."

"Are you crazy to-night, Tord?"

Tord spoke without knowing what words he was using. His shyness had left him all at once, speech seemed to flow from his lips. "They were white monks, as pale as corpses. And their clothes are spotted with blood. They draw their hoods down over their foreheads, but I can see the wound shining there. The great, yawning, red wound from the axe."

"Tord," said the giant, pale and deeply grave, "the Saints alone know why you see wounds of axe thrusts. I slew the monk with a knife."

Tord stood before Berg trembling and wringing his hands. "They demand you of me. They would compel me to betray you."

"Who? The monks?"

"Yes, yes, the monks. They show me visions. They show me Unn. They show me the open, sunny ocean. They show me the camps of the fishermen, where there is dancing and merriment. I close my eyes, and yet I can see it all. 'Leave me,' I say to them. 'My friend has committed a murder, but he is not bad. Leave me alone, and I will talk to him, that he may repent and atone. He will see the wrong he has done, and he will make a pilgrimage to the Holy Grave.' "

"And what do the monks answer?" asked Berg. "They do not want to pardon me. They want to torture me and to burn me at the stake."

" 'Shall I betray my best friend?' I ask them. He is all that I have in the world. He saved me from the bear when its claws were already at my throat. We have suffered hunger and cold together. He covered me with his own garments while I was ill. I have brought him wood and water, I have watched over his sleep, and led his enemies off the trail. Why should they think me a man who betrays his friend? My friend will go to the priest himself, and will confess to him, and then together we will seek absolution?"

Berg listened gravely, his keen eyes searching in Tord's face. "Go to the priest yourself, and tell him the truth. You must go back again among mankind."

"What does it help if I go alone? The spirits of the dead follow me because of your sin. Do you not see how I tremble before you? You have lifted your hand against God himself. What crime is like unto yours? Why did you tell me about the just God? It is you yourself who compel me to betray you. Spare me this sin. Go to the priest yourself." He sank down on his knees before Berg.

The murderer laid his hand on his head and looked at him. He measured his sin by the terror of his comrade, and it grew and grew to monstrous size. He saw himself in conflict with the Will that rules the world. Remorse entered his heart.

"Woe unto me that I did what I did," he said. "And is not this miserable life, this life we lead here in terror, and in deprivation, is it not atonement enough? Have I not lost home and fortune? Have I not lost friends, and all the joys that make the life of a man? What more?"

As he heard him speak thus, Tord sprang up in wild terror. "You can repent!" he cried. "My words move your heart? Oh, come with me, come at once. Come, let us go while yet there is time."

Berg the Giant sprang up also. "You—did it—?"

"Yes, yes, yes. I have betrayed you. But come quickly. Come now, now that you can repent. We must escape. We will escape."

The murderer stooped to the ground where the battle-ax of his fathers lay at his feet. "Son of a thief," he hissed. "I trusted you—I loved you."

But when Tord saw him stoop for the axe, he knew that it was his own life that was in peril now. He tore his own axe from his girdle, and thrust at Berg before the latter could rise. The Giant fell headlong to the floor, the blood spurting out over the cave. Between the tangled masses of hair Tord saw the great, yawning, red wound of an axe thrust.

Then the peasants stormed into the cave. They praised his deed and told him that he should receive full pardon.

Tord looked down at his hands, as if he saw there the fetters that had drawn him on to kill the man he loved. Like the chains of the Fenrir wolf, they were woven out of empty air. They were woven out of the green light amid the reeds, out of the play of shadows in the woods, out of the song of the storm, out of the rustling of the leaves, out of the magic vision of dreams. And he said aloud: "God is great."

He crouched beside the body, spoke amid his tears to the dead, and begged him to awake. The villagers made a litter of their spears, on which to carry the body of the free peasant to his home. The dead man aroused awe in their souls, they softened their voices in his presence. When they raised him on to the bier, Tord stood up, shook the hair from his eyes, and spoke in a voice that trembled:

"Tell Unn, for whose sake Berg the Giant became a murderer, that Tord the fisherman, whose father plunders wrecks, and whose mother is a witch—tell her that Tord slew Berg because Berg had taught him that justice is the corner-stone of the world."

hands and feet were white as marble, and the nails carefully polished. He did not wipe the sweat from his forehead with a fold of his garment, as did the other disciples, but drew out always a long Roman handkerchief. His beardless, well-looking face, with its small, sedate, intelligent eyes, was altogether that of the sober, discreet man of property.

. . . .

He stole away softly behind the cottage on the road to Jerusalem, while his green head-cloth fluttered among the twisted black olive trees. He smote himself on the forehead and spoke half-aloud, and it was not difficult to divine his thoughts.

What does it lead to, thought he, if one follow this man who forbids us to work and to think of the future, and upon whose head they have finally set a price? Have not I, year by year and day by day, saved coin after coin? There lack but thirty pieces of silver—but thirty!—and I shall be sitting under my own fig-tree.

Then Christ, the Proclaimer of Brotherhood, arose in the lighted doorway.

"Thou art still young," he called out. "Thy first thought upon thine own fig-tree shall go forth and sell me."

Meanwhile the ravine became so dark that nothing could any longer be distinguished. All sank back into the Orient's indescribable stillness, a stillness that has brought forth prophets. But from that evening I understood those who desire that no man shall possess an own fig-tree.

❋ ❋ ❋

PELLE MOLIN
(1864-1896)

THIS gifted Swedish author has to his credit a number of powerful stories that entitle him to a permanent position in his country's literature.

Bear Solomon is an excellent example of his vivid and vigorous style. This story translated by Lisa Lindquist and Mary S. Walker appeared in the *Scandinavian American Review* and is here reprinted by permission of the editor.

BEAR SOLOMON

IN the middle of the night Solomon of Nysvedjan ran along the irregular road over Horse Mountain. From the Laplanders he had learned the soft knee-walk, and it stood him in good stead now. But the road seemed interminable, for his hurry was great. There was still

VERNER VON HEIDENSTAM
(1859-   )

OF all native writers, von Heidenstam exercised most influence i
Sweden at the beginning of the twentieth century. He began hi
career with a volume of poetry in 1888. He led the reaction agains
realism and was the first to turn back to romantic idealism in his nove
and lovely stories collected in 1897.

The Fig-Tree, translated by Charles W. Stork, appeared in T
Pagan magazine, and is here reprinted by permission of the editor.

THE FIG-TREE

WELCOME, thou cool evening, welcome! After the h
thou art as a pitcher of water after a ride in the desert.
art as a pale young wife, who, from the hill beckons ho
sweating toiler of the fields. Thou art like the Tartar jeweler's o
thy colour shifts between the white of milk and the glowing red o
in the same manner as thy joy shifts between healthful, strengt
repose and enflaming jollity.

With this apostrophe I saluted the evening and reined up m
in a small ravine which clambered up toward Jerusalem. The city
a height, with its surrounding wall and its cupolaed houses, like
cornered basket full of eggs. Before the city gate, white-clad
were sitting motionless at the graves of their husbands, mirror
great, quiet, colourless pool.

All at once came the dusk. The road of the ravine became
people—for the time of the Passover was drawing near.

.   .   .   .

At the door of a small cottage, where women were prepar
Last Supper, was seated Christ, the Proclaimer of Brotherhoo
though His face could not be wholly distinguished, because the
an oil-lamp within the house fell upon His back, yet one coul
once who He was. His dark hair hung in rough luxuriance dow
knees. His white prophet's garment was frayed. His feet stair
travel. With His left hand He held shut the nozzle of a leat
of wine. Whenever one of the friends who were sitting with
legs in a circle about Him, attempted to rise, He pressed him ba
place again and offered him a drink. No cares, no thought of lab
to disturb the still evening joy.

Then arose, unnoticed, Judas, the Jew of Jews. His we

some distance to the village, and beyond the village he had three miles more to go.

"What was that?"

Something stirred in the dry twigs, like a heavy body moving. Solomon heard, but paused not a moment. It would be two hours before he could reach the house of the slow and hard-to-wake woman. He knew from previous experience how hard she was to wake. Hundreds of excited men had knocked at her walls and doors, while perspiration cold from anguish made light tracks in unwashed faces. Yes, she took their calls in a professional manner, turned over in her warm bed, and wondered which one of the wives' turn it might be this time.

"Sh, what was that?"

A loud noise broke the mighty peace of the forest. Solomon understood now, but he kept on, his knees pliant as steel springs. He was not going to wait at the woman's door to-night as patiently as he had waited before. No, there was danger at home in the new cottage, and he was prepared to break the woman's windows and drag her by the hair of her head out of her professional calmness. God in heaven! A human life was at stake! Why should he wait? He would not. Let the woman complain afterwards to the trustees of the village, but no—now she should come at once.

A furious grumble passed with a coughing howl a few feet ahead of him. A moment ago, Solomon had understood that a bear was in the vicinity, but so near and of that size! He came to a sudden stop.

"I'll give her time to quiet down and get away," he thought.

Just then a she-bear rose up on her hind legs, showing her white teeth and an open jaw, red as blood.

"So you're of that kind!" said Solomon, and with a cat-like spring he reached a dry spruce twig, looked around with quick eyes, and ran to a big pine. Things were not right. What had burnt the bear's fur and made her so furious? What had roused her?

"She'll be quiet in a minute," muttered Solomon crossly. But the bear came straight at him, growling furiously. This seemed, after all a serious matter. Thank God for the pine tree! It was worth all to an unarmed man. Would his eyes be quick enough and his feet accurate enough? Otherwise the outcome would be uncertain. A bear is not always a slow, heavy body. When it is in a fury, its powerful legs throw it forward quickly and in great leaps, and a man must indeed be sinewy and quick-footed to escape it.

Now the bear dashed through the forest. Twigs and dry branches broke under her huge feet, trees and stumps flew like dust, and small spruces bent like straws. For a lone man in the forest, at a time like this, it is all over in two blood-red minutes—unless God has pity. The crofter had barely reached the pine tree before the bear was so close to his heels that the brute's breath whistled about him. Solomon was now standing in the lee of the tree, and with his quick, light blue eyes on guard, he was ready to elude the embrace. Like lightning he would run in a circle around the tree, always keeping the trunk between himself and the enemy.

Then the dance began. Solomon felt the cords in his knees snap like bent steel. His hand did not show a sign of tremor. Now came the hairy one, on with full speed. A jumping half-circle, and the bear whipped by, scarcely a foot away. The miscalculated jump ended with a sudden stop in the moss, where the bear's nose ploughed a little path. A noisy roar, and the moss flew like a cloud. Back she rushed in blind fury, but came to a sudden stop at the tree. When she saw Solomon draw back she rushed after him again, but could not keep to the small circle that Solomon moved in. Her body was too long, and so she rushed back and forth in sharp angles, making sudden stops and turns like a frightened pig, and growling furiously. Twigs cracked, and all the little rocks cried and rattled at the turmoil.

The sun had been down for quite an hour, but it was broad daylight. It was the season following midsummer when, in the northern part of Sweden, there is no night, though the sun sleeps for two hours. The atmosphere was light yellow, with fine-edged little clouds in the west. Solomon and the bear danced in the witching light their passionate circle dance on Horse Mountain, one boiling and noisy, the other quick and silent. And Solomon's wife—"Mother," he called her—was home in agony.

In all that neighbourhood Solomon was known among bear hunters; even away off to Doutea parish there was no one who had had such luck and skill in the bear forest. Up to the present time Solomon had killed twenty bears; he himself said twenty-four, and even that might be true. But to-night, even while his mind was so occupied with suffering and distress and haste, he knew that he had never seen a bear like this one. He could not explain the unaccountable fury of the stubborn, running beast. Was the bear hunted and wounded? Was it a mother bear robbed of her young? No, there was not a drop of blood in the brown fur. Not a shot had been heard in the forest since the birds had ceased their evening song. Now—well, there was only one thing to do, and that was to look out for one's skin.

The bear's small piercing eyes glowed, the hair on her back lay tight and smooth, and her ears were drawn back flat on her head. Without a minute's rest, she chased the thin crofter around and around the tree. The bear's huge body made it impossible for her to turn like poor Solomon, and the angles necessary at every turn prevented a sudden end to the dance. No matter how hard she tried, she could not make the circles so as to get straight at her enemy. Solomon's poor hands began to burn from the uninterrupted rubbing of the pine's coarse bark. They had been circling the tree for ten minutes, more or less.

"Will no one come?" thought Solomon, "and Mother at home fighting death too. Help, help!" he called loudly. After a few seconds of silence he heard the dogs from the village, where they were sitting on the stoops listening to one another's barking, bark in answer to his call. First one answered, then another, until he could hear a dozen. The deep voice of Namden, moose dog, he heard again and again. Then the long, howling, melancholy, death-prophesying bark of his own bitch. It was like a long string without knots and ends.

Would not some wake up? If only a single peasant would wake up from under his sheep-skin blanket and come out to quiet the dogs! Perhaps the peasant could learn from the dogs that something was going on only a mile and a half from the village, away up in the forest. Solomon called again: "Help!" Would no one come to the rescue?

The bear paused not for one moment. Could anyone understand such fury? At times she came so close to the tree that her hair rubbed off, but Solomon was always a few inches on the other side. His skin shivered, but perspiration was running in little streams all over his body. He could feel it under his clothes. His bark shoes at first had made big holes in the fine moss. Now they were completely torn away, and he was running in a round, evenly-trodden circle of bare soil. One of the shoes had fallen off altogether. The other still hung on, but it was torn and showed his bleeding toes. And Mother was waiting, waiting!

Suddenly the bear changed tactics. Instead of running incessantly, she began to throw herself, dash and wheel about, whirl on her hind legs, as bears do in pursuit of a hunter who gets behind a tree and whom they are unable to reach by a jump on all fours. At least, so it has been told. The bear now threw herself alternately on her fore feet, then on her hind feet, between jumps keeping her sharp, furious eyes on Solomon.

The crofter from Nysvedjan was raging, too, not alone from fear of the bear, but from the terrible worry for mother, home in the log house, waiting, with three crying children about her and the sickening expectation of another, which—well, it is not easy to be alone and poor. So thought Solomon, in the deep forest, far from human help, in his hour of distress. Well, God have mercy on those who are poor in this world!

So, as Solomon slid around the tree, his thoughts, too, were sliding. When he left home running, with his ears full of groans and his soul trembling in restless waves of anxiety, he had felt like a rolling witchball thrown forward by magic formulas and invisible hands along a dark and mysterious path. On this light midsummer night there had been something within him that threw him forward; and *now* he was nailed to Horse Mountain, his own old Horse Mountain, where he had experienced so much of danger and of luck!

The bear rolled herself again, and Solomon slid with his arms around the pine. It was just like that time—he could see the place from here—when he had saved himself with a shot as the bear reached the end of his skis.

Or that other time when he had found a bear lying on a young cow just attacked and chewing her udder while she was still alive. The cow had thrown back her head so that her bell jingled, but with a strange sound not like that from a feeding or ruminating animal. The bear had shown his teeth, but had run away into the forest, only to come back growling a moment later toward Solomon and his companion. That day Solomon had thrust a dry spruce branch down the bear's throat, as his frightened comrade, swearing profanely, raised their only weapon, an axe, when the bear turned back into the forest. Never had Solomon seen such "bear fright" as his companion showed on the way home. The trembling wretch saw a bear behind every tree and rock in the autumn night. He looked continually to the right and to the left and murmured again and again. "There he is, Solomon," and "God have mercy on us." Certainly there were times of excitement up here in the forest.

All this time the bear continued to rage. Pine needles and moss hung on her fur coat, which fairly steamed. Suddenly a bird chirped. It seemed to say, "What is the matter? Who are you that you cannot sleep the short while the sun sleeps in this wonderful midsummer night?"

The bear now sat down on her hind legs for an instant, but was spurred on again by the fury in her blood, and now she walked, walked like a man toward the tree, and stopped with loud breathing a few inches from Solomon. It seemed to be her intention to scare the uncatchable man away from his firm protection. Her jaw grinned, half open, and her breath came like steam in the somewhat chilly air. Solomon had a cold, creepy feeling down his back as his skin shrank. Unconsciously he seized his sheath-knife. Must he give his life at last? The bear put her head close to the tree. Solomon's hand was only two feet above, and it was not ten inches between him and the bear's jaws. The bear seemed to know that if she could separate the man from the tree, the rest could be finished in a minute.

Solomon held on to the tree firmly with his left hand and, with a quick motion, drove his long-bladed knife into the bear's left eye. At the same time, something warm and red poured over his arm. What could it be? Yes, there was a burning sensation in his shoulder, and while the bear, dazed by the sting of the knife, jumped high in the air like a ball, Solomon was conscious that his coat was torn and his skin scratched. He knew now that the play would not end before one of them was lying there cold and still. If there had been ever so little chance a moment ago for a friendly settlement, now there was none. Solomon had become known as "Bear Solomon." Was he to remain "Bear Solomon?" *One* must lose his life, and it would hardly be the bear. The fight was too uneven for that.

"It is not I who will become a widower to-night, but Mother will become a widow, Mother who is waiting," thought Solomon.

The bear danced like mad. She frothed noisily and screamed, but she did not run any longer. She stood erect by the tree and bit after the crofter first on one side and then on the other. The bark was torn off and fell to the ground in big pieces under the even scratching of the claws. Solomon's torn clothes got their share. His shoulder was half bare and wet with blood, but the hand that held the knife moved uninterruptedly and was always ready. The sun rose. The peak toward the south, visible from Horse Mountain, stood violet and dreamed; only the top was awake and shining red with the sun. Solomon knew that he ought to be home in the cottage by this time with the help—the cottage which would now be more lonely than ever. The children would be turned out in the neighbourhood to beg and suffer, for Father was gone for ever! It would be a story from the *fjaell*, a dark story from the wilderness on Horse Mountain.

What now took place happened with whirling speed. Once more the bear started to throw herself; she rolled, jumped, and did venturesome gymnastics. Solomon's eyes were as blue and cold as a frosty night sky, and they did not for one second leave the jumping beast, the beast who, whenever she came within reach, was met by a knife darting like lightning.

Solomon's bark shoe was worn out and had slid up on his ankle, where it turned around and around and made red circles on his skin. His left hand, the slide hand and support, was swollen and full of blisters; some were high and full and others burst, empty and burning. Solomon slipped and fell down on his knee, and the beast was barely two feet away, but he was up again only to feel the stream of hot air as the bear opened and shut her jaw with a crash. At that moment Solomon almost lost his grip of the protecting pine. It grew black and red before his eyes; he began to slide backwards, and thought his death minute had come. But his knife moved, and he cut something soft and—Bear Solomon was on his feet again.

The bear now got down from her standing position and rushed blindly twice around the tree. Her speed was too great, for when she tried to turn she finished in too long a run. She came to a sudden stop and growled. Some intestines hung from a wound; they were discolored by dust and dirt, moss and pine needles, and looked like grey rags on a brown coat. The sun had now reached the pine tops at the scene of destruction. The bear rose again on her hind legs and walked toward the crofter, who stepped to the other side of the tree. The beast encircled the tree with her huge paws as if to tear it out of the earth. Solomon got hold of the bear's right paw, leaned to the right and sunk the knife once, twice, three times between the ribs, aiming for the heart. Solomon's lips were blue and shrunken, the tongue in his mouth was parched, but his eyes sparkled. He was *yet* "Bear Solomon."

The bear dropped and rolled backwards, but got up again and ran in a whirling circle to the underbrush, which bent like straw. She came back once more erect and tasted again the long knife. Solomon was in a strange mood. Within him he felt red, trembling waves, and the ground rocked under him; his eyes blurred, and he could not see straight.

"It would be foolish to faint now," he thought, and he took a deep breath. "I must not weaken now for Mother's sake." Just then something moved in the top of the tree. "It's a bold bird that sits there," thought Solomon, as he cut again between the bear's ribs.

What happened from now on Solomon was never able to describe accurately when he sometimes told the story. The bear, he said, tumbled over like a bag of hay, then jumped and groaned aloud. The unhurt eye glistened like a coal of fire, but the other was hidden by a clot of blood. At every step and every breath the blood poured in a thick stream, like a shaft of blood, Solomon said. He explained that this happened because the bear did not stop for a second to pull the skin over the wound and to twist the hairs, as they often do when wounded.

The sun had risen high. A shimmering gold stream stole through the leaves and needles to the pine of the conflict, as though to see what was going on. The birds were awake and singing everywhere. The grouse whistled, and the crane called from the marsh. To-day the wind was from the village.

Once more the bear stood erect by the tree, but the mouth she opened was full of blood from pierced lungs. Once more Solomon stole in a half circle, and once more did he use the knife; it hit the throat. Once more it struck the heart, and the dripping, bleeding, hairy body received one furious cut after the other—in the breast, in the head, in the paws, in the side. "This is for you," shouted Solomon, cursing, "this is for you—there—there—there, you beast. More, more, you get this for Mother, this for the children, this for the whole night, you devil, you limb of Satan! You wanted to die, did you, did you, did you?"

The bear choked in his last growl, and Solomon saw, through his own tears and perspiration, as if looking through the window pane at an autumn rain, the beast get up again, fall, get up, tremble in convulsions, fall once more, and lie still. When the bear dropped for the last time, Solomon, too, sank at the foot of the pine.

He was tired to death, and his joints were stiff. He felt it now. His right hand hung as if dead, although it still held the knife. Some sun rays found Solomon in this position and kissed him on the cheek. He winked and tried to chase away the sleep. He was thinking, would he continue on his errand? He might, yes; or would he return home and weep over the corpse? There was deep anguish within him. He could not escape misfortune to-day. The poor are certainly reminded of their existence in this world. Well, whom would he get to carry the corpse through the forest next Saturday? It would be expensive; the casket would have to be unpainted, as poor people's caskets usually are. The judge had boards at the Lillsjö mill, but the judge was the stingiest man in the world. Then, yes surely, there are several men carrying a long box over the bridge Langmyrans! Who is in the box that they dare throw it down like that and run around a tree after a bear? It is Mother who is waiting for them. She will have to wait—and Solomon lost consciousness.

About half an hour later something moved in the top of the pine tree. A head is thrust out, draws back, and appears on the other side of the tree. It is the dead bear's cub. He cannot understand the meaning of the deep silence after the long turmoil. But he sees that his mother has made peace—at least she does not stir, and the other one, too, is quiet; and he wants to get away from this place. He has been very much frightened up in the pine tree, so he puts his paws on the trunk and commences to slide down. He starts slowly——

Solomon was not sane when he was awakened by a heavy bundle falling on top of him. Like a hunted animal he sprang up and rushed down to the village, mumbling something, with wits half scared, about "a grey bundle with a tail between its legs." Indeed, there was little left of the hero of the night, of "Bear Solomon." It was only a starved crofter, stripped of his clothing, and running for his poor life, who tottered into the village.

ROUMANIA

Introduction

WHILE Roumanian literature in its widest application dates back to the seventeenth century, its important development with regard to the novel and the short story form had its beginnings about the middle of the nineteenth century. Under the influence of Maiorescu, a group of national writers gathered around the newly founded periodical, *Convorbiri Literare.* Among them were I. Creanga, who embodied in his tales the spirit of the Moldavian peasantry; Caragiale, who, besides several dramas, wrote two volumes of short stories of unsurpassed craftsmanship. Popovici-Banatseanu describes the humble life of Banat, while Beza presents the romantic natives in the mountains of Macedonia. Bratescu-Voinesti produced several volumes of short stories remarkable for their blending of humor and subdued pathos. In recognition of his contribution to his native literature, he was awarded the prize of the Roumanian Academy. Michael Sadoveanu is one of the most prolific Roumanian writers of short stories that give a very vivid insight into the countryside.

❋ ❋ ❋

I. L. CARAGIALE
(1852-1912)

CARAGIALE began his literary career by contributing stories to *Convorbiri Literare.* These immediately attracted attention of Maiorescu, Roumania's distinguished critic, and assured Caragiale a place of importance among his contemporaries. He is the author of several comedies, sketches and short stories. A cosmopolitan in views, he has injected Western ideas and manners into his works which satirize his countrymen.

A Great Invention, translated by A. Kraushaar, is reprinted from *The Pagan* Magazine, copyright, 1918, by permission of the publisher.

A GREAT INVENTION

O N a Sunday morning Satan sought God, found him, and said to him: "Holiest of the Holiest! Why do you worry over mankind? . . . Don't you see what good-for-nothings they are? . . . Give them to me and be done with them! A useless care they are; bad and stupid!"

But God—at that moment uninclined to any palavering—answered somewhat roughly: "Get out of here, blackguard and fiend, I do not want to listen, to-day of all days, to such vile accusations."

"Holiest of . . ."

"Holiest nothing! How can they be stupid if I created them in my likeness? How can they?"

"You did create them after your likeness, but you made their heads wrong,—if Your Sanctity will permit my saying so——"

"Keep still! Begone! . . . you . . . pessimist!" God exclaimed, with austerity. "Do not make me angry! . . . Why do you come here with such lies and tales? How are my creatures stupid? . . . I don't see them as stupid!"

"Well," said the Evil One, "Your Holiness does not see them because you do not go among them since—well, a thousand pardons for daring to mention it—you remember . . . when they dishonored Your Holy Countenance?"

"What? . . . Dishonored my countenance? . . . When?" asked God, frowning, and feigning forgetfulness—or, who knows? He may really have forgotten, for anything is possible with God.

"Don't You remember? With those two thieves . . . on Golgotha Hill, when . . ."

"All right! All right!" said God, trying to change the subject . . . "Have you been there, among the people, lately?"

"Why,—how else do I make my living, Almighty? I am with them, day and night, even in their sleep. . . . Who rears them? Who takes care of them? . . . Who shows them the straight path? But they are so stupid! It's a long time I have been teaching them, but all in vain; they are such thickheads!"

"Now, now!" interfered Saint Peter, seeing God was getting angry; "we know you too well! God wants proofs, not mere words. . . . Come! don't stuff our ears with your chatter. . . . Take yourself off before I get hold of your ears and stretch them for you!"

What was poor Satan to do? He took to his heels, realising that Saint Peter was not joking, but said to himself: "Proofs you want? Proofs you shall have . . . and a-plenty!"

So he continued on his way till he came, as the sun was setting, to a

German city lying peacefully between two rivers. As he passed through the city-gate he heard the Angelus. Satan shivered all over and stopped. . . . There he stood, his tail curled up and his nails biting into the quick of his palms, till the last echo died away in the evening air. Then he tiptoed into the city, and presently accosted a man with a beard reaching to his belt.

"*Guten Abend! Guten Abend! Wie geht's, wie steht's, Herr von Guttenberg!* (Good evening! How are things, Mr. Guttenberg?)

(You see, the Evil-one knew the man's language and name!)

And . . . they became friends. From one thing to another,—they finally drifted into a bier-keller. Here they talked, and talked. . . . But what Satan whispered to the good man only Satan knows. Suffice it to say that the Deutsche lost his sleep that night, thinking. And other nights, too . . . the poor man could not close an eye. He fought with ideas, and plans, turning, twisting, throwing away good ones, picking up bad ones, many a day and many a night, till, finally, after much torment he invented the *Printing-Press!*

Then . . . hold fast, paper! Print . . . and print . . . and print!

At first it went rather slow. But Satan has ideas! He sees the wheels are turning too slowly to suit him, so he curls his tail into the spokes, and lo!—Speed! . . . He does not stop till he gets a million pages an hour, all printed, numbered, addressed, and stamped, ready for the mail, and on to the railroad; here, again, he puts his tail to the wheels to make ninety miles an hour; such is his hurry to distribute his goods.

Shortly after, Saint Peter hears a fearful tumult at the Gate to Paradise, as if the Tartars themselves were there . . . such a whistling and shouting, and singing . . . and what a smoke!

What is it? . . . What is it? . . .

It is Satan, with a milk-train full of *Bibles, Philosophies, Laws, Papers, Magazines new and old.* The Evil One unloads them all, and rushes to God with them.

Says God again: "Good-for-nothing! Are you here again?"

"Again, Almighty!"

"What news do you bring?"

"A mere trifle, Your Holiness; I come with these rags; you wanted proofs, and proofs I have brought you. Look! Do me the pleasure, Saint Peter! Put on your glasses and look . . ." Satan showed all his goods to God and Saint Peter.

God looks on, Saint Peter looks on, and both scratch their beards, gazing deep into each other's eyes.

"Am I right, Almighty?" asks Satan.

God does not answer.

"Am I right, Saint Peter?"

Saint Peter likewise—nothing.

"Well, what of it?" asks God after a while.

"Give them to me, as bargained."

"Huh! Take them, and let me alone!" cries God, annoyed.

Jumping with joy, Satan starts to go.

"Wait! . . . Where are you going, Evil-one?"

"Going to take them."

"What? . . . and leave all this rubbish here? . . . Take it away!
. . . And if I see you here with such stuff again I will order Saint Peter
to cut off your tail! Do you hear me?"

So Satan rushed off, with his tail between his legs, taking his goods
with him.

Thus mankind learned to build Libraries and Academies, for fear
Master Time might destroy their wisdom.

❊ ❊ ❊

MICHAEL SADOVEANU
(18 ?-1926)

SADOVEANU is one of the most prolific writers of short stories. He
has published many collections, the last of these, *A Mill on the Siret*,
appearing in 1925. This volume is considered by critics the best of
Sadoveanu's work. It contains vivid pictures of the country and masterly descriptions.

The Wanderers, translated by Lucy Byng, appeared in *Roumanian Stories*, published in 1921 by John Lane, by whose permission,
and that of the translator, it is here reprinted.

THE WANDERERS

A HOUSE stood isolated in the middle of a garden, separated from
the main group about the market place.

It was an old house, its veranda was both high and broad
and had big whitewashed pillars. The pointed roof was tiled and green
with moss. In front of the veranda, and facing south, stood two beautiful round lime-trees throwing out their shade.

One day in the month of August, the owners, Vladimir Savicky and
Ana, his wife, were sitting in the veranda. Both were old, weather-
beaten by the storms of many journeys and the misfortunes of life. The
old man wore a long white beard and long white hair, which was parted
down the middle and smooth on the top; he smoked a very long pipe,

and his blue eyes gazed towards the plains which stretched away towards the sunset. The old woman, Ana, selected a nosegay of flowers from a basket. He was tall and vigorous still, she was slight with gentle movements. Forty years ago they left their ruined Poland, and settled in our country. They kept an adopted daughter, and had a son of thirty years of age, a bachelor, and a good craftsman. They had lived for thirty years here in the old house, busying themselves with market-gardening; for thirty years they had lived a sad, monotonous life in this place. They had been alone with their adopted child, with Magdalena; Roman, their boy, had been roaming through the world for the last ten years.

Old Vladimir puffed away at his pipe as he stroked his beard; the warmth of the afternoon had made him lay aside his blue jacket. The old wife was choosing her flowers. A gentle breeze, laden with fragrance, came from the garden, from the trees heavy with fruit, and from the gay-coloured flowers. Shafts of light penetrated through the leafy limes, little patches of white light came from above, and played over the bright grass, green as the tree-frog. From time to time the quivering foliage sent a melodious rustle into the peaceful balcony.

At intervals the soft notes of a song floated through the open window.

Suddenly a resounding noise broke the stillness of the day. What was it? A carriage. The old man started, put down his pipe, and rose. The old woman put her head, wrapped in a white shawl, out over the railings. The rumbling vehicle, an ugly Jew upon the box, drew nearer and pulled up outside the door of the old house. A strong, broad shouldered young man descended, a big bundle in his right hand, a cas in his left.

"Roman! Roman!" cried the old lady in a feeble voice. She tried to rise but fell softly back beside the flowers.

"There, there, old lady, it is Roman," murmured the old man gaily, as he went down the stairs.

"Mr. Roman!" cried a gentle voice, and Magdalena's fair head appeared at the window.

Roman had let fall the bundle and thrown himself into his father's arms.

"Yes, old lady, it is Roman!" murmured Vladimir Savicky, with tears in his eyes. He embraced his son, and pressed him to his heart. "Yes, old lady, it is Roman!" That was all he could find to say.

"Mother," cried the young man, "I have not seen you for ten years."

The old mother cried silently, her son strained her to his breast, while the old man wandered round murmuring tearfully into his beard: "Yes, yes, old lady, it is our Roman."

As Roman Savicky straightened his strong frame and turned round, he saw a white face with blue eyes in the doorway. He stood transfixed with astonishment; the girl watched him, smiling shyly.

"Ha! ha!" laughed old Savicky, "how now? Do you not know each other? Ah! Kiss each other, you have known Magdalena ever since she was a child."

The young people approached each other in silence, the girl offered her cheek with eyelids lowered, and Roman kissed her.

"I did not recognise her," said Roman, "she has grown so big."

His mother laughed softly. "You, too, Roman, you have grown much bigger—and handsome."

"Naturally *our* Roman is handsome," said the old man, "our own Roman, old lady."

Again the mother kissed her son. Roman seated himself upon a chair in the veranda, the old man placed himself on his right, and the mother on the left; they watched him, feasting their eyes upon him.

"My darling! my darling!" he said to the old woman, "it is long since I have seen you."

In the end they grew silent, looking intently at one another, smiling. The gentle rustle of the lime trees broke the heat and stillness of the August day.

"Whence do you come, Roman?" questioned the old man suddenly.

"From Warsaw," said his son, raising his head.

The old man opened wide his eyes, then he turned towards Ana.

"Do you hear that, old lady, from Warsaw?"

The old lady nodded her head, and said wonderingly:

"From Warsaw!"

"Yes," said Roman, "I have journeyed throughout Poland, full of bitterness, and I have wandered among our exiled brothers in all parts of the world."

Profound misery rang in his powerful voice. The old people looked smilingly at him, lovingly, but without understanding him. All acute feeling for their country had long ago died away in their hearts. They sat looking happily into the blue eyes of their Roman, at his fair, smooth face, at his beautiful luxuriant hair.

The young man began to speak. Gradually his voice rose, it rang powerfully, full of sorrow and bitterness. Where had he not been! He had been everywhere, and everywhere he had met exiled Poles, pining away among strangers, dying far from the land of their fathers. Everywhere the same longing, everywhere the same sorrow. Tyrants ruled over the old hearth, the cry of the oppressed rent the air, patriots lay in chains or trod the road to Siberia, crowds fled from the homes of their fathers, strangers swept like a flood into their places.

"Roman, Roman!" said the old woman, bursting into tears, "how beautifully you talk."

"Beautifully talks our Roman, old lady," said Vladimir Savicky sadly, "beautifully, but he brings us sad tidings."

And in the old man's soul old longings and bitter memories began to stir. On the threshold Magdalena stood dismayed and shuddered as she looked at Roman.

Suddenly two old men entered by the door. One had thick, grizzled whiskers, the other a long beard in which shone silver threads.

"Ah," cried the old Savicky, "here comes Palchevici, here comes Rujancowsky. Our Roman has come! Here he is!"

"We know," said Rujancowsky gravely, "we have seen him."

"Yes, yes, we have seen him," murmured Palchevici.

They both approached and shook Roman warmly by the hand.

"Good day and welcome to you! See, now all the Poles of this town are met together in one place," said Rujancowsky.

"What?" questioned Roman. "Only these few are left?"

"The others have passed away," said old Savicky sadly.

"Yes, they have passed away," murmured Palchevici, running his fingers through his big grey whiskers.

They were all silent for a time.

"Old lady," said Vladimir Savicky, "go and fetch a bottle of wine and get something to eat too, perhaps Roman is hungry. But where are you? Where is Ana?" asked the old man, looking at Magdalena.

"Do not worry, she has gone to get things ready," replied the girl smilingly.

" 'Tis well! 'tis well!" Then turning towards the two Poles, "You do not know how Roman can talk. You should hear him. Roman, you must say it again."

The old wife came with wine and cold meat. She placed meat in front of her boy, and the wine before the older men. They all began to talk. But Roman's voice sounded melancholy in the stillness of the summer day. Then they began to drink to Roman's health, to the health of each one of them.

"To Poland!" cried Roman, excitedly, striking the table with his fist. And then he began to speak:

"Do you realise how the downtrodden people begin to murmur and to agitate? Soon there will rise a mighty storm which will break down the prison walls, the note of liberty will ring through our native land! Ah, you do not know the anguish and the bitterness *there!* Stranger-ridden and desolate! Since Kosciusko died there are exiles and desolation everywhere! Mother," cried Roman, then turning towards the old woman, "give me the case from over there, I must sing something to you."

With these words his eyes darkened and he stared into space. The old people looked at him, much moved, their heads upon their breasts, not speaking a word. Quiet reigned in the old house, and in the garden there was peace; a fiery sunset, crowned with clouds of flame, was merging into the green sea of the woods. Golden rays penetrated into the old veranda and shone on Roman's hair.

His mother handed him the case.

"Well," said the young man, "I will sing you something with my cithern. I will sing of our grief."

Then, beneath his fingers, the strings began to murmur as though awaking from sleep. Roman bent forward and began, the old people sat motionless round him.

Sad tones vibrated through the quiet of the old house, notes soft and sorrowful like some remote mournful cry, notes deep with the tremor of affliction; the melody rose sobbing through the clear sunset like the flight of some bird of passage.

In the souls of the old people there rose like a storm the clamour of past sorrows. The song lamented the ruin of fair lands; they seemed to listen, as in a sad dream, to the bitter tears of those dying for their native land. They seemed to see Kosciusko, worn with the struggle, covered in blood, kneeling with a sword in hand.

Finis Poloniæ! Poland is no more! Ruin everywhere, death all around; a cry of sorrow rose; the children were torn from their unhappy land to pine away and die on alien soil!

The chords surged, full of grief, through the clear sunset. Then slowly, slowly, the melody died away as though tired with sorrow until the final chord finished softly, like a distant tremor, ending in deathlike silence.

The listeners seemed turned to stone. Roman leant his head upon his hand, and his eyes, full of pain, turned towards the flaming sunset. His chin trembled; his mind was full of bitter memories. The old men sat as though stunned, like some wounded creatures, their heads upon their breasts; the old mother cried softly, sighing, her eyes upon her Roman. As the young man turned his eyes towards the door he saw two bright tears in Magdalena's blue eyes; amid a deep silence his own eyes gazed into the girl's while the last crimson rays faded away from the woods.

ing into the green sea of the woods. Golden rays penetrated into the old
veranda and shone on Roman's harp.

His mother handed him the case.

"Well," said the young man, "I will sing you something with my
cithern. I will sing of our grief."

Then, beneath his fingers, the strings began to murmur as though
awaking from sleep. Roman bent forward and began, the old people
sat motionless round him.

Sad tones vibrated through the quiet of the old house; notes soft
and sorrowful like some remote mournful cry; notes deep with the tremor
of affliction; the melody rose, sobbing, through the clear sunset like the
flight of some bird of passage.

In the souls of the old people there rose like a storm the clamour of
past sorrows. The song lamented the ruin of fair lands; they seemed
to listen, as in a sad dream, to the bitter tears of those dying for their
native land. They seemed to see Kosciuszko, worn with the struggle, covered in blood, kneeling with a sword in hand.

Finis Poloniae! Poland is no more! Ruin everywhere; death all
around; a cry of sorrow rose; the children were torn from their one
happy land to pine away and die on alien soil.

The chords surged, full of grief, through the clear sunset. Then
slowly, slowly, the melody died away as though tired with sorrow, until
the final chord finished softly, like a distant tremor, ending in deathlike
silence.

The listeners seemed turned to stone. Roman leant his head upon
his hand, and his eyes, full of pain, turned towards the flaming sunset.
His chin trembled; his mind was full of bitter memories. The old men
sat as though stunned, like some wounded creatures, their heads upon
their breasts; the old mother cried softly, sighing, her eyes upon her
Roman. As the young man turned his eyes towards the door he saw two
bright tears in Magdalena's blue eyes; amid a deep silence his own eyes
gazed into the girl's while the last crimson rays faded away from the
woods.

INDICES

INDEX OF STORIES

About Myself and Others 913
Apple-Tree, The 445
Apple-Tree, The 957
Ares and Aphrodite 9
Assignation, The 816
At the Fair 1081

Bear Solomon 1106
Beast, The 511
Beggar Boy at Christ's Christmas Tree, The 759
Bel and the Dragon 37
Bella-Flor 195
Bill-Collecting, The 1042
Birth of Sinfjotli, the Son of Sigmund 1052
Black Cat, The 874
"Blow Up with the Brig!" 359
Blue Beard 93
Blue Murder 734
Book of Esther, The 28
Broken Pitcher, The 465
Butter-blinded Brahman, The 21

Candaules' Folly 12
Caprice 787
Cask of Amontillado, The 578
Celebrated Jumping Frog of Calaveras County, The 612
Chicken 922
City Hunter, The 895
Clerk's Quest, The 382
Cnemon's Story 14
Coffin-maker, The 745
Constant Guinard 150
Convict's Return, The 352
Cordovans in Crete 199

Dancing Bear, The 835
Darkening Shadows 841
Darling, The 769
Death in the Woods 716
Debt, The 677

Devasmita 23
Donkey's Revenge, The 1011
Doomdorf, Mystery, The 706
Doomed Prince, The 3
Dowry, The 154
Do You Remember? 809
Dr. Faust Arranges a Marriage.... 461
Drifting Crane 648

Empty Drum, The 763
Ensign, The 141
Eulenspiegel Carries Off the Parson's Horse.... 459
Eva 851
Executioner, The 116

Farm Magnate, The 926
Ferid 988
Feridun and His Three Sons.... 56
Fidelity 1074
Fig-Tree, The 1105
First Prize, The 209
Flowers 505
Friends, The 479
Funeral, A 1086

Glass House, The 892
Grass of Lohina, The.... 824
Great Invention, A.... 1114

Half-brothers, The 342
Happiness 973
Healer, The 937
Her Lover 782
Heroism of Dr. Hallidonhill, The.... 137
Horse Fair at Opdorp, The.... 899
Horse of Genghis Khan, The 160
How Lazaro Served a Priest.... 172
Hubert and Minnie.... 447
Husband Who Was Blind of an Eye, The.... 91

Il Conde 391
In Defence of His Right.... 309
Irene Holm 1065
Island, The 965

Jar of Olives and the Boy Kazi, The.... 75
Jealous Wife, The 223
Jeannot and Colin 97

Jewish Child, A 882
Johannes Attends a Party................................... 903

LEGEND, THE 800
Lie, The 792
Livelihood, A 863
Lodger for the Night, A................................... 954
Lost Stars, The 148
Love Triumphant 231

MAID OF THE DAUBER, THE................................ 144
Man with the Ragged Soul, The............................ 991
Man Who Tamed a Shrew, The............................. 168
Marble Bust, The 948
Markheim 369
Mary with the High Hand................................. 409
Mere Formality, A 261
Military Service 868
Mirrors 282
Mock Aunt, The 181
Mrs. Beelbrow's Lions 438
Municipal Report, A 664

NEW ENGLAND NUN, A.................................... 653
New-Year's Night of an Unhappy Man, The................. 463
Nights in Talca 950

OCCURRENCE AT OWL CREEK BRIDGE, AN.................. 631
Of a Dancing Girl 1018
Omphale: A Rococo Story................................. 129
One Hundred Dollar Bill, The............................. 692
Orderly, The 247
Our Lady's Tumbler 83
Outlaws, The 1091

PADDY AT SEA 335
Papago Wedding 688
Pardoner's Tale, The 294
Paul Turns Beggar 192
Peter Rugg, the Missing Man.............................. 524
Plague at Bergamo, The................................... 1058
Postmistress of Laurel Run, The........................... 617
Pyramus and Thisbe 40

QUALITY 420

RAILWAY ACCIDENT, A 513
Rappaccini's Daughter 554

Raspberry Water, The 751
Reincarnated Melody, A 846
Rip-rip 943
Room with Forty-Eight Stars, The 820
Rumpelstiltskin 488

SACRIFICE OF YANG CHIAO-AI, THE 1000
Sir Simon Eyer 297
Slap, The 285
Soliman II 105
Sphinx Without a Secret, The 386
Stolen Bacillus, The 403
Stone of Invisibility, The 215
Story of a Chicken, The 1077
Story of the Saint Joseph's Ass 238
Stout Gentleman, The 546
Stub-book, The 204

TAKING OF THE REDOUBT, THE 125
Tale of Negative Gravity, A 595
Talkative Tortoise, The 19
Three Robbers, The 49
Tom Varnish 318
Treasure of Mansur, The 68
Trimalchio's Dinner 43
Tsugaru Strait 1033
Turlendana Returns 254
Twilight 813
Two Blue Birds 425

USURER'S WILL, THE 219

VICTIM, THE 497
Virgin and the Nun, The 491
Vouya Goes a-Wooing 979

WANDERER'S, THE 1117
Wandering Willie's Tale 320
What the Old Man Does Is Always Right 1054
What Was It? 584
White Dog, The 777
Winter Wolves 887

ZENOBIA'S INFIDELITY 639

INDEX OF AUTHORS

ADAM, VILLIERS DE L'ISLE 137
Alarcón, Pedro Antonio 204
Aleichem, Sholom 851
Amicis, Edmondo de 247
Andersen, Hans Christian 1054
Anderson, Sherwood 716
Andreyev, Leonid 792
Apocrypha, The 37
Apuleius 49
Ash, Sholom 882
Aumonier, Stacy 438
Austin, Mary Hunter 688
Austin, William 524

BALZAC, HONORÉ DE 116
Bang, Hermann Joachim 1065
Bársony, Etienne 835
Bazan, Emilia 209
Berdyczewski, Micah Joseph 868
Bennett, Arnold 409
Bierce, Ambrose 631
Biro, Louis 841
Björnson, Björnstjerne 1074
Boccaccio, Giovanni 215
Bontempelli, Massimo 282
Bunner, H. C. 639

CABALLERO, FERNAN 195
Çalzini, Raffaele 285
Čapek, Karel 965
Caragiale, I. L. 1114
Čech, Svatopluk 957
Cervantes, Miguel 181
Chaucer, Geoffrey 294
Chekhov, Anton 769
Cinthio, Giovanbatista Giraldi 231
Collins, Wilkie 359
Conrad, Joseph 391
Couperus, Louis 913

D'ANNUNZIO, GABRIELE 254
Daudet, Alphonse 141
Defoe, Daniel 309
Deloney, Thomas 297
De Maupassant, Guy 154
De Mendoza, Diego Hurtado 172
De Navarre, Marguerite 91
De Quevedo, Francisco 192
Dickens, Charles 352
Dostoievsky, Feodor 759

FIALLO, FABIO 948
Firdawsi, Abul 56
Freeman, Mary Wilkins 653

GALSWORTHY, JOHN 420
Garland, Hamlin 648
Gaskell, Elizabeth C. 342
Gautier, Théophile 129
Glishich, Milovan 979
Gorky, Maxim 782
Grazzini, Anton-Francesco 223
Grimm, Jacob and Wilhelm 488
Gutiérrez-Nájera, Manuel 943

HARTE, FRANCIS BRET 617
Hawthorne, Nathaniel 554
Hearn, Lafcadio 1018
Heijermans, Herman 922
Heliodorus 14
Henry, O. 664
Herodotus 12
Homer 9
Huxley, Aldous 447

IRVING, WASHINGTON 546

JACOBSEN, JENS PETER 1058
Jokai, Maurus 820

KAFU, NAGAI 1042
Keller, Gottfried 491
Kielland, Alexander 1081
Kisfaludi, Karoly 816
Krasinsky, Zygmunt 800
Kuprin, Alexander 787

LAGERLÖF, SELMA 1091
Lawrence, D. H. 425

Lemmonier, Camille 892
Lie, Jonas 1077
Lobato, Monteiro 926
Lover, Samuel 335

Mann, Thomas 513
Mansfield, Katherine 445
Manuel, Juan 168
Marmontel, J. F. 105
Mendès, Catulle 148
Mérimée, Prosper 125
Mesko, Francis Xavier 991
Mikszath, Koloman 824
Molin, Pelle 1106
Moore, George 382
Morand, Paul 160

Neruda, Jan 954

Opotawshu, Joseph 887
O'Brien, Fitz-James 584
Old Testament 28
Orzeszkowa, Eliza 809
Ovid 40

Panov, Tedor 973
Peretz, Isaac Loeb 846
Perrault, Charles 93
Petronius 43
Pinski, David 874
Pirandello, Luigi 261
Poe, Edgar Allan 578
Post, Melville Davisson 706
Pushkin, Alexander 745

Reymont, Wladyslaw 813
Richepin, Jean 150
Richter, Jean Paul 463
Rodenbach, Georges 895

Sadoveanu, Michael 1117
Schnitzler, Arthur 505
Scott, Sir Walter 320
Sologub, Feodor 777
Somadeva 23
Steele, Richard 318
Steele, Wilbur Daniel 734
Steinberg, Judah 863

Stevenson, Robert Louis 369
Stockton, Frank R. 595
Straparola, Giovan-Francesco 219
Strindberg, August 1086
Sudermann, Hermann 497
Sung-Ling, P'u 1011

TARKINGTON, BOOTH 692
Tieck, Johann Ludwig 479
Tolstoy, Leo 763
Toson, Shimazaki 1033
Trescec, Vladimir 988
Turgenev, Ivan 751
Twain, Mark 612

UGARTE, MANUEL 937

VALERA, DON JUAN 199
Van Eeden, Frederick W. 903
Verga, Giovanni 238
Verhaeren, Emile 899
Voltaire 97
Von Heidenstam, Verner 1105

WASSERMANN, JACOB 511
Wells, H. G. 403
Wharton, Edith 677
Wilde, Oscar 386

ZEGRI, ARMANDO 950
Zola, Émile 144
Zschokke, Heinrich 465